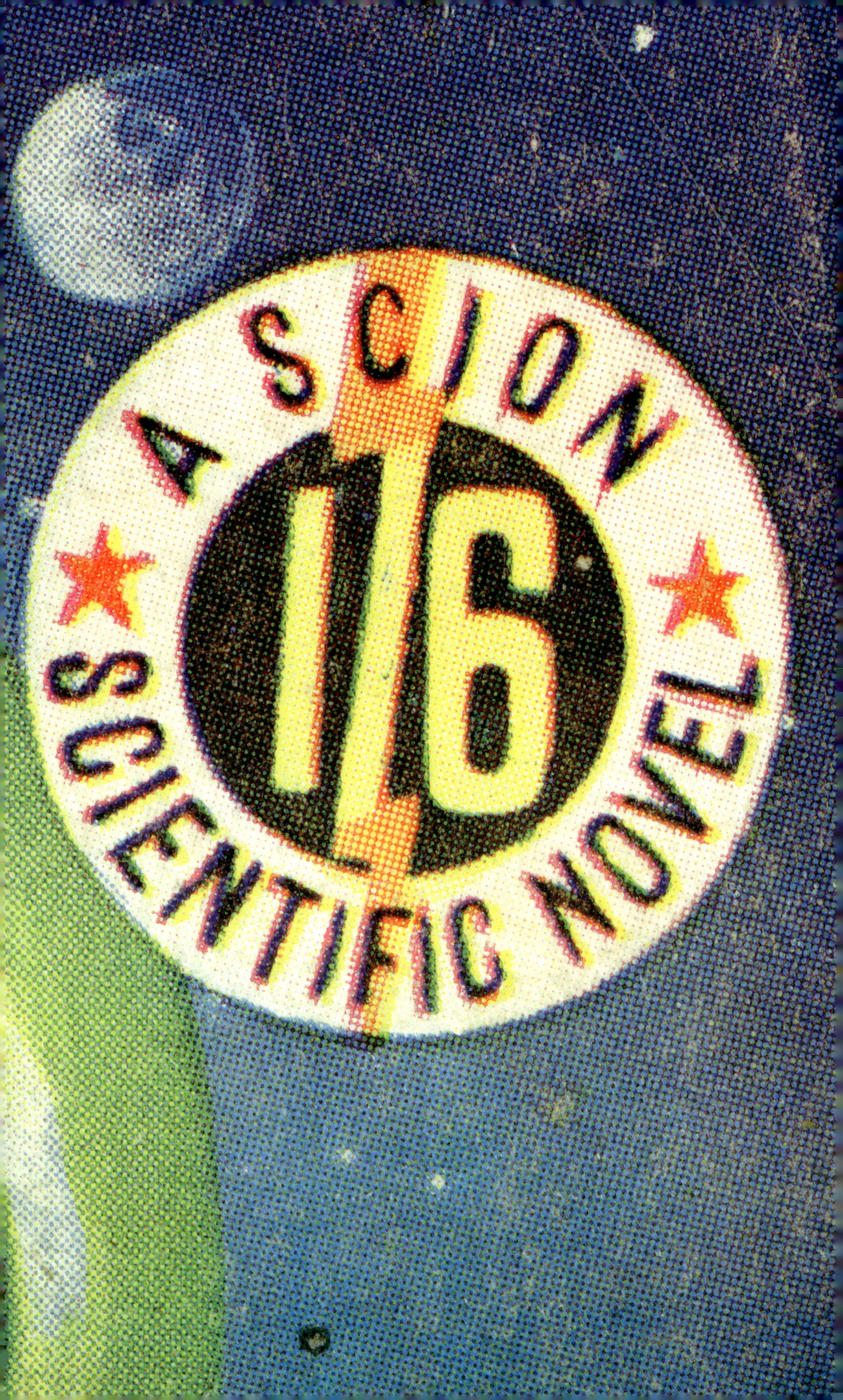
A SCION
1/6
SCIENTIFIC NOVEL

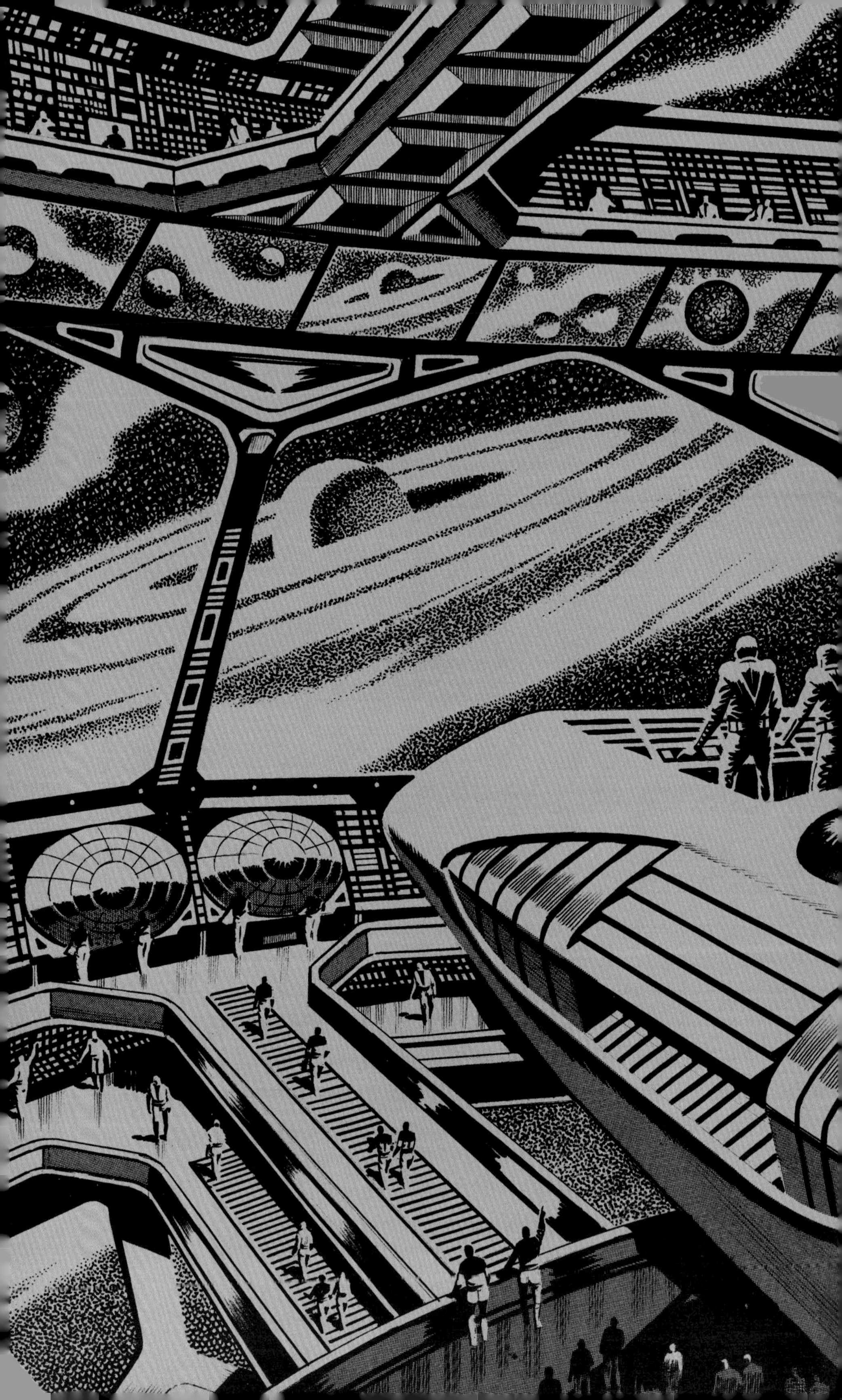

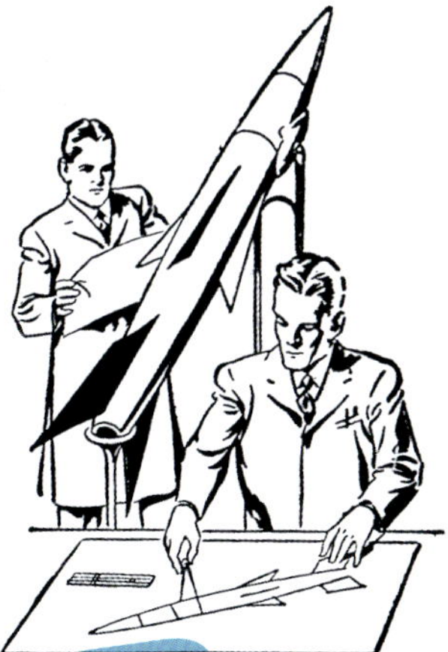

EDITED AND DESIGNED BY

RIAN HUGHES

RAYGUNS & ROCKETSHIPS

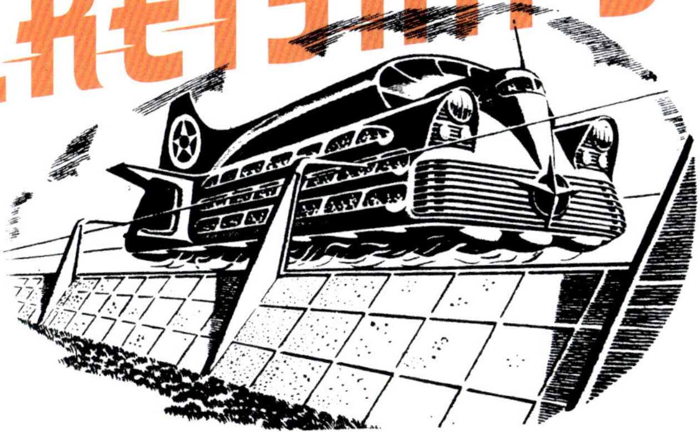

KORERO PRESS

Published by Korero Press Limited
www.koreropress.com

First published in 2022
ISBN-13: 978-1-912740-04-8
Revised edition published in 2024
ISBN-13: 978-1-912740-33-8

 A CIP catalogue record of this book is available from The British Library.

10 9 8 7 6 5 4 3 2
Printed in China
Set in Aurore Grotesque, a Device font
Book design by Rian Hughes at Device
Science Service approved
www.devicefonts.co.uk
www.rianhughes.com

Thank you to the following people for information, insight, and scans of rare items:
John Lawrence, Ron Turner's agent
Rob Liano at Josh Kirby Art
Doug Ellis
Bruce Pennington
Morgan Wallace: https://spectrelibrary.wordpress.com
Steve Holland, for his introduction. Follow him at his Bear Alley blog: bearalley.blogspot.com
Shane Agnew, author of the Badger Books illustrated bibliography
For pseudonym information and the afterword:
Phil Harbottle, author of *Vultures of the Void – The Legacy* and his 1950s British sf YouTube channel: https://tinyurl.com/42ce4vac
For captioning assistance: Rahid Khan
For additional artist identification: David Roach, Rog Peyton
Special thanks to Colin Larkin, author of *Cover Me: the Vintage Art of Pan Books*, Telos Publishing, for the use of his Pan cover art

An earlier version of the foreword appeared in *The Private Library*, seventh series, volume 2 number 3

Despite our best efforts there was still doubt about certain attributions. If you spot any errors or omissions in this book the publisher will gratefully correct them in any future edition.

Endpapers, art details on pages 2, 3 (bottom), 8-9, 34-35: Ron Turner

Also by Rian Hughes

The Black Locomotive
XX
Typodiscography
Logo-a-Gogo
I Am a Number
Soho Dives, Soho Divas
Cult-ure: Ideas can be Dangerous
Yesterday's Tomorrows
Lifestyle Illustration of the '50s
Lifestyle Illustration of the '60s
Custom Lettering of the '20s and '30s
Custom Lettering of the '40s and '50s
Custom Lettering of the '60s and '70s
On the Line
Tales from Beyond Science
Art, Commercial
Dare
The Science Service

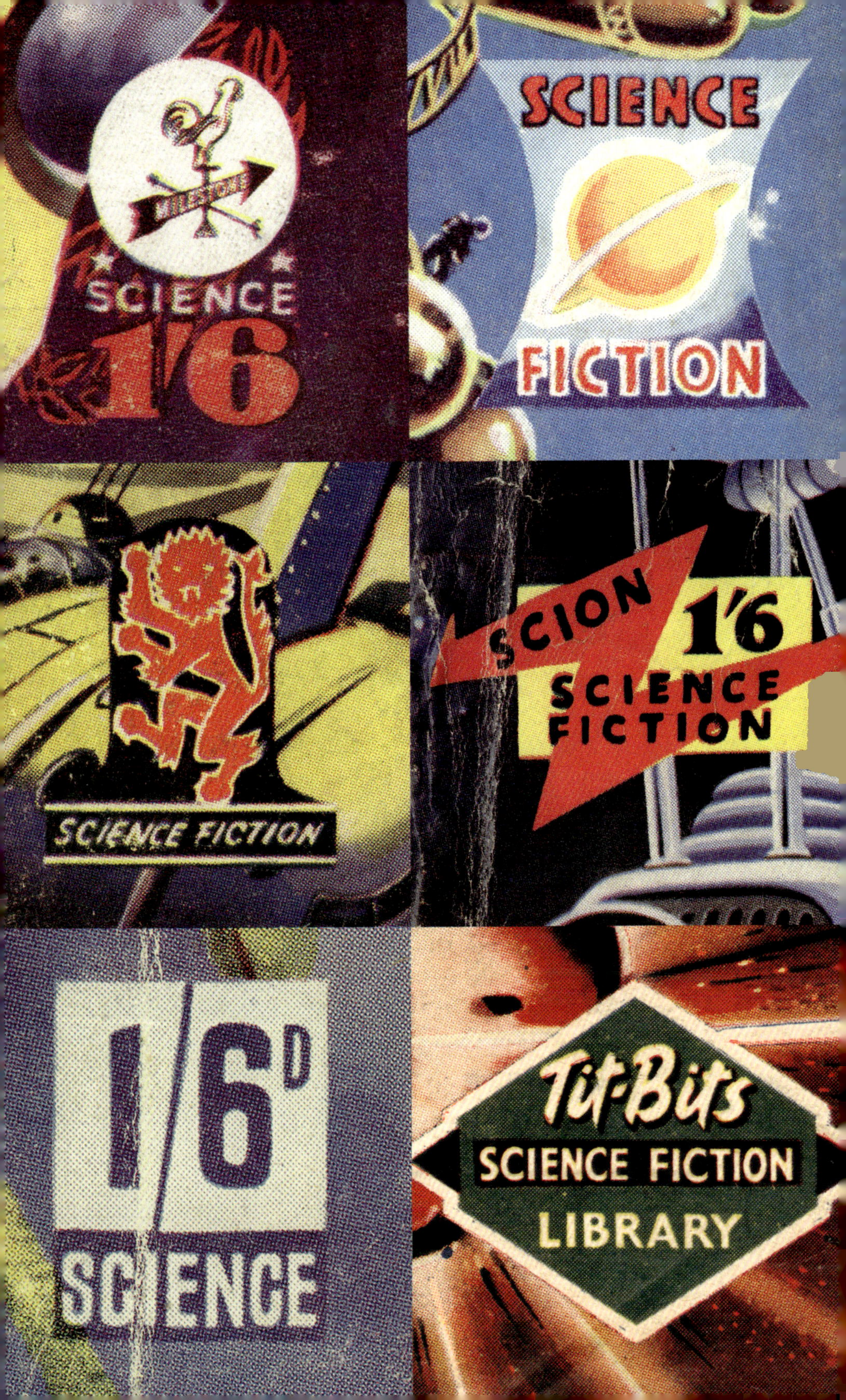

SCIENCE
1/6
SCIENCE
FICTION
SCIENCE FICTION
SCION
1/6
SCIENCE
FICTION
1/6D
SCIENCE
Tit-Bits
SCIENCE FICTION
LIBRARY

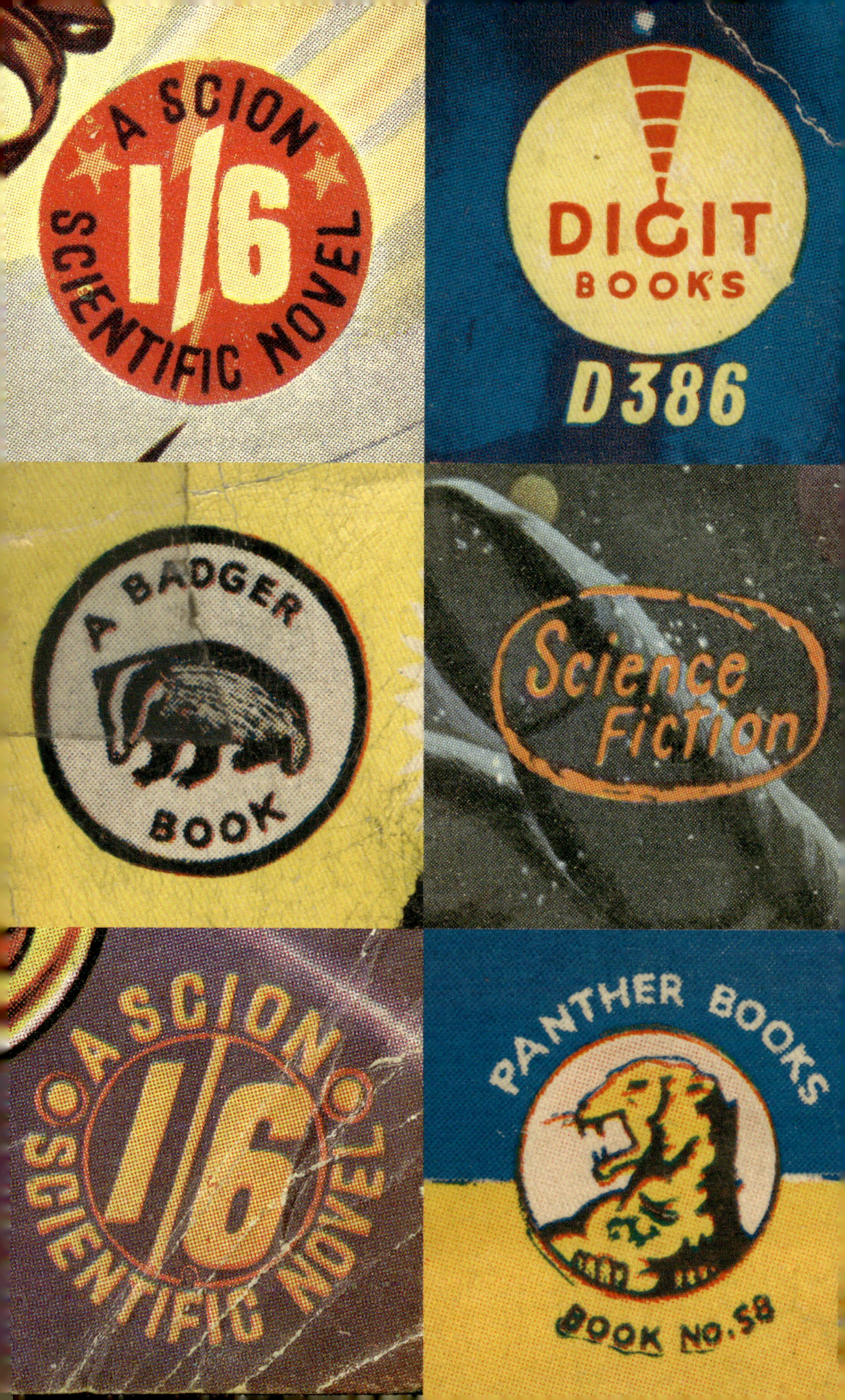
A SCION
1/6
SCIENTIFIC NOVEL
DIGIT
BOOKS
D386
A BADGER
BOOK
Science
Fiction
A SCION
1/6
SCIENTIFIC NOVEL
PANTHER BOOKS
BOOK NO.58

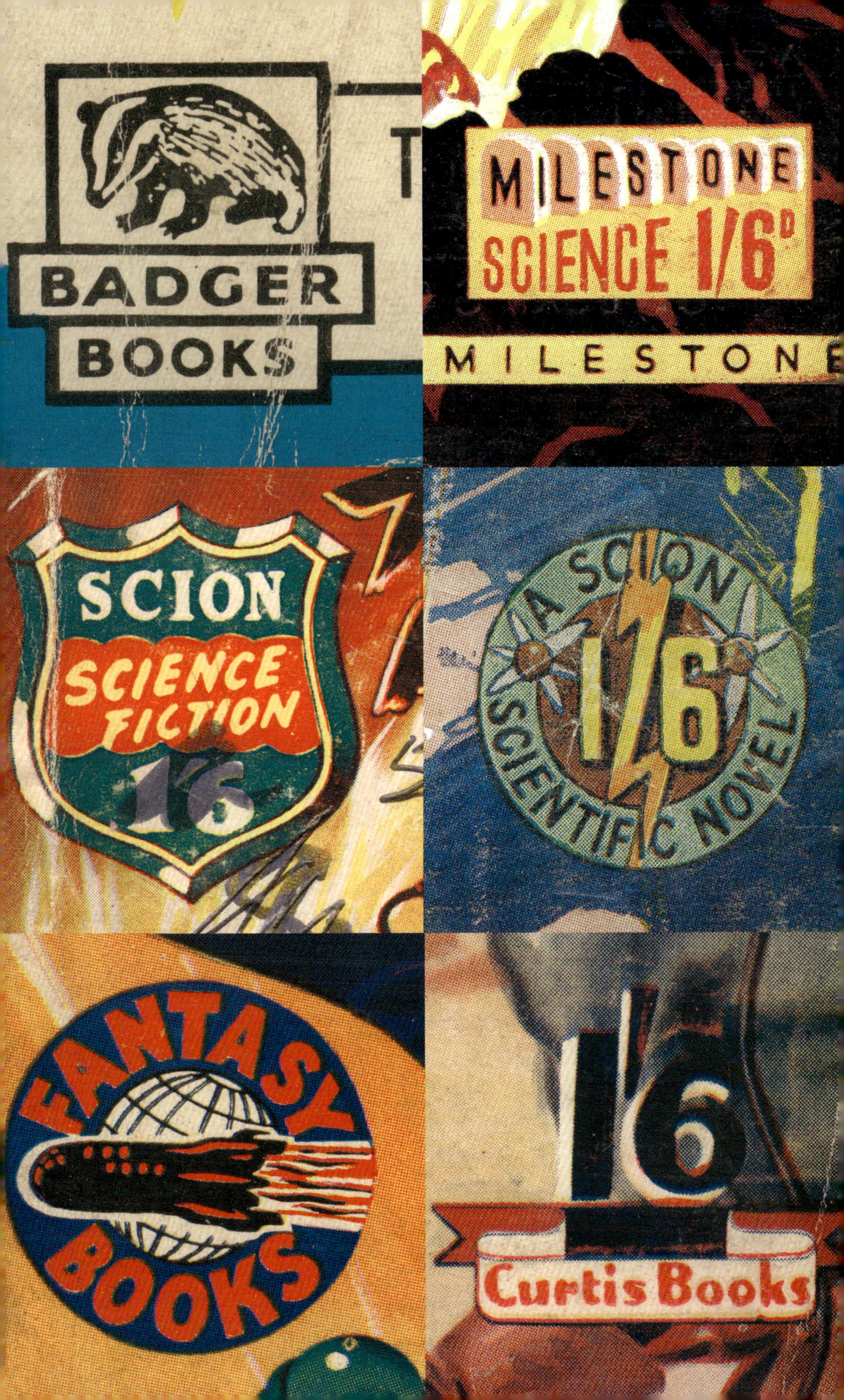
BADGER BOOKS
MILESTONE SCIENCE 1/6d
MILESTONE
SCION SCIENCE FICTION 1/6
A SCION SCIENTIFIC NOVEL 1/6
FANTASY BOOKS
1/6
Curtis Books

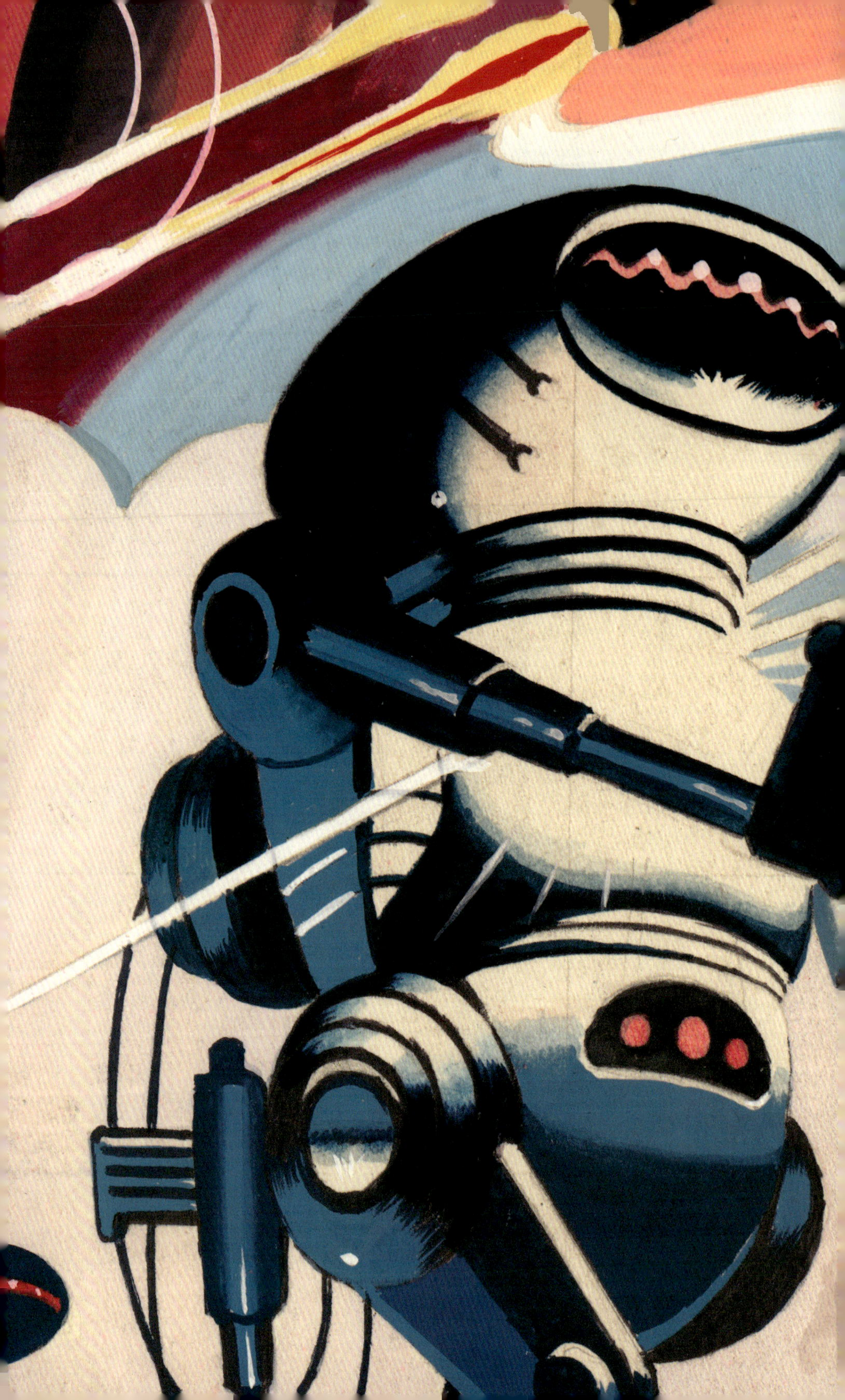

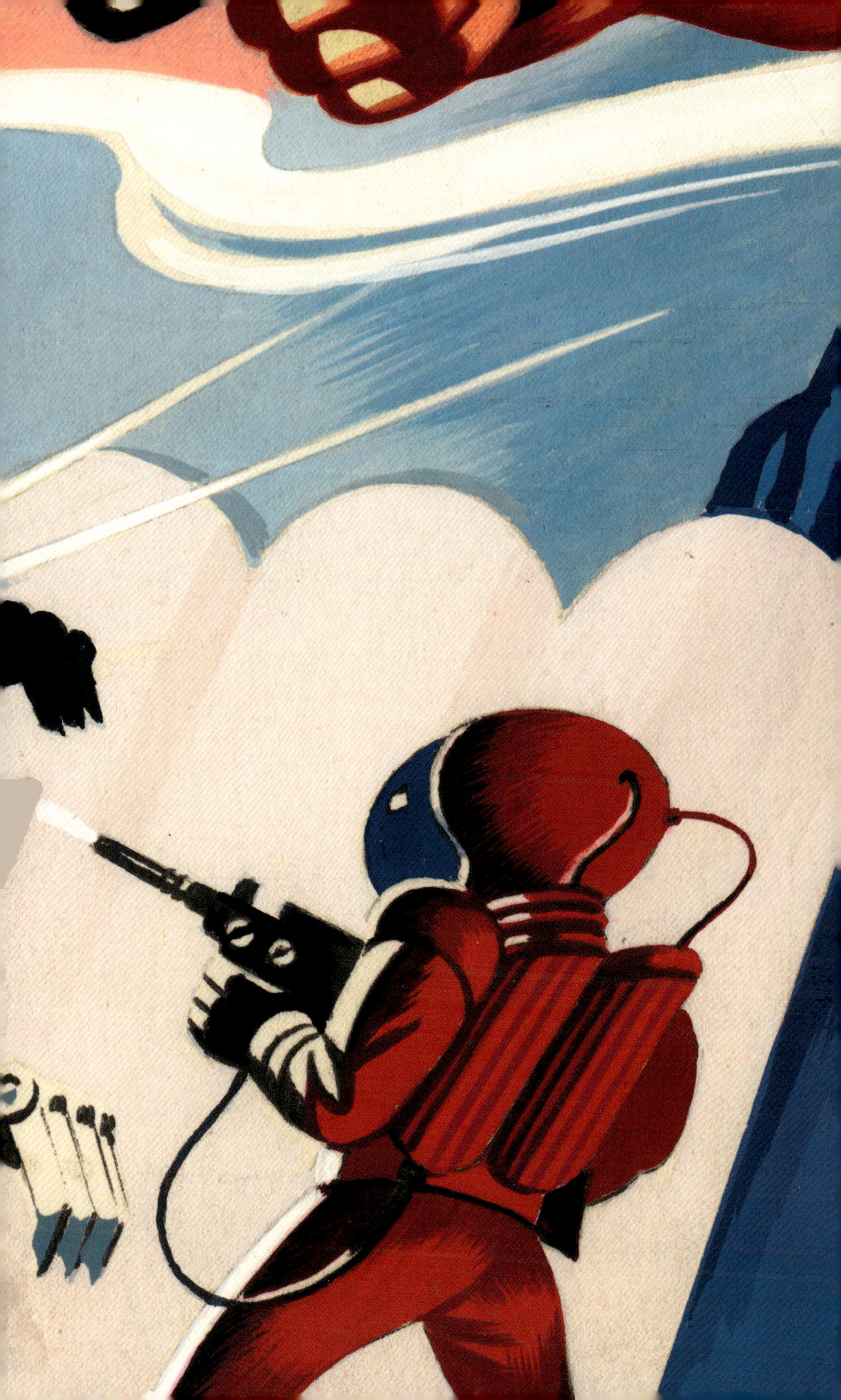

FOREWORD by STEVE HOLLAND

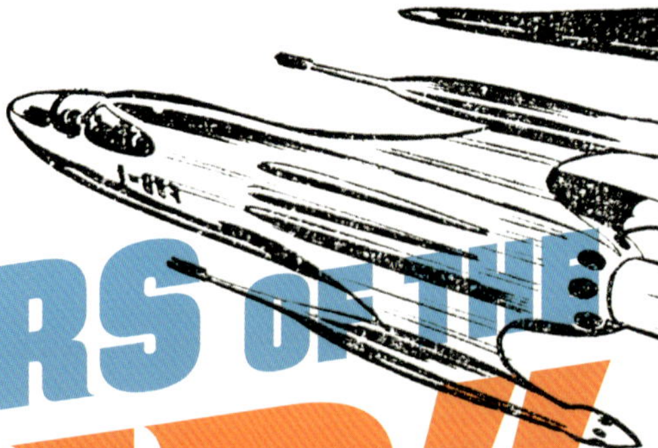

"CRUISERS OF THE VOID"

FLYING FACTORIES AND HAND-CRAFTED SPACESHIPS

"A narrow football of steel, the Inter-Planetary Vessel Arcturus stood upright in her berth in the dock like an egg in its cup. A hundred feet across and a hundred and seventy feet deep was that gigantic bowl, its walls supported by the structural steel and concrete of the dock and lined with hard-packed bumper-layers of hemp and fibre. High into the air extended the upper half of the ship of space—a sullen grey expanse of fifty-inch hardened steel armour, curving smoothly upward to a needle prow. Countless hundreds of fine vertical scratches marred every inch of her surface, and here and there the stubborn metal was grooved and scored to a depth of inches—each scratch and score the record of an attempt of some wandering cosmic body to argue the right-of-way with the stupendous mass of that man-made cruiser of the void."

Now *that's* a spaceship. Back in 1974, my eyes were firmly set on the future – BBC television's *Tomorrow's World* was introducing us to digital watches, and presenter James Burke was predicting the widespread use of home computers. The steady progress of space exploration would, I was certain, give us regular trips to the Moon and Mars by the time I was old enough to buy a ticket.

My 25p pocket money (more if I did some slave labour mowing the lawn or weeding the vegetables) was already stretched when I spotted a new magazine on the shelf at the village newsagents: *Speed & Power*. Two jets flew over a speedboat on the cover and, inside, there were heavily illustrated articles on cars, planes, boats and trains. But what really grabbed my attention were the illustrations that accompanied a reprint of an Arthur C. Clarke short story, *Summertime on Icarus*. An astronaut in a tiny space pod crashes onto the rugged surface of an asteroid. I had to wait a fortnight to discover if he survived the approaching sunrise that threatened to burn him to a cinder.

Two weeks later, *Into the Comet* was illustrated by the lumpiest spaceship I'd ever seen. Michael Whittlesea's illustration looked like an uprooted factory: clusters of rocket tubes and vast, bulky habitat blocks. No surface was free of antennae or the interlaced spider-web of spokes and struts. Lettering adorned the hull like the decals from an Airfix Spitfire.

School was a bus ride away, but sometimes I'd cycle, save the bus fare, and use it to buy books from J. H. Clarke's, where I discovered Chris Foss and the illustrators who followed his comet-like overthrow of sixties abstract British sf paperback art.

Foss also painted lumpy spaceships. They looked like battleships in space, bristling with weapons, or pods, or rockets. Between these covers there was a pulp boom – novels by authors who had debuted in the thirties were being reprinted, which introduced me to the *Lensmen* and *Skylark* novels of E. E. "Doc" Smith, the *Legion of Space* series by Jack Williamson, and the crew of

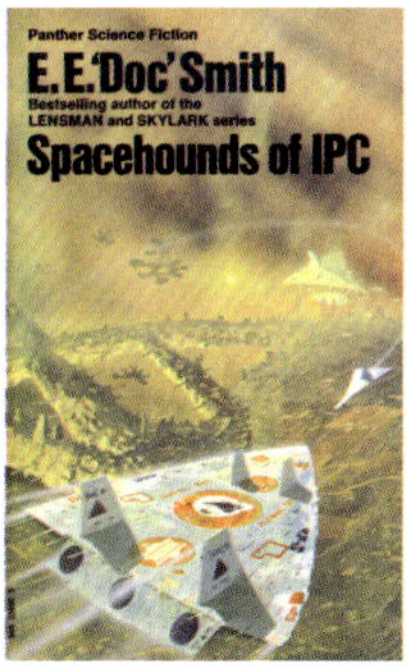

1

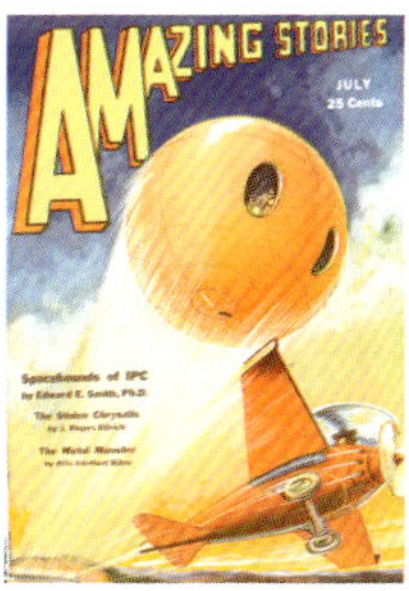

2

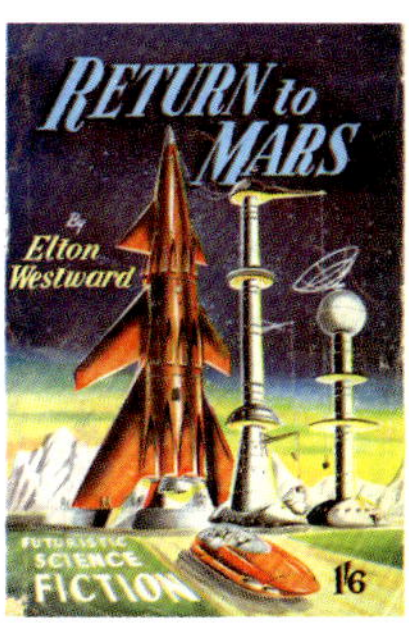

3

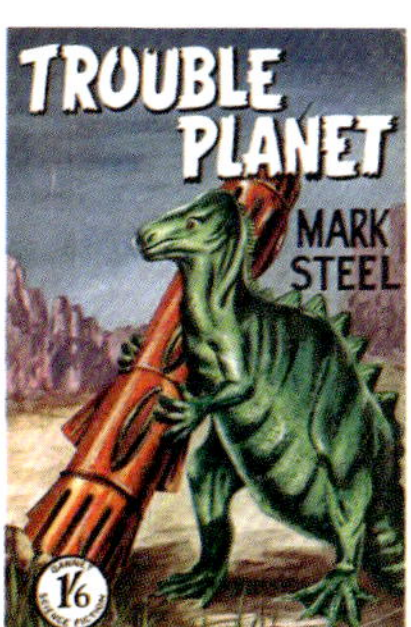

4

the Space Beagle and A. E. Van Vogt. Foss's covers for Van Vogt led me to his work on James Blish's *Cities in Flight,* to Asimov's *Foundation* series, and the discovery of sf magazines via poster-mag *Science Fiction Monthly*.

The paragraph quoted above is from E. E. "Doc" Smith's epic *Spacehounds of IPC* [1], first published in *Amazing Stories* way back in July 1931 [2, art by Leo Morey]. It opens with the IPV *Arcturus* heading out to Mars. The pilot and assistants run through safety checks and tests to make sure the vast space liner will reach its destination.

Compare this, from the pages of Elton Westward's *Return to Mars* [3, art by Gordon C. Davies], published 23 years later:

"Lars Denmoon gave the big nut on the starboard strut a final turn, then dropped the wrench, sat down on the tool-box he found right behind him, and craned his neck to look up at the shining sides of Brent Sellers' ship. She was enormous; she was swell, and she'd gone through her space trials like a well-trained animal—only much more intelligently."

Our hero is literally tightening nuts and bolts on a home-made spaceship, hand-crafted by two twenty-six-year-olds, that is meant to carry a crew to Mars. Reaching the red planet, the ship swoops over the red dust of a flat plain and settles gently on anti-grav engines amongst the knee-high red grass. Brent and Lars, who have taken along a couple of blondes to assist them, crush out their cigarettes, drop lightweight, self-assembly jeeps to the ground and are soon kicking up red dust with their jet motors as they purr along a Martian road.

This was *not* the kind of science fiction I would recommend to anyone. The paucity of ideas, the dismal plotting and writing, and the faux American dialogue will stop you in your dusty red tracks and make you wonder how something so terrible could be foisted on the public.

The *cover,* on the other hand, promises so much. A robust red rocket sits on its tail, three sets of fins sweeping back like a modern-day jet-fighter. A sleek car with no visible wheels floats towards it. A gantry tower has swung aside. Against a backdrop of icy mountains, gleaming in the sunrise – or sunset – tiny men are about to climb up a ladder into the rocket. Never, you might think, has a cover promised so much, and a novel delivered so little.

Um . . . actually, there are dozens more that deliver in similar tiny measures. I'm a science fiction fan, and I'll defend the genre ferociously, but in the pages of this book I spy a fair number of titles that are indefensible. Their only saving grace is the colourful, often magnificent cover that disguises a worthless story, churned out to earn a living by an author with little knowledge of science fiction.

Occasionally this worked in reverse: a novel of some merit might lurk behind a cover so utterly inappropriate that it would put a potential reader off. I will let you decide whether Mark Steel's *Trouble Planet* [4, art by Gerald Facey] is better or worse for having a dinosaur attacking a spaceship on the cover, there being no such scene in the book.

Brian Aldiss complained that 19 out of 20 paperback editions of his novel *Non-Stop* featured a spaceship on the cover, which undercut the whole point of the story – that the characters are not aware they are trapped inside a starship.

I'm in two minds about this. My youthful desire to discover what was behind the often interchangeable paperback covers of the seventies meant that I was exposed to a range of science fiction authors I might not have otherwise read. John Wyndham and Ursula Le Guin shared the same cover artist, although *Stowaway to Mars* and *The Left Hand of Darkness* are worlds apart as novels.

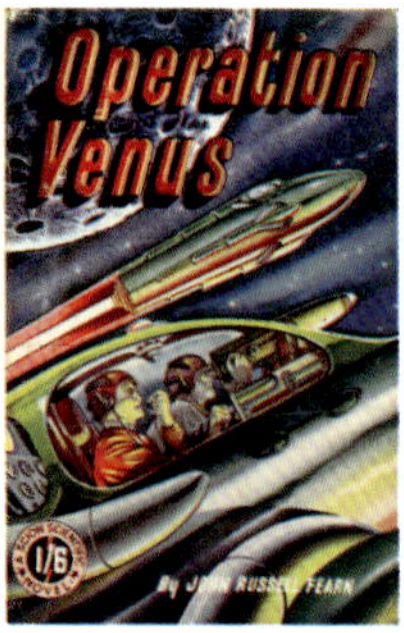

5

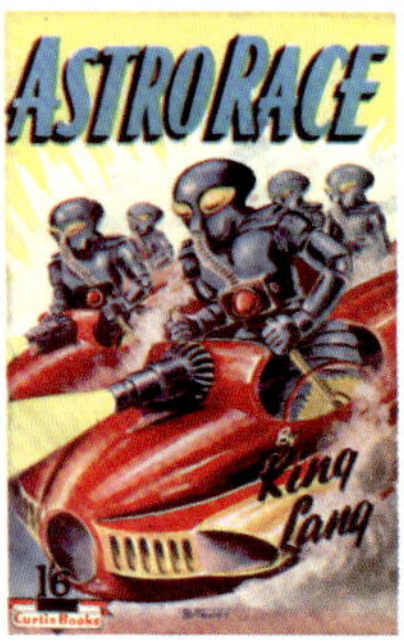

6

Indeed, I should add that the guy who painted the covers to many a book by Arthur C. Clarke and Robert A. Heinlein was the very same artist whose cover for *Return to Mars* outshone its contents so greatly. Gordon C. Davies straddled both the literary and cheap ends of the market, and his colourful covers rescued a great many novels from being entirely worthless. (Fair warning: as you work your way through this book, marvelling at Davies' many covers, you will eventually reach Bryan Berry's *Dread Visitor*, which is a rare stinker.)

Of all the artists of those cheaply produced paperbacks of the fifties, the finest was Ron Turner. Plenty of praise has been heaped on Turner's shoulders – and rightly so. He was my gateway artist into these novels. A school project took me to Dagenham, where the Science Fiction Foundation housed its library at North East London Polytechnic. Browsing the shelves I stumbled upon Vargo Statten, the pen name of prolific pulpster John Russell Fearn, and Turner's richly painted images: a spacesuited man shooting a dinosaur-like alien, sleek vehicles flying over a futuristic city, all in bold, bright colours. Others were understated and evocative, Turner being one of the few artists to have access to the novels he was illustrating, which allowed him to compose more expressive, abstract covers and restrained montages, hinting at more thoughtful content.

There was no such subtlety in the covers of Norman Light. Almost garish in comparison, Light painted space battles like no other artist — light beams slicing through space and spacecraft, fire flaming into the void. His covers showed plenty of invention – as a fan of science fiction, he was well versed in the pulp tradition. It is a shame that Light was first sidelined into comics (as was Turner) and then into the pub trade, as he could well have become one of Britain's finest sf artists.

Both Turner and Light embraced the pulp aesthetic with creativity and technical skill, while others would appear to have knocked out covers with little consideration for an adult audience. In 1950, a relaxation in paper supply caused a flurry of activity from publishers already flooding the crime and western markets. The sf magazine *New Worlds* was launched in 1949, and a handful of paperback novels pointed the way. In April 1950 John Spencer launched four interchangeable magazines at the same time as *Eagle*, home of Dan Dare, the comic that reached a million schoolboys. Scion published John Russell Fearn's *Operation Venus* [5, art by Ron Turner] in May, before Fearn became Vargo Statten, and the floodgates opened.

Sales must have made science fiction seem an attractive prospect; between them Curtis Warren, Hamilton & Co. and Gaywood Distributors published a dozen sf novels by the end of the year, and that number exploded in 1951. Low rates of pay meant that they were authored by newcomers and hacks already used to hammering out a manuscript to order. A contemporary review by fan Ken Slater summed up the flood: "This sort of stuff will give sf a bad name."

Science fiction's reputation may have been further tarnished by Gerald Facey and Ray Theobald's juvenile and sometimes poorly executed covers. Theobald seemed to struggle with the human form, but could occasionally produce a striking image, for example *Astro Race* [6] and *Task Flight*, both by King Lang, while the best that could be said of Facey is that his work was colourful. This may be unfair, as Facey was actually a capable artist when working outside the field, eventually turning to fine art and abstract landscapes.

Facey worked for the early John Spencer magazines, which were radically improved when Norman Light, Ron Turner and Ron Embleton began producing covers. The content, on the other hand, did not. A one-man operation, the publisher switched to novels, a small team of writers pounding out book after

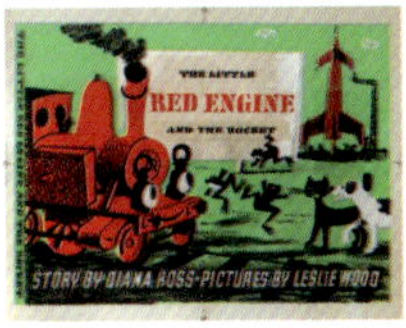

7

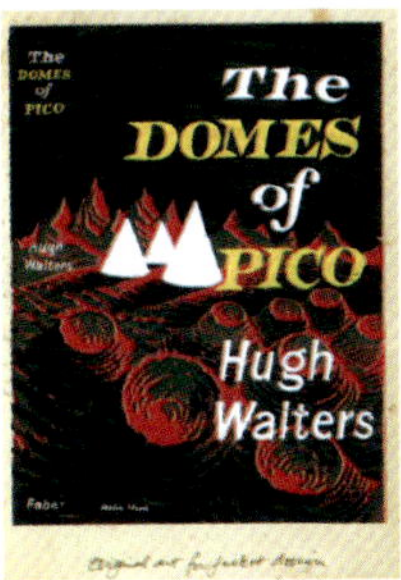

8

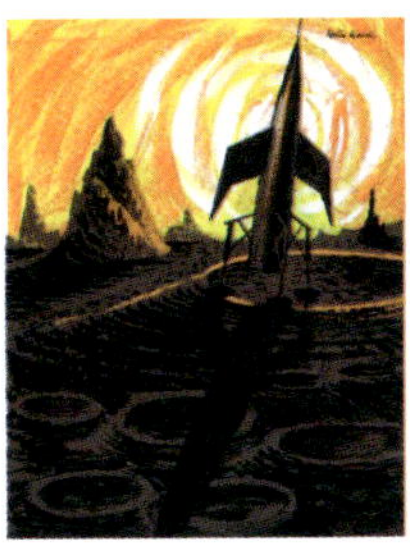

9

book to fill the company's schedule. Under the John Spencer, Cobra Books and Badger Books imprints, Spencers published some 700 novels and collections, plus non-fiction books, magazines and comics. Almost 500 of them were by just three authors: John S. Glasby, R. Lionel Fanthorpe and John F. Watt. Badger's chief artist was Henry Fox, whose striking images gave the novels a uniformity that most publishers lacked.

Another fifties survivor, Brown Watson, published over 1,400 books under their Digit Books imprint between 1956 and 1967, mixing originals with reprints. There was little quality control over the original sf novels, which meant Asimov, Van Vogt and Aldiss rubbed shoulders with Luan Ranzetta and Graeme de Timms. Luan — her real name the more down-to-earth Valerie — was one of only a handful of female writers penning science fiction for the original paperback market. Others included Doreen Ellis, Mildred Danforth and Ellen Redknap, although the extensive use of pen names may hide others. Digit relied heavily on the artistic talents of its art director, Robert A. Osborne, who (unlike Gordon Davies) never really escaped the cheaper end of the market, although RAO, as he often signed himself, also worked for Corgi. His early work, as "Leroi", made distinctive use of the airbrush on spaceships and robots.

One of the best artists to emerge from the rash of cheap paperbacks was John Richards, who earned his spurs in the pages of *Authentic Science Fiction* before becoming art director for Corgi. Their range of reprints was far more selective, and Richards' often abstract covers graced the works of Ray Bradbury, Charles Eric Maine, Richard Matheson and Arthur C. Clarke.

The juvenile market is represented by Patrick Moore, Angus MacVicar and Hugh Walters, with covers by Patricia Cullen, the emerging talent of David A. Hardy, and the versatile *Punch* and *Little Red Engine* illustrator Leslie Wood [7, original art for *The Little Red Engine and the Rocket*; 8, *The Domes of Pico* and 9, *Operation Columbus* by Hugh Walters].

The artwork collected here is sometimes vivid and gauche, at other times expressive and eloquent. It represents an era when science fiction was finding its feet in the UK, unsure whether it was a juvenile or adult medium, and, if the two could coexist, where the line between them should be drawn. Publishers with no clue bumped alongside those who were trying to raise the genre to the more sophisticated heights of the American market. To my eye, the more symbolic graphic covers of the late sixties, featuring close-ups of light bulbs or oscilloscope sine waves (shown at the end of this volume) were no match for even the gaudiest illustrations of the fifties. Thankfully they were soon replaced by the work of Chris Foss, Peter Elson, Tony Roberts, Colin Hay, Angus McKie, Bob Layzell, Jim Burns, Chris Moore and others. Like those covers of the cheap paperbacks, the gargantuan spaceships and towering cities were used interchangeably, but young fans like myself, we didn't care. We soon learned that the spaceship was just a gateway image into a world of imagination.

The wildest science fiction dreams of our youth are unlikely to come to pass. You are more likely to be replaced by a robot at your workplace than murdered by one that travels through time; inter-dimensional invaders are going to find our resources exhausted, the lush forests burned down, the ice caps melted and the oceans full of microplastics; and bikini-clad women would freeze to death instantly in the vacuum of space instead of wriggling seductively when kidnapped by bug-eyed aliens.

My chances of a trip to Mars grow more distant with time, but there are a couple of tech billionaires out there, wrenches in hand, tightening the nuts on their new spacecraft, who just might make commercial space flight possible in my lifetime. I may need to mow a few more lawns and weed a few extra vegetable patches to raise the ticket price, but sign me up!

Follow Steve Holland over at his Bear Alley blog, where he delves into the secret history of British science fiction paperbacks and comics.

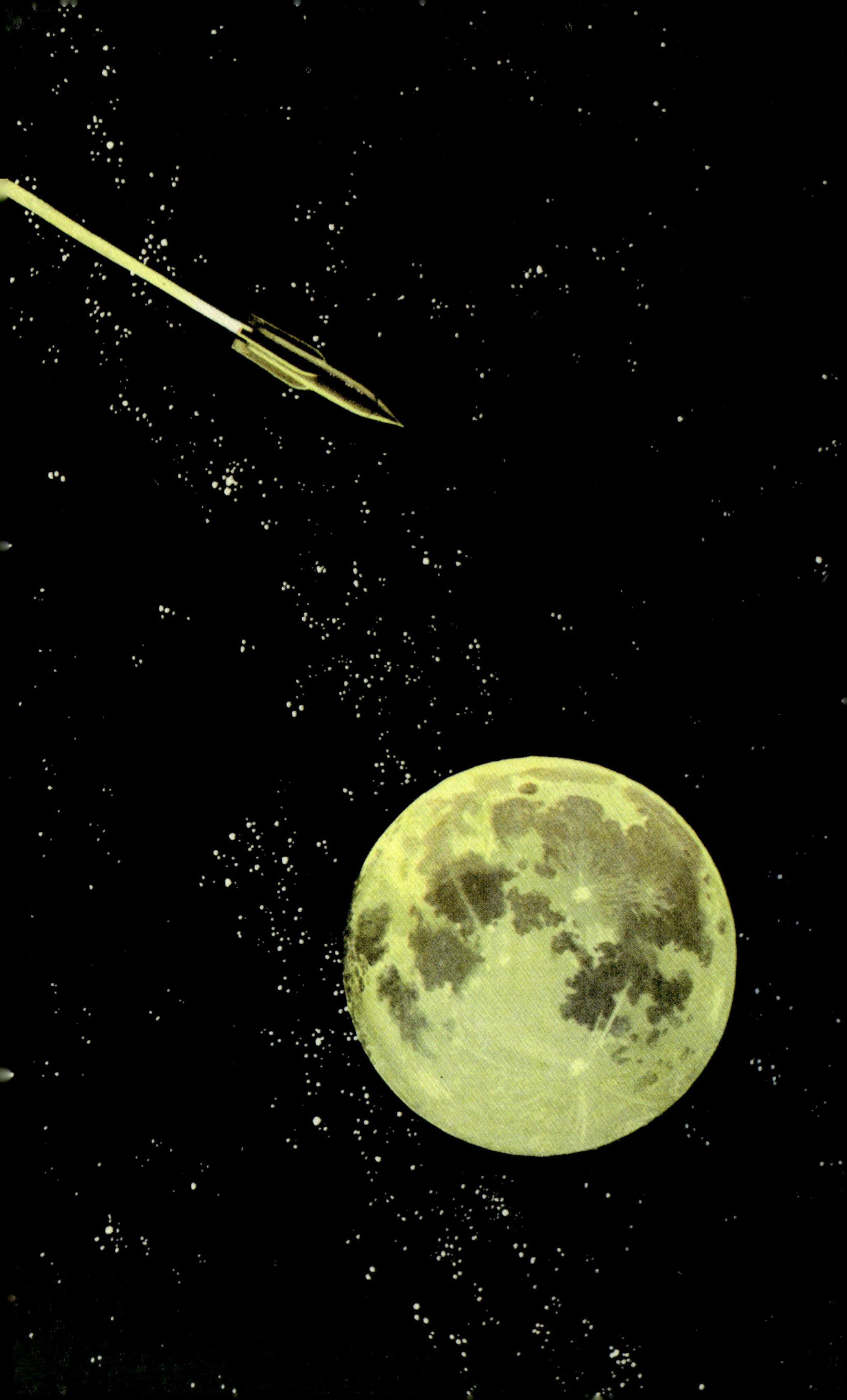

HIS RAYGUN SPAT ATOMIC FIRE...”

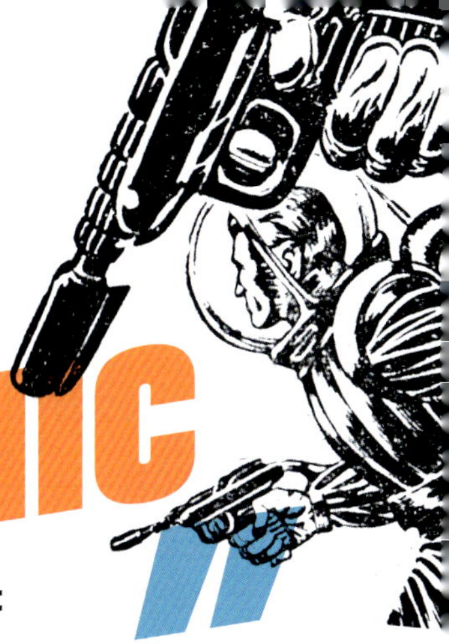

NTRODUCTION by RIAN HUGHES

BRITISH SCIENCE FICTION BOOK COVER ART

As an avid reader of the coming-of-age tales of Andre Norton and the transformative hard science fiction of Arthur C. Clarke, I was already a sf aficionado when I was given Robert Holdstock's *Encyclopaedia of Science Fiction* (Octopus, 1975) as a youngster. For me, this was the book that laid out the history of the genre, in detail, for the first time.

In the margins were small reproductions of vintage magazine and paperback covers, each only around 25mm (1in) high, but still large enough to read the titles of stories I had never read by authors I had never heard of. *The Incubi of Parallel X, The Cosmic Relic, The Woman in Skin 13, Dark Eternity, Planet of the Knob-Heads* and other forgotten literary gems evoked stupendous tales of mind-bending adventure, grand ideas played out on cosmos-sized canvases. Many collectors recall a key event, a trigger that crystallised an interest that would become a lifelong passion – this was to be one of mine. Maybe "passion" is too strong a term, but "hobby" sounds needlessly lacklustre; how one might describe needlework, or golf.

In reality many of these tales were workmanlike at best, and anything of note was later collected into anthologies that save the reader ploughing through pages and pages of rough pulp paper, but of course I didn't know that. Most of those stories I will never read, but years later I would channel that remembered sense of anticipation into my novel *XX*, part of which is told in the typographical and literary style of a mid-sixties Jack Vance or Philip K. Dick serial. Laid out in two columns, just like those magazines, I filled the vacant space after each chapter with an advertisement for the next issue, listing my own imagined stories by fictional authors.

A short while later I came across Brian Aldiss' large-format book *Science Fiction Art* (New English Library, 1975) in a remainder bookshop in Charing Cross Road. Remainder bookshops were a haven for any youngster of limited means interested in comics, science fiction, art or design – for 50 pence you could pick up obscure American titles you'd not find in regular British bookshops, even at full price. Aldiss' book was an overview of the artists who worked or were still working on the science fiction magazines, and included many beautiful full-page reproductions, some larger than the originals. At the back was a gallery of covers – titles that ran for many decades shown alongside other obscure magazines that only lasted an issue or three. These were rare treasures from another time and place, and I had still to see any of them in the flesh.

Then I came across a bookstall in Seven Dials, London. If memory serves, it looked like a converted gipsy carriage: big wheels, wooden shelves of books, and an awning from which magazines hung from bulldog clips. They had a fine selection of comics, American paperbacks from publishers Ace and DAW, and, one day, a copy of *Future Science Fiction* [1, British Edition

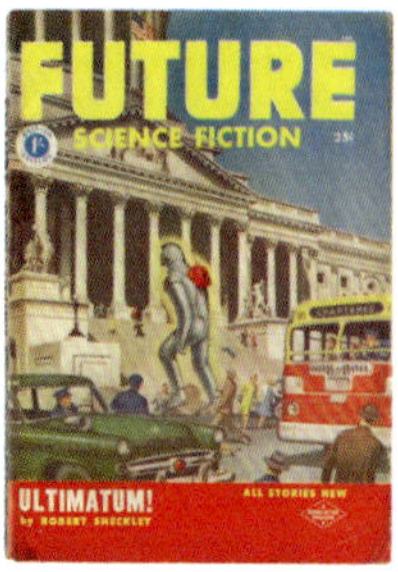

1

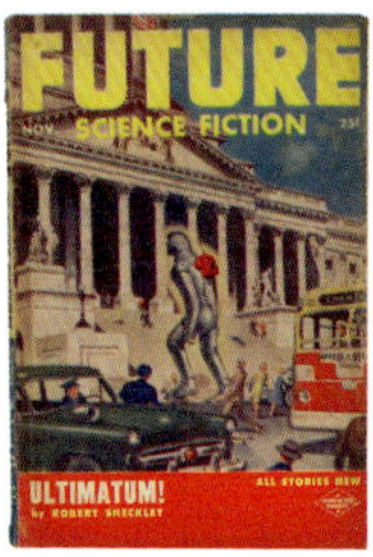

2

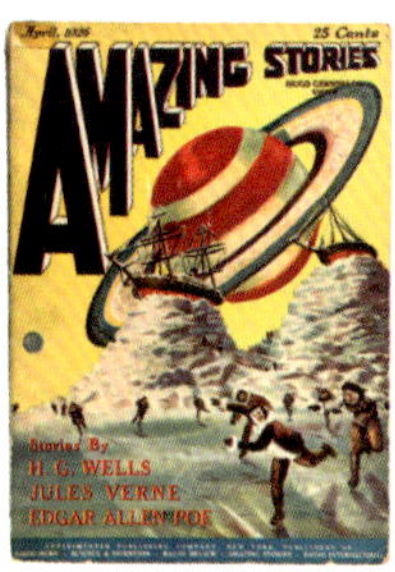

3

Nº14, June 1954, and for comparison 2, the original US edition, Vol. 4 Nº4, November 1953]. This very issue had appeared as a full-page in Aldiss' book, printed twice its original size. It had a cover by Alex Schomburg, in his immediately identifiable clean and precise airbrush style, showing a robot marching up the steps of the Capitol Building. I stood in awe, feeling a thrill course through my extremities. Here, at last, was an original copy of a pulp magazine, exuding a retro-futuristic fifties glamour, an apport from another time and place. I paid two pounds for it.

New York was the birthplace of the modern science fiction magazine, the first issue of Hugo Gernsback's *Amazing Stories* [3] being published in bedsheet-size format back in 1926. It reprinted stories by H. G. Wells and Jules Verne, and had a cover by Frank R. Paul, who would go on to paint the covers for almost all of Gernsback's later magazines – *Science Wonder Stories* [4, Vol. 1 Nº10, March 1930], *Air Wonder Stories* [5, Vol. 1 Nº5, November 1929], the two titles later combined as *Wonder Stories,* and others – for the next thirty-odd years. If his figures could be somewhat stiff and lacking in dynamism, his architecture and hardware were beyond reproach, upholding Gernsback's claims as to the educational and prophetic nature of the genre.

The best regarded of the early pulps was *Astounding* (later *Analog*). Founded in 1930 as *Astounding Stories of Super-Science*, its title morphed over the years from *Astounding Stories* to *Astounding Science Fiction* to (in very small letters) *Astounding* (and in much larger) *Science Fiction* as it incrementally sought to reposition itself as a more literary magazine. Editor John W. Campbell planned to drop "Astounding" entirely, but a new magazine called simply *Science Fiction* beat him to it. The period that begins with Campbell's editorship in 1938 is often referred to as the Golden Age of Science Fiction.

The June 1936 issue [6, art by Howard V. Brown] is notable for the first publication of H. P. Lovecraft's *The Shadow Out of Time,* and contains three evocative black-and-white interior illustrations, also by Brown. An early story by Edgar Rice Burroughs, Arthur C. Clarke or J. G. Ballard can lift the desirability and value of a magazine, but I'm still surprised that later hardback "first" editions of the very same tale can fetch far more – maybe this is due to a particular bias from collectors and dealers. This can also be true of sf paperbacks, in which the cheap edition (often as part of a back-to-back format Ace Double, of which more later) might precede the hardback. Others are sought out for different reasons: the March 1954 issue [7*:* this copy is actually a UK reprint of the October 1953 US edition] features a cover by Kelly Freas that was later adapted for Queen's album *News of the World* (1977).

The story of the science fiction magazine is long and convoluted, and several exhaustive overviews have been written, prime among them Michael Ashley's four-volume *The History of the Science Fiction Magazine* (New English Library, 1977). Suffice to say, from a nascent collector's point of view, I had no idea how large these very early sf magazines were: bedsheet-size is an impressive 216×298mm (8.5×11.75in). The pulps of the forties and fifties were generally smaller at 177×254mm (7×10in), still a reasonable size for an artist to work with; then, sometime in the fifties, most sf magazines shrank to "digest" size – at 140×210mm (5.5×8.25in), it was akin to the switch from LP to CD. Many short-lived magazines appeared in this format, a kind of halfway house between magazine and paperback. These smaller editions were more robust and the paper stock less prone to crumbling around the edges, a perennial problem with the untrimmed pulp format. This made them easier to find, sometimes turning up in jumble sales or Popular Book Centres, though I soon learned that most of these were not

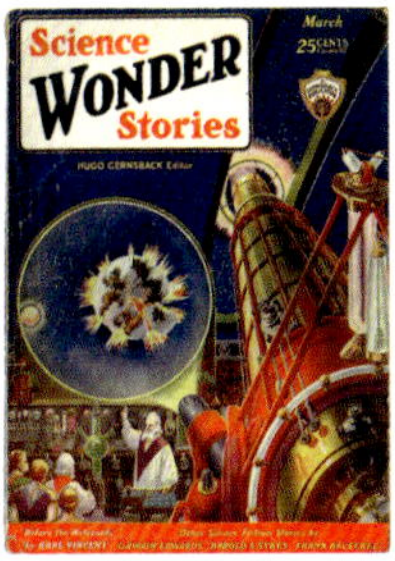

4

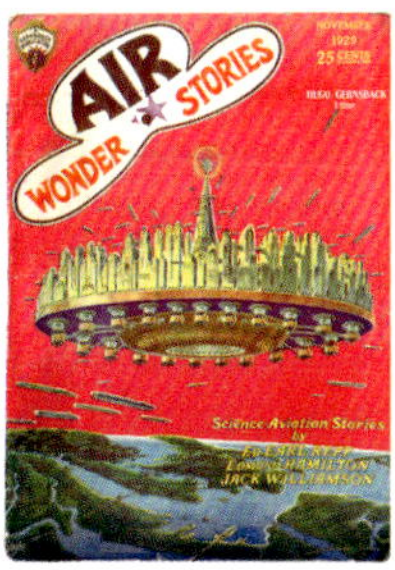

5

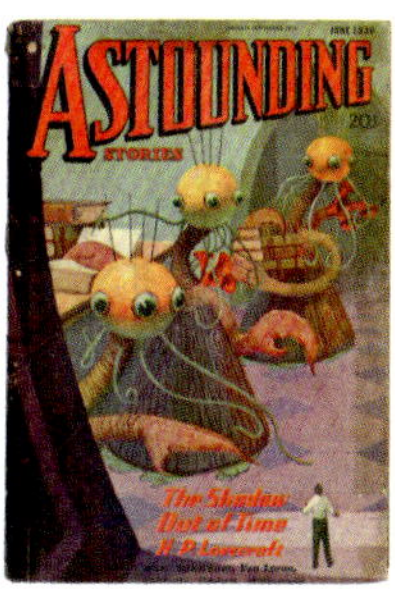

6

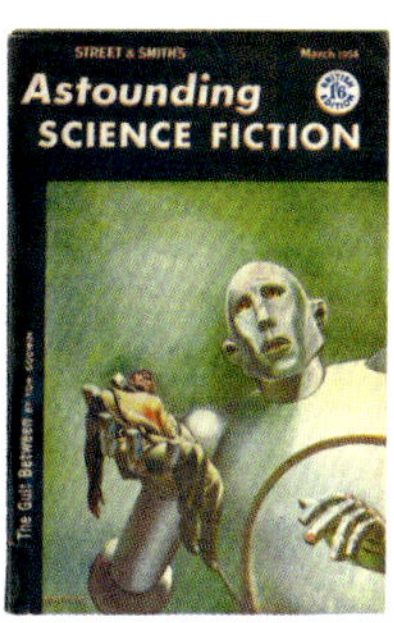

7

original editions but UK reprints, which often omitted stories and are thus of little interest to serious aficionados.

That issue of *Future Science Fiction* [1] was also a UK reprint, though at the time I was too thrilled to care very much. I now have both the UK and the US versions [2], and it is interesting to note that the UK reprint is larger. The date has been replaced by a blue circle with "British Edition" and the price in shillings, but as the plates themselves could not be enlarged the UK reprint has an extra inch or so of illustration that is lost to the crop on the US original. Sometimes the UK reprints are hard to spot, as they often retained the US cents price to give them an air of authenticity. This was especially the case for UK gangster and sleaze paperbacks from the post-war "mushroom" publishers, which would often sport a price in cents alongside a price in shillings even though they were UK originals, not reprints. Other than checking the indicia, the obvious give-away is often the advertisement on the back cover, which might have a coupon with a British address.

Sometime in the early eighties I saw an advertisement for London's Fantasy Centre bookshop in the back of a magazine – probably *Starburst*, or a newspaper-format fanzine. Without a firm idea where it was, a school friend and I took ourselves off to find it one Saturday. Walking up the Holloway Road for what seemed like an age, my friend gave up and turned back. I walked on a while longer, and there it was – a vast emporium of vintage sf books and magazines. It was, and remains, my favourite bookshop of all time, and when it finally closed in 2010 or thereabouts, it was the end of a regular pilgrimage I'd try and make at least once a year. The front of the shop was stocked with more recent paperbacks, but a section at the back was given over to vintage magazines: long runs of *Analog, Fantasy and Science Fiction* or *Amazing Stories,* most of which were well out of my price range, and a selection of Ace Doubles, the unusual back-to-back double-novel paperbacks with a cover on each side that ran from 1952 to 1973 (then to 1975 in a more traditional single-cover format). Soho's Vintage Magazine Centre, originally at Cambridge Circus, was pricier – I recall coveting a copy of *Scientific Detective Monthly,* a short-lived Gernsback experiment that managed fifteen issues beginning in 1930. Their UK reprint copies of *Startling Stories* and *Astounding Science Fiction* were not much cheaper.

I graduated from my design degree, began working as a comic artist, graphic designer, typographer and illustrator, and found myself with a bit more money to spare. I'd pick up the odd item in second-hand bookshops or provincial market stalls, or acquire cast-offs – Dave Gibbons, the artist on *Watchmen,* kindly gave me his old copies of *Astounding Science Fiction.* Fast-forward to the present day and many of these can now be bought in clean condition for under ten pounds on eBay. For a magazine from the fifties, that's something of a bargain. A modern-day design magazine might be more expensive.

I'd acquire more vintage paperbacks and magazines, usually in ones or twos, from a market stall shelf or a cardboard box on the floor of a bookshop in Worthing or Bath or Brighton. Dealers at book fairs might have bigger selections, either bagged and labelled or just piled up with detective paperbacks, comics, vintage T&A or Sexton Blake digests. But, on rare occasions, I'd come across entire collections for sale. This happened to me recently in Charing Cross Road – usually I find that these centrally located bookshops, right on the tourist thoroughfares, have been picked clean of anything remotely interesting. Then, on my way to a book signing at Forbidden Planet (the sf and comic shop, for which I designed the logo way back when) I noticed an early copy of *Amazing Stories* high up on a shelf in a shop window, something I've only seen once or twice in my life. Inside were a couple of shelves' worth of pulps and books, ranging from the thirties to the

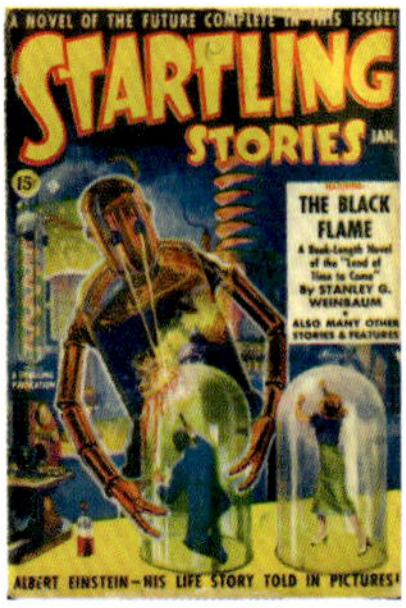

8

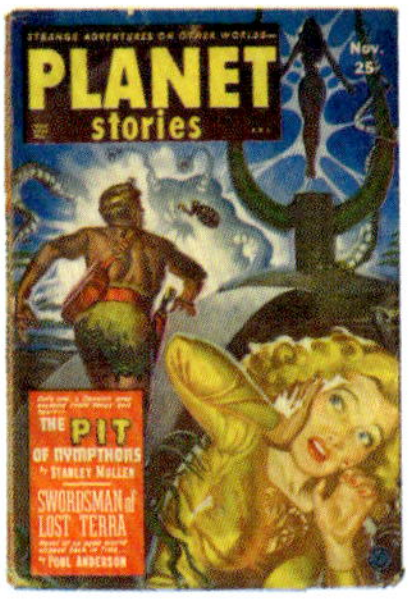

9

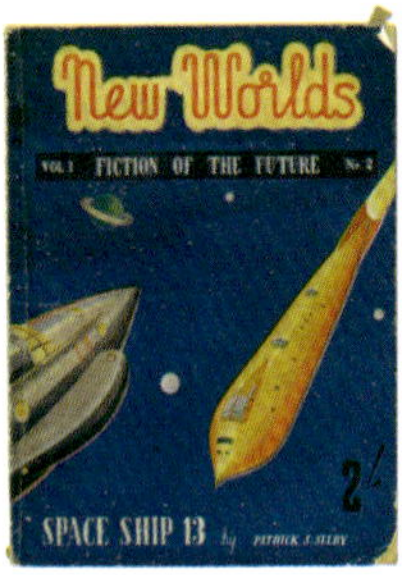

10

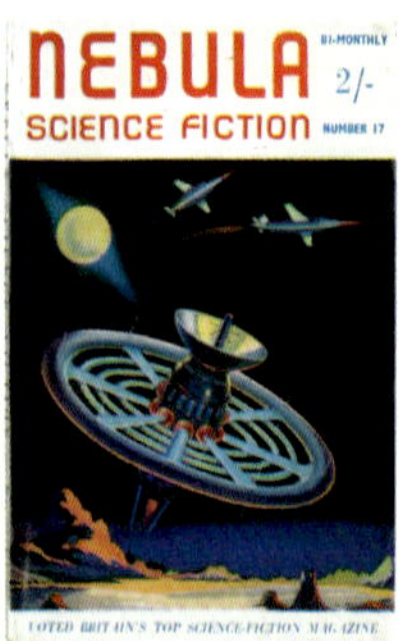

11

fifties, in reasonable condition at a reasonable price. Taking a selection to the till, I asked if they had any more.

They did. Downstairs, an entire room was given over to them – yard upon yard, covering pretty much every title ever published. Given that I was supposed to be signing books in fifteen minutes just up the road, I made a swift appraisal and bought three big bags' worth – copies of *Startling Stories* [8, the first issue, January 1939, art by Howard V. Brown], *Amazing Stories, Astounding Science Fiction, Planet Stories* [9, Vol. 5 Nº3, 1951, art by Allan Anderson], third-rate UK paperbacks from John Spencer & Co., and a smattering of other, lesser-known titles. I have a recurring dream in which I come across some motherlode, but circumstances mean I have no time to look through them all – this was that dream!

I went back a week later for a second, more thorough pass, and picked out another thirty or so from several hundred. I'm sure I missed out on some of the choicest items, but any one of the issues would have been a celebrated find in other circumstances. This surfeit of wonders can present a problem – whereas one or two, even in less than perfect condition, might be picked up without much thought, encountering hundreds or even thousands at once can make even the most dedicated reexamine their collecting criteria. I'm not much of a completist – most of the magazines and books I buy seduce me because of the cover art or design, and in cases like this you can't buy them all (and you probably wouldn't want to). So once you've recovered from the initial excitement, a peculiar readjustment comes upon you – you pass over things you'd otherwise jump at, and your selection criteria all of a sudden become more stringent. Rarity imparts a certain desirability which availability tends to undermine – or, I've come to realise, it refocusses your attention on what's important: the inherent properties of the item itself. An interest that began with a genuine love for the source material, honed through the pleasures of the hunt, needs recalibration in this world of easy internet access. Ordering that last issue online from across the other side of the world means it arrives in a padded envelope, delivered directly to your door, without any of the backstory, without the thrill of discovery in some out-of-the-way bookshop or market stall. Where's the romance in that? eBay has, for the most part, both raised availability and pushed down prices – though certain items now attract the attention of a bigger pool of buyers, some with much deeper pockets.

The chap at the till told me they were still pricing up the collection and to come back the next day when they had rotated their stock. I did – and true to his word, the basement room had been refilled with even more books and magazines. This time they were mostly the smaller, digest-sized issues that long-running titles like *Astounding* and *Amazing* adopted from the mid-fifties, newer titles such as *Galaxy* or *Fantasy and Science Fiction* being printed in this format from the outset. Again, hundreds of issues presented a problem of excess, so I applied four vague criteria: the cover artwork, the authors within, the condition (no-one likes rusty staples or flakes of brittle paper in their lap), and the issue number. I picked up the first six or seven issues of *The Magazine of Fantasy* (retitled *The Magazine of Fantasy and Science Fiction* from issue 2, it is still being published today), *Cosmos, Fantasy Fiction, Imagination – Stories of Science and Fantasy, Venture Science Fiction, If, Galaxy* and lesser-known titles like *Satellite Science Fiction, Orbit, Beyond, Fantastic Universe, Other Worlds* and *Universe. Venture* (from the same publisher as *Fantasy and Science Fiction*) also warranted an English edition, which had undistinguished typographic covers. *Satellite Science Fiction* can be treasured for the covers by Alex Schomburg, while even the pulpier titles could occasionally feature the likes of Ray Bradbury or Philip K. Dick.

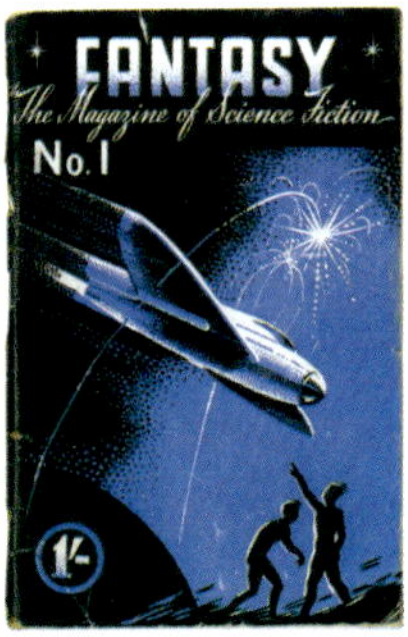

12

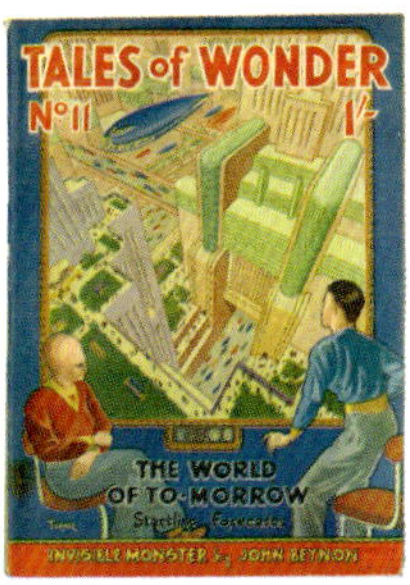

13

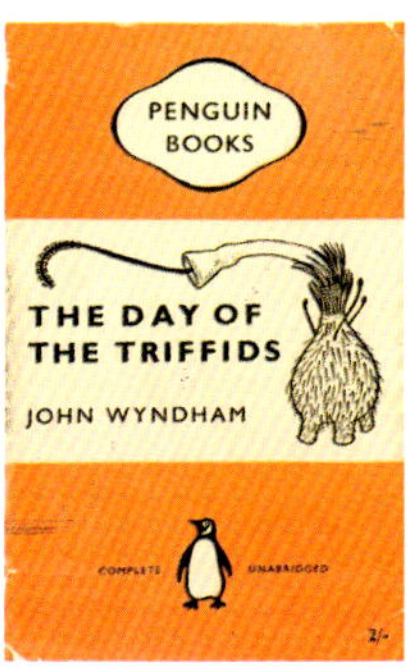

14

Most of these were US editions. In the UK, the magazine market was always much smaller, with paperbacks taking up the majority of publishers' lists by the mid-sixties. Originally edited by John Carnell, *New Worlds* [10, Vol. 1 Nº2, October 1946] evolved from an earlier fanzine into a pioneering digest-sized magazine. Edited by Michael Moorcock from 1964 to around 1970, it eventually became a paperback anthology. Other long-running titles with interesting cover art were *Science-Fantasy,* which often featured the mid-century modern, surrealist influenced art of Brian Lewis (who was also a well-respected comic artist) and *Nebula* [11, Nº17, July 1956], many of whose covers were painted in a sleek airbrush style by James Stark. Edited by Walter Gillings, the two-colour cover for the first issue of *Fantasy – The Magazine of Science Fiction* [12, Nº1] is a more sober English affair, lacking the manly drama and Hollywood glamour of an Earle Bergey *Thrilling Wonder Stories* or an Allen Anderson *Planet Stories* cover. This may be why it ran for just three issues, from December 1946 to August 1947. Publication of *Tales of Wonder* [13, Nº11, Summer 1940, art by Harry Turner] was interrupted by WW2, but it still ran early stories by John Beynon, later to find mainstream success under the name John Wyndham with *The Midwich Cuckoos* and *The Day of the Triffids* [14, the Penguin edition in the classic Edward Young design]. The title also published Arthur C. Clarke's first work.

The origin of the modern paperback format is often traced back to 1932 and German publisher Albatross, whose first tranche of affordably priced titles included works by James Joyce, Virginia Woolf and Aldous Huxley. Hans Mardersteig, then art director of the Italian printers Mondadori, designed their covers using clean, consistent typography (Futura, centred), no illustrations, and colour-coded genres – yellow for psychological novels and essays, orange for short stories and humour, red for adventure and crime – innovations that proved enormously popular.

This did not go unnoticed in Britain. Allen Lane, director of The Bodley Head, proposed setting up a joint venture with Albatross. When this proved to be unworkable due to copyright issues, he instead launched Penguin Books, which borrowed many of Albatross' ideas – the seabird logo, the size of the books, the modern typographic design and the colour-coding. Albatross were also instrumental in publishing genre novels in the format via the Albatross Crime Club and Albatross Mystery Club imprints, both in close collaboration with UK publisher Collins.

However, the UK's experiments with affordable paperback novels (as opposed to serialised fiction periodicals or hardbacks) go back further to *The Boys' Friend Library,* a small, squarish format (around the size of today's *Commando Picture Library*) title founded by W. H. "Willy" Back in September 1906 [pages 37-40]. Published by Amalgamated Press, four novels were issued each month, mostly reprinted from Amalgamated's weekly story-papers *Champion, Pluck, Chums, Magnet, The Modern Boy* and others, though it also ran original material and novels licensed from other publishers. The series ran to 1,440 titles over two numbered series, and as well as science fiction contained the usual boy's paper mix of school stories, crime, mystery and adventure. Initially running to 144 pages, then dropping to 120 and eventually 96 pages, they still managed to contain 60,000 words of tiny print by well-known authors like Jules Verne, Leslie Charteris (creator of the Saint), Biggles' W. E. Johns and Billy Bunter's Charles Hamilton. Wartime paper shortages eventually ended its run in 1940.

It was after WW2 that the paperback format really came into its own in the UK. The post-war boom saw a slew of opportunistic "mushroom" publishers, fired up by the availability of cheaper paper, pump out hundreds of gangster, romance, sleaze, western and science fiction paperbacks. This period has been thoroughly documented by Steve Holland in *The*

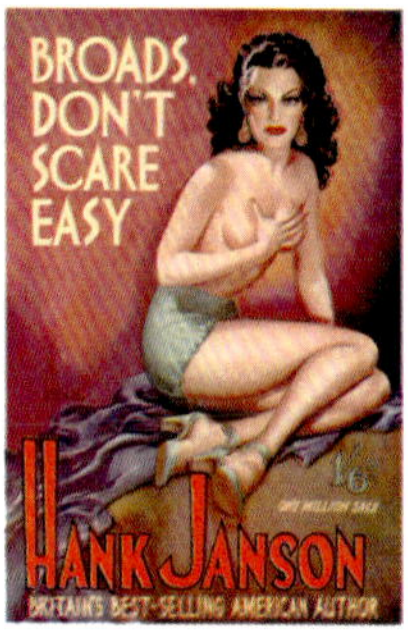

15

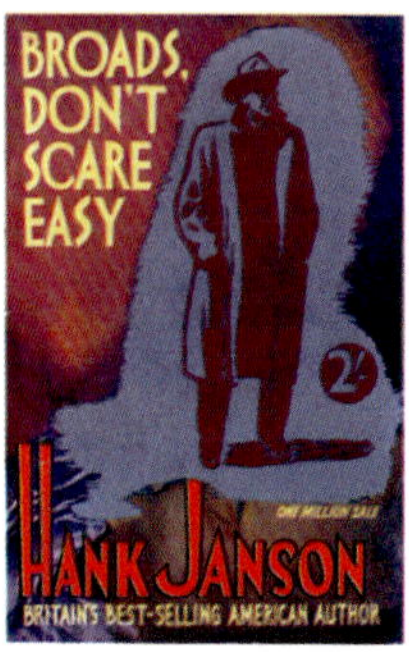

16

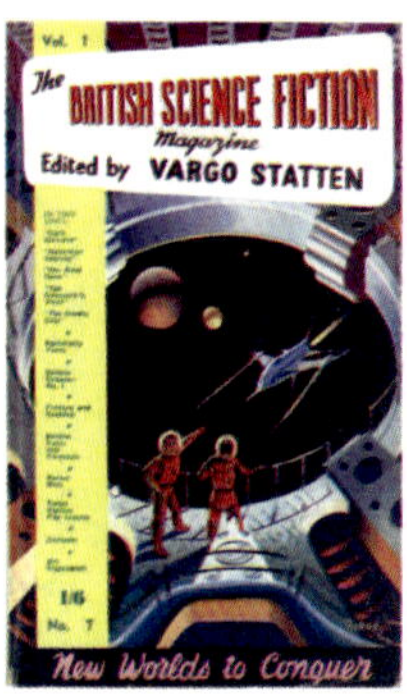

17

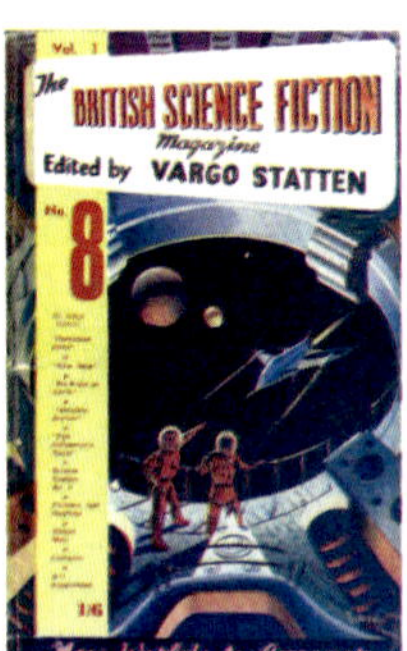

18

Mushroom Jungle (Zardoz Books), to which I refer readers whose taste might stretch to authors with names like Jeff Bogar, Jack Cairo, Johnny Dark, Dirk Saxon, Michael Storme and Ace Capelli. I first encountered this publishing phenomenon through two series, both notorious for different reasons. The Hank Janson books, produced to fill the demand for hard-boiled American fiction in a Chandleresque vein, were reputedly written by a "tough Chicago reporter", in reality the prolific and British Stephen Daniel Frances. Beginning with *When Dames Get Tough* (1946), some five million copies of the series had been sold by 1954. Titles like *Honey, Take My Gun*, *Slay-Ride for Cutie*, *Baby Don't Dare Squeal*, *This Dame Dies Soon* and *Skirts Bring Me Sorrow* sported fabulous covers by Reginald Heade, master of silk stockings and décolletage, which is probably why they eventually fell victim to the early fifties Home Office crackdown on "obscene" paperbacks. Recalled copies were overprinted with silver ink to hide the offending art and bump up the price [15, 16], but Heade left to paint more respectable (and far less interesting) covers for Pan Books and the series never recovered. Holland's *The Trials of Hank Janson* (Telos, 2005) has the full story.

The prolific John Russell Fearn wrote novels under the names Volsted Gridban and Vargo Statten for publisher Scion, many adapted from stories he'd already sold years previously to American magazines. So interchangeable were these pseudonyms that they were both inadvertently used on the same book – *The Grand Illusion* [19, Scion, 1954].

A surviving Scion contract with author Norman Lazenby states their requirements: two novels a month, each of 40-50,000 words, for which they would pay 30 shillings per thousand words for all rights, due six weeks after delivery. No extra fees were paid for reprints or foreign resales, and they were not permitted to write for anyone else. Pseudonyms were to be chosen by the publisher, and remain their property. Even so, with the average wage less than £30 a month, if you could meet those deadlines it was still an attractive offer. Some couldn't cope – an unnamed publisher withheld payment from an author in order to encourage him to work harder. He had no other way to pay for his medication, and subsequently died.

One publisher kept a writer in a cellar. Author Gordon Landsborough, the first editor of *Authentic Science Fiction*, wouldn't name names for fear of libel – even in 1970, decades later – but describes a room at the end of a stone passage where a wasted individual typed from morning till night, including weekends, at a small kitchen table under a naked, low-wattage bulb. He was expected to write two books a week – 70,000 words, 10,000 a day. He slept in the same room, on a hospital bed under overcoats and army blankets, for which the publisher deducted £2 and 10 shillings from his £7 and 10 shillings wages. He was once seen crying outside the publisher's office, pleading for money because he was hungry. The publisher was shouting through the locked door, ordering him to go away and work if he didn't want to starve.

Landsborough witnessed a publisher who refused to pay for work he had commissioned chased around his desk by an author with a fireman's axe. Another nameless publisher was in the habit of breaking into his own warehouse, parcelling up books and selling them on. He'd leave a window open, then crawl in on a decorator's plank he'd propped against the wall beforehand. His wife, who was also the company accountant, knew nothing of this until he was caught in the act one night by a London policeman. These stories, and more, are related in Phil Harbottle's revealing and indispensable history *Vultures of the Void* (Cosmos Books, 2011).

Key to Scion's sales success were the covers by the incomparable Ron Turner. Born in Norwich, England, Turner became interested in science fiction at an early age through the novels of H. G. Wells, Edgar Rice Burroughs and Jules Verne, serials and films such as *Metropolis* and *Things to Come*,

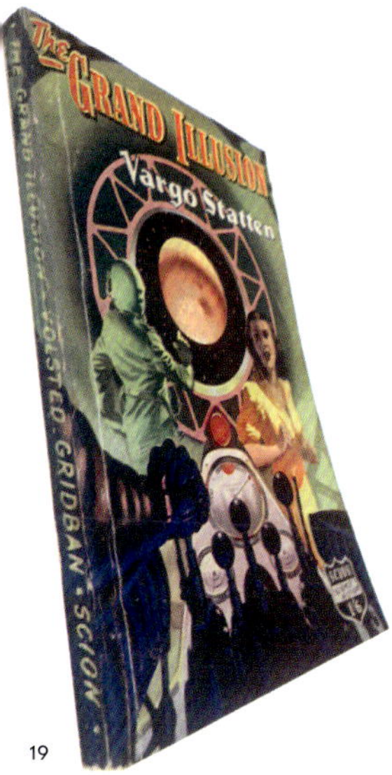

19

and Alex Raymond's *Flash Gordon* comic strip. In 1936, at the age of 14, Turner first got work as an apprentice at Odhams, a London art studio and publishing house, and by 1938 he was providing illustrations for the British magazine *Modern Wonder.* Returning to professional illustration after serving in WW2 he drew the comic strip adventures of the *Atomic Mole* for Scion, a company for which he would go on to produce a long run of covers for their Vargo Statten, Volsted Gridban and E. C. Tubb sf paperbacks. These earned him similar commissions from other publishers, and his gift for sleek and stylish craft painted in fluorescent, eye-catching colours made him the premier British artist of the period. A typical Turner cover had a sense of design that ran from the sculptural hardware to the type on the dials of a spacecraft's dashboard and the hand-lettered book title itself, which, for illustrators of this period, was all part of the job. If you were a professional illustrator, apprenticed in the art agencies of the day, you learned to do it all. Much of Turner's original art does not survive, but he would sometimes recreate them as commissions in later life.

Vargo Statten was so popular that eventually a magazine was launched under his pseudonymous editorship, though Alistair Paterson edited the first seven issues until Fearn took over. The budget was tiny, and so the same cover art was sometimes used on two different issues, a move that must have confused readers and reduced sales. Numbers 7 and 8 [17, 18, 1954, 1955] both feature the same John Richards painting, as do 6 and 9 [pages 346-347], the repeats adding a large red number as if to announce "This is a new issue, honest!" After Scion incurred a hefty fine in 1954 for publishing a pornographic gangster novel, the title passed to their printers, Dragon Press, and changed its name to *The British Science Fiction Magazine.* The final seven issues all used the same Turner art and design, the only differentiating factor being the colour behind the text.

Turner also slummed it with John Spencer & Co. on their pre-Badger output (producing small black-and-white chapter heading vignettes that are reproduced on the endpapers of this book), Kaye Publications and Brown Watson, but produced some of his best work for the short-lived *Tit-Bits Science Fiction Library.* These were short, 64-page novelettes by the likes of John Rackham, who went on to write *Man From U.N.C.L.E.* novelisations, and Steve Future, which we can safely assume is another pseudonym. Turner's *Into Space with Ace Brave* [page 144] is a beautiful three-colour pop-up book, usually found in a dilapidated state.

Turner was also a distinguished comic artist. In 1953 he spoke to the publisher of *Tit-Bits* about the possibility of producing his own comic book series, and the result was *Tit-Bits Science Fiction Comics,* a 64-page monthly written, drawn and lettered by Turner. It quickly became apparent that the workload was too onerous for one person, so Turner brought in other artists to meet deadlines, eventually producing seven issues, the last of which has only ever appeared in French. For Fleetway's *Super-Detective Picture Library* he produced superlative black-and-white strips starring space sleuth Rick Random, though for some reason he did not paint all the covers, an uncredited Fleetway stalwart providing art for *Rick Random and the Kidnapped Planet* [page 438]. Here, his aliens, rayguns, space stations, craft and couture were all impeccably delineated in his trademark stark shadows and clean, precise linework. These stories, plus others, have been reprinted in one fat volume, *Rick Random, Space Detective* (Prion Books Ltd., 2008) and more recently by Book Palace Books. The late fifties and early sixties saw him illustrating covers and interiors for *Practical Mechanics* [pages 200-211], a long-running science and do-it-yourself magazine published by George Newnes Ltd., known for *The Strand Magazine* (where the earliest Sherlock Holmes stories appeared) and the groundbreaking

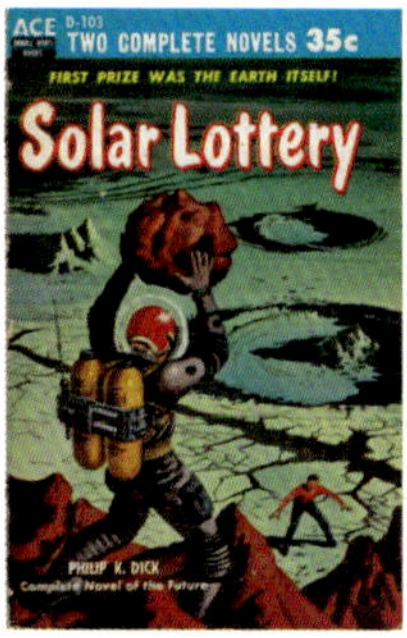

21

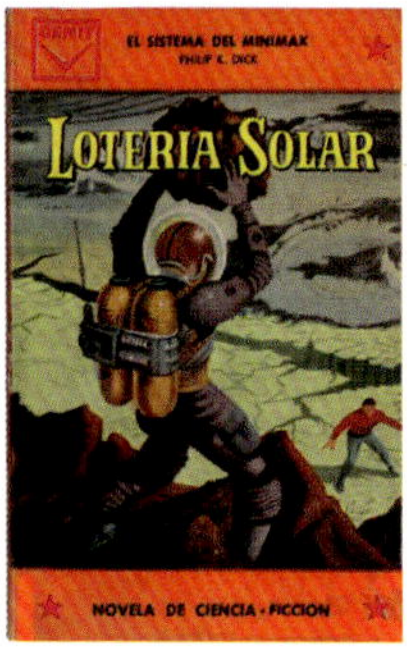

22

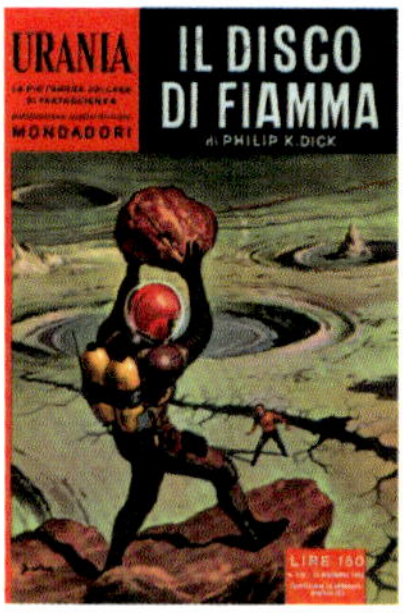

23

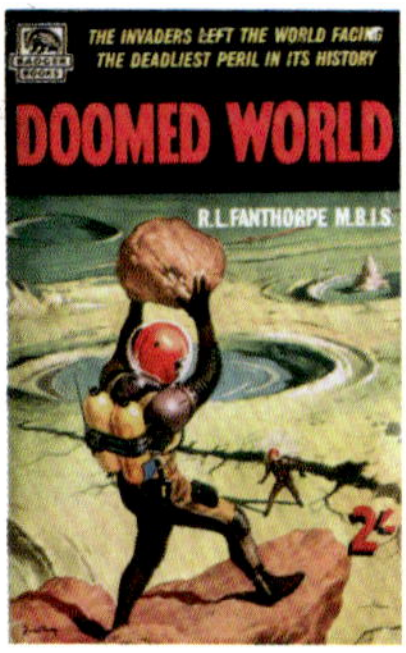

24

woman's magazine *Nova*. In these his attention to mechanical detail came to the fore, lending then-current predictions on space flight, communication satellites, giant hovercraft, space stations, and even the Channel Tunnel a gloss of believability. From 1966 to 1967 he drew the back page *Daleks* strip for the weekly photogravure Gerry Anderson comic *TV21*, and was still producing work for the long-running *2000AD* well into the seventies.

Other Scion artists also worked for a range of publishers – Norman Light's spaceships were full of intricate detail, even if they sometimes resembled toys. Light was also a sometime comic artist, publishing fifteen issues of *Spaceman* between 1953 and 1954, though his main outlet for cover work was Scion's competitor, the aforementioned John Spencer & Co., of Hammersmith, West London.

Primarily known for their science fiction and supernatural paperback series, Spencer also published war, western and romance titles. Set up by Samuel Assael in 1947, their early output consisted of interchangeable juvenile sf anthologies – *Futuristic Science Stories, Tales of Tomorrow* and *Wonders of the Spaceways* each featured a half dozen or so short stories written under house pseudonyms. Described by David Kyle in *Science Fiction Ideas and Dreams* (Hamlyn, 1978) as "the leading choice for the worst sf publications of the last fifty years", these paperback magazines had "forgettable stories by unknown writers". By 1951 the British market was already suffering under a glut of fly-by-night publishers, and between 1950 and 1955 at least thirteen went out of business; John Spencer, publishing under their Badger imprint, somehow managed to last until 1967.

Using a range of pseudonyms, almost all of those "forgettable stories" were written by just two men: John Glasby, who wrote over 300 novels and short stories, and Robert Lionel Fanthorpe, who wrote over 200. Fanthorpe often used anagrammatical pen names – Lionel Roberts, Trebor Thorpe, Pel Torro, Leo Brett, Bron Fane – or the shared "house" pseudonyms Victor La Salle, John E. Muller or Karl Zeigfreid. As one dealer told me at the occasional Pulp and Paperback Fair in Russell Square, London, his favourite author as a youngster had been Karl Ziegfried; he would read everything he wrote. Discovering that your literary hero is actually a shared house pseudonym may be a revelation from which it's hard to recover.

Fanthorpe himself confesses he can't always recall whether a certain story was by him or someone else, but, as critic and author David Langford notes, he remains happy to sign them anyway. In one three-year period he wrote eighty-nine Badger books, which works out at a rate of one 158-page, 45,000-word novel every twelve days; for each of these he was paid £22 and ten shillings. Sequestered under a blanket so he didn't disturb other family members, Fanthorpe dictated the stories directly into a tape recorder and then passed them to a pool of typists. This approach could cause particular problems: sometimes words or phrases would be accidentally transliterated, or a character would die at the end of one chapter only to reappear, with no explanation, later on. Some are object lessons in padding, or the author, finding he was rapidly approaching the prescribed word count, would quickly wrap up using some unlikely *deus ex machina*. Each Badger title had a couple of pages of ads somewhere in the middle touting a "miracle vegetable cream" that could apparently do amazing things for breasts. One wonders if, for an extra shilling, the opportunistic proprietors would come over and apply it themselves [page 473].

The publishers seemed to do their best to ensure that any authorial pretensions were extinguished at the outset. Covers would be chosen first, either bought in from Ace Books in the US, Italian sf magazine *Urania*, published since 1952 by Arnoldo Mondadori Editore and still going strong, or Spanish publisher Toray's sf series *Espacio – El Mundo Futuro*, who

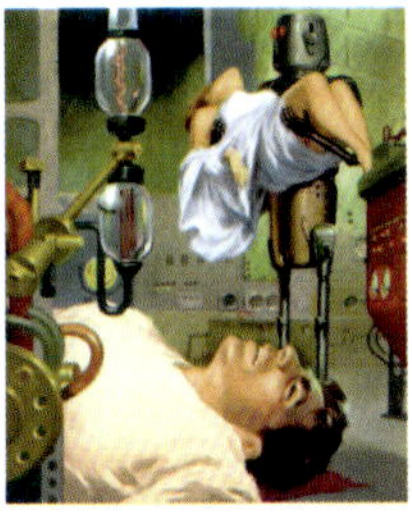
25

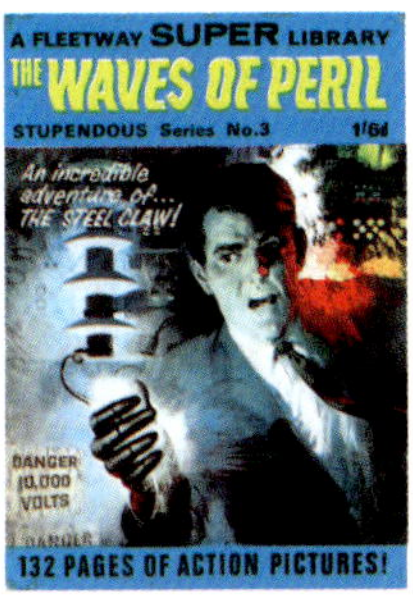

26

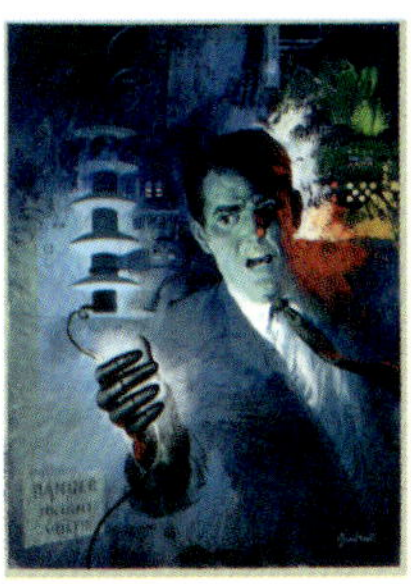
27

used an artist who signed his work Cha' Bril, a pseudonym for the prolific Joaquín Chacopino Fabré. A title and short byline would then be chosen from a proposed shortlist, and the novel written around it. Numbers were popular: *Galaxy 666, Uranium 235, U.F.O. 517, Barrier 346.* Comparisons between the original book covers and the UK repurposings show that literal interpretations were the order of the day: Ed Emshwiller's cover for John Brunner's *Slavers of Space* becomes R. L. Fanthorpe's *The Hand of Doom*; Ed Valigursky's cover for Philip K. Dick's *The Cosmic Puppets* becomes Leo Brett's *The Microscopic Ones*; Ed Emshwiller's cover for James White's *The Secret Visitors* becomes Lionel Roberts' *The Face of X*; Ed Emshwiller's cover for Andrew North's (a pseudonym for Andre Norton) *Voodoo Planet* becomes Trebor Thorpe's (Lionel Fanthorpe) *Lightning World*; Cha' Bril's cover for H. S. Thiel's *Persecución En La Órbita* becomes A. J. Merak's (John S. Glasby) *Hydrosphere*; and Ed Emshwiller's cover for Harlan Ellison's *The Man With Nine Lives* becomes Murray Leinster's *The Brain Stealers* – even though the same novel had already been published, with a different cover, as one half of the Ace Double D-79 [pages 24-25, 62]. Curtin Warren added a further wrinkle by not supplying the cover till the novel was half-written, requiring some creative contortions from the author.

More upmarket publishers were not above similar practices. Panther Books would re-appropriate covers by Richard Powers from US paperback house Avon Books – Abraham Merritt's *Ship of Ishtar,* for example, can be found on the UK edition of John Taine's *Seeds of Life* [1956, 1959, page 25]. It also worked the other way around: early Badger covers were reinterpreted for Barcelona-based publisher Cenit's Spanish editions [published from 1960-1964], and art by Fred Wolff from Martin Caidin's *Worlds in Space* (Sigwick and Jackson, 1954) inspired covers for *Más Allá,* chiefly an Argentinian edition of US digest *Galaxy* [1955, page 25].

Sometimes the covers were repainted almost exactly: Valigursky's dramatic illustration of a spacesuited figure about to throw a rock at a cowering (and unspacesuited) civilian for Philip K. Dick's *Solar Lottery* [21], an Ace Double first edition from 1955, was reproduced fairly closely for Cenit's *Colección Novela de Ciencia Ficción Nº4,* the Spanish edition from 1960 [22]. The colours have shifted – though that may be due to the vagaries of printing – and the rocks in the foreground have turned into putty. It is uncredited. *Urania* produced a more successful pastiche for their 1958 translation [23], in some aspects even improving on the original. The astronaut's feet are planted further apart, making for a more dramatic silhouette, and the large crater now circles his head. His torso leans further back and his left arm is more realistically bent forwards, both lending his stance more force. The second figure has been moved towards the centre, and though smaller is perhaps more prominent, framed as he is by the foreground figure and the promontory he is standing on. For the Badger publication of *Doomed World* [SF series Nº25, 1960] by Lionel Fanthorpe – here writing under his real name – the small figure has been given a matching red-helmeted spacesuit [24, page 58].

This version is signed. The versatile and prolific Italian illustrator Carlo Jacono was born in Milan in 1929, going on to study at the Brera Academy of Fine Arts. In 1950 Alberto Tedeschi commissioned the then twenty-one-year-old to produce the covers for *Il Giallo Mondadori,* a long-running series of noir and detective novels; he would go on to paint more than 3000. Jacono also illustrated the first hundred covers of the sf weekly *Urania,* doing much to popularise science fiction in Italy. In its pages, writers of the calibre of Asimov, Dick, LeGuin and others were translated for the first time. [25, original art for *Urania* Nº161, 1957, reused on *Black Abyss* by J. L. Powers, a pseudonym of John S. Glasby, Badger Books 1960]. Jacono also

Art source comparisons

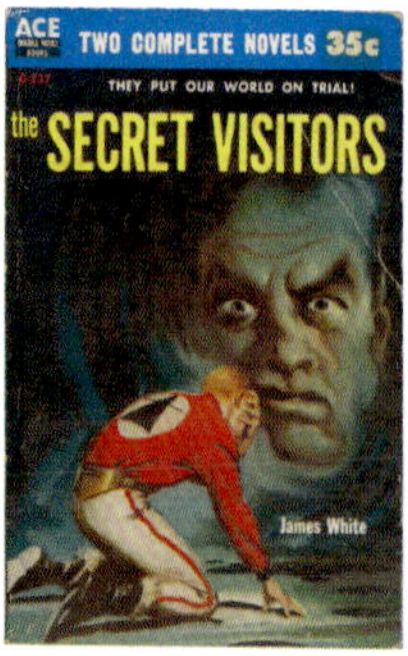

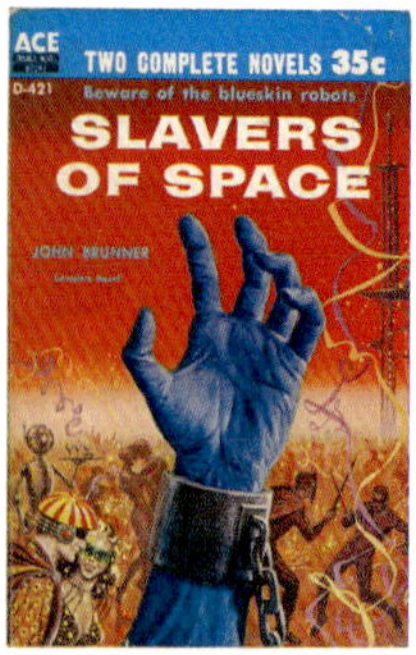

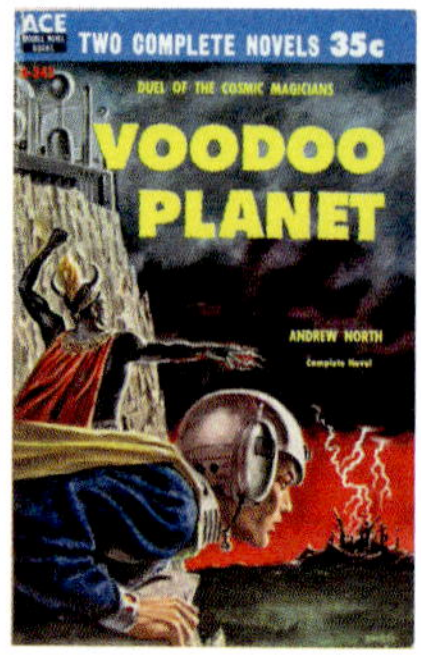

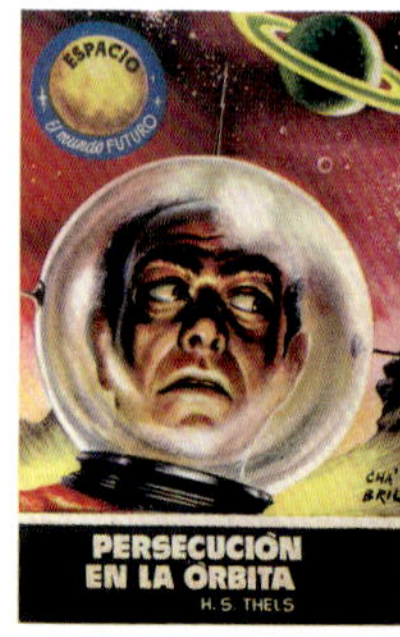

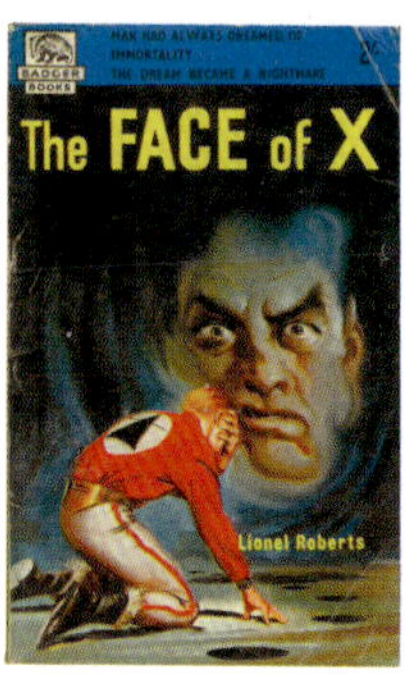

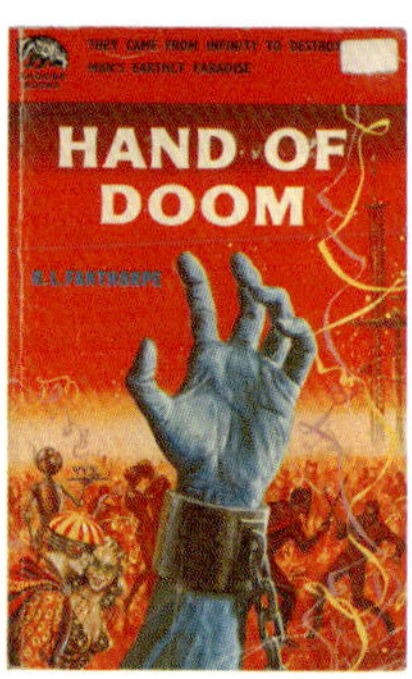

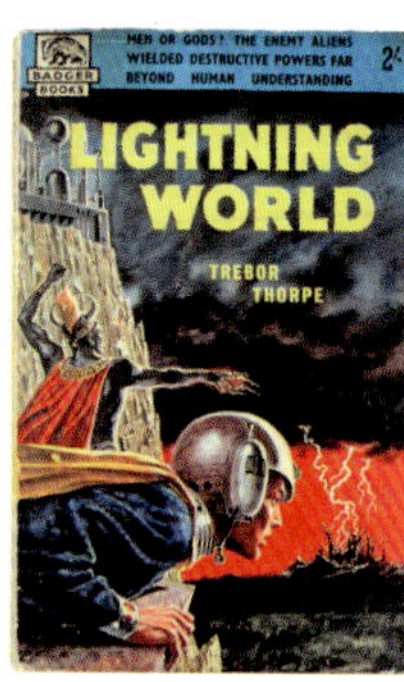

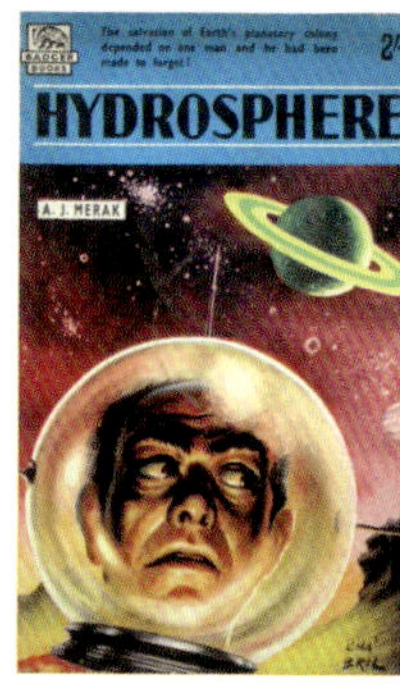

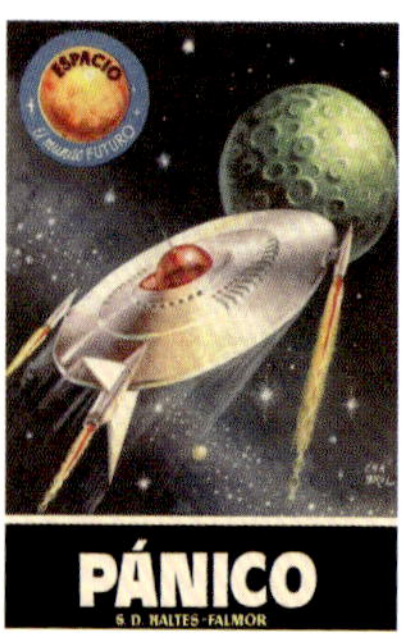

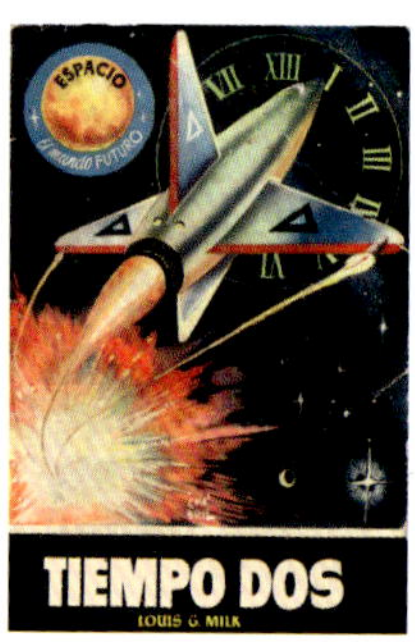

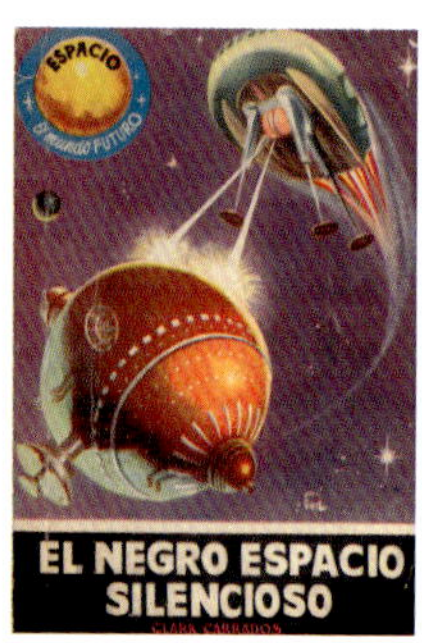

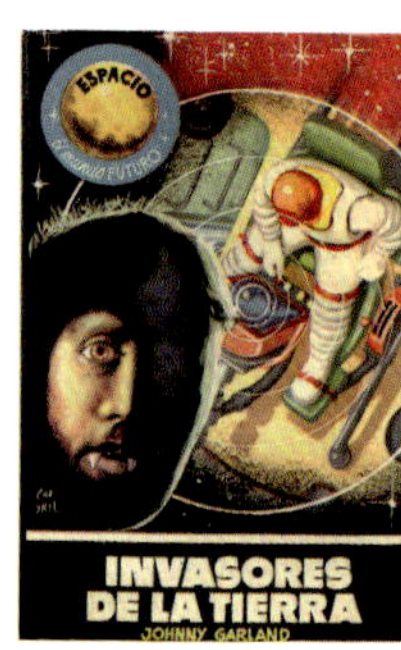

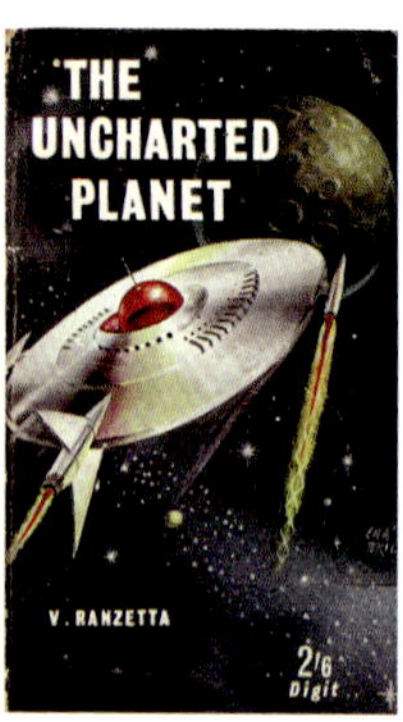

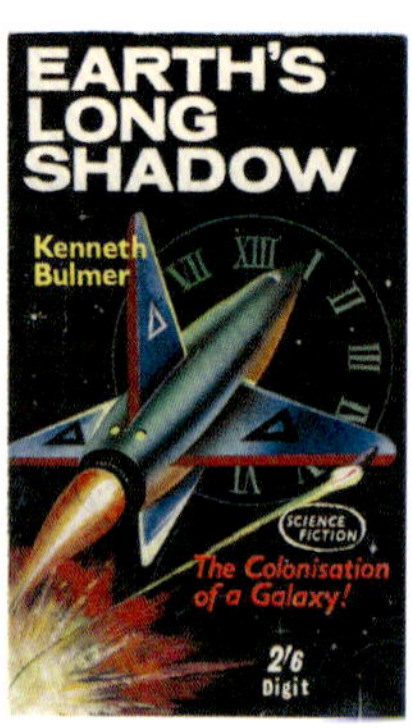

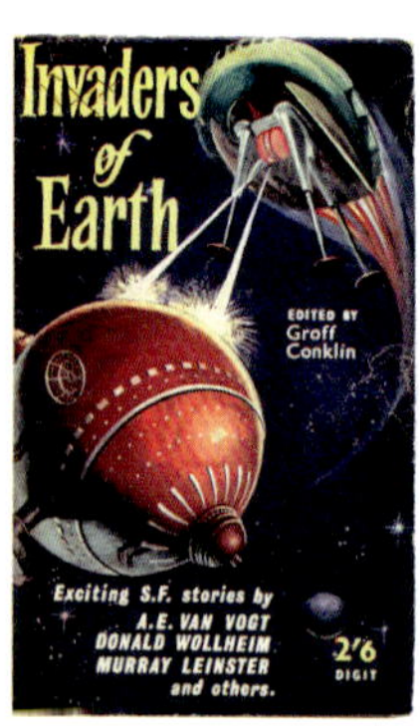

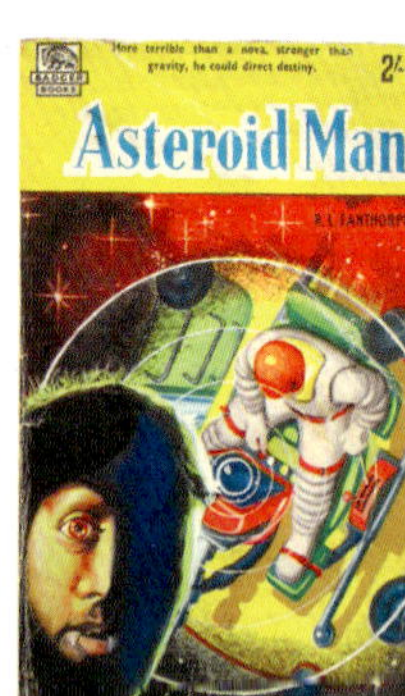

Third row, first two by Fred Wolff from *Worlds in Space*, Martin Caidin, Sidgwick and Jackson 1954
All other art credits in main text

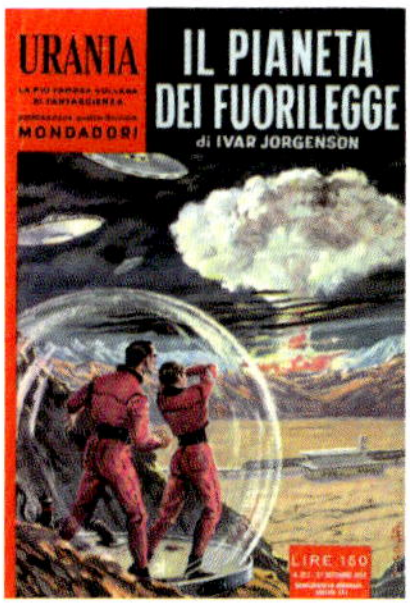

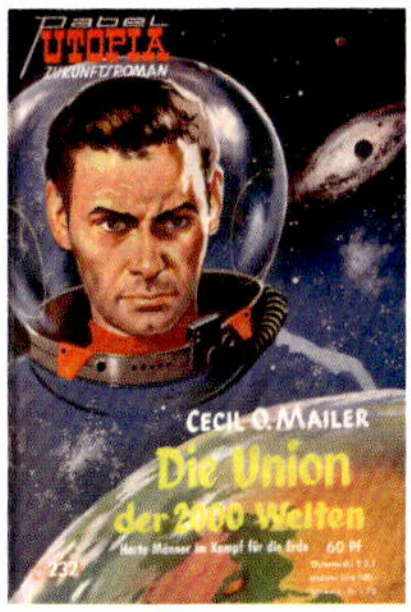

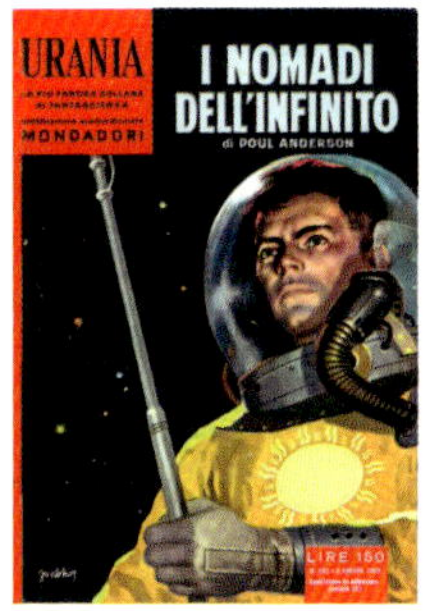

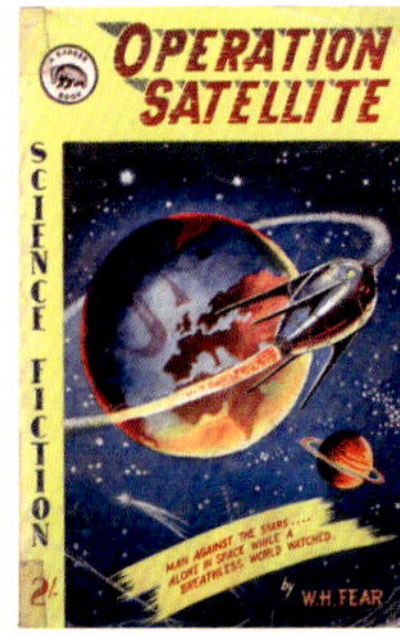

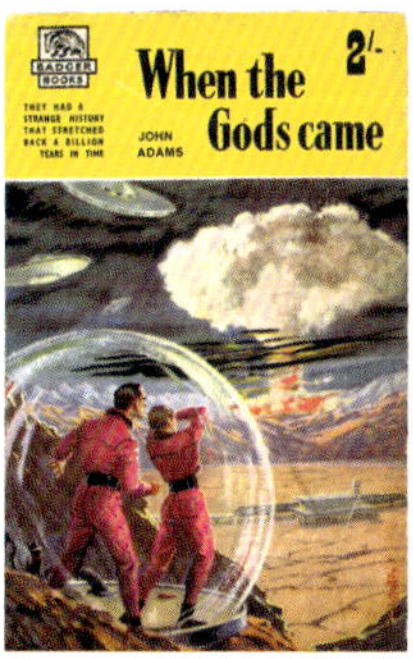

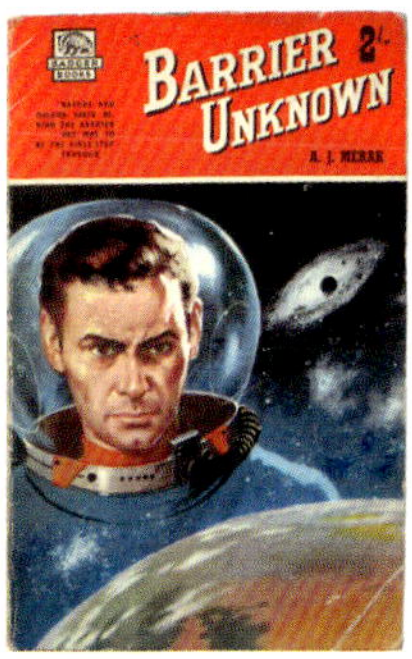

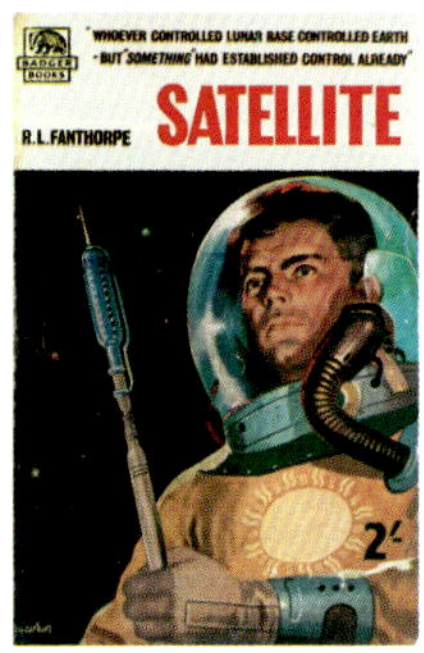

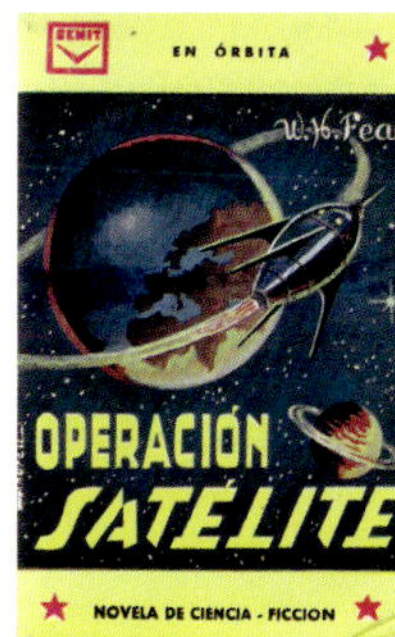

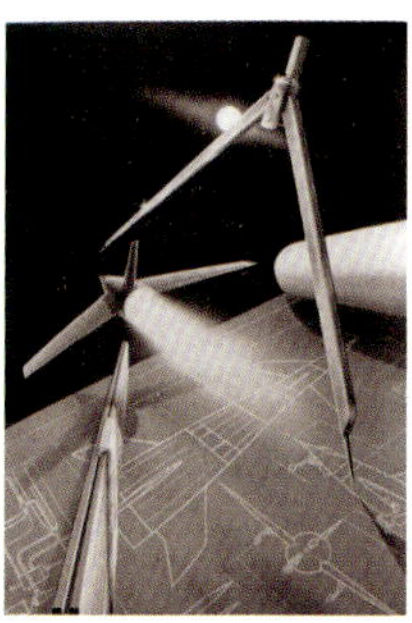
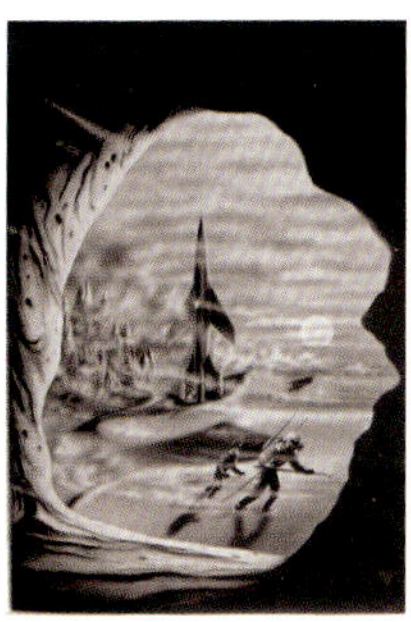
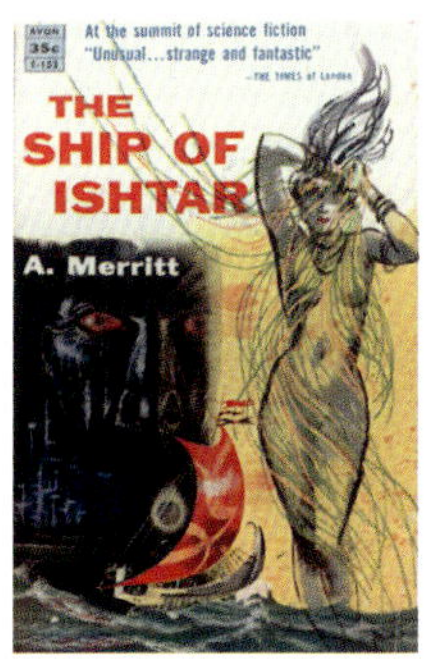

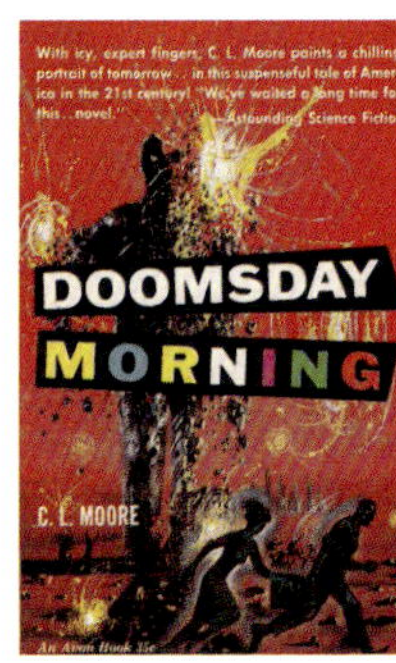

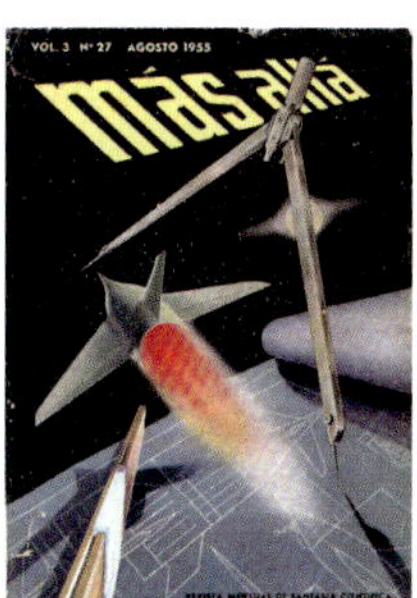

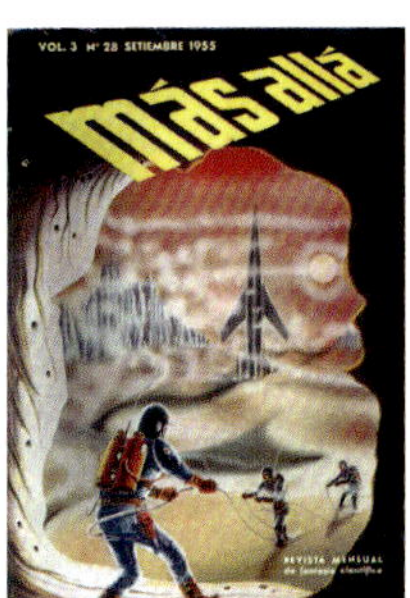

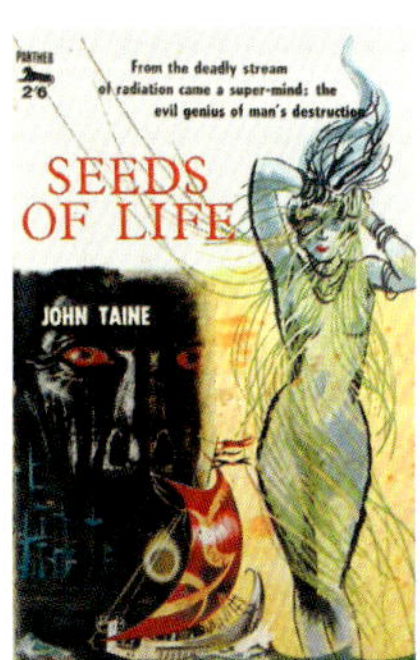

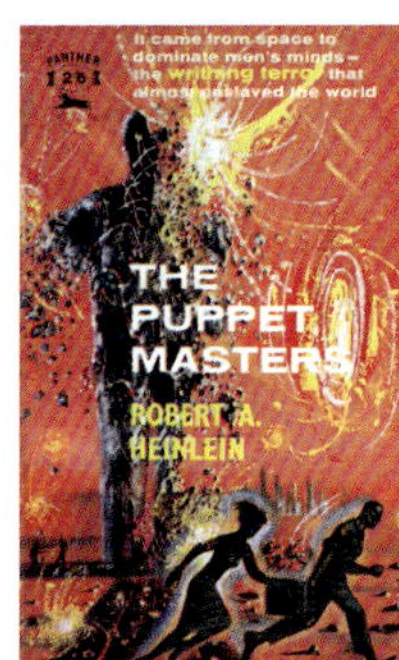

worked directly for the Swedish, Norwegian, American and British markets, painting covers for comic and magazine publisher Fleetway's *Steel Claw* [26, Fleetway Super Library Nº3 1967, 27, original art]. In 1970 he was awarded the Illustrazionel'olio Prize. He passed away in 2000.

Badger reused several of Jacono's covers in the early years, before Henry Fox became the regular artist on their *Supernatural* and *Science Fiction* series. Not much is known about Fox – Steve Holland traces his early output for Arrow Books, Ward and Locke and Pan, though he wasn't shy about producing work for the cheaper end of the market: Modern Fiction, Comyns, Alexander Moring and even Mills and Boon. By the sixties, in parallel with his Badger work Fox was painting covers for the *Sexton Blake Library,* the war libraries, and Amalgamated Press' children's titles *Once Upon a Time, Treasure* and *Look and Learn.* By the end of Badger's long run he had painted over 200 covers, efficiently working his way through a wide range of genre clichés.

Some of Badger's literary output is not quite as godawful as you might imagine. Though unapologetically produced at speed and without pretension, Fanthorpe often draws on literary or historical themes or digresses into page-padding philosophical discussions, and I get the impression that the Reverend could actually write well, should he choose to – which, for the most part, he didn't. The first Badger I came across, in a local jumble sale, was *Rodent Mutation* [page 70]. Giant beavers threaten London, so our heroes seek out the help of a certain Professor Septimus Harbottle, an expert in beaver lore. I can picture the author walking across his study, hefting the relevant volume of the *Encyclopaedia Britannica,* then proceeding to read from it verbatim, interspersing the occasional "the professor explained" or "'I see,' the investigator nodded" as required. This goes on for an entire chapter. For those who have far better things to do than read Badger books from cover to cover, excerpts of the best (or most egregious, depending on your point of view) passages have been collected in *Down the Badger Hole* by Debbie Cross (Wrigley Cross Books, 1995), which includes the immortal first chapter of *March of the Robots* [page 74], probably the most extensive use of a thesaurus in literary history:

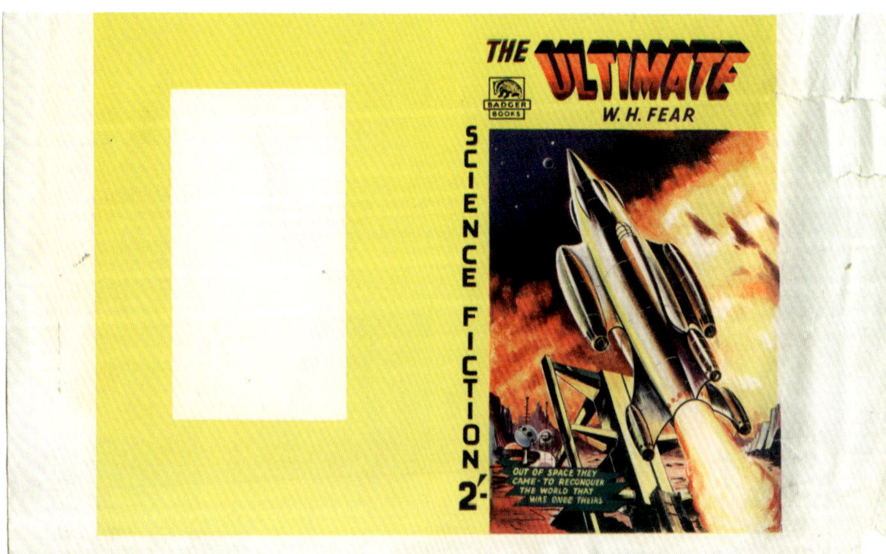

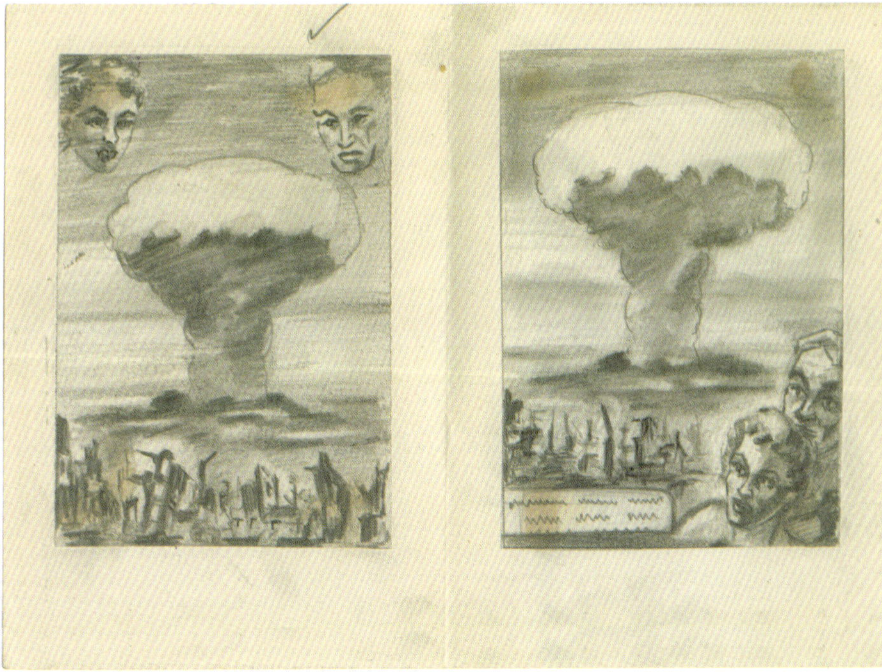

29

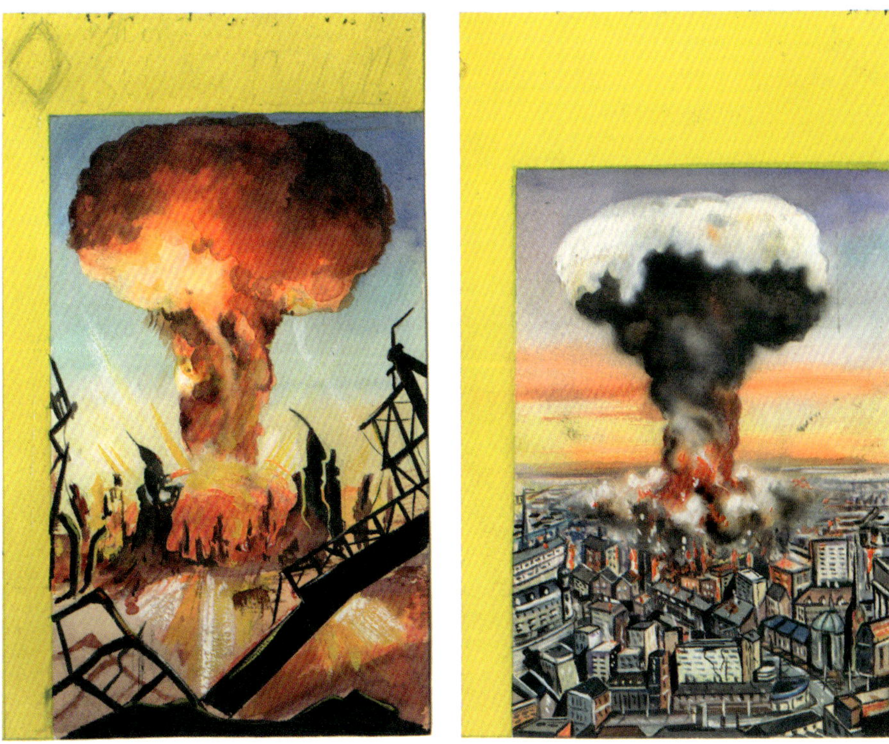

30

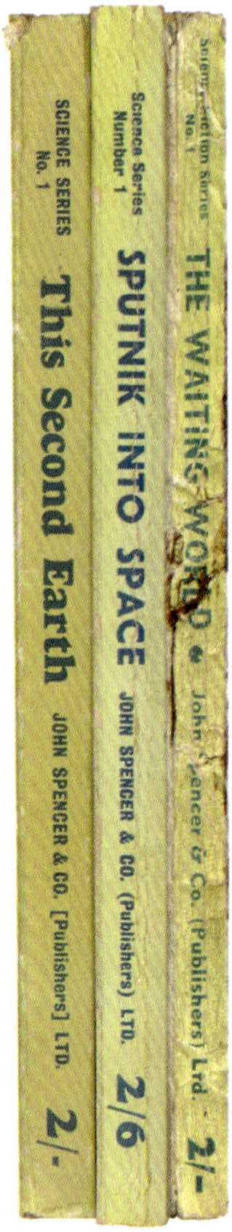

31

"The robots had arrived . . .

There were strange flickering lights all around the ship. Terrifying lights, weird lights, uncanny lights, awful lights, inhuman lights, alien lights, robot lights; and all around a great hemispherical glowing shield sprang up. A thing with a pale, grey blue luminescence. An electronic thing, a mechanical thing. A thing that was part of the robot genius. A thing that was as strange as the ship and its occupants. A force field, a glowing greenish-blue force field . . .

The city slept. Men slept. Women slept. Children slept. Dogs and cats slept."

Badger books are easy to spot because of their yellow spines (there are a few rogue titles in pink, green or blue), the number at the top and the Badger logo, and are still relatively cheap, though the early numbers are becoming more expensive. SF Nº1 [page 45], the first of the science fiction series, can fetch a few hundred pounds on eBay, even though earlier, unnumbered John Spencer titles are still cheaper. I blame the collector's penchant for completing sets — the same numeric weakness that comic book publishers, with their periodic "first issue collector's item" reboots, have been exploiting for decades.

Badger's publishing schedule was complex and full of inconsistencies, as was the case for many of these small, opportunistic publishers. A case in point: in the *Science Fiction* series, so far as anyone is aware, there are two number 3s and no number 2, 8 or 108. Steve Holland theorises that John C. Maxwell's *The World Makers* (one of the two number 3s) [page 46] was misnumbered and should be number 2, while W. H. Fear's *The Ultimate* (the other number 3) [28] was intended to be SF 8. Number 16 of another series, *Futuristic* [page 99], was issued in February 1958 and could be SF 3, mislabelled. Typographically, this seems plausible – the design of the spine and the Badger logo is similar to numbers 7 and 9, which would have been published directly before and after.

Records are almost non-existent, and you might ask yourself why anyone would be interested in such barrel-scraping literary puzzles in the first place. But then, on eBay, I bid on and won a small package of illustrations and cover roughs by an artist called Stanley Nicholson. Nicholson drew many of the early Badger covers, and though not as accomplished as Fox, he does have a certain pulpy charm. The listing

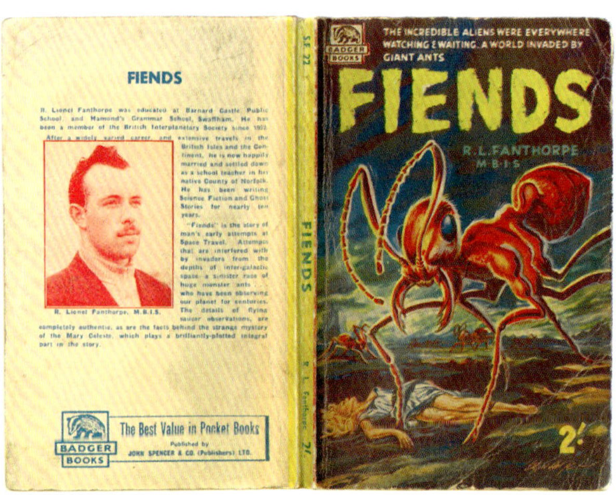

32

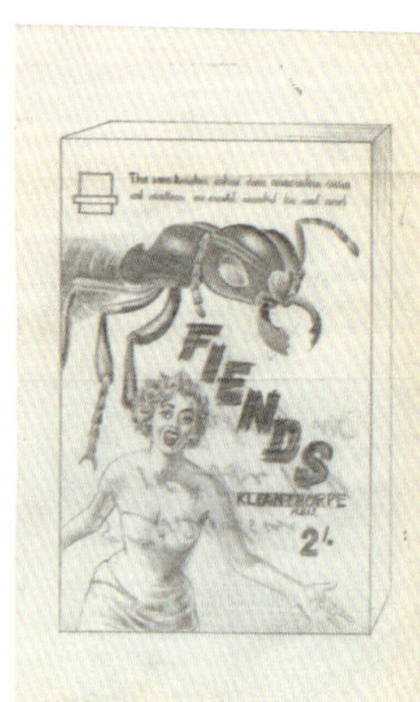

33

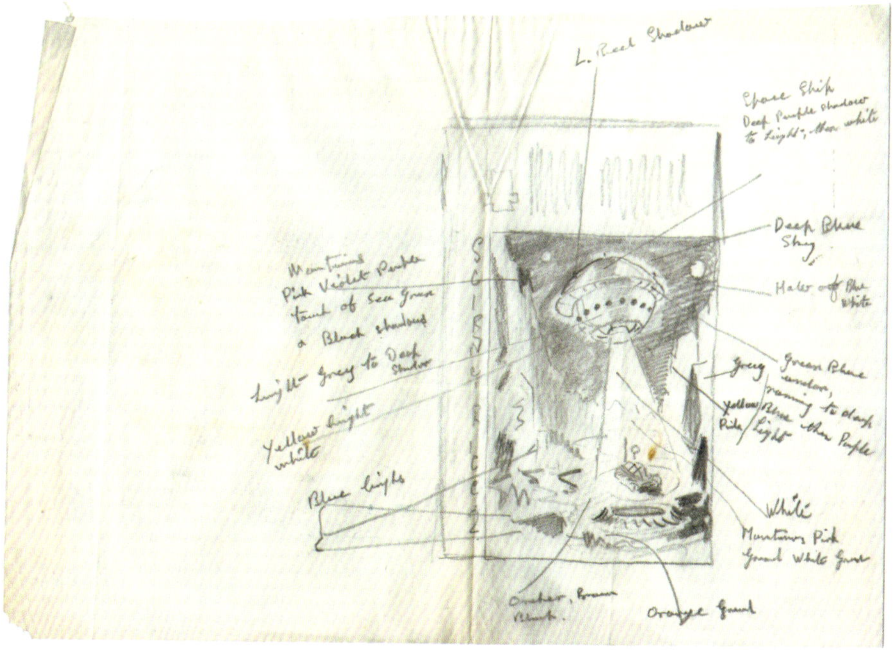

34

showed a couple of cover roughs, in colour, and some flat printer's proofs [28]. These proofs are missing the back and spine copy, which were probably added later as a separate pass on the press using hot-metal letterpress. The seller told me he had some other sketches by the same artist, and sent them along, gratis. In this second package were some personal watercolours of boats, tigers and Degas dancers, plus some interesting pencil roughs. A couple of these were for a Badger war title, while others were preliminary layouts and colour roughs [29, 30] for R. L. Bowers's (another John S. Glasby pseudonym) *This Second Earth* [page 44], the first and only sf title issued under John Spencer's Cobra Books imprint. None of these, it has to be said with all honesty, are top-flight examples of the illustrators' art; but nostalgia, and the collectors' gene, can help one overlook such considerations, and they do shed light on the evolution of the design through several different pencil sketches to the final art. Labelled "Science Series Nº1" on the spine [31], *This Second Earth* actually predates "Science Fiction Series Nº1" (later just "SF"), the first book in the Badger science fiction series proper. My guess is that, like the pseudonymous authors, the publisher was pretending to be several different imprints rather than just the one. To confuse things further, there was yet another "Science Series", this one running to four non-fiction titles beginning with *Sputnik into Space* in 1958 [page 95].

Another pencil rough was for R. L. Fanthorpe's *Fiends* [33], though the final, published cover art is signed by Edgar Hodges [32]. The book's back cover gives us a glimpse of the young Fanthorpe, looking dapper in 'tasche and roll-neck jumper. Whether the rough is by Nicholson or Hodges (it is certainly more polished than the rough for *This Second Earth,* especially the faces), written on the reverse is Nicholson's name and address: a flat above a shop in The Mall, Ealing Broadway. In another of those peculiar coincidences, I grew up in Ealing and attended Ealing Green High School, a comprehensive just south of the Broadway, and The Mall is very familiar

35

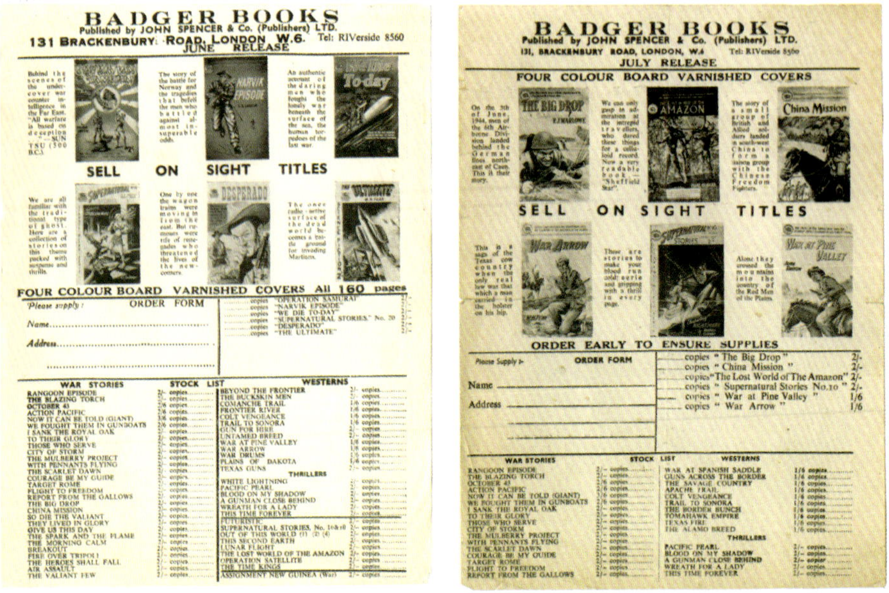

36

to me – it turns out his address is a few doors down from a toy shop, Confiserie Française, that I frequented as a boy. Stanley Nicholson might have moved on by the time I was pooling pocket money for an onion-shaped pencil topper, but it's strange to think that, only a short distance away, this illustrator had been painting covers for books I would later collect.

In that second batch of roughs was another sketch, this time for a cover I couldn't place [34]. The lettering down the left-hand side tells us it's certainly a Badger science fiction title, and I wondered if it could possibly be for a book in the series that no-one had seen before. Could this be the first clue to the identity of the elusive, presumed non-existent number 8? There are a few details that allow us to place it in the publication schedule. Note that you can tell from the sketch that it has the yellow border that runs down the left-hand side and across the top, with "Science Fiction" and the price, 2/-, written within. This device was only used up to number 14. We can narrow it down further: the Badger logo on the sketch is square. This version replaced the previous round one, which was only used up to number 7. So this cover must have been for a book numbered between 8 (if it exists!) and 14. The transition from the round Badger logo to the square one also allows us to say which of the two number 3s was published after the other. Of course, none of these books carry anything useful like a publication date or an ISBN which would conclusively provide the order of publication, and even if they did, the dates might be no more reliable than the numbering. So, the actual number 3 should have a circular logo, and is, as suggested, most likely *The World Makers* by John C. Maxwell – but this could *still* be

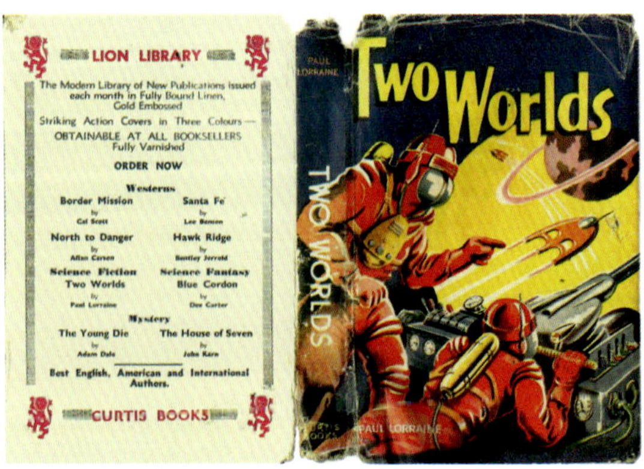

37

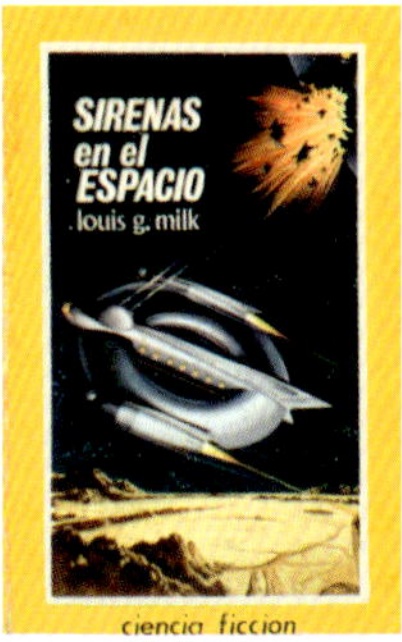

38

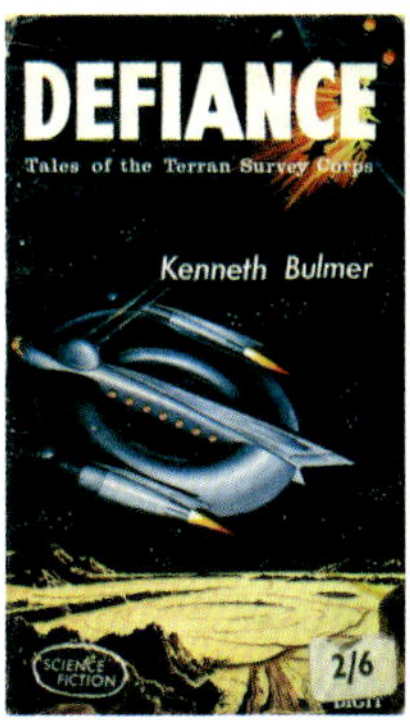

39

the missing number 2, just misnumbered. The other number 3, *The Ultimate* by W. H. Fear, has a square logo. It's unlikely that they would change to the more polished (here, that is a relative term) square design [35] and then back again, so it does seem likely that this book is actually number 8.

But back to the rough. If the scribble at the top is more than just a scribble, it looks like the title has two words, a shorter word and a longer word. Though several titles between 9 and 14 have two words in the title, none of them resemble a short word followed by a long word (discounting titles that begin with a very short "the"). But it *does* feature a flying saucer over an alien landscape, so could it be W. H. Fear's *Return to Space,* number 9 in the series [page 48]? The sketches for *This Second Earth* show several variations on a theme, so it's entirely possible the published cover turned out slightly differently.

There is one more clue. Also included were two sales sheets, set in some of the most amateurish hot-metal typography ever committed to paper [36]. The June sheet lists SF series titles up to and including *Lunar Flight,* number 7, though here they are not numbered. The second sheet is from July, the month after. This is the month that SF number 8, our mystery title, should have been published. Conclusive proof may finally be to hand! But though a *Supernatural* title, №10, does get a mention, there doesn't seem to be an SF section listed at all — just war, westerns and thrillers. Perhaps it's from the previous July. There are fewer war titles listed, and the June sheet lists later *Supernatural Stories,* 16 and 18. The puzzle remains.

Possibly surpassing Badger at the low end of the market, Curtis Warren published gangster, western, foreign legion and science fiction paperbacks throughout the late forties and early fifties. The sf line used peculiar, sometimes nonsensical titles that sound like the product of one of those online random name generators: *Solar Gravita, Brain Palaeo, Trans Mercurian, Elektron Union, Stella Radium Discharge* (straight to the doctor with that, please) and *Bio-Muton* [page 190], though they did publish John Brunner's first novel, *Galactic Storm,* under the byline Gill Hunt in 1951 [page 184]. Many of these were also released in hardback under the Lion Library imprint [37], the larger dust jacket showing more of the cover art. This, by Gordon C. Davies, Ray Theobald and others, is mostly undistinguished.

Other British paperback houses also made use of previously published American, Italian and Spanish art. Digit Books, an imprint of Brown Watson, first appeared in 1956 and reprinted several covers from Ace, sometimes for the same title – Kenneth Bulmer's *The Changeling Worlds* (1959) [page 115] by Ed Valigursky, for example – but more often than not seemingly at random: Frederick Pohl and C. M. Kornbluth's *Search the Sky* (Digit, 1959) [page 120] uses Poul Anderson's *We Claim These Stars!,* half of an Ace Double with Robert Silverberg's *The Planet Killers* (1959). They also reprinted *Espacio*'s Cha' Bril and shared covers with Ediciones Toray – Robert A. Osborne's cover for Louis G. Milk's *Sirenas en el Espacio* (1966) first appeared on Kenneth Bulmer's *Defiance* in 1963 [38, 39]. They even used the same art on two completely different books – *Split Worlds* by Tyrone C. Barr in 1959 and *The United Planets* by Victor Wadey in 1962 [page 115]. These titles are polar opposites, which makes using the same art on both something of a feat. Whereas Badger would attempt to mimic the typographic style of the original, often using hand-drawn lettering, Digit's covers sometimes suffer from the poor application of foundry typefaces in small sizes, which, by comparison, lack the requisite drama.

Authentic Science Fiction blurs the categories of paperback and magazine. Beginning in 1951 as a series of standalone fortnightly novels, it switched to a monthly schedule the same year, and began featuring short

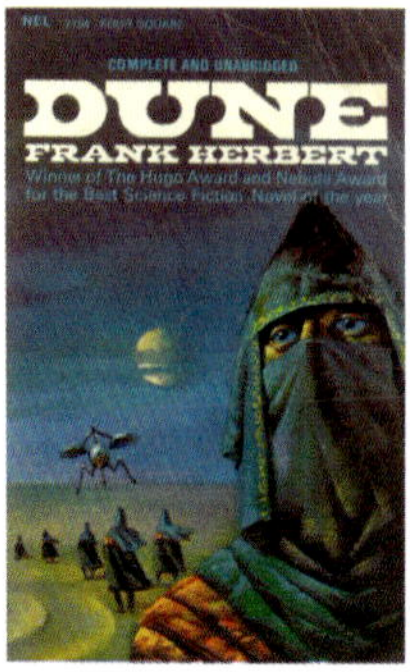

40

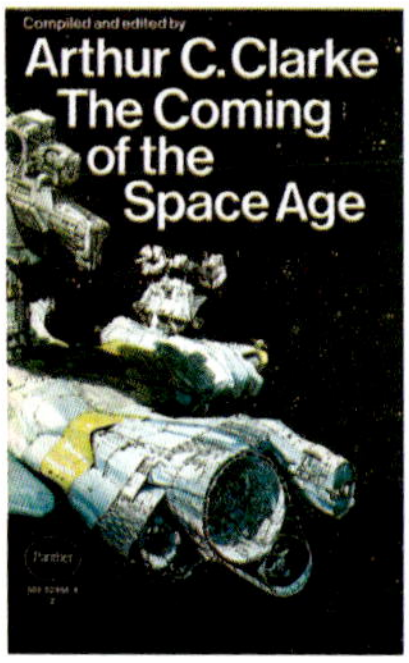

41

fiction soon thereafter. Their first title, *Mushroom Men from Mars* [page 269] by Lee Stanton (a pseudonym for Richard Conroy), announces the imprint's pulpy agenda – at £1 per 1,000 words, they could not hope to attract the best writers. When E. C. Tubb took over from H. J. Campbell as editor in 1956, he found that the quality of submissions was so poor that he often had to fill out the magazine himself under a series of pseudonyms. *Authentic*'s cover art improved enormously over its run, a highlight being a series of polished space scenes by John Richards (signing himself "Davis"), who produced an unbroken run from №30 to 55. Richards began his career painting covers for Scion's Volsted Gridban novels (*Reverse Universe*, *De Bracy's Drug*, 1952-3) [pages 227, 246] before Ron Turner overshadowed him, but matured into a polished illustrator with a fine sense of layout and symbolism, providing many covers for Panther and Corgi. Though these later, digest-sized "magazine" issues of *Authentic* technically fall outside this book's remit, they are included here.

Authentic's publisher Hamiltons also ran the paperback imprint Panther, which in time became a respectable publisher of mainstream quality science fiction, switching from original material to reprints of best-selling hardbacks from other publishers. One of the few success stories of this period, by 1968 Panther was part of Granada Group Ltd., and in 1983 was absorbed by William Collins, Sons & Co., now part of Harper Collins. Like *Authentic*, Panther's roots were unapologetically pulpy – Ron Turner launched the series in his signature style with his cover for Roy Sheldon's (a pseudonym of both Herbert J. Campbell and E. C. Tubb) *Two Days of Terror* in 1952 [page 156]. Many titles were also issued as hardback "library editions".

Outlasting most of its rivals at the bottom of the market, Badger finally ceased publication in 1967, by which time paperback sf had begun to gain a modicum of respectability. Josh Kirby, for example, was giving Richard Powers a run for his money with his fantastical paintings for Corgi. Citing Hieronymus Bosch, Pieter Bruegel and muralist Frank Brangwyn as influences, he started with the novel *Cee-Tee Man* by Dan Morgan [Panther, 1955, page 174] and photo-referenced covers for the last issues of *Authentic Science Fiction*. Kirby would go on to paint covers for Isaac Asimov, Ian Fleming, Alfred Hitchcock, Guy de Maupassant, Jack Kerouac and, most famously, Terry Pratchett's long-running *Discworld* series, illustrating no less than twenty-six of these before his death in 2001.

The cut-off point for this volume is around 1970. By then, science fiction was gaining more mainstream credibility and the covers reflected these changing attitudes. A foretaste of this can be seen here, on the jackets that foreground design and photography or lean towards the more symbolic and less representational. The days of rocketships and rayguns were fading into a post-atomic twilight – or so it seemed. Seven years later, *Star Wars* would place them front and centre all over again.

Sf paperback cover art in the seventies and early eighties would be dominated by two artists who began their careers in the late sixties: Bruce Pennington and Chris Foss, who inspired a legion of copyists, some of whom occasionally outpaced them. Pennington leaned towards mystical landscapes and fantastical creatures, his luminous colour sense lending them a suitably otherworldly atmosphere. His cover for *Dune* [40, New English Library, 1968, page 408] is a classic, the blue eyes of the Fremen gazing out over Arrakis, desert planet and source of the space-warping spice Melange. If Pennington dealt in high fantasy, Chris Foss cornered the more realistic, "hard" sf market. His battle-weary spaceships look like they have been patched together from junkyard leftovers, and he single-handedly started a trend for hyper-detailed science fiction illustration [41, *The Coming of The Space Age*, Panther, 1970]. He began his career painting spitfires, bombers

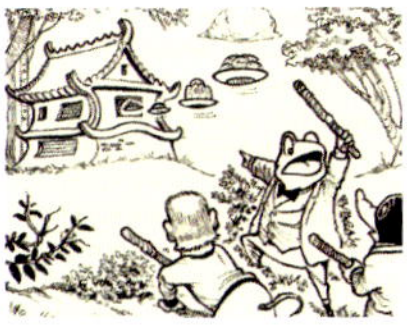

42

and submarines for war and espionage novels, and this provided him with the wherewithal to make even extraterrestrial hardware believable. Though known for his Asimov, Clarke and Perry Rhodan covers (which he admits to never reading), his most widely seen work was *The Joy Of Sex,* for which he provided delicate pencil drawings of naked beardy men and hairy women getting it on (see Titan Books' *Hardware: The Definitive SF Works of Chris Foss* by Rian Hughes and Imogene Foss, 2011).

Much of the original artwork is long lost to publisher bankruptcies, moves, amalgamations and warehouse clear-outs. For a long time it was considered to have no intrinsic value, and as it would mount up in the editorial offices, week after week, issue after issue, space considerations meant that regular purges were inevitable. Today's standard publishing practice is to return artwork to the artist, but as the vast majority is now produced digitally for ease of delivery and printing, there is little real, physical art to lose.

Back in the early nineties I was delivering pages of a strip for *2000AD,* the long-running British weekly. Home of Judge Dredd, it featured early breakthrough work by such luminaries as Alan Moore, Brian Bolland, Dave Gibbons and Mike McMahon. When it was launched in the post-*Star Wars* boom for all things sf in 1977, I'd imagine the editorial team didn't think it would still be going strong today, a futuristic title now named after a date two decades in the past. When I worked for them it was run from the old IPC offices in King's Reach Tower, and on this occasion the lift doors opened in the ground-floor reception to reveal piles and piles of original art, all on Crown-sized boards. Two men with a wheelbarrow were taking it out and around the back, where there was a skip in the car park. This was already full of original art – hundreds of pages, going right back to the forties and earlier. I began sorting through it, finally having to climb in and stand on the art itself to see everything. The two workmen were not happy. As they loaded more and more in, I was taking more and more out. In the end, I saved as much as I could carry – two armfuls, around 25-35 pages, mostly by obscure artists from long-forgotten publications. The highlights were several fairy-tale pages by Ron Embleton, best known for his work on *Stingray* and *Captain Scarlet* for *TV21* and *Oh! Wicked Wanda!* for *Penthouse* magazine, and some *Wind in the Willows* pages from Playhour by Peter Woolcock. These are surreal, depicting Mole, Ratty and Toad chasing floating trifles through an idealised English countryside [detail, 42]. Some friends went to have a look the next day, but I must have worn out the workmen's patience – they'd turned a hose on it, filling the skip with soggy pulp to prevent any more being rescued.

I will still search out the odd volume. Recently I was in Detroit for the ICON illustration conference, and of course looked up the local second-hand bookshops. One in particular stood out: it was listed as the largest in the state, and the "Nº2 Book Store in the World" (who is Nº1, I wonder?) Detroit is depopulated, and gives the impression that every third or fourth building has vanished, even in some downtown areas. Standing on its own, John King Books is a huge warehouse with the name written in flaking block capitals all around the top storey. I knew I was on to something when the hot air wafting out the front door carried the aroma of old paper, and in their sf section they had several sixties Ace Doubles with familiar-looking covers by Emsh and Valigursky. Before the internet any one of these would have been a rare find in the UK, the original price probably covered over by a two-shilling Thorpe and Porter sticker.

I held one under my nose. It was a Proustian moment: I here confess that I can recognise an Ace Double simply by the smell.

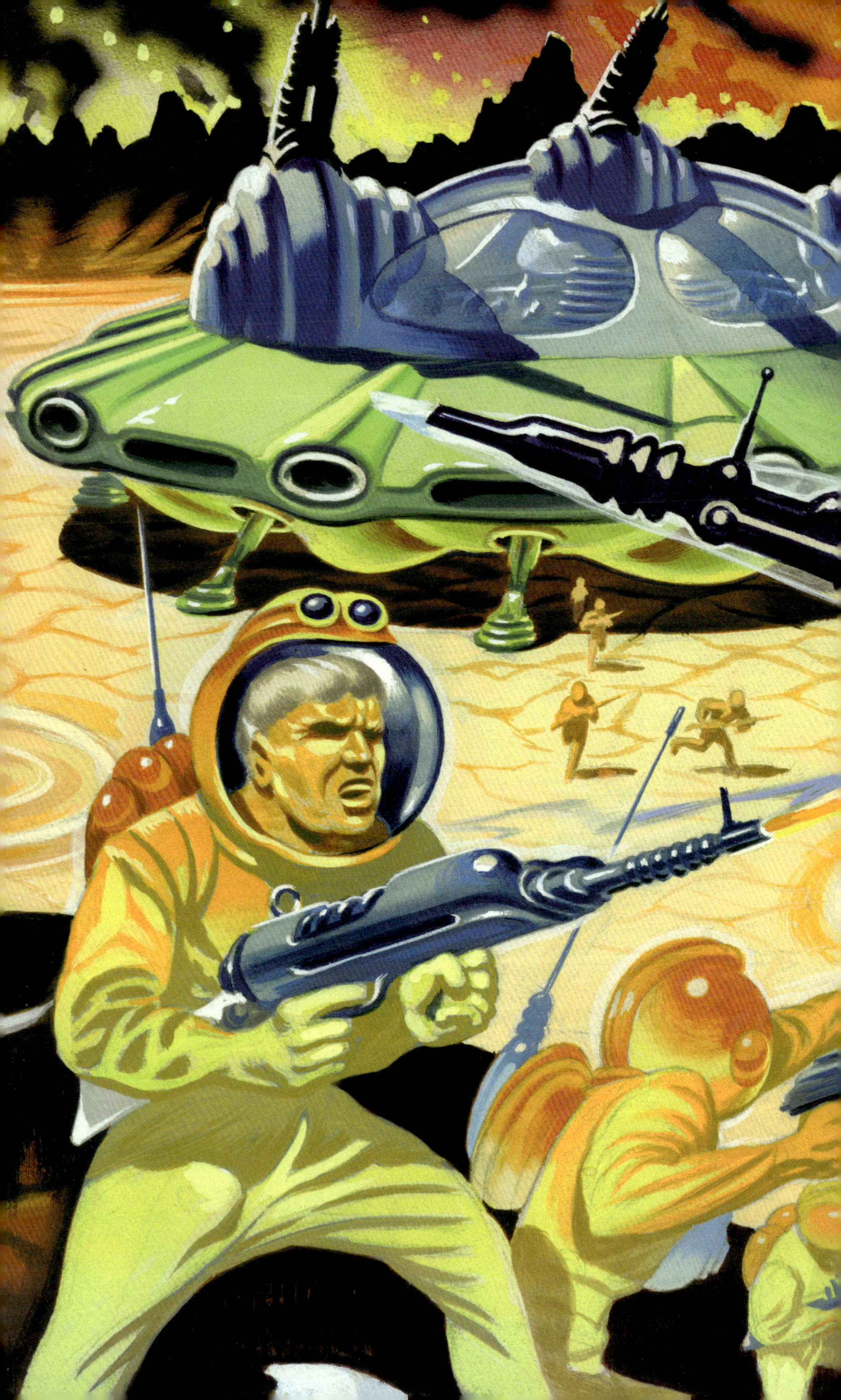

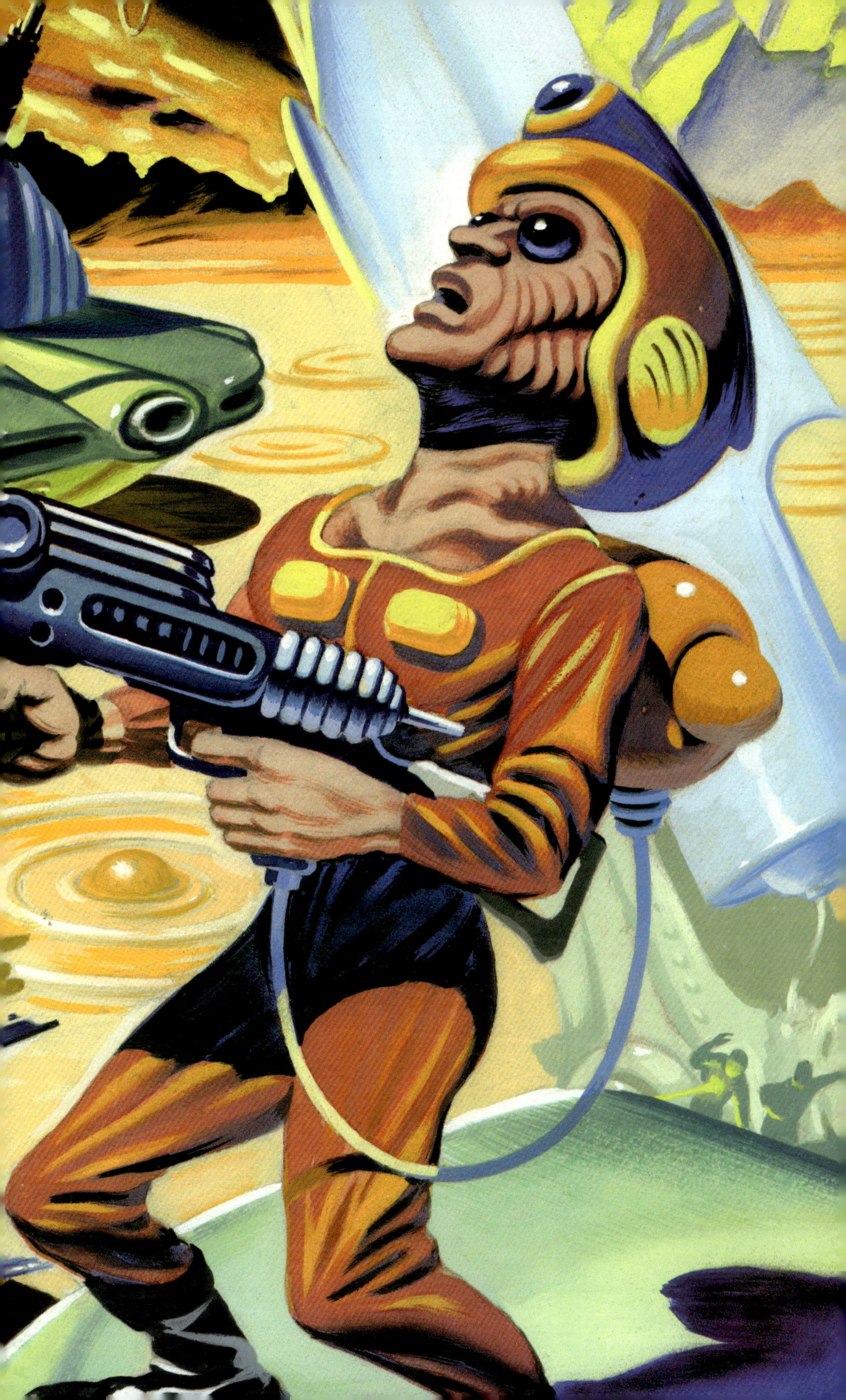

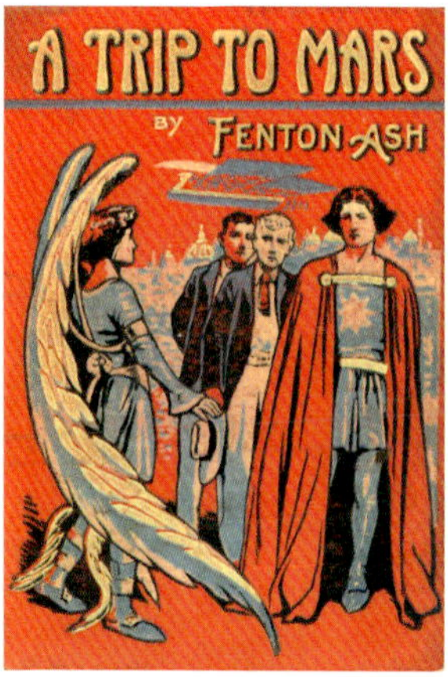

Fenton Ash (Francis Henry Atkins)
A Trip to Mars
W. & R. Chambers, Limited, 1909 | Art **Unknown**

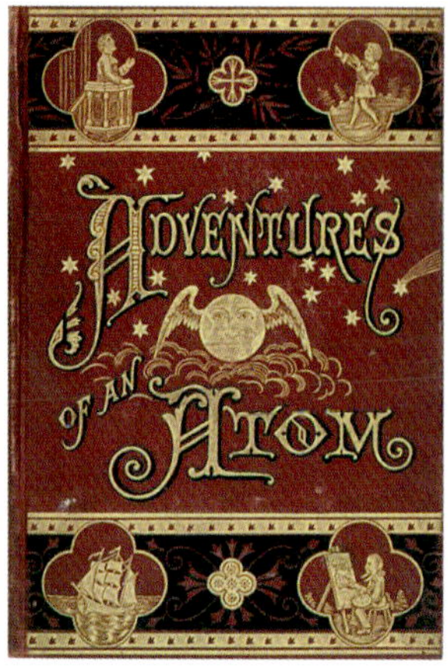

The Adventures of an Atom;
Its Autobiography, by Itself
Hurst & Co., 1880 | Art **Unknown**

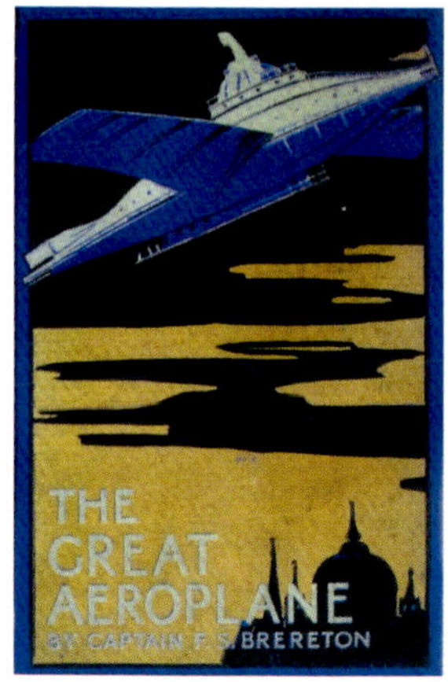

Frederick Sadleir Brereton
The Great Aeroplane
Blackie & Son, 1916 | Art **Unknown**

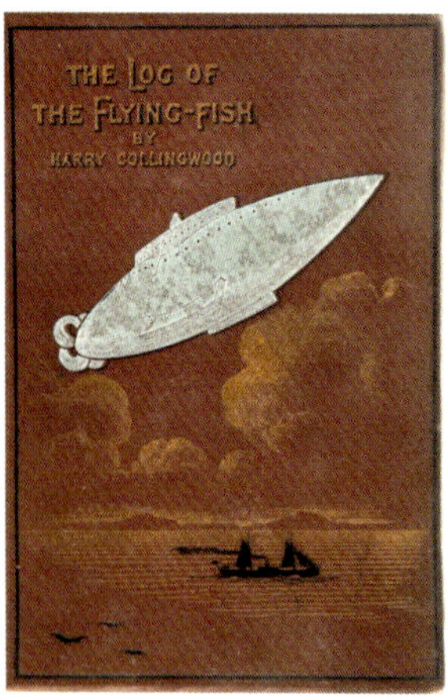

Harry Collingwood | *The Log of the Flying-Fish*
Blackie & Son, 1887 | Art **Unknown**

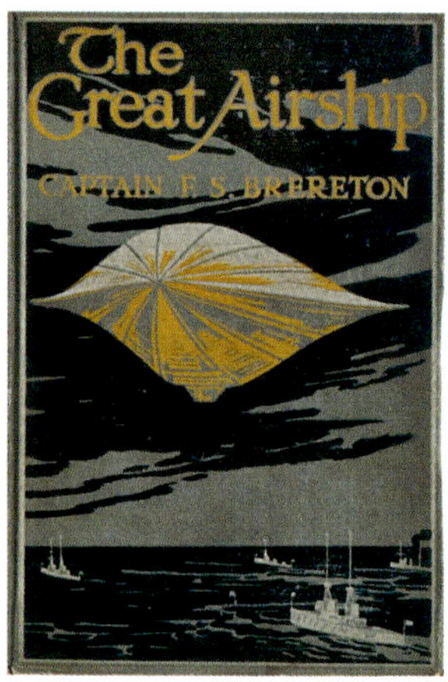

Captain F. S. Brereton | *The Great Airship*
Blackie & Son, 1918 | Art **Unknown**

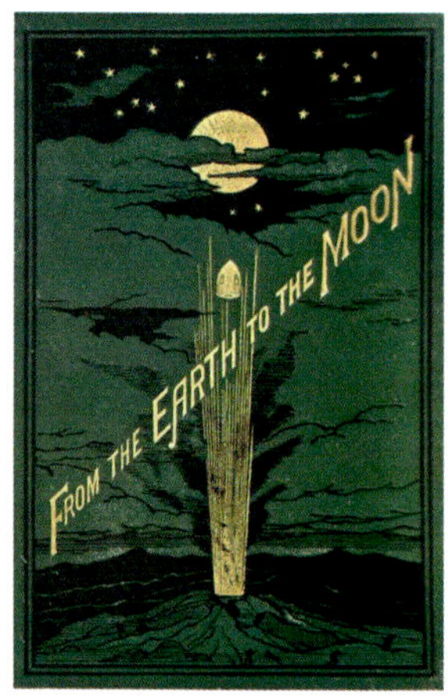

Jules Verne | *From the Earth to the Moon*
Sampson Low, 1873 | Art **Unknown**

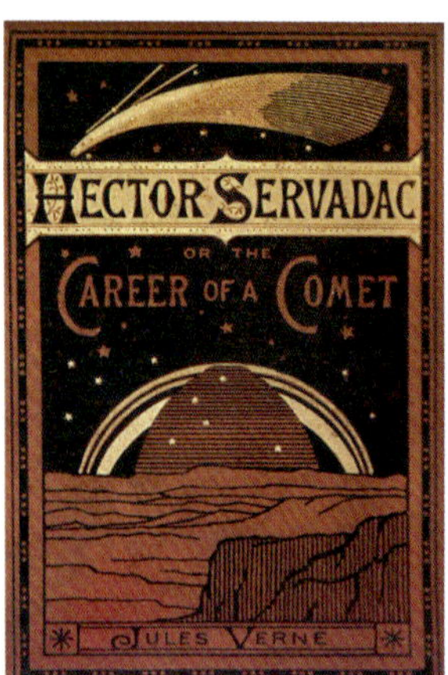

Jules Verne
Hector Servadac or the Career of a Comet
Sampson Low, 1878 | Art **Unknown**

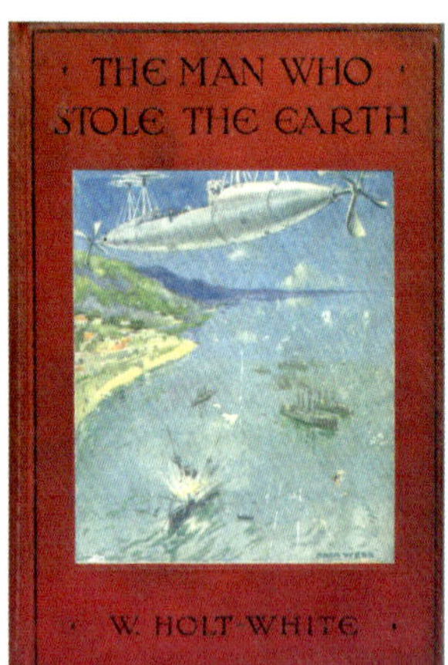

William Holt-White
The Man Who Stole The Earth
T. Fisher Unwin, 1909 | Art **Arch Webb**

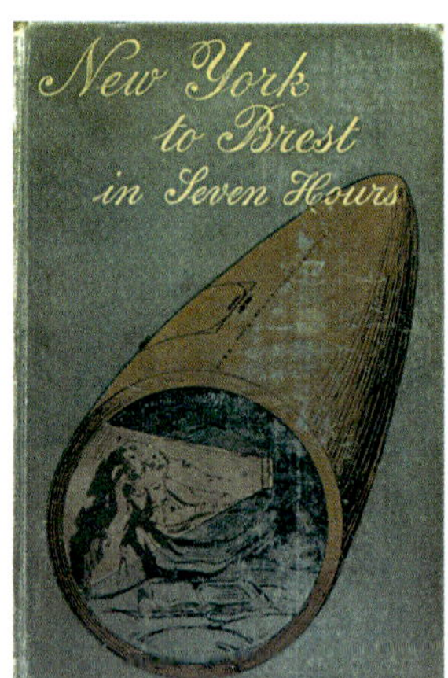

André Laurie (Paschal Grousset)
New York To Brest In Seven Hours
Sampson Low, 1890 | Art **Unknown**

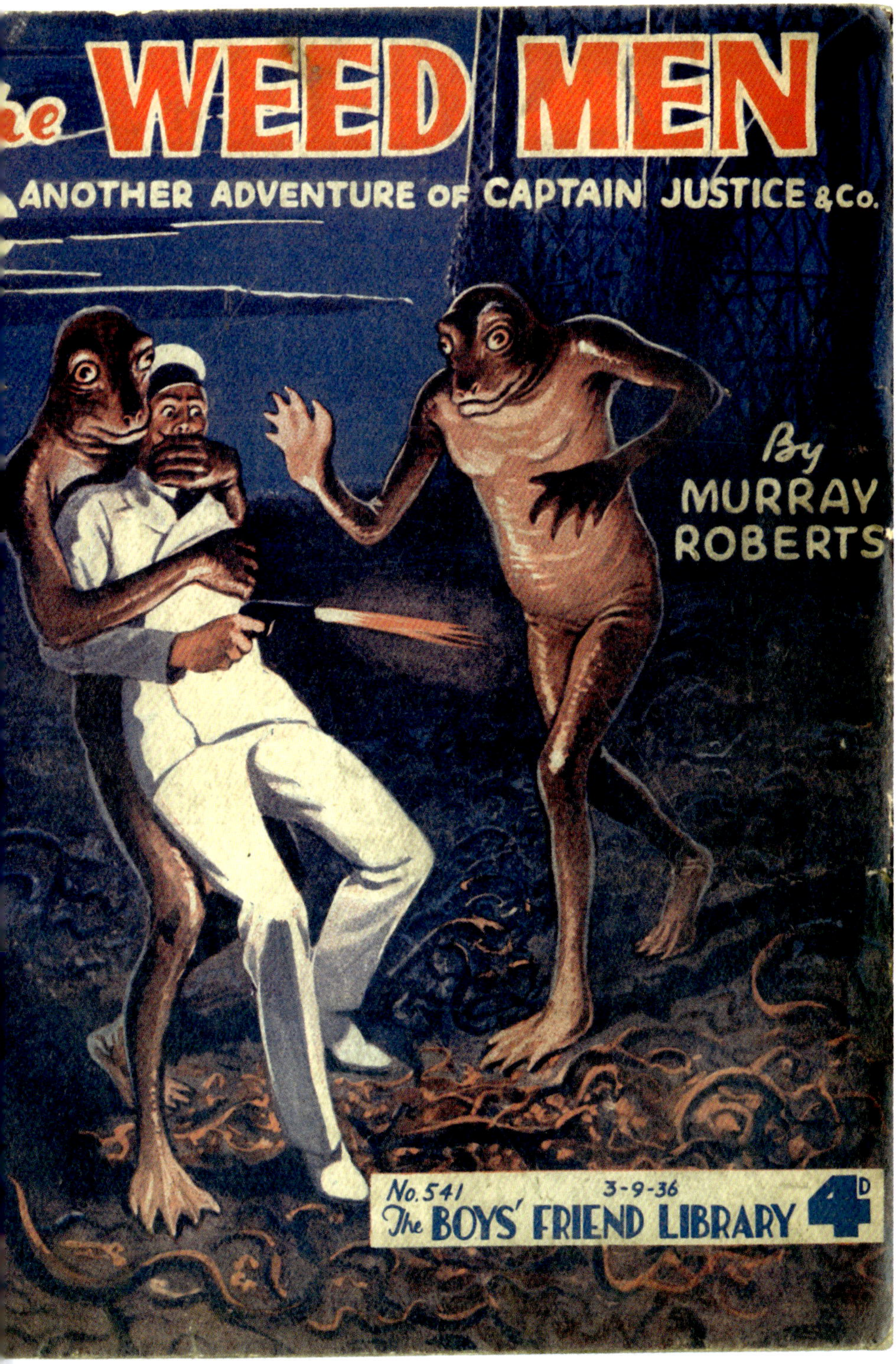

Murray Roberts | *The Weed Men*
Boys' Friend Library 541, 1936 | Art **Unknown**

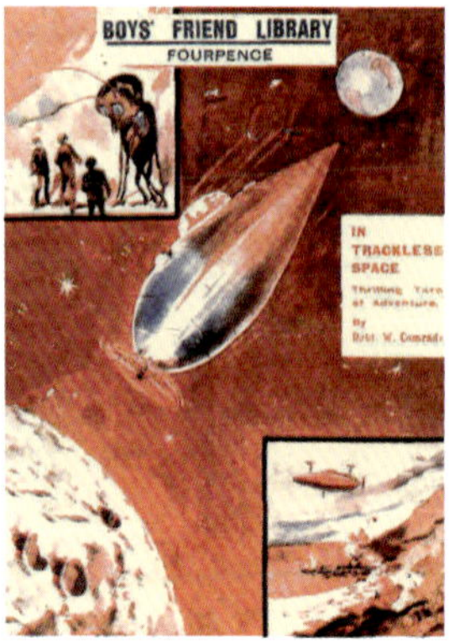

Robert W. Comrade (Edwy Searles Brooks)
In Trackless Space
Boys' Friend Library 504, 1920 | Art **Unknown**

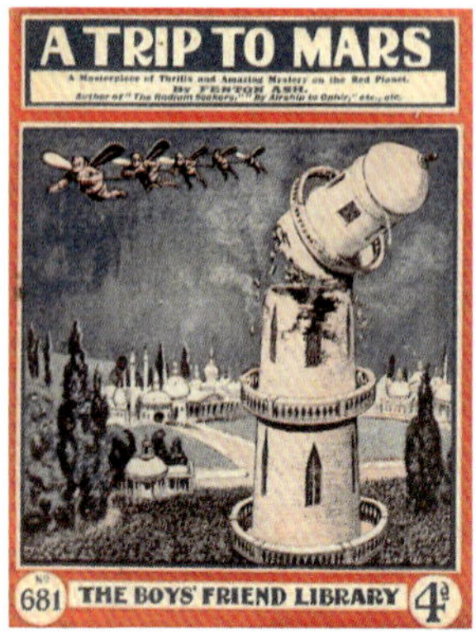

Fenton Ash (Francis Henry Atkins, Sr.)
A Trip to Mars
Boys' Friend Library 681, 1923 | Art **Unknown**

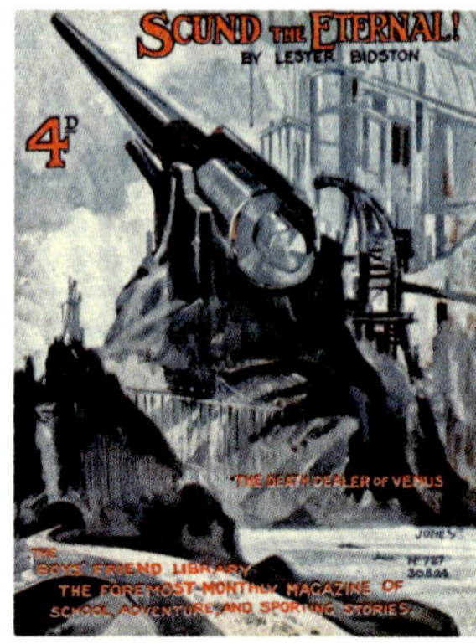

Lester Bidston
Scund the Eternal!
Boys' Friend Library 727, 1924 | Art **Arthur Jones**

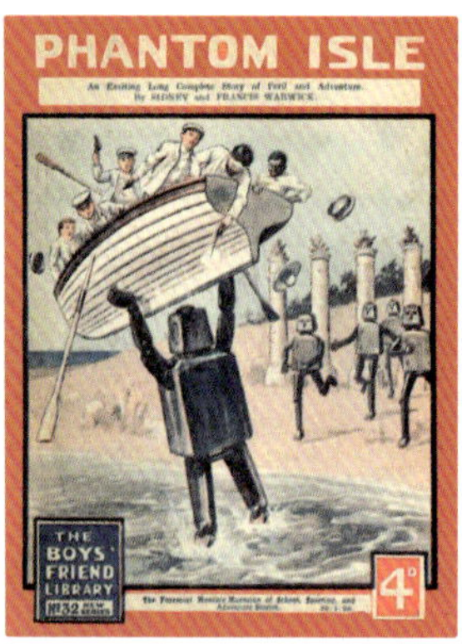

Sidney and Francis Warwick | *Phantom Isle*
Boys' Friend Library (New Series) 32, 1926
Art **Unknown**

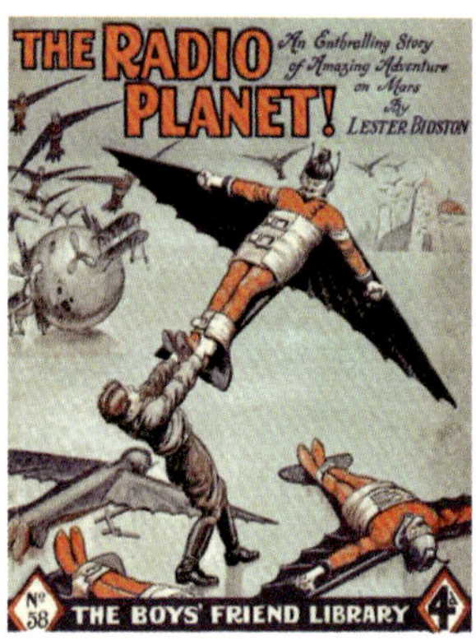

Lester Bidston
The Radio Planet!
Boys' Friend Library 58, 1926 | Art **Unknown**

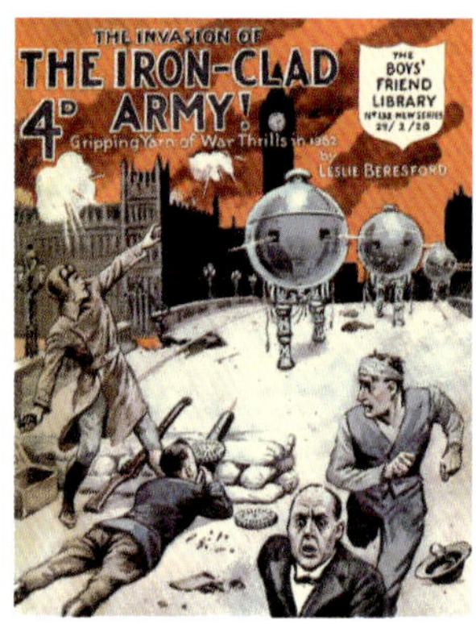

Leslie Beresford
The Invasion of the Iron-Clad Army!
Boys' Friend Library 132, 1928 | Art **Unknown**

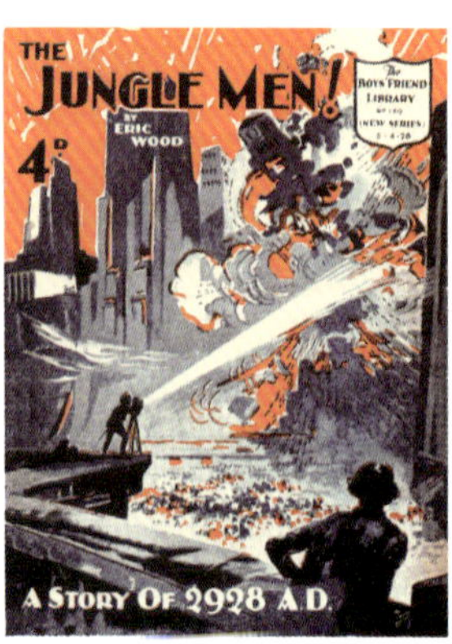

Eric Wood (Francis Knowles Campling)
The Jungle Men!
Boys' Friend Library 139, 1928 | Art **Unknown**

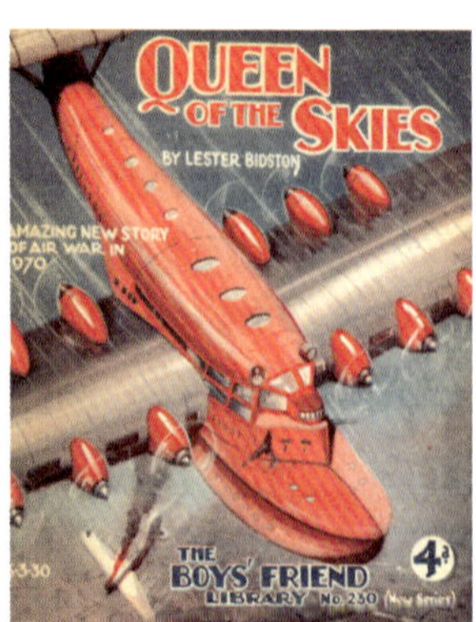

Lester Bidston
Queen of the Skies
Boys' Friend Library 230, 1930 | Art **Unknown**

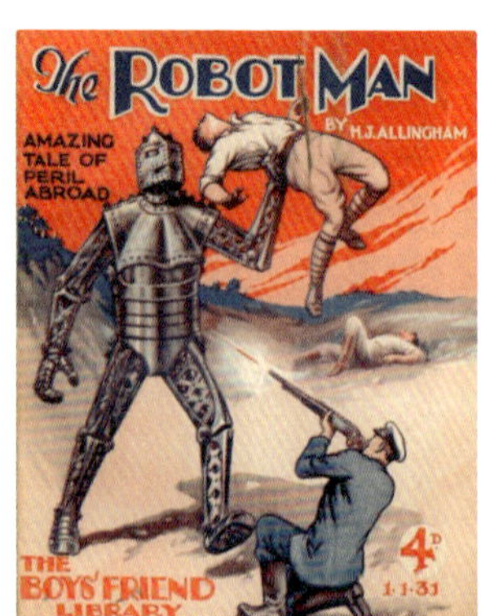

H. J. Allingham
The Robot Man
Boys' Friend Library 271, 1931 | Art **Unknown**

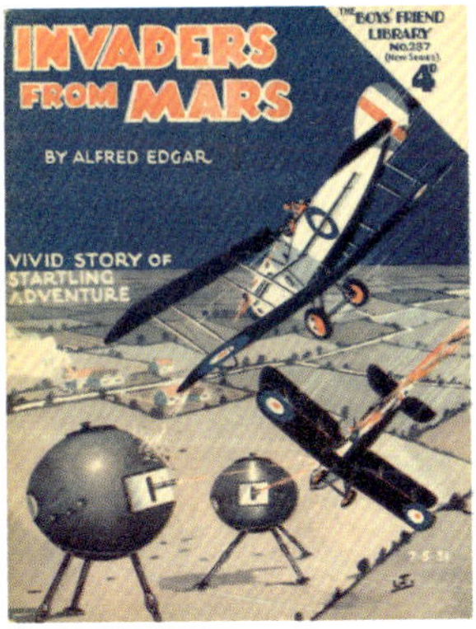

Alfred Edgar
Invaders From Mars
Boys' Friend Library 287, 1931 | Art **L. J.**

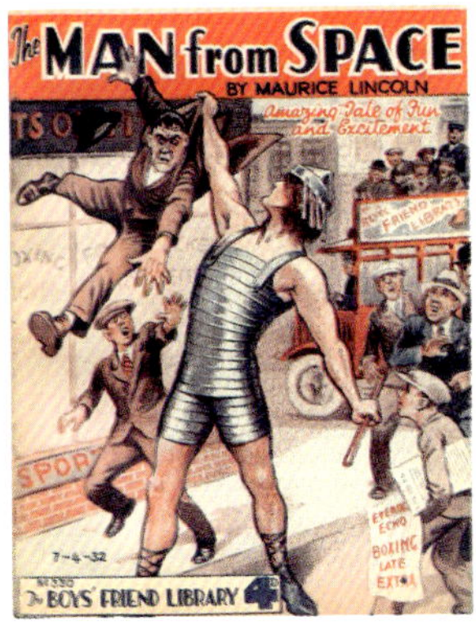

Maurice Lincoln
The Man from Space
Boys' Friend Library 330, 1932 | Art **Unknown**

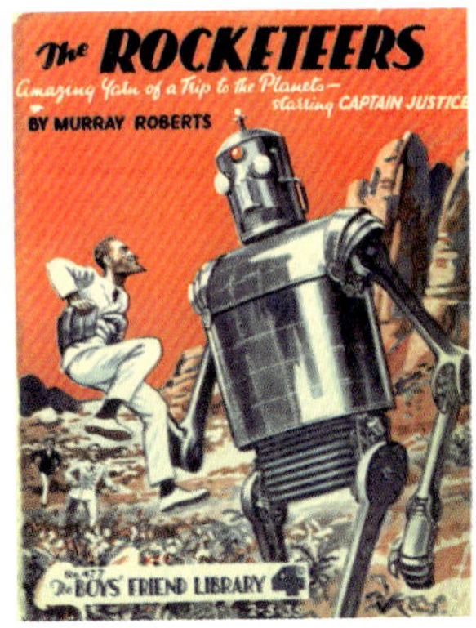

Murray Roberts
The Rocketeers
Boys' Friend Library 477, 1935 | Art **Unknown**

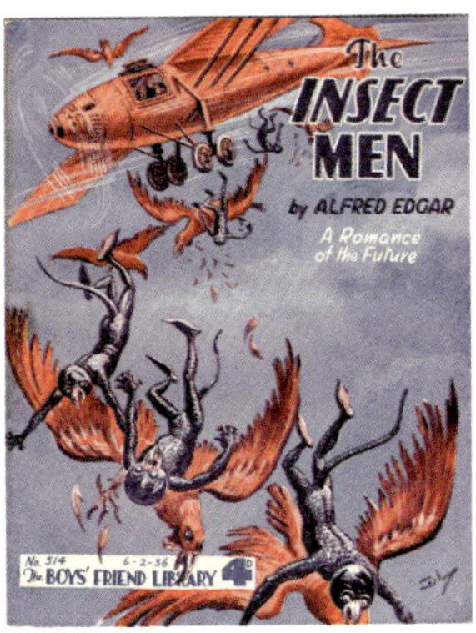

Alfred Edgar
The Insect Men
Boys' Friend Library 514, 1936 | Art **Unknown**

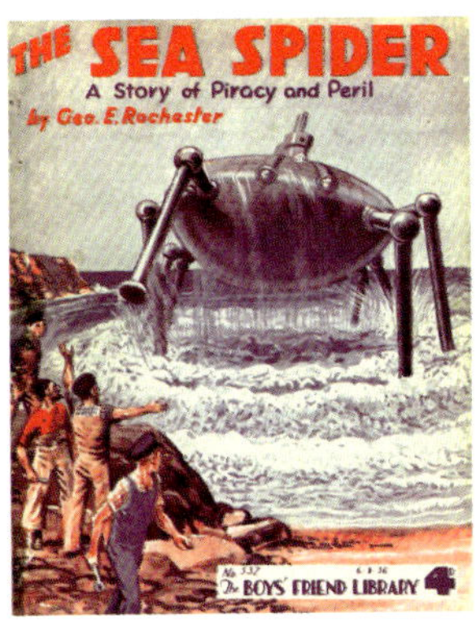

George Ernest Rochester
The Sea Spider
Boys' Friend Library 537, 1936 | Art **Unknown**

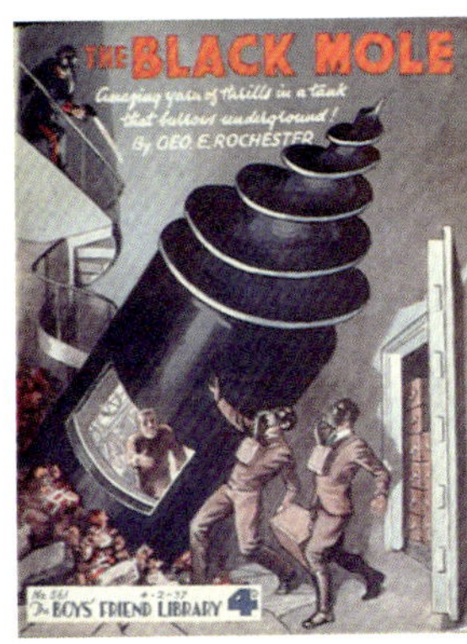

George Ernest Rochester
The Black Mole
Boys' Friend Library 561, 1937 | Art **Unknown**

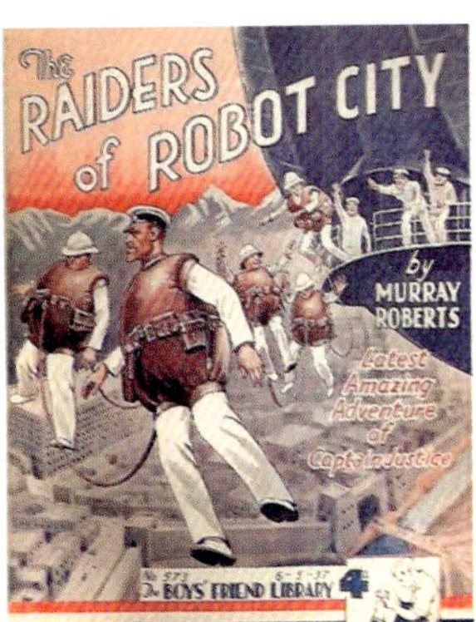

Murray Roberts
The Raiders of Robot City
Boys' Friend Library 573, 1937 | Art **Unknown**

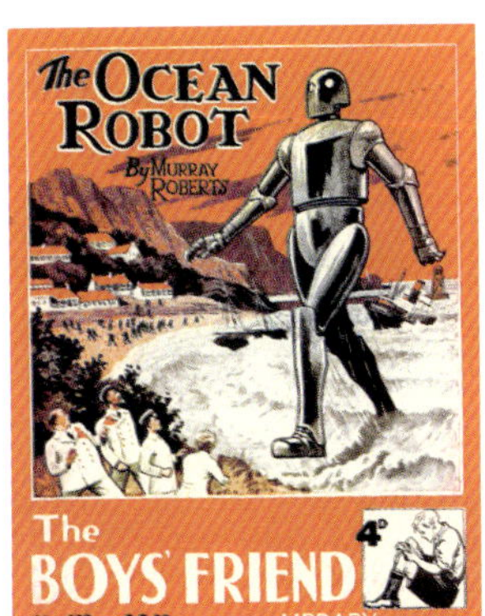

Murray Roberts
The Ocean Robot
Boys' Friend Library 629, 1938 | Art **Unknown**

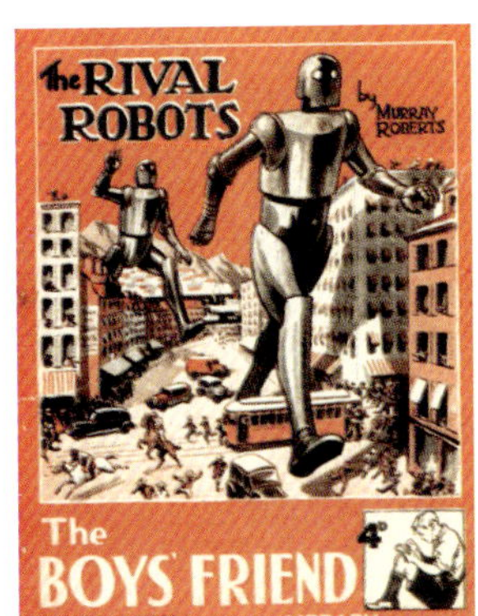

Murray Roberts
The Rival Robots
Boys' Friend Library 633, 1938 | Art **Unknown**

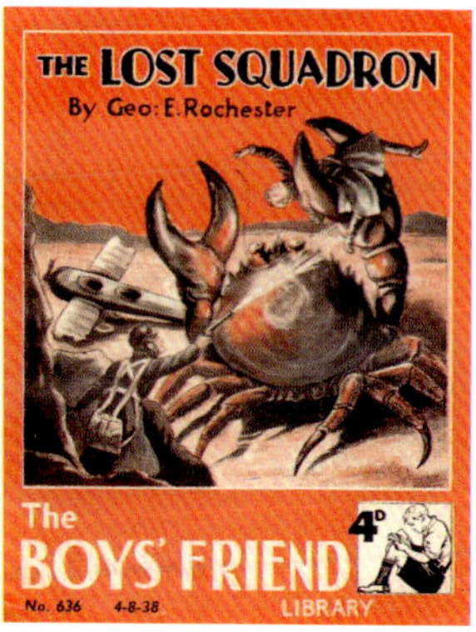

George Ernest Rochester
The Lost Squadron
Boys' Friend Library 636, 1938 | Art **Unknown**

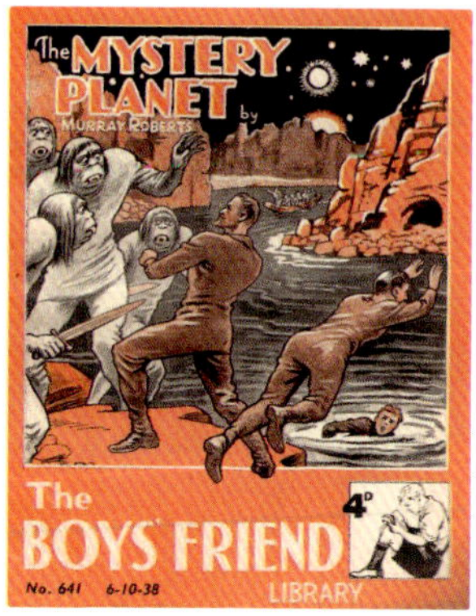

Murray Roberts
The Mystery Planet
Boys' Friend Library 641, 1938 | Art **Unknown**

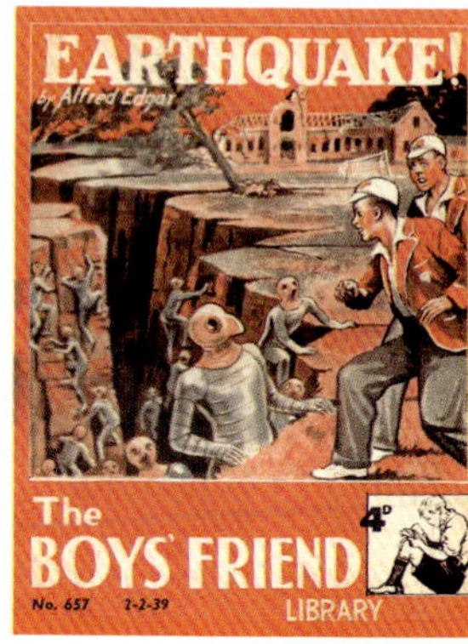

Alfred Edgar
Earthquake!
Boys' Friend Library 657, 1939 | Art **Unknown**

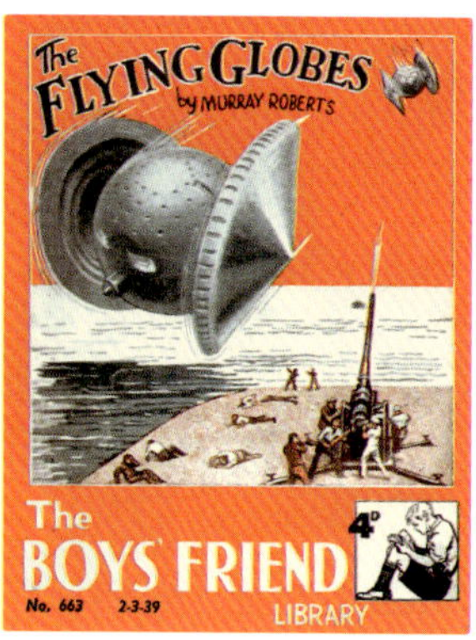

Murray Roberts
The Flying Globes
Boys' Friend Library 663, 1939 | Art **Unknown**

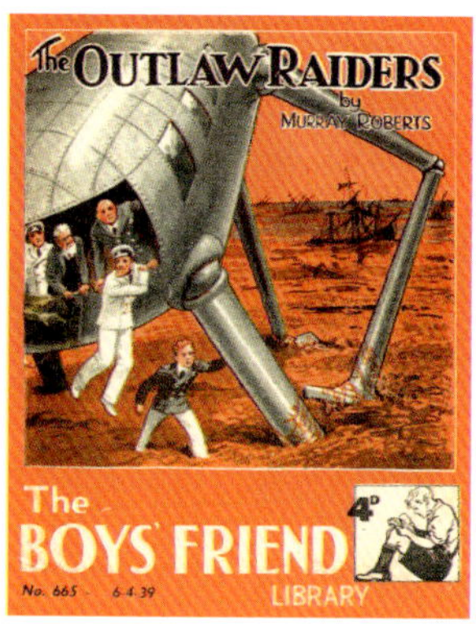

Murray Roberts
The Outlaw Raiders
Boys' Friend Library 665, 1939 | Art **Unknown**

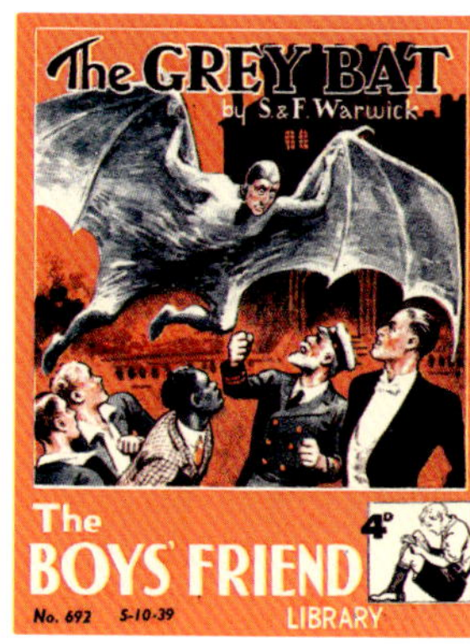

Sidney and Francis Warwick
The Grey Bat
Boys' Friend Library 692, 1939 | Art **Unknown**

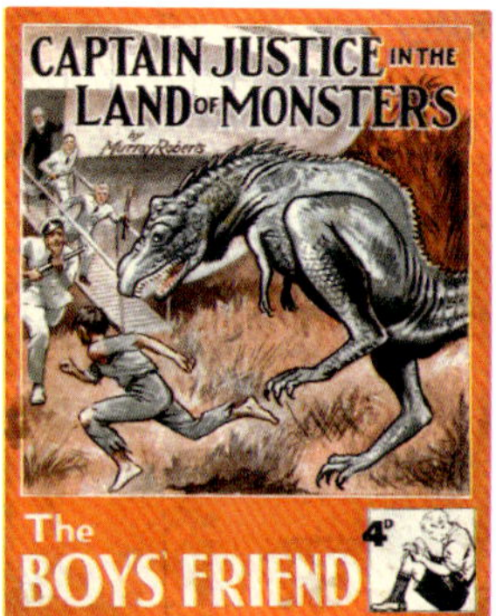

Murray Roberts
Captain Justice in the Land of Monsters
Boys' Friend Library 697, 1939 | Art **Unknown**

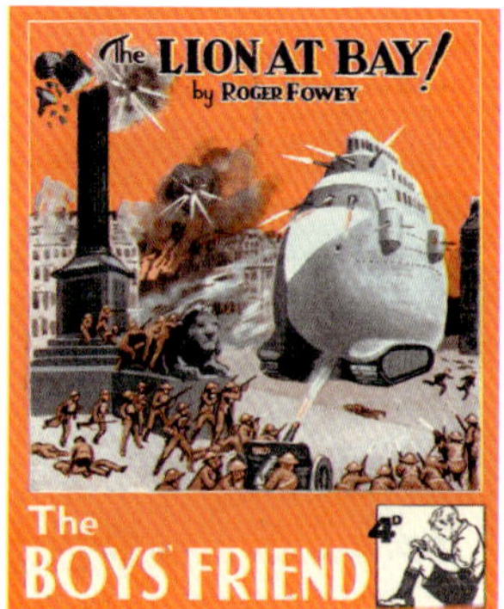

Roger Fowey (Alfred Edgar)
The Lion at Bay!
Boys' Friend Library 679, 1939 | Art **Unknown**

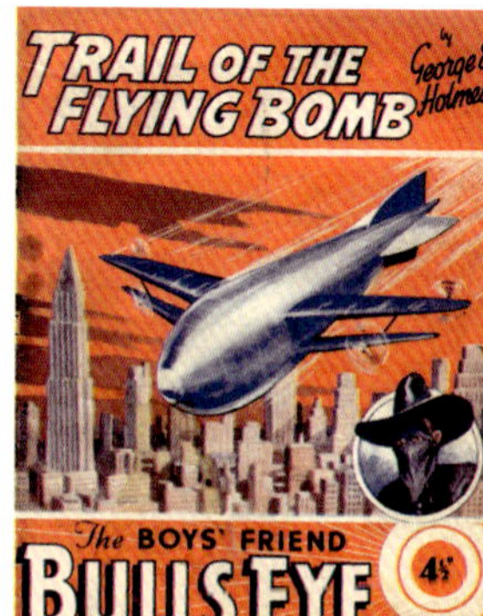

George E. Holmes (George Ernest Rochester)
Trail of the Flying Bomb
Boys' Friend Library 701, 1940 | Art **Unknown**

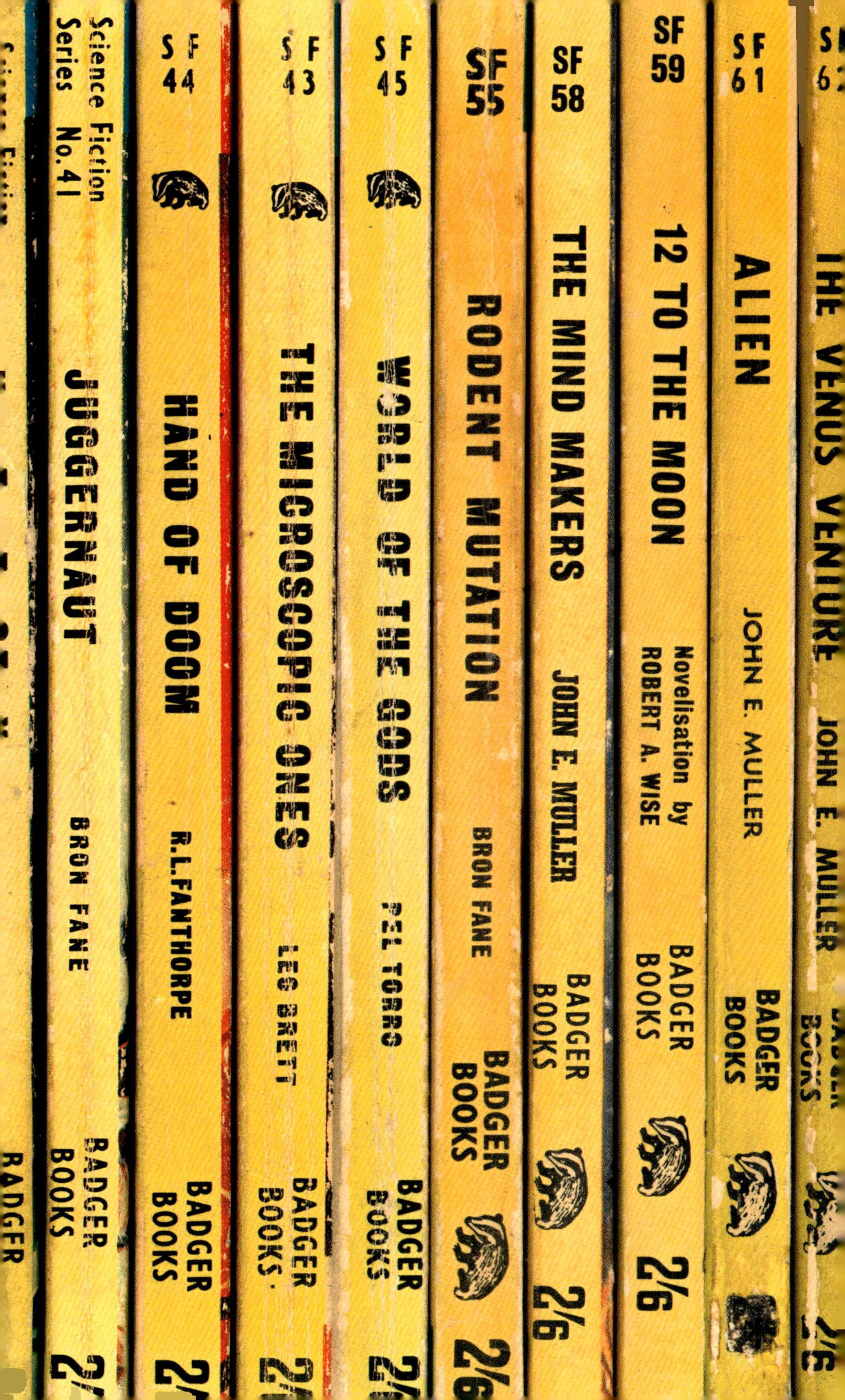
Science Fiction Series No.41
JUGGERNAUT
BRON FANE
BADGER BOOKS
SF 44
HAND OF DOOM
R.L.FANTHORPE
BADGER BOOKS
SF 43
THE MICROSCOPIC ONES
LEO BRETT
BADGER BOOKS
SF 45
WORLD OF THE GODS
PEL TORRO
BADGER BOOKS
SF 55
RODENT MUTATION
BRON FANE
BADGER BOOKS
2/6
SF 58
THE MIND MAKERS
JOHN E. MULLER
BADGER BOOKS
2/6
SF 59
12 TO THE MOON
Novelisation by ROBERT A. WISE
BADGER BOOKS
2/6
SF 61
ALIEN
JOHN E. MULLER
BADGER BOOKS
THE VENUS VENTURE
JOHN E. MULLER

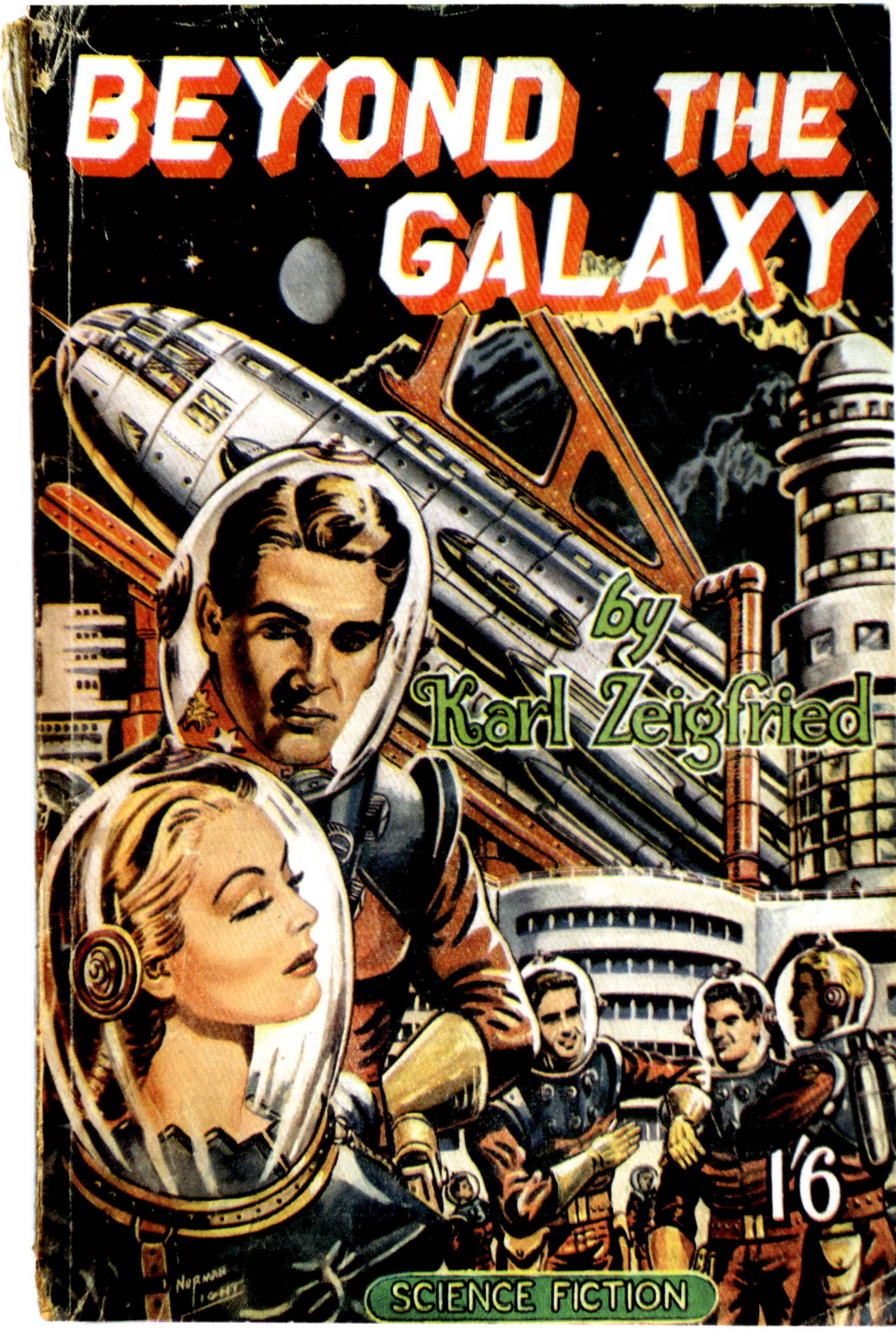

Karl Zeigfried (Tom W. Wade) | *Beyond the Galaxy*
John Spencer & Co., 1953 | Art **Norman Light**

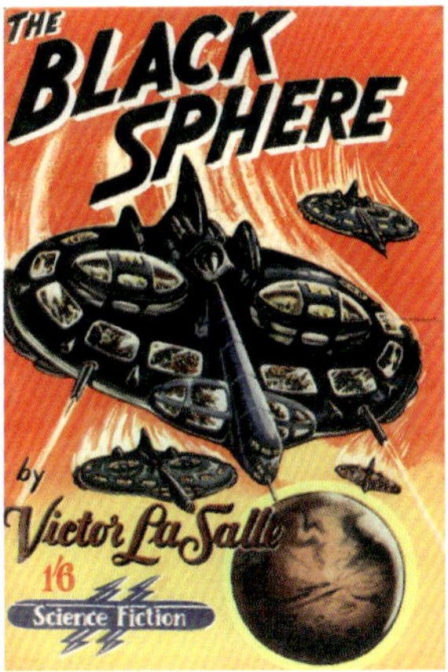

Victor La Salle (Gerald Evans)
The Black Sphere
John Spencer & Co., 1952 | Art **Norman Light**

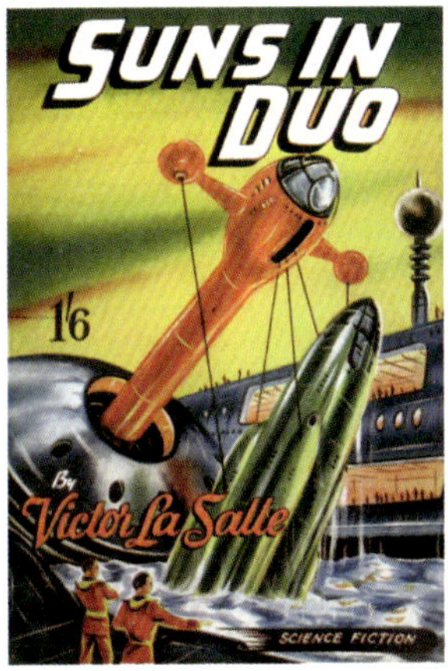

Victor La Salle (Tom W. Wade)
Suns in Duo
John Spencer & Co., 1953 | Art **Gordon C. Davies**

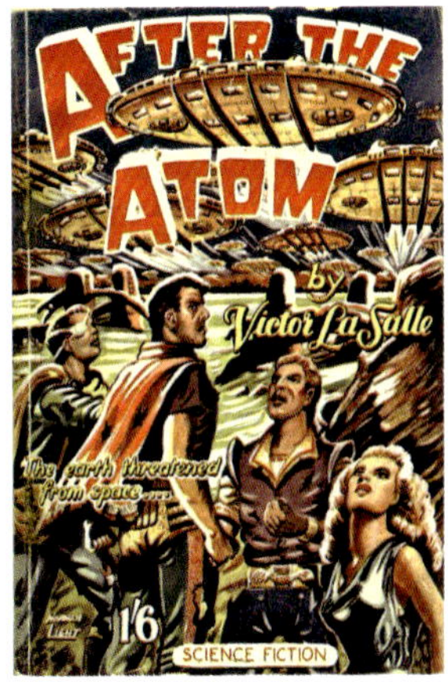

Victor La Salle (Leonard G. Fish)
After the Atom
John Spencer & Co., 1953 | Art **Norman Light**

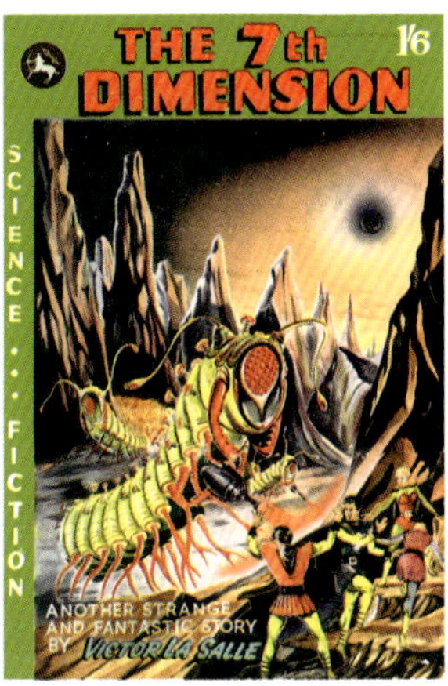

Victor La Salle (Tom W. Wade)
The 7th Dimension
John Spencer & Co., 1953 | Art **Gordon C. Davies**

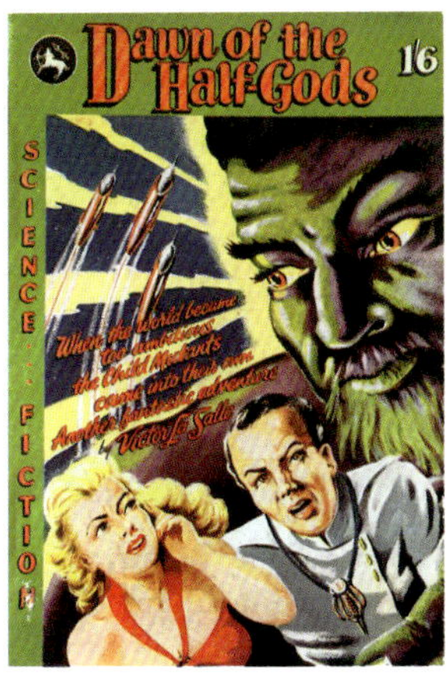

Victor La Salle (John Glasby)
Dawn of the Half-Gods
John Spencer & Co., 1953 | Art **Ray Theobald**

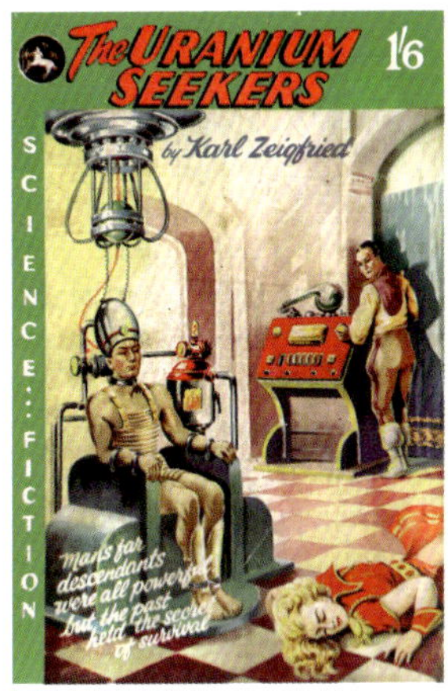

Karl Zeigfried (John Glasby)
The Uranium Seekers
John Spencer & Co., 1953 | Art **Ray Theobald**

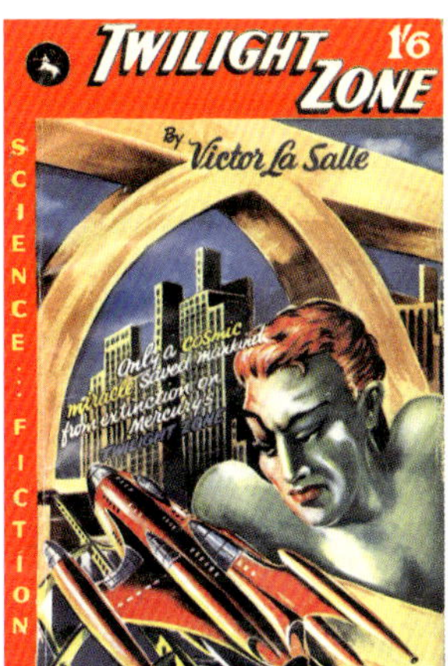

Victor La Salle (John Glasby)
Twilight Zone
John Spencer & Co., 1954 | Art **Ray Theobald**

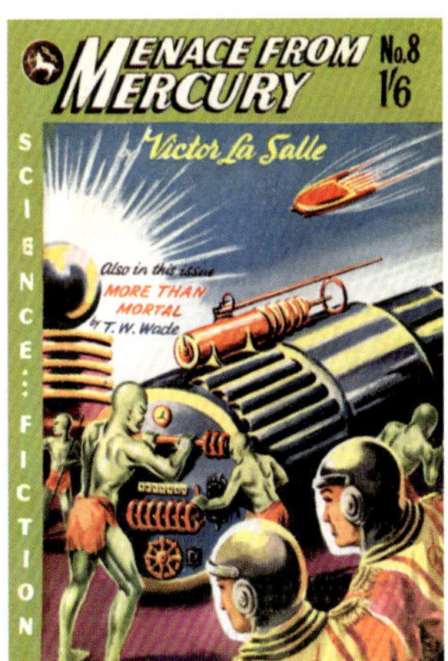

Victor La Salle (R. L. Fanthorpe)
Menace from Mercury
John Spencer & Co., 1954 | Art **Ray Theobald**

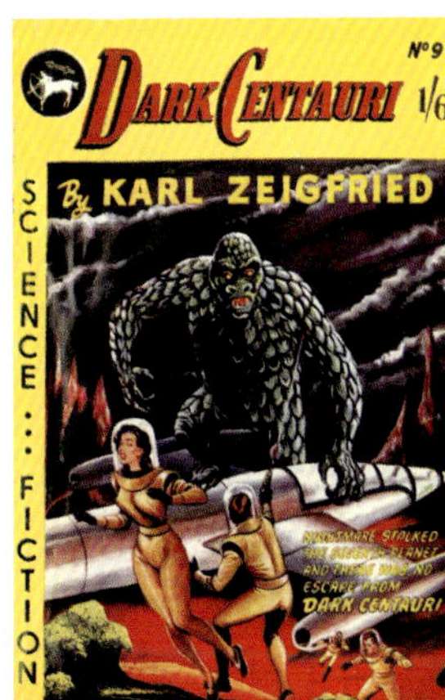

Karl Zeigfried (John Glasby)
Dark Centauri
John Spencer & Co., 1954 | Art **Ron Embleton**

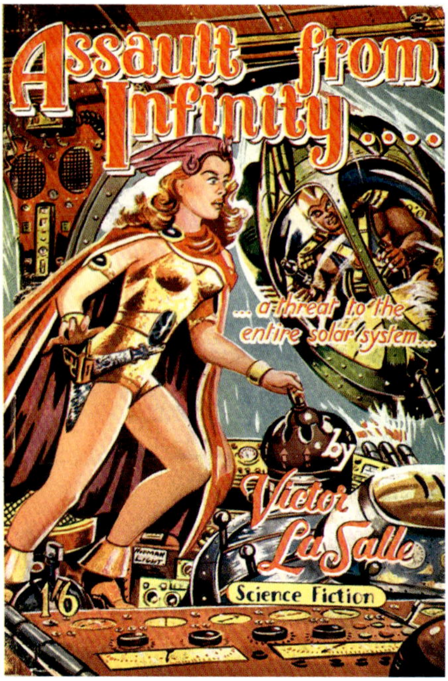

Victor La Salle (Tom W. Wade) | *Assault from Infinity*
John Spencer & Co., 1953 | Art **Norman Light**

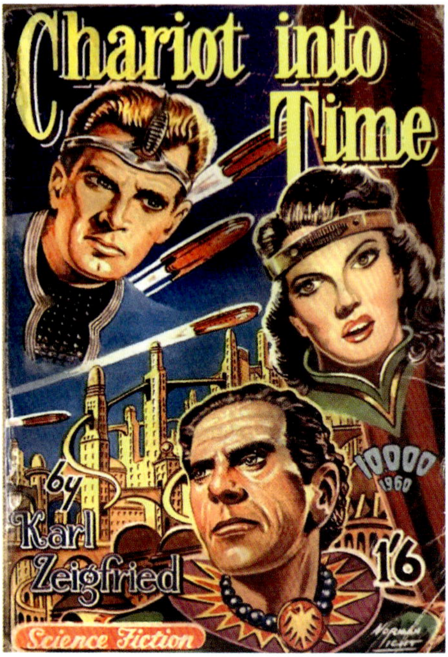

Karl Zeigfried (Tom W. Wade) | *Chariot Into Time*
John Spencer & Co., 1953 | Art **Norman Light**

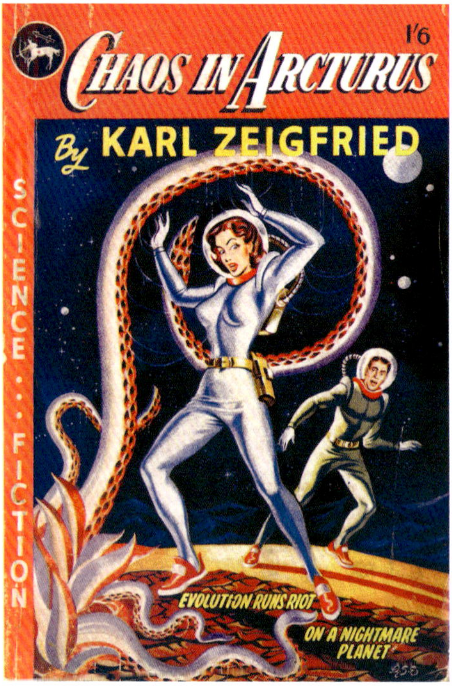

Karl Zeigfried (Tom W. Wade) | *Chaos in Arcturus*
John Spencer & Co., 1953 | Art **Ron Embleton**

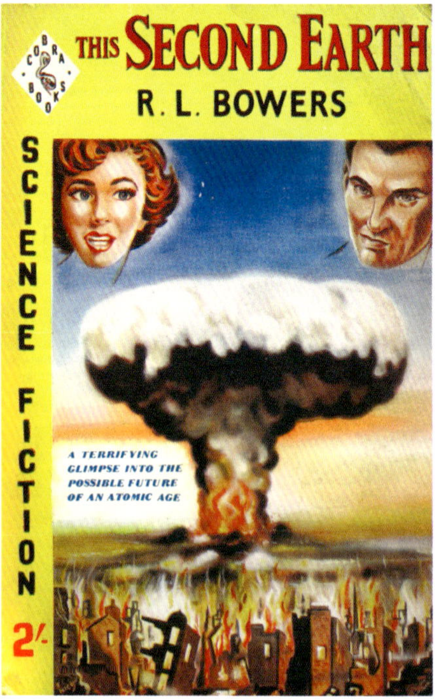

R. L. Bowers (John Glasby) | *This Second Earth*
Cobra Books Science Series No.1, 1957 | Art **Stanley Nicholson**

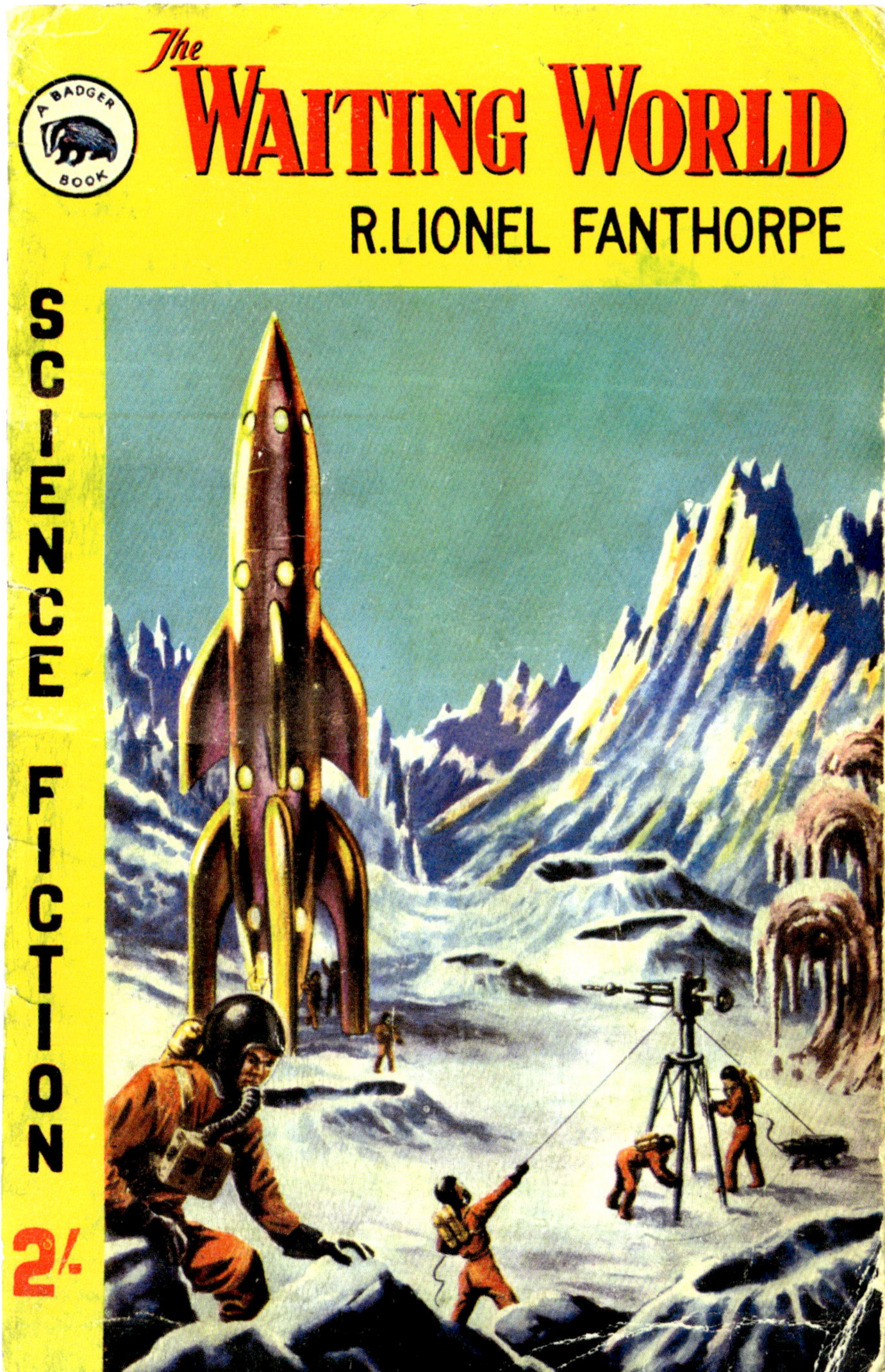

R. Lionel Fanthorpe | *The Waiting World*
Badger Books Science Fiction Series No. 1 (SF1), 1958 | Art **Stanley Nicholson**

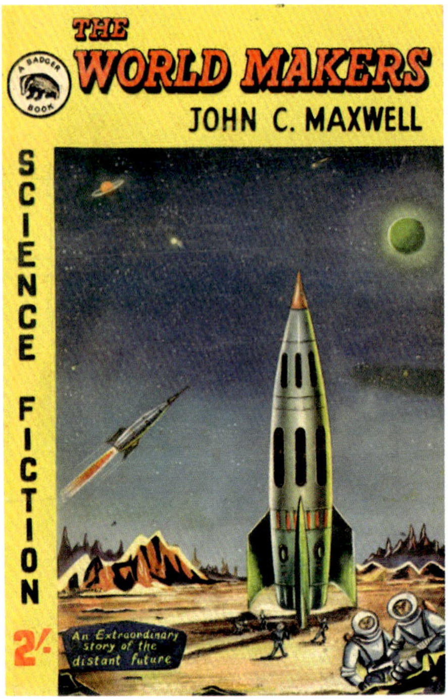

John C. Maxwell (John Glasby) | *The World Makers*
Badger Books SF3, 1958 | Art **Gordon C. Davies**

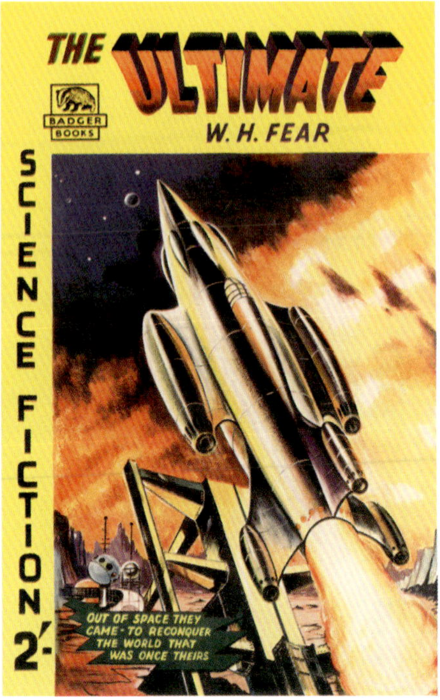

W. H. Fear | *The Ultimate*
Badger Books SF3 1958 | Art **Stanley Nicholson** or **Gerald Facey**

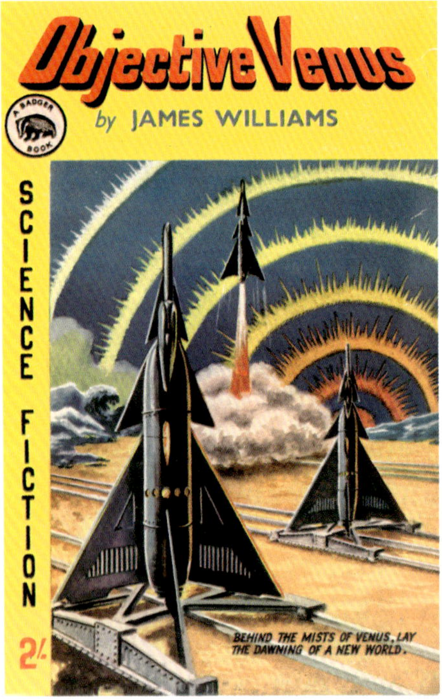

James Williams (Tom W. Wade) | *Objective Venus*
Badger Books SF4, 1958 | Art **Stanley Nicholson**

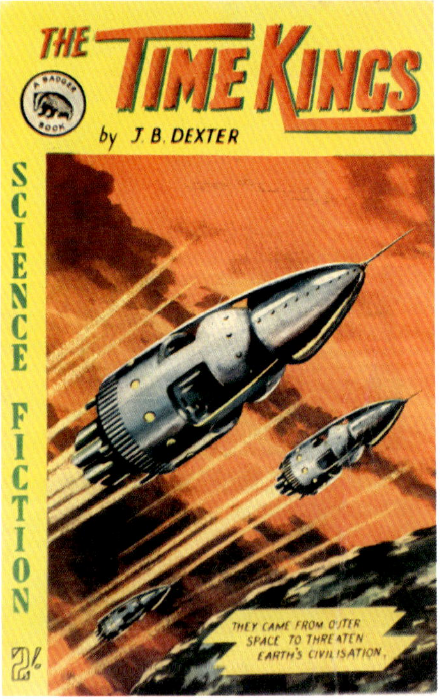

J. B. Dexter | *The Time Kings*
Badger Books SF6, 1958 | Art **Stanley Nicholson** or **Ray Theobald**

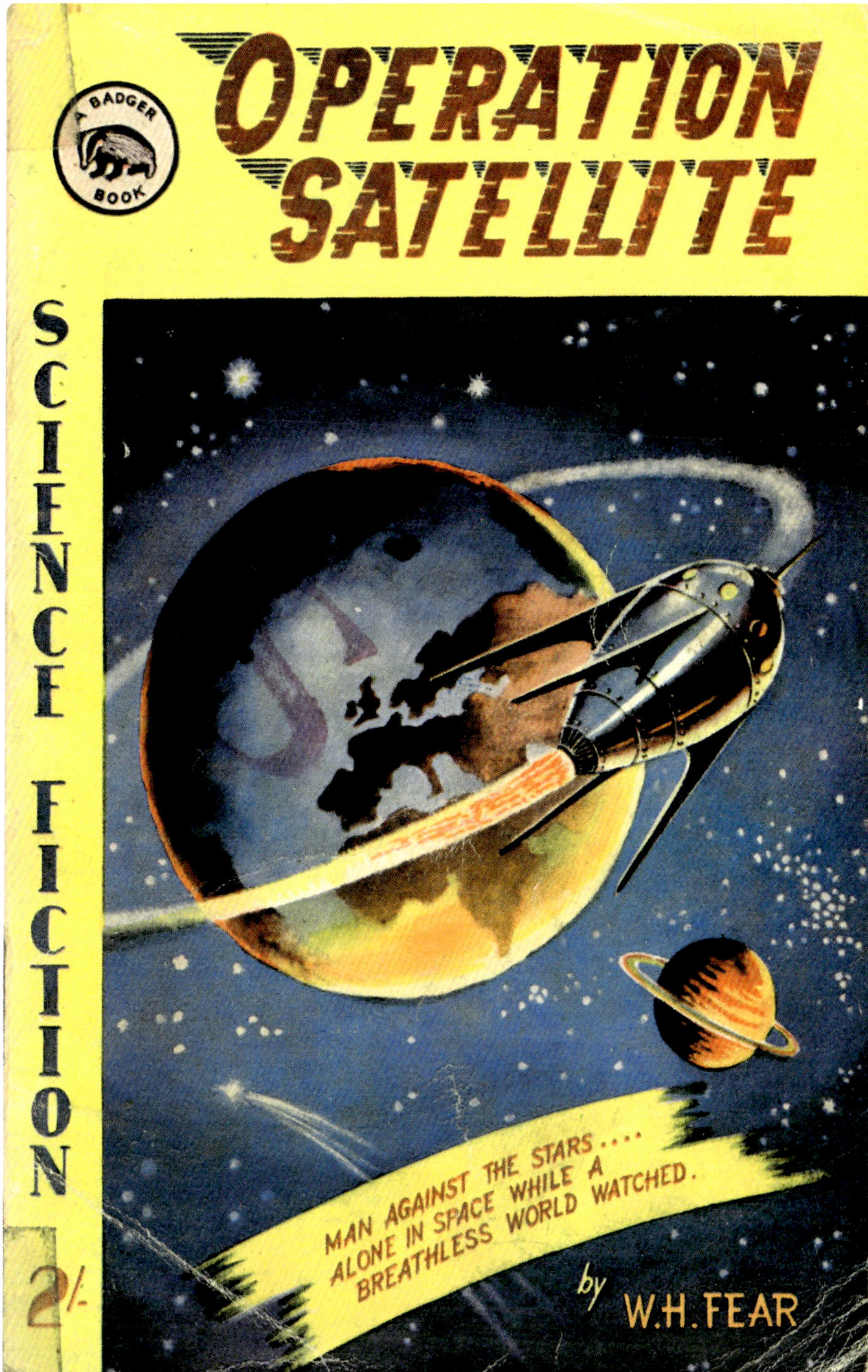

W. H. Fear | *Operation Satellite*
Badger Books SF5, 1958 | Art **Stanley Nicholson**

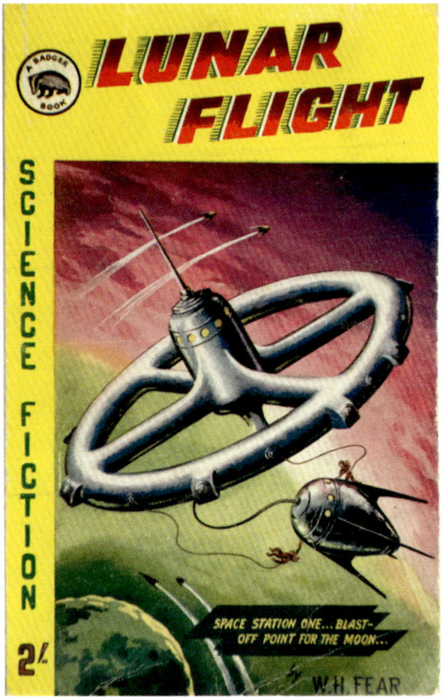

W. H. Fear | *Lunar Flight*
Badger Books SF7, 1958 | Art **Stanley Nicholson**

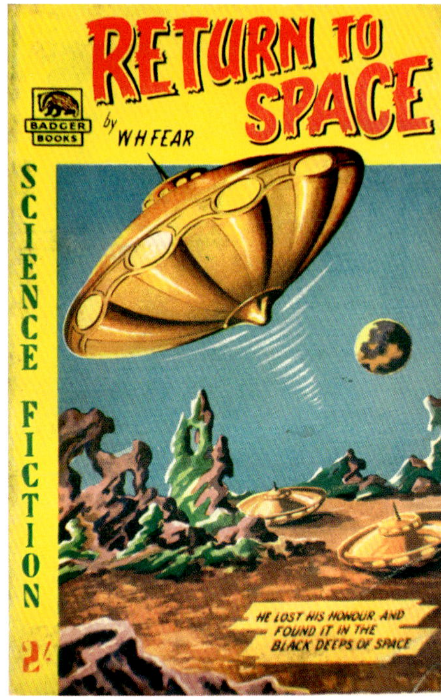

W. H. Fear | *Return to Space*
Badger Books SF9, 1958 | Art **Stanley Nicholson**

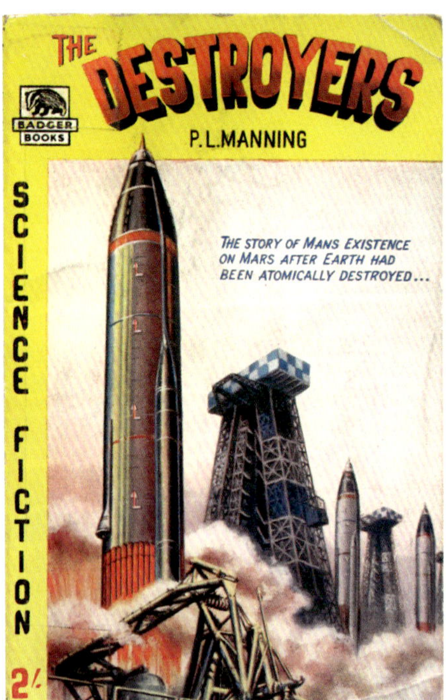

P. L. Manning (John Glasby) | *The Destroyers*
Badger Books SF11, 1958 | Art **Stanley Nicholson** or **Ray Theobald**

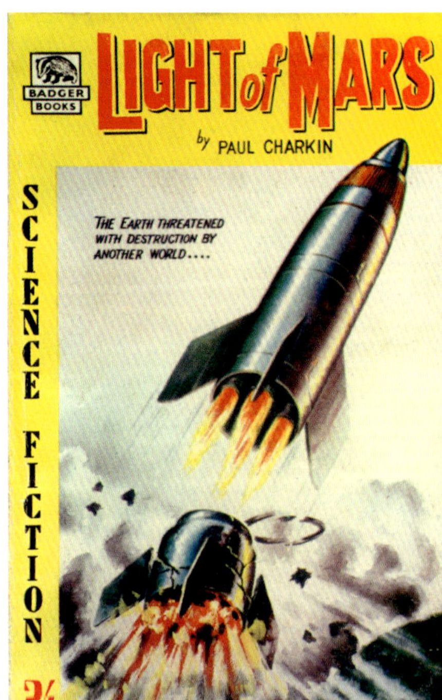

Paul Charkin | *Light of Mars*
Badger Books SF12, 1959 | Art **Stanley Nicholson** or **Ray Theobald**

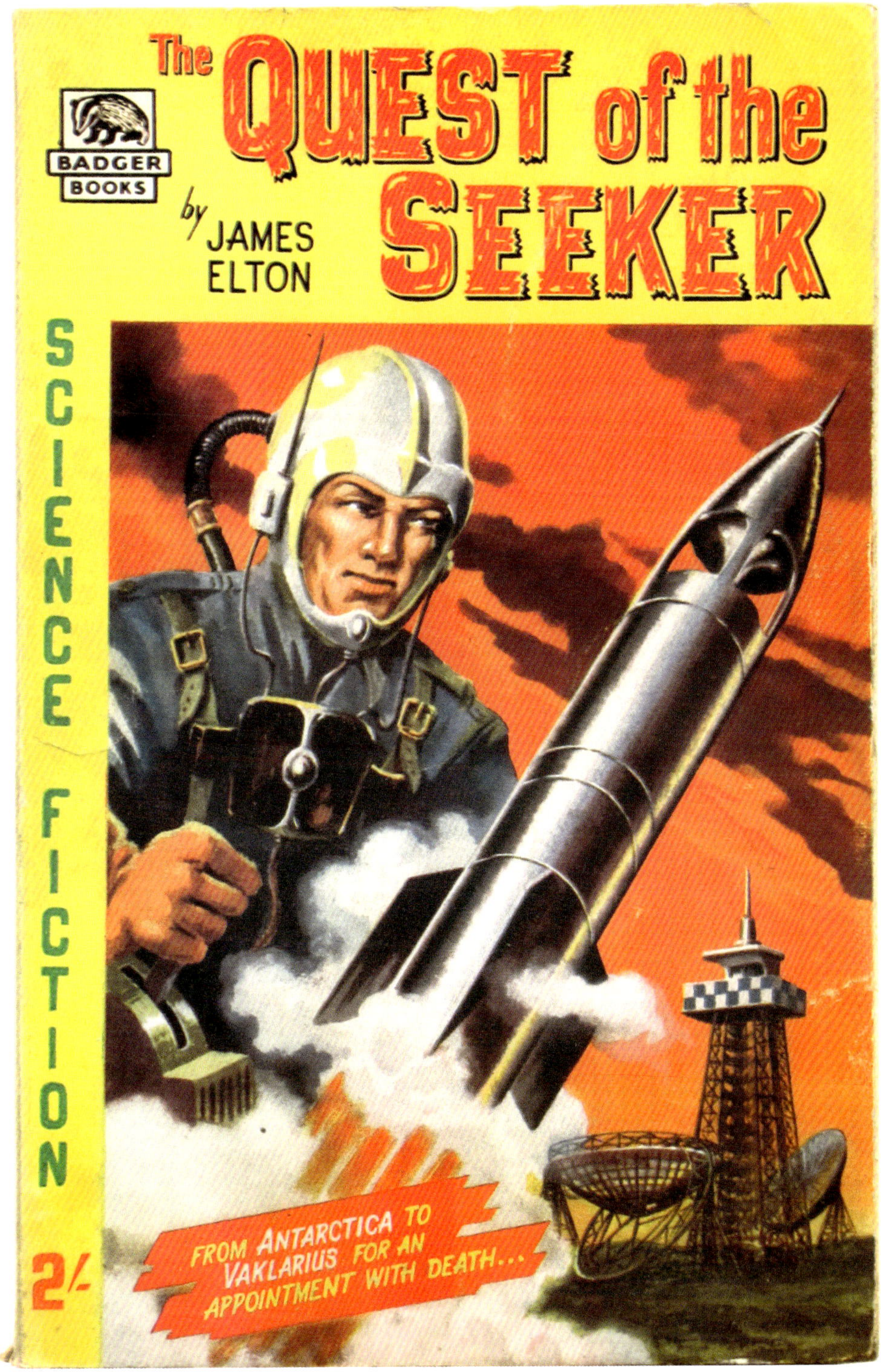

James Elton (W. H. Fear) | *The Quest of the Seeker*
Badger Books SF10, 1958 | Art **Stanley Nicholson** or **Ray Theobald**

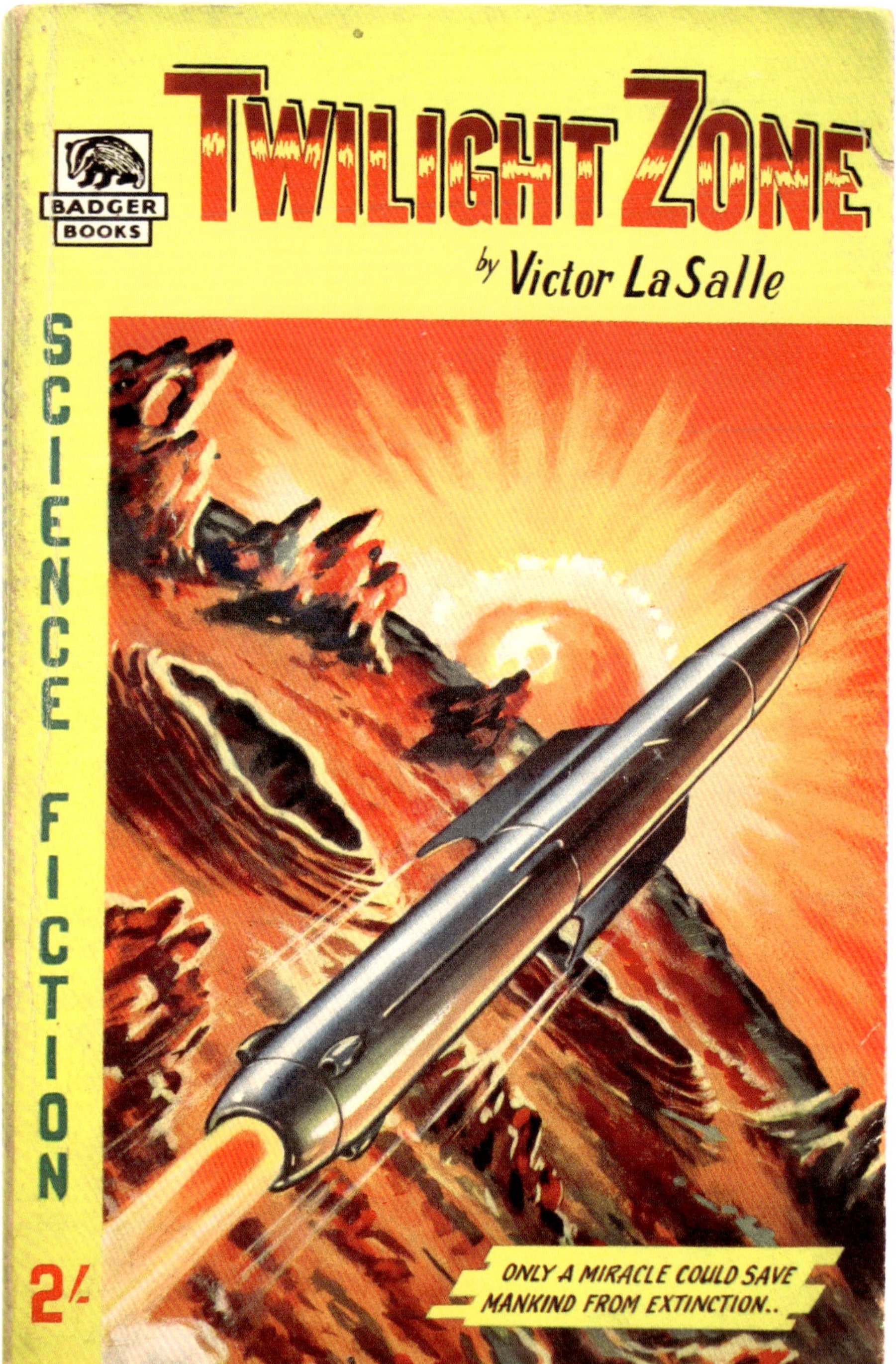

Victor La Salle (John Glasby) | *Twilight Zone*
Badger Books SF13, 1959 | Art **Stanley Nicholson**

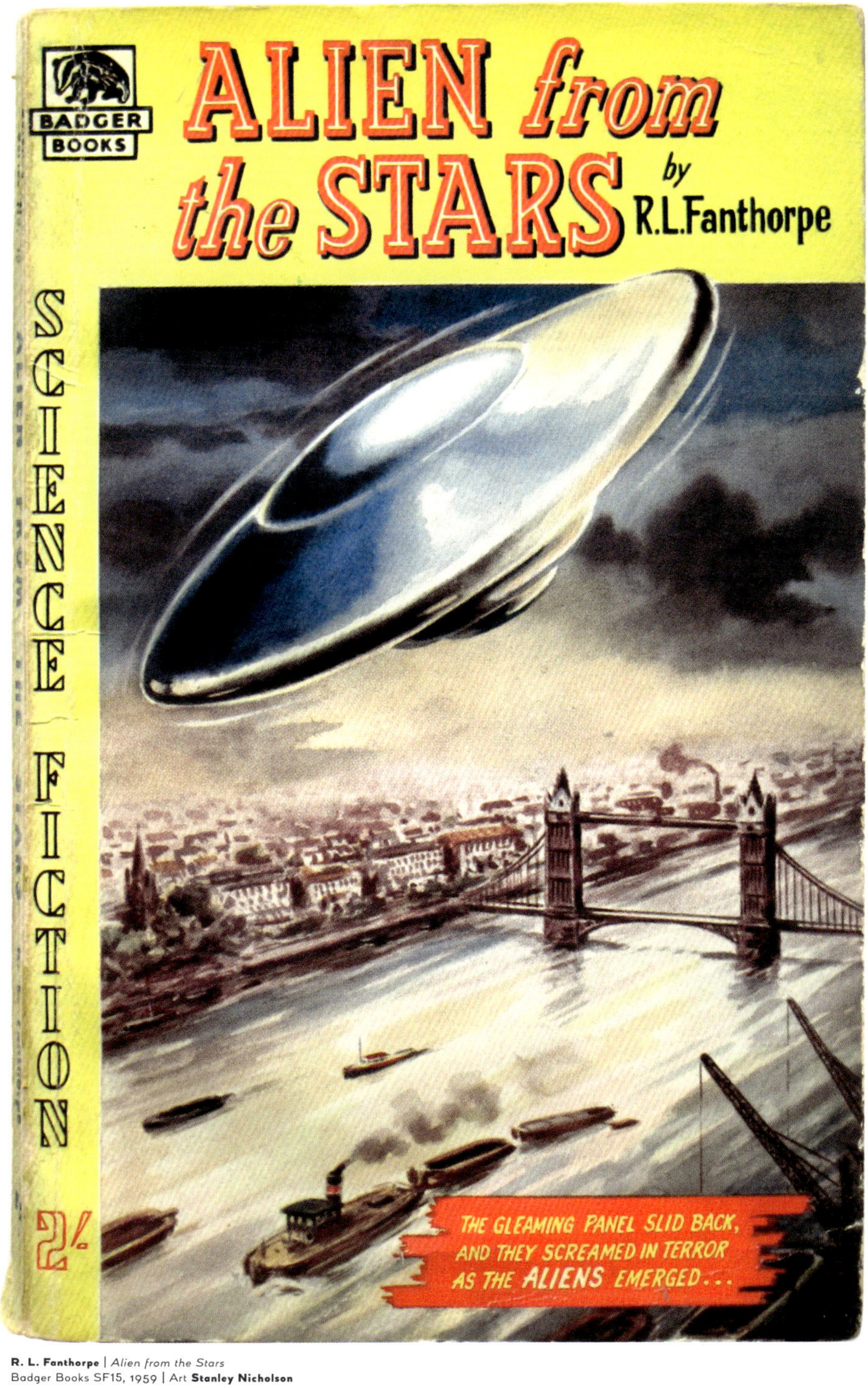

R. L. Fanthorpe | *Alien from the Stars*
Badger Books SF15, 1959 | Art **Stanley Nicholson**

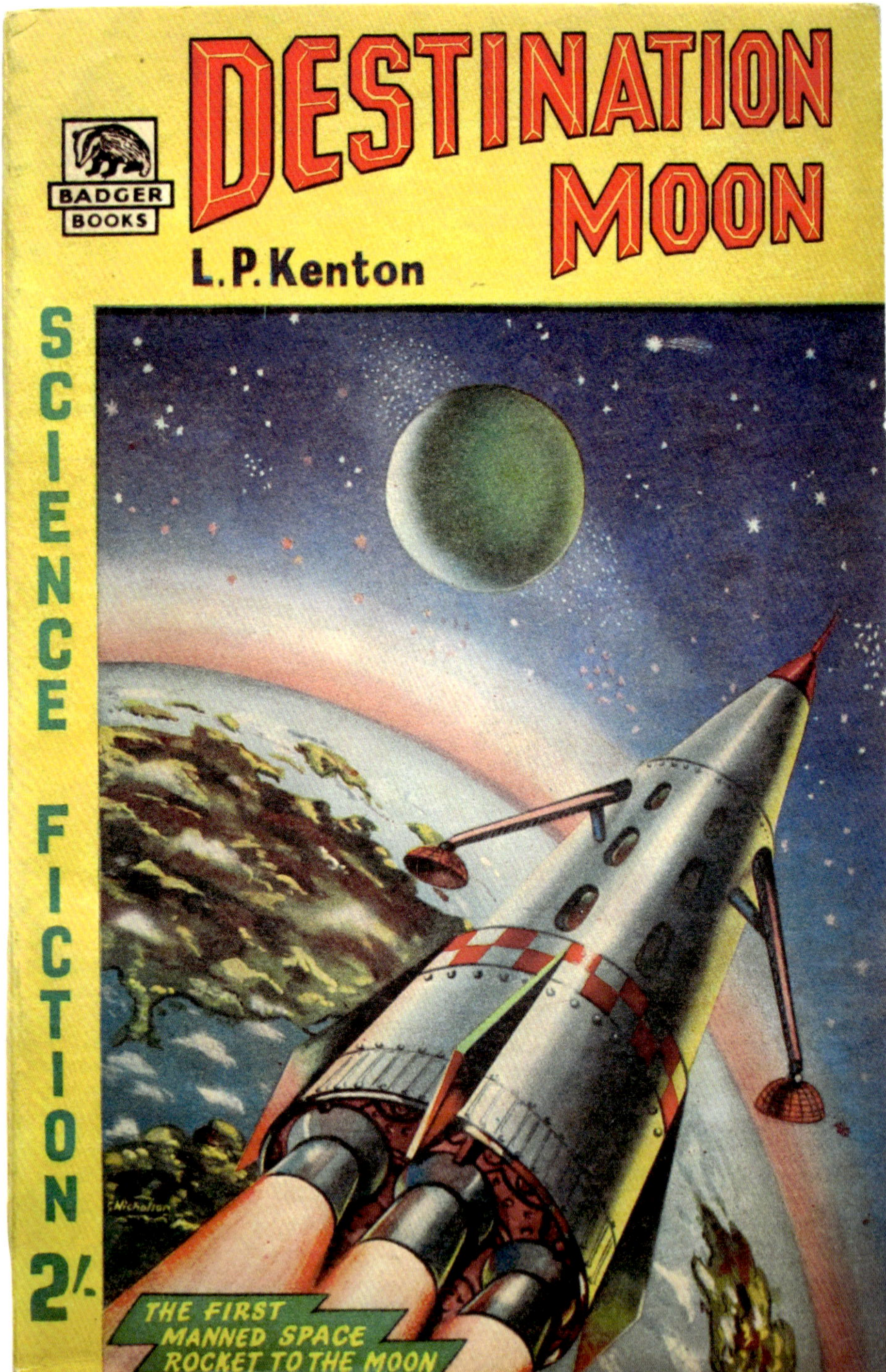

L. P. Kenton (R. L. Fanthorpe) | *Destination Moon*
Badger Books SF13, 1959 | Art **Stanley Nicholson**

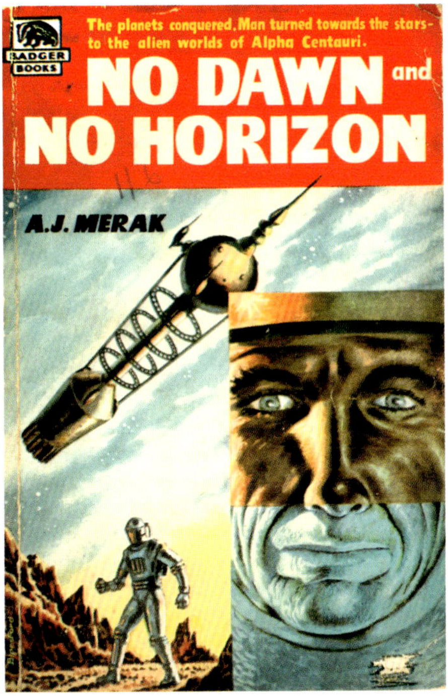

A. J. Merak (John Glasby) | *No Dawn and No Horizon*
Badger Books SF16, 1959 | Art **Ed Blandford**

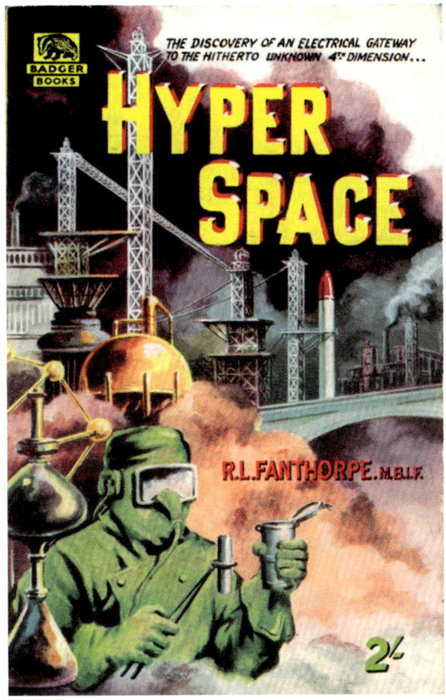

R. L. Fanthorpe M. B. I. F. | *Hyper Space*
Badger Books SF17, 1959 | Art **Ray Theobald**

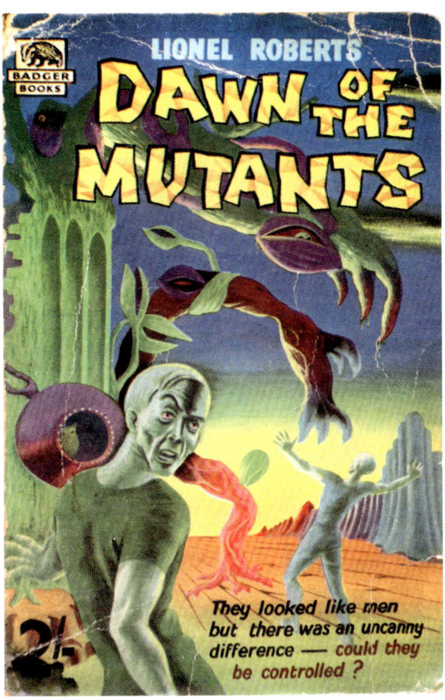

Lionel Roberts (R. L. Fanthorpe) | *Dawn of the Mutants*
Badger Books SF18, 1959 | Art **Unknown**

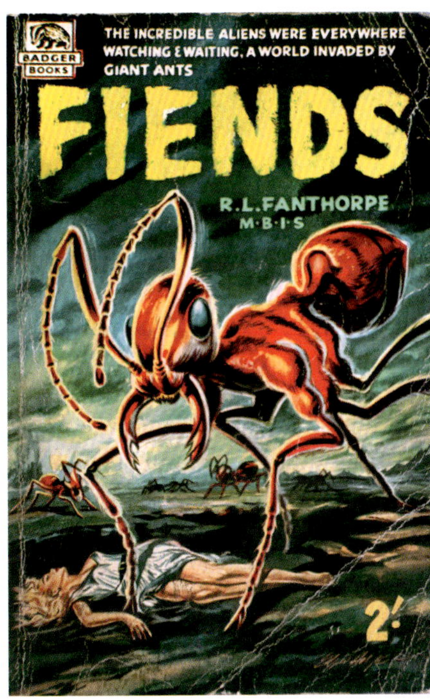

R. L. Fanthorpe M. B. I. S. | *Fiends*
Badger Books SF22, 1959 | Art **Edgar Hodges**

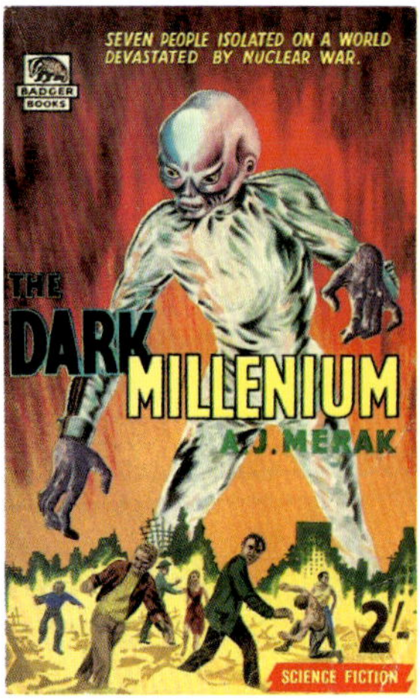

A. J. Merak (John Glasby)
The Dark Millen(n)ium
Badger Books SF19, 1959 | Art **Unknown**

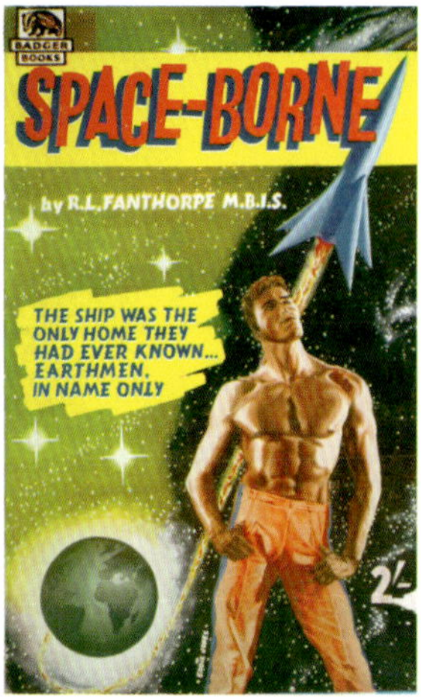

R. L. Fanthorpe M. B. I. S.
Space-Borne
Badger Books SF20, 1959 | Art **Eddie Jones**

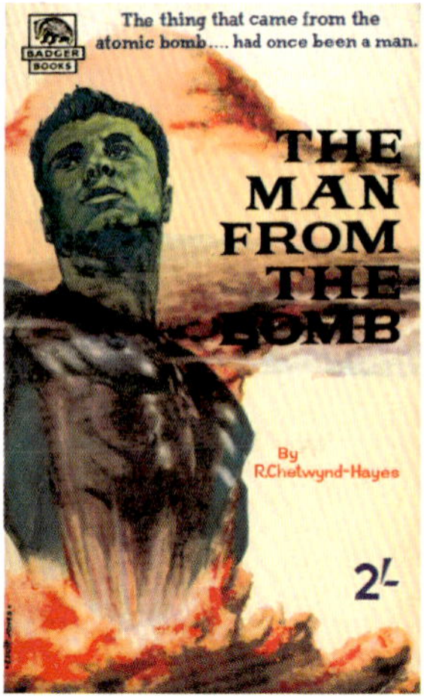

R. Chetwynd-Hayes
The Man from the Bomb
Badger Books SF21, 1959 | Art **Eddie Jones**

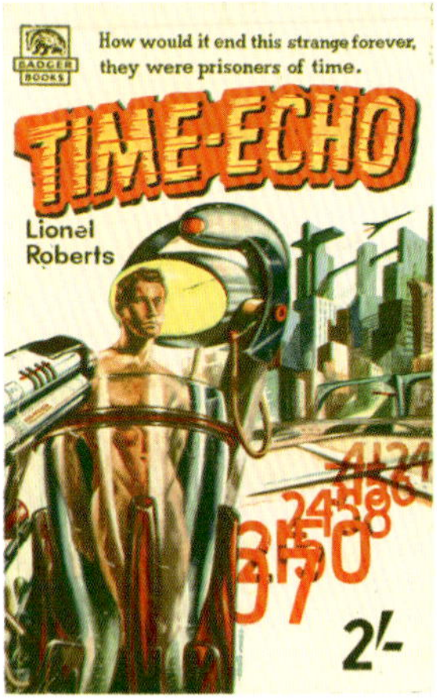

Lionel Roberts (R. L. Fanthorpe)
Time-Echo
Badger Books SF23, 1959 | Art **Eddie Jones**

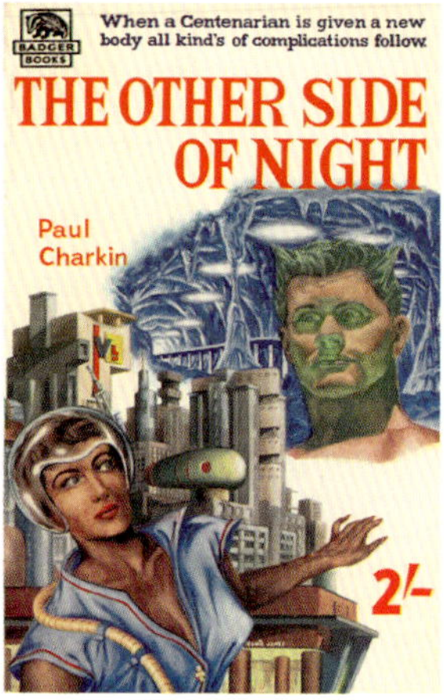

Paul Charkin
The Other Side of Night
Badger Books SF24, 1961 | Art **Eddie Jones**

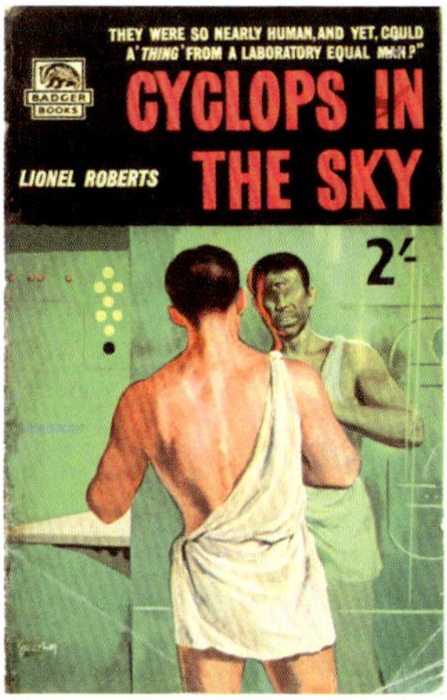

Lionel Roberts (R. L. Fanthorpe)
Cyclops in the Sky
Badger Books SF26, 1960 | Art **Carlo Jacono**

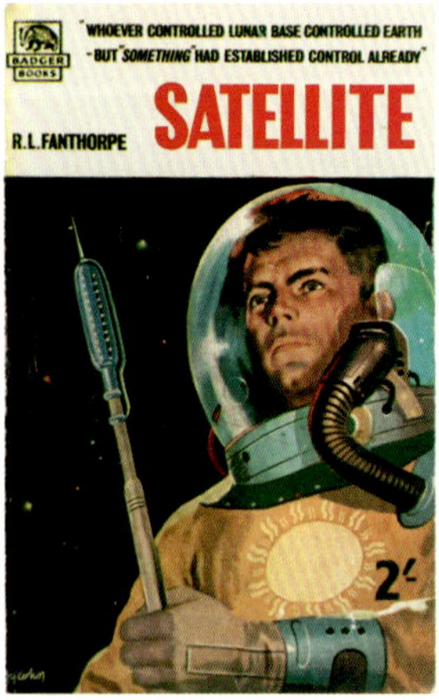

R. Lionel Fanthorpe
Satellite
Badger Books SF27, 1960 | Art **Carlo Jacono**

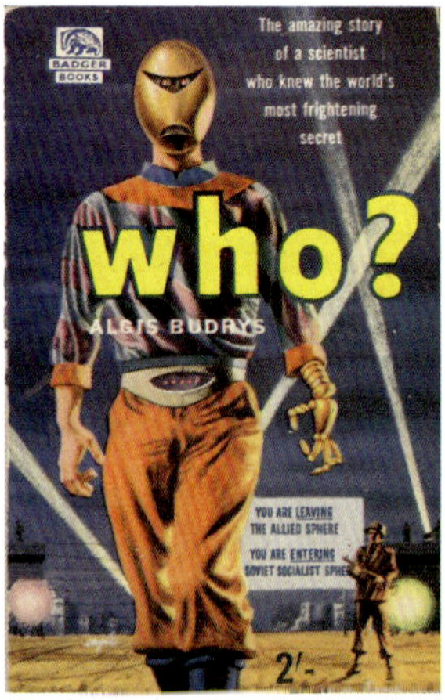

Algis Budrys
Who?
Badger Books SF28, 1960 | Art **Robert Engle**

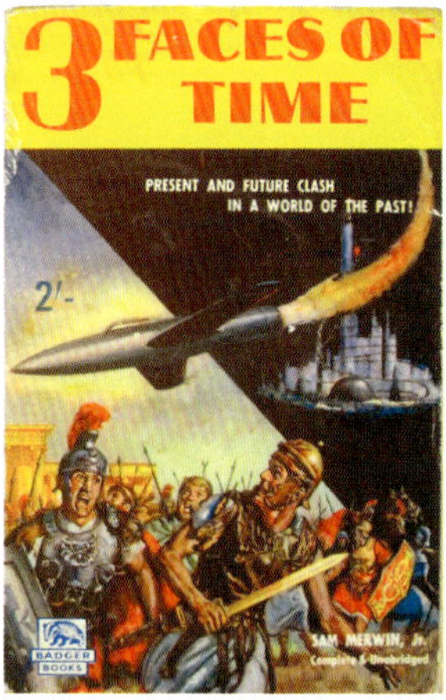

Sam Merwin, Jr.
3 Faces of Time
Badger Books SF29, 1960 | Art **Ed Valigursky**

Algis Budrys | *Who?*
Badger Books SF28, 1960 | Original art **Robert Engle**

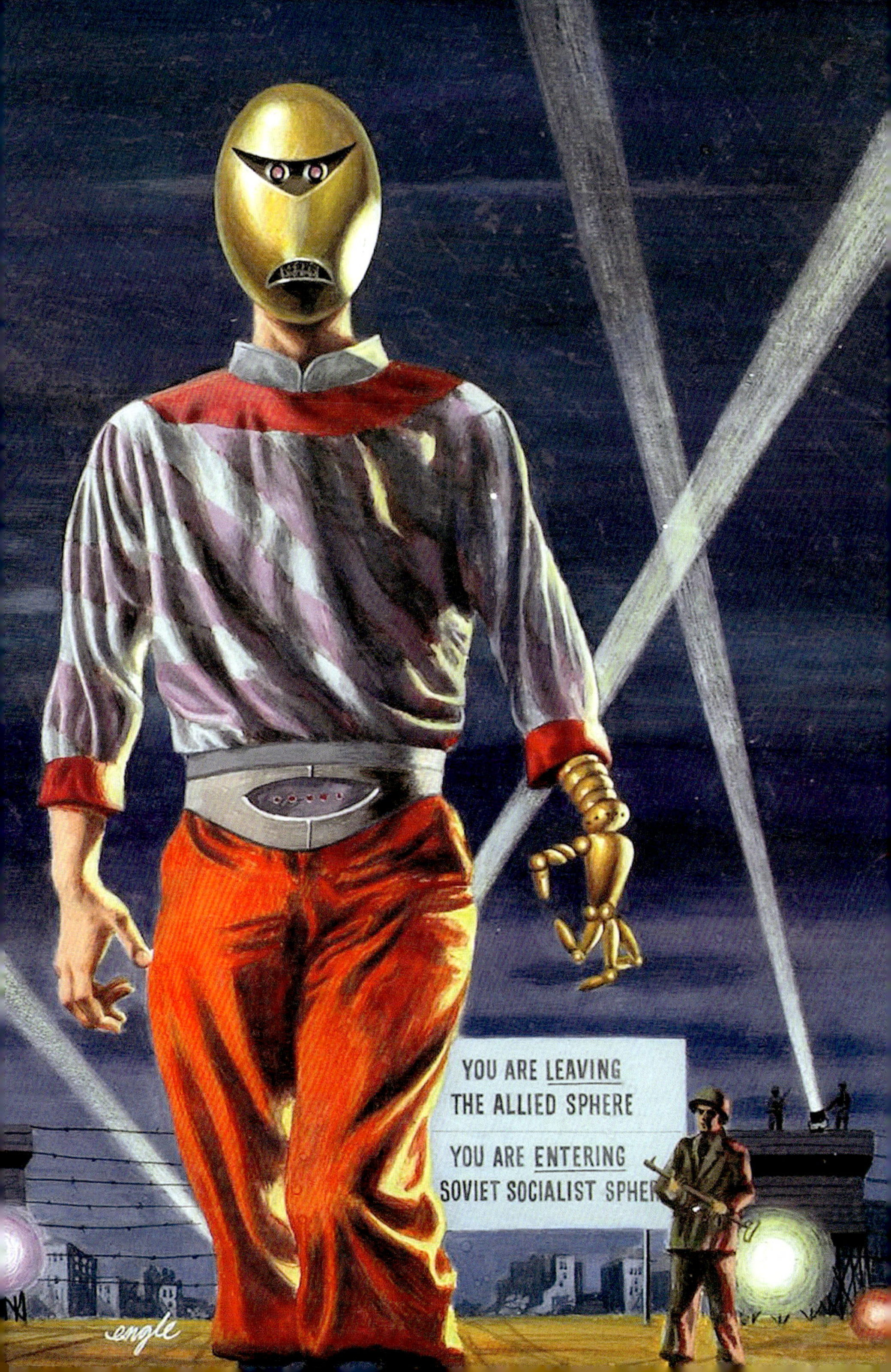

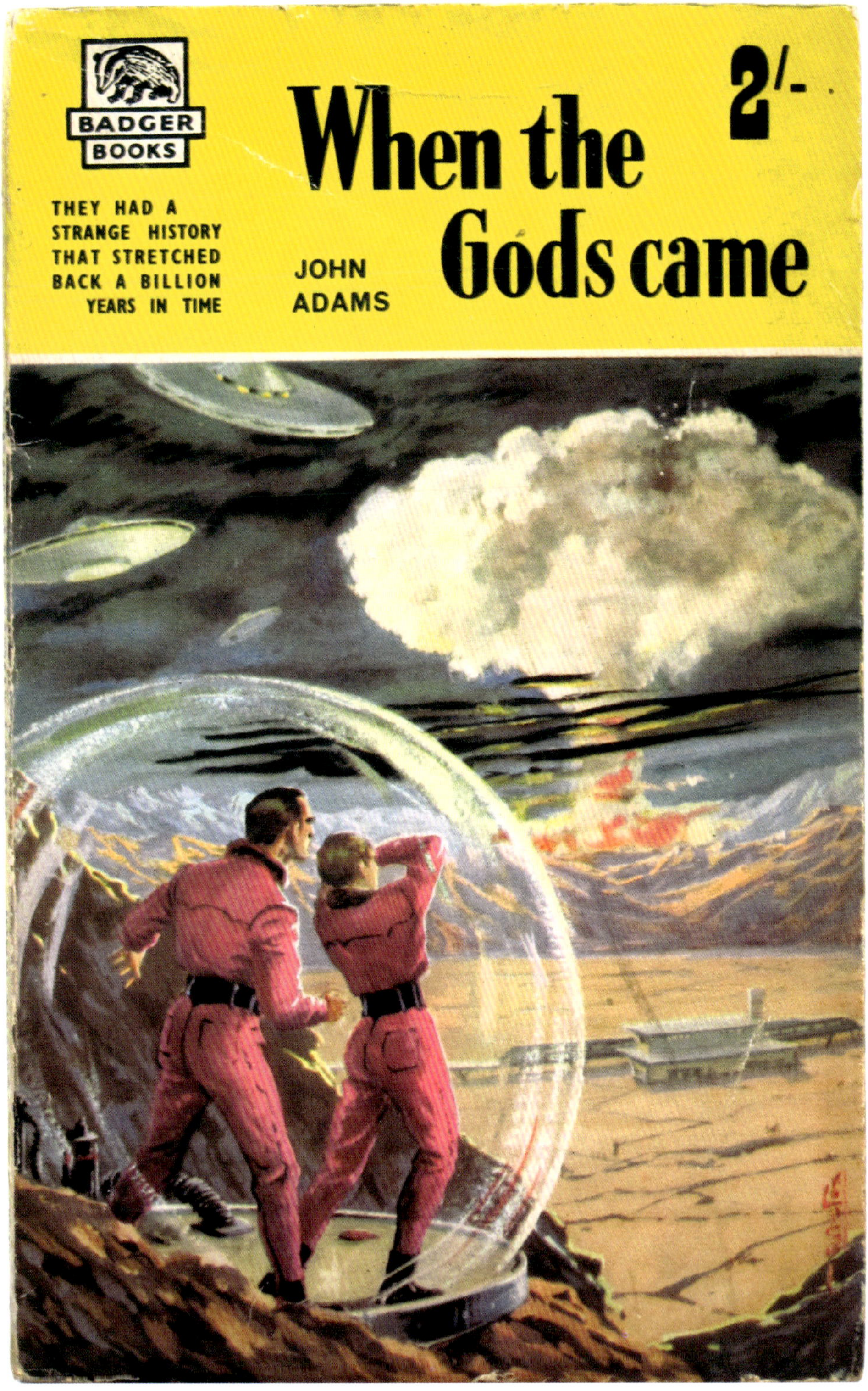

John Adams (John Glasby) | *When the Gods Came*
Badger Books SF31, 1961 | Art **Mario D'Antona**

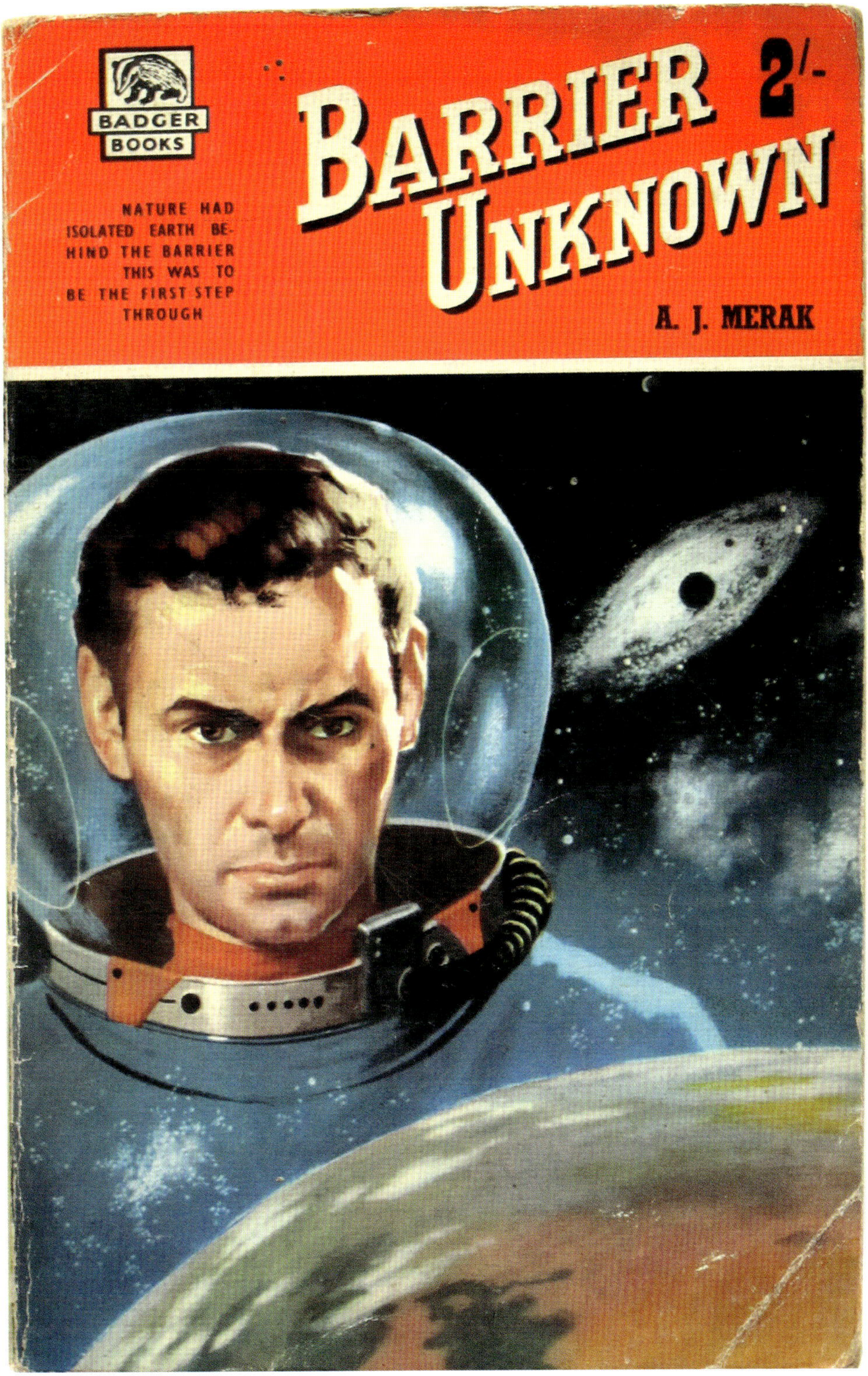

A. J. Merak (John Glasby) | *Barrier Unknown*
Badger Books SF30, 1960 | Art **Carlo Jacono**

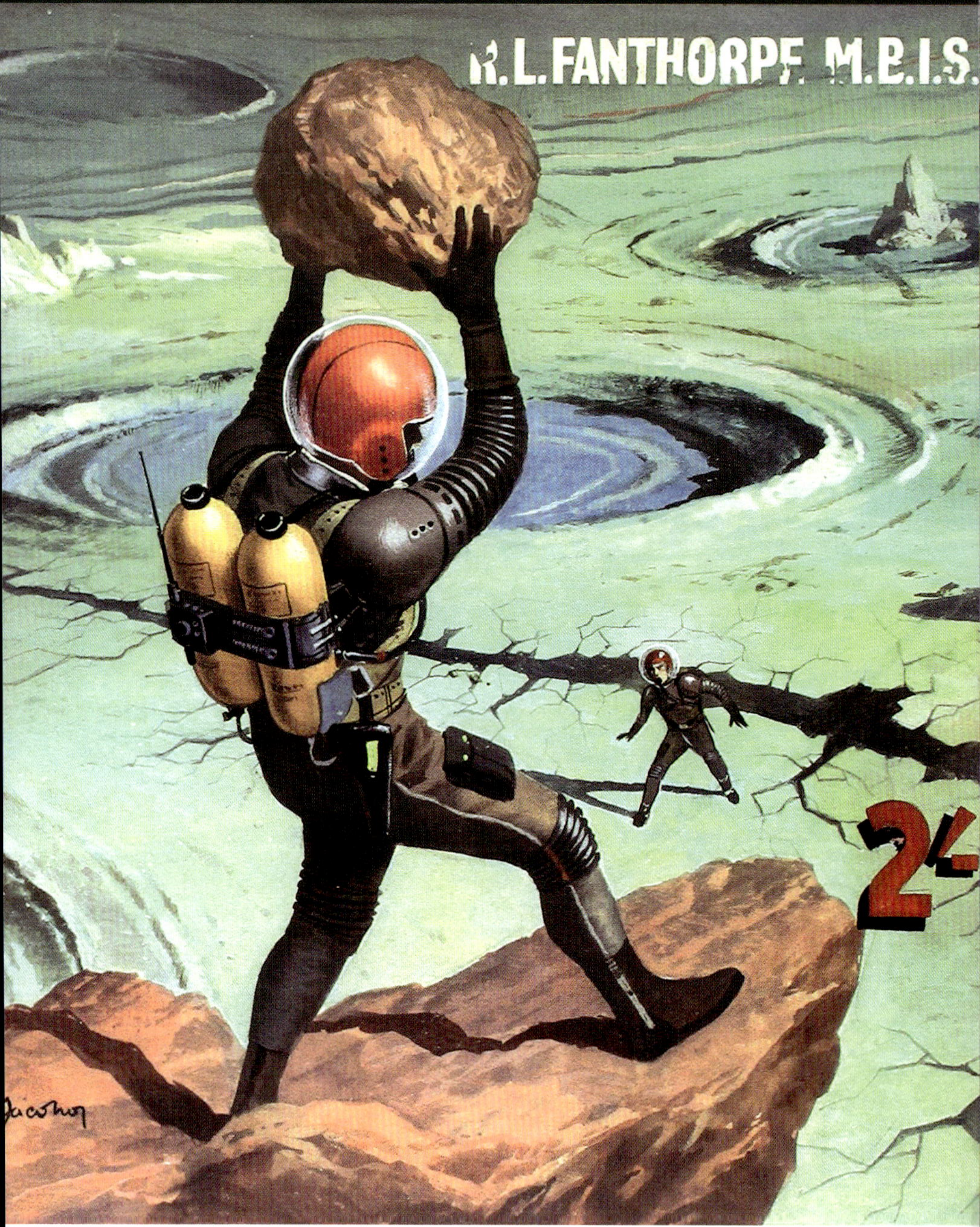

R. Lionel Fanthorpe, M.B.I.S. | *Doomed World*
Badger Books SF25, 1960 | Original art **Carlo Jacono**

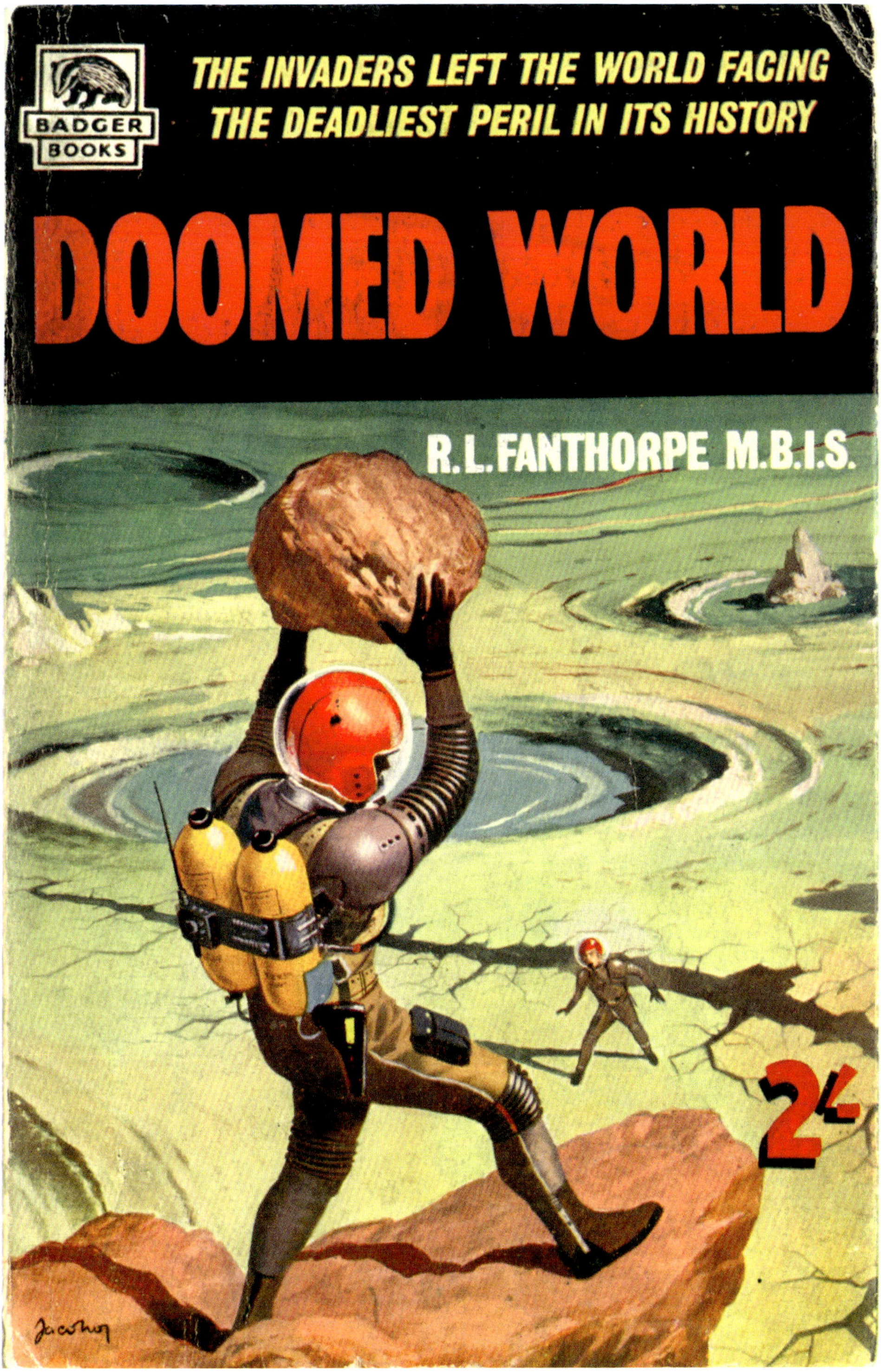

R. Lionel Fanthorpe, M.B.I.S. | *Doomed World*
Badger Books SF25, 1960 | Art **Carlo Jacono**

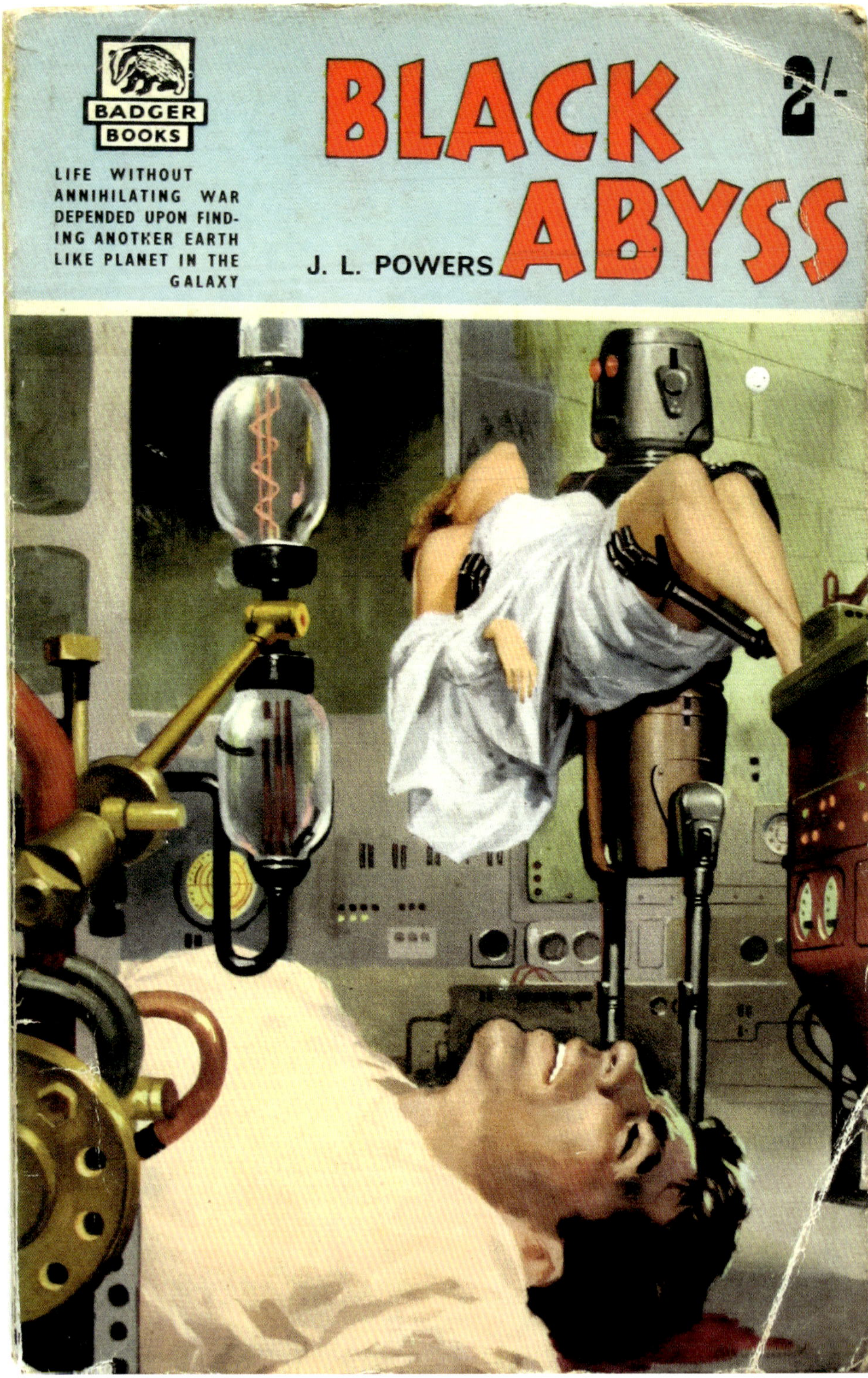

J. L. Powers | *Black Abyss*
Badger Books SF32, 1960 | Art **Carlo Jacono**

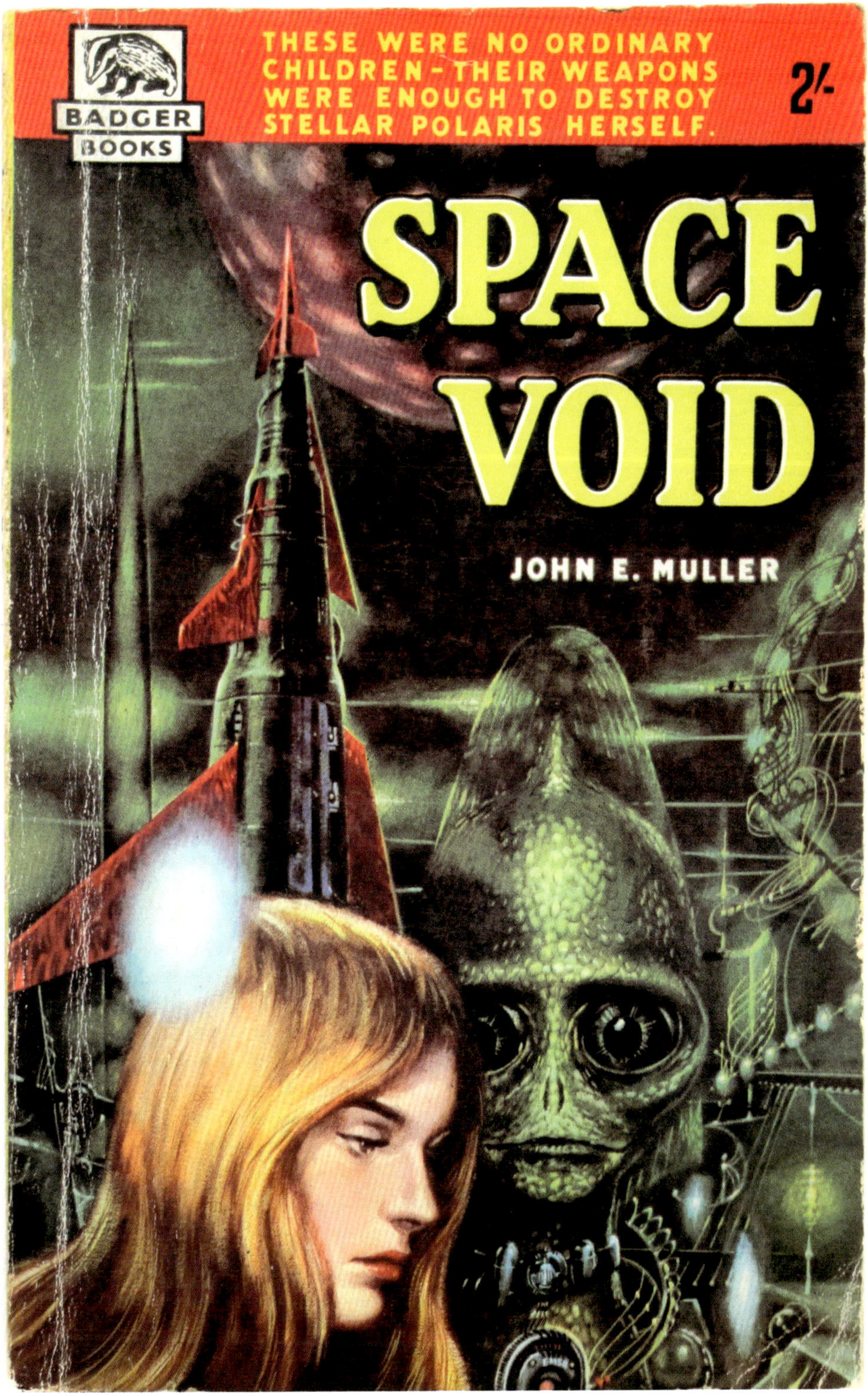

John E. Muller | *Space Void*
Badger Books SF34, 1960 | Art **Ed Emshwiller**

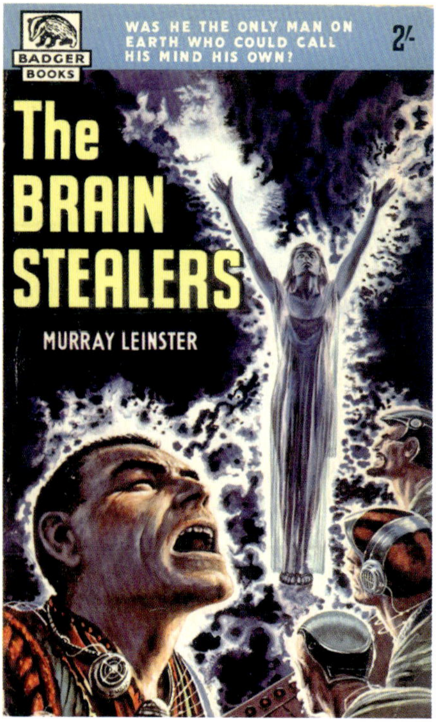

Murray Leinster | *The Brain Stealers*
Badger Books SF33 1960 | Art **Ed Emshwiller**

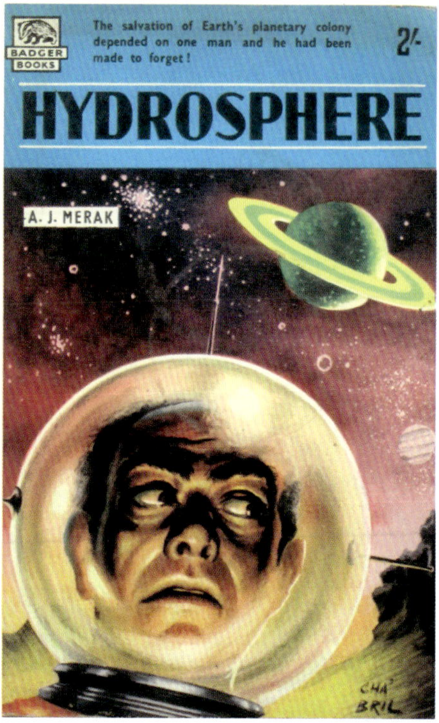

A. J. Merak (John Glasby) | *Hydrosphere*
Badger Books SF36, 1960 | Art **Cha' Bril**

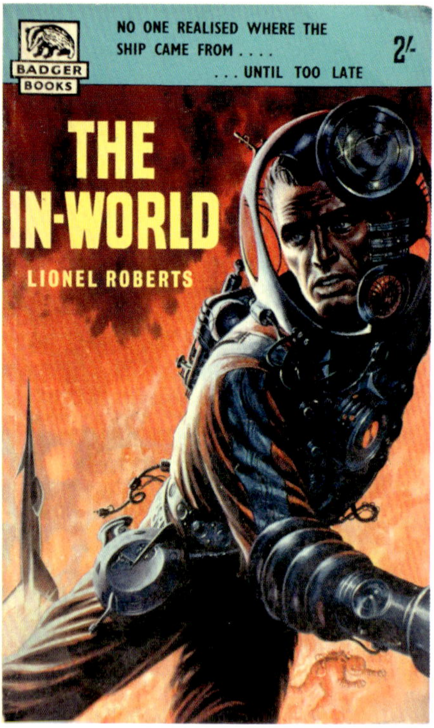

Lionel Roberts (R. L. Fanthorpe) | *The In-World*
Badger Books SF37, 1960 | Art **Ed Emshwiller**

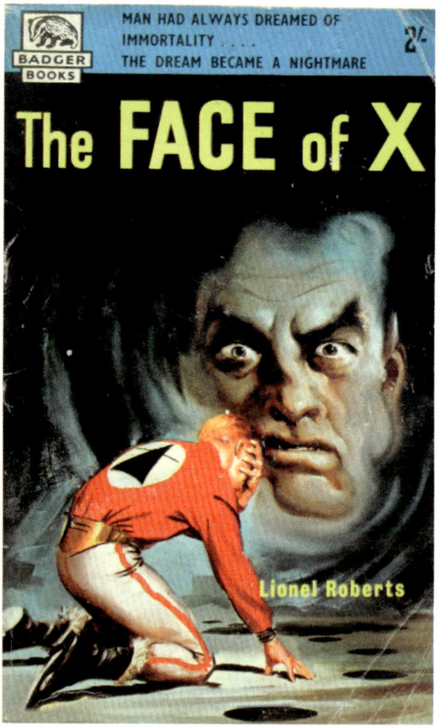

Lionel Roberts (R. L. Fanthorpe) | *The Face of X*
Badger Books SF39, 1960 | Art **Ed Emshwiller**

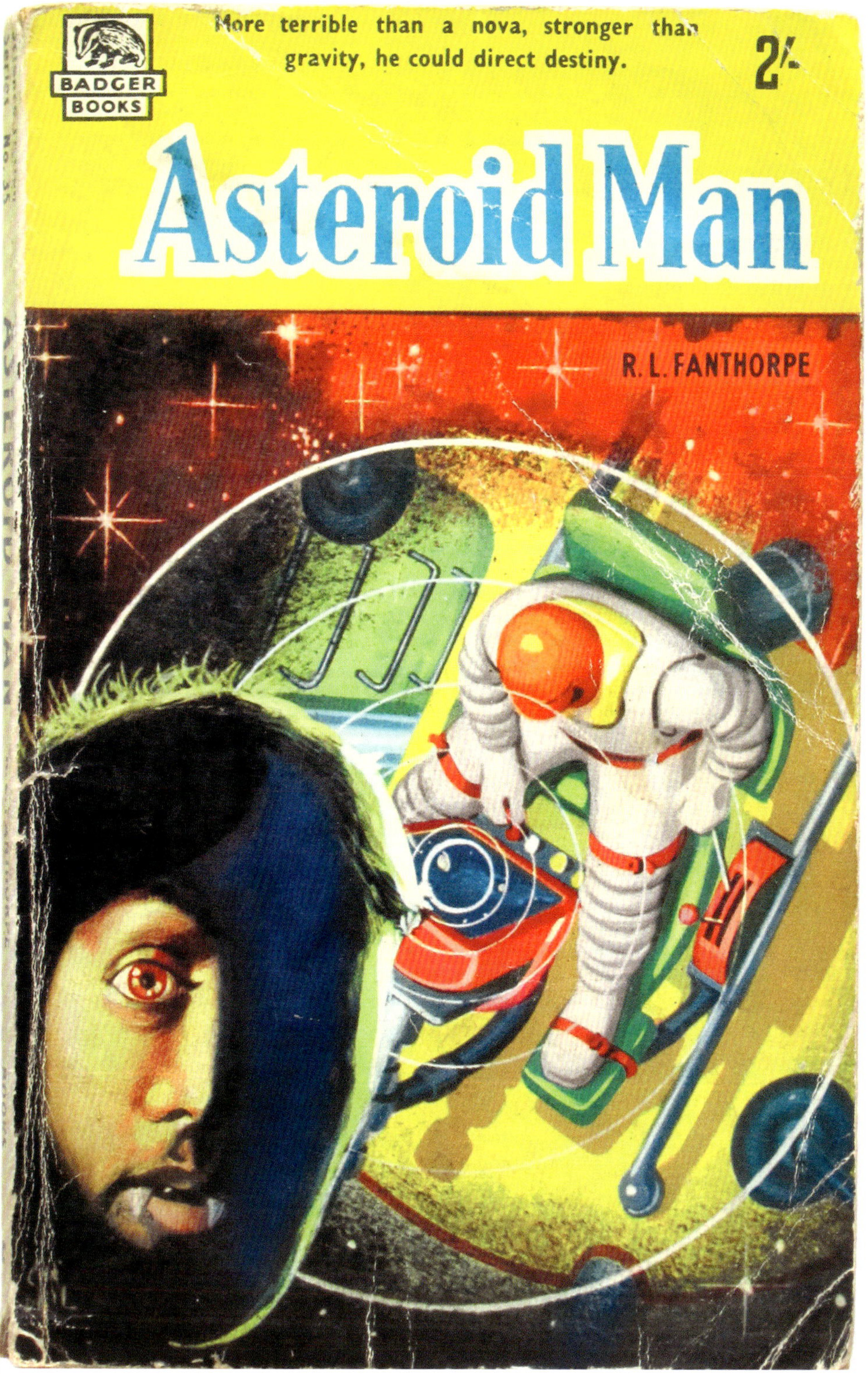

R. Lionel Fanthorpe | *Asteroid Man*
Badger Books SF35, 1960 | Art **Cha' Bril**

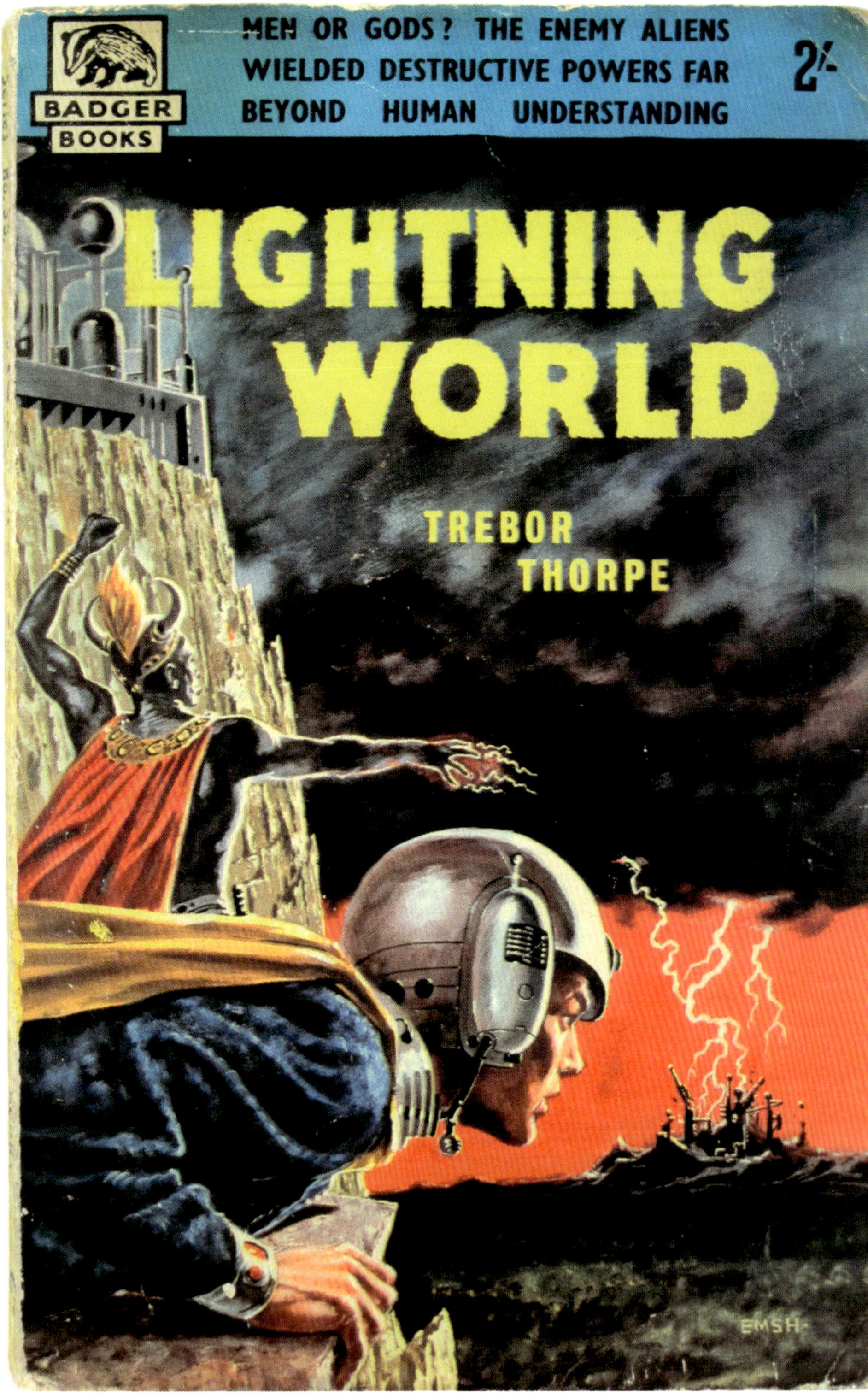

Trebor Thorpe (R. L. Fanthorpe) | *Lightning World*
Badger Books SF38, 1960 | Art **Ed Emshwiller**

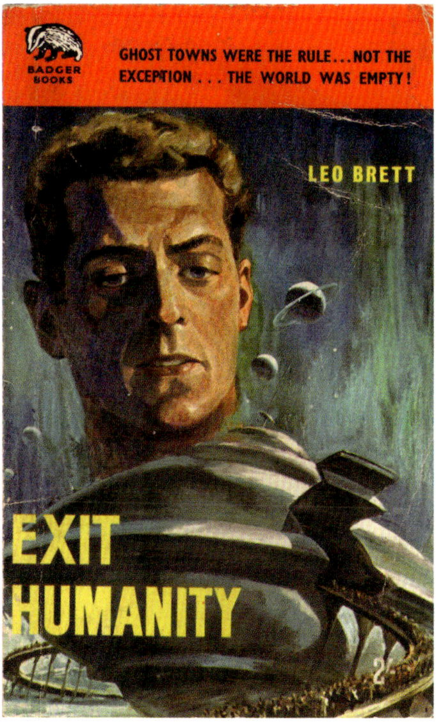

Leo Brett (R. L. Fanthorpe) | *Exit Humanity*
Badger Books SF40, 1960 | Art **Unknown**

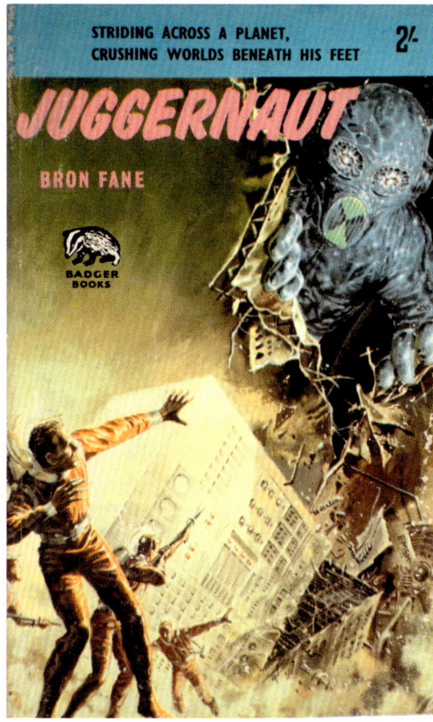

Bron Fane (R. L. Fanthorpe) | *Juggernaut*
Badger Books SF41, 1960 | Art **Ed Emshwiller**

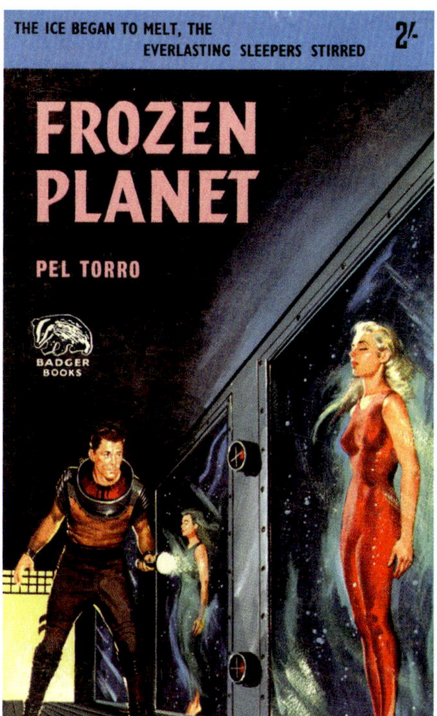

Pel Torro (R. L. Fanthorpe) | *Frozen Planet*
Badger Books SF42, 1960 | Art **Ed Valigursky**

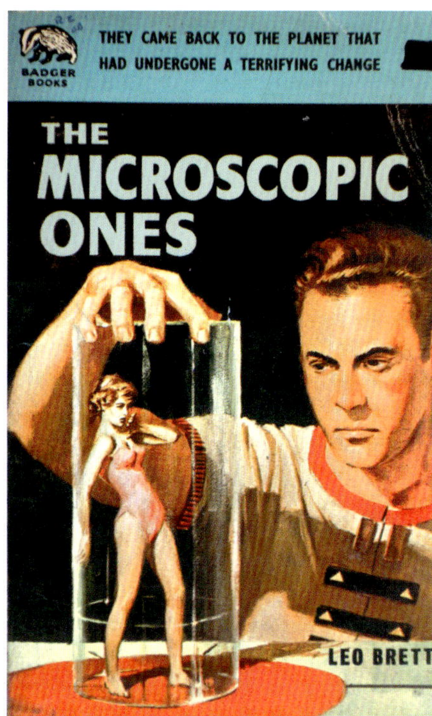

Leo Brett (R. L. Fanthorpe) | *The Microscopic Ones*
Badger Books SF43, 1960 | Art **Ed Valigursky**

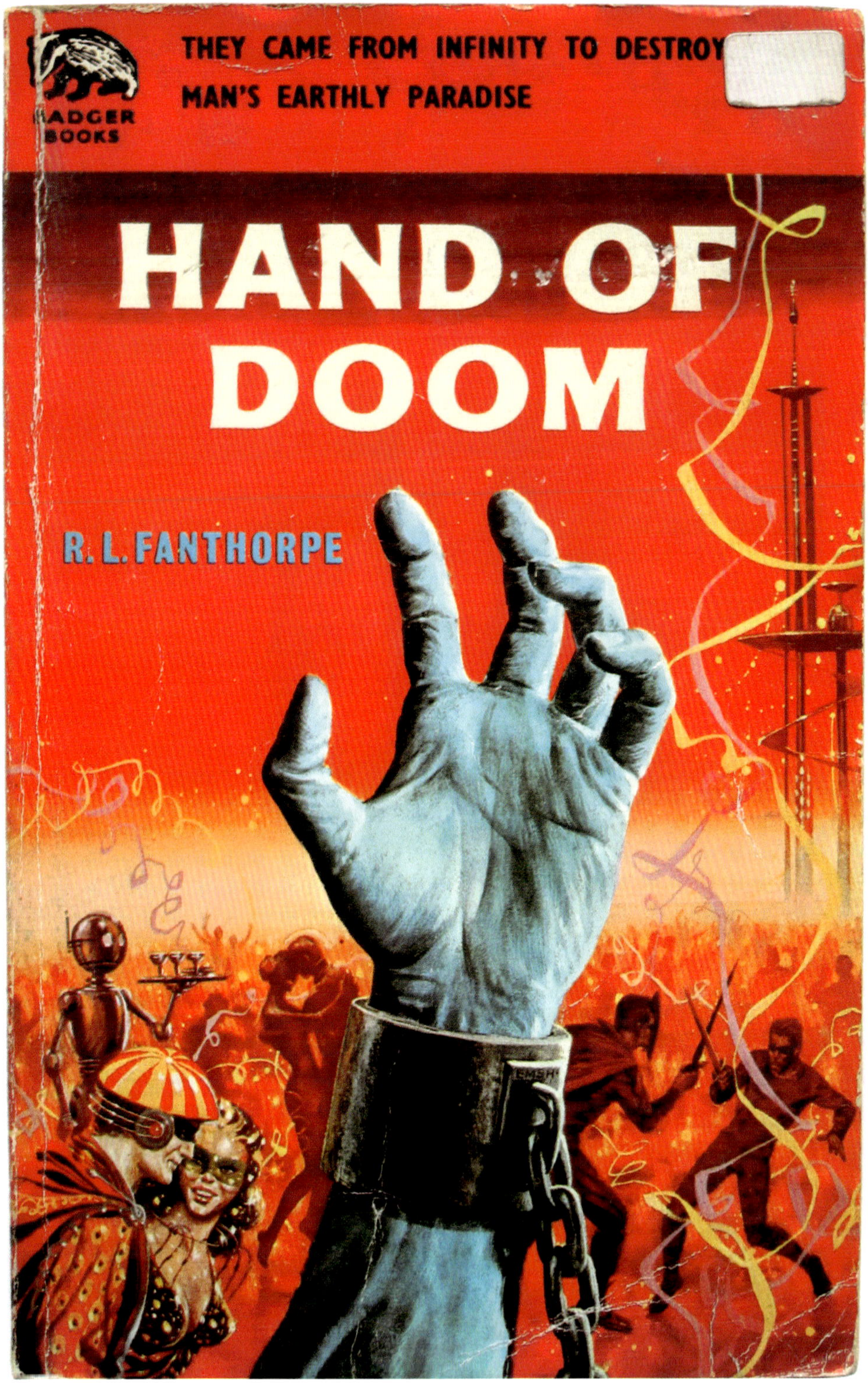

R. L. Fanthorpe | *Hand of Doom*
Badger Books SF44, 1960 | Art **Ed Emshwiller**

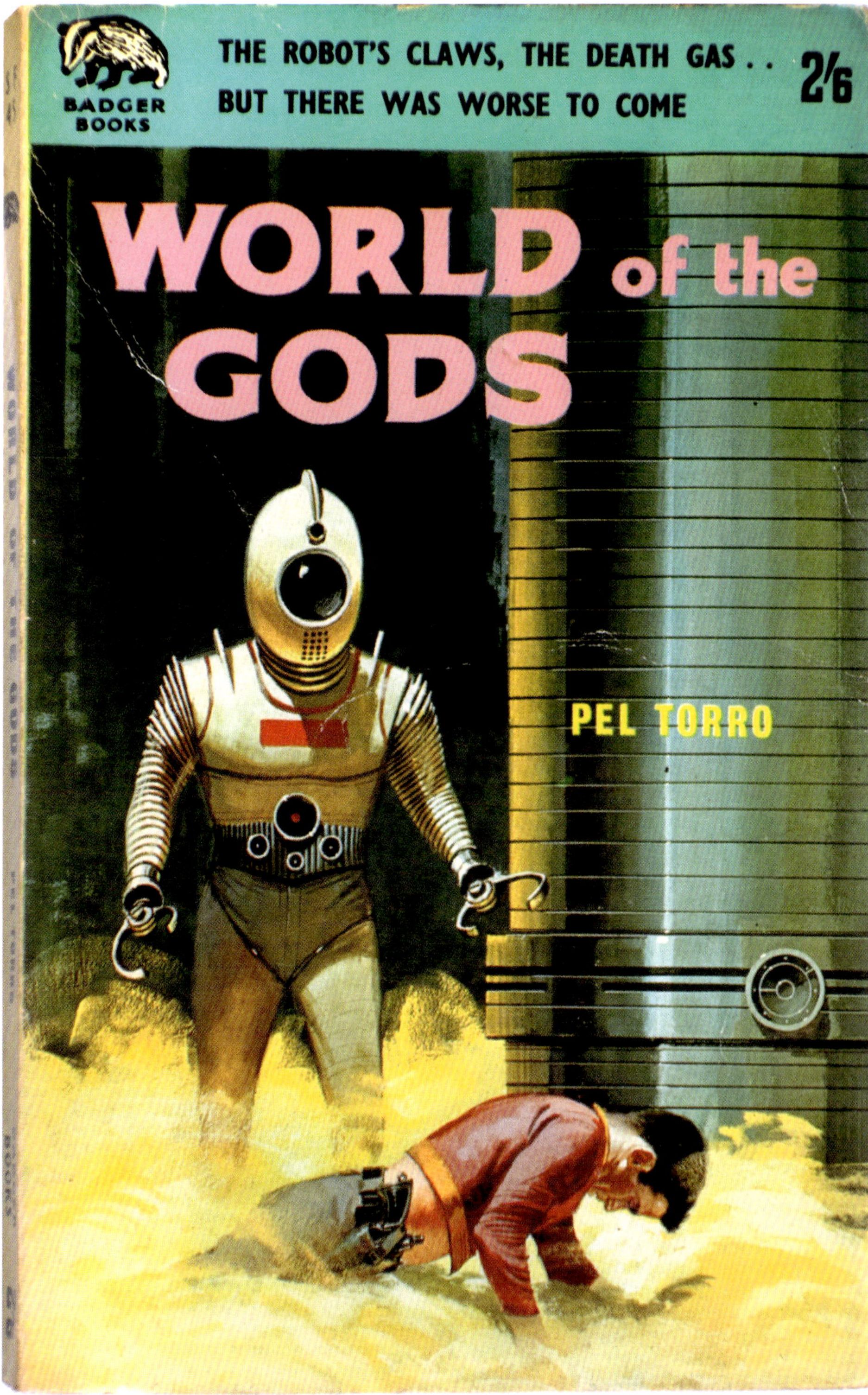

Pel Torro (R. L. Fanthorpe) | *World of the Gods*
Badger Books SF45, 1960 | Art **Ed Valigursky**

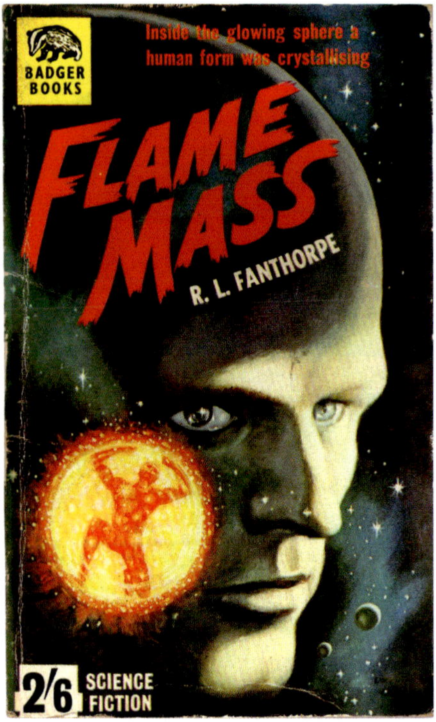

R. L. Fanthorpe | *Flame Mass*
Badger Books SF49 1961 | Art **Ed Emshwiller**

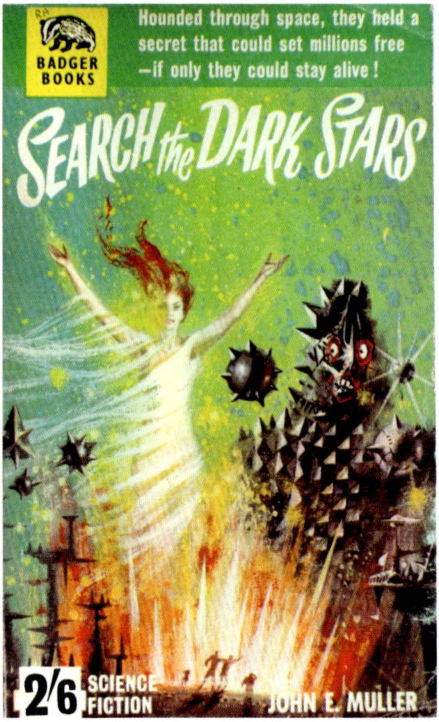

John E. Muller (R. L. Fanthorpe) | *Search the Dark Stars*
Badger Books SF48, 1960 | Art **Richard Powers**

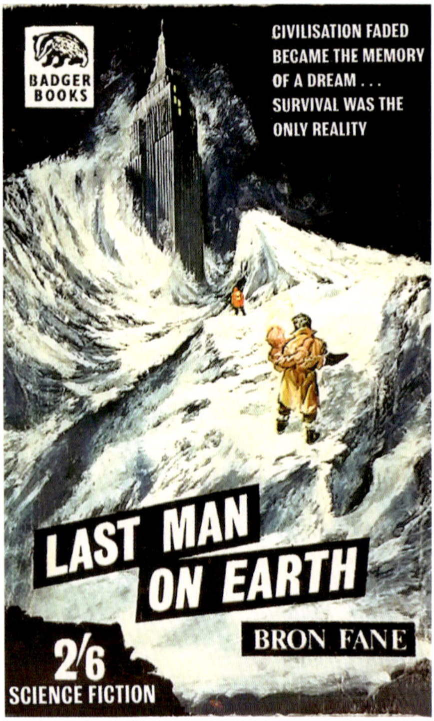

Bron Fane (R. L. Fanthorpe) | *Last Man on Earth*
Badger Books SF46, 1960 | Art **Unknown**

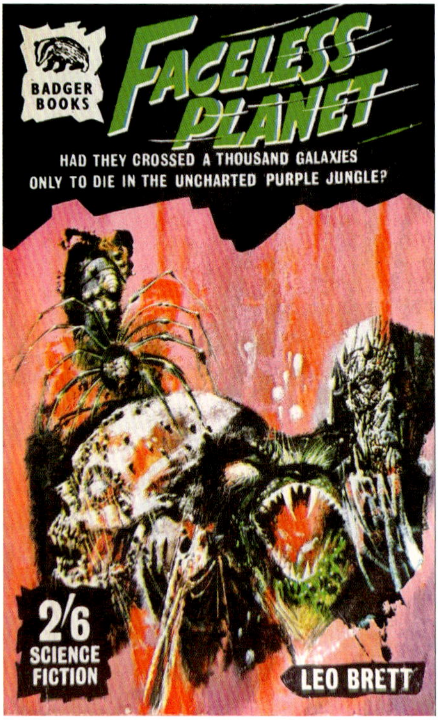

Leo Brett (R. L. Fanthorpe) | *Faceless Planet*
Badger Books SF47, 1960 | Art **Richard Powers**

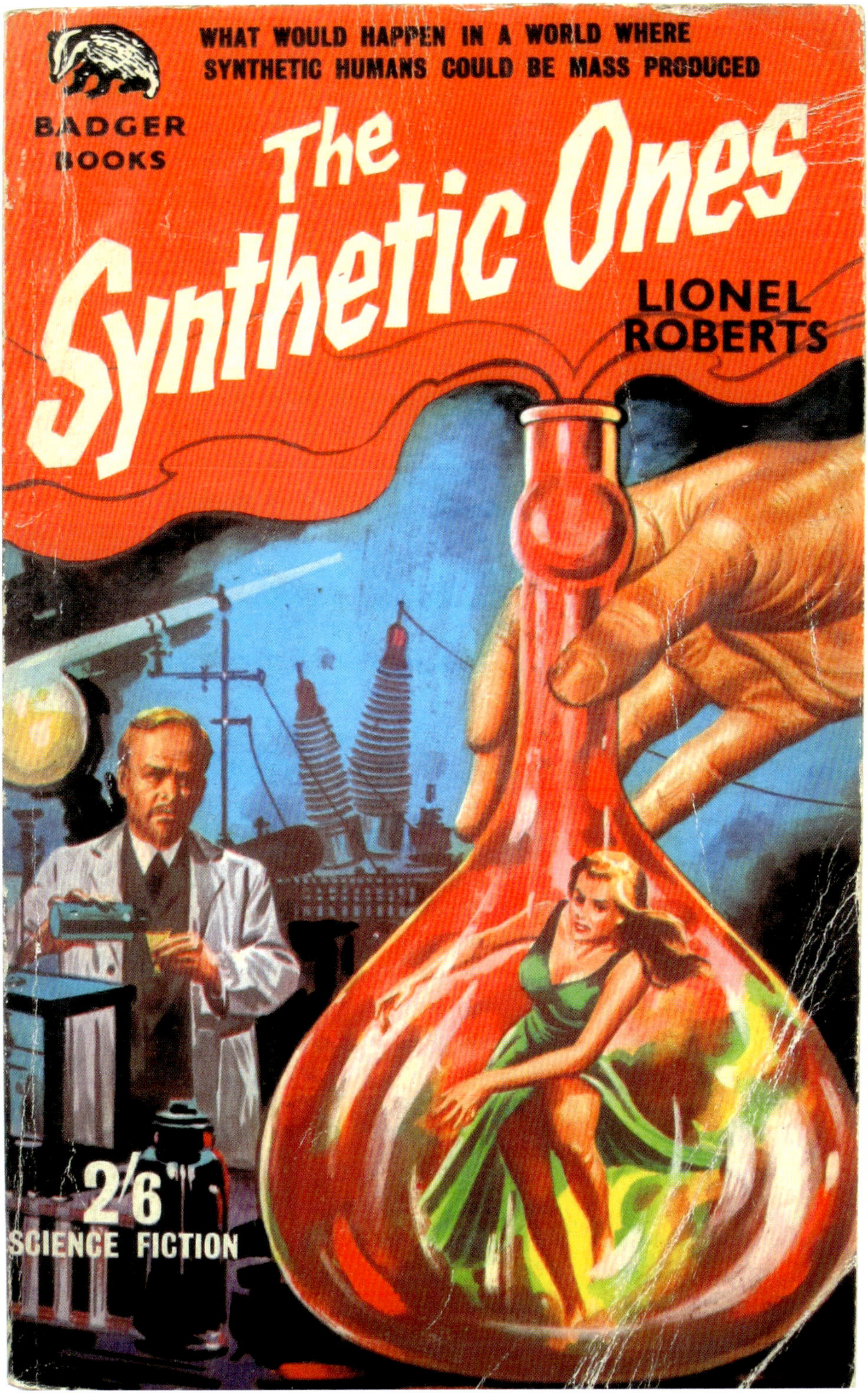

Lionel Roberts (R. L. Fanthorpe) | *The Synthetic Ones*
Badger Books SF52, 1961 | Art **Henry Fox**

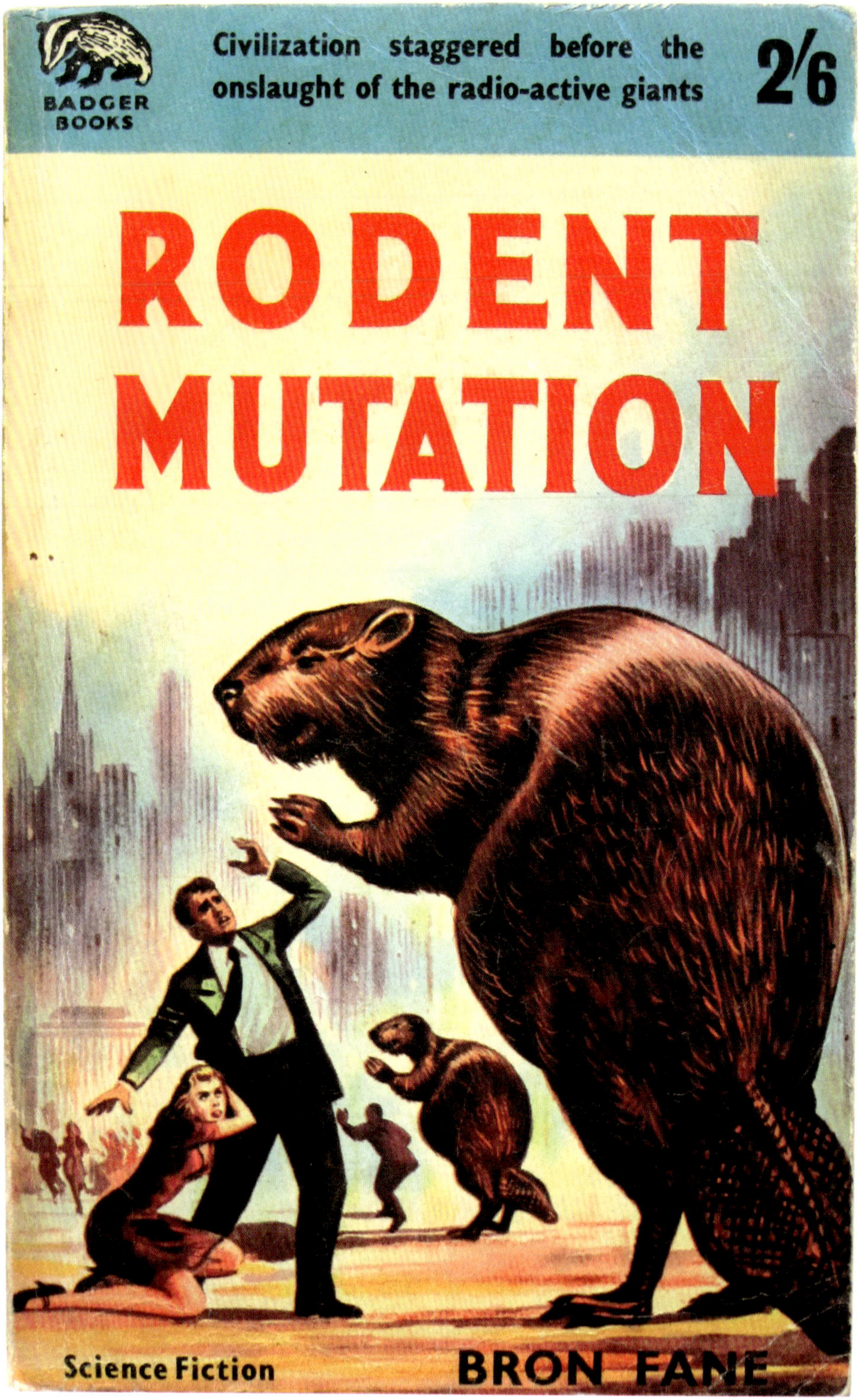

Bron Fane (R. L. Fanthorpe) | *Rodent Mutation*
Badger Books SF55, 1961 | Art **Henry Fox**

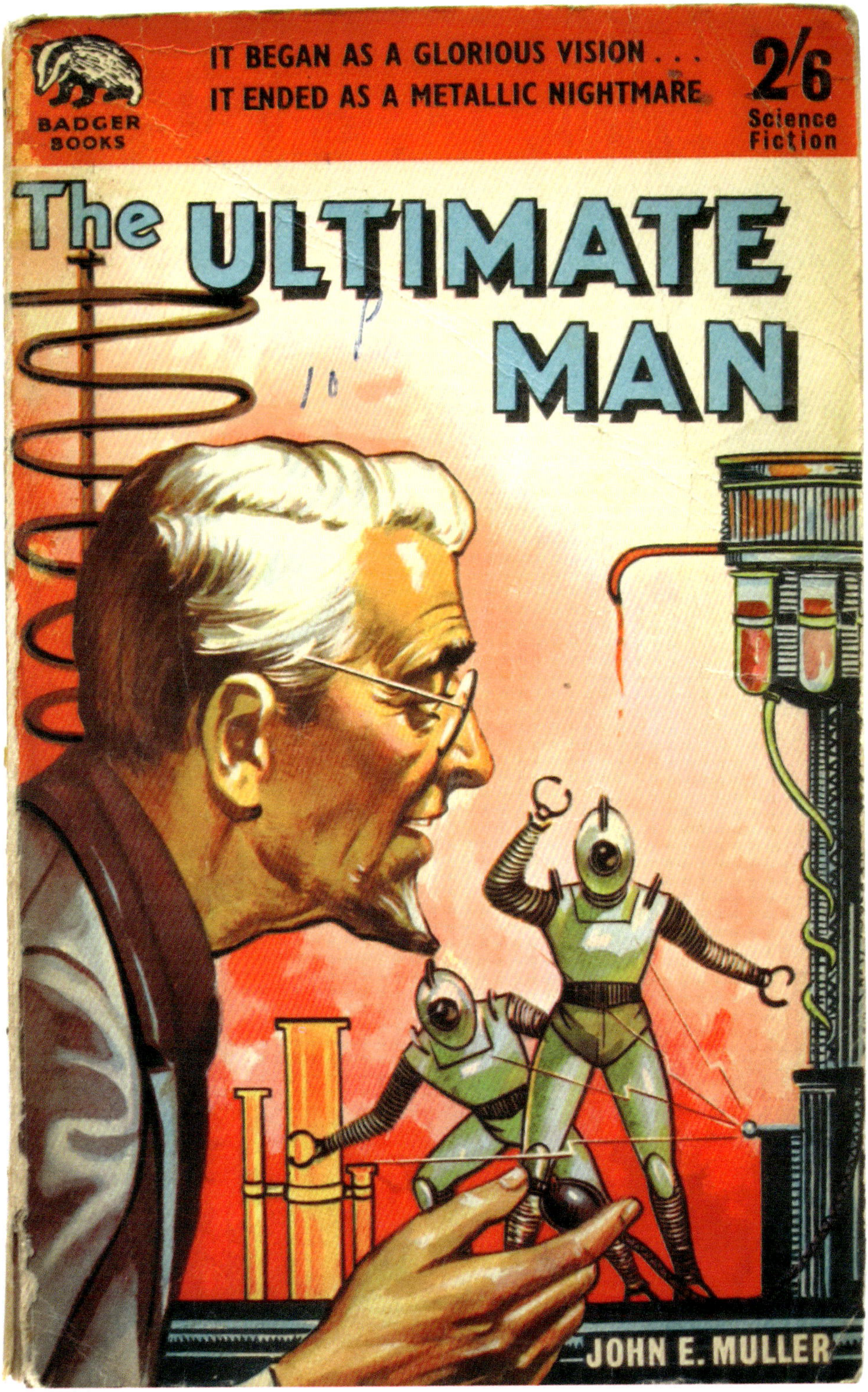

John E. Muller (R. L. Fanthorpe) | *The Ultimate Man*
Badger Books SF56, 1961 | Art **Henry Fox**

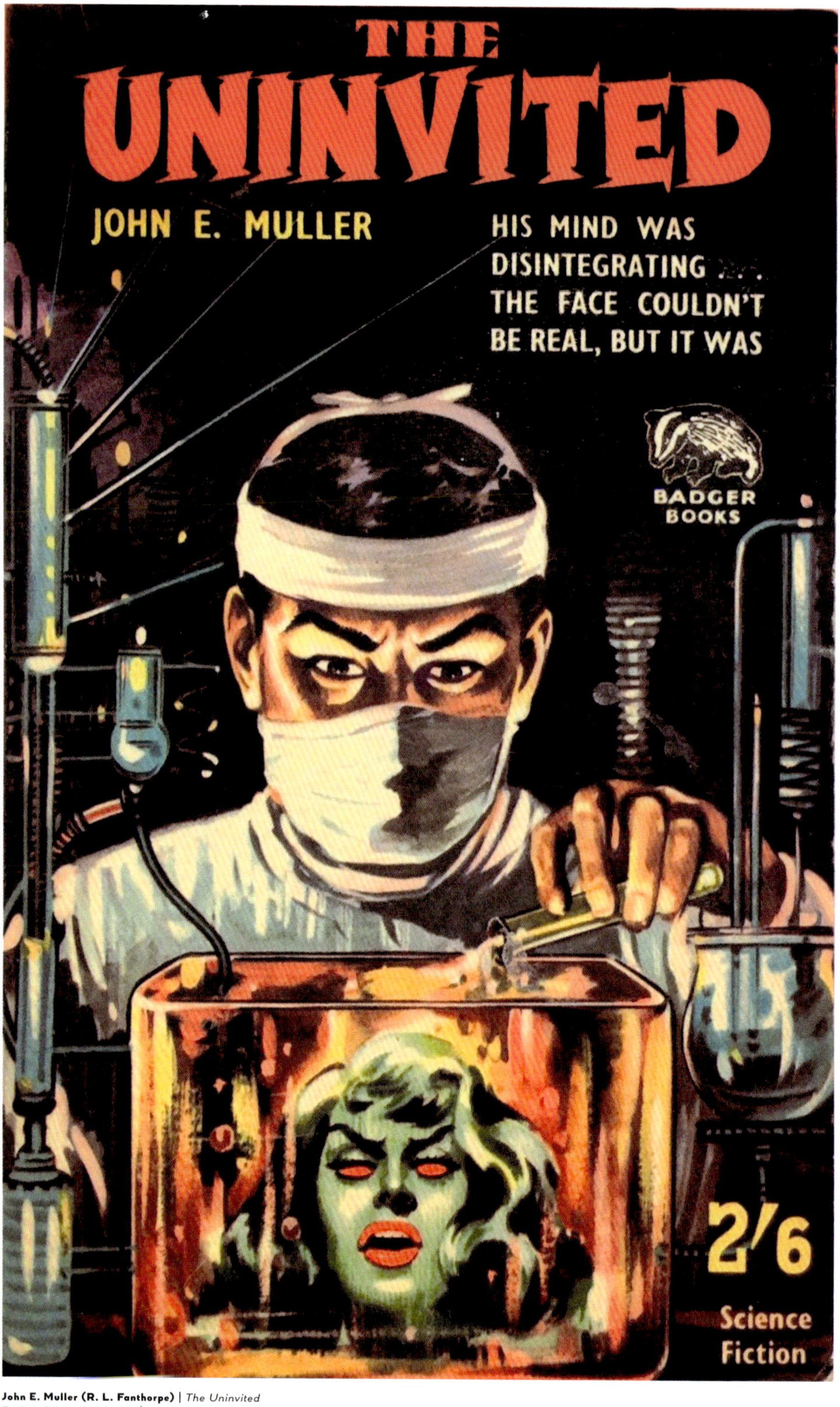

John E. Muller (R. L. Fanthorpe) | *The Uninvited*
Badger Books SF57, 1961 | Art **Henry Fox**

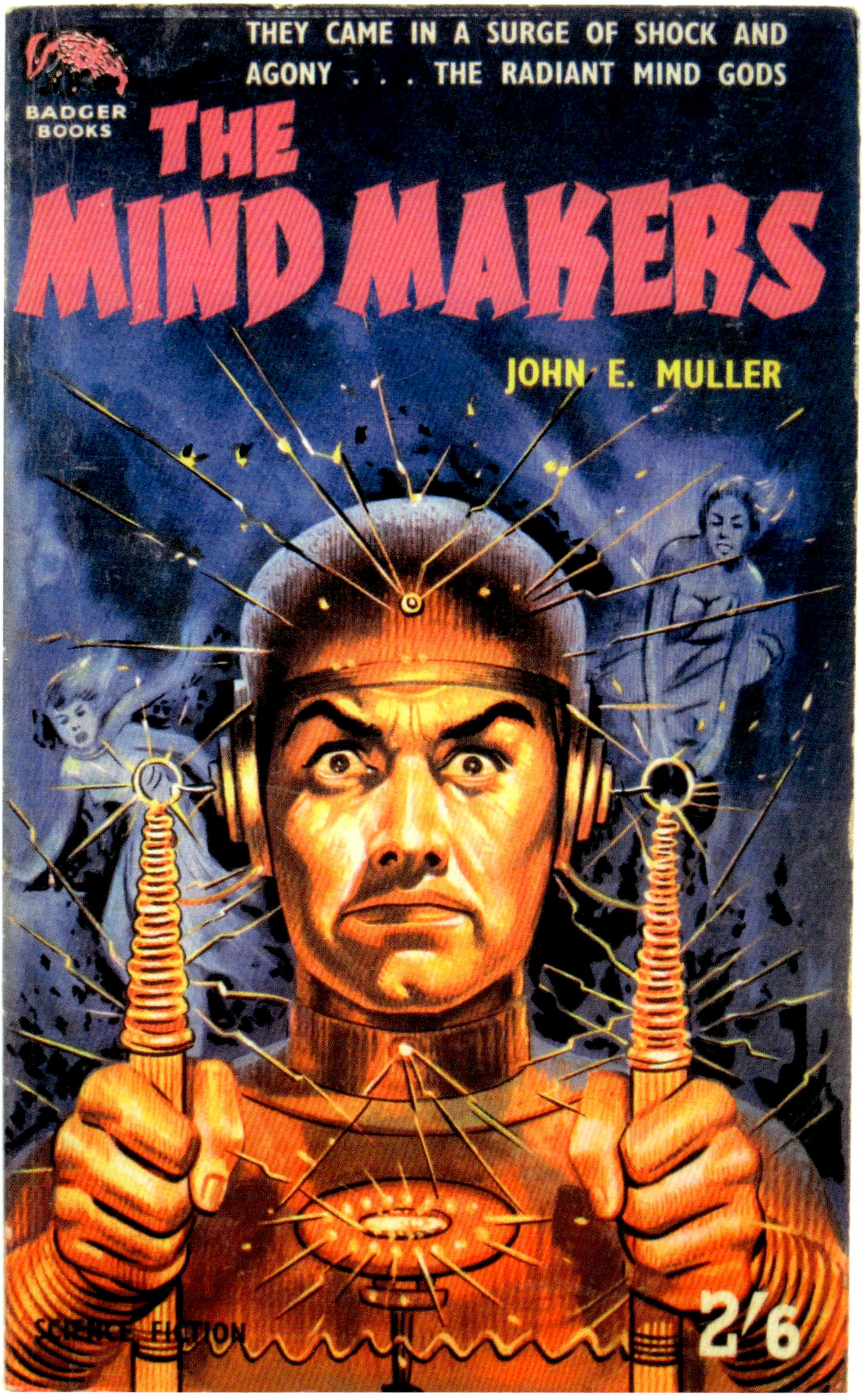

John E. Muller (R. L. Fanthorpe) | *The Mind Makers*
Badger Books SF58, 1961 | Art **Henry Fox**

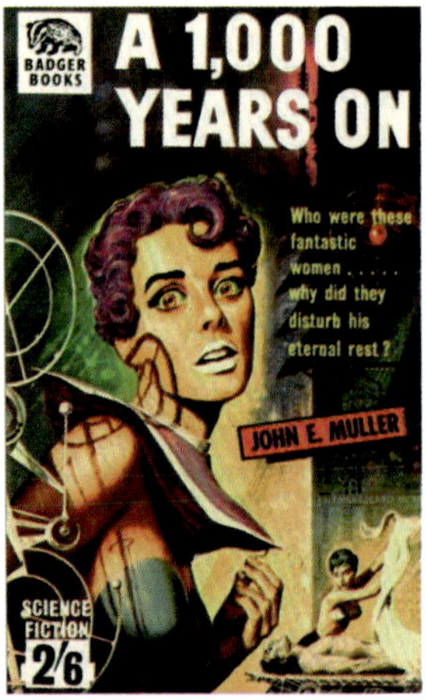

John E. Muller (R. L. Fanthorpe)
A 1,000 Years On
Badger Books SF50, 1961 | Art **Ed Emshwiller**

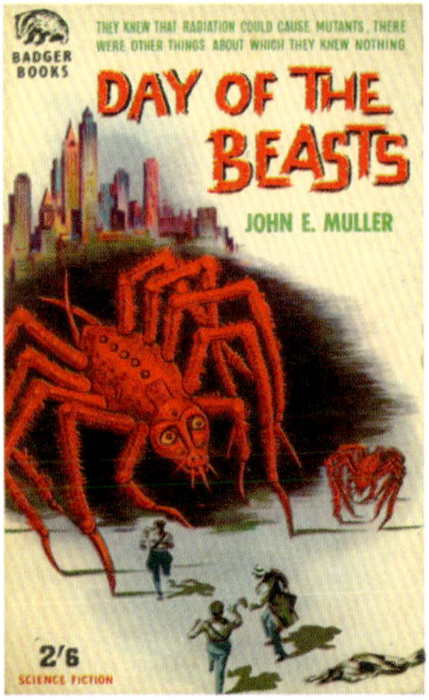

John E. Muller (R. L. Fanthorpe)
Day of the Beasts
Badger Books SF51, 1961 | Art **Henry Fox**

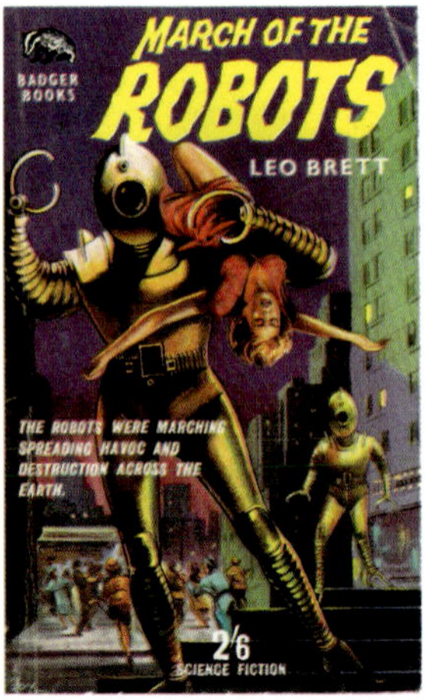

Leo Brett (R. L. Fanthorpe)
March of the Robots
Badger Books SF53, 1961 | Art **Henry Fox**

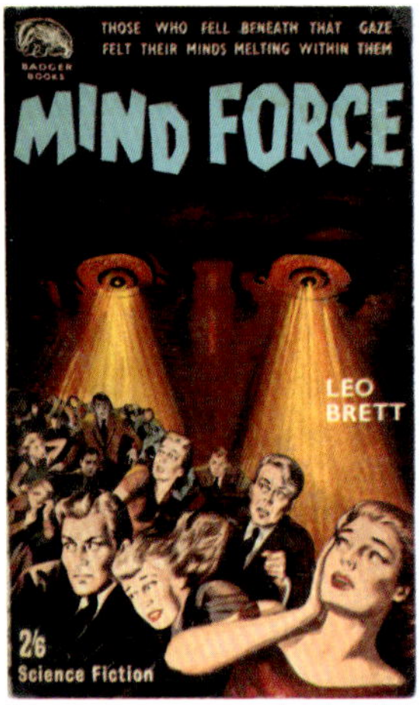

Leo Brett (R. L. Fanthorpe)
Mind Force
Badger Books SF54, 1961 | Art **Unknown**

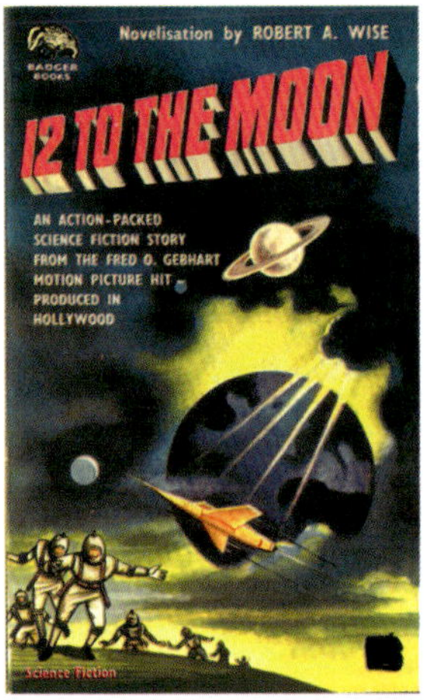

Robert A. Wise
12 to the Moon
Badger Books SF58, 1961 | Art **Henry Fox**

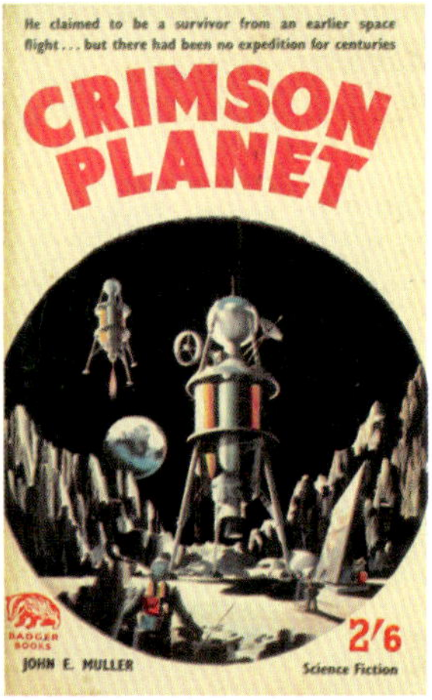

John E. Muller (R. L. Fanthorpe)
Crimson Planet
Badger Books SF60 1961 | Art **John Richards**

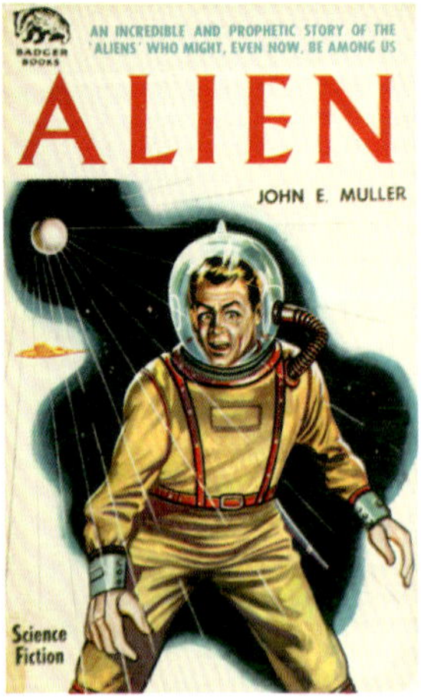

John E. Muller (John Glasby)
Alien
Badger Books SF61, 1961 | Art **Henry Fox**

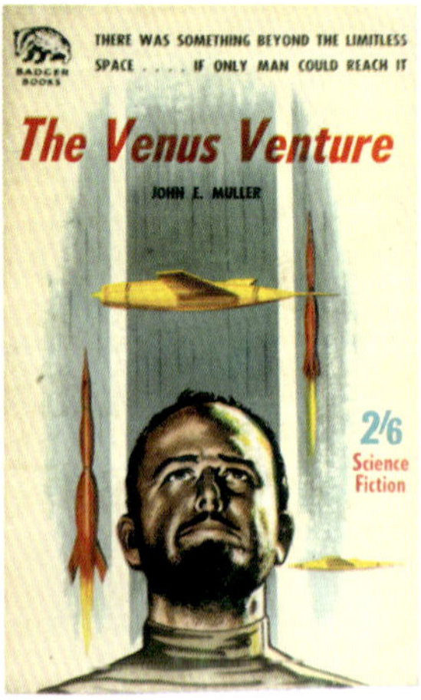

John E. Muller (R. L. Fanthorpe)
The Venus Venture
Badger Books SF62, 1961 | Art **Henry Fox**

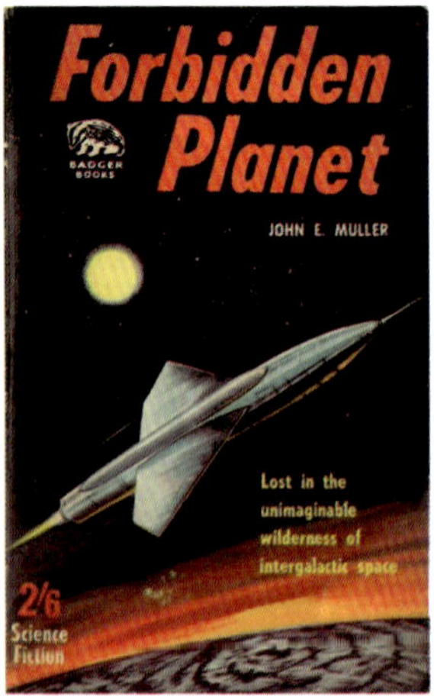

John E. Muller (R. L. Fanthorpe)
Forbidden Planet
Badger Books SF63, 1961 | Art **Unknown**

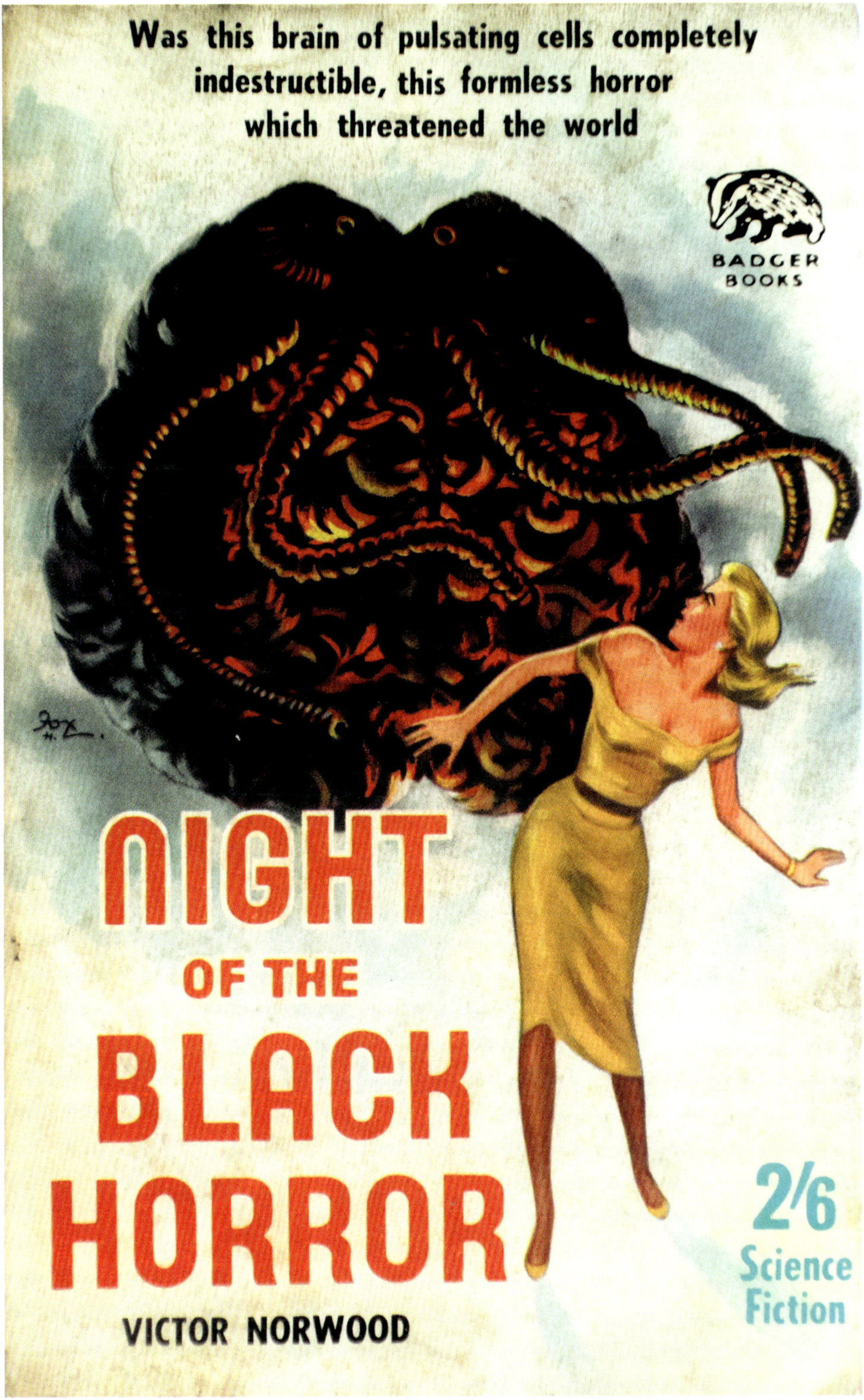

Victor Norwood | *Night of the Black Horror*
Badger Books SF64, 1961 | Art **Henry Fox**

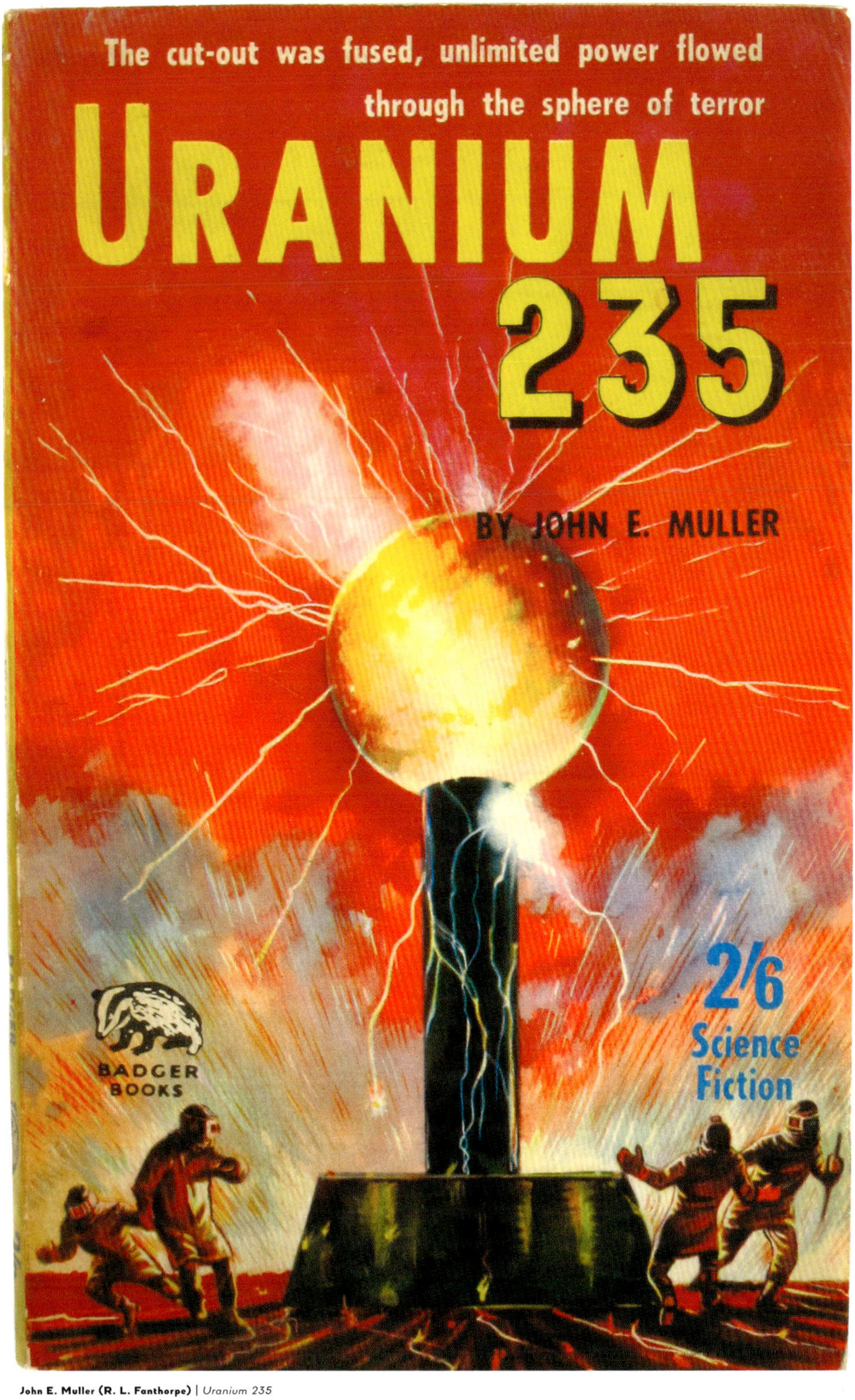

John E. Muller (R. L. Fanthorpe) | *Uranium 235*
Badger Books SF67, 1962 | Art **Henry Fox**

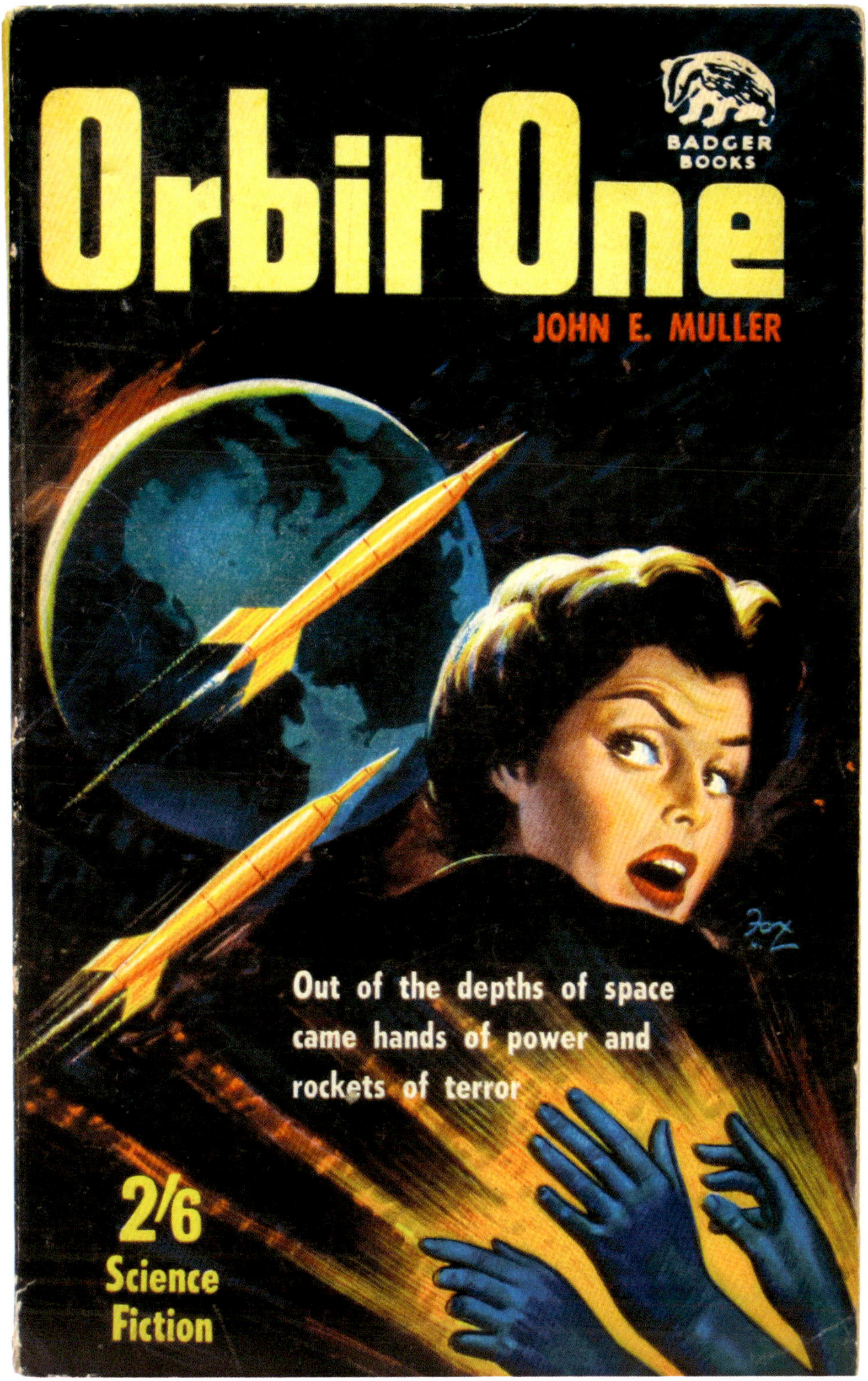

John E. Muller (R. L. Fanthorpe) | *Orbit One*
Badger Books SF69, 1962 | Art **Henry Fox**

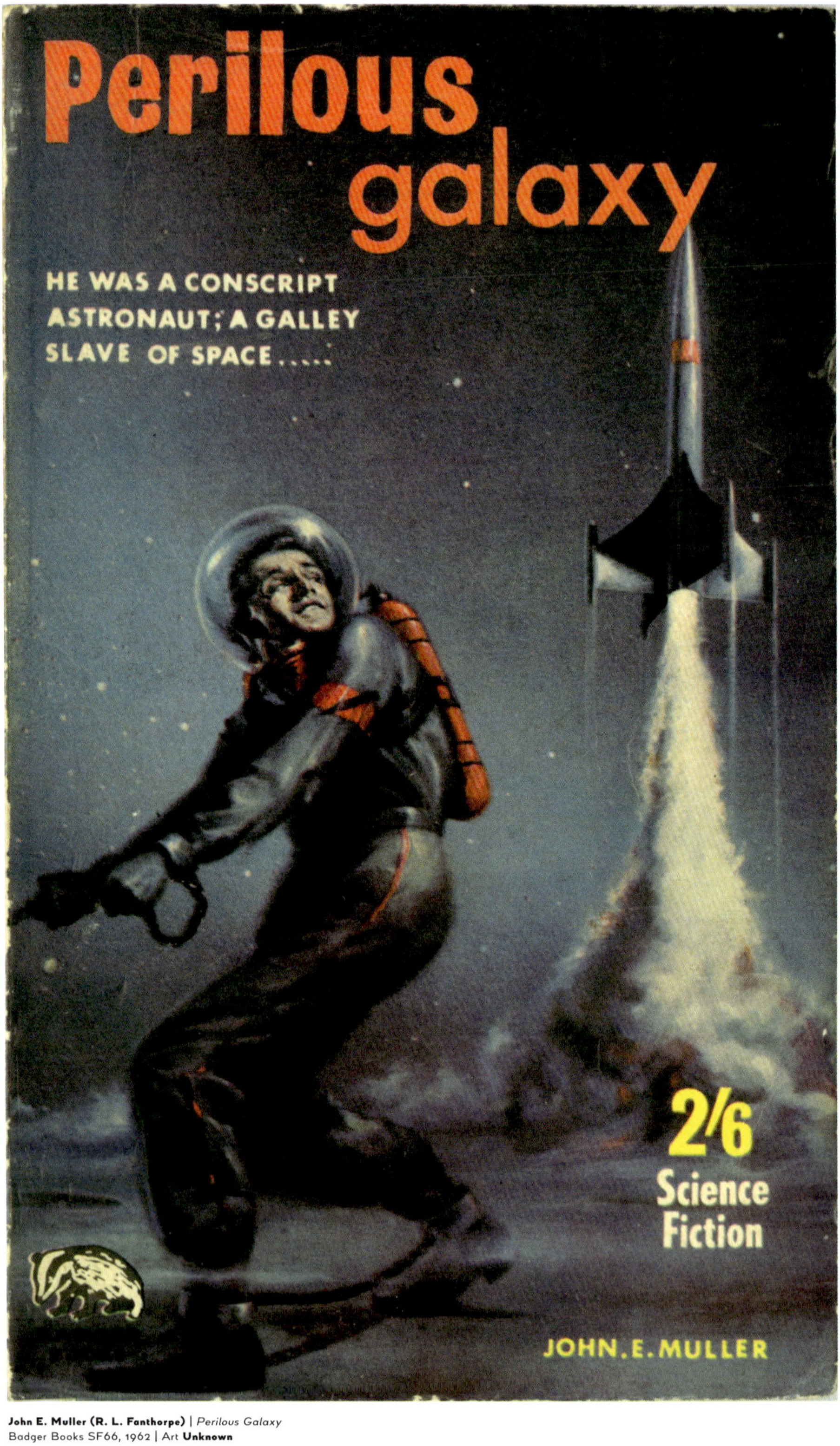

John E. Muller (R. L. Fanthorpe) | *Perilous Galaxy*
Badger Books SF66, 1962 | Art **Unknown**

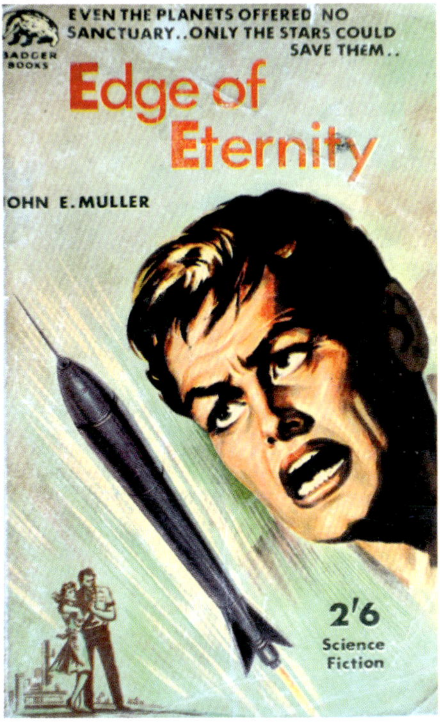

John E. Muller (R. L. Fanthorpe) | *Edge of Eternity*
Badger Books SF65, 1962 | Art **Henry Fox**

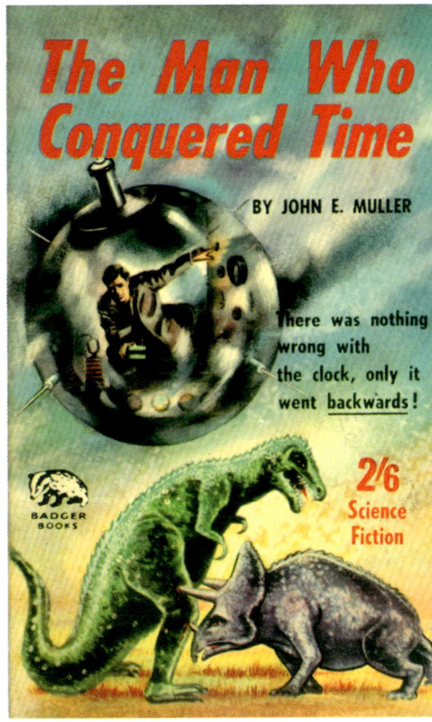

John E. Muller (R. L. Fanthorpe) | *The Man Who Conquered Time*
Badger Books SF68, 1962 | Art **Henry Fox**

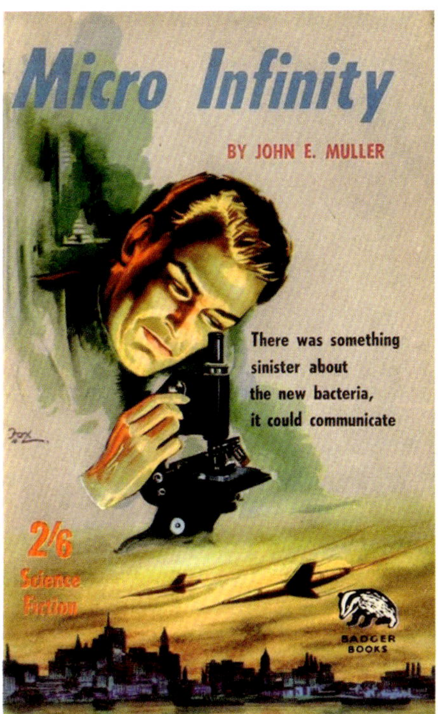

John E. Muller (R. L. Fanthorpe) | *Micro Infinity*
Badger Books SF70, 1962 | Art **Henry Fox**

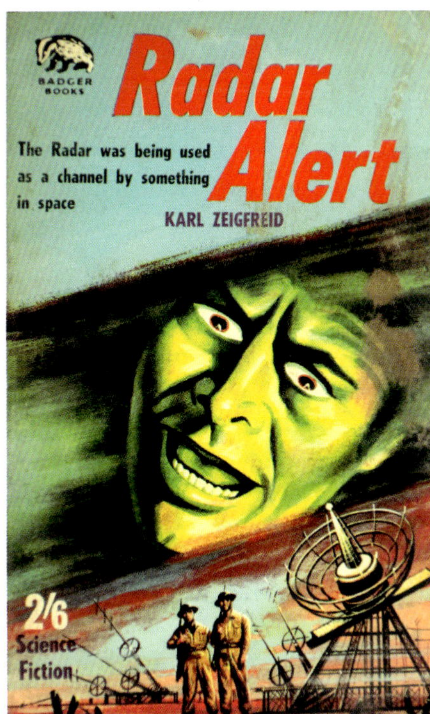

Karl Zeigfreid (R. L. Fanthorpe) | *Radar Alert*
Badger Books SF83, 1963 | Art **Henry Fox**

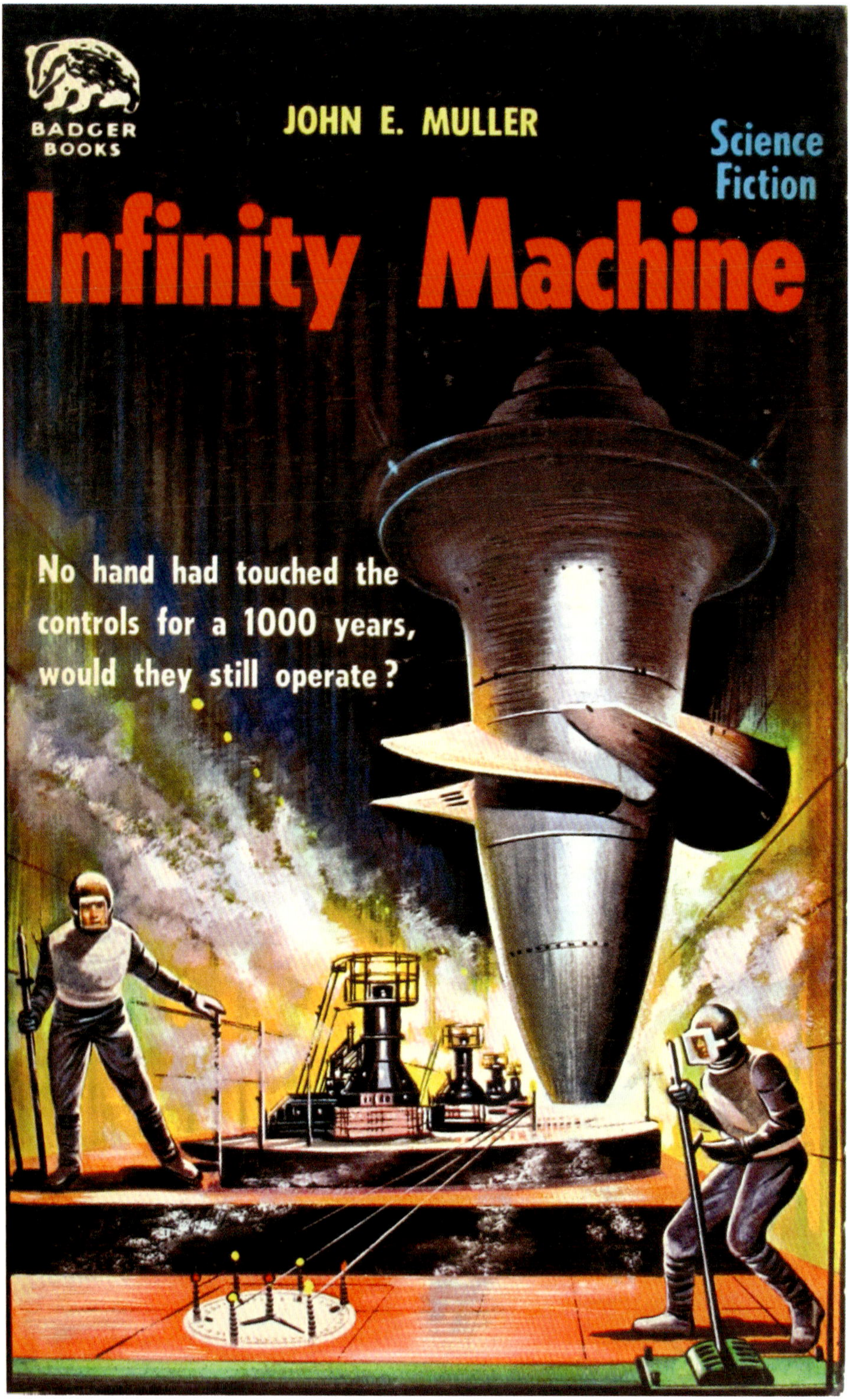

John E. Muller (R. L. Fanthorpe) | *Infinity Machine*
Badger Books SF72, 1962 | Art **Henry Fox**

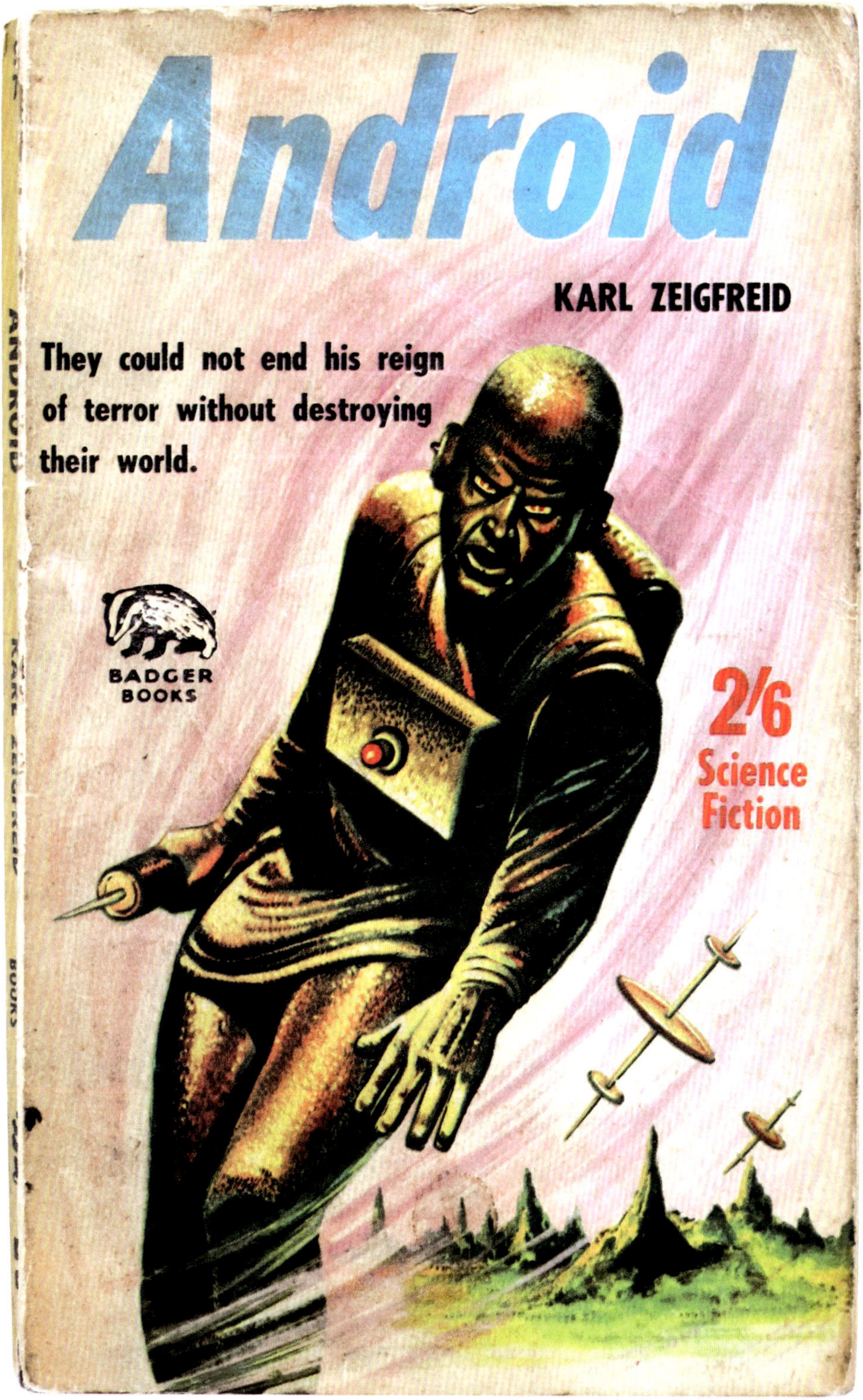

Karl Zeigfreid (R. L. Fanthorpe) | *Android*
Badger Books SF79, 1962 | Art **Henry Fox**

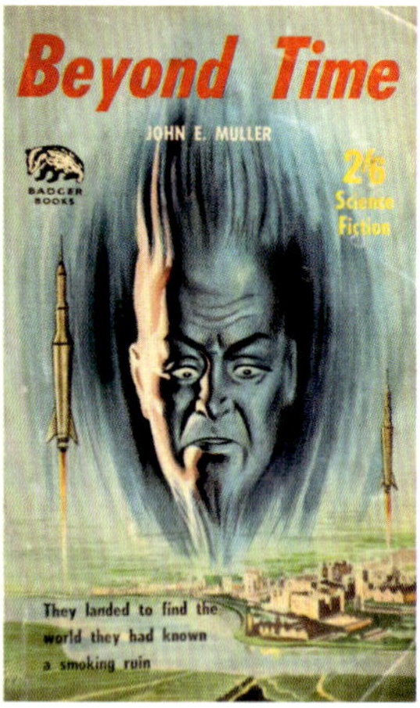

John E. Muller (R. L. Fanthorpe)
Beyond Time
Badger Books SF71, 1962 | Art **Henry Fox**

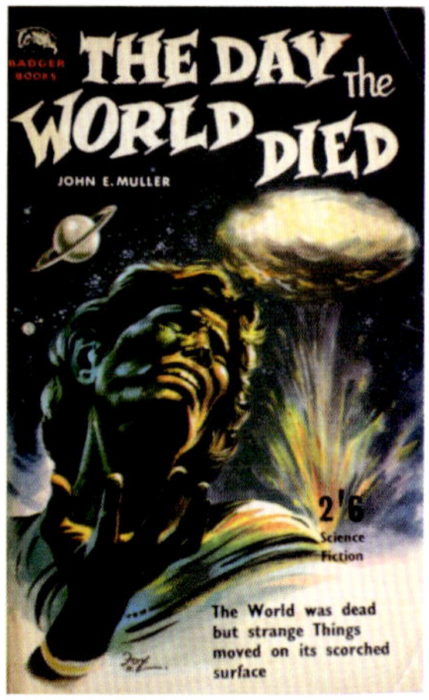

John E. Muller (R. L. Fanthorpe)
The Day the World Died
Badger Books SF73, 1962 | Art **Henry Fox**

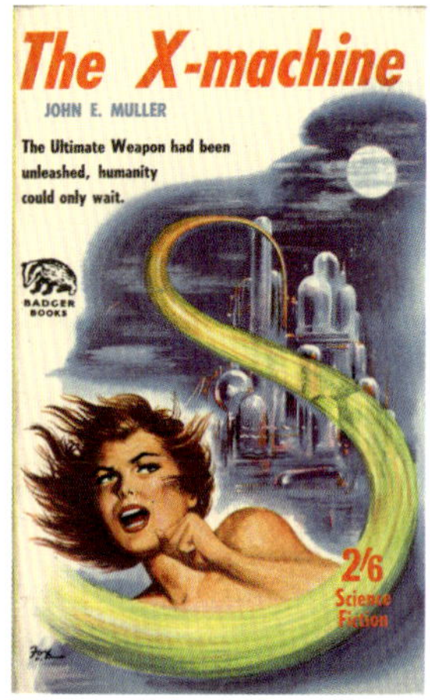

John E. Muller (R. L. Fanthorpe)
The X-Machine
Badger Books SF74, 1962 | Art **Henry Fox**

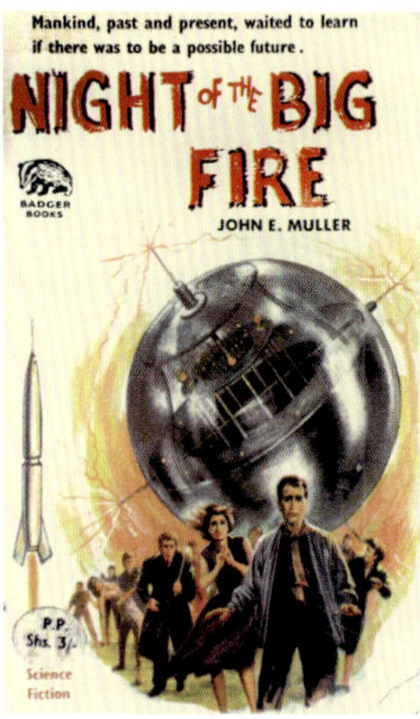

John E. Muller (R. L. Fanthorpe)
Night of the Big Fire
Badger Books SF75, 1962 | Art **Henry Fox**

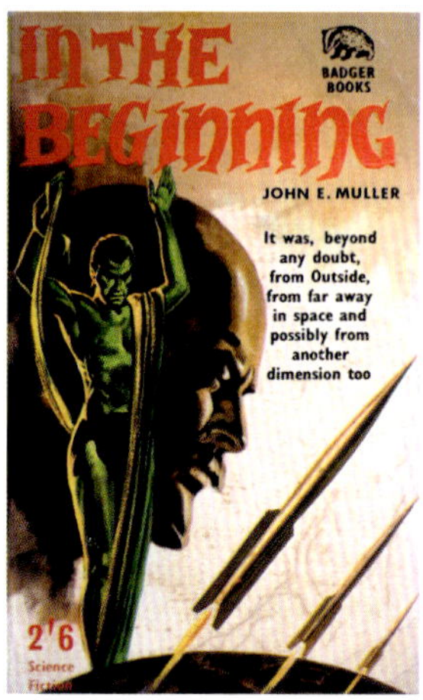

John E. Muller (R. L. Fanthorpe)
In the Beginning
Badger Books SF76, 1962 | Art **Henry Fox**

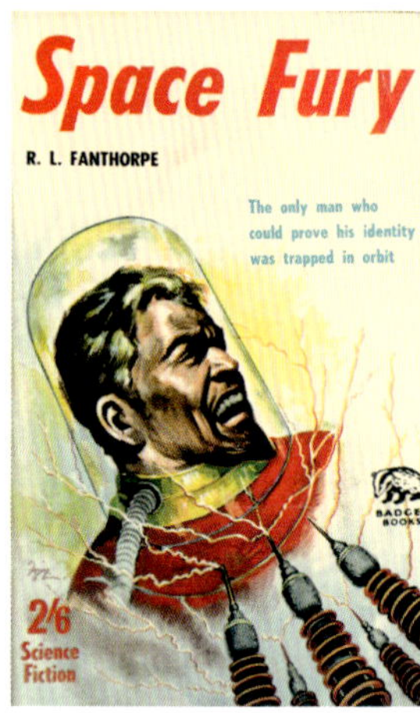

R. L. Fanthorpe
Space Fury
Badger Books SF77, 1962 | Art **Henry Fox**

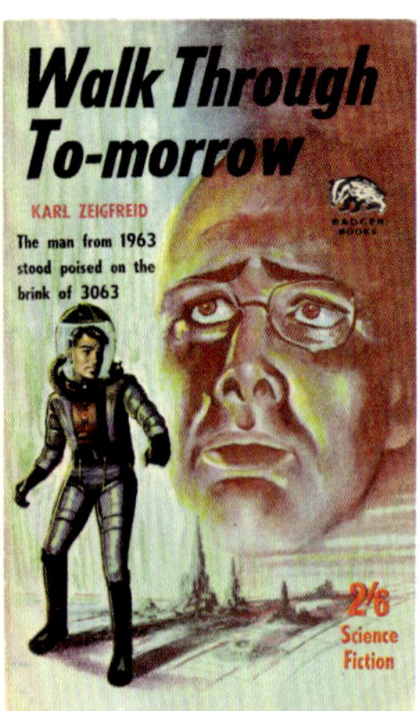

Karl Zeigfreid (R. L. Fanthorpe)
Walk Through To-Morrow
Badger Books SF78, 1962 | Art **Henry Fox**

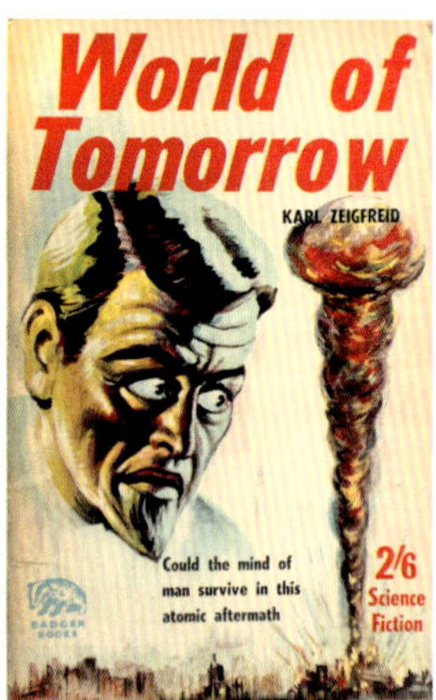

Karl Zeigfreid (R. L. Fanthorpe)
World of Tomorrow
Badger Books SF84, 1963 | Art **Henry Fox**

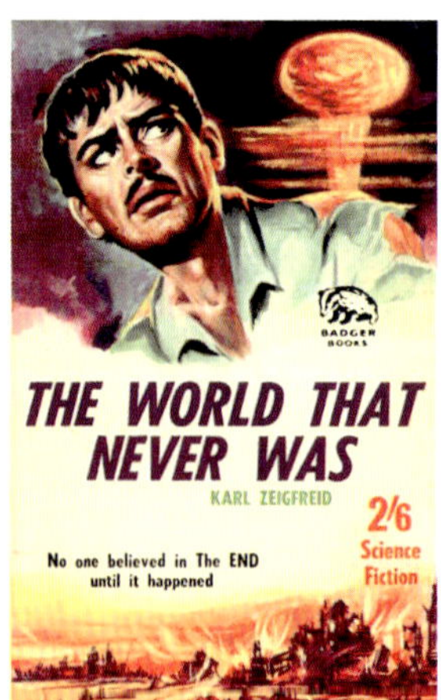

Karl Zeigfreid (R. L. Fanthorpe)
The World That Never Was
Badger Books SF85, 1963 | Art **Henry Fox**

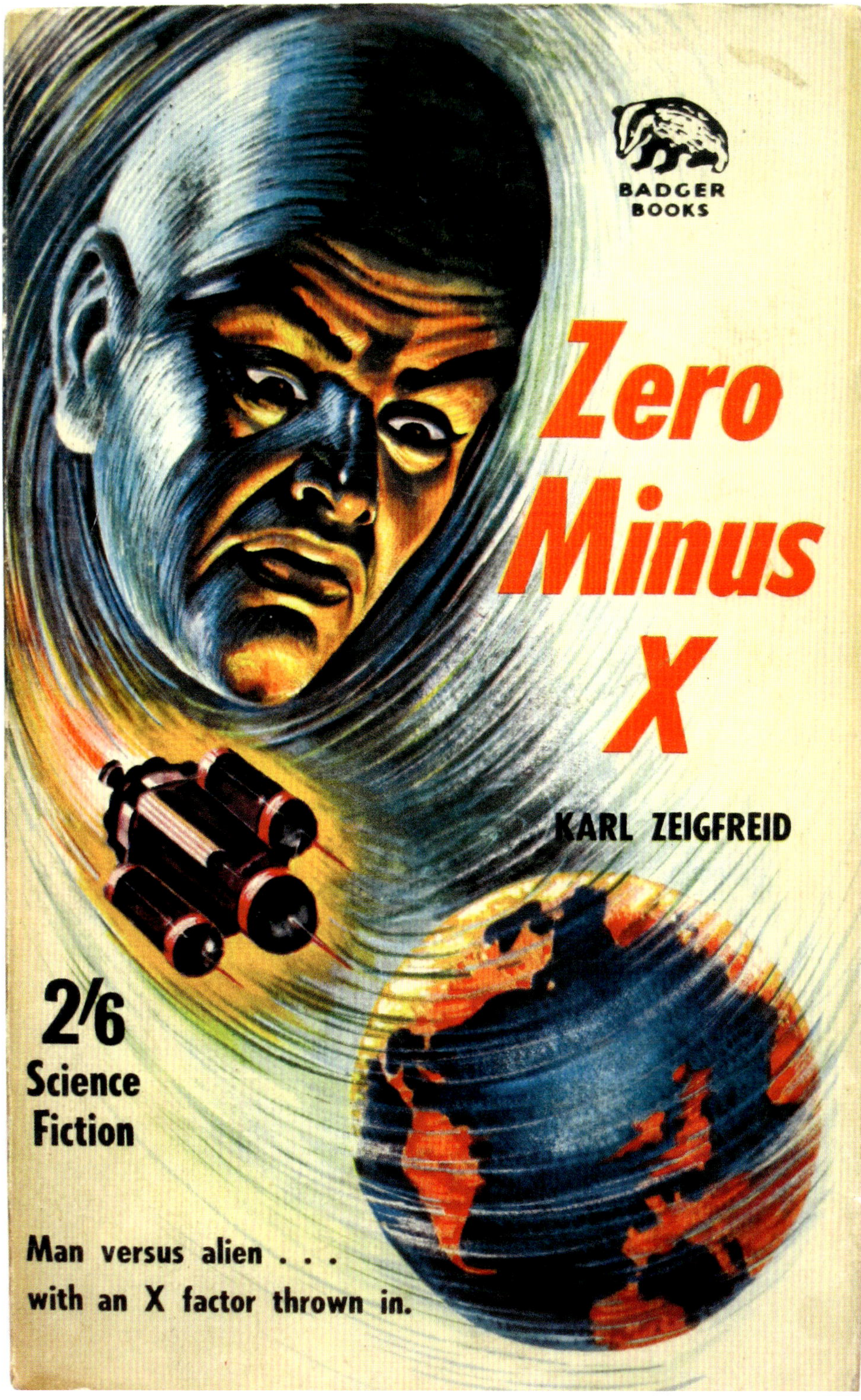

Karl Zeigfreid (R. L. Fanthorpe) | *Zero Minus X*
Badger Books SF81, 1962 | Art **Henry Fox**

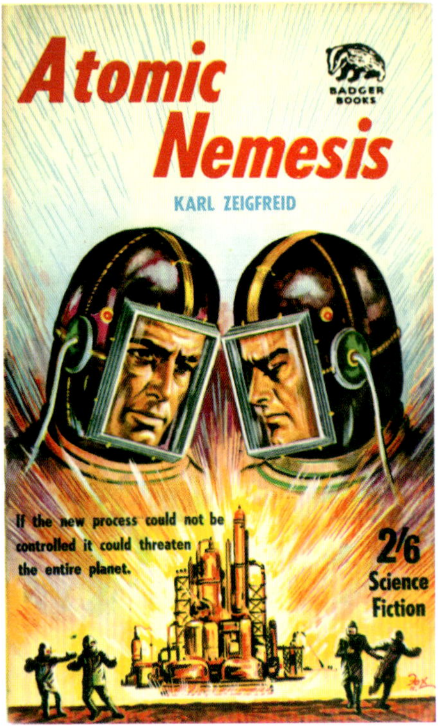

Karl Zeigfreid (R. L. Fanthorpe) | *Atomic Nemesis*
Badger Books SF80, 1962 | Art **Henry Fox**

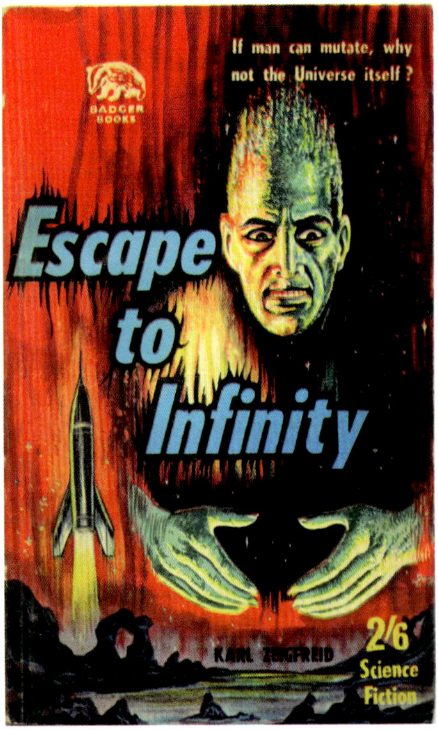

Karl Zeigfreid (R. L. Fanthorpe) | *Escape to Infinity*
Badger Books SF82, 1963 | Art **Henry Fox**

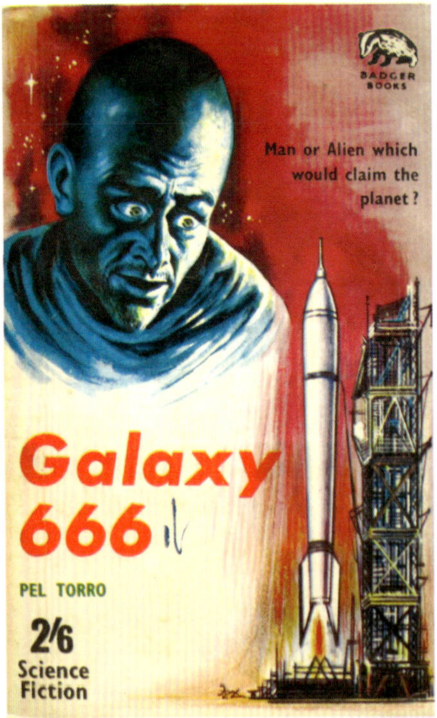

Pel Torro (R. L. Fanthorpe) | *Galaxy 666*
Badger Books SF86, 1963 | Art **Henry Fox**

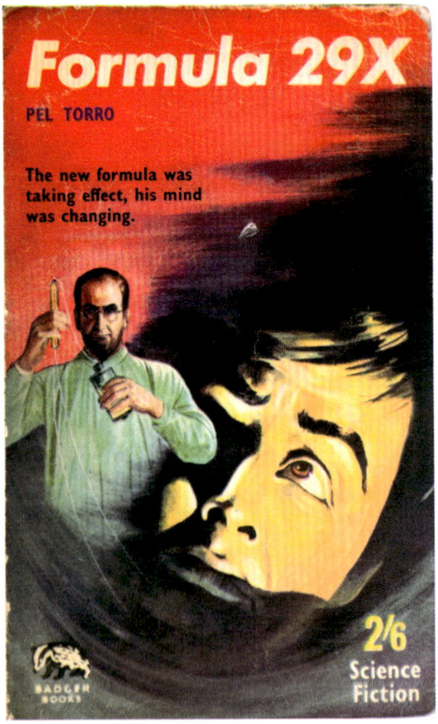

Pel Torro (R. L. Fanthorpe) | *Formula 29X*
Badger Books SF87, 1963 | Art **Henry Fox**

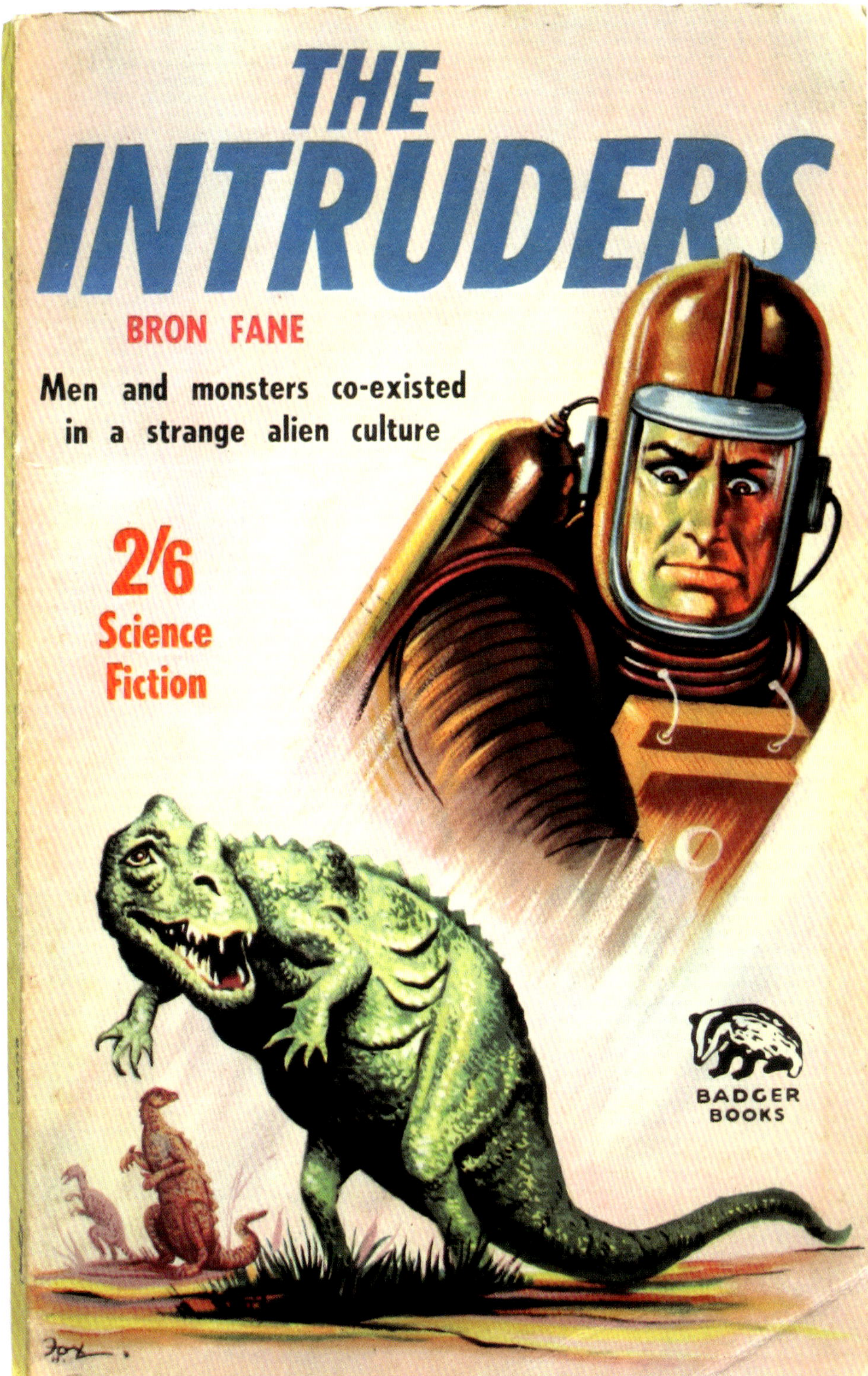

Bron Fane (R. L. Fanthorpe) | *The Intruders*
Badger Books SF89, 1963 | Art **Henry Fox**

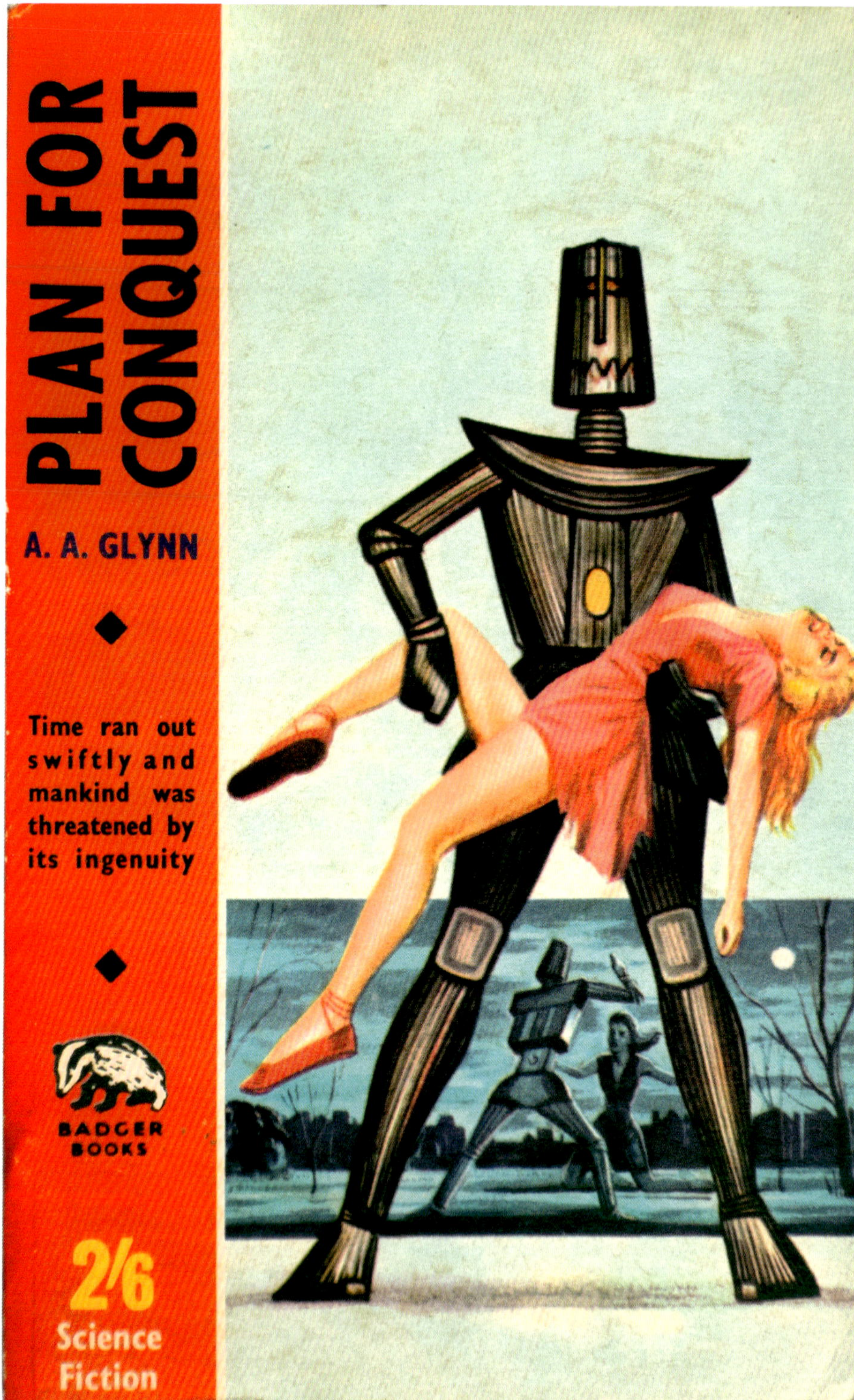

A. A. Glynn | *Plan for Conquest*
Badger Books SF90, 1963 | Art **Henry Fox**

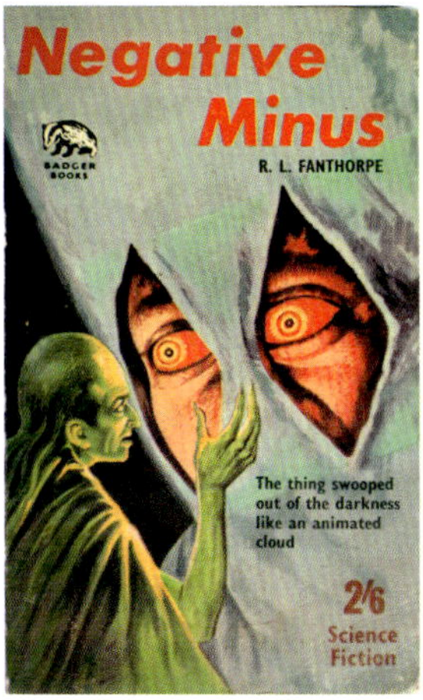

R. L. Fanthorpe
Negative Minus
Badger Books SF88, 1963 | Art **Henry Fox**

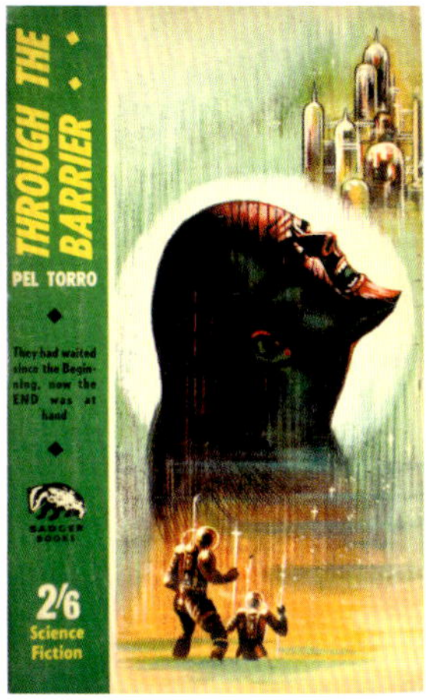

Pel Torro (R. L. Fanthorpe)
Through the Barrier
Badger Books SF91, 1963 | Art **Henry Fox**

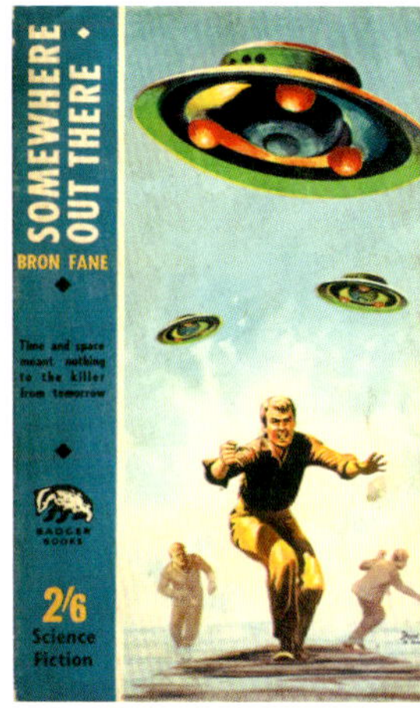

Bron Fane (R. L. Fanthorpe)
Somewhere Out There
Badger Books SF92, 1963 | Art **Henry Fox**

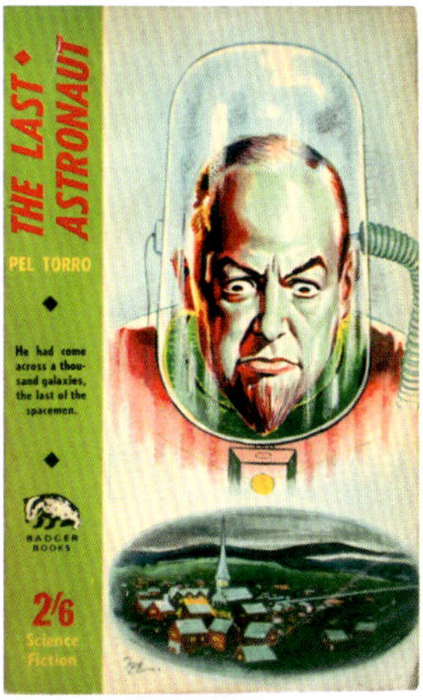

Pel Torro (R. L. Fanthorpe)
The Last Astronaut
Badger Books SF93, 1963 | Art **Henry Fox**

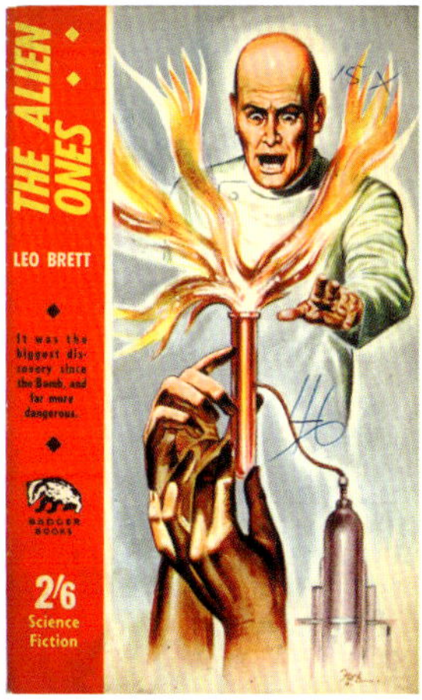

Leo Brett (R. L. Fanthorpe)
The Alien Ones
Badger Books SF94, 1963 | Art **Henry Fox**

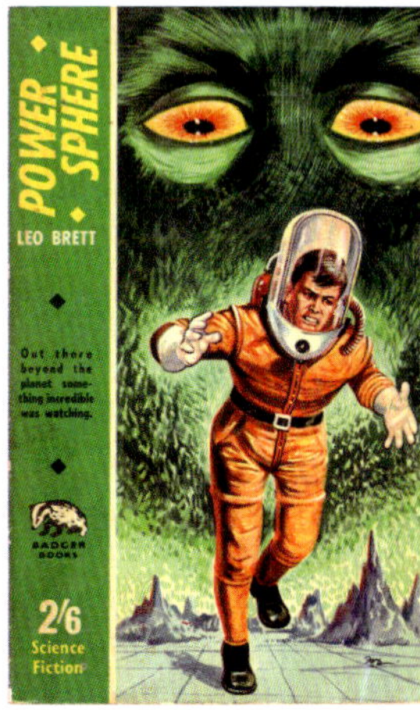

Leo Brett (R. L. Fanthorpe)
Power Sphere
Badger Books SF95, 1963 | Art **Henry Fox**

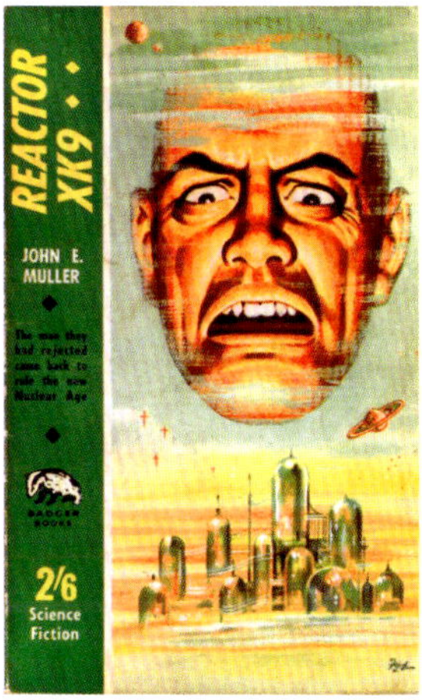

John E. Muller (R. L. Fanthorpe)
Reactor XK9
Badger Books SF96, 1963 | Art **Henry Fox**

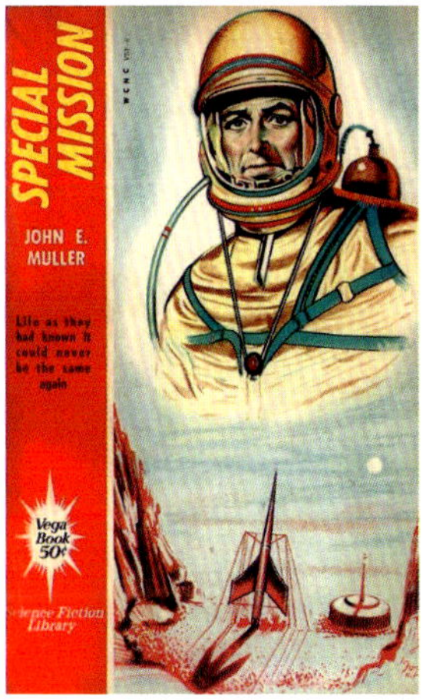

John E. Muller (R. L. Fanthorpe)
Special Mission (Vega Books 8 US edition)
Badger Books SF97, 1963 | Art **Henry Fox**

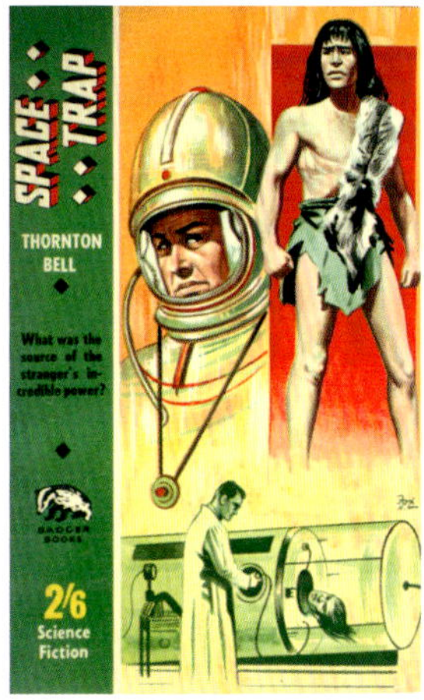

Thornton Bell (R. L. Fanthorpe)
Space Trap
Badger Books SF98, 1964 | Art **Henry Fox**

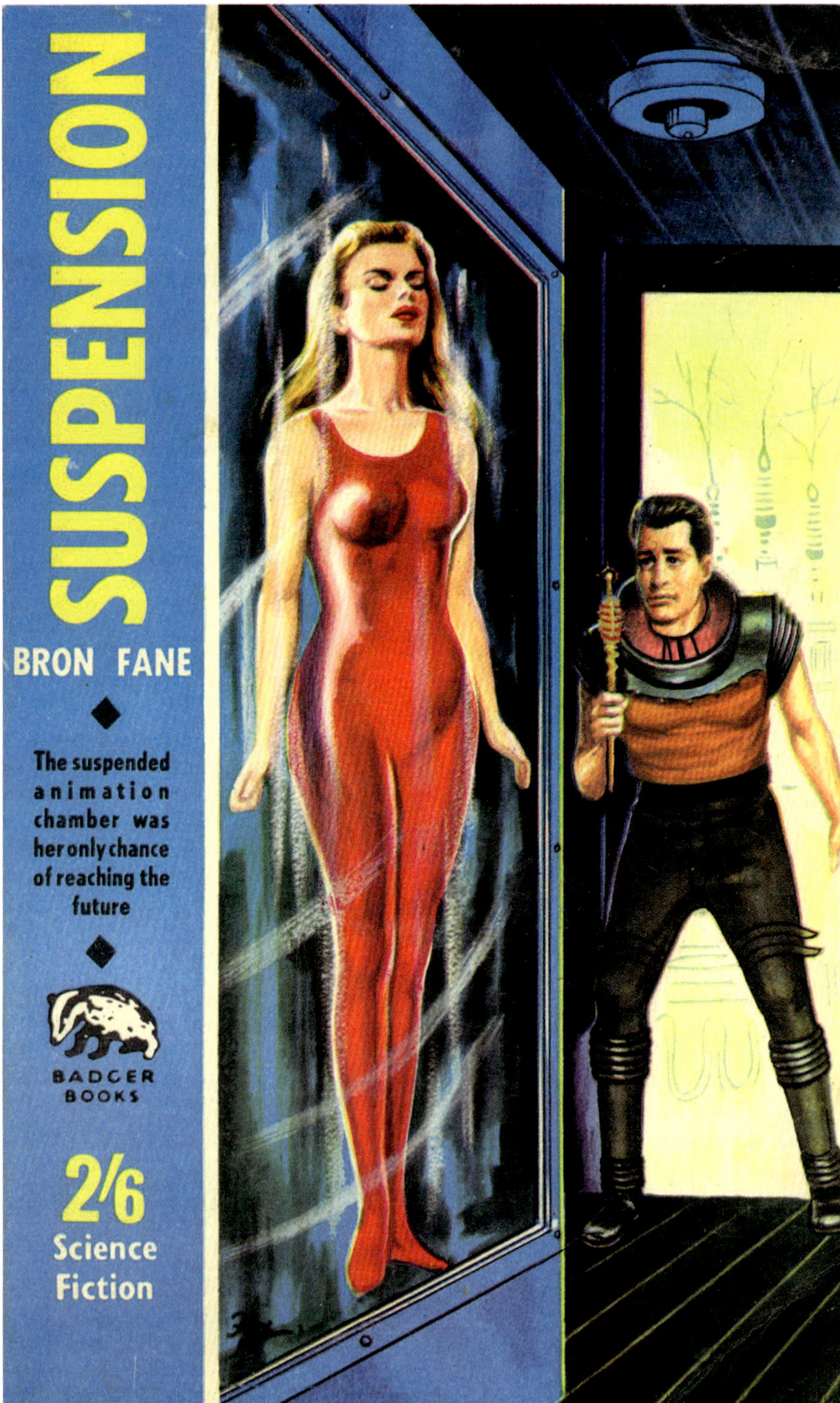

Bron Fane (R. L. Fanthorpe) | *Suspension*
Badger Books SF102, 1964 | Art **Henry Fox** after **Ed Emshwiller** (SF42)

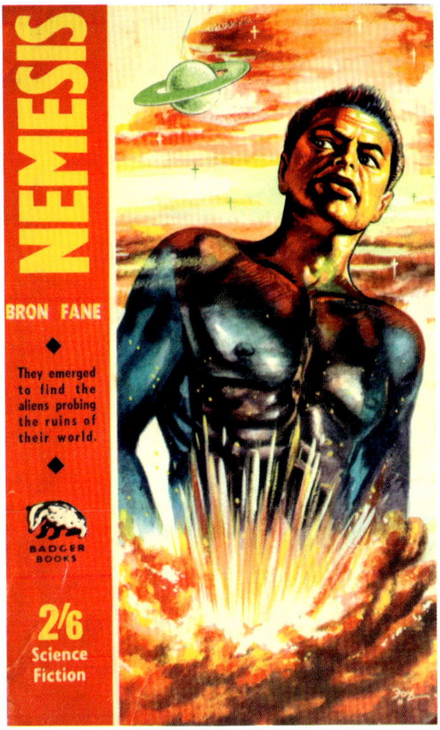

Bron Fane (R. L. Fanthorpe) | *Nemesis*
Badger Books SF100, 1964 | Art **Henry Fox** after **Eddie Jones** (SF21)

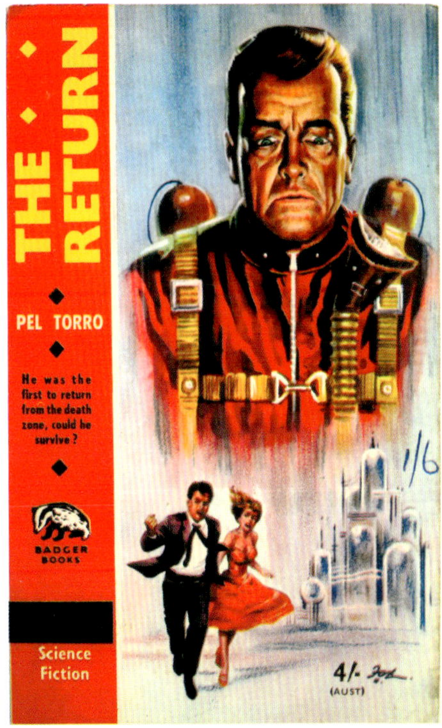

Pel Torro (R. L. Fanthorpe) | *The Return* (Australian edition)
Badger Books SF101, 1964 | Art **Henry Fox**

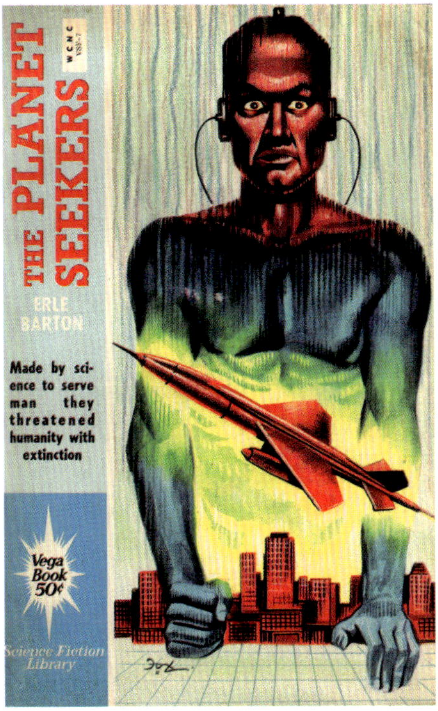

Erle Barton (R. L. Fanthorpe) | *The Planet Seekers*
(Vega Books 7 US edition) Badger Books SF99, 1964 | Art **Henry Fox**

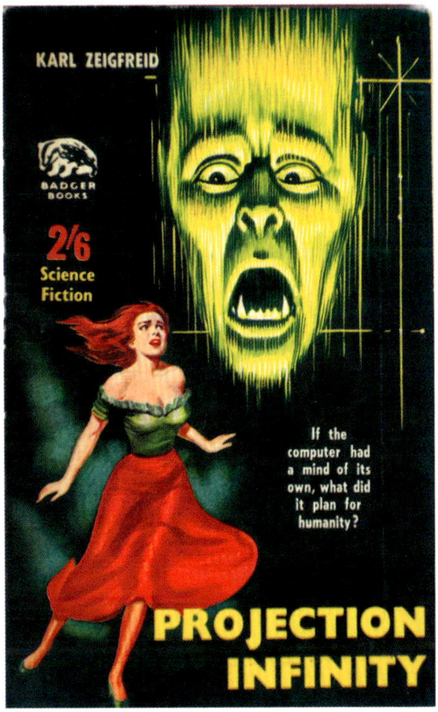

Karl Zeigfreid (R. L. Fanthorpe) | *Projection Infinity*
Badger Books SF103, 1964 | Art **Henry Fox**

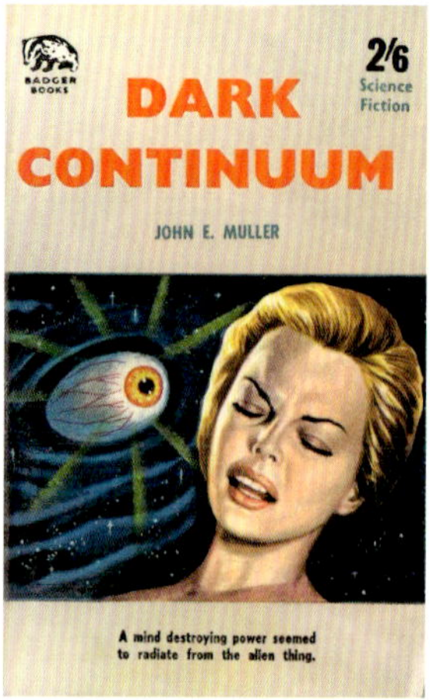

John E. Muller (R. L. Fanthorpe)
Dark Continuum
Badger Books SF104, 1964 | Art **Henry Fox**

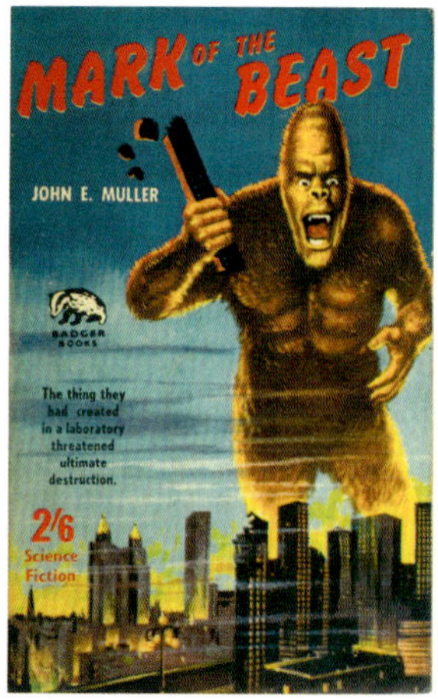

John E. Muller (R. L. Fanthorpe)
Mark of the Beast
Badger Books SF105, 1964 | Art **Henry Fox**

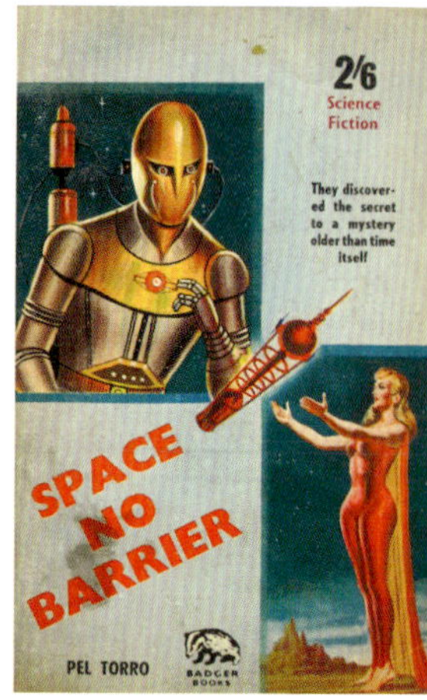

Pel Torro (R. L. Fanthorpe)
Space No Barrier
Badger Books SF106, 1964 | Art **Henry Fox**

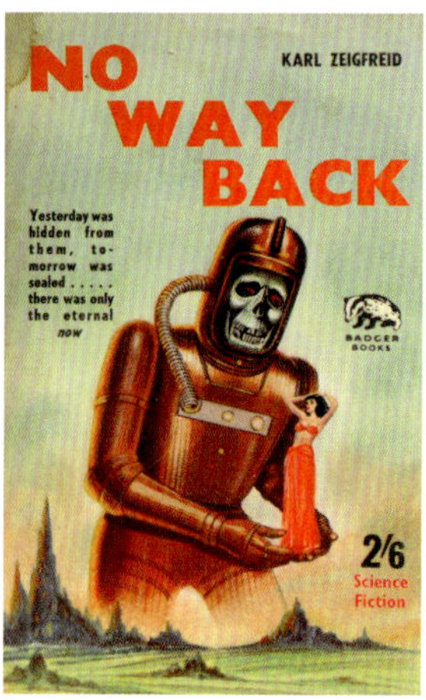

Karl Zeigfreid (R. L. Fanthorpe)
No Way Back
Badger Books SF107, 1964 | Art **Henry Fox**

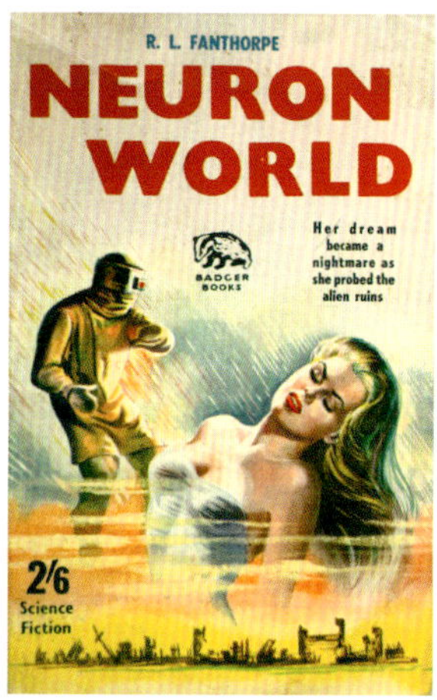

R. L. Fanthorpe
Neuron World
Badger Books SF108, 1965 | Art **Henry Fox**

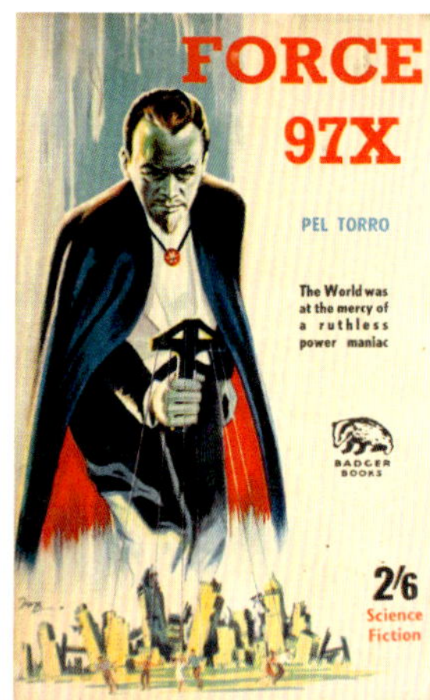

Pel Torro (R. L. Fanthorpe)
Force 97X
Badger Books SF110, 1965 | Art **Henry Fox**

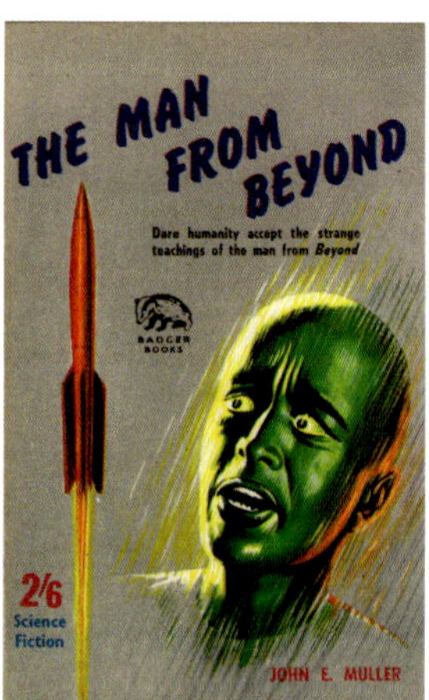

John E. Muller (R. L. Fanthorpe)
The Man from Beyond
Badger Books SF111, 1965 | Art **Henry Fox**

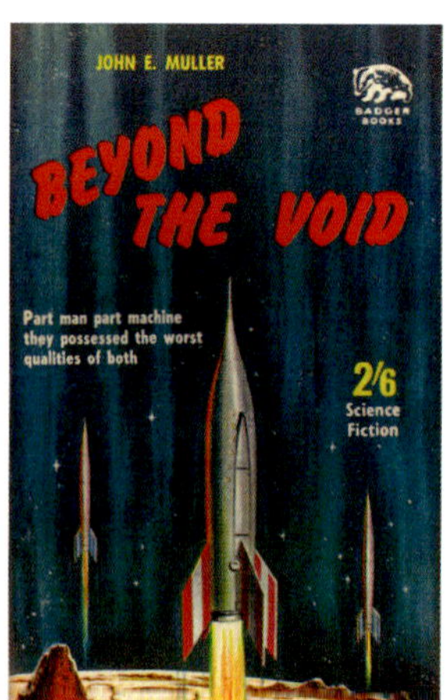

John E. Muller (R. L. Fanthorpe)
Beyond the Void
Badger Books SF112, 1965 | Art **Henry Fox**

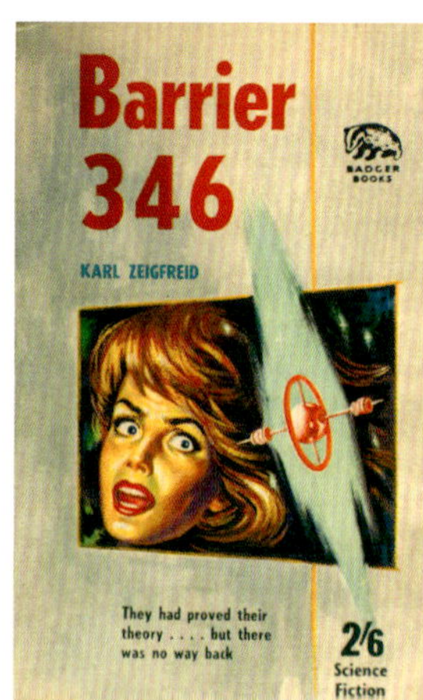

Karl Zeigfreid (R. L. Fanthorpe)
Barrier 346
Badger Books SF113, 1965 | Art **Henry Fox**

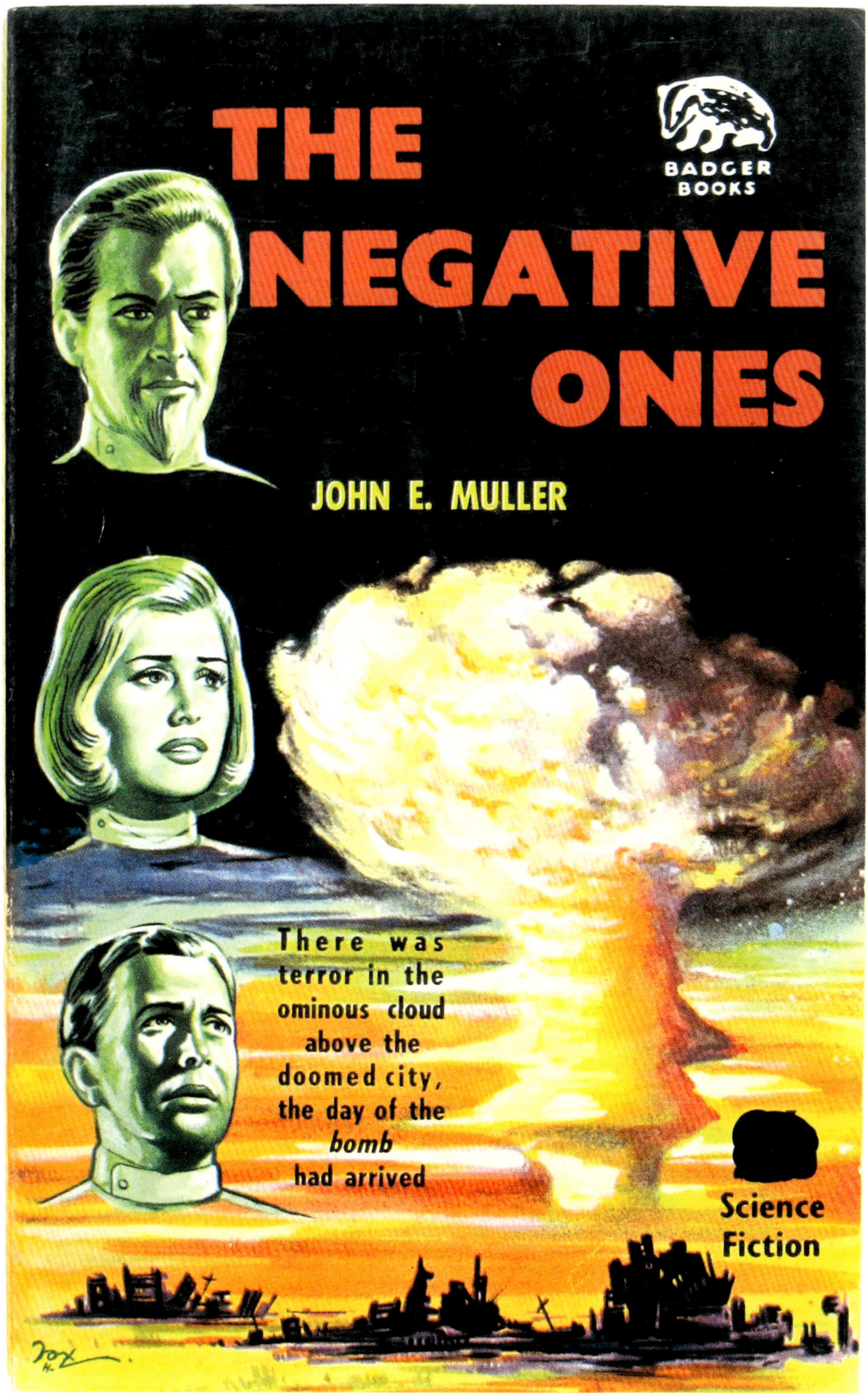

John E. Muller (R. L. Fanthorpe) | *The Negative Ones*
Badger Books SF109, 1965 | Art **Henry Fox**

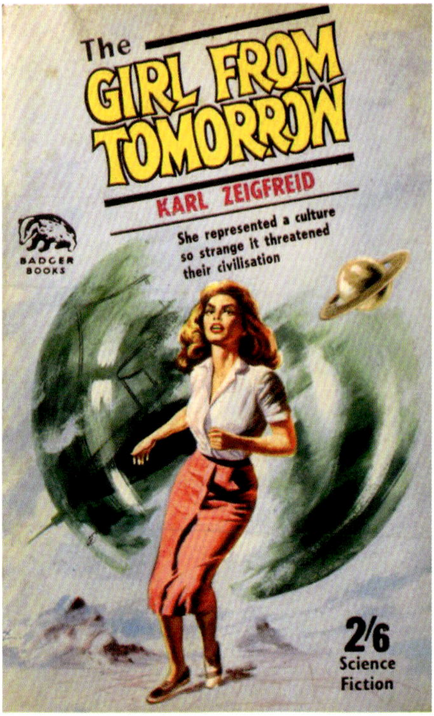

Karl Zeigfreid (R. L. Fanthorpe) | *The Girl from Tomorrow*
Badger Books SF114, 1965 | Art **Henry Fox**

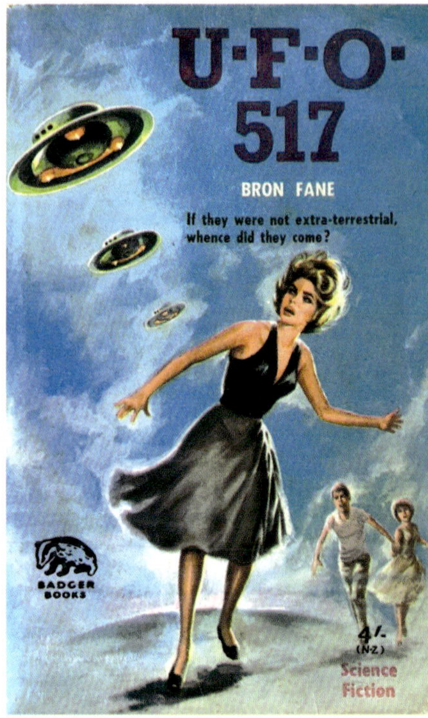

Bron Fane (R. L. Fanthorpe) | *U.F.O. 517* (New Zealand edition)
Badger Books SF115, 1965 | Art **Henry Fox**

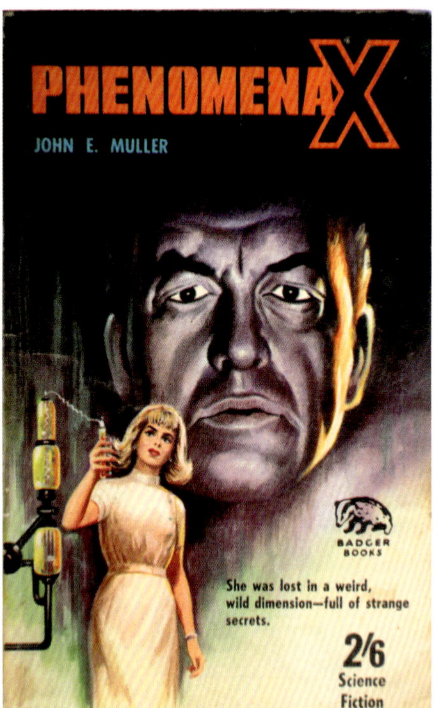

John E. Muller (R. L. Fanthorpe) | *Phenomena X*
Badger Books SF116, 1966 | Art **Henry Fox**

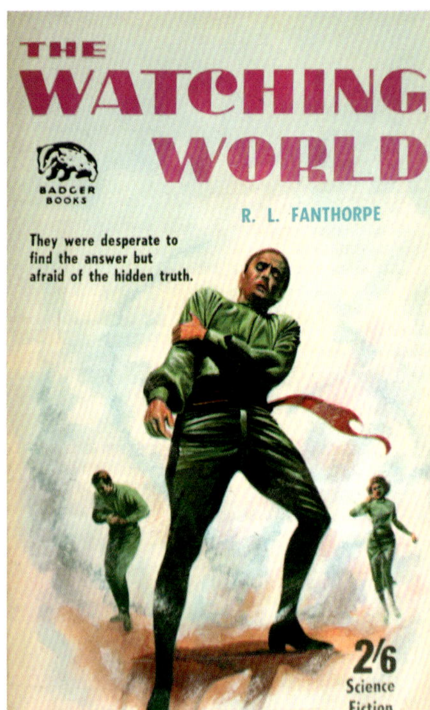

R. L. Fanthorpe | *The Watching World*
Badger Books SF118, 1966 | Art **Henry Fox**

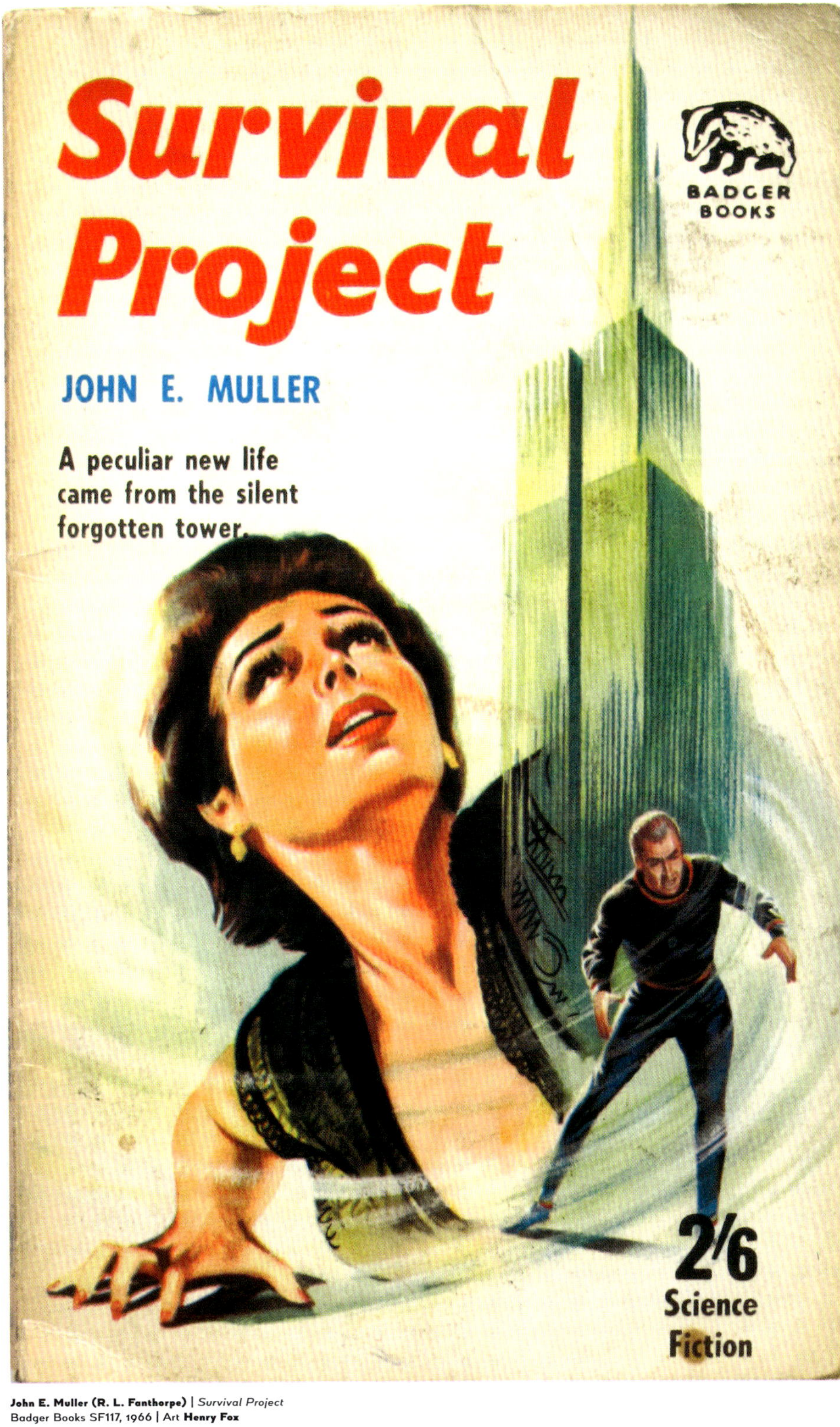

John E. Muller (R. L. Fanthorpe) | *Survival Project*
Badger Books SF117, 1966 | Art **Henry Fox**

THROUGH THE BARRIER

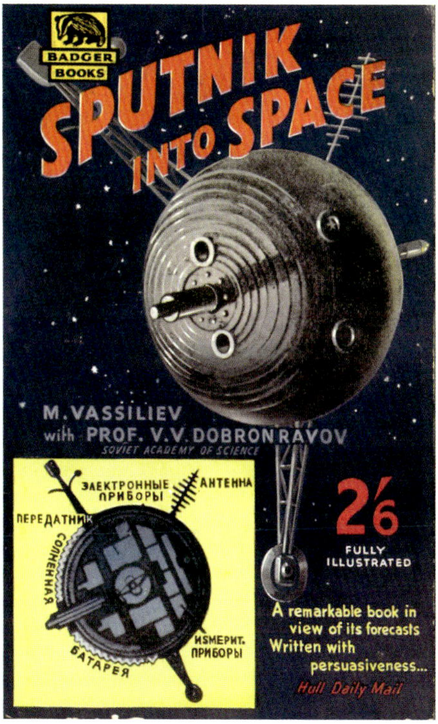

M Vassiliev | *Sputnik into Space*
Badger Books SS1, 1958 | Art **Unknown**

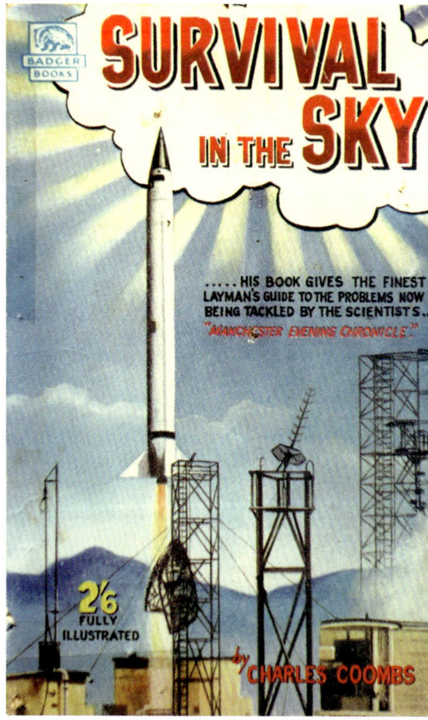

Charles Coombs | *Survival in the Sky*
Badger Books SS2, 1958 | Art **Unknown**

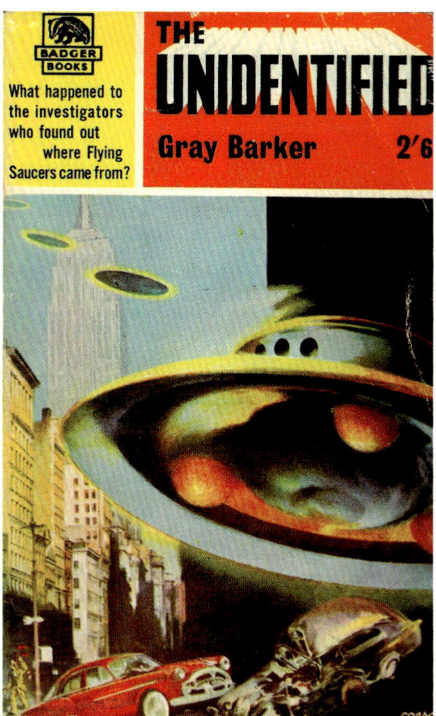

Gray Barker | *The Unidentified*
Badger Books SS3, 1960 | Art **Kurt Caesar**

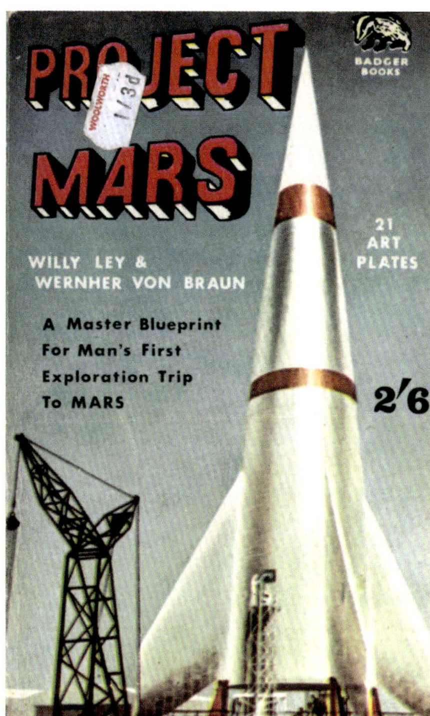

Wernher von Braun, Willy Ley | *Project Mars*
Badger Books SS4, 1961 | Art **Chesley Bonestell**

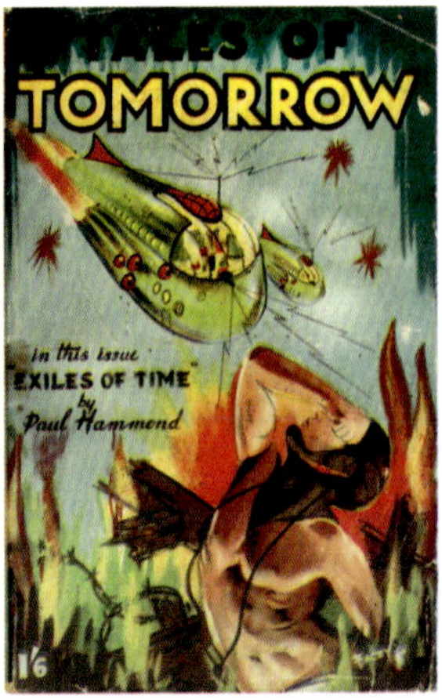

Tales of Tomorrow #1
John Spencer & Co., 1950
Art **Gerald Facey**

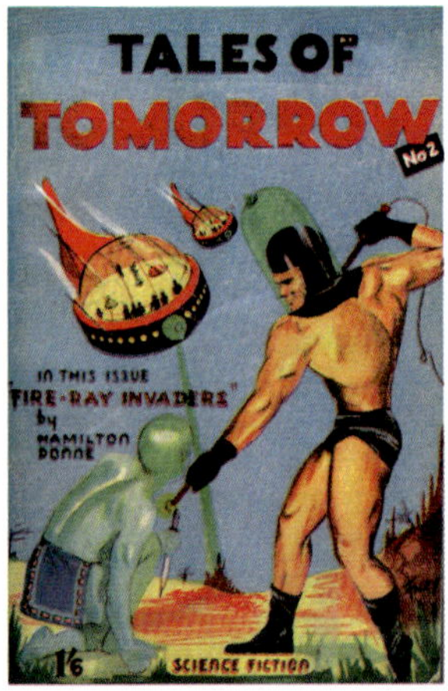

Tales of Tomorrow #2
John Spencer & Co., 1950
Art **Gerald Facey**

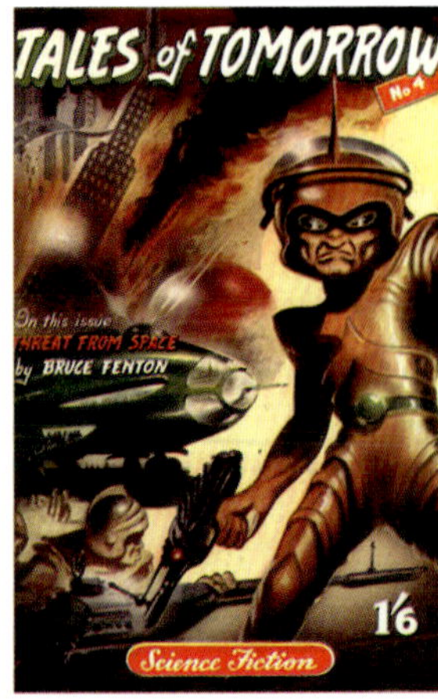

Tales of Tomorrow #4
John Spencer & Co., 1952
Art **Unknown (Ron Turner?)**

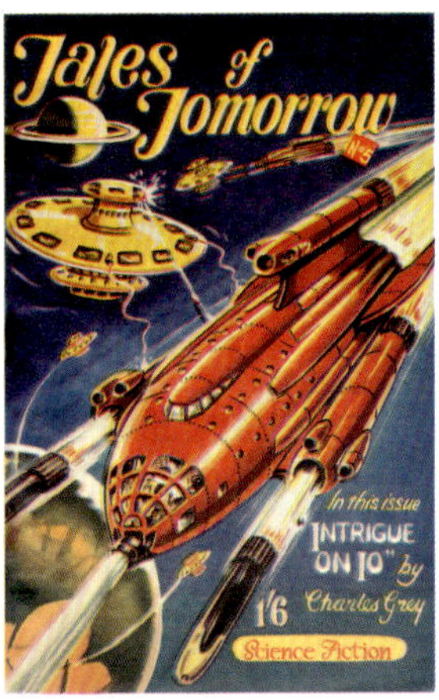

Tales of Tomorrow #5
John Spencer & Co., 1952
Art **Norman Light**

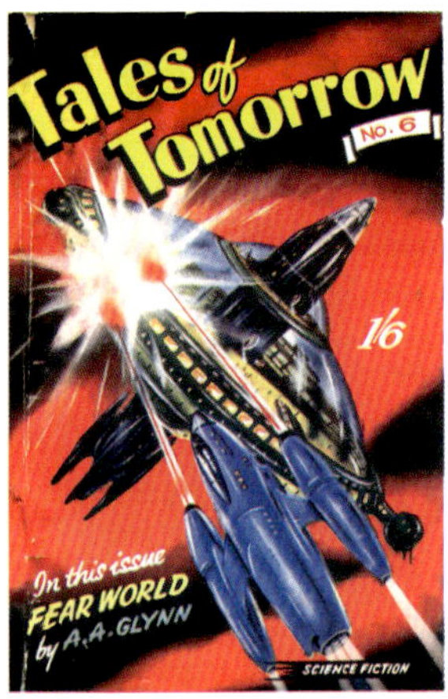

Tales of Tomorrow #6
John Spencer & Co., 1953
Art **Gordon C. Davies**

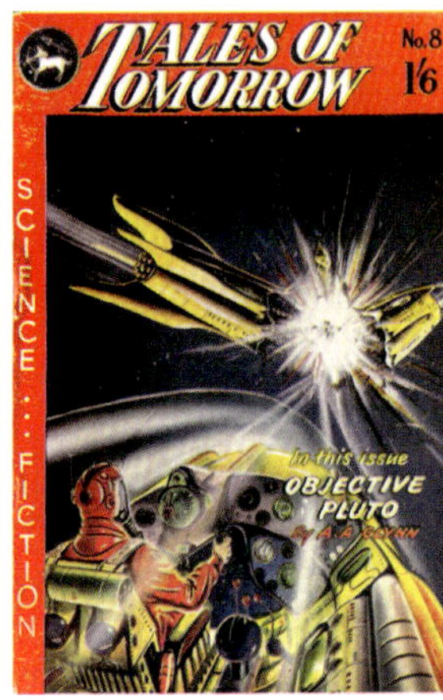

Tales of Tomorrow #8
John Spencer & Co., 1953
Art **Gordon C. Davies**

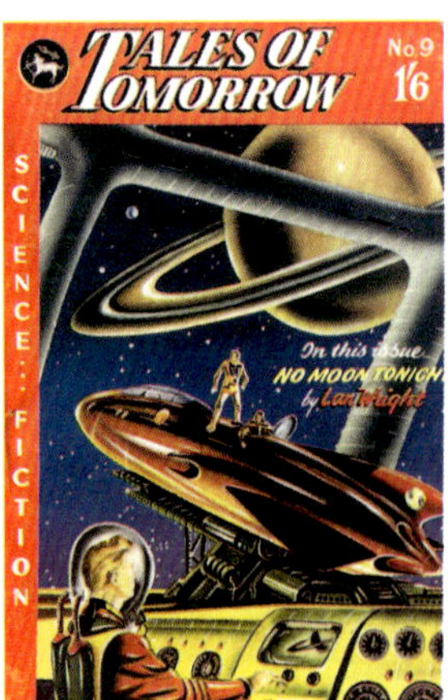

Tales of Tomorrow #9
John Spencer & Co., 1953
Art **Gordon C. Davies**

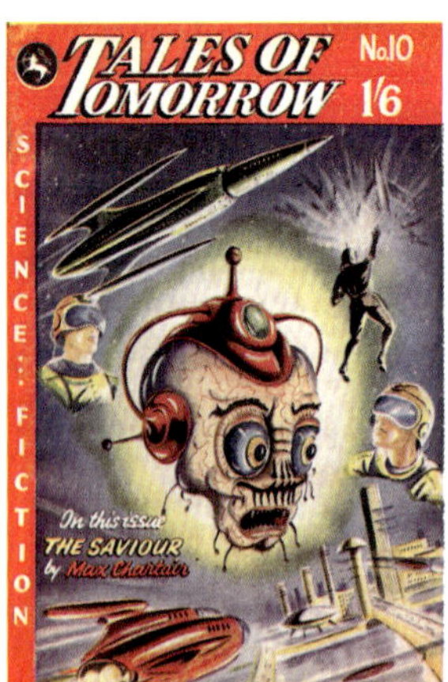

Tales of Tomorrow #10
John Spencer & Co., 1954
Art **Gordon C. Davies**

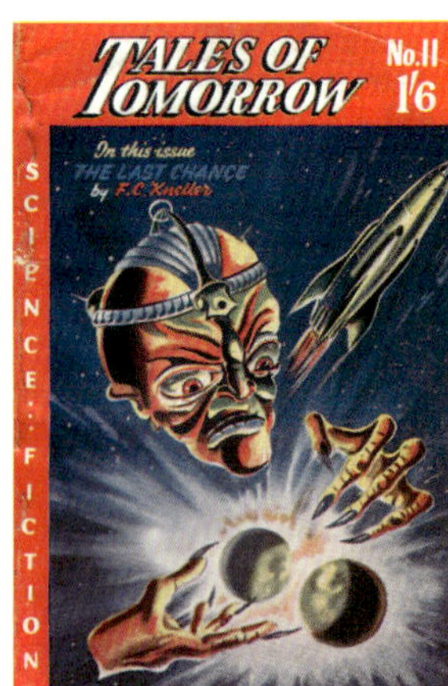

Tales of Tomorrow #11
John Spencer & Co., 1954
Art **Gordon C. Davies**

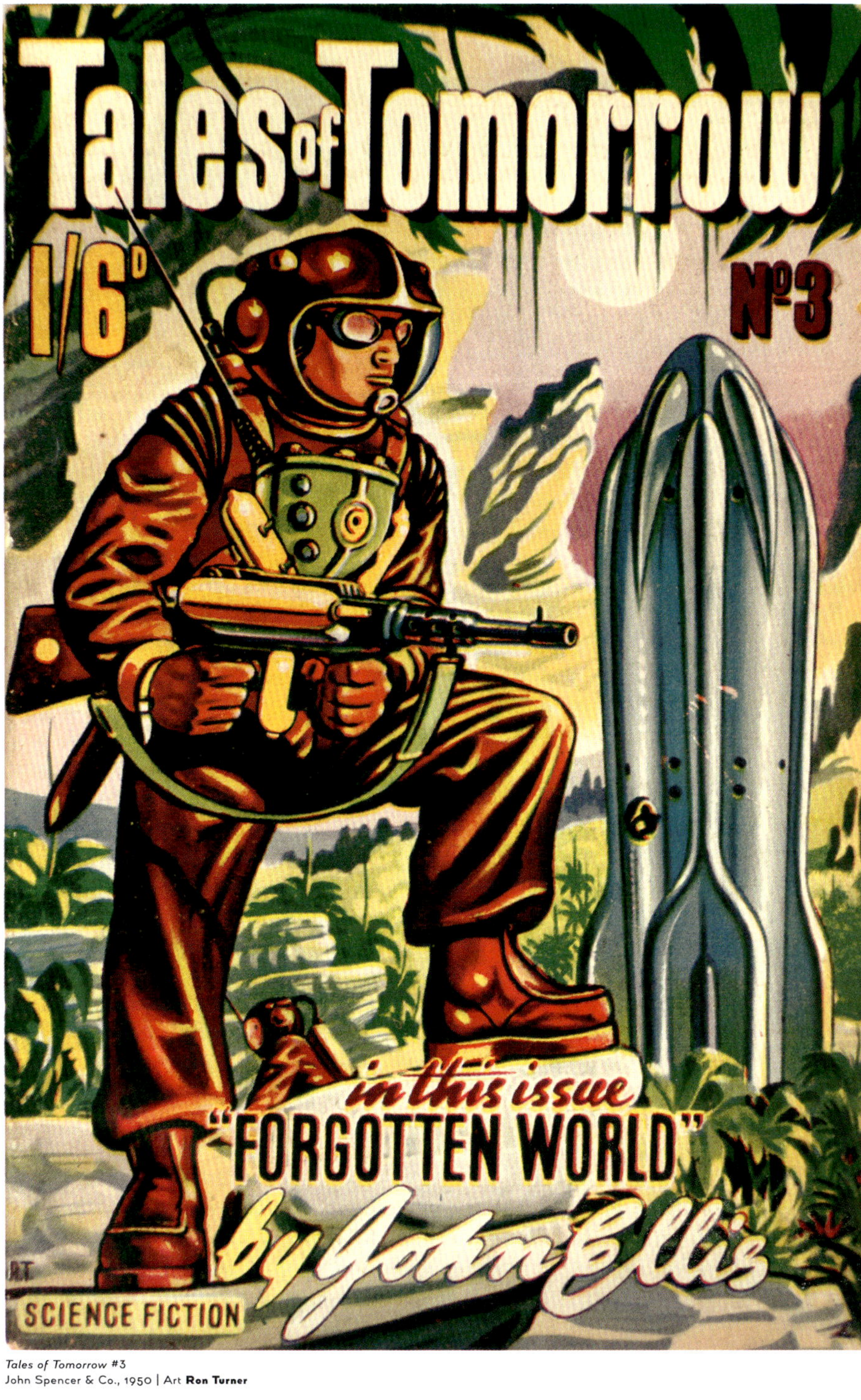

Tales of Tomorrow #3
John Spencer & Co., 1950 | Art **Ron Turner**

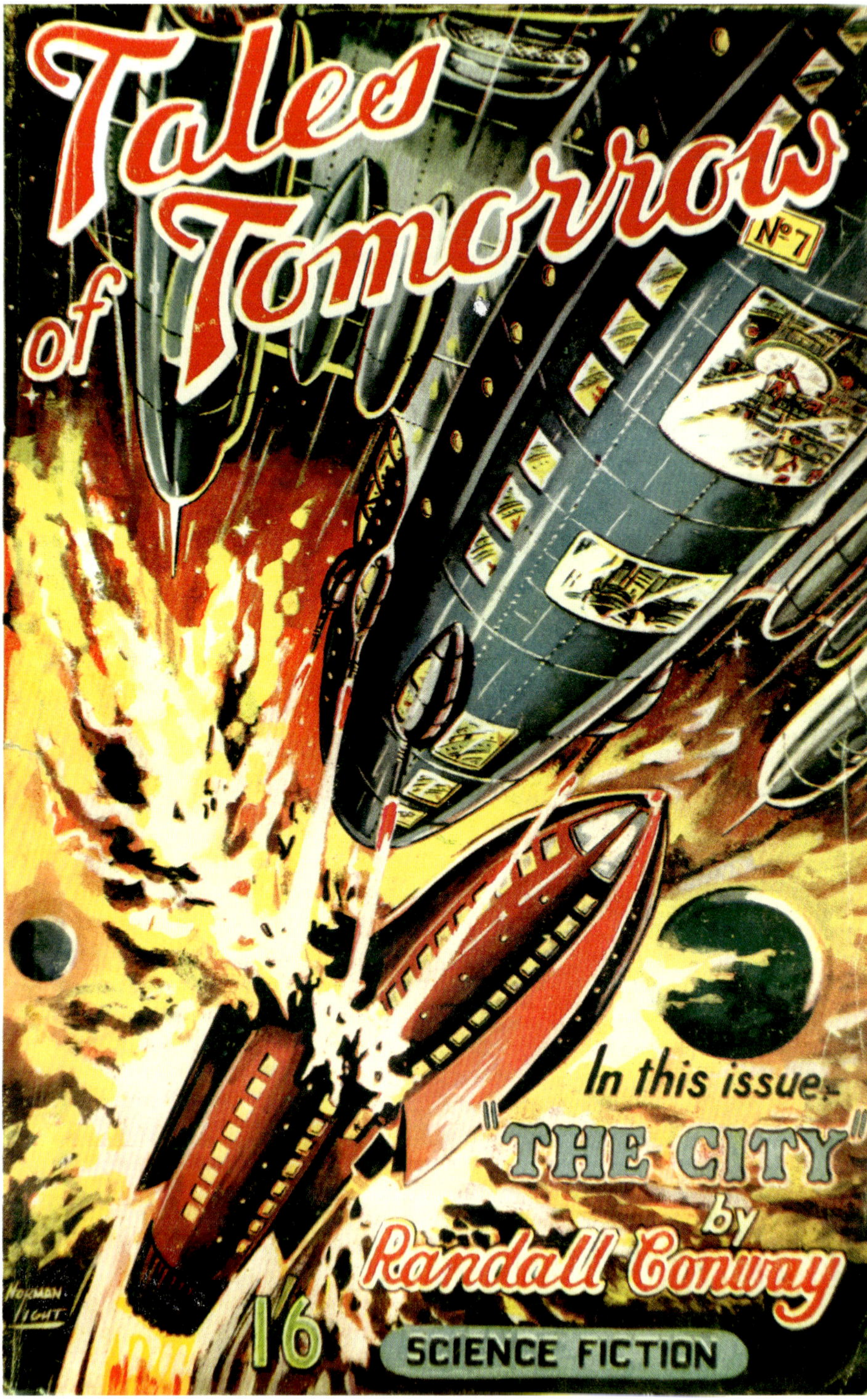

Tales of Tomorrow #7
John Spencer & Co., 1953 | Art **Norman Light**

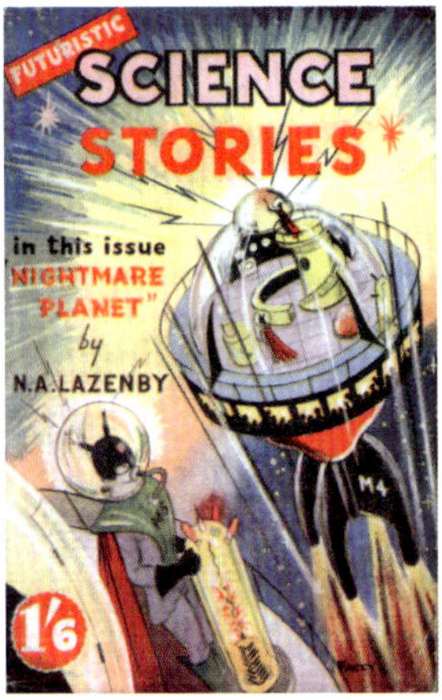

Futuristic Science Stories #1
John Spencer & Co., 1950
Art **Gerald Facey**

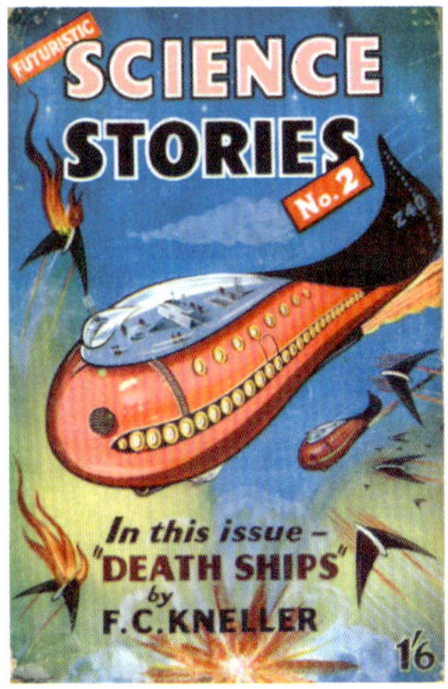

Futuristic Science Stories #2
John Spencer & Co., 1950
Art **Gerald Facey**

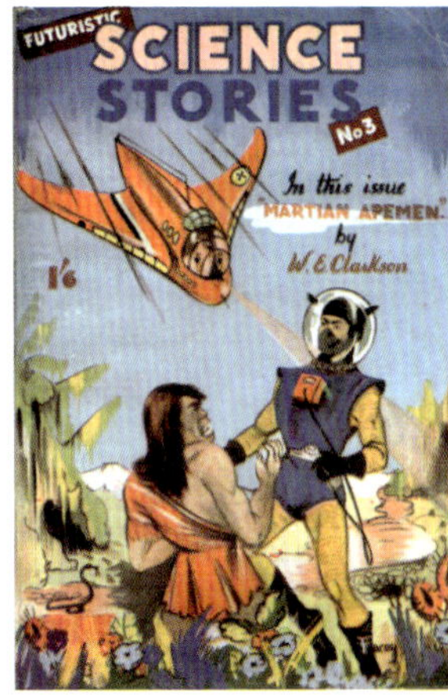

Futuristic Science Stories #3
John Spencer & Co., 1950
Art **Gerald Facey**

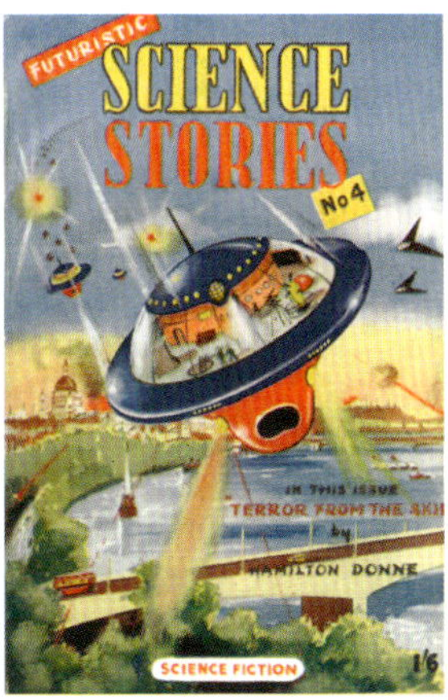

Futuristic Science Stories #4
John Spencer & Co., 1951
Art **Gerald Facey**

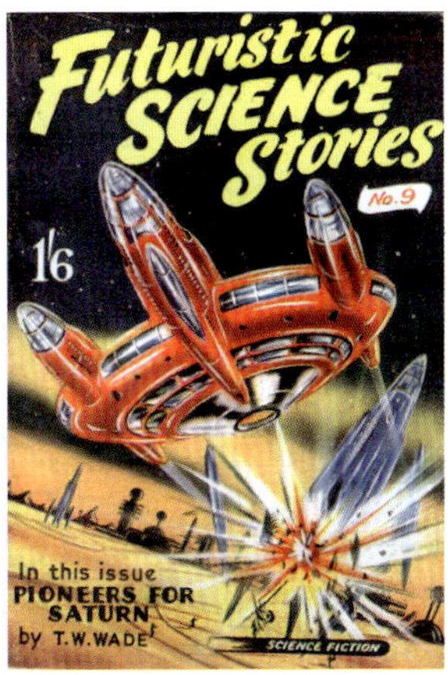

Futuristic Science Stories #9
John Spencer & Co., 1953
Art **Gordon C. Davies**

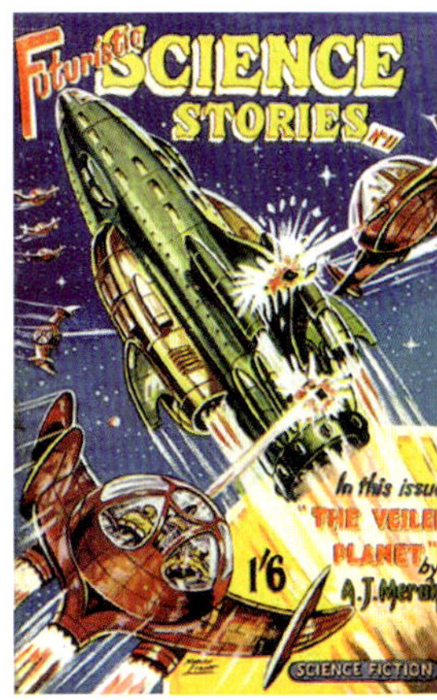

Futuristic Science Stories #11
John Spencer & Co., 1953
Art **Norman Light**

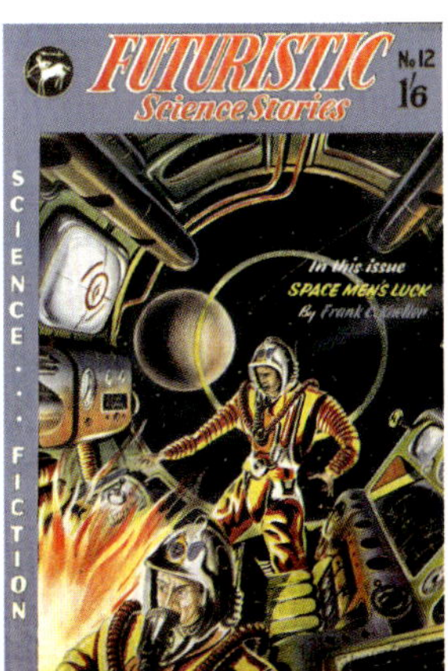

Futuristic Science Stories #12
John Spencer & Co., 1953
Art **Gordon C. Davies**

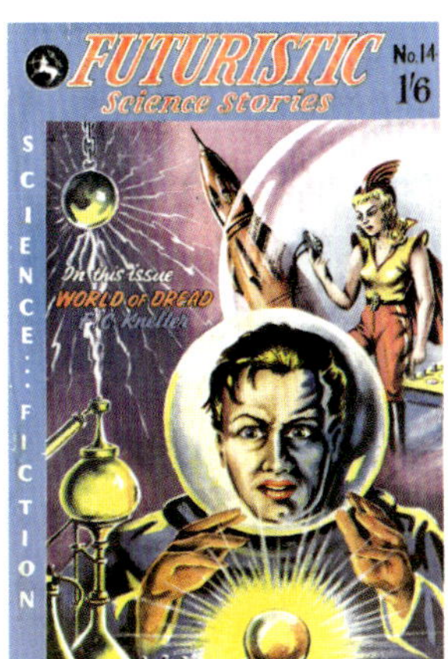

Futuristic Science Stories #14
John Spencer & Co., 1954
Art **Ray Theobald**

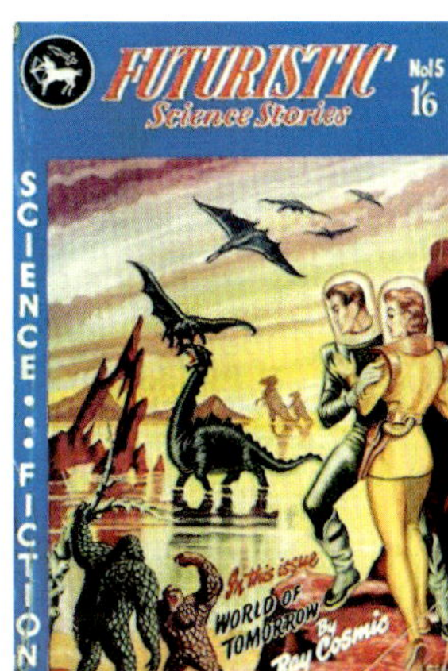

Futuristic Science Stories #15
John Spencer & Co., 1954
Art **Ron Embleton**

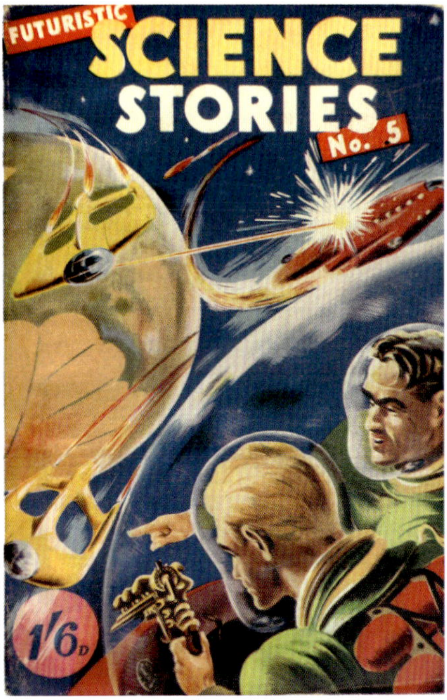

Futuristic Science Stories #5
John Spencer & Co., 1951 | Art **Unknown (George Ratciffe?)**

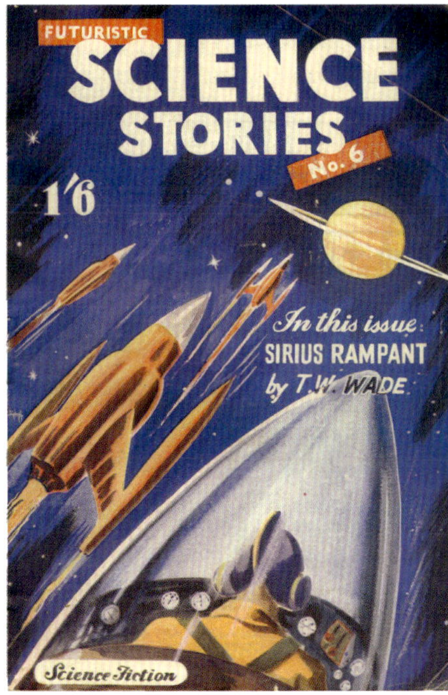

Futuristic Science Stories #6
John Spencer & Co., 1952 | Art **Unknown (George Ratciffe?)**

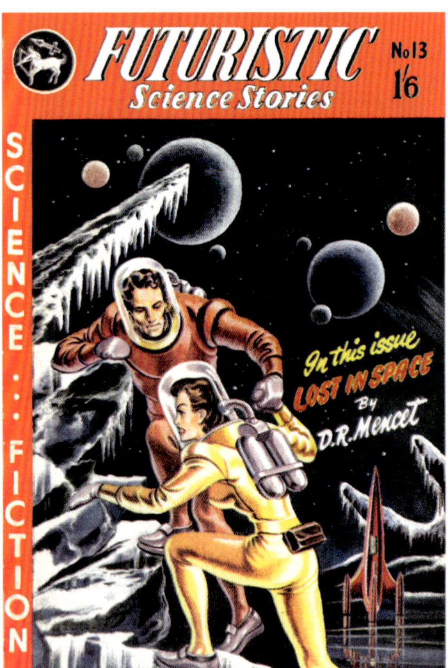

Futuristic Science Stories #13
John Spencer & Co., 1953 | Art **Ron Embleton**

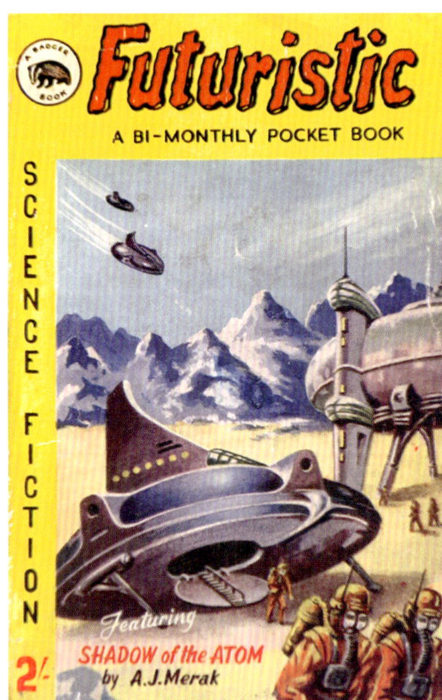

Futuristic Science Stories #16
John Spencer & Co., 1958 | Art **Ray Theobald**

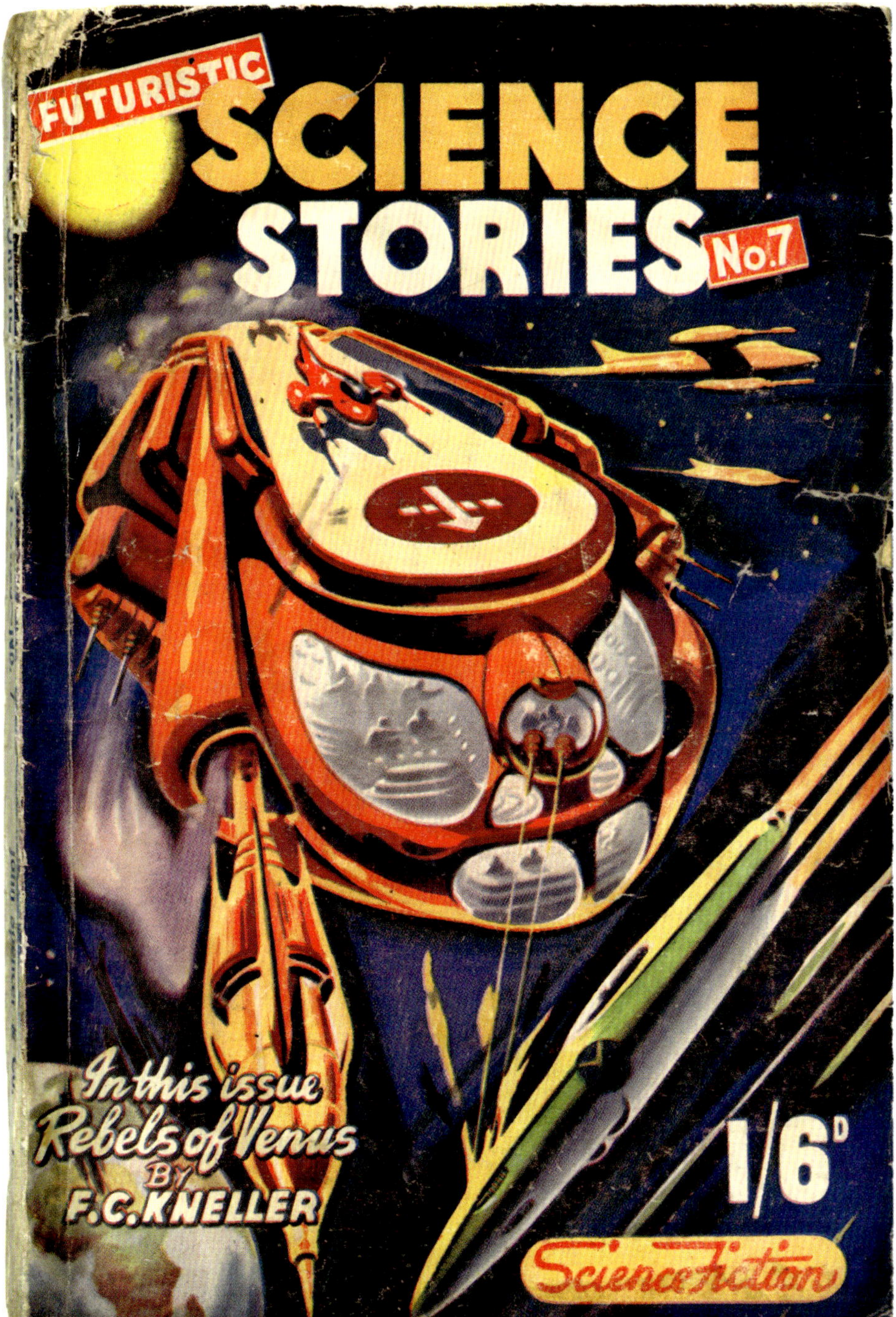

Futuristic Science Stories #7
John Spencer & Co., 1952 | Art **Ron Turner**

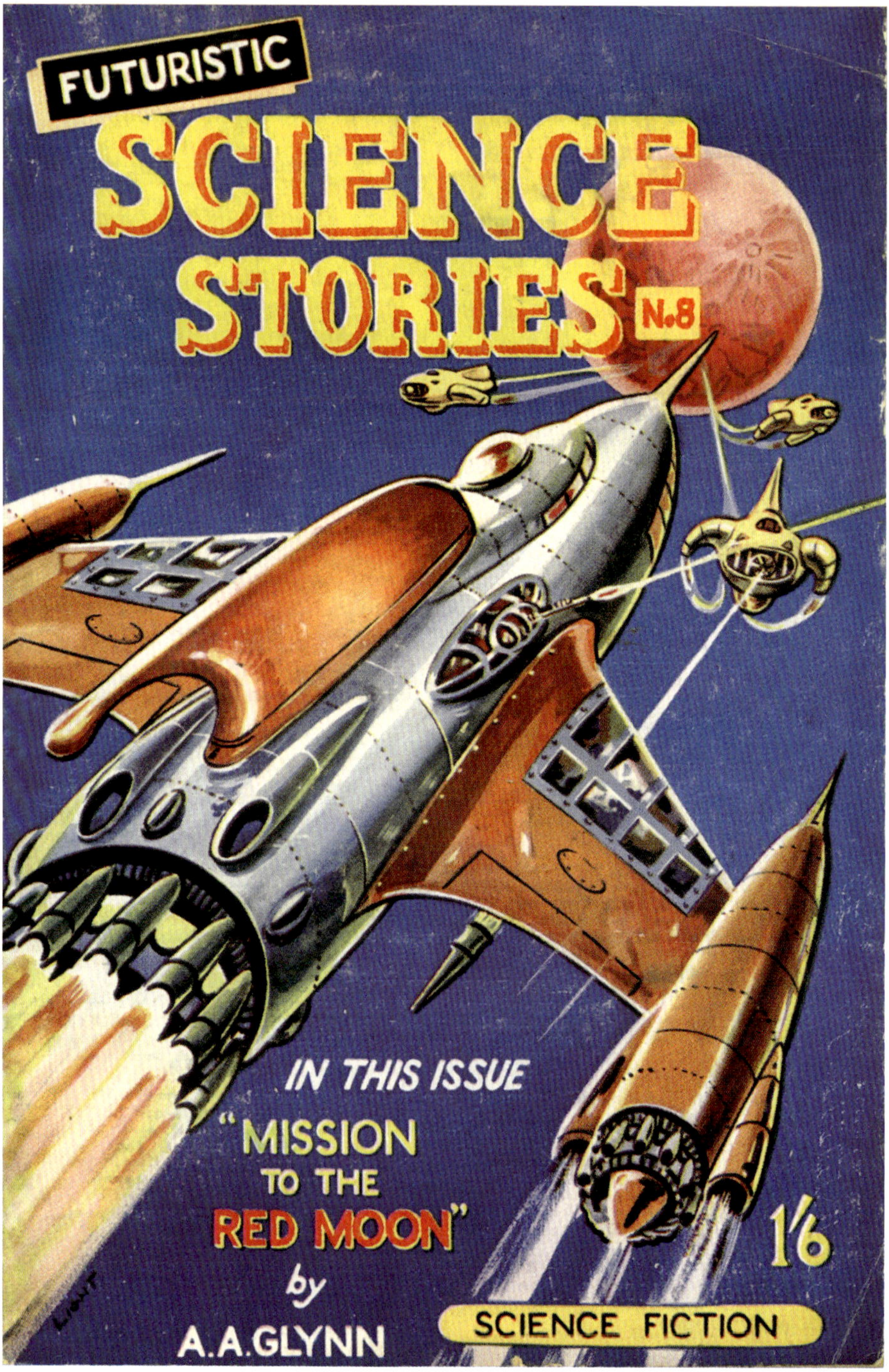

Futuristic Science Stories #8
John Spencer & Co., 1952 | Art **Norman Light**

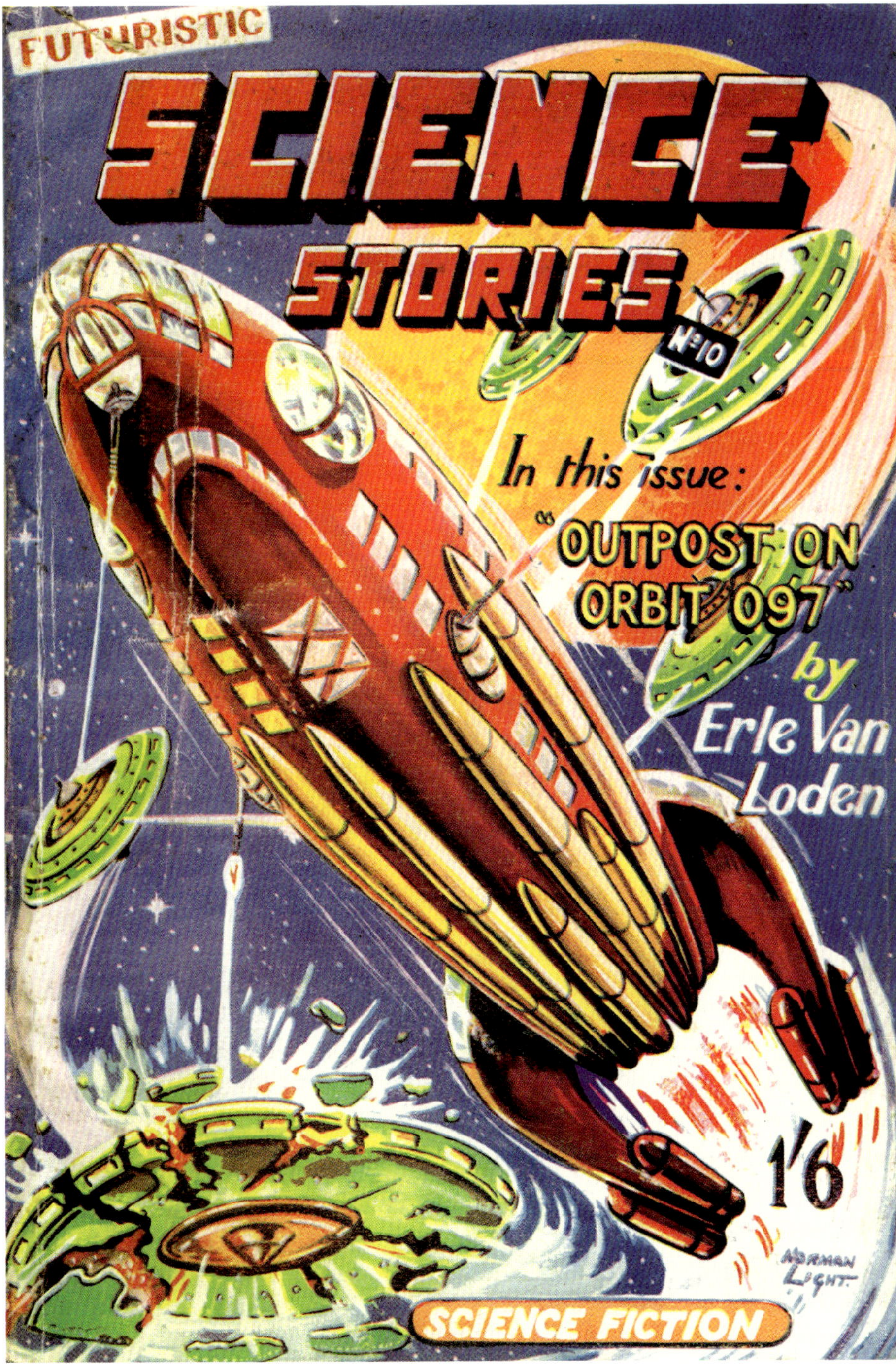

Futuristic Science Stories #11
John Spencer & Co., 1953 | Art **Norman Light**

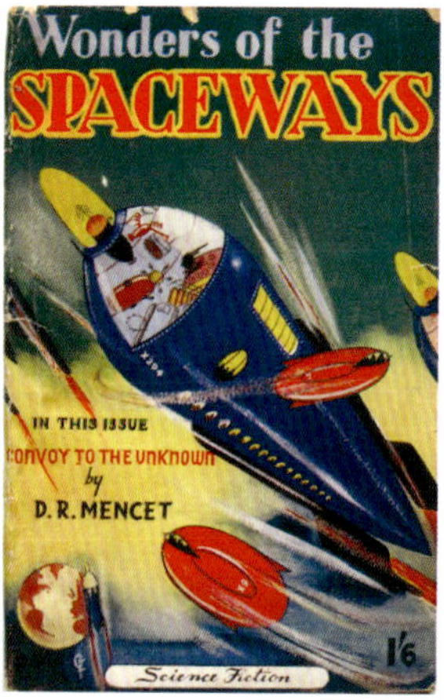

Wonders of the Spaceways #1
John Spencer & Co., 1950
Art **Gerald Facey**

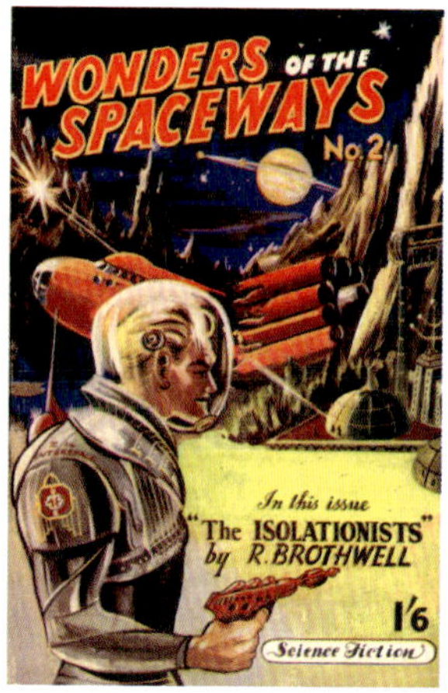

Wonders of the Spaceways #2
John Spencer & Co., 1952
Art **Gerald Facey**

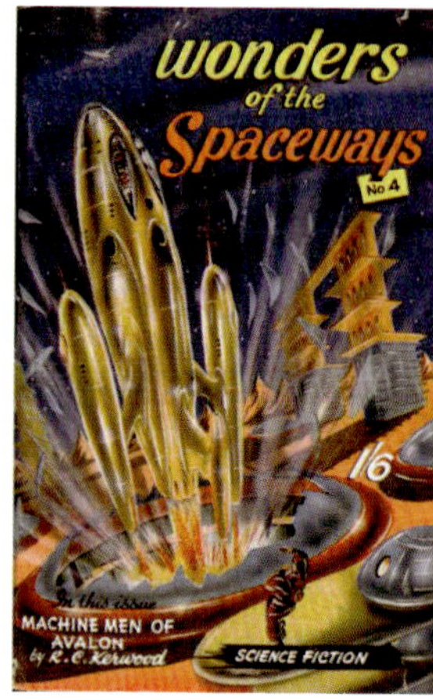

Wonders of the Spaceways #4
John Spencer & Co., 1952
Art **Gordon C. Davies**

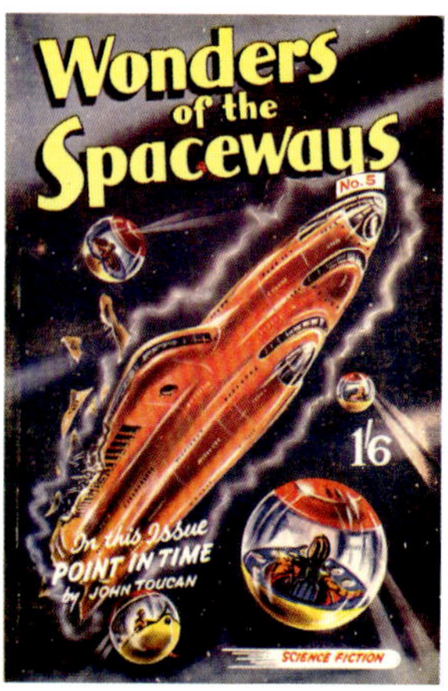

Wonders of the Spaceways #5
John Spencer & Co., 1952
Art **Gordon C. Davies**

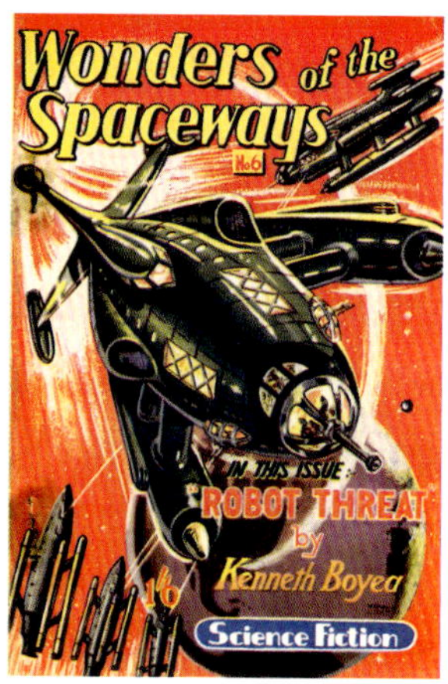

Wonders of the Spaceways #6
John Spencer & Co., 1953
Art **Norman Light**

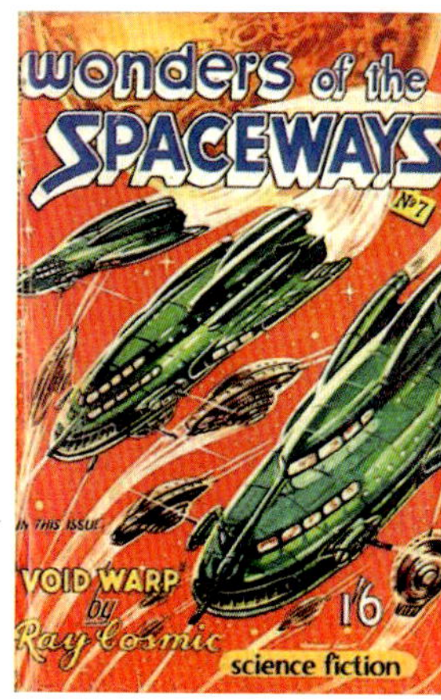

Wonders of the Spaceways #7
John Spencer & Co., 1953
Art **Norman Light**

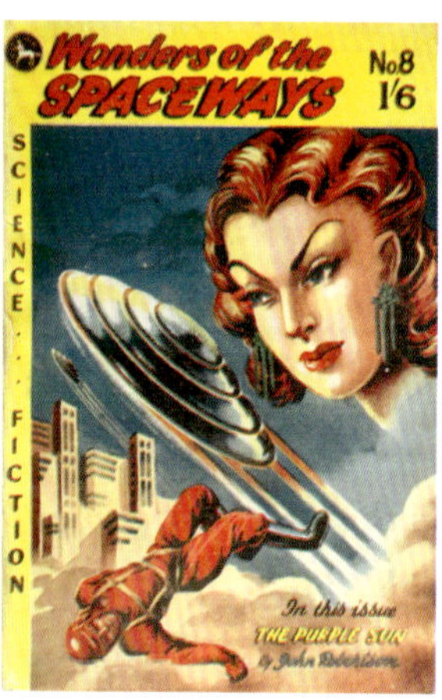

Wonders of the Spaceways #8
John Spencer & Co., 1953
Art **Ray Theobald**

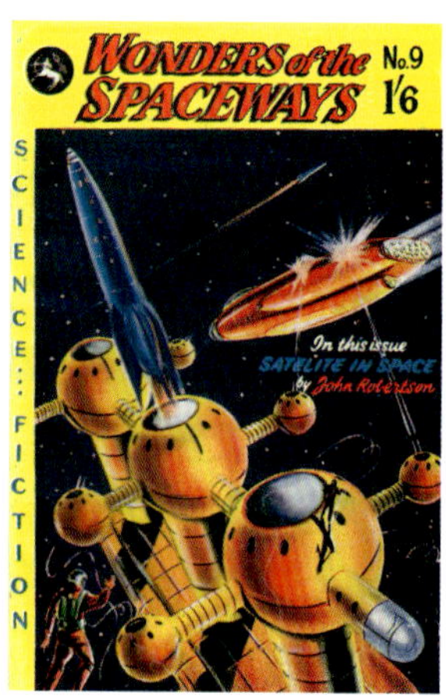

Wonders of the Spaceways #9
John Spencer & Co., 1954
Art **Gordon C. Davies**

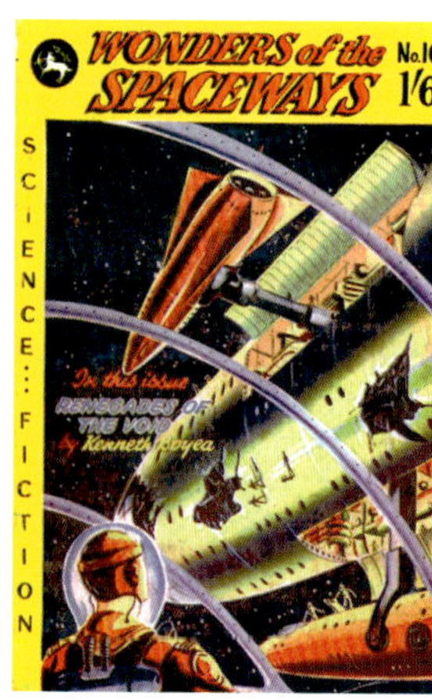

Wonders of the Spaceways #10
John Spencer & Co., 1954
Art **Gordon C. Davies**

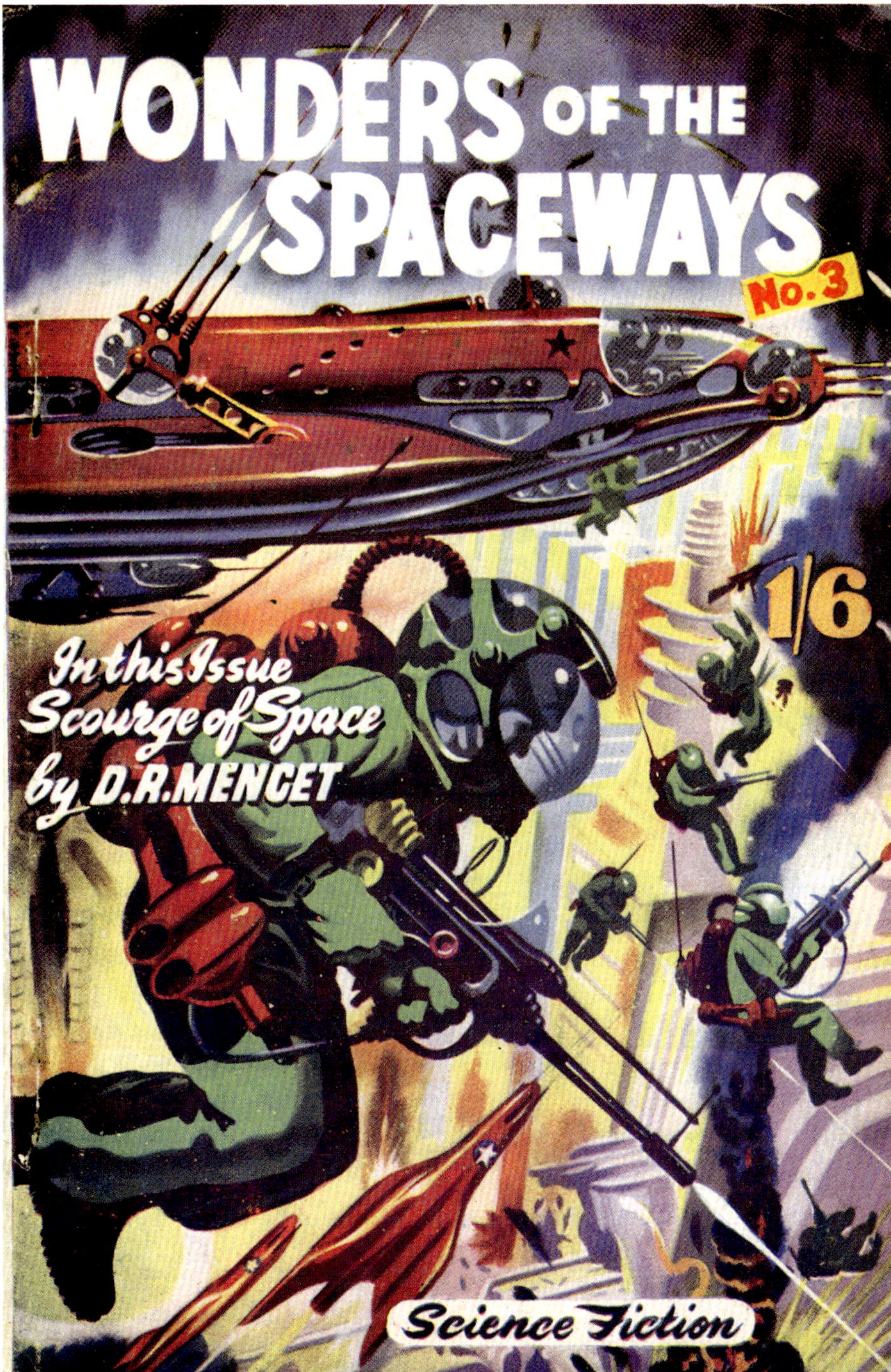

Wonders of the Spaceways #3
John Spencer & Co., 1952 | Art **Ron Turner**

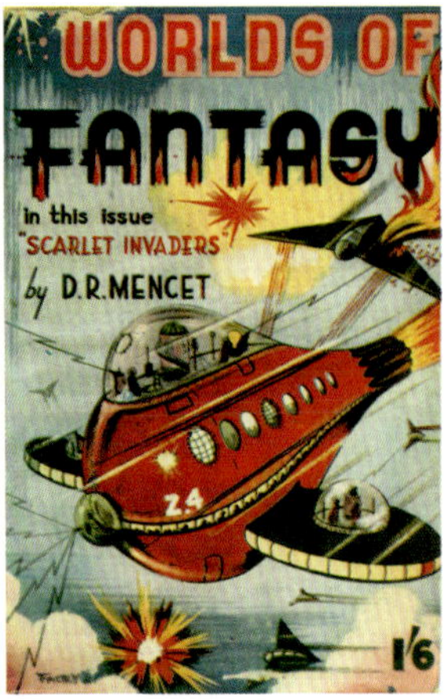

Worlds of Fantasy #1
John Spencer & Co., 1950
Art **Gerald Facey**

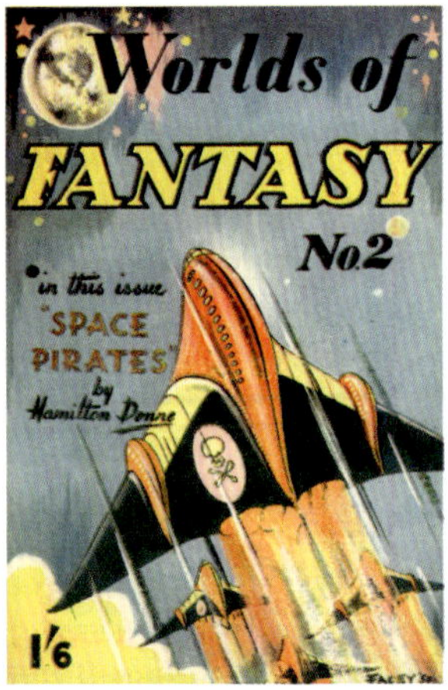

Worlds of Fantasy #2
John Spencer & Co., 1950
Art **Gerald Facey**

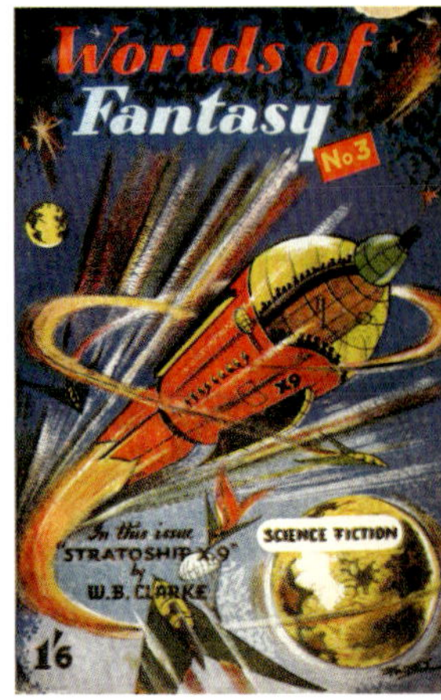

Worlds of Fantasy #3
John Spencer & Co., 1950
Art **Gerald Facey**

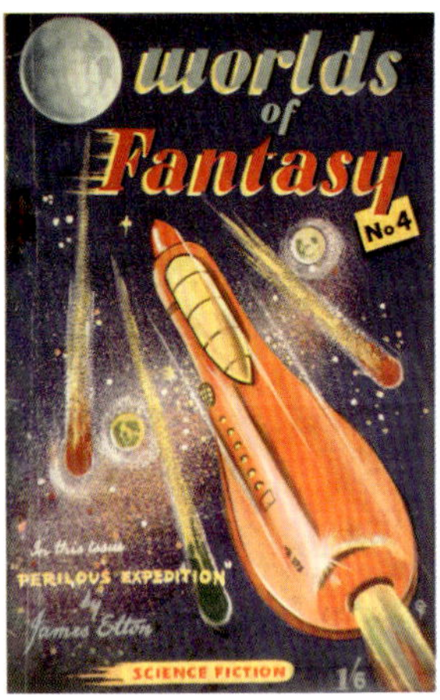

Worlds of Fantasy #4
John Spencer & Co., 1951
Art **Gerald Facey**

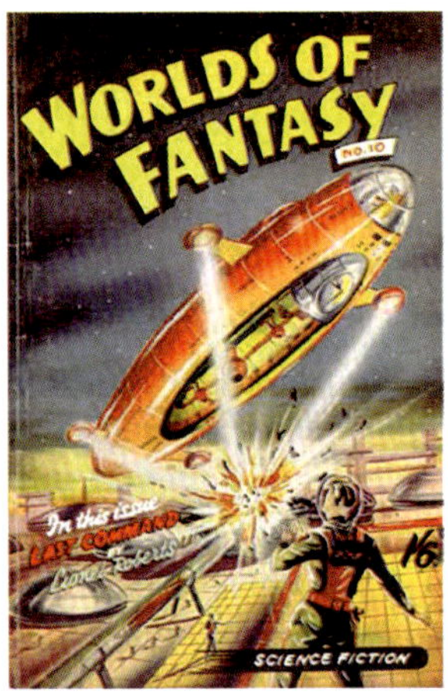

Worlds of Fantasy #10
John Spencer & Co., 1953
Art **Gordon C. Davies**

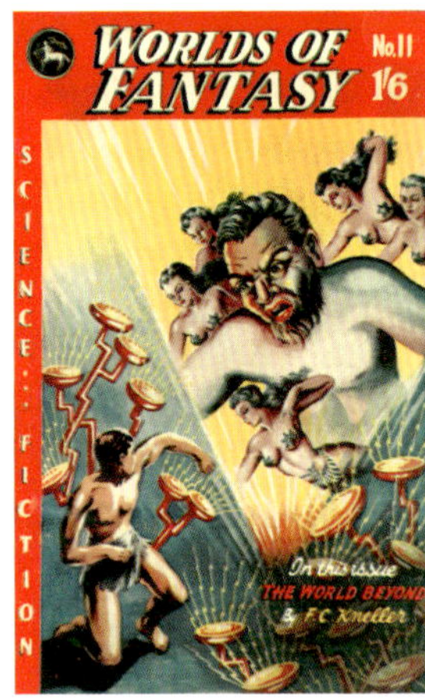

Worlds of Fantasy #11
John Spencer & Co., 1951
Art **Ray Theobald**

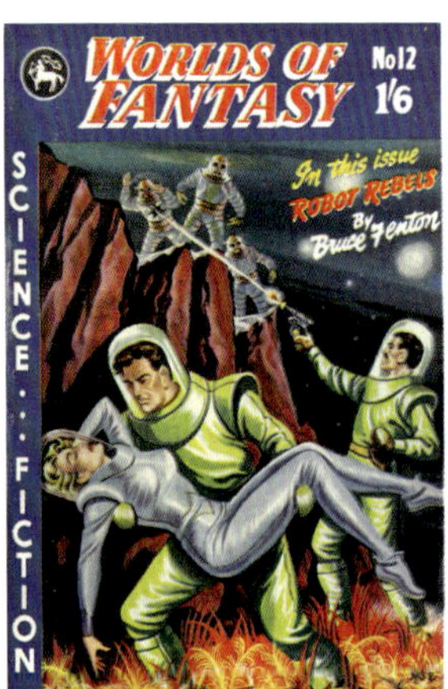

Worlds of Fantasy #12
John Spencer & Co., 1954
Art **Ron Embleton**

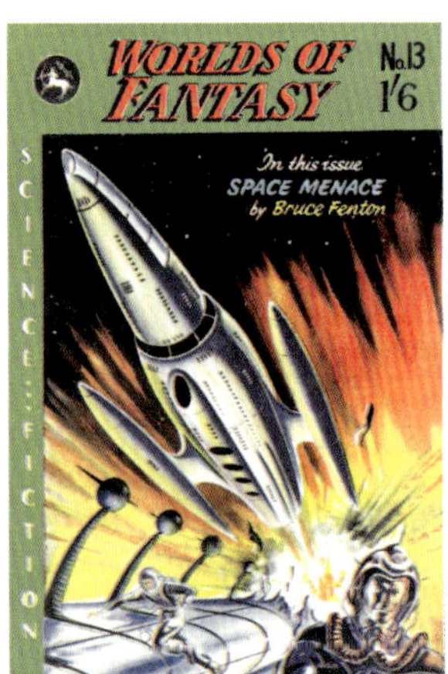

Worlds of Fantasy #13
John Spencer & Co., 1954
Art **Gordon C. Davies**

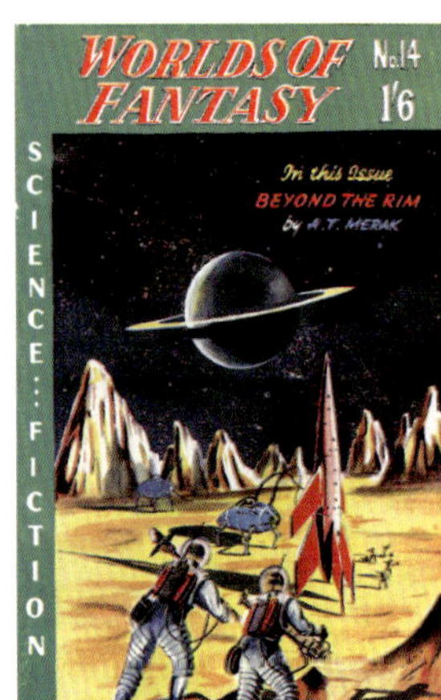

Worlds of Fantasy #14
John Spencer & Co., 1954
Art **Ray Theobald**

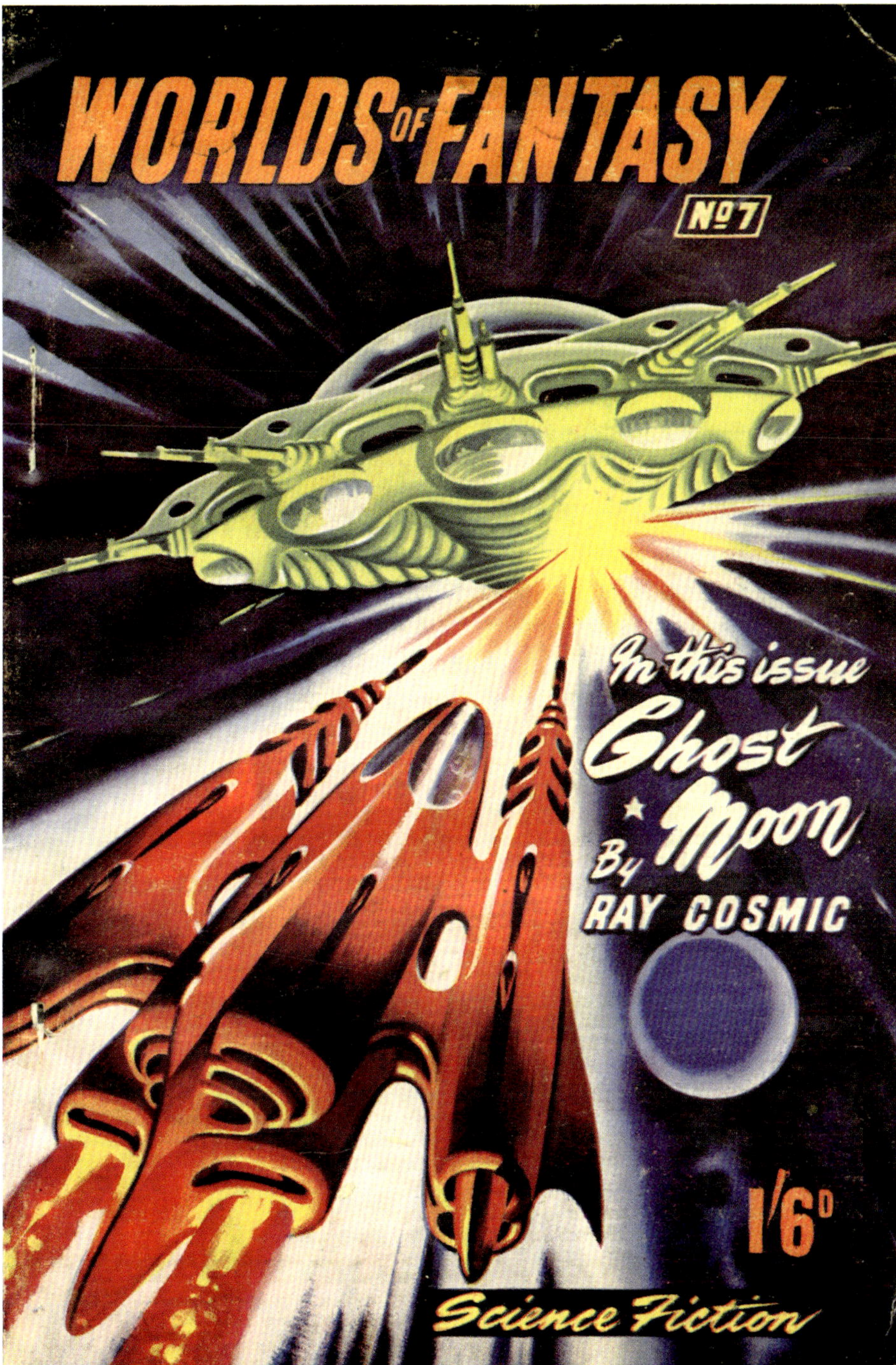

Worlds of Fantasy #7
John Spencer & Co., 1952 | Art **Ron Turner**

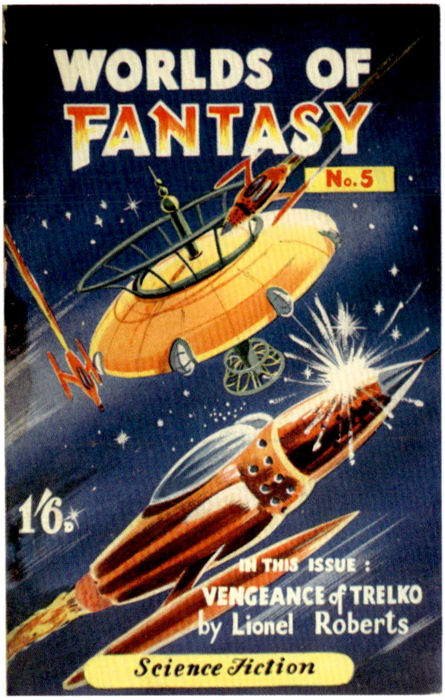

Worlds of Fantasy #5
John Spencer & Co., 1952 | Art **Unknown (George Ratcliffe?)**

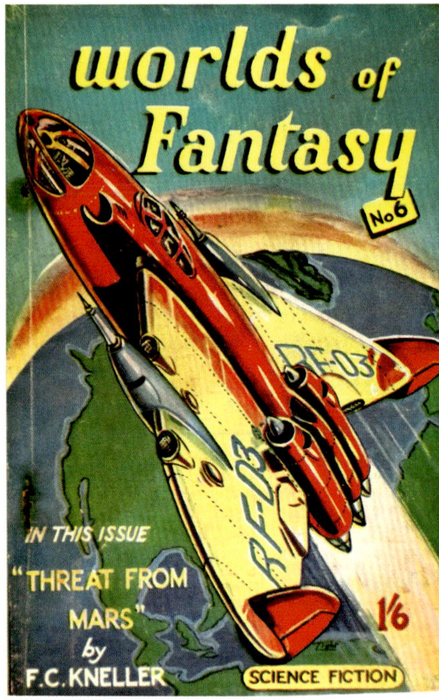

Worlds of Fantasy #6
John Spencer & Co., 1952 | Art **Norman Light**

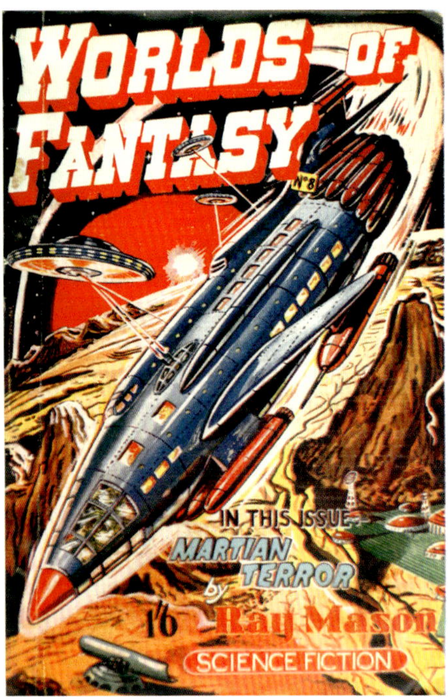

Worlds of Fantasy #8
John Spencer & Co., 1953 | Art **Norman Light**

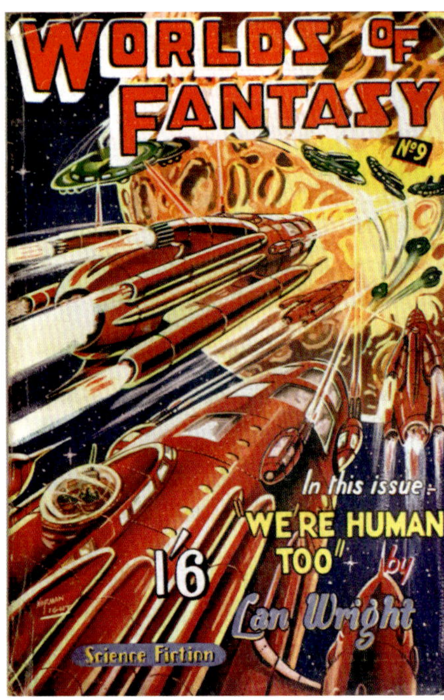

Worlds of Fantasy #9
John Spencer & Co., 1953 | Art **Norman Light**

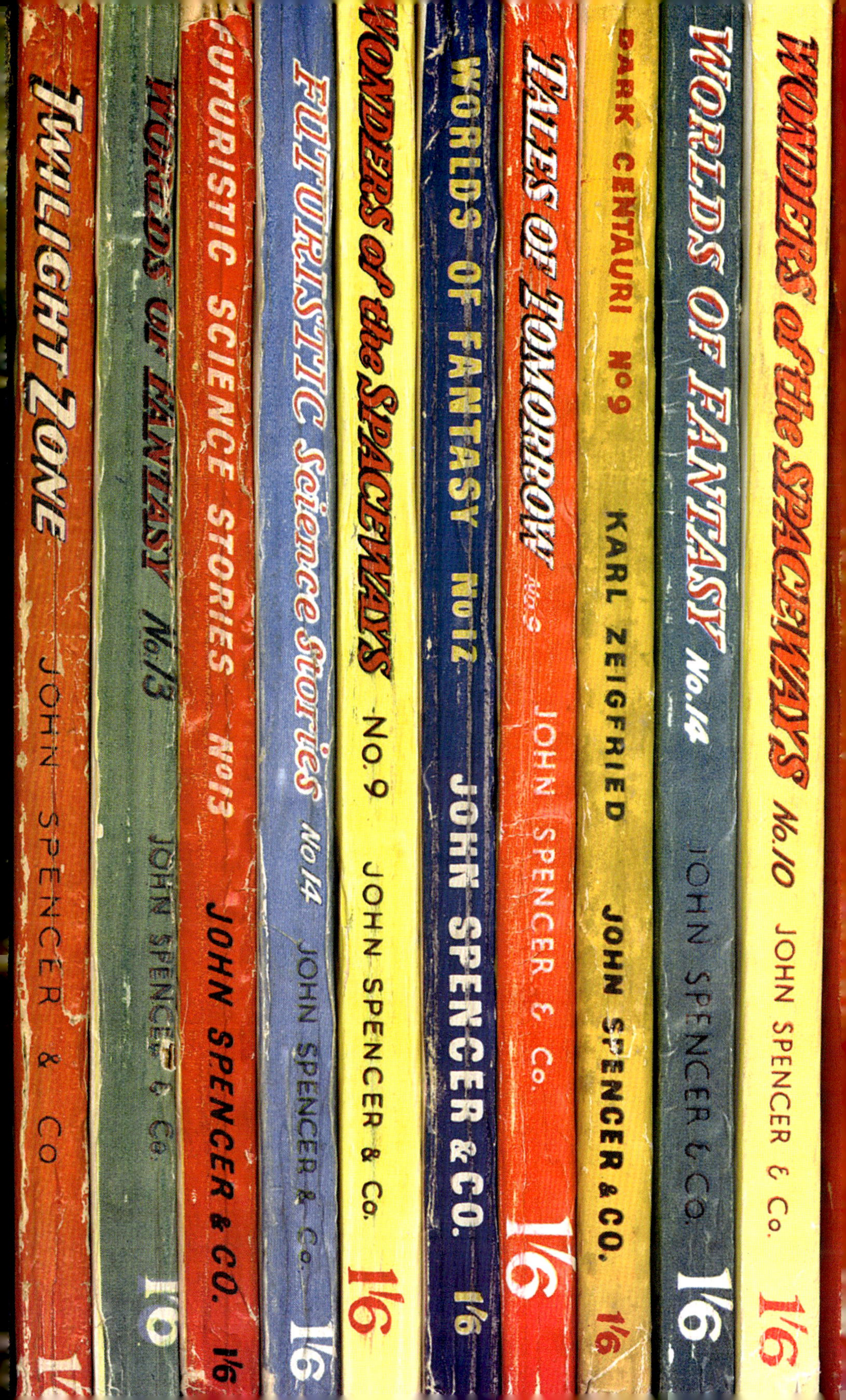
TWILIGHT ZONE
JOHN SPENCER & CO
WORLDS OF FANTASY No.13
JOHN SPENCER & Co.
FUTURISTIC SCIENCE STORIES No13
JOHN SPENCER & CO.
1/6
FUTURISTIC Science Stories No14
JOHN SPENCER & Co.
1/6
WONDERS of the SPACEWAYS
No.9
JOHN SPENCER & Co.
1/6
WORLDS OF FANTASY No12
JOHN SPENCER & CO.
1/6
TALES OF TOMORROW
JOHN SPENCER & Co.
1/6
DARK CENTAURI No9
KARL ZEIGFRIED
JOHN SPENCER & CO.
1/6
WORLDS OF FANTASY No.14
JOHN SPENCER & Co.
1/6
WONDERS of the SPACEWAYS
No.10
JOHN SPENCER & Co.
1/6

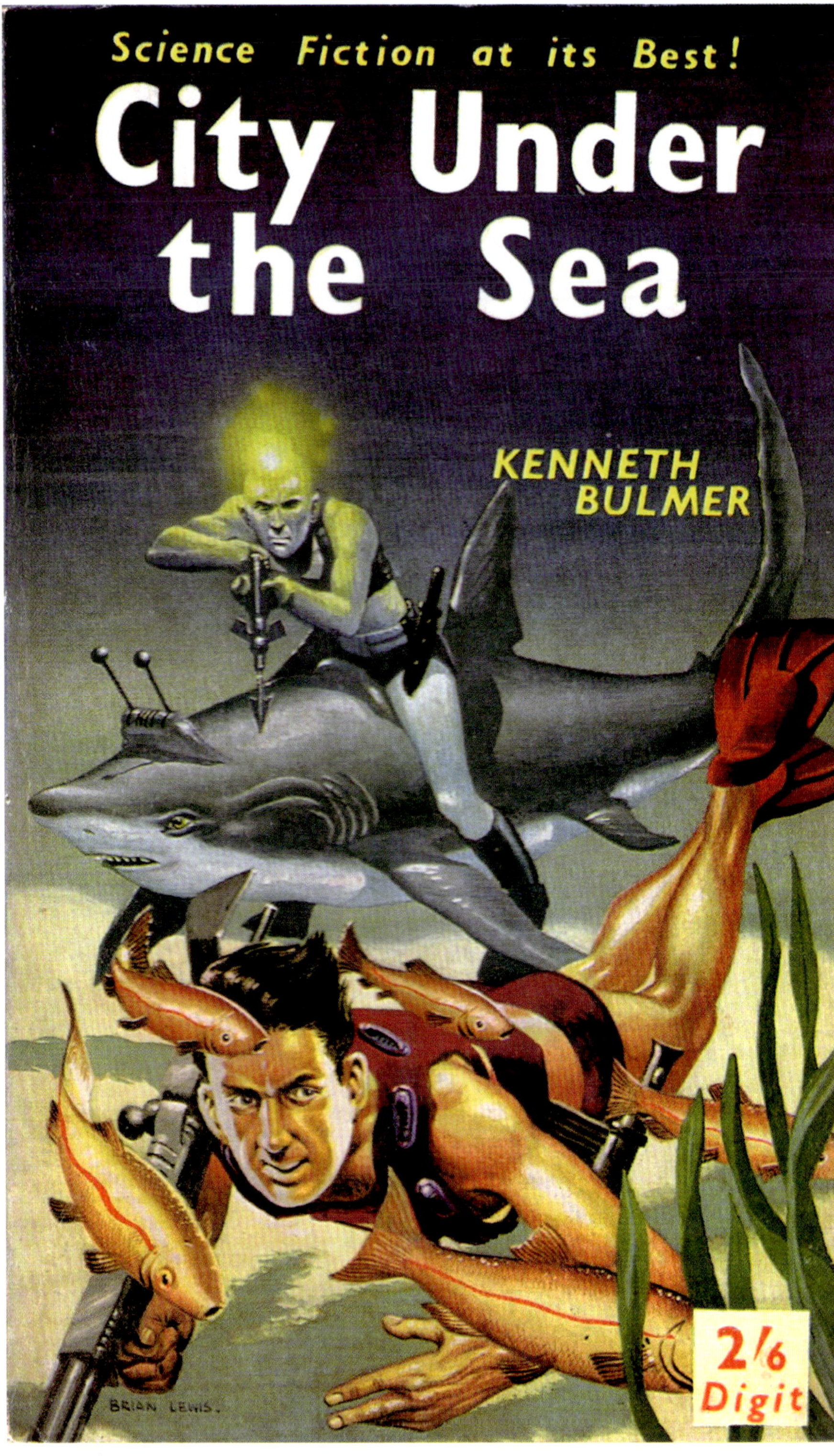

Kenneth Bulmer | *City Under The Sea*
Digit Books R505, 1961 | Art **Brian Lewis**

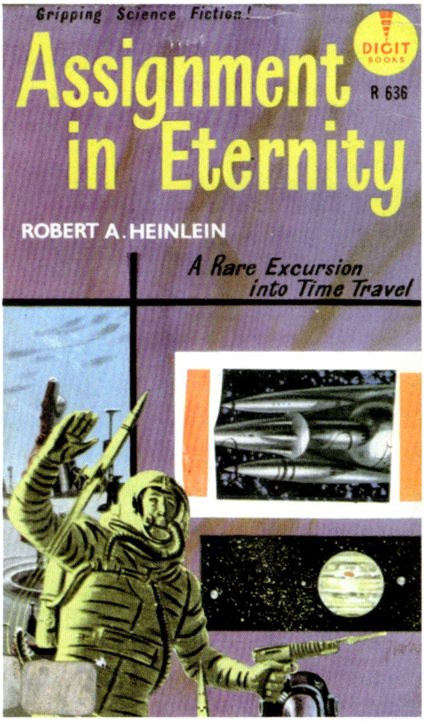

Robert A. Heinlein | *Assignment in Eternity*
Digit Books, 1962 | Art **Richard Powers**

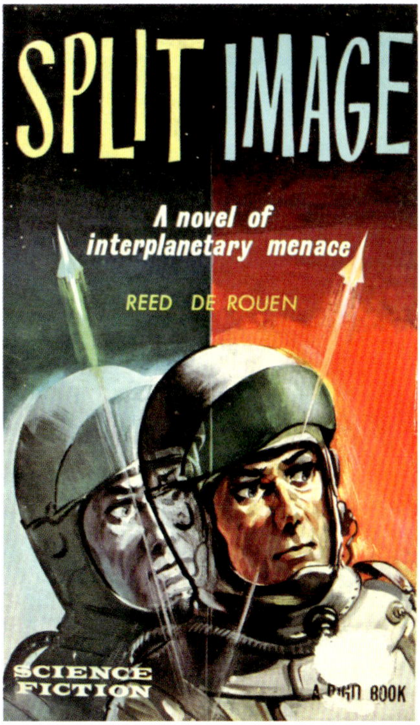

Reed De Rouen | *Split Image*
Digit Books, 1963 | Art **Unknown**

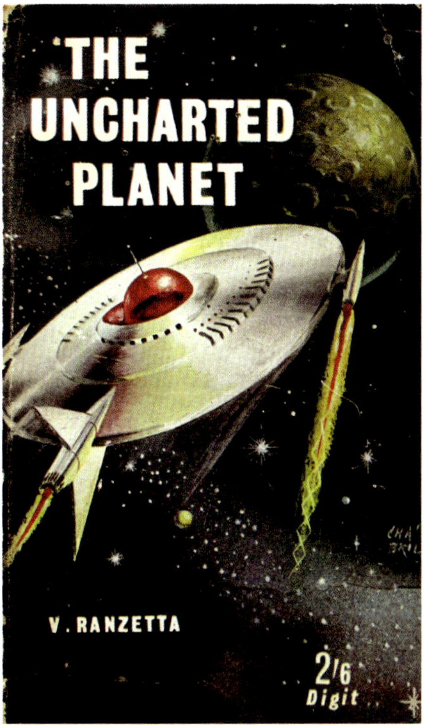

Valerie (Luan) Ranzetta | *The Uncharted Planet*
Digit Books, 1962 | Art **Cha' Bril**

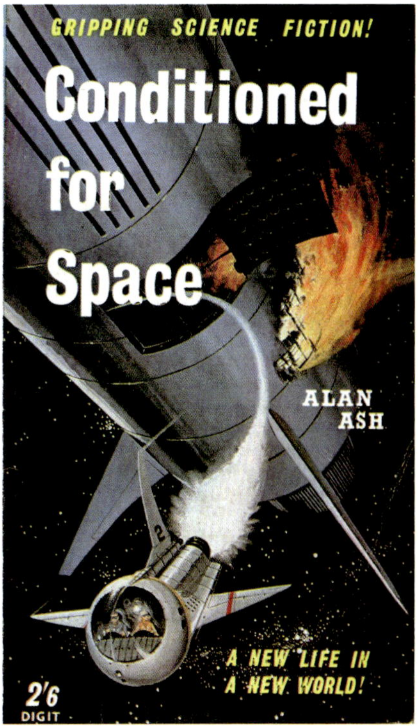

Alan Ash | *Conditioned for Space*
Digit Books, 1961 | Art **Ed Valigursky**

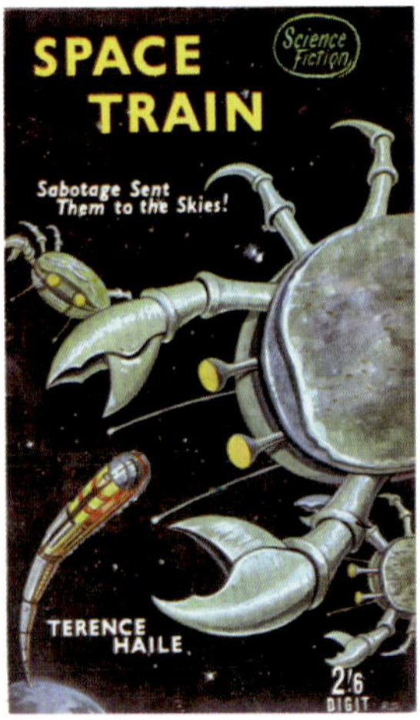

Terence Haile | *Space Train*
Digit Books R584, 1962 | Art **Davies**

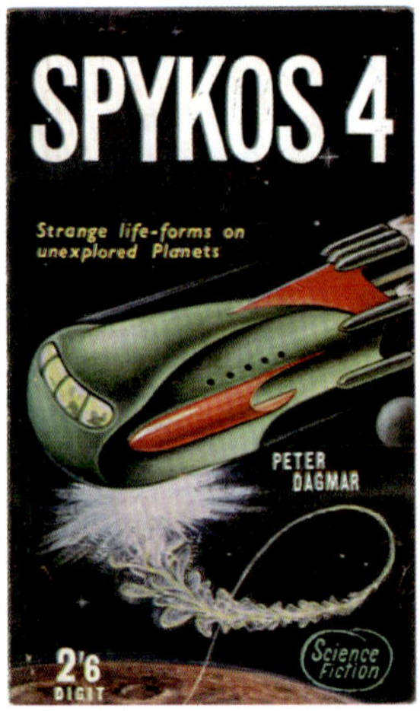

Peter Dagmar | *Spykos 4*
Digit Books R609, 1962 | Art **Cha' Bril**

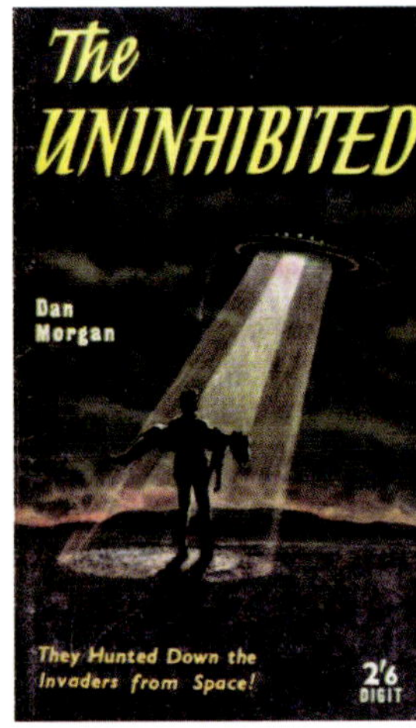

Dan Morgan | *The Uninhibited*
Digit Books R532, 1961 | Art **Unknown**

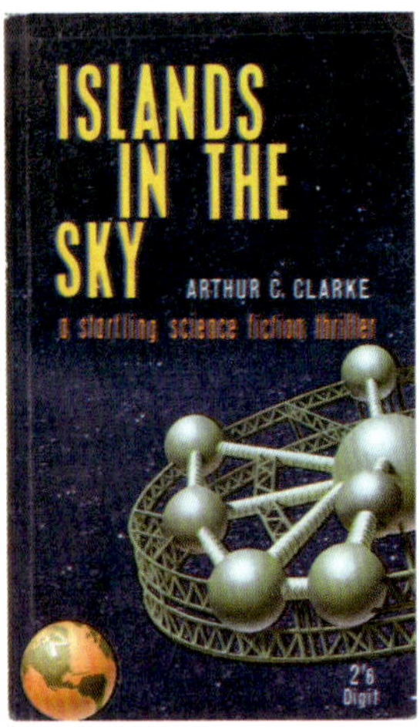

Arthur C. Clarke | *Islands in the Sky*
Digit Books R802, 1964 | Art **Unknown**

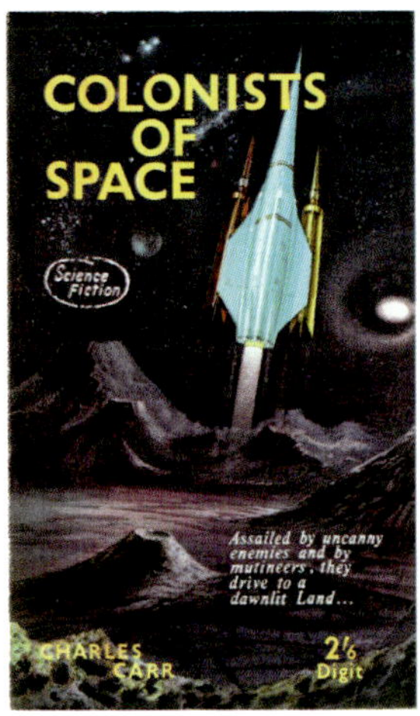

Charles Carr | *Colonists of Space*
Digit Books R617, 1962 | Art **Norman Adams**

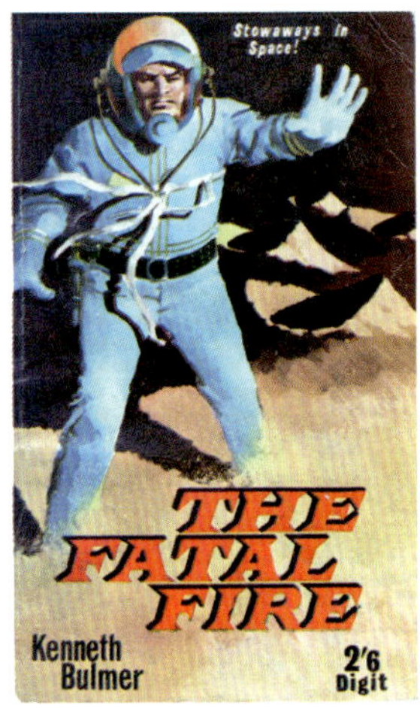

Kenneth Bulmer | *The Fatal Fire*
Digit Books R597, 1962 | Art **Unknown**

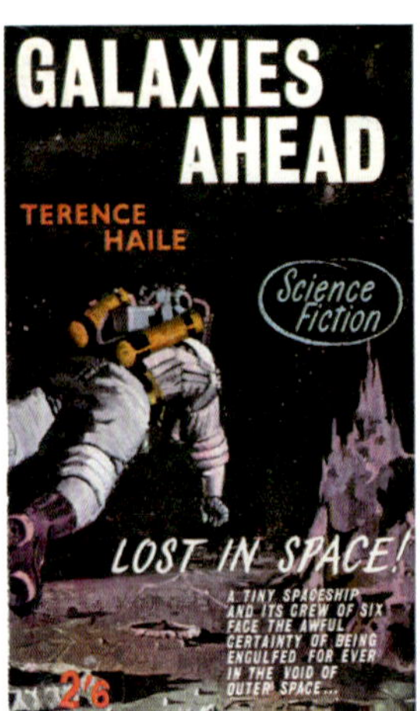

Terence Haile | *Galaxies Ahead*
Digit Books R652, 1962 | Art **Unknown**

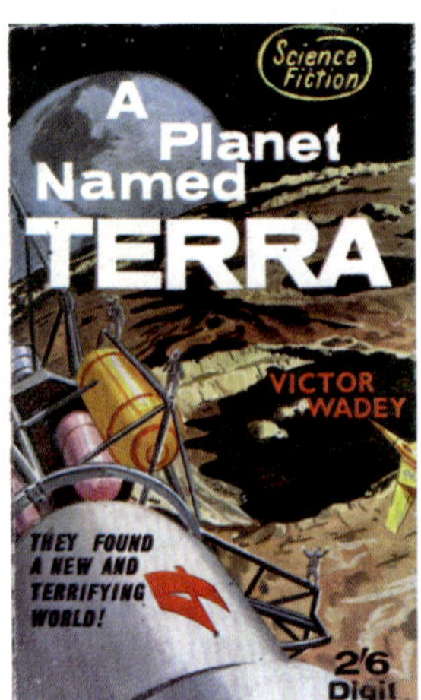

Victor Wadey | *A Planet Named Terra*
Digit Books R588, 1962 | Art **Unknown**

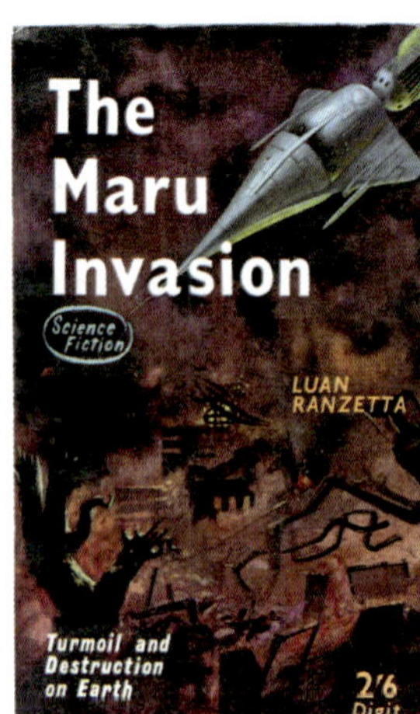

Luan Ranzetta | *The Maru Invasion*
Digit Books R606, 1962 | Art **Unknown**

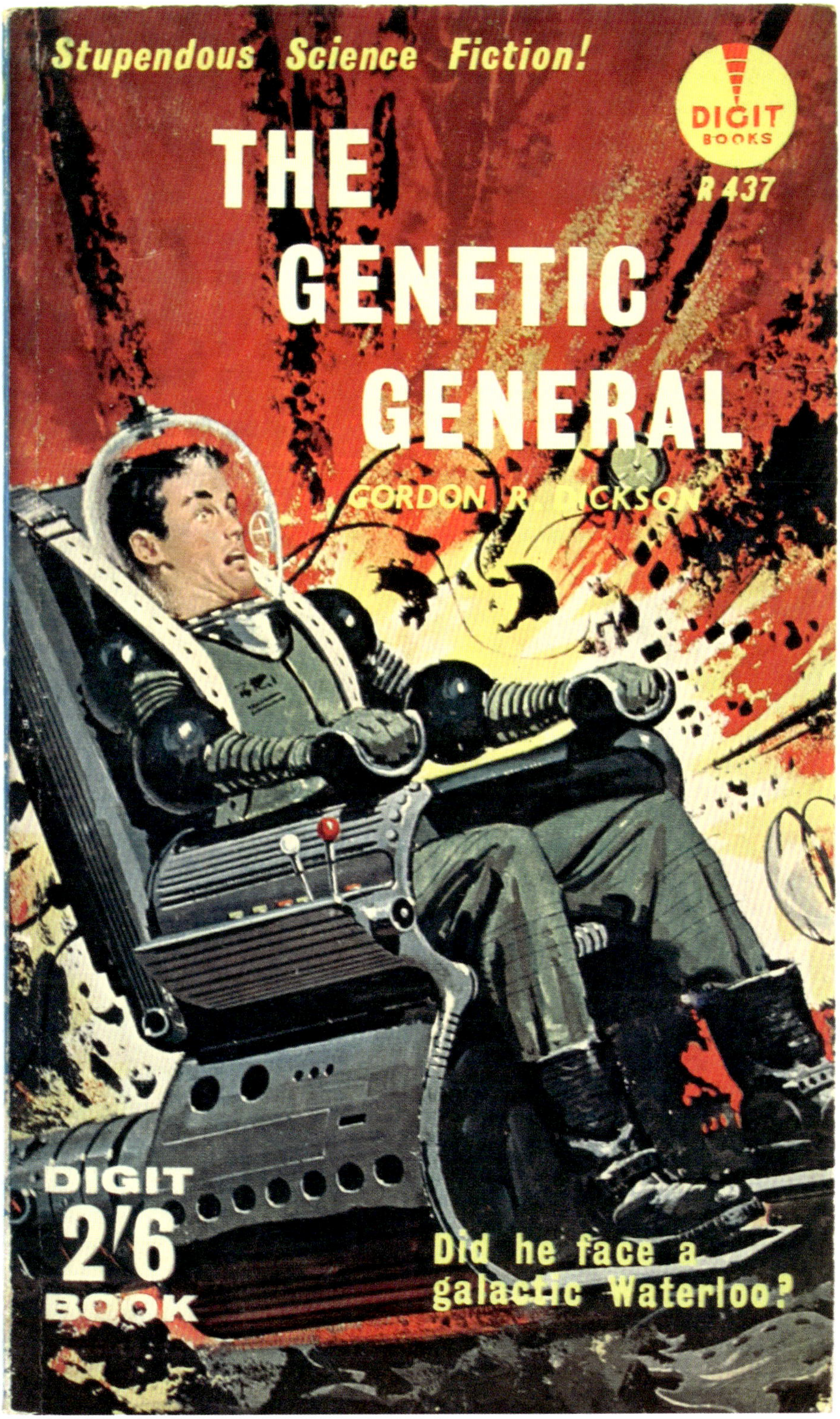

Gordon R. Dickson | *The Genetic General*
Digit Books R437, 1961 | Art **Ed Valigursky**

Kenneth Bulmer | *The Changeling Worlds*
Ace Books, 1959 | Original art **Ed Valigursky**

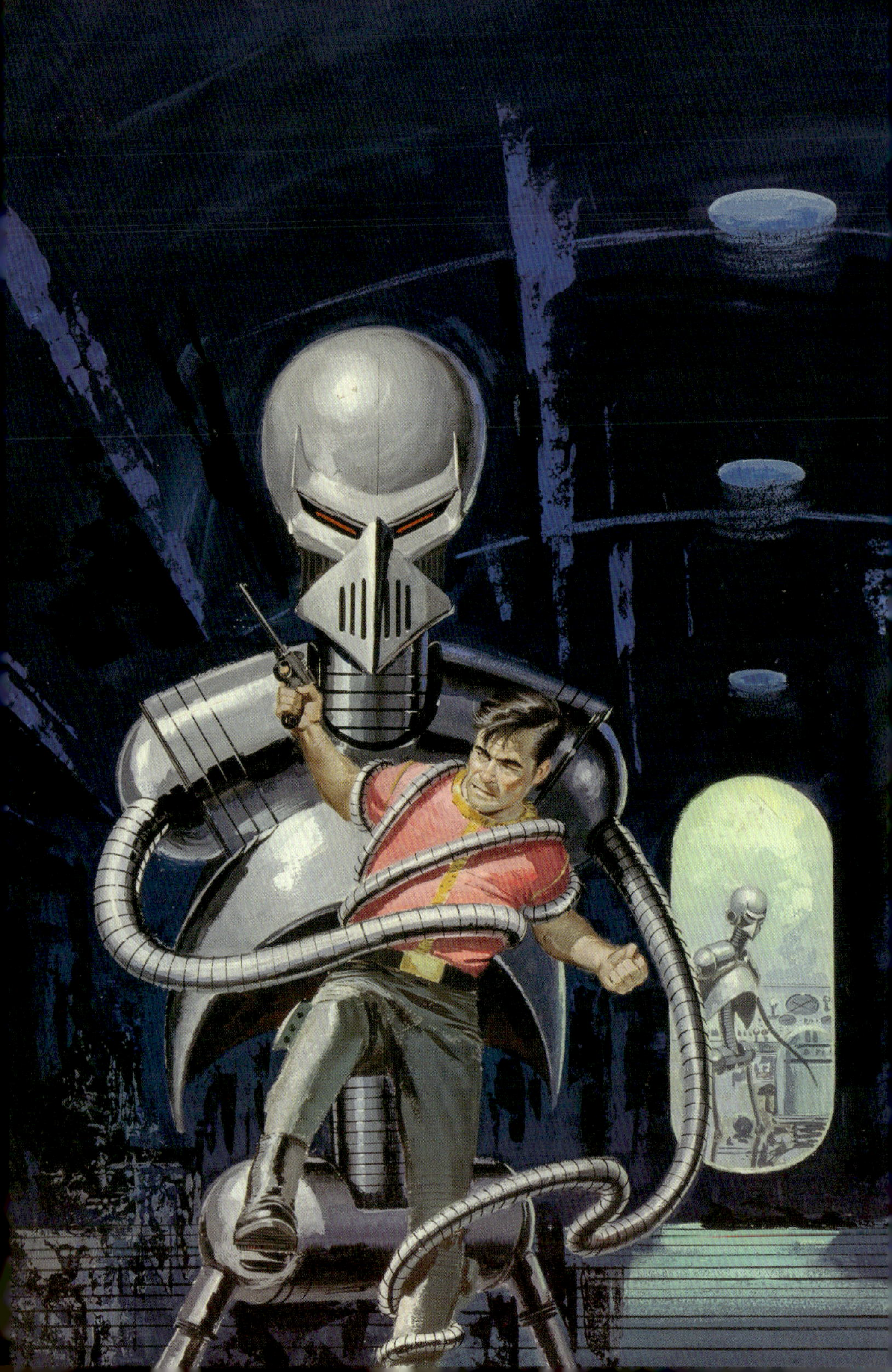

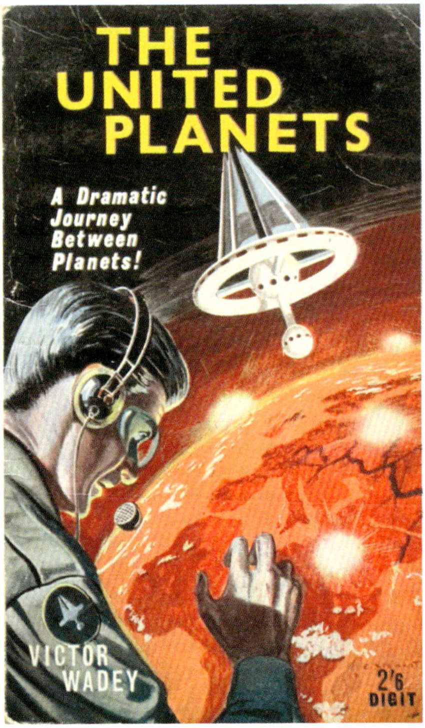

Victor Wadey | *The United Planets*
Digit Books R590, 1962 | Art **C. Stewart**

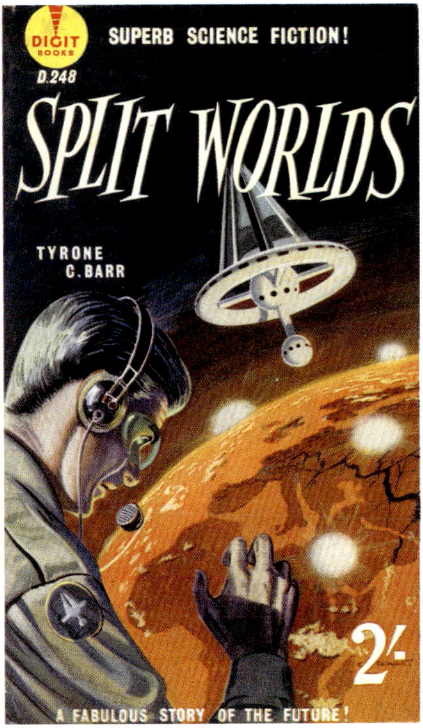

Tyrone C. Barr | *Split Worlds*
Digit Books D248, 1959 | Art **C. Stewart**

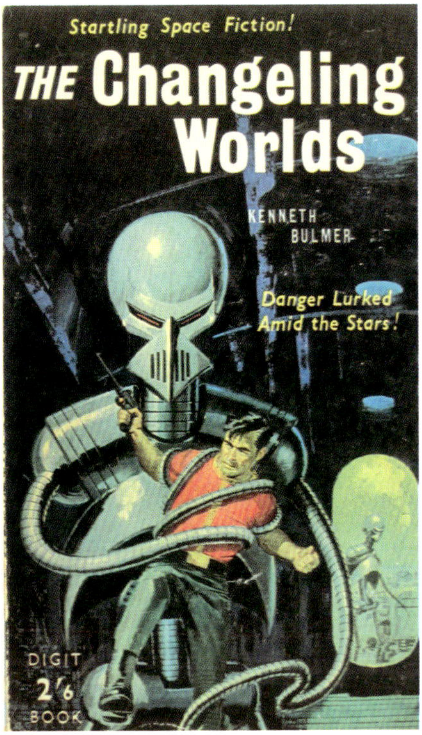

Kenneth Bulmer | *The Changeling Worlds*
Digit Books R466, 1961 | Art **Ed Valigursky**

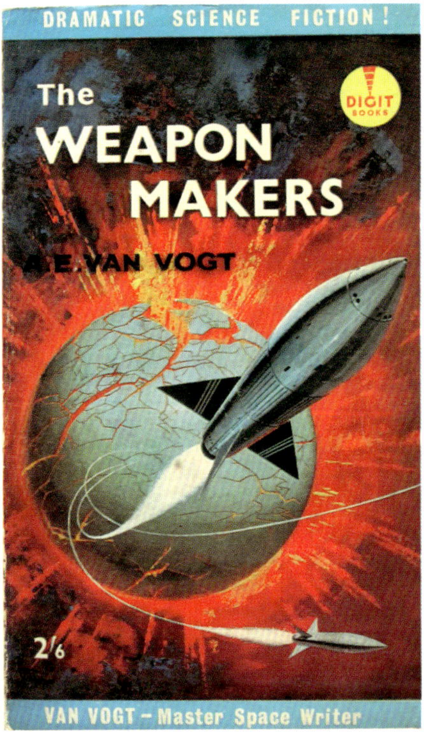

A. E. van Vogt | *The Weapon Makers*
Digit Books R454, 1961 | Art **Ed Valigursky**

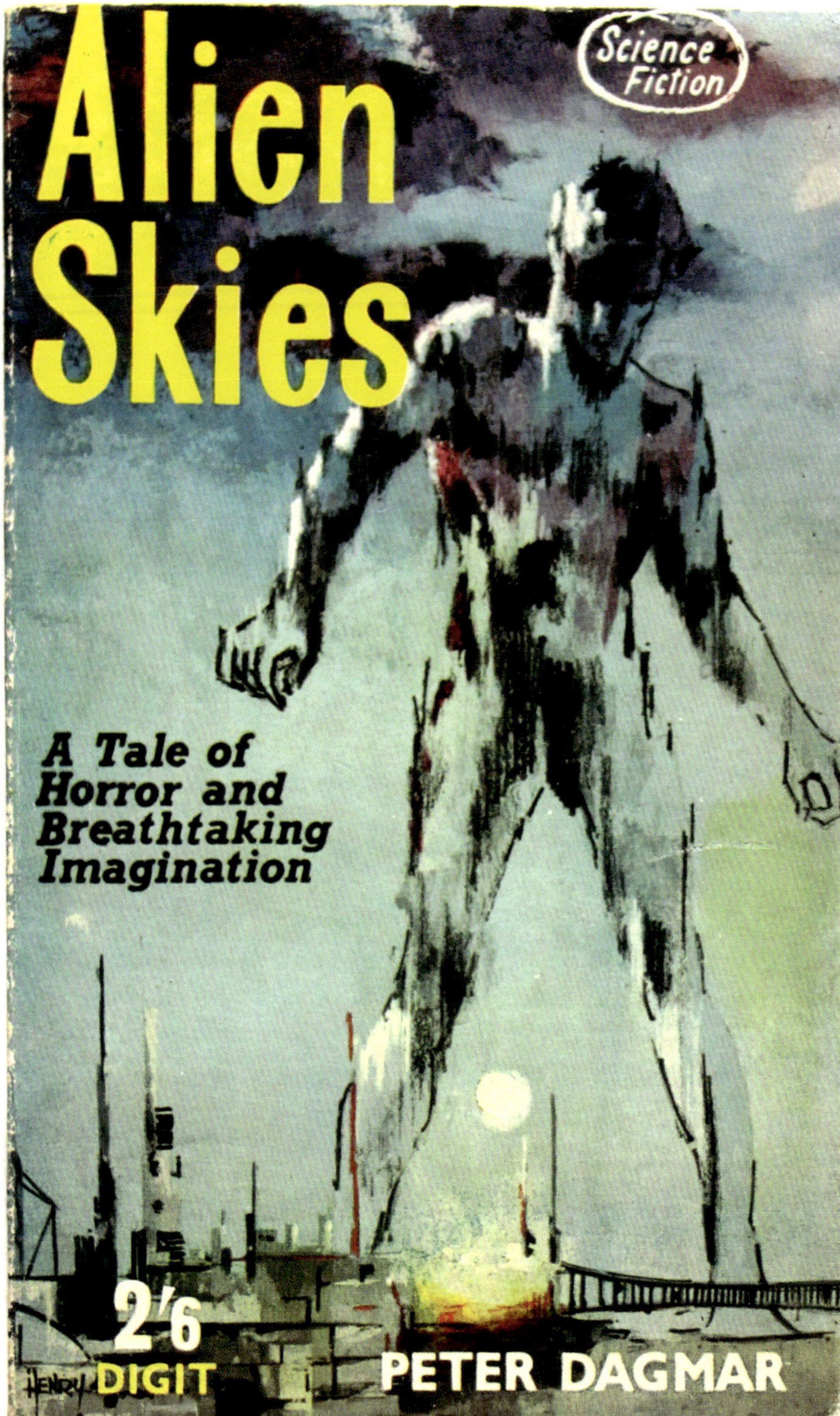

Peter Dagmar | *Alien Skies*
Digit Books R605, 1962 | Art **Henry (Enric Torres-Prat)**

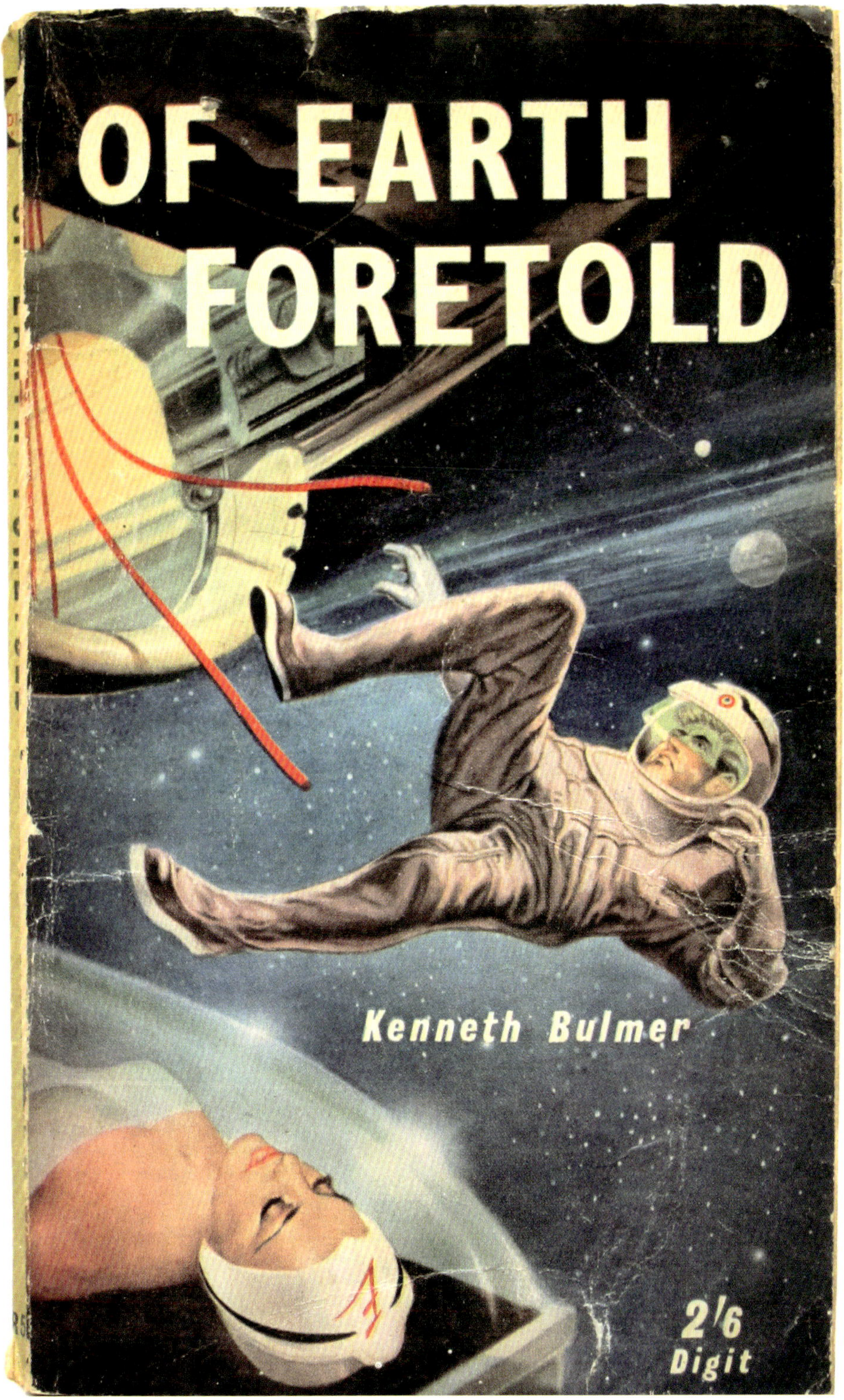

Kenneth Bulmer | *Of Earth Foretold*
Digit Books R539, 1961 | Art **Unknown**

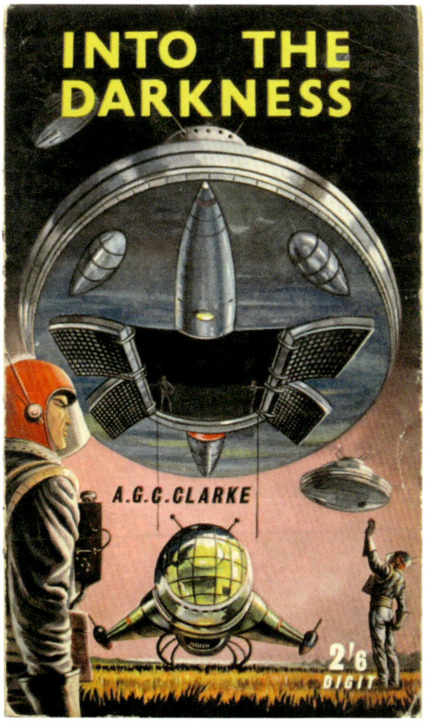

A. G. C. Clarke | *Into the Darkness*
Digit Books D164, 1961 | Art **Unknown**

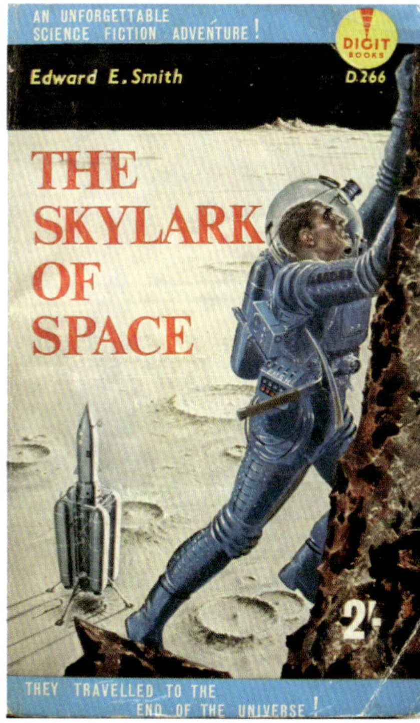

Edward E. Smith | *The Skylark of Space*
Digit Books D266, 1959 | Art **Ed Emshwiller**

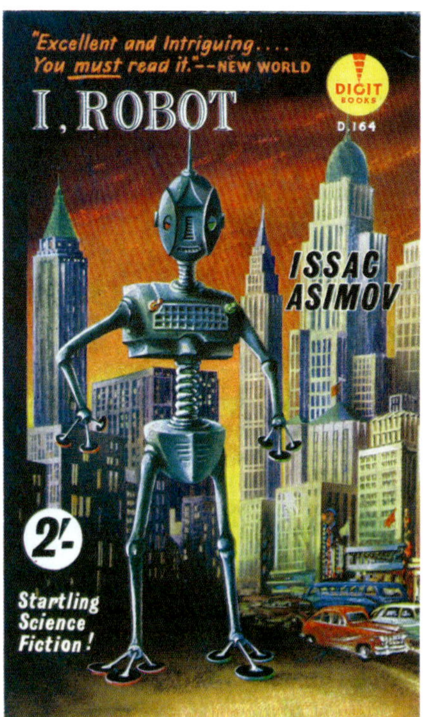

Isaac Asimov | *I, Robot*
Digit Books D164, 1958 | Art **Unknown**

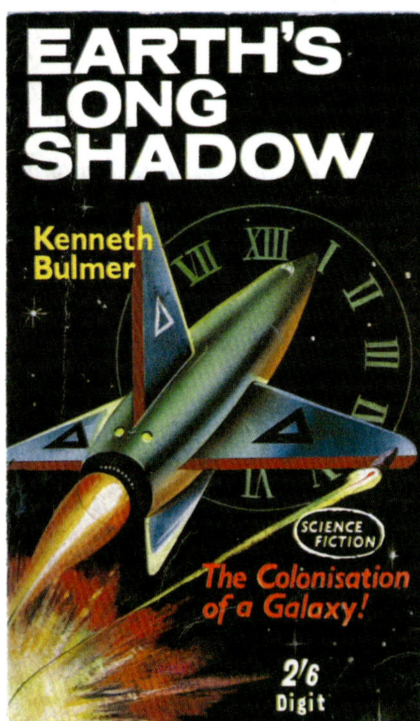

Kenneth Bulmer | *Earth's Long Shadow*
Digit Books R572, 1962 | Art **Cha' Bril**

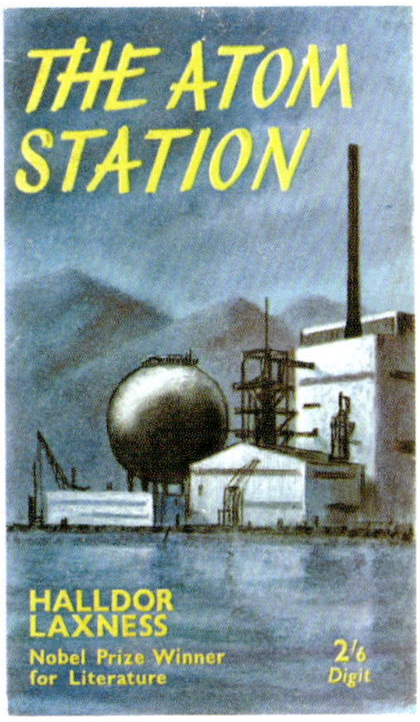

Halldor Laxness | *The Atom Station*
Digit Books R578, 1961
Art **Unknown**

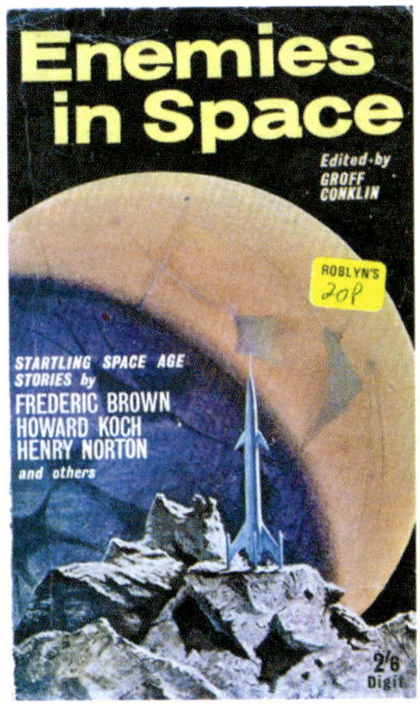

Groff Conklin | *Enemies in Space*
Digit Books R577, 1961
Art **Unknown**

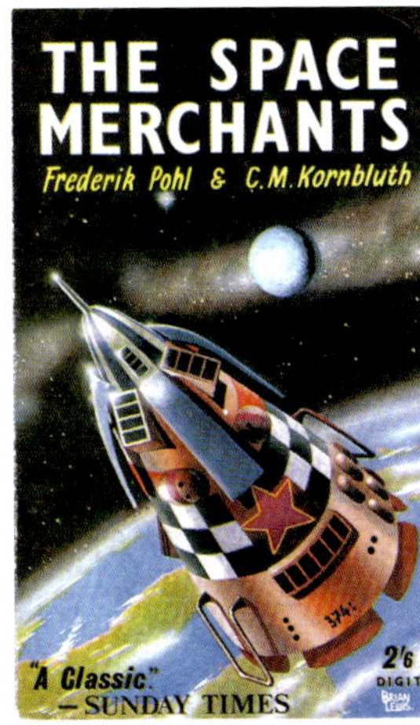

C. M. Kornbluth, Frederik Pohl
The Space Merchants
Digit Books R499, 1961 | Art **Brian Lewis**

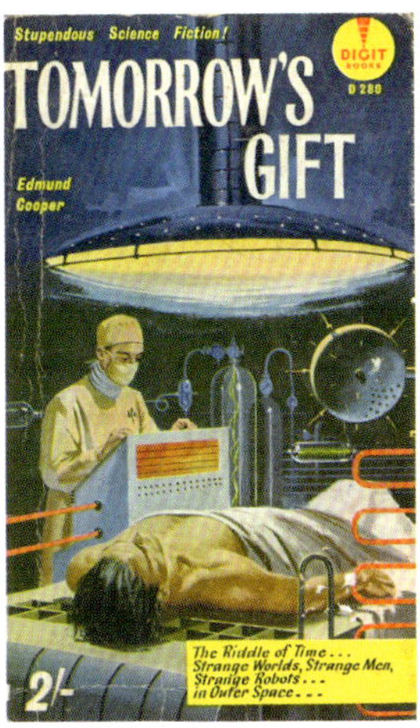

Edmund Cooper | *Tomorrow's Gift*
Digit Books D280, 1958 | Art **Ed Valigursky**

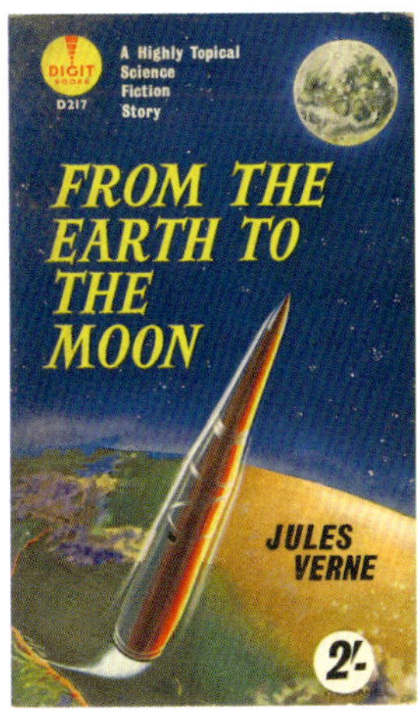

Jules Verne | *From Earth to the Moon*
Digit Books D217, 1958 | Art **Unknown**

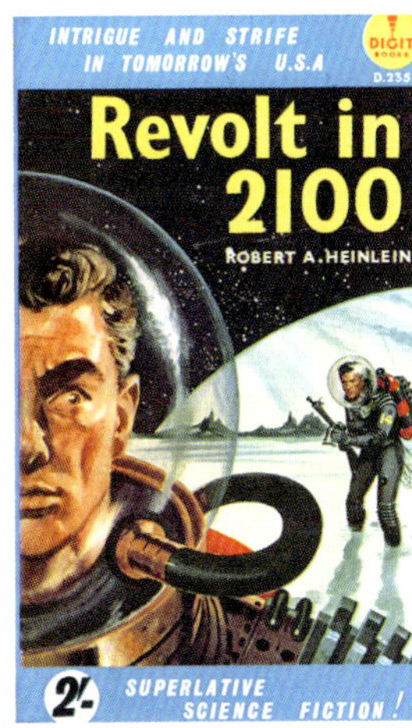

Robert A. Heinlein | *Revolt in 2100*
Digit Books D235, 1959 | Art **Ed Valigursky**

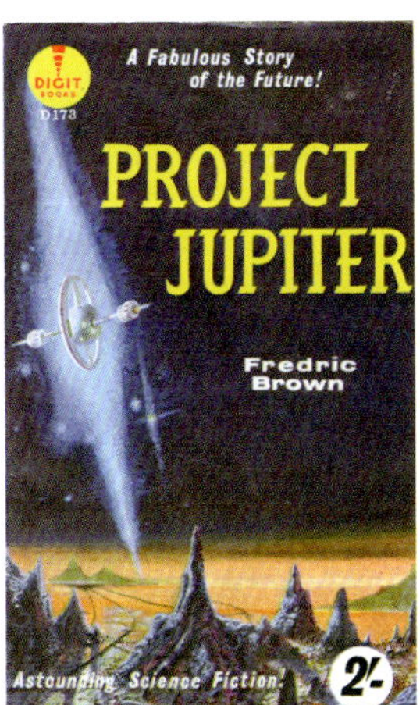

Fredric Brown | *Project Jupiter*
Digit Books D173, 1958 | Art **Unknown**

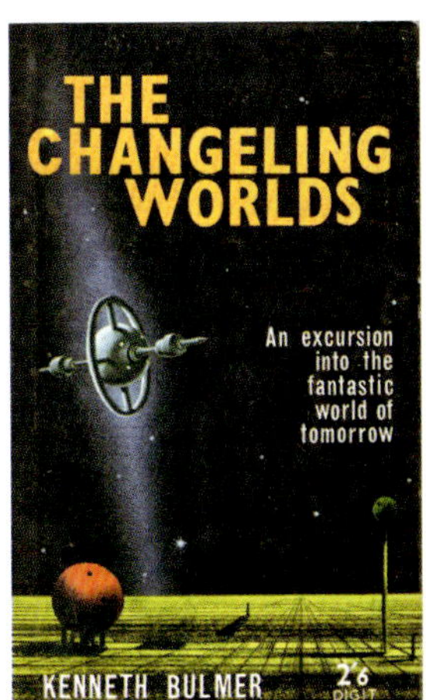

Kenneth Bulmer | *The Changeling Worlds*
Digit Books R758, 1963 | Art **Unknown**

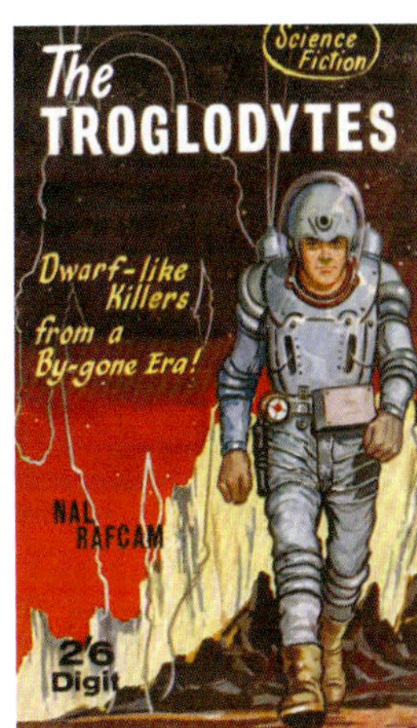

Nal Rafcam | *The Troglodytes*
Digit Books 587, 1962 | Art **Unknown**

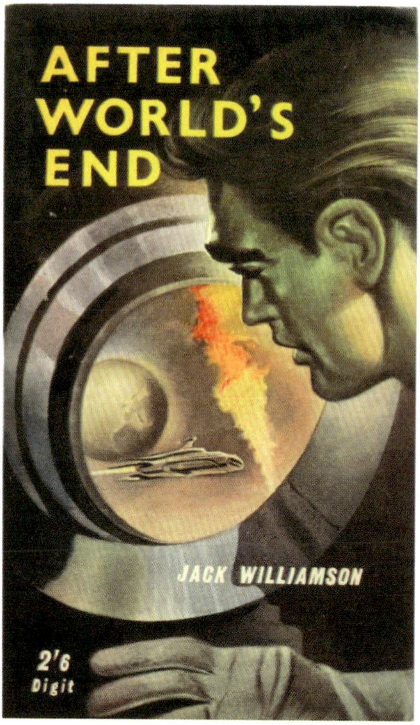

Jack Williamson | *After World's End*
Digit Books R538, 1961 | Art **Unknown**

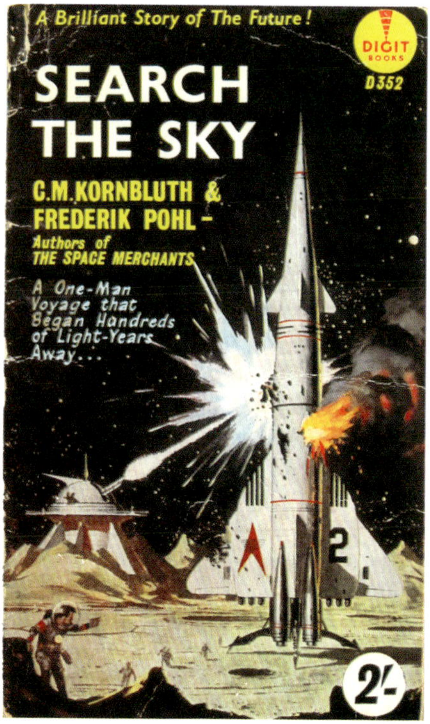

C. M. Kornbluth, Frederik Pohl | *Search the Sky*
Digit Books D352, 1959 | Art **Ed Valigursky**

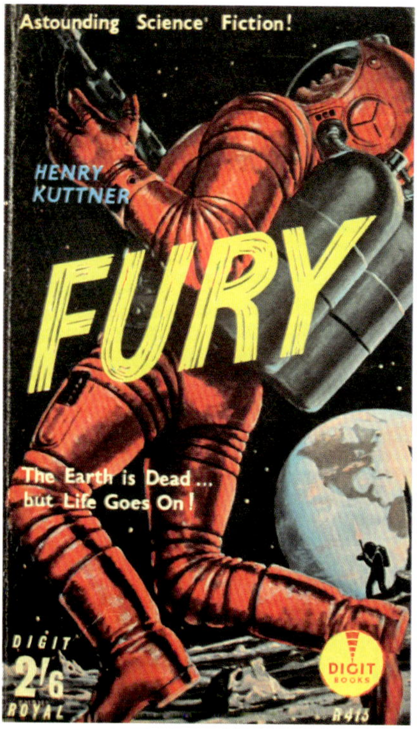

Henry Kuttner | *Fury*
Digit Books R413, 1960 | Art **Ed Emshwiller**

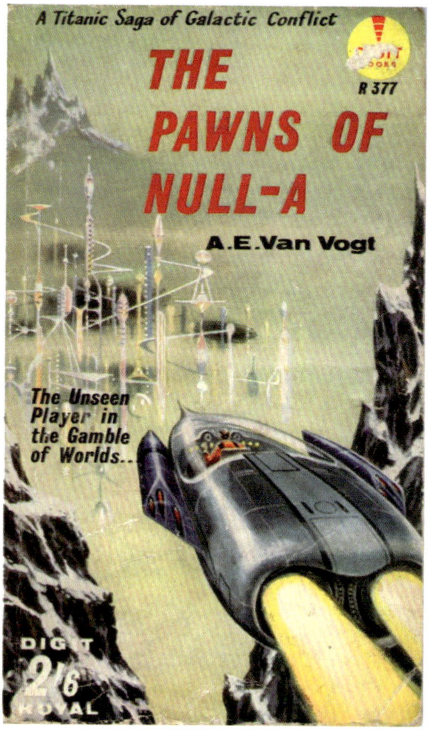

A. E. van Vogt | *The Pawns of Null-A*
Digit Books R377, 1960 | Art **Ed Emshwiller**

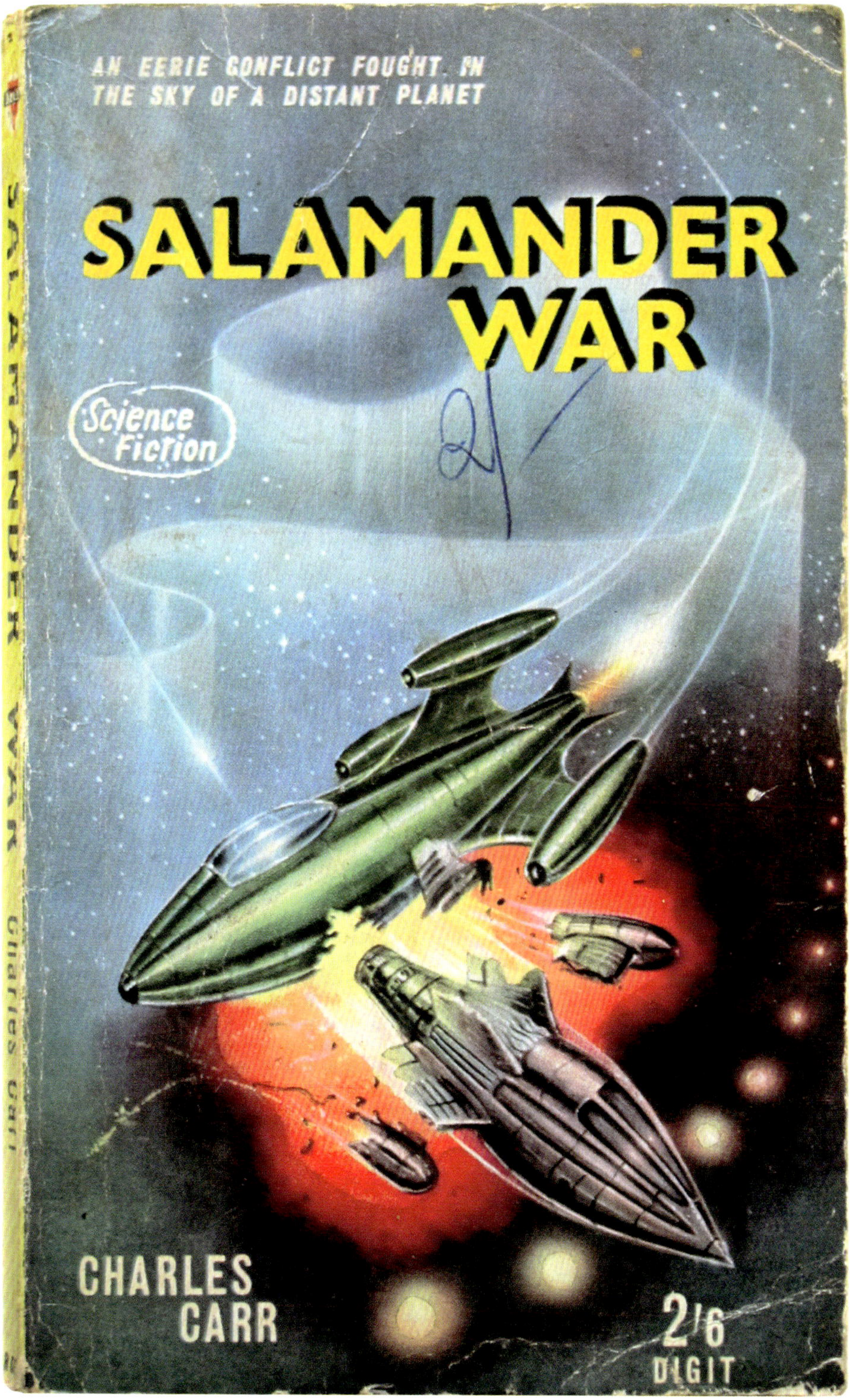

Charles Carr | *Salamander War*
Digit Books R616, 1962 | Art **Unknown**

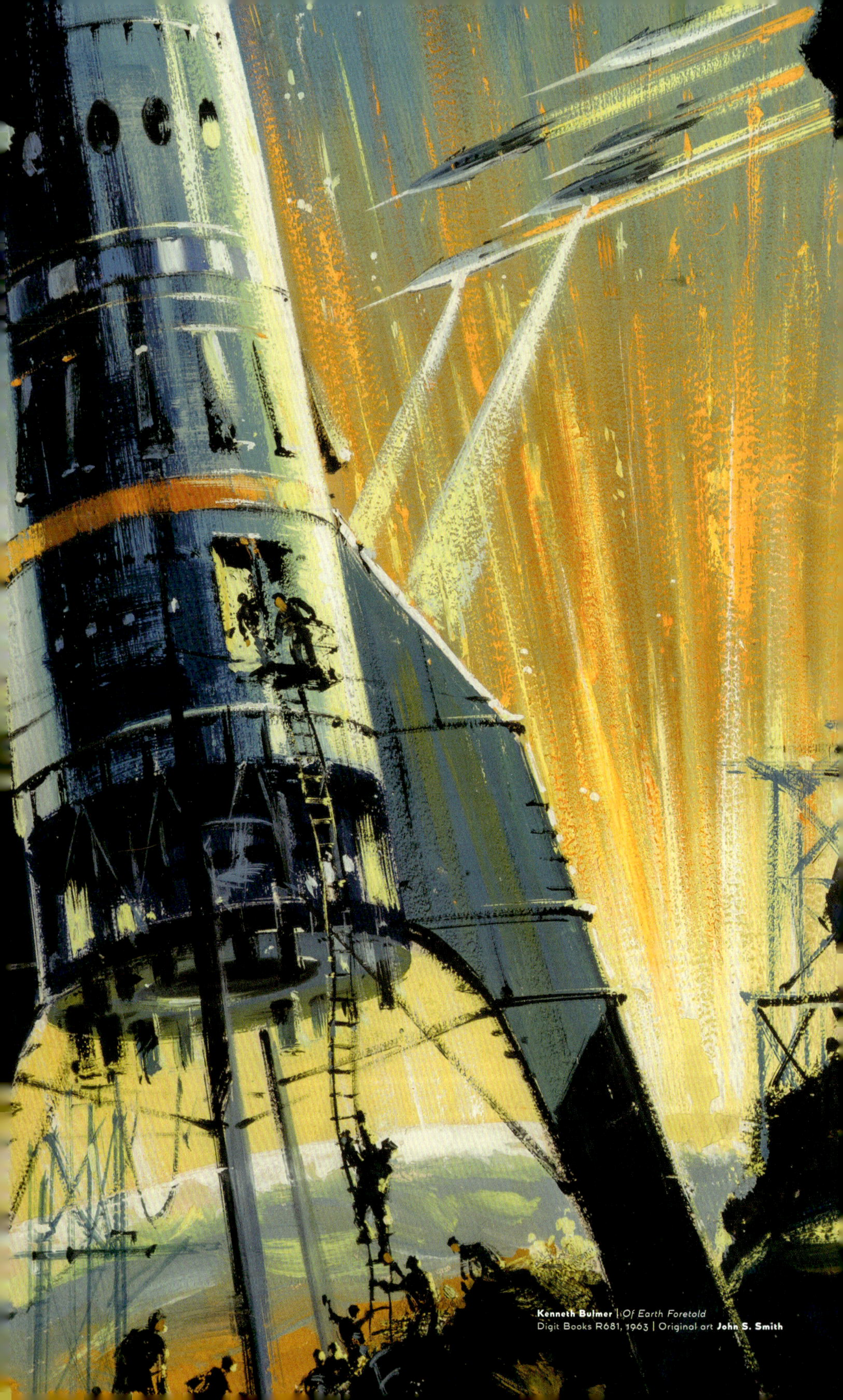

Kenneth Bulmer | *Of Earth Foretold*
Digit Books R681, 1963 | Original art **John S. Smith**

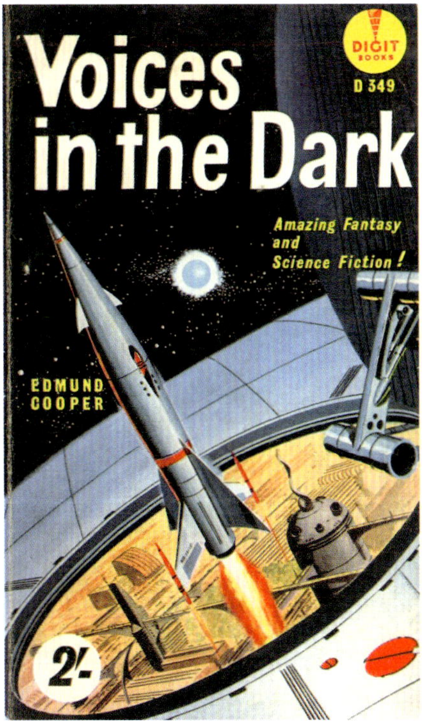

Edmund Cooper | *Voices in the Dark*
Digit Books D349, 1960 | Art **Ed Valigursky**

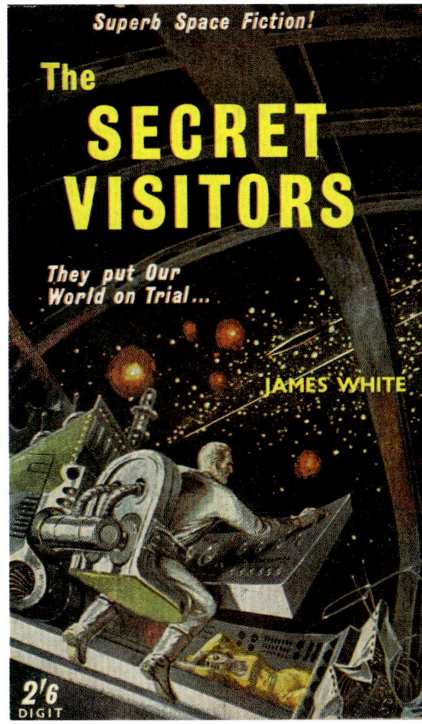

James White | *The Secret Visitors*
Digit Books R479, 1961 | Art **Ed Emshwiller**

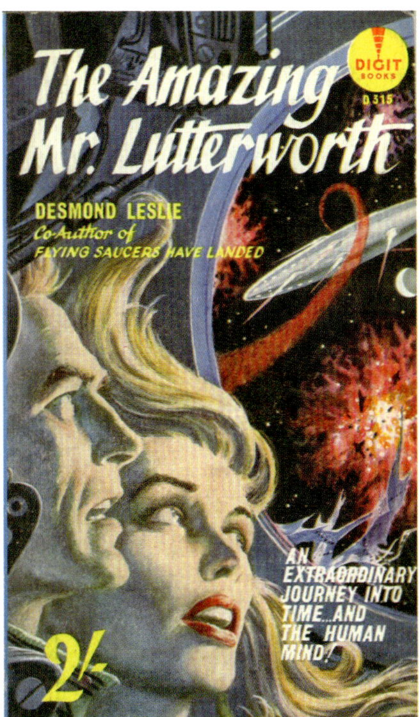

Desmond Leslie | *The Amazing Mr. Lutterworth*
Digit Books D315, 1960 | Art **Ed Emshwiller**

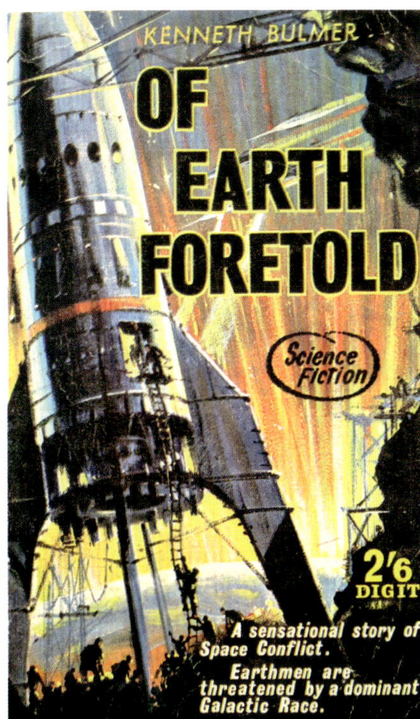

Kenneth Bulmer | *Of Earth Foretold*
Digit Books R681, 1963 | Art **John S. Smith**

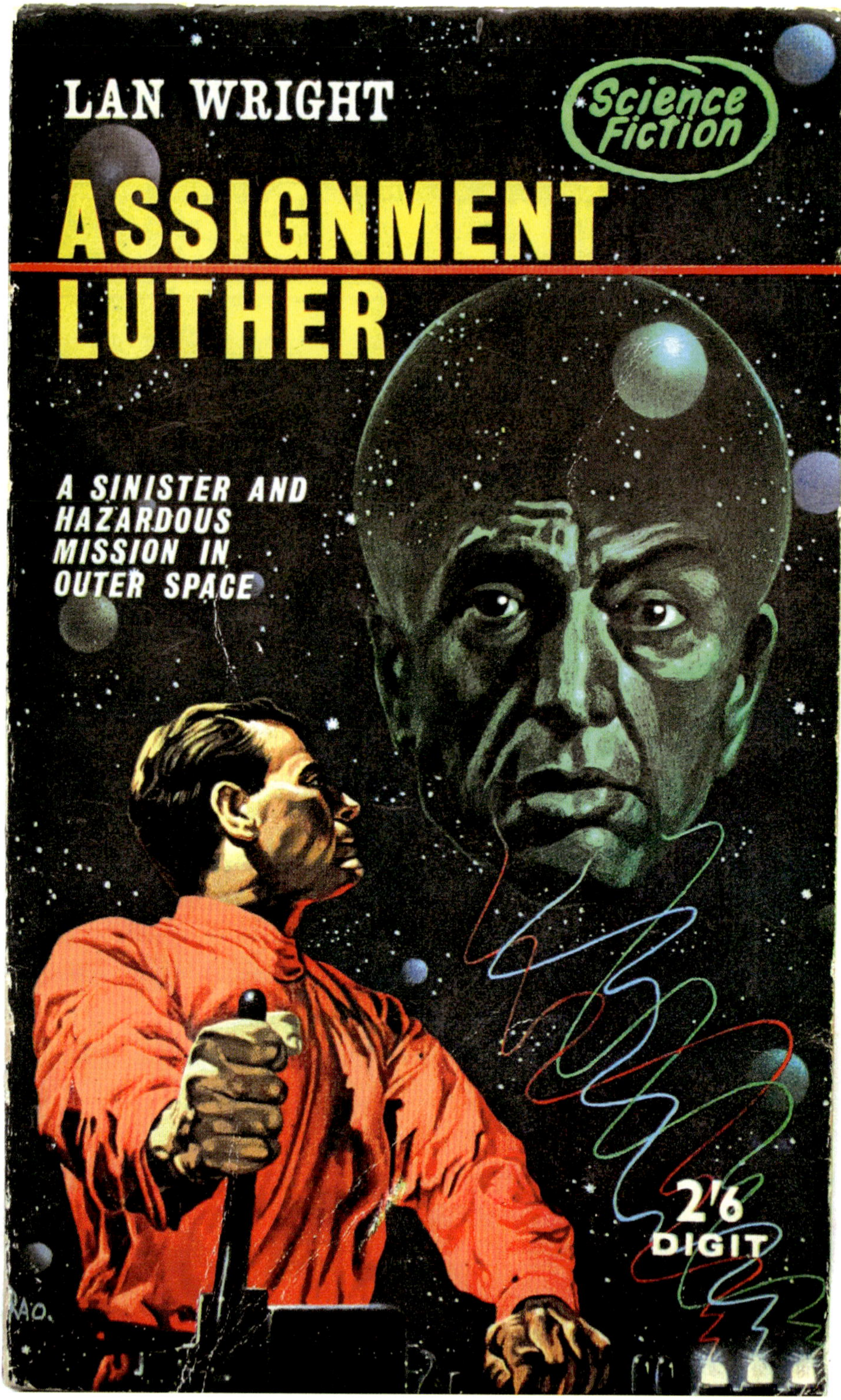

Lan Wright | *Assignment Luther*
Digit Books R686, 1963 | Art **Robert A. Osborne**

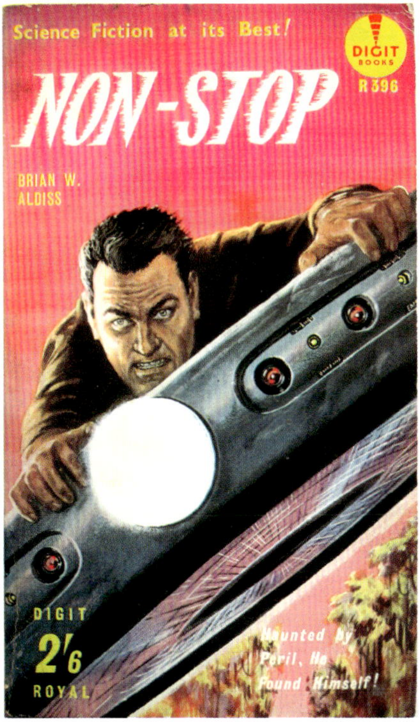

Brian W. Aldiss | *Non-Stop*
Digit Books R396, 1959 | Art **Ed Emshwiller**

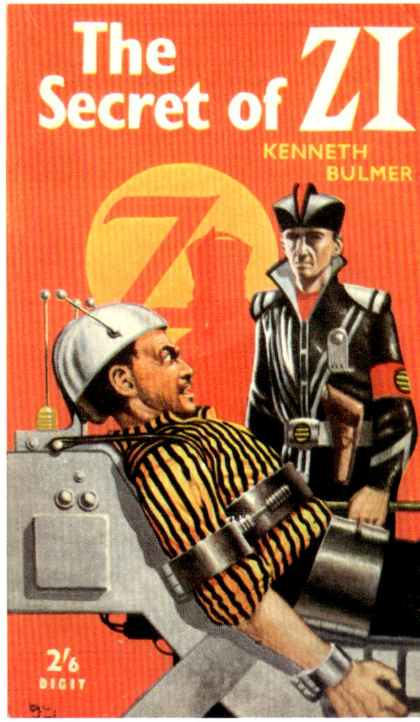

Kenneth Bulmer | *The Secret of ZI*
Digit Books R515, 1961 | Art **Brian Lewis**

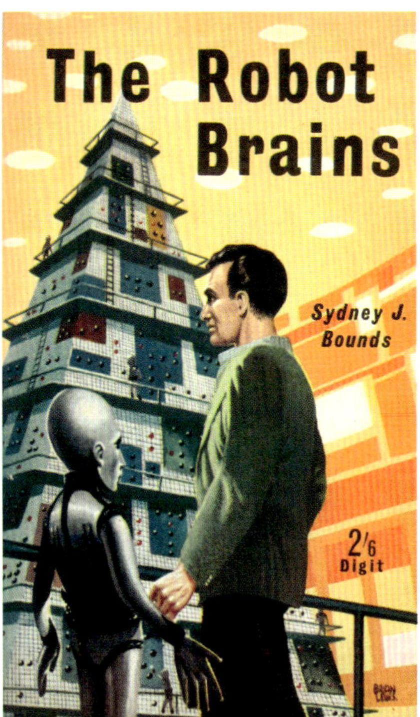

Sydney James Bounds | *The Robot Brains*
Digit Books R521, 1961 | Art **Brian Lewis**

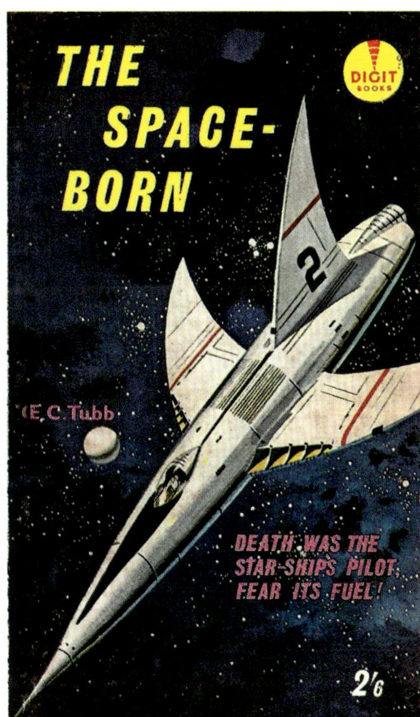

E. C. Tubb | *The Space-Born*
Digit Books R449, 1961 | Art **Ed Valigursky**

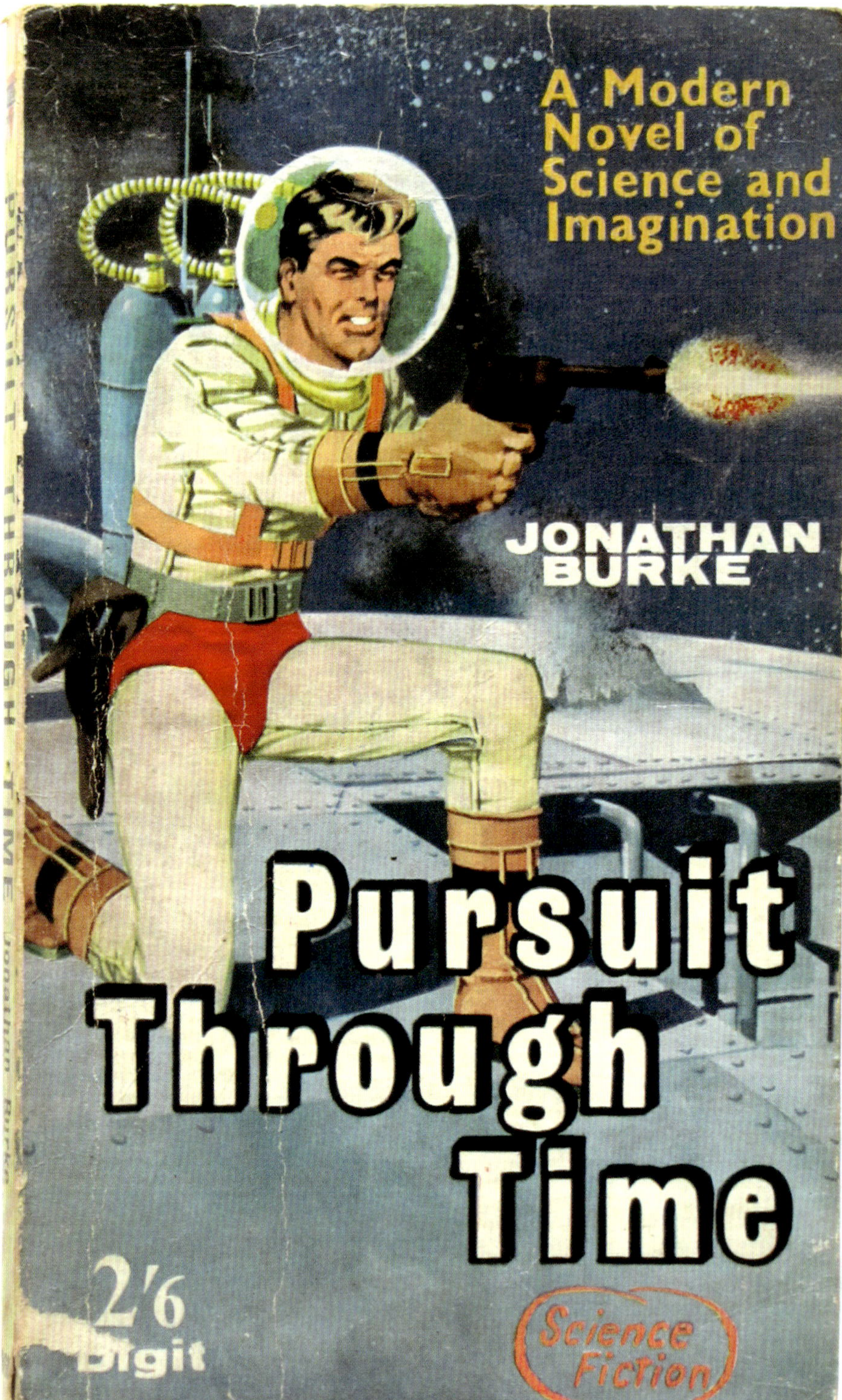

Jonathan Burke | *Pursuit Through Time*
Digit Books R612, 1962 | Art **Unknown**

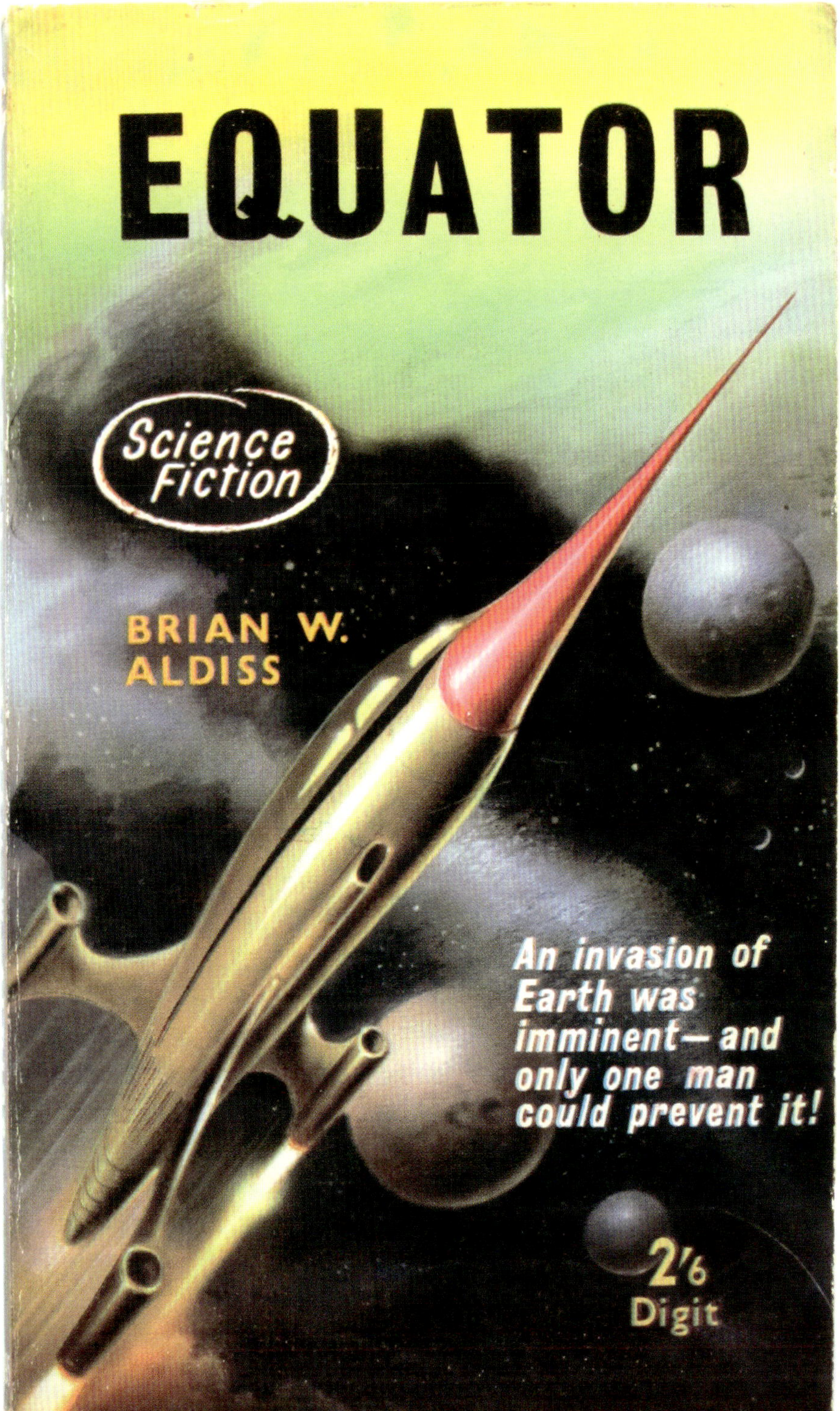

Brian W. Aldiss | *Equator*
Digit Books R695, 1963 | Art **Unknown**

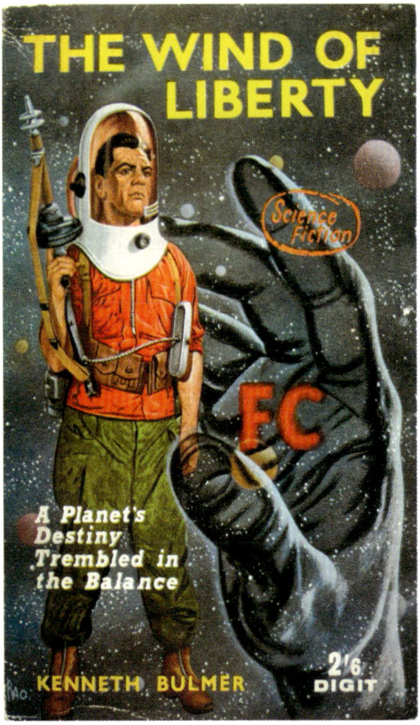

Kenneth Bulmer | *The Wind of Liberty*
Digit Books R607, 1962 | Art **Robert A. Osborne**

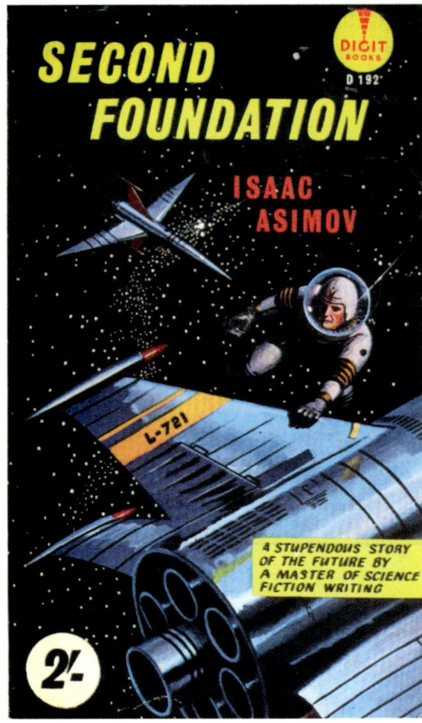

Isaac Asimov | *Second Foundation*
Digit Books D192, 1958 | Art **Ed Valigursky**

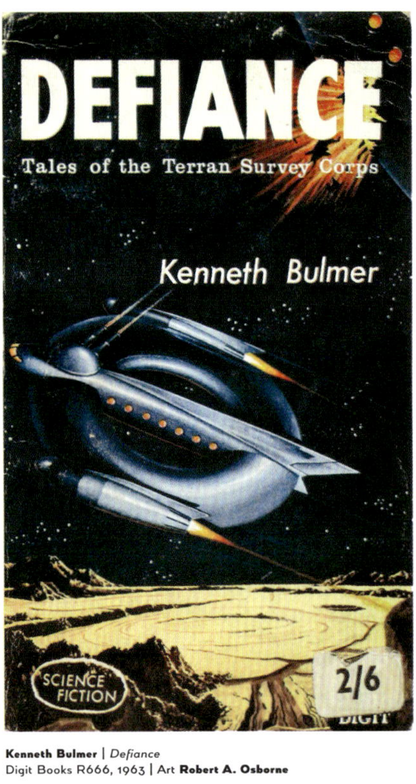

Kenneth Bulmer | *Defiance*
Digit Books R666, 1963 | Art **Robert A. Osborne**

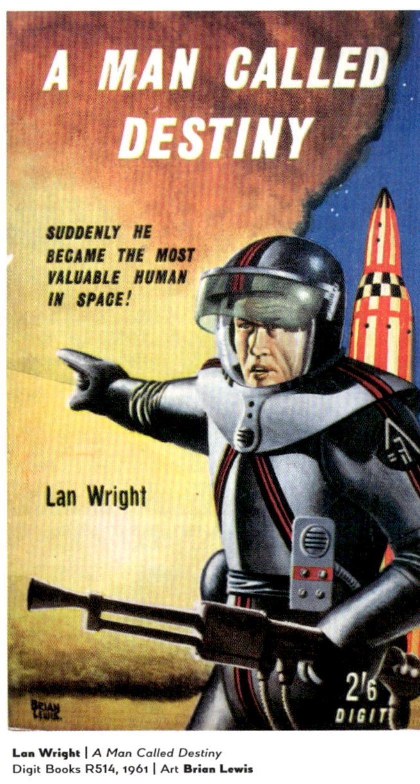

Lan Wright | *A Man Called Destiny*
Digit Books R514, 1961 | Art **Brian Lewis**

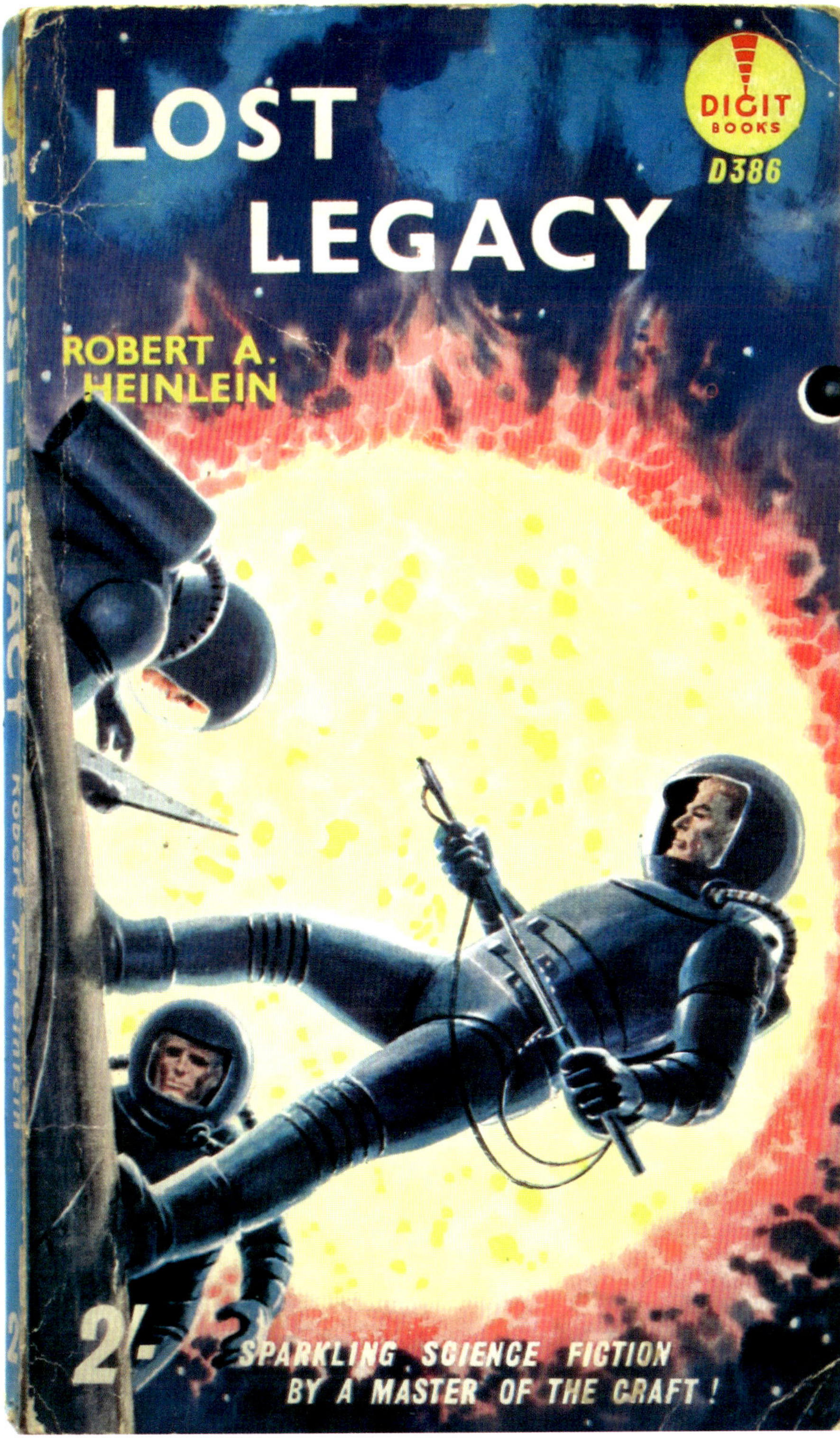

Robert A. Heinlein | *Lost Legacy*
Digit Books D386, 1960 | Art **Ed Emshwiller**

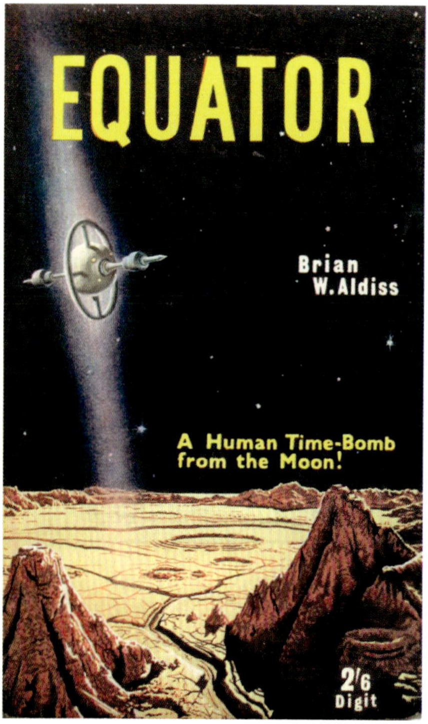

Brian W. Aldiss | *Equator*
Digit Books R533, 1961 | Art by **Chesley Bonestell**

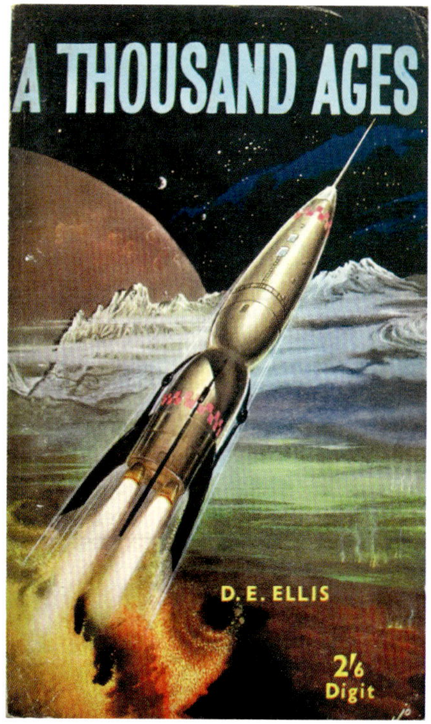

D. E. Ellis | *A Thousand Ages*
Digit Books R549, 1961 | Art **Carlo Jacono**

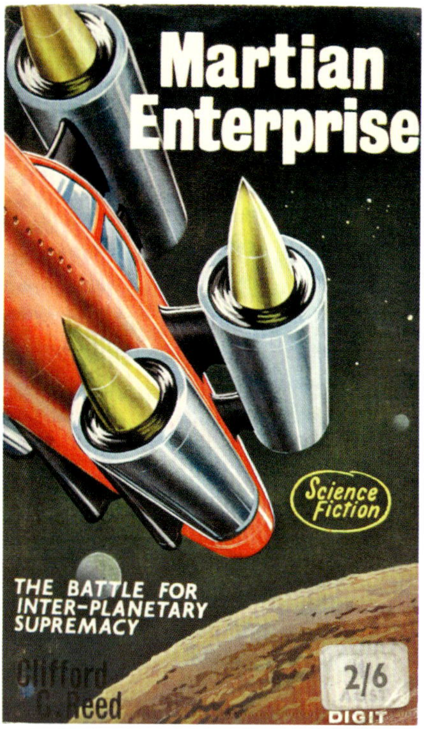

Clifford C. Reed | *Martian Enterprise*
Digit Books R638, 1962 | Art **Cha' Bril**

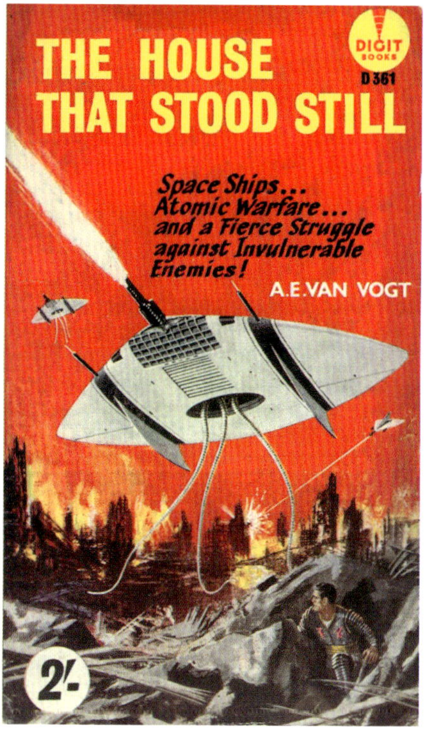

A. E. van Vogt | *The House That Stood Still*
Digit Books D361, 1960 | Art **Ed Valigursky**

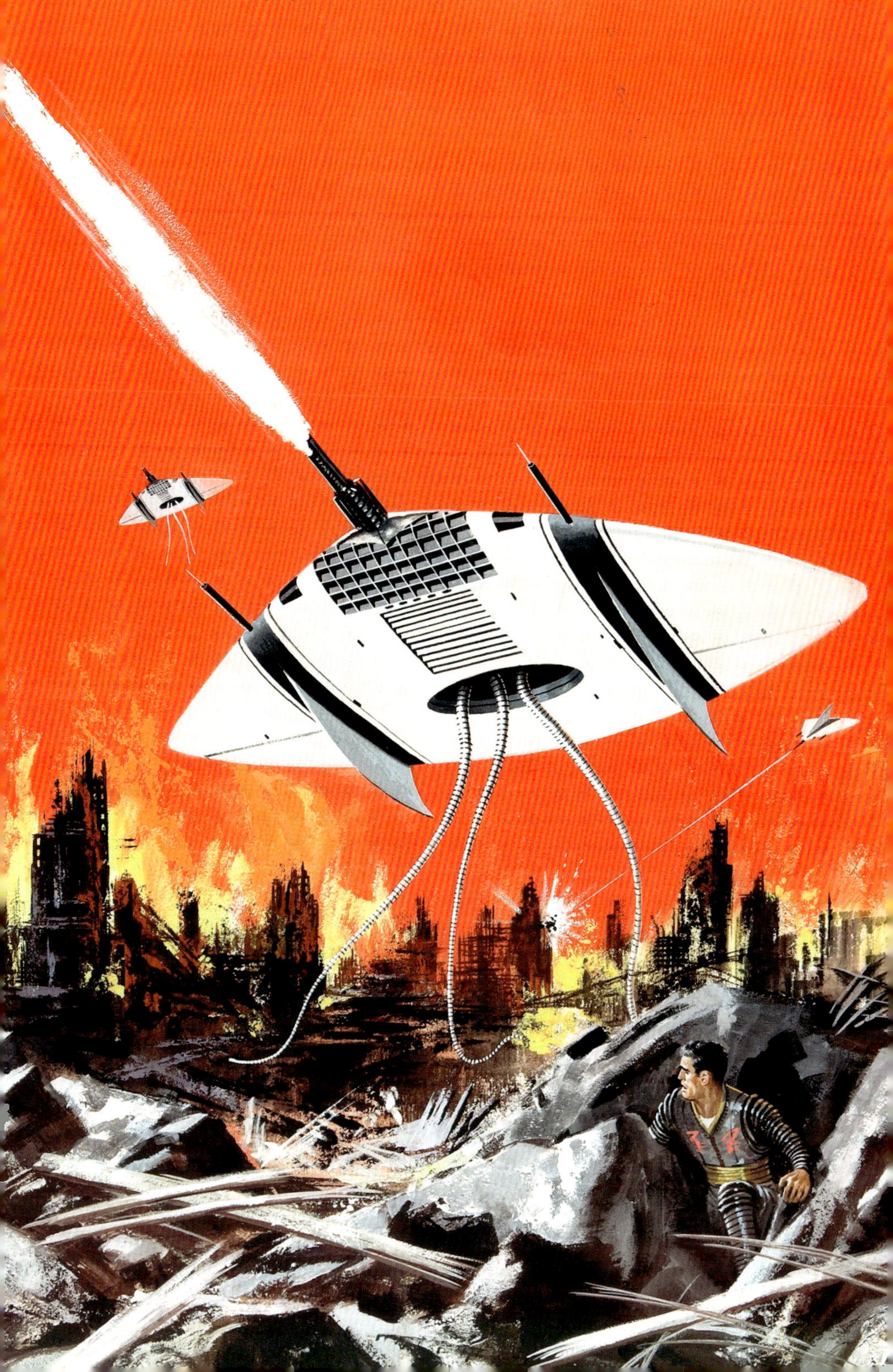

A. E. van Vogt | *A Touch of Infinity*
Ace Books, 1960 | Original art **Ed Valigursky**

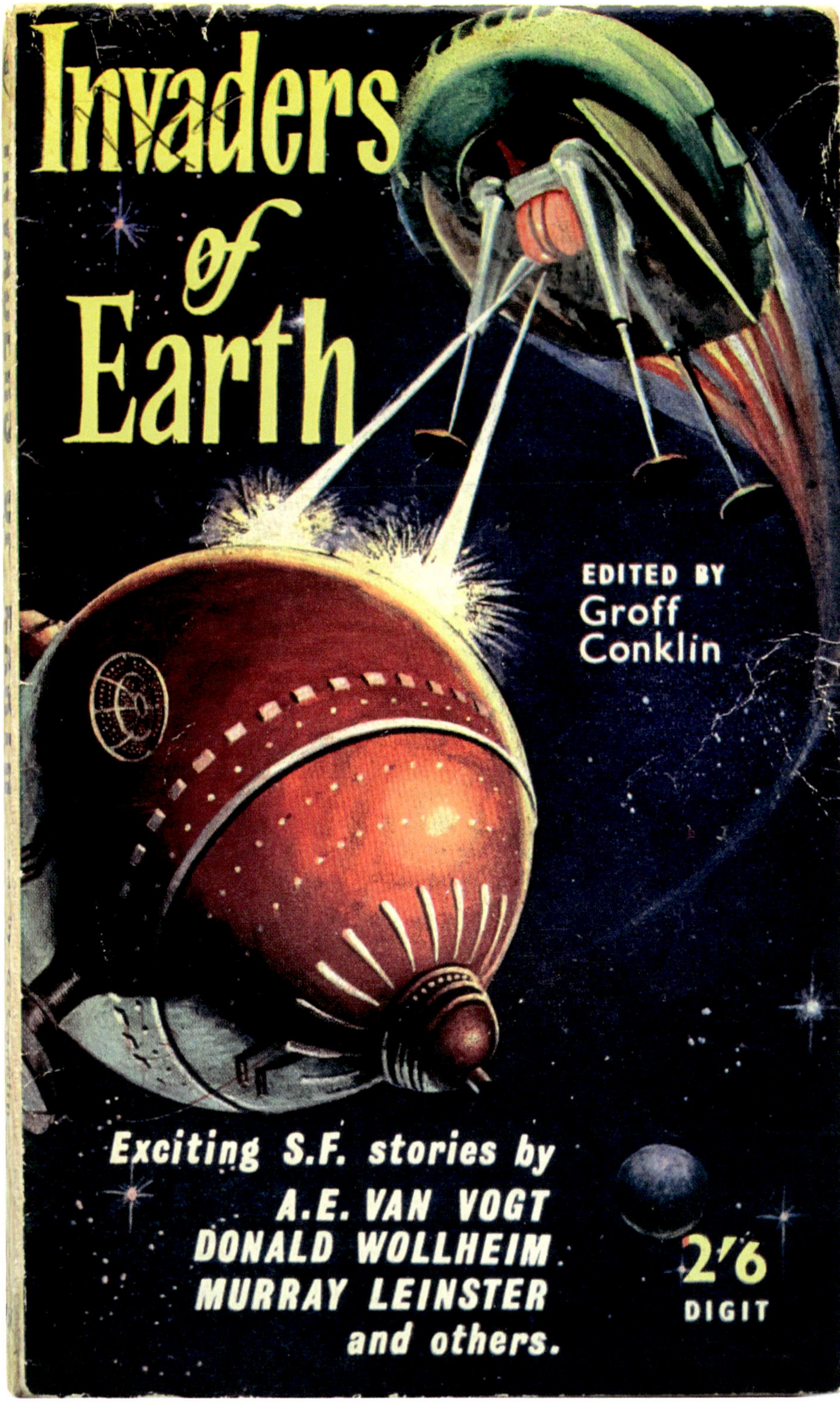

Groff Conklin | *Invaders of Earth*
Digit Books R562, 1962 | Art **Unknown**

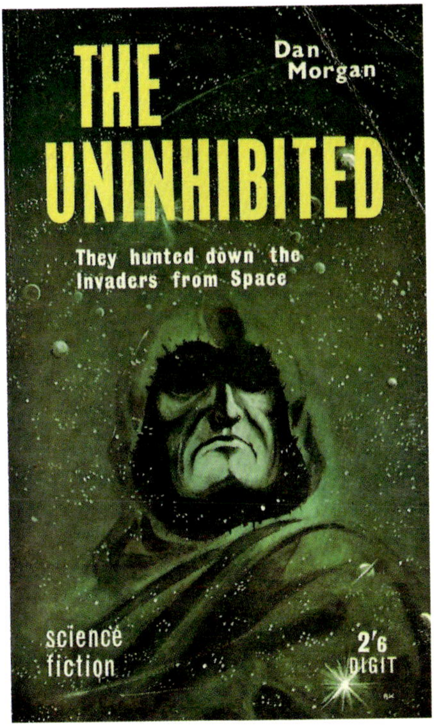

Dan Morgan | *The Uninhibited*
Digit Books R771, 1963 | Art **A. W.**

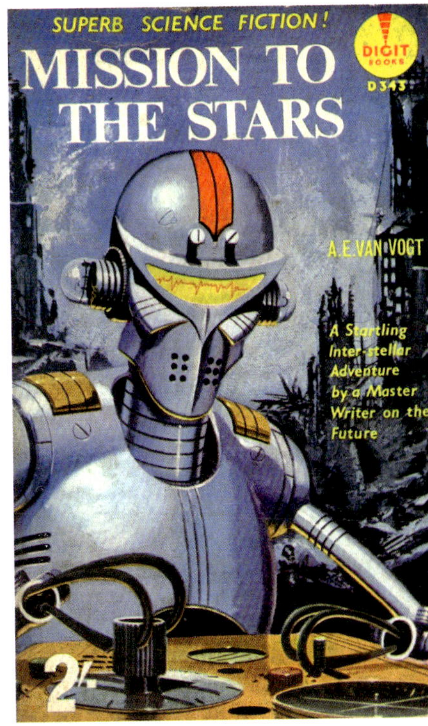

A. E. van Vogt | *Mission to the Stars*
Digit Books D343, 1962 | Art **Ed Valigursky**

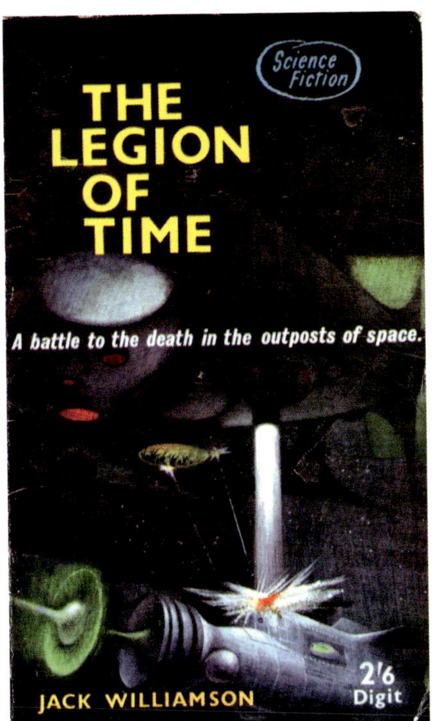

Jack Williamson | *The Legion of Time*
Digit Books R703, 1963 | Art **Unknown**

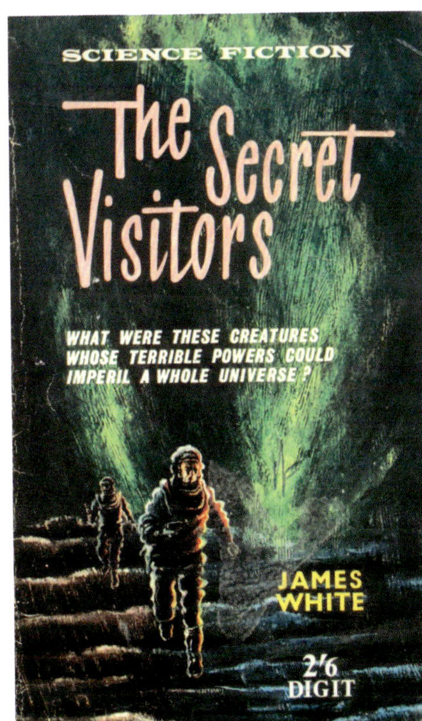

James White | *The Secret Visitors*
Digit Books R725, 1963 | Art **Unknown**

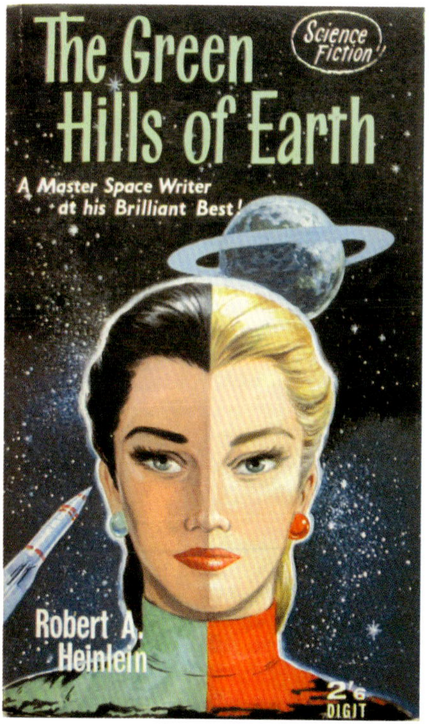

Robert A. Heinlein | *The Green Hills of Earth*
Digit Books R583, 1962 | Art **Davies**

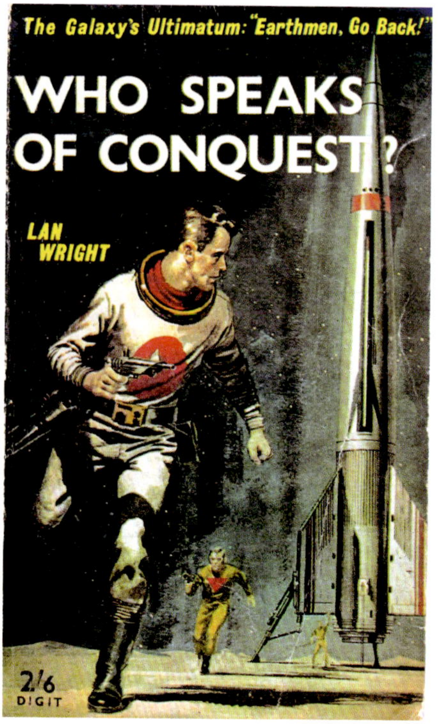

Lan Wright | *Who Speaks of Conquest?*
Digit Books R490, 1961 | Art **Ed Valigursky**

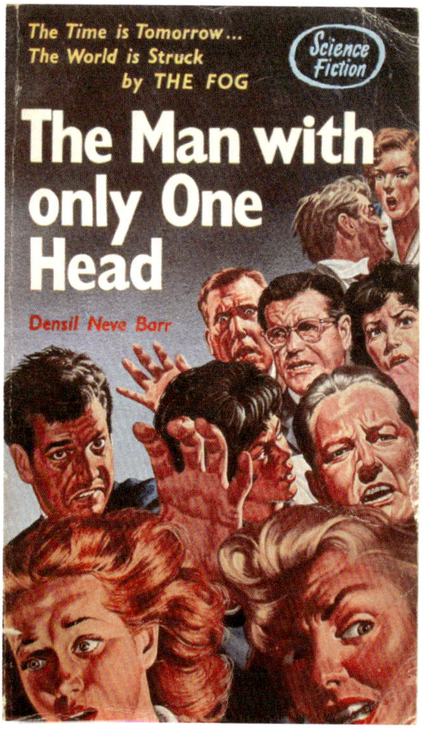

Densil Neve Barr | *The Man with Only One Head*
Digit Books R558, 1962 | Art **Robert A. Osborne**

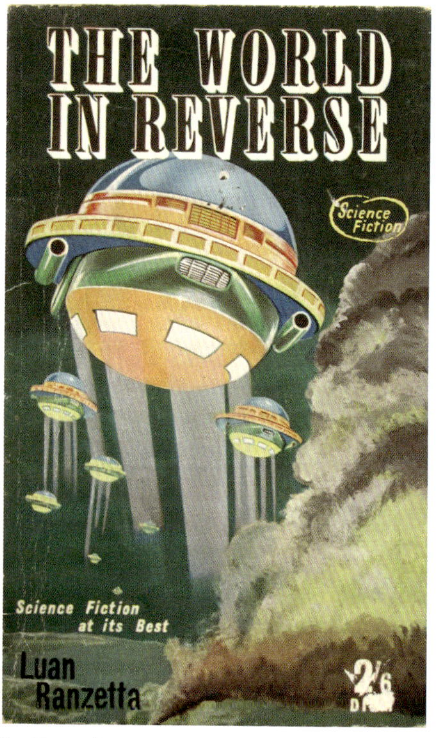

Luan Ranzetta | *The World in Reverse*
Digit Books R618, 1962 | Art **Unknown**

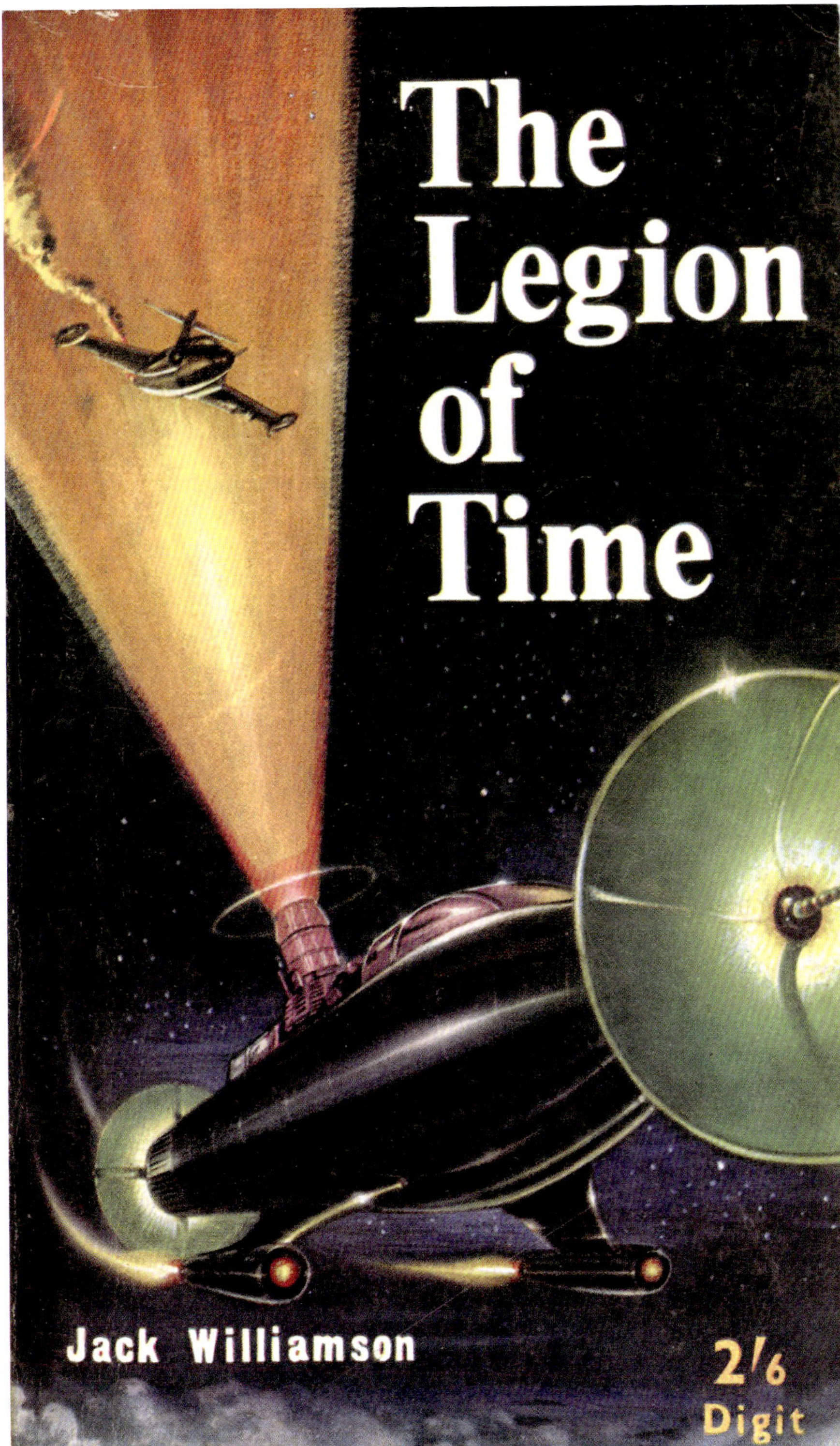

Jack Williamson | *The Legion of Time*
Digit Books R522, 1961 | Art **Unknown**

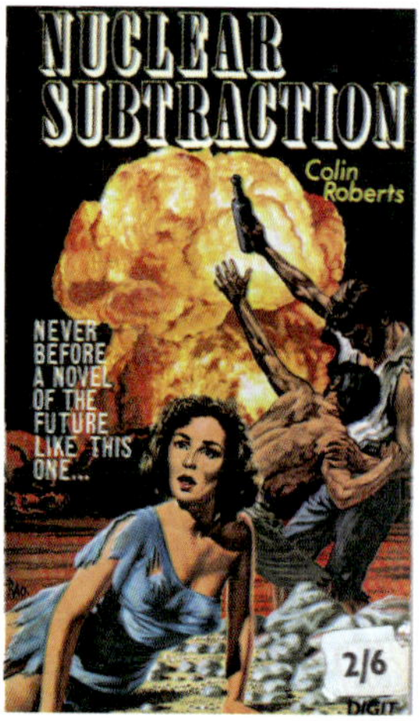

Colin Roberts | *Nuclear Subtraction*
Digit Books R683, 1963 | Art **R. A. Osborne**

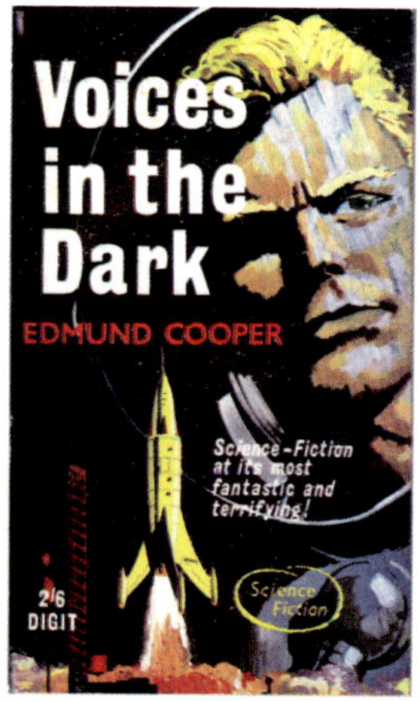

Edmund Cooper | *Voices in the Dark*
Digit Books R663, 1963 | Art **Unknown**

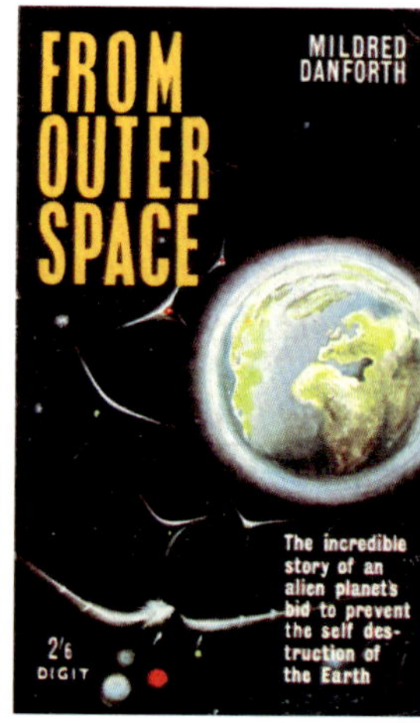

Mildred E. Danforth | *From Outer Space*
Digit Books R760, 1963 | Art **Unknown**

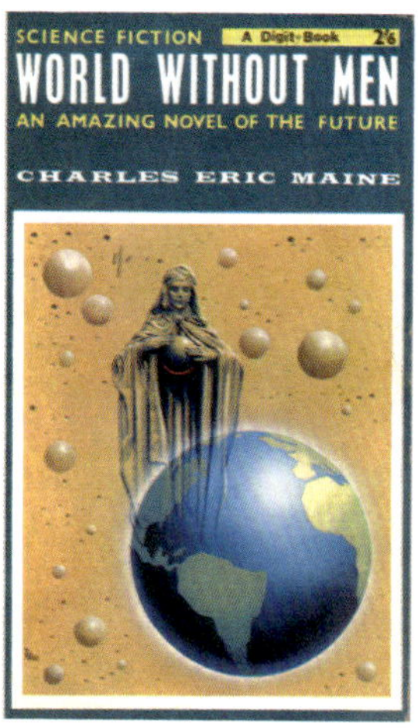

Charles Eric Maine | *World Without Men*
Digit Books R808, 1963 | Art **R. A. Osborne**

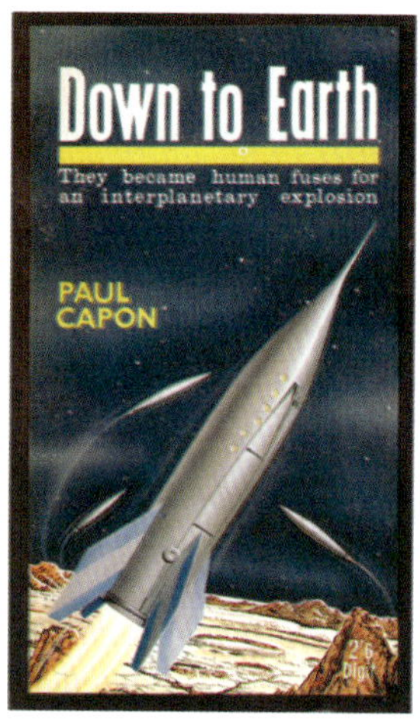

Paul Capon | *Down to Earth*
Digit Books R842, 1964 | Art **R. A. Osborne**

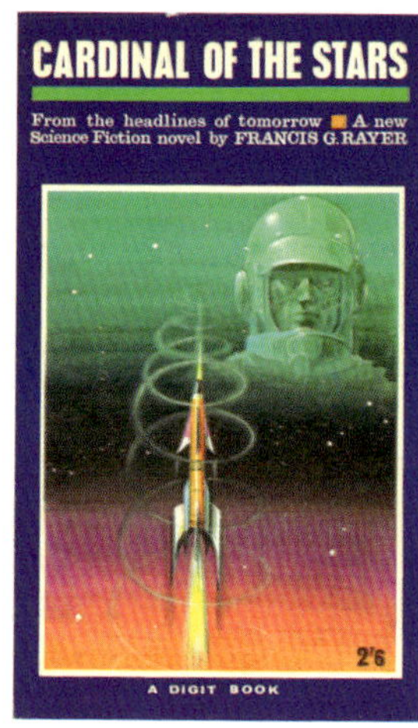

Francis G. Rayer | *Cardinal of the Stars*
Digit Books R851, 1964 | Art **Unknown**

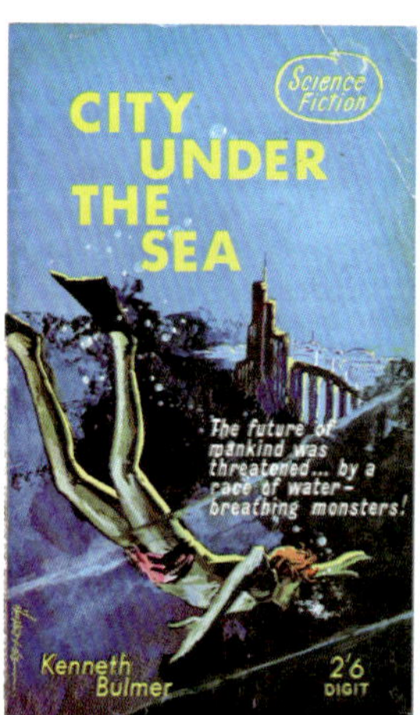

A Kenneth Bulmer | *City Under the Sea*
Digit Books R672, 1963 | Art **Enric Torres-Prat**

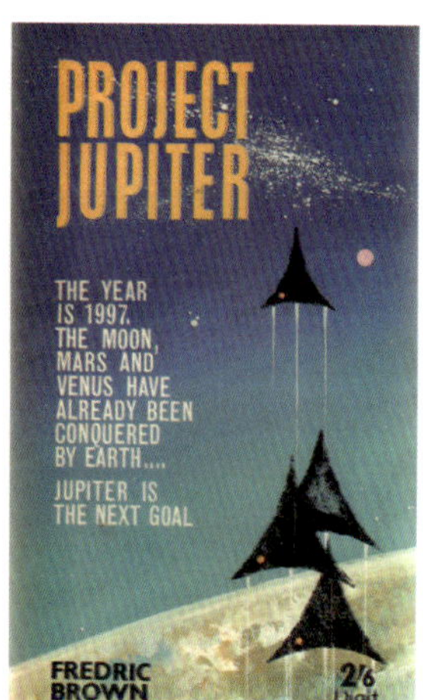

Fredric Brown | *Project Jupiter*
Digit Books R828, 1964 | Art **Enric Torres-Prat**

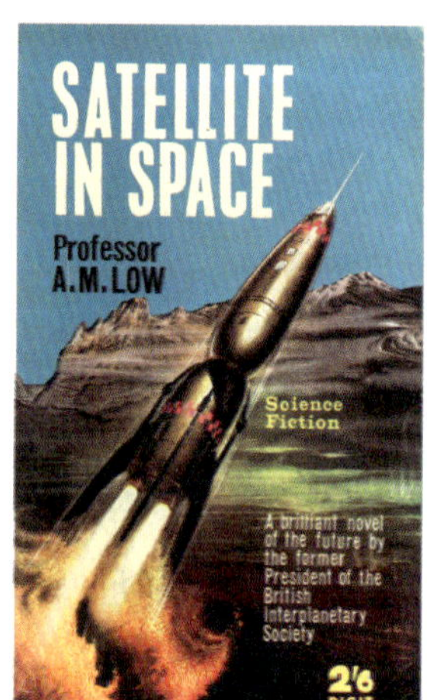

Professor A. M. Low | *Satellite in Space*
Digit Books R734, 1963 | Art **Carlo Jacono**

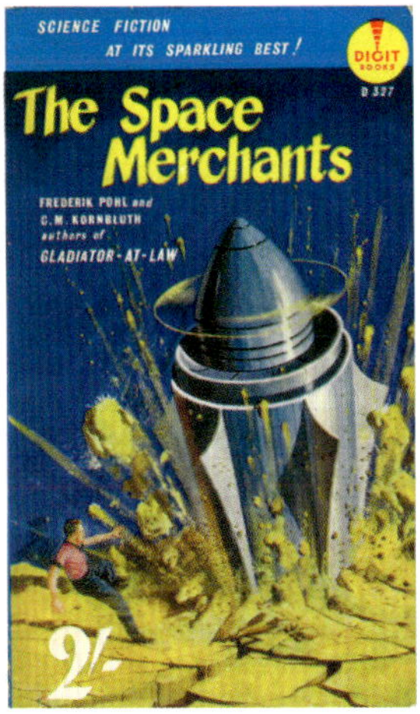

Kornbluth, Pohl | *The Space Merchants*
Digit Books R327, 1960 | Art **Ed Valigursky**

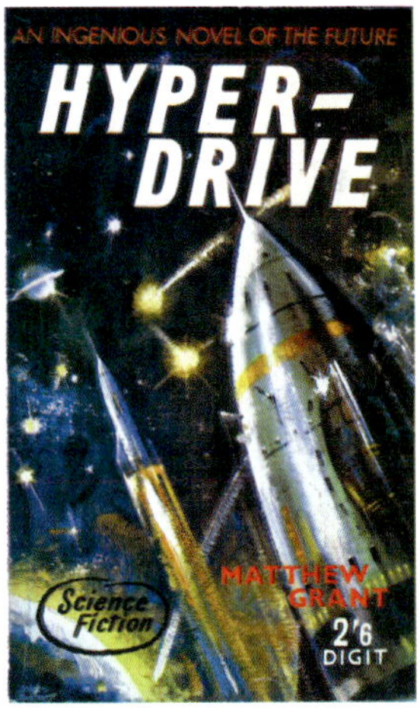

Matthew Grant | *Hyper-Drive*
Digit Books R673, 1962 | Art **John S. Smith**

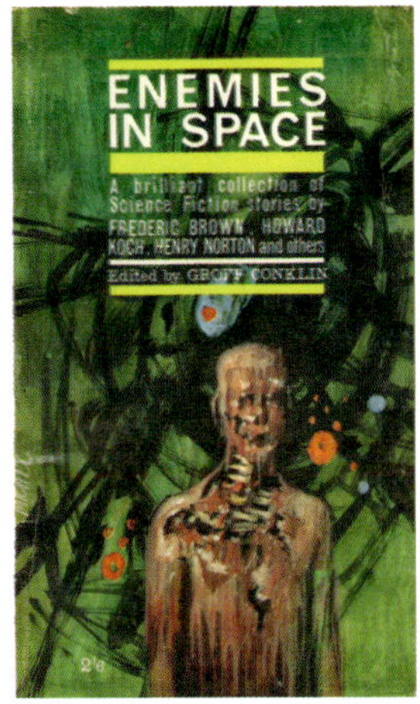

Groff Conklin | *Enemies in Space*
Digit Books R883, 1964 | Art **Michal Atkinson**

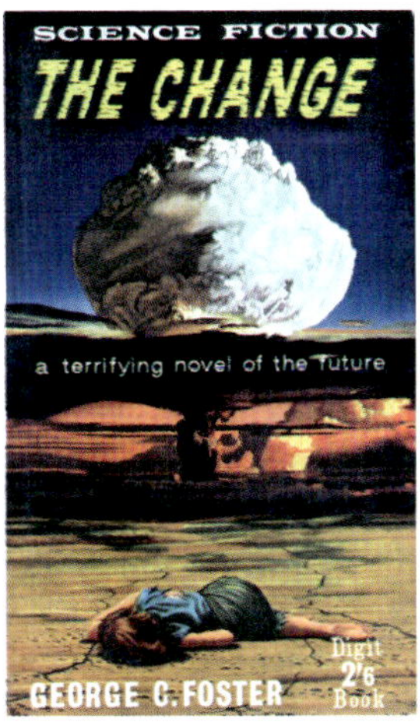

George C. Foster | *The Change*
Digit Books R721, 1963 | Art **R. A. Osborne**

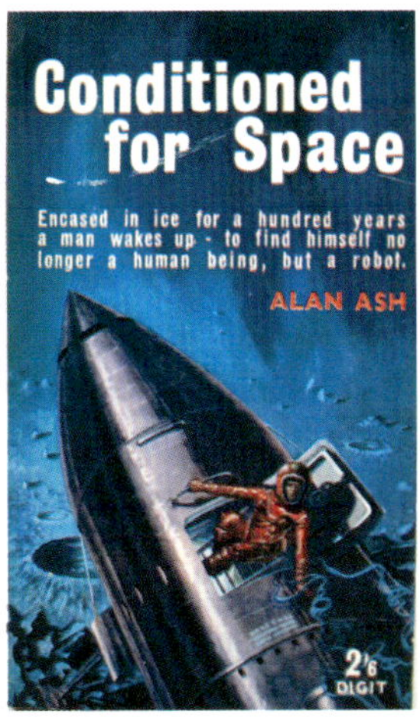

Alan Ash | *Conditioned for Space*
Digit Books R754, 1963 | Art **Unknown**

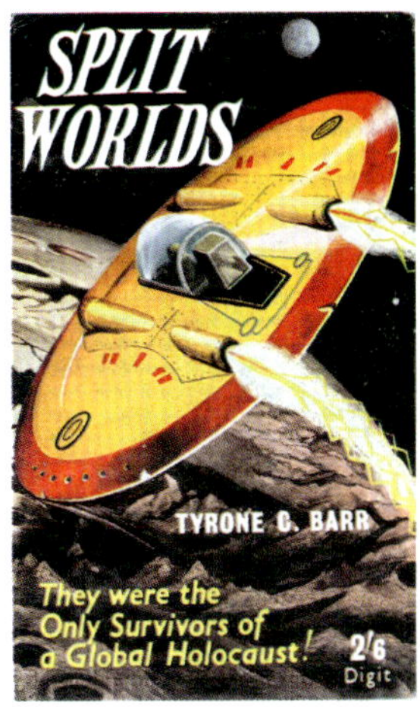

Tyrone C. Barr | *Split Worlds*
Digit Books R563, 1962 | Art **Cha' Bril**

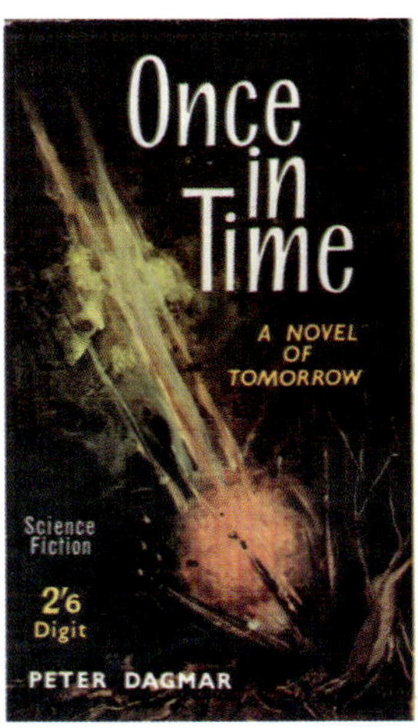

Peter Dagmar | *Once in Time*
Digit Books R746, 1963 | Art **Unknown**

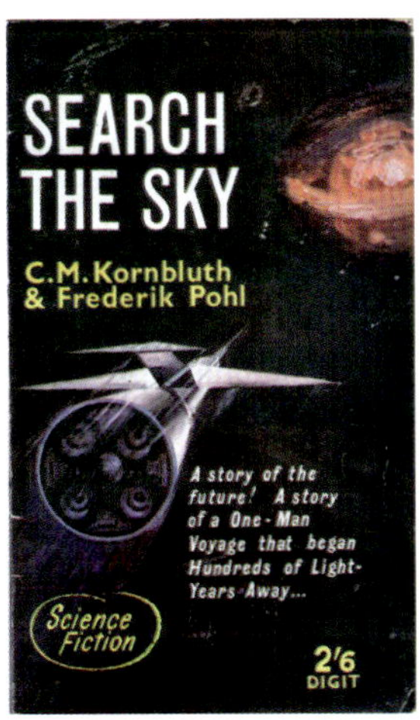

Kornbluth, Pohl | *Search the Sky*
Digit Books R662, 1963 | Art **Unknown**

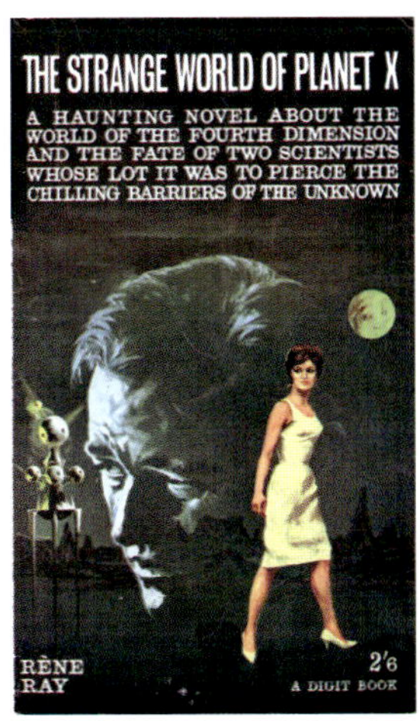

René Ray | *The Strange World of Planet X*
Digit Books R735, 1963 | Art **Robert A. Osborne**

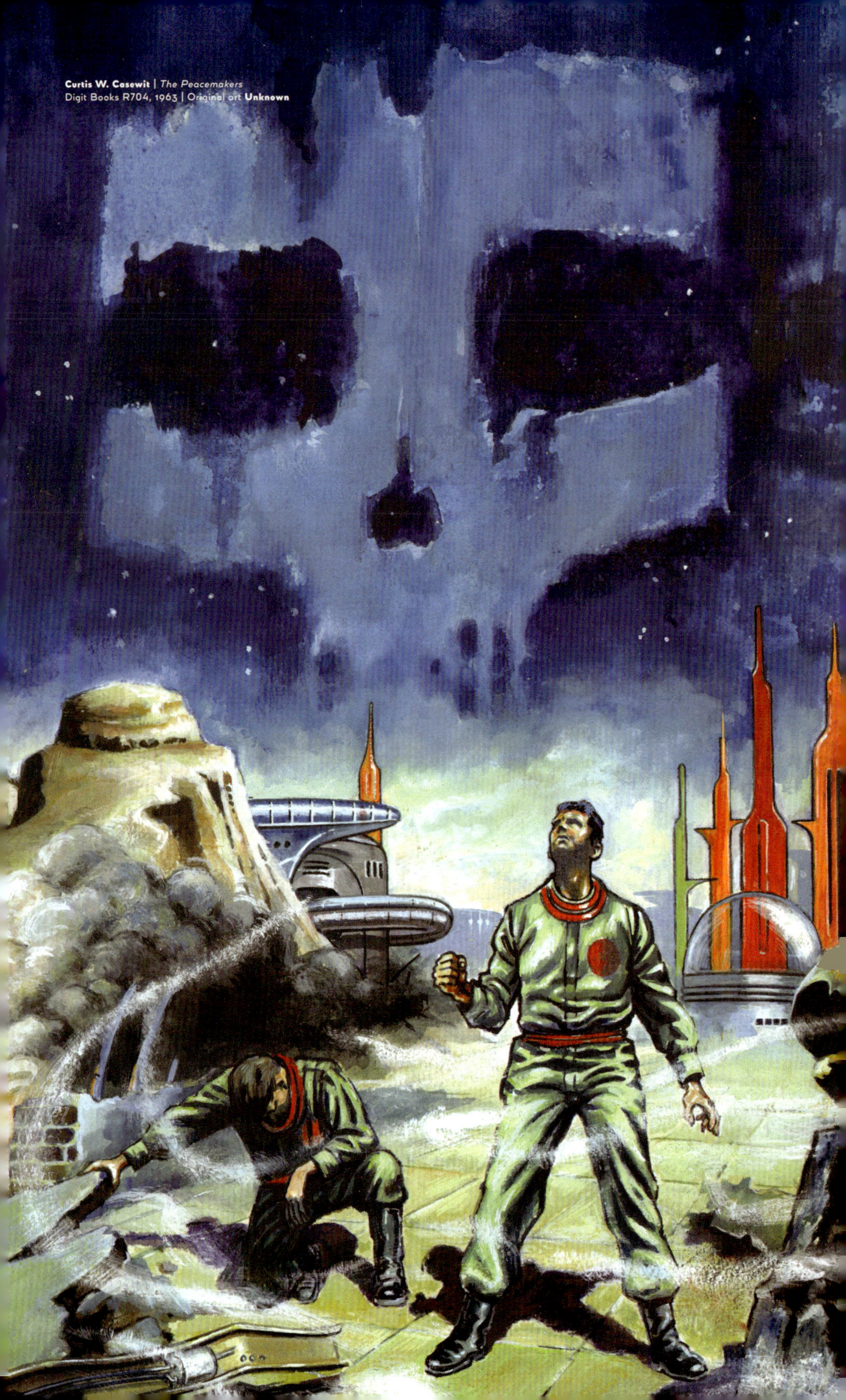

Curtis W. Casewit | *The Peacemakers*
Digit Books R704, 1963 | Original art **Unknown**

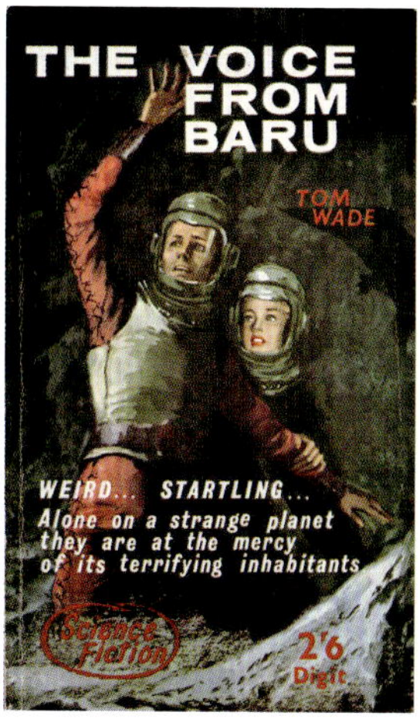

Tom Wade | *The Voice from Baru*
Digit Books R661, 1962 | Art **Unknown**

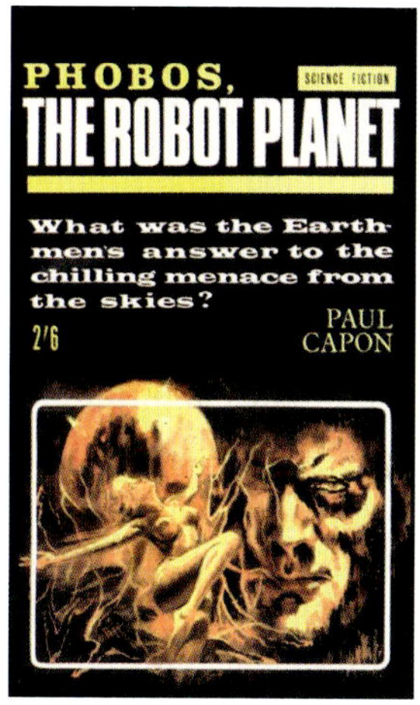

Paul Capon | *Phobos, the Robot Planet*
Digit Books R887, 1965 | Art **Sam Peffer**

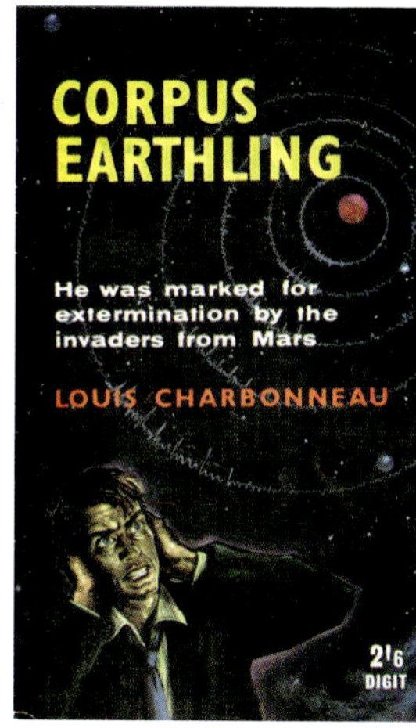

Louis Charbonneau | *Corpus Earthling*
Digit Books R753, 1963 | Art **Unknown**

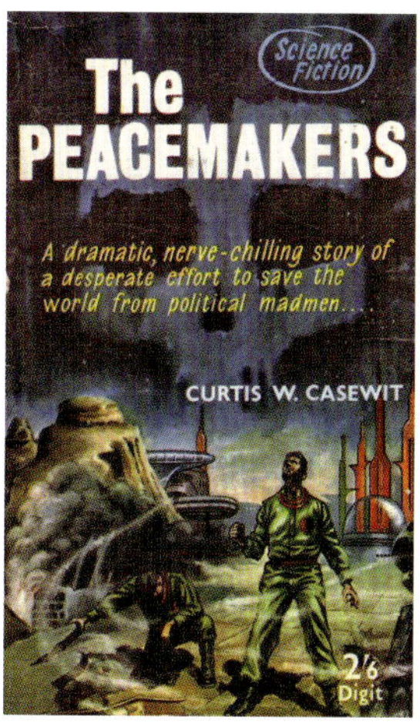

Curtis W. Casewit | *The Peacemakers*
Digit Books R704, 1963 | Art **Unknown**

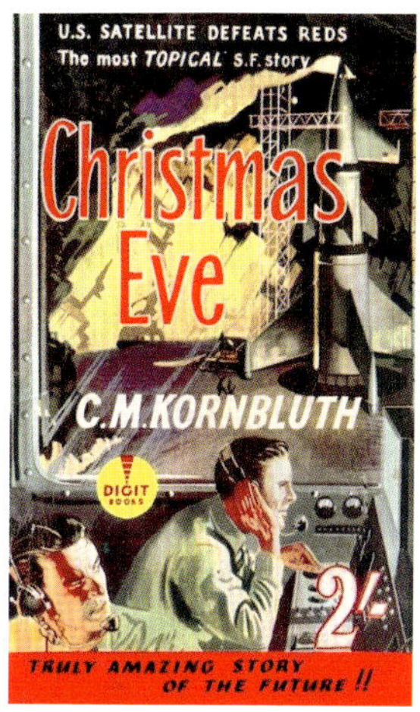

C. M Kornbluth | *Christmas Eve*
Digit Books, 1957 | Art **Unknown**

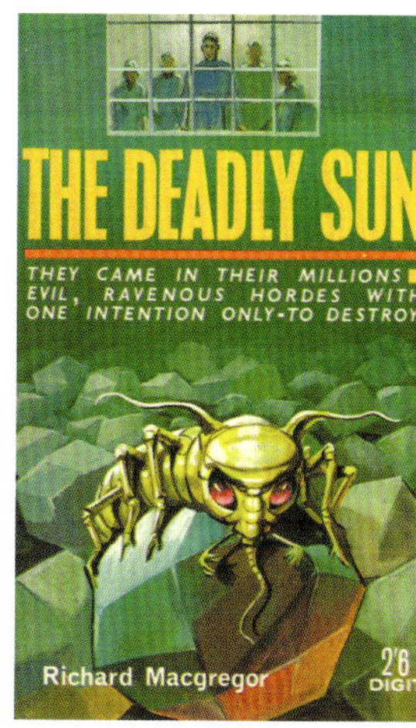

Richard Macgregor | *The Deadly Sun*
Digit Books R856, 1965 | Art **Unknown**

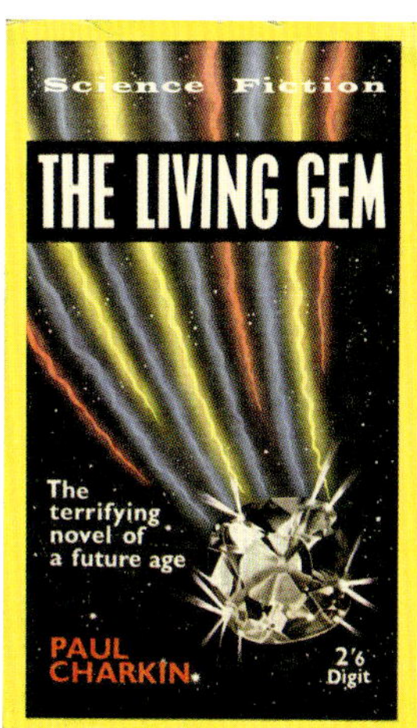

Paul Charkin | *The Living Gem*
Digit Books R782, 1963 | Art **Unknown**

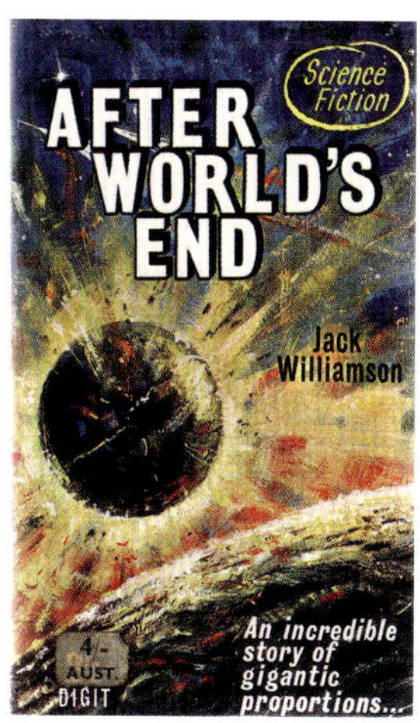

Jack Williamson | *After World's End*
Digit Books R671, 1963 | Art **Unknown**

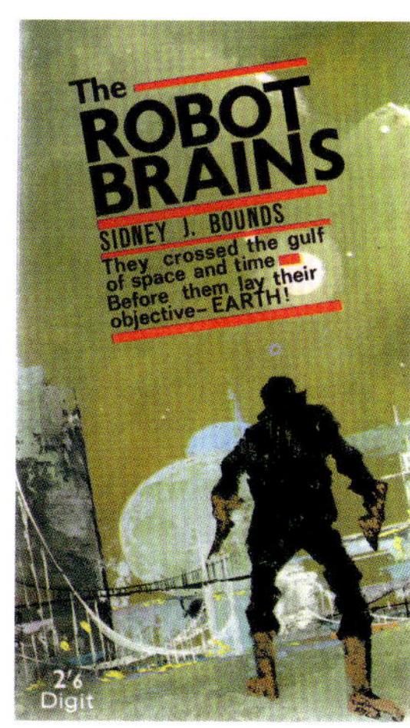

Sidney (Sydney) J. Bounds | *The Robot Brains*
Digit Books R819, 1964 | Art **Enrich**

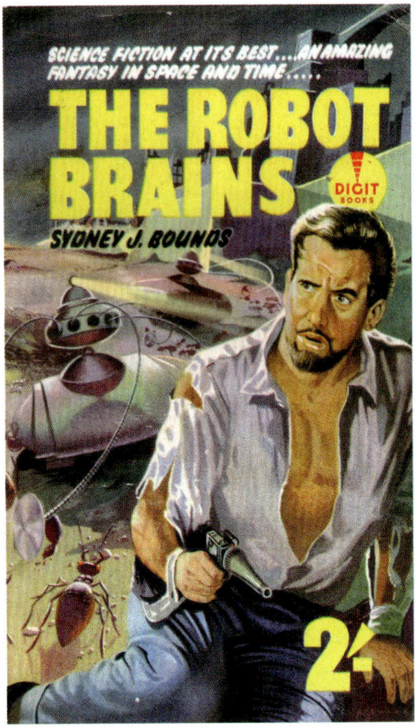

Sydney J. Bounds | *The Robot Brains*
Digit Books, 1957 | Art **Glen Steward**

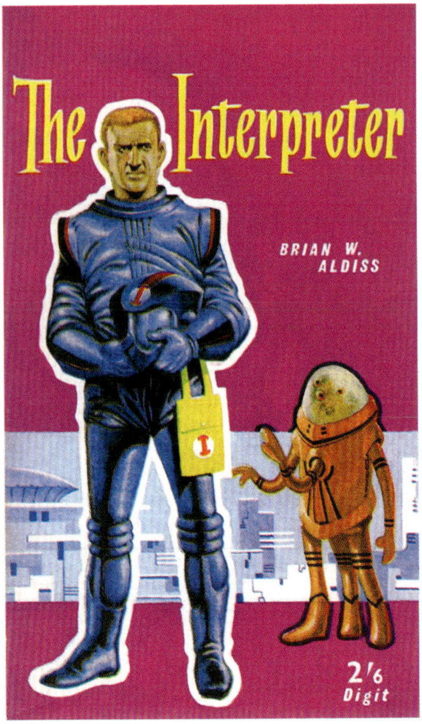

Brian W. Aldiss | *The Interpreter*
Digit Books R506, 1961 | Art **Brian Lewis**

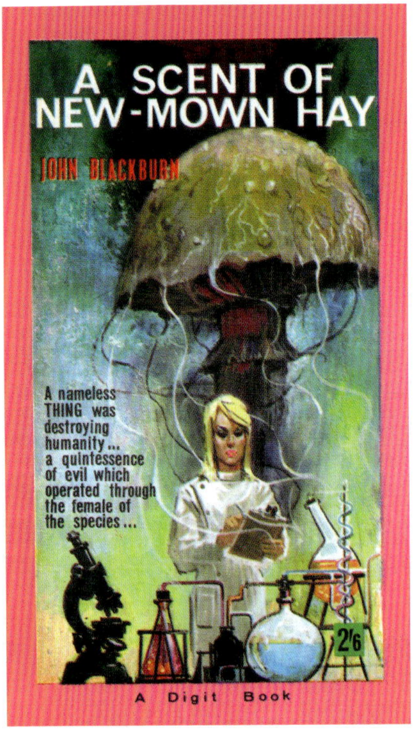

John Blackburn | *A Scent of New-Mown Hay*
Digit Books R846, 1964 | Art **Unknown**

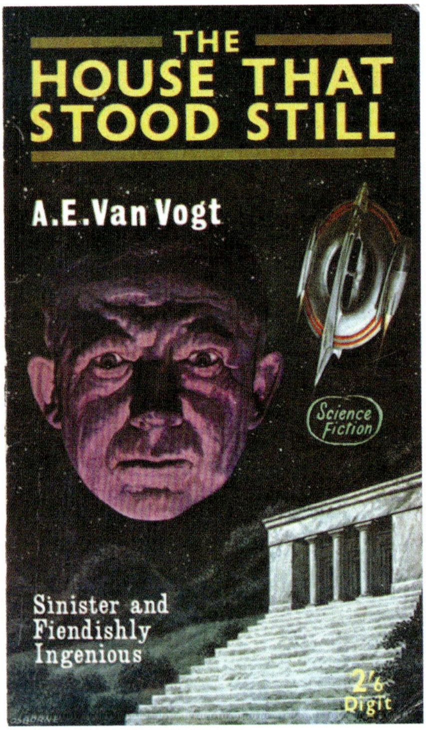

A. E. van Vogt | *The House That Stood Still*
Digit Books R623, 1962 | Art **Robert A. Osborne**

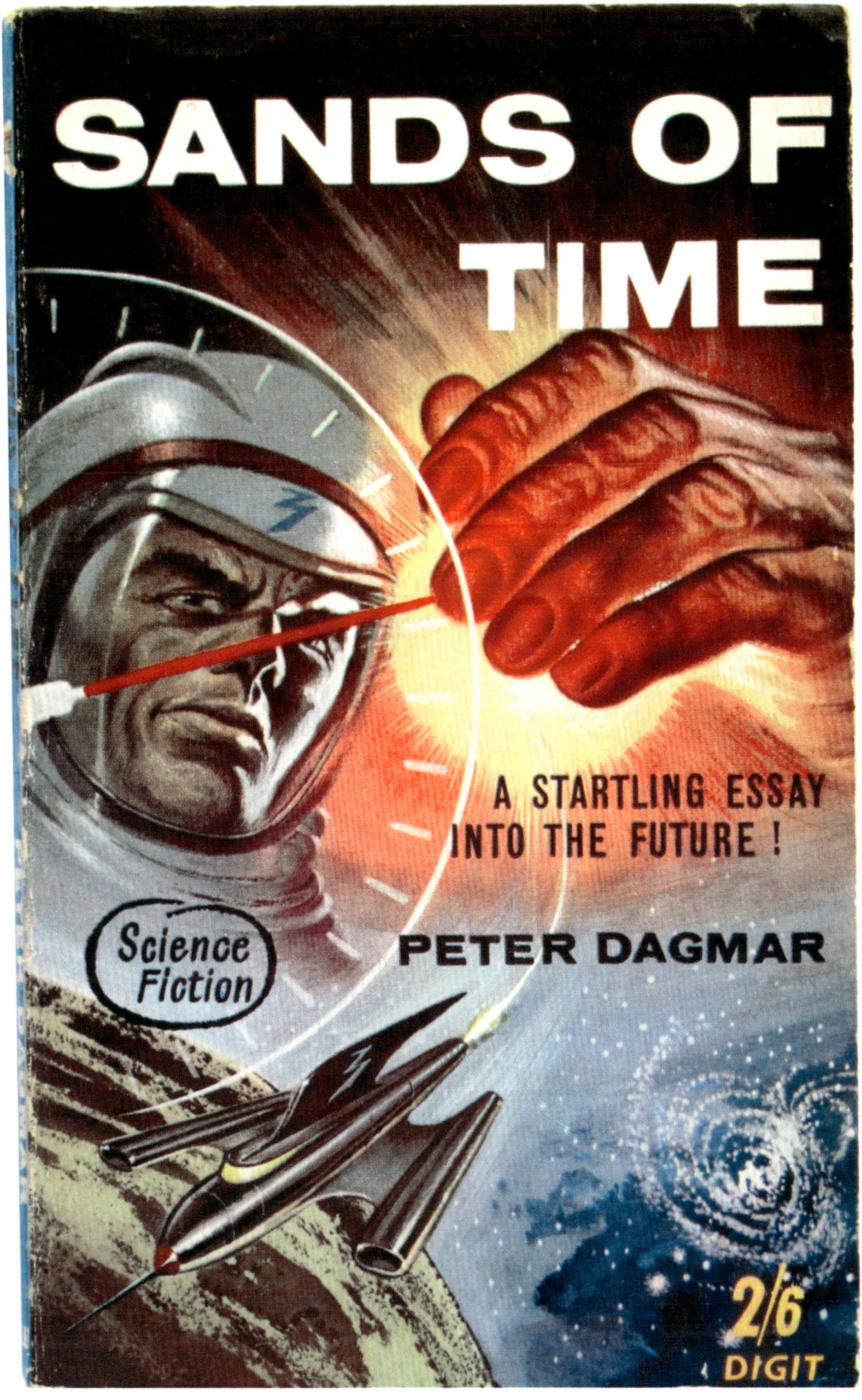

Peter Dagmar | *Sands of Time*
Digit Books R696, 1963 | Art **Unknown**

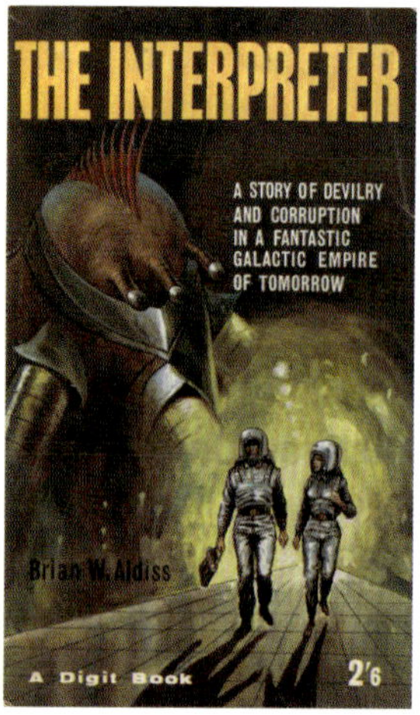

Brian W. Aldiss | *The Interpreter*
Digit Books R766, 1963 | Art **Unknown**

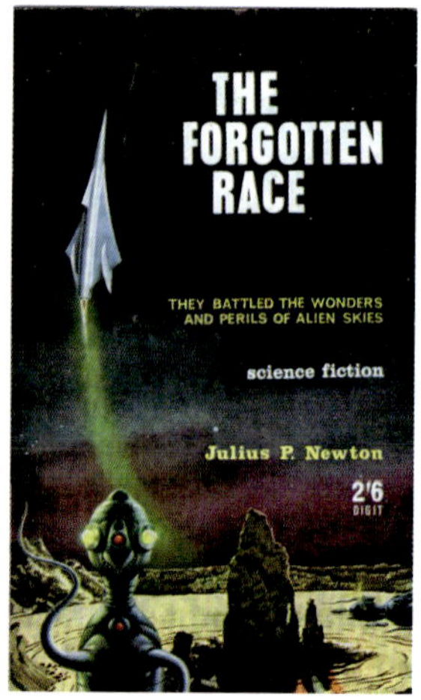

Julius P. Newton | *The Forgotten Race*
Digit Books R747, 1963 | Art **Unknown**

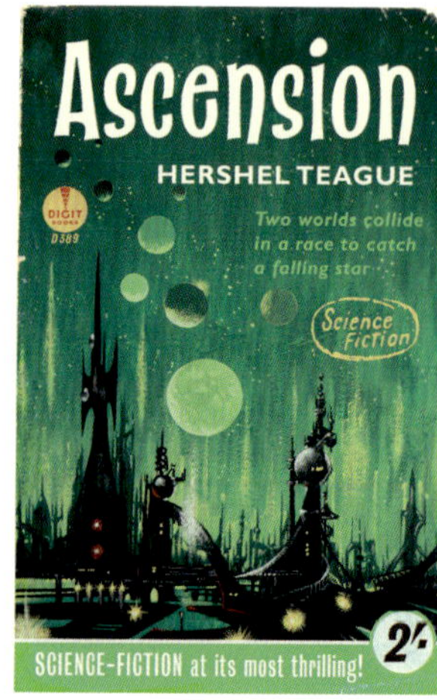

Herschel Teague | *Ascension*
Digit Books D389, 1960 | Art **Unknown**

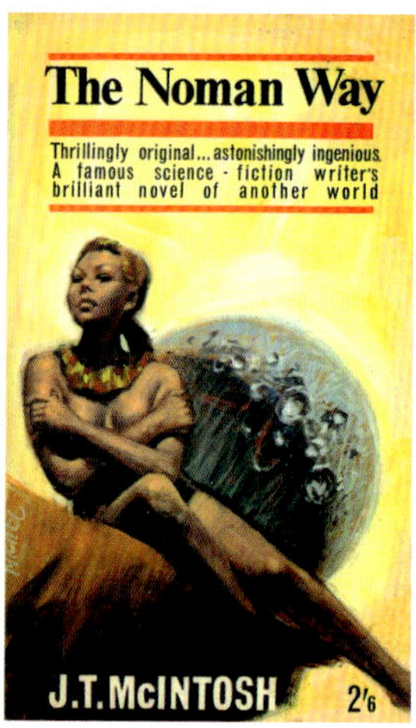

J. T. McIntosh | *The Noman Way*
Digit Books R882, 1964 | Art **Michael Atkinson**

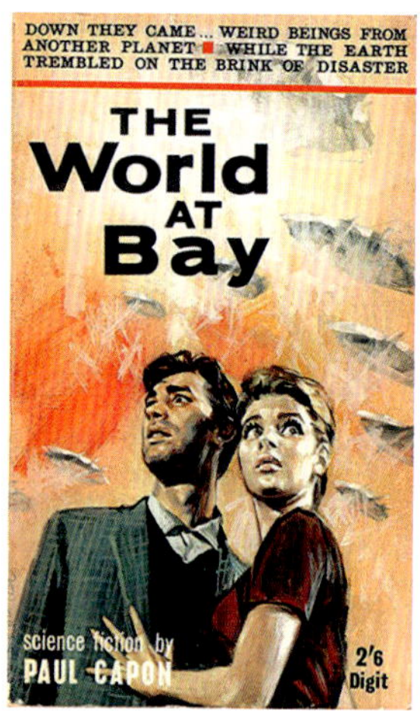

Paul Capon | *The World at Bay*
Digit Books R863, 1964 | Art **Michel Atkinson**

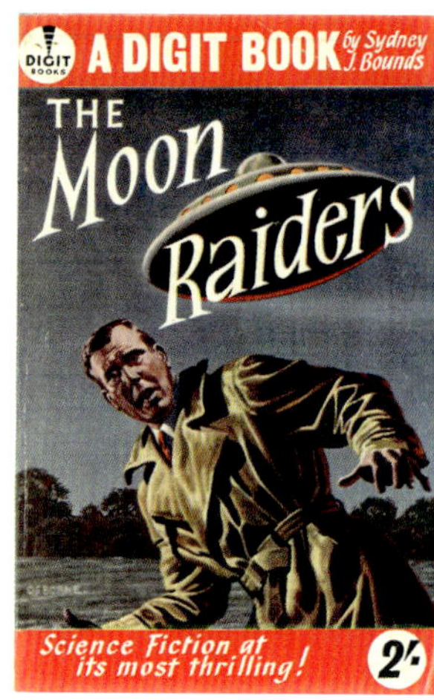

Sydney J. Bounds | *The Moon Raiders*
Digit Books, 1958 | Art **Robert A. Osborne**

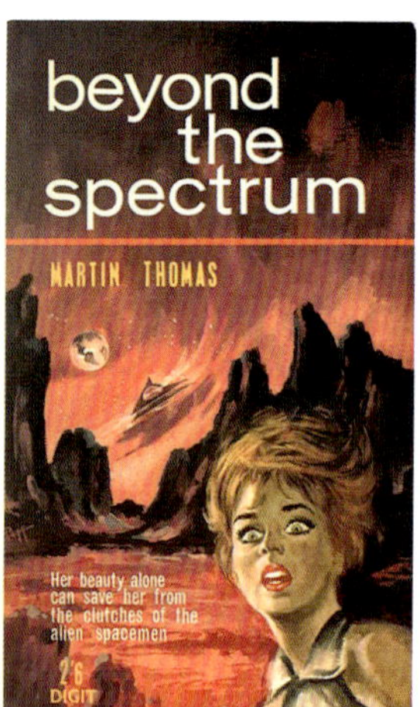

Martin Thomas | *Beyond the Spectrum*
Digit Books R864, 1964 | Art **Sam Peffer**

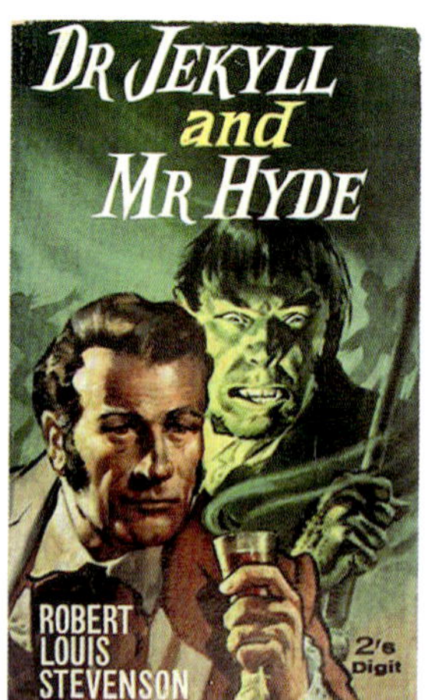

Robert Louis Stevenson | *Dr Jekyll and Mr Hyde*
Digit Books R581, 1962 | Art **James McConnell**

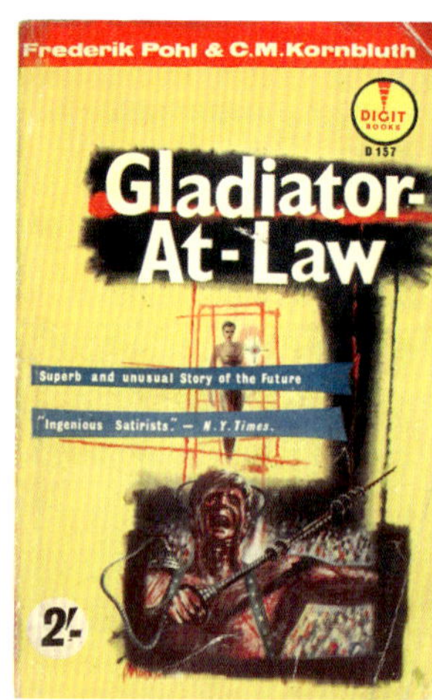

C. M. Kornbluth, Frederik Pohl | *Gladiator-at-Law*
Digit Books D157, 1958 | Art **Richard Powers**

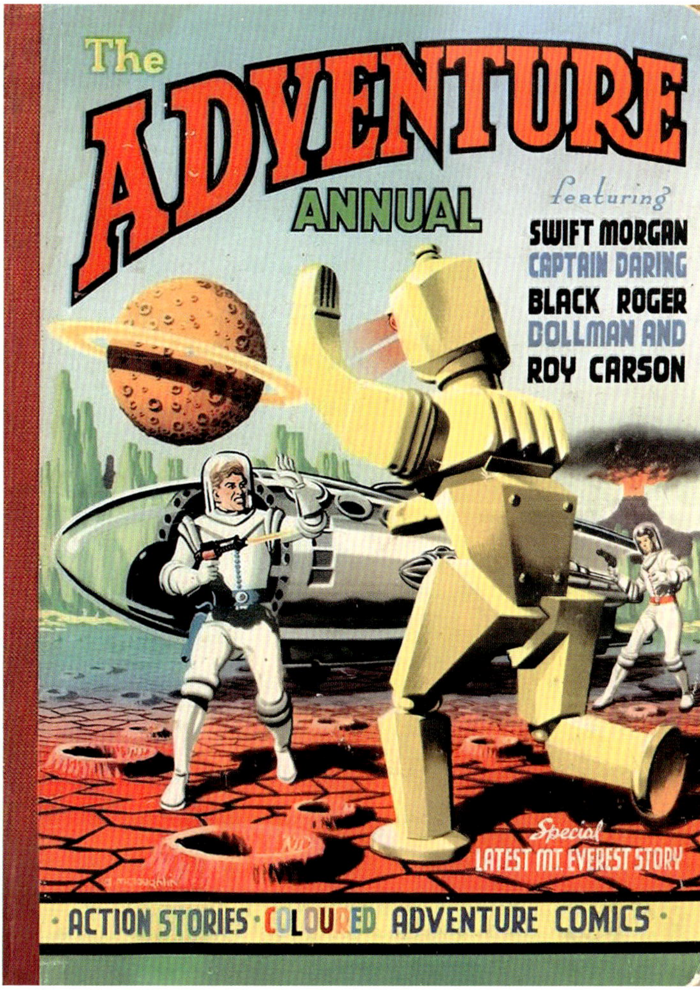

T. V. Boardman | *The Adventure Annual*
The Popular Press Ltd., 1953 | Art **Denis McLoughlin**

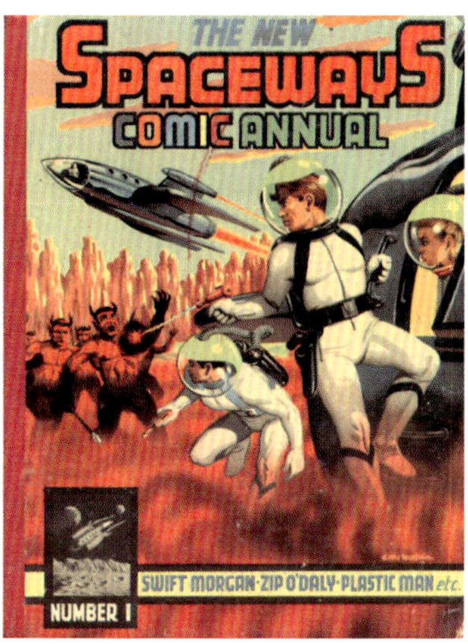

T. V. Boardman | *New Spaceways Comic Annual #1*
The New Popular Press Ltd., 1954 | Art **Denis McLoughlin**

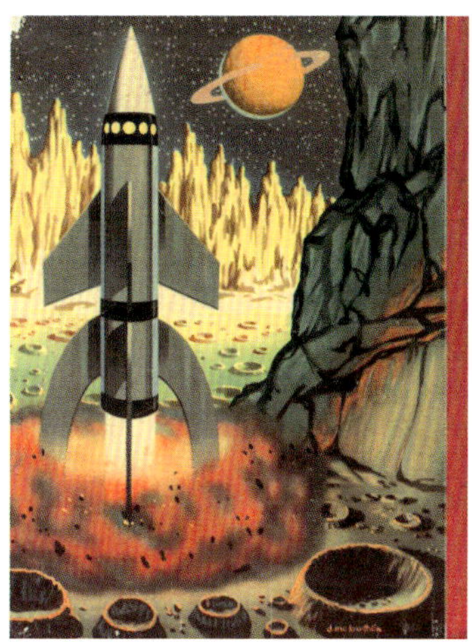

T. V. Boardman | *New Spaceways Comic Annual #1*
The New Popular Press Ltd., 1954 | Art **Denis McLoughlin**

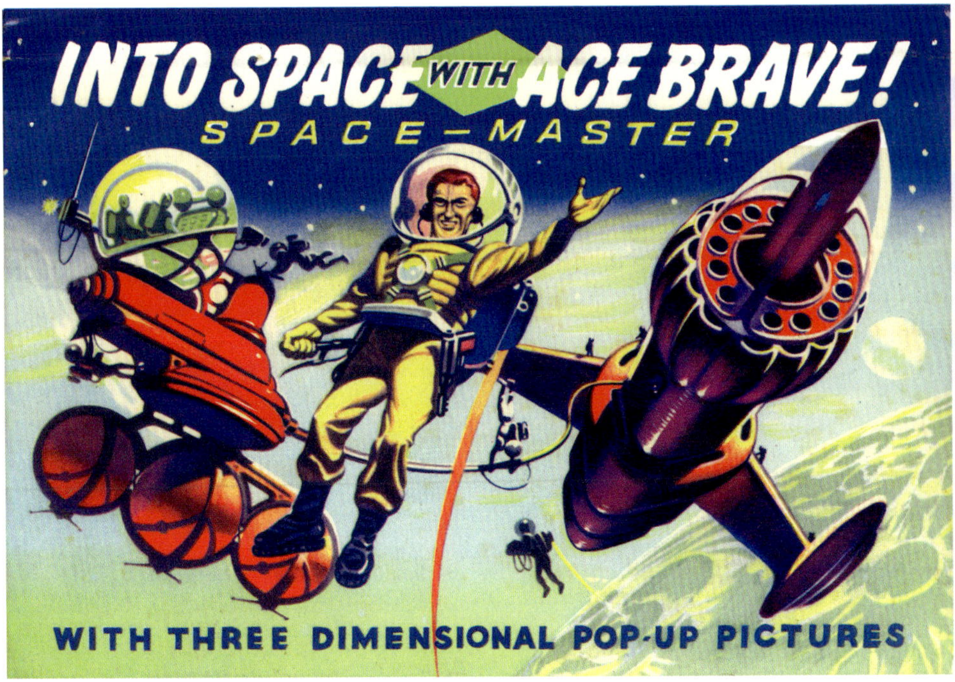

Into Space with Ace Brave, Space-Master
Birn Brothers Ltd., 1955 | Art **Ron Turner**

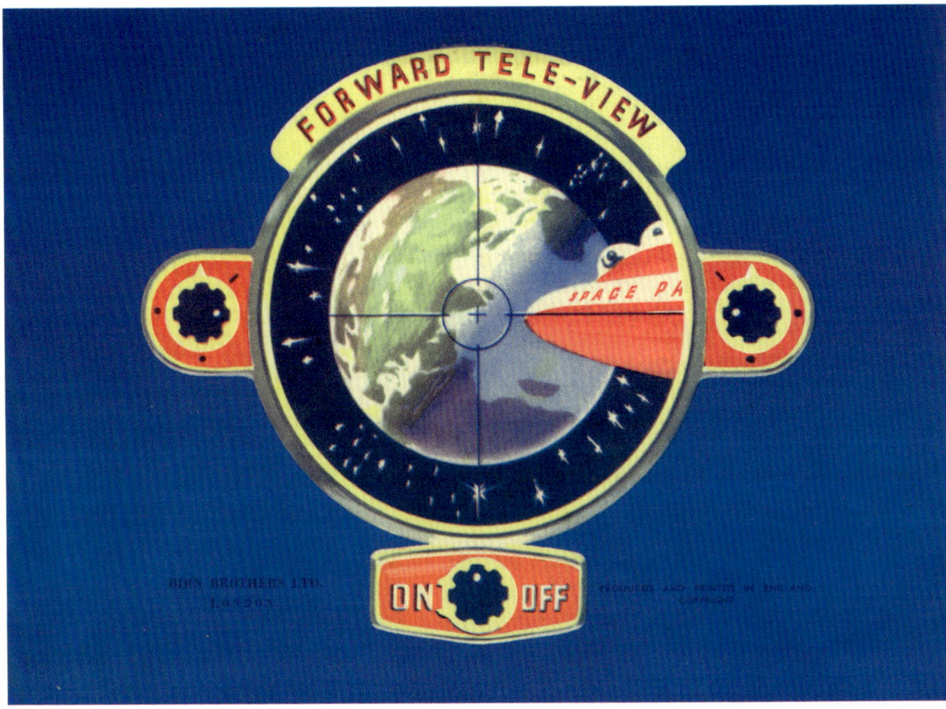

Into Space with Ace Brave, Space-Master
Birn Brothers Ltd., 1955 | Art **Ron Turner**

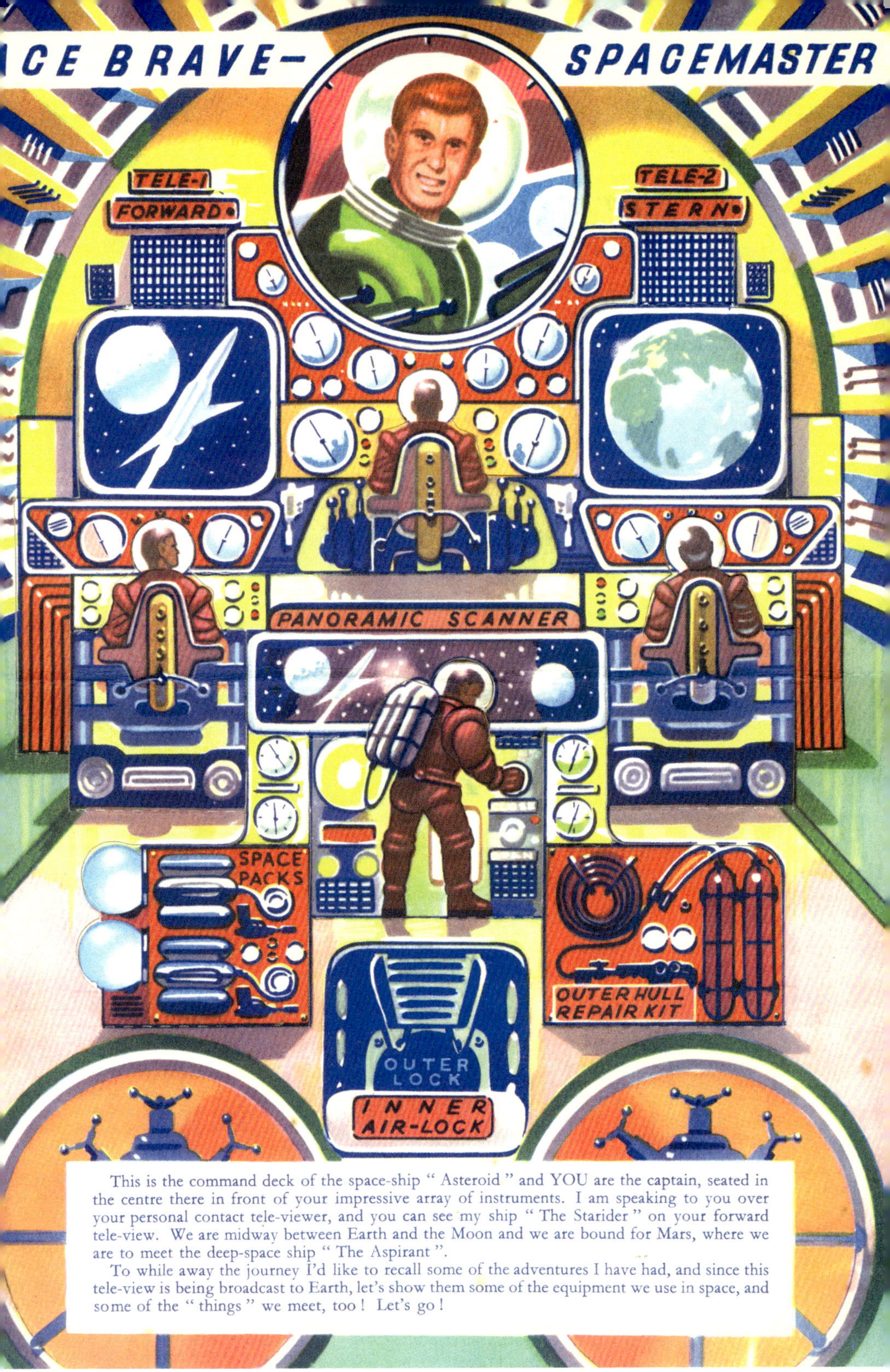

Into Space with Ace Brave, Space-Master
Birn Brothers Ltd., 1955 | Art **Ron Turner**

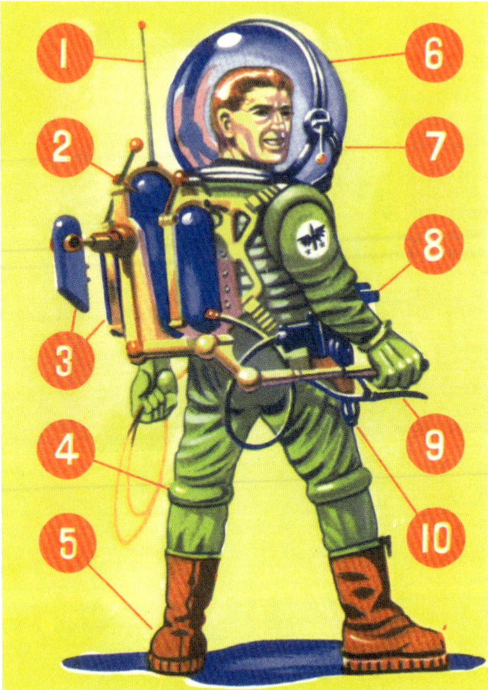

THE SPACE SUIT

First things first, and the first thing you need in space is a suit. Apart from its necessity for working on space pr (building space stations, etc.) it is absolutely vital for exam the outside of your ship in case of damage from meteorite It may even be necessary to abandon ship, in extreme cases in this event your very existence depends upon its efficiency. see me here in a self-contained, total-vacuum, mark-seven Below you will find listed some of its most important feat

(1) Radio mast of ultra short-wave radio.

(2) Compressed air cylinder of closed-circuit air supply.

(3) Jet on universal mounting and chemical-fuel containe

(4) All joints reinforced. A punctured space suit means d

(5) Reinforced plastic boots with electro-magnetic soles.

(6) Large universal-vision, anti-cosmic " Plastilight " helm

(7) Sealing ring to visor, metal with rubber " hose " l inflated from air supply.

(8) Miniature tele-view tray (referred to as the " T " tray

(9) Control stick to jet (3). Twist grip rotates jet for manœu in space.

(10) Hydro-ammonal container and feed line to flame gun.

THE WEAPONS OF SPACE

A. This is the Hydramatic Mark 4 Flame Gun, which you see me toting with the space suit above. It was developed by Professor Maklin Devonport of The Interplanetary Research Institute in 1995. The Hydramatic takes its name from the fact that it operates on a liquid hydro-ammonal compound, which is contained in a cylinder and fed to the gun via a feed line, which couples onto the gun at (a). Its lethal range in space is 2,000 yards – a useful weapon.

B. This is the Atomatic. It is rather bulkier than the " Hydra " but it has the great advantage of being self-contained. It fires .20-calibre atomic bullets; of course a .20 bullet in the old days would have been just about useless, but these, having atomic heads, produce spectacular results. I once saw a pirate ship (which was attacking transports on the Earth–Mars run) torn completely apart by a burst from one of these atom guns. The burst had penetrated the hull and hit the power plant; the pirates never knew what hit them!

C. Another type of atomic weapon, but working on the controlled-fission principle, the Radiumatic projects a concentrated radiation beam. Another " brain child " of our brilliant Professor Devonport, it is a much heavier weapon than the previous two, but proportionately more effective.

There is no recoil with this weapon or the flame gun and therefore great accuracy is obtainable.

The Radiumatic, when the front hand grip is removed and the tripod screwed into its place, is converted into an ideal weapon for ground use – in positions of defence, for instance.

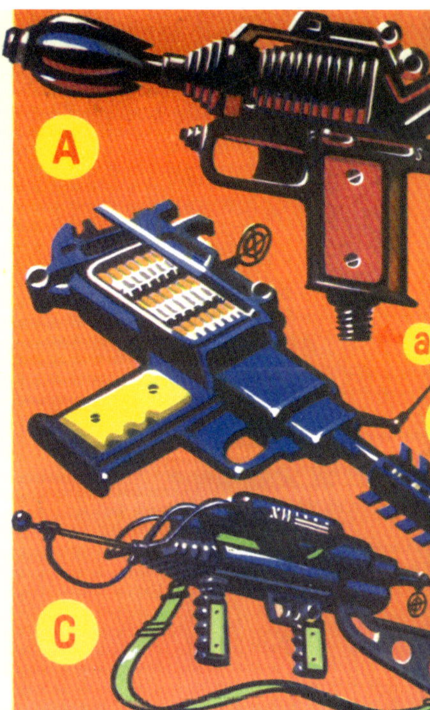

Into Space with Ace Brave, Space-Master
Birn Brothers Ltd., 1955 | Art **Ron Turner**

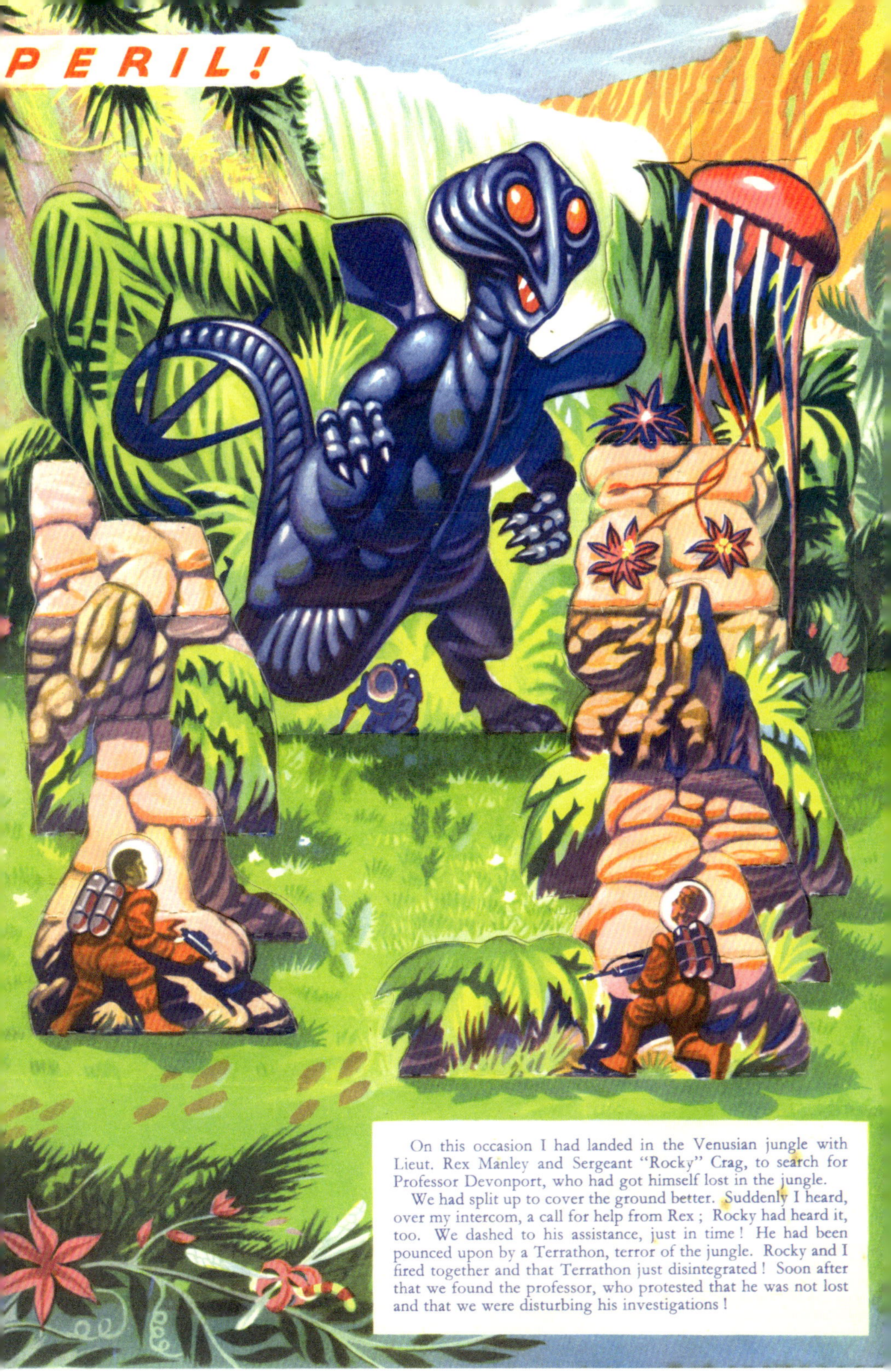

Into Space with Ace Brave, Space-Master
Birn Brothers Ltd., 1955 | Art **Ron Turner**

LIFE ON OTHER PLANETS—MERCURY

I led an exploratory force of three inter-orbital ships to Mercury in the latter part of 1991. An atomic fire broke out in one of the ships, when we had covered half the fifty-seven million miles. I transferred the crew to my ship when the fire got beyond control. In spite of this I decided to press on.

We reached Mercury without further trouble and circled the planet at orbiting distance. We were carrying with us a small satellite ship which was to make the actual landing. I boarded this with Lieutenant Manley and Sergeant Crag and we began the descent.

We landed on the termination line, where the temperature is more or less bearable. Mercury always keeps one half of her surface facing the sun, which is only 36,000,000 miles away, and the temperature on this side is that of molten lead!

Imagine our feelings then when we saw, marching out of the blazing horizon, a group of seemingly human figures! Mercurians! As we now know, they are a friendly, cheerful race, and considering the conditions under which they live this is remarkable.

Manley, Crag and myself soon made friends with them although, at this stage, we were only able to converse in signs. Now, of course, nine years after that first meeting, the people of Earth and the iron men of Mercury are firm friends.

Iron men is very nearly literally true, for the outer skin of these strange chaps is a thick tissue with a metallic base, protection against the intense heat.

The canopy and cape worn by the Mercurian on the right are used by them when Mercury makes its nearest approach to the sun, when even they need some extra protection.

That's me, sweating in the background in an asbestos suit!

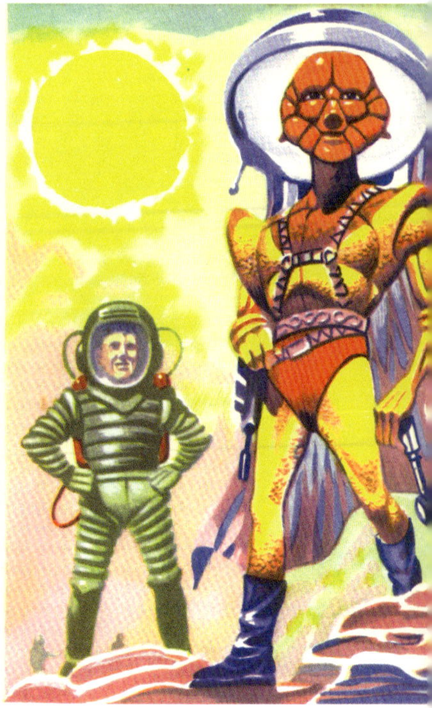

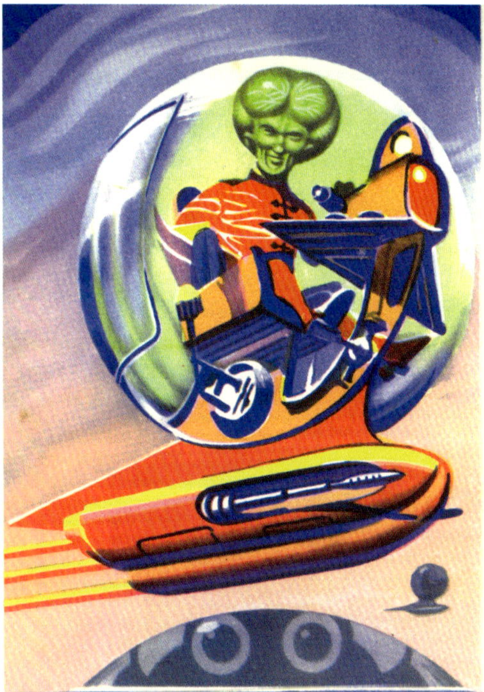

VENUS

We first visited Venus in 1982. This trip was made under leadership of Professor Maklin Devonport. I was with the Force Rocket Research Section at the time and was assigne the project. Sergeant Crag was on it, too. That's how I him and we've stuck together ever since.

The outward journey took us eight weeks; at the end of time we were circling down through the dense cloud layers w surround the planet. We orbited Venus ten times, emplo the dense atmosphere as an air brake to reduce speed for lanc

Suddenly we were frozen into immobility by a voice, gr and metallic, on our intercom system: "Hello, men of E Follow me and no harm will come to you. Do as I comman Then we saw them, six bubble-like craft which suddenly surrou us. The Professor decided to obey, wisely as it turned out wards, for the Venusians could have blasted us out of existe

We landed with the Venusians on the perimeter of a vast dc transparent structure, within which lay a city, Metharon, prin city of Venus and seat of Government.

Here we were interviewed by the Imperator, elected ove of Venus. He gave us to understand that the Venusians kne about Earth, had in fact visited it in the past, and now moni our radio broadcasts. "Go back to Earth," said the Impe "and tell them that whenever men come in peace we shall wel them but, at the first sign of hostility they will be destr utterly!"

Since then we have treated the Venusians with the respect merit and we have never regretted it.

Into Space with Ace Brave, Space-Master
Birn Brothers Ltd., 1955 | Art **Ron Turner**

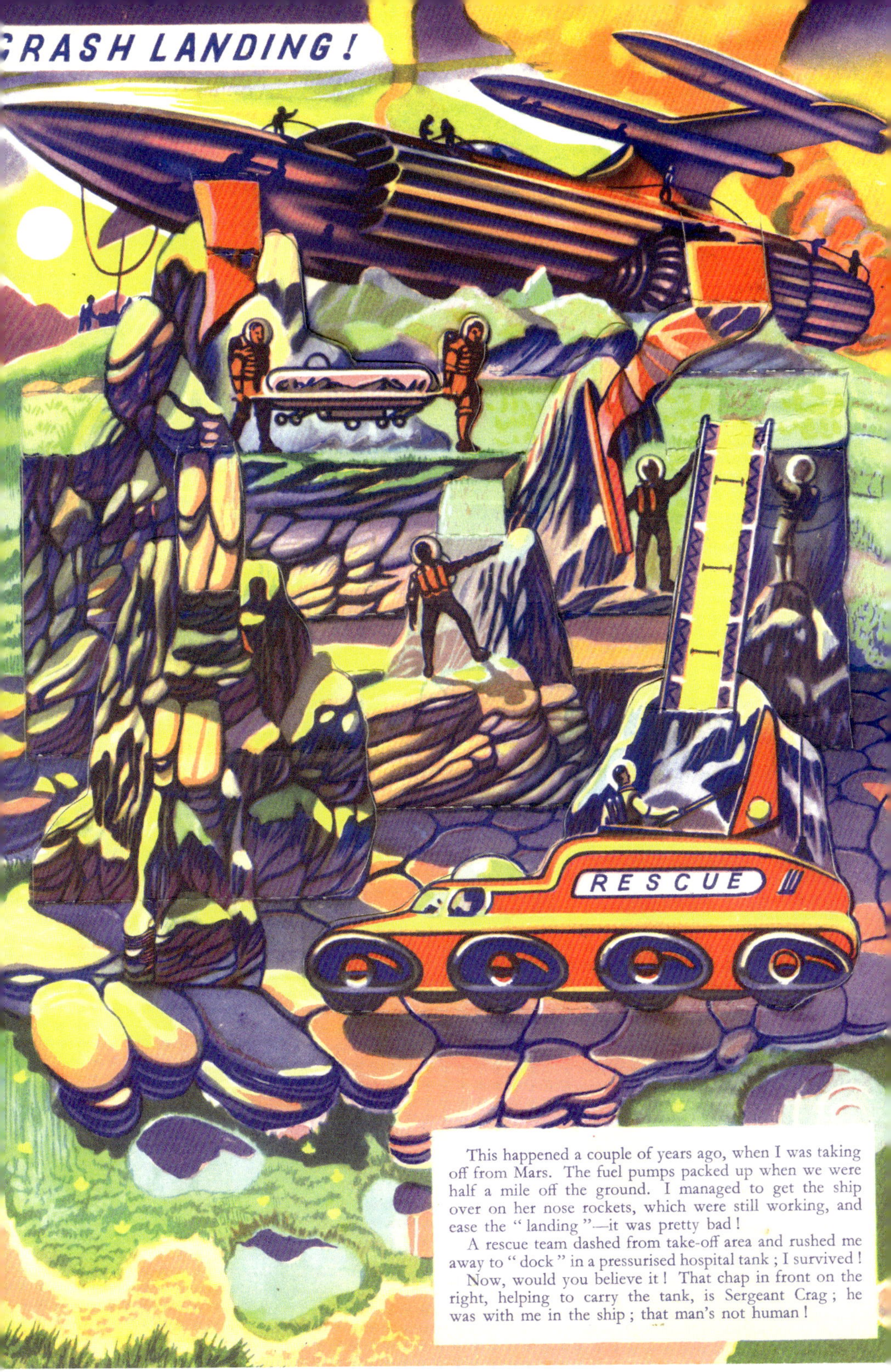

Into Space with Ace Brave, Space-Master
Birn Brothers Ltd., 1955 | Art **Ron Turner**

MARS

We visited Mars in 1982 for the first time. The expedition was made by three ships of the Space Fleet and I was placed in command as Space-master.

On this trip we had to face the peril of the planetoids. These planetoids are the scattered fragments of what was once Gylon, another planet having an orbit between Earth and Mars.

Countless ages ago this planet was blown up, scattering its debris in space just outside the Earth's orbit. The fragments vary in diameter from a few feet to, in the case of Ceres, 480 miles. When you are moving at anything up to 150 miles per second these obstacles in space can prove disastrous. One of our ships, the " Pallantine ", struck a small planetoid and vaporized before our horrified gaze. A hazard of space !

I decided to push on with two ships, and two weeks later we landed on Mars. The only sign of life was a thin scrub of vegetation which mottled the red sand. Then, in the distance, we saw a mushroom-like creature on stilted legs, with tentacled arms and a three-lensed eye—a Martian !

He raised a tentacle to his gun, then lowered it again and just stood staring while more of his fellows appeared.

The Martians surrounded our ships and for three days remained there, silent and unmoving ; the tension was horrible ! At the end of the third day the leading Martian thought : " Now we know you, Earthmen, welcome to Alkmenos." This was telepathy ; although he hadn't spoken we all knew what he had thought. The Martians had been studying our minds and it seemed we had passed the test. The Martians are good friends, but they would be formidable enemies !

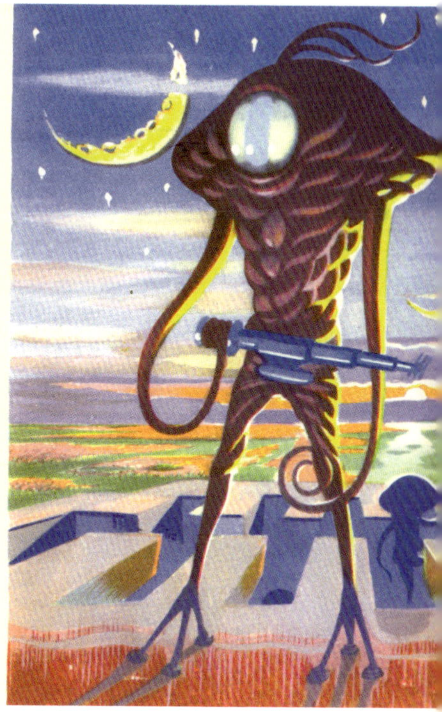

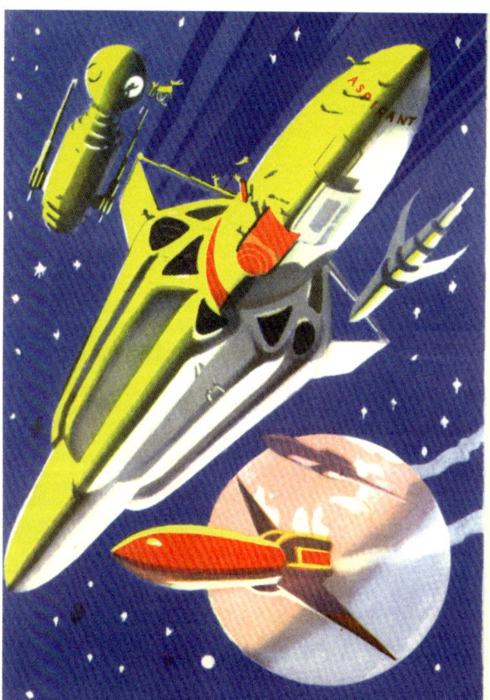

WHAT LIES BEYOND ?

Well, here we are at last ! There is Mars and there is the de space ship " The Aspirant ". As we draw near we see that is surrounded by space-suited men ; two transport ships are bring in last-minute supplies.

I am joining " The Aspirant " as commander. I know her w for I have watched her being built here in space on the Mars o I have just returned from a last-minute council meeting on Ear now we are all set to go on " Operation Deep Space ", the explo tion of the outer planets—Jupiter, Saturn, Uranus, Neptune Pluto.

Much of the credit for the design of " The Aspirant " must to the Martians and Venusians. Neither of these races had sp ships when we first visited them. Oh, they knew how, but no longer had a use for them ! You see, it was the Venus and the Martians who blew up Gylon. The Gylons had ideas ab conquering the Solar system but they didn't get very far. Venusians and Martian space fleets struck ; five thousand So bombs rained down on Gylon and the planet disintegrated.

To the victors, space ships were now no longer necessary ; other planet was even remotely far enough advanced to thre their security and they stopped building them. They looked u our aspirations with amused tolerance, but they supplied designs certain components for " The Aspirant "—and what a ship is !

Well, the cargo you brought from Earth in your ship " Asteroid " has been loaded into " The Aspirant " and you are ab to return to Earth. In twenty-four hours " The Aspirant " b into deep space. One day I'll be back to tell you—what beyond !

Into Space with Ace Brave, Space-Master
Birn Brothers Ltd., 1955 | Art **Ron Turner**

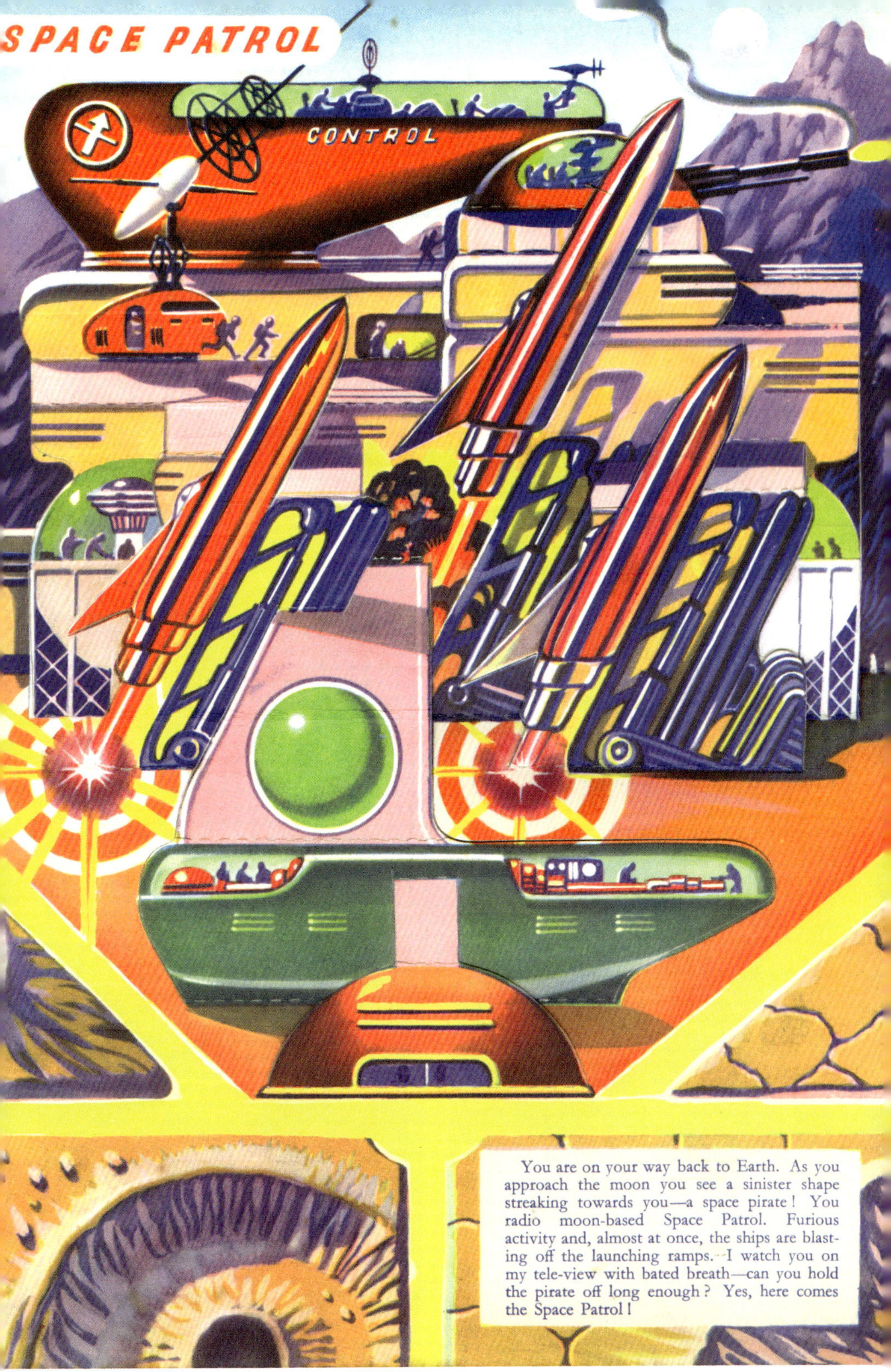

Into Space with Ace Brave, Space-Master
Birn Brothers Ltd., 1955 | Art **Ron Turner**

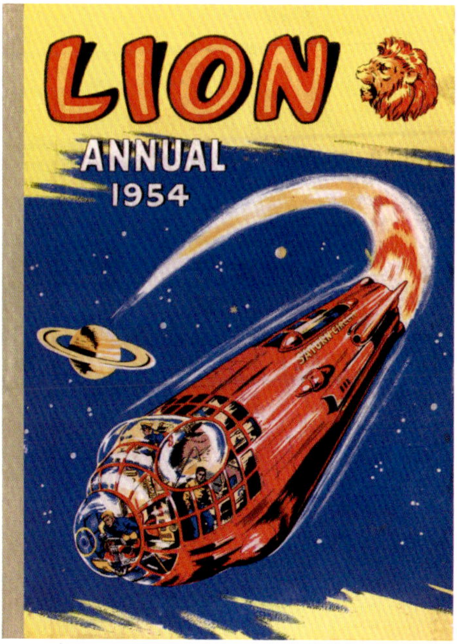

Lion Annual 1954
Fleetway, 1954 | Art **Ron Forbes**

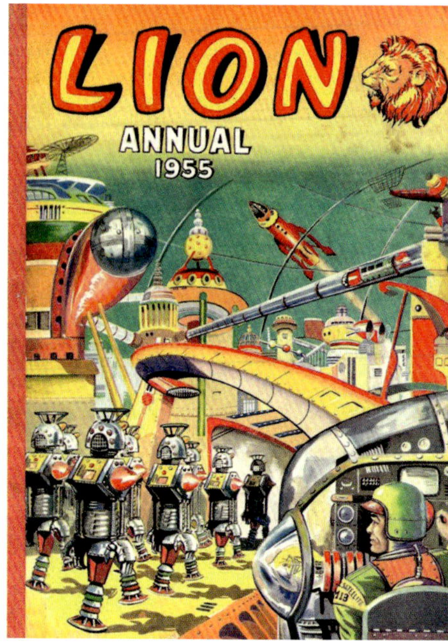

Lion Annual 1955
Fleetway, 1955 | Art **Ron Forbes**

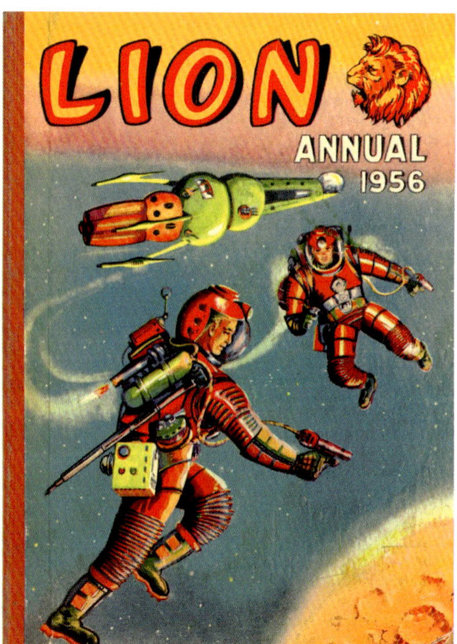

Lion Annual 1956
Fleetway, 1956 | Art **Ron Forbes**

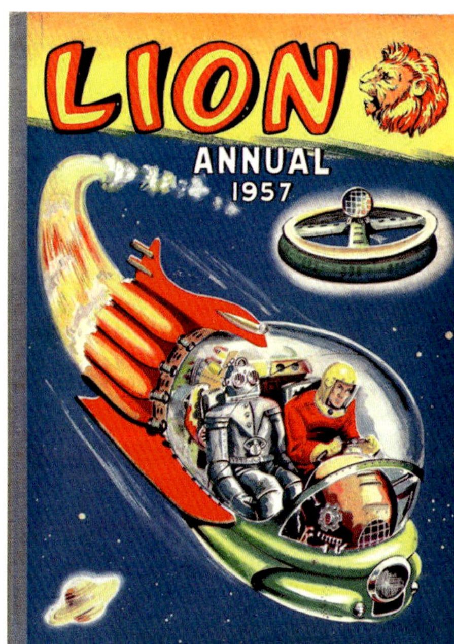

Lion Annual 1957
Fleetway, 1957 | Art **Ron Forbes**

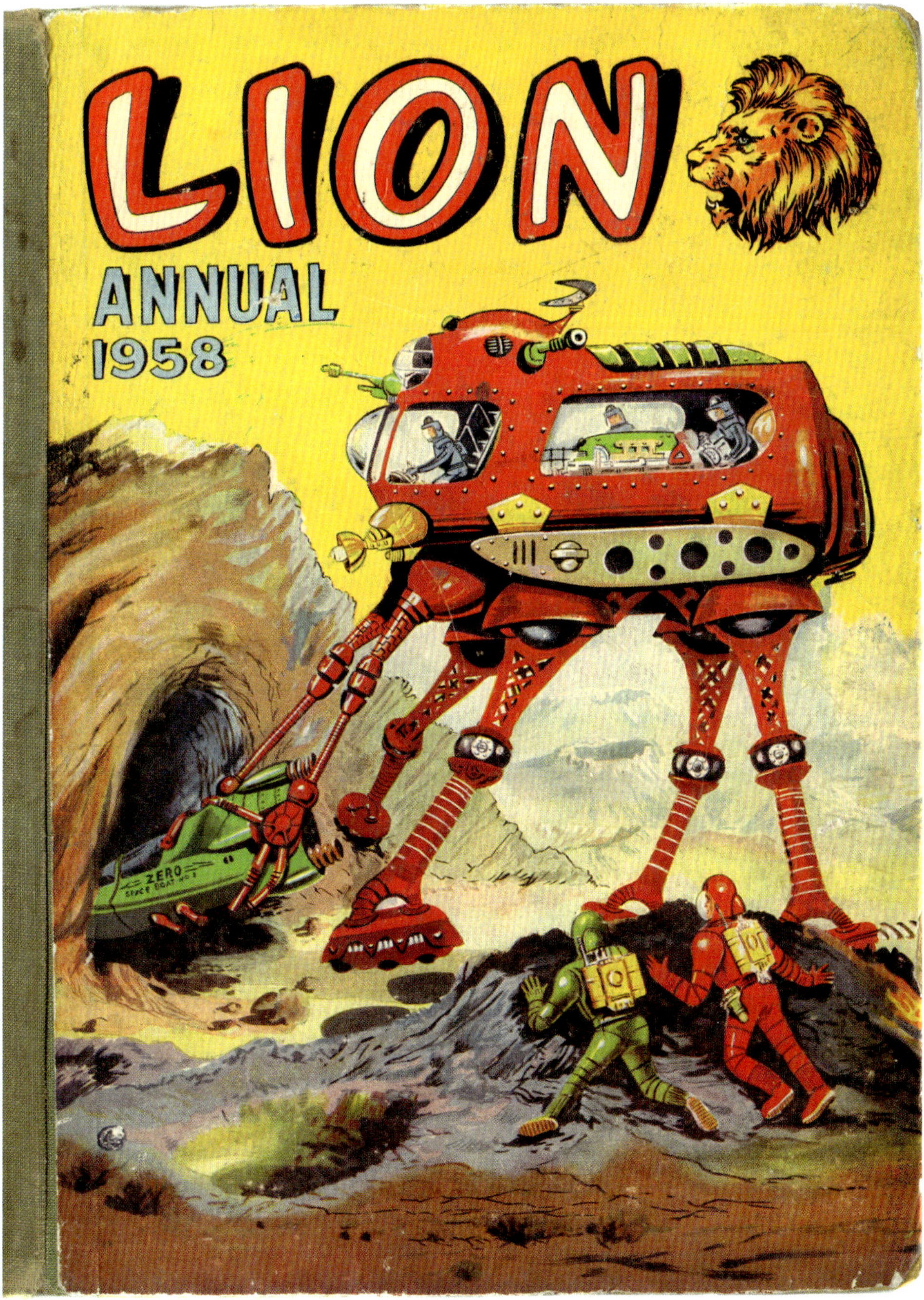

Lion Annual 1958
Fleetway, 1958 | Art **Ron Forbes**

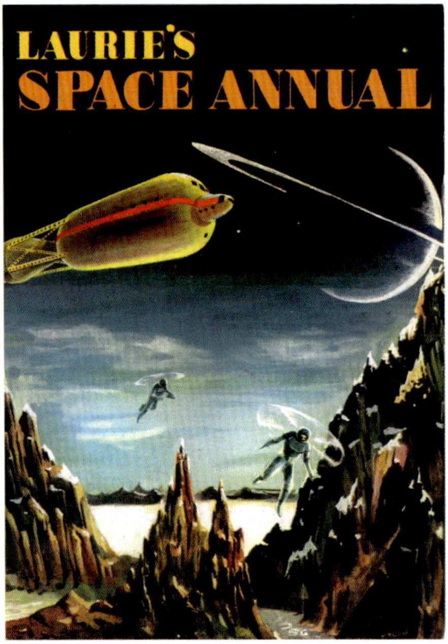

Laurie's Space Annual
T. Werner Laurie Ltd., 1953 | Art **Terry Maloney**

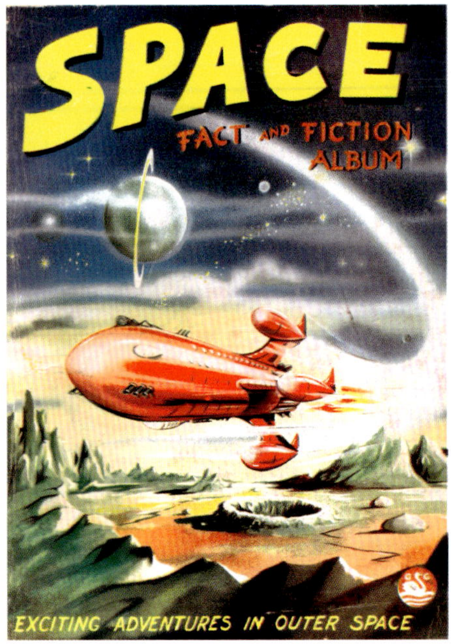

Space Fact and Fiction Album
Gerald Swan, c1954 | Art **David Williams**

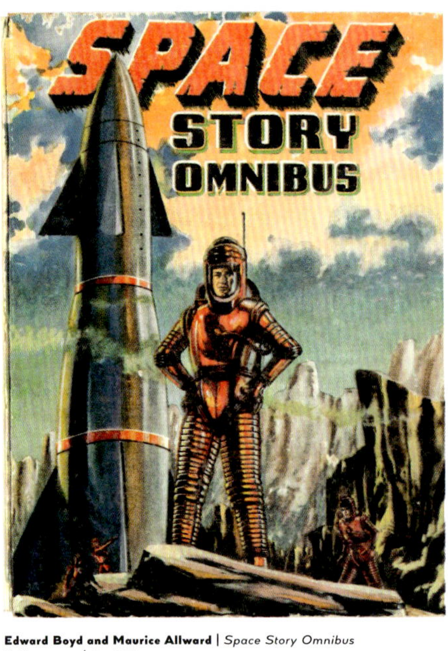

Edward Boyd and Maurice Allward | *Space Story Omnibus*
Collins, 1955 | Art **Unknown**

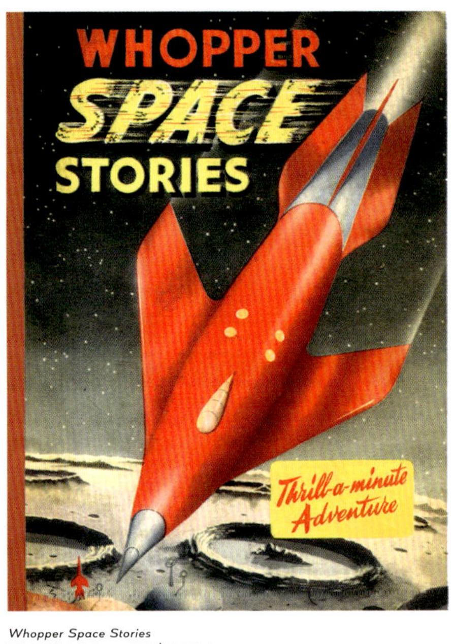

Whopper Space Stories
World Distributors, 1955 | Art **Unknown**

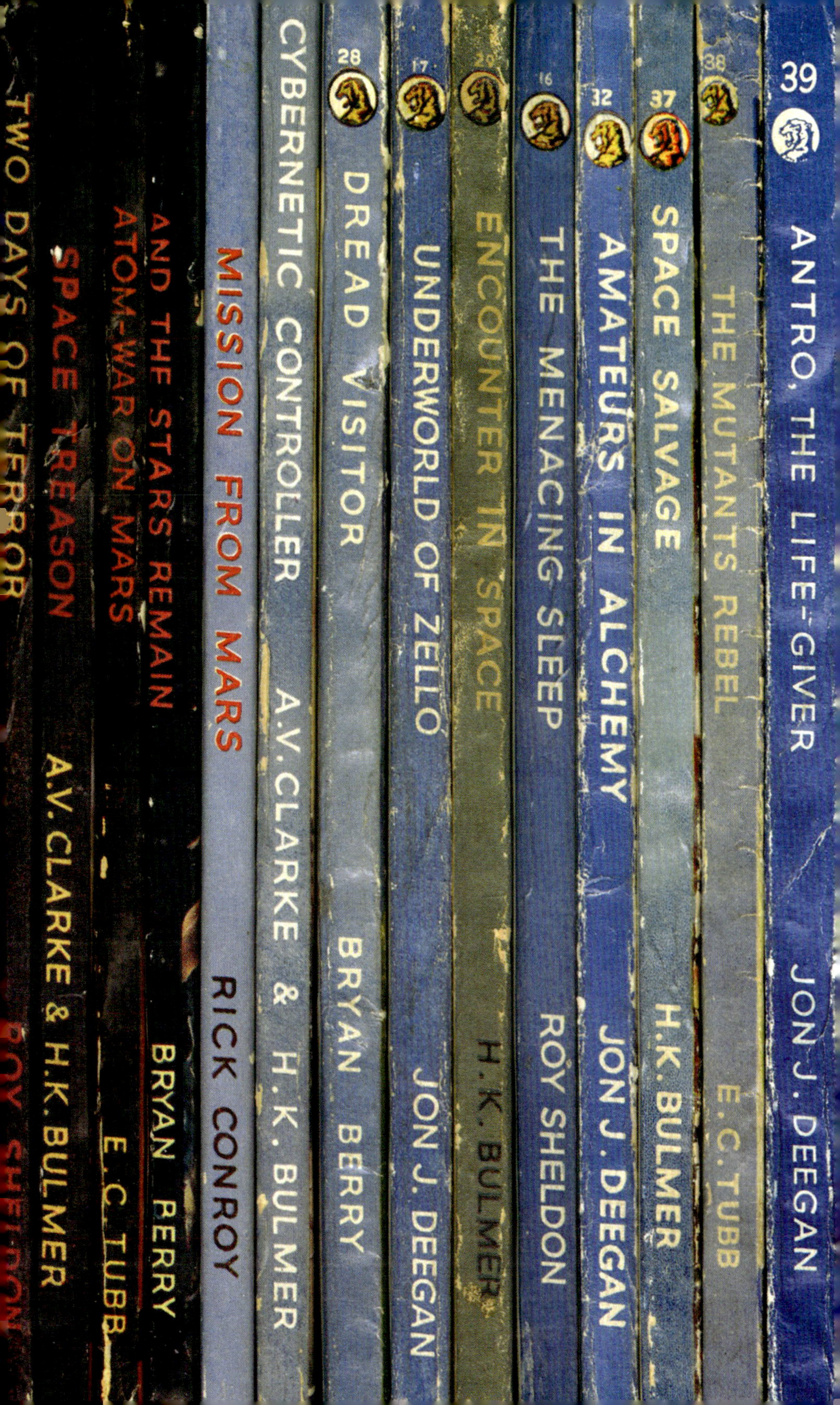

TWO DAYS OF TERROR
SPACE TREASON
A.V. CLARKE & H.K. BULMER
ATOM-WAR ON MARS
E.C. TUBB
AND THE STARS REMAIN
BRYAN BERRY
MISSION FROM MARS
RICK CONROY
CYBERNETIC CONTROLLER
A.V. CLARKE & H.K. BULMER
28
DREAD VISITOR
BRYAN BERRY
17
UNDERWORLD OF ZELLO
JON J. DEEGAN
29
ENCOUNTER IN SPACE
H.K. BULMER
16
THE MENACING SLEEP
ROY SHELDON
32
AMATEURS IN ALCHEMY
JON J. DEEGAN
37
SPACE SALVAGE
H.K. BULMER
38
THE MUTANTS REBEL
E.C. TUBB
39
ANTRO, THE LIFE-GIVER
JON J. DEEGAN

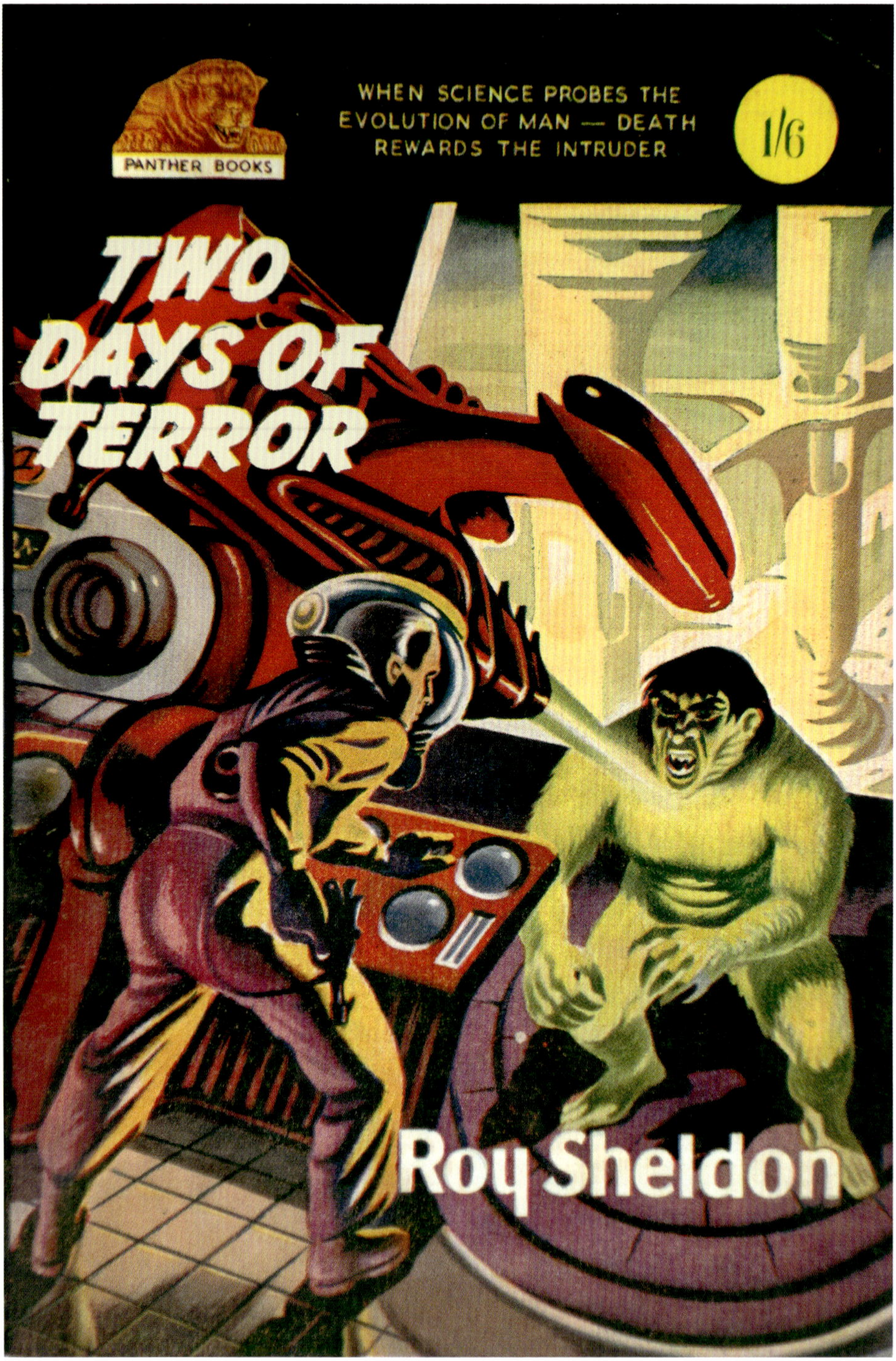

Roy Sheldon (H. J. Campbell) | *Two Days of Terror*
Panther Books, no number (#1), 1951 | Art **Ron Turner**

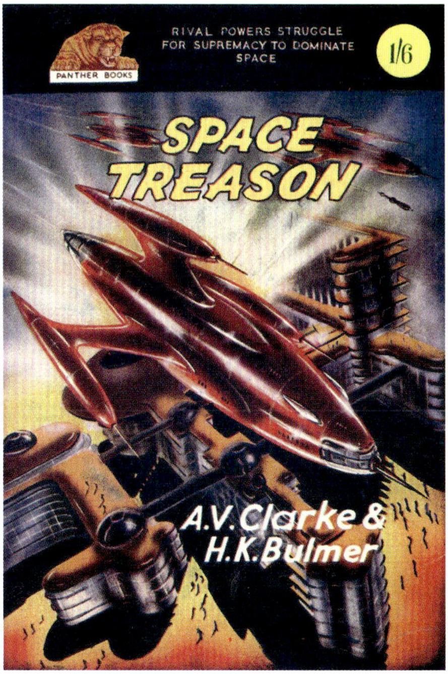

H. K. Bulmer, A. V. Clarke | *Space Treason*
Panther Books, nn, 1952 | Art **Gordon C. Davies**

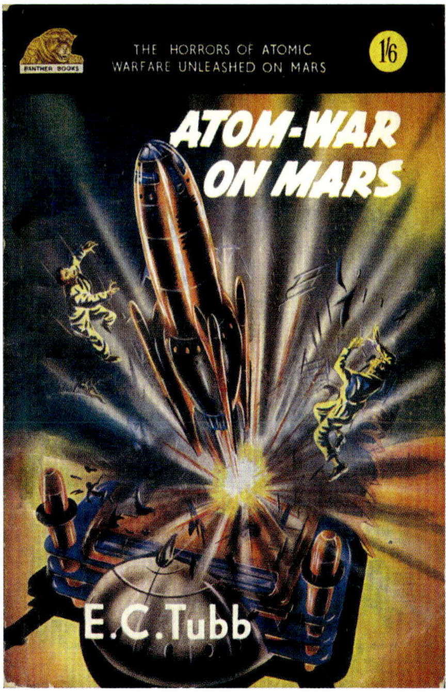

E. C. Tubb | *Atom War on Mars*
Panther Books, nn, 1952 | Art **Gordon C. Davies**

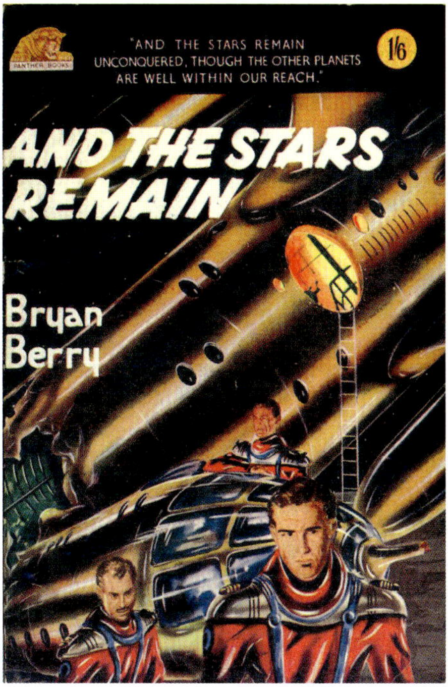

Bryan Berry | *And the Stars Remain*
Panther Books, nn, 1952 | Art **Gordon C. Davies**

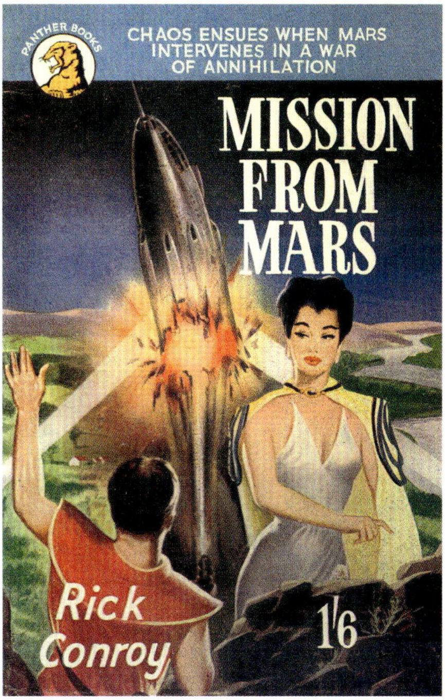

Rick Conroy (Richard Conroy)| *Mission from Mars*
Panther Books, nn, 1952 | Art **John Pollack**

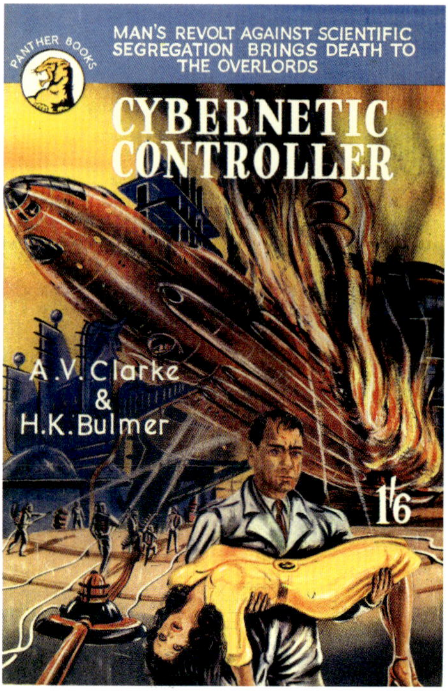

H. K. Bulmer, A. V. Clarke | *Cybernetic Controller*
Panther Books, nn, 1952 | Art **Gordon C. Davies**

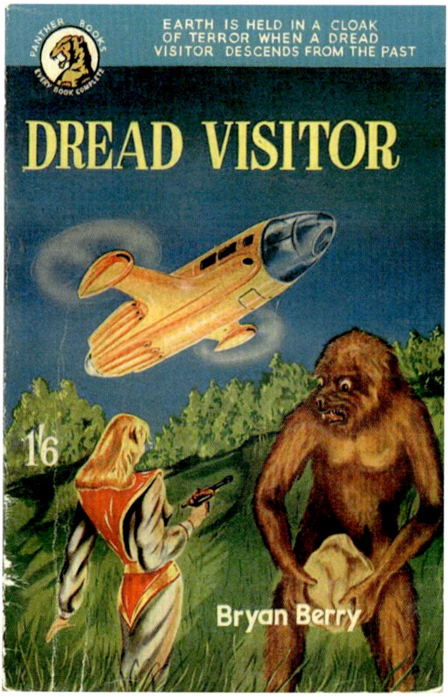

Bryan Berry | *Dread Visitor*
Panther Books, nn, 1952 | Art **Gordon C. Davies**

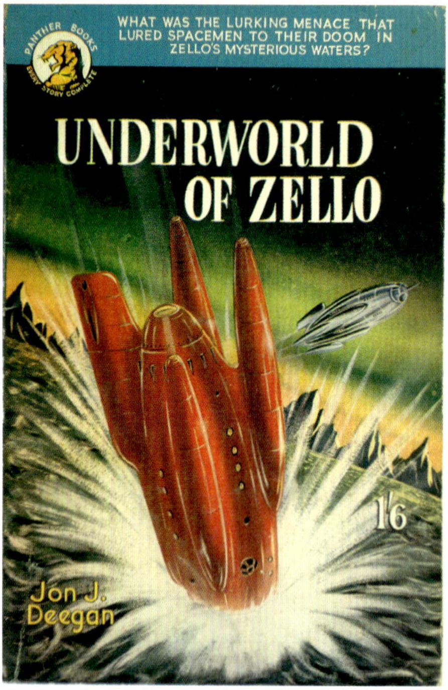

Jon J. Deegan (Robert G. Sharp) | *Underworld of Zello*
Panther Books, #17, 1952 | Art **Gordon C. Davies**

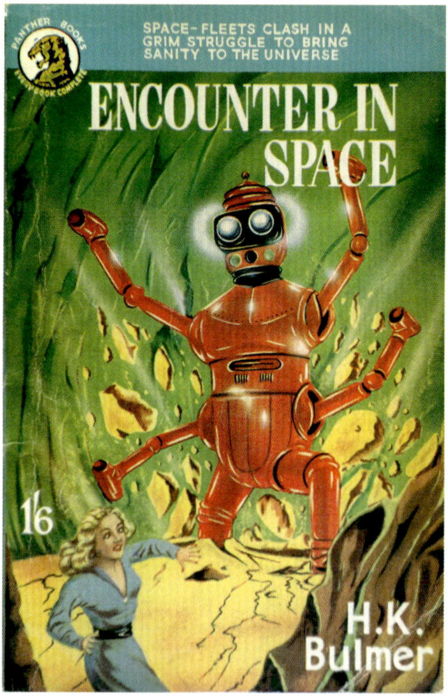

H. K. Bulmer | *Encounter in Space*
Panther Books, #29, 1952 | Art **Gordon C. Davies**

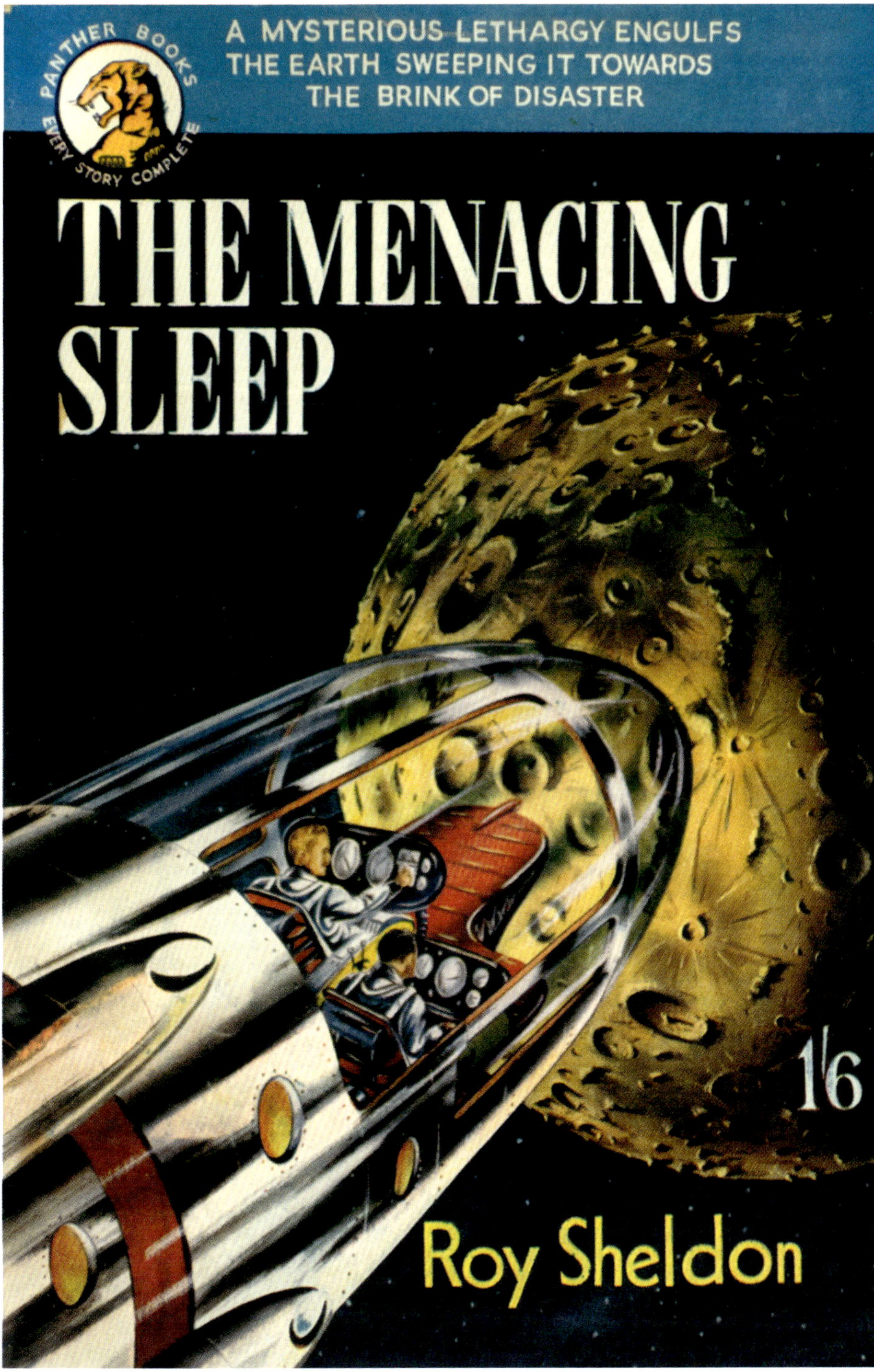

Roy Sheldon (H. J. Campbell) | *The Menacing Sleep*
Panther Books #16, 1952 | Art **Gordon C. Davies**

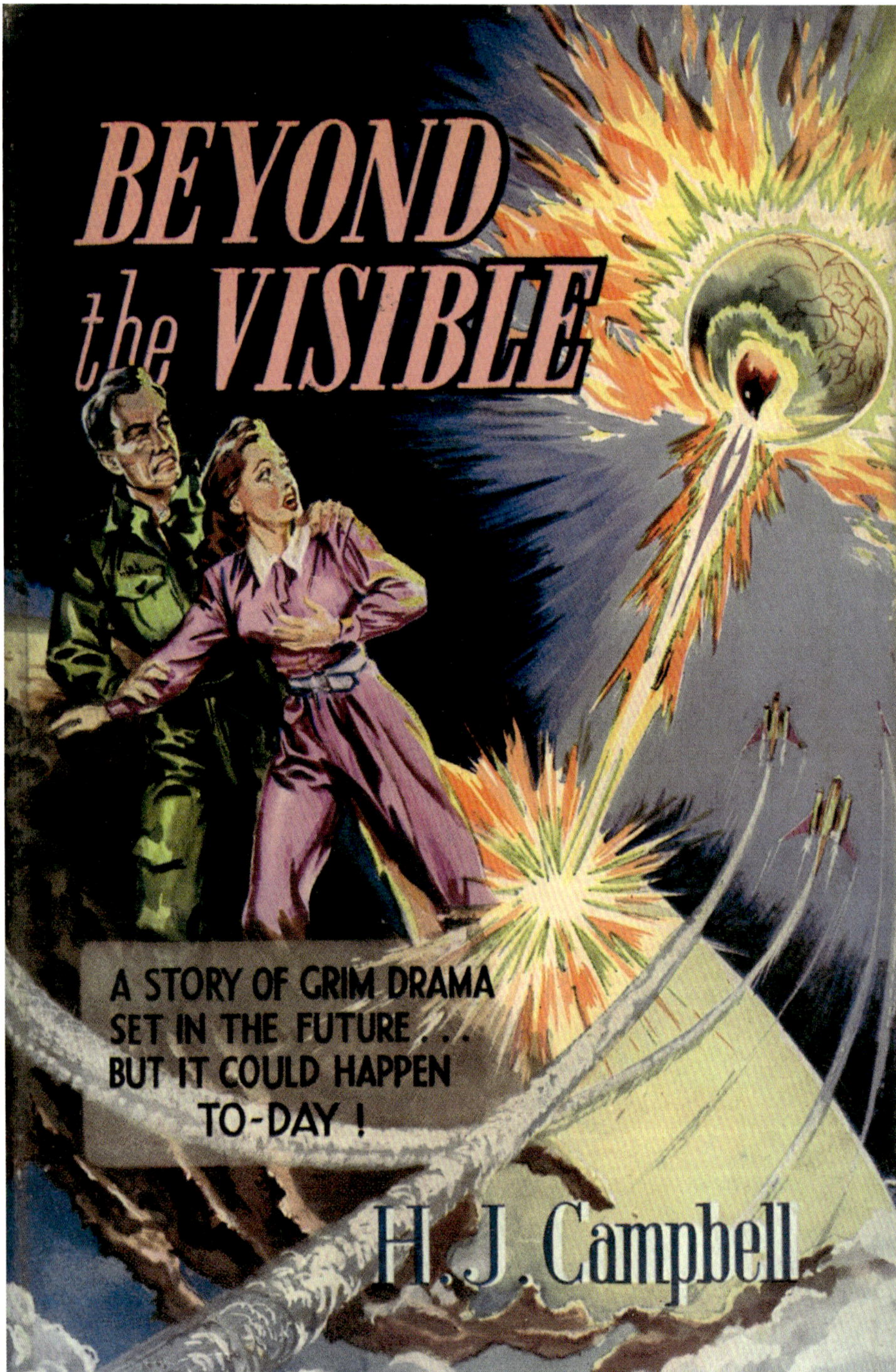

H. J. Campbell | *Beyond the Visible*
Hamilton & Co. (non-numbered Panther?), 1952 | Art **George Ratcliffe**

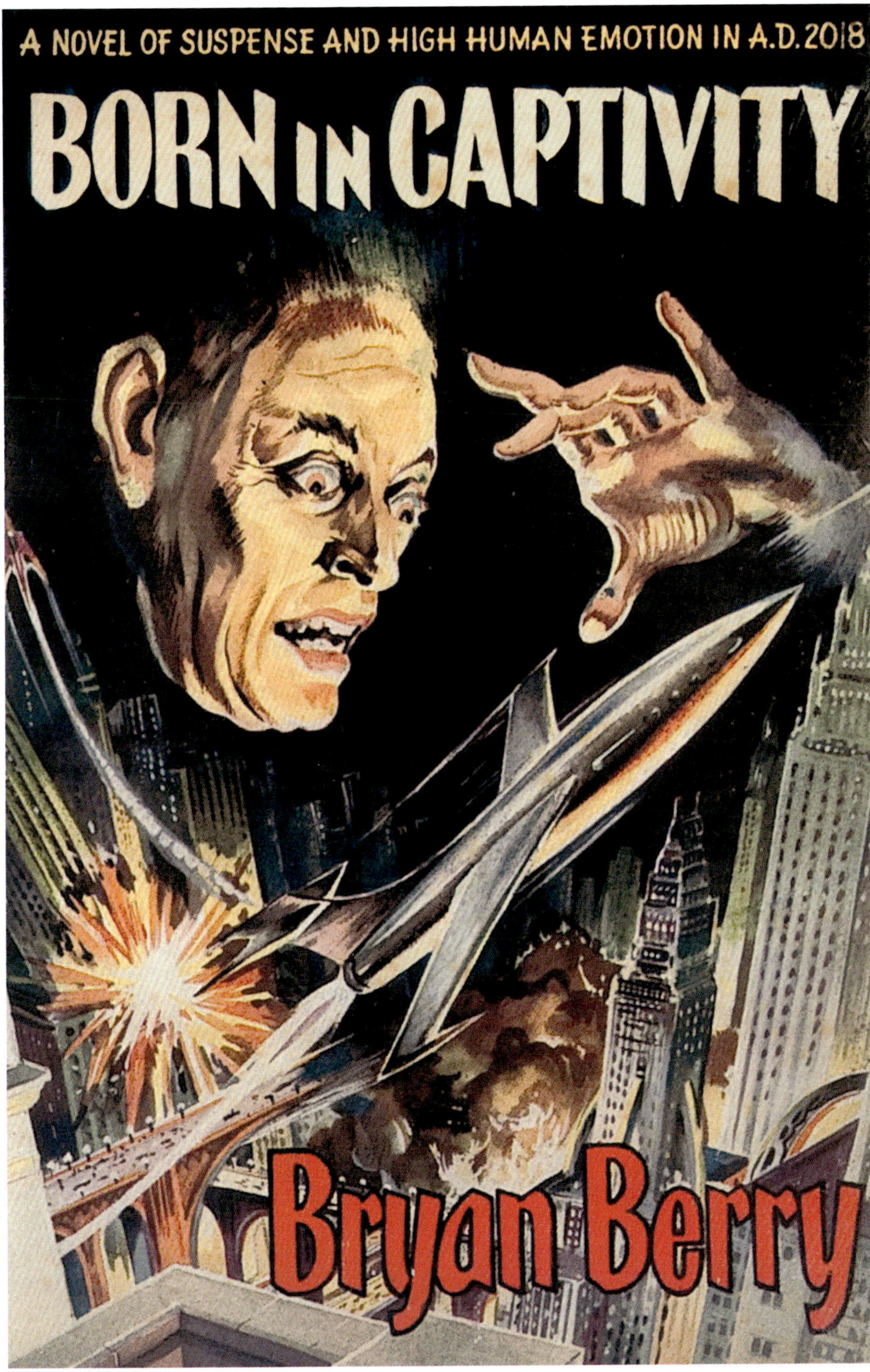

Bryan Berry | *Born in Captivity*
Hamilton & Co. (non-numbered Panther?), 1952 | Art **George Ratcliffe**

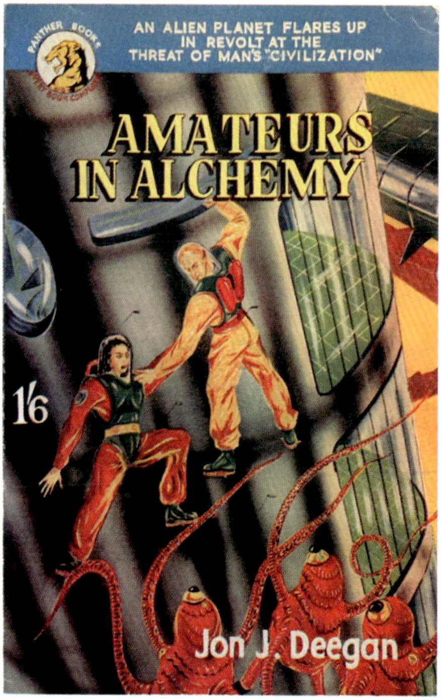

Jon J. Deegan (Robert G. Sharp) | *Amateurs in Alchemy*
Panther Books #32, 1952 | Art **Gordon C. Davies**

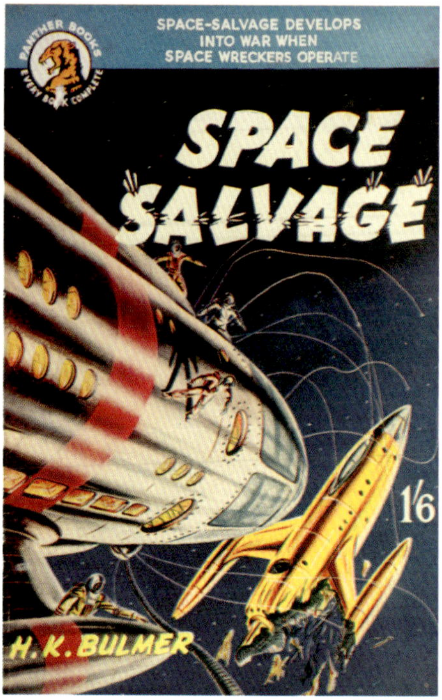

H. K. Bulmer | *Space Salvage*
Panther Books #37, 1953 | Art **Gordon C. Davies**

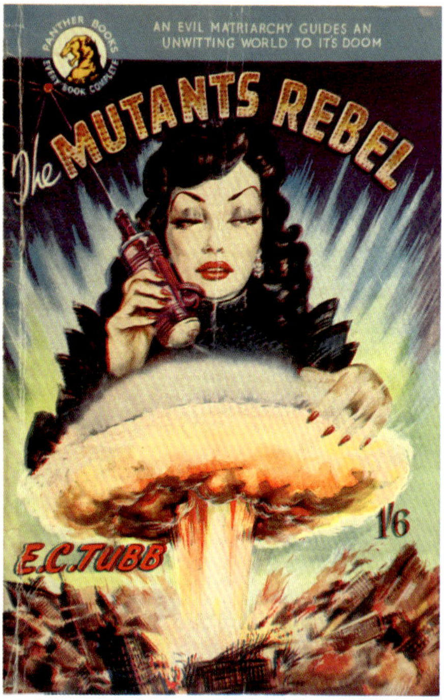

E. C. Tubb | *The Mutants Rebel*
Panther Books #38, 1953 | Art **Vann**

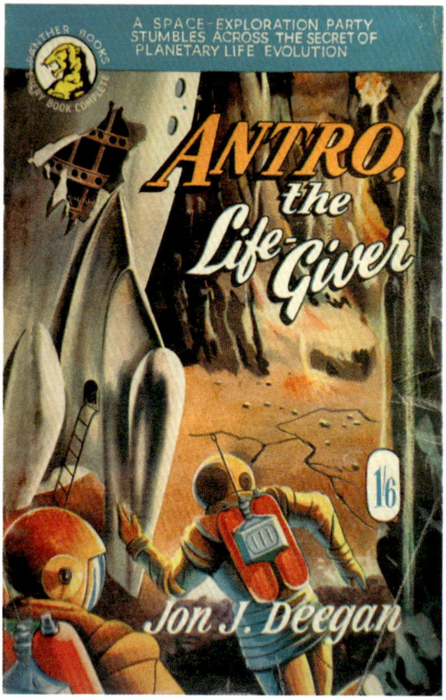

Jon J. Deegan (Robert G. Sharp) | *Antro, the Life-Giver*
Panther Books #39, 1953 | Art **George Ratcliffe**

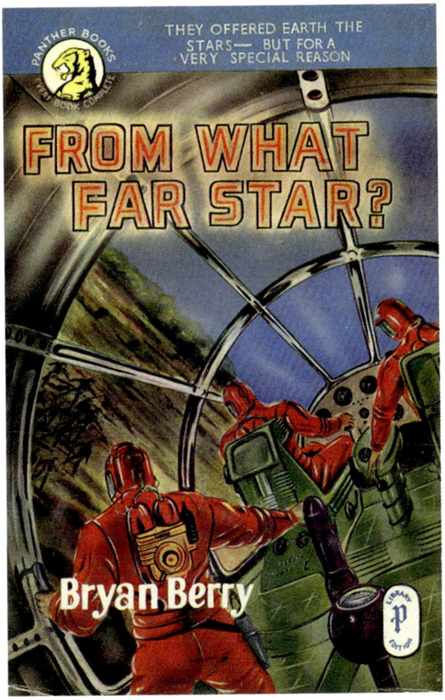

Bryan Berry | *From What Far Star?*
Panther Books #40, 1953 | Art **Gordon C. Davies**

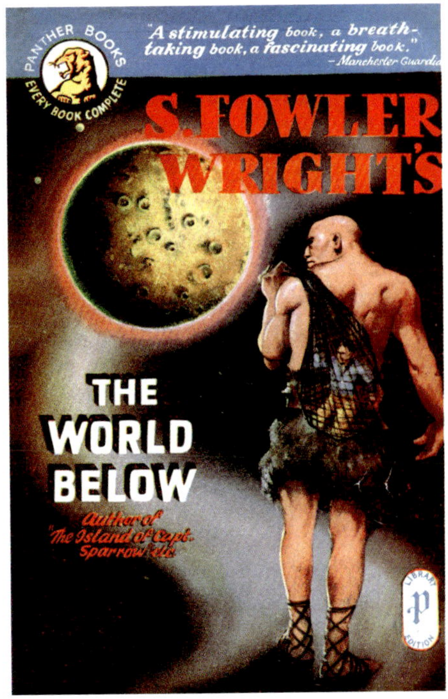

S. Fowler Wright | *The World Below*
Panther Books #44, 1953 | Art **John Richards**

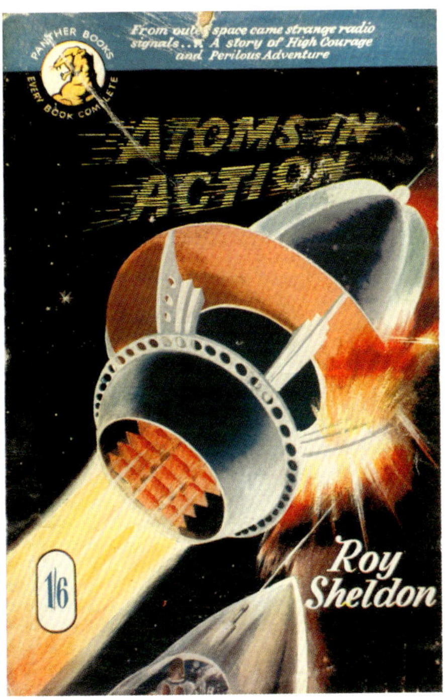

Roy Sheldon (H. J. Campbell) | *Atoms in Action*
Panther Books #47, 1953 | Art **Gordon C. Davies**

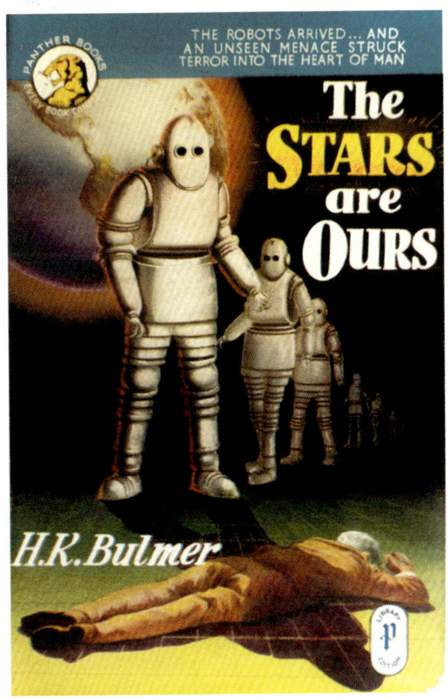

H. K. Bulmer | *The Stars Are Ours*
Panther Books #48, 1953 | Art **John Richards**

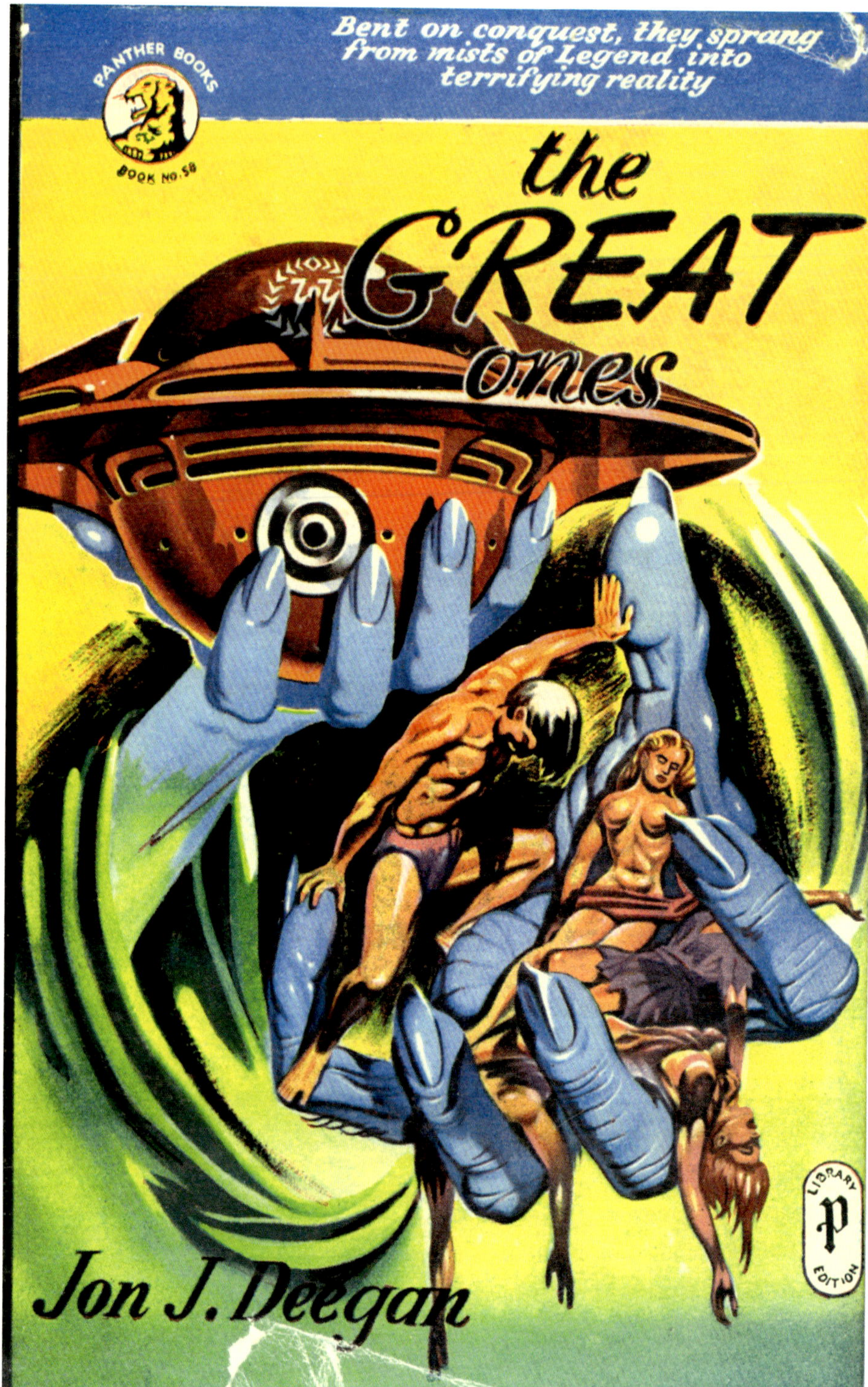

Jon J. Deegan (Robert G. Sharp) | *The Great Ones*
Panther Books #58, 1953 | Art **Ron Turner**

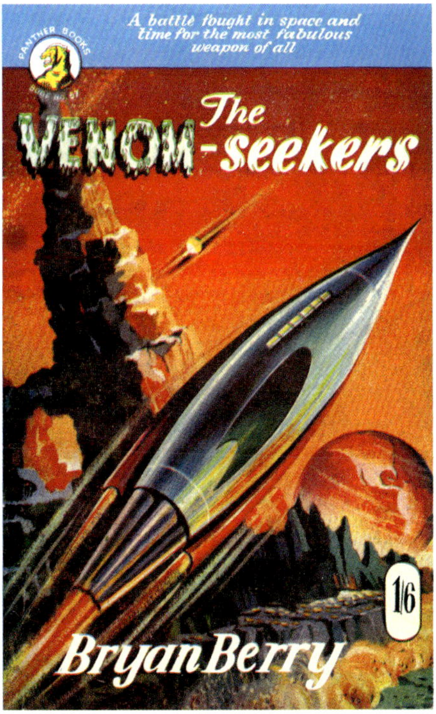

Bryan Berry | *The -Seekers*
Panther Books #57, 1953 | Art **George Ratcliffe**

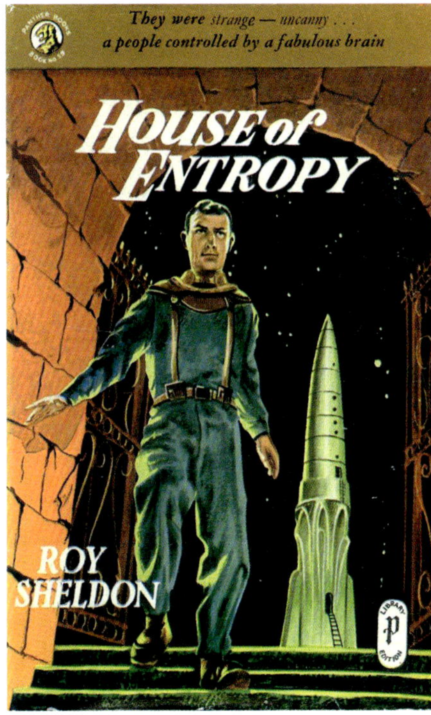

Roy Sheldon (H. J. Campbell) | *House of Entropy*
Panther Books #59, 1953 | Art **John Richards**

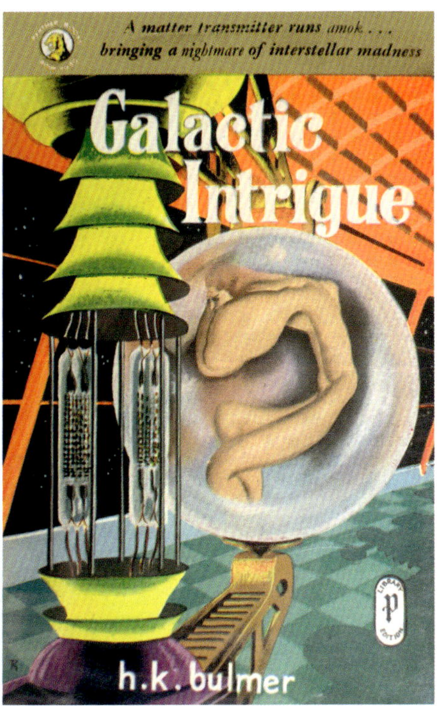

H. K. Bulmer | *Galactic Intrigue*
Panther Books #60, 1953 | Art **John Richards**

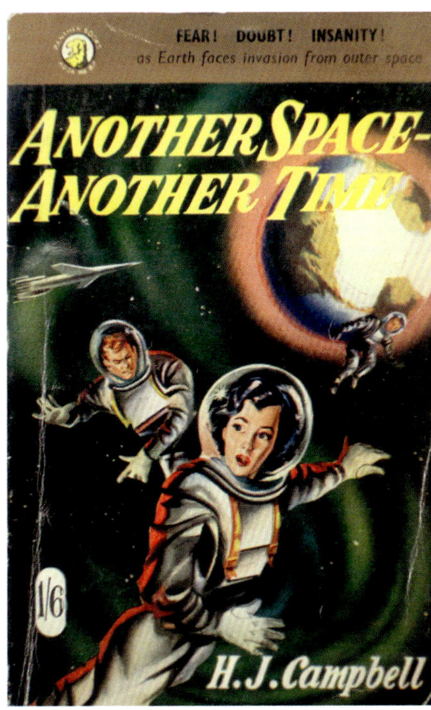

H. J. Campbell | *Another Space - Another Time*
Panther Books #67, 1953 | Art **John Richards**

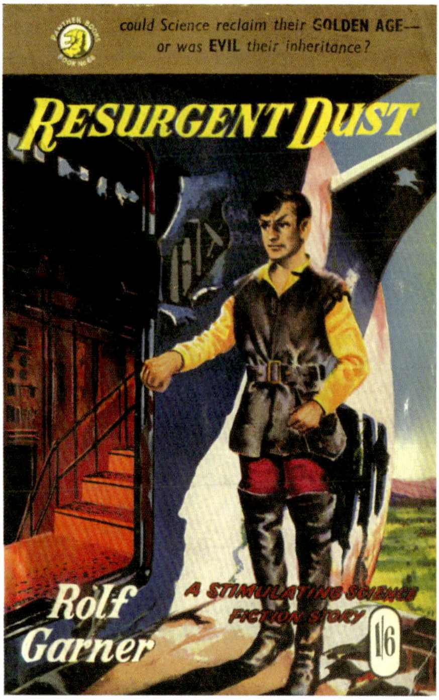

Rolf Garner (Bryan Berry) | *Resurgent Dust*
Panther Books #68, 1953 | Art **John Richards**

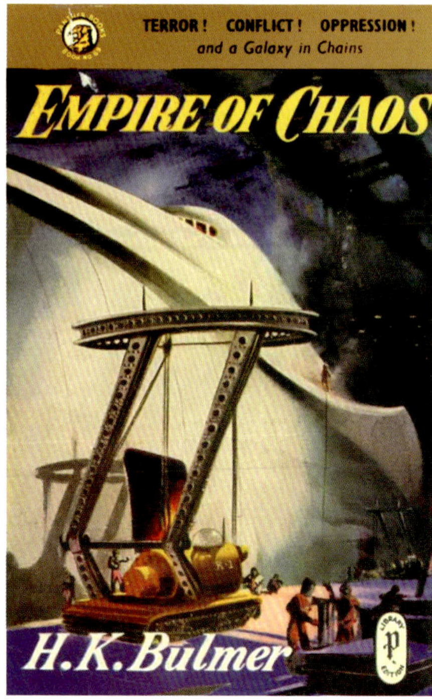

H. K. Bulmer | *Empire of Chaos*
Panther Books #69, 1952 | Art **John Richards**

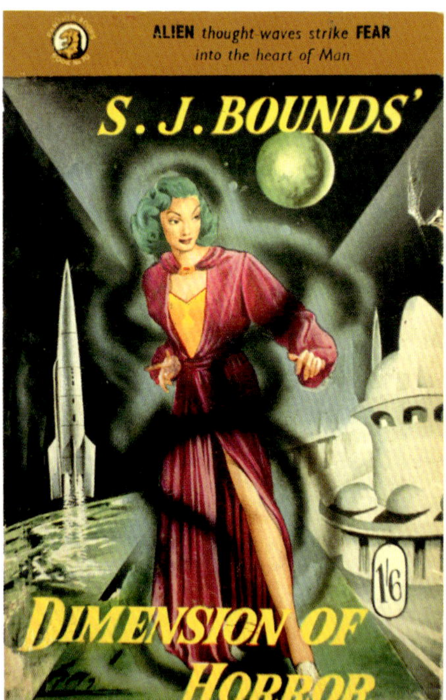

Sydney J. Bounds | *Dimension of Horror*
Panther Books #70, 1953 | Art **John Richards**

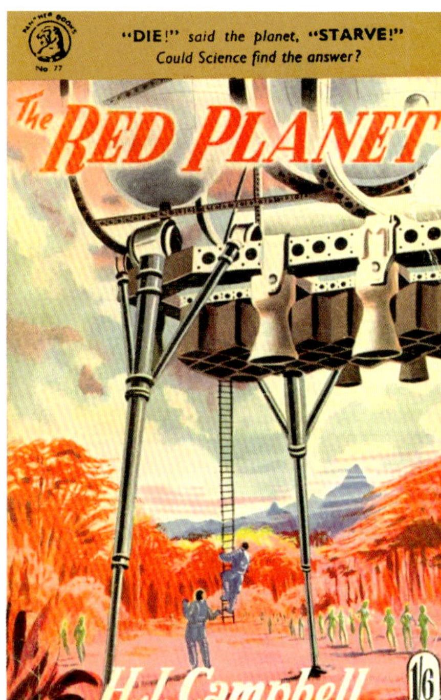

H. J. Campbell | *The Red Planet*
Panther Books #77, 1953 | Art **John Richards**

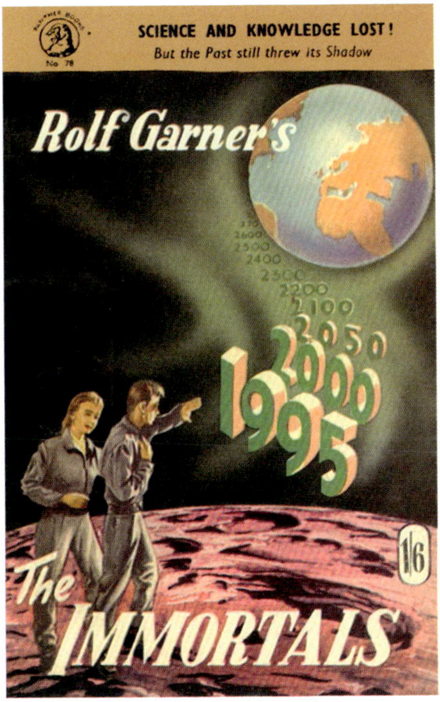

Rolf Garner (Bryan Berry) | *The Immortals*
Panther Books #78, 1953 | Art **John Richards**

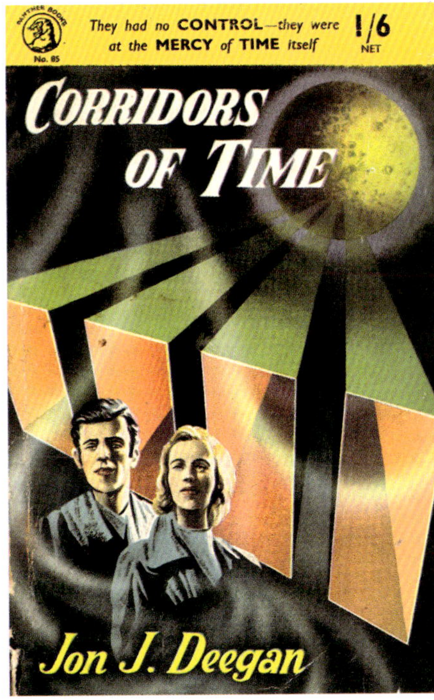

Jon J. Deegan (Robert G. Sharp) | *Corridors of Time*
Panther Books #85, 1953 | Art **John Richards**

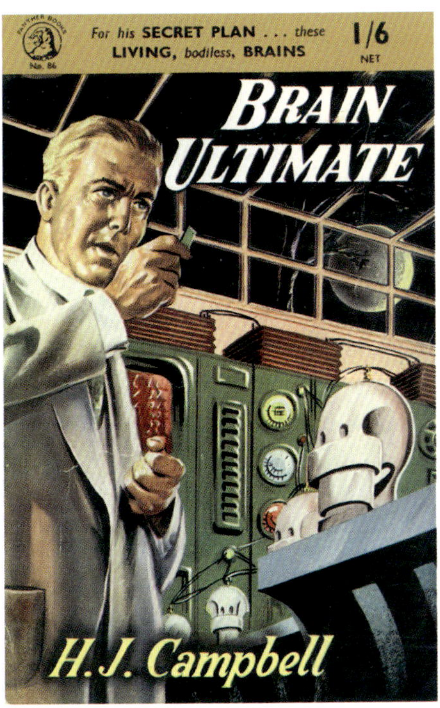

H. J. Campbell | *Brain Ultimate*
Panther Books #86, 1953 | Art **John Richards**

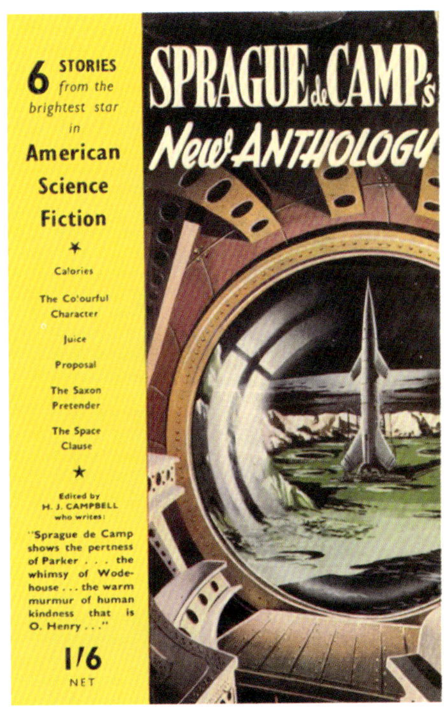

L. Sprague de Camp | *Sprague de Camp's New Anthology*
Panther Books # 92, 1953 | Art **John Richards**

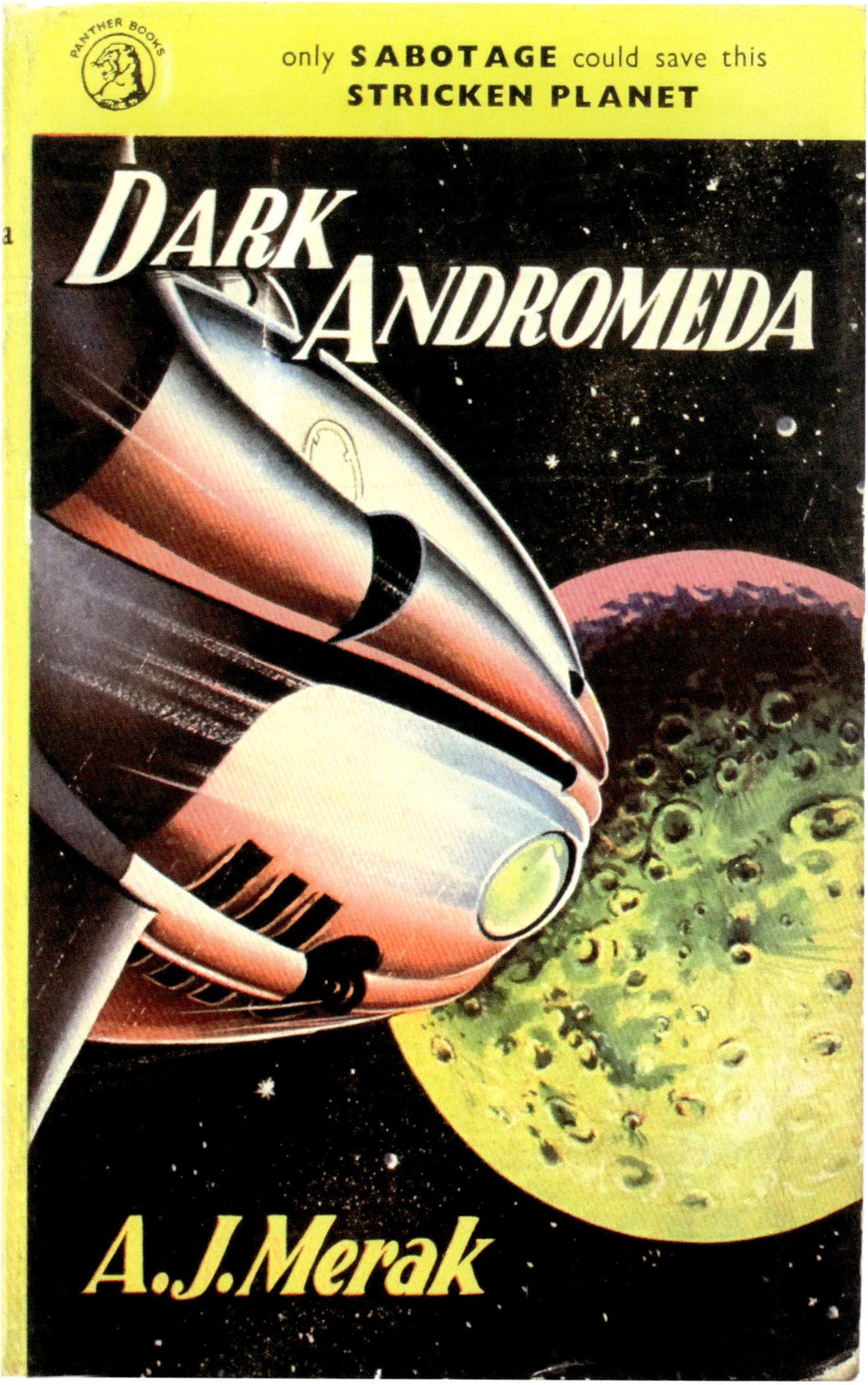

A. J. Merak (John Glasby) | *Dark Andromeda*
Panther Books #95, 1954 | Art **John Richards**

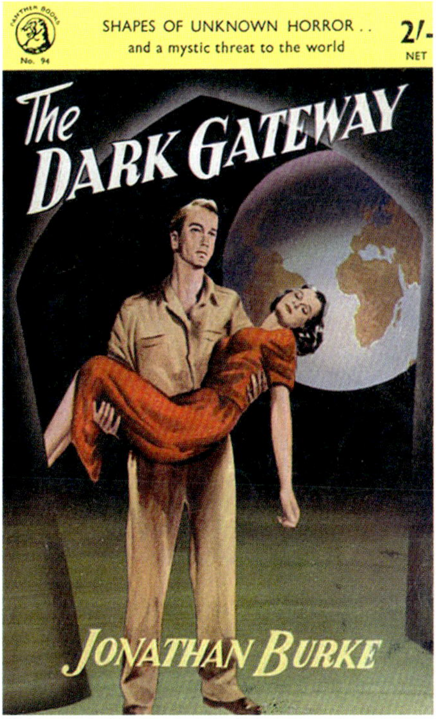

Jonathan Burke | *The Dark Gateway*
Panther Books #94, 1953 | Art **John Richards**

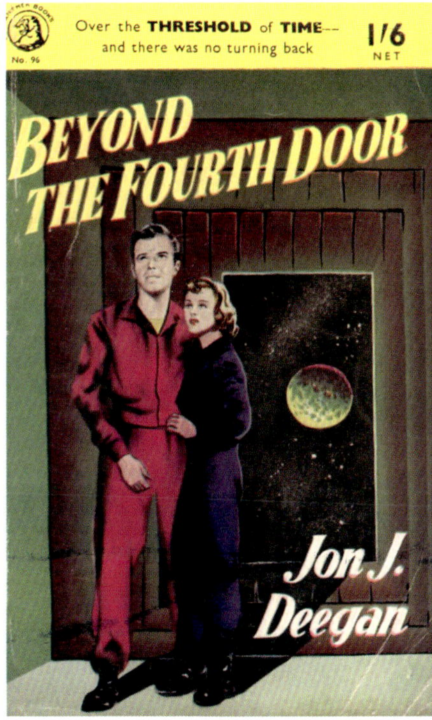

Jon J. Deegan (Robert G. Sharp) | *Beyond the Fourth Door*
Panther Books #96, 1954 | Art **John Richards**

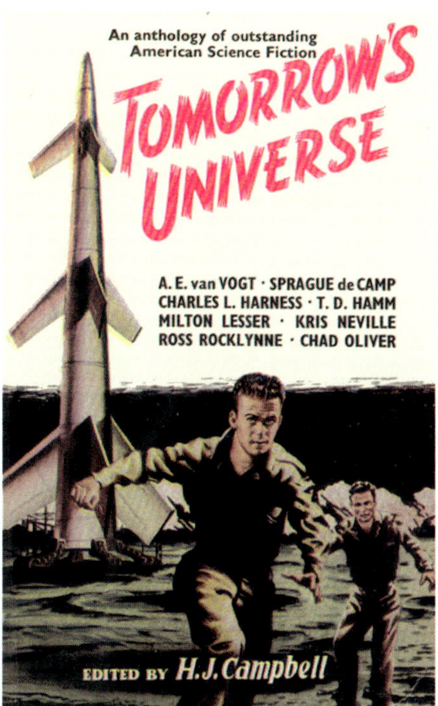

H. J. Campbell | *Tomorrow's Universe*
Panther Books #101, 1953 | Art **John Richards**

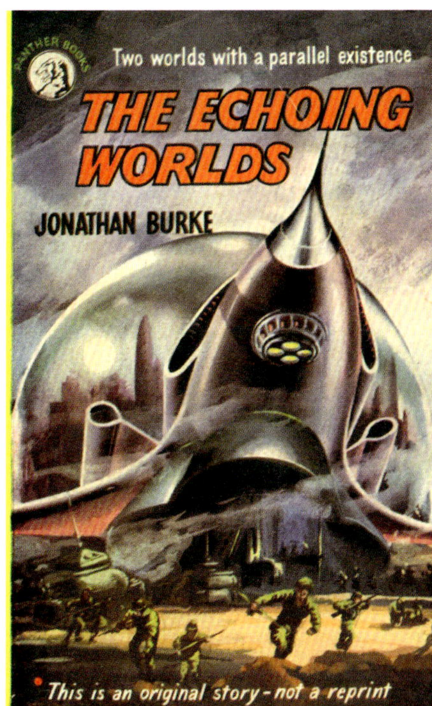

Jonathan Burke | *The Echoing Worlds*
Panther Books #103, 1953 | Art **John Richards**

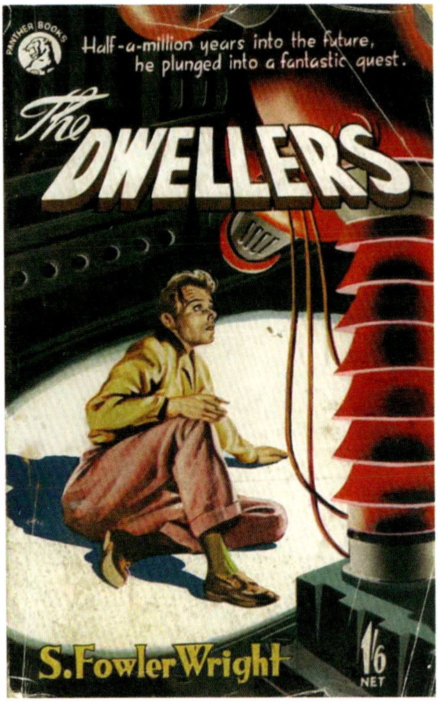

S. Fowler Wright | *The Dwellers*
Panther Books, nn, 1954 | Art **John Richards**

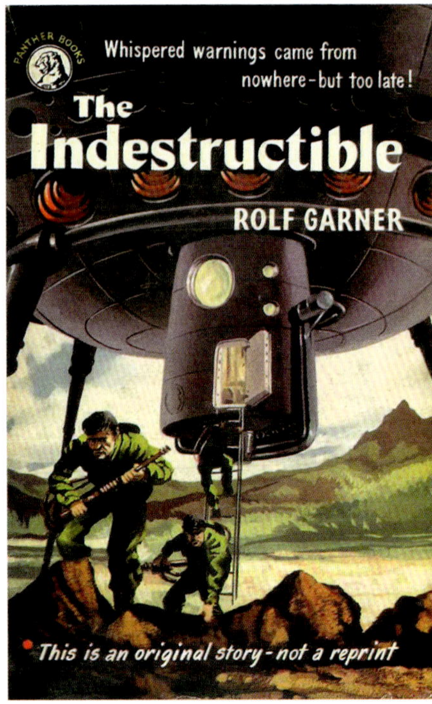

Rolf Garner (Bryan Berry) | *The Indestructible*
Panther Books #104, 1954 | Art **John Richards**

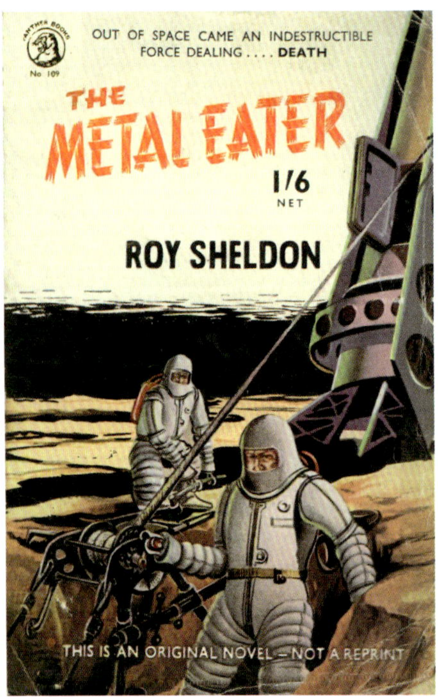

Roy Sheldon (E. C. Tubb) | *The Metal Eater*
Panther Books #109, 1954 | Art **John Richards**

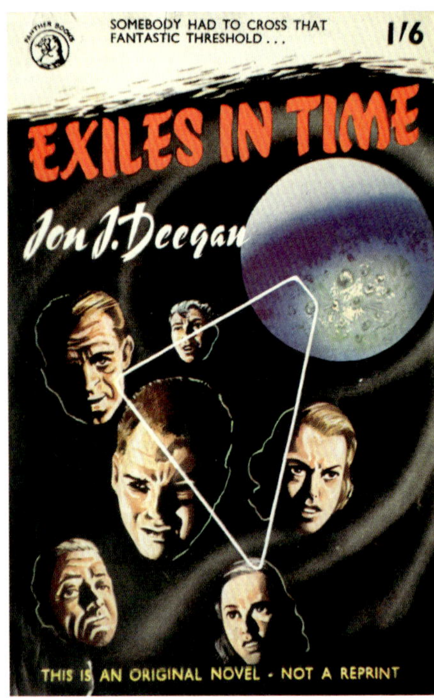

Jon J. Deegan (Robert G. Sharp) | *Exiles in Time*
Panther Books #117, 1954 | Art **John Richards**

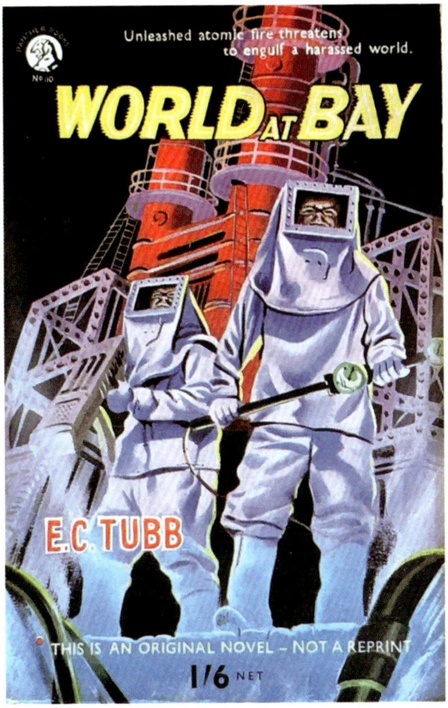

E. C. Tubb | *World at Bay*
Panther Books #110, 1954 | Art **John Richards**

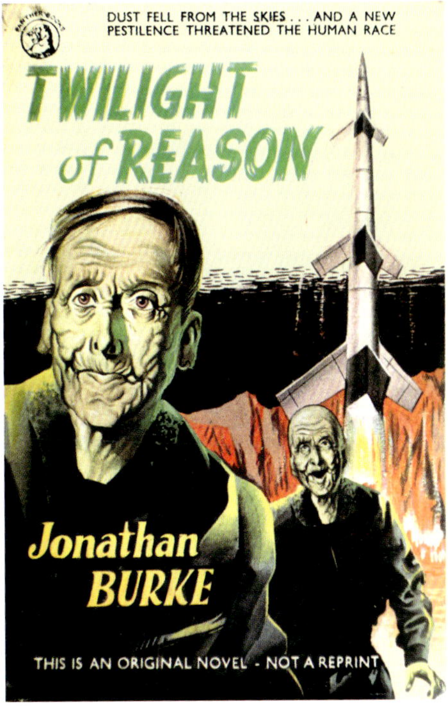

Jonathan Burke | *Twilight of Reason*
Panther Books #118, 1954 | Art **John Richards**

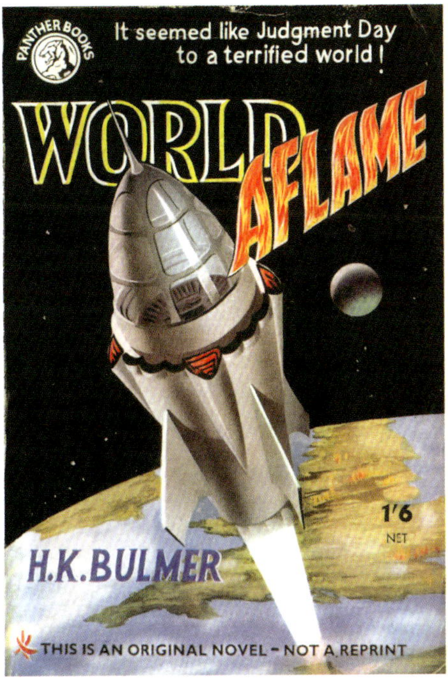

H. K. Bulmer | *World Aflame*
Panther Books #159, 1954 | Art **John Richards**

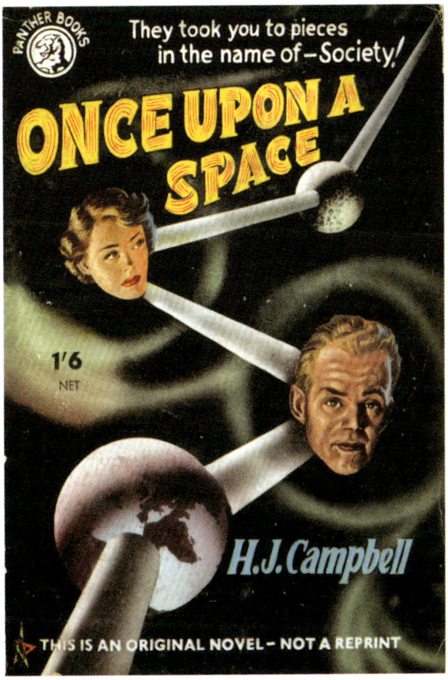

H. J. Campbell | *Once Upon a Space*
Panther Books #160, 1954 | Art **John Richards**

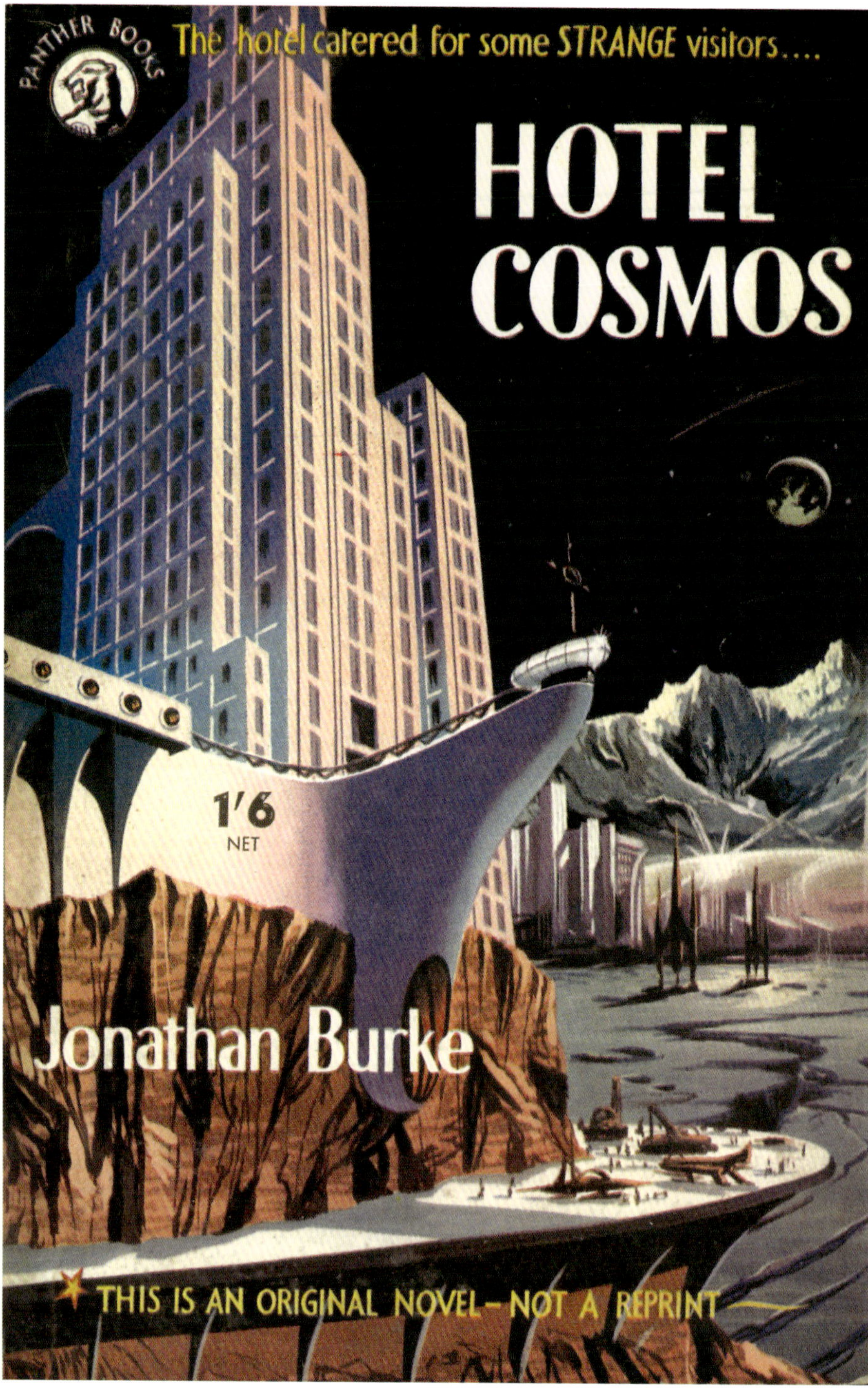

Jonathan Burke | *Hotel Cosmos*
Panther Books #135, 1954 | Art **John Richards**

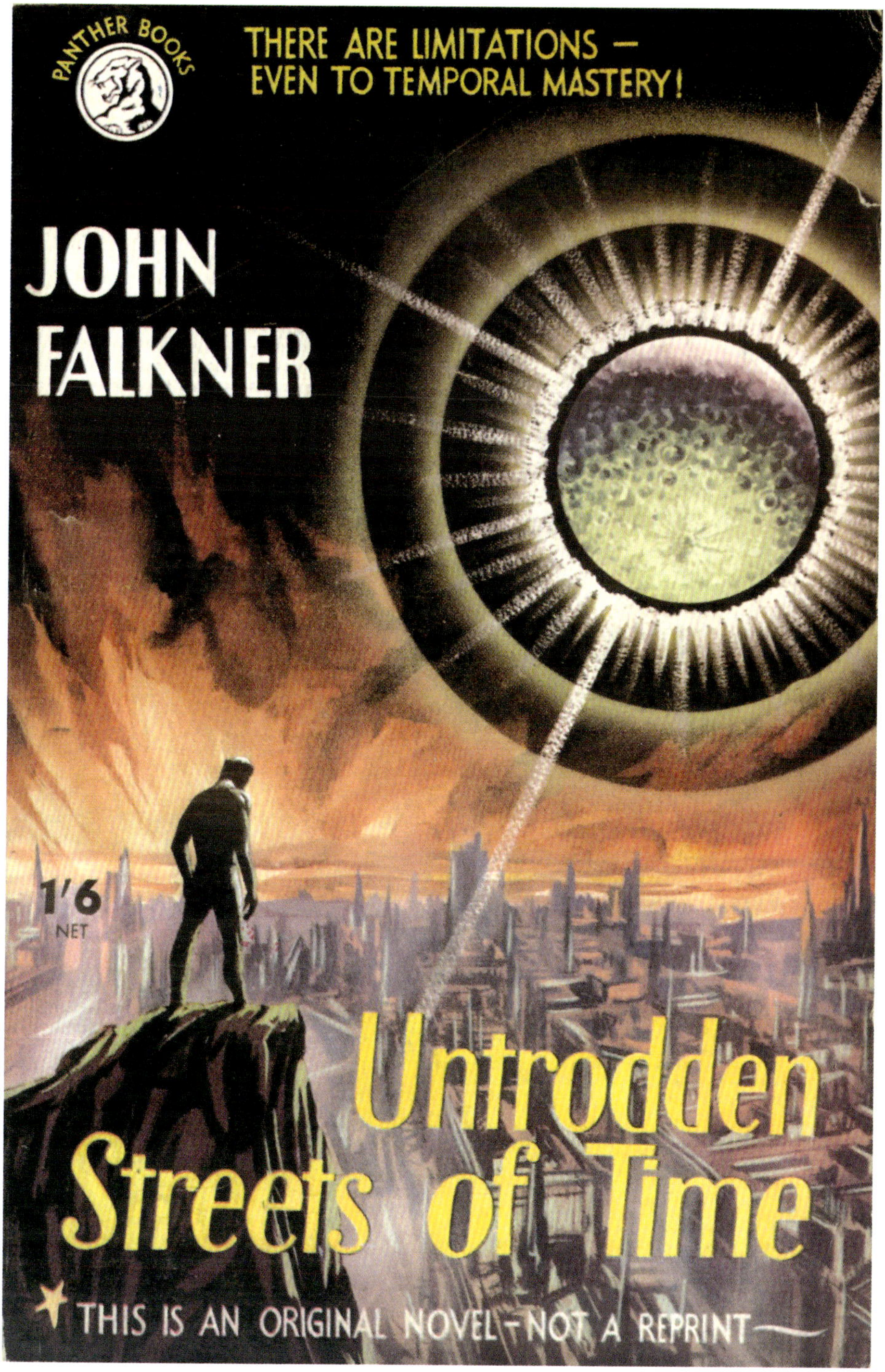

John Falkner (E. F. Gayle) | *Untrodden Streets of Time*
Panther Books #136, 1954 | Art **John Richards**

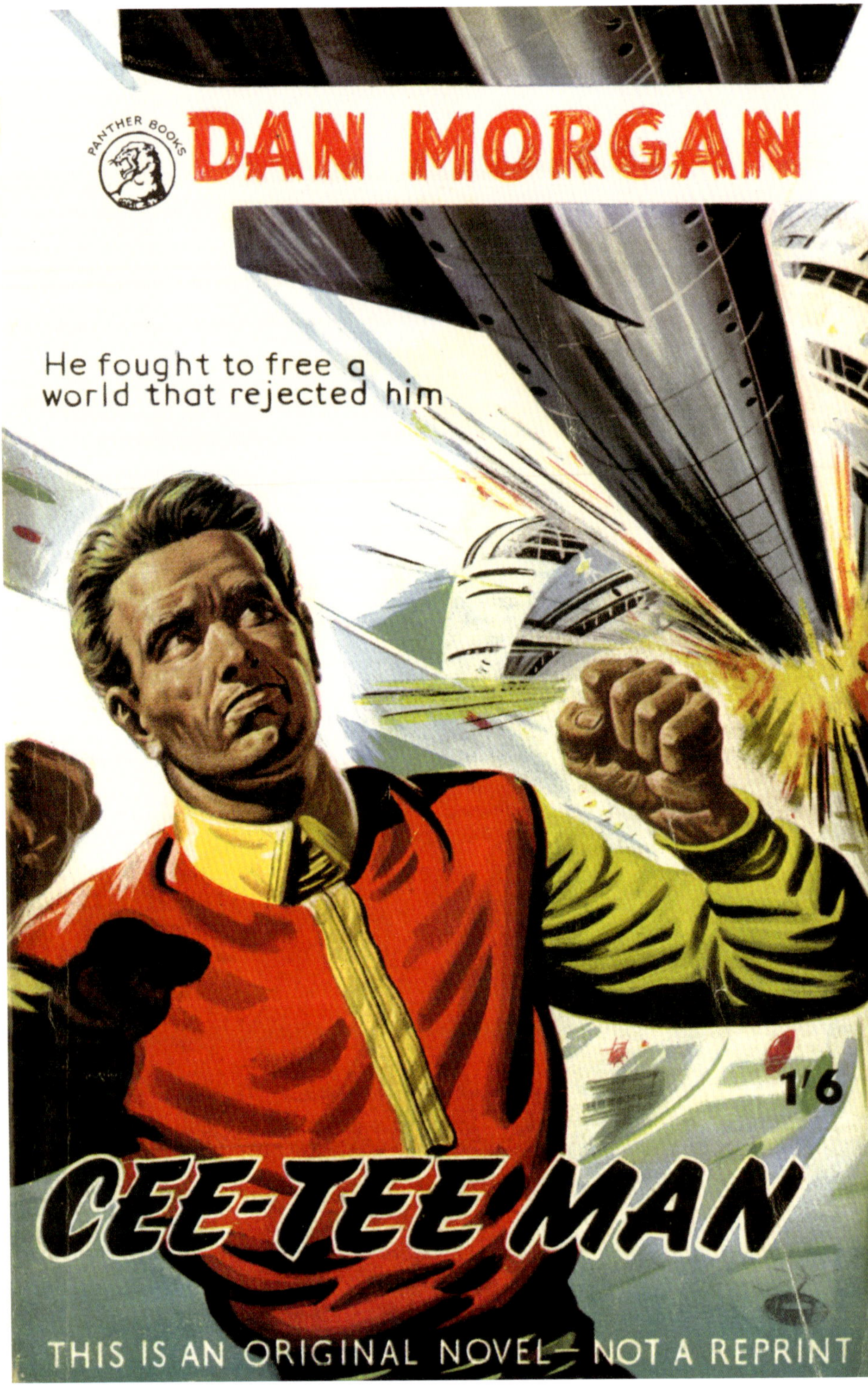

Dan Morgan | *Cee-Tee Man*
Panther Books #181, 1955 | Art **Josh Kirby** | This is Kirby's first published book cover

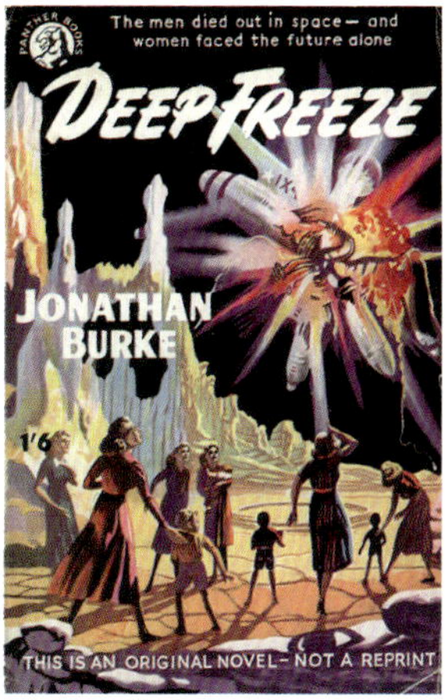

Jonathan Burke | *Deep Freeze*
Panther Books #182, 1955 | Art **Ron Turner**

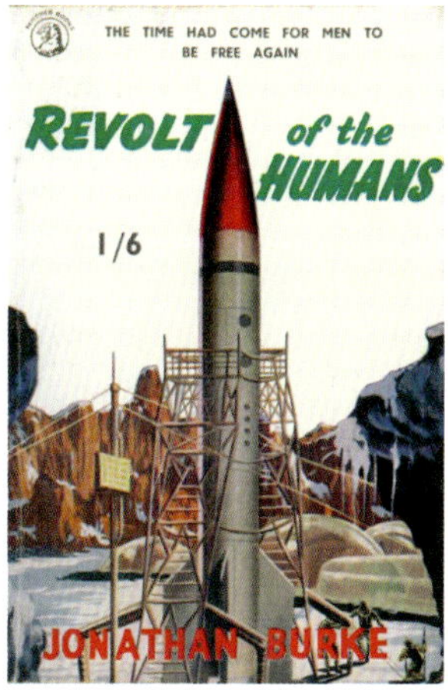

Jonathan Burke | *Revolt of the Humans*
Panther Books #192, 1955 | Art **John Richards**

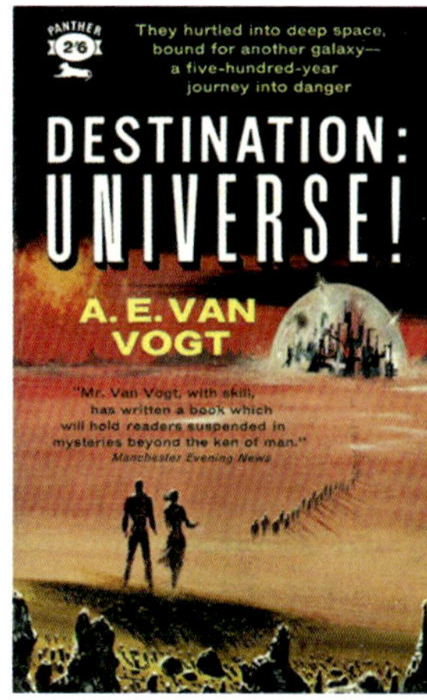

A. E. van Vogt | *Destination: Universe!*
Panther Books #1063, 1960 | Art **Richard Powers**

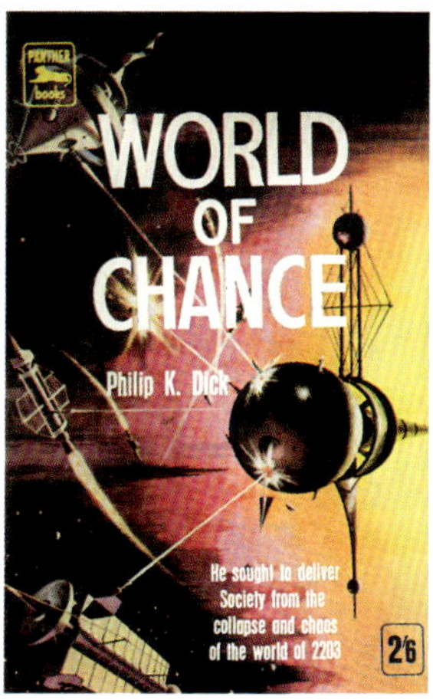

Philip K. Dick | *World of Chance*
Panther Books #785, 1959 | Art **Unknown**

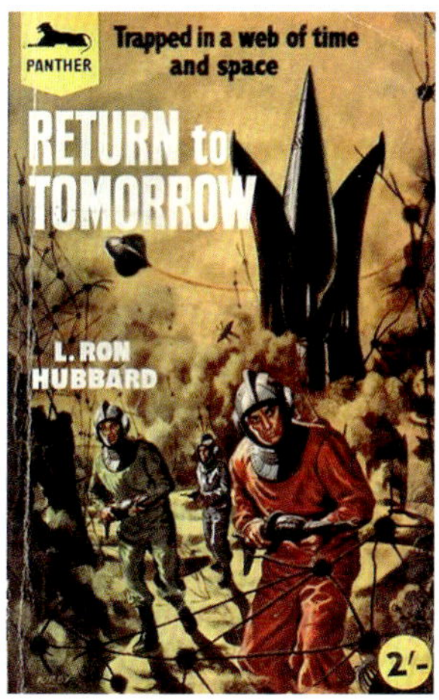

L. Ron Hubbard | *Return to Tomorrow*
Panther Books #692, 1957 | Art **Josh Kirby**

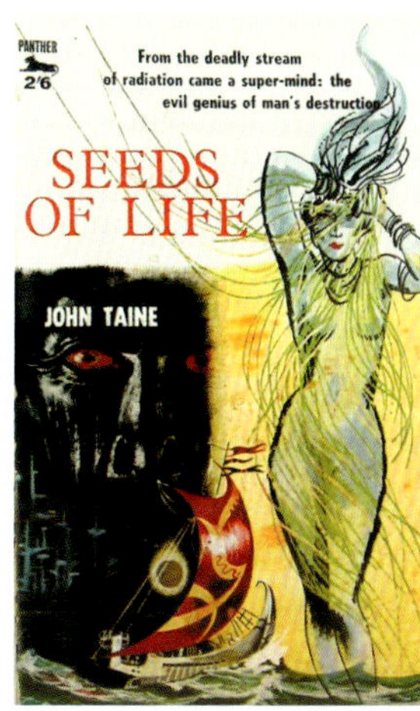

John Taine | *Seeds of Life*
Panther Books #784, 1959 | Art **Richard Powers**

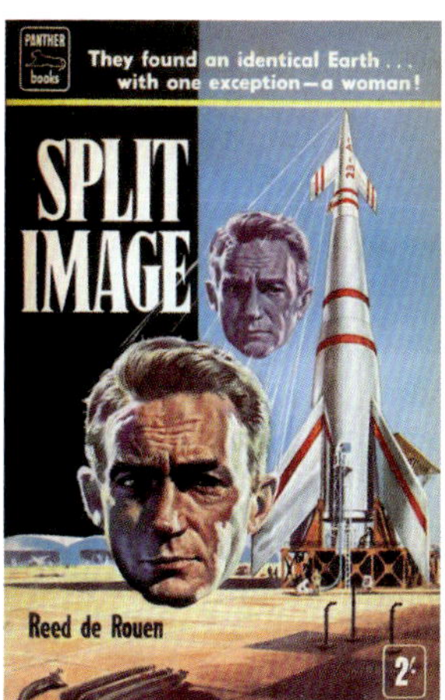

Reed De Rouen | *Split Image*
Panther Books #763, 1958 | Art **Josh Kirby**

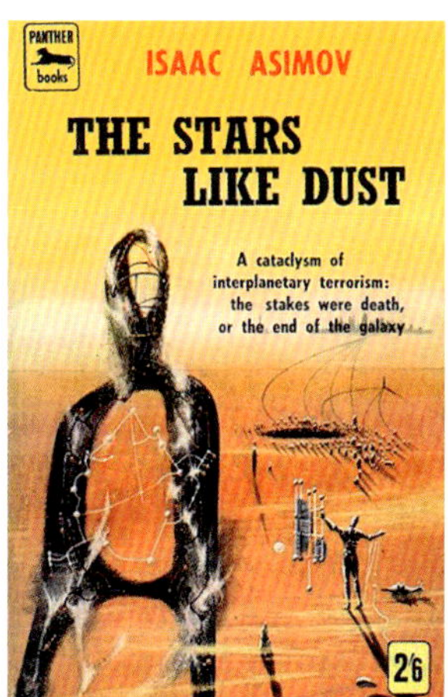

Isaac Asimov | *The Stars Like Dust*
Panther Books #863, 1958 | Art **Richard Powers**

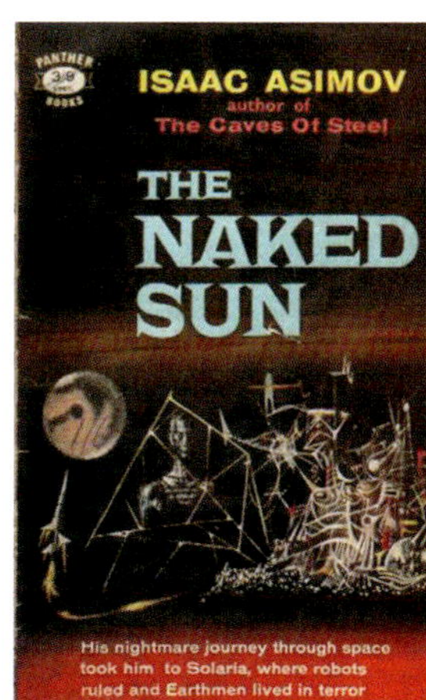

Isaac Asimov | *The Naked Sun*
Panther Books #1016, 1960 | Art **Richard Powers**

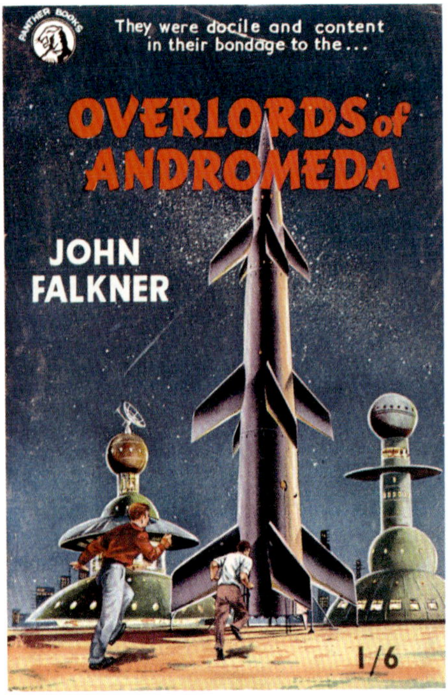

John Falkner (E. F. Gayle) | *Overlords of Andromeda*
Panther Books #193, 1955 | Art **John Richards**

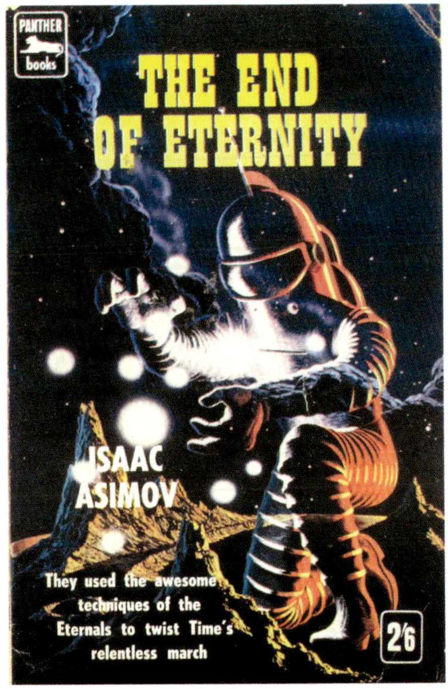

Isaac Asimov | *The End of Eternity*
Panther Books #881, 1959 | Art **Mel Hunter**

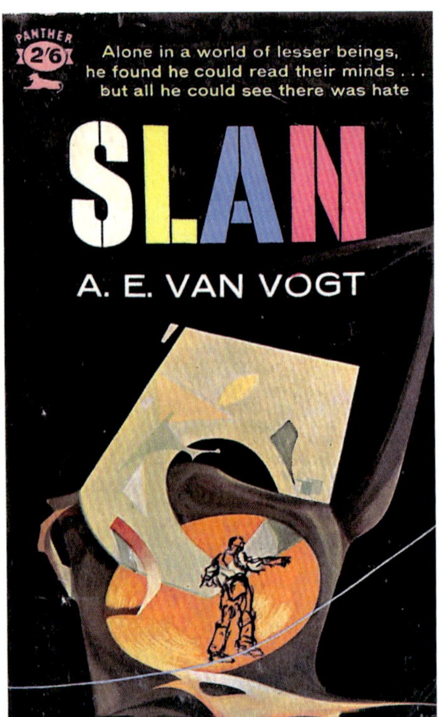

A. E. van Vogt | *Slan*
Panther Books #1132, 1962 | Art **Arthur Sussman**

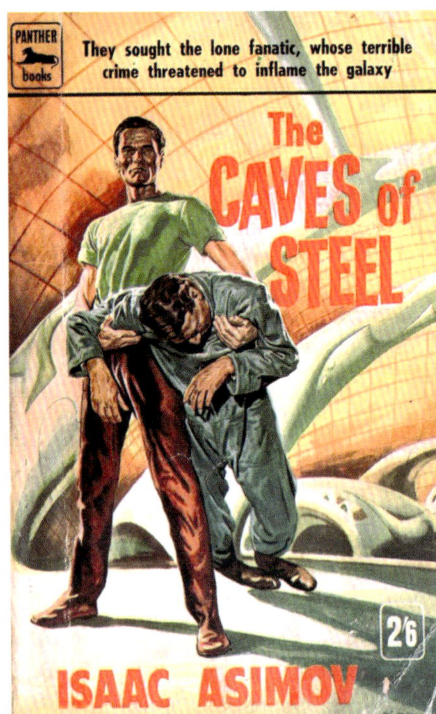

Isaac Asimov | *The Caves of Steel*
Panther Books #835, 1958 | Art **Josh Kirby**

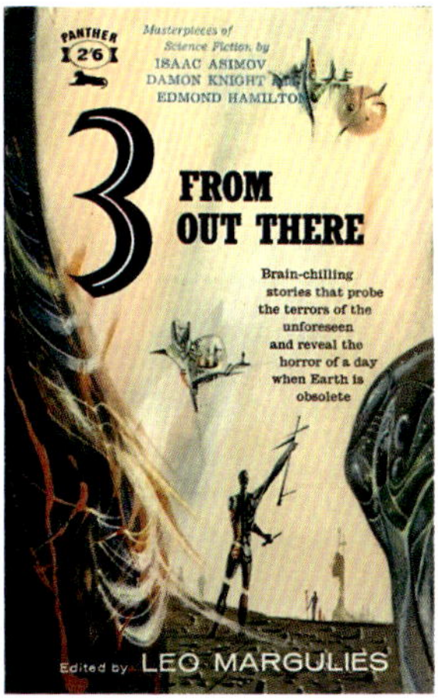

Leo Margulies, ed. | *3 from Out There*
Panther Books #1057, 1960 | Art **Richard Powers**

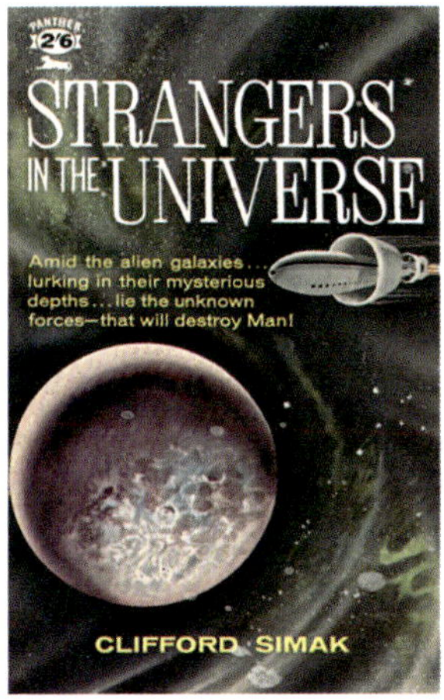

Clifford Simak | *Strangers in the Universe*
Panther Books #1332, 1962 | Art **John Richards**

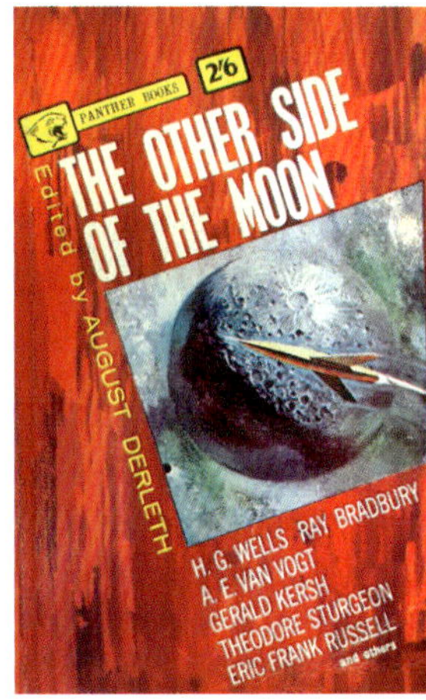

August Derleth, ed. | *The Other Side of the Moon*
Panther Books #1541, 1963 | Art **Unknown**

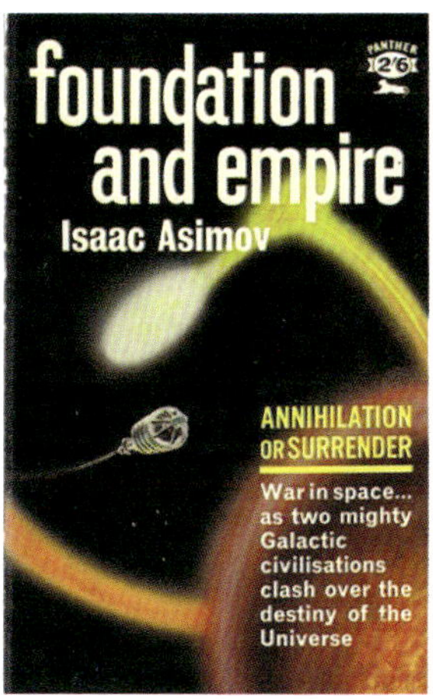

Isaac Asimov | *Foundation and Empire*
Panther Books #1962 | Art **John Richards**

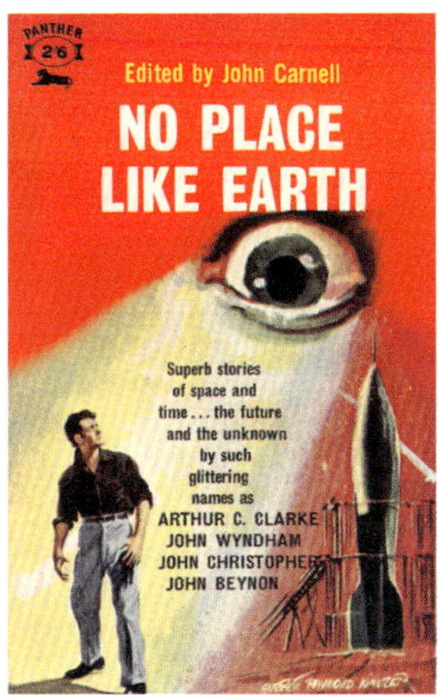

John Carnell, ed. | *No Place Like Earth*
Panther Books #1252, 1961 | Art **Everett Kinstler**

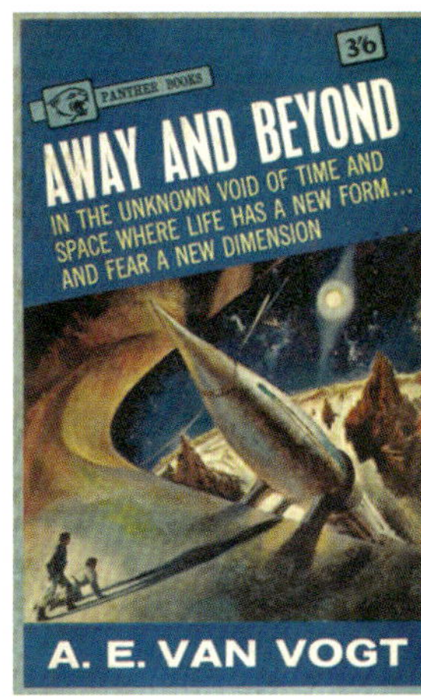

A. E. van Vogt | *Away and Beyond*
Panther Books #1569, 1963 | Art **Charles Binger**

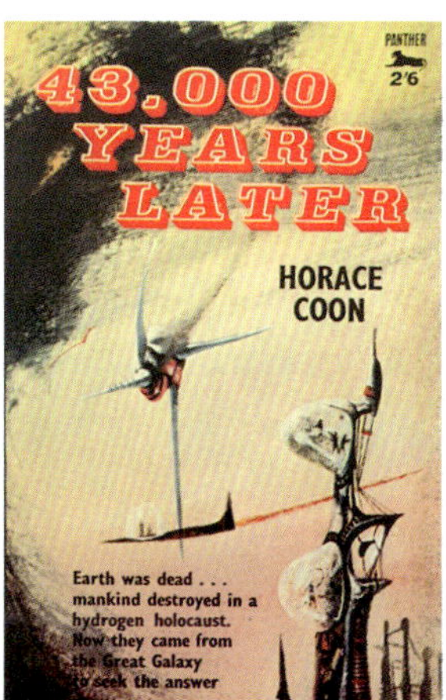

Horace Coon | *43,000 Years Later*
Panther Books #975, 1959 | Art **Richard Powers**

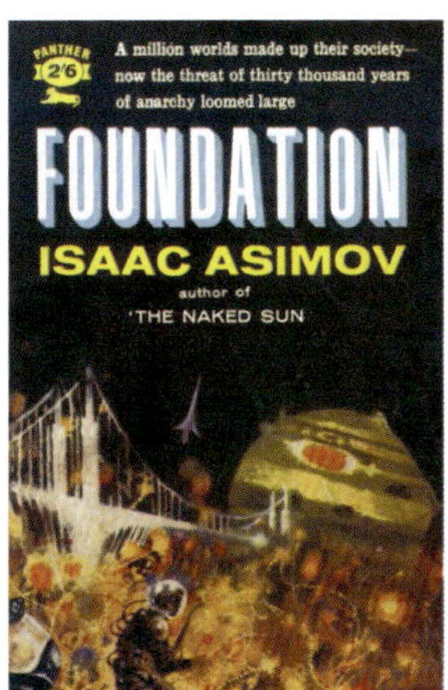

Isaac Asimov | *Foundation*
Panther Books #1080, 1962 | Art **Richard Powers**

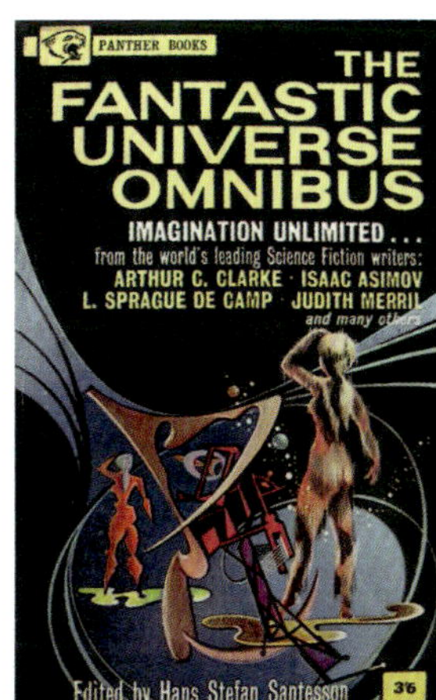

H. Santesson | *The Fantastic Universe Omnibus*
Panther Books #1414, 1962 | Art **Arthur Sussman**

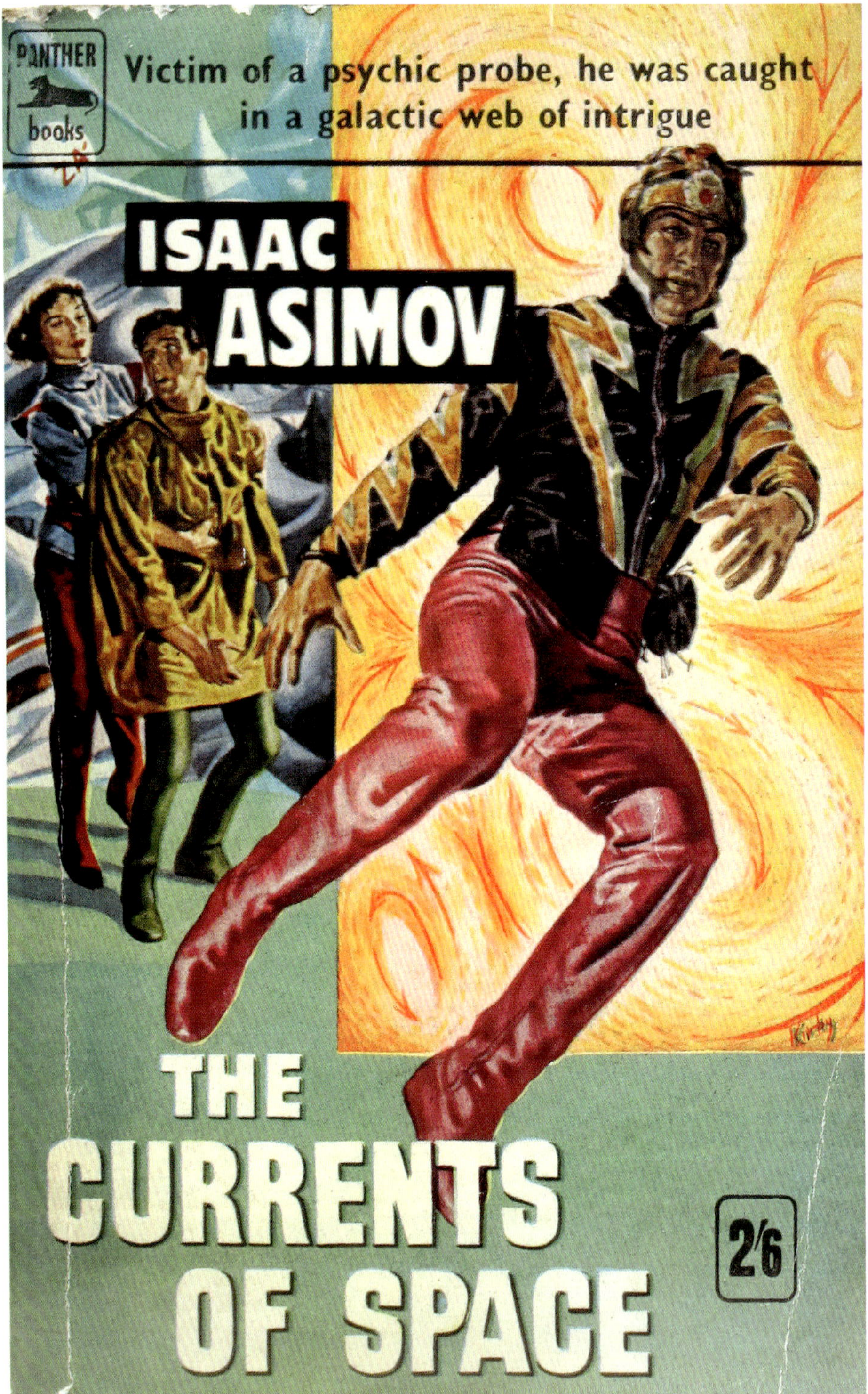

Isaac Asimov | *The Currents of Space*
Panther Books #824, 1958 | Art **Josh Kirby**

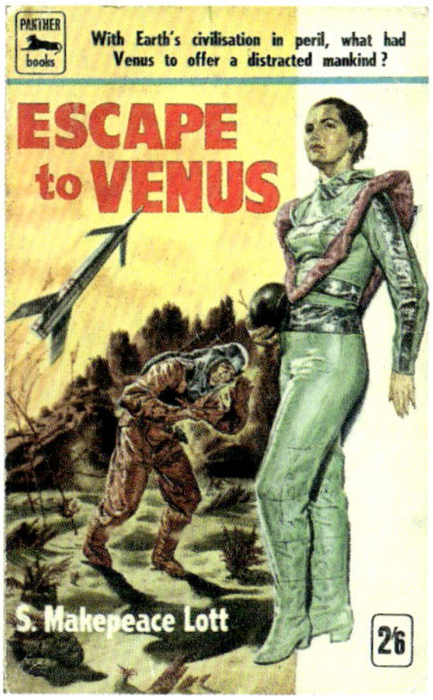

S. Makepeace Lott | *Escape to Venus*
Panther Books, nn, 1958 | Art **Josh Kirby**

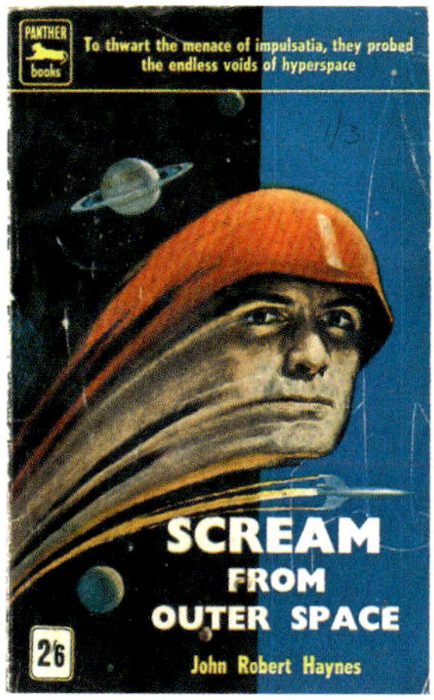

John Robert Haynes | *Scream From Outer Space*
Panther Books #852, 1955 | Art **Unknown**

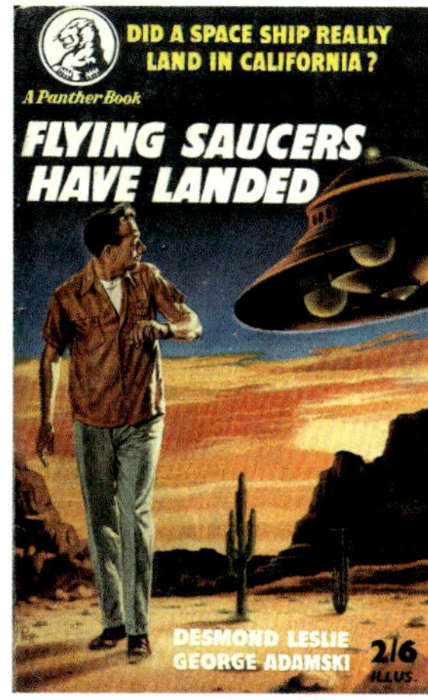

Leslie & Adamski | *Flying Saucers Have Landed*
Panther Books #4663, 1957 | Art **Sam Peffer**

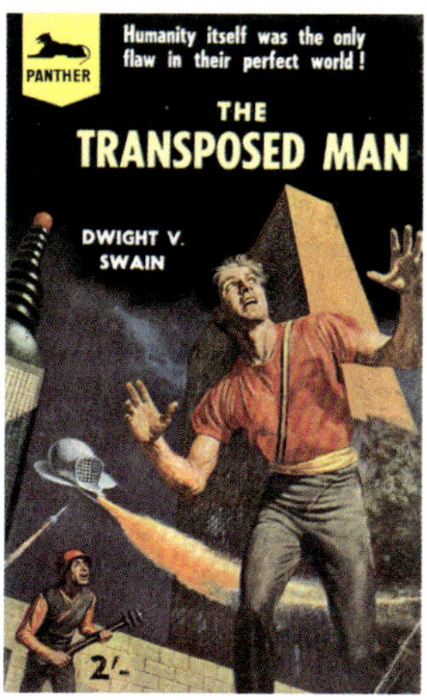

Dwight V. Swain | *The Transposed Man*
Panther Books #696, 1957 | Art **Ed Valigursky**

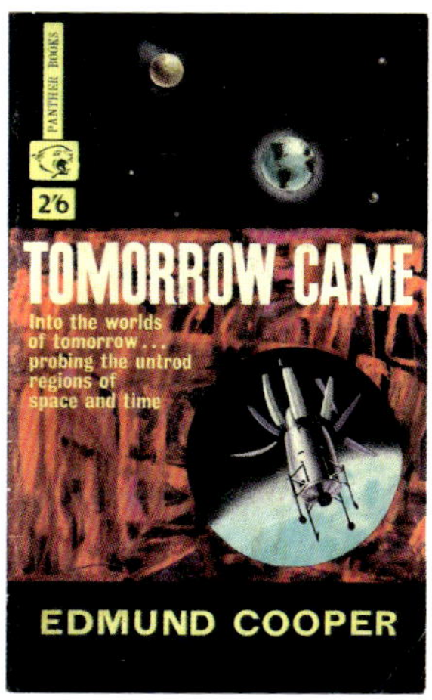

Edmund Cooper | *Tomorrow Came*
Panther Books #1511, 1963 | Art **Unknown**

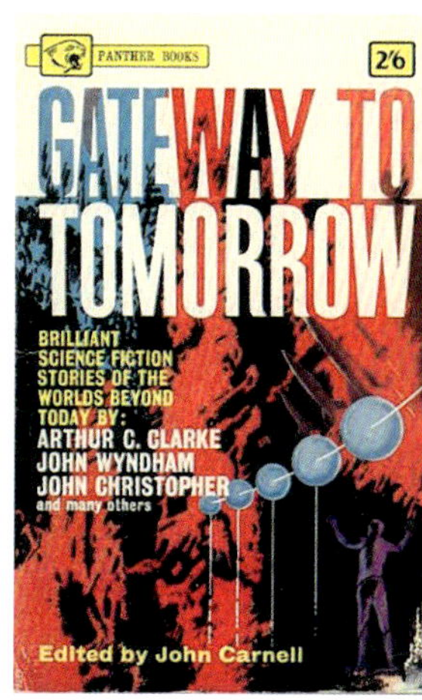

John Carnell | *Gateway to Tomorrow*
Panther Books #1460, 1963 | Art **Peter Green**

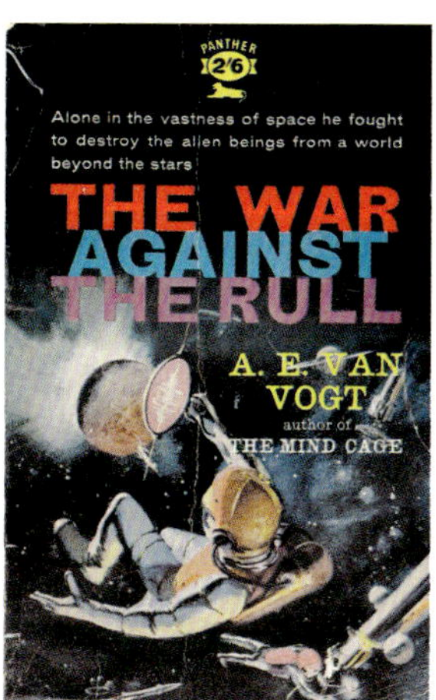

A. E. van Vogt | *The War Against the Rull*
Panther Books #1168, 1962 | Art **Stanley Meltzoff**

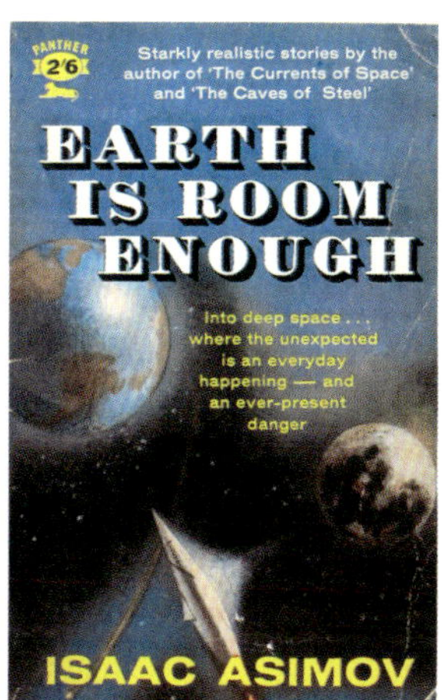

Isaac Asimov | *Earth Is Room Enough*
Panther Books #1042, 1960 | Art **Unknown**

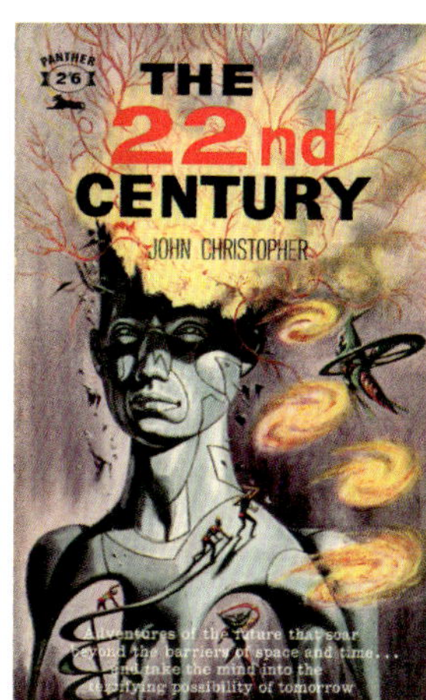

John Christopher | *The 22nd Century*
Panther Books #1142, 1960 | Art **Josh Kirby**

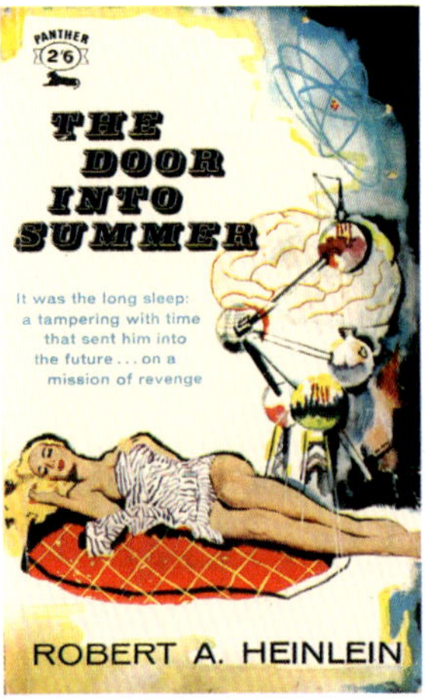

Robert A. Heinlein | *The Door into Summer*
Panther Books #1021, 1960 | Art **Richard Powers**

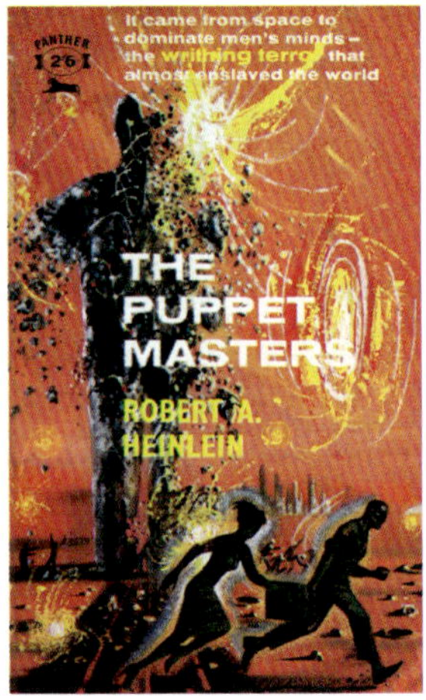

Robert A. Heinlein | *The Puppet Masters*
Panther Books #1001, 1960 | Art **Richard Powers**

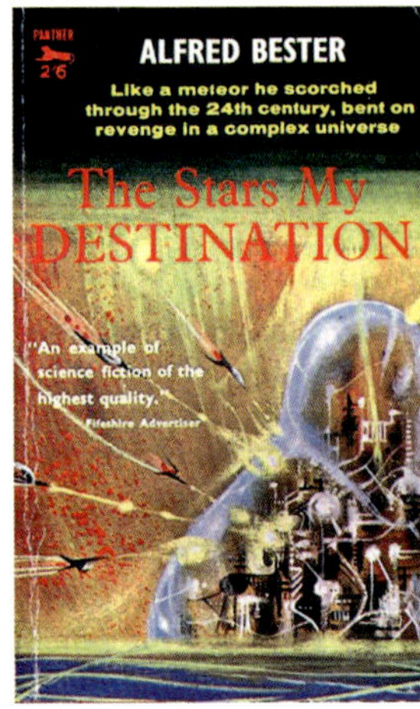

Alfred Bester | *The Stars My Destination*
Panther Books #973, 1962 | Art **Richard Powers**

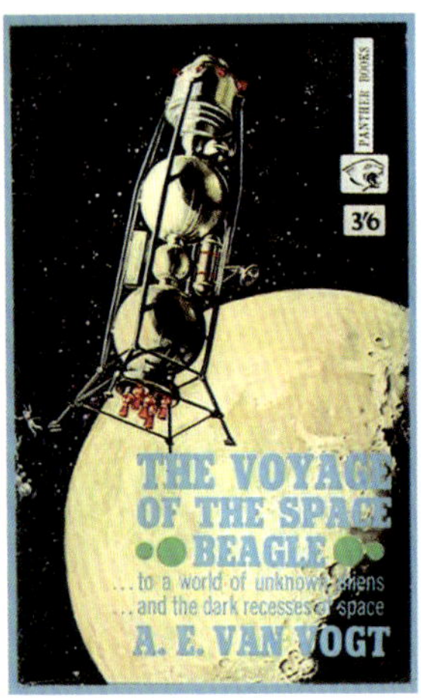

A. E. van Vogt | *The Voyage of the Space Beagle*
Panther Books #990, 1963 | Art **Jack Fargasso**

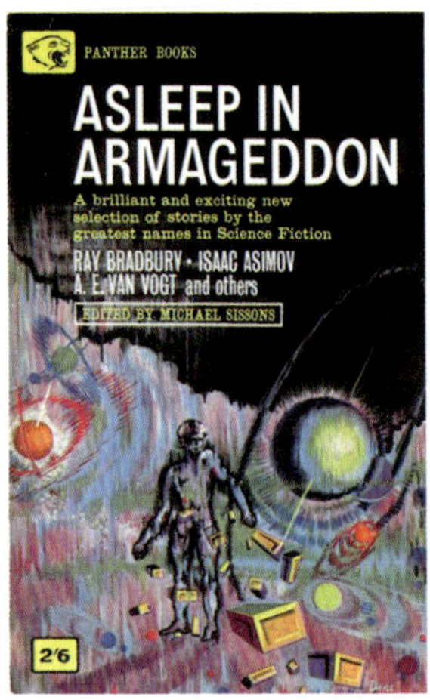

Michael Sissons, Ed. | *Asleep in Armageddon*
Panther Books #1379, 1962 | Art **Dayle**

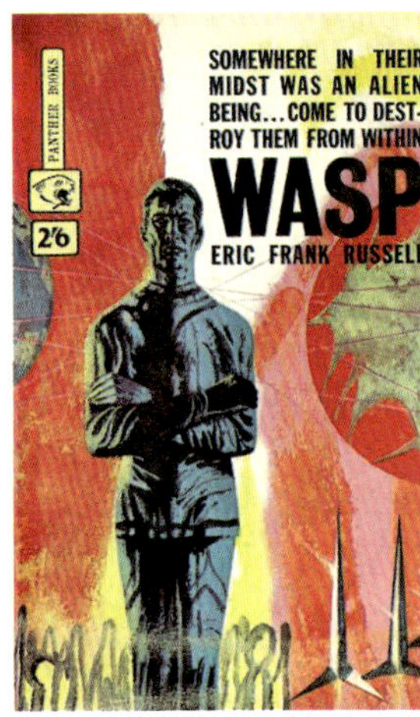

Eric Frank Russell | *Wasp*
Panther Books #1487, 1963 | Art **Richard Powers**

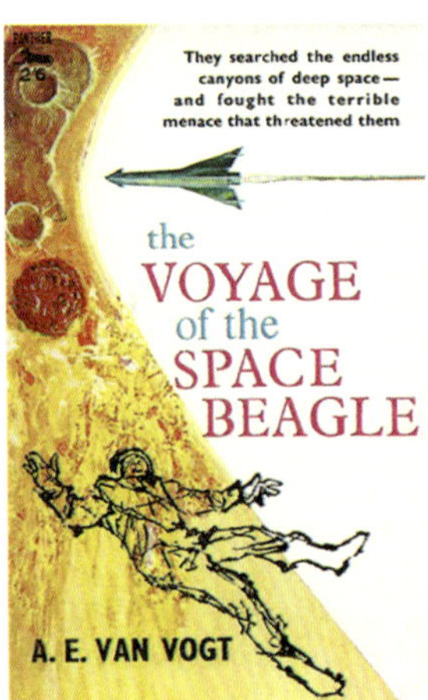

A. E. van Vogt | *The Voyage of the Space Beagle*
Panther Books #990, 1959 | Art **Arthur Sussman**

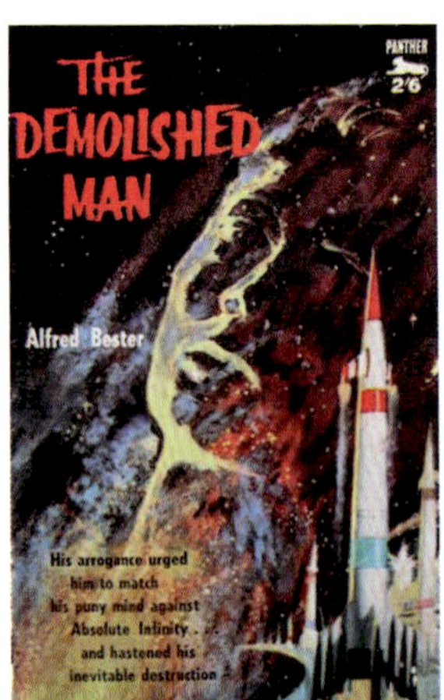

Alfred Bester | *The Demolished Man*
Panther Books #933, 1959 | Art **Unknown**

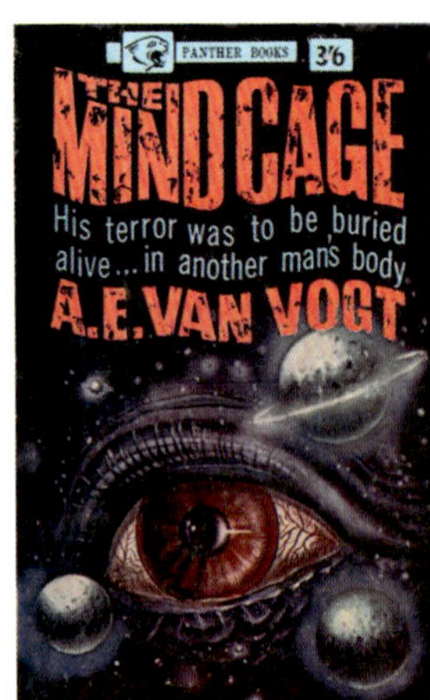

A. E. van Vogt | *The Mind Cage*
Panther Books #1112, 1963 | Art **Unknown**

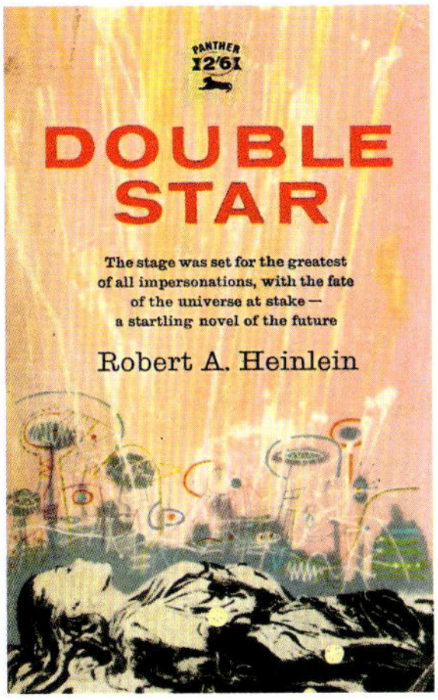

Robert A. Heinlein | *Double Star*
Panther Books #1120, 1960 | Art **Richard Powers**

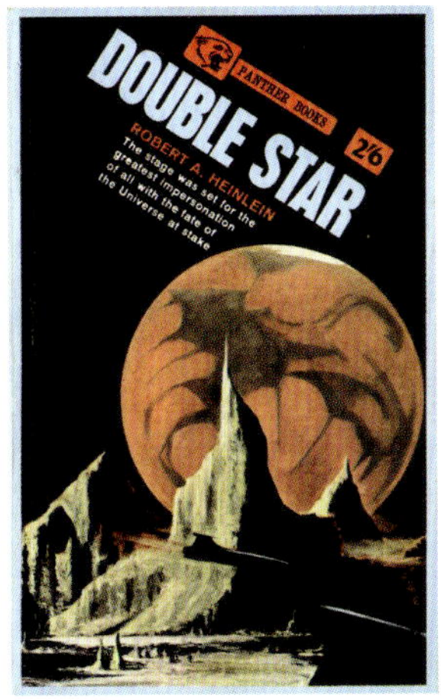

Robert A. Heinlein | *Double Star*
Panther Books #1120, 1963 | Art **Unknown**

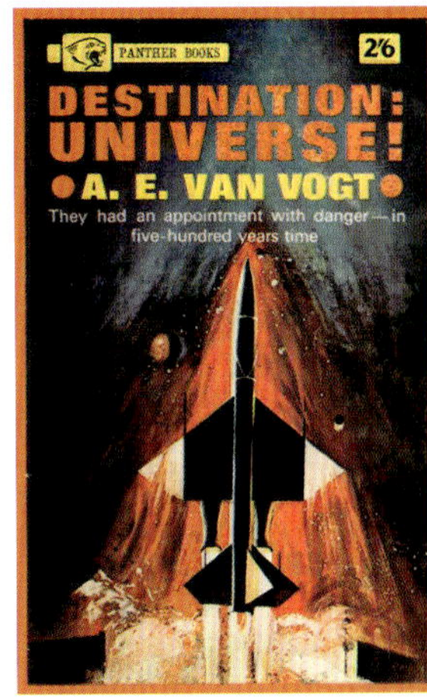

A. E. van Vogt | *Destination: Universe!*
Panther Books #1063, 1963 | Art **Unknown**

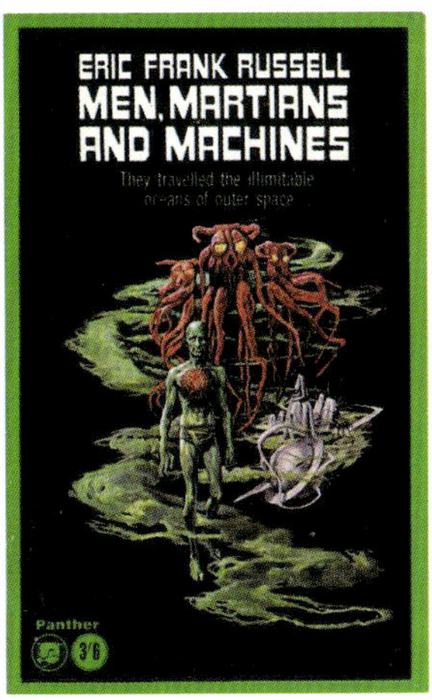

Eric Frank Russell | *Men, Martians & Machines*
Panther Books #1890, 1965 | Art **Josh Kirby**

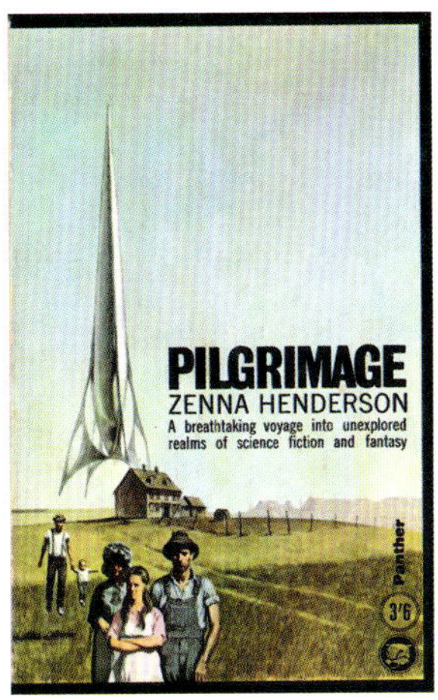

Zenna Henderson | *Pilgrimage*
Panther Books #1971, 1965 | Art **Michael Leonard**

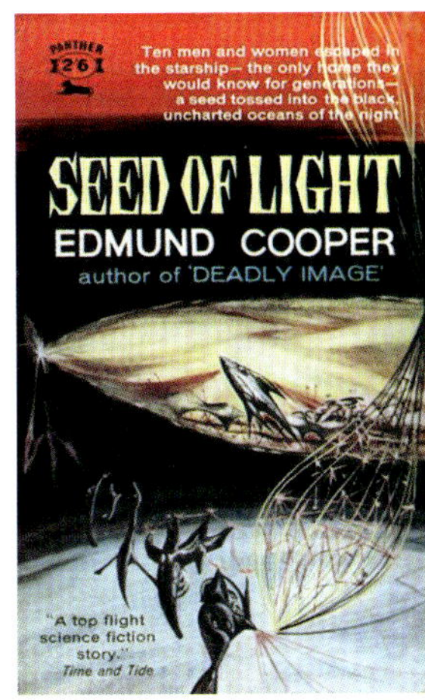

Edmund Cooper | *Seed of Light*
Panther Books #1094, 1960 | Art **Josh Kirby**

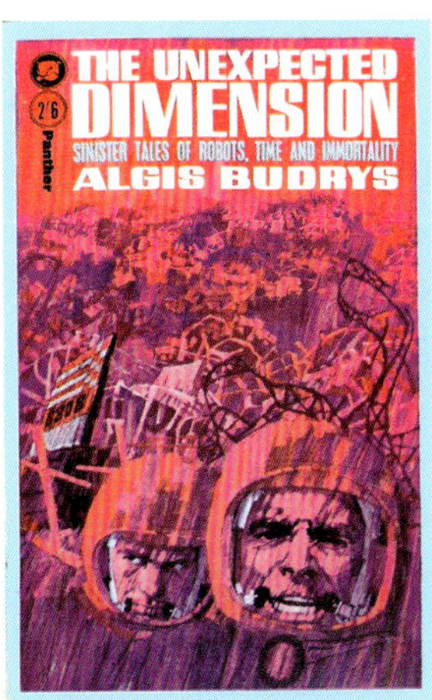

Algis Budrys | *The Unexpected Dimension*
Panther Books #1649, 1964 | Art **Pino Dell'Orco**

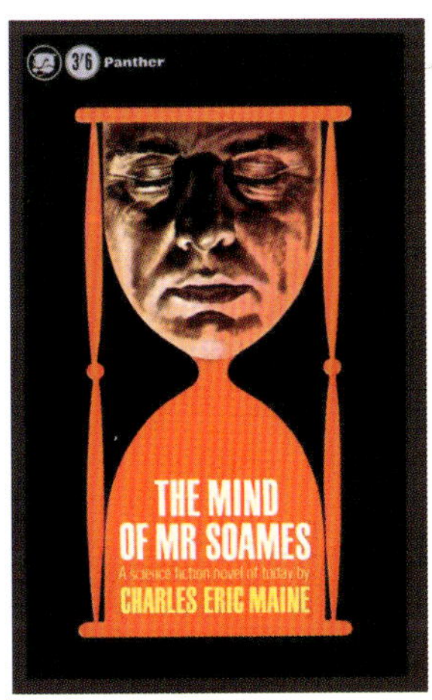

Charles Eric Maine | *The Mind of Mr Soames*
Panther Books #1700, 1964 | Art **Unknown**

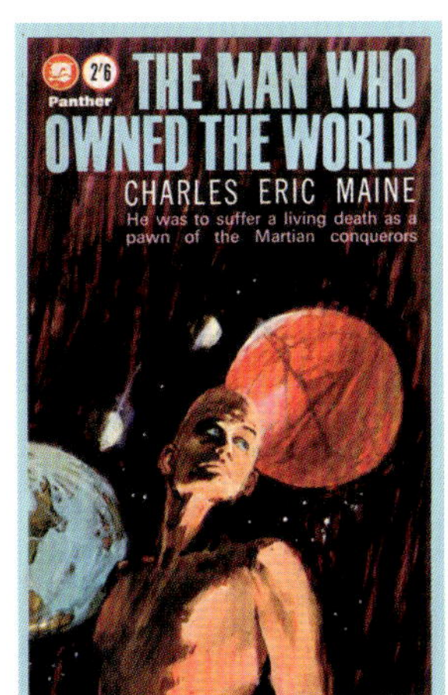

C. E. Maine | *The Man Who Owned the World*
Panther Books #1610, 1963 | Art **Neil Boyle**

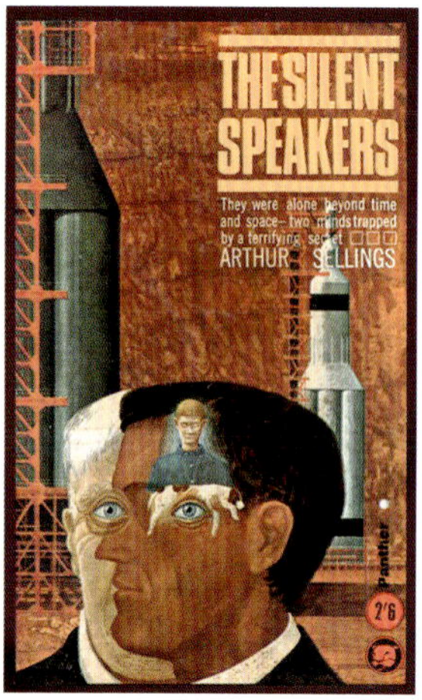

Arthur Sellings | *The Silent Speakers*
Panther Books, 1965 | Art **Unknown**

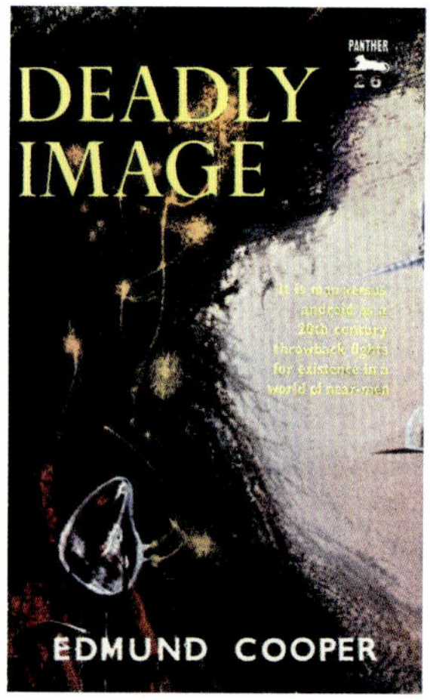

Edmund Cooper | *Deadly Image*
Panther Books 1001, 1960 | Art **Richard Powers**

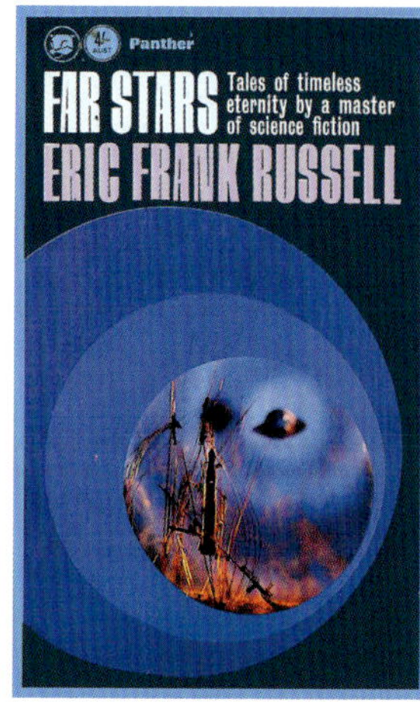

Eric Frank Russell | *Far Stars*
Panther Books, 1964 | Art **Unknown**

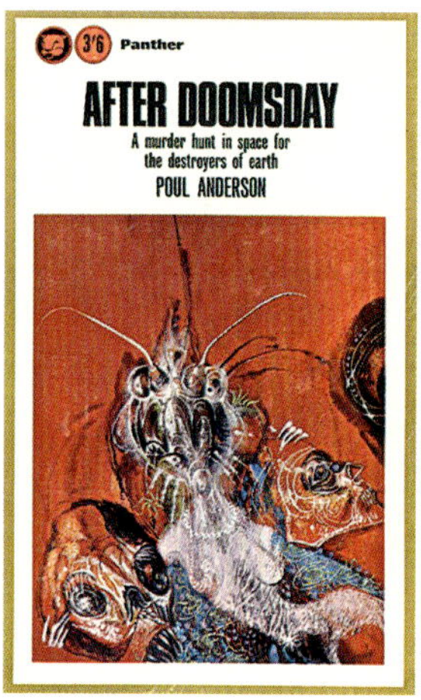

Poul Anderson | *After Doomsday*
Panther Books, 1964 | Art **Richard Powers**

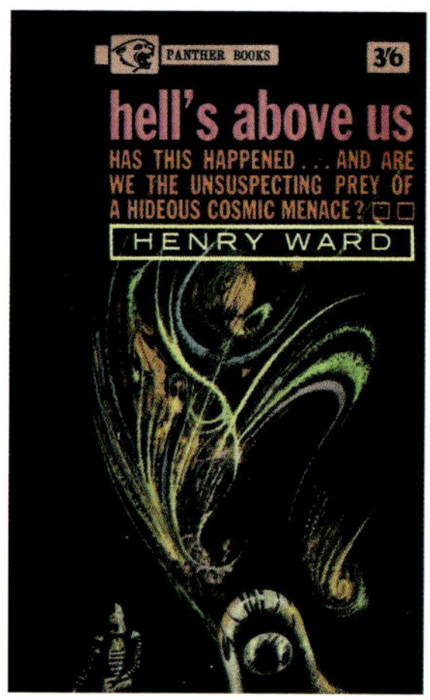

Henry Ward | *Hell's Above Us*
Panther Books, 1963 | Art **Richard Powers**

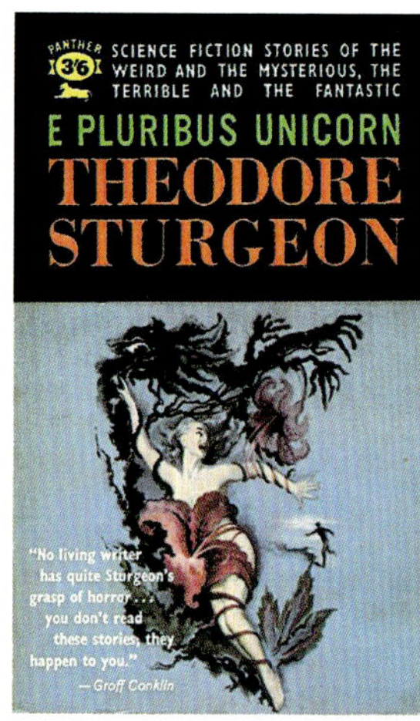

Theodore Sturgeon | *E Pluribus Unicorn*
Panther Books, 1961 | Art **Bill Rose**

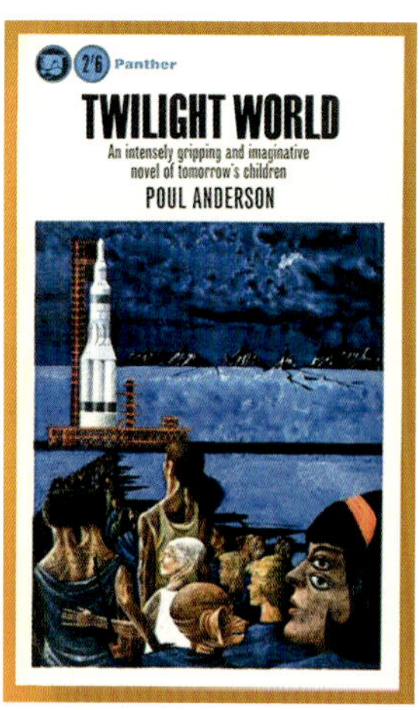

Poul Anderson | *Twilight World*
Panther Books, 1965 | Art **Unknown**

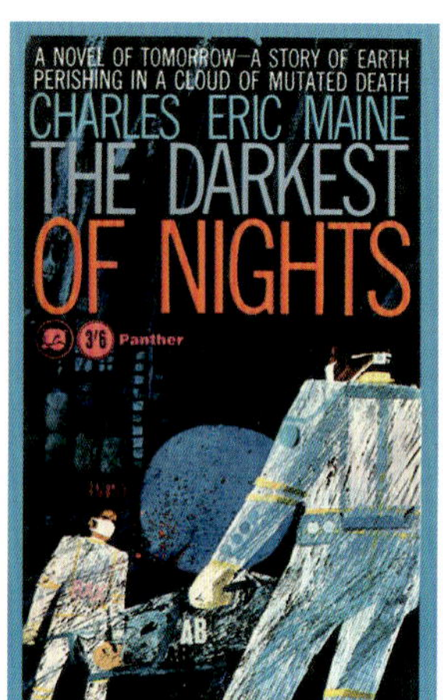

Charles Eric Maine | *The Darkest of Nights*
Panther Books, 1965 | Art **Unknown**

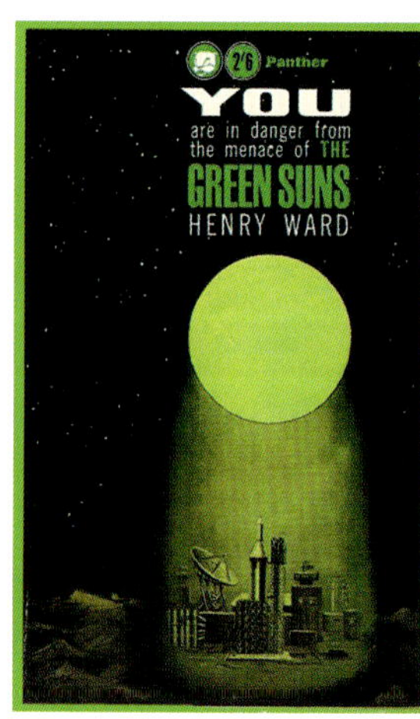

Henry Ward | *The Green Suns*
Panther Books, 1963 | Art **Unknown**

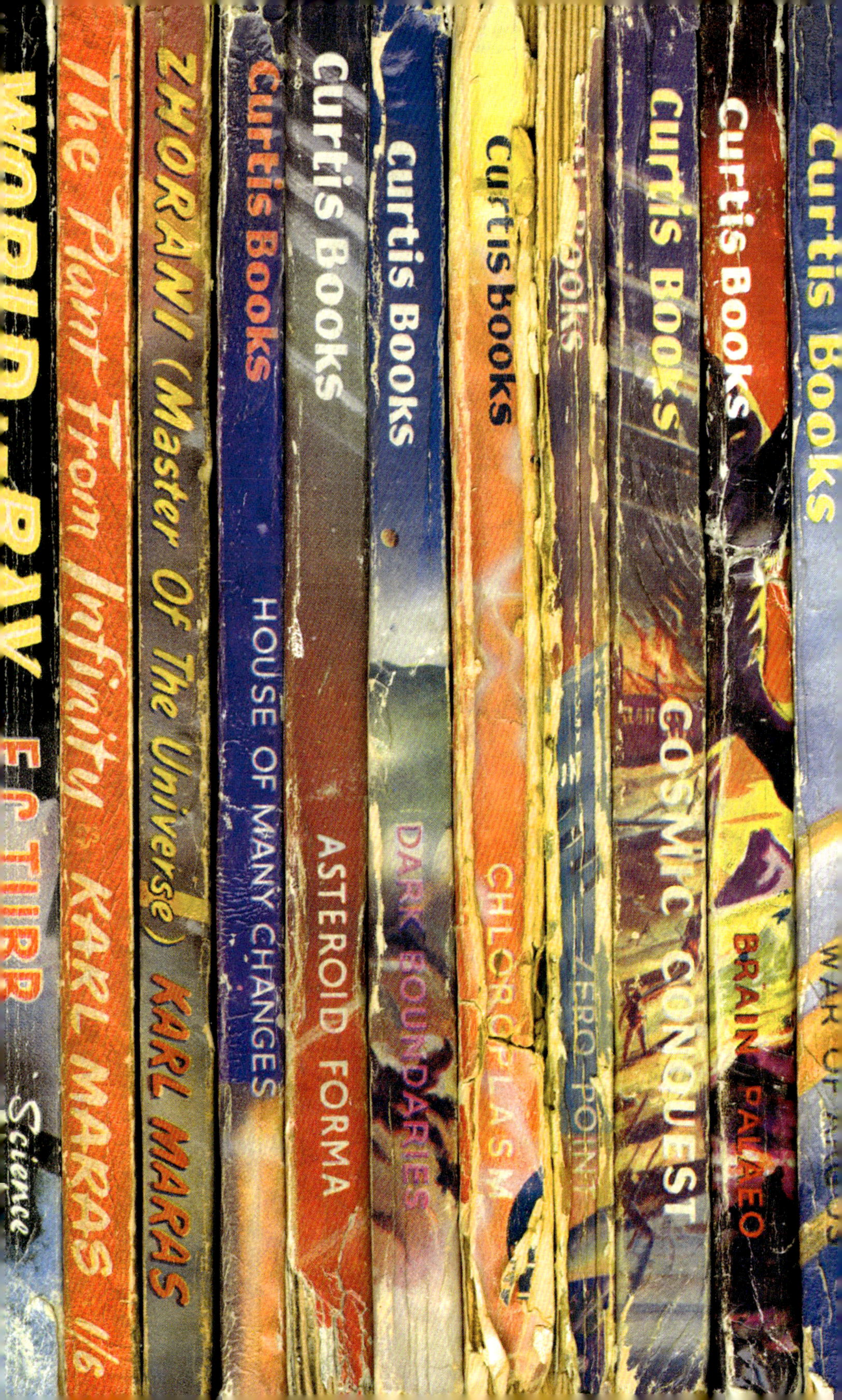

E C TUBB
Science
The Plant From Infinity
KARL MARAS
1/6
ZHORANI (Master Of The Universe)
KARL MARAS
Curtis Books
HOUSE OF MANY CHANGES
Curtis Books
ASTEROID FORMA
Curtis Books
DARK BOUNDARIES
Curtis Books
CHLOROPLASM
ZERO POINT
Curtis Books
COSMIC CONQUEST
Curtis Books
BRAIN PALAEO
Curtis Books

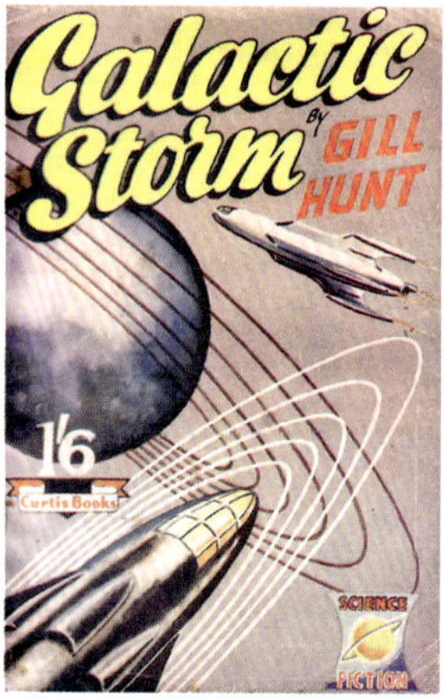

Gill Hunt (John Brunner) | *Galactic Storm*
Curtis Books, 1951 | Art **Ray Theobald**

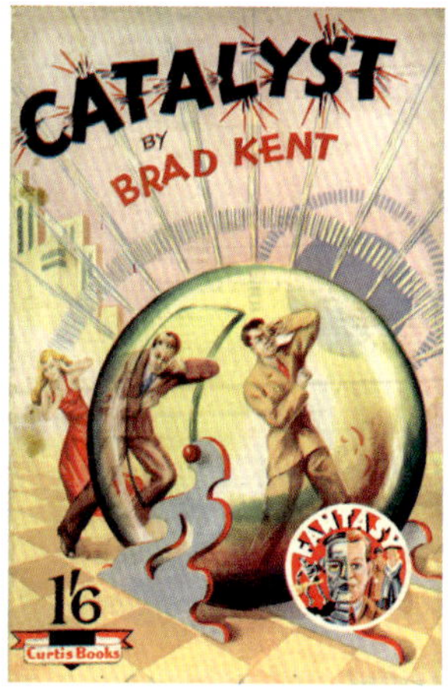

Brad Kent (Denis Hughes) | *Catalyst*
Curtis Books, 1952 | Art **Ray Theobald**

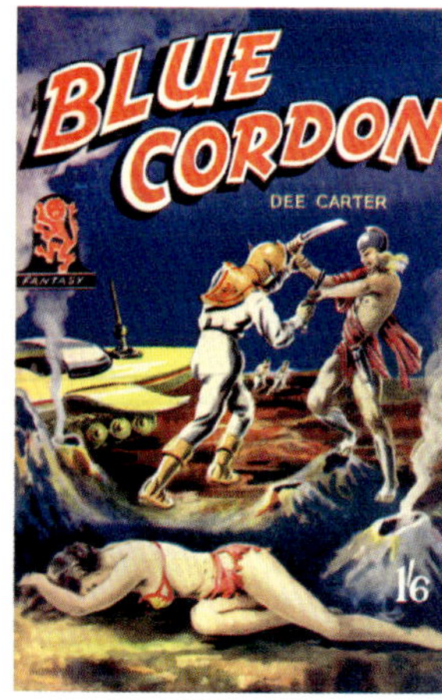

Dee Carter (Denis Hughes) | *Blue Cordon*
Curtis Books, 1952 | Art **Ray Theobald**

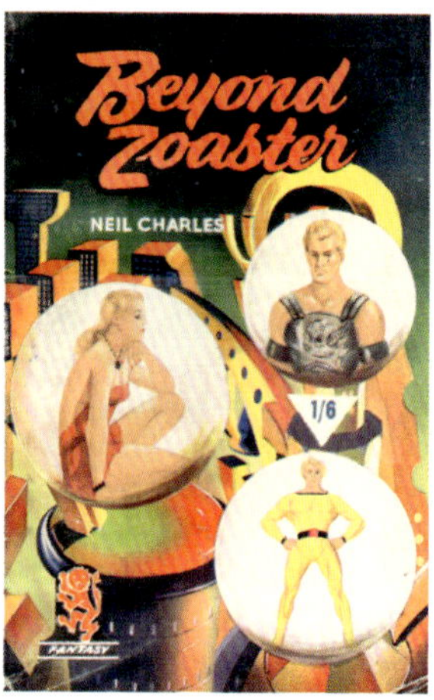

Neil Charles (Denis Hughes) | *Beyond Zoaster*
Curtis Books, 1953 | Art **Gordon C. Davies**

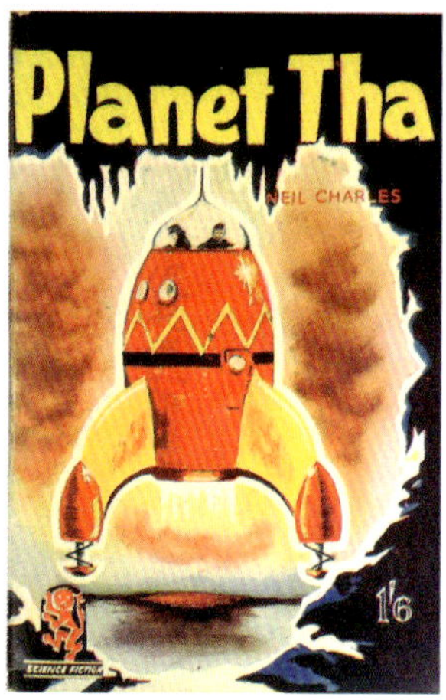

Neil Charles (Brian Holloway) | *Planet Tha*
Curtis Books, 1953 | Art **Gerald Facey**

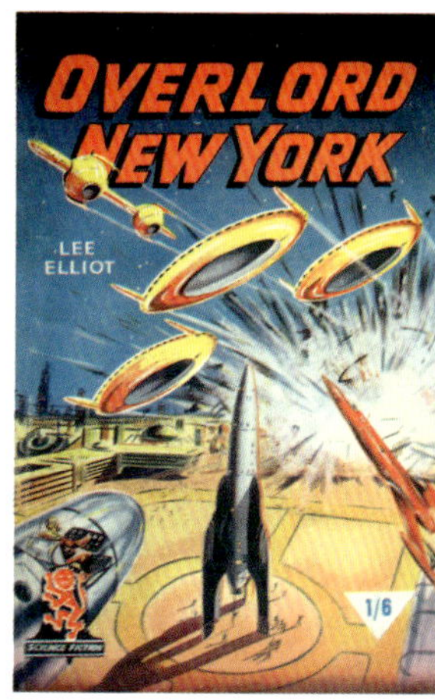

Lee Elliot | *Overlord New York*
Curtis Books, 1953 | Art **Gordon C. Davies**

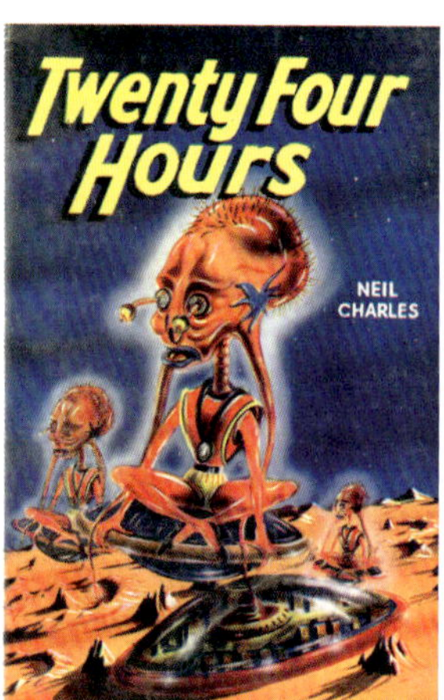

Neil Charles (Denis Hughes) | *Twenty-Four Hours*
Curtis Books, 1952 | Art **Gordon C. Davies**

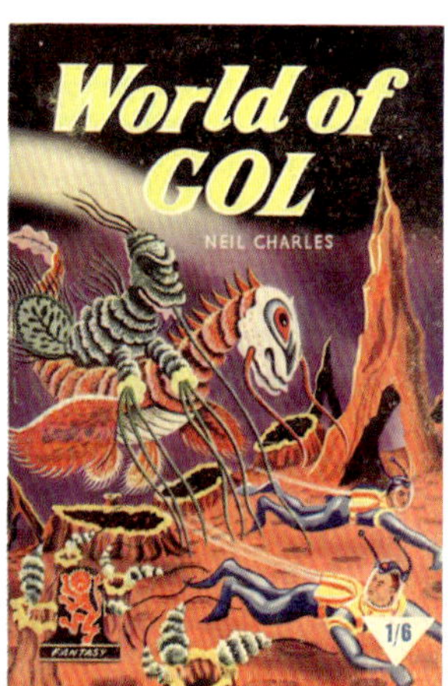

Neil Charles (Denis Hughes) | *World of Gol*
Curtis Books, 1953 | Art **Gordon C. Davies**

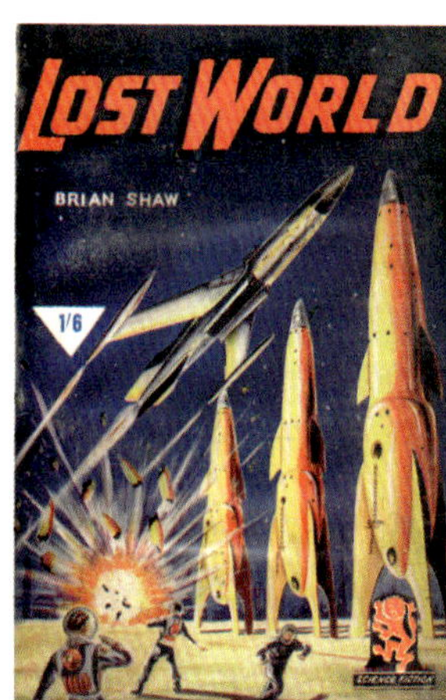

Brian Shaw (Brian Holloway) | *Lost World*
Curtis Books, 1953 | Art **Gordon C. Davies**

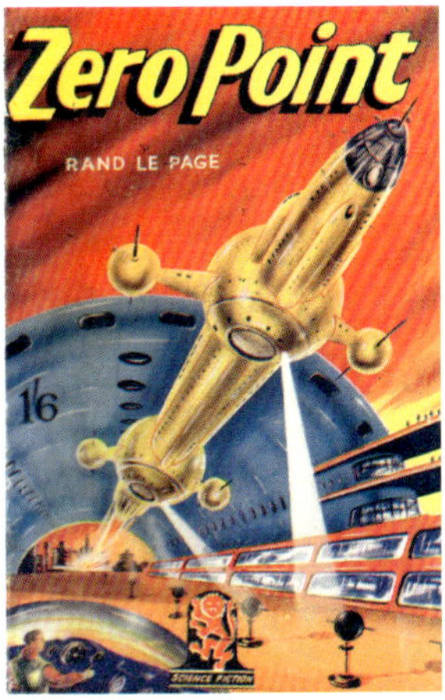

Rand Le Page (John Glasby) | *Zero Point*
Curtis Books, 1952 | Art **Gordon C. Davies**

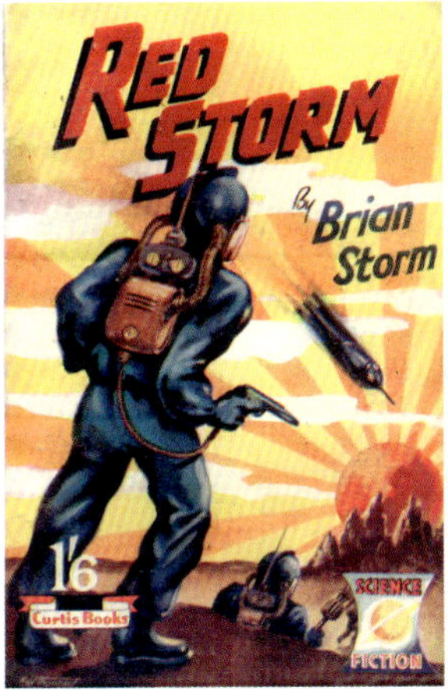

Brian Storm (Brian Holloway) | *Red Storm*
Curtis Books, 1952 | Art **Ray Theobald**

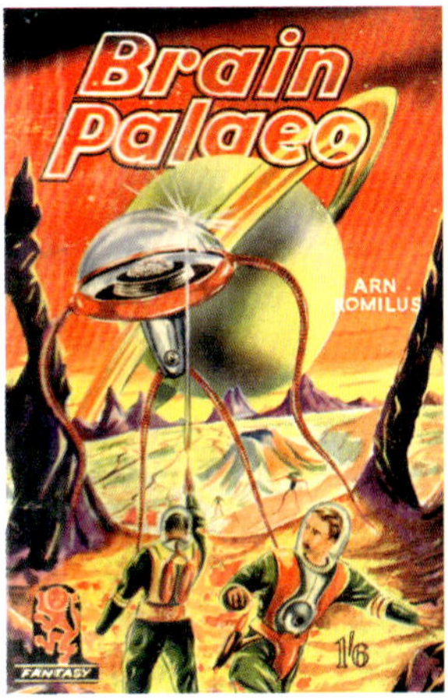

Arn Romilus (Denis Hughes) | *Brain Palaeo*
Curtis Books, 1953 | Art **Gordon C. Davies**

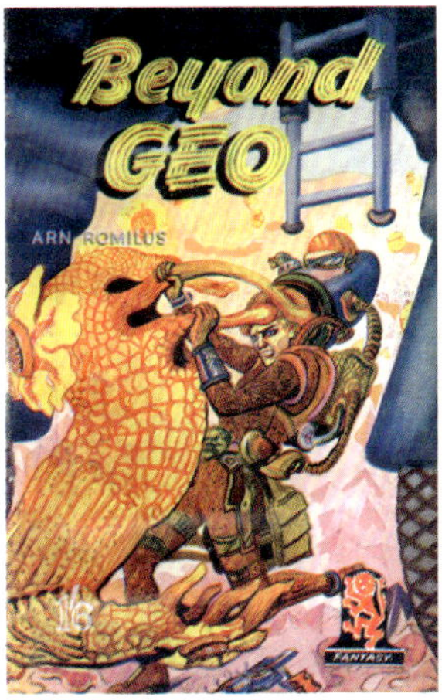

Arn Romilus (Brian Holloway) | *Beyond Geo*
Curtis Books, 1953 | Art **Gerald Facey**

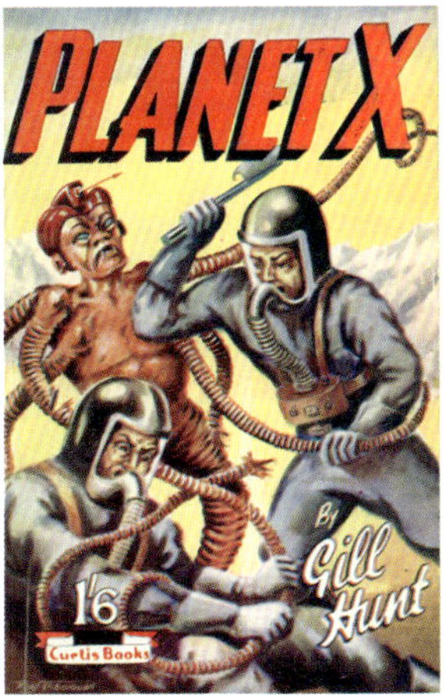

Gill Hunt (Denis Hughes) | *Planet X*
Curtis Books, 1951 | Art **Ray Theobald**

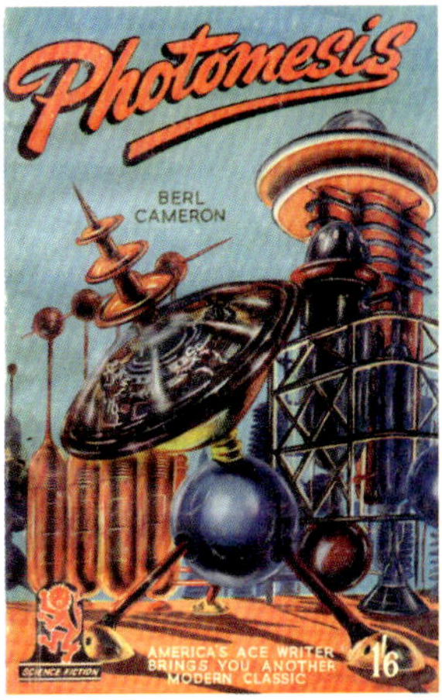

Berl Cameron (David O'Brien) | *Photomesis*
Curtis Books, 1952 | Art **Gordon C. Davies**

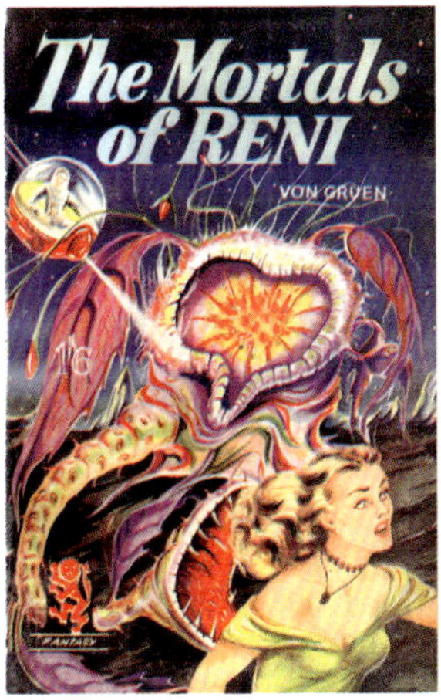

Von Gruen (Brian Holloway)
The Mortals of Reni
Curtis Books, 1953 | Art **Ray Theobald**

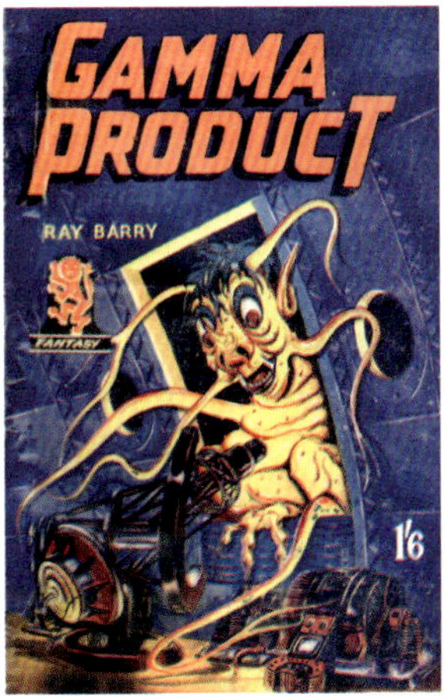

Ray Barry (Denis Hughes)
Gamma Product
Curtis Books, 1952 | Art **Gordon C. Davies**

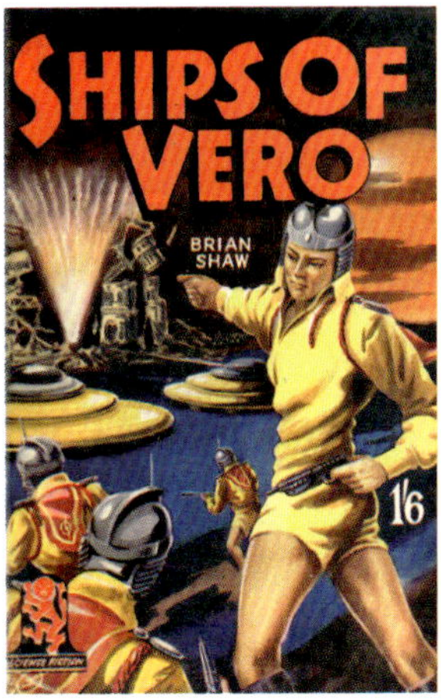

Brian Shaw (Brian Holloway) | *Ships of Vero*
Curtis Books, 1952 | Art **Ray Theobald**

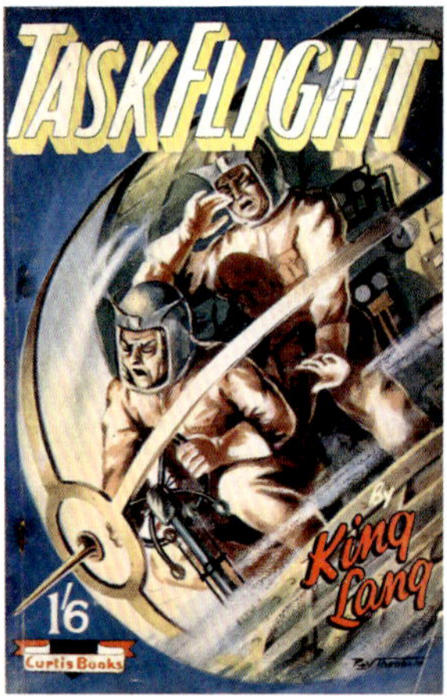

King Lang (David A. Griffiths) | *Task Flight*
Curtis Books, 1951 | Art **Ray Theobald**

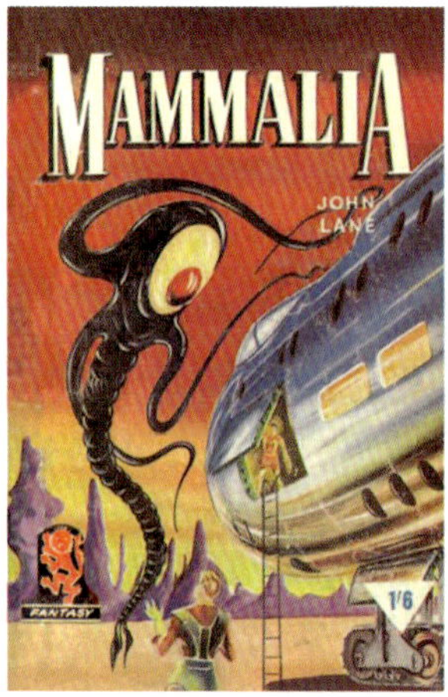

John Lane (Denis Hughes) | *Mammalia*
Curtis Books, 1953 | Art **Gordon C. Davies**

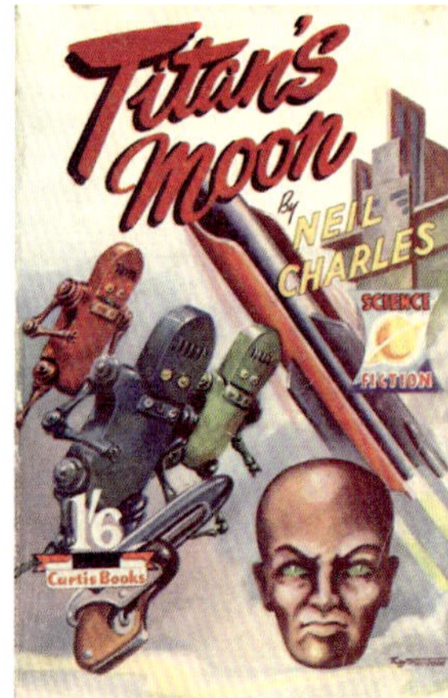

Neil Charles (Brian Holloway) | *Titan's Moon*
Curtis Books, 1952 | Art **Ray Theobald**

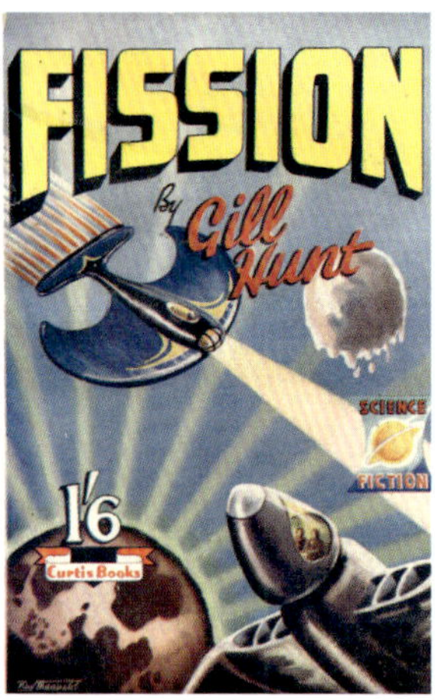

Gill Hunt (David A. Griffiths) | *Fission*
Curtis Books, 1952 | Art **Ray Theobald**

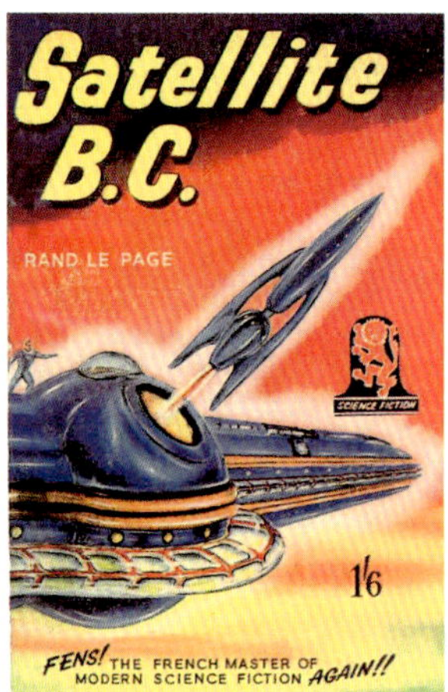

Rand Le Page (John Glasby) | *Satellite B.C.*
Curtis Books, 1952 | Art **Gordon C. Davies**

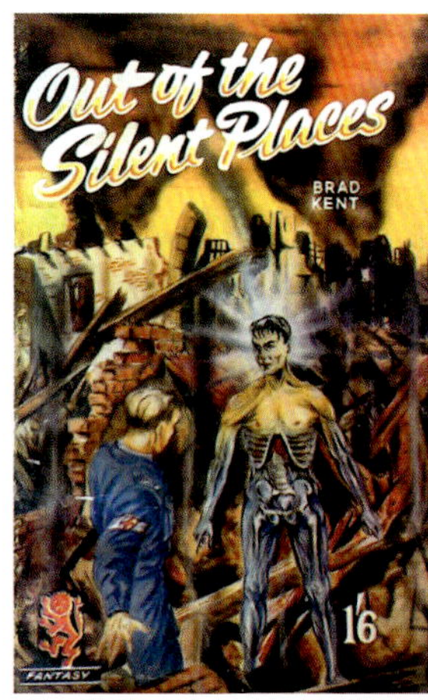

Brad Kent (Maurice G. Hugi)
Out of the Silent Places
Curtis Books, 1952 | Art **Gordon C. Davies**

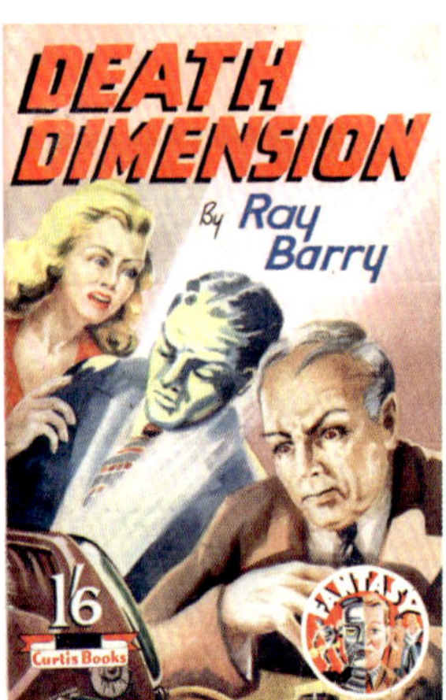

Ray Barry (Denis Hughes) | *Death Dimension*
Curtis Books, 1952 | Art **Ray Theobald**

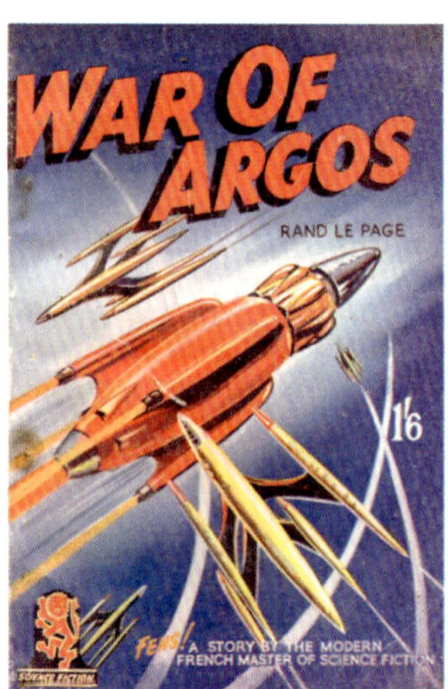

Rand Le Page (William Bird) | *War of Argos*
Curtis Books, 1952 | Art **Gordon C. Davies**

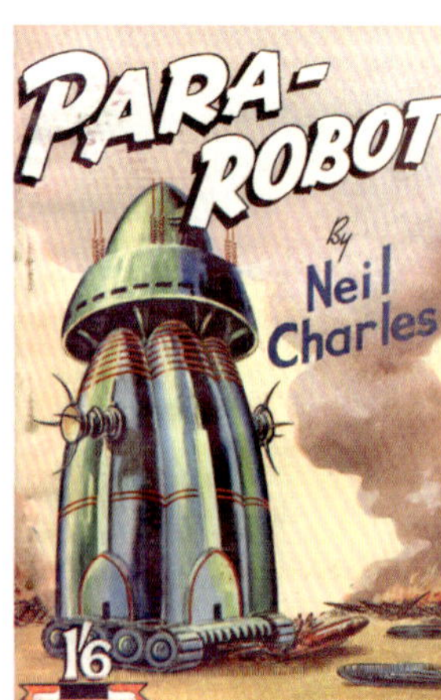

Neil Charles (John Jennison) | *Para-Robot*
Curtis Books, 1952 | Art **Ray Theobald**

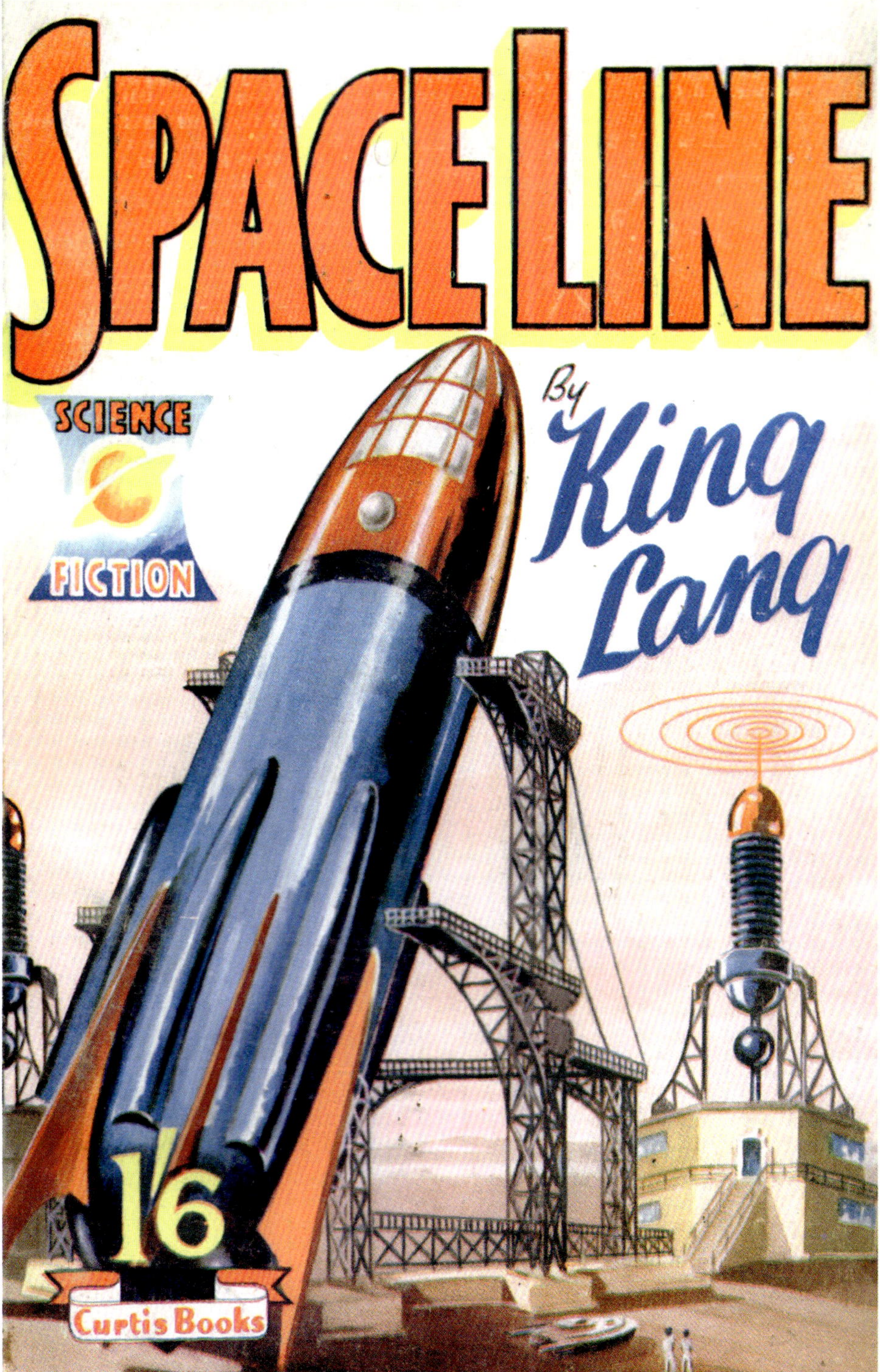

King Lang (John Jennison) | *Space Line*
Curtis Books, 1952 | Art **Ray Theobald**

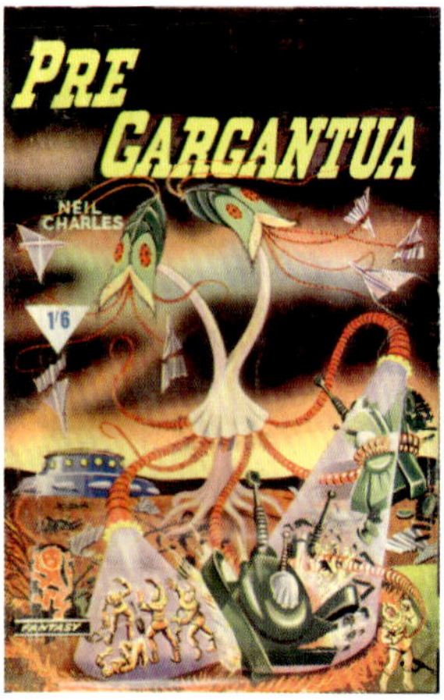

Neil Charles (Denis Hughes) | *Pre Gargantua*
Curtis Books, 1953 | Art **Gordon C. Davies**

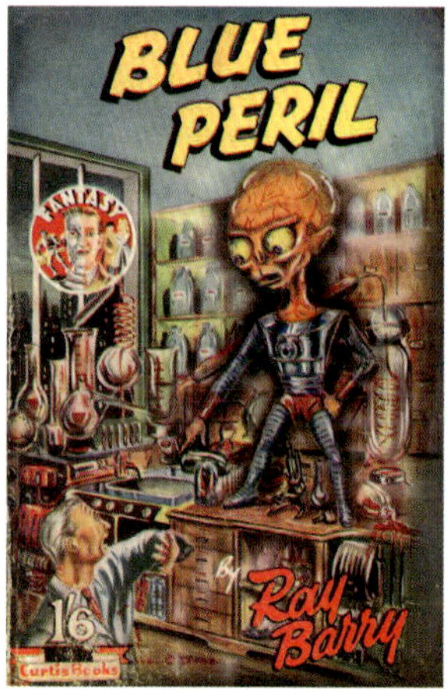

Ray Barry (Denis Hughes) | *Blue Peril*
Curtis Books, 1952 | Art **Gordon C. Davies**

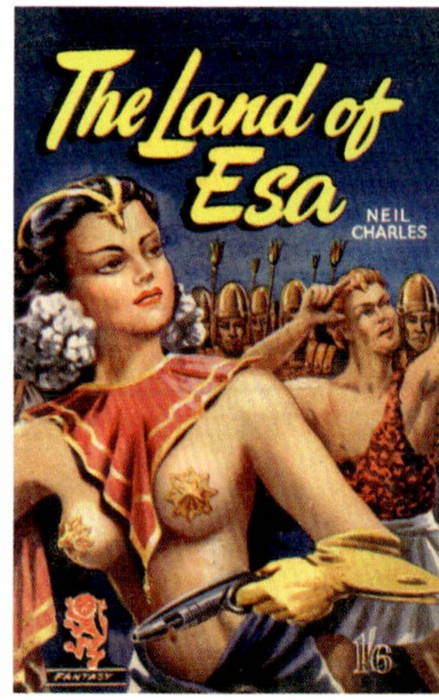

Neil Charles (Denis Hughes) | *The Land of Esa*
Curtis Books, 1952 | Art **Ray Theobald**

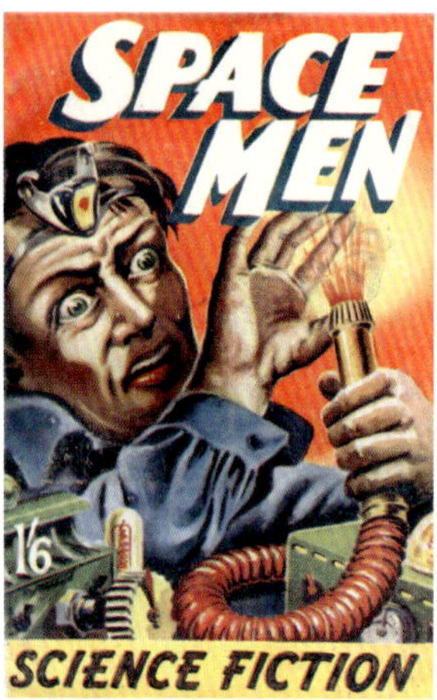

David Shaw (David A. Griffiths)
Space Men
Curtis Books, 1951 | Art **Ray Theobald**

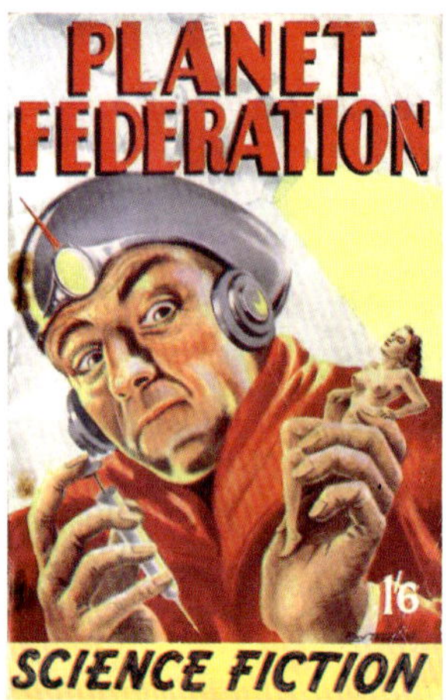

David Shaw (David A. Griffiths)
Planet Federation
Curtis Books, 1950 | Art **Ray Theobald**

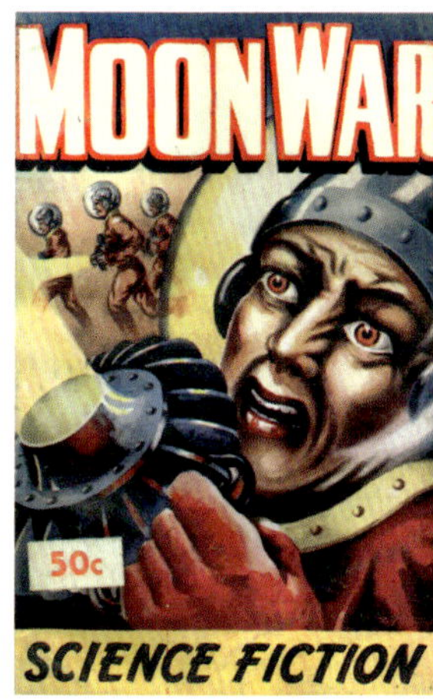

Denis Hughes | *Moon War*
Curtis Books, 1951 | Art **Ray Theobald**

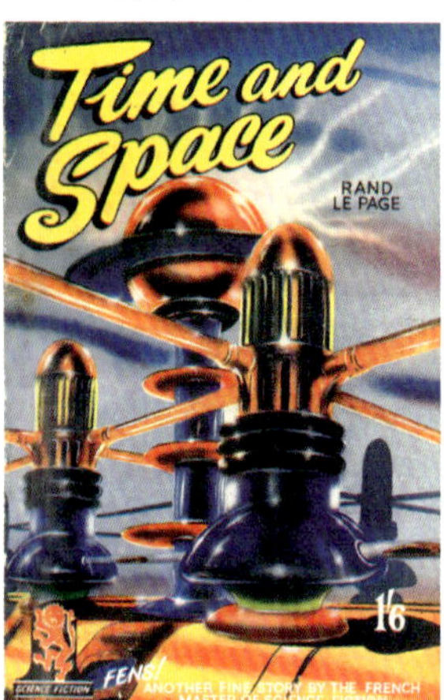

Rand Le Page (John Glasby, Arthur Roberts)
Time and Space
Curtis Books, 1952 | Art **Gordon C. Davies**

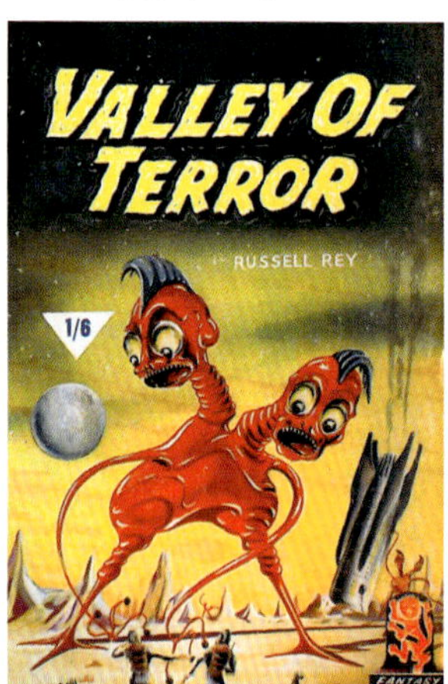

Russell Rey (Denis Hughes) | *Valley of Terror*
Curtis Books, 1953 | Art **Gordon C. Davies**

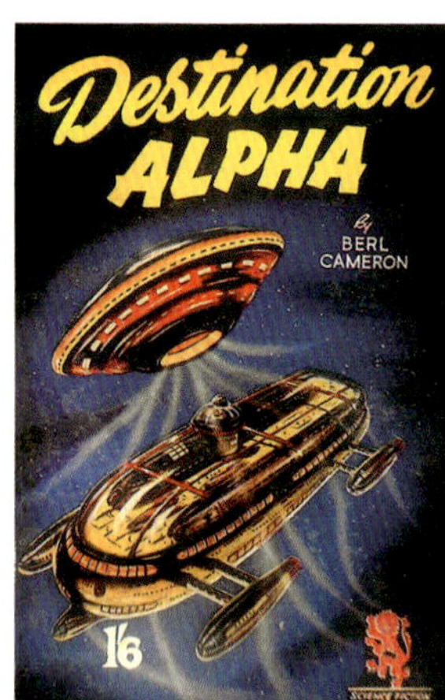

Berl Cameron (Brian Holloway)
Destination Alpha
Curtis Books, 1952 | Art **Gordon C. Davies**

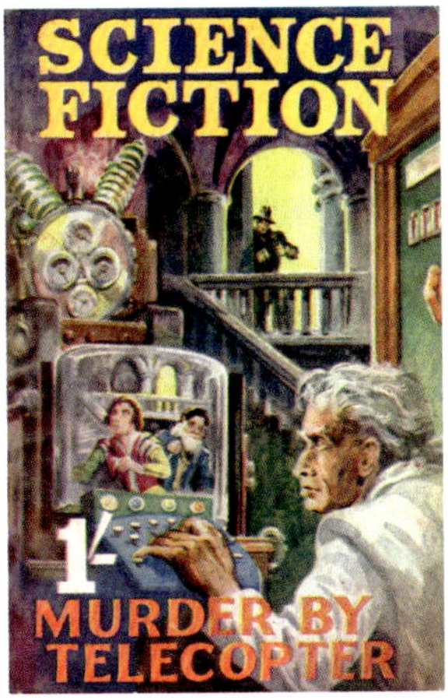

Denis Hughes | *Murder by Telecopter*
Curtis Books, 1950 | Art **George Ratcliffe**

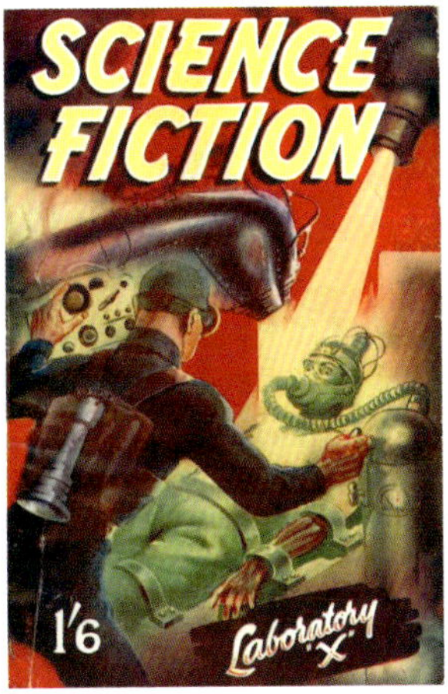

David Shaw | *Laboratory "X"*
Curtis Books, 1950 | Art **Terry Maloney**

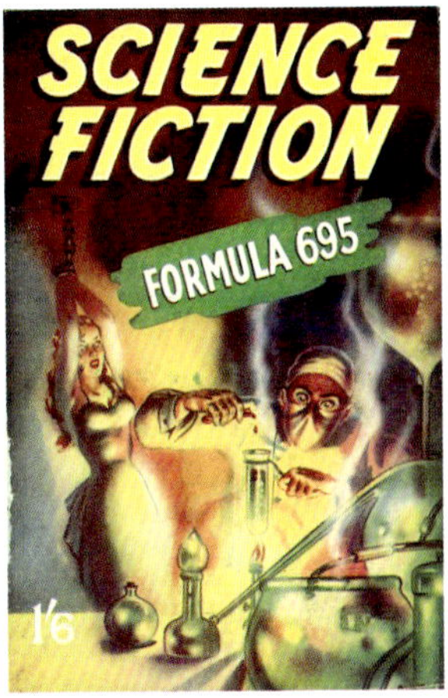

Denis Hughes | *Formula 695*
Curtis Books, 1950 | Art **Terry Maloney**

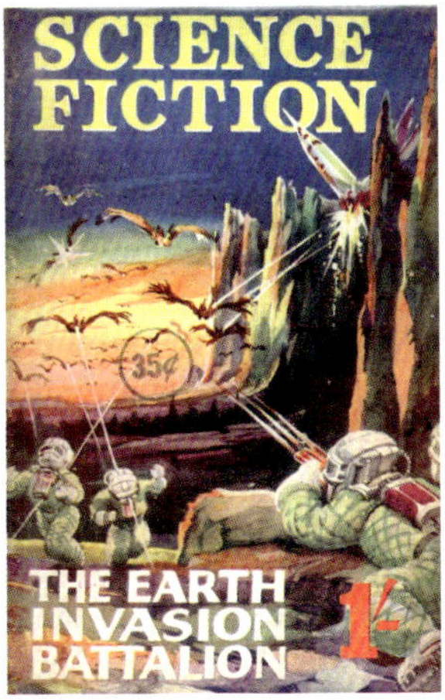

Denis Hughes | *The Earth Invasion Battalion*
Curtis Books, 1950 | Art **George Ratcliffe**

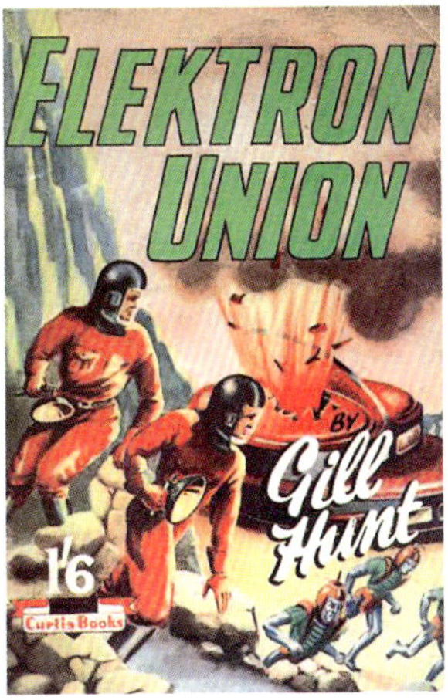

Gill Hunt (Denis Hughes) | *Elektron Union*
Curtis Books, 1951 | Art **Ray Theobald**

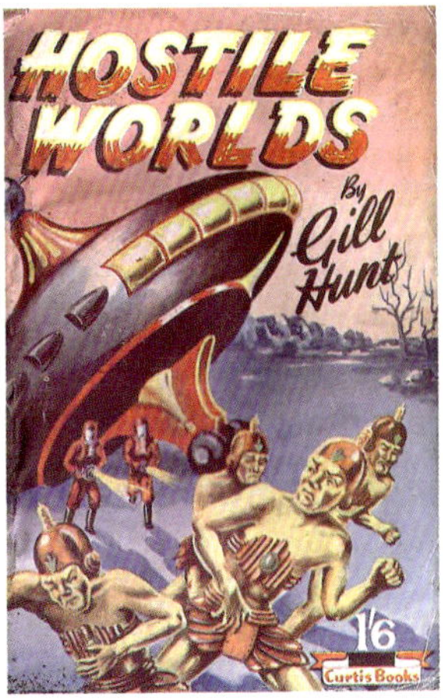

Gill Hunt (Denis Hughes) | *Hostile Worlds*
Curtis Books, 1951 | Art **Ray Theobald**

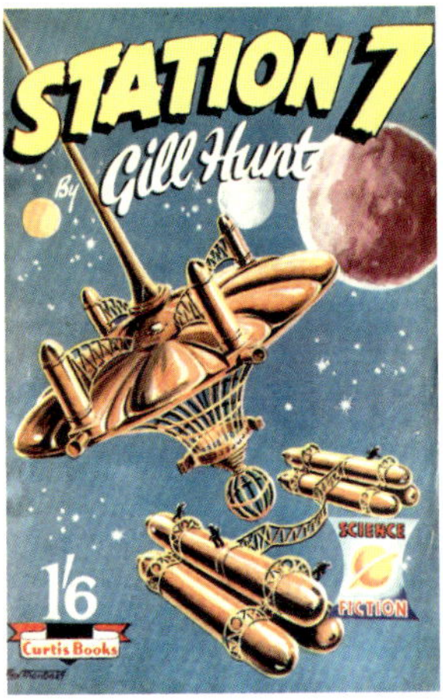

Gill Hunt (John Jennison) | *Station 7*
Curtis Books, 1952 | Art **Ray Theobald**

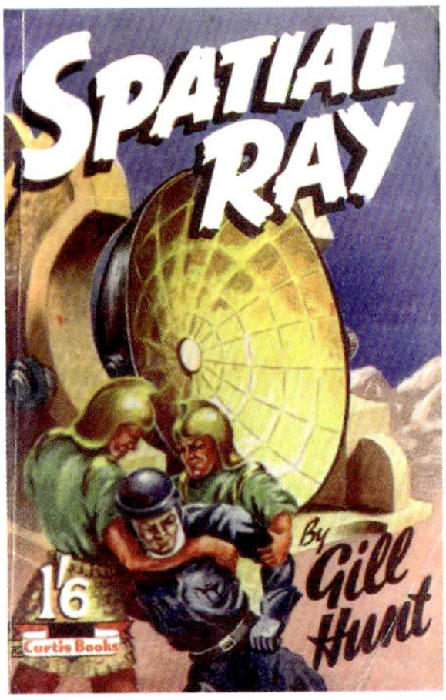

Gill Hunt (Denis Hughes) | *Spatial Ray*
Curtis Books, 1951 | Art **Ray Theobald**

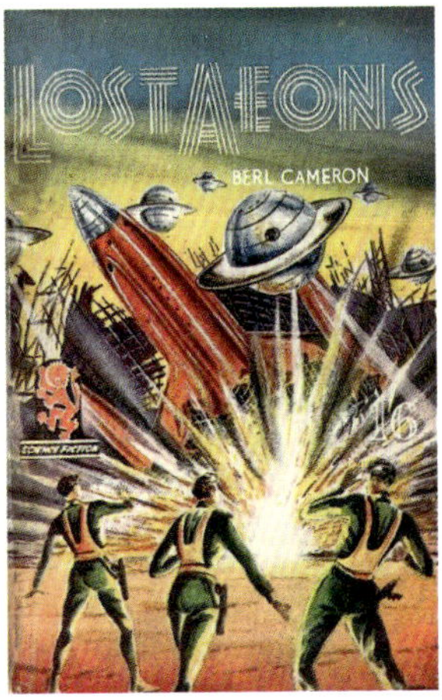

Berl Cameron (Denis Hughes) | *Lost Aeons*
Curtis Books, 1953 | Art **Gordon C. Davies**

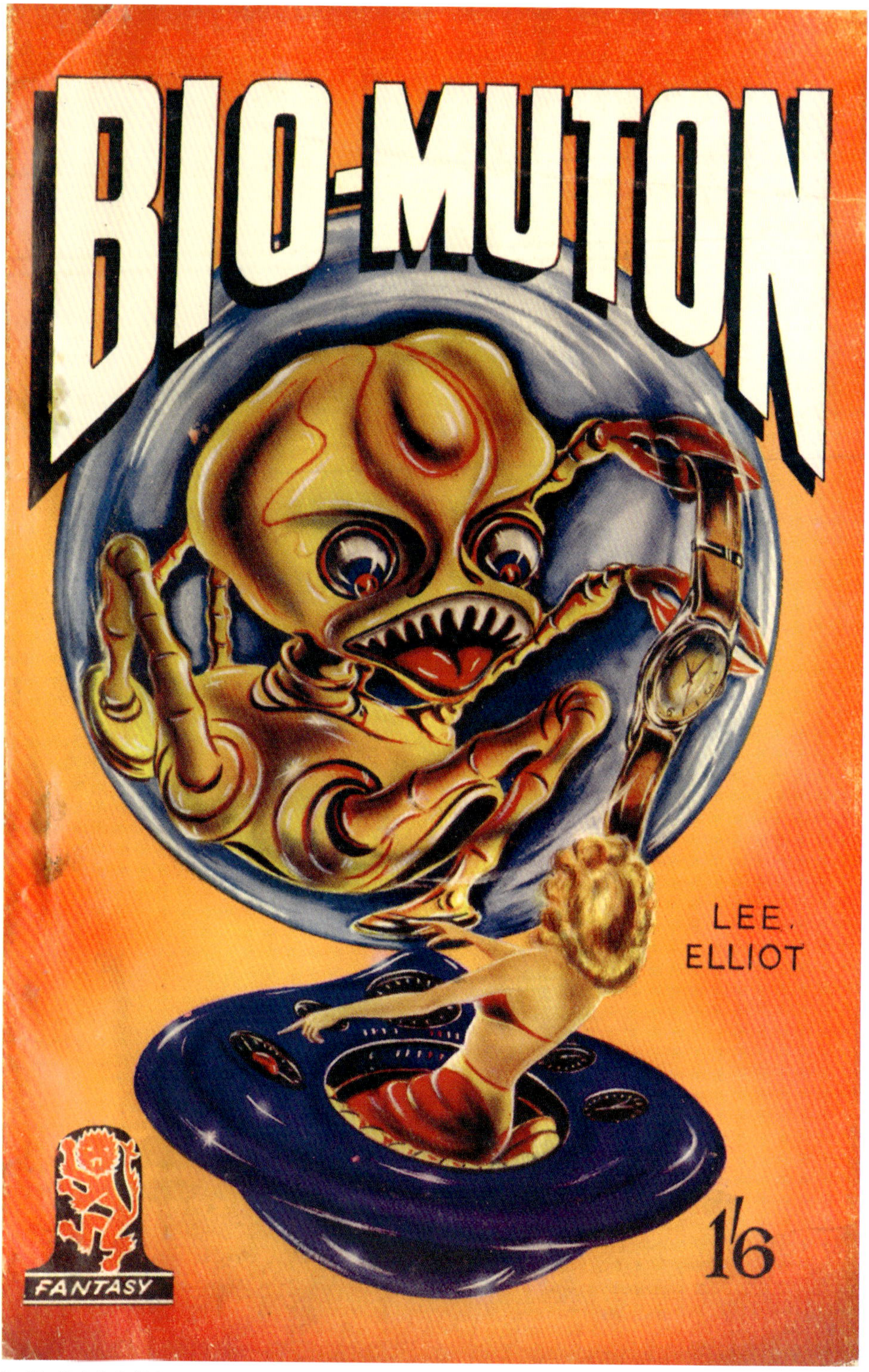

Lee Elliot (Denis Hughes) | *Bio-Muton*
Curtis Books, 1952 | Art **Gordon C. Davies**

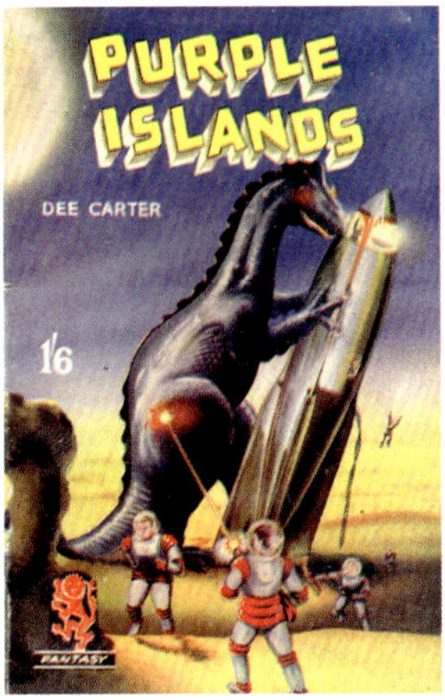

Dee Carter (Denis Hughes) | *Purple Islands*
Curtis Books, 1953 | Art **Gerald Facey**

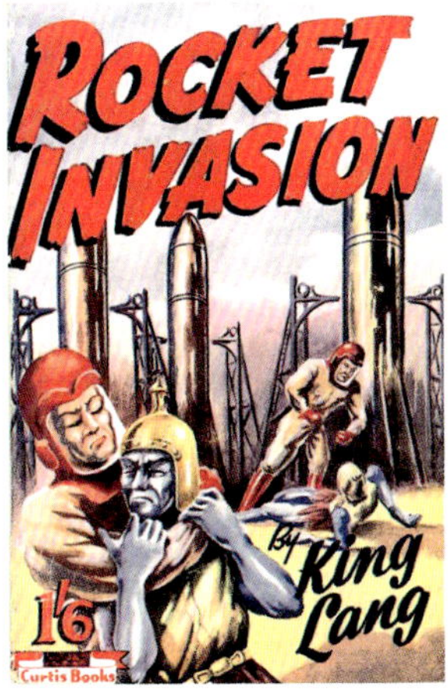

King Lang (David A. Griffiths)
Rocket Invasion
Curtis Books, 1951 | Art **Ray Theobald**

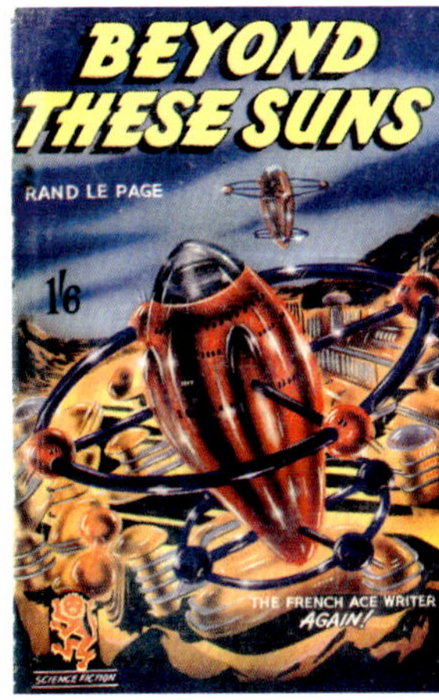

Rand Le Page (Cyril Protheroe)
Beyond These Suns
Curtis Books, 1952 | Art **Gordon C. Davies**

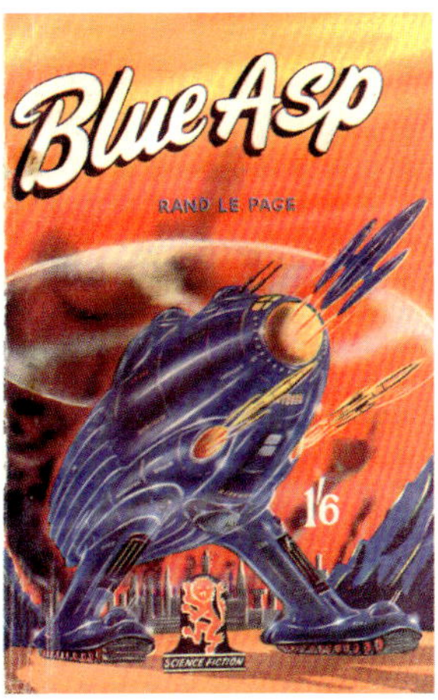

Rand Le Page (David O'Brien) | *Blue Asp*
Curtis Books, 1952 | Art **Gordon C. Davies**

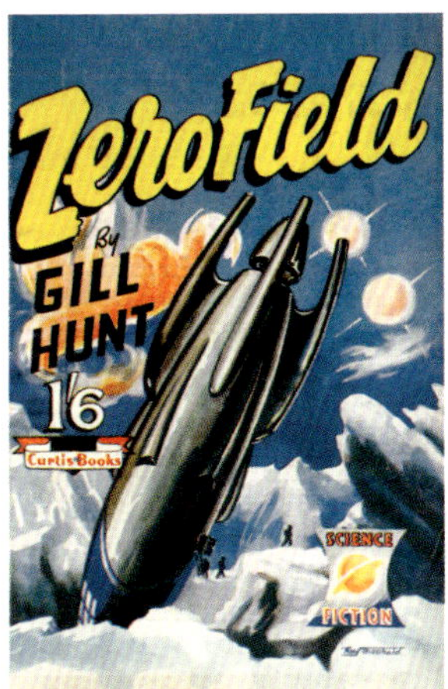

Gill Hunt (John Jennison) | *Zero Field*
Curtis Books, 1952 | Art **Ray Theobald**

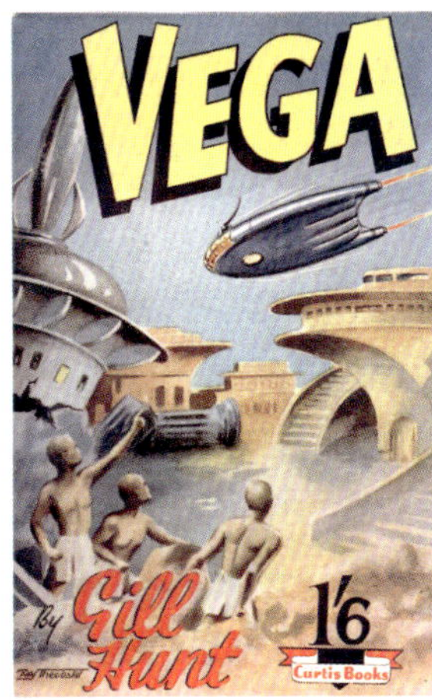

Gill Hunt (David A. Griffiths) | *Vega*
Curtis Books, 1951 | Art **Ray Theobald**

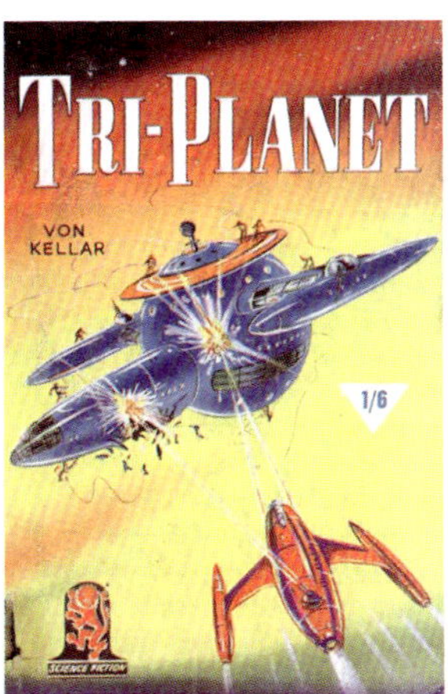

Von Kellar (Denis Hughes) | *Tri-Planet*
Curtis Books, 1953 | Art **Gordon C. Davies**

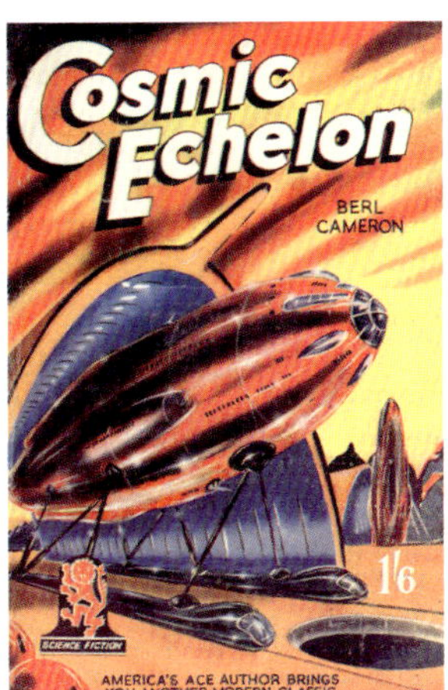

Berl Cameron (John Glasby, Arthur Roberts)
Cosmic Echelon
Curtis Books, 1952 | Art **Gordon C. Davies**

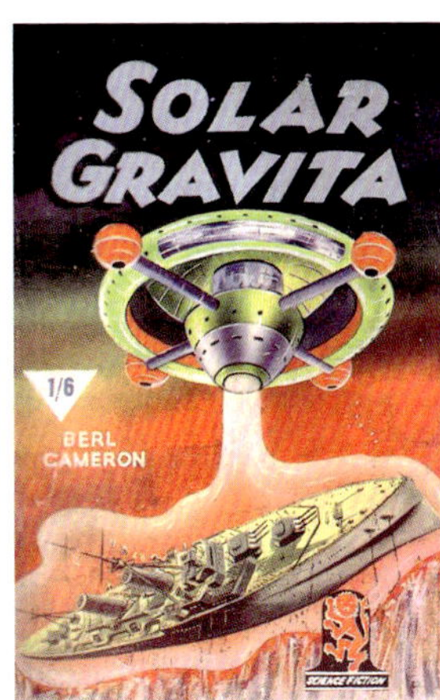

Berl Cameron | *Solar Gravita*
Curtis Books, 1953 | Art **Gordon C. Davies**

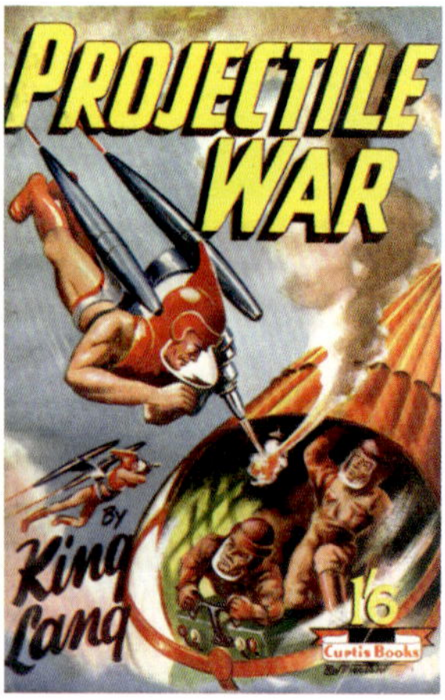

King Lang (David A. Griffiths) | *Projectile War*
Curtis Books, 1951 | Art **Ray Theobald**

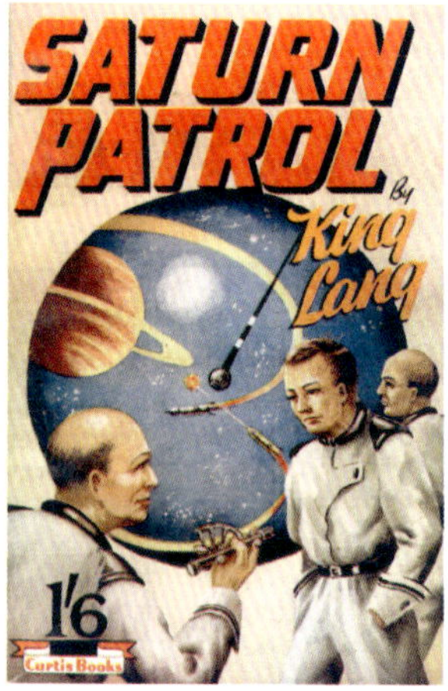

King Lang (E. C. Tubb) | *Saturn Patrol*
Curtis Books, 1951 | Art **Ray Theobald**

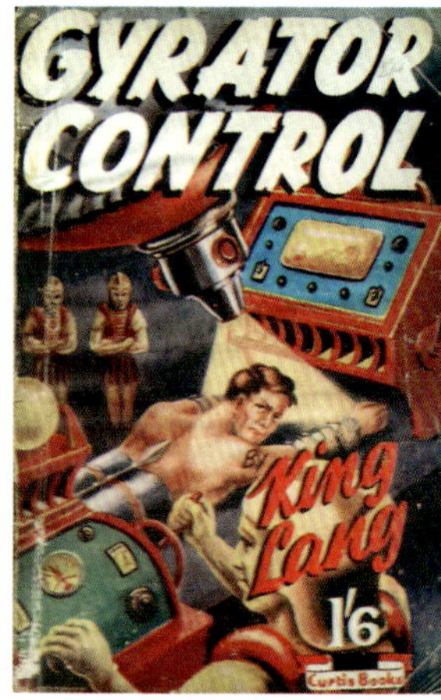

King Lang (David A. Griffiths) | *Gyrator Control*
Curtis Books, 1951 | Art **Ray Theobald**

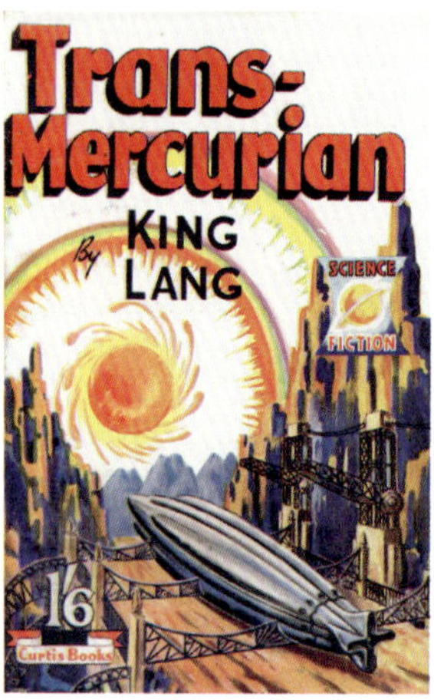

King Lang (Brian Holloway) | *Trans-Mercurian*
Curtis Books, 1952 | Art **Ray Theobald**

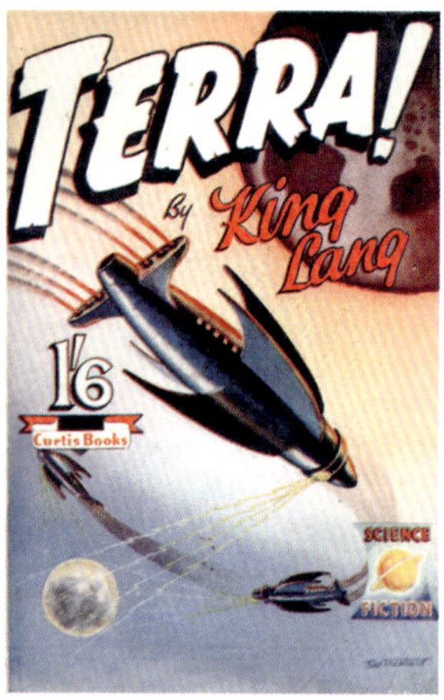

King Lang (George Hay) | *Terra!*
Curtis Books, 1952 | Art **Ray Theobald**

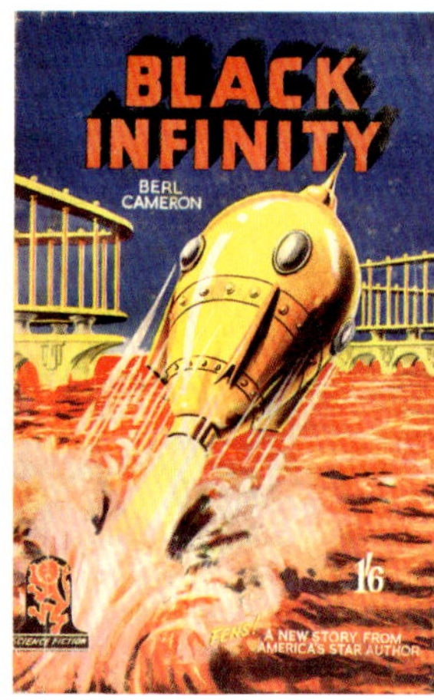

Berl Cameron (David O'Brien) | *Black Infinity*
Curtis Books, 1952 | Art **Unknown**

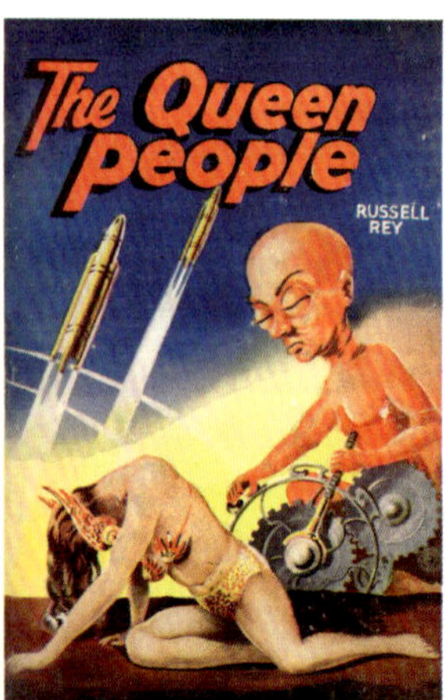

Russell Rey (Denis Hughes)
The Queen People
Curtis Books, 1952 | Art **Ray Theobald**

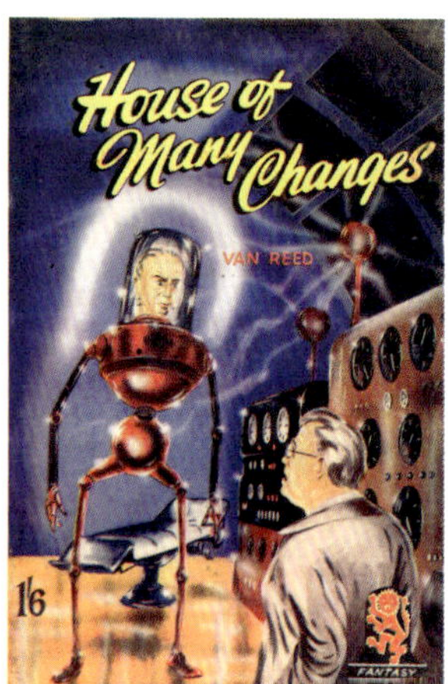

Van Reed (Denis Hughes)
House of Many Changes
Curtis Books, 1952 | Art **Gordon C. Davies**

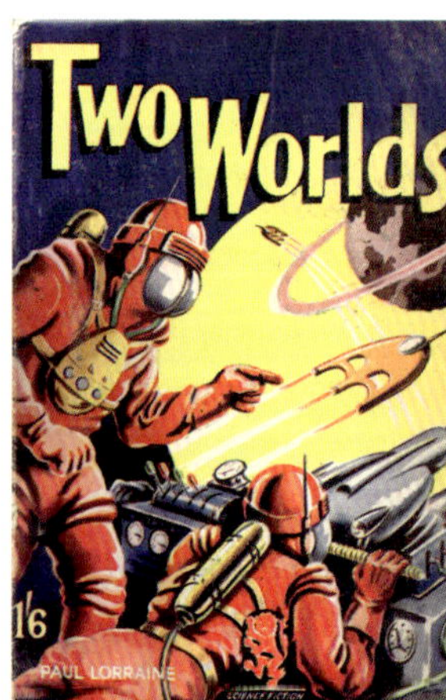

Paul Lorraine (William Bird) | *Two Worlds*
Curtis Books, 1952 | Art **Ray Theobald**

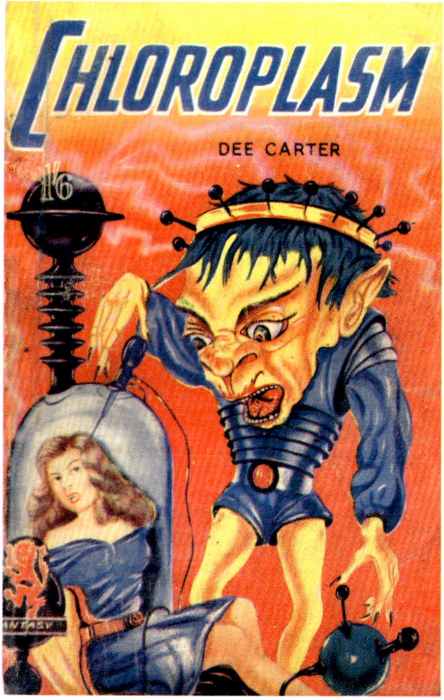

Dee Carter (Denis Hughes) | *Chloroplasm*
Curtis Books, 1952 | Art **Gordon C. Davies**

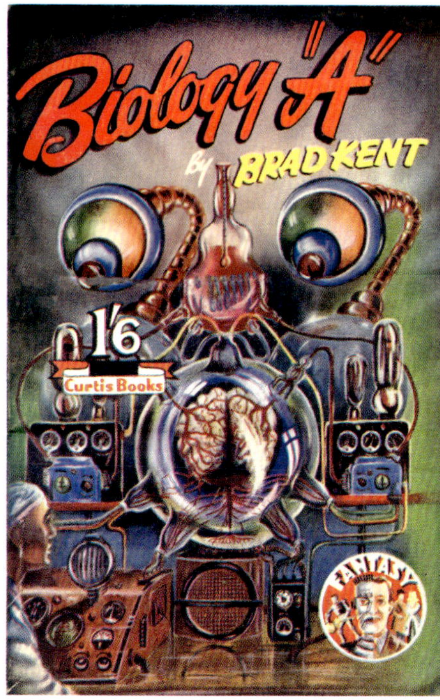

Brad Kent (Denis Hughes) | *Biology "A"*
Curtis Books, 1952 | Art **Gordon C. Davies**

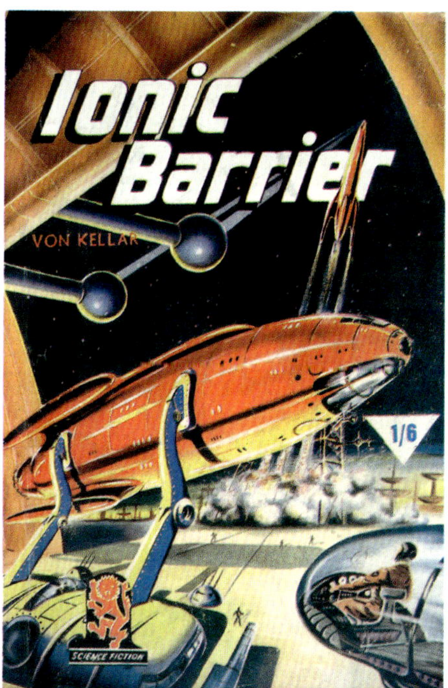

Von Kellar (Denis Hughes) | *Ionic Barrier*
Curtis Books, 1953 | Art **Gordon C. Davies**

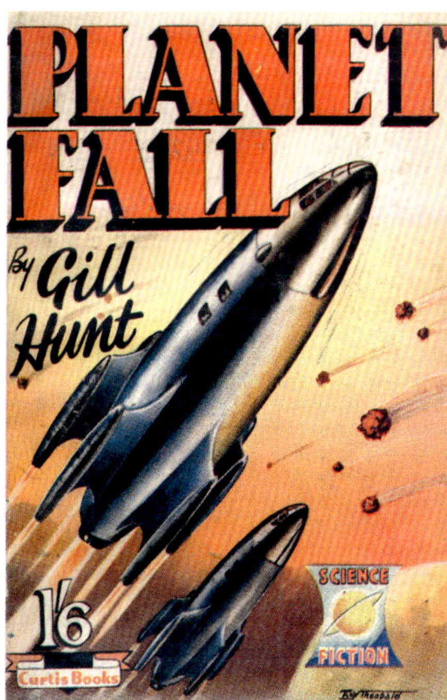

Gill Hunt (E. C. Tubb) | *Planetfall*
Curtis Books, 1951 | Art **Ray Theobald**

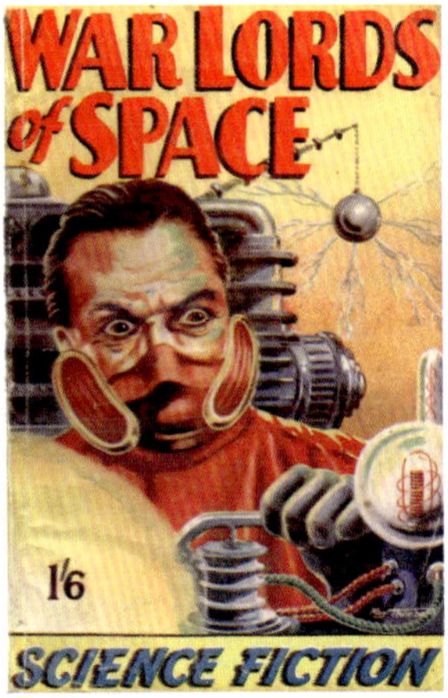

Denis Hughes | *War Lords of Space*
Curtis Books, 1950 | Art **Ray Theobald**

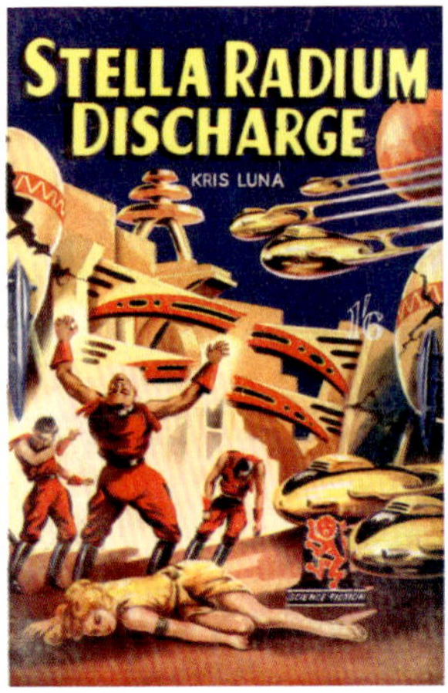

Kris Luna (David O'Brien)
Stella Radium Discharge
Curtis Books, 1952 | Art **Ray Theobald**

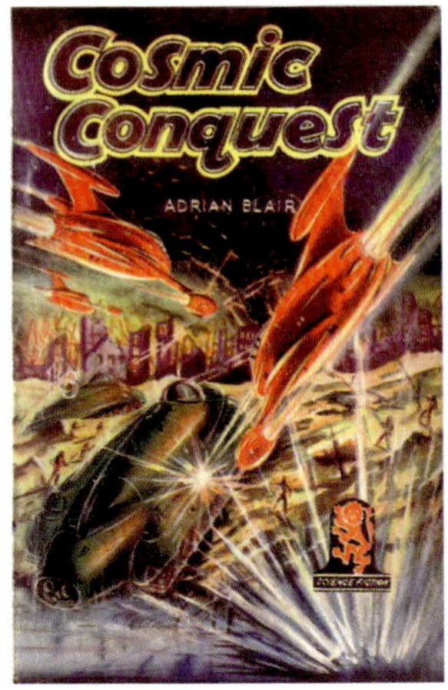

Adrian Blair (William Bird) | *Cosmic Conquest*
Curtis Books, 1953 | Art **Gordon C. Davies**

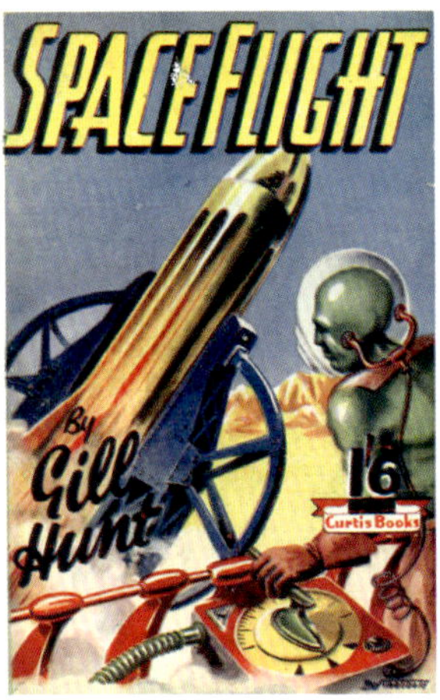

Gill Hunt (Denis Hughes) | *Space Flight*
Curtis Books, 1951 | Art **Ray Theobald**

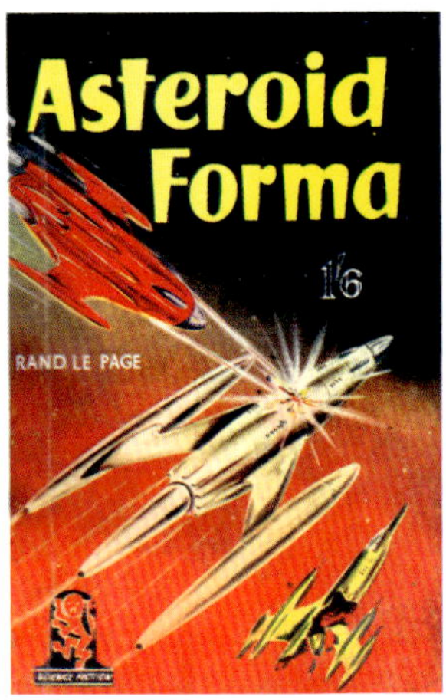

Rand Le Page (Denis Hughes) | *Asteroid Forma*
Curtis Books, 1953 | Art **Gordon C. Davies**

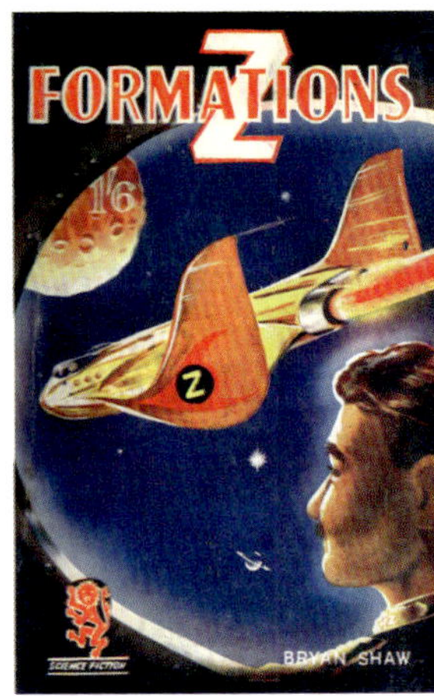

Brian Shaw (John Russell Fearn) | *Z-Formations*
Curtis Books, 1953 | Art **Gerald Facey**

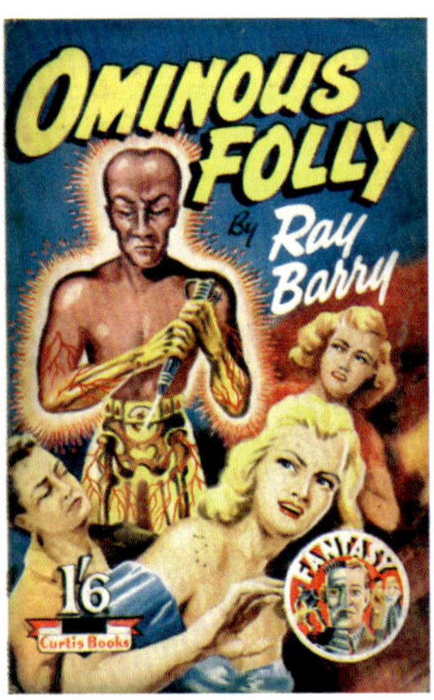

Ray Barry (Denis Hughes)
Ominous Folly
Curtis Books, 1952 | Art **Ray Theobald**

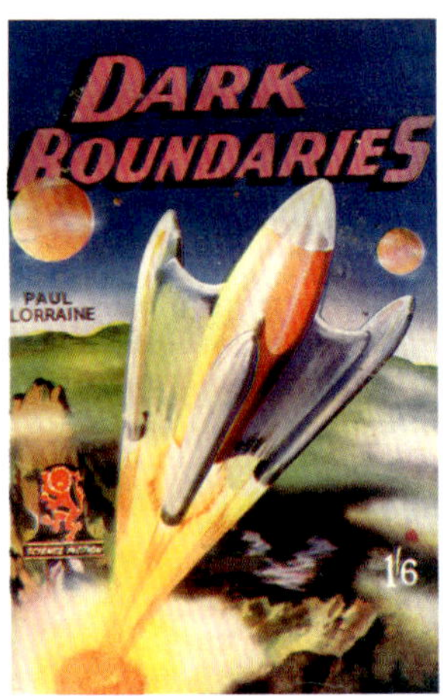

Paul Lorraine (John Russell Fearn)
Dark Boundaries
Curtis Books, 1953 | Art **Gerald Facey**

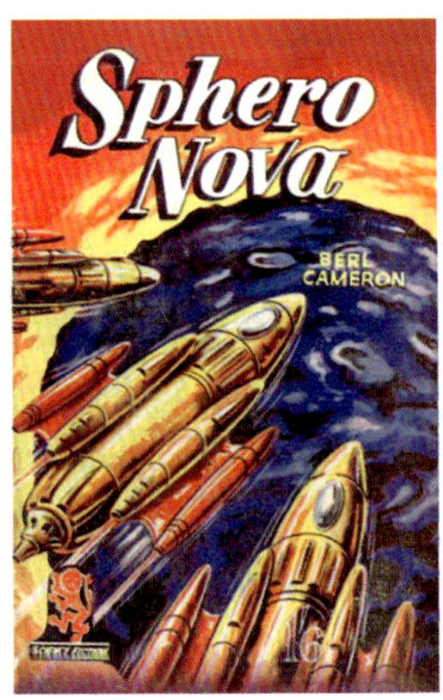

Berl Cameron (John Glasby, Arthur Roberts)
Sphero Nova
Curtis Books, 1952 | Art **Ray Theobald**

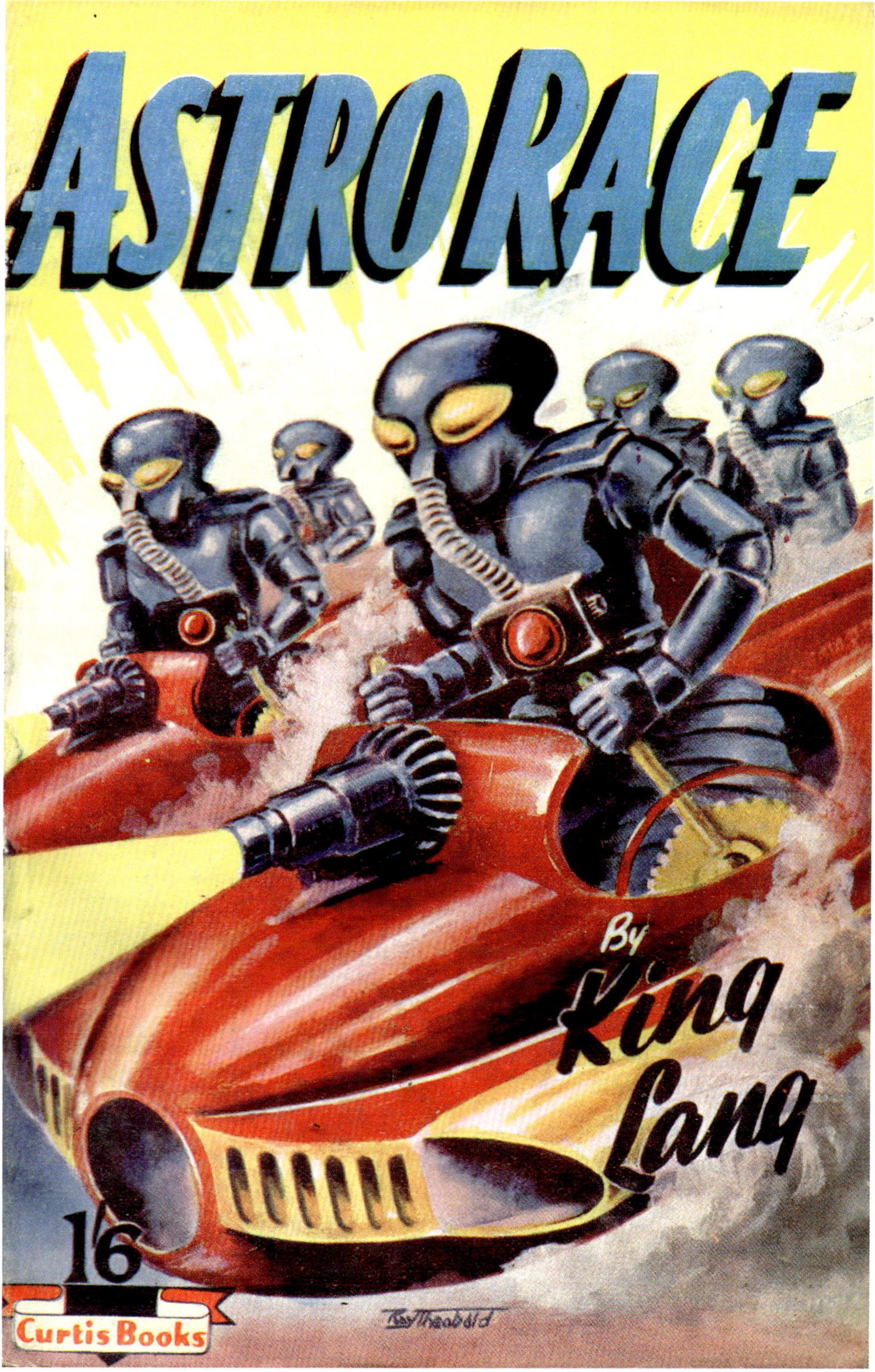

King Lang (David A. Griffiths) | *Astro Race*
Curtis Books, 1951 | Art **Ray Theobald**

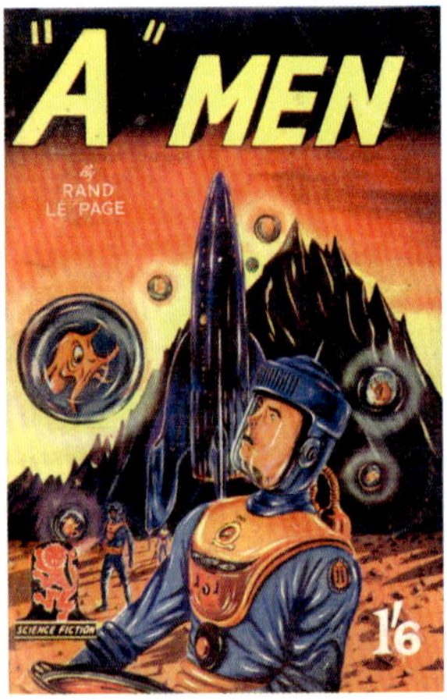

Rand Le Page (Brian Holloway) | *"A" Men*
Curtis Books, 1952 | Art **Gordon C. Davies**

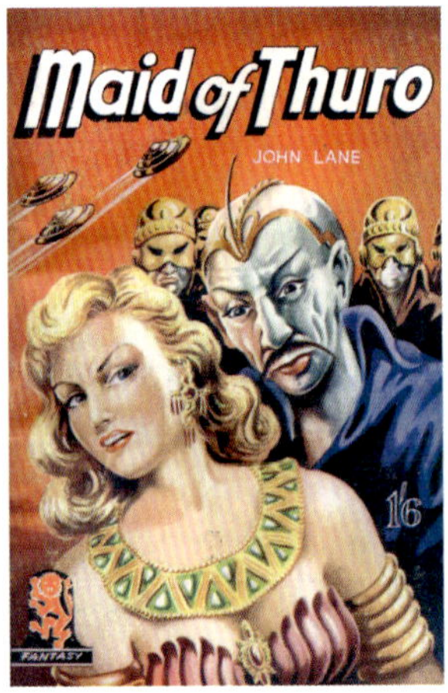

John Lane (Denis Hughes) | *Maid of Thuro*
Curtis Books, 1952 | Art **Ray Theobald**

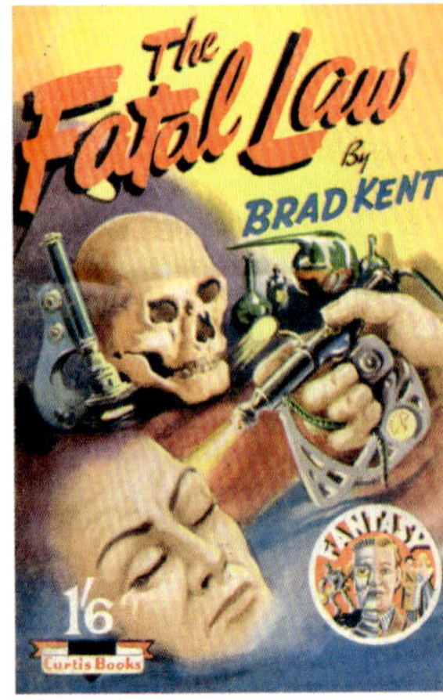

Brad Kent (Denis Hughes) | *The Fatal Law*
Curtis Books, 1952 | Art **Ray Theobald**

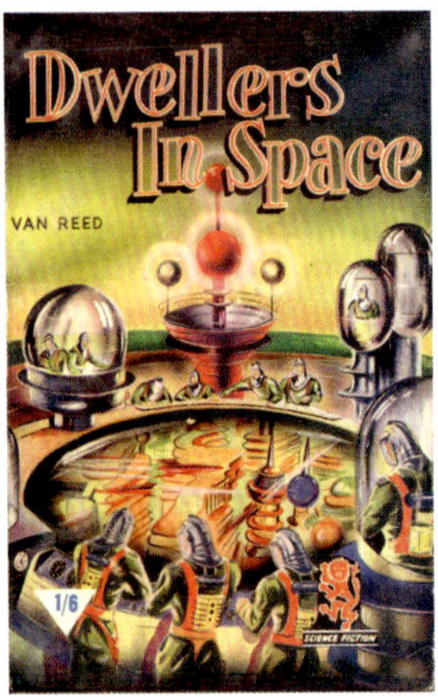

Van Reed | *Dwellers in Space*
Curtis Books, 1953 | Art **Gordon C. Davies**

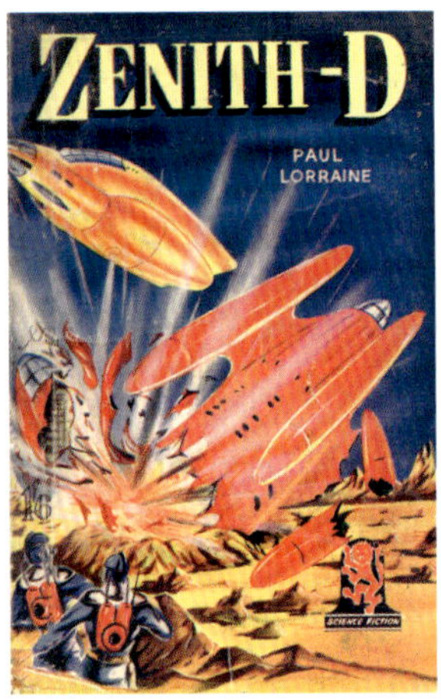

Paul Lorraine (John Glasby, Arthur Roberts)
Zenith-D
Curtis Books, 1952 | Art **Gordon C. Davies**

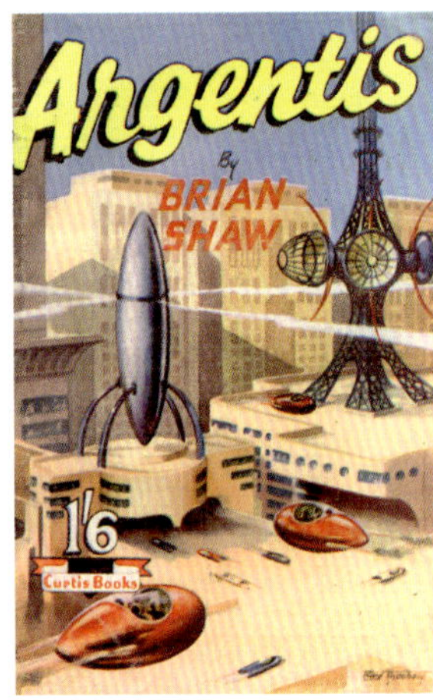

Brian Shaw (E. C. Tubb) | *Argentis*
Curtis Books, 1952 | Art **Ray Theobald**

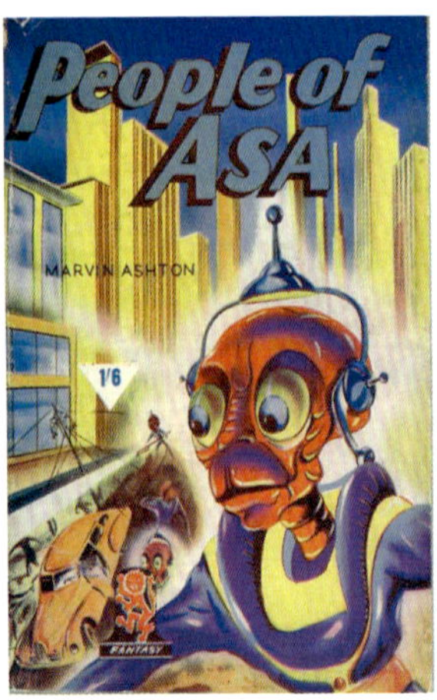

Marvin Ashton (Denis Hughes) | *People of Asa*
Curtis Books, 1953 | Art **Gordon C. Davies**

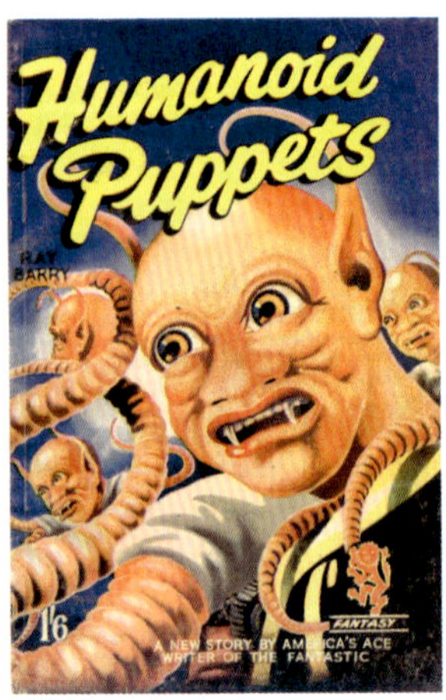

Ray Barry (Denis Hughes) | *Humanoid Puppets*
Curtis Books, 1952 | Art **Ray Theobald**
Possibly inspired by H. R. Van Dongen's October 1951 *Astounding Science Fiction* cover

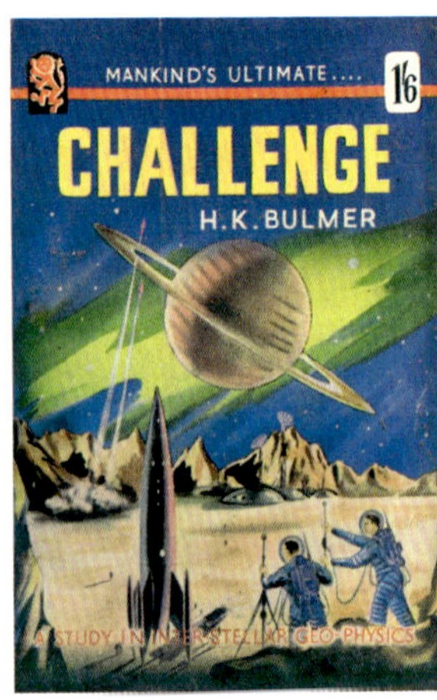

H. K. Bulmer | *Challenge*
Curtis Books, 1954 | Art **Gordon C. Davies**

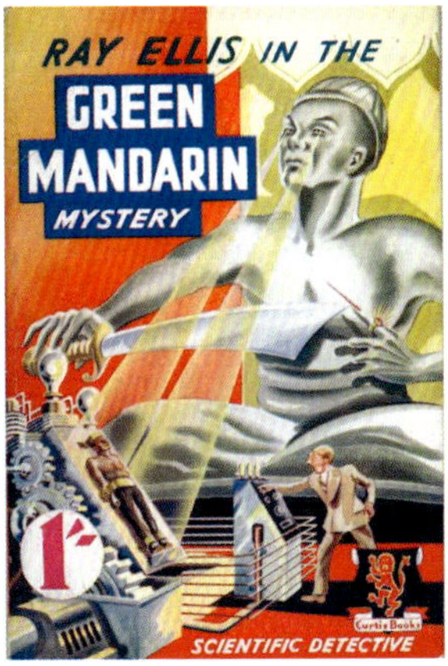

Grant Malcolm (Denis Hughes)
The Green Mandarin Mystery
Curtis Books, 1950 | Art **Ray Theobald**

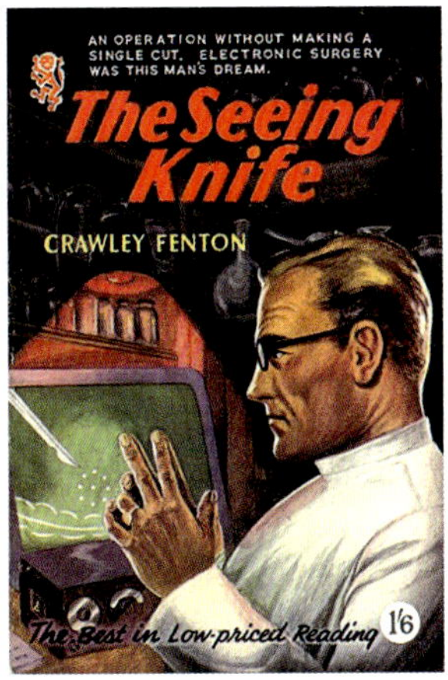

Crawley Fenton | *The Seeing Knife*
Curtis Books, 1954 | Art **Gordon C. Davies**

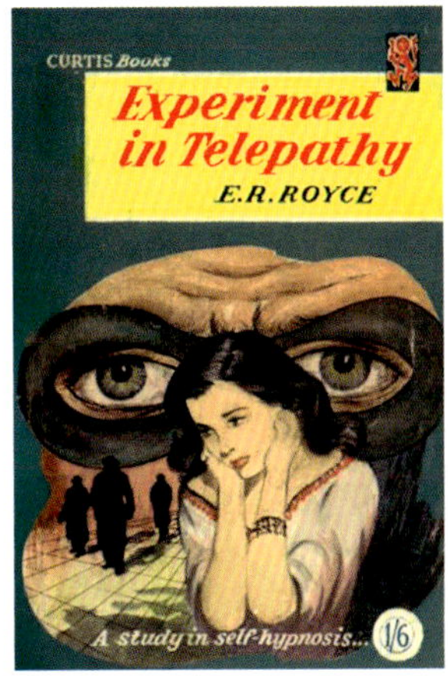

E. R. Royce | *Experiment in Telepathy*
Curtis Books, 1954 | Art **Unknown**

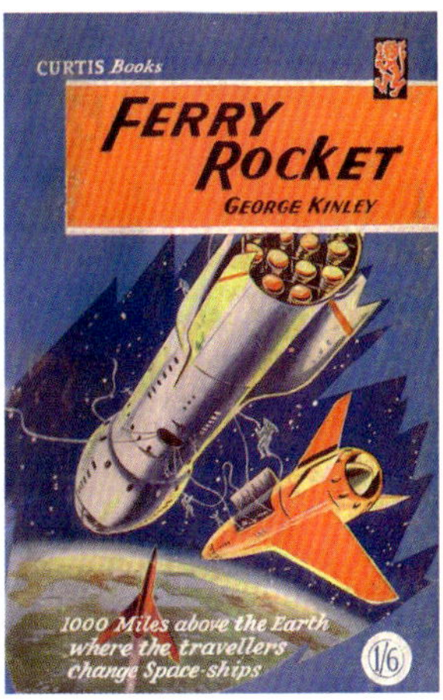

George Kinley (Edmund Cooper) | *Ferry Rocket*
Curtis Books, 1954 | Art **Gordon C. Davies**

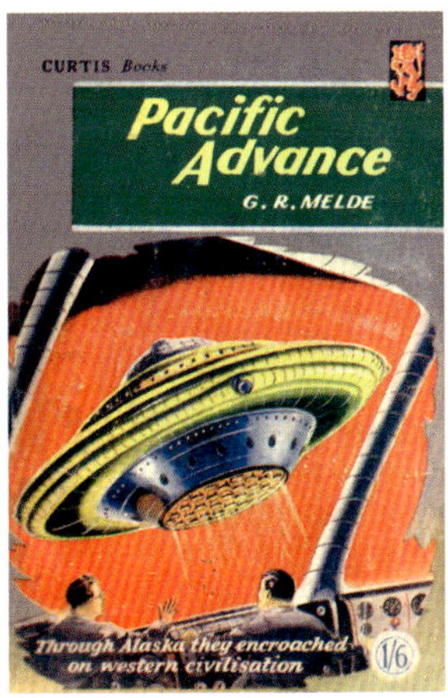

G. R. Melde (Denis Hughes) | *Pacific Advance*
Curtis Books, 1954 | Art **Gordon C. Davies**

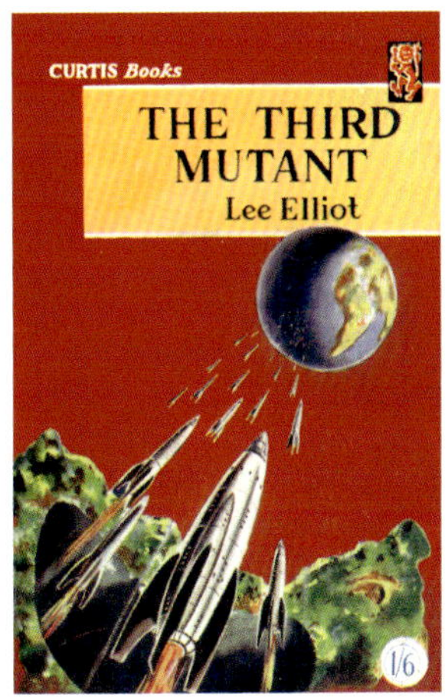

Lee Elliot (William Bird) | *The Third Mutant*
Curtis Books, 1952 | Art **Gordon C. Davies**

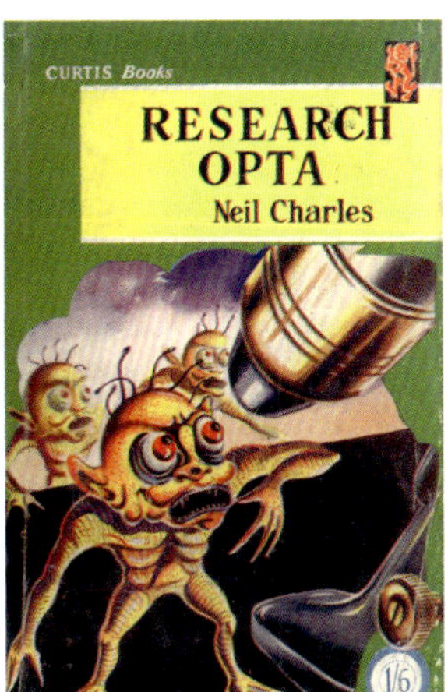

Neil Charles (Denis Hughes) | *Research Opta*
Curtis Books, 1953 | Art **Gordon C. Davies**

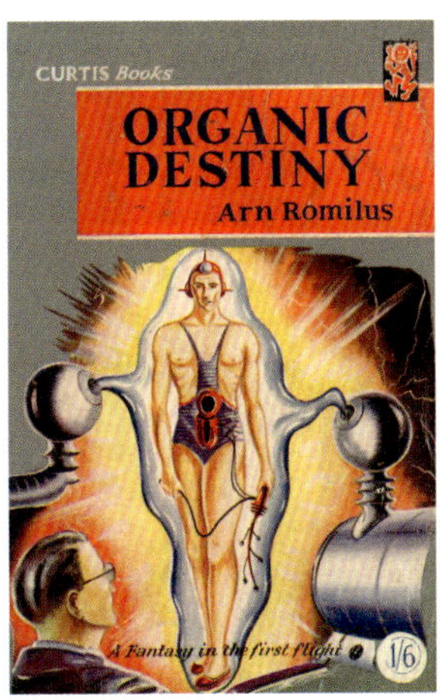

Arn Romilus (Denis Hughes) | *Organic Destiny*
Curtis Books, 1953 | Art **Gordon C. Davies**

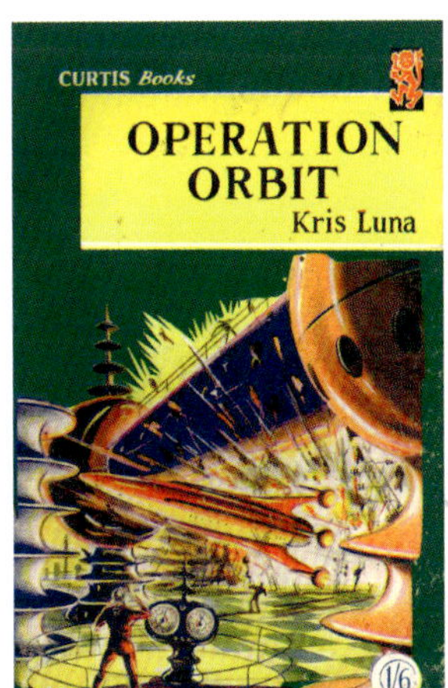

Kris Luna (William Bird) | *Operation Orbit*
Curtis Books, 1953 | Art **Gordon C. Davies**

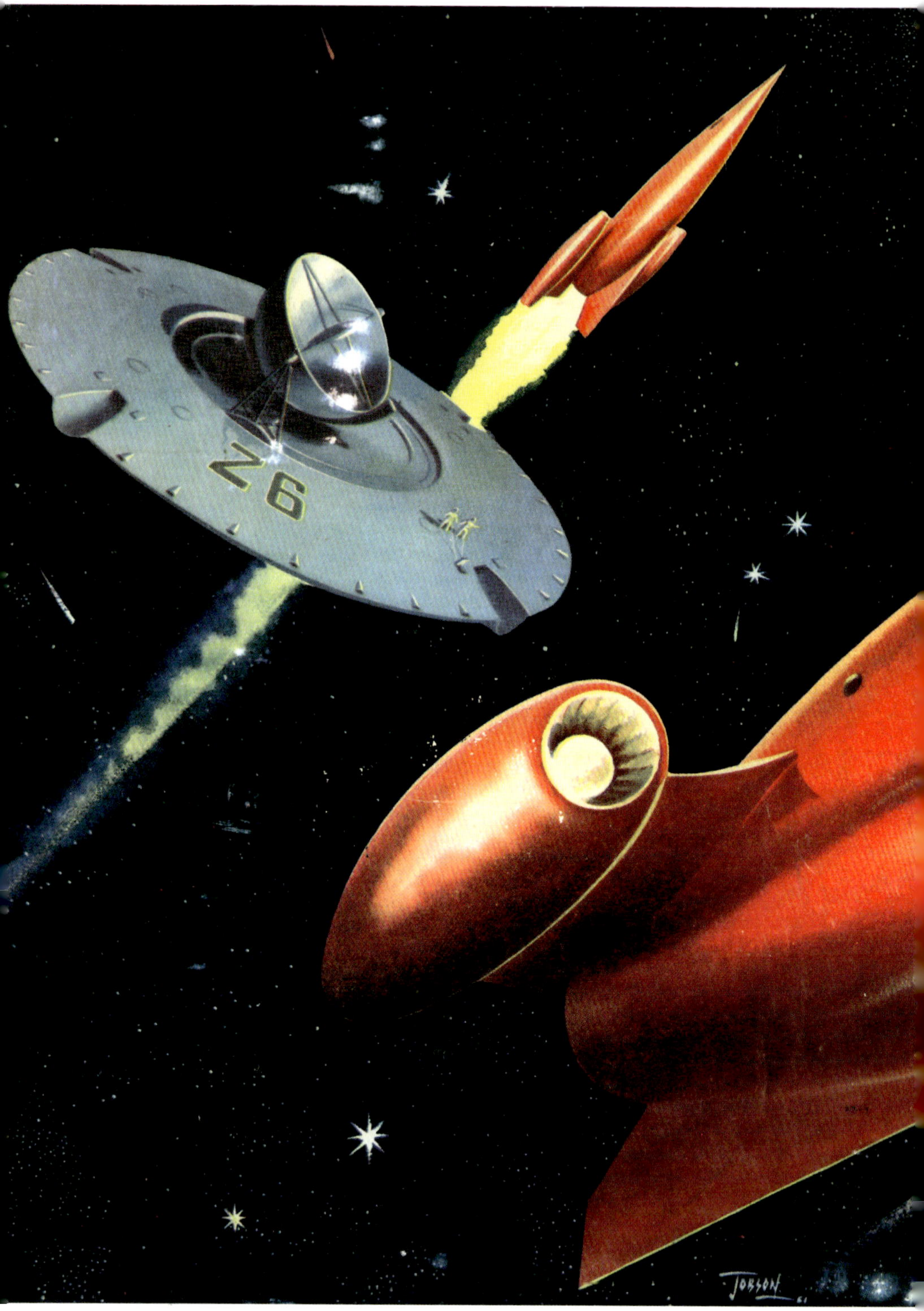

Ray Sonin | *The Adventures of Captain Space Kingley*
Sampson Low, Marston & Co Ltd., 1951 | Art **Ron Jobson**

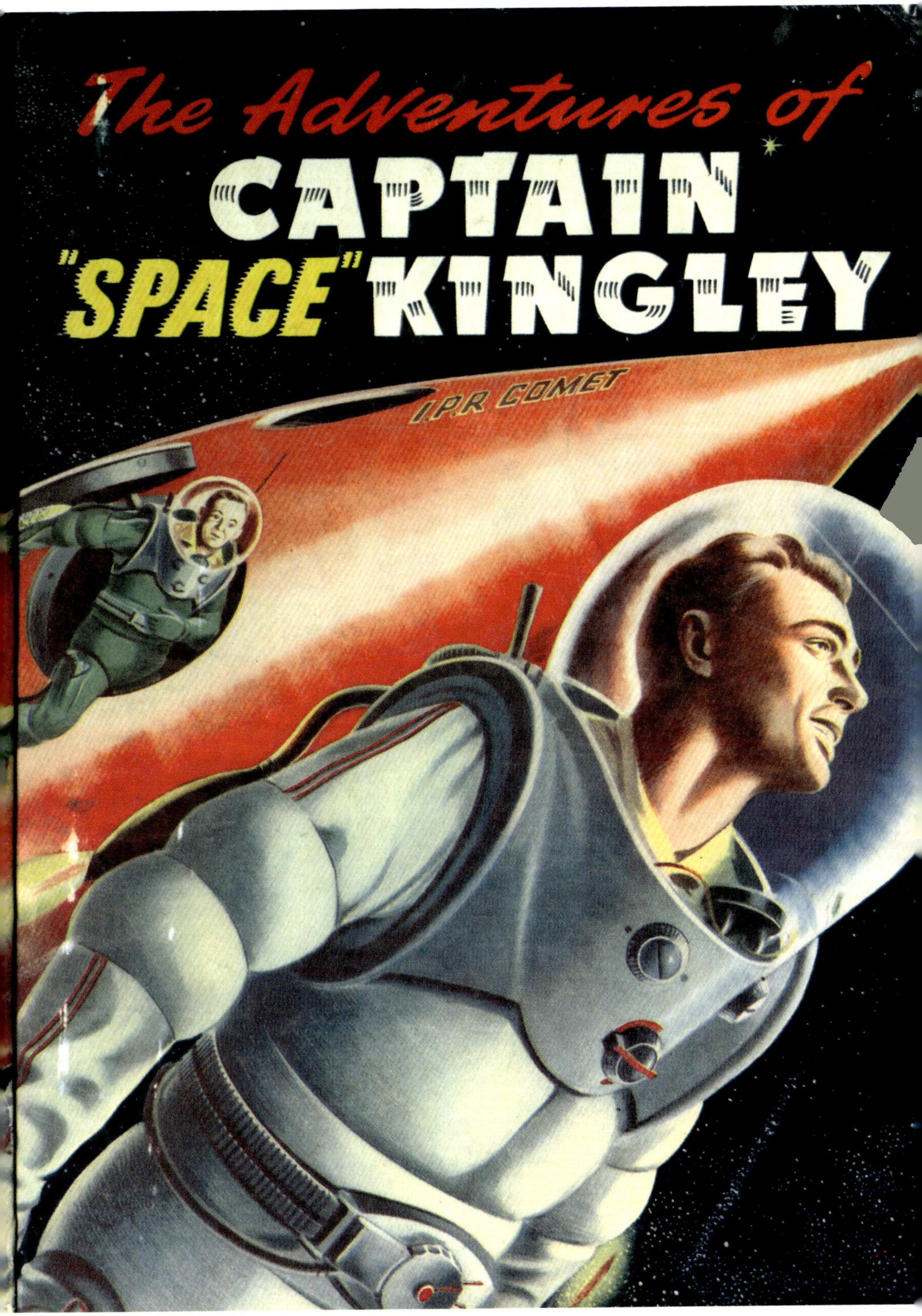
The Adventures of
CAPTAIN
"SPACE" KINGLEY
I.P.R COMET

opposite: Practical Mechanics
George Newnes Ltd., 1962 | Art **Ron Turner**

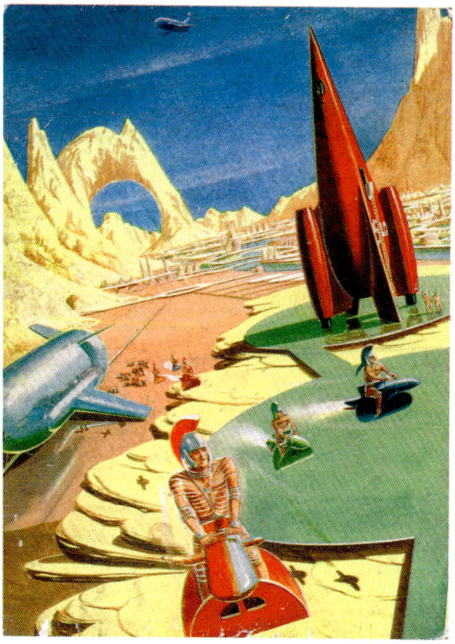

Ray Sonin | *Space Kingley and the Secret Squadron* (back cover)
Sampson Low, Marston & Co Ltd., 1951 | Art **Ron Jobson**

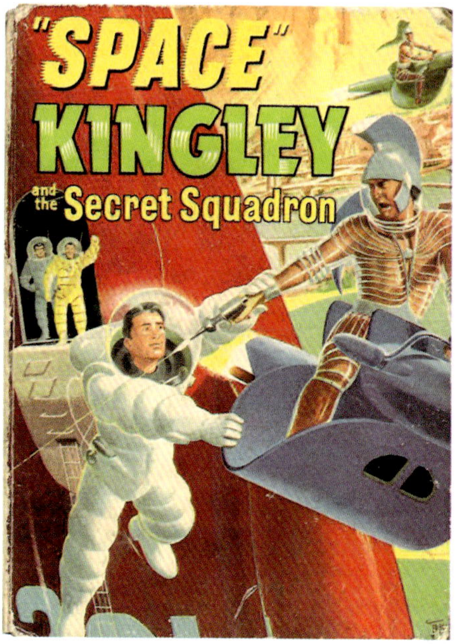

Ray Sonin | *Space Kingley and the Secret Squadron*
Sampson Low, Marston & Co Ltd., 1951 | Art **Ron Jobson**

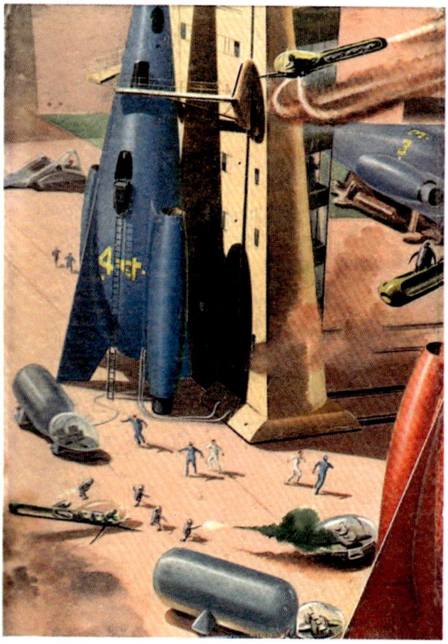

Ray Sonin | *The Space Kingley Annual* (back cover)
Sampson Low, Marston & Co Ltd., 1951 | Art **Ron Jobson**

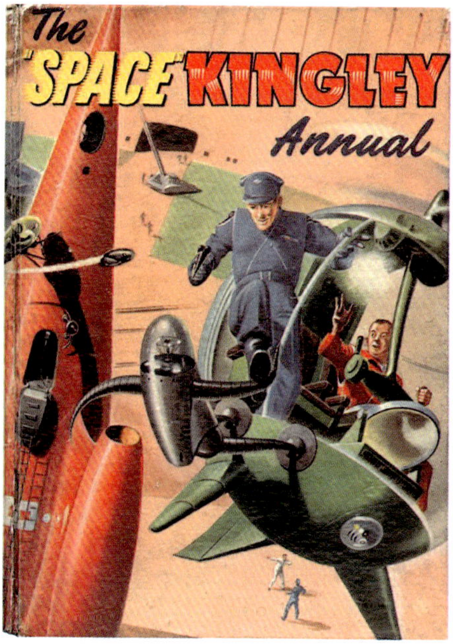

Ray Sonin | *The Space Kingley Annual*
Sampson Low, Marston & Co Ltd., 1951 | Art **Ron Jobson**

Practical MECHANICS

1'6

JAN—1962

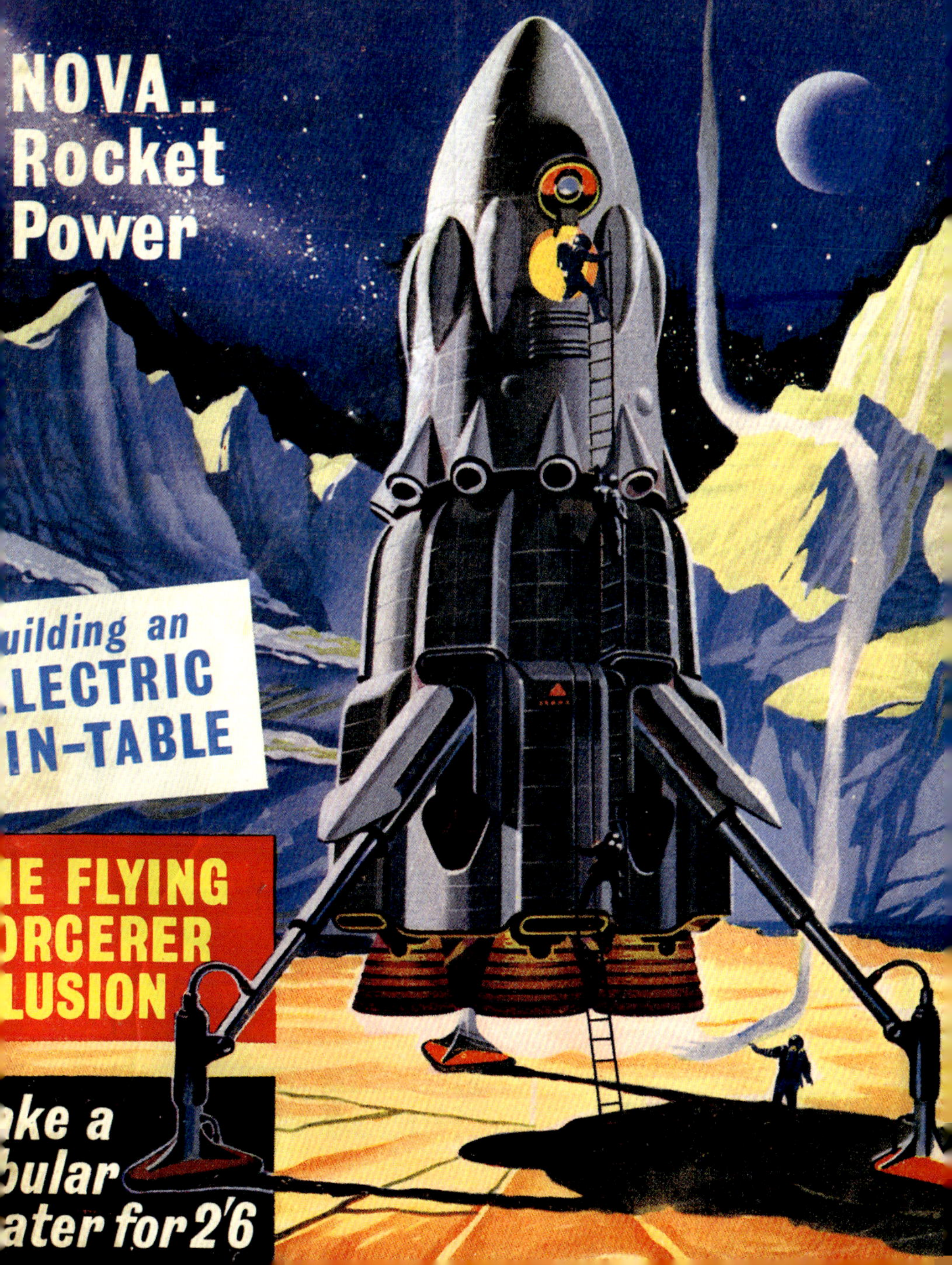

NOVA.. Rocket Power

uilding an LECTRIC IN-TABLE

IE FLYING ORCERER LUSION

ake a bular ater for 2'6

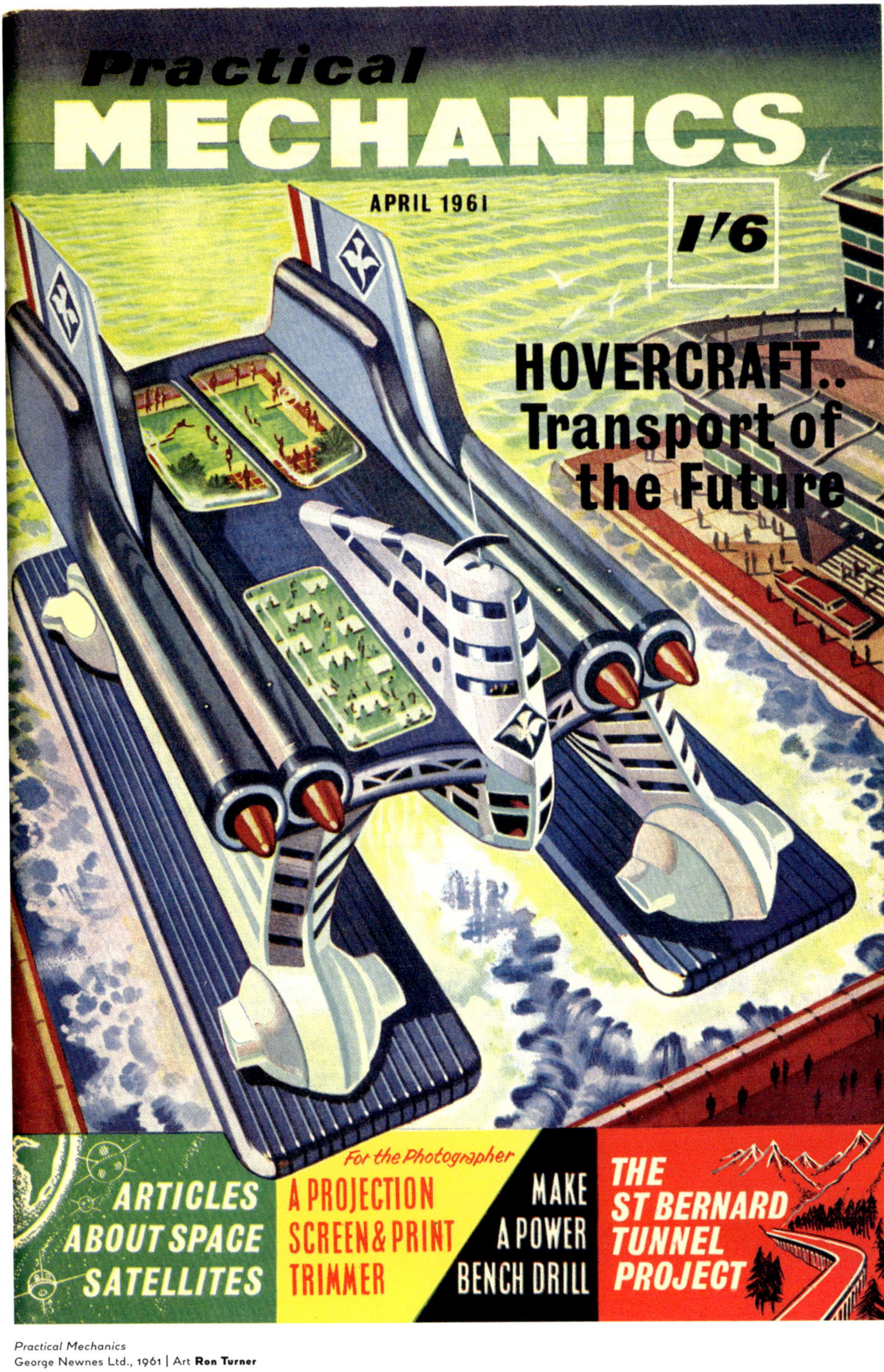

Practical Mechanics
George Newnes Ltd., 1961 | Art **Ron Turner**

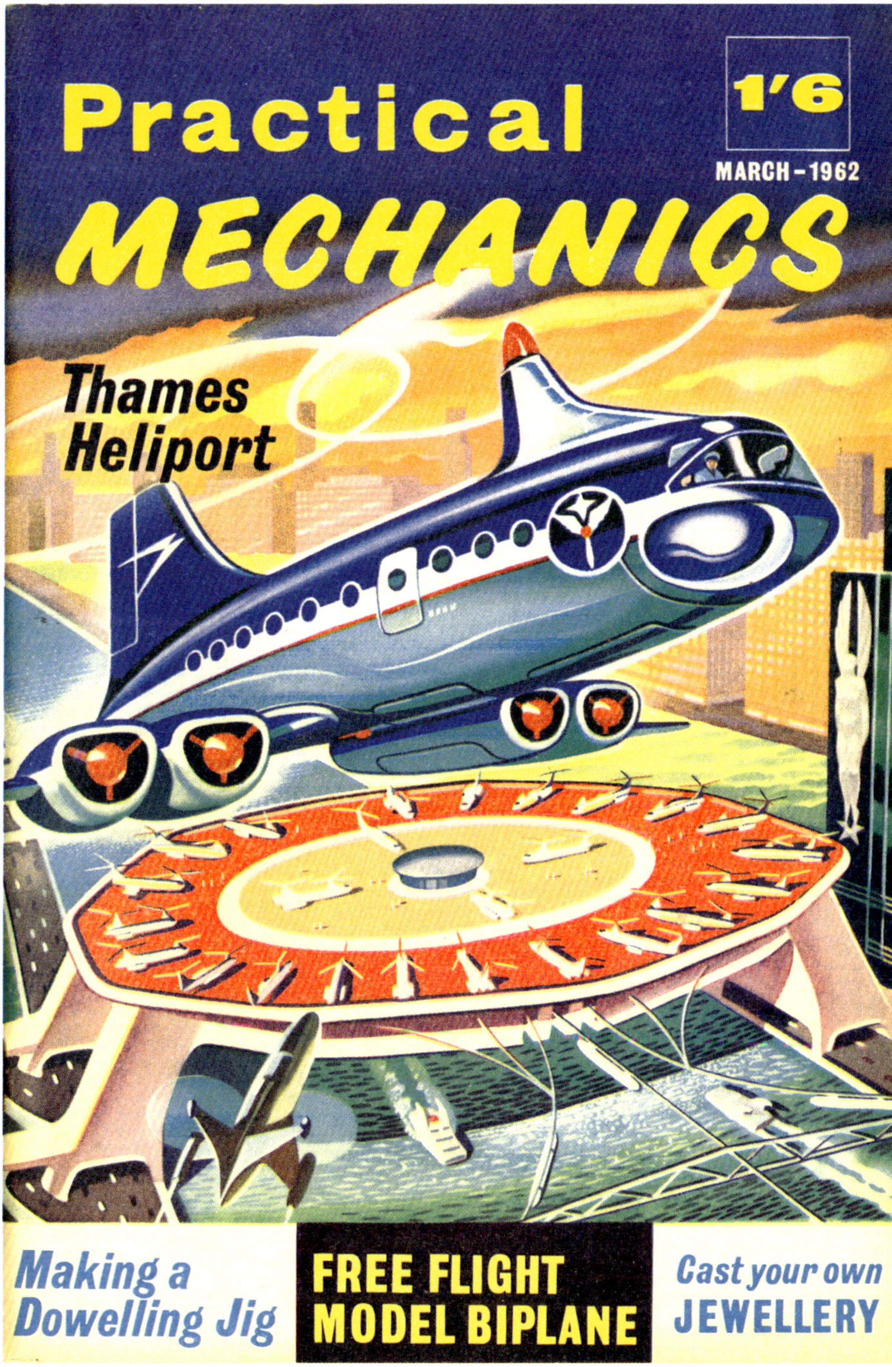

Practical Mechanics
George Newnes Ltd., 1962 | Art **Ron Turner**

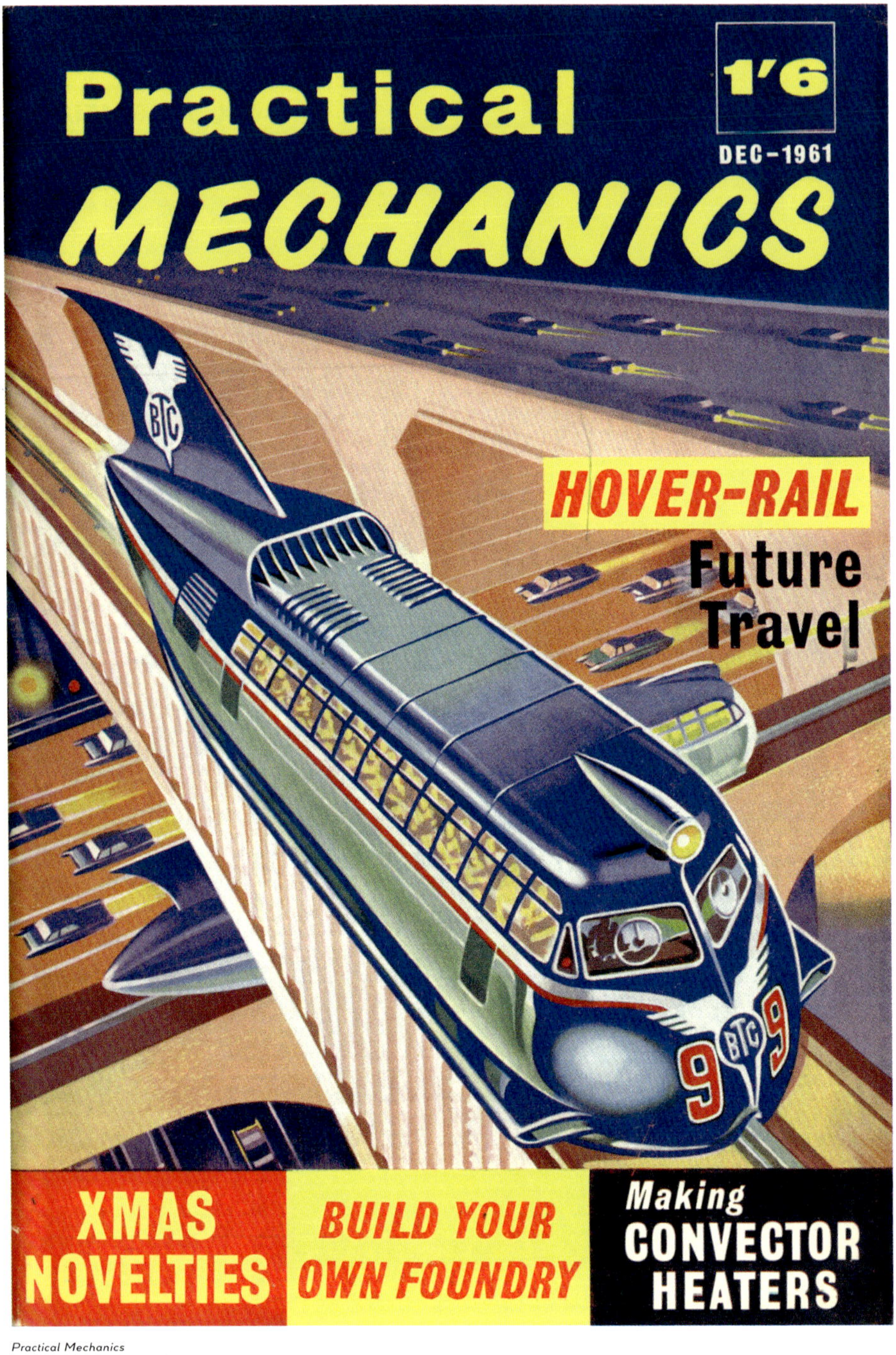

Practical Mechanics
George Newnes Ltd., 1961 | Art **Ron Turner**

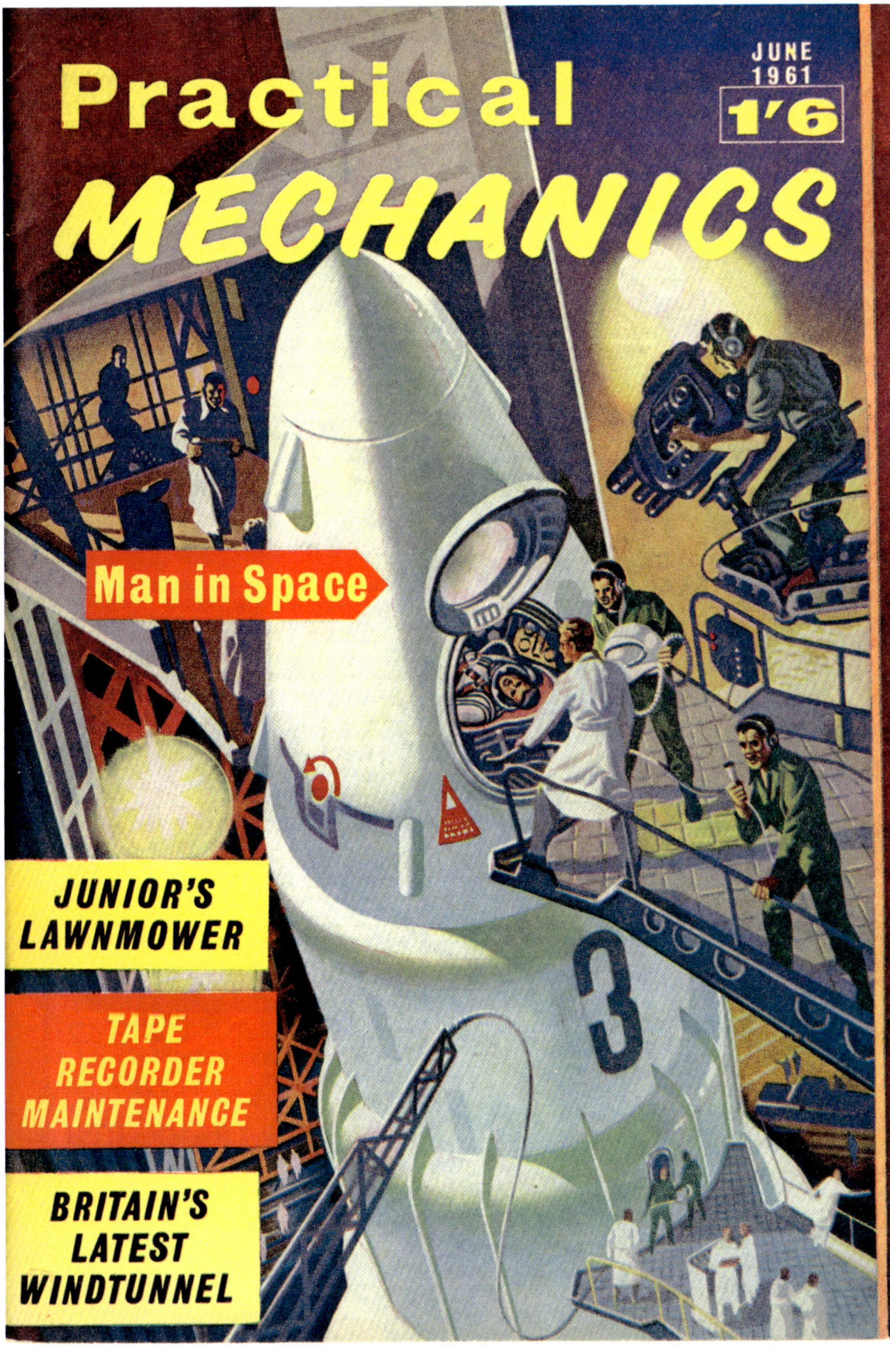

Practical Mechanics
George Newnes Ltd., 1961 | Art **Ron Turner**

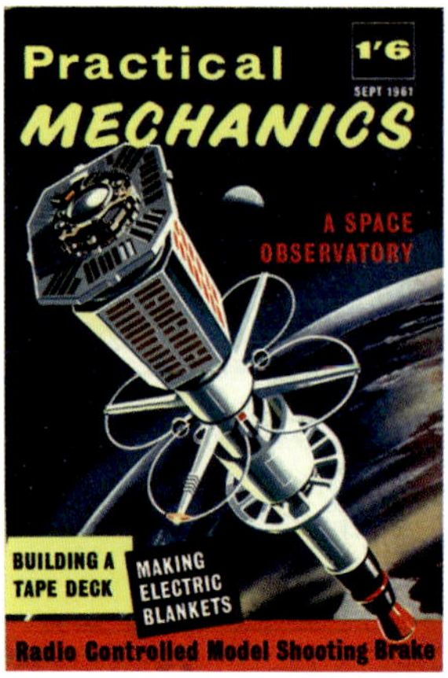

Practical Mechanics
George Newnes Ltd., 1961 | Art **Ron Turner**

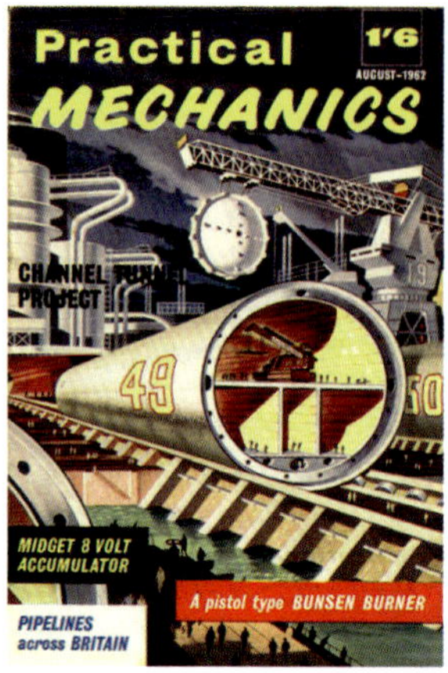

Practical Mechanics
George Newnes Ltd., 1962 | Art **Ron Turner**

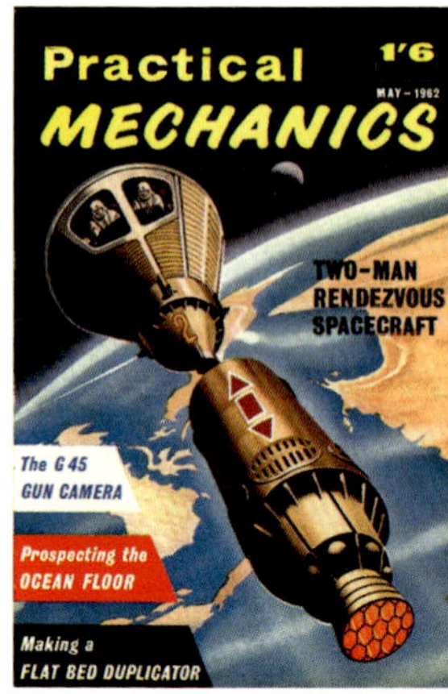

Practical Mechanics
George Newnes Ltd., 1962 | Art **Ron Turner**

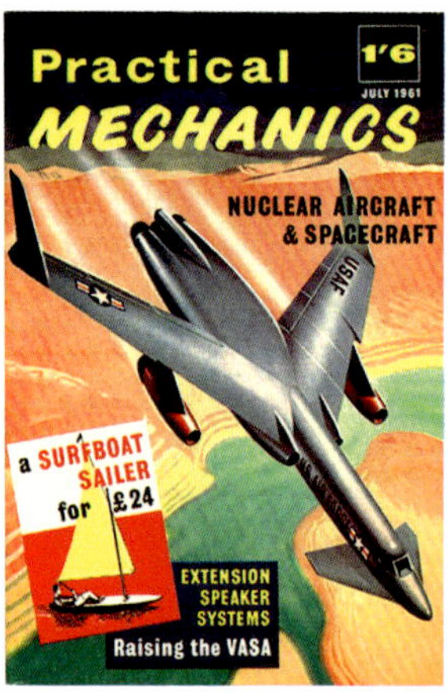

Practical Mechanics
George Newnes Ltd., 1961 | Art **Ron Turner**

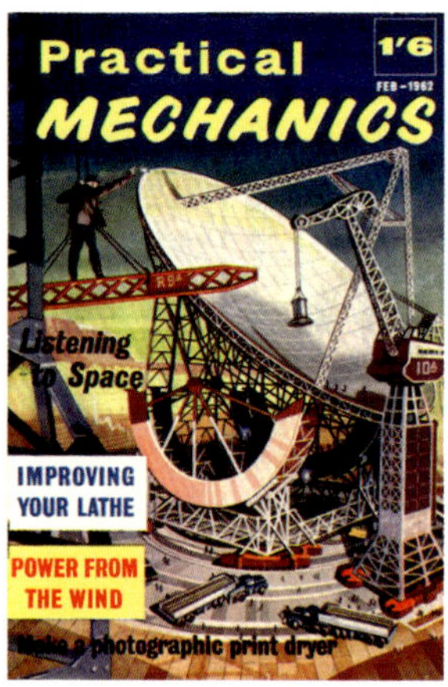

Practical Mechanics
George Newnes Ltd., 1962 | Art **Ron Turner**

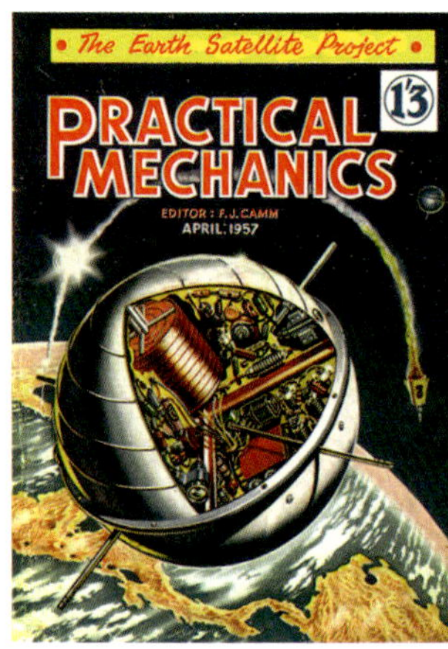

Practical Mechanics
George Newnes Ltd., 1957 | Art **Ron Turner**

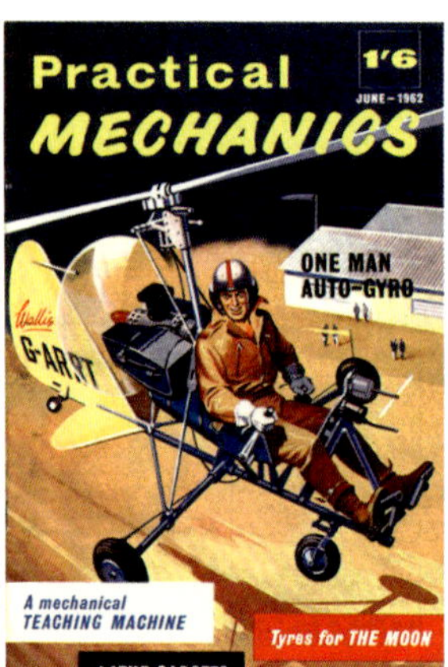

Practical Mechanics
George Newnes Ltd., 1962 | Art **Ron Turner**

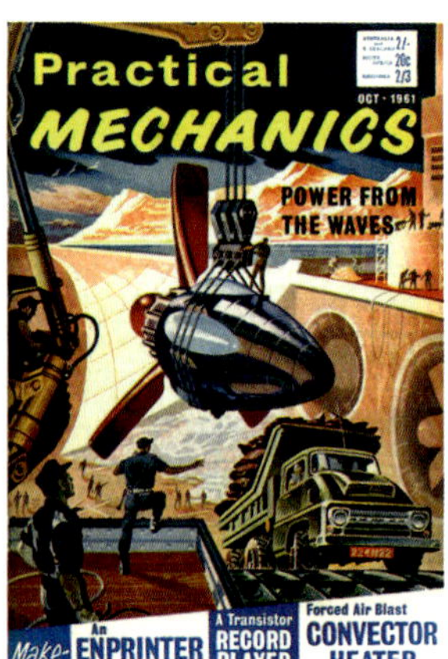

Practical Mechanics
George Newnes Ltd., 1961 | Art **Ron Turner**

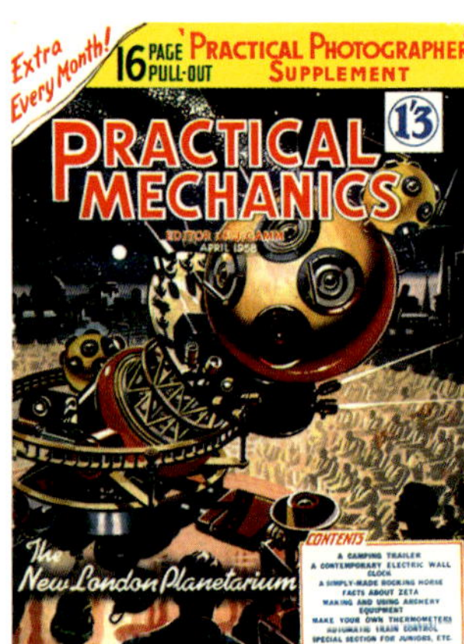

Practical Mechanics
George Newnes Ltd., 1958 | Art **Ron Turner**

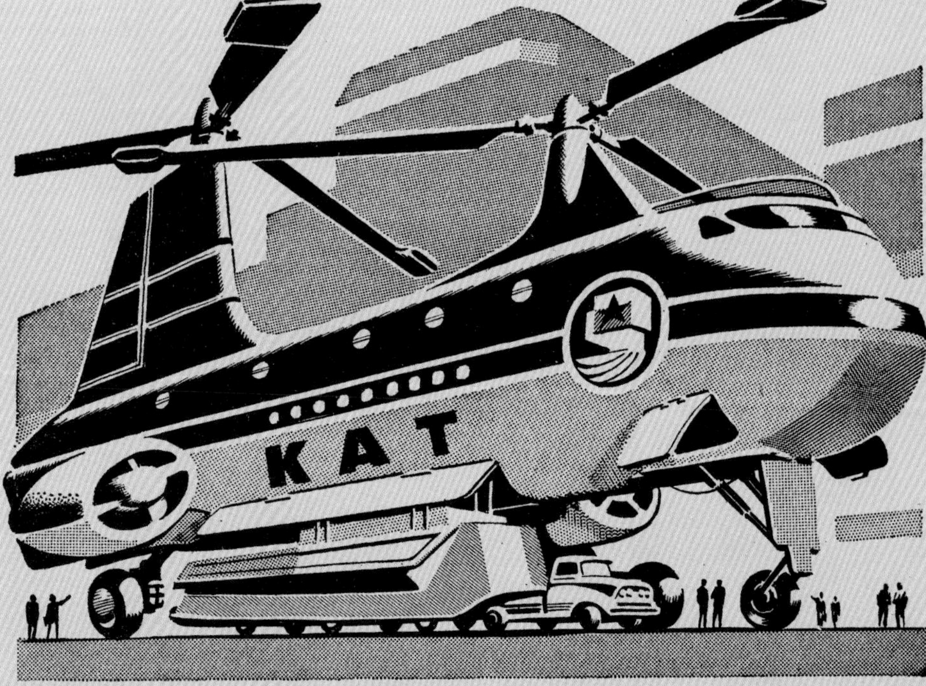

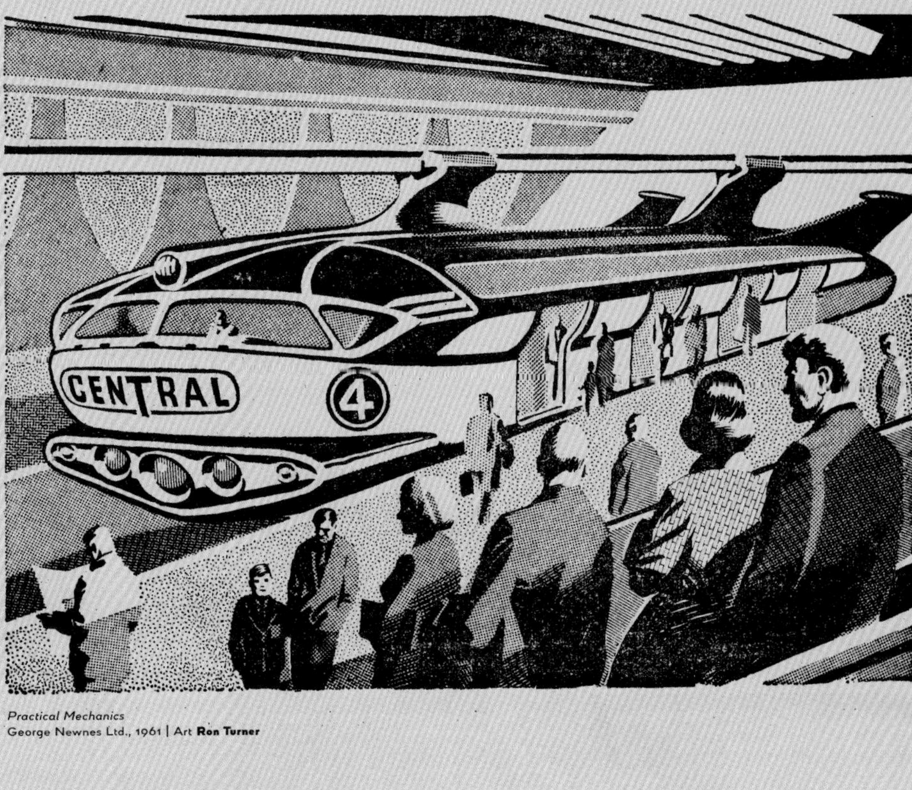

Practical Mechanics
George Newnes Ltd., 1961 | Art **Ron Turner**

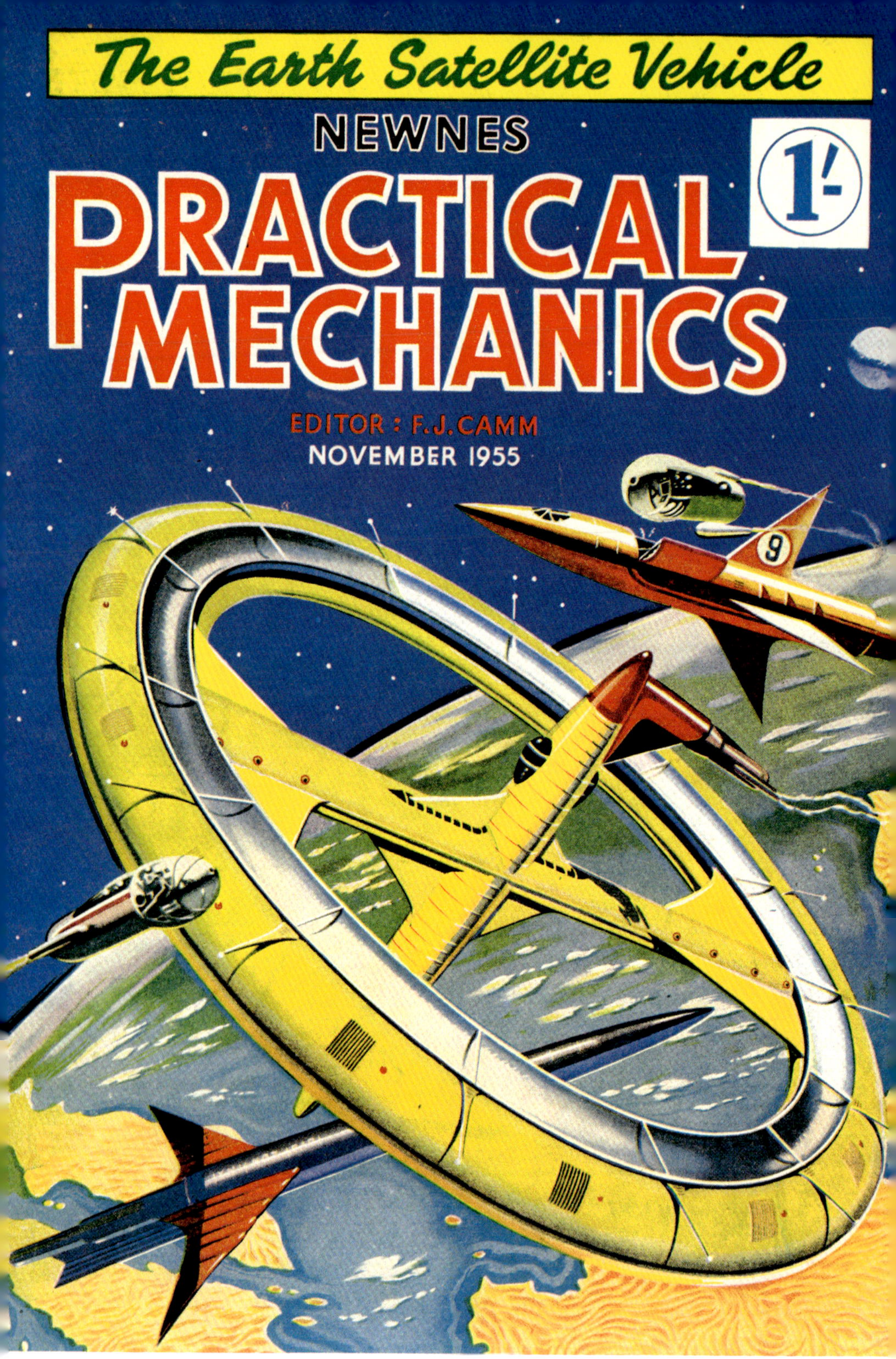

Practical Mechanics
George Newnes Ltd., 1955 | Art **Ron Turner**

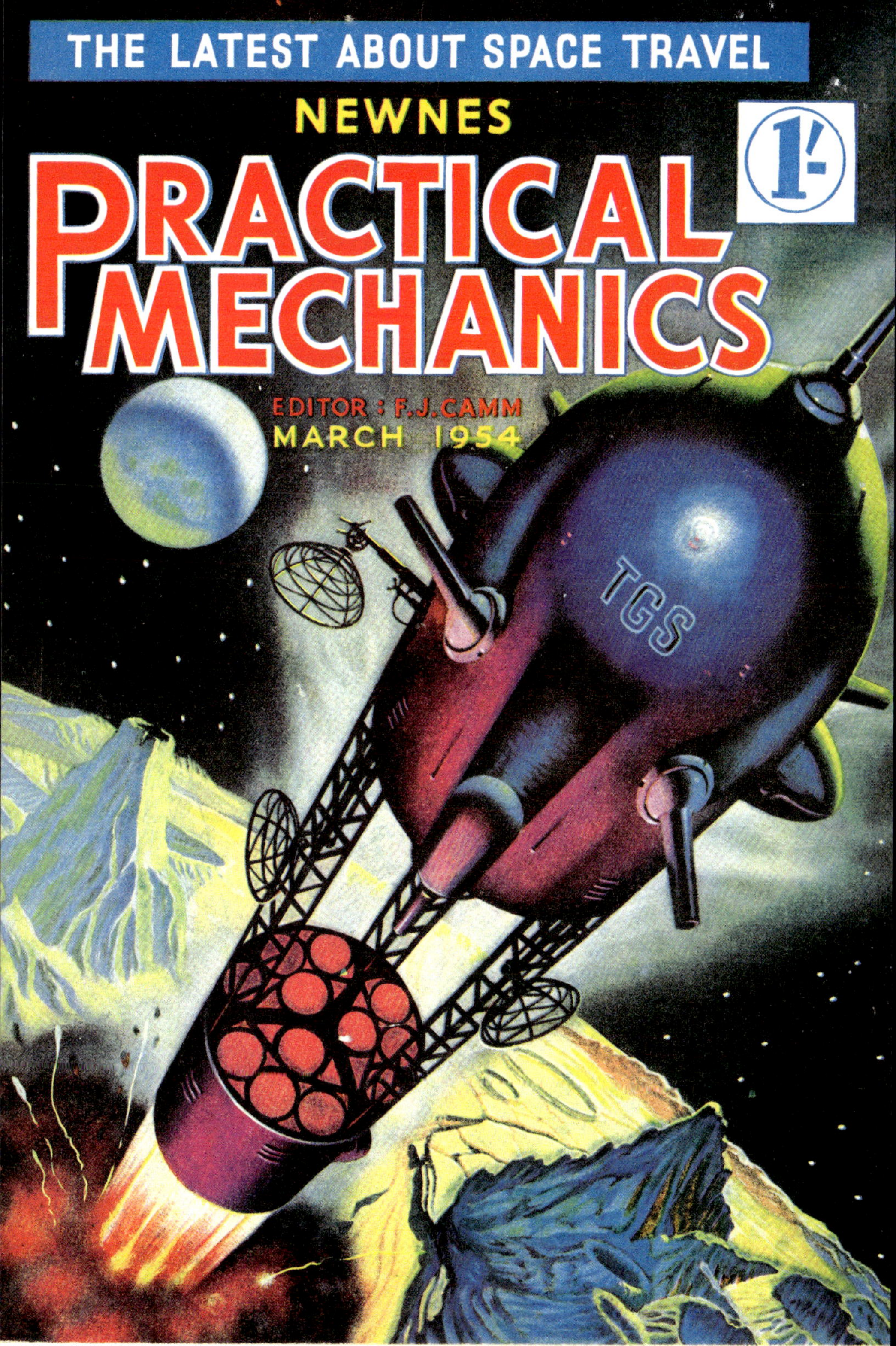

Practical Mechanics
George Newnes Ltd., 1954 | Art **Ron Turner**

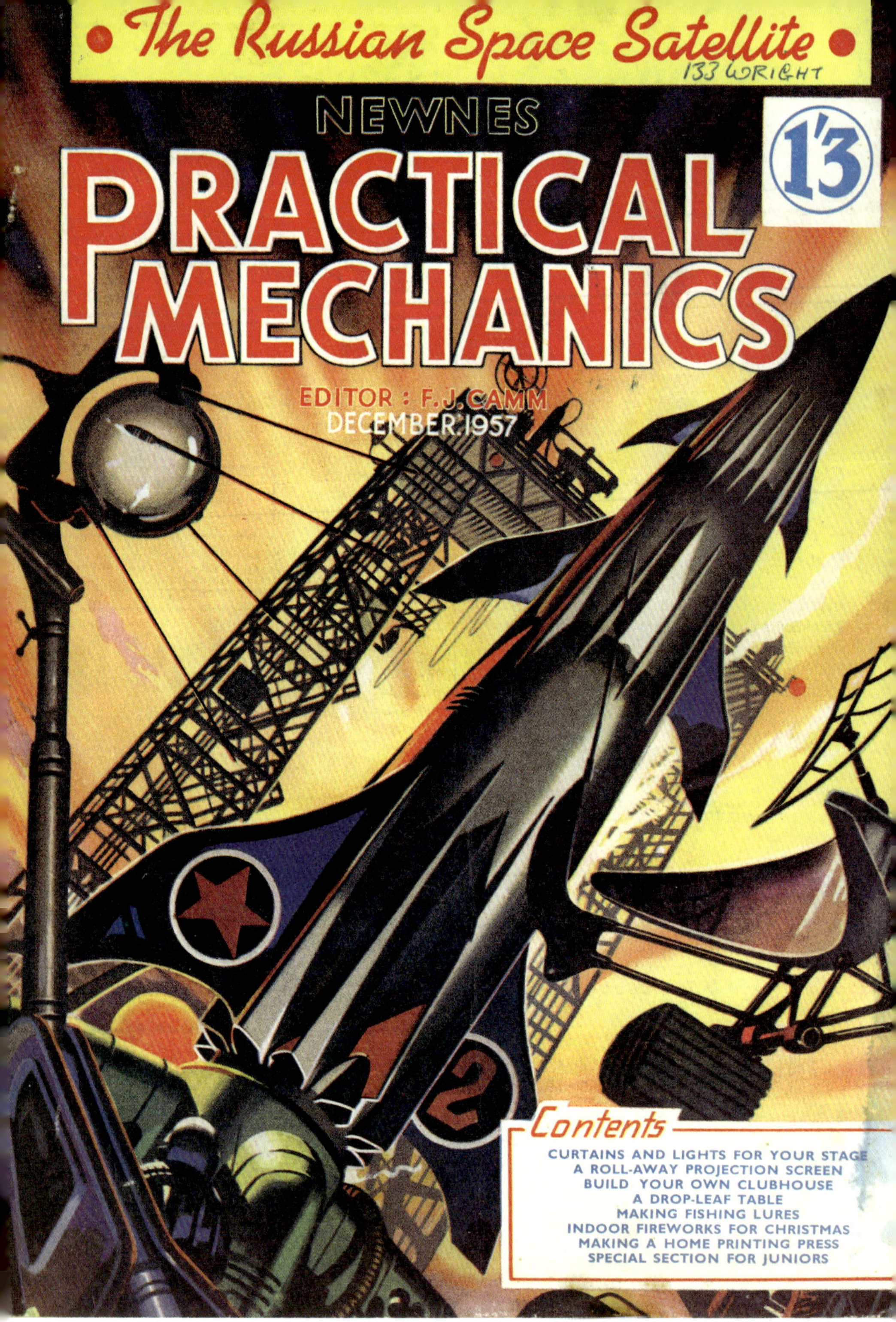

Practical Mechanics
George Newnes Ltd., 1957 | Art **Ron Turner**

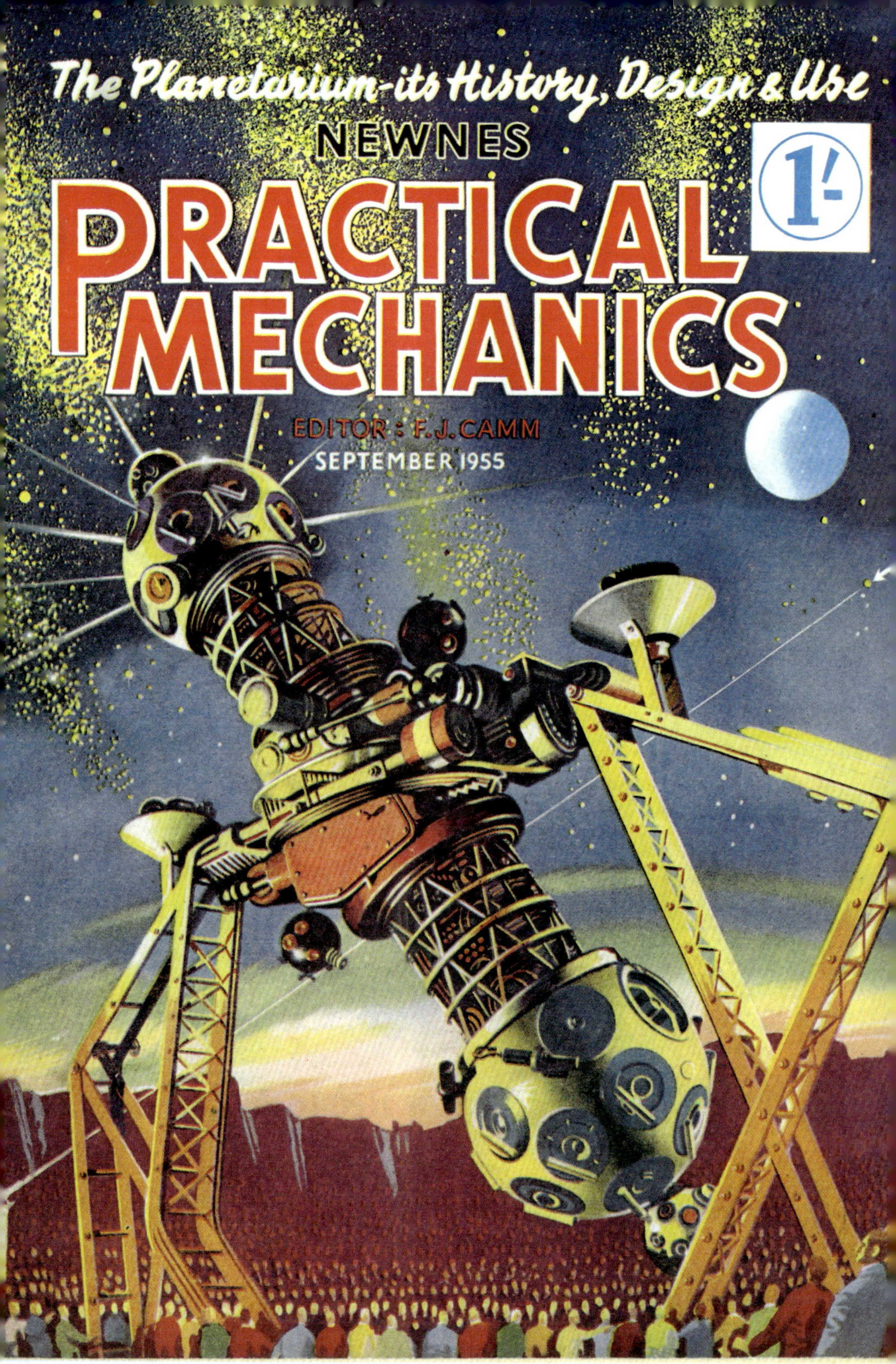

Practical Mechanics
George Newnes Ltd., 1955 | Art **Ron Turner**

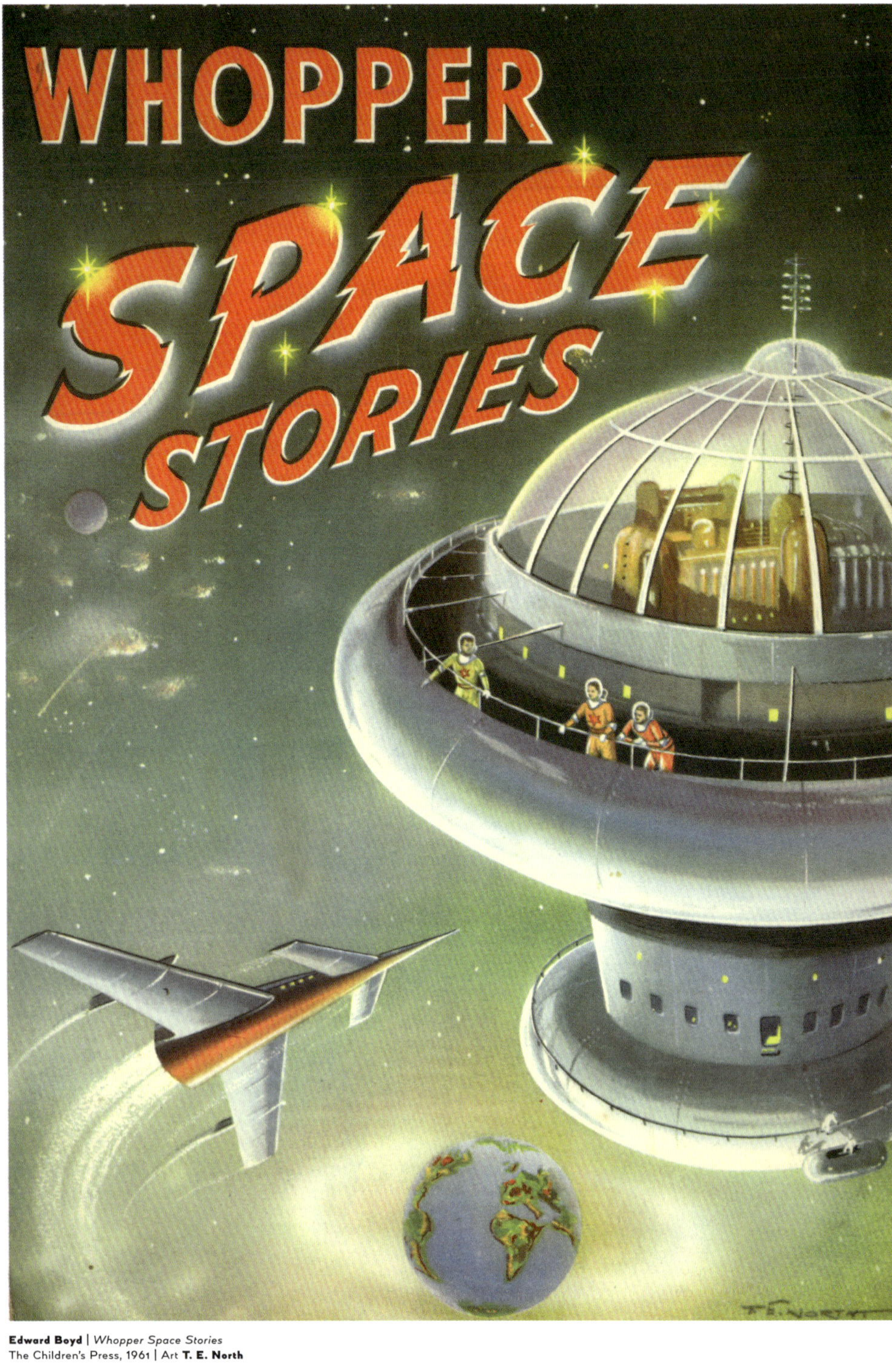

Edward Boyd | *Whopper Space Stories*
The Children's Press, 1961 | Art **T. E. North**

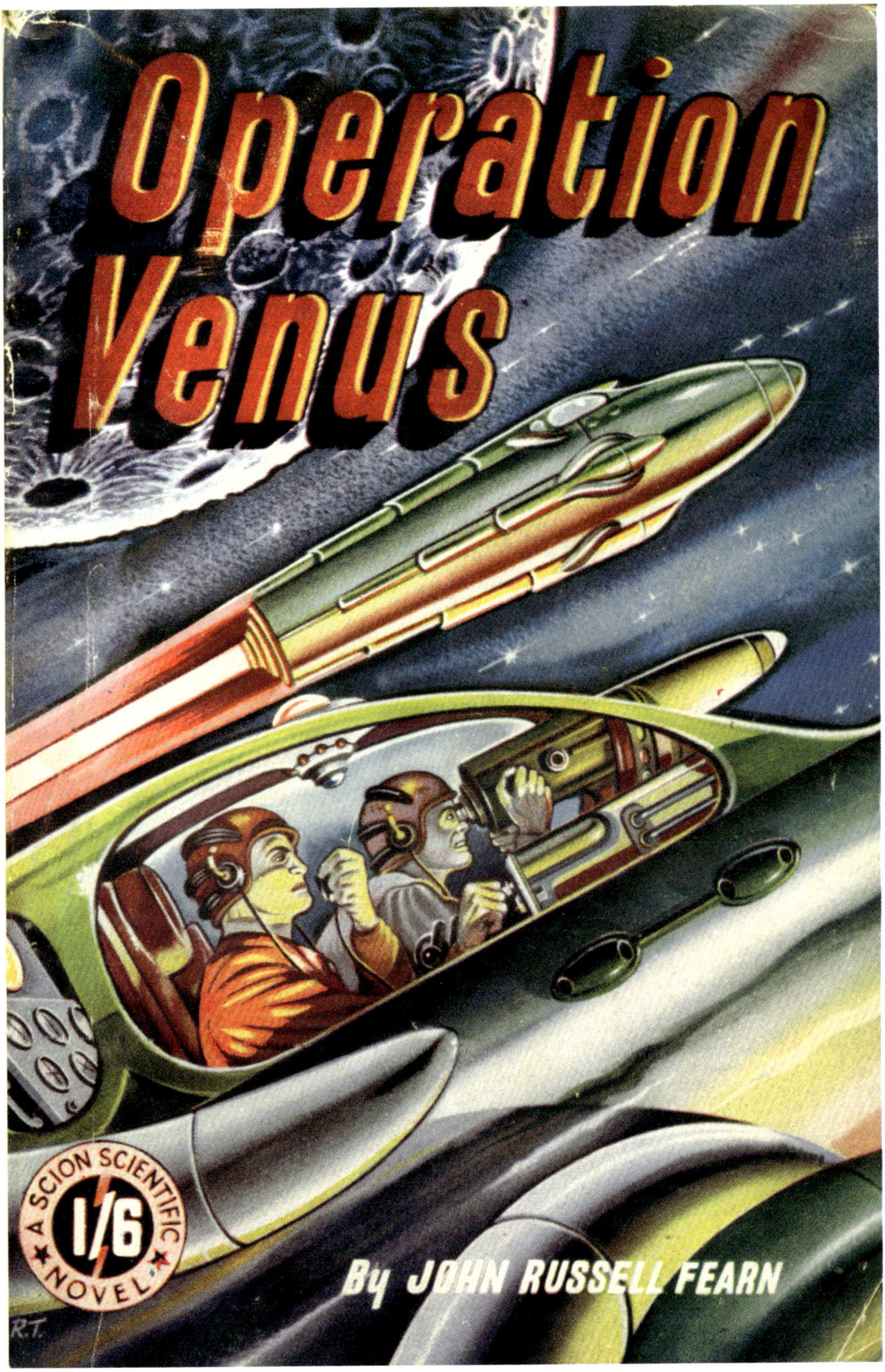

John Russell Fearn | *Operation Venus*
Scion Ltd., 1950 | Art **Ron Turner**

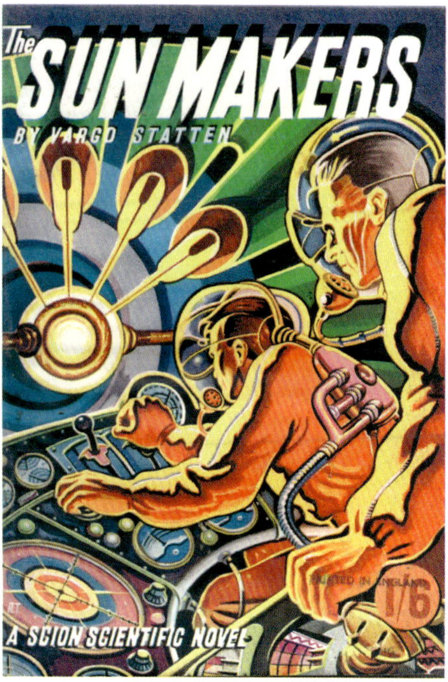

Vargo Statten (John Russell Fearn) | *The Sun Makers*
Scion Ltd., 1950 | Art **Ron Turner**

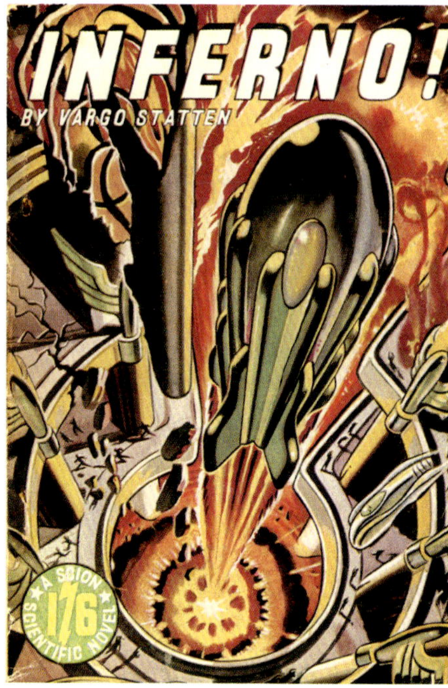

Vargo Statten (John Russell Fearn) | *Inferno!*
Scion Ltd., 1950 | Art **Ron Turner**

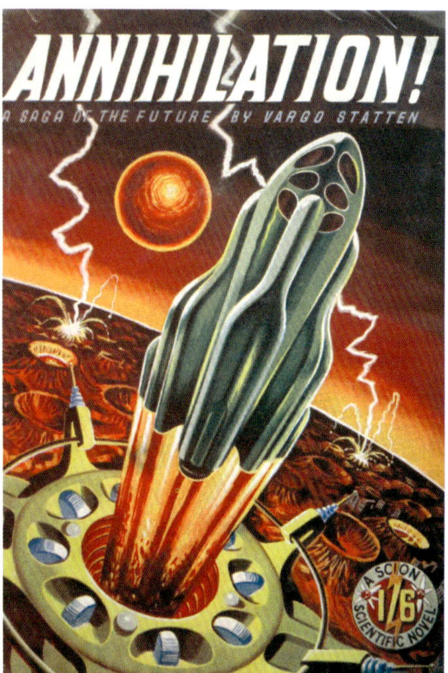

Vargo Statten (John Russell Fearn) | *Annihilation!*
Scion Ltd., 1950 | Art **Ron Turner**

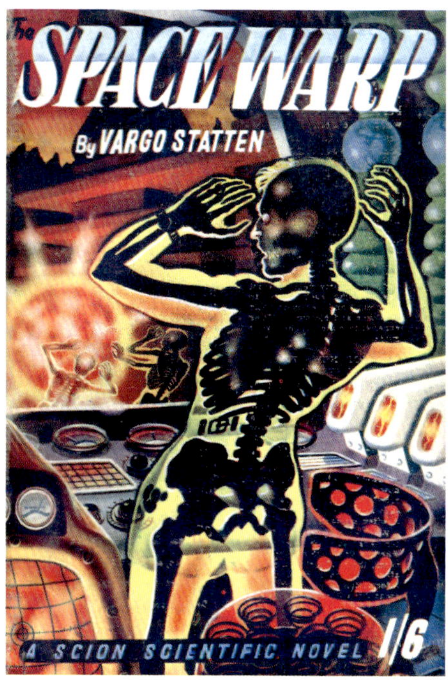

Vargo Statten (John Russell Fearn) | *The Space Warp*
Scion Ltd., 1952 | Art **Ron Turner**

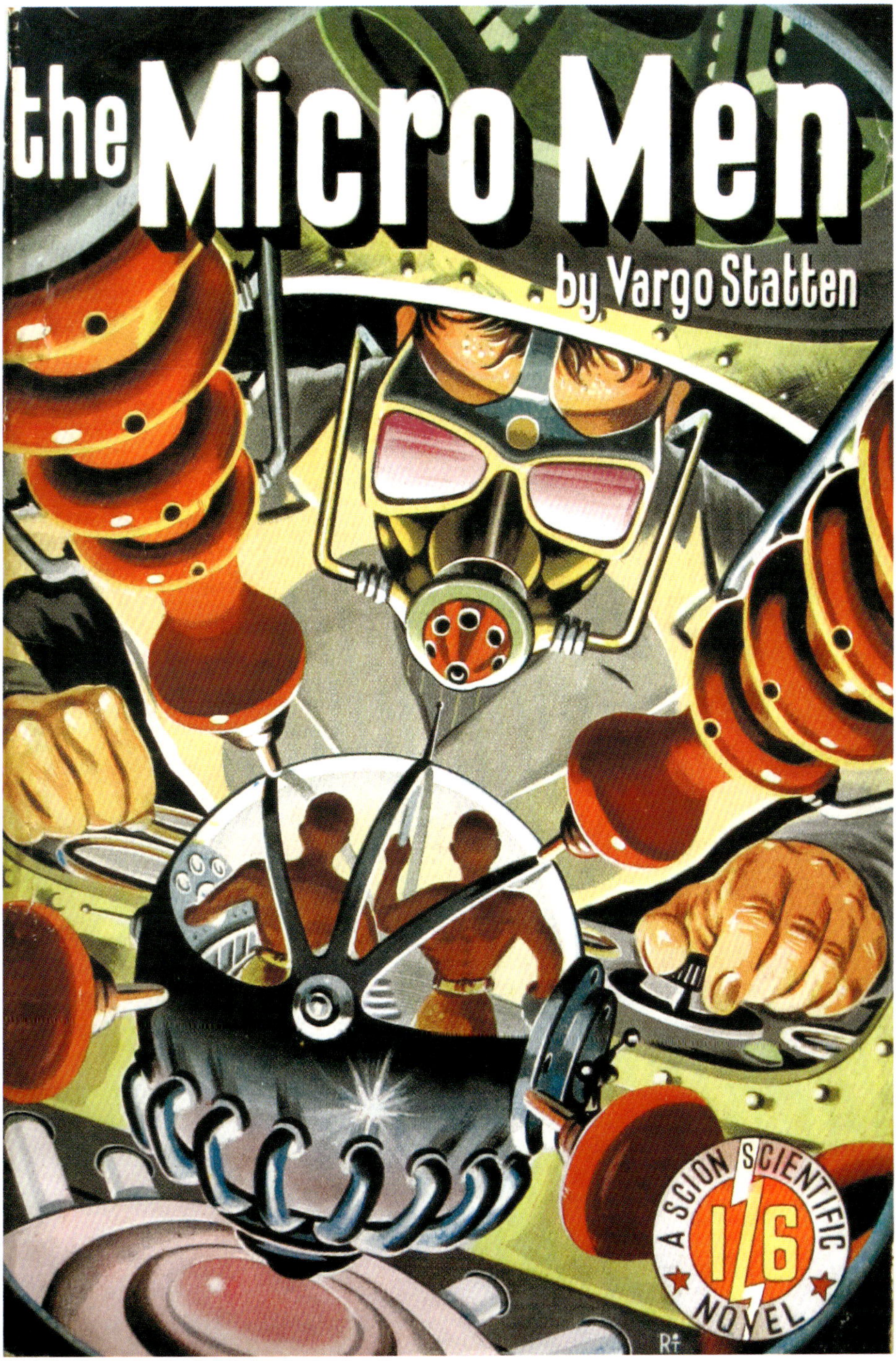

Vargo Statten (John Russell Fearn) | *The Micro Men*
Scion Ltd., 1950 | Art **Ron Turner**

opposite: **Vargo Statten (John Russell Fearn)** | *Deadline to Pluto* (recreation, 1980s)
Scion Ltd., 1951 | Art **Ron Turner**

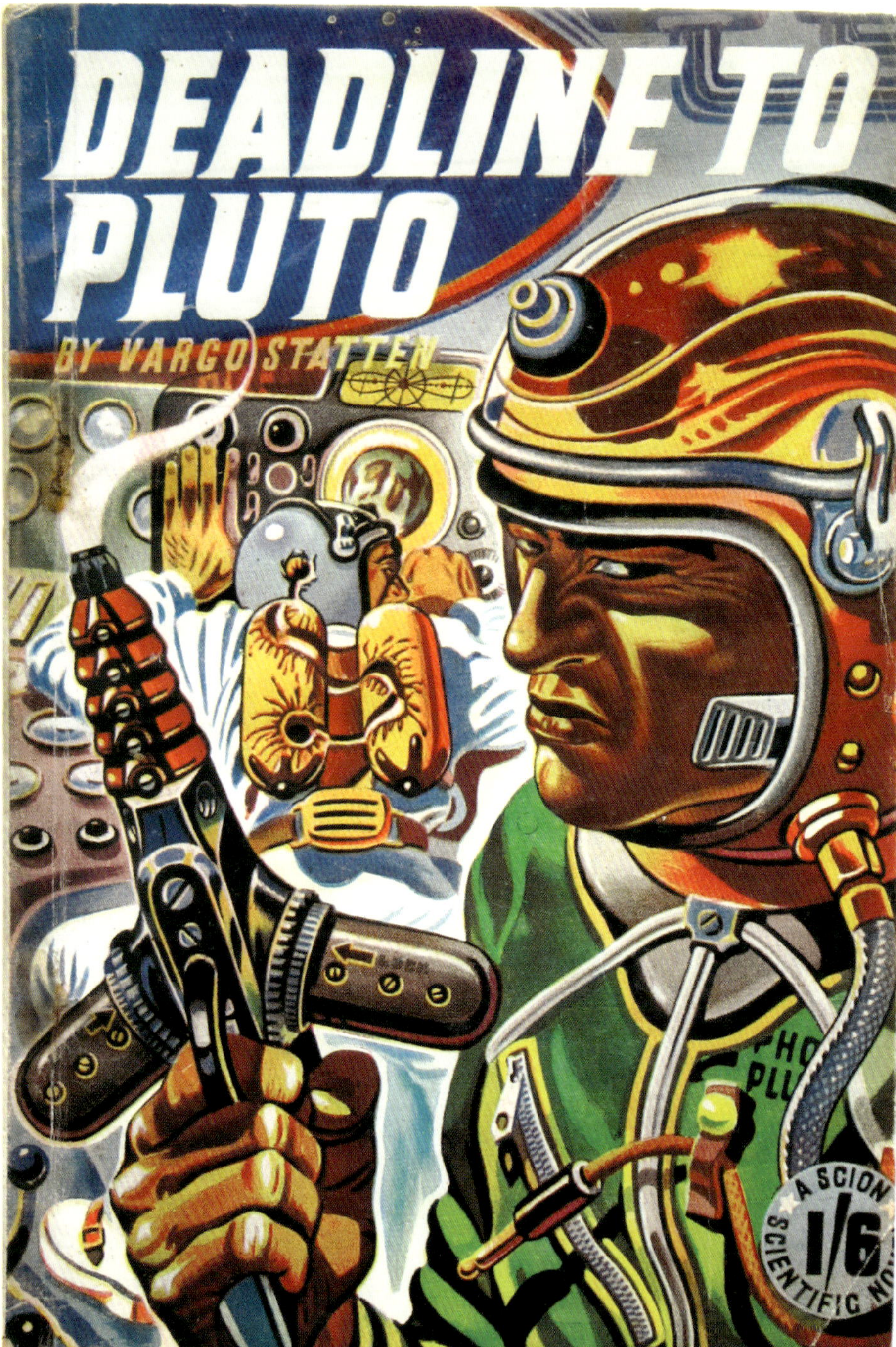

Vargo Statten (John Russell Fearn) | *Deadline to Pluto*
Scion Ltd., 1951 | Art **Ron Turner**

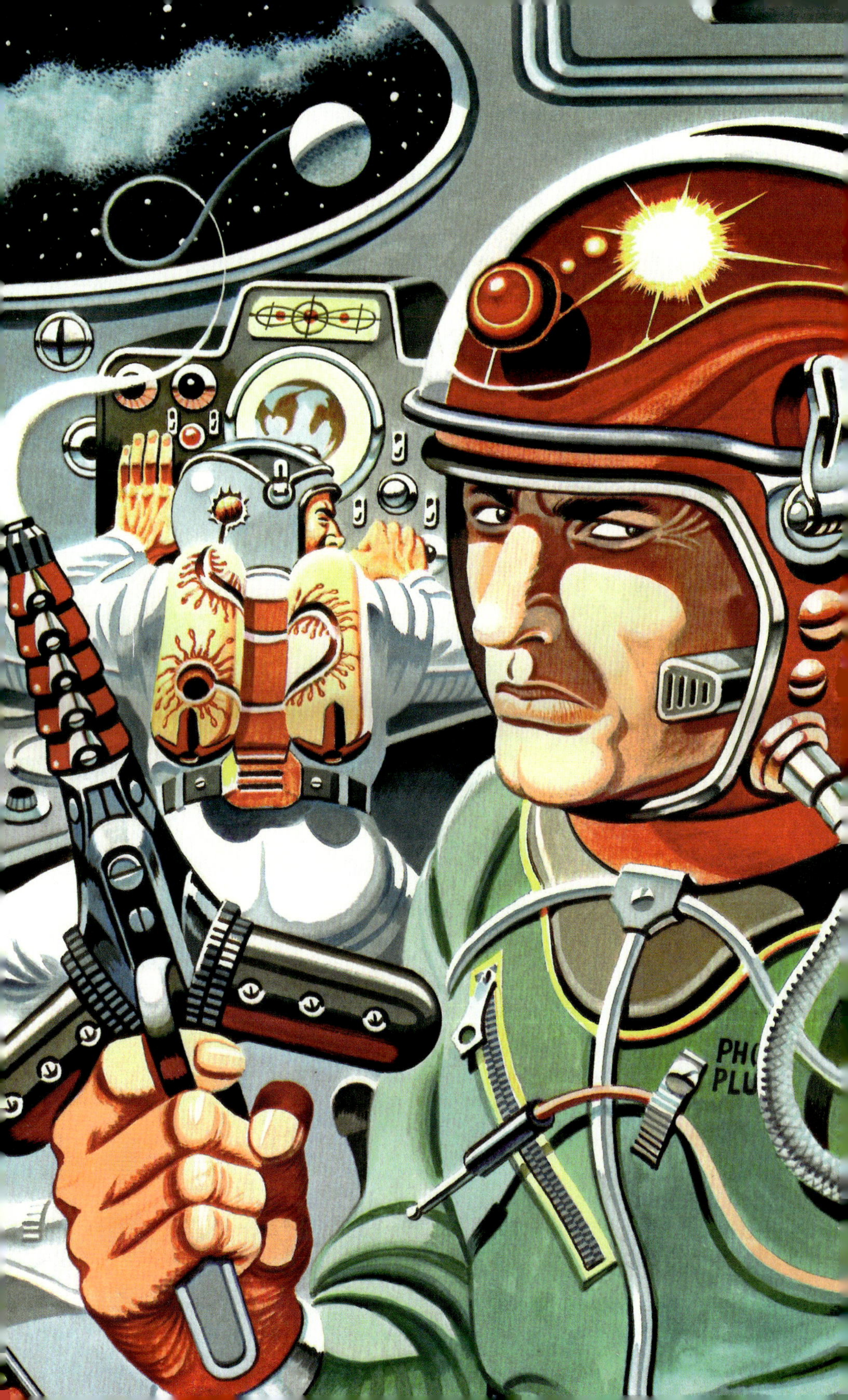

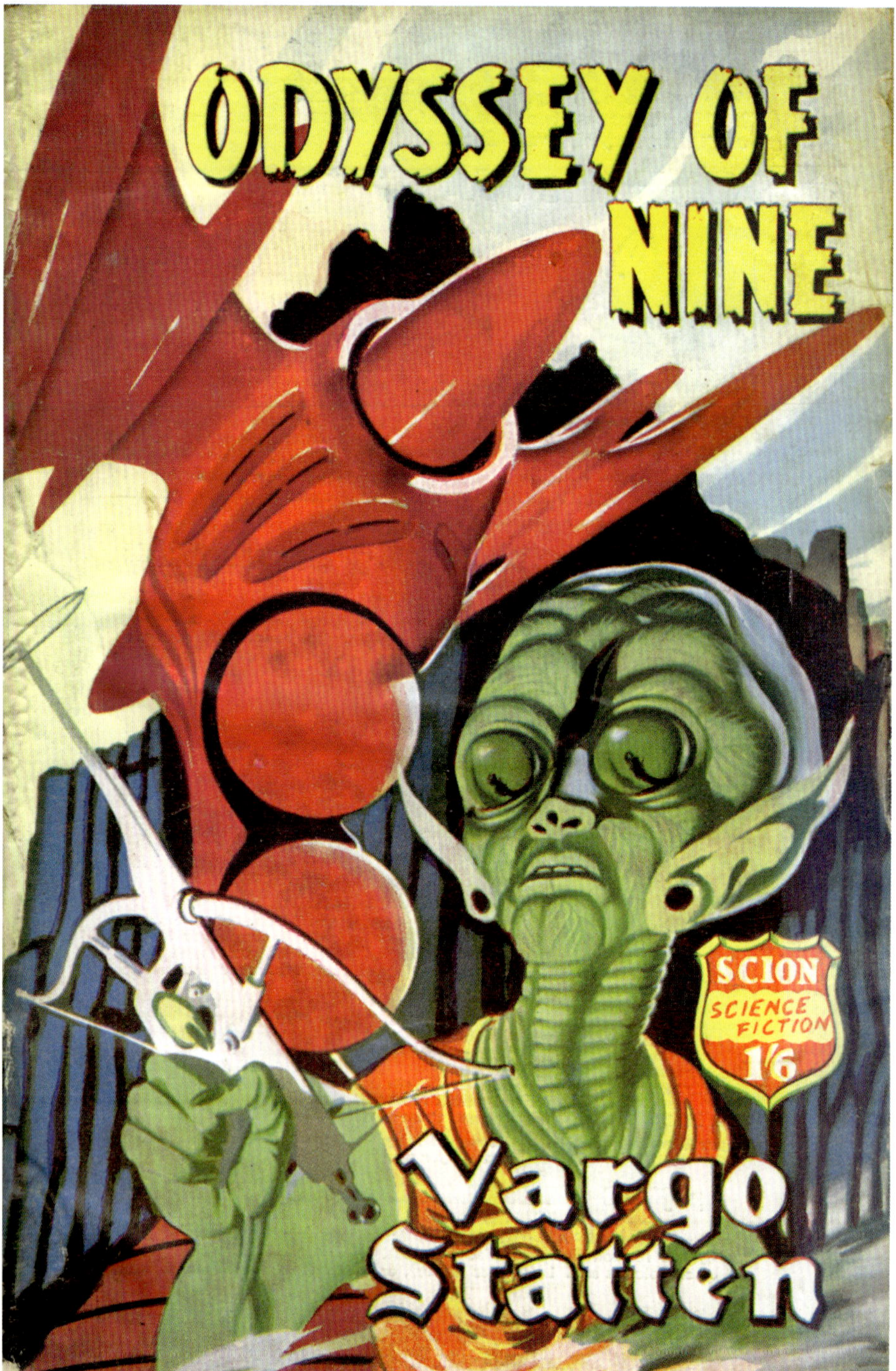

Vargo Statten (John Russell Fearn) | *Odyssey of Nine*
Scion Ltd., 1953 | Art **Ron Turner**

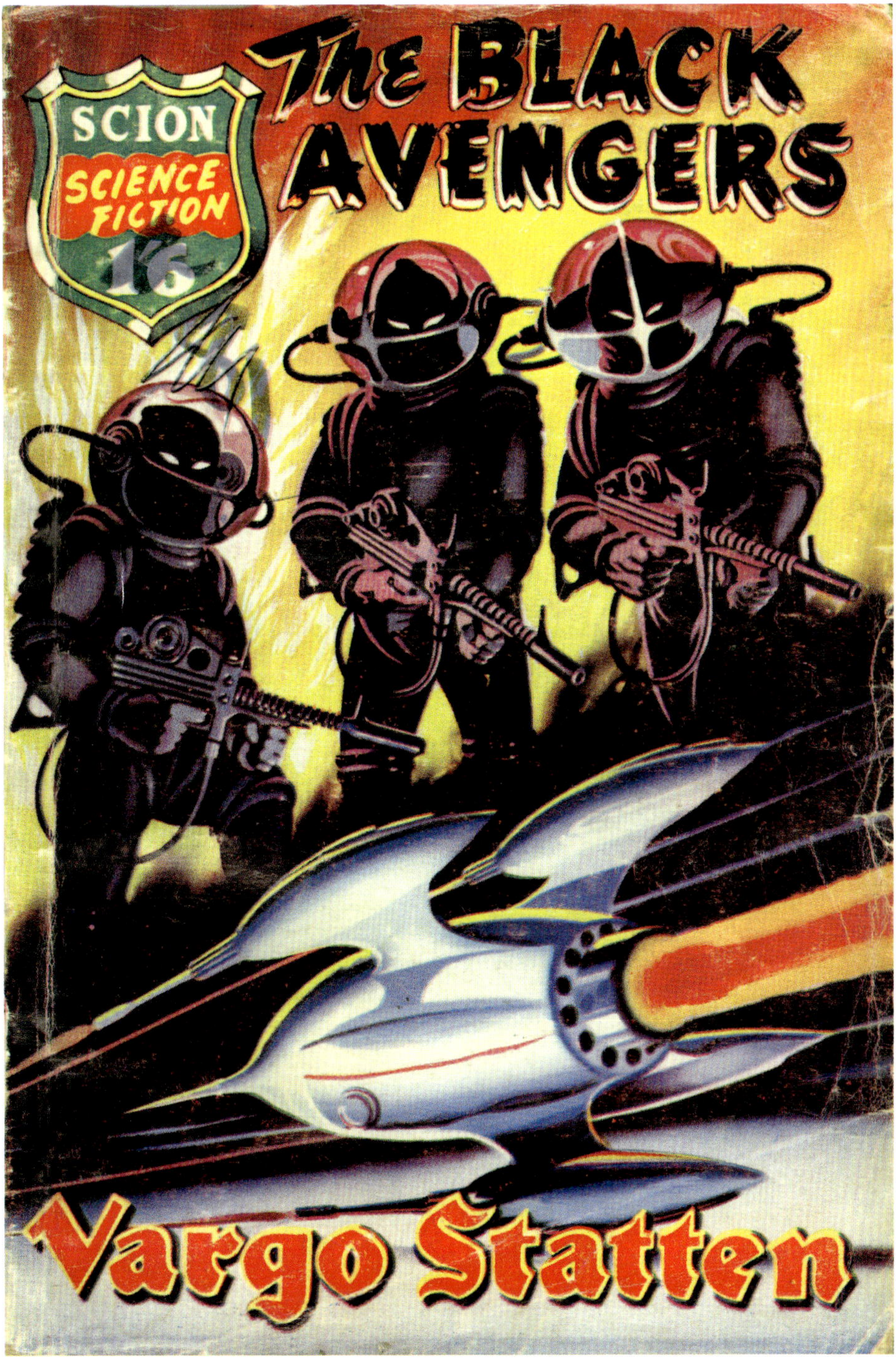

Vargo Statten (John Russell Fearn) | *The Black Avengers*
Scion Ltd., 1953 | Art **Ron Turner**

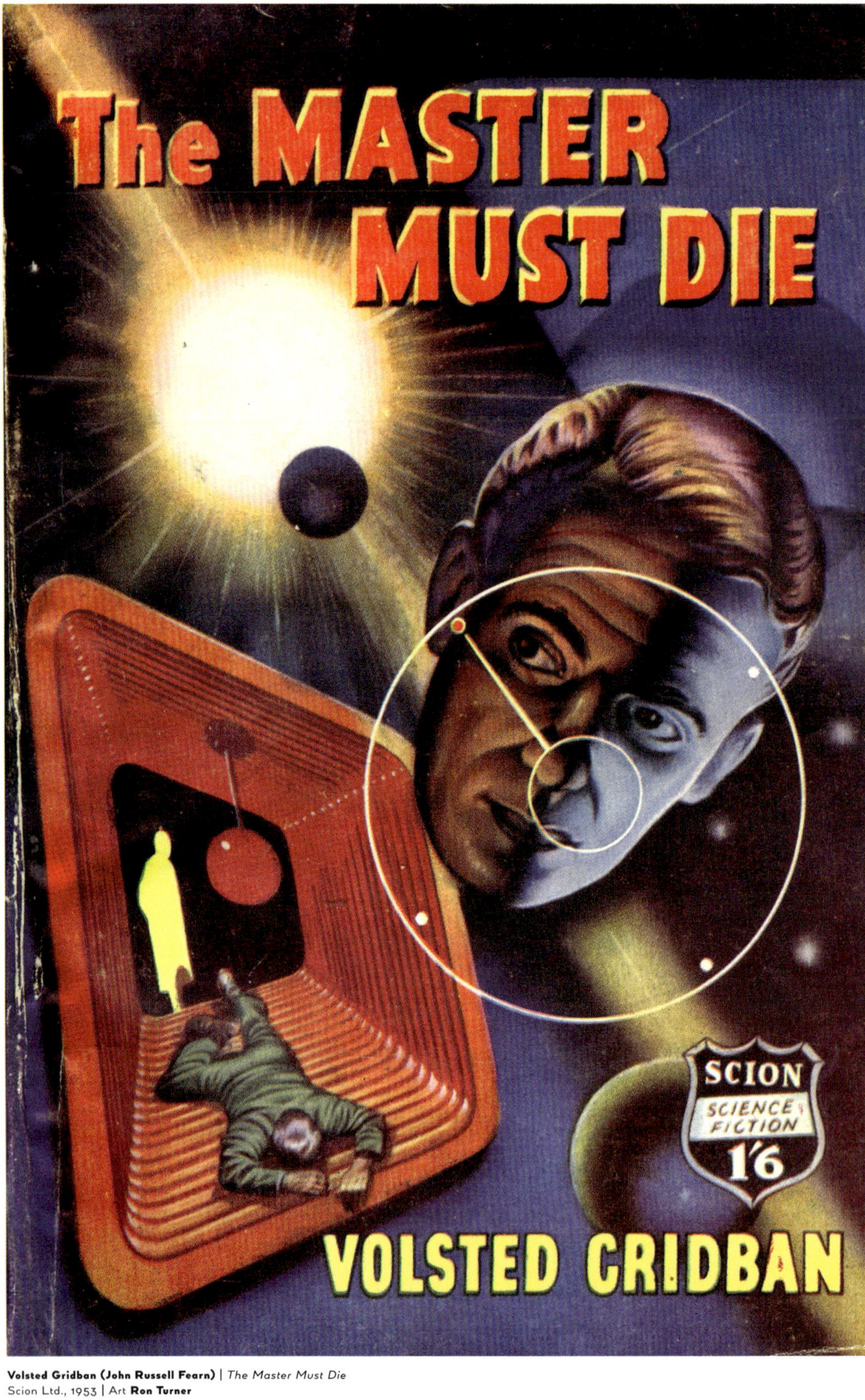

Volsted Gridban (John Russell Fearn) | *The Master Must Die*
Scion Ltd., 1953 | Art **Ron Turner**

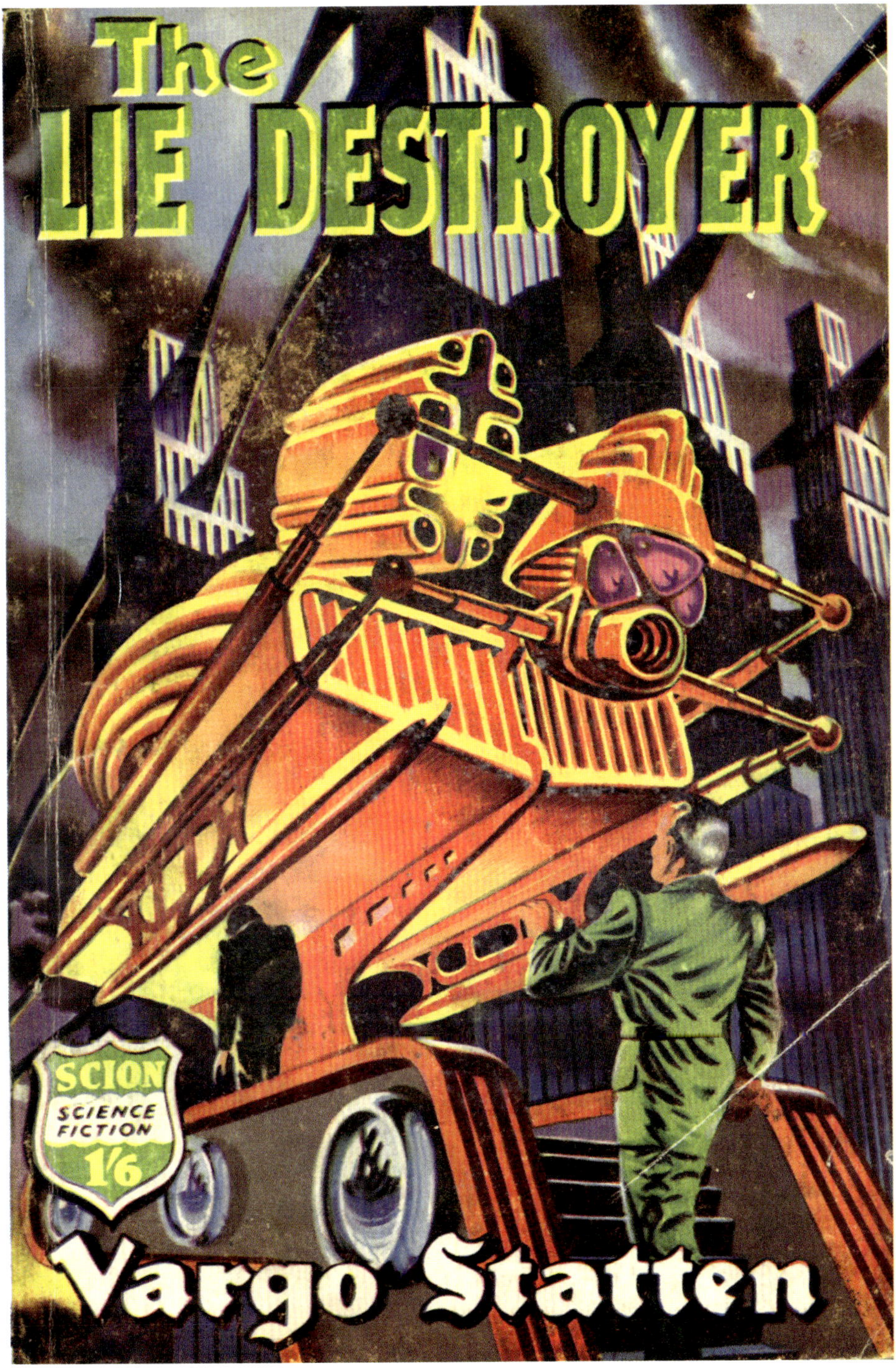

Vargo Statten (John Russell Fearn) | *The Lie Destroyer*
Scion Ltd., 1953 | Art **Ron Turner**

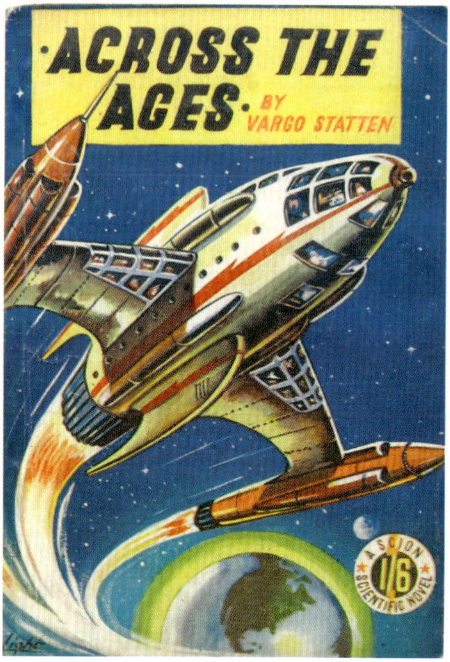

Vargo Statten (John Russell Fearn) | *Across the Ages*
Scion Ltd., 1952 | Art **Norman Light**

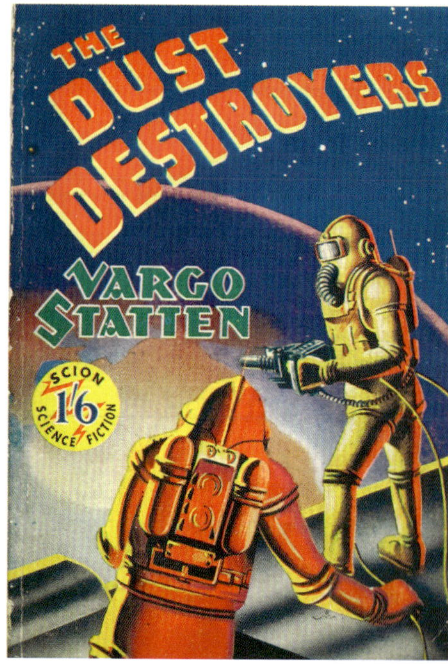

Vargo Statten (John Russell Fearn) | *The Dust Destroyers*
Scion Ltd., 1953 | Art **John Richards**

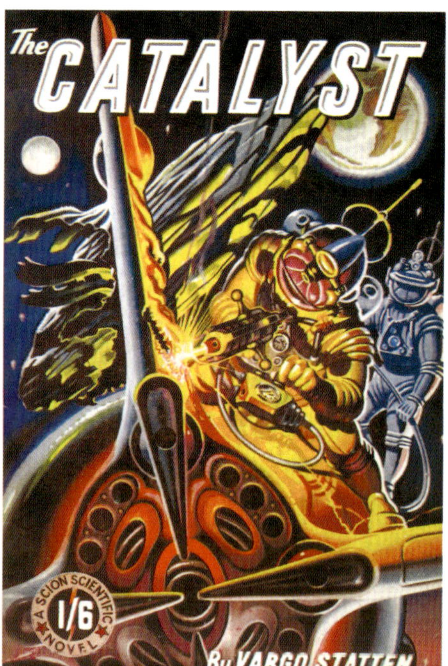

Vargo Statten (John Russell Fearn) | *The Catalyst*
Scion Ltd., 1951 | Art **Ron Turner**

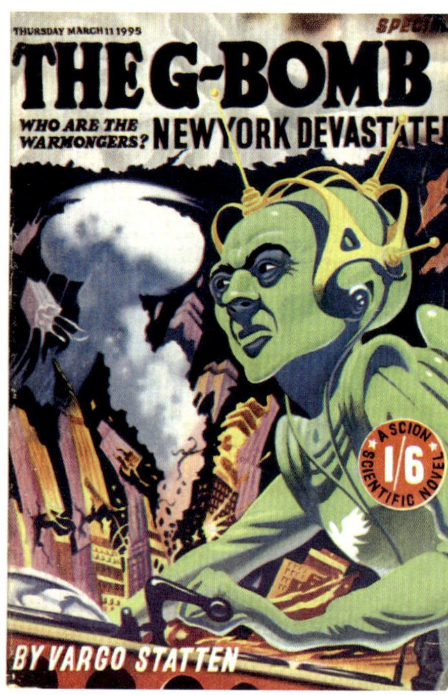

Vargo Statten (John Russell Fearn) | *The G-Bomb*
Scion Ltd., 1952 | Art **Ron Turner**

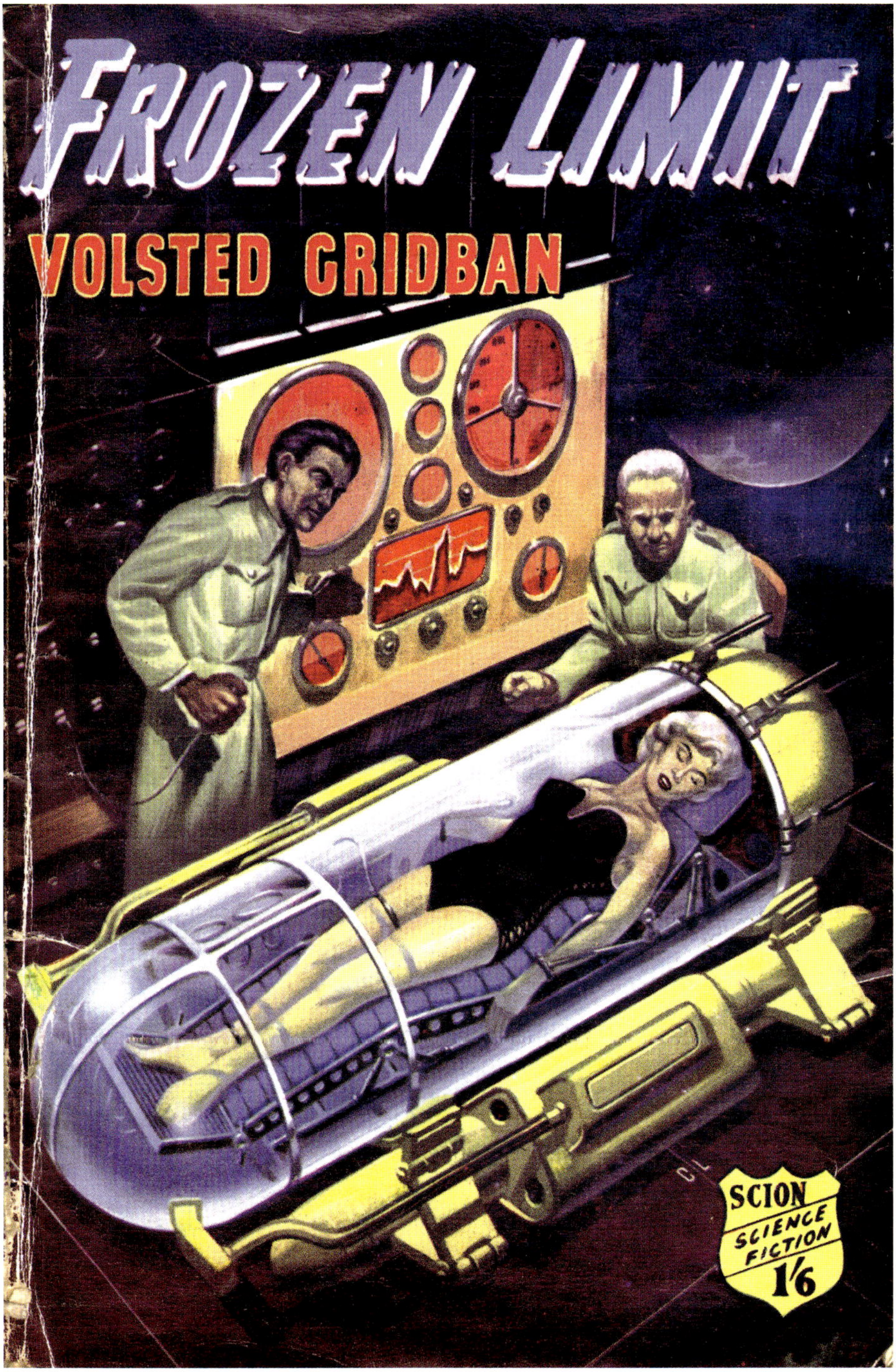

Volsted Gridban (John Russell Fearn) | *Frozen Limit*
Scion Ltd., 1954 | Art **Ron Turner**

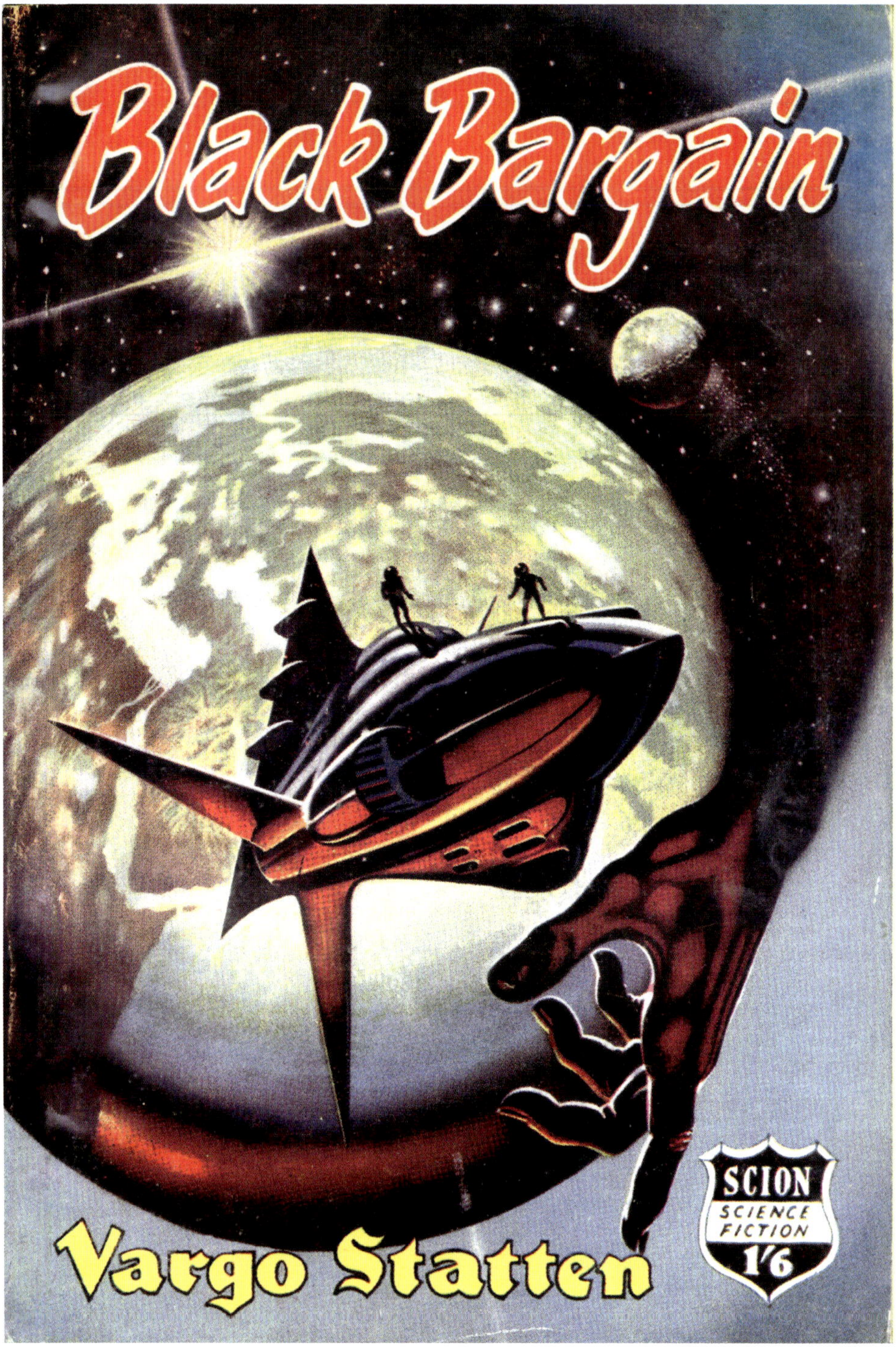

Vargo Statten (John Russell Fearn) | *Black Bargain*
Scion Ltd., 1953 | Art **Ron Turner**

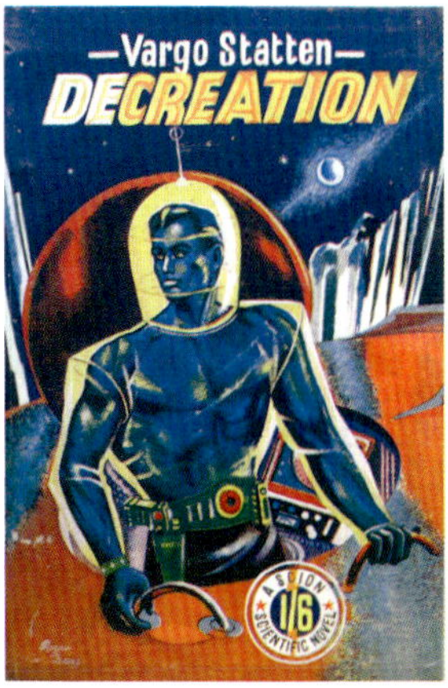

Vargo Statten (John Russell Fearn)
Decreation
Scion Ltd., 1952 | Art **Roger Davis**

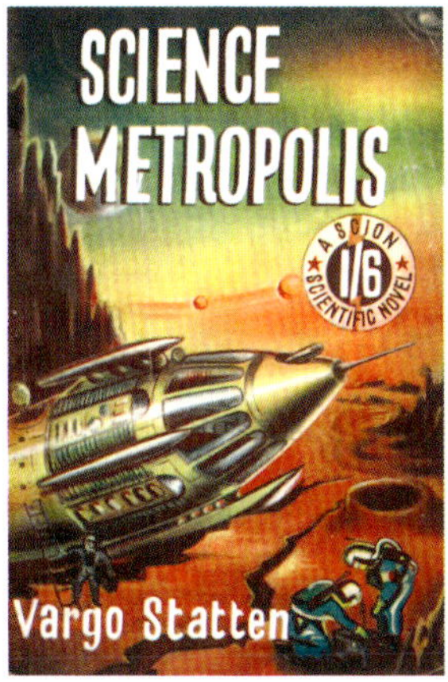

Vargo Statten (John Russell Fearn)
Science Metropolis
Scion Ltd., 1952 | Art **Philip Mendoza**

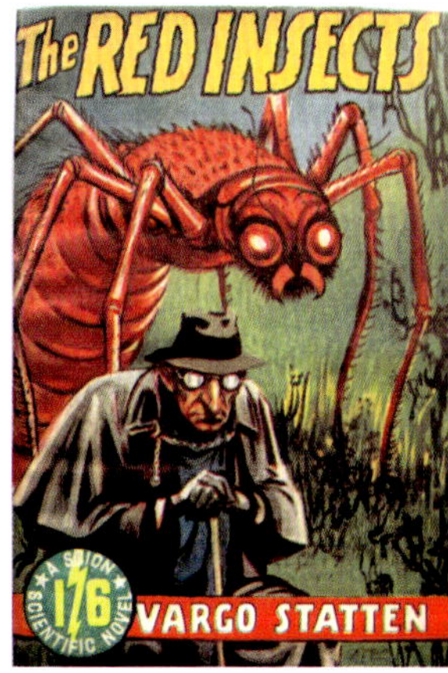

Vargo Statten (John Russell Fearn)
The Red Insects
Scion Ltd., 1951 | Art **Zero (Philip Mendoza)**

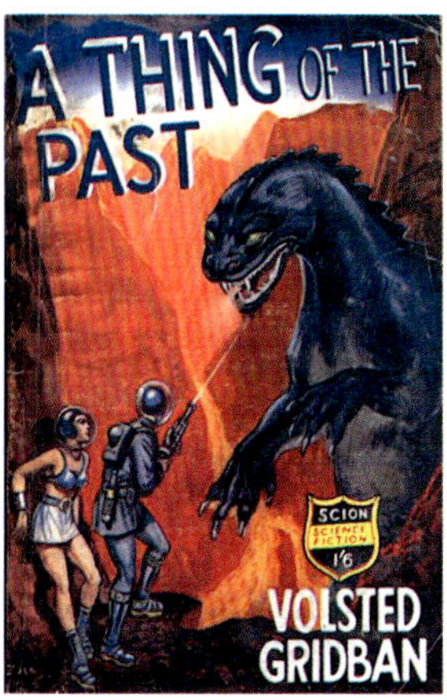

Volsted Gridban (John Russell Fearn)
A Thing of the Past
Scion Ltd., 1953 | Art **Philip Mendoza**

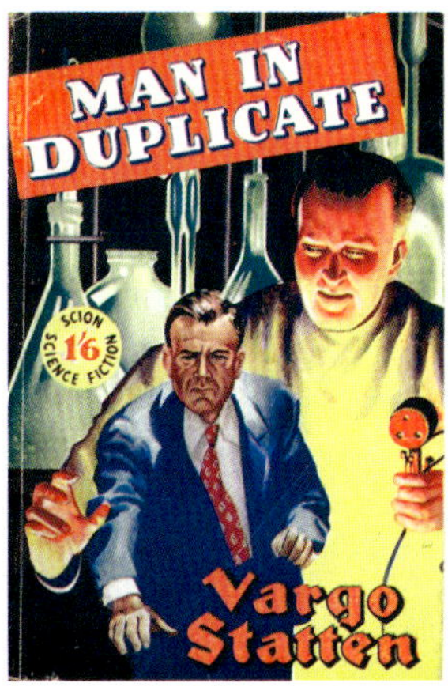

Vargo Statten (John Russell Fearn)
Man in Duplicate
Scion Ltd., 1953 | Art **John Richards**

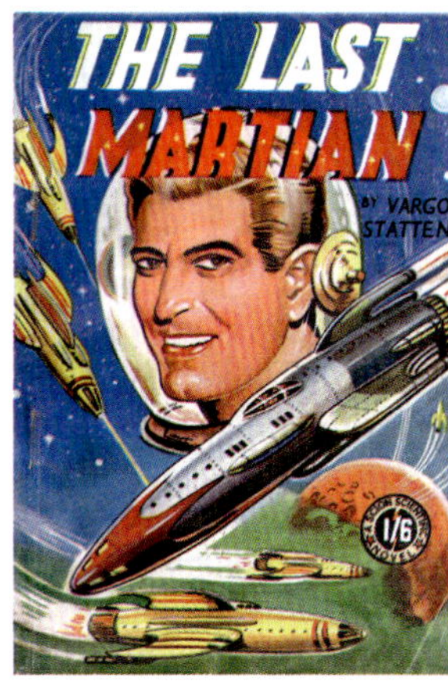

Vargo Statten (John Russell Fearn)
The Last Martian
Scion Ltd., 1952 | Art **Norman Light**

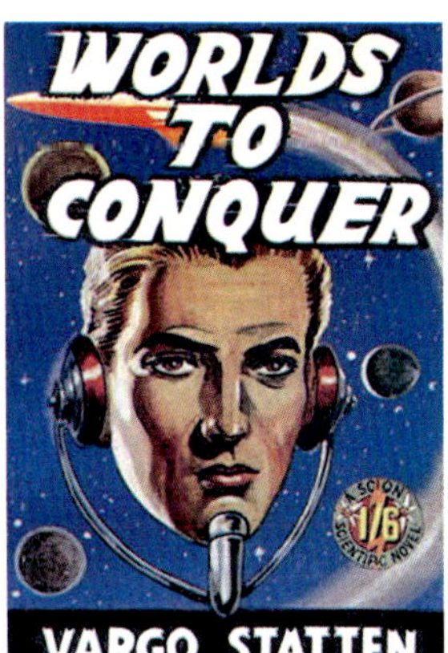

Vargo Statten (John Russell Fearn)
Worlds to Conquer
Scion Ltd., 1952 | Art **Norman Light**

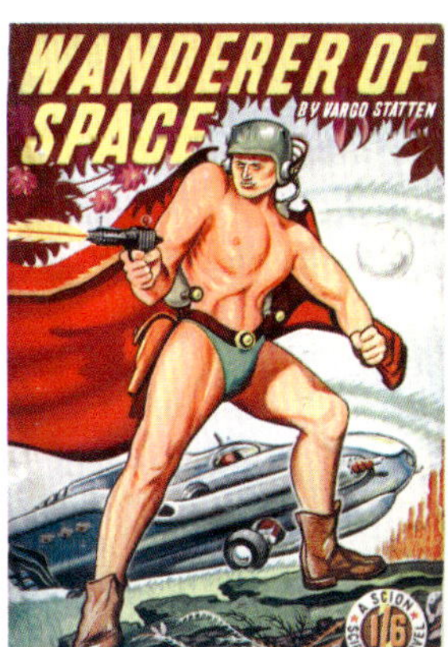

Vargo Statten (John Russell Fearn)
Wanderer of Space
Scion Ltd., 1950 | Art **Ron Turner**

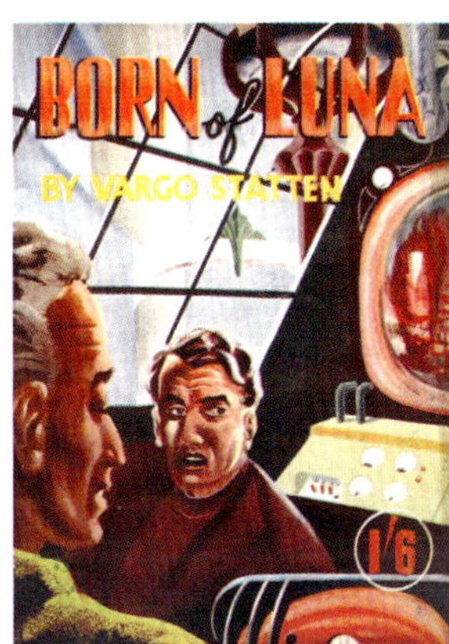

Vargo Statten (John Russell Fearn)
Born of Luna
Scion Ltd., 1951 | Art **George Ratcliffe**

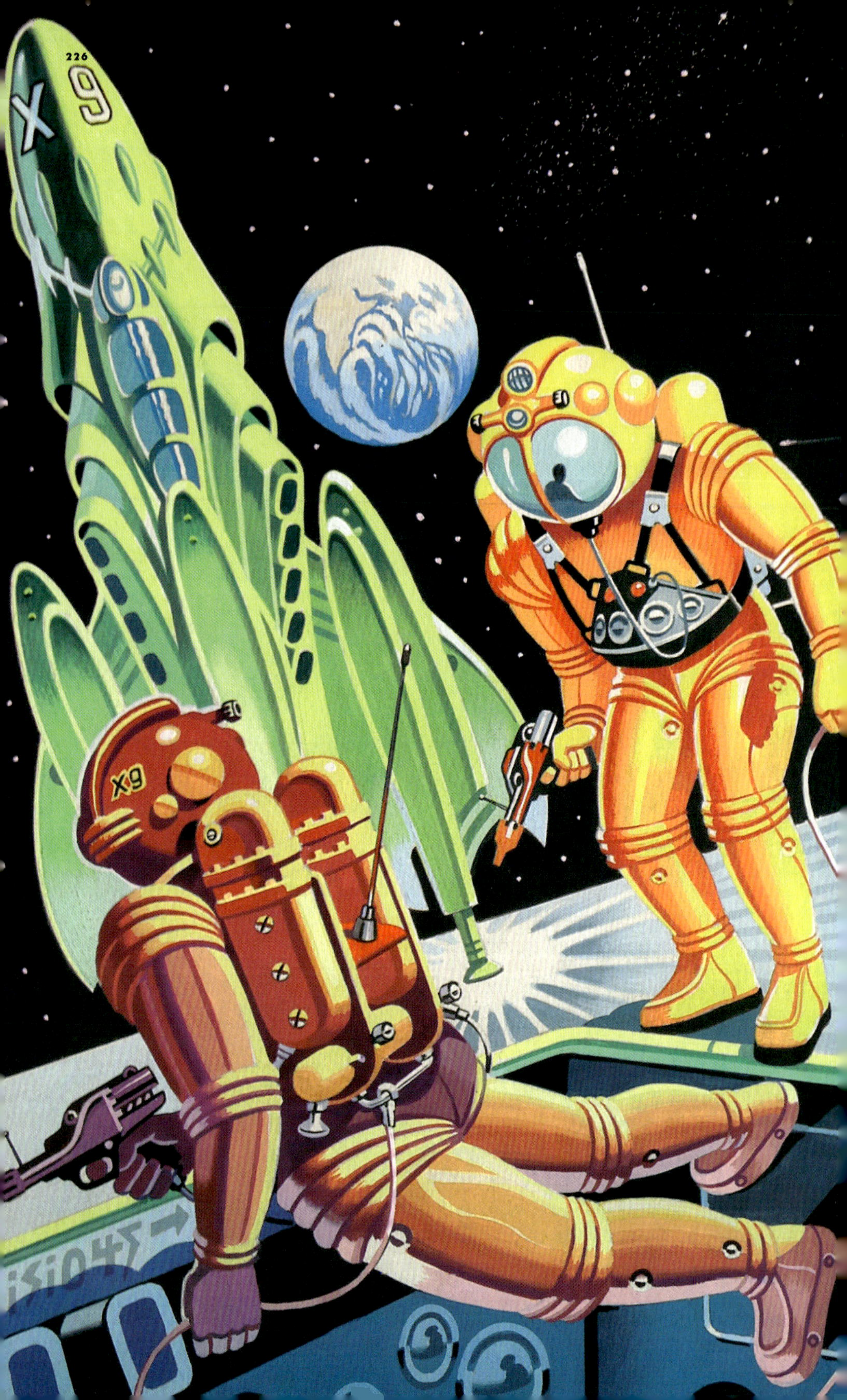
X 9
X9

opposite **Vargo Statten (John Russell Fearn)** | *The New Satellite*
Scion Ltd., 1951 | Art recreation, c1980s **Ron Turner**

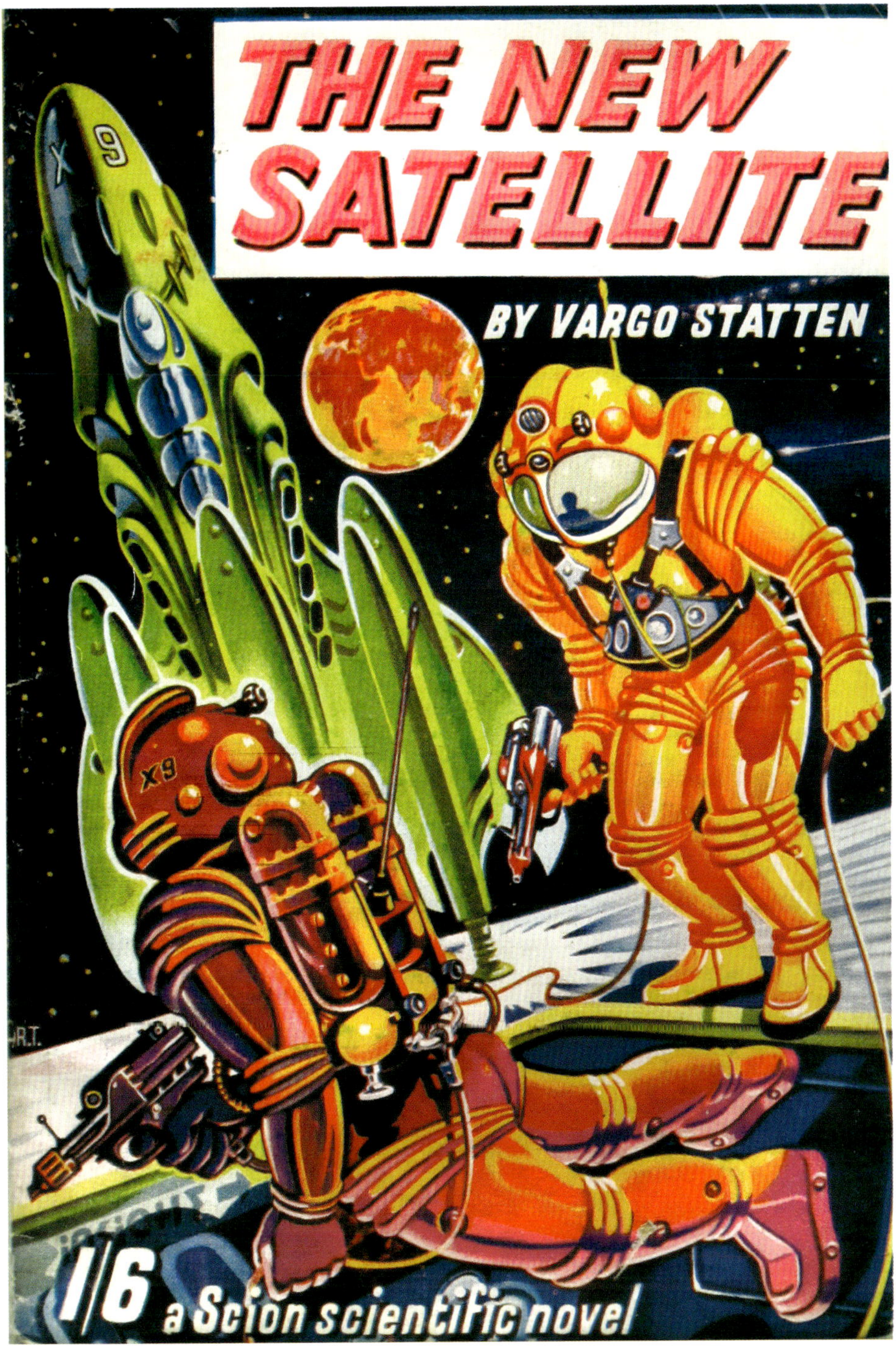

Vargo Statten (John Russell Fearn) | *The New Satellite*
Scion Ltd., 1951 | Art **Ron Turner**

John Lawrence, Ron Turner's agent: *"If Ron was really pleased with a particular cover he would sign it, though ironically, as 'Roland', as he thought it sounded a bit more 'up market' than plain Ron. Eventually, with his work much sought after, he realised that it's the quality of the work that matters, not the name."*

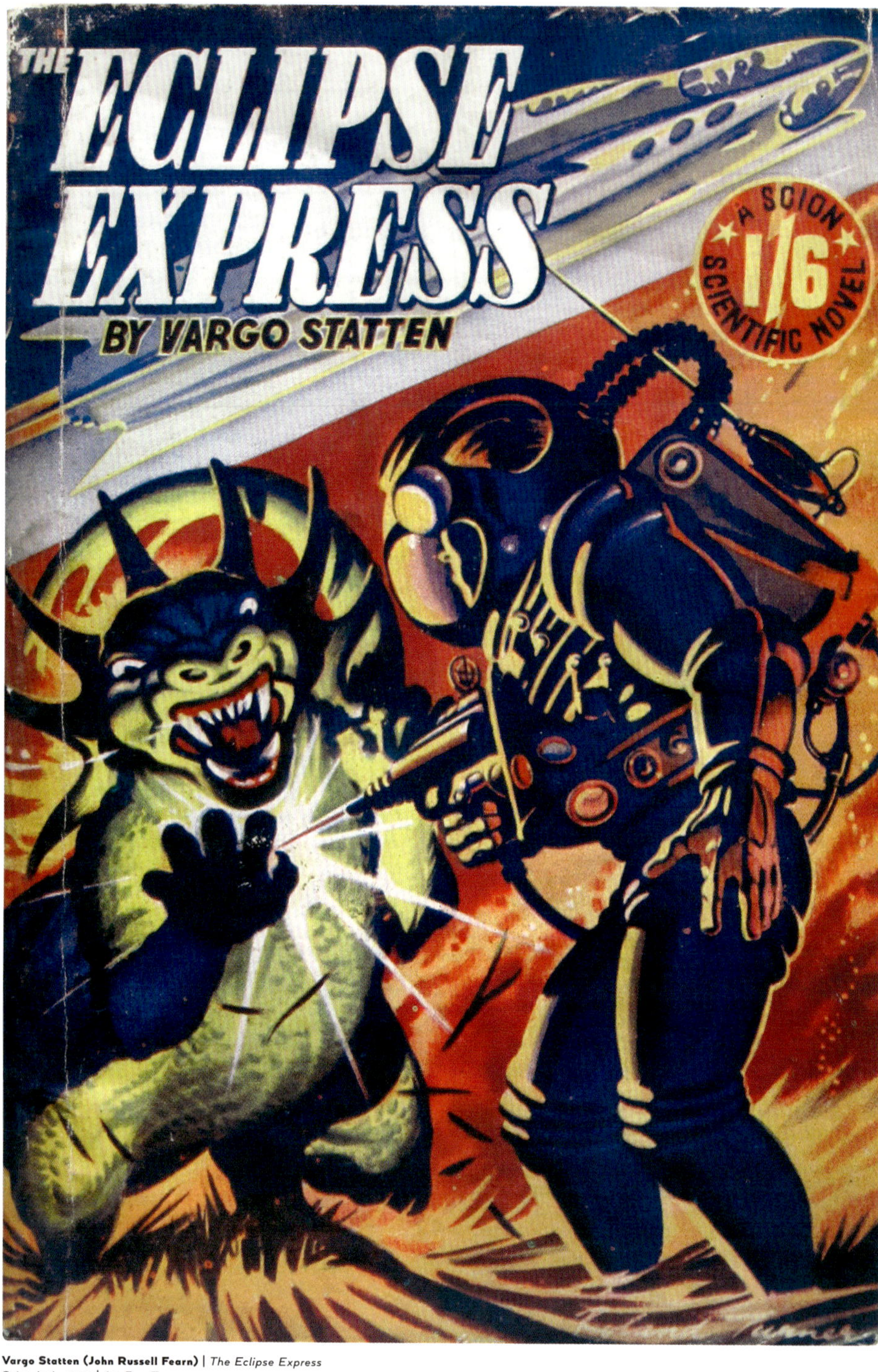

Vargo Statten (John Russell Fearn) | *The Eclipse Express*
Scion Ltd., 1952 | Art **Ron Turner**

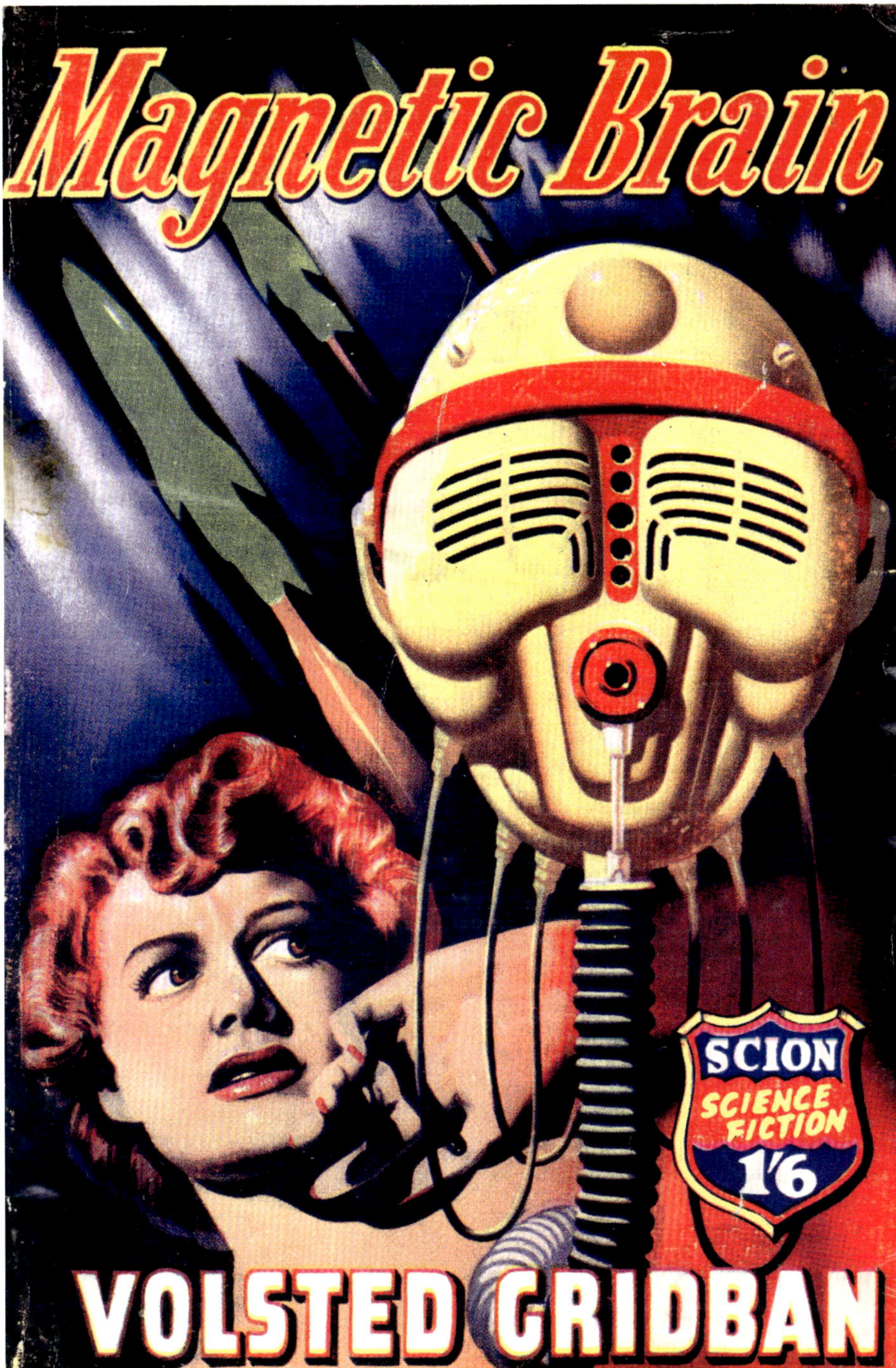

Volsted Gridban (John Russell Fearn) | *Magnetic Brain*
Scion Ltd., 1953 | Art **Ron Turner**

opposite **Vargo Statten (John Russell Fearn)** | *The Grand Illusion*
Scion Ltd., 1954 | Art recreation, c1980s **Ron Turner**

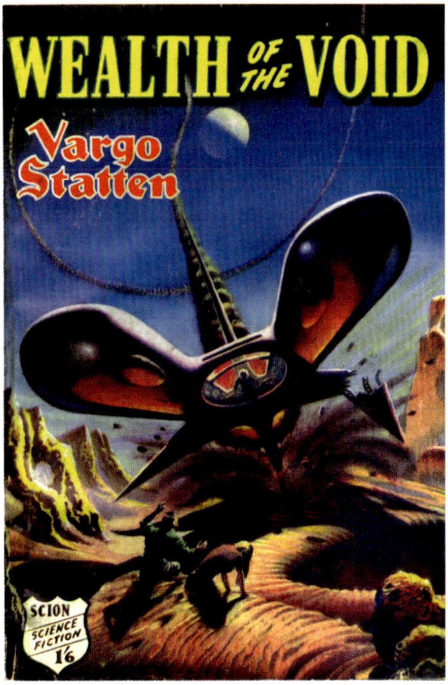

Vargo Statten (John Russell Fearn) | *Wealth of the Void*
Scion Ltd., 1954 | Art **Ron Turner**

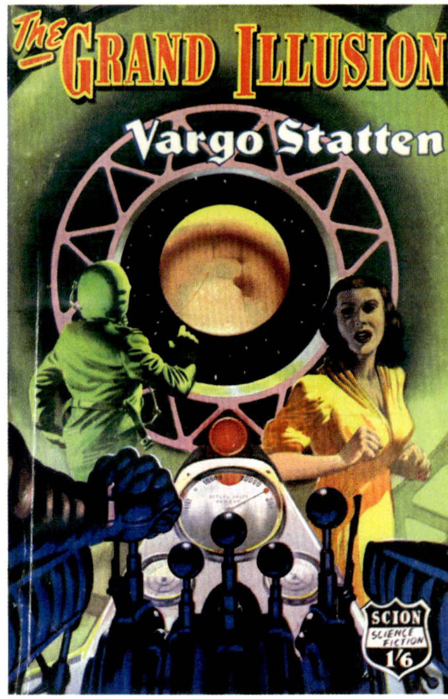

Vargo Statten (John Russell Fearn) | *The Grand Illusion*
Scion Ltd., 1954 | Art **Ron Turner**

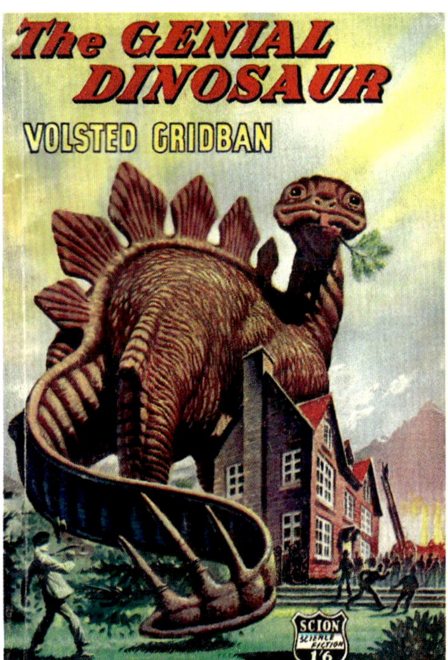

Volsted Gridban (John Russell Fearn) | *The Genial Dinosaur*
Scion Ltd., 1954 | Art **Ron Turner**

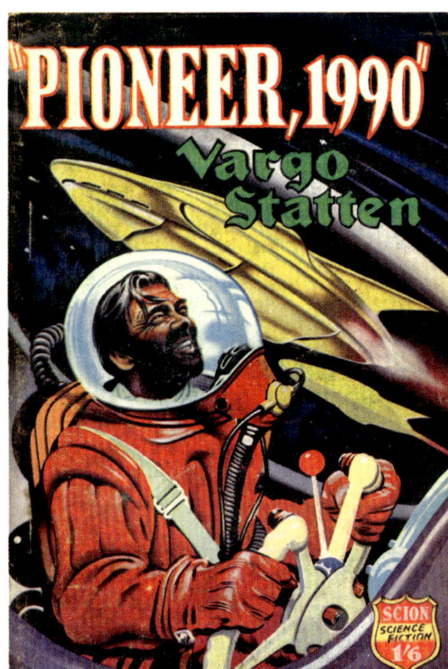

Vargo Statten (John Russell Fearn) | *Pioneer, 1990*
Scion Ltd., 1953 | Art **Ron Turner**

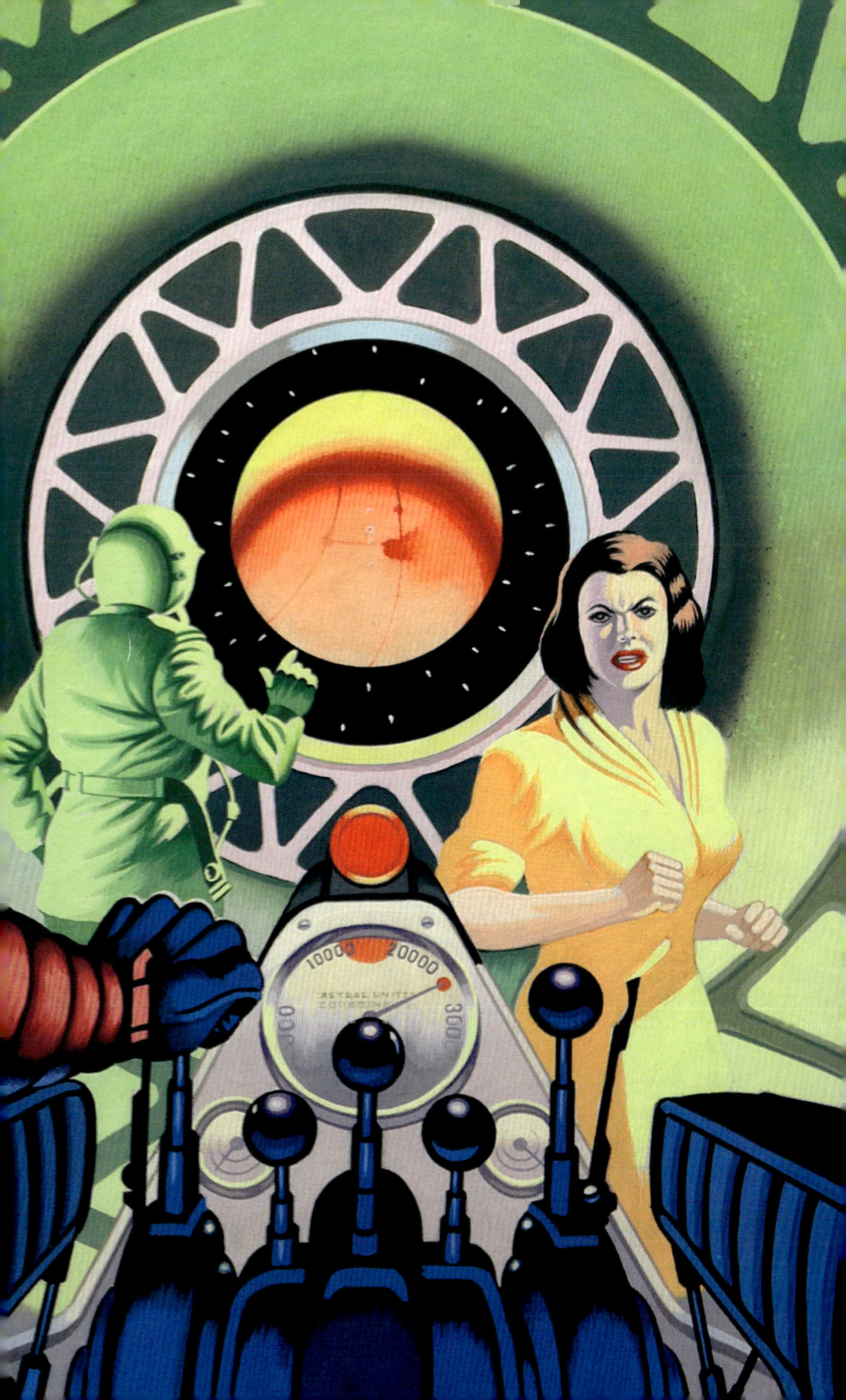
10000
20000

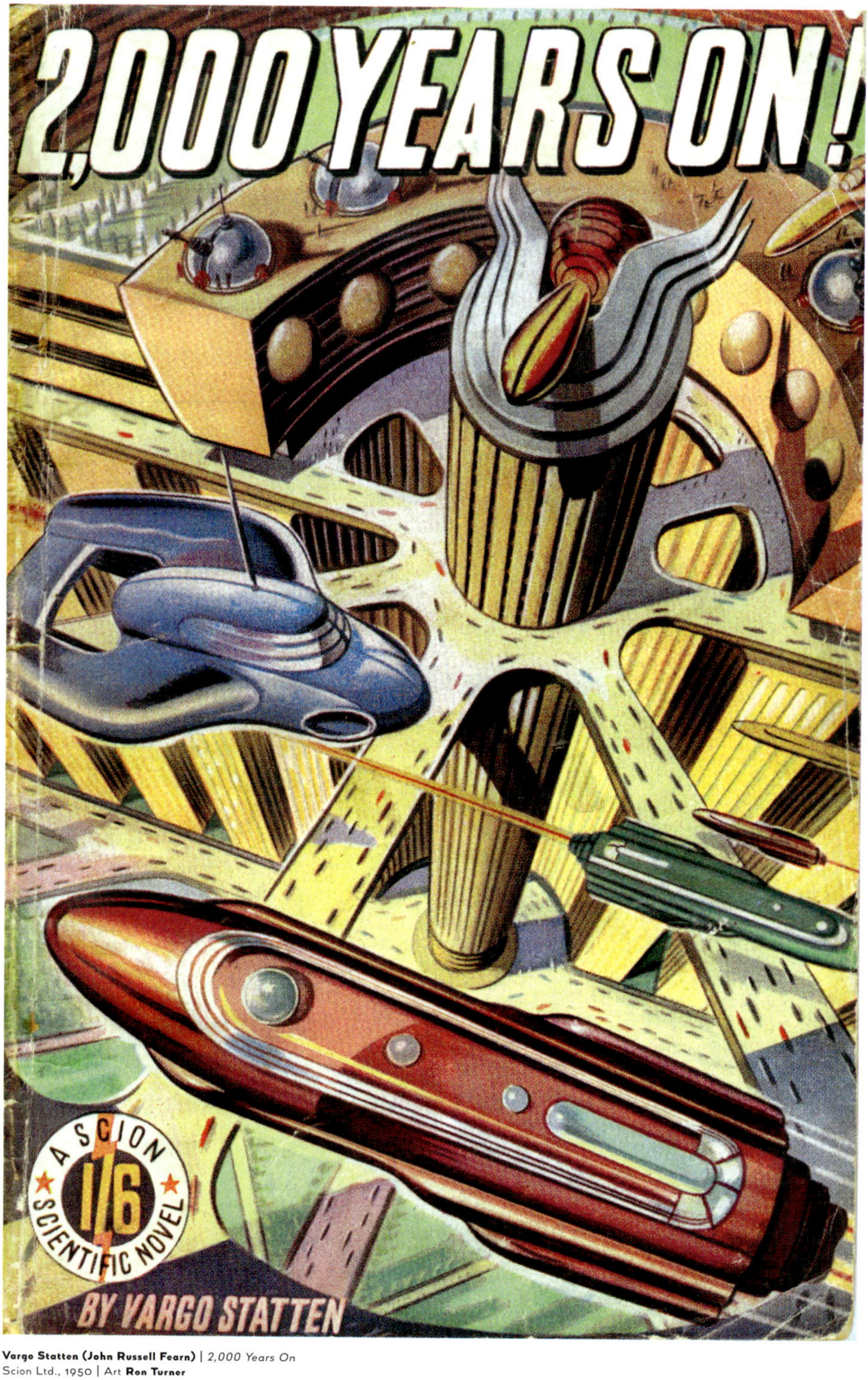

Vargo Statten (John Russell Fearn) | *2,000 Years On*
Scion Ltd., 1950 | Art **Ron Turner**

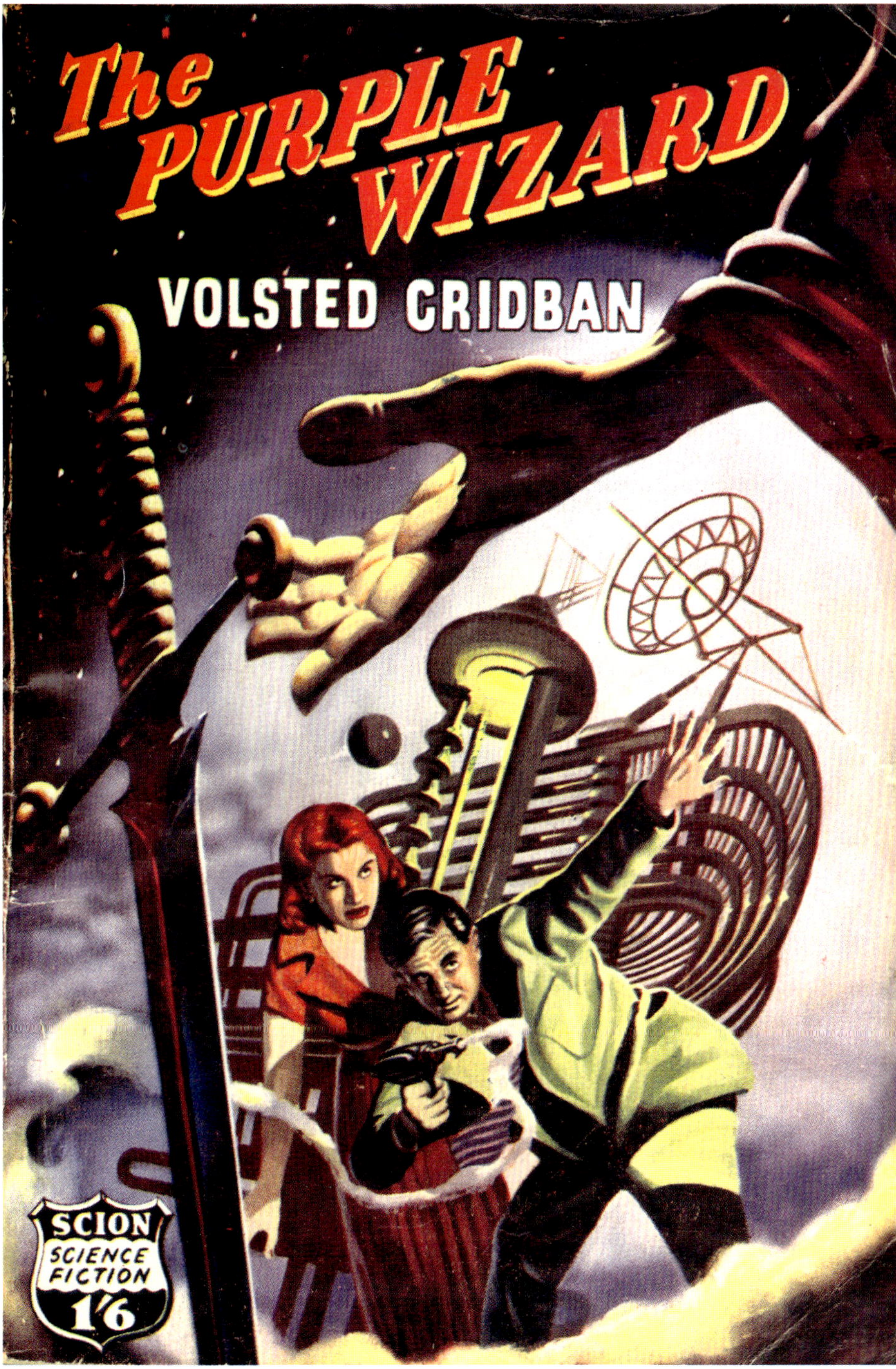

Volsted Gridban (John Russell Fearn) | *The Purple Wizard*
Scion Ltd., 1954 | Art **Ron Turner**

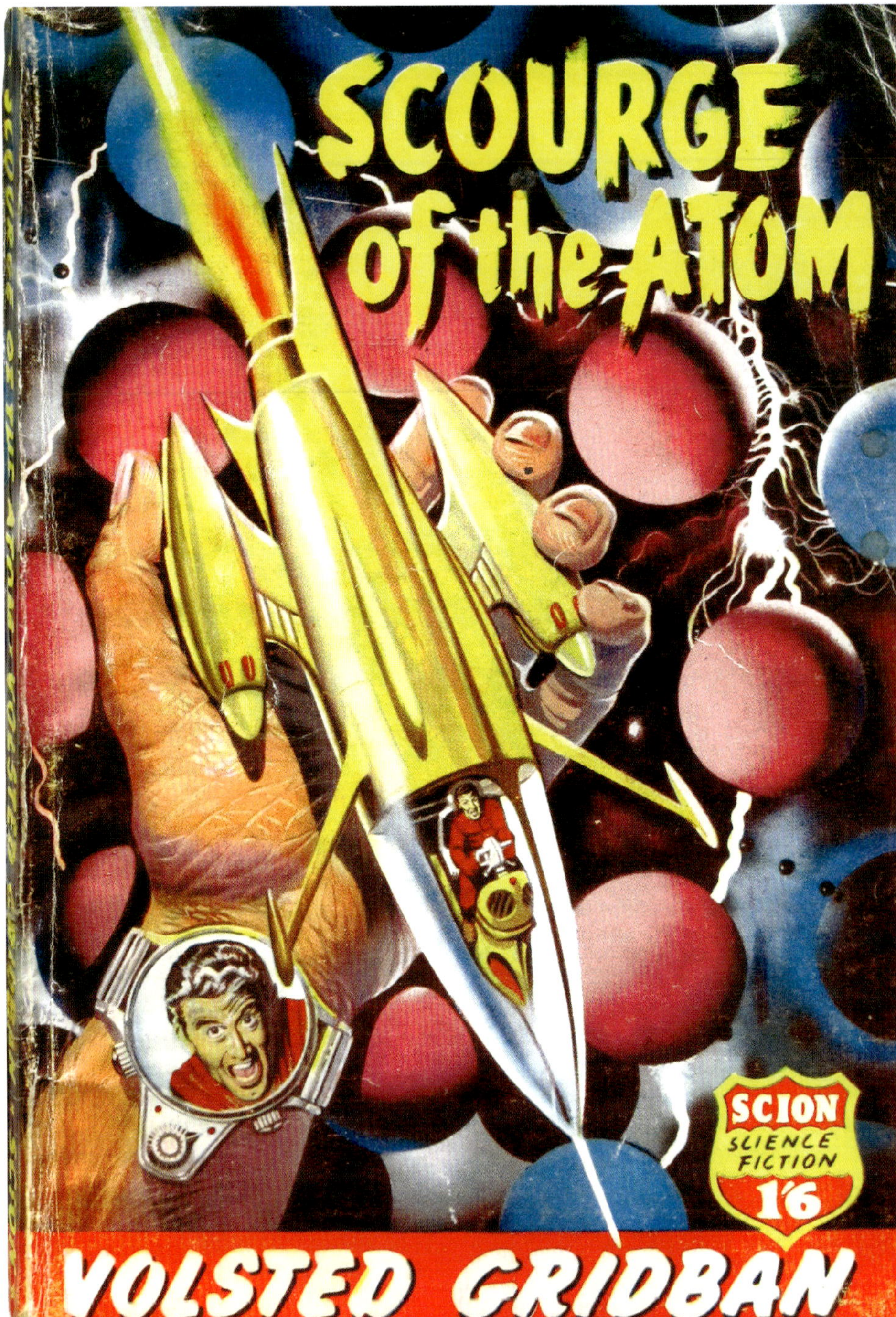

Volsted Gridban (John Russell Fearn) | *Scourge of the Atom*
Scion Ltd., 1953 | Art **Ron Turner**

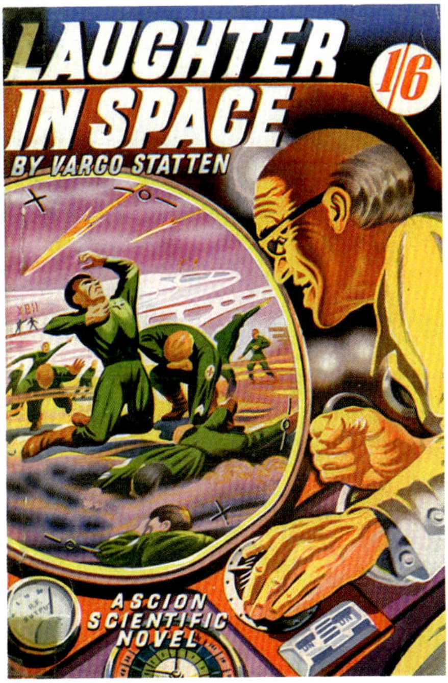

Vargo Statten (John Russell Fearn) | *Laughter in Space*
Scion Ltd., 1952 | Art **Ron Turner**

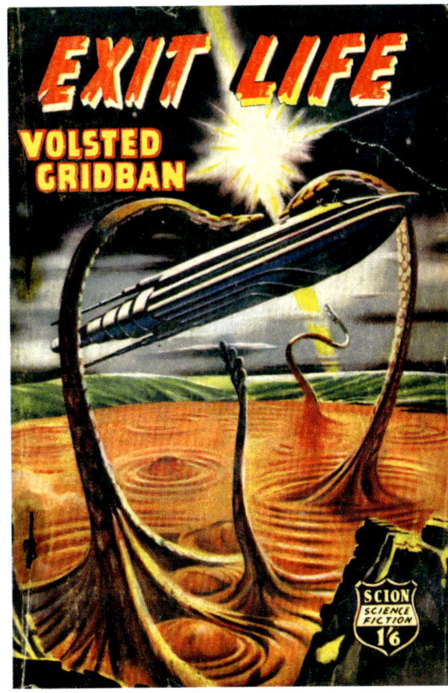

Volsted Gridban (John Russell Fearn) | *Exit Life*
Scion Ltd., 1953 | Art **Ron Turner**

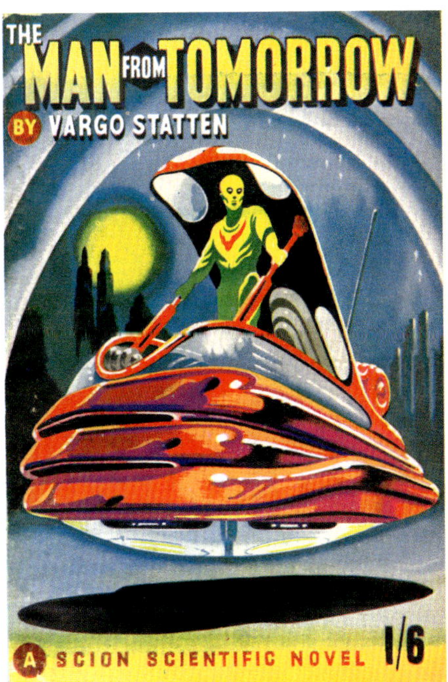

Vargo Statten (John Russell Fearn) | *The Man from Tomorrow*
Scion Ltd., 1952 | Art **Ron Turner**

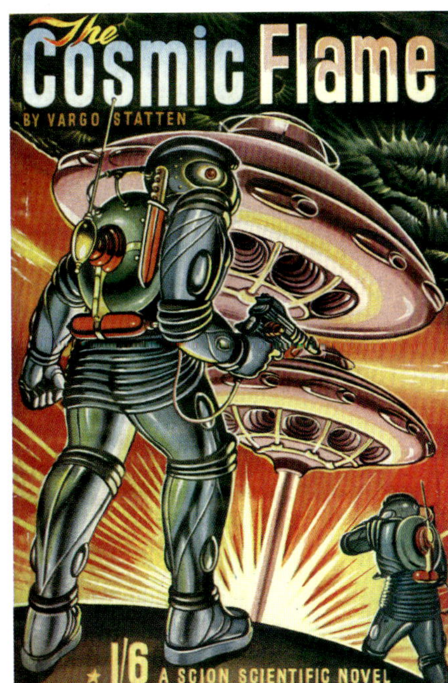

Vargo Statten (John Russell Fearn) | *The Cosmic Flame*
Scion Ltd., 1950 | Art **Ron Turner**

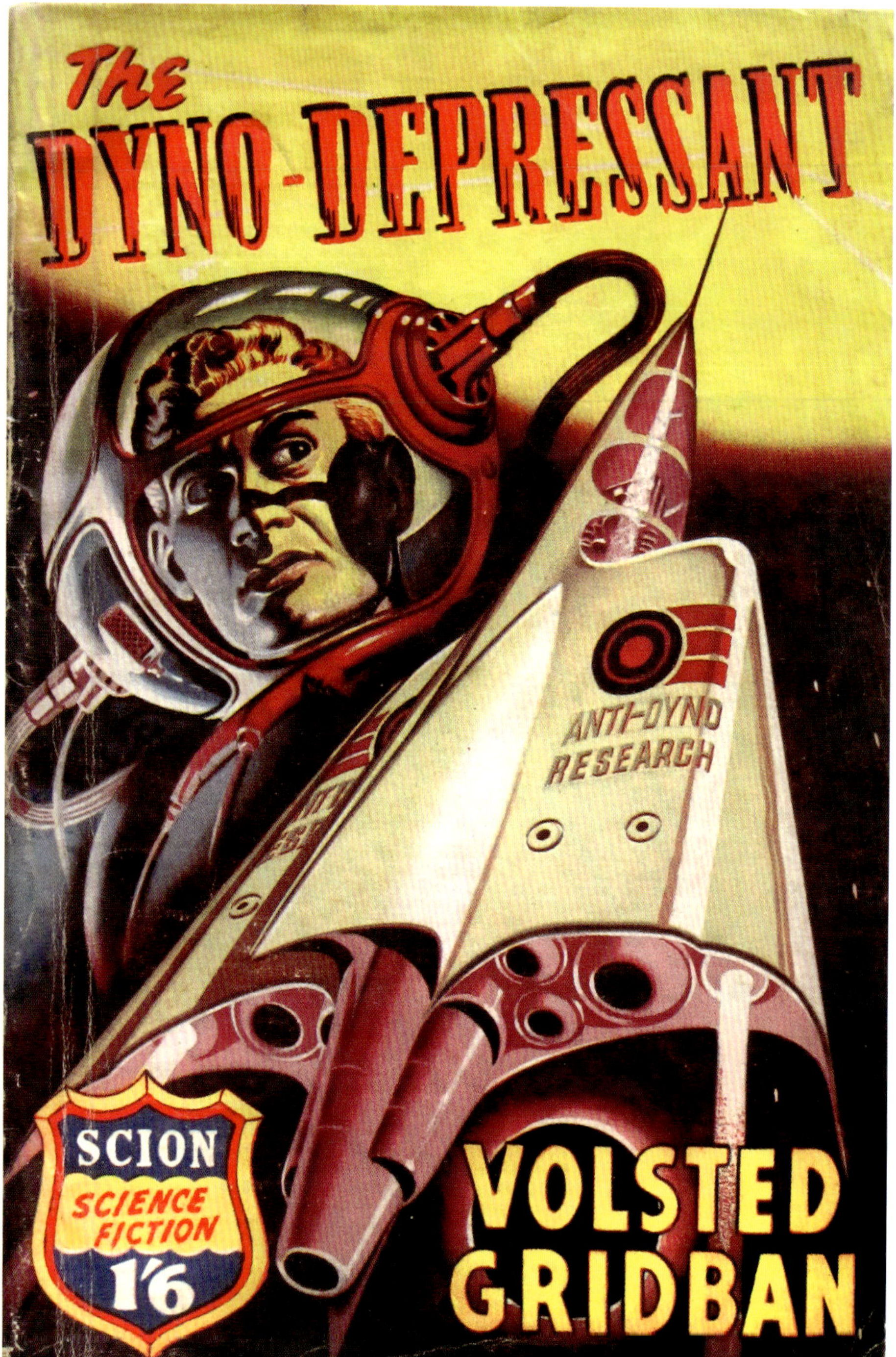

Volsted Gridban (John Russell Fearn) | *The Dyno-Depressant*
Scion Ltd., 1953 | Art **Ron Turner**

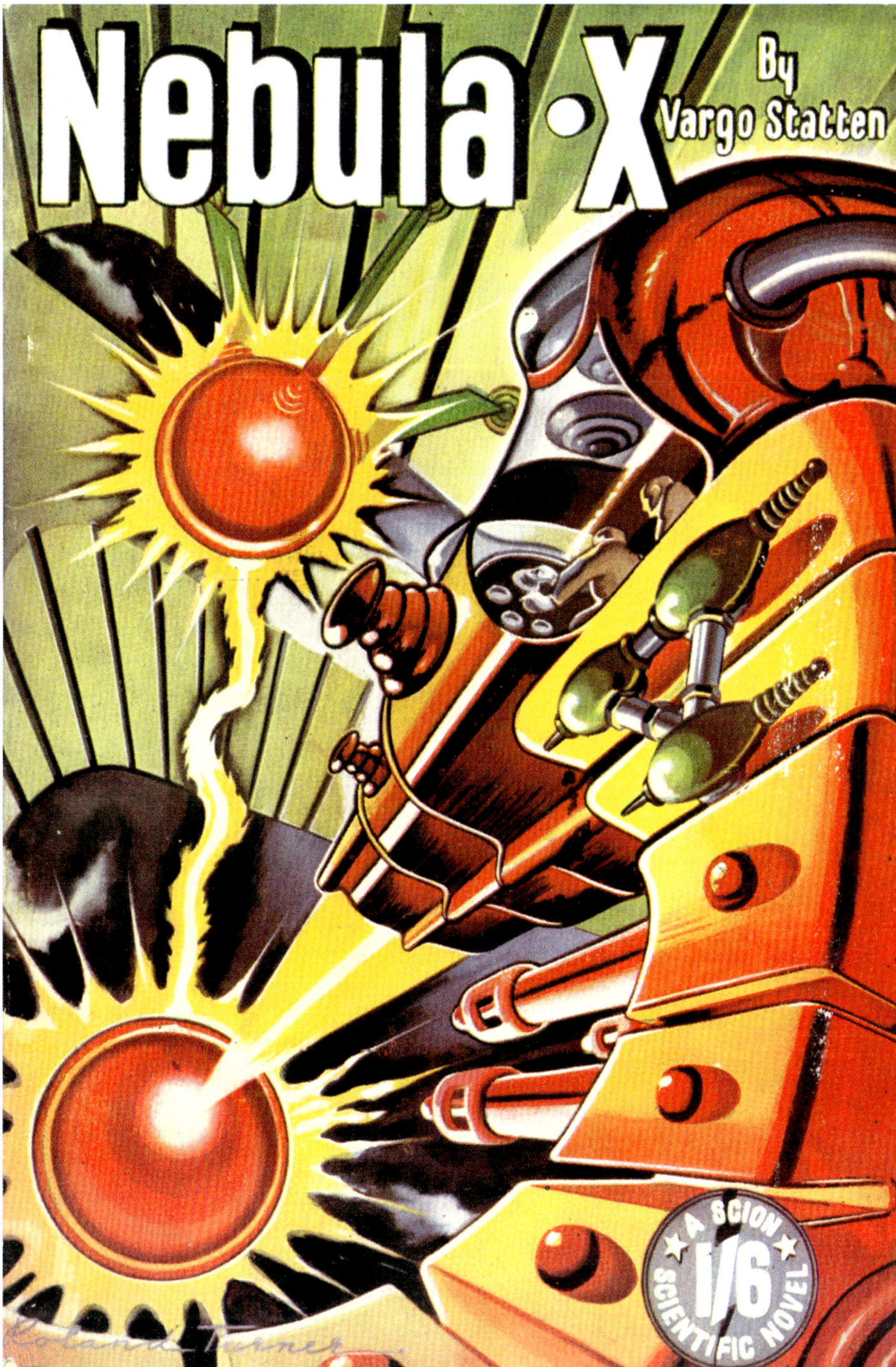

Vargo Statten (John Russell Fearn) | *Nebula X*
Scion Ltd., 1950 | Art **Ron Turner**

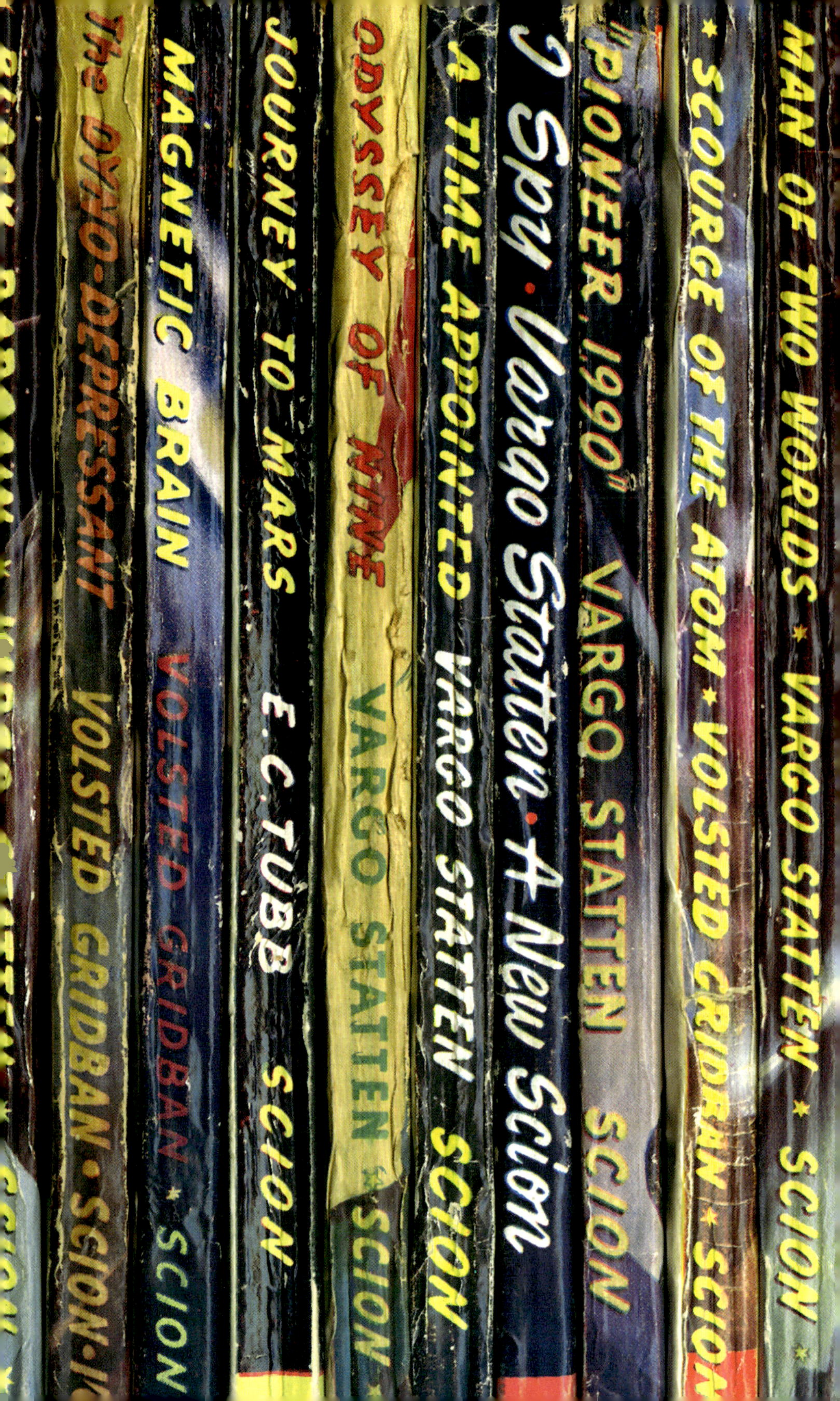

The DYNO-DEPRESSANT
VOLSTED GRIDBAN • SCION
MAGNETIC BRAIN
VOLSTED GRIDBAN * SCION
JOURNEY TO MARS
E.C. TUBB
SCION
ODYSSEY OF NINE
VARGO STATTEN
SCION
A TIME APPOINTED
VARGO STATTEN
SCION
I Spy • Vargo Statten • A New Scion
"PIONEER 1990"
VARGO STATTEN
SCION
SCOURGE OF THE ATOM • VOLSTED GRIDBAN • SCION
MAN OF TWO WORLDS * VARGO STATTEN * SCION

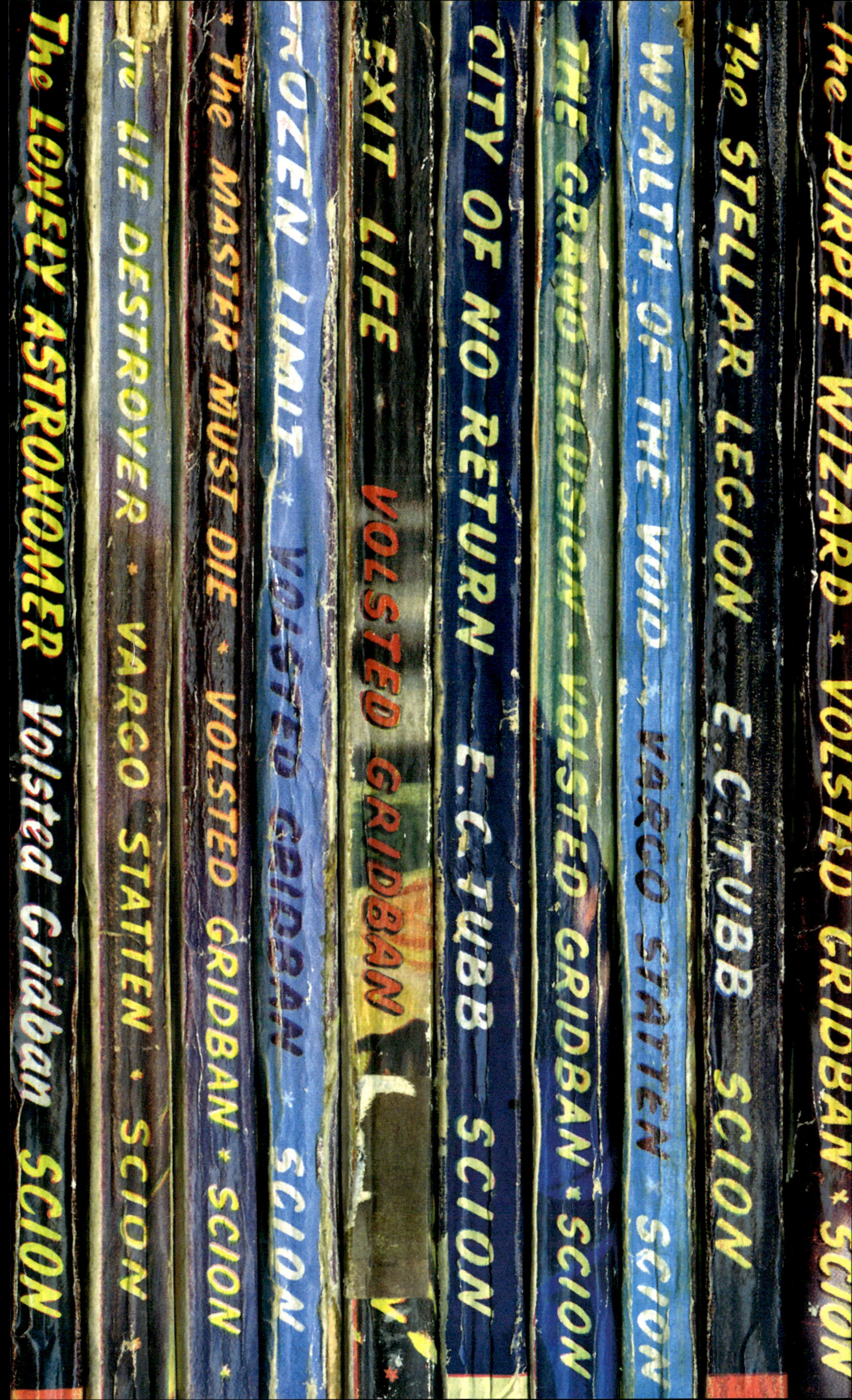

The LONELY ASTRONOMER Volsted Gridban SCION
LIE DESTROYER · VARGO STATTEN · SCION
The MASTER MUST DIE · VOLSTED GRIDBAN · SCION
ROZEN LIMIT · VOLSTED GRIDBAN · SCION
EXIT LIFE VOLSTED GRIDBAN
CITY OF NO RETURN E.C.TUBB SCION
THE GRAND ILLUSION · VOLSTED GRIDBAN · SCION
WEALTH OF THE VOID VARGO STATTEN · SCION
The STELLAR LEGION E.C.TUBB SCION
The PURPLE WIZARD · VOLSTED GRIDBAN · SCION

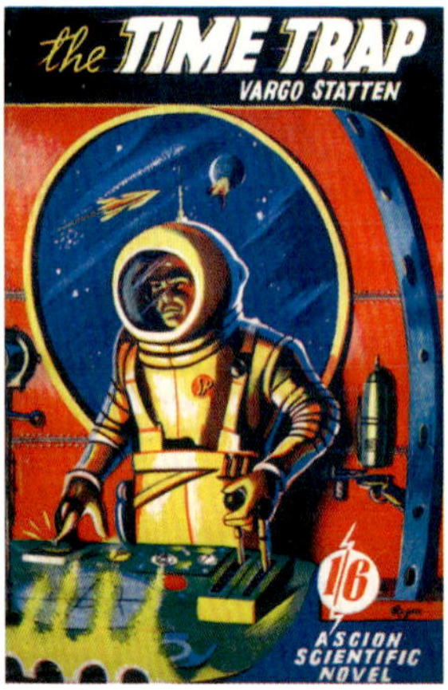

Vargo Statten (John Russell Fearn)
The Time Trap | Scion Ltd., 1952
Art **Roger Davis**

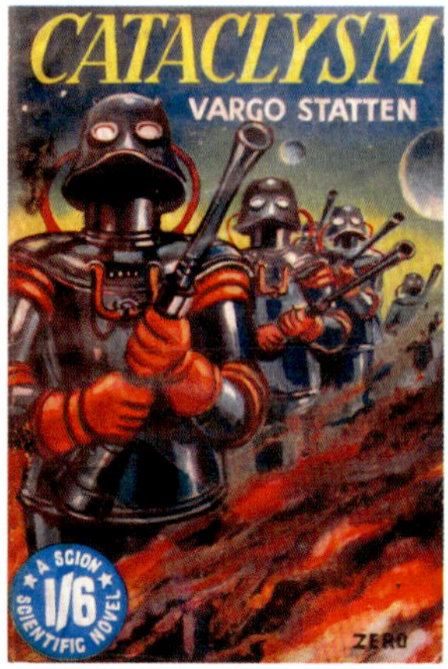

Vargo Statten (John Russell Fearn)
Cataclysm
Scion Ltd., 1951 | Art **Zero (Philip Mendoza)**

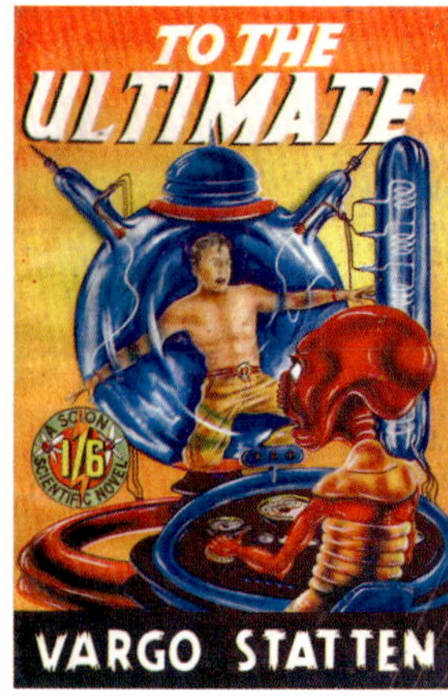

Vargo Statten (John Russell Fearn)
To the Ultimate
Scion Ltd., 1952 | Art **Gordon C. Davies**

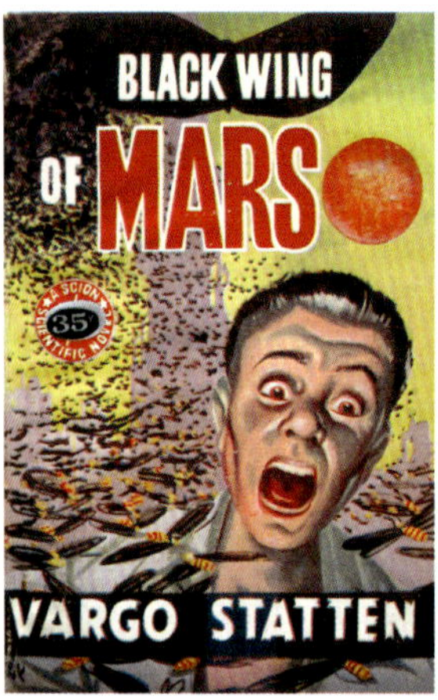

Vargo Statten (John Russell Fearn)
Black Wing of Mars
Scion Ltd., 1953 | Art **John Richards**

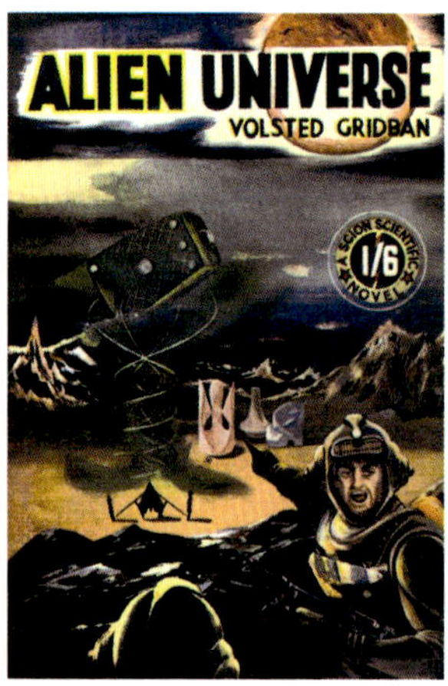

Volsted Gridban (E. C Tubb)
Alien Universe
Scion Ltd., 1952 | Art **George Ratcliffe**

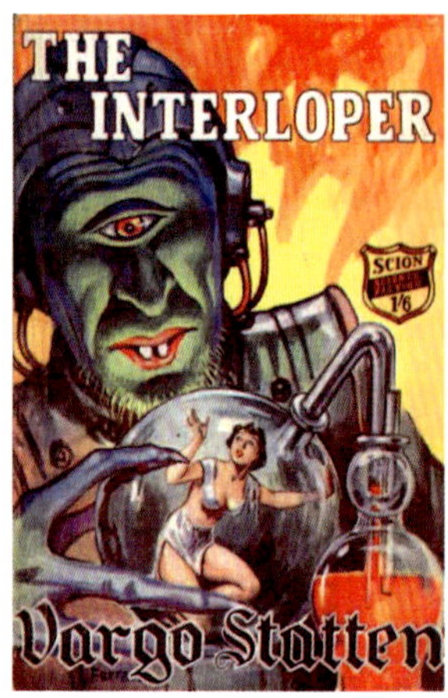

Vargo Statten (John Russell Fearn)
The Interloper
Scion Ltd., 1953 | Art **Philip Mendoza**

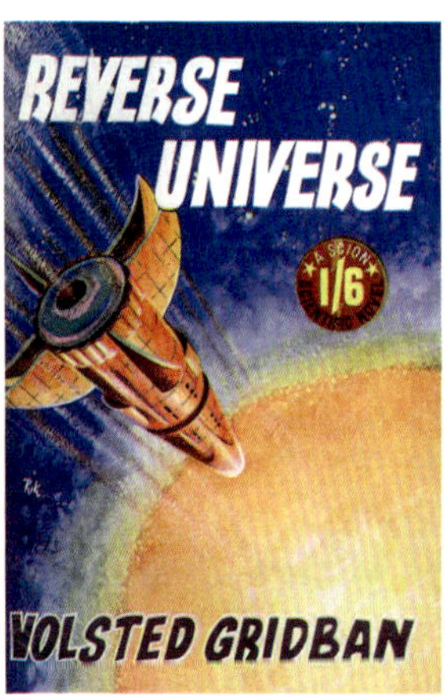

Volsted Gridban (E. C. Tubb)
Reverse Universe
Scion Ltd., 1952 | Art **Rik (John Richards)**

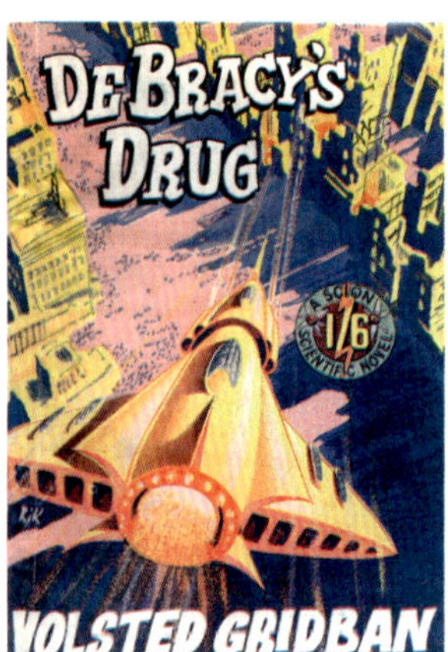

Volsted Gridban (E. C. Tubb)
De Bracy's Drug
Scion Ltd., 1953 | Art **Rik (John Richards)**

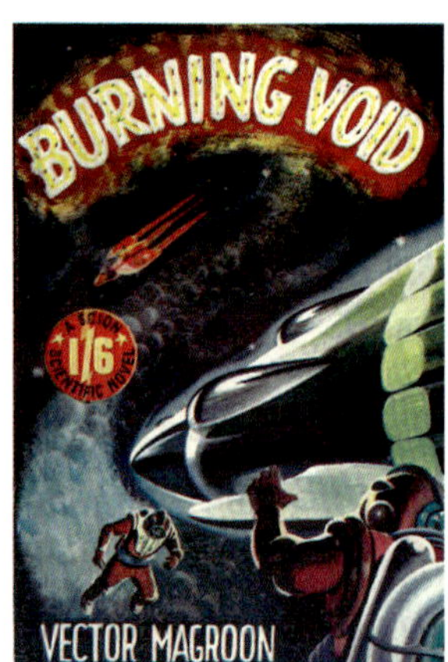

Vector Magroon (Julian Franklyn)
Burning Void
Scion Ltd., 1952 | Art **George Ratcliffe**

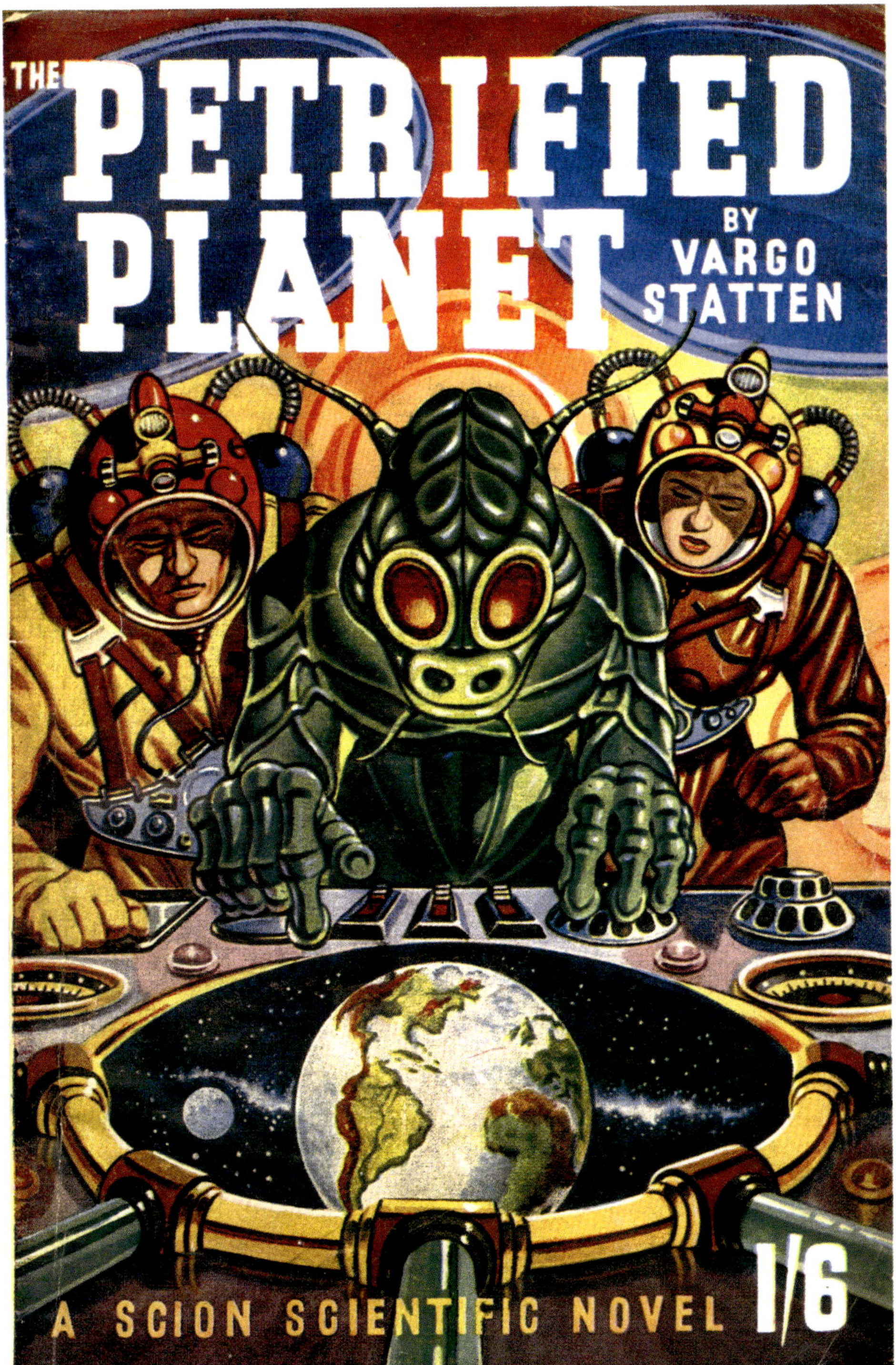

Vargo Statten (John Russell Fearn) | *The Petrified Planet*
Scion Ltd., 1951 | Art **Ron Turner**

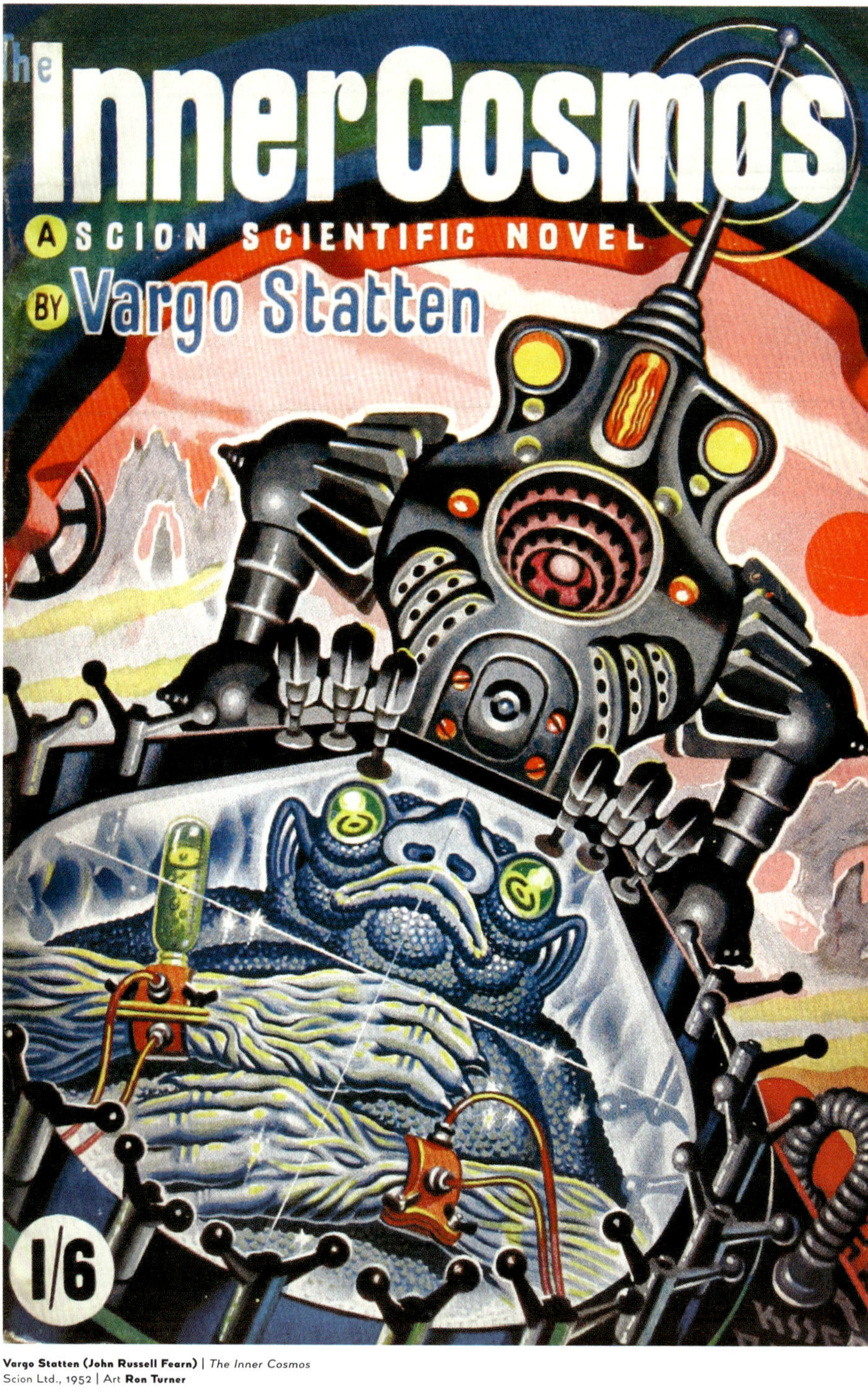

Vargo Statten (John Russell Fearn) | *The Inner Cosmos*
Scion Ltd., 1952 | Art **Ron Turner**

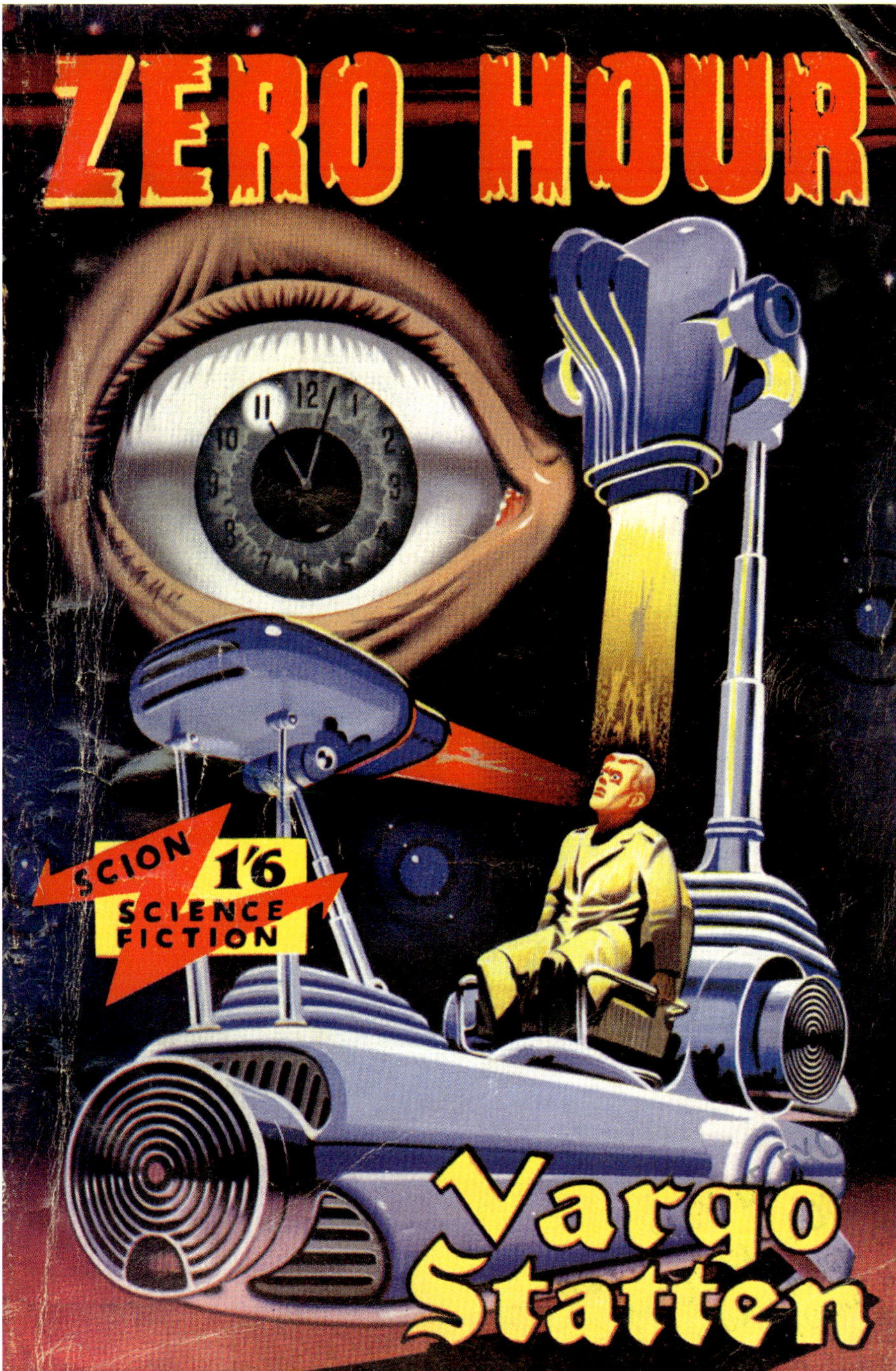

Vargo Statten (John Russell Fearn) | *Zero Hour*
Scion Ltd., 1953 | Art **Ron Turner**

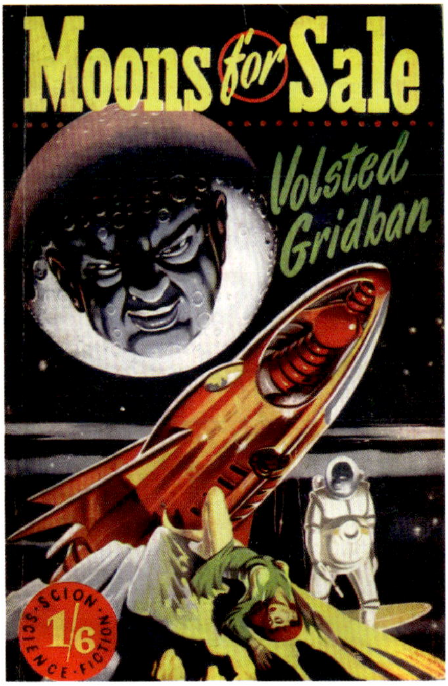

Volsted Gridban (John Russell Fearn) | *Moons for Sale*
Scion Ltd., 1953 | Art **Ron Turner**

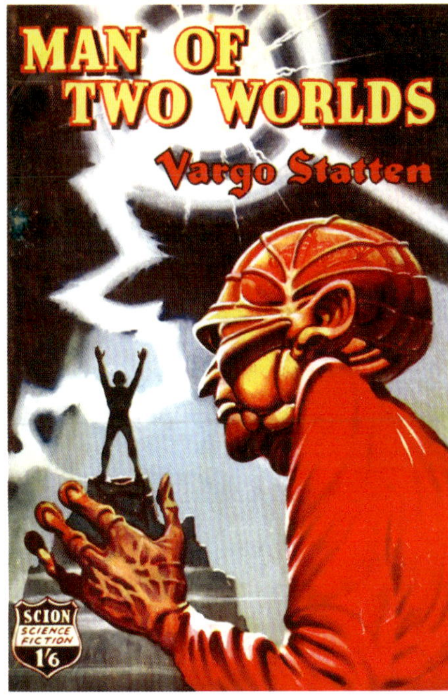

Vargo Statten (John Russell Fearn) | *Man of Two Worlds*
Scion Ltd., 1953 | Art **Ron Turner**

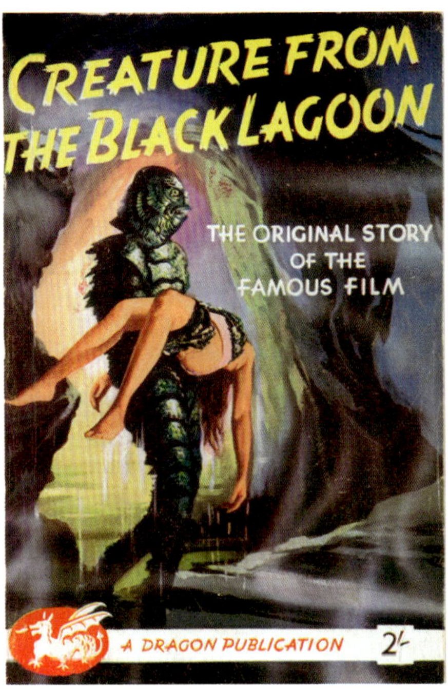

Vargo Statten (John Russell Fearn) | *Creature from the Black Lagoon*
Dragon Publications (Scion Ltd.), 1954 | Art **John Richards**

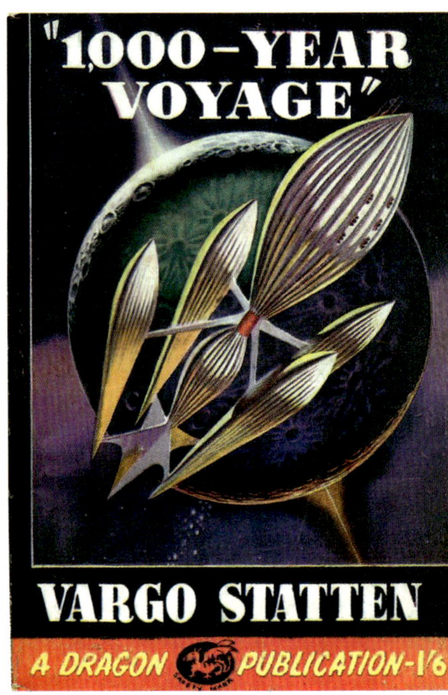

Vargo Statten (John Russell Fearn) | *1,000-Year Voyage*
Dragon Publications (Scion Ltd.), 1954 | Art **Ron Turner**

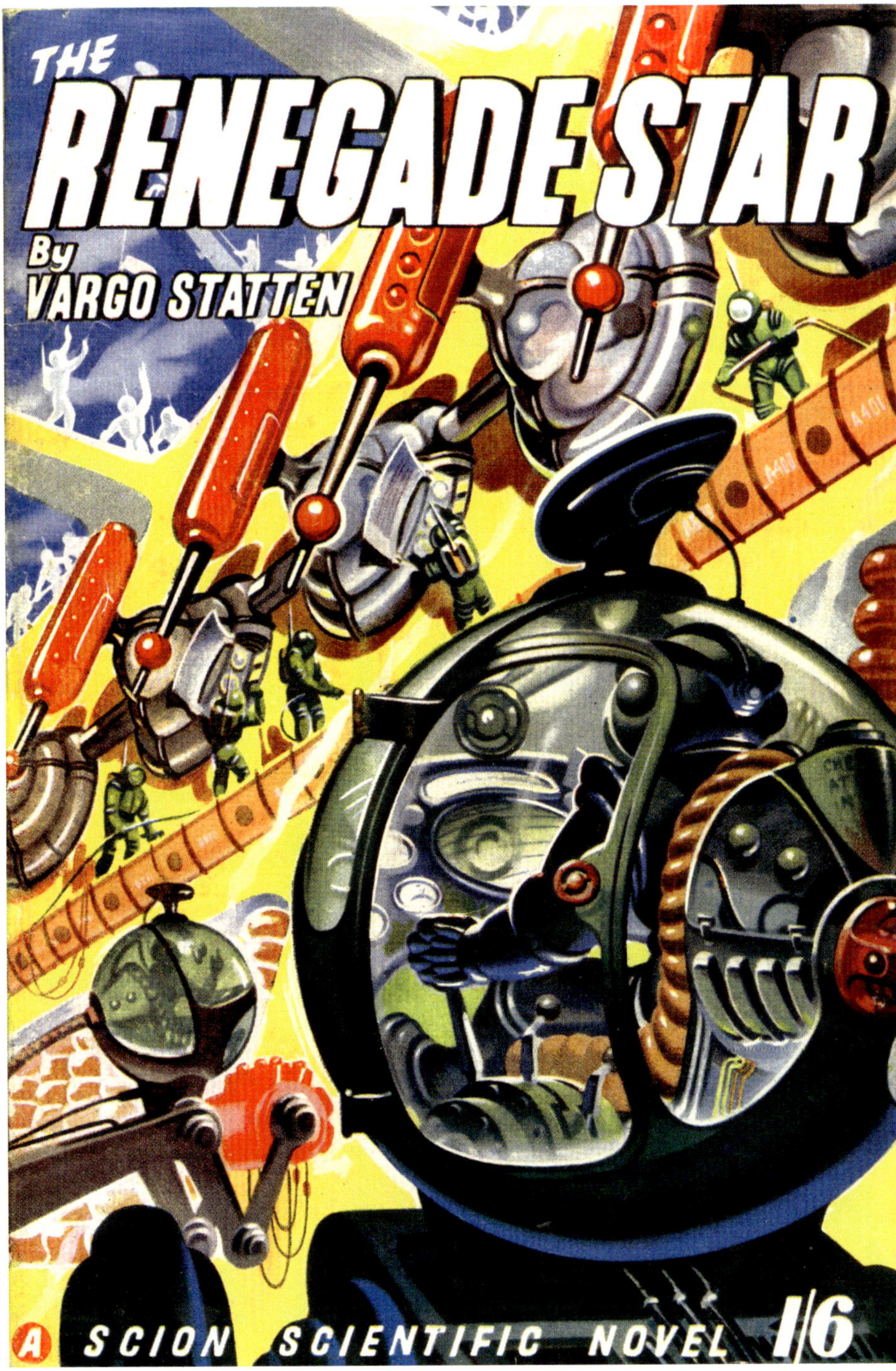

Vargo Statten (John Russell Fearn) | *The Renegade Star*
Scion Ltd., 1951 | Art **Ron Turner**

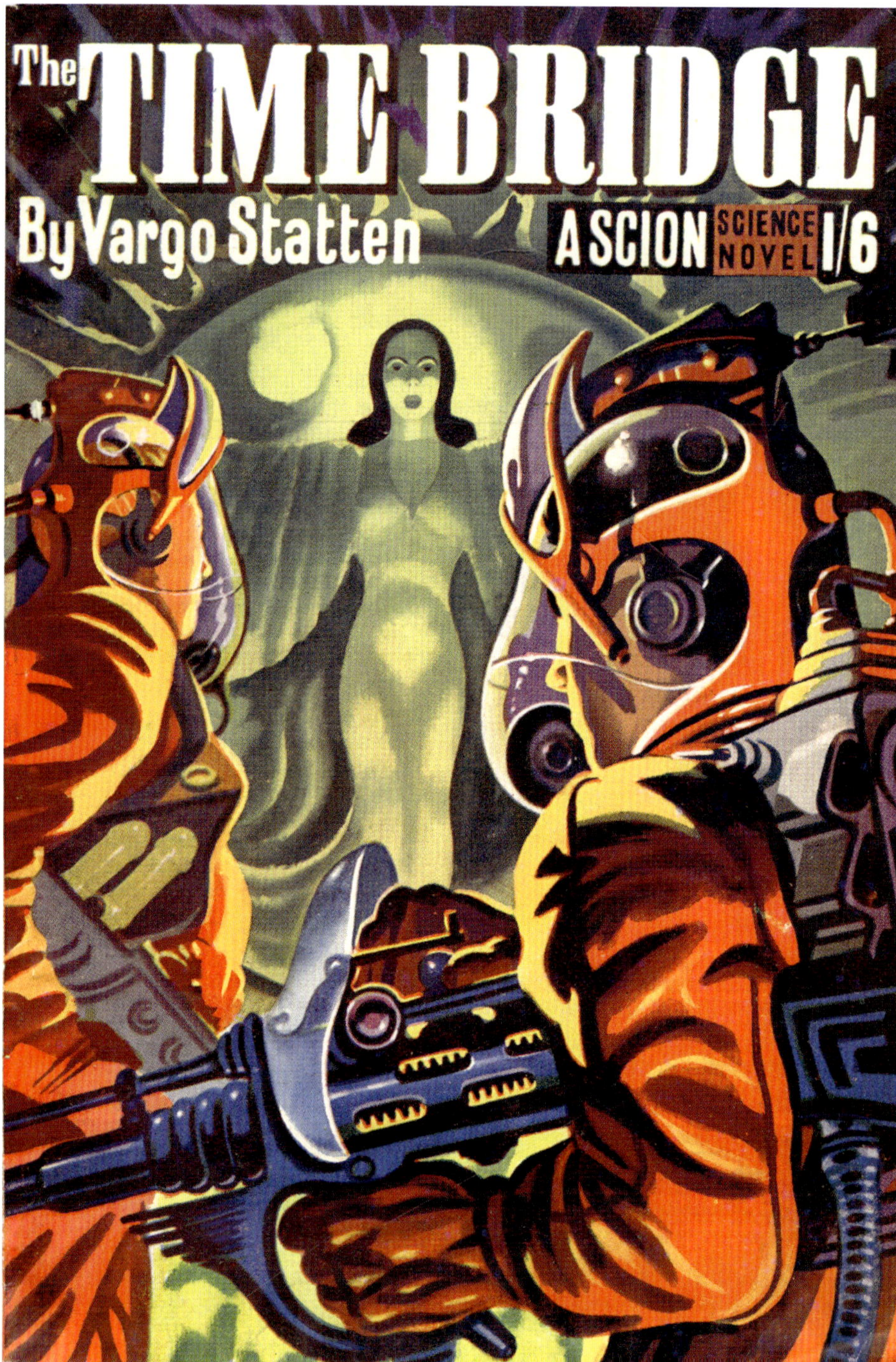

Vargo Statten (John Russell Fearn) | *The Time Bridge*
Scion Ltd., 1952 | Art **Ron Turner**

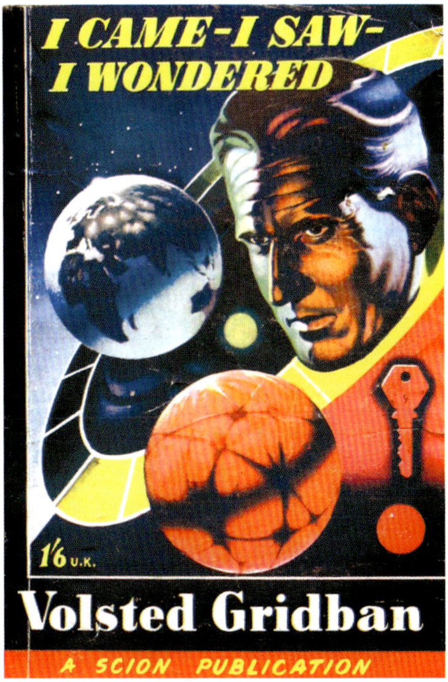

Volsted Gridban (John Russell Fearn) | *I Came - I Saw - I Wondered*
Scion Ltd., 1954 | Art **Ron Turner**

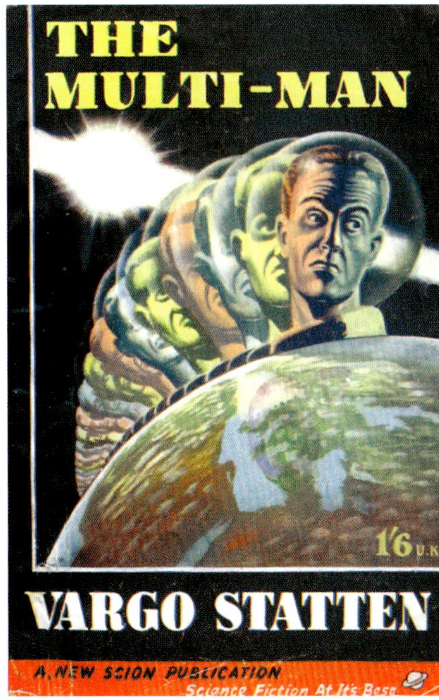

Volsted Gridban (John Russell Fearn) | *The Multi-Man*
Scion Ltd., 1954 | Art **Ron Turner**

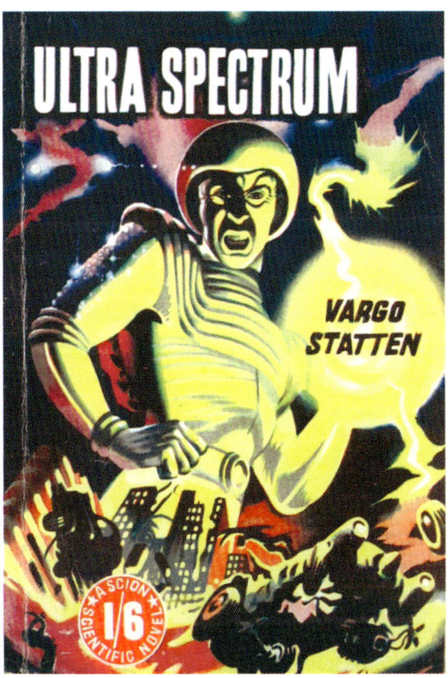

Vargo Statten (John Russell Fearn) | *Ultra Spectrum*
Scion Ltd., 39799, 1953 | Art **Ron Turner**

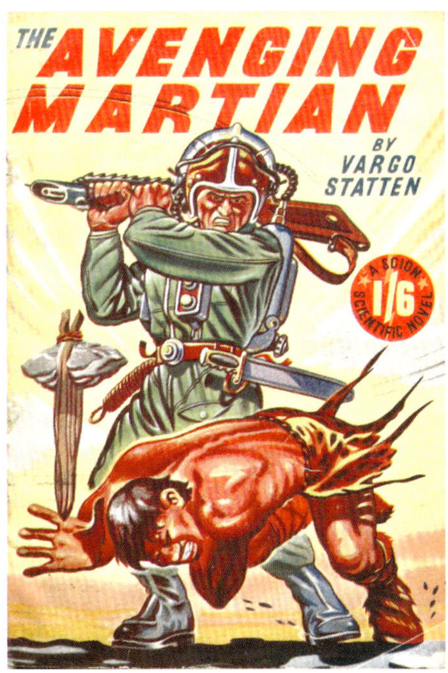

Vargo Statten (John Russell Fearn) | *The Avenging Martian*
Scion Ltd., 1951 | Art **Ron Turner**

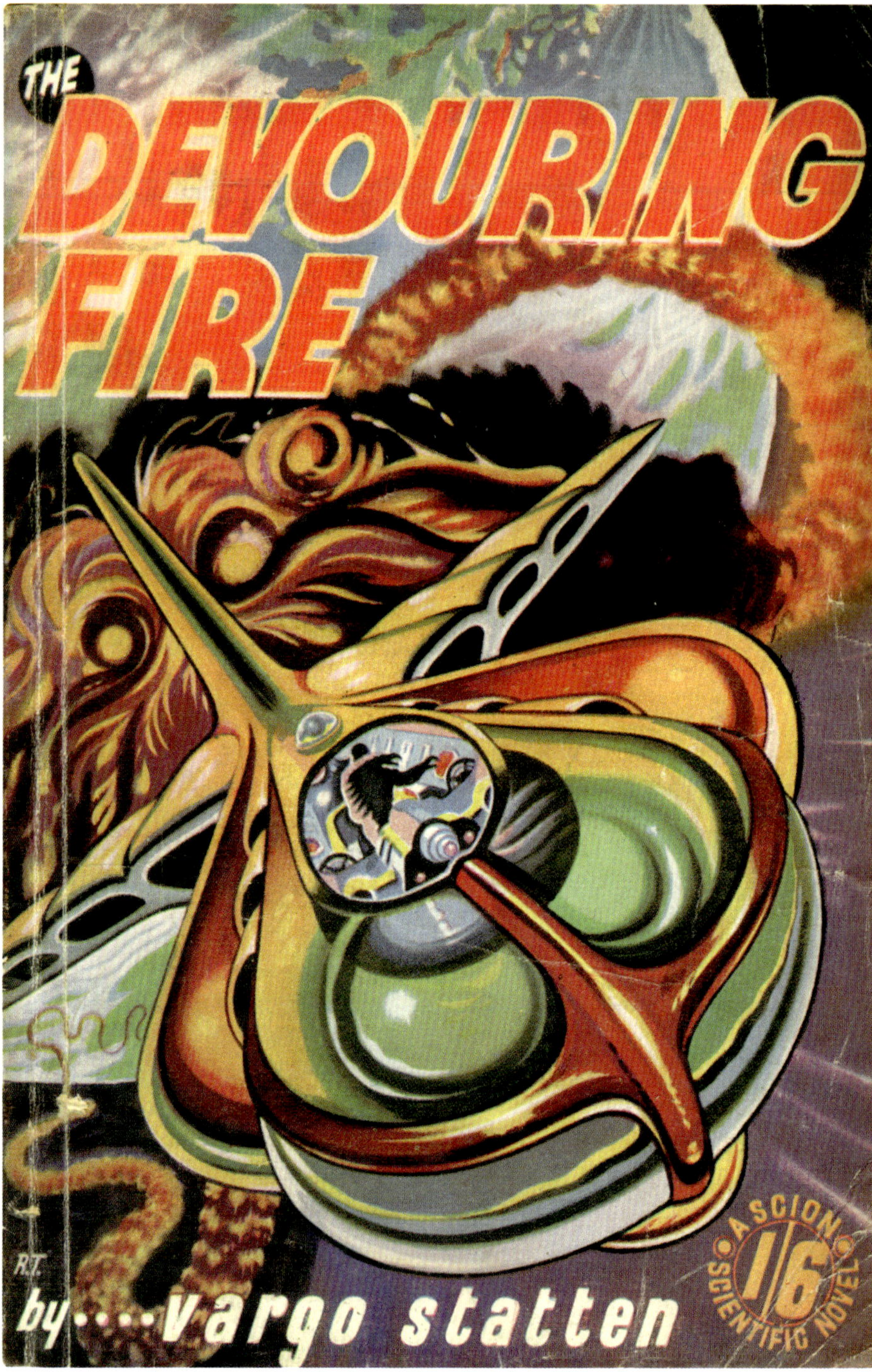

Vargo Statten (John Russell Fearn) | *The Devouring Fire*
Scion Ltd., 1951 | Art **Ron Turner**

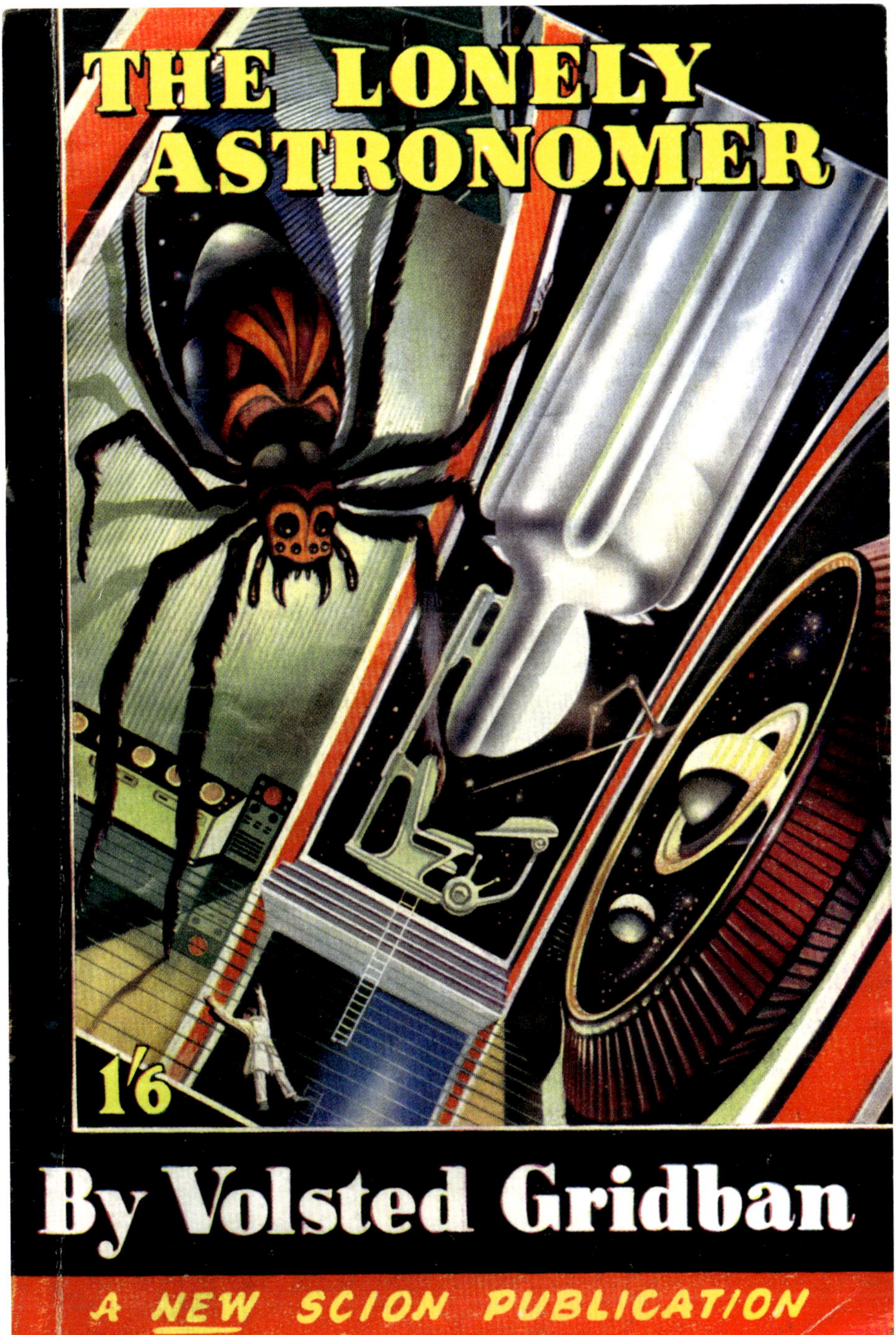

Volsted Gridban (John Russell Fearn) | *The Lonely Astronomer*
Scion Ltd., 1954 | Art **Ron Turner**

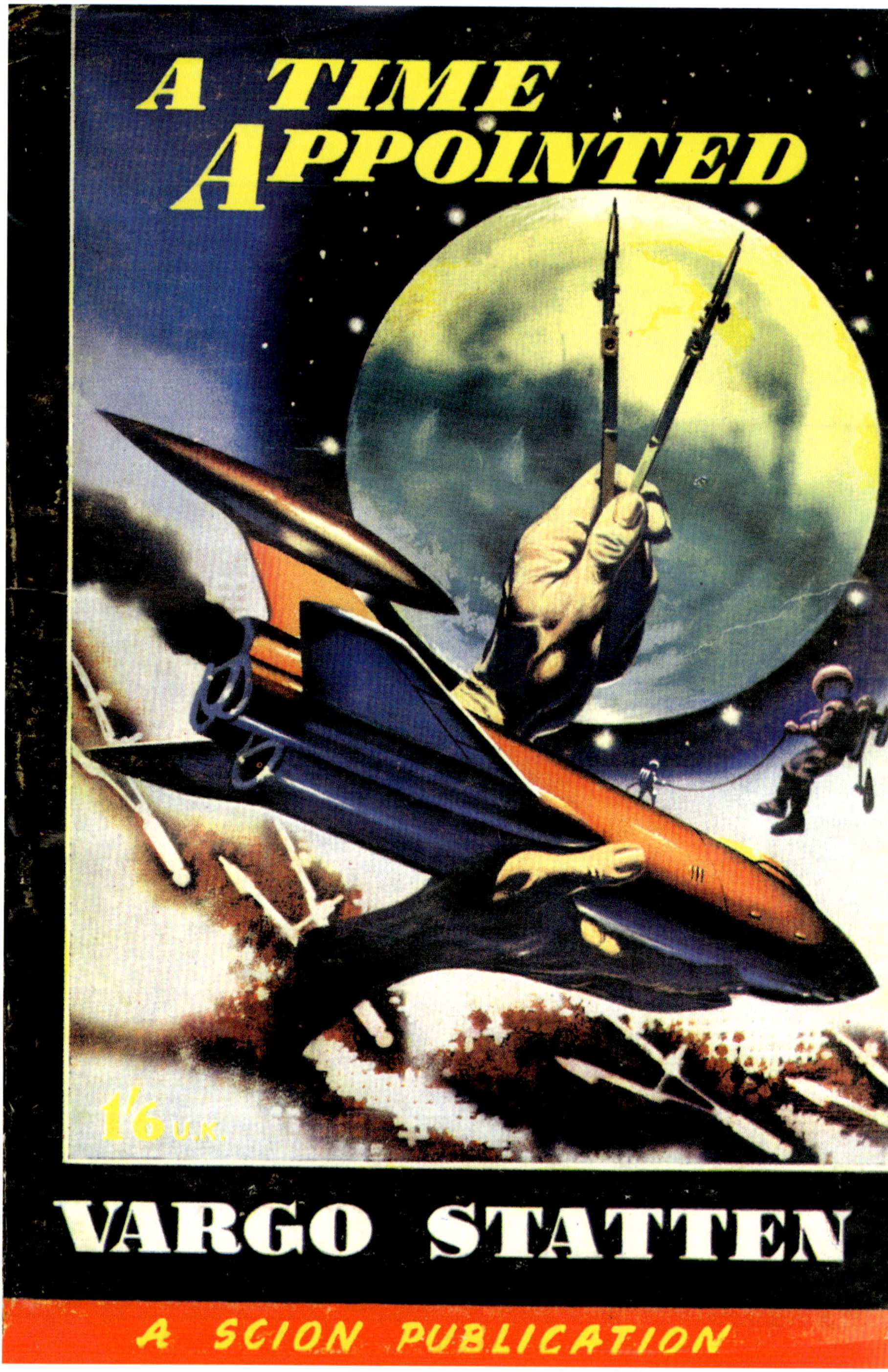

Vargo Statten (John Russell Fearn) | *A Time Appointed*
Scion Ltd., 1954 | Art **Ron Turner**

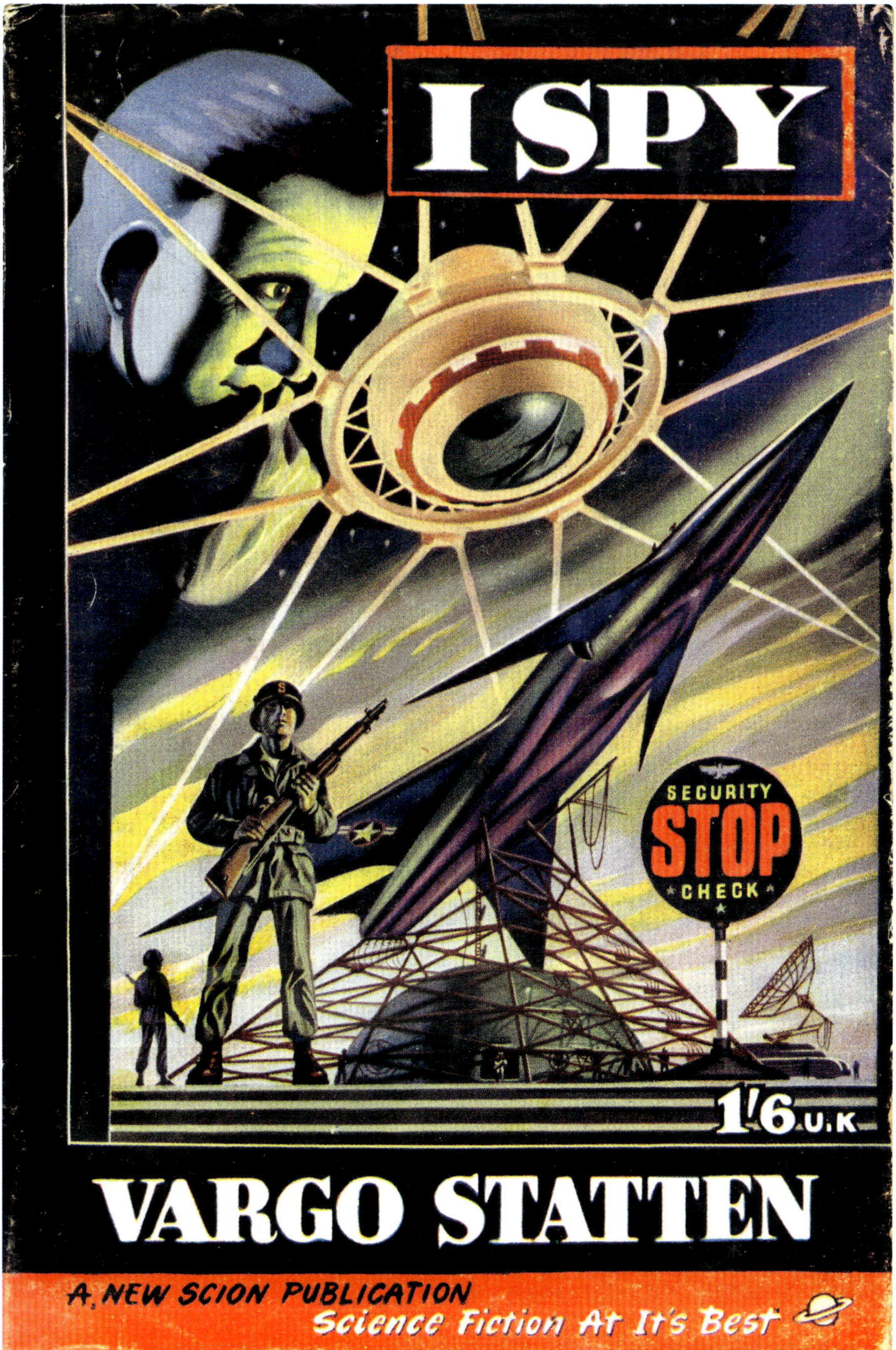

Vargo Statten (John Russell Fearn) | *I Spy*
Scion Ltd., 1954 | Art **Ron Turner**

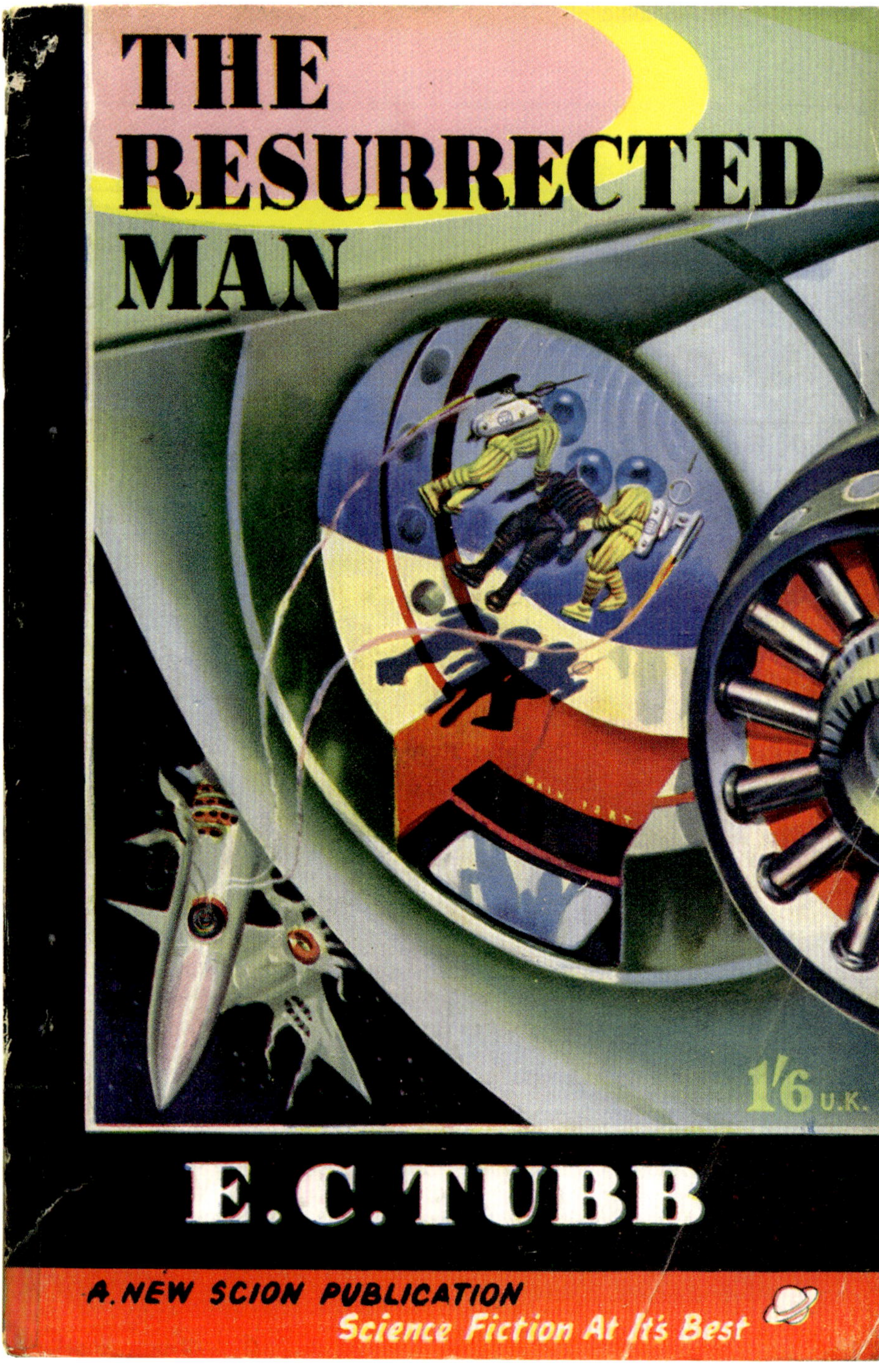

E. C. Tubb | *The Resurrected Man*
Scion Ltd., 1954 | Art **Ron Turner**

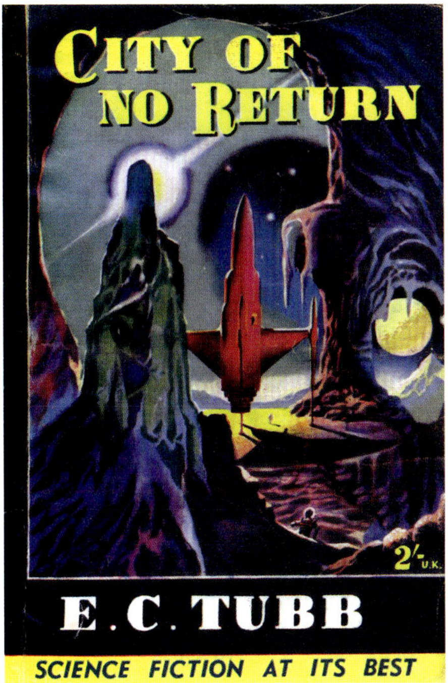

E. C. Tubb | *City of No Return*
Scion Ltd., 1954 | Art **Ron Turner**

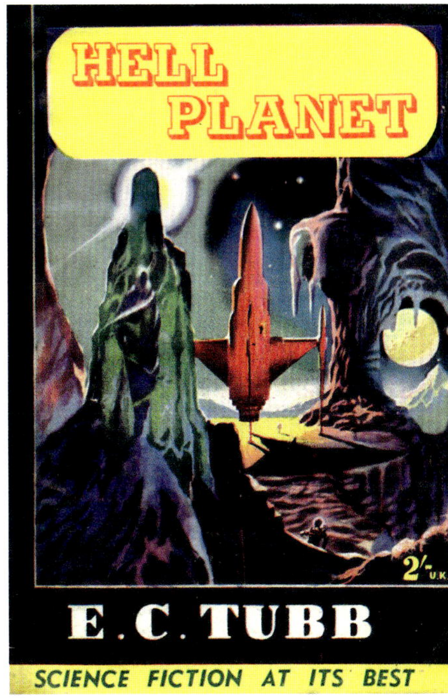

E. C. Tubb | *Hell Planet*
Scion Ltd., 1954 | Art **Ron Turner**

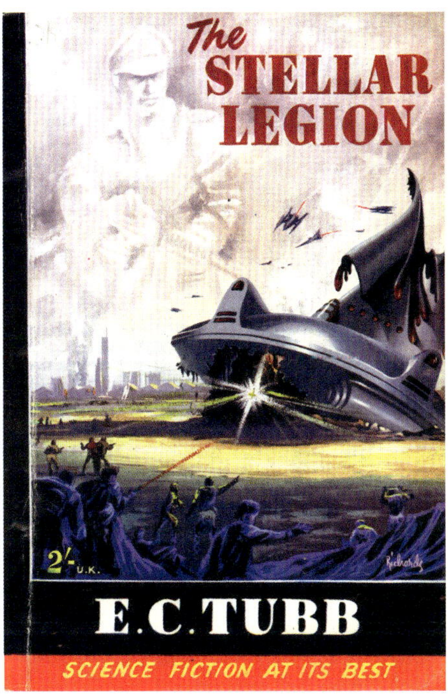

E. C. Tubb | *The Stellar Legion*
Scion Ltd., 1954 | Art **John Richards**

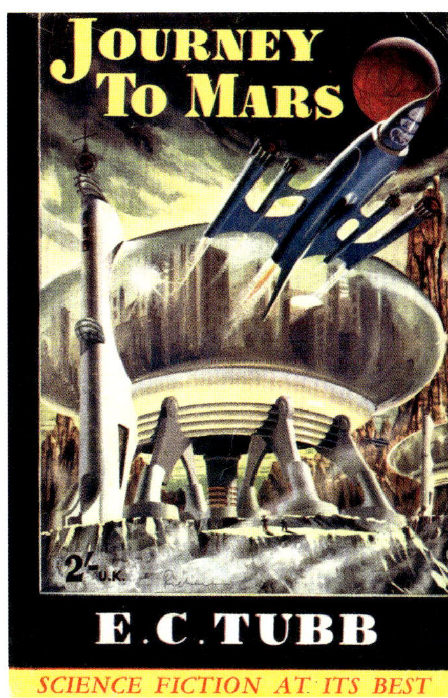

E. C. Tubb | *Journey to Mars*
Scion Ltd., 1954 | Art **John Richards**

opposite **Gerald Kepps** | *Adventures In Space*
Ward, Lock & Co. Ltd., 1955 | Art **I. Teece**

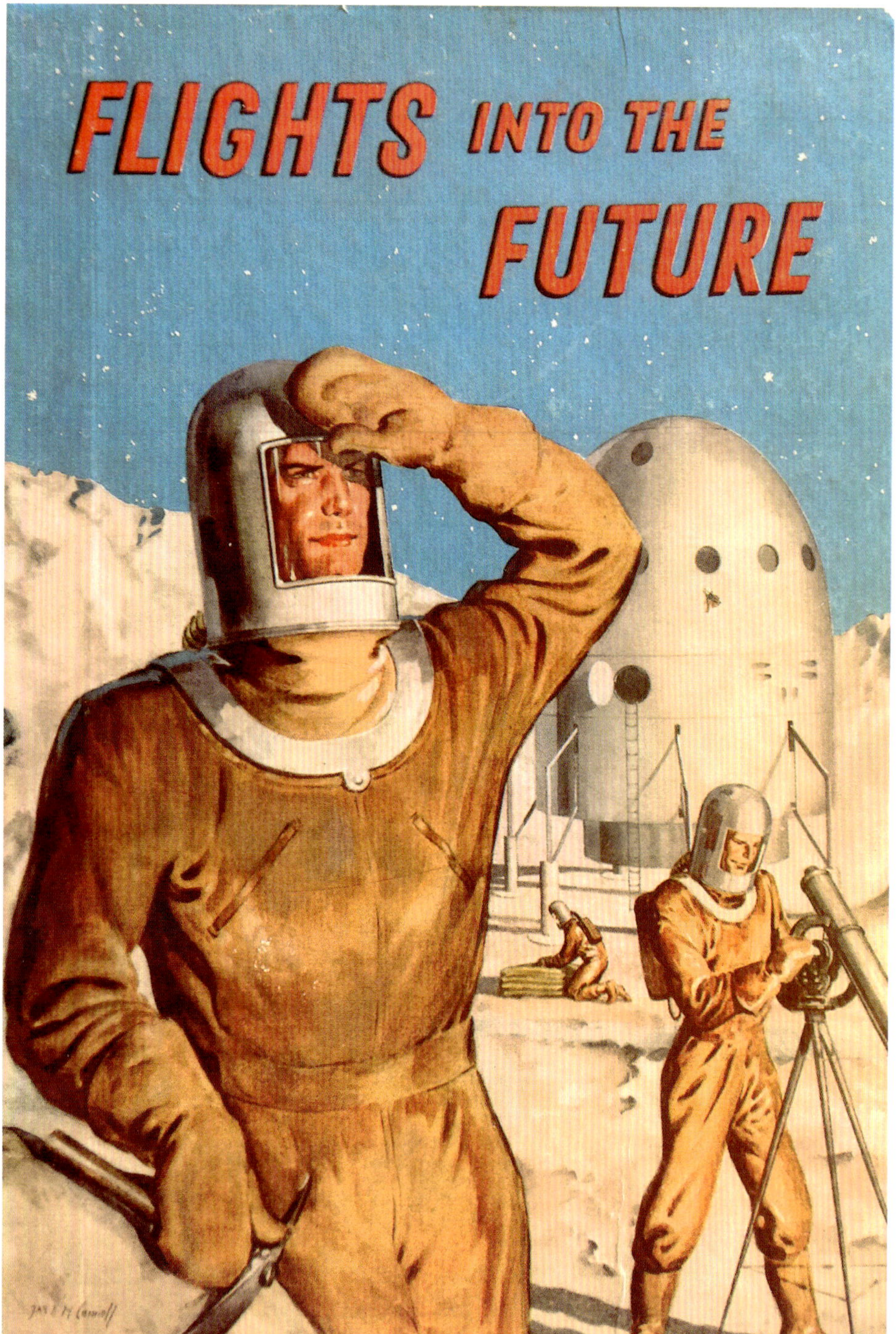

Professor A. M. Low, Harry Harper, Sir Arthur Conan Doyle, Jules Verne | *Flights into the Future*
The Thames Publishing Co., 1953 | Art **Jas E. M'Connell**

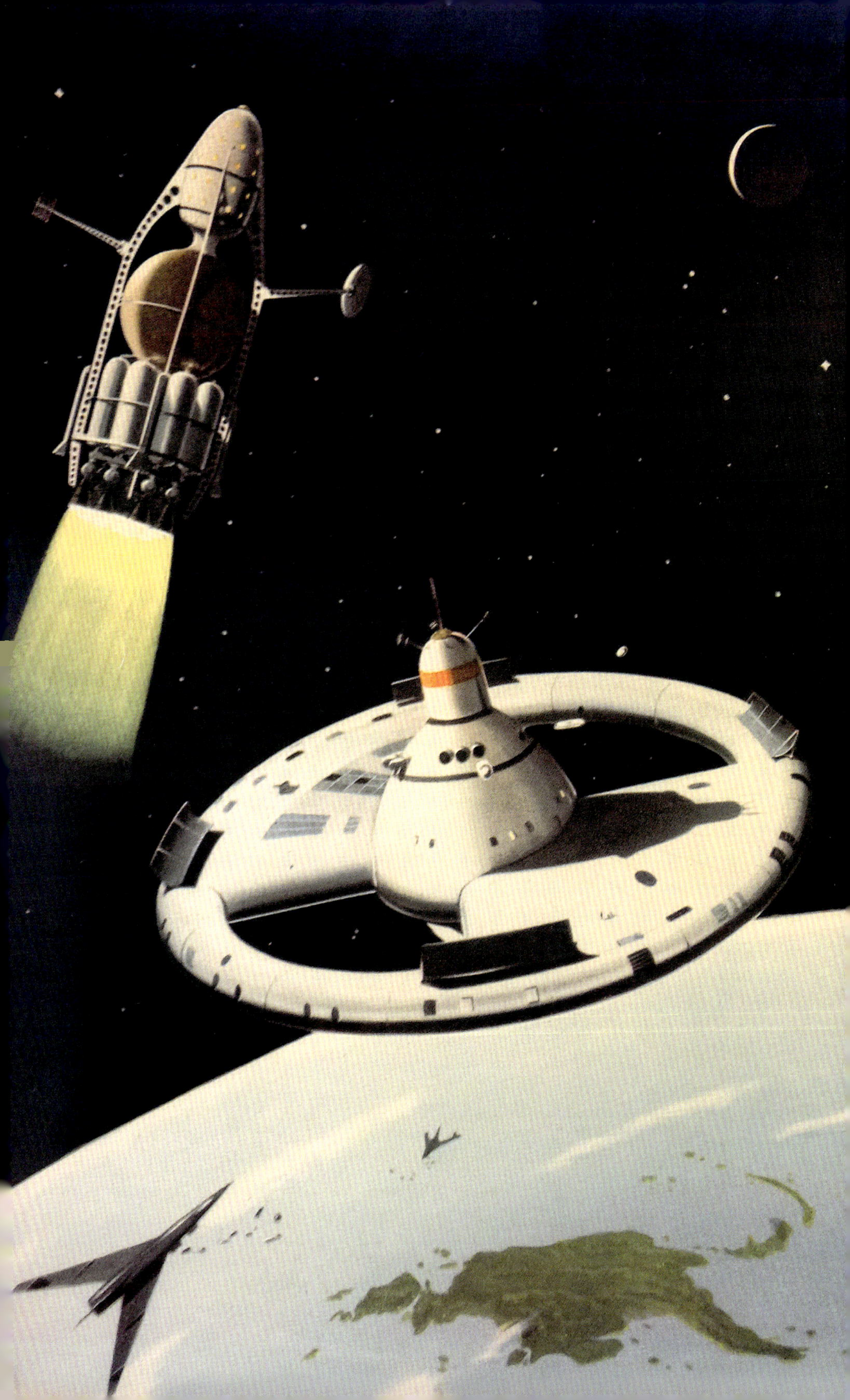

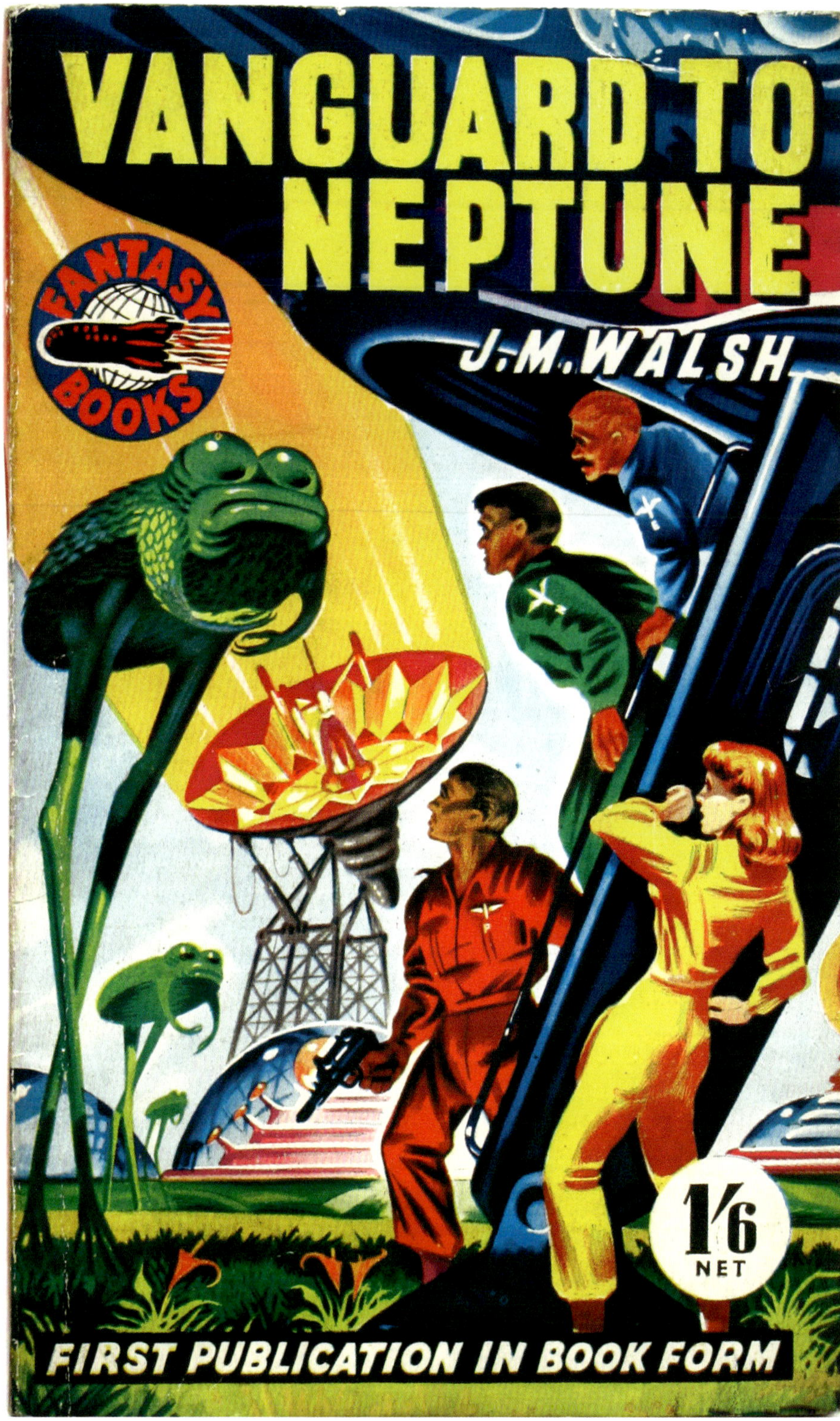

J. M. Walsh | *Vanguard To Neptune*
Cherry Tree / Fantasy Books 410, 1953 | Art **Ron Turner**

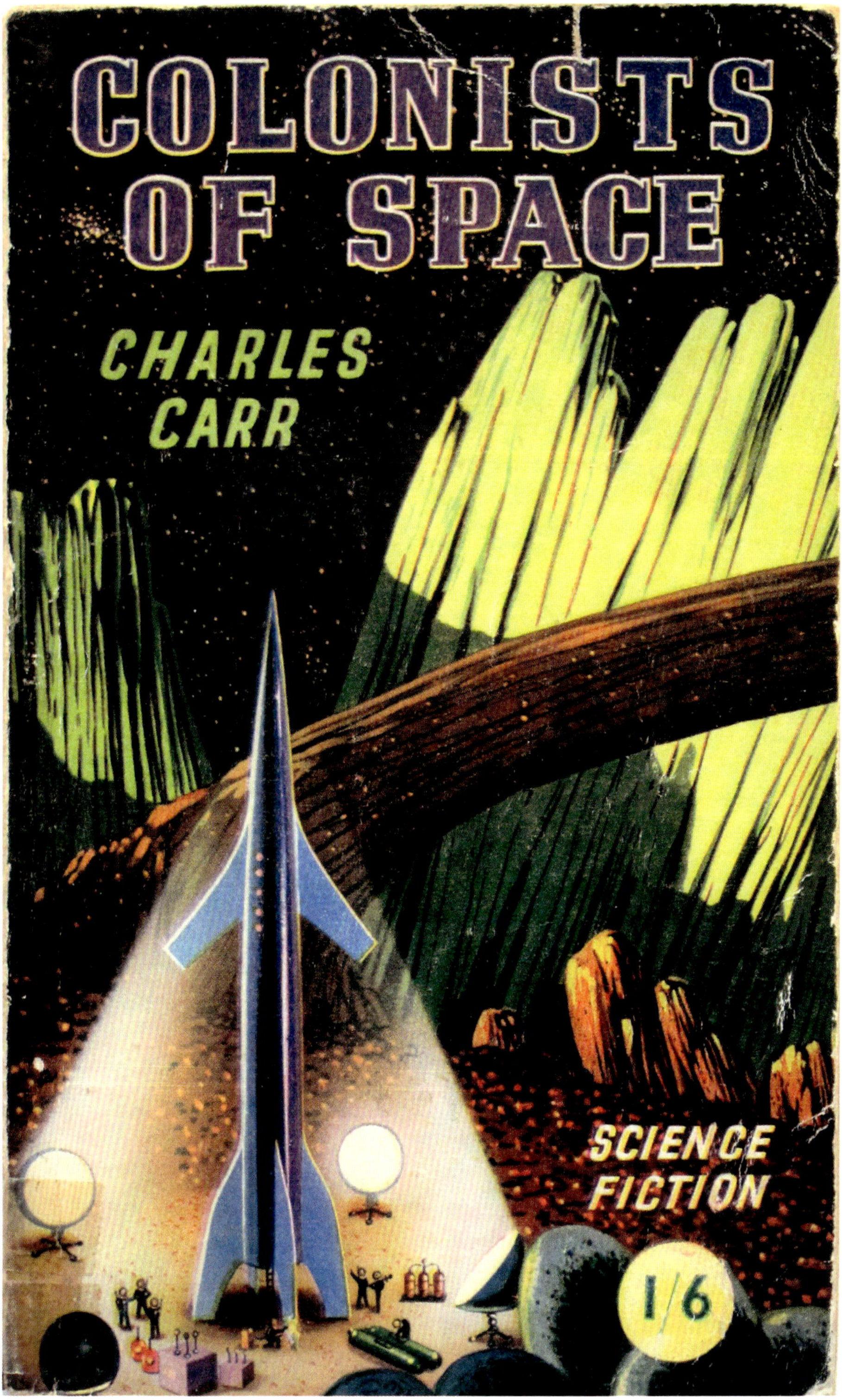

Charles Carr | *Colonists of Space*
Ward Lock & Co. 25, 1955 | Art **Harold Johns**

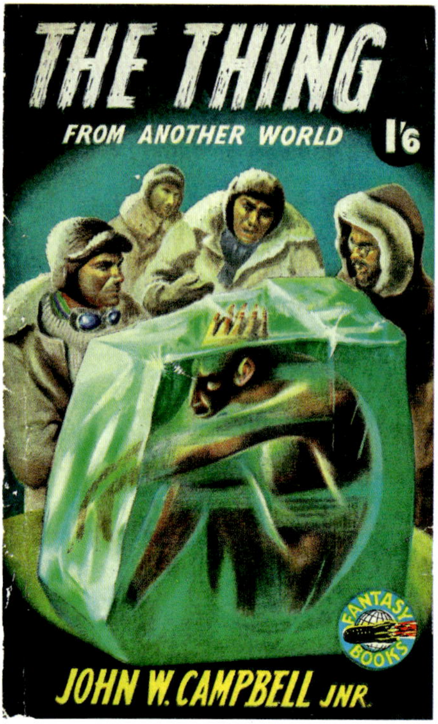

John W. Campbell, Jr. | *The Thing from Another World*
Cherry Tree / Fantasy Books 408, 1952 | Art **Terry Maloney**

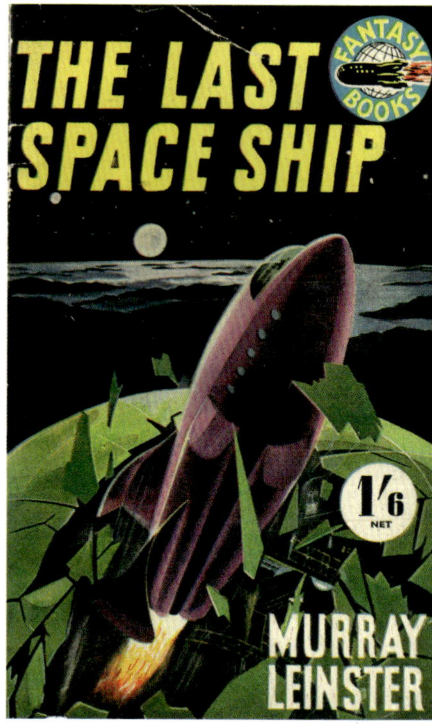

Murray Leinster | *The Last Space Ship*
Cherry Tree / Fantasy Books 404, 1952 | Art **Terry Maloney**

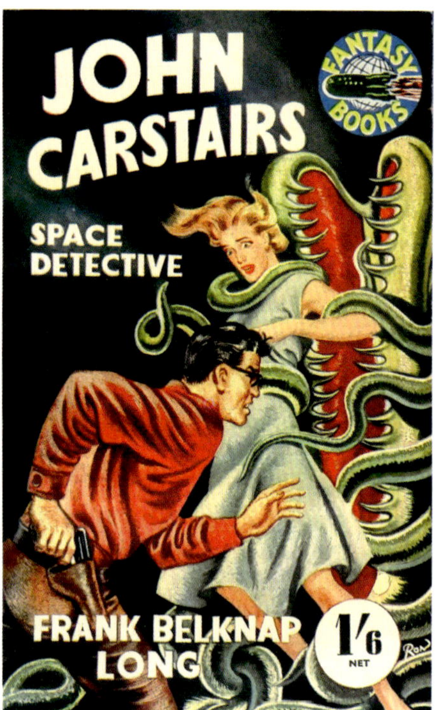

Frank Belknap Long | *John Carstairs: Space Detective*
Cherry Tree / Fantasy Books 400, 1951 | Art **Ron Embleton**

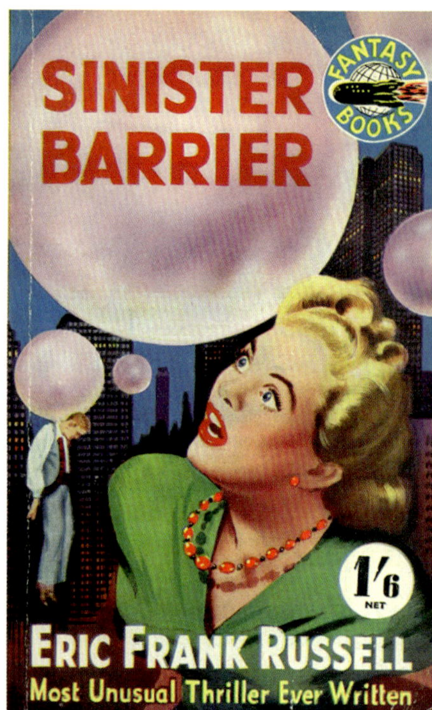

Eric Frank Russell | *Sinister Barrier*
Cherry Tree / Fantasy Books 407, 1952 | Art **Terry Maloney**

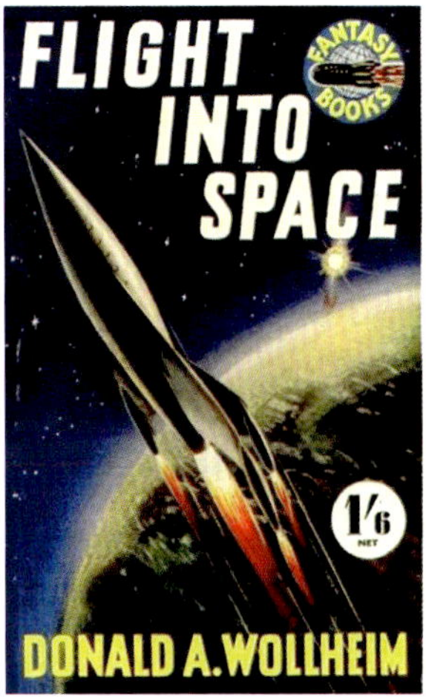

Donald A. Wollheim | *Flight Into Space*
Cherry Tree / Fantasy Books 403, 1951
Art **Terry Maloney**

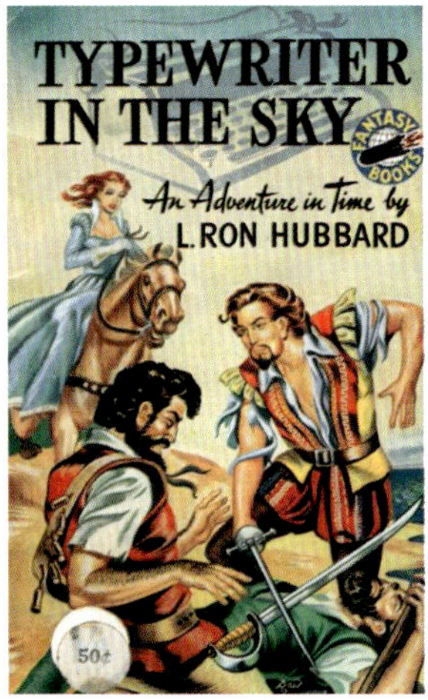

L. Ron Hubbard | *Typewriter in the Sky*
Cherry Tree / Fantasy Books 409, 1953
Art **Ron Embleton**

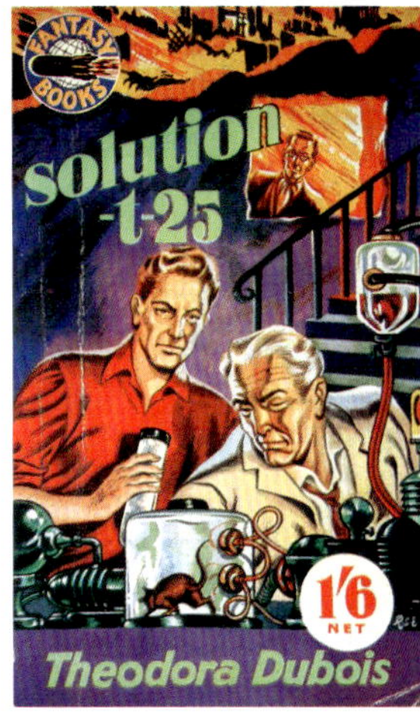

Theodora Dubois | *Solution T-25*
Cherry Tree / Fantasy Books 411, 1953
Art **Ron Embleton**

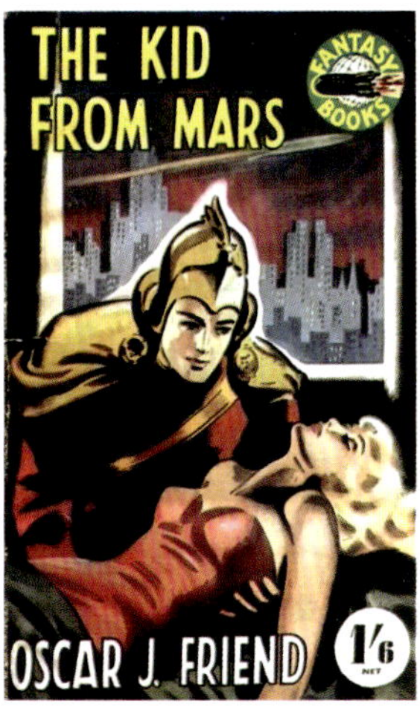

Oscar J. Friend | *The Kid from Mars*
Cherry Tree / Fantasy Books 401, 1951
Art **Terry Maloney**

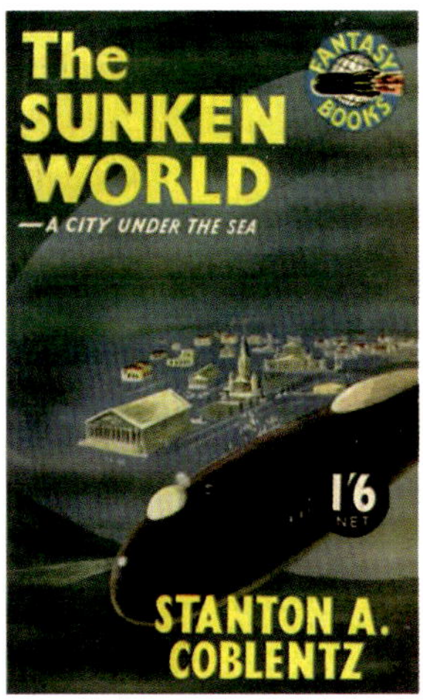

Stanton A. Coblentz | *The Sunken World*
Cherry Tree / Fantasy Books 402, 1951
Art **Terry Maloney**

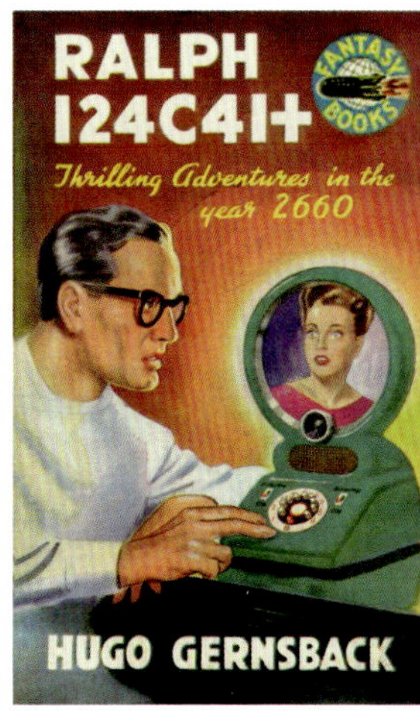

Hugo Gernsback | *Ralph 124C41+*
Cherry Tree / Fantasy Books 406, 1951
Art **Unknown**

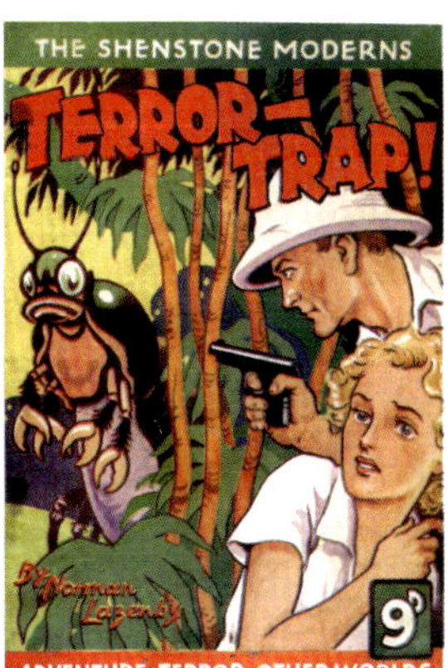

Norman Lazenby | *Terror-Trap!*
Shenstone, 1949 | Art **Unknown**

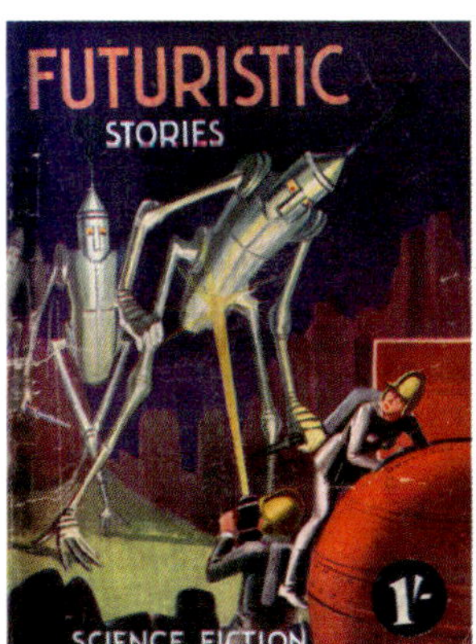

Dennis H. Pratt, ed. | *Futuristic Stories 1*
Hamilton & Co., 1946
Art **H. W. Perl**

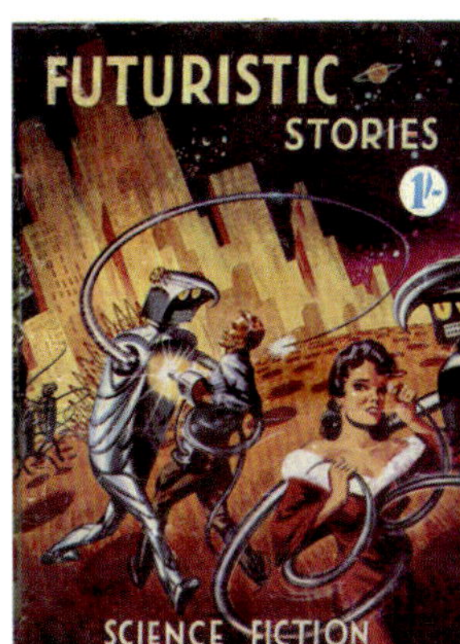

Dennis H. Pratt, ed. | *Futuristic Stories 2*
Hamilton & Co., 1946
Art **Brabbins**

opposite: **Hugh Walters** | *Expedition Venus*
Faber and Faber, 1962 | Art **Leslie Wood**

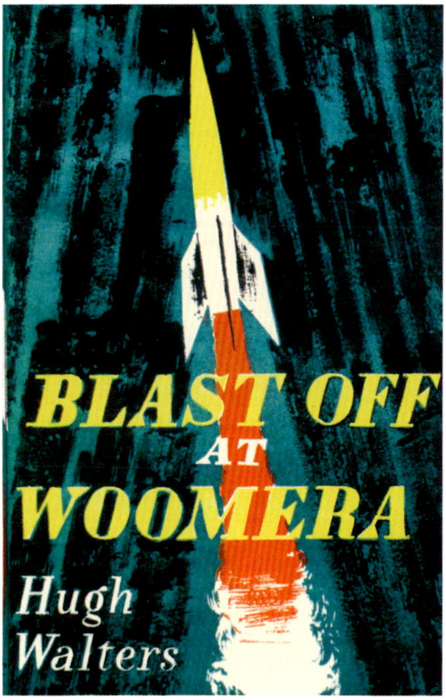

Hugh Walters | *Blast Off at Woomera*
Faber and Faber, 1957 | Art **Leslie Wood**

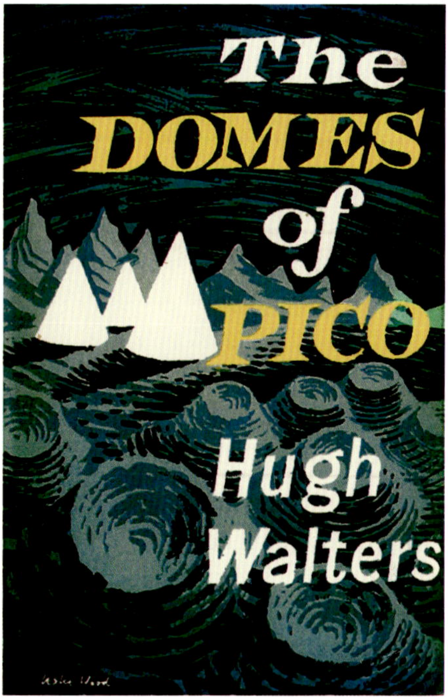

Hugh Walters | *The Domes of Pico*
Faber and Faber, 1958 | Art **Leslie Wood**

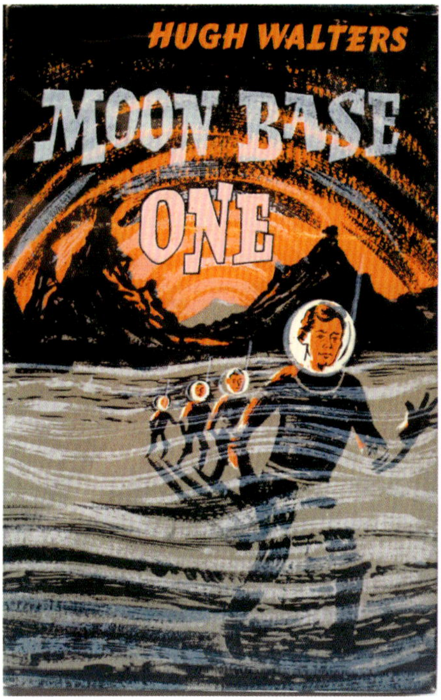

Hugh Walters | *Moon Base One*
Faber and Faber, 1961 | Art **Leslie Wood**

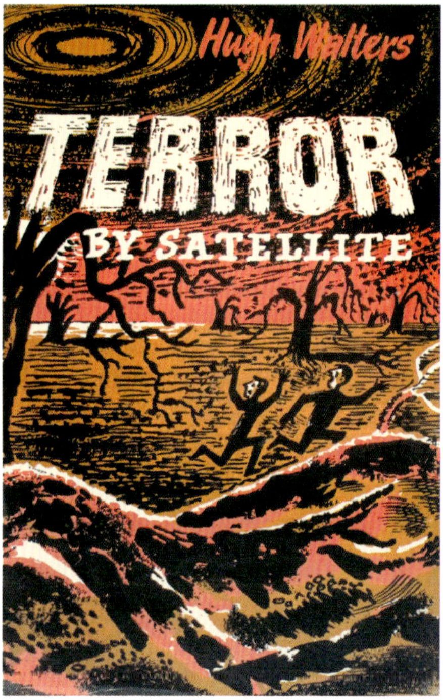

Hugh Walters | *Terror by Satellite*
Faber and Faber, 1964 | Art **Leslie Wood**

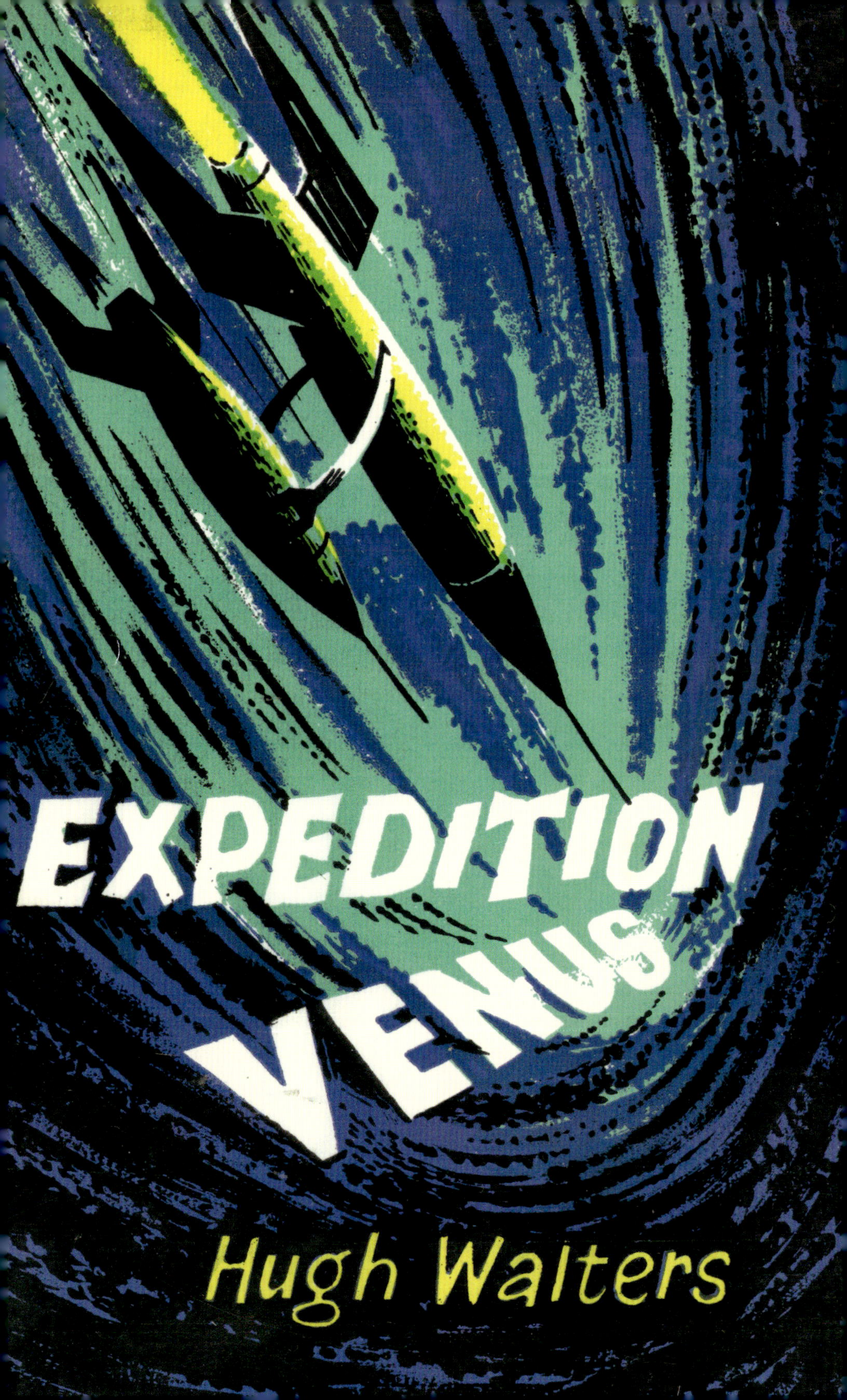
EXPEDITION
VENUS
Hugh Walters

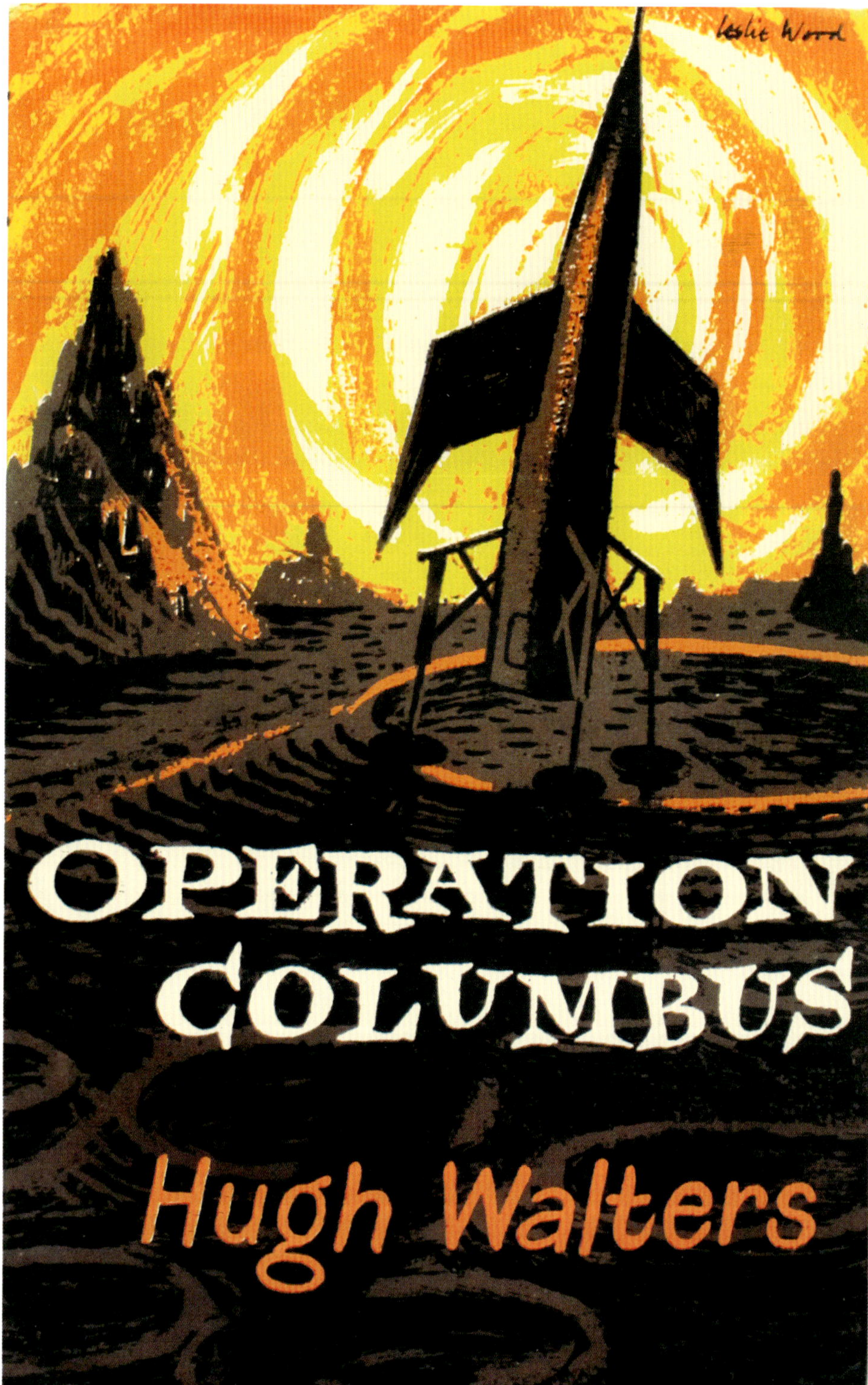

Hugh Walters | *Operation Columbus*
Faber and Faber, 1960 | Art **Leslie Wood**

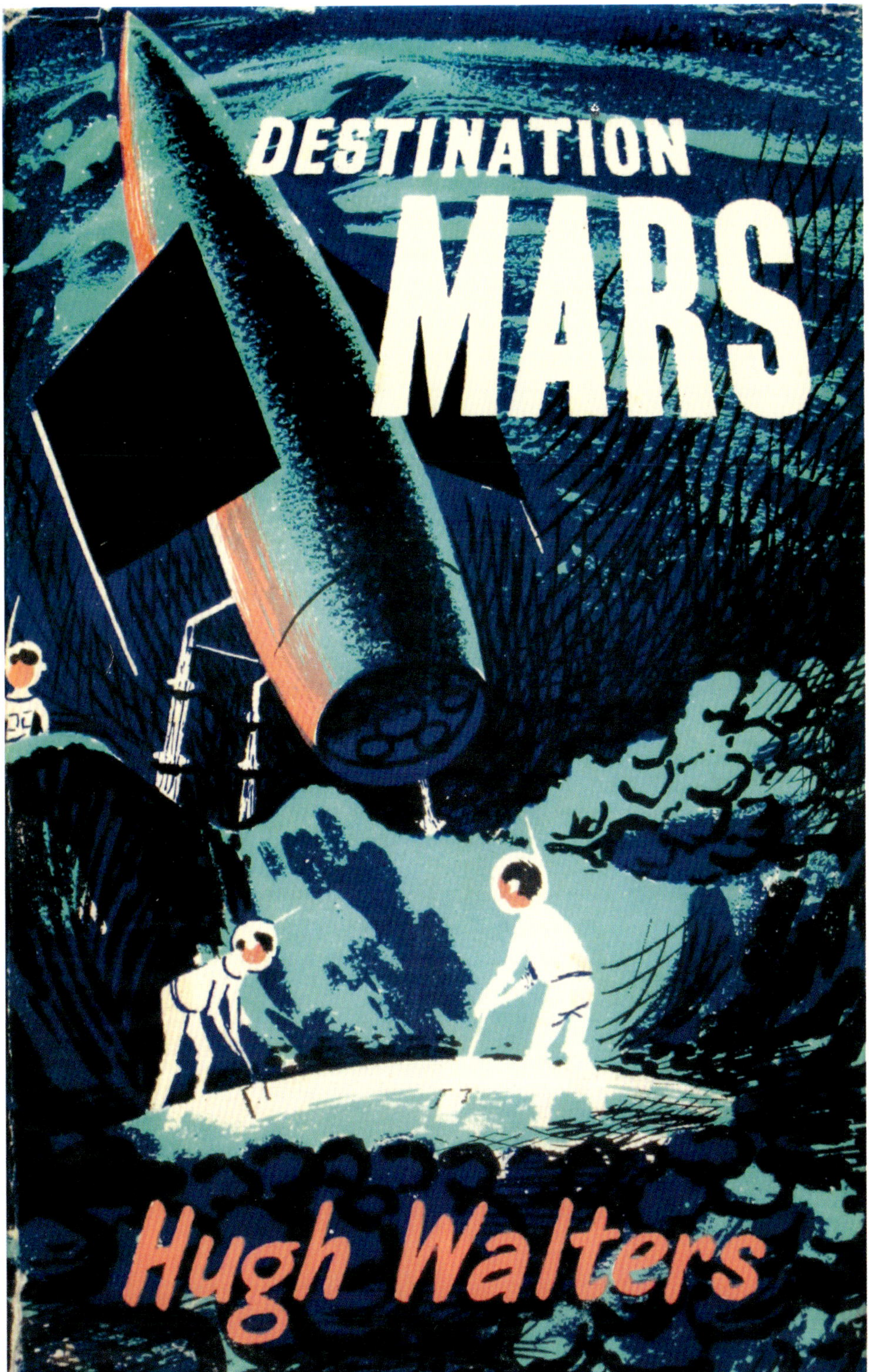

Hugh Walters | *Destination Mars*
Faber and Faber, 1963 | Art **Leslie Wood**

opposite: **Hugh Walters** | *Spaceship to Saturn*
Faber and Faber, 1965 | Art **Leslie Wood**

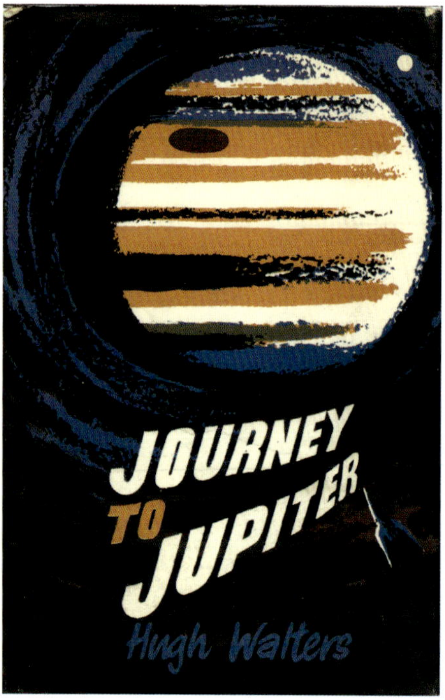

Hugh Walters | *Journey to Jupiter*
Faber and Faber, 1965 | Art **Leslie Wood**

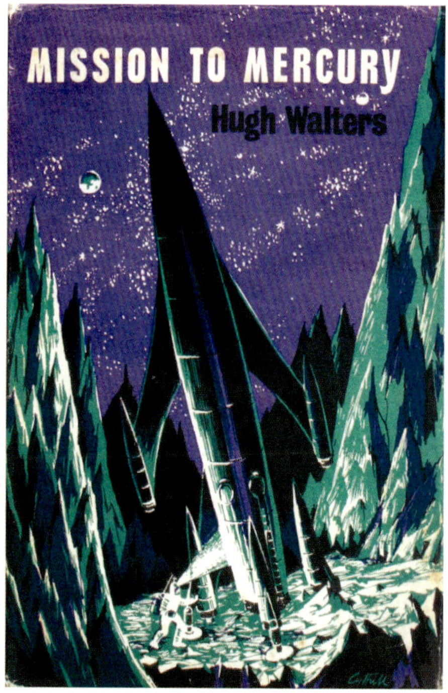

Hugh Walters | *Mission to Mercury*
Children's Book Club, 1965 | Art **Cuthill**

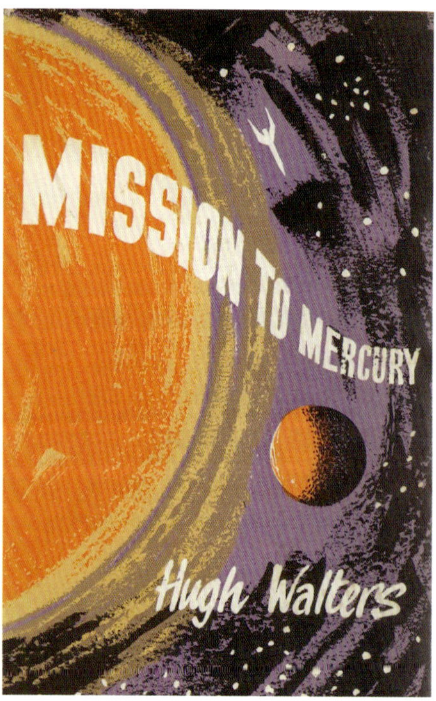

Hugh Walters | *Mission to Mercury*
Faber and Faber, 1965 | Art **Leslie Wood**

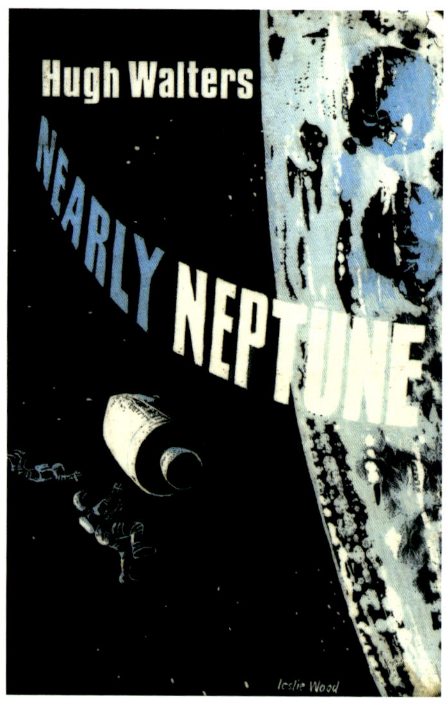

Hugh Walters | *Nearly Neptune*
Faber and Faber, 1969 | Art **Leslie Wood**

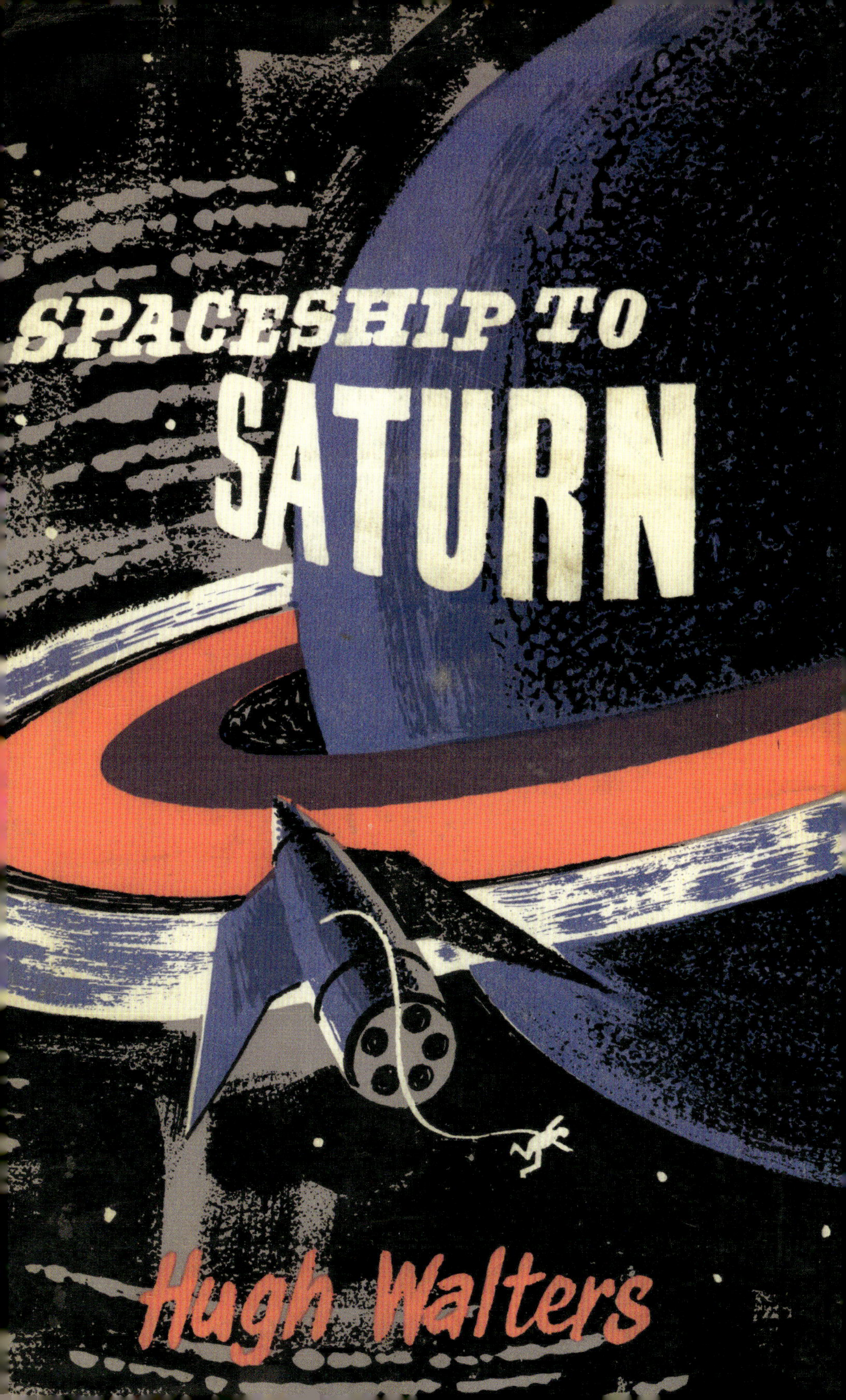
SPACESHIP TO
SATURN
Hugh Walters

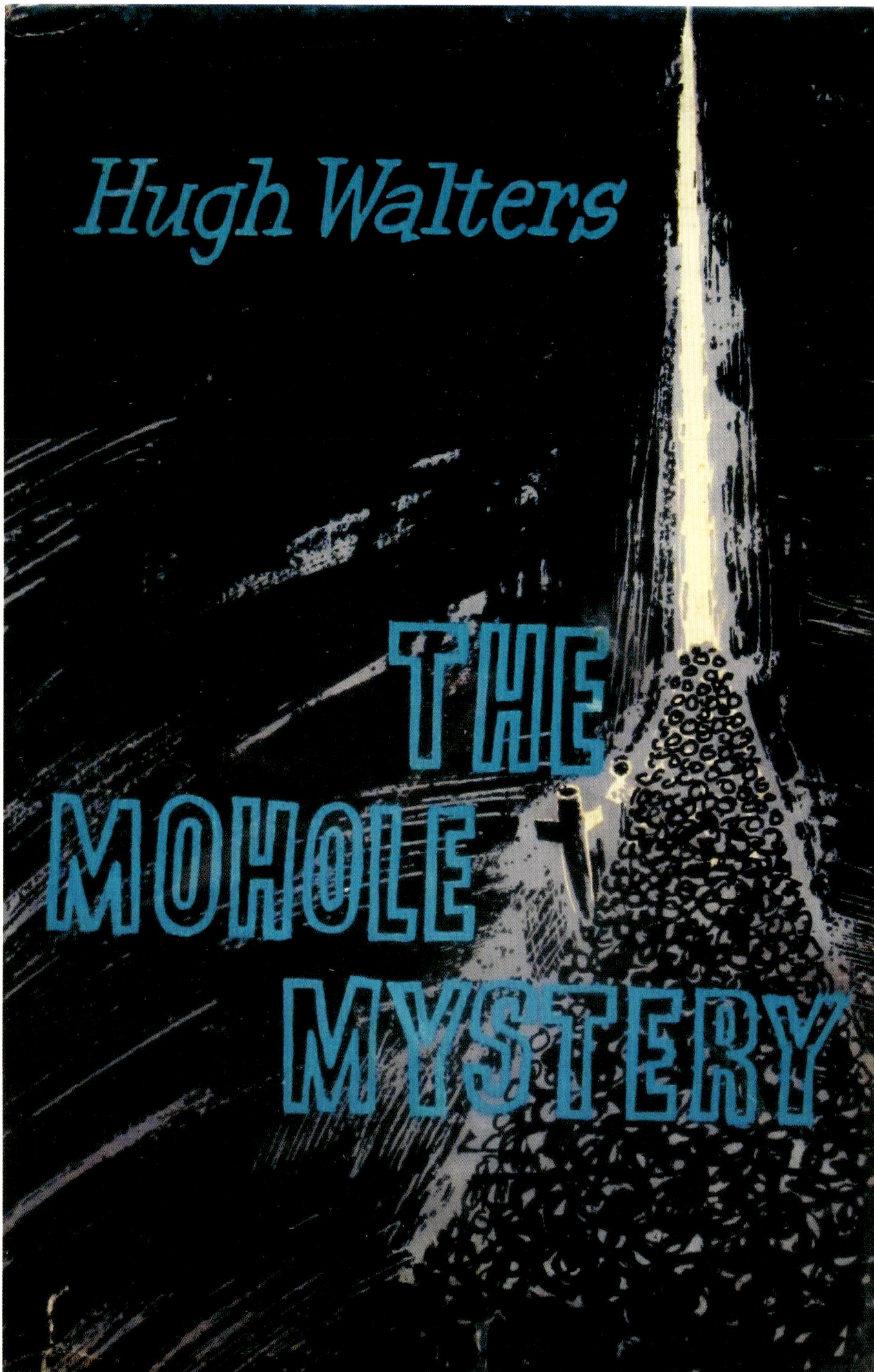

Hugh Walters | *The Mohole Mystery*
Faber and Faber, 1968 | Art **Leslie Wood**

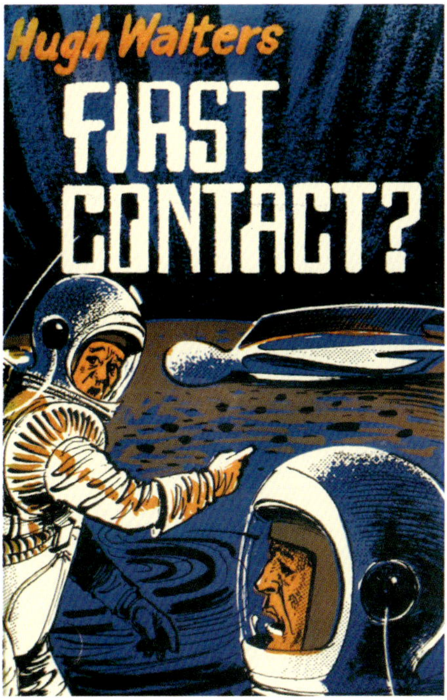

Hugh Walters | *First Contact?*
Faber and Faber, 1971 | Art **Leslie Wood**

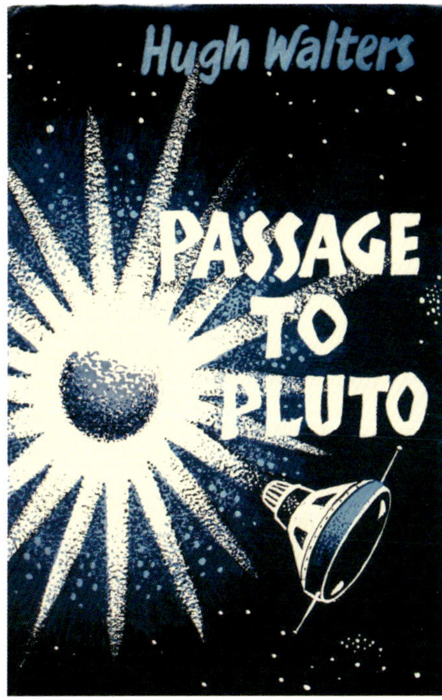

Hugh Walters | *Passage To Pluto*
Faber and Faber, 1973 | Art **Leslie Wood**

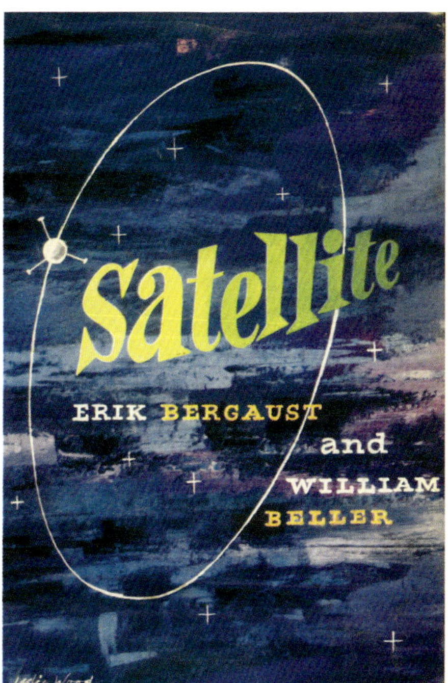

Erik Bergaust and William Beller | *Satellite*
The Scientific Book Club, 1957 | Art **Leslie Wood**

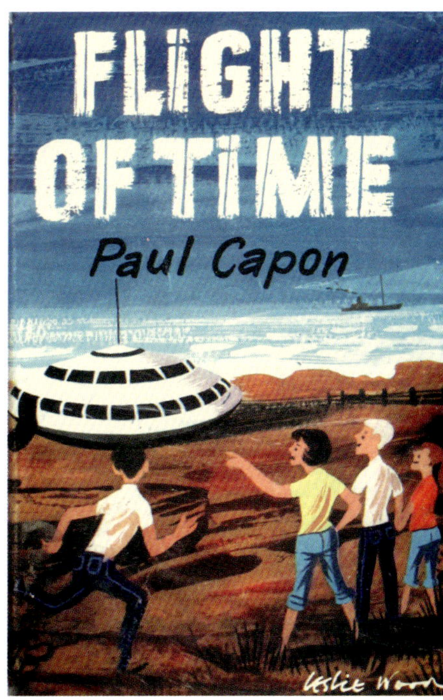

Paul Capon | *Flight of Time*
Children's Book Club, 1961 | Art **Leslie Wood**

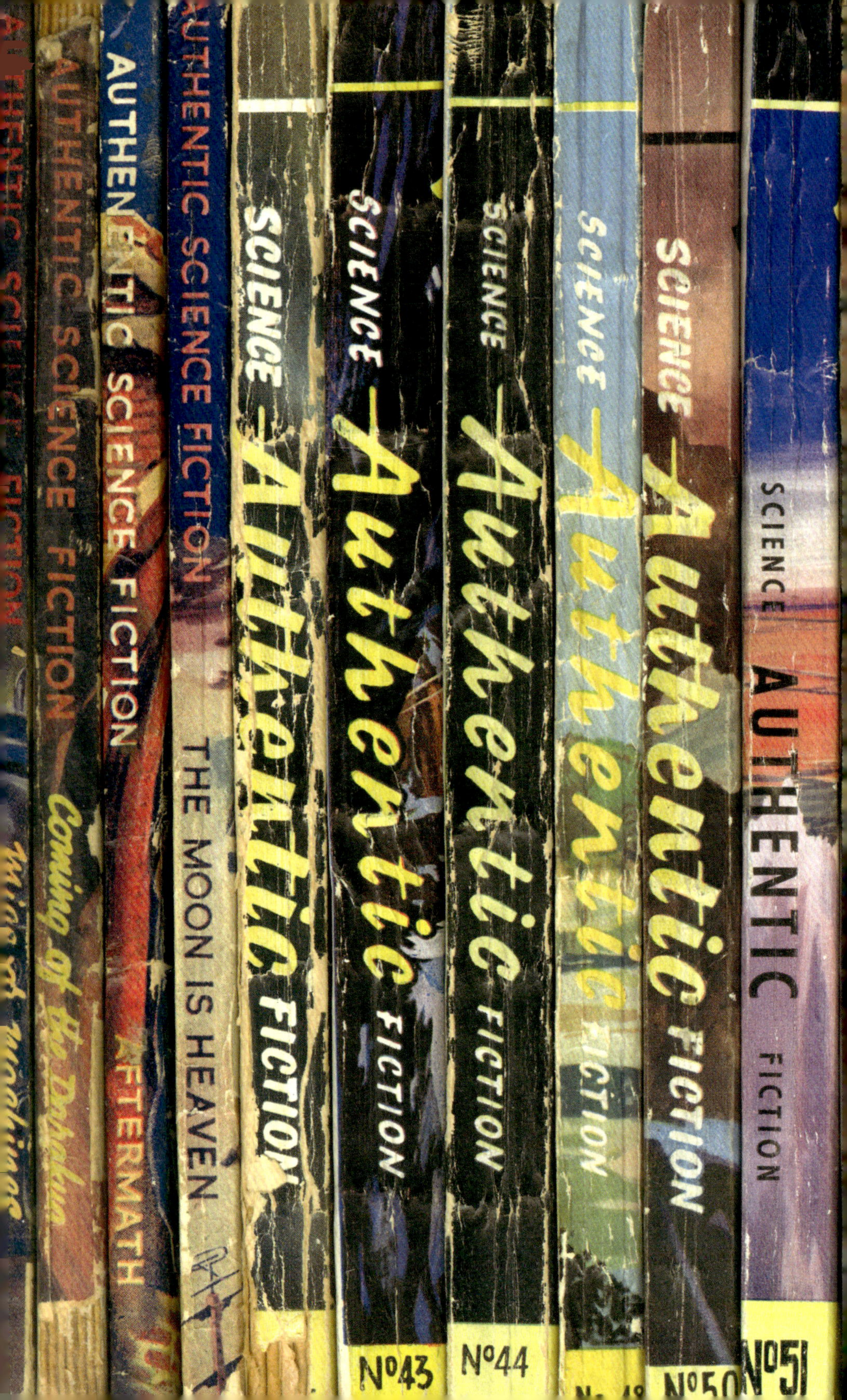
AUTHENTIC SCIENCE FICTION
AUTHENTIC SCIENCE FICTION
AUTHENTIC SCIENCE FICTION
AFTERMATH
AUTHENTIC SCIENCE FICTION
THE MOON IS HEAVEN
SCIENCE Authentic FICTION
SCIENCE Authentic FICTION
Nº43
SCIENCE Authentic FICTION
Nº44
SCIENCE Authentic FICTION
SCIENCE Authentic FICTION
Nº50
SCIENCE AUTHENTIC FICTION
Nº51

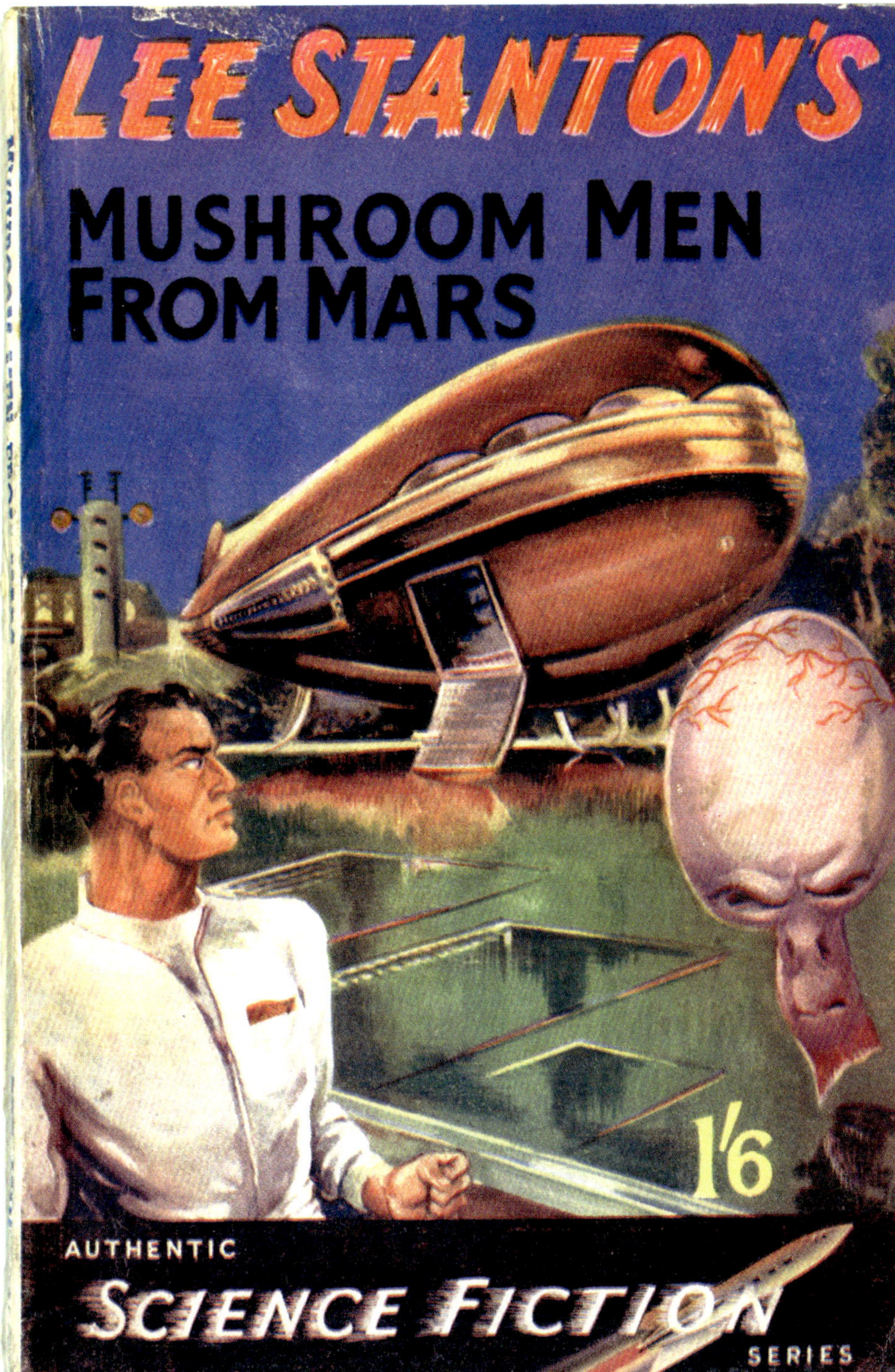

Lee Stanton (Richard Conroy) *Mushroom Men from Mars*
Authentic Science Fiction Series #1 | Hamilton & Co., 1951 | Art **D. L. W.**

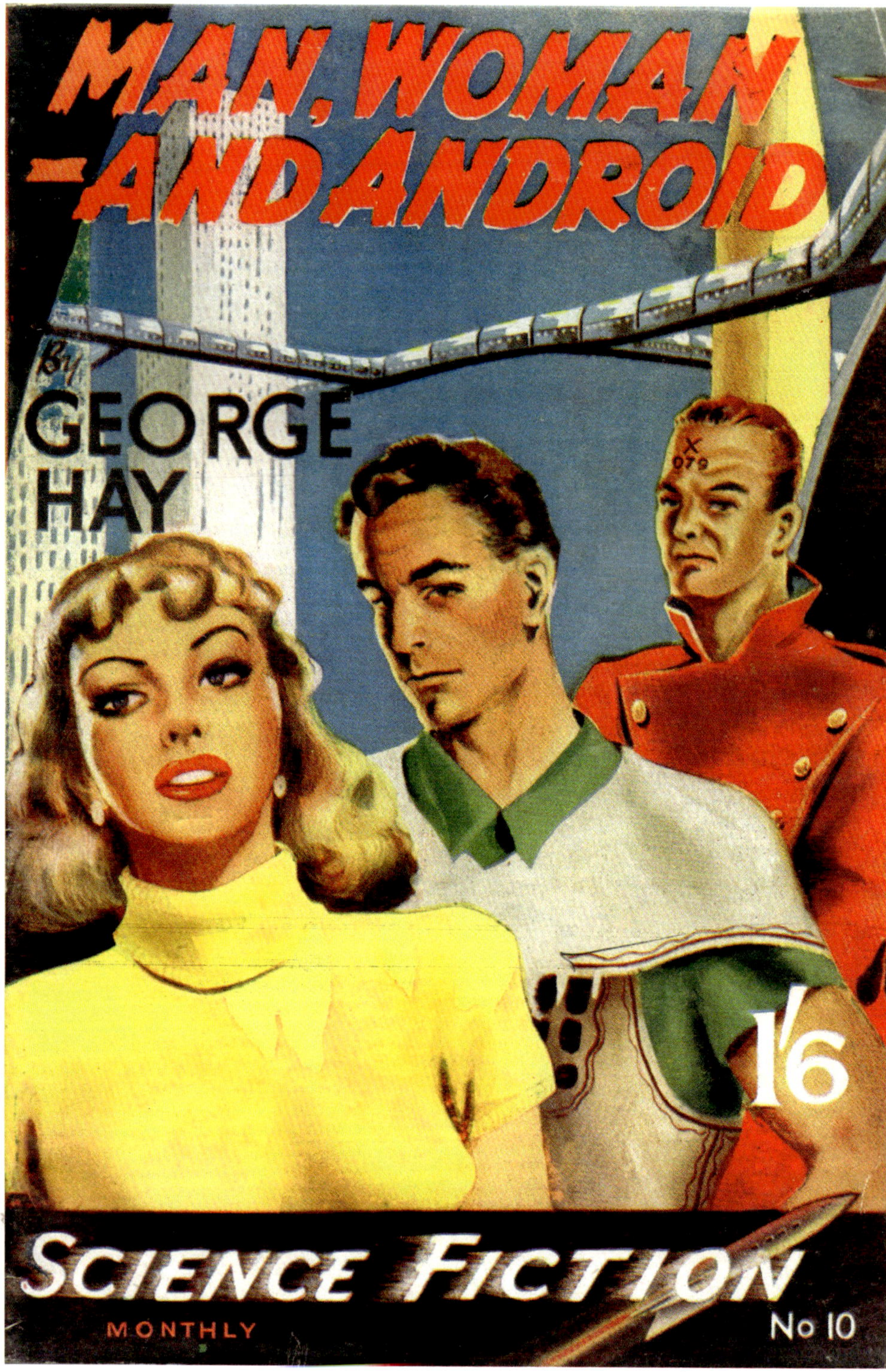

George Hay | *Man, Woman – and Android*
Science Fiction Monthly #10
Hamilton & Co., 1951 | Art **George Ratcliffe**

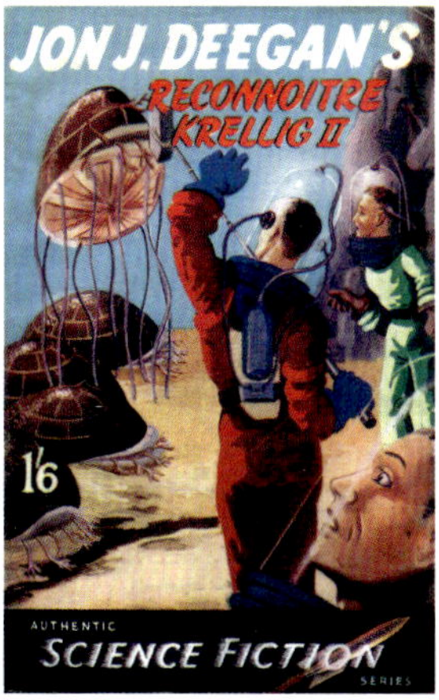

Jon J. Deegan (Robert G. Sharp)
Reconnoitre Krellig II
Authentic Science Fiction Series #2
Hamilton & Co., 1951 | Art **D. L. W.**

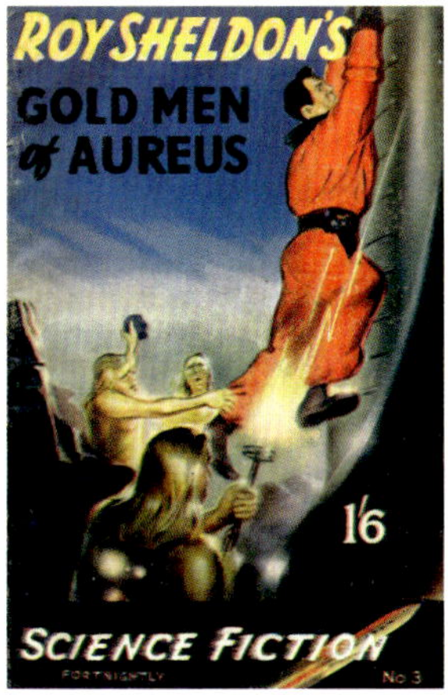

Roy Sheldon | *Gold Men of Aureus*
Science Fiction Fortnightly #3
Hamilton & Co., 1951 | Art **D. L. W.**

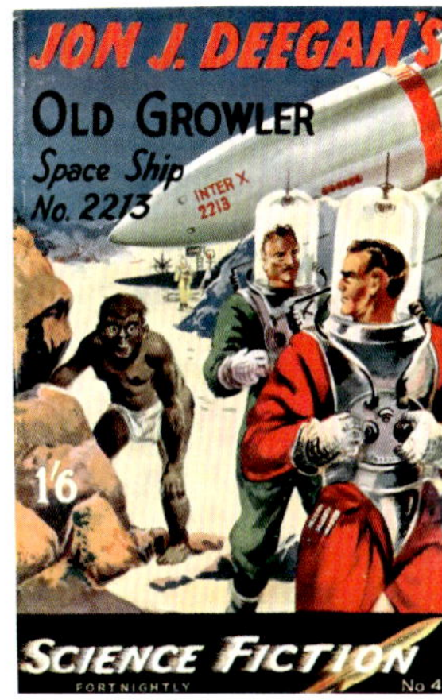

Jon J. Deegan (Robert G. Sharp)
Old Growler Space Ship No. 2213
Science Fiction Fortnightly #4
Hamilton & Co., 1951 | Art **D. L. W.**

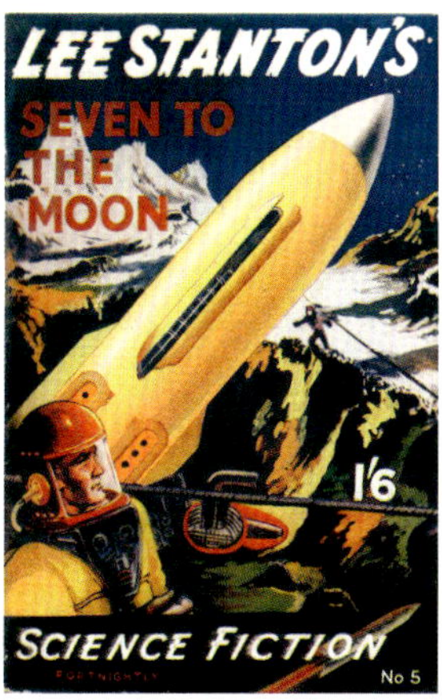

Lee Stanton (Richard Conroy)
Seven to the Moon
Science Fiction Fortnightly #5
Hamilton & Co., 1951 | Art **D. L. W.**

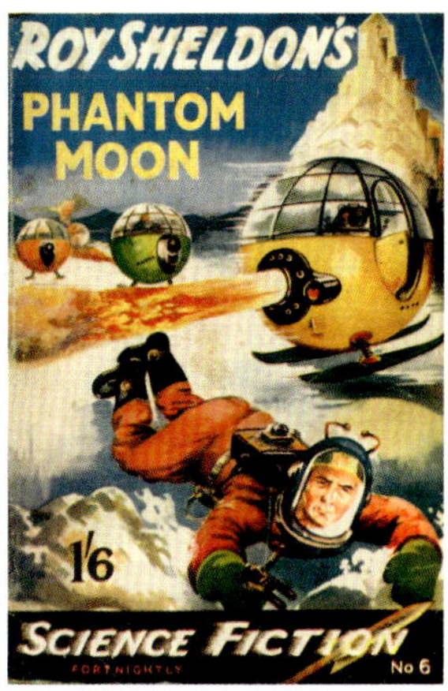

Roy Sheldon (H. J. Campbell)
Phantom Moon
Science Fiction Fortnightly #6
Hamilton & Co., 1951 | Art **D. L. W.**

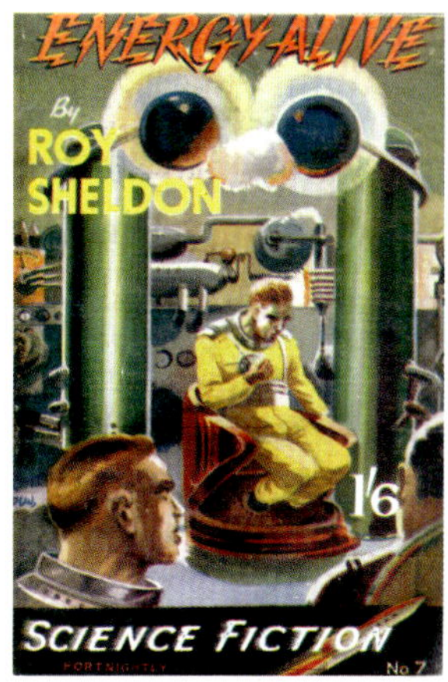

Roy Sheldon (H. J. Campbell) | *Energy Alive*
Science Fiction Fortnightly #7
Hamilton & Co., 1951 | Art **D. L. W.**

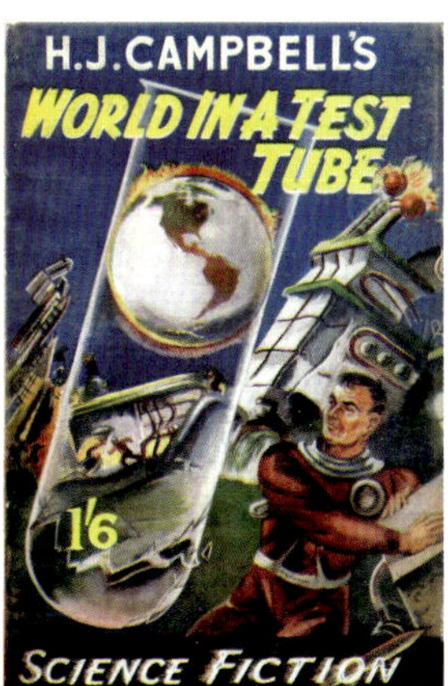

H. J. Campbell | *World in a Test Tube*
Science Fiction Fortnightly #8
Hamilton & Co., 1951 | Art **D. L. W.**

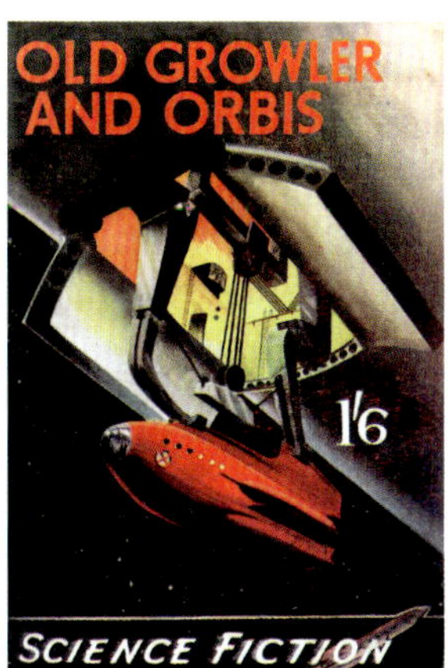

Jon J. Deegan | **(Robert G. Sharp)**
Old Growler and Orbis
Science Fiction Monthly #9
Hamilton & Co., 1951 | Art **George Ratcliffe**

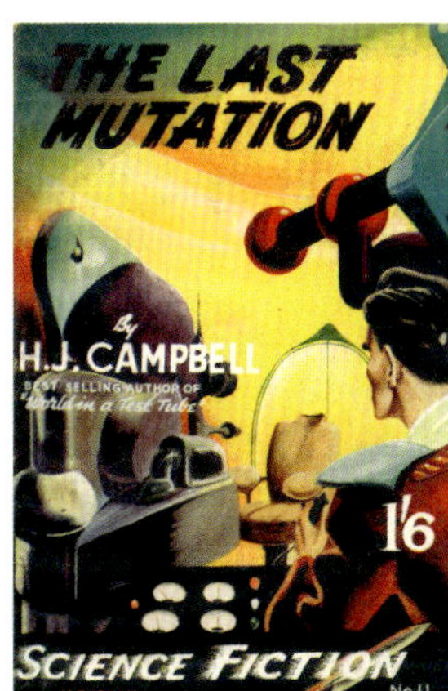

H. J. Campbell | *The Last Mutation*
Science Fiction Monthly #11
Hamilton & Co., 1951 | Art **George Ratcliffe**

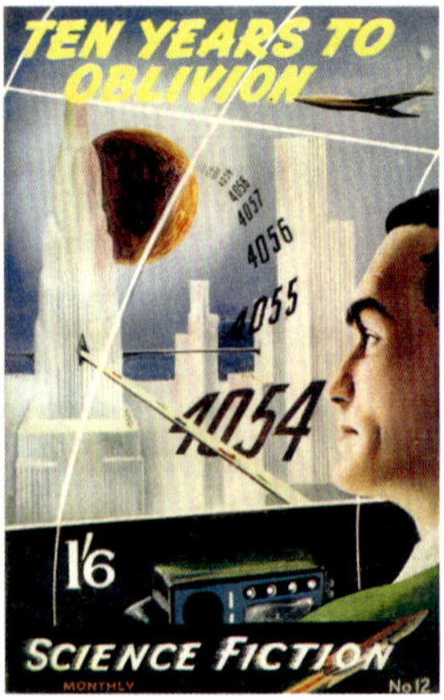

Clem Macartney (William David Flackes)
Ten Years to Oblivion
Science Fiction Monthly #12
Hamilton & Co., 1951 | Art **George Ratcliffe**

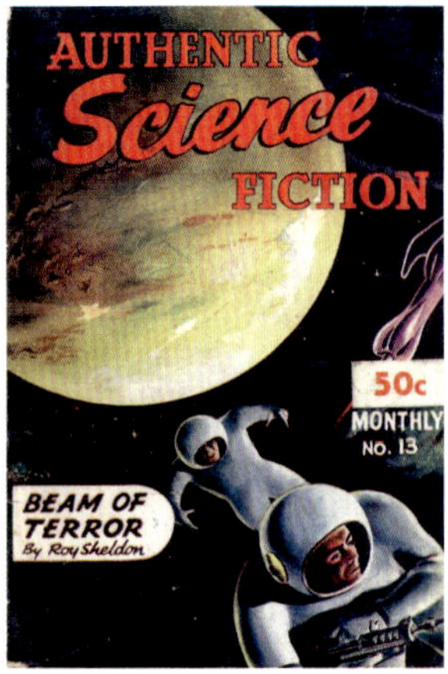

Roy Sheldon (H. J. Campbell) | *Beam of Terror*
Authentic Science Fiction #13
Hamilton & Co., 1951 | Art **D. L. W.**

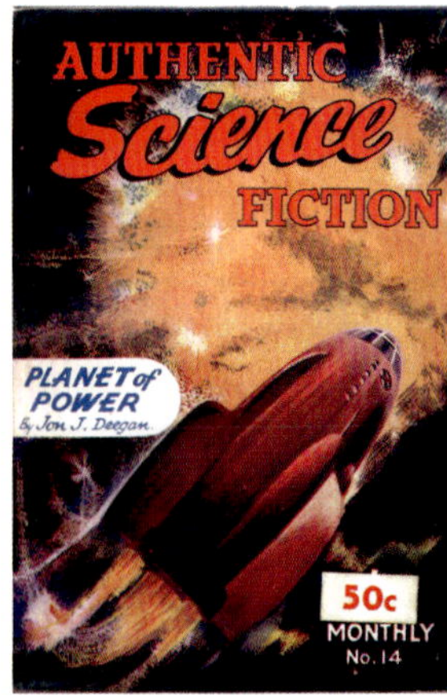

Jon J. Deegan (Robert G. Sharp)
Planet of Power
Authentic Science Fiction #14
Hamilton & Co., 1951 | Art **D. L. W.**

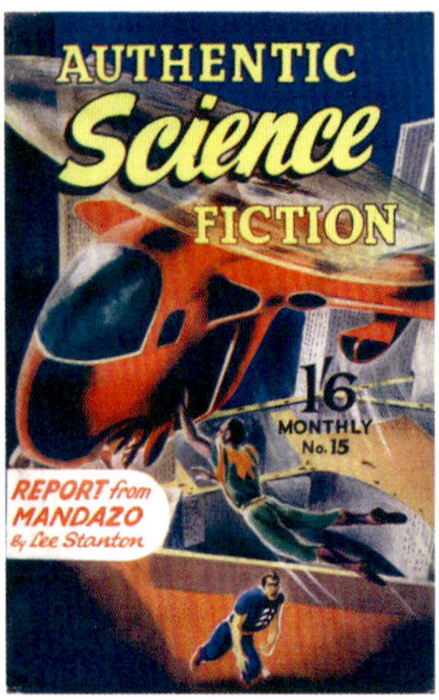

Lee Stanton (Richard Conroy)
Report from Mandazo
Authentic Science Fiction #15
Hamilton & Co., 1951 | Art **D. L. W.**

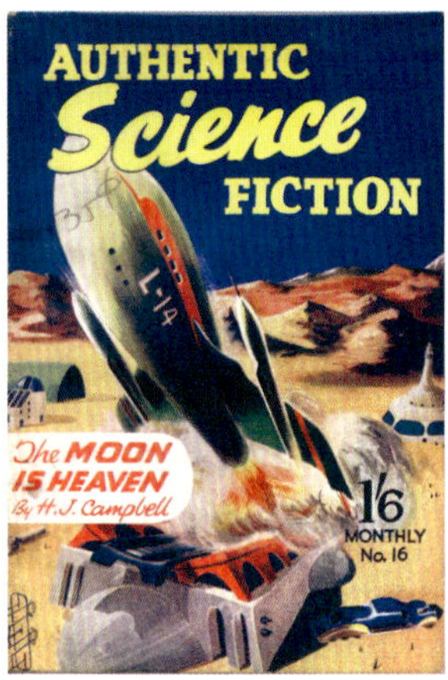

H. J. Campbell | *The Moon is Heaven*
Authentic Science Fiction #16
Hamilton & Co., 1951 | Art **D. L. W.**

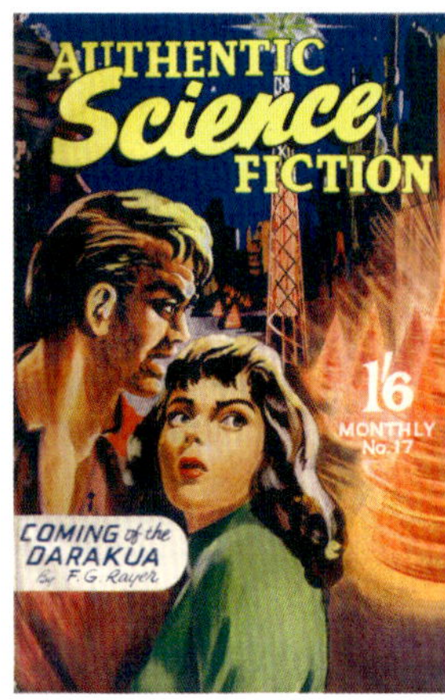

F. G. Rayer | *Coming of the Darakua*
Authentic Science Fiction #17
Hamilton & Co., 1952 | Art **D. L. W.**

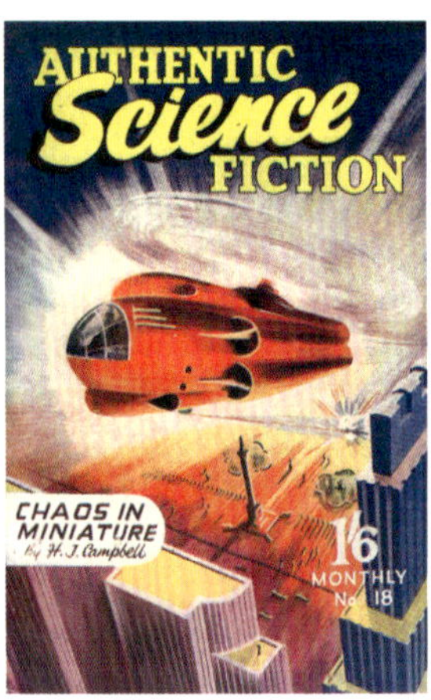

H. J. Campbell | *Chaos in Miniature*
Authentic Science Fiction #18
Hamilton & Co., 1952 | Art **D. L. W.**

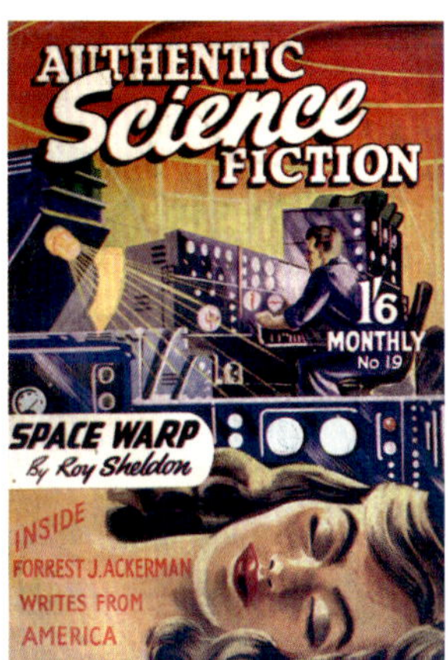

Roy Sheldon | *Space Warp*
Authentic Science Fiction #19
Hamilton & Co., 1952 | Art **D. L. W.**

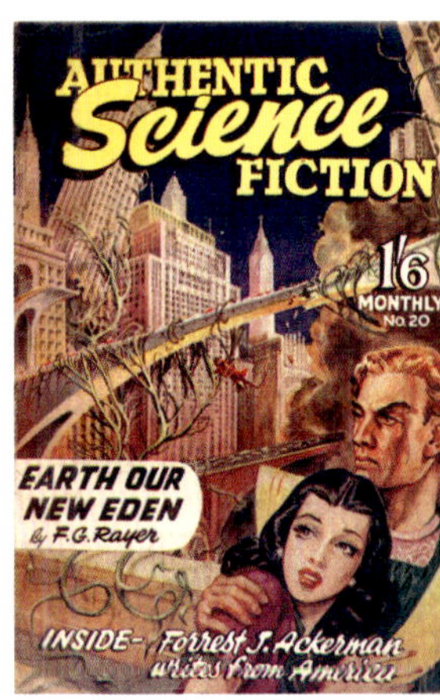

F. G. Rayer | *Earth our New Eden*
Authentic Science Fiction #20
Hamilton & Co., 1952 | Art **Vann**

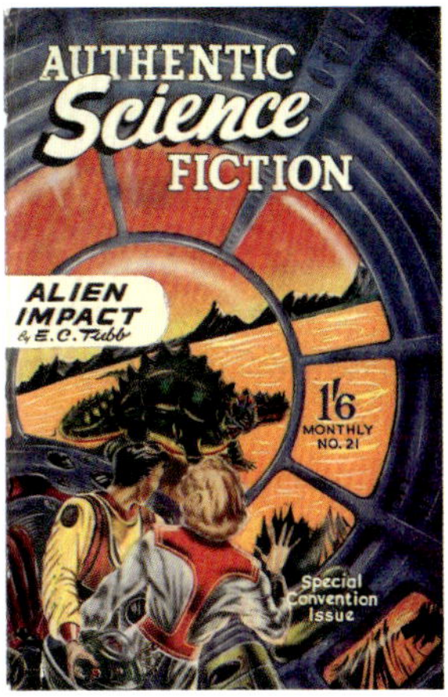

E. C. Tubb | *Alien Impact*
Authentic Science Fiction #21
Hamilton & Co., 1952 | Art **Gordon C. Davies**

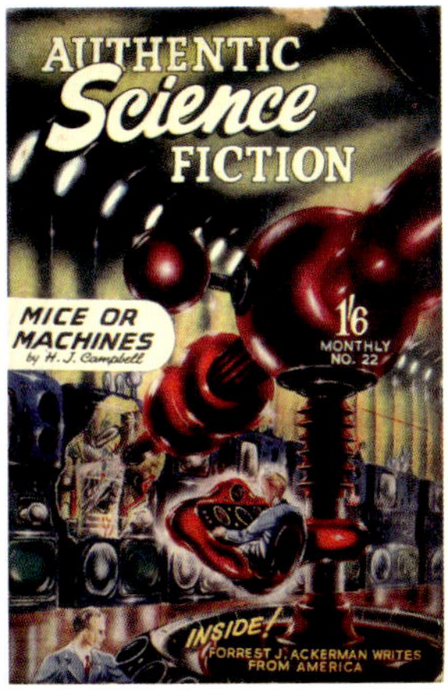

H. J. Campbell | *Mice or Machines*
Authentic Science Fiction #22
Hamilton & Co., 1952 | Art **Gordon C. Davies**

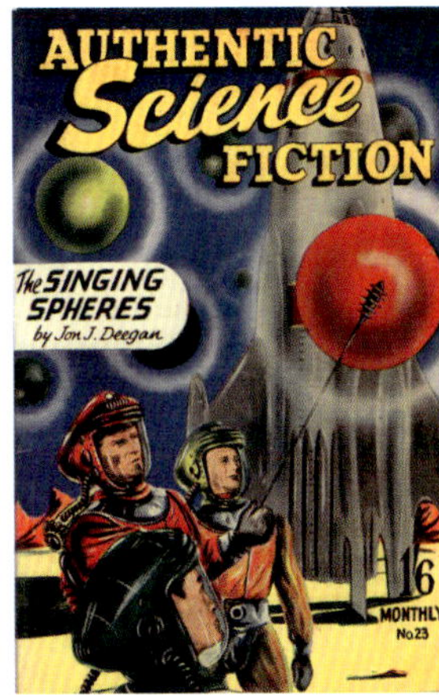

Jon J. Deegan (Robert G. Sharp)
The Singing Spheres
Authentic Science Fiction #23
Hamilton & Co., 1952 | Art **Gordon C. Davies**

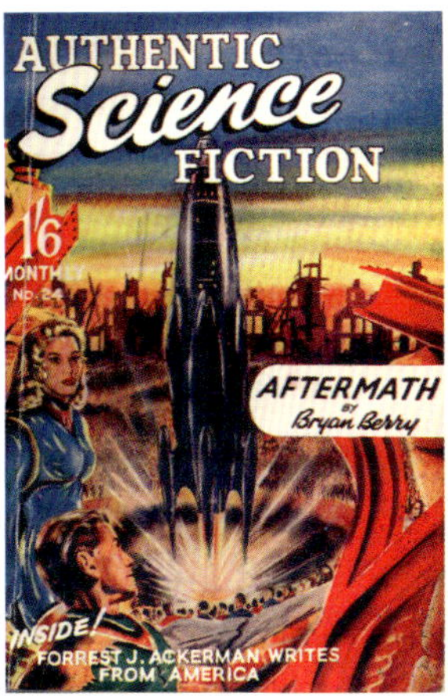

Bryan Berry | *Aftermath*
Authentic Science Fiction #24
Hamilton & Co., 1952 | Art **Gordon C. Davies**

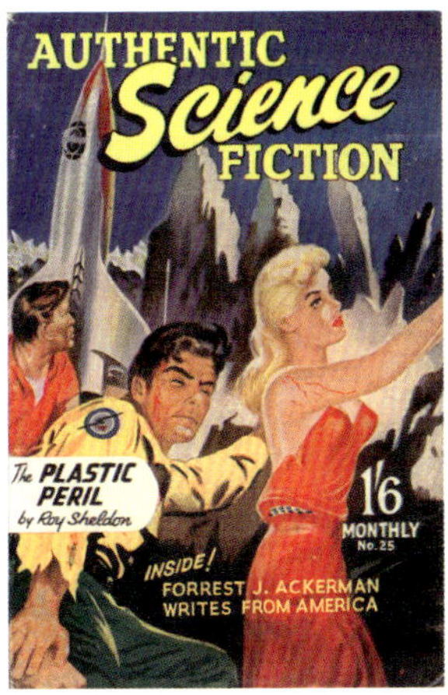

Roy Sheldon (H. J. Campbell) | *The Plastic Peril*
Authentic Science Fiction #25
Hamilton & Co., 1952 | Art **John Pollack**

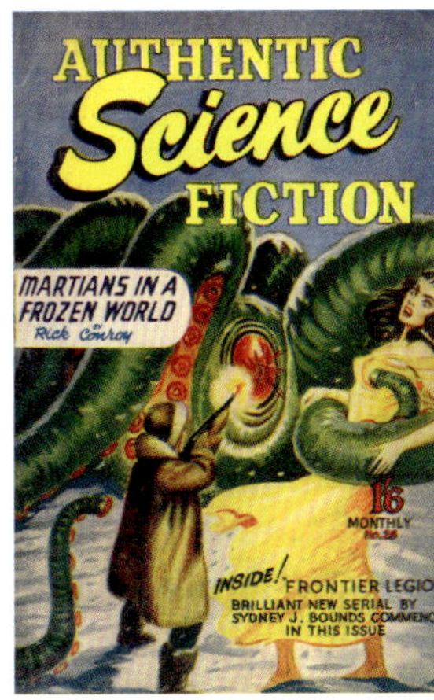

Rick Conroy | *Martians in a Frozen World*
Authentic Science Fiction #26
Hamilton & Co., 1952 | Art **D. L. W.**

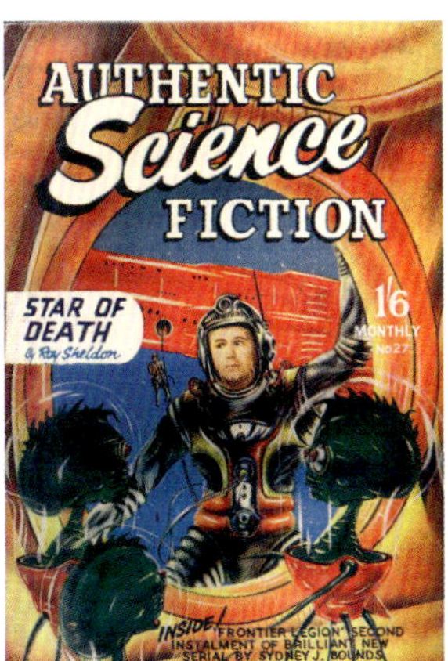

Roy Sheldon (H. J. Campbell) | *Star of Death*
Authentic Science Fiction #27
Hamilton & Co., 1952 | Art **Gordon C. Davies**

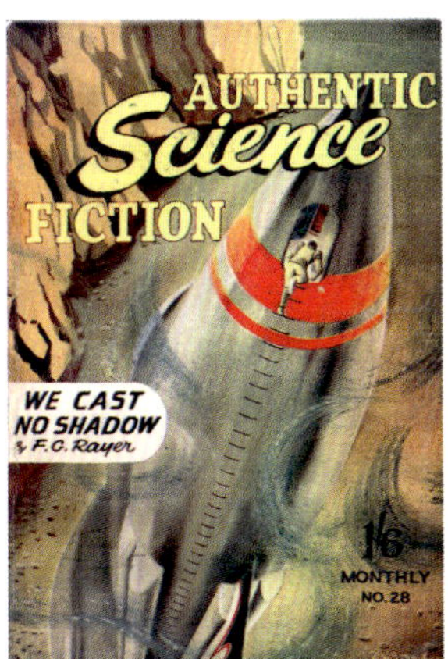

F. G. Rayer | *We Cast No Shadow*
Authentic Science Fiction #28
Hamilton & Co., 1952 | Art **Vann**

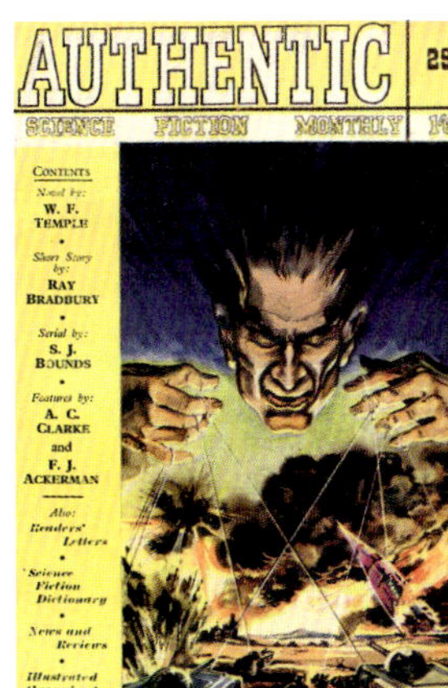

Herbert J. Campbell, ed.
Authentic Science Fiction Monthly #29
Hamilton & Co., 1953 | Art **Vann**

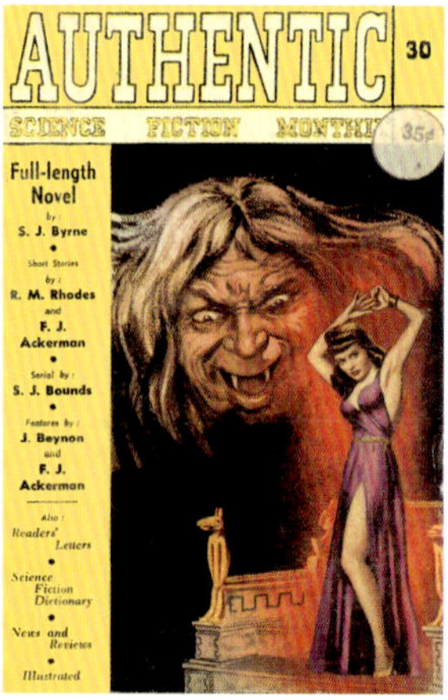

Herbert J. Campbell, ed.
Authentic Science Fiction Monthly #30
Hamilton & Co., 1953 | Art **John Richards**

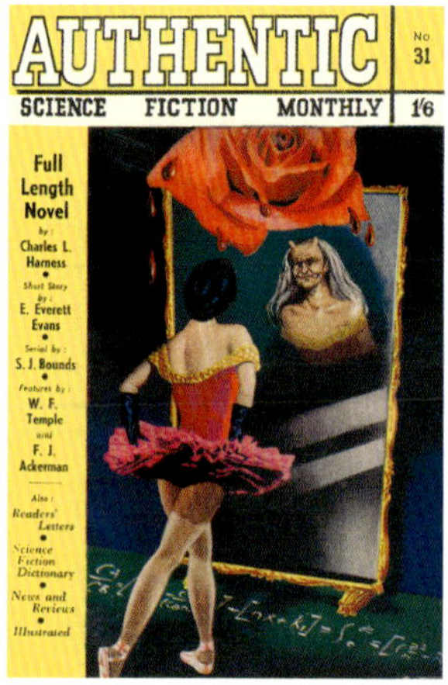

Herbert J. Campbell, ed.
Authentic Science Fiction Monthly #31
Hamilton & Co., 1953 | Art **John Richards**

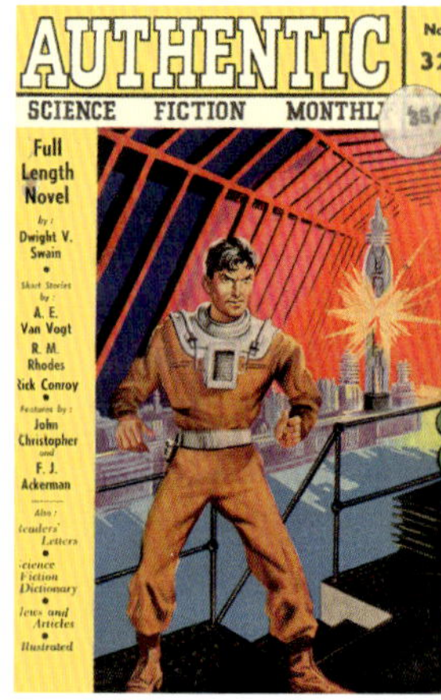

Herbert J. Campbell, ed.
Authentic Science Fiction Monthly #32
Hamilton & Co., 1953 | Art **John Richards**

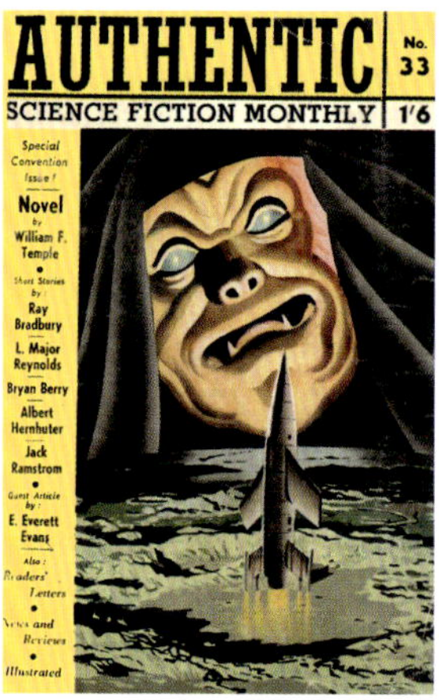

Herbert J. Campbell, ed.
Authentic Science Fiction Monthly #33
Hamilton & Co., 1953 | Art **John Richards**

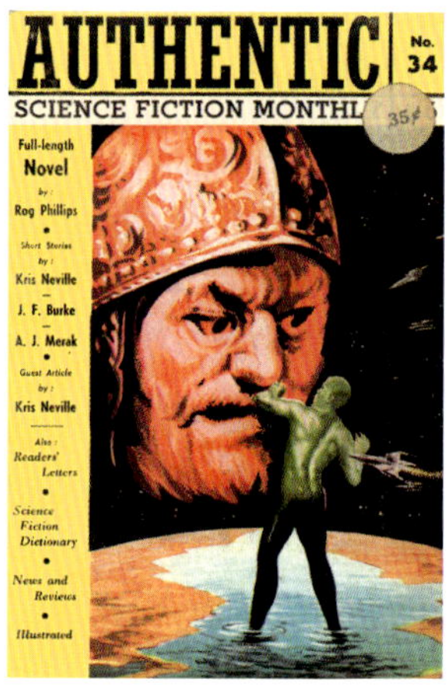

Herbert J. Campbel, ed.
Authentic Science Fiction Monthly #34
Hamilton & Co., 1953 | Art **John Richards**

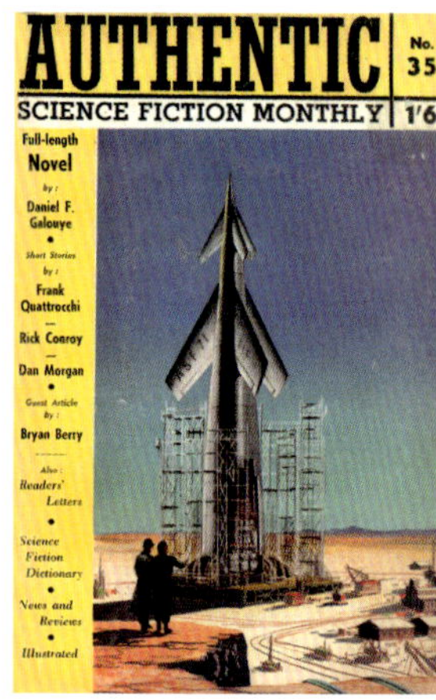

Herbert J. Campbell, ed.
Authentic Science Fiction Monthly #35
Hamilton & Co., 1953 | Art **John Richards**

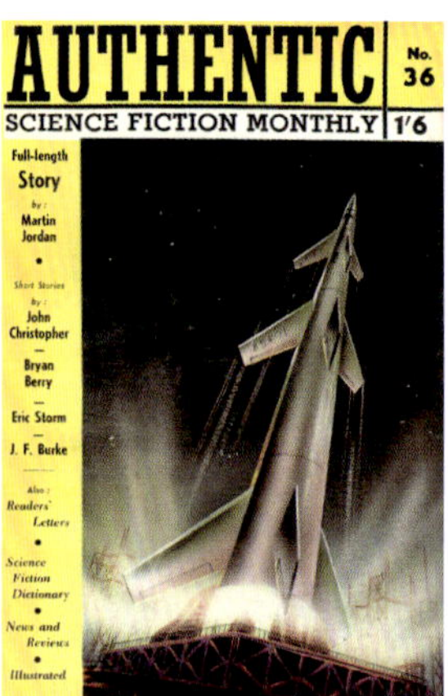

Herbert J. Campbell, ed.
Authentic Science Fiction Monthly #36
Hamilton & Co., 1953 | Art **John Richards**

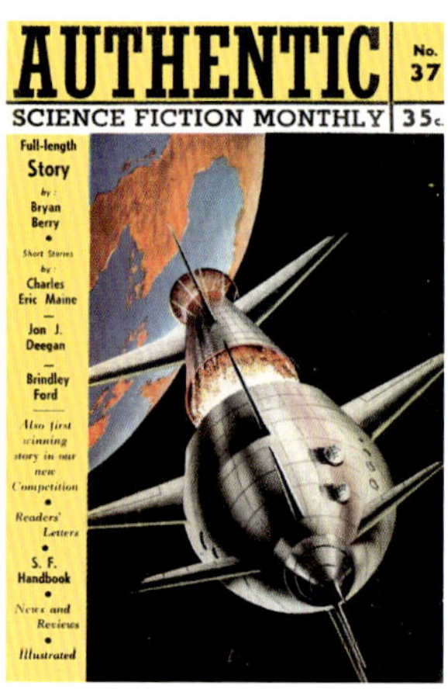

Herbert J. Campbell, ed.
Authentic Science Fiction Monthly #37
Hamilton & Co., 1953 | Art **John Richards**

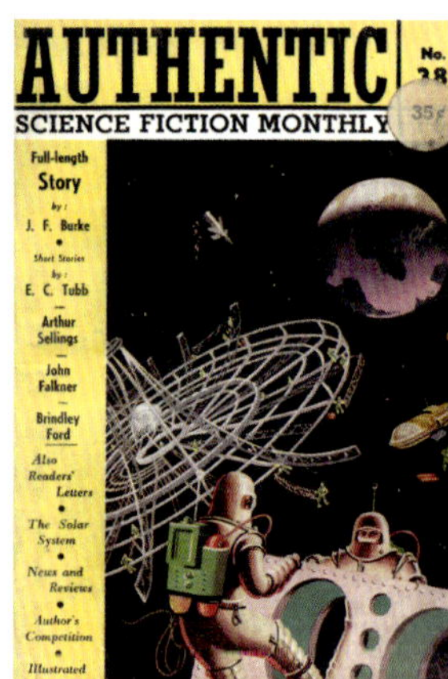

Herbert J. Campbell, ed.
Authentic Science Fiction Monthly #38
Hamilton & Co., 1953 | Art **John Richards**

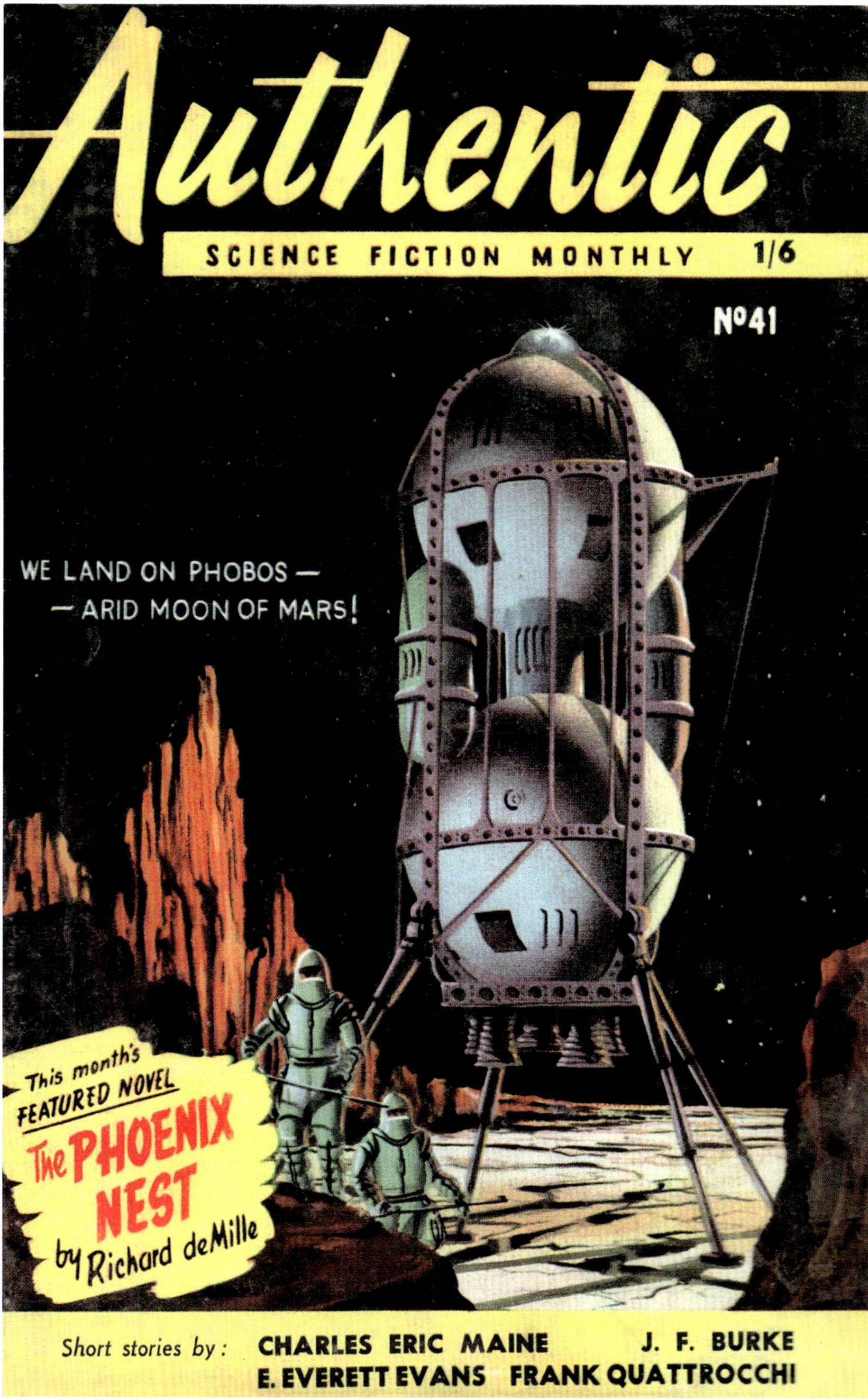

Herbert J. Campbell, ed. | Authentic Science Fiction Monthly #41
Hamilton & Co., 1954 | Art **John Richards**

opposite: **Herbert J. Campbell, ed.** | *Authentic Science Fiction Monthly #40*
Hamilton & Co., 1954 | Art **John Richards**

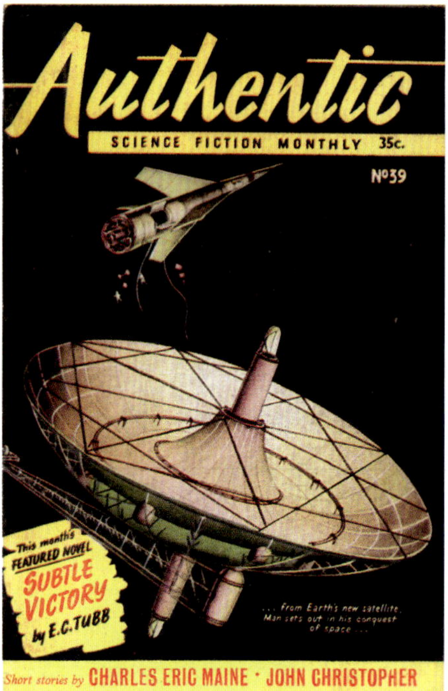

Herbert J. Campbell, ed. | Authentic Science Fiction Monthly #39
Hamilton & Co., 1953 | Art **John Richards**

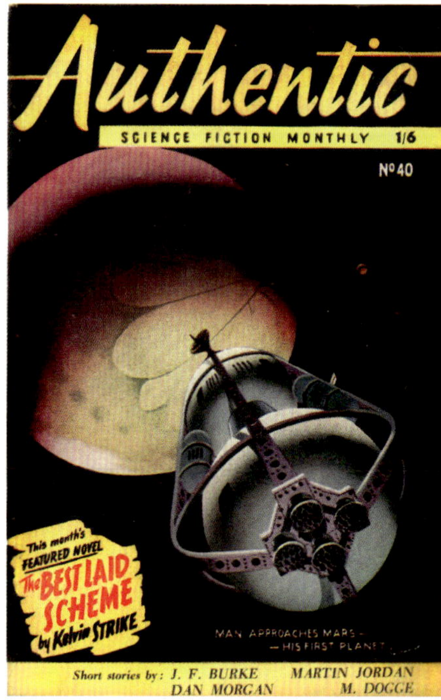

Herbert J. Campbell, ed. | Authentic Science Fiction Monthly #40
Hamilton & Co., 1953 | Art **John Richards**

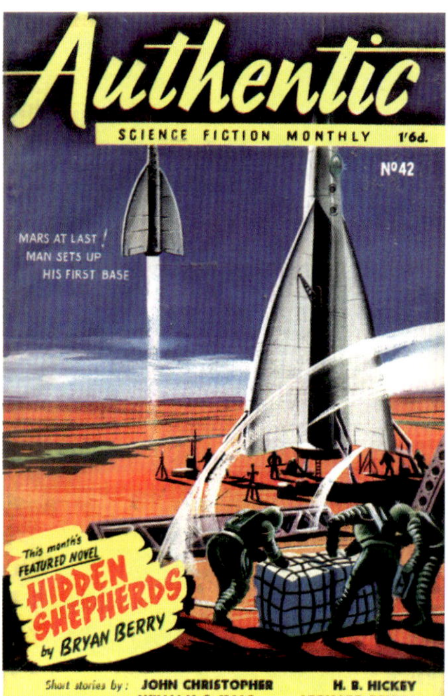

Herbert J. Campbell, ed. | Authentic Science Fiction Monthly #42
Hamilton & Co., 1954 | Art **John Richards**

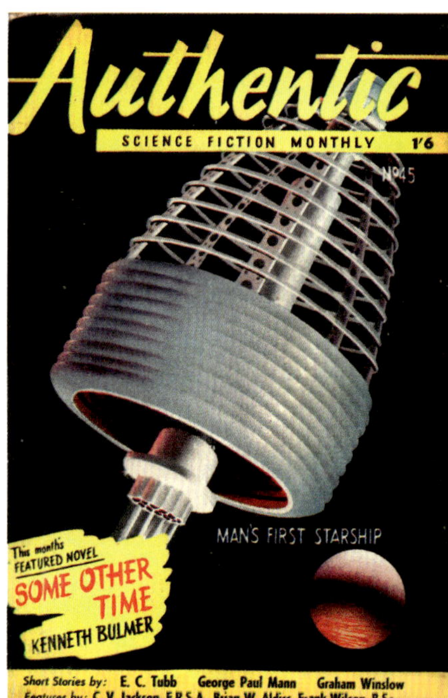

Herbert J. Campbell, ed. | Authentic Science Fiction Monthly #45
Hamilton & Co., 1954 | Art **John Richards**

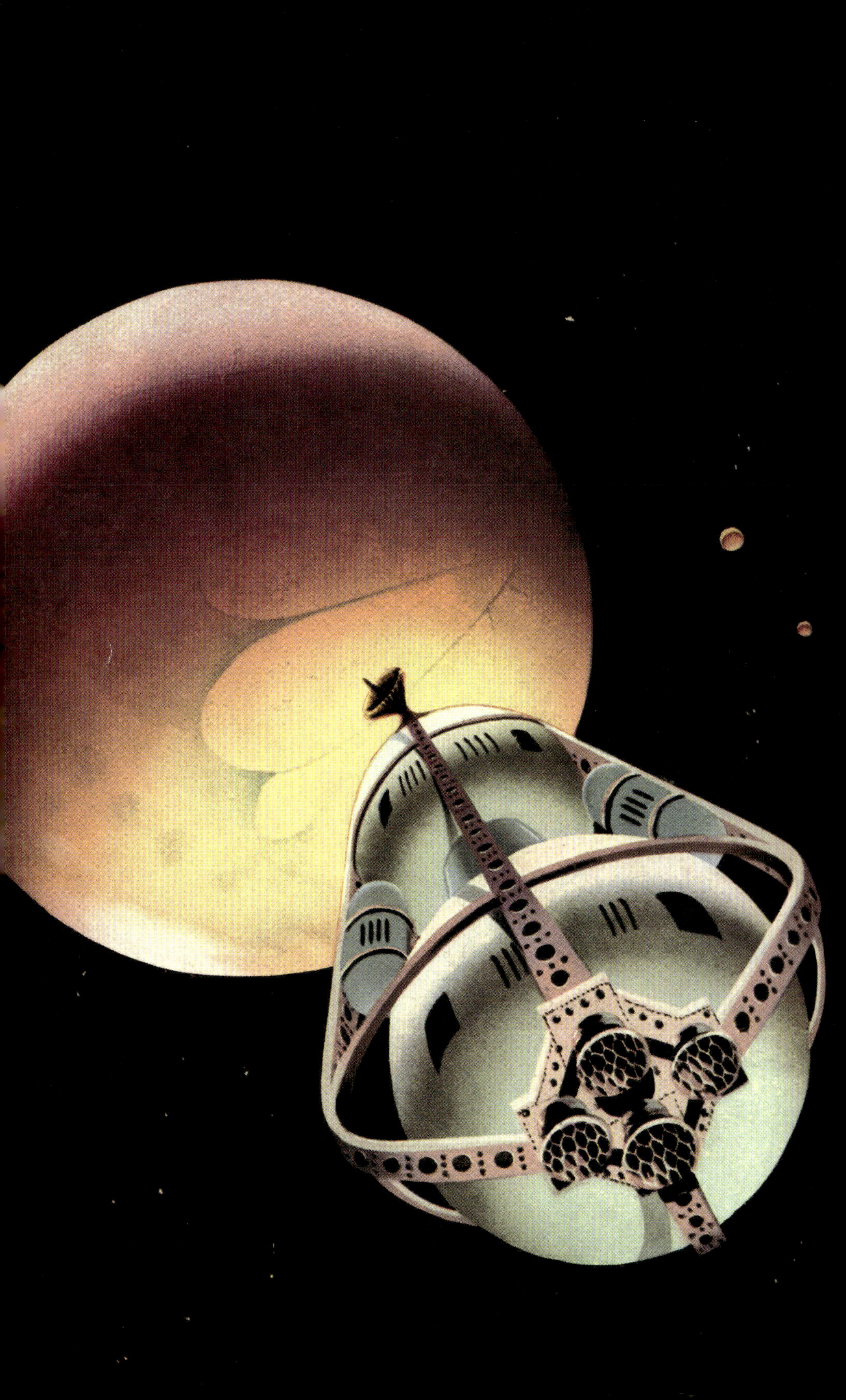

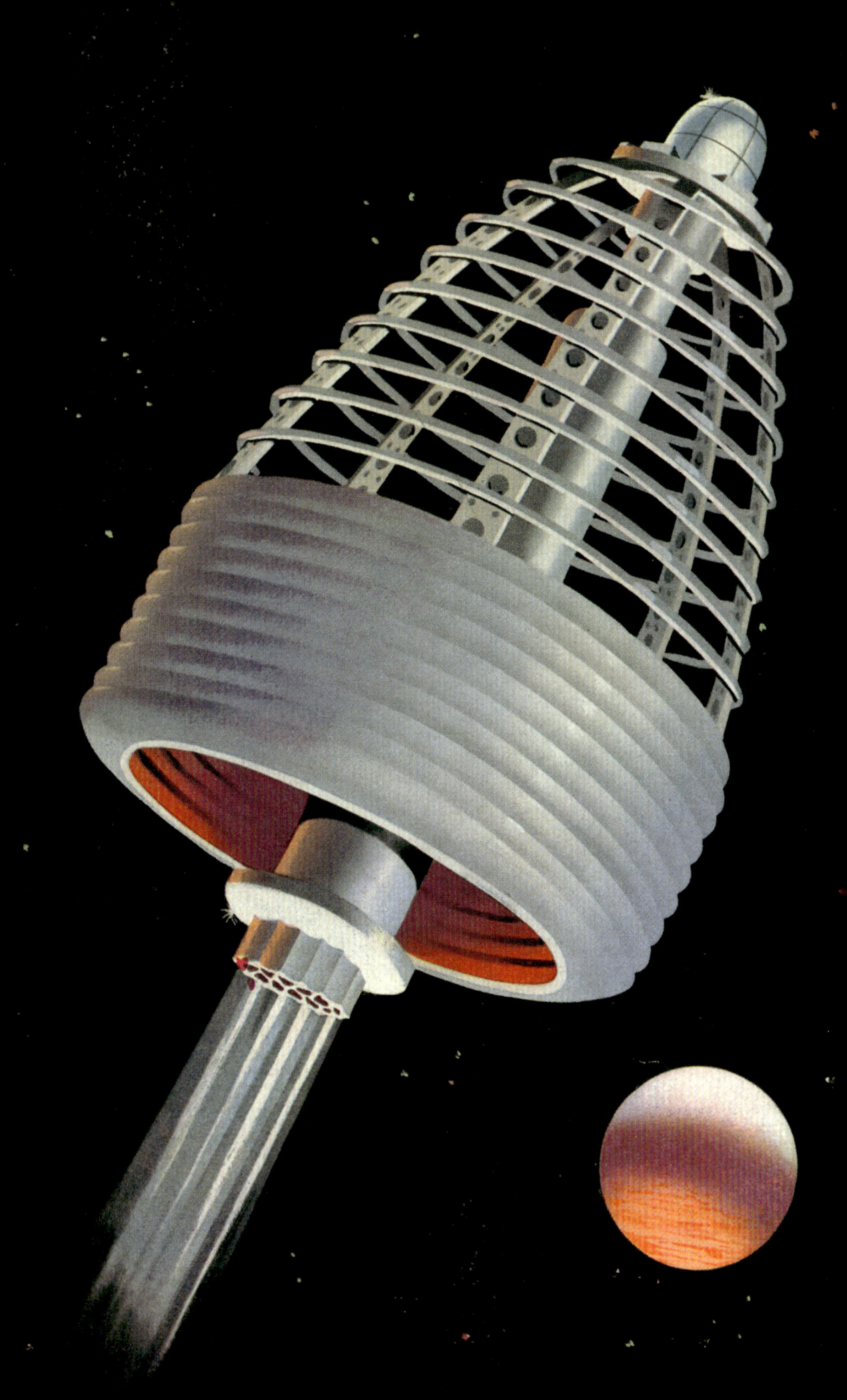

opposite: **Herbert J. Campbell, ed.** | *Authentic Science Fiction Monthly* #45
Hamilton & Co., 1954 | Art **John Richards**

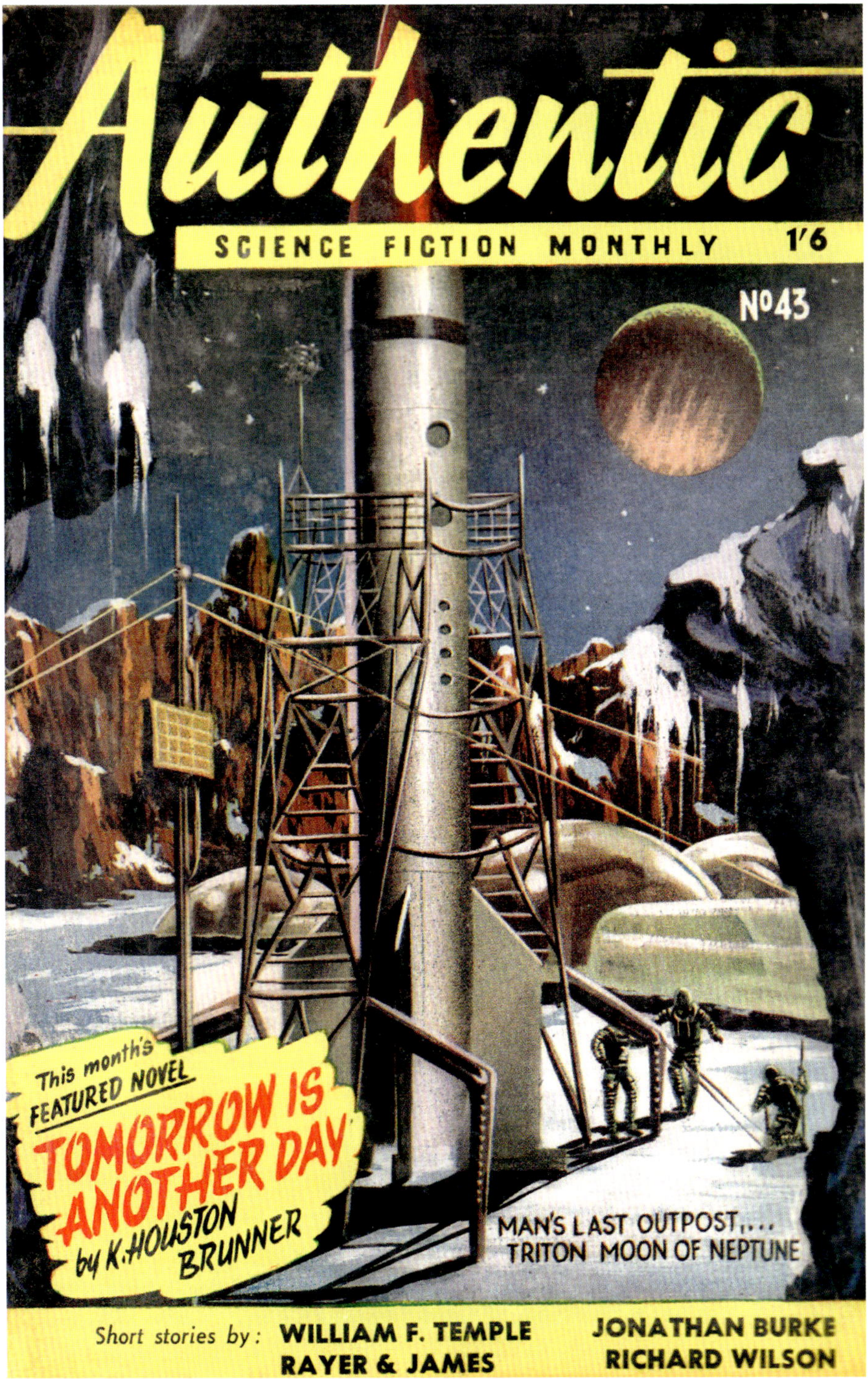

Herbert J. Campbell, ed. | Authentic Science Fiction Monthly #43
Hamilton & Co., 1954 | Art **John Richards**

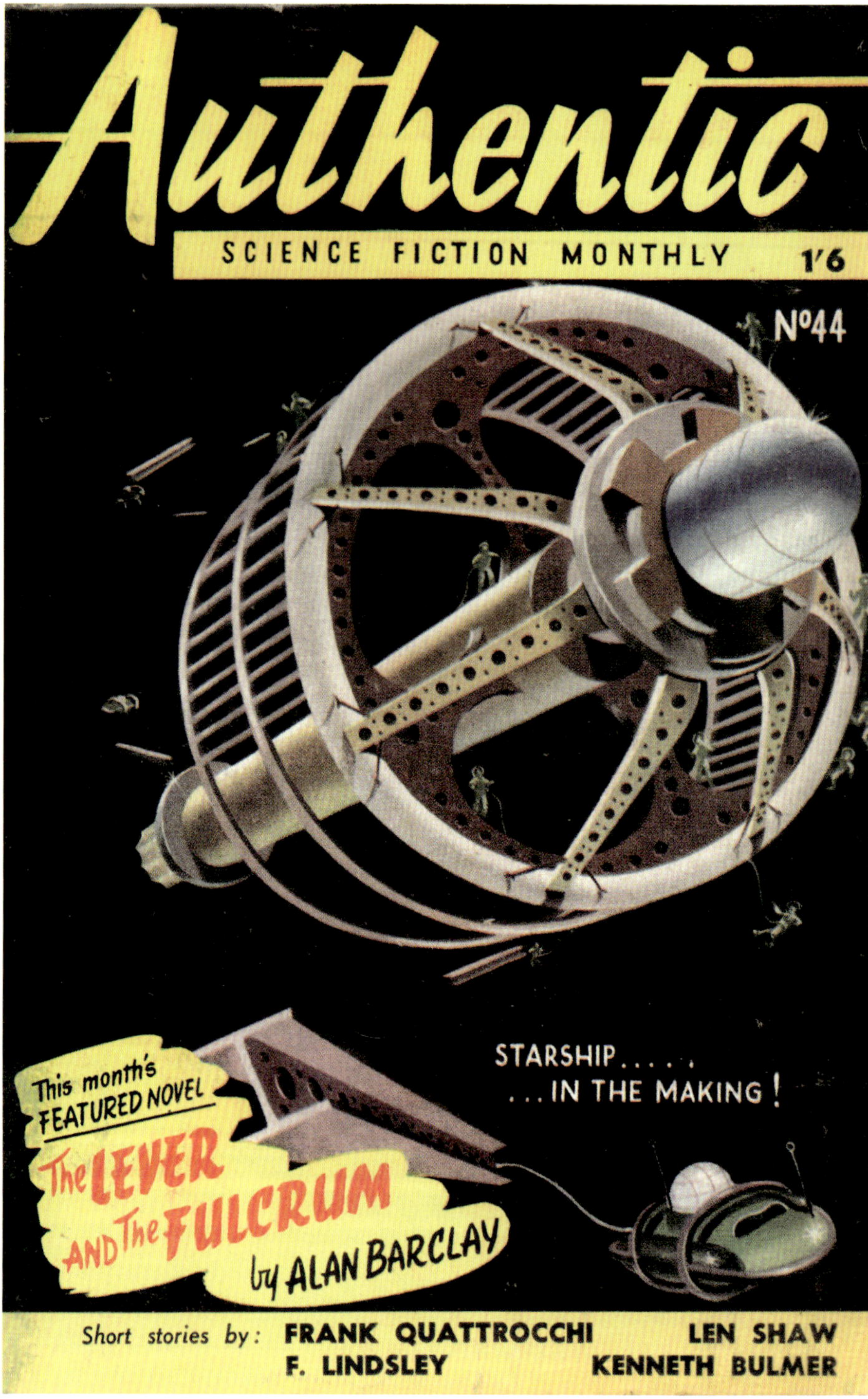

Herbert J. Campbell, ed. | Authentic Science Fiction Monthly #44
Hamilton & Co., 1954 | Art **John Richards**

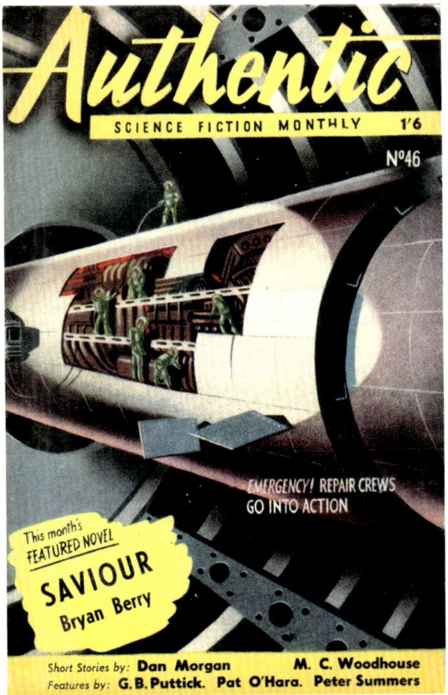

Herbert J. Campbell, ed. | Authentic Science Fiction Monthly #46
Hamilton & Co., 1954 | Art **John Richards**

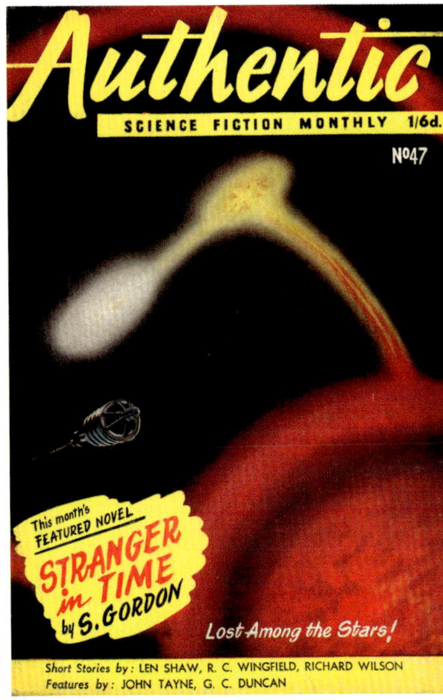

Herbert J. Campbell, ed. | Authentic Science Fiction Monthly #47
Hamilton & Co., 1954 | Art **John Richards** (see page 173)

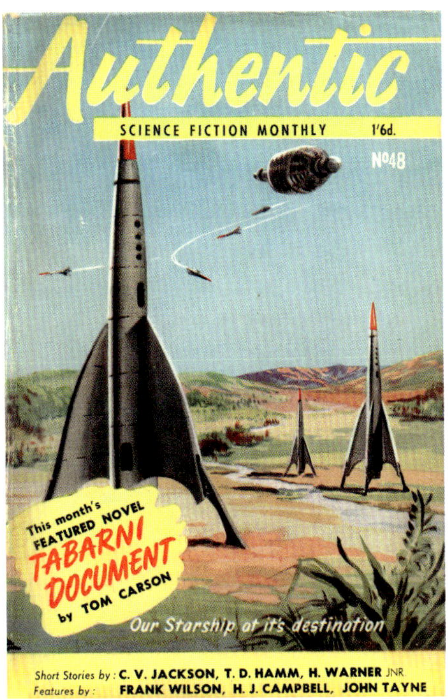

Herbert J. Campbell, ed. | Authentic Science Fiction Monthly #48
Hamilton & Co., 1954 | Art **John Richards**

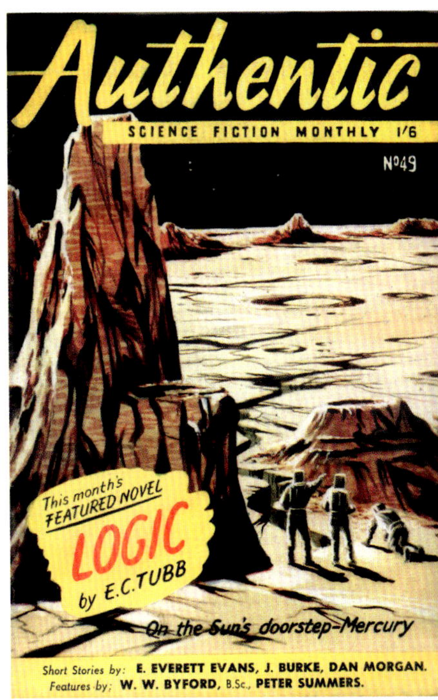

Herbert J. Campbell, ed. | Authentic Science Fiction Monthly #49
Hamilton & Co., 1954 | Art **John Richards**

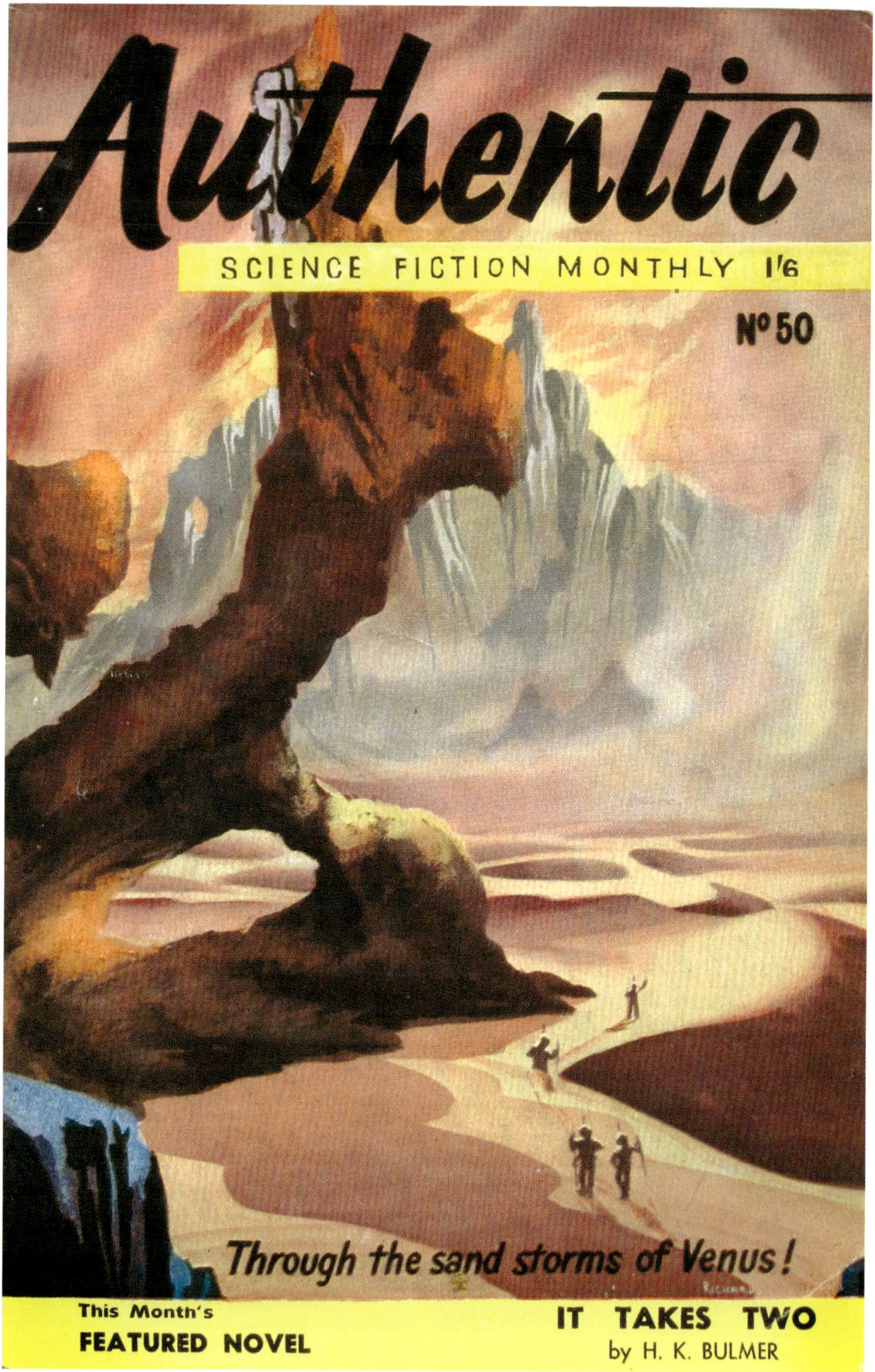

Herbert J. Campbell, ed. | Authentic Science Fiction Monthly #50
Hamilton & Co., 1954 | Art **John Richards**

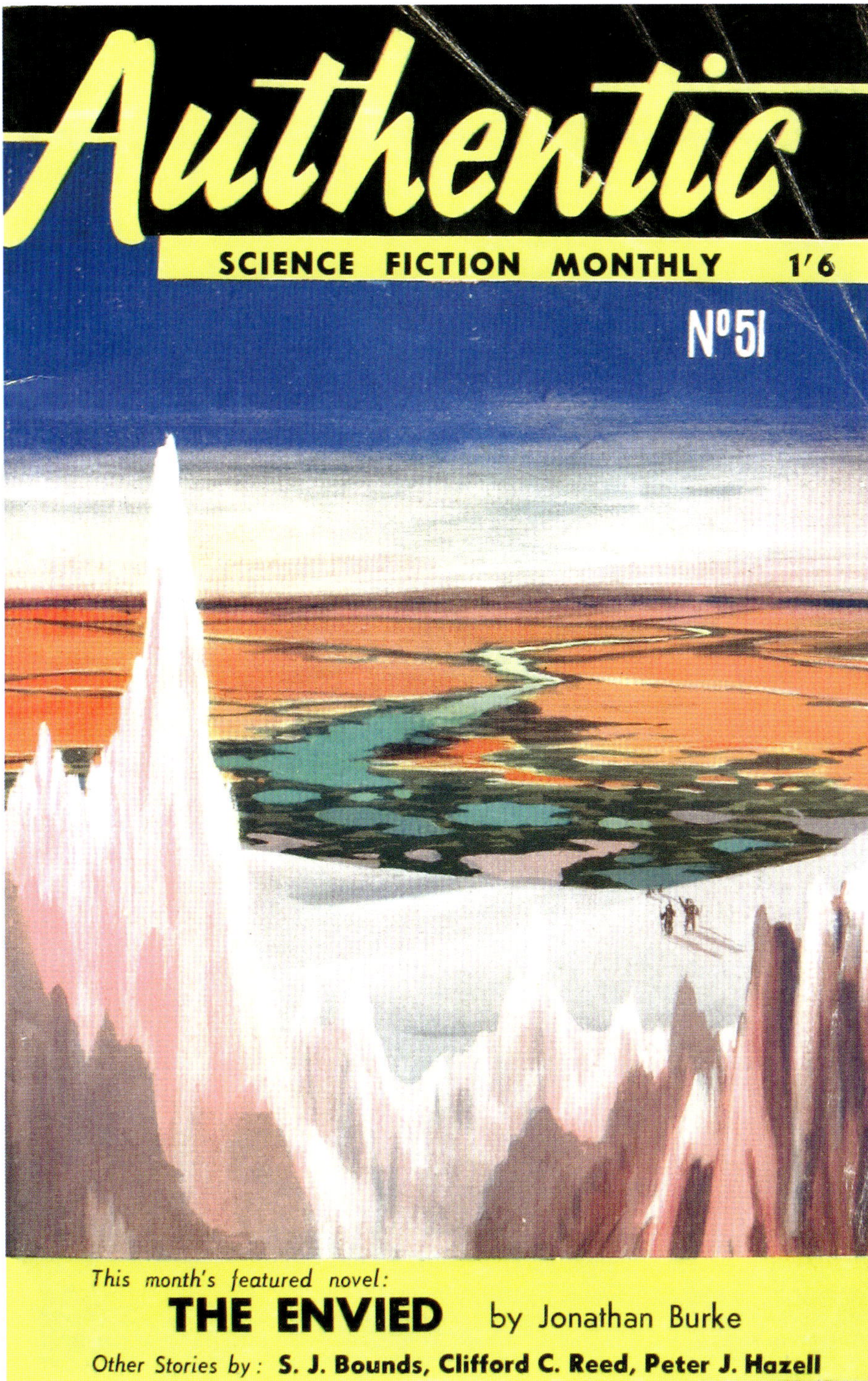

Herbert J. Campbell, ed. | Authentic Science Fiction Monthly #51
Hamilton & Co., 1954 | Art **John Richards**

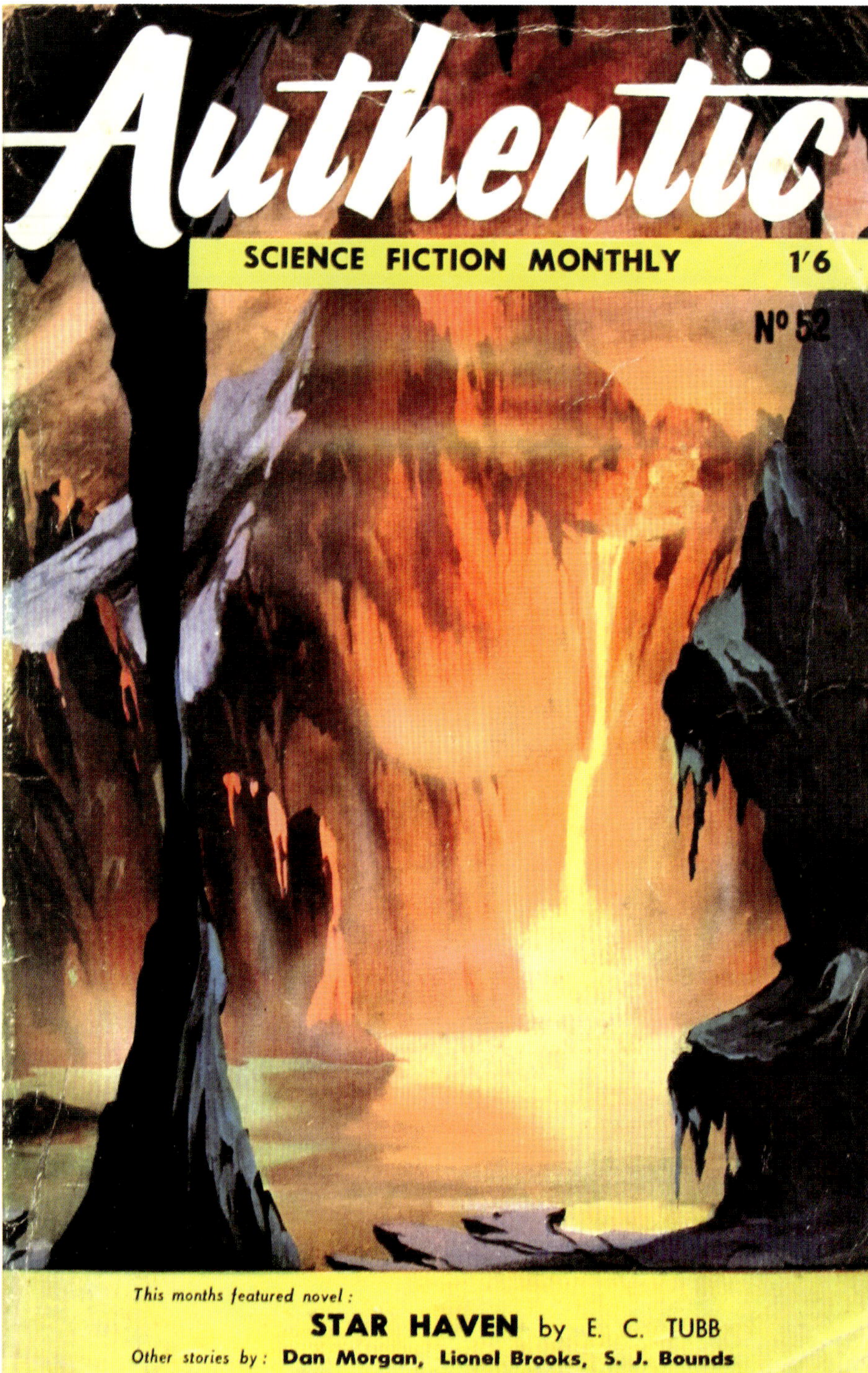

Herbert J. Campbell, ed. | Authentic Science Fiction Monthly #52
Hamilton & Co., 1954 | Art **John Richards**

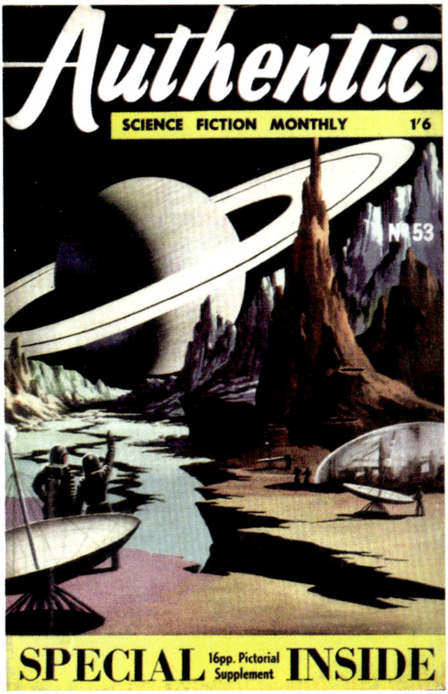

Herbert J. Campbell, ed. | Authentic Science Fiction Monthly #53
Hamilton & Co., 1955 | Art **John Richards**

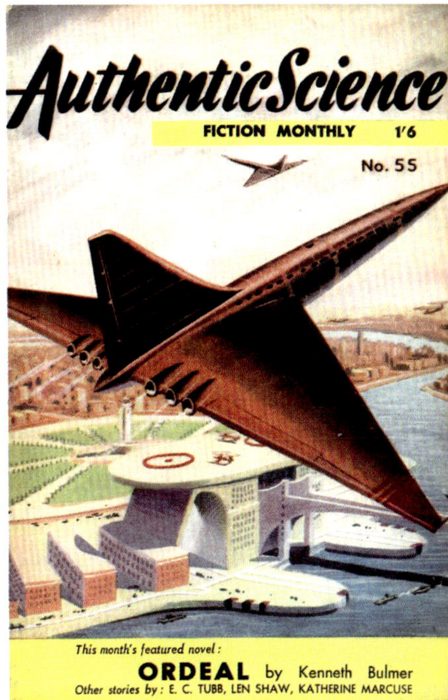

Herbert J. Campbell, ed. | Authentic Science Fiction Monthly #55
Hamilton & Co., 1955 | Art **John Richards**

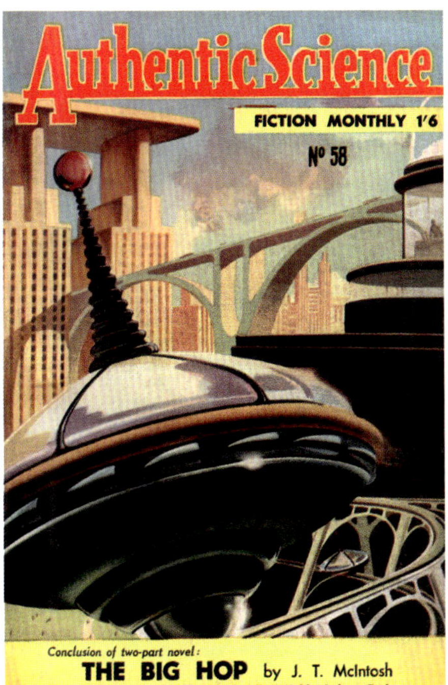

Herbert J. Campbell, ed. | Authentic Science Fiction Monthly #58
Hamilton & Co., 1955 | Art **John Richards**

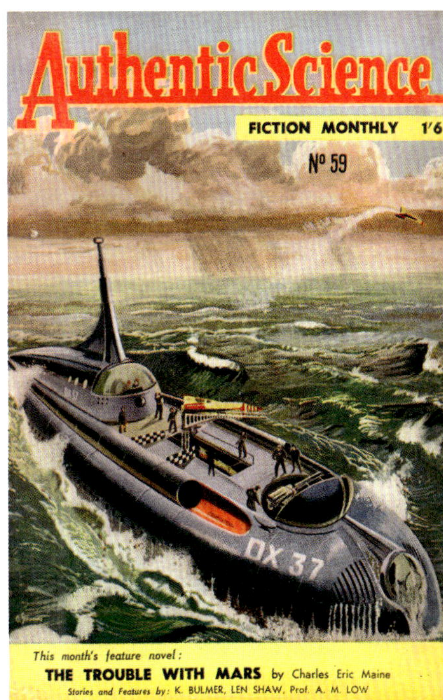

Herbert J. Campbell, ed. | Authentic Science Fiction Monthly #59
Hamilton & Co., 1955 | Art **John Stewart**

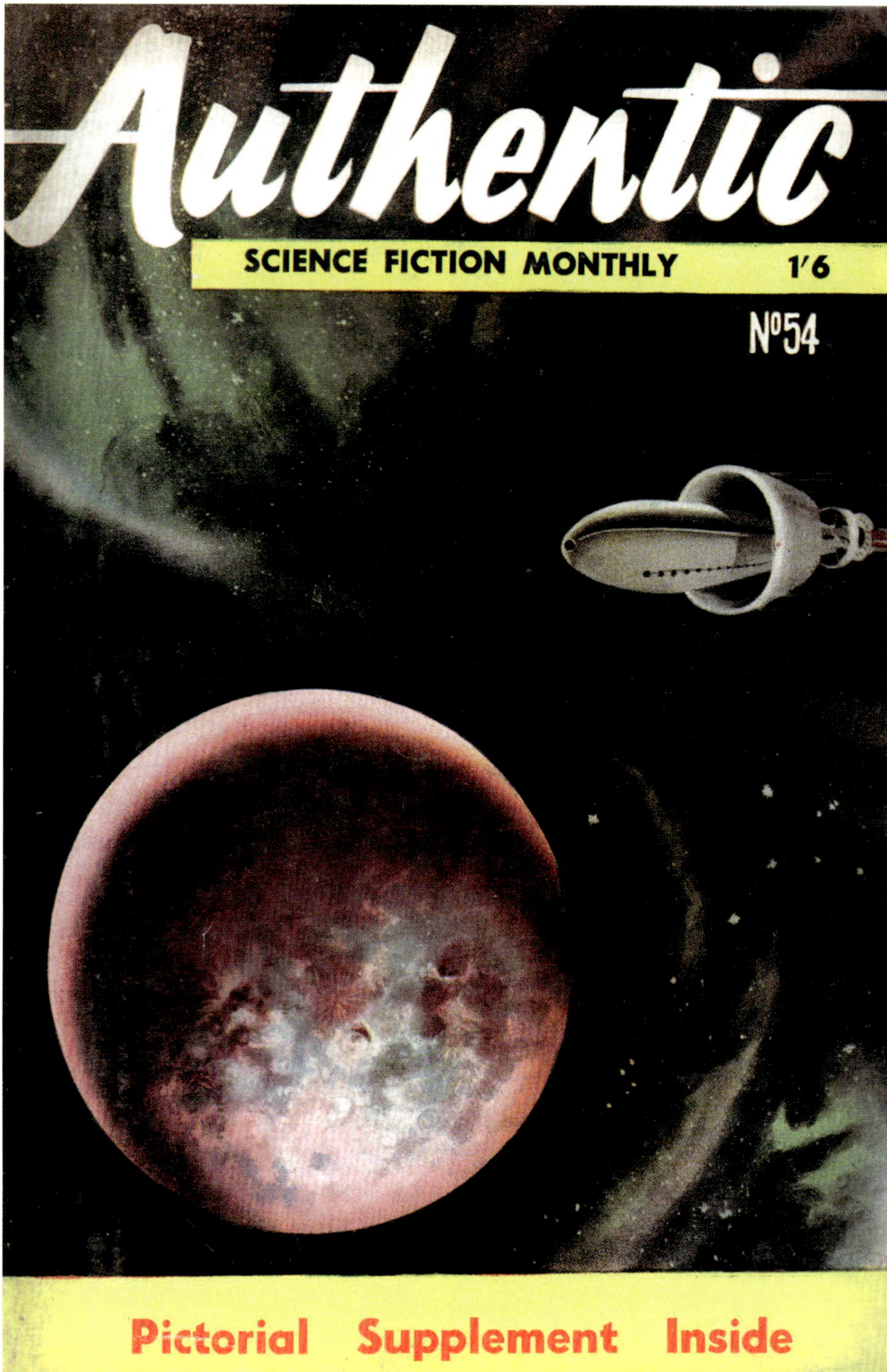

Herbert J. Campbell, ed. | Authentic Science Fiction Monthly #54
Hamilton & Co., 1955 | Art **John Richards** (see page 173)

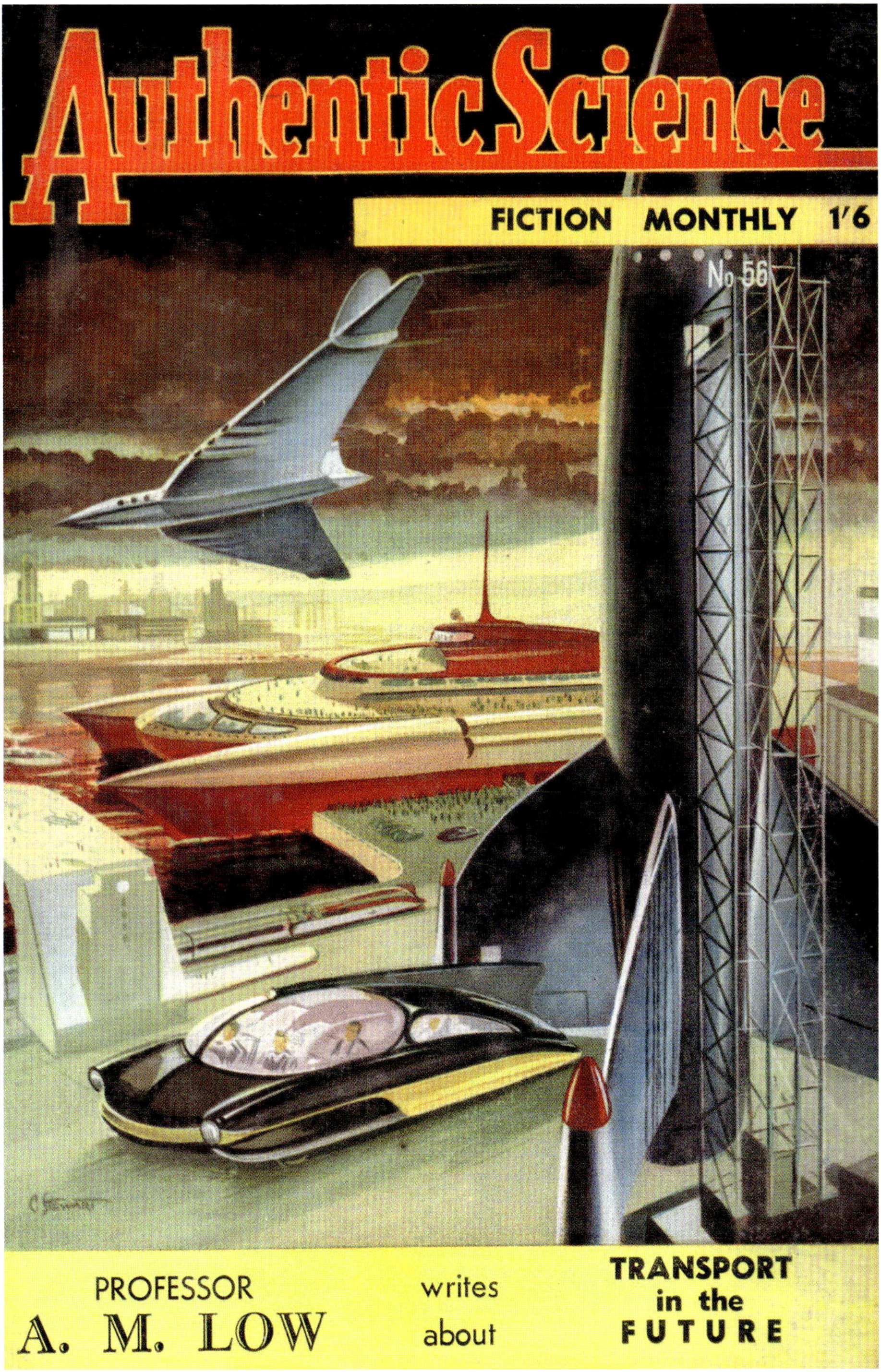

Herbert J. Campbell, ed. | Authentic Science Fiction Monthly #56
Hamilton & Co., 1955 | Art **John Stewart**

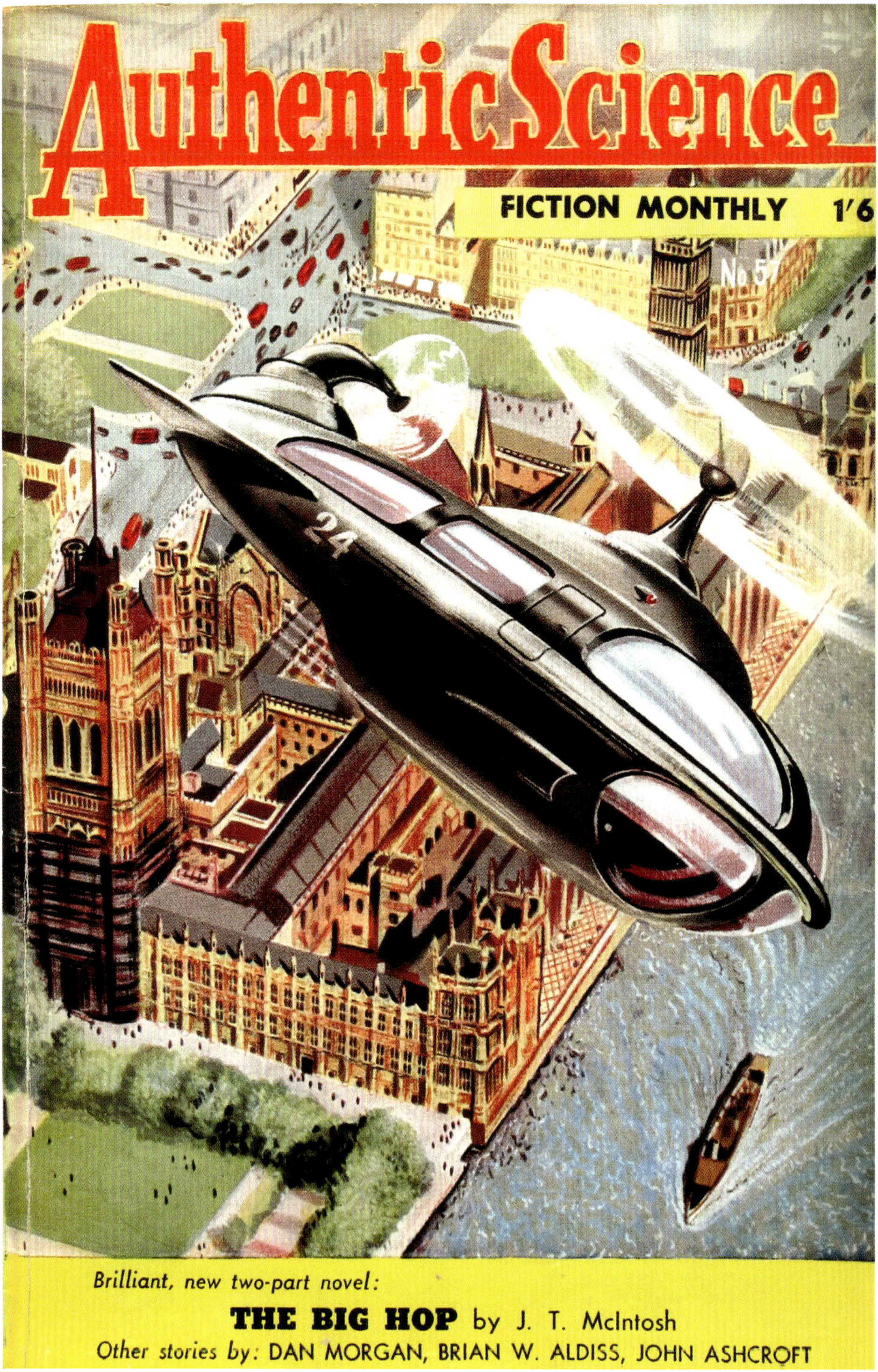

Herbert J. Campbell, ed. | Authentic Science Fiction Monthly #57
Hamilton & Co., 1955 | Art **John Richards**

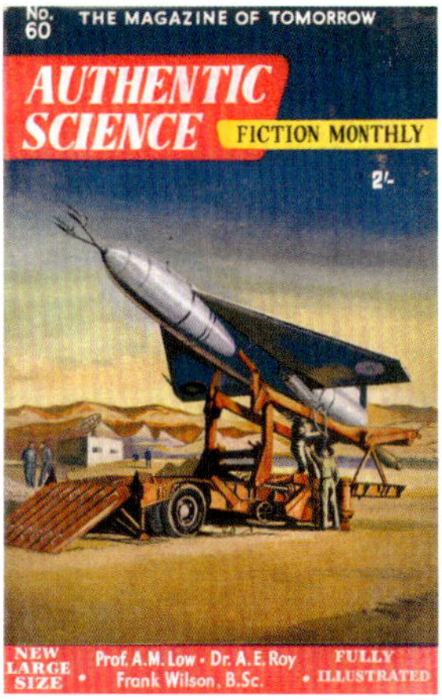

Herbert J. Campbell, ed.
Authentic Science Fiction Monthly #60
Hamilton & Co., 1955 | Art **Slater**

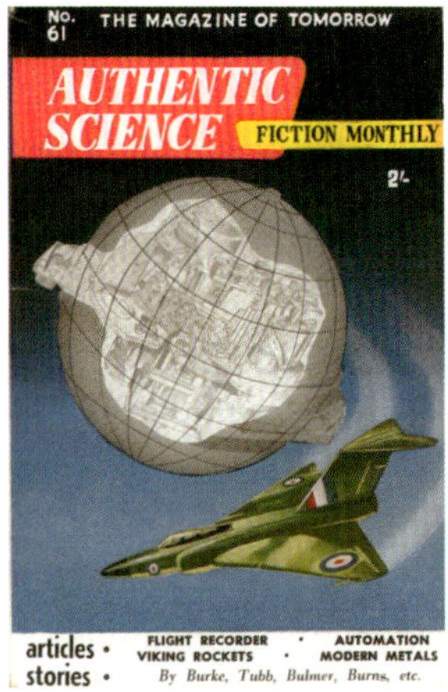

Herbert J. Campbell, ed.
Authentic Science Fiction Monthly #61
Hamilton & Co., 1955 | Art **Unknown**

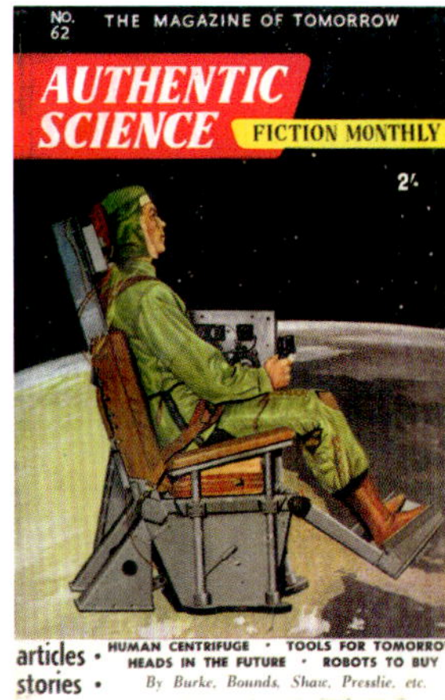

Herbert J. Campbell, ed.
Authentic Science Fiction Monthly #62
Hamilton & Co., 1955 | Art **Derek A. Stowe**

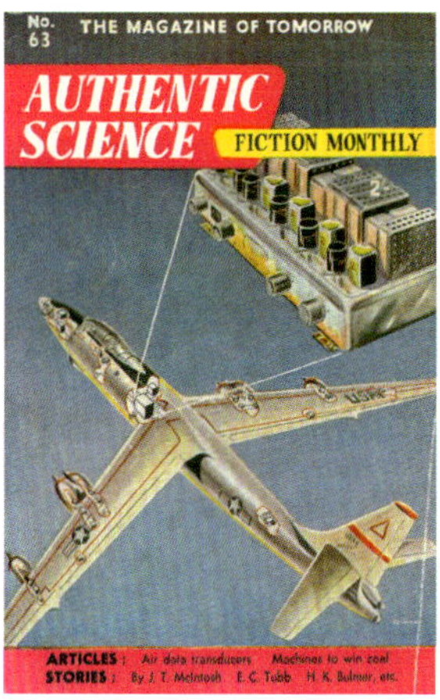

Herbert J. Campbell, ed.
Authentic Science Fiction Monthly #63
Hamilton & Co., 1955 | Art **Gordon C. Davis**

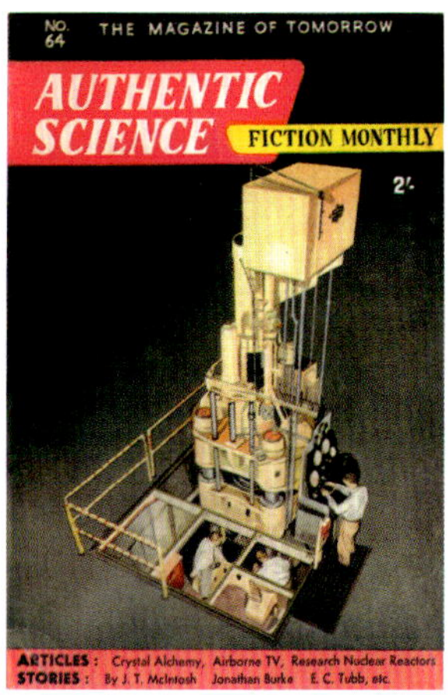

Herbert J. Campbell, ed.
Authentic Science Fiction Monthly #64
Hamilton & Co., 1956 | Art **Derek. A. Stowe**

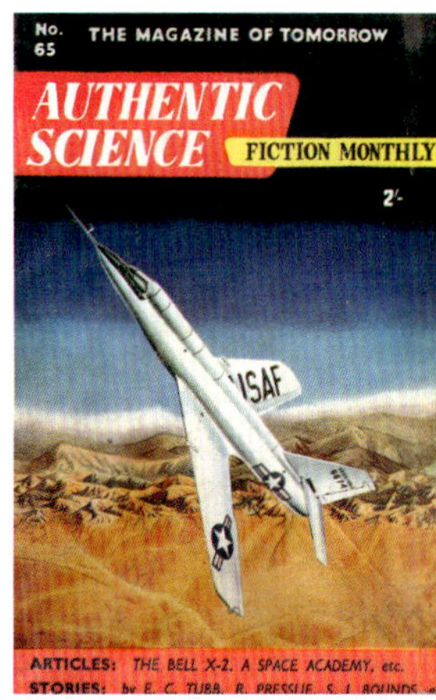

Herbert J. Campbell, ed.
Authentic Science Fiction Monthly #65
Hamilton & Co., 1956 | Art **Ken Woodward**

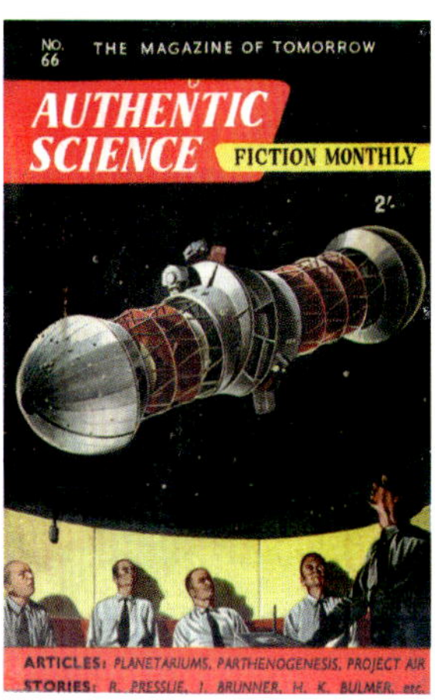

E. C. Tubb, ed.
Authentic Science Fiction Monthly #66
Hamilton & Co., 1956 | Art **Ken Woodward**

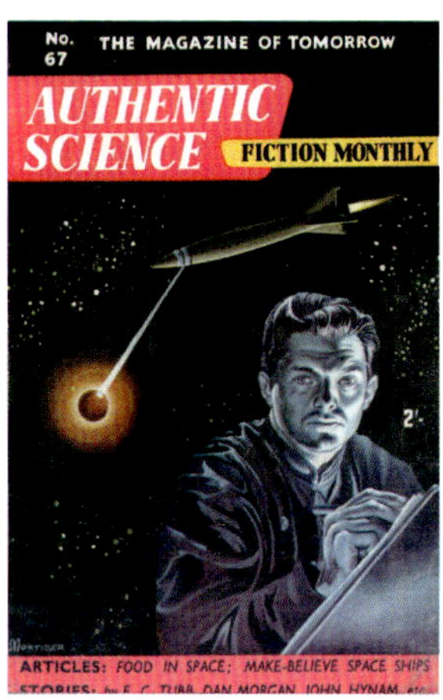

E. C. Tubb, ed.
Authentic Science Fiction Monthly #67
Hamilton & Co., 1956 | Art **John E. Mortimer**

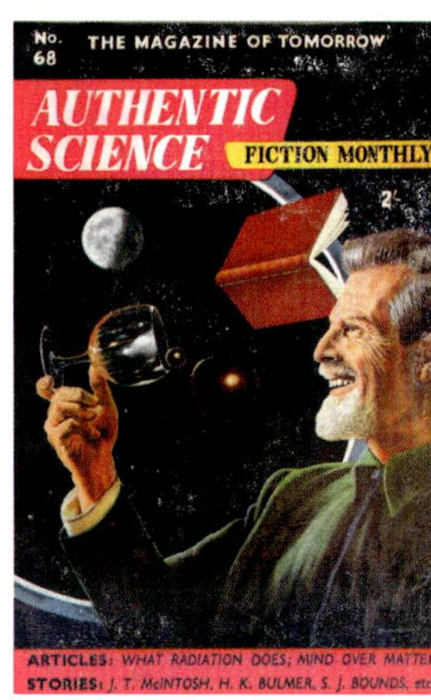

E. C. Tubb, ed.
Authentic Science Fiction #68
Hamilton & Co., 1956 | Art **E. L. Blandford**

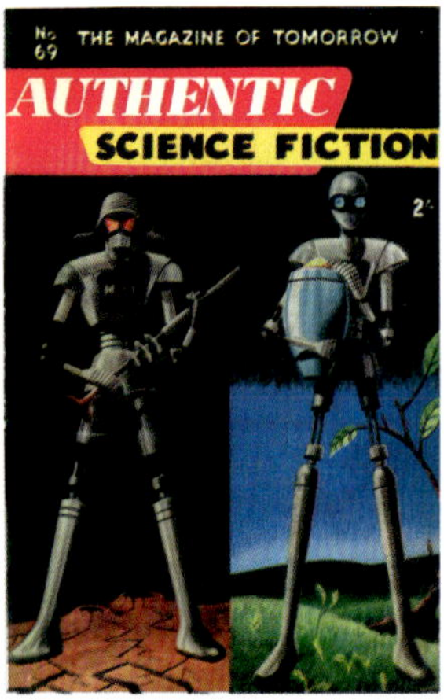

E. C. Tubb, ed. | Authentic Science Fiction #69
Hamilton & Co., 1956 | Art **John E. Mortimer**

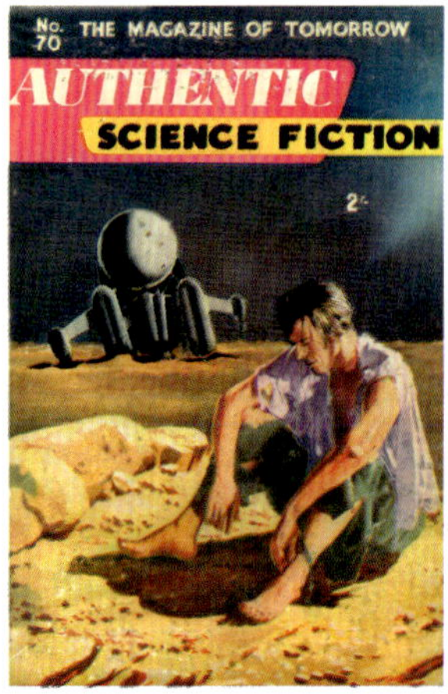

E. C. Tubb, ed. | Authentic Science Fiction #70
Hamilton & Co., 1956 | Art **E. L. Blandford**

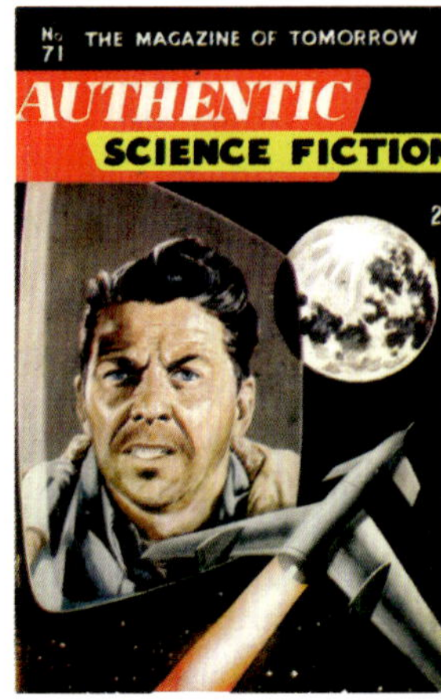

E. C. Tubb, ed. | Authentic Science Fiction #71
Hamilton & Co., 1956 | Art **E. L. Blandford**

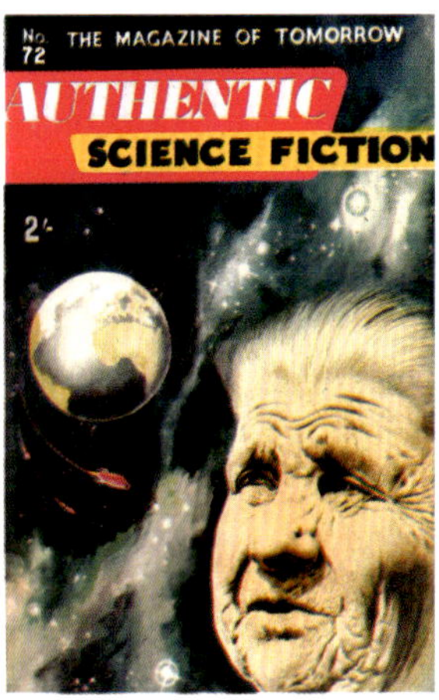

E. C. Tubb, ed. | Authentic Science Fiction #72
Hamilton & Co., 1956 | Art **E. L. Blandford**

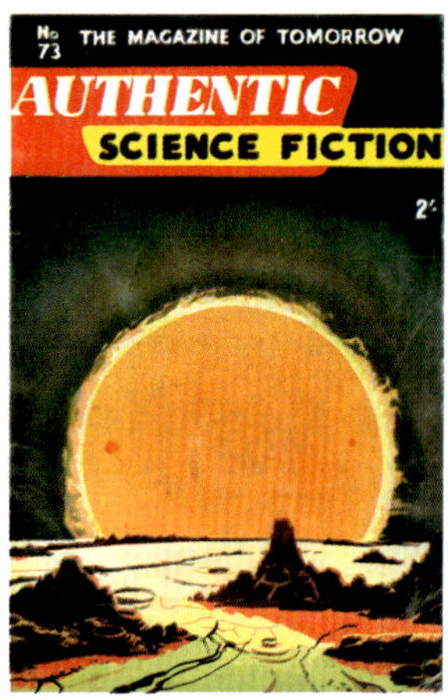

E. C. Tubb, ed. | Authentic Science Fiction #73
Hamilton & Co., 1956 | Art **E. L. Blandford**

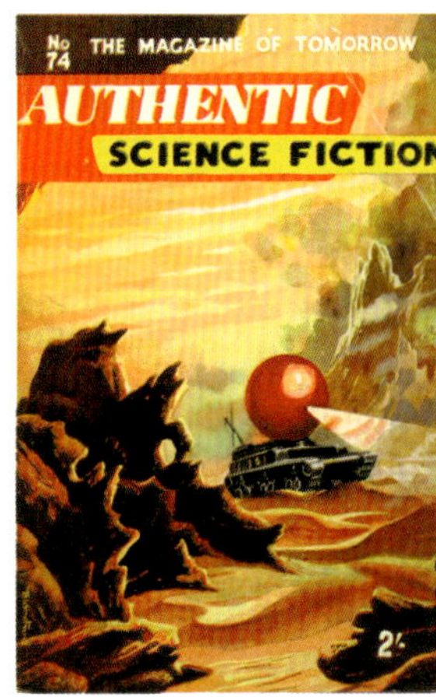

E. C. Tubb, ed. | Authentic Science Fiction #74
Hamilton & Co., 1956 | Art **E. L. Blandford**

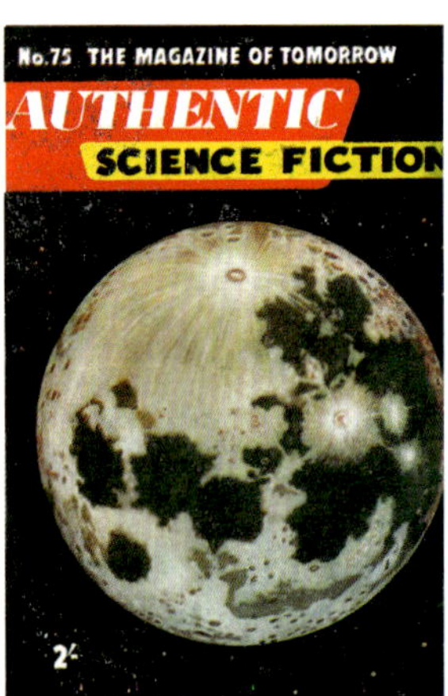

E. C. Tubb, ed. | Authentic Science Fiction #75
Hamilton & Co., 1956 | Art **John E. Mortimer**

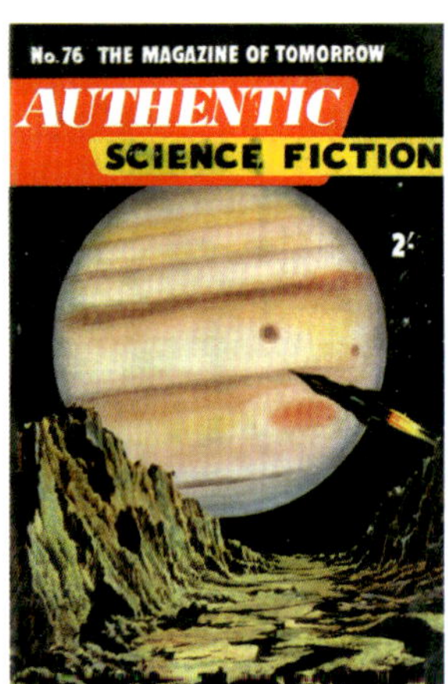

E. C. Tubb, ed. | Authentic Science Fiction #76
Hamilton & Co., 1957 | Art **E. L. Blandford**

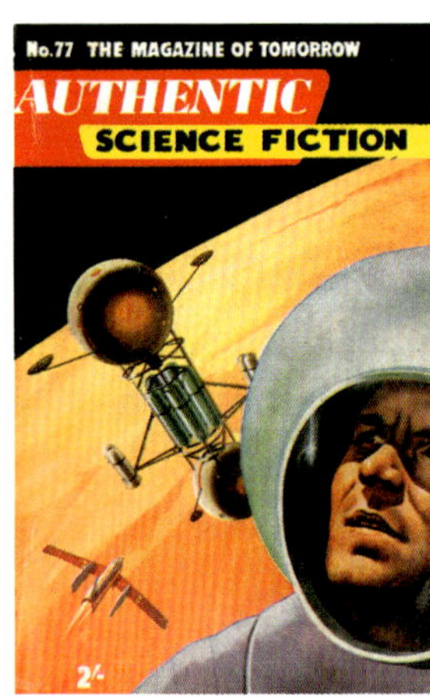

E. C. Tubb, ed. | Authentic Science Fiction #77
Hamilton & Co., 1957 | Art **E. L. Blandford**

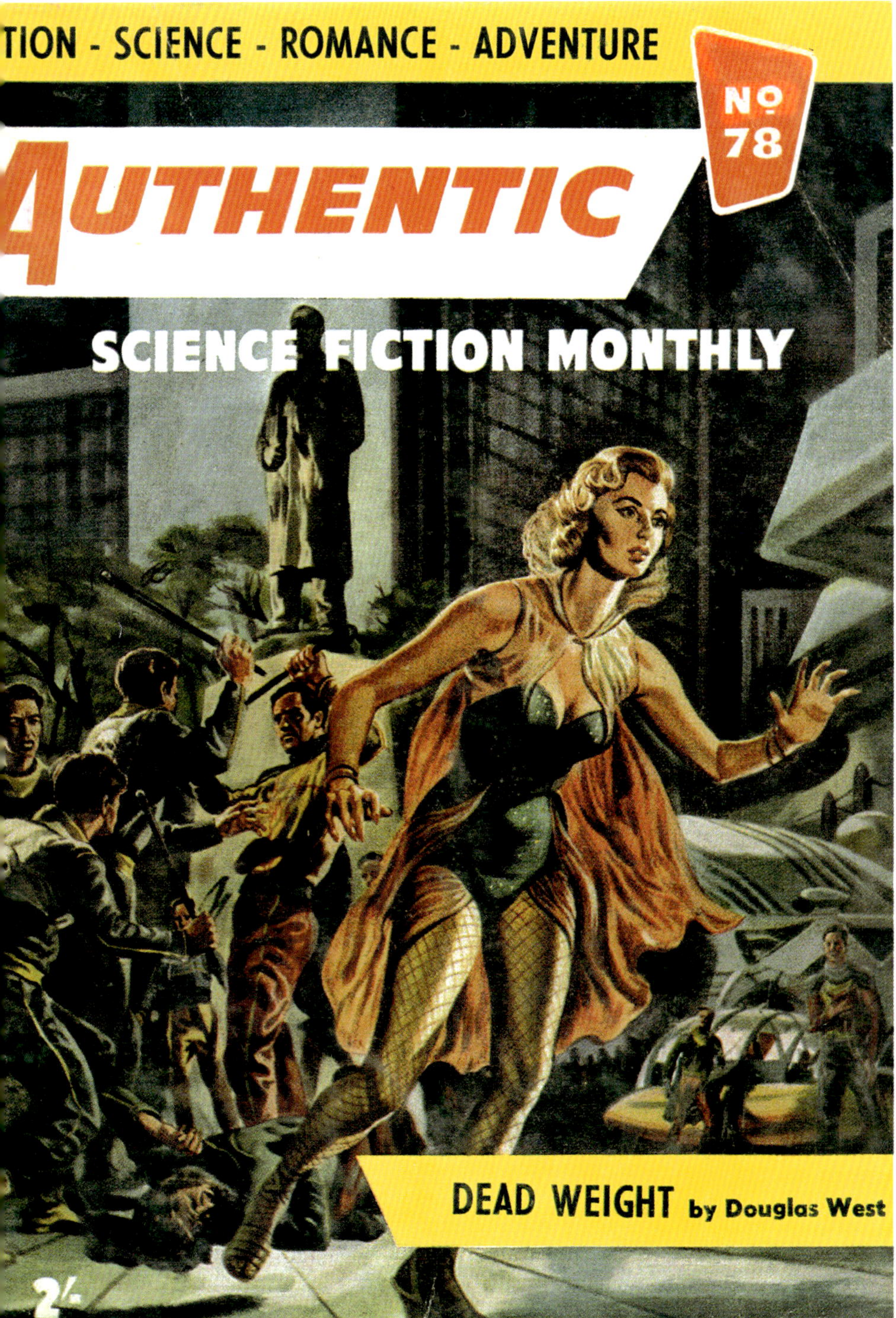

E. C. Tubb, ed. | Authentic Science Fiction Monthly #78
Hamilton & Co., 1957 | Art **Josh Kirby**

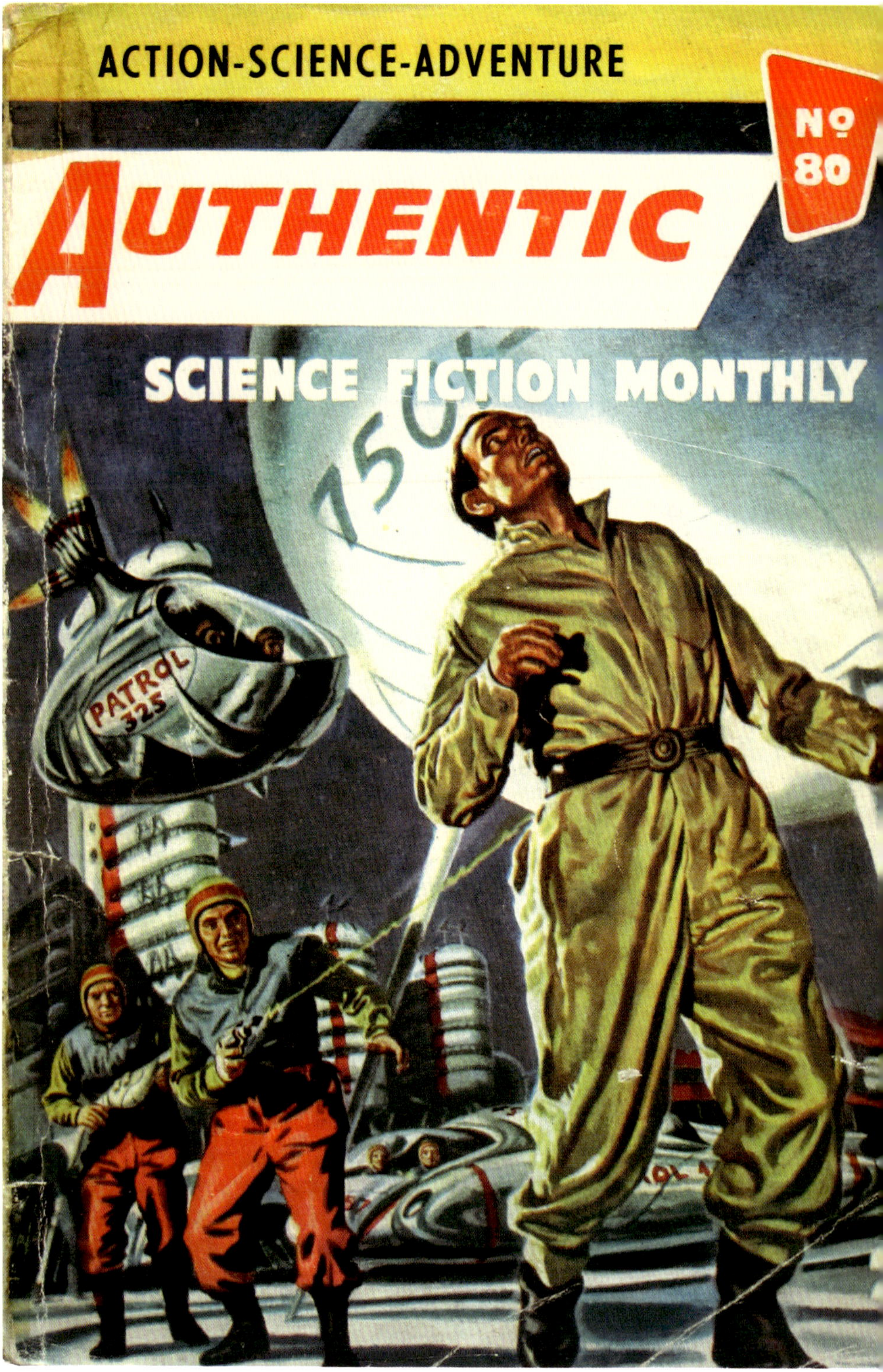

E. C. Tubb, ed. | Authentic Science Fiction Monthly #80
Hamilton & Co., 1957 | Art **Josh Kirby**

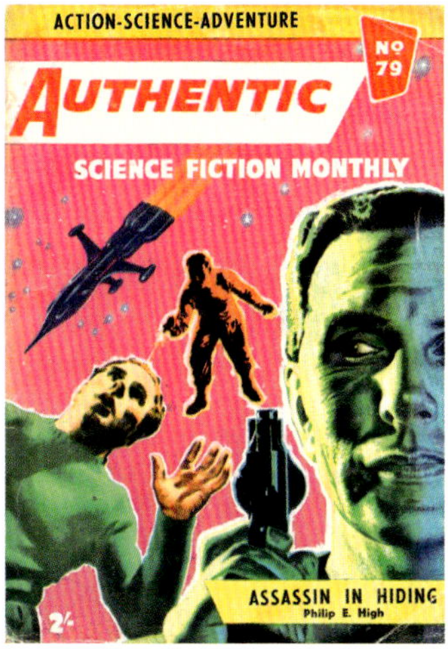

E. C. Tubb, ed. | Authentic Science Fiction #79
Hamilton & Co., 1957 | Art **E. L. Blandford**

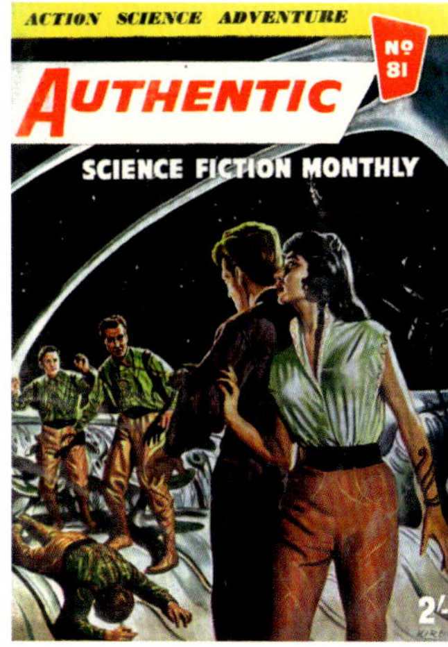

E. C. Tubb, ed. | Authentic Science Fiction Monthly #81
Hamilton & Co., 1957 | Art **Josh Kirby**

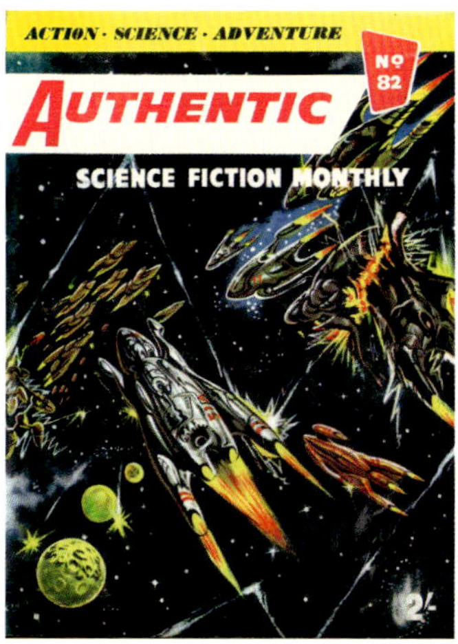

E. C. Tubb, ed. | Authentic Science Fiction Monthly #82
Hamilton & Co., 1957 | Art **Josh Kirby**

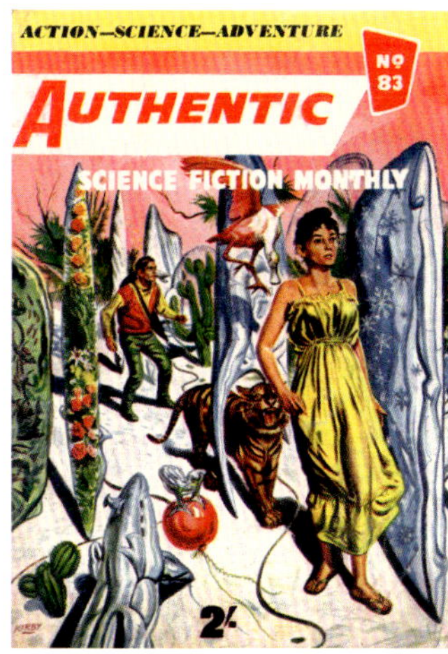

E. C. Tubb, ed. | Authentic Science Fiction Monthly #83
Hamilton & Co., 1957 | Art **Josh Kirby**

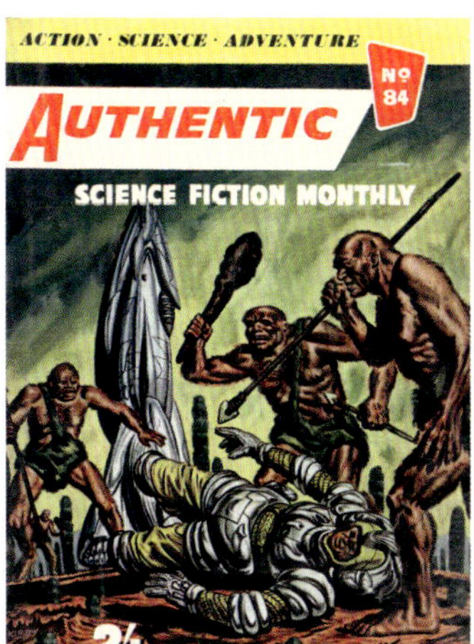

E. C. Tubb, ed. | Authentic Science Fiction Monthly #84
Hamilton & Co., 1957 | Art **Josh Kirby**

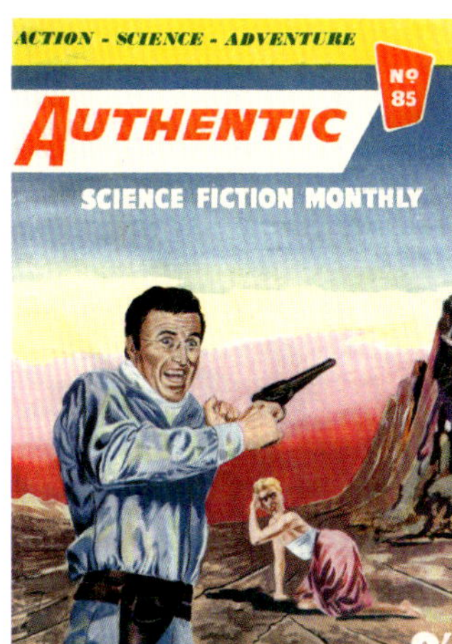

E. C. Tubb, ed. | Authentic Science Fiction Monthly #85
Hamilton & Co., 1957 | Art **P. R. Green**

opposite **Jack Coggins and Fletcher Pratt** | *By Space Ship to the Moon*
Publicity Products, 1952 | Art **Jack Coggins**

H. J. Campbell, ed. | *Authentic Science Book of Space*
Hamilton & Co., 1954 | Art **John Richards**

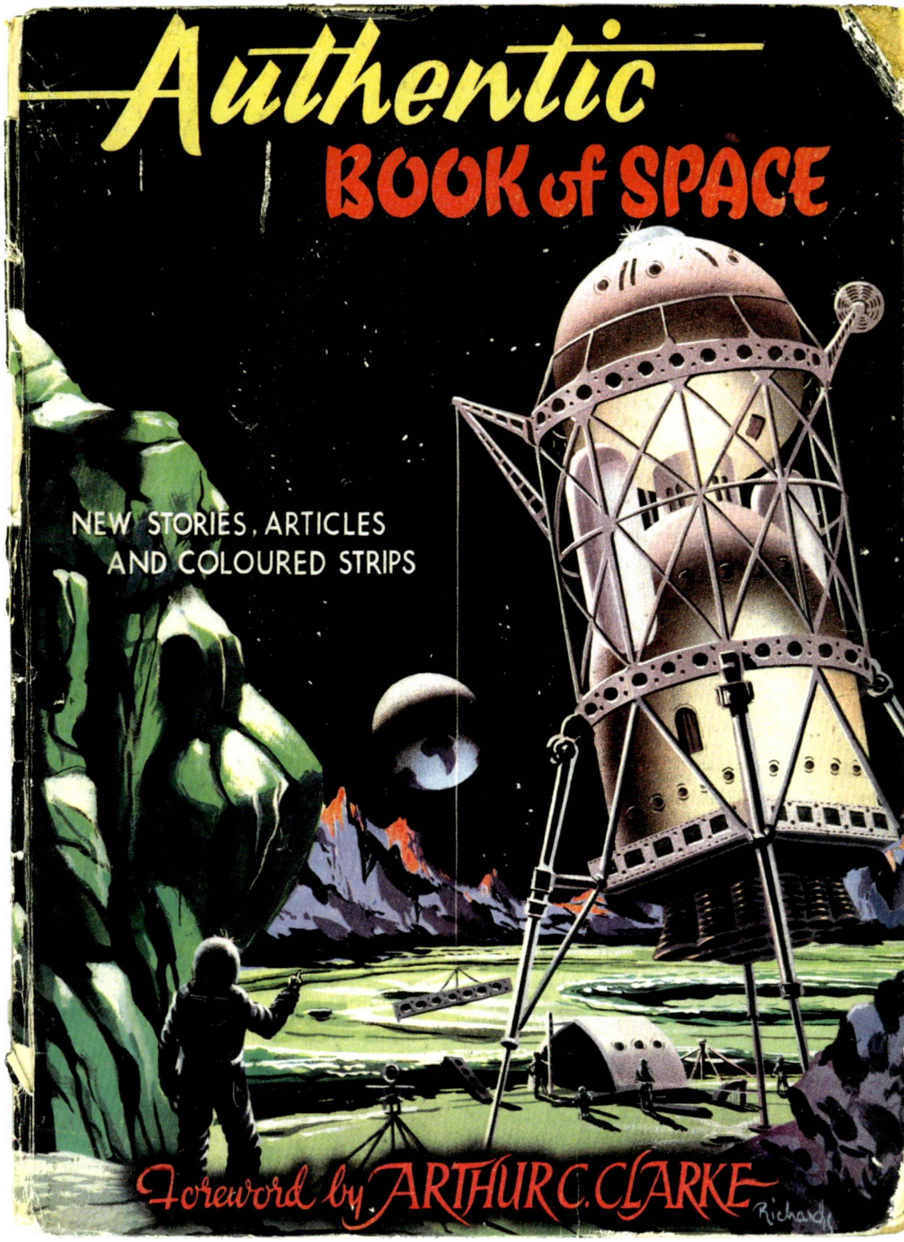

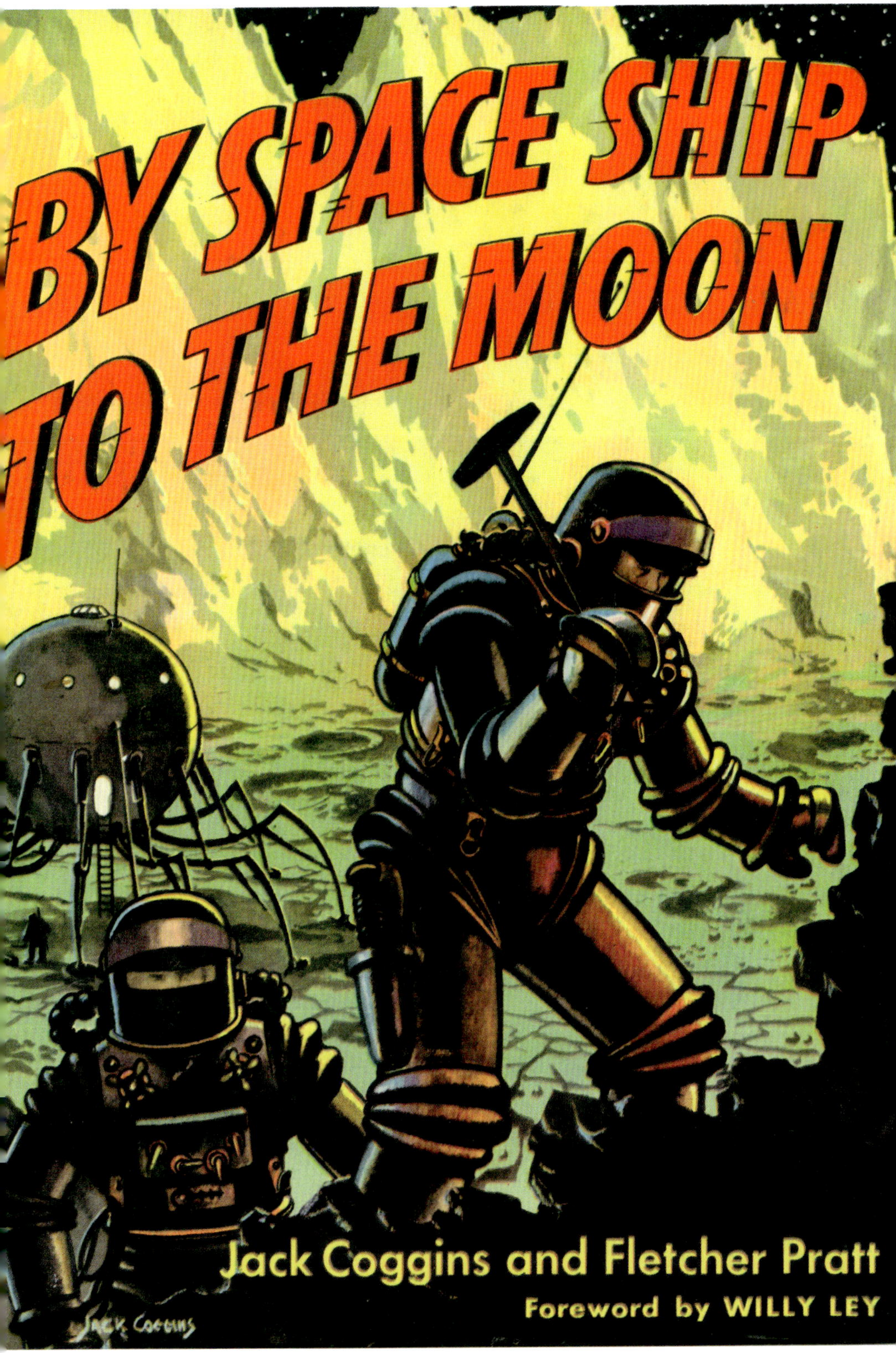
BY SPACE SHIP TO THE MOON
Jack Coggins and Fletcher Pratt
Foreword by WILLY LEY
JACK COGGINS

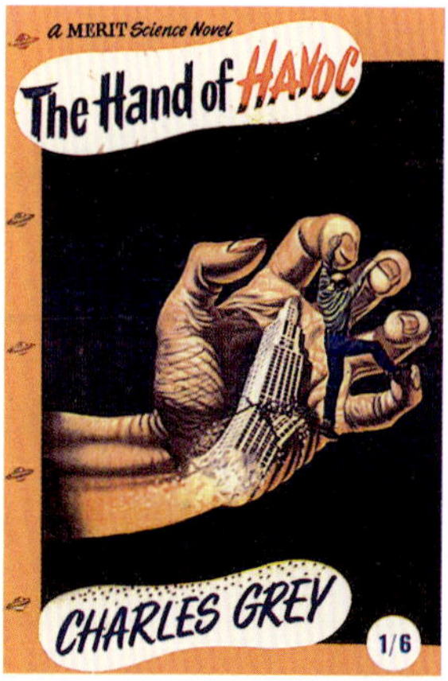

Charles Grey (E. C. Tubb) | *The Hand of Havoc*
Merit Books (Milestone), 1954 | Art **Ron Turner**

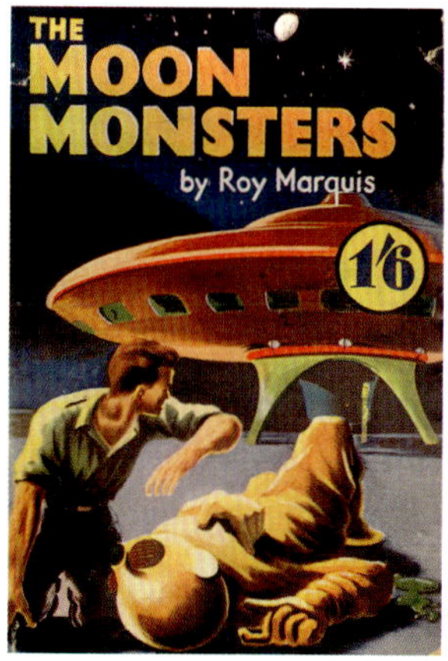

Roy Marquis | *The Moon Monsters*
Barrington Gray, 1951 | Art **Unknown**

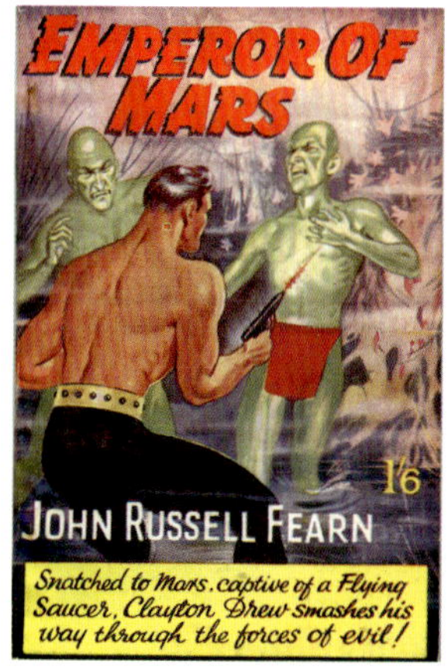

John Russell Fearn | *Emperor of Mars*
Hamiltons, 1950 | Art **Terry Maloney**

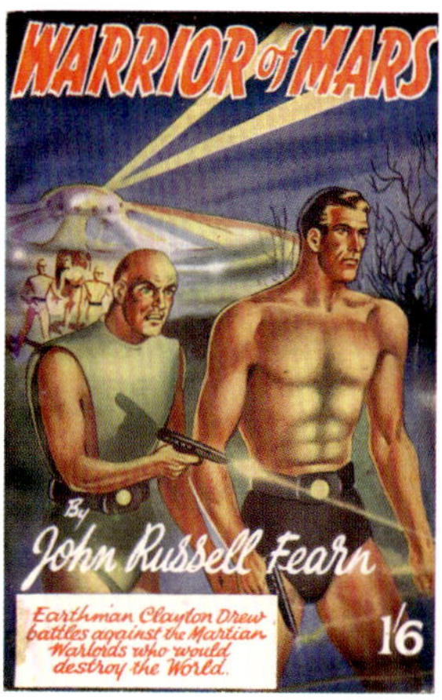

John Russell Fearn | *Warrior of Mars*
Hamiltons, 1950 | Art **Terry Maloney**

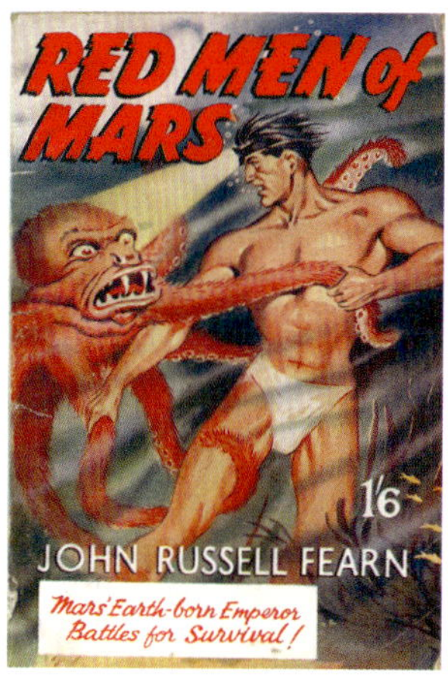

John Russell Fearn | *Red Men of Mars*
Hamiltons, 1950 | Art **Terry Maloney**

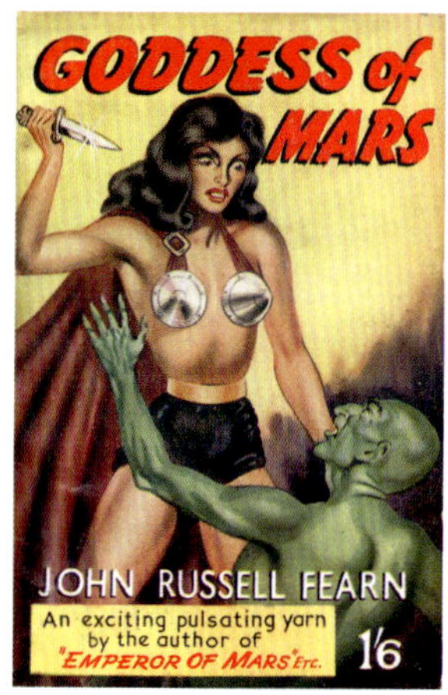

John Russell Fearn | *Goddess of Mars*
Hamiltons, 1950 | Art **Terry Maloney**

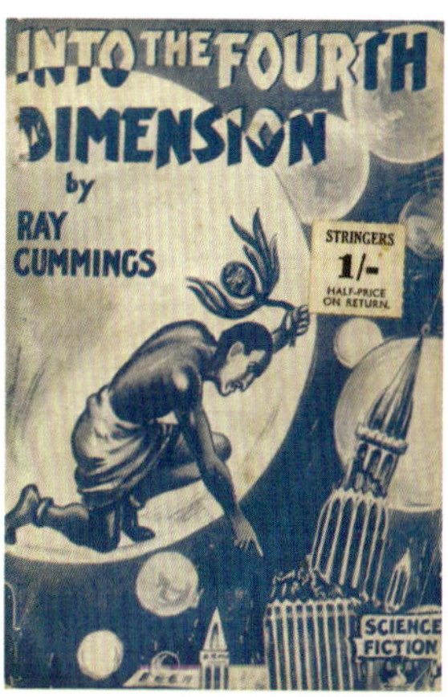

Ray Cummings | *Into the Fourth Dimension*
Gerald G. Swan, 1942 | Art **Jock McCail**

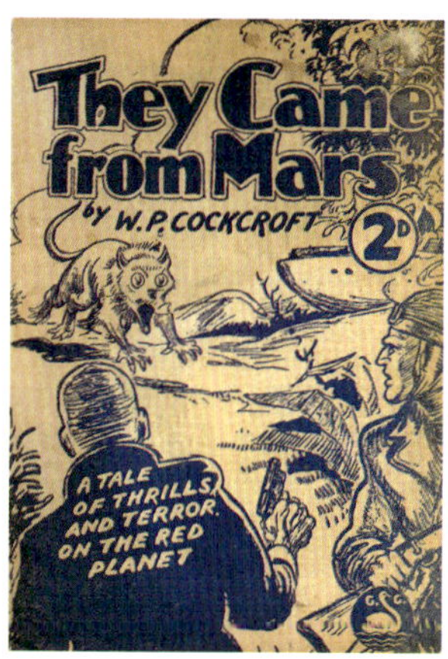

W. P. Cockroft | *They Came From Mars*
Gerald G. Swan, 1944 | Art **Jock McCail**

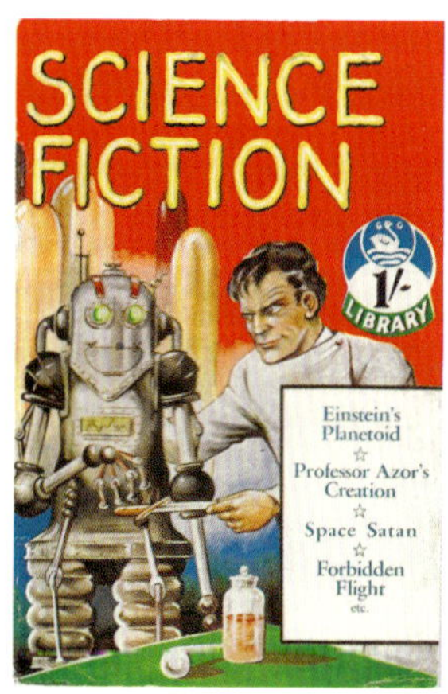

Science Fiction #1
Gerald G. Swan, 1960 | Art **David Williams**

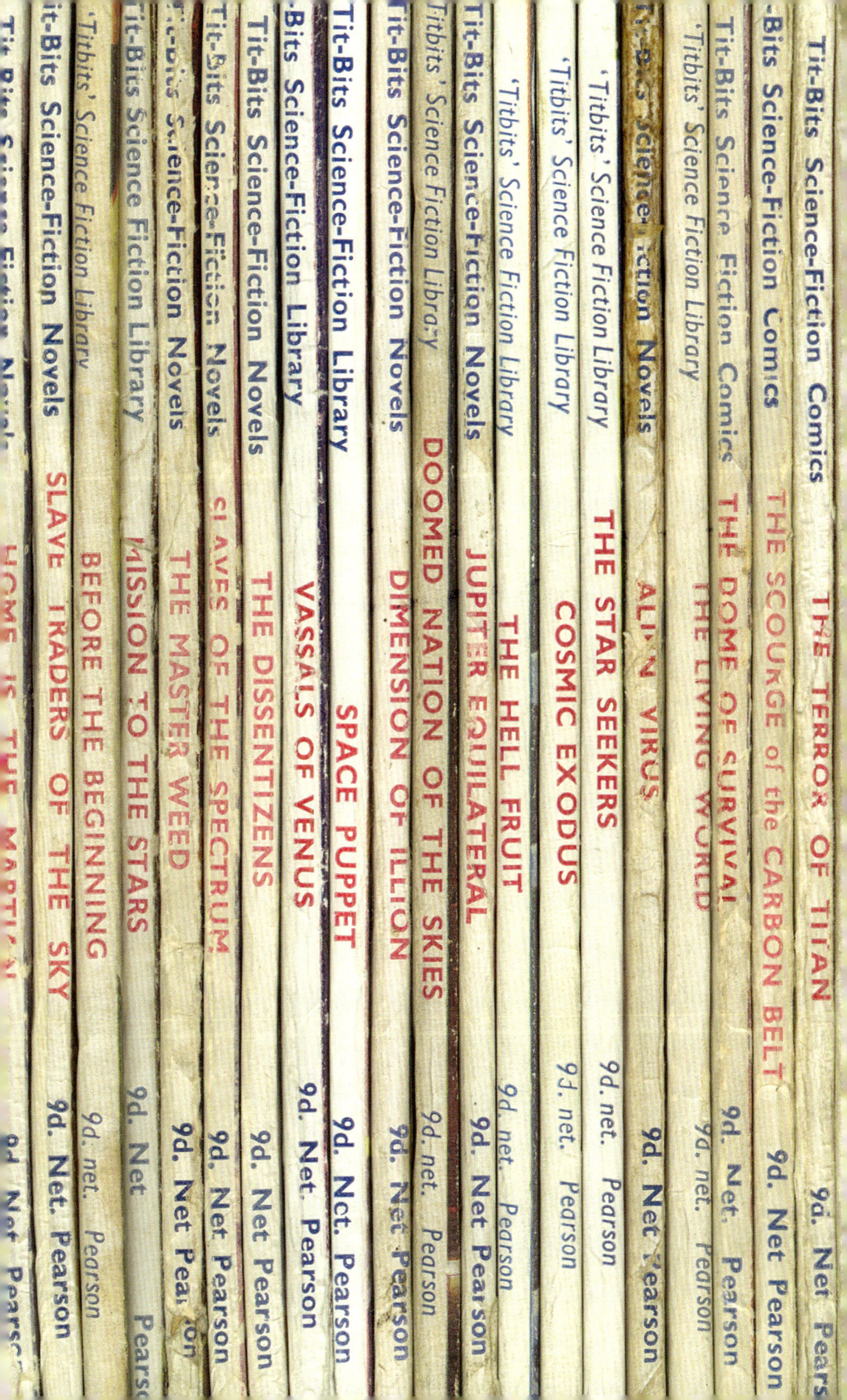
Tit-Bits Science-Fiction Novels
SLAVE TRADERS OF THE SKY
9d. Net. Pearson
'Titbits' Science Fiction Library
BEFORE THE BEGINNING
9d. net. Pearson
Tit-Bits Science Fiction Library
MISSION TO THE STARS
9d. Net
Tit-Bits Science-Fiction Novels
THE MASTER WEED
9d. Net
Tit-Bits Science-Fiction Novels
SLAVES OF THE SPECTRUM
9d. Net Pearson
Tit-Bits Science-Fiction Novels
THE DISSENTIZENS
9d. Net Pearson
Tit-Bits Science-Fiction Library
VASSALS OF VENUS
9d. Net. Pearson
Tit-Bits Science-Fiction Library
SPACE PUPPET
9d. Nct. Pearson
Tit-Bits Science-Fiction Novels
DIMENSION OF ILLION
9d. Net Pearson
'Titbits' Science Fiction Library
DOOMED NATION OF THE SKIES
9d. net. Pearson
Tit-Bits Science-Fiction Novels
JUPITER EQUILATERAL
9d. Net Pearson
'Titbits' Science Fiction Library
THE HELL FRUIT
9d. net. Pearson
'Titbits' Science Fiction Library
COSMIC EXODUS
9d. net. Pearson
'Titbits' Science Fiction Library
THE STAR SEEKERS
9d. net. Pearson
Novels
VIRUS
9d. Net
'Titbits' Science Fiction Library
THE LIVING WORLD
9d. net. Pearson
Tit-Bits Science Fiction Comics
THE DOME OF SURVIVAL
9d. Net. Pearson
Tit-Bits Science-Fiction Comics
THE SCOURGE of the CARBON BELT
9d. Net Pearson
Tit-Bits Science-Fiction Comics
THE TERROR OF TITAN
9d. Net

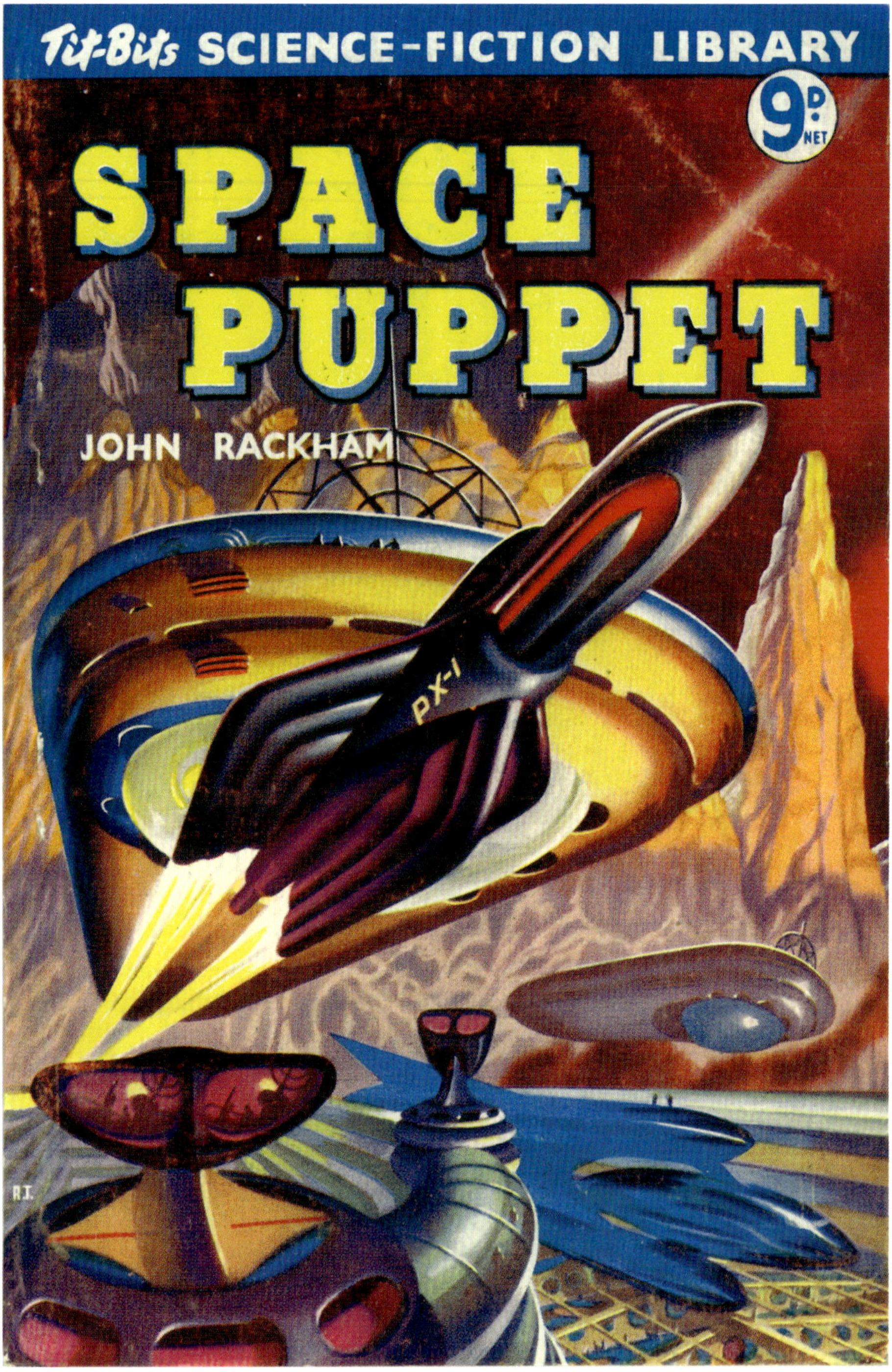

John Rackham (John T. Phillifent) | *Space Puppet*
Tit-Bits Science Fiction Library, 1954 | Art **Ron Turner**

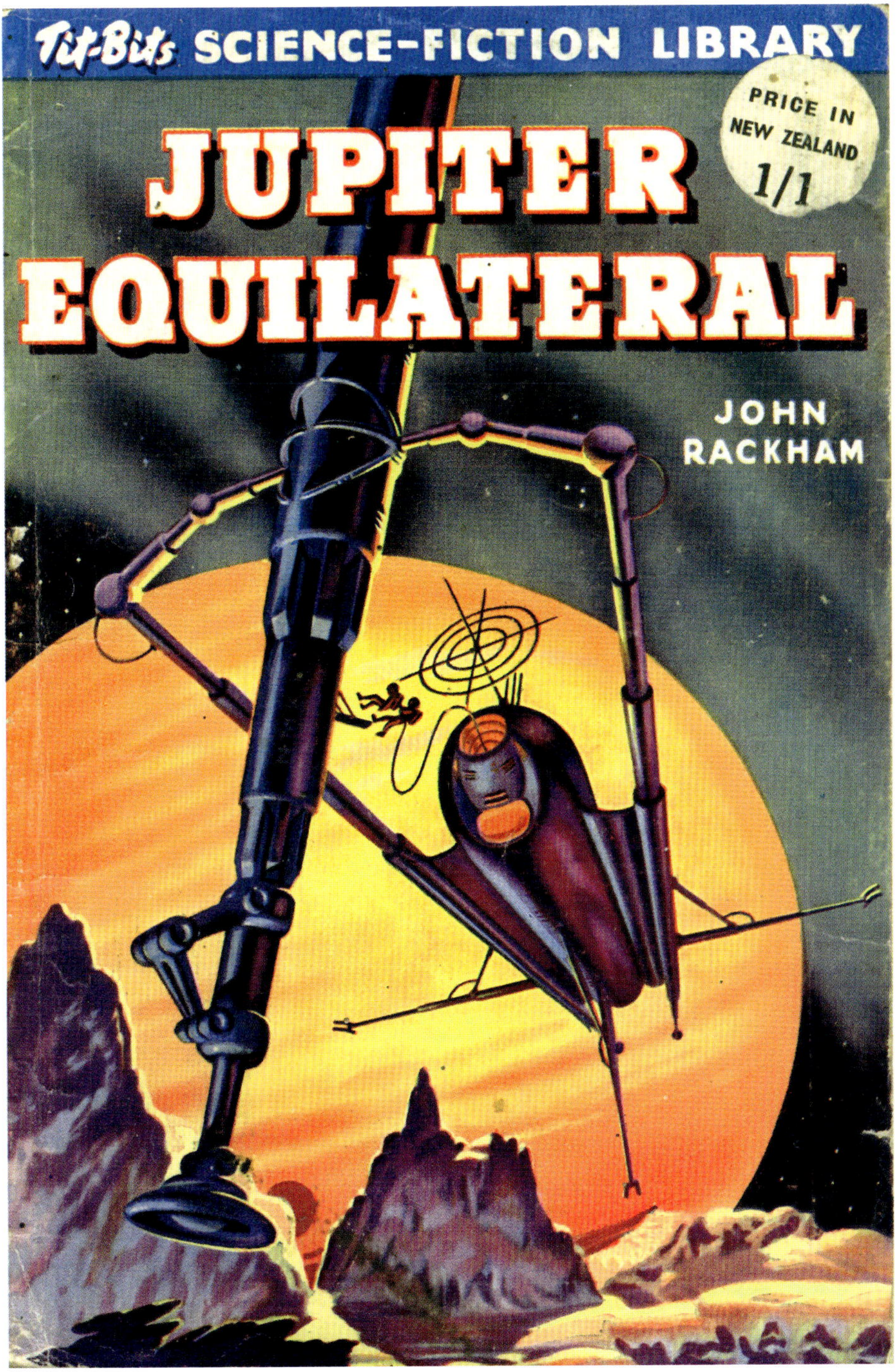

John Rackham (John T. Phillifent) | *Jupiter Equilateral*
Tit-Bits Science Fiction Library, 1954 | Art **Ron Turner**

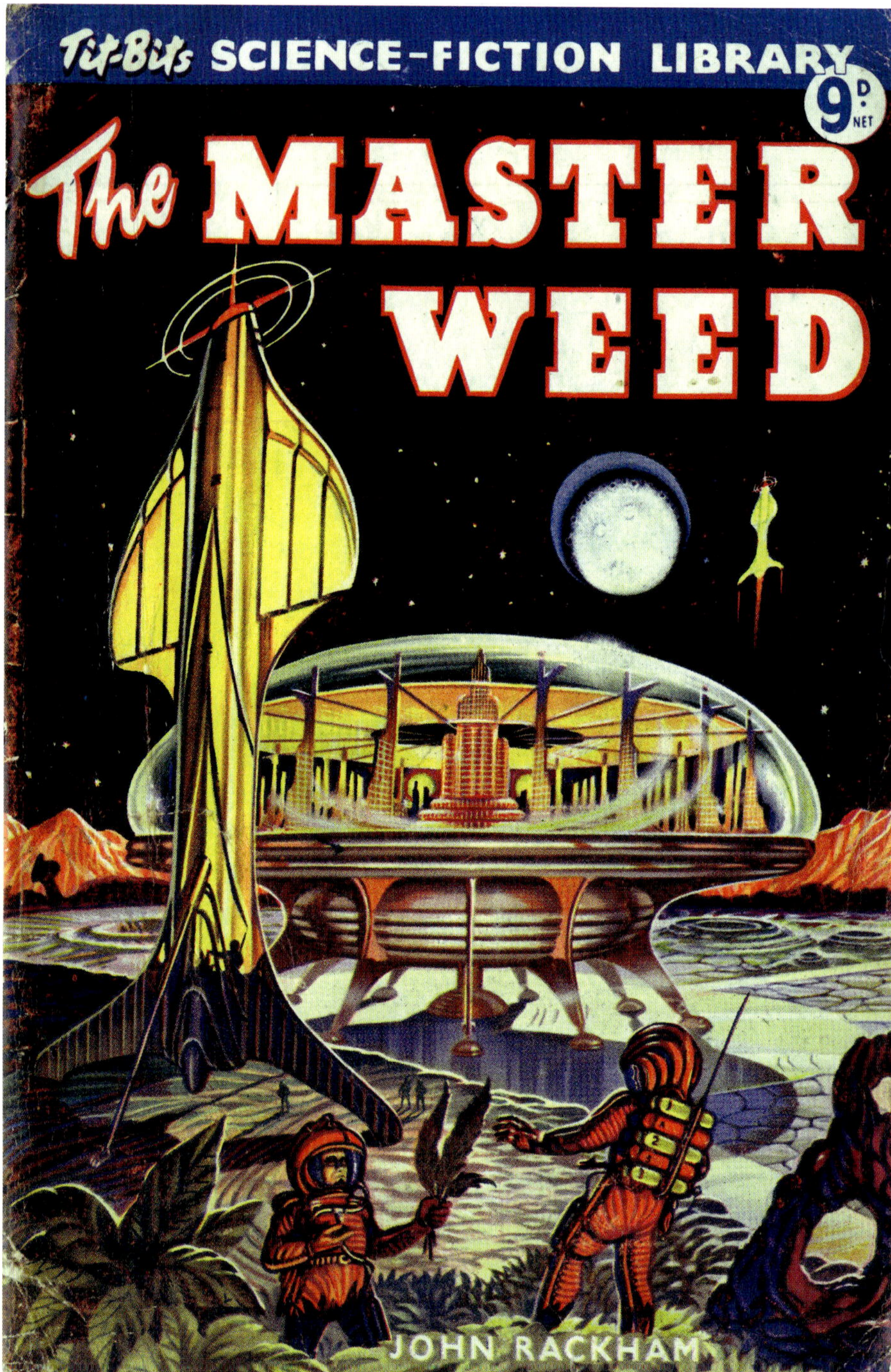

John Rackham (John T. Phillifent) | *The Master Weed*
Tit-Bits Science Fiction Library, 1954 | Art **Ron Turner**

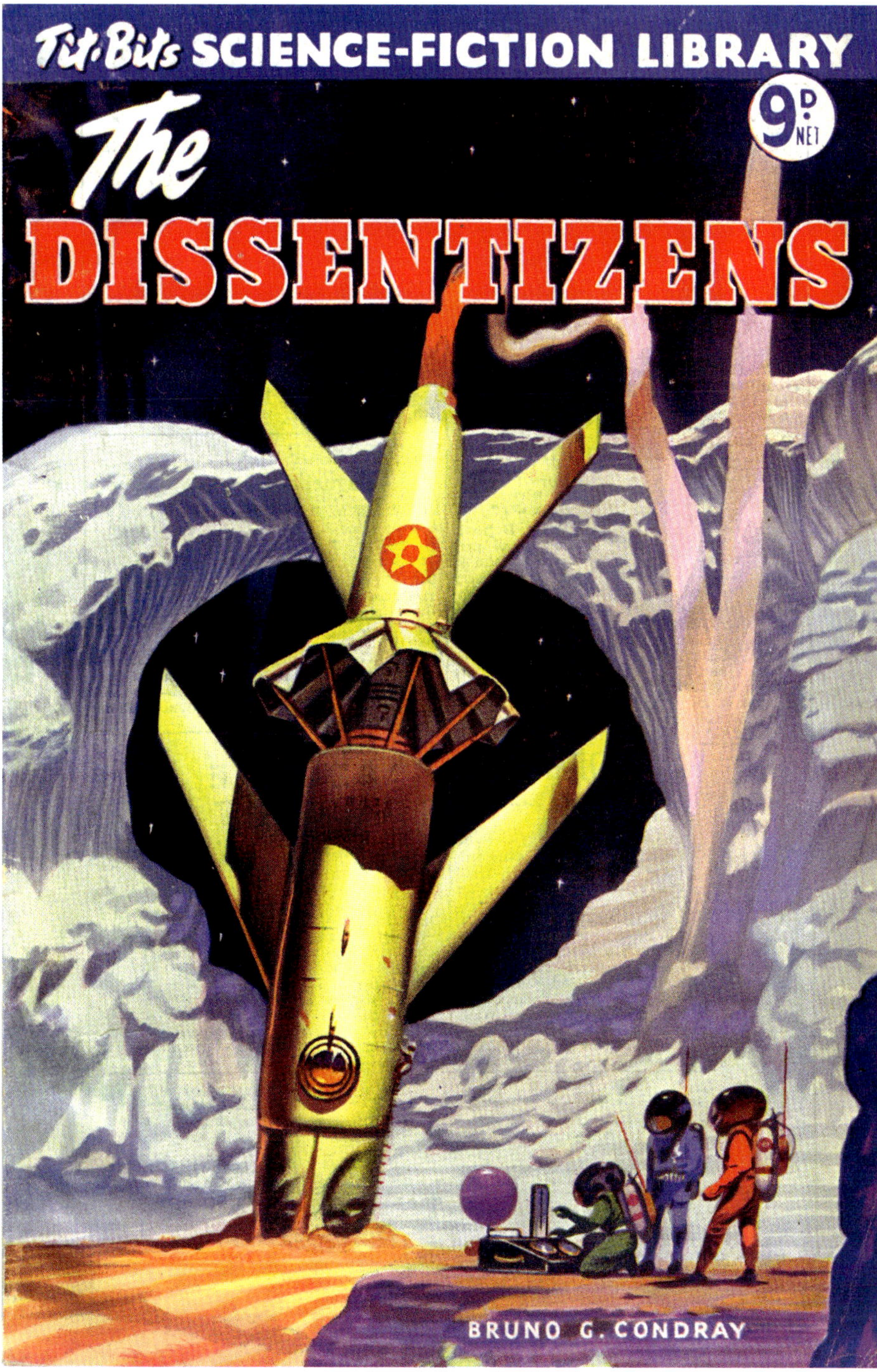

Bruno G. Condray (Leslie G. Humphrys) | *The Dissentizens*
Tit-Bits Science Fiction Library, 1954 | Art **Ron Turner**

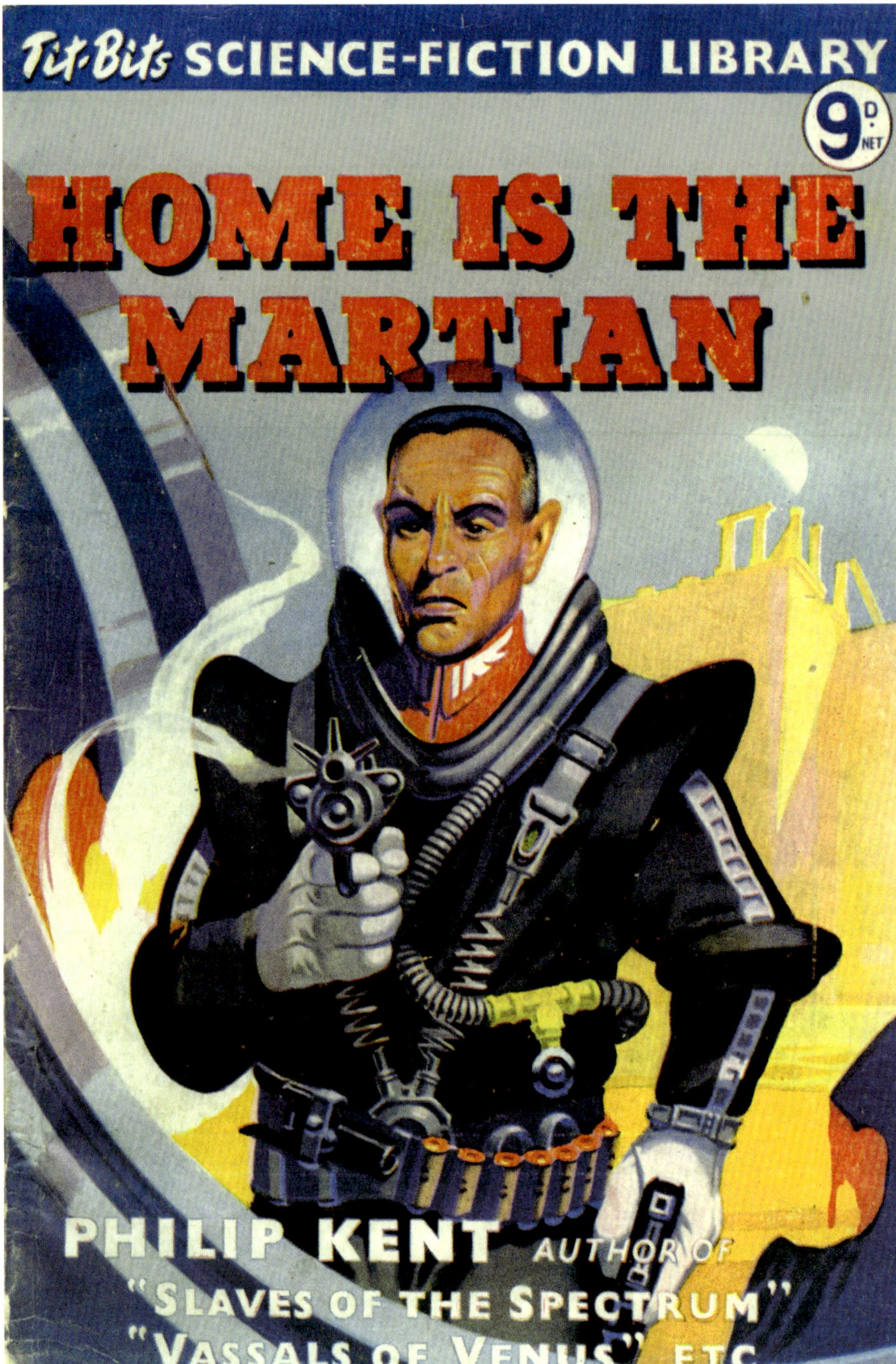

Philip Kent (H. K. Bulmer) | *Home Is the Martian*
Tit-Bits Science Fiction Library, 1954 | Art **Ron Turner**

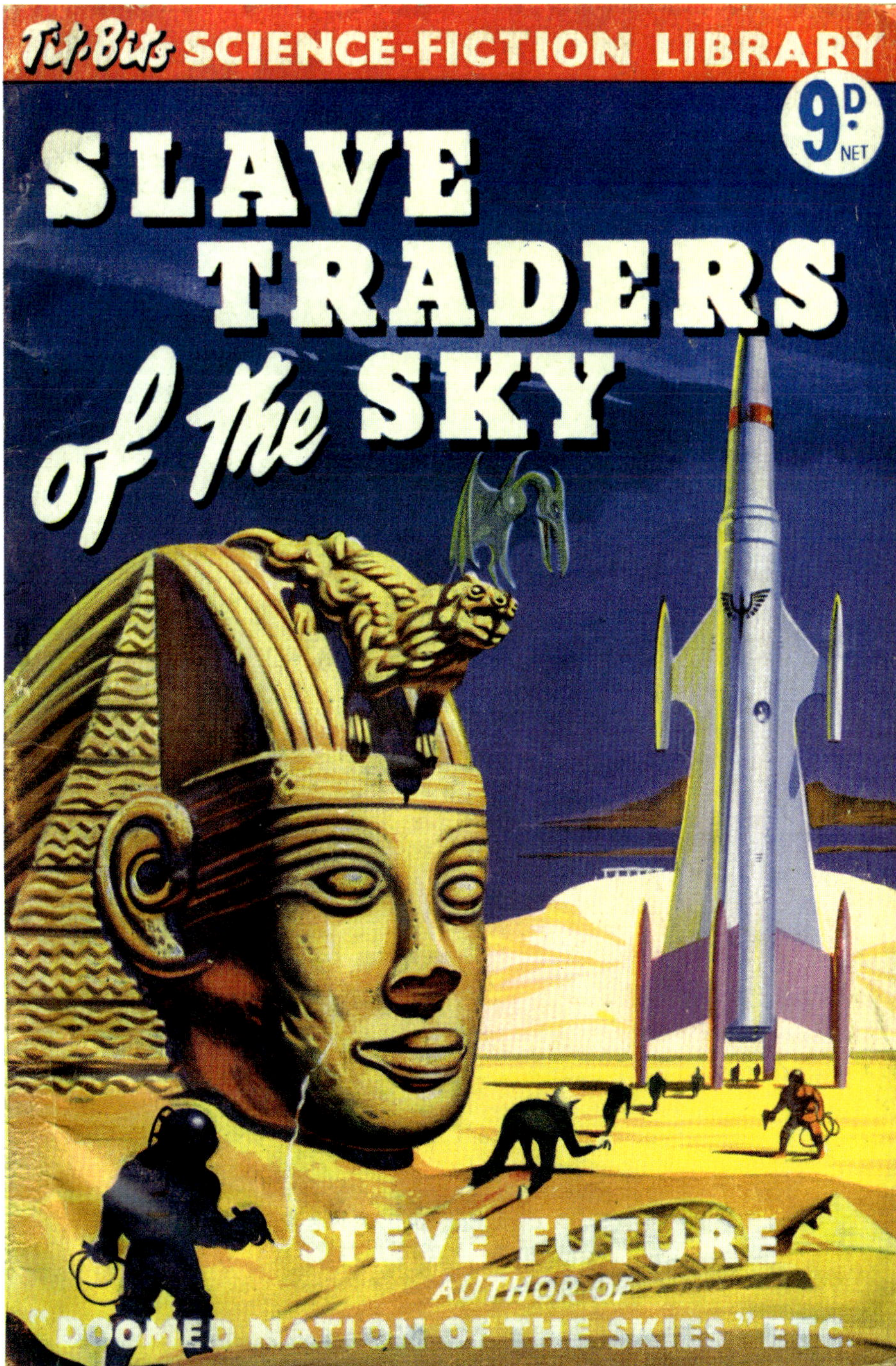

Steve Future | *Slave Traders of the Sky*
Tit-Bits Science Fiction Library, 1954 | Art **Ron Turner**

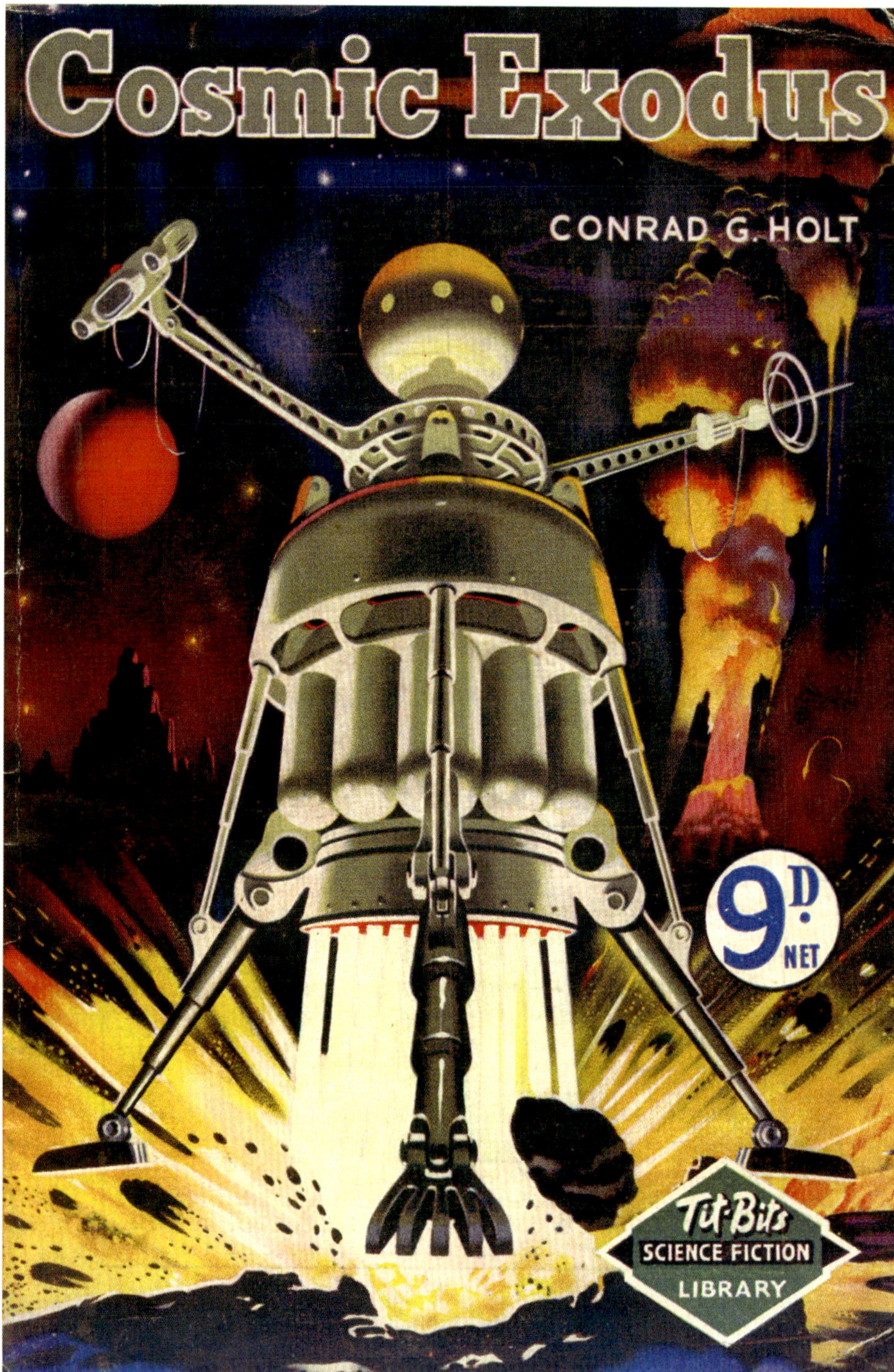

Conrad G. Holt (John Russell Fearn) | *Cosmic Exodus*
Tit-Bits Science Fiction Library, 1953 | Art **Ron Turner**

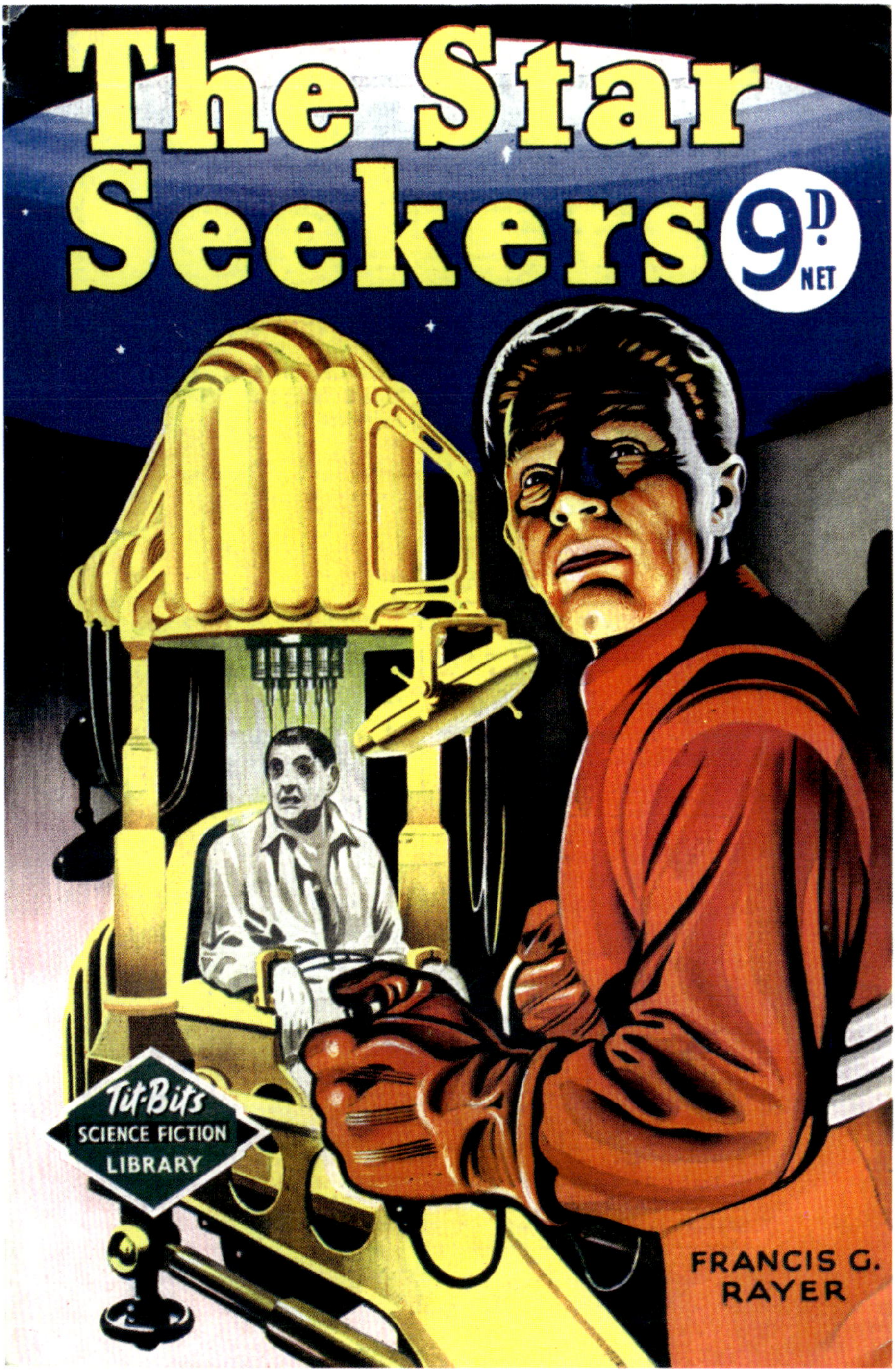

Francis G. Rayer | *The Star Seekers*
Tit-Bits Science Fiction Library, 1953 | Art **Ron Turner**

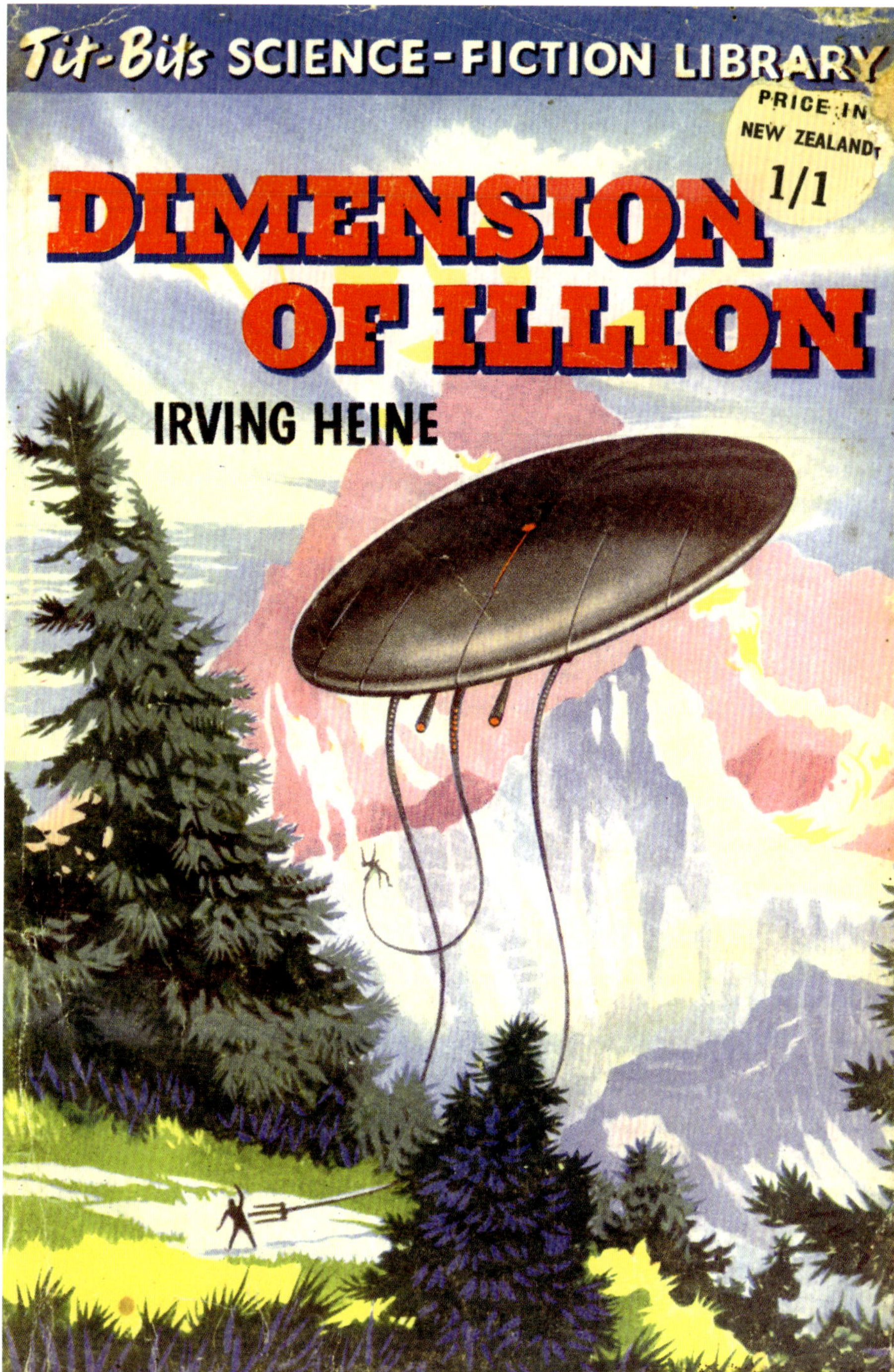

Irving Heine (Denis Hughes) | *Dimension of Illion*
Tit-Bits Science Fiction Library, 1955 | Art **Ron Turner**

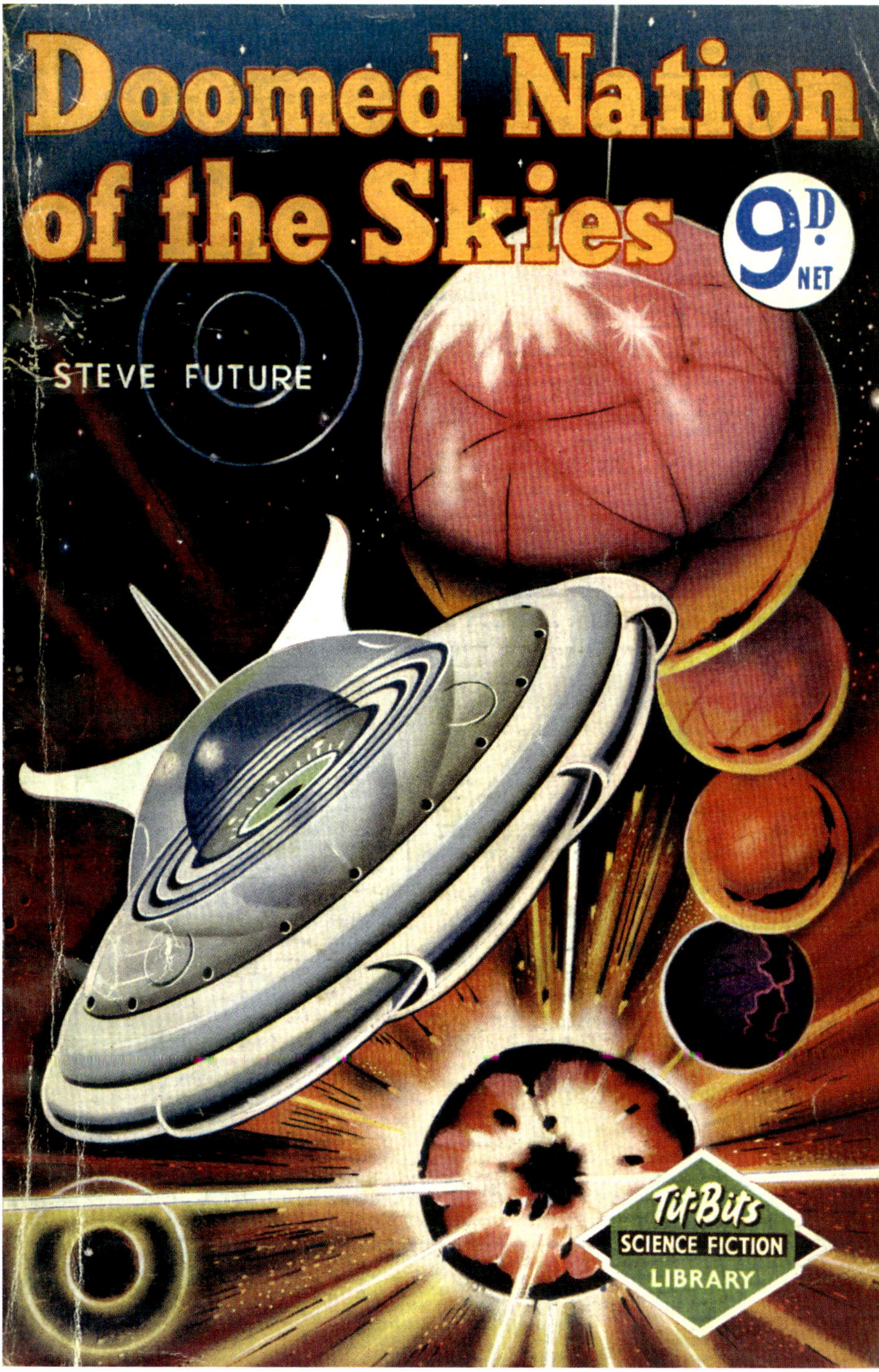

Steve Future | *Doomed Nation of the Skies*
Tit-Bits Science Fiction Library, 1953 | Art **Ron Turner**

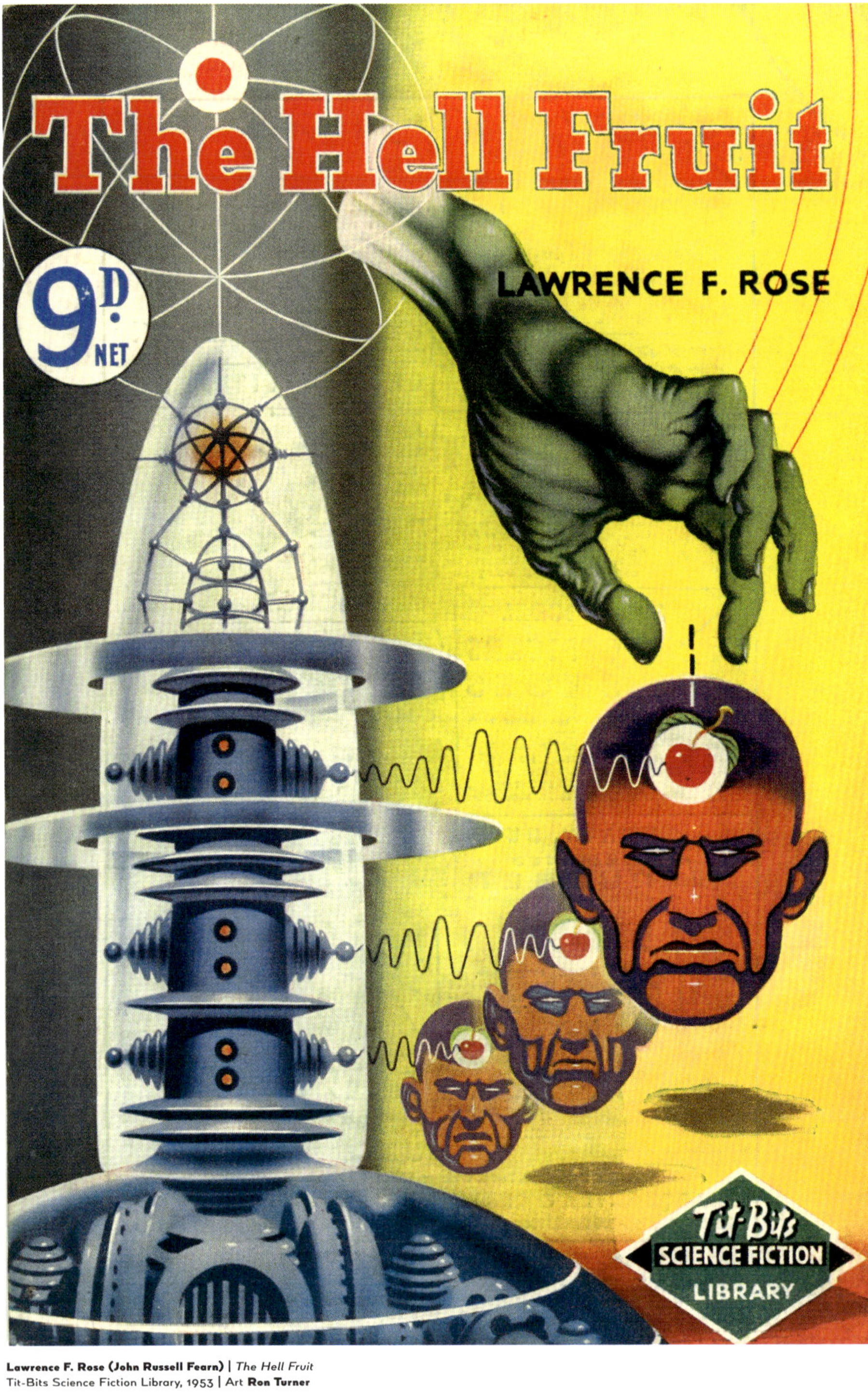

Lawrence F. Rose (John Russell Fearn) | *The Hell Fruit*
Tit-Bits Science Fiction Library, 1953 | Art **Ron Turner**

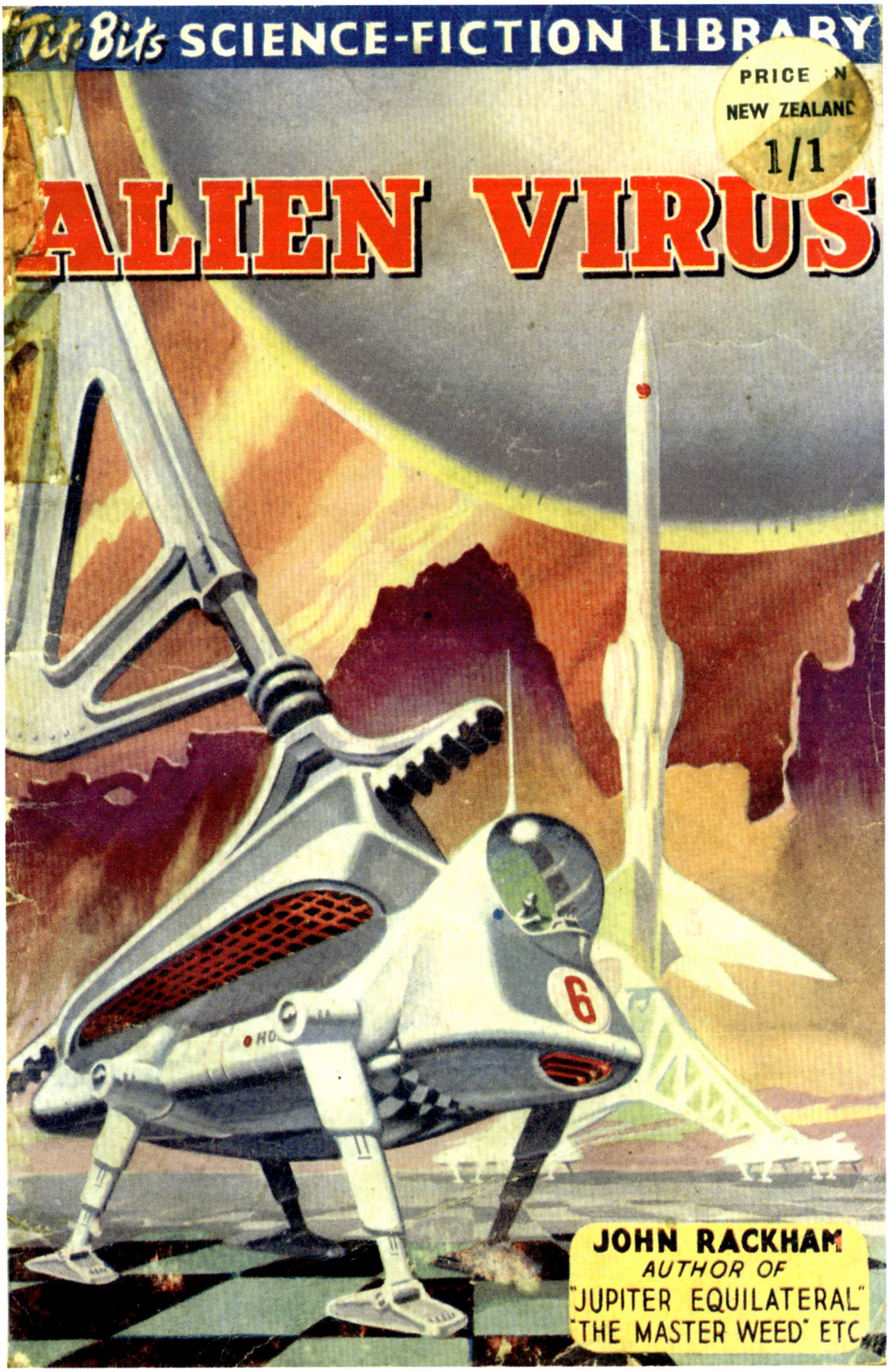

John Rackham (John T. Phillifent) | *Alien Virus*
Tit-Bits Science Fiction Library, 1955 | Art **Ron Turner**

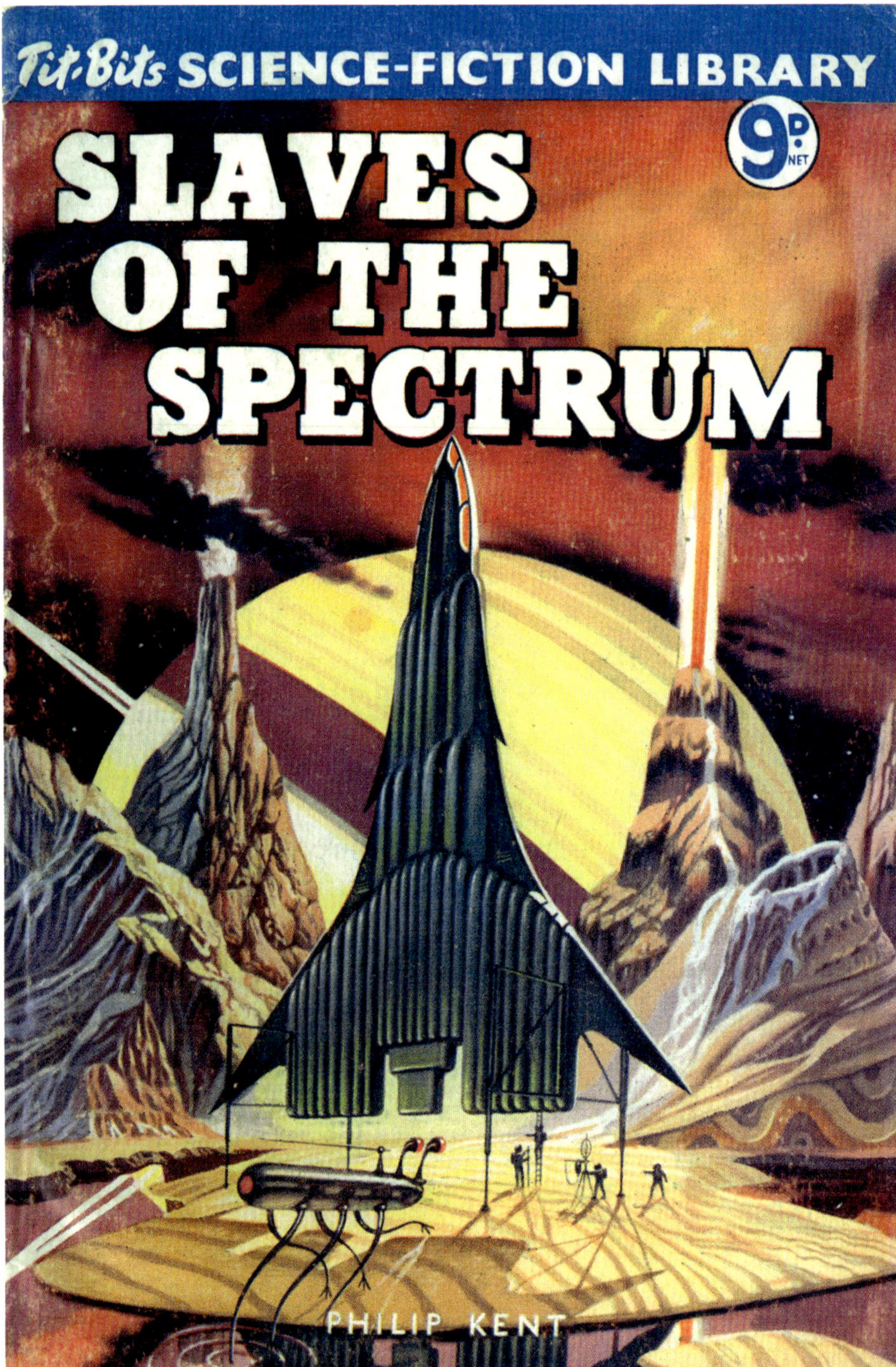

Philip Kent (H. K. Bulmer) | *Slaves of the Spectrum*
Tit-Bits Science Fiction Library, 1954 | Art **Ron Turner**

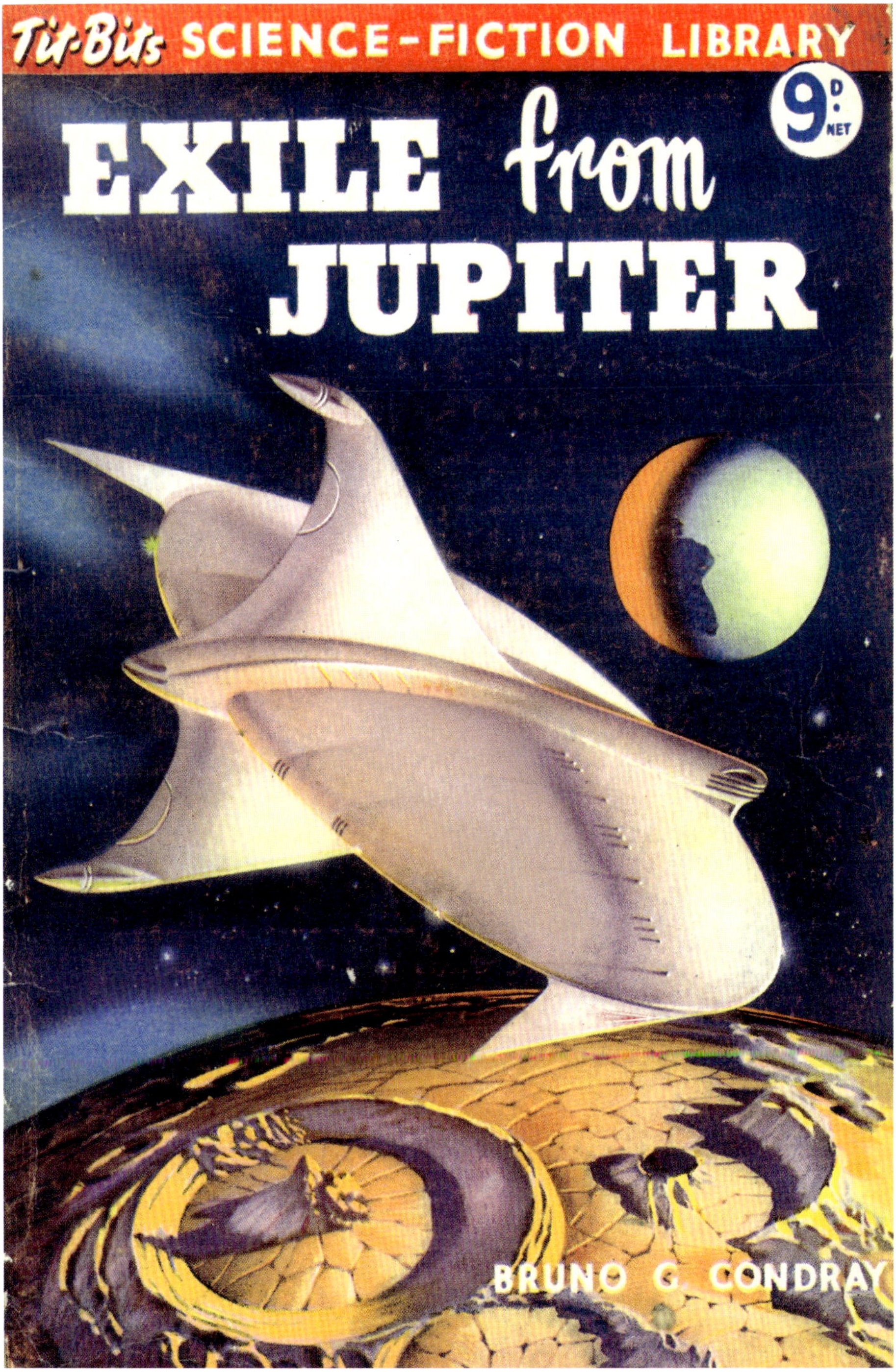

Bruno G. Condray (Leslie G. Humphrys) | *Exile from Jupiter*
Tit-Bits Science Fiction Library, 1955 | Art **Ron Turner**

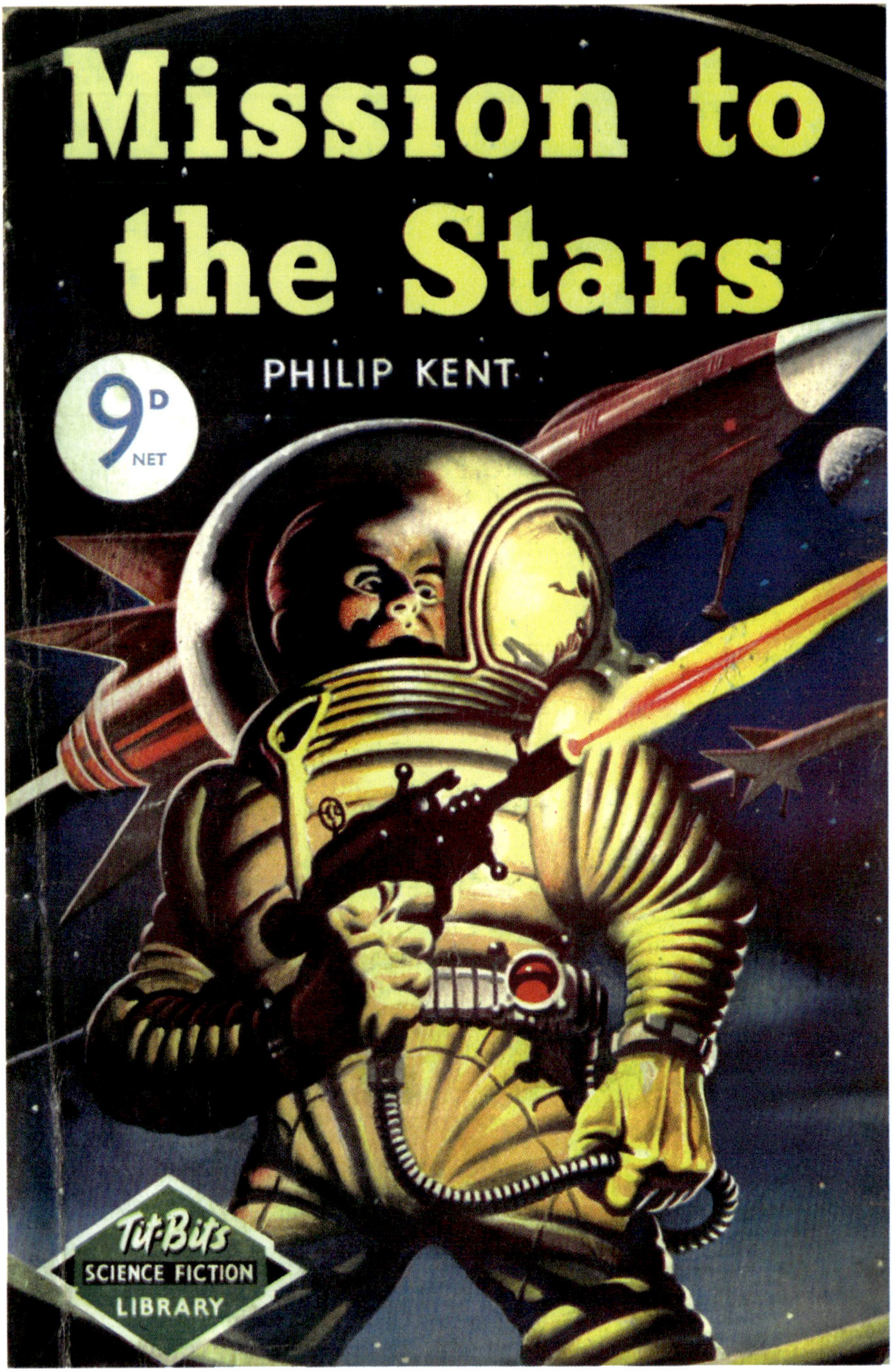

Philip Kent (H. K. Bulmer) | *Mission to the Stars*
Tit-Bits Science Fiction Library, 1954 | Art **Ron Turner**

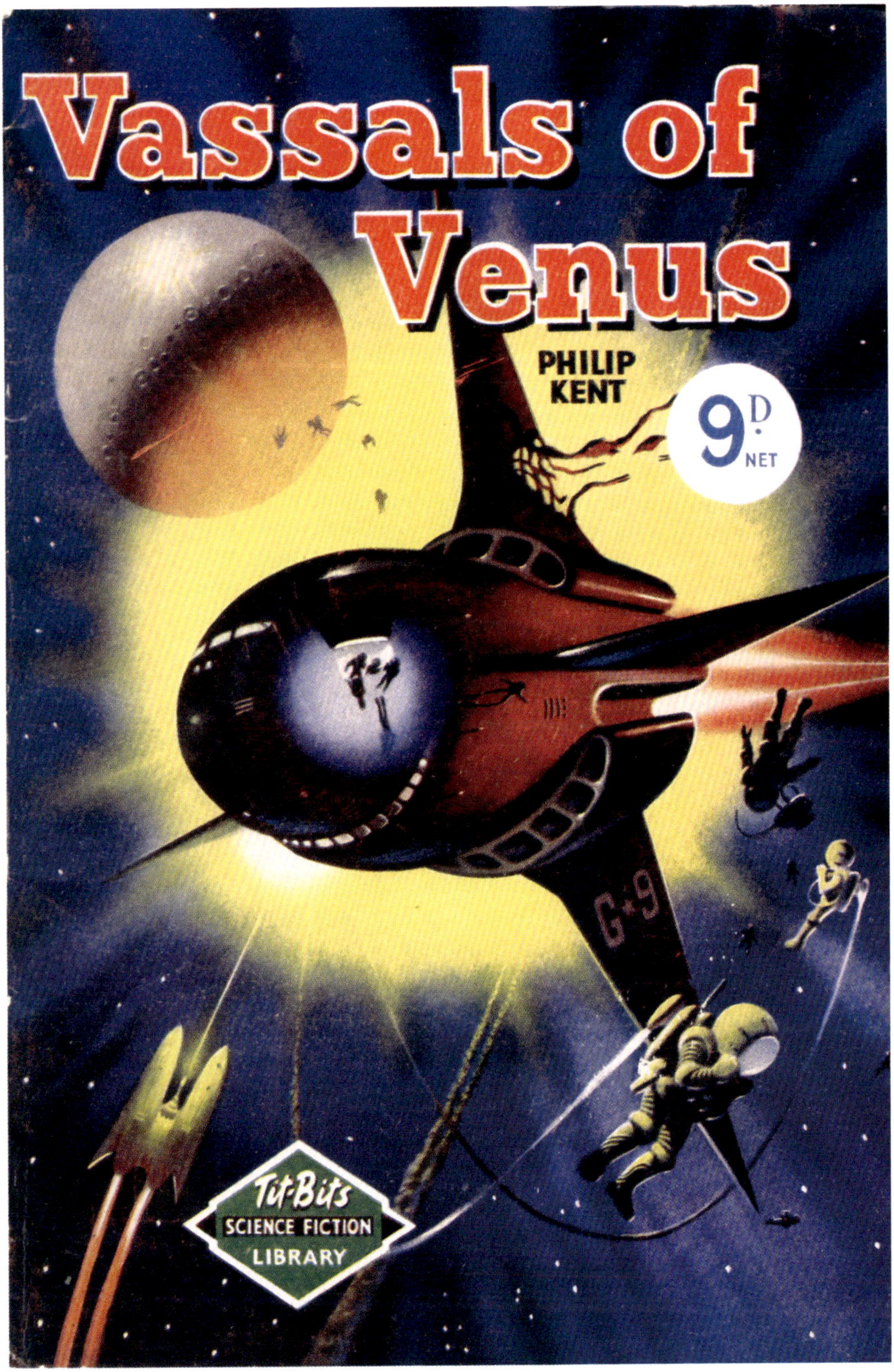

Philip Kent (H. K. Bulmer) | *Vassals of Venus*
Tit-Bits Science Fiction Library, 1954 | Art **Ron Turner**

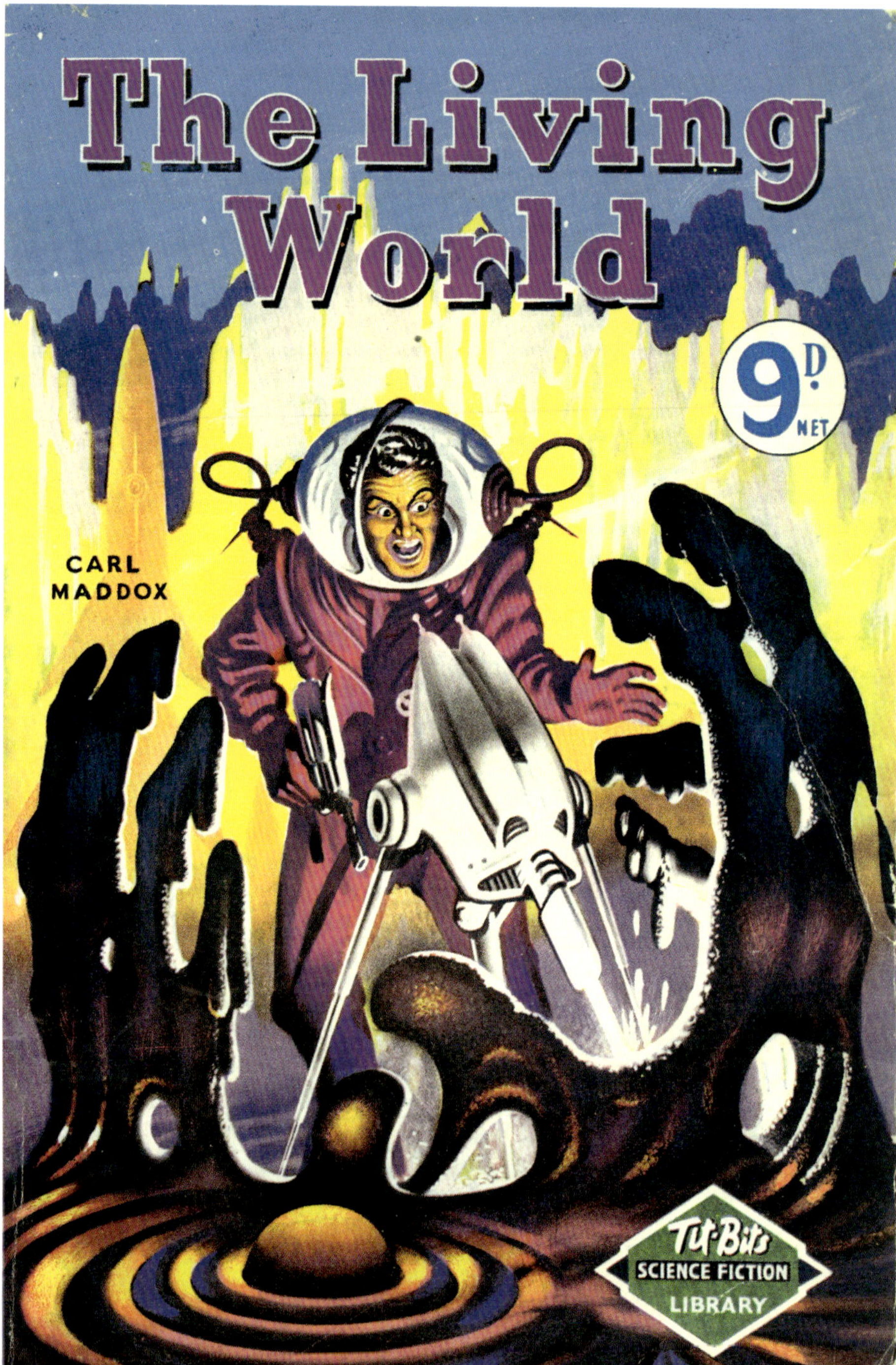

Carl Maddox (E. C. Tubb) | *The Living World*
Tit-Bits Science Fiction Library, 1954 | Art **Ron Turner**

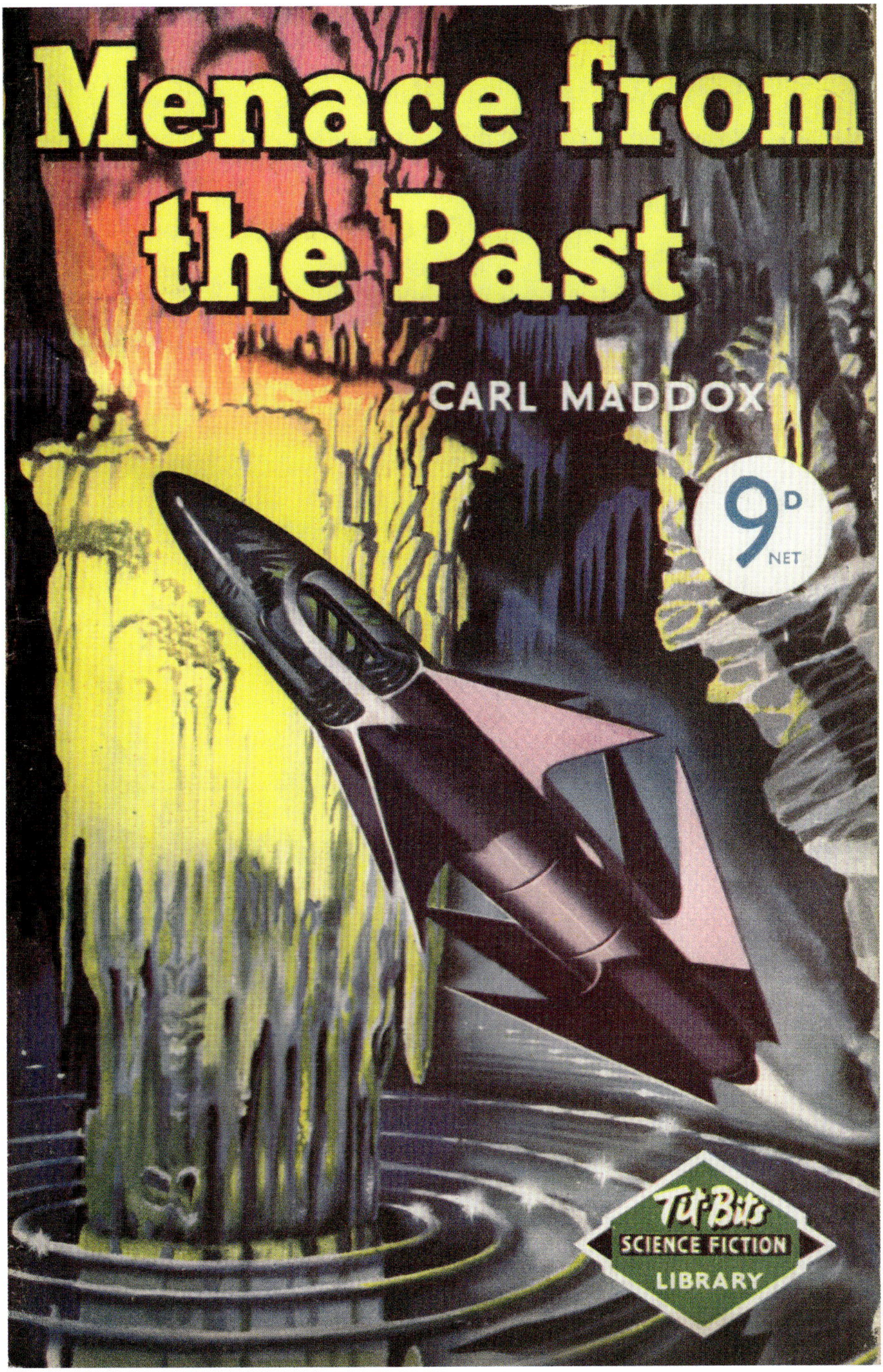

Carl Maddox (E. C. Tubb) | *Menace from the Past*
Tit-Bits Science Fiction Library, 1954 | Art **Ron Turner**

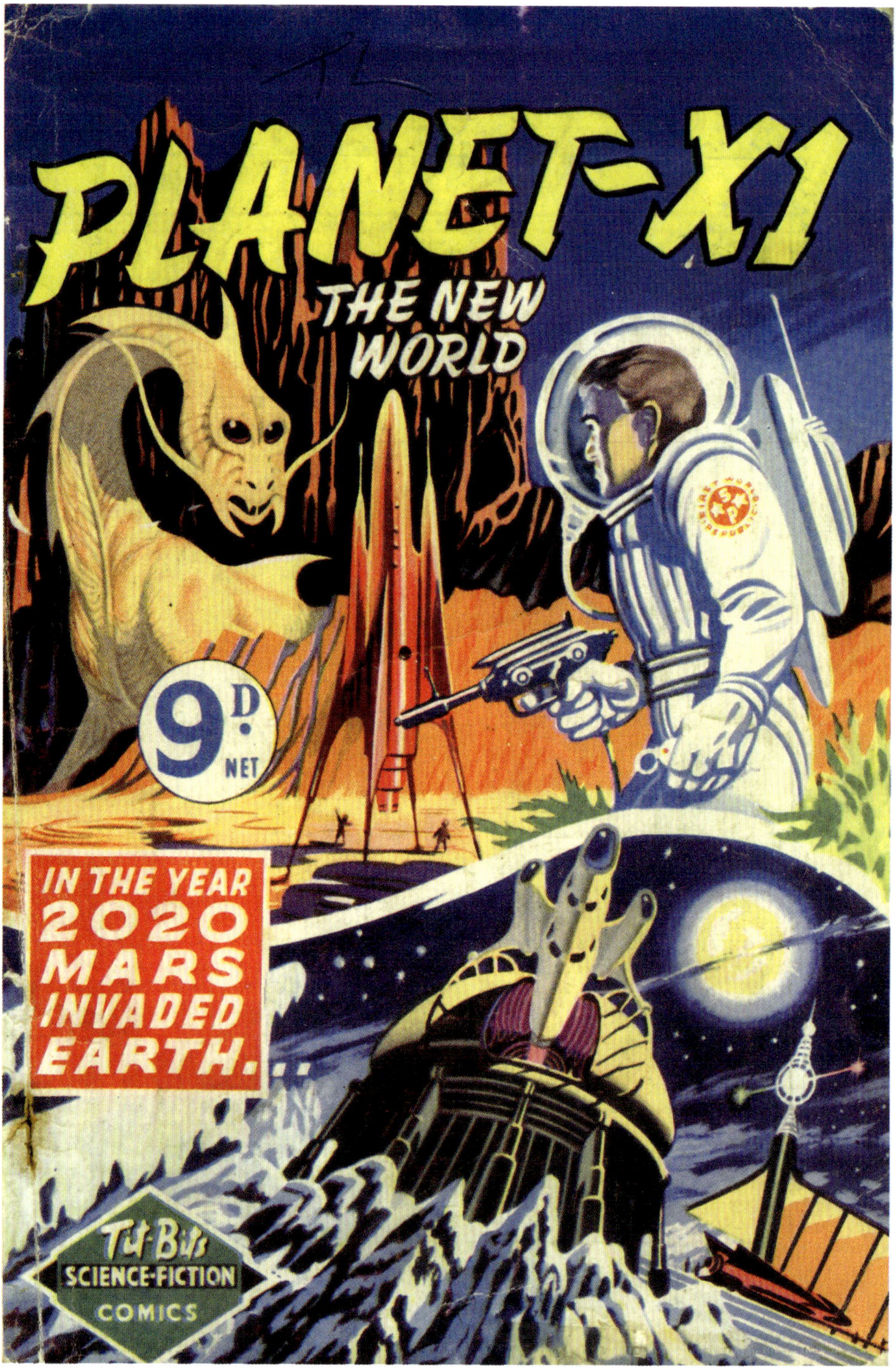

Planet-X1 The New World
Tit-Bits Science Fiction Comics, 1954 | Art **Ron Turner**

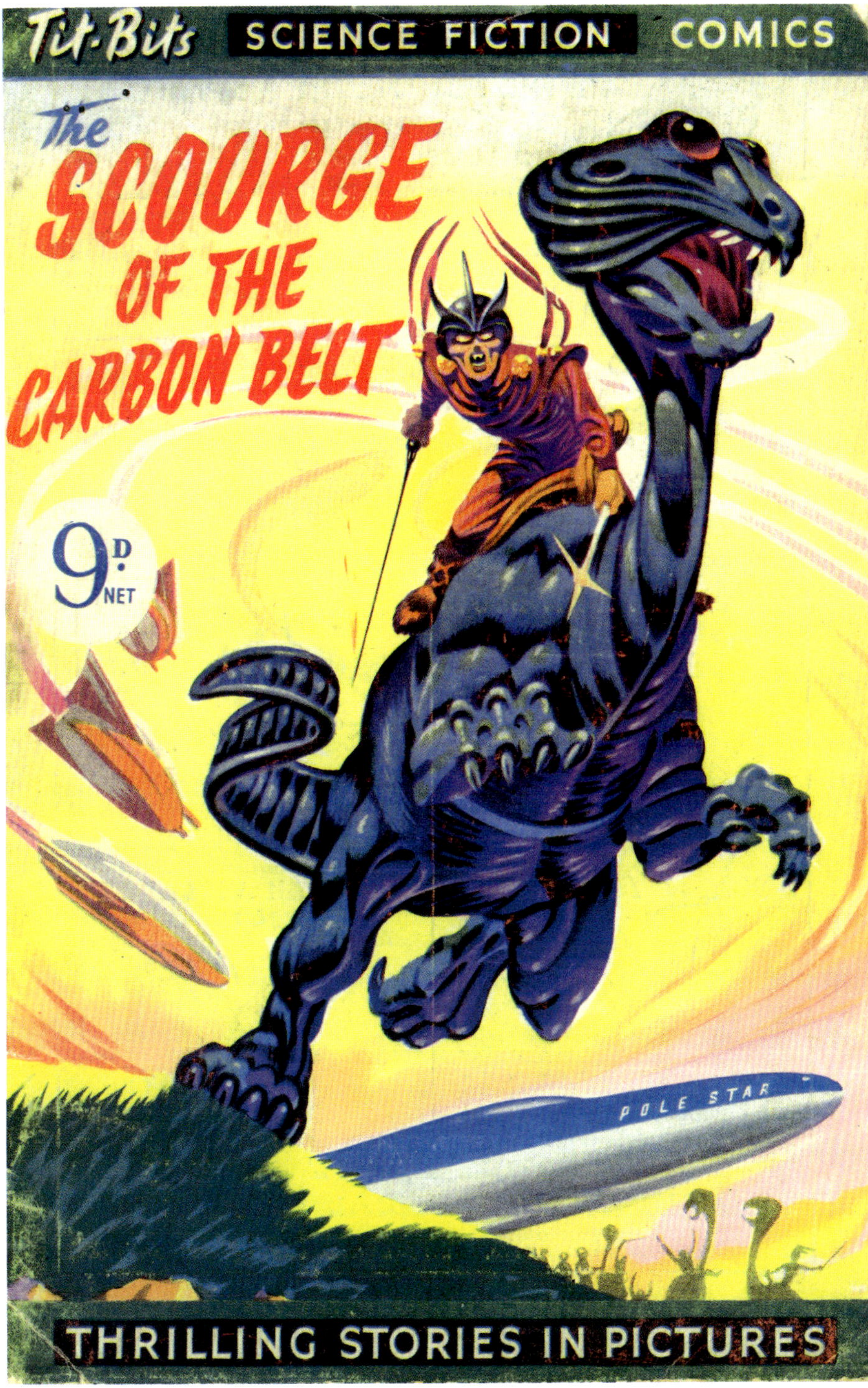

The Scourge of The Carbon Belt
Tit-Bits Science Fiction Comics, 1954 | Art **Ron Turner**

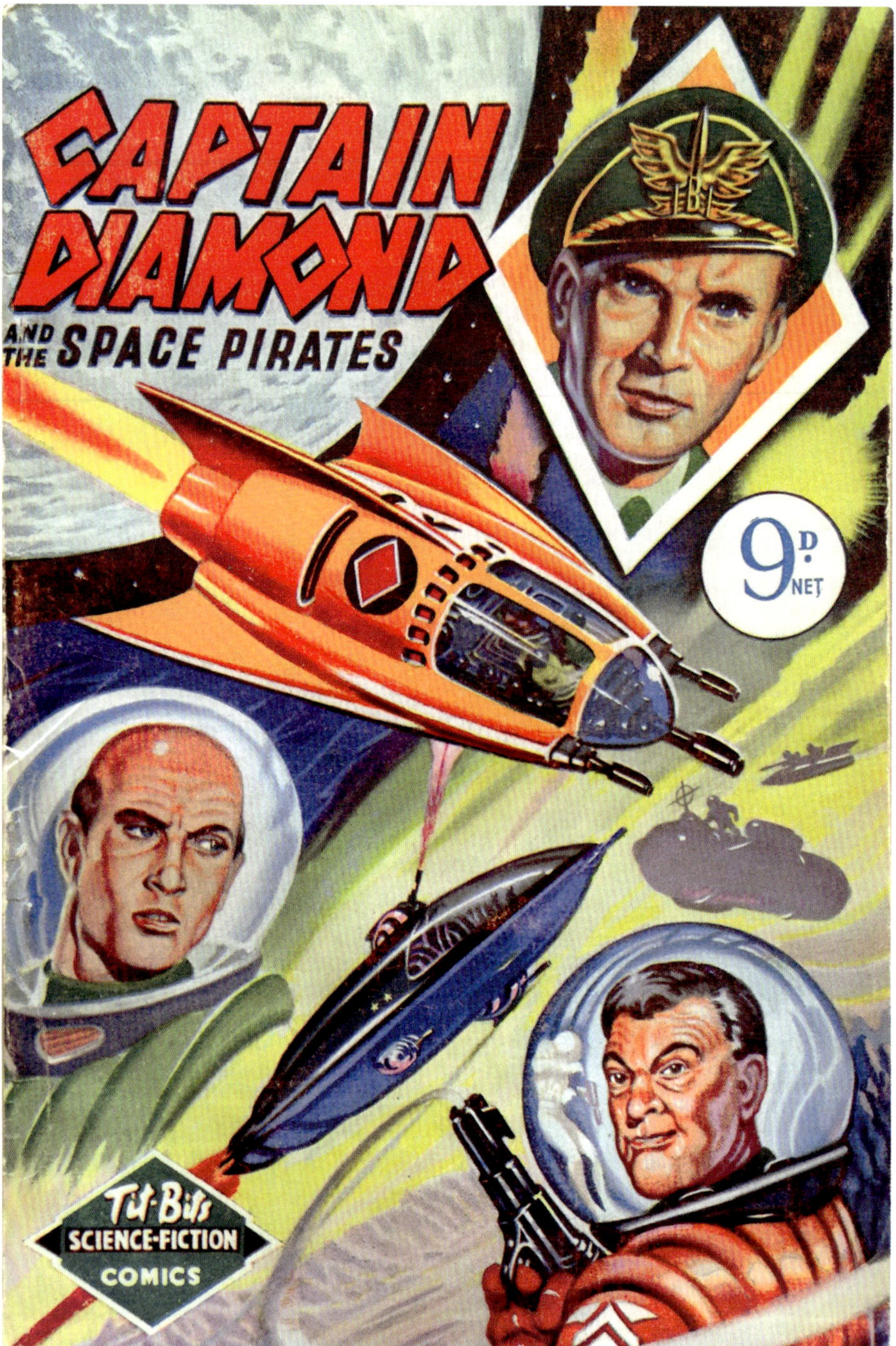

Captain Diamond and the Space Pirates
Tit-Bits Science Fiction Comics, 1954 | Art **Ron Turner**

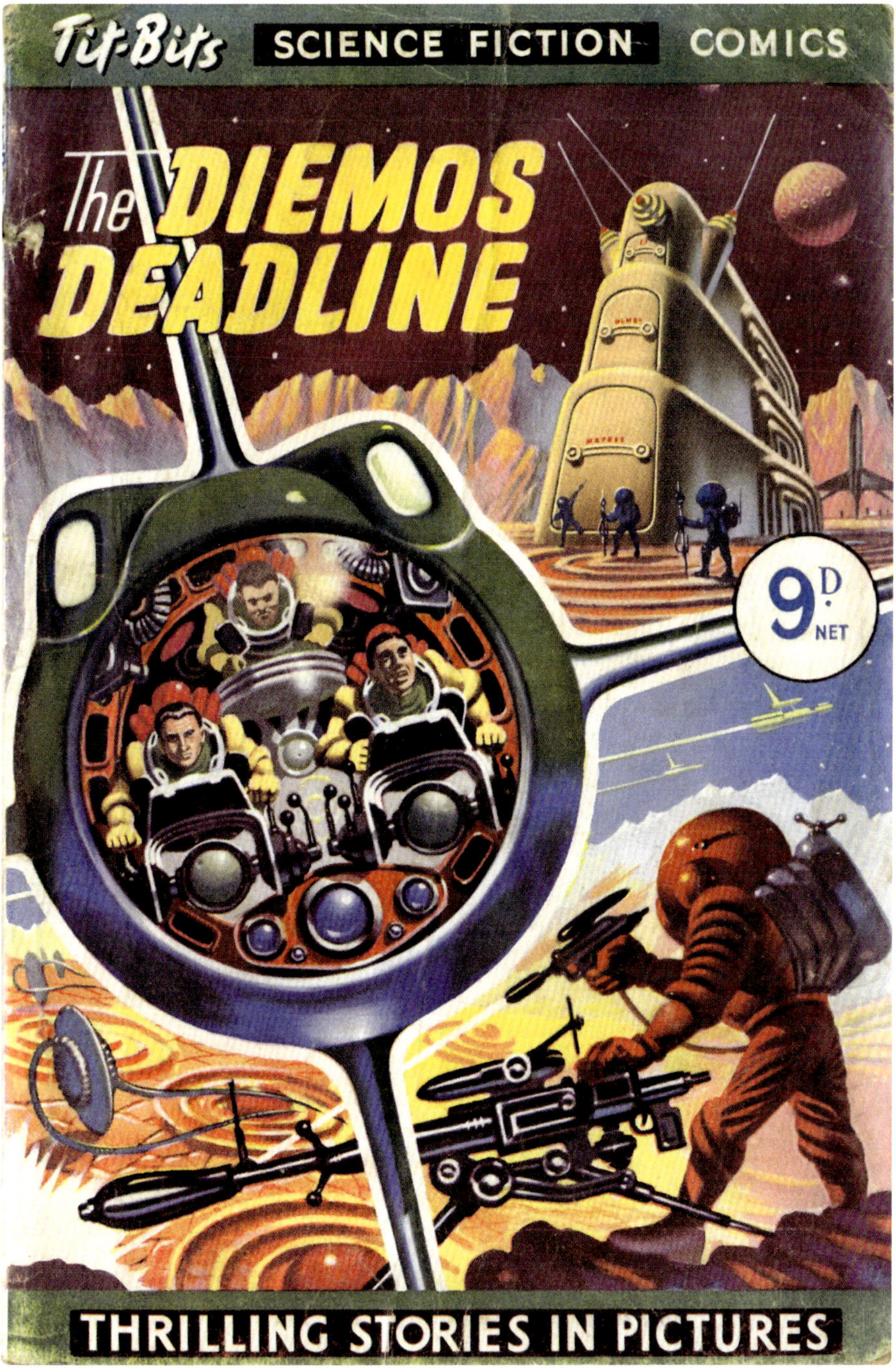

The Diemos Deadline
Tit-Bits Science Fiction Comics, 1954 | Art **Ron Turner**

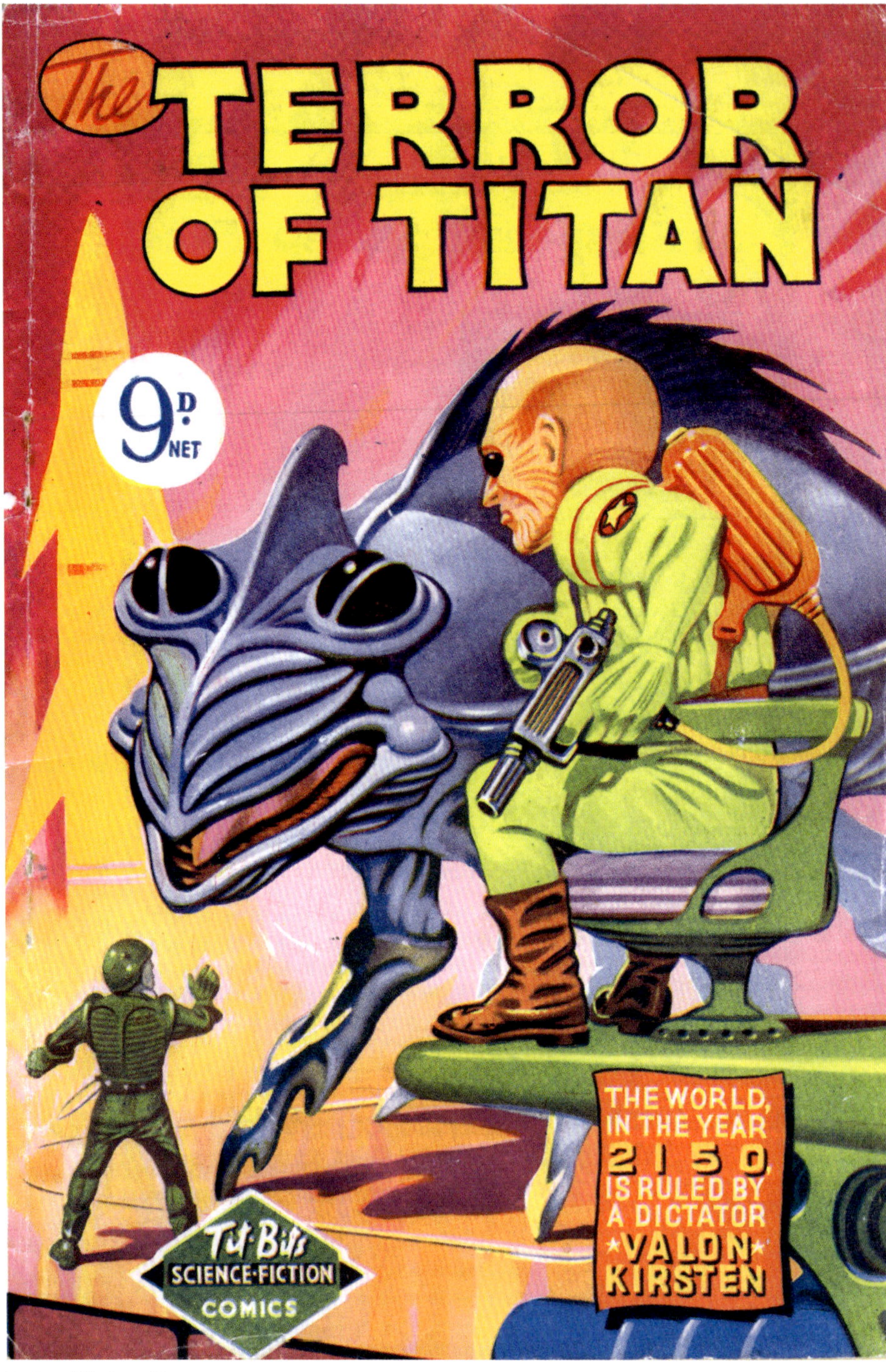

Ron Turner | *The Terror of Titan*
Tit-Bits Science Fiction Comics, 1954 | Art **Ron Turner**

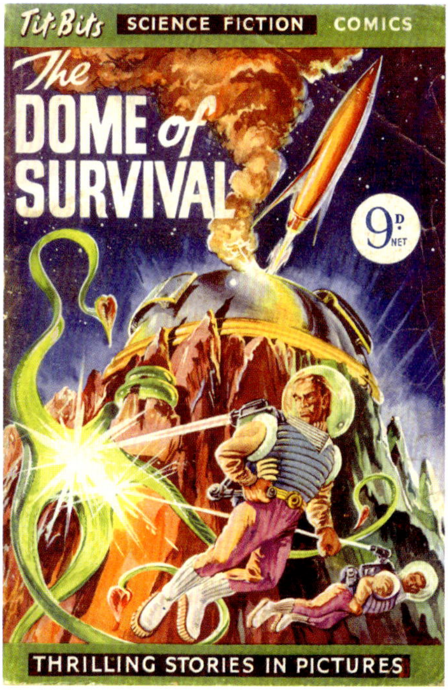

The Dome of Survival
Tit-Bits Science Fiction Comics, 1954 | Art **George Ratcliffe**

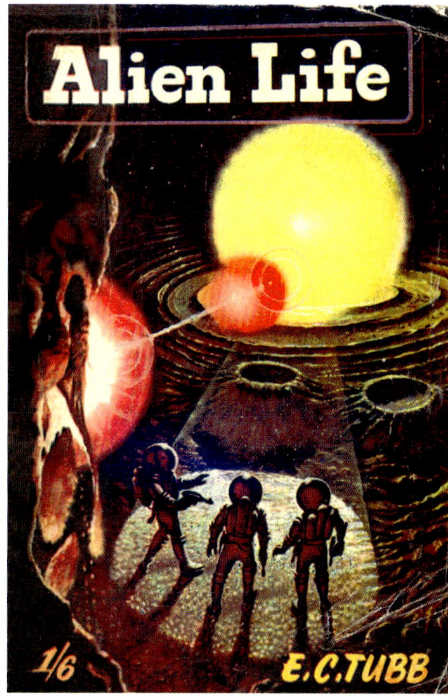

E. C. Tubb | *Alien Life*
Paladin Press, 1954 | Art **Ron Turner**

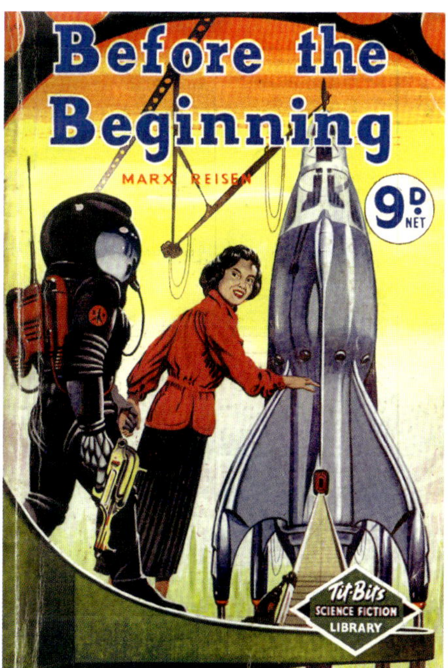

Marx Reisen | *Before the Beginning*
Tit-Bits Science Fiction Library, 1954 | Art **Ron Turner**

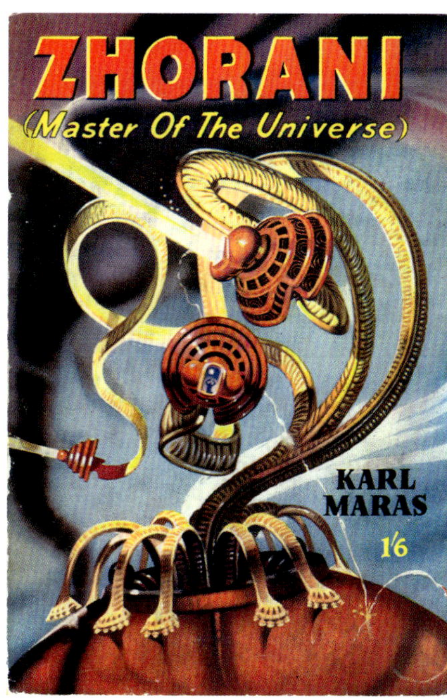

Karl Maras (H. K. Bulmer) | *Zhorani (Master of the Universe)*
Comyns Ltd., 1953 | Art **Ron Turner**

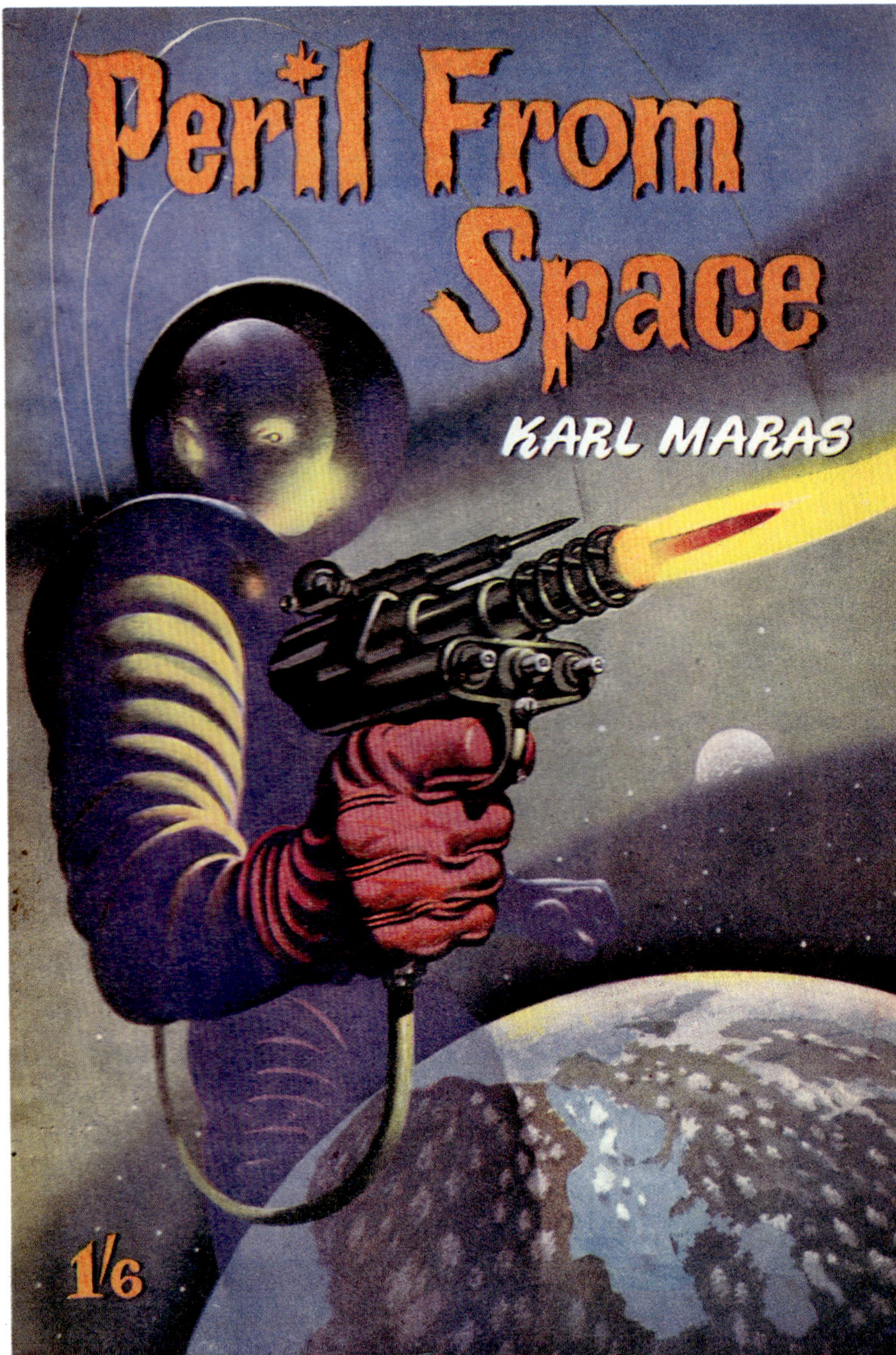

Karl Maras (H. K. Bulmer) | *Peril from Space*
Comyns Ltd., 1954 | Art **Ron Turner**

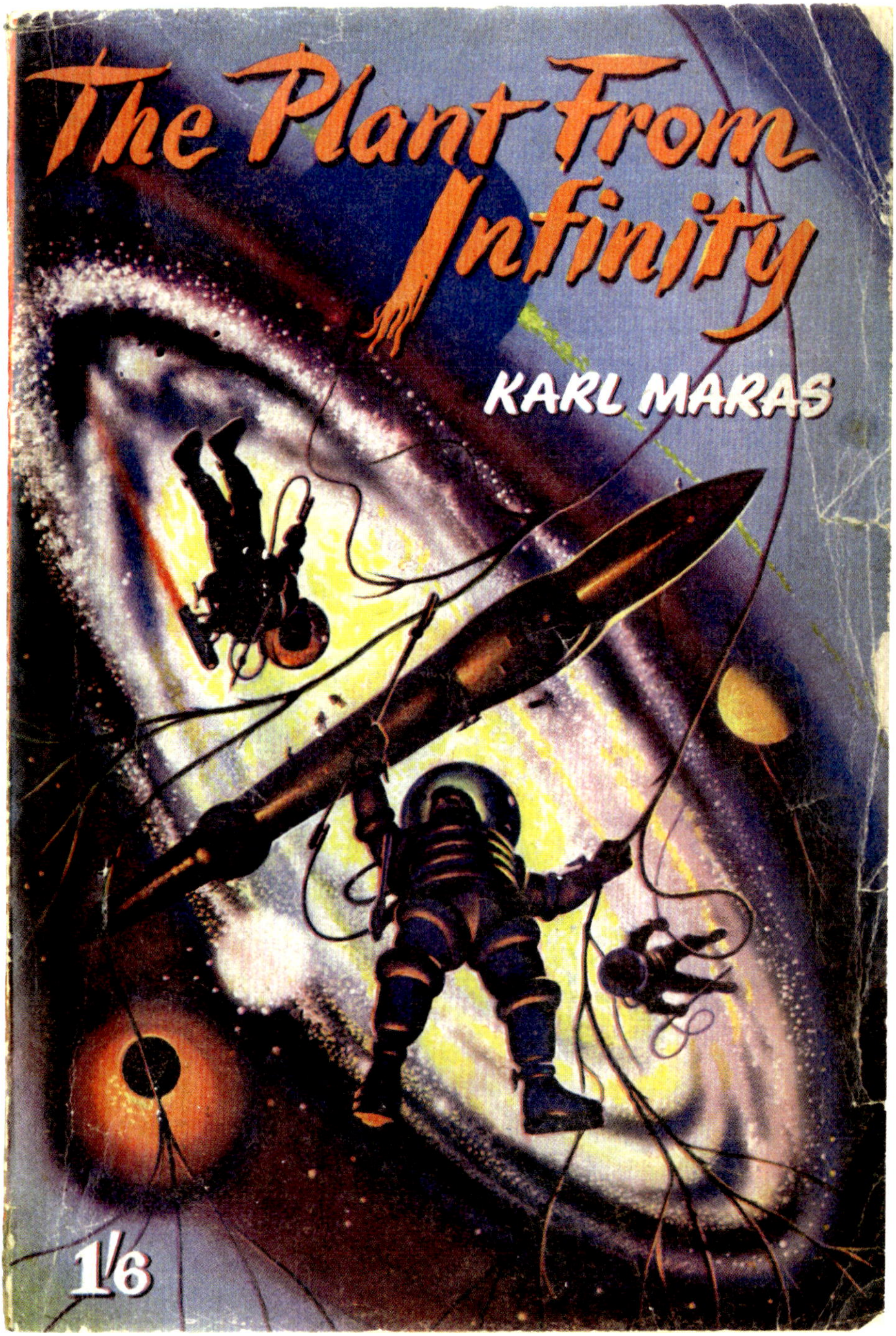

Karl Maras (Peter Hawkins) | *The Plant from Infinity*
Paladin Press, 1954 | Art **Ron Turner**

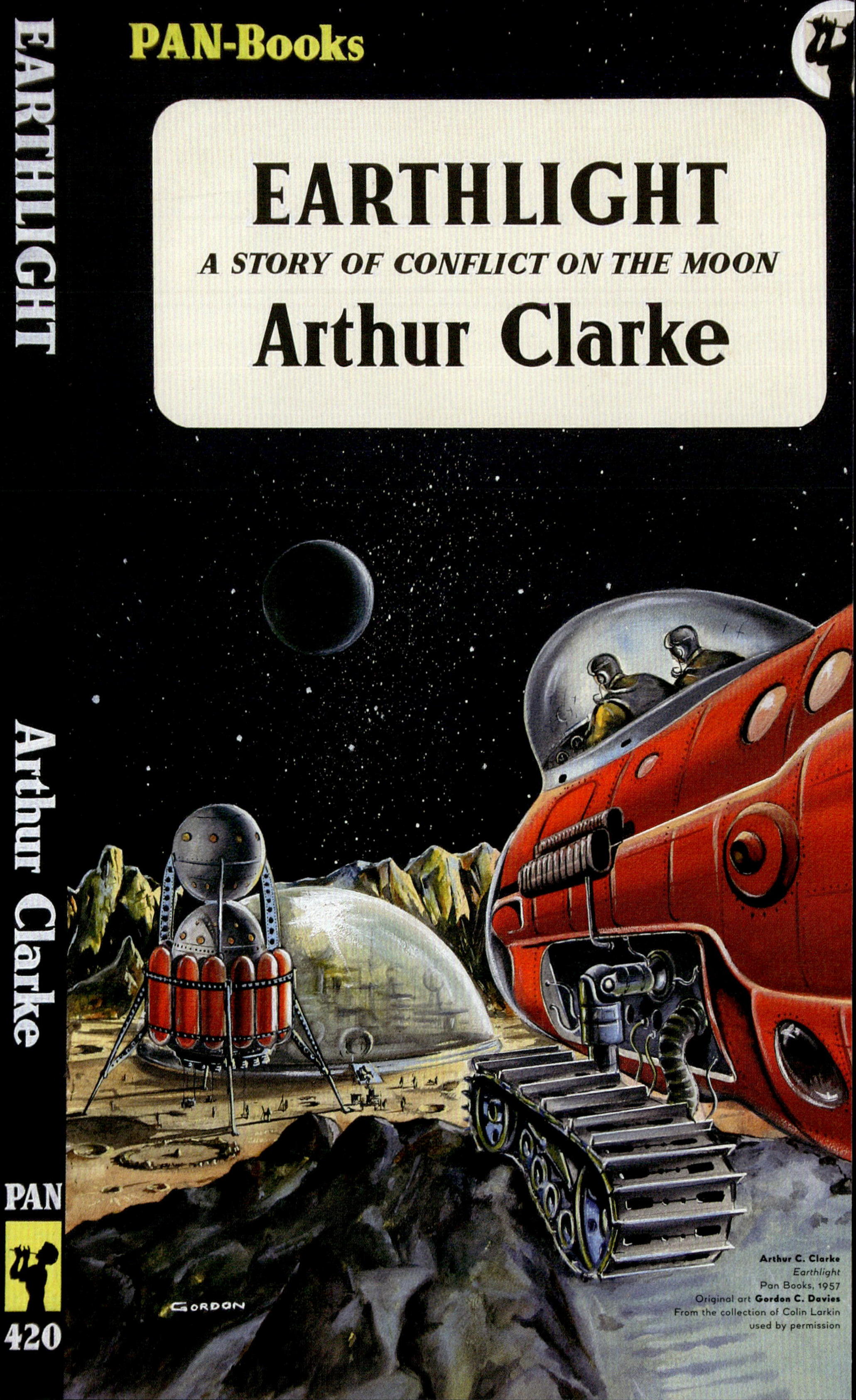

Arthur C. Clarke
Earthlight
Pan Books, 1957
Original art **Gordon C. Davies**
From the collection of Colin Larkin
used by permission

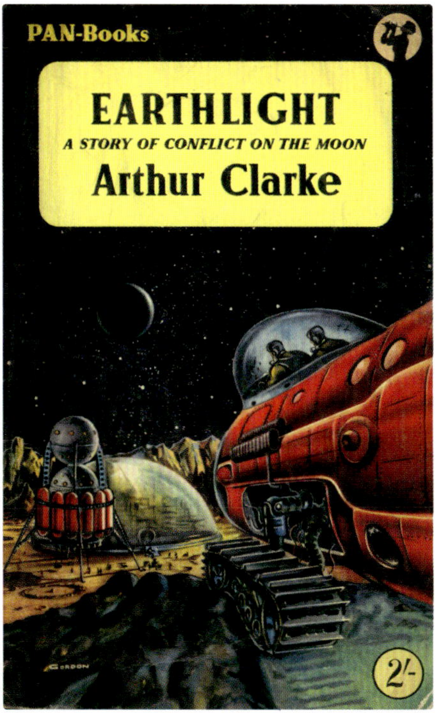

Arthur C. Clarke | *Earthlight*
Pan Books, 1957 | Art **Gordon C. Davies**

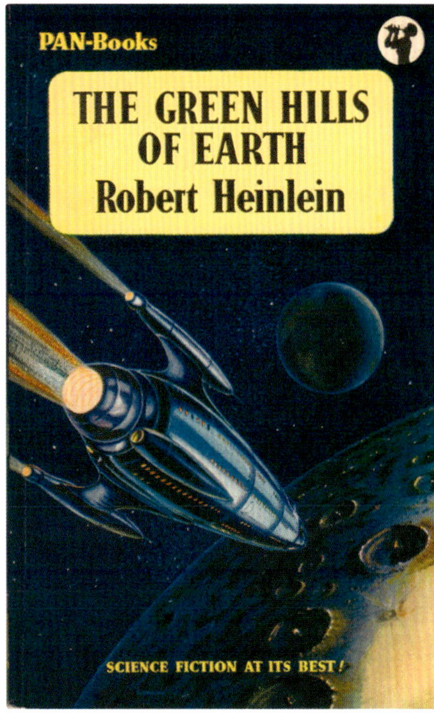

Robert Heinlein | *The Green Hills of Earth*
Pan Books, 1956 | Art **Gordon C. Davies**

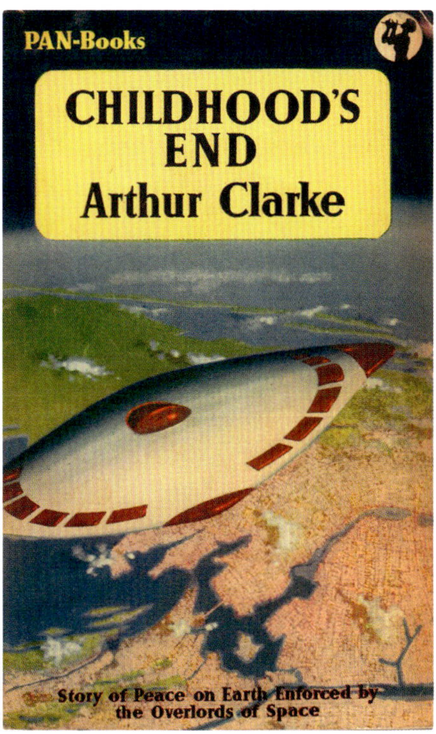

Arthur C. Clarke | *Childhood's End*
Pan Books, 1956 | Art **Gerard Quinn**

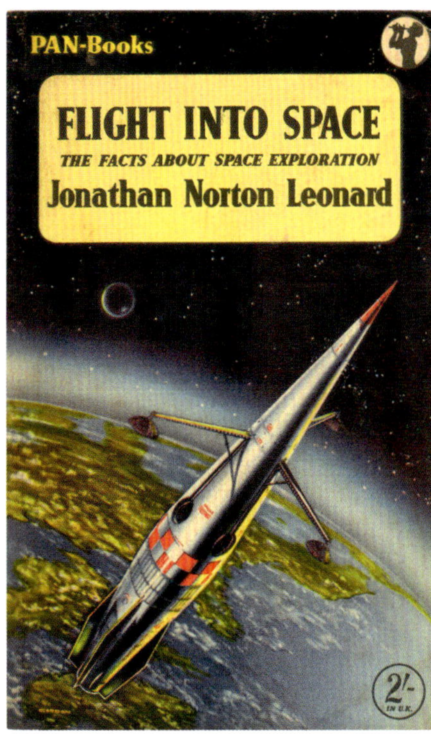

Jonathan Norton Leonard | *Flight Into Space*
Pan Books, 1956 | Art **Gordon C. Davies**

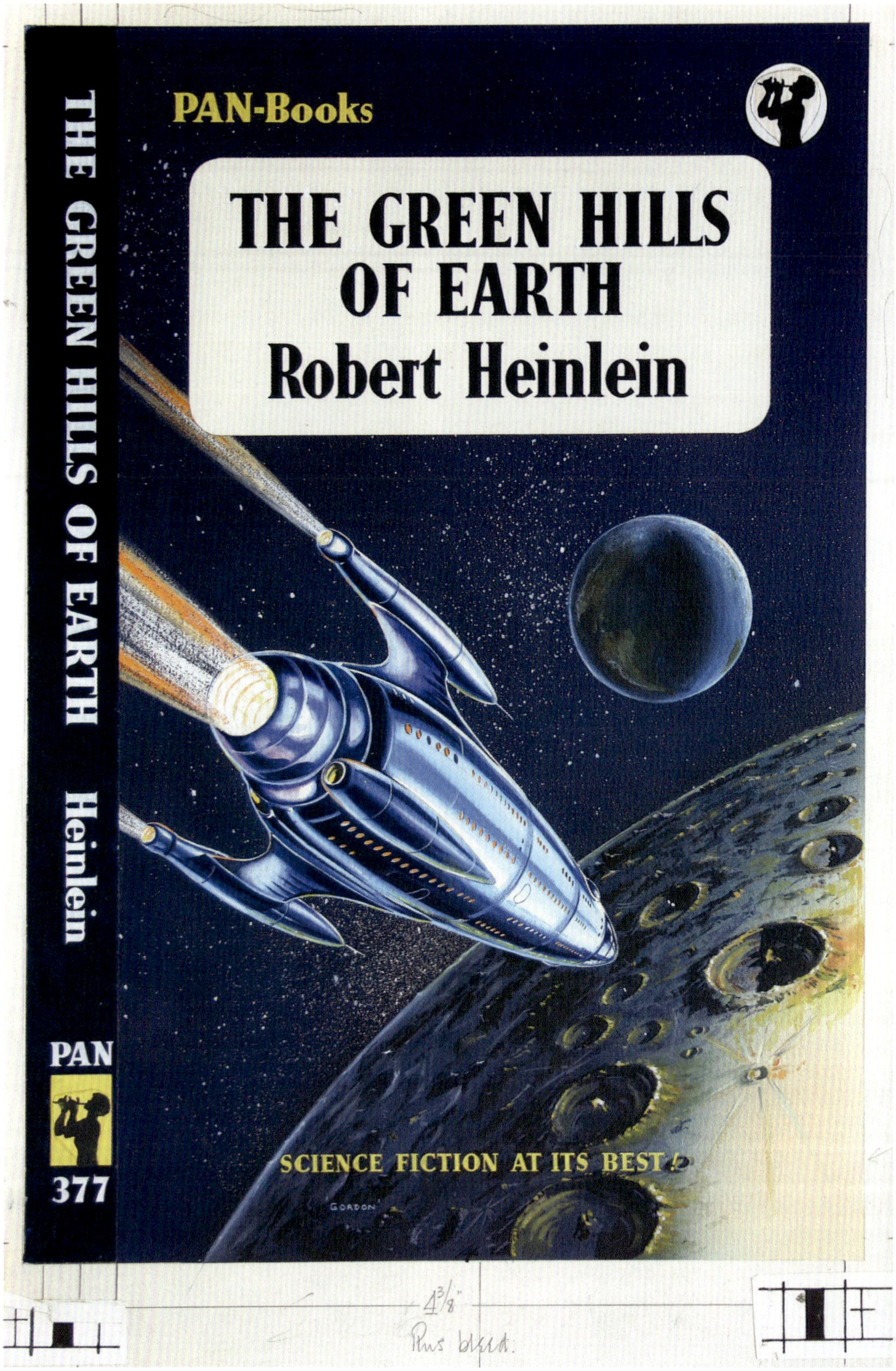

Robert Heinlein | *The Green Hills of Earth*
Pan Books, 1956 | Original art **Gordon C. Davies**
From the collection of Colin Larkin, used by permission

opposite: **Jonathan Norton Leonard** | *Flight Into Space*
Pan Books, 1956 | Original art **Gordon C. Davies**
From the collection of Colin Larkin, used by permission

PAN-Books

FLIGHT INTO SPACE

THE FACTS ABOUT SPACE EXPLORATION

Jonathan Norton Leonard

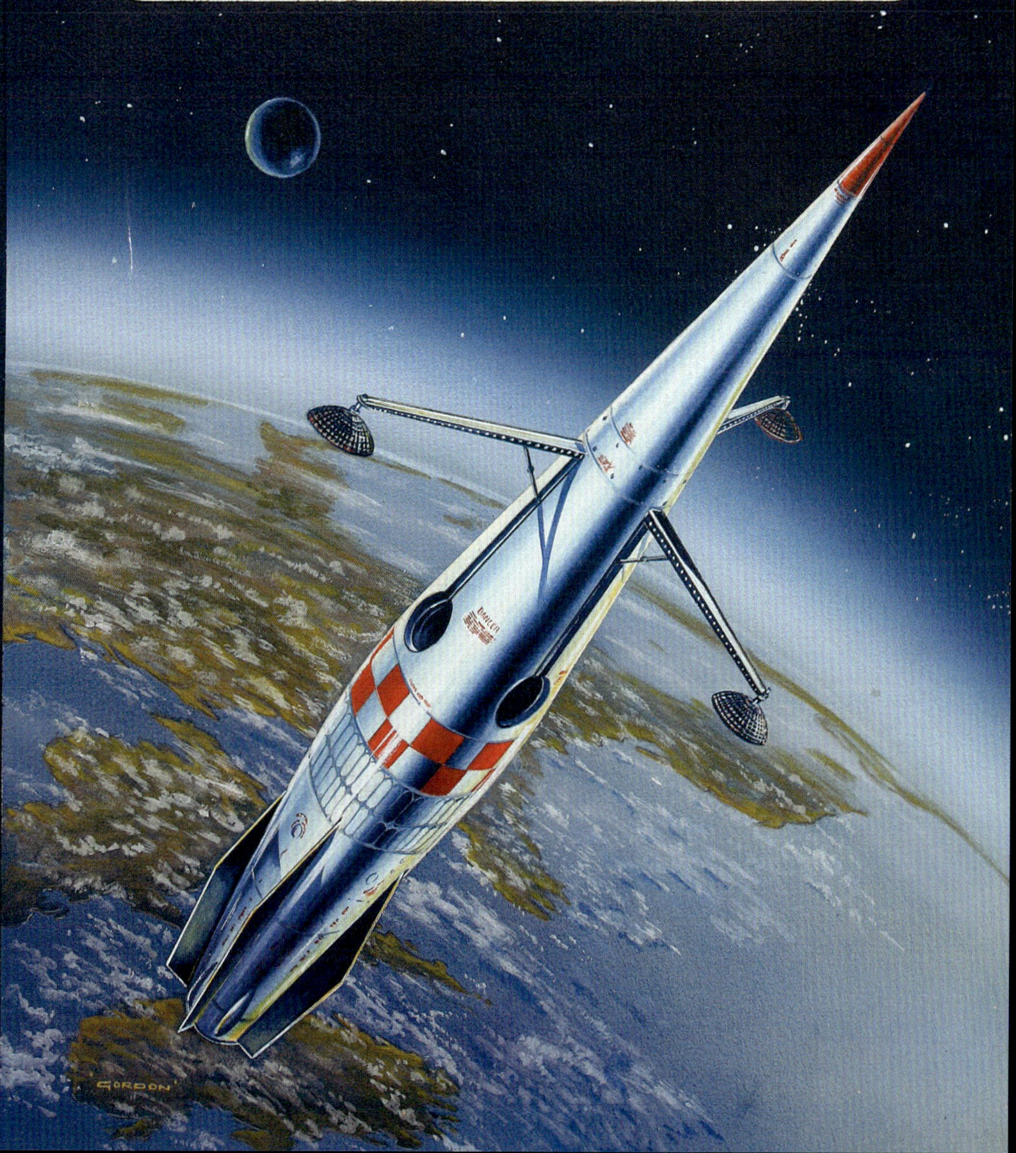

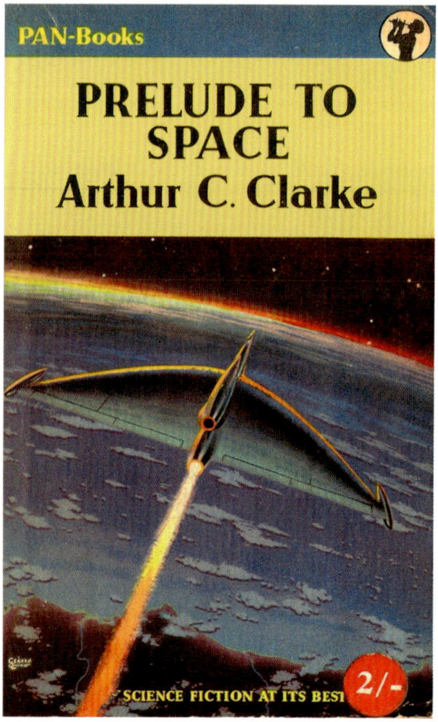

Arthur C. Clarke | *Prelude to Space*
Pan Books, 1954 | Art **Gerard Quinn**

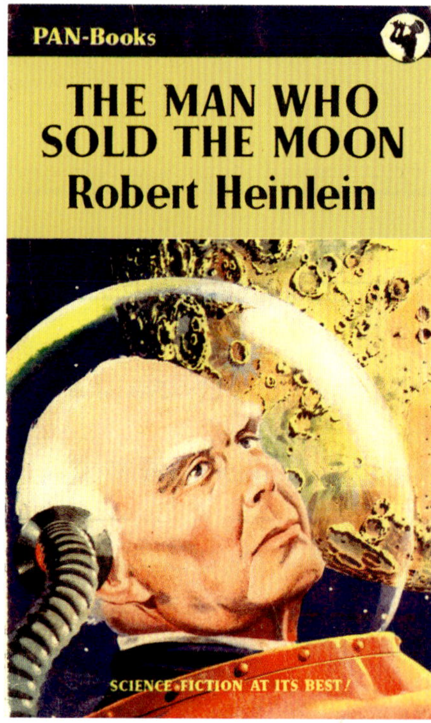

Robert Heinlein | *The Man Who Sold the Moon*
Pan Books, 1955 | Art **Gerard Quinn**

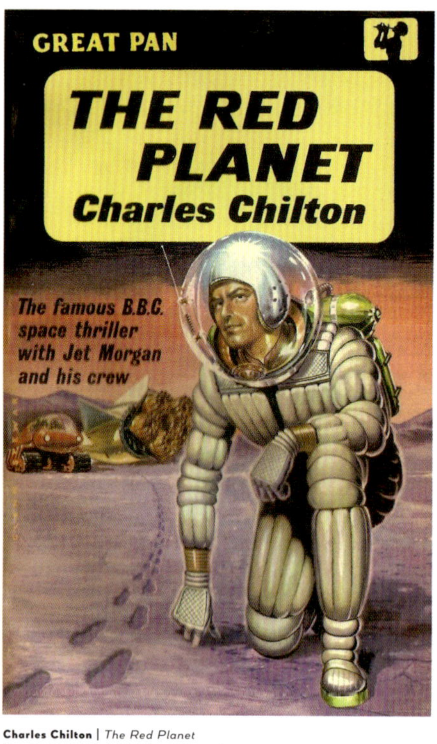

Charles Chilton | *The Red Planet*
Pan Books, 1960 | Art **Glenn Steward**

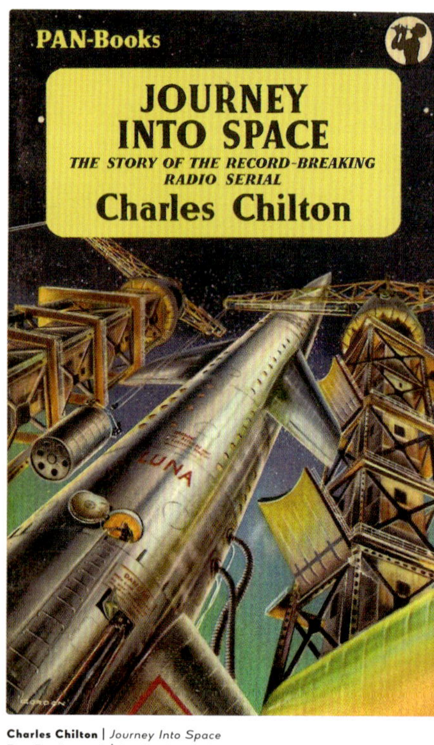

Charles Chilton | *Journey Into Space*
Pan Books, 1958 | Art **Gordon C. Davies**

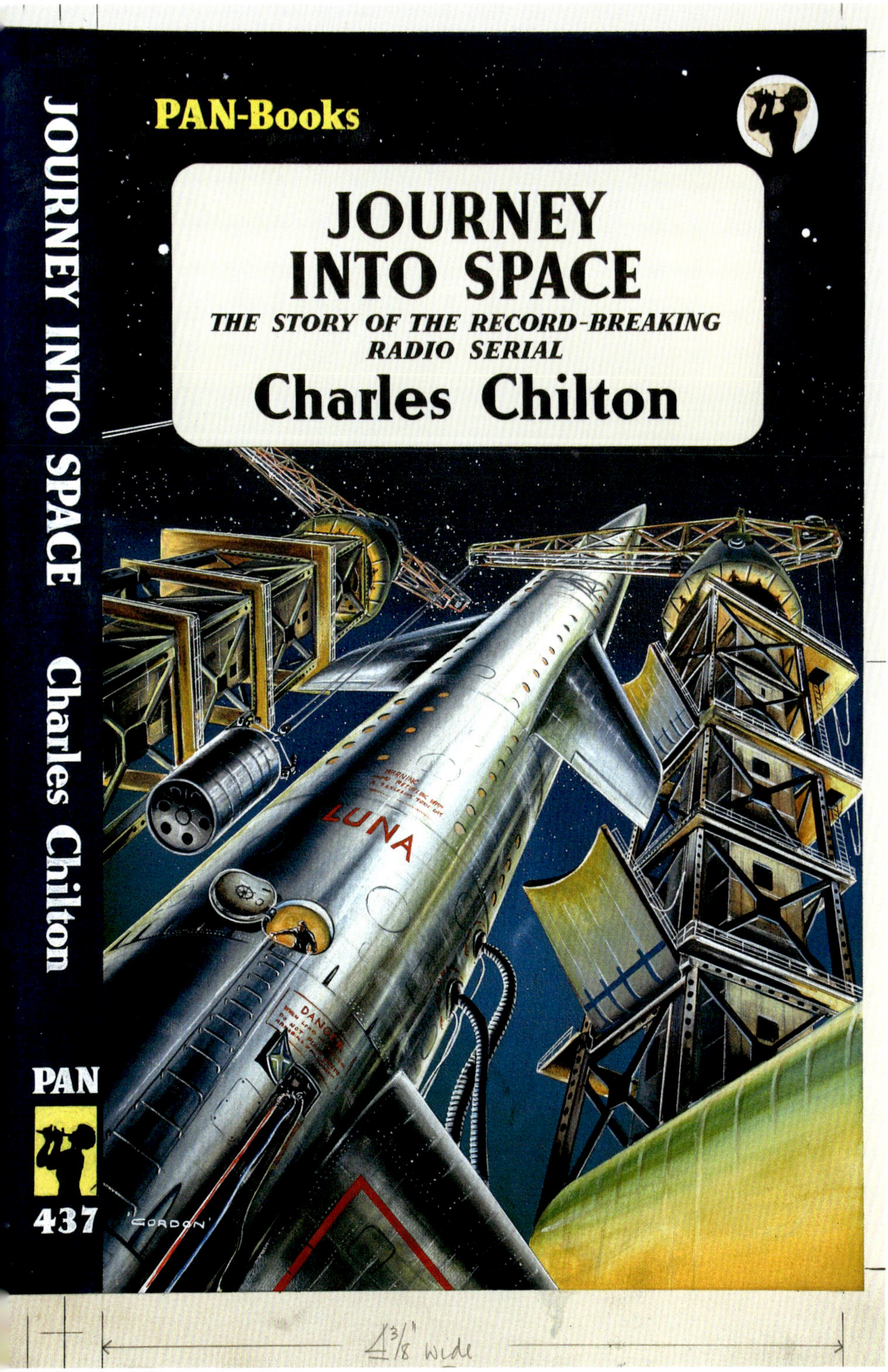

Charles Chilton | *Journey Into Space*
Pan Books, 1958 | Original art **Gordon C. Davies**

From the collection of Colin Larkin used by permission

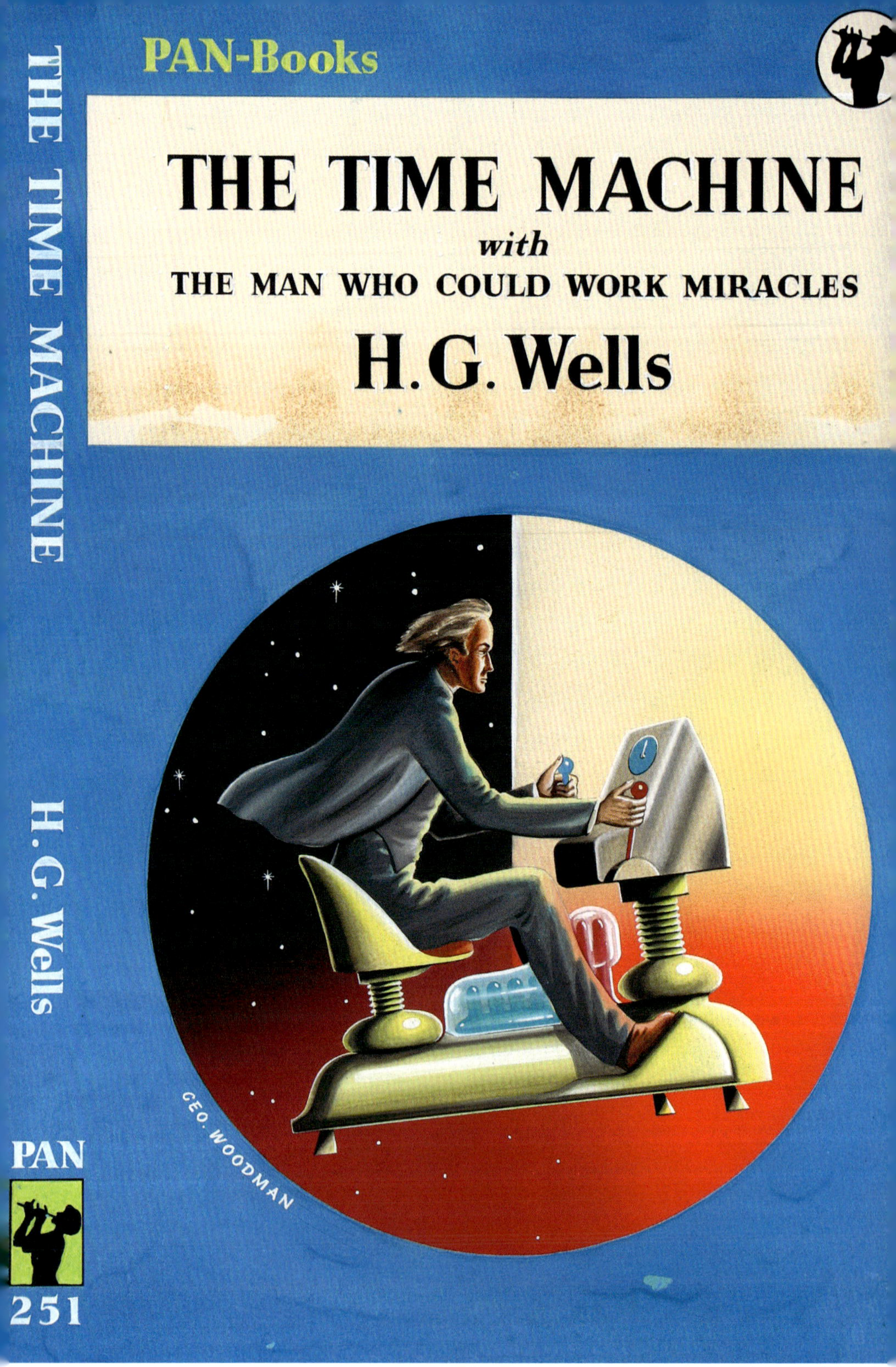

H. G. Wells | *The Time Machine with The Man Who Could Work Miracles* | Pan Books, 1953
Original art **George Woodman** | From the collection of Colin Larkin, used by permission

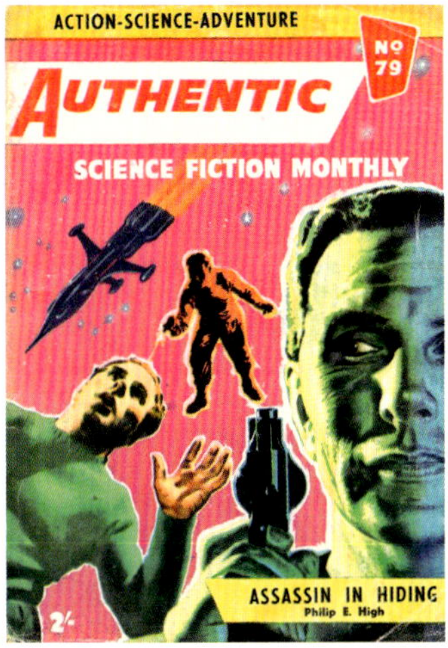

E. C. Tubb, ed. | Authentic Science Fiction #79
Hamilton & Co., 1957 | Art **E. L. Blandford**

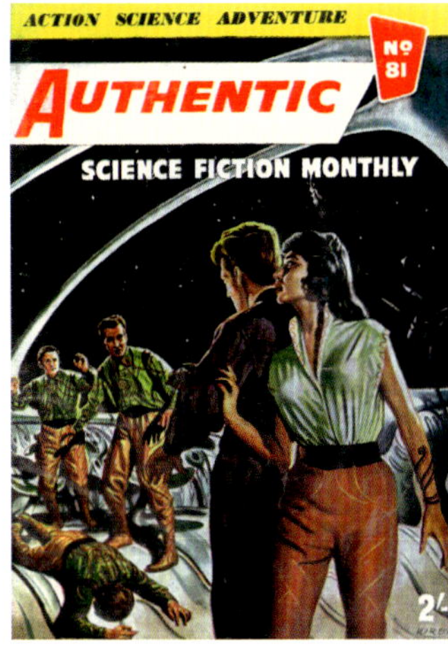

E. C. Tubb, ed. | Authentic Science Fiction Monthly #81
Hamilton & Co., 1957 | Art **Josh Kirby**

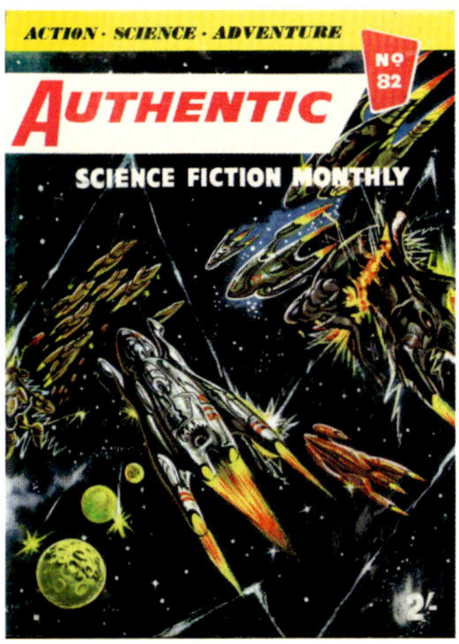

E. C. Tubb, ed. | Authentic Science Fiction Monthly #82
Hamilton & Co., 1957 | Art **Josh Kirby**

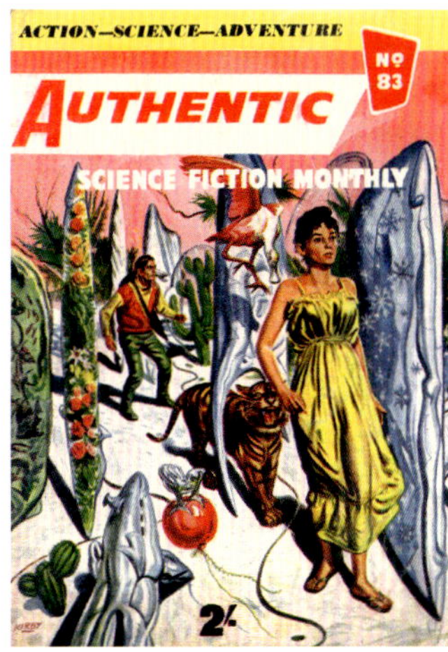

E. C. Tubb, ed. | Authentic Science Fiction Monthly #83
Hamilton & Co., 1957 | Art **Josh Kirby**

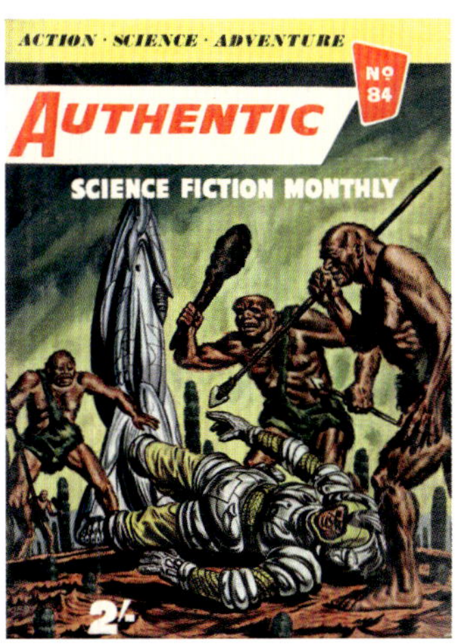

E. C. Tubb, ed. | Authentic Science Fiction Monthly #84
Hamilton & Co., 1957 | Art **Josh Kirby**

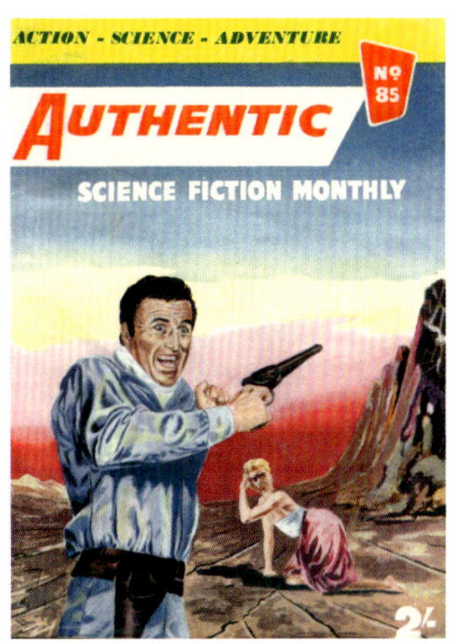

E. C. Tubb, ed. | Authentic Science Fiction Monthly #85
Hamilton & Co., 1957 | Art **P. R. Green**

opposite **Jack Coggins and Fletcher Pratt** | *By Space Ship to the Moon*
Publicity Products, 1952 | Art **Jack Coggins**

H. J. Campbell, ed. | *Authentic Science Book of Space*
Hamilton & Co., 1954 | Art **John Richards**

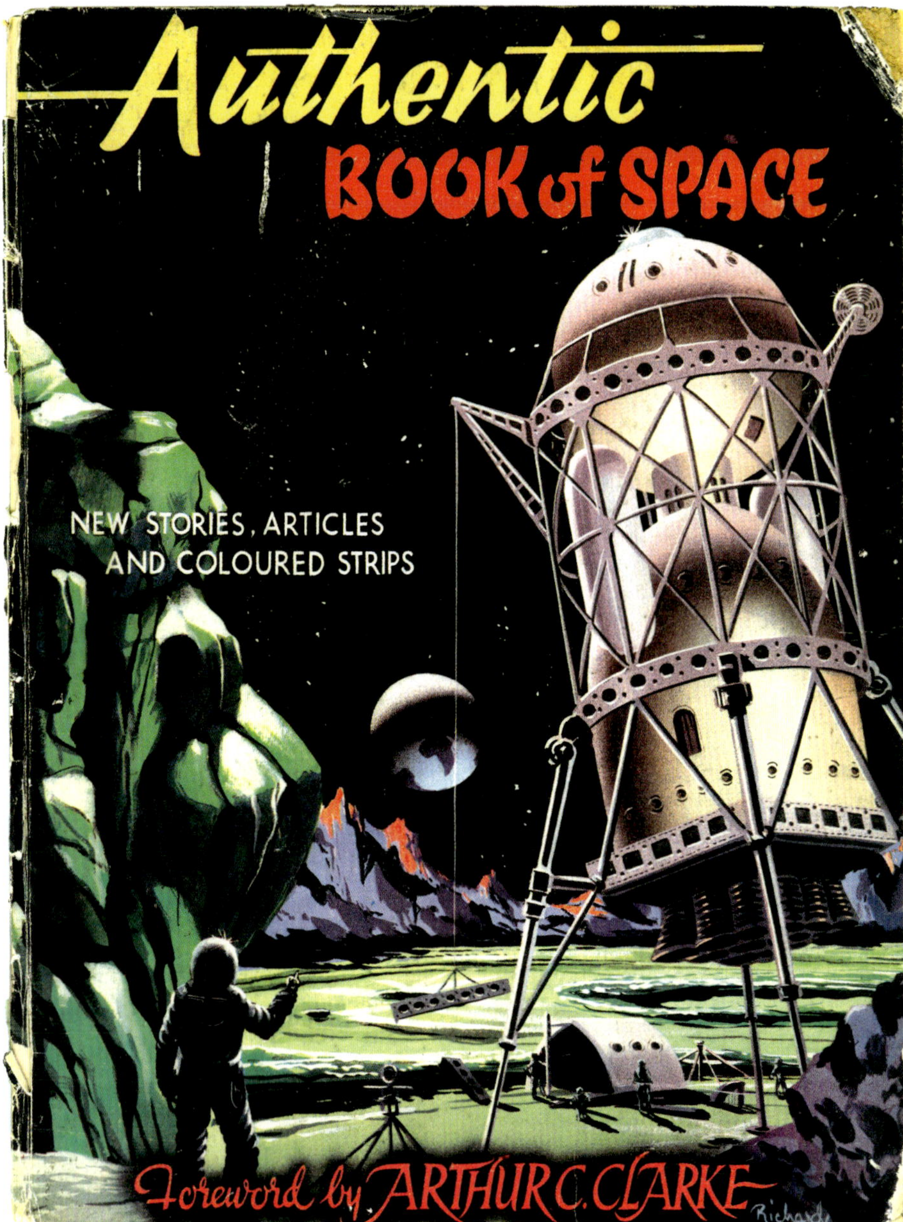

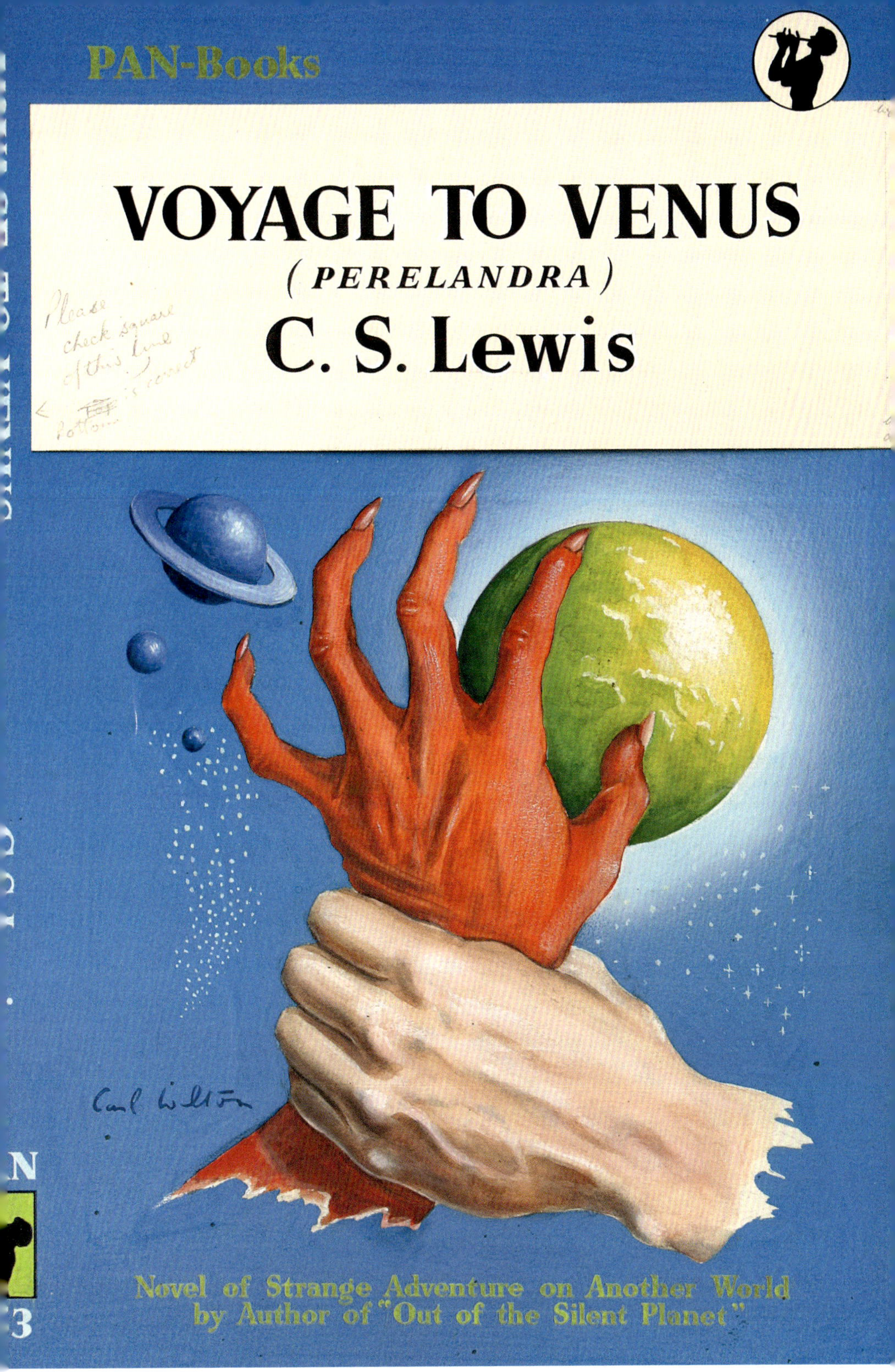

C. S. Lewis | *Voyage to Venus (Perelandra)* | Pan Books, 1953
Original Art **Carl Wilton** | From the collection of Colin Larkin, used by permission

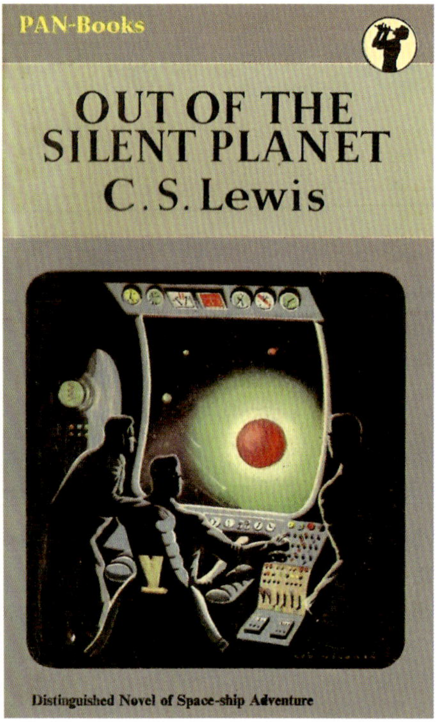

C. S. Lewis | *Out of the Silent Planet*
Pan Books, 1952 | Art **George Woodman**

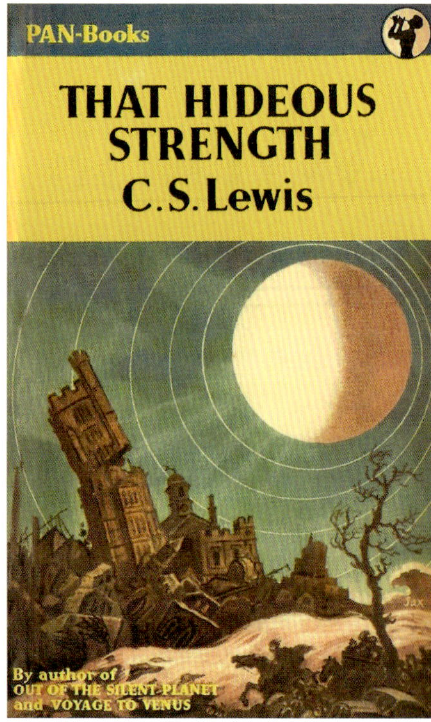

C. S. Lewis | *That Hideous Strength*
Pan Books, 1955 | Art **Sax**

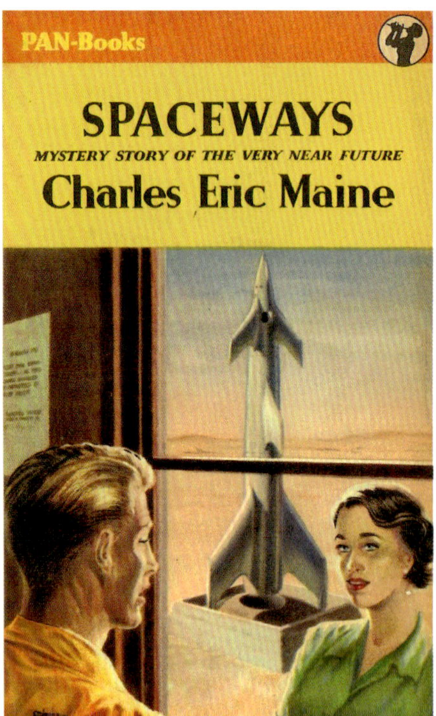

Charles Eric Maine | *Spaceways*
Pan Books, 1954 | Art **Gerard Quinn**

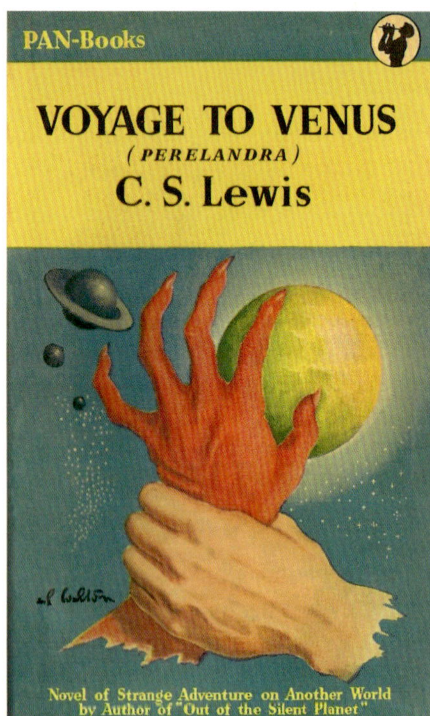

C. S. Lewis | *Voyage to Venus*
Pan Books, 1953 | Art **Carl Wilton**

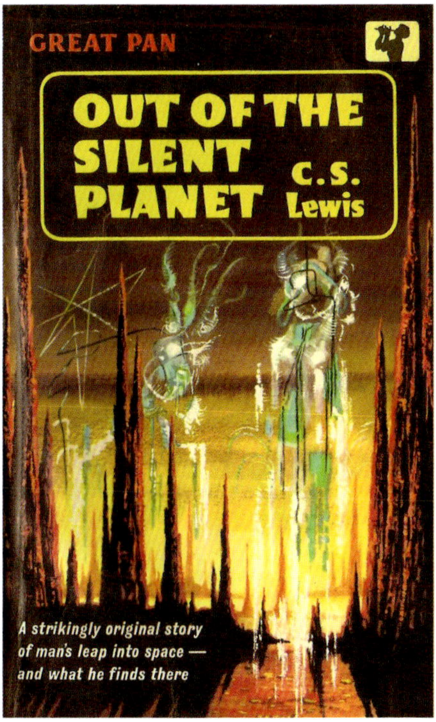

C. S. Lewis | *Out of the Silent Planet*
Pan Books, 1960 | Art by **S. R. Boldero**

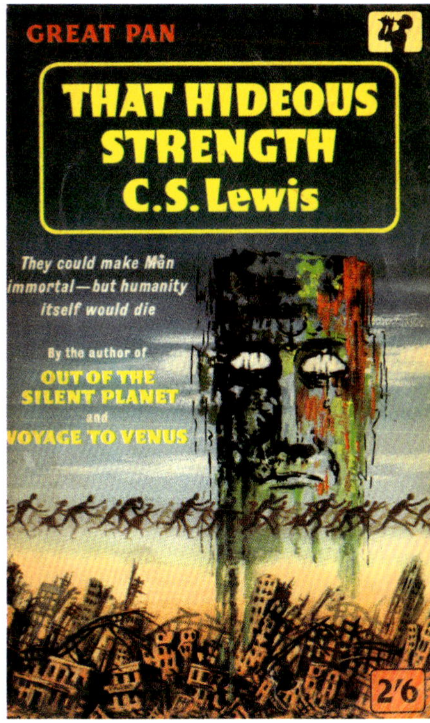

C. S. Lewis | *That Hideous Strength*
Pan Books, 1955 | Art **S. R. Boldero**

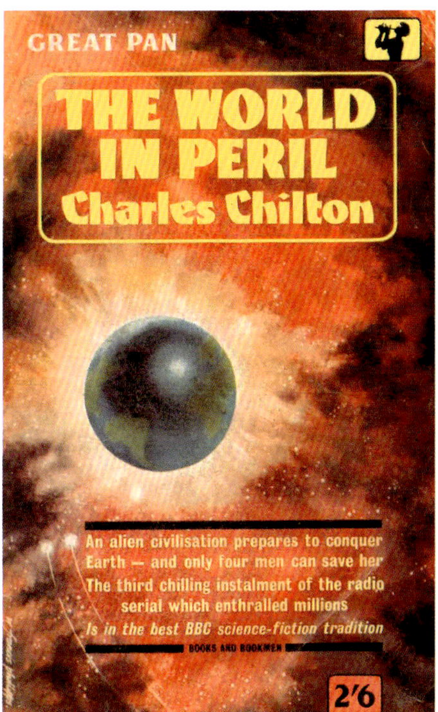

Charles Chilton | *The World in Peril*
Pan Books, 1962 | Art by **William Francis Phillipps**

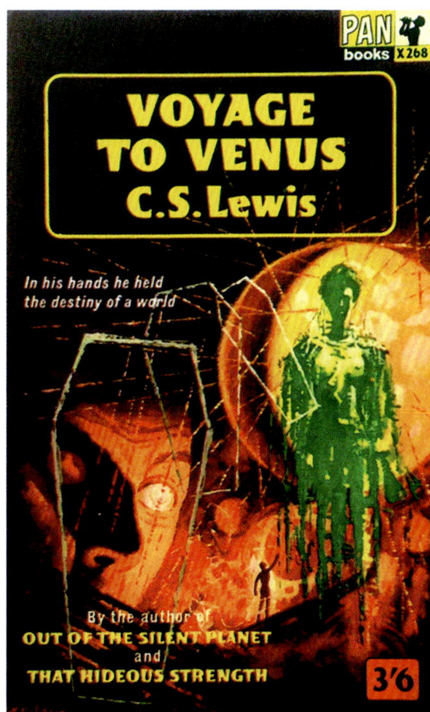

C. S. Lewis | *Voyage to Venus*
Pan Books, 1963 | Art **S. R. Boldero**

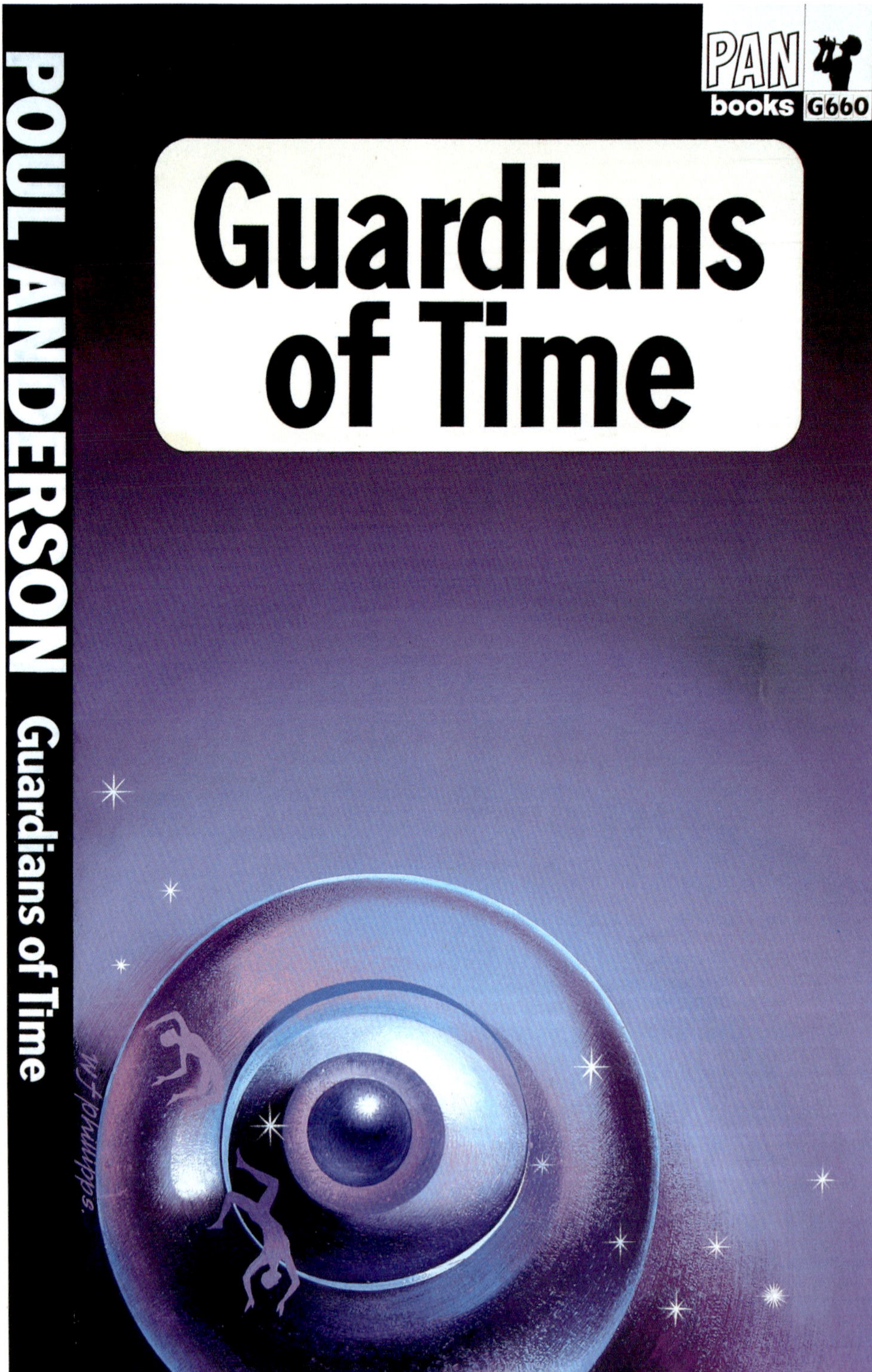

Poul Anderson | *Guardians of Time*
Pan Books, 1964 | Original art **William F. Phillipps**

From the collection of Colin Larkin
used by permission

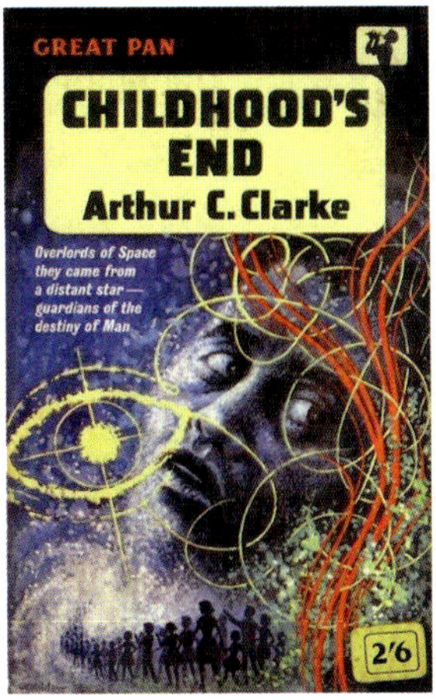

Arthur C. Clarke | *Childhood's End*
Pan Books, 1961 | Art **S. R. Boldero**

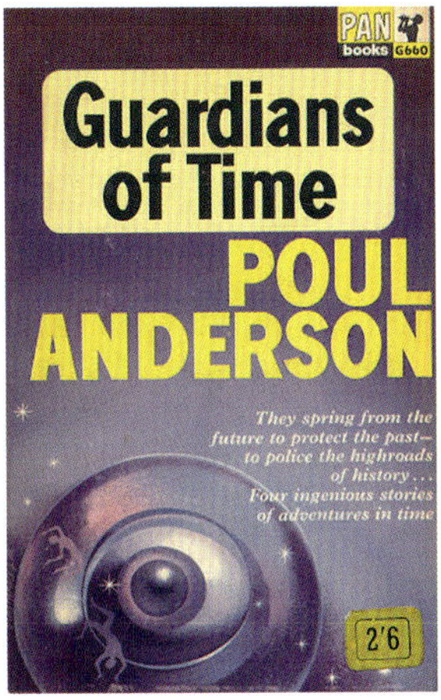

Poul Anderson | *Guardians of Time*
Pan Books, 1964 | Art **William F. Phillipps**

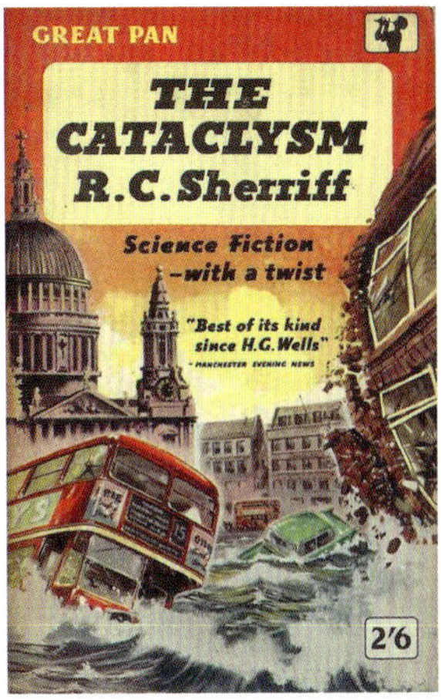

R. C. Sherriff | *The Cataclysm*
Pan Books, 1958 | Art **Glenn Steward**

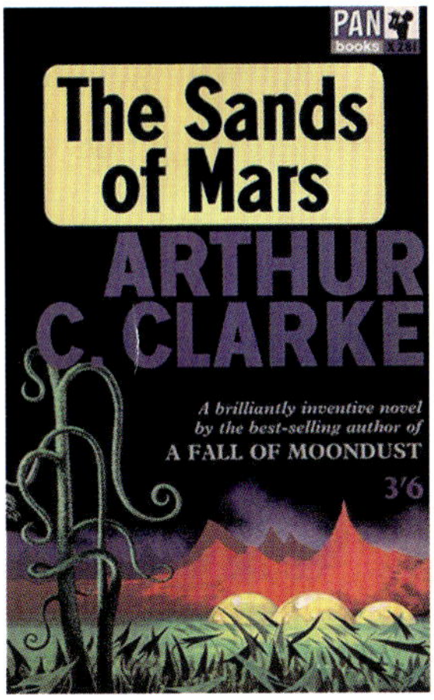

Arthur C. Clarke | *The Sands of Mars*
Pan Books, 1964 | Art **William F. Phillipps**

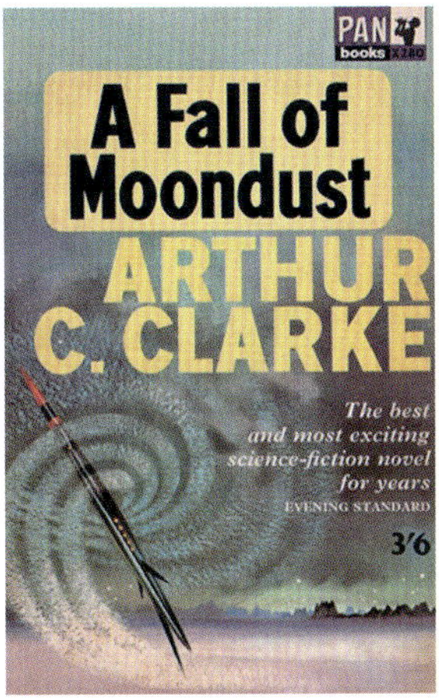

Arthur C. Clarke | *A Fall of Moondust*
Pan Books, 1964 | Art **William F. Phillipps**

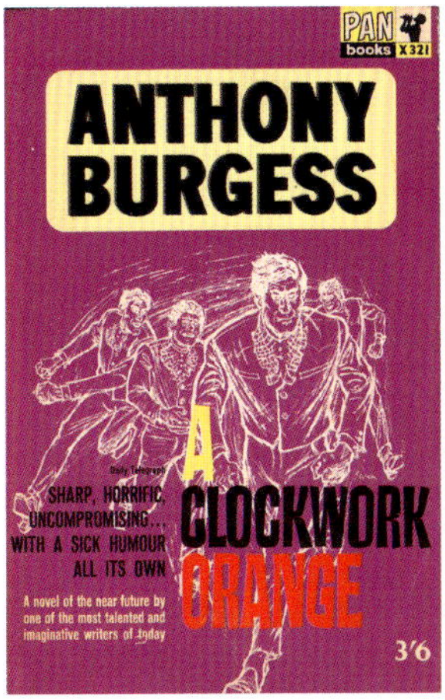

Anthony Burgess | *A Clockwork Orange*
Pan Books, 1964 | Art **Pat Owen**

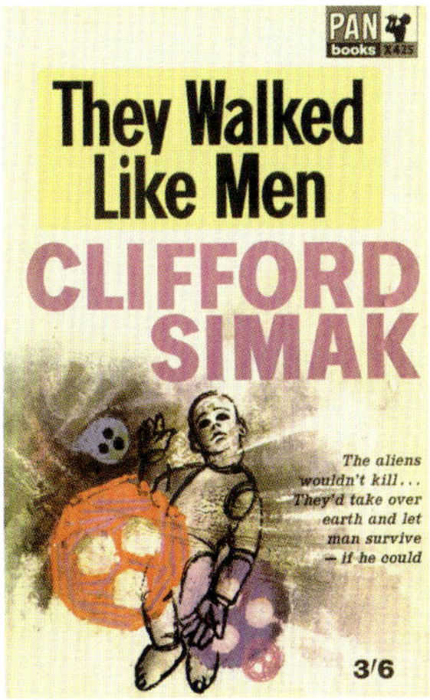

Clifford D. Simak | *They Walked Like Men*
Pan Books, 1965 | Art **William F. Phillipps**

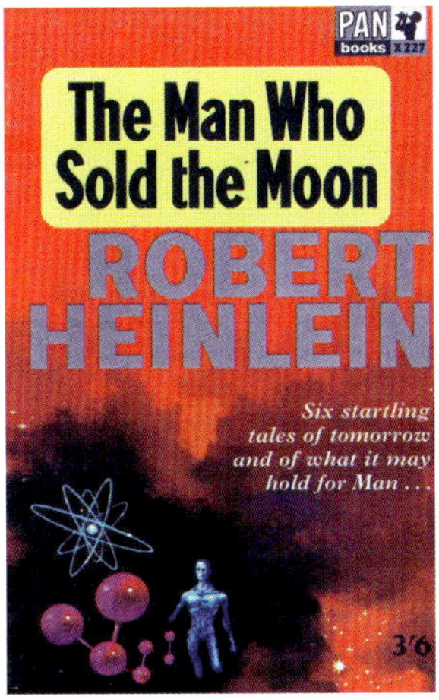

Robert Heinlein | *The Man Who Sold the Moon*
Pan Books, 1963 | Art **William F. Phillipps**

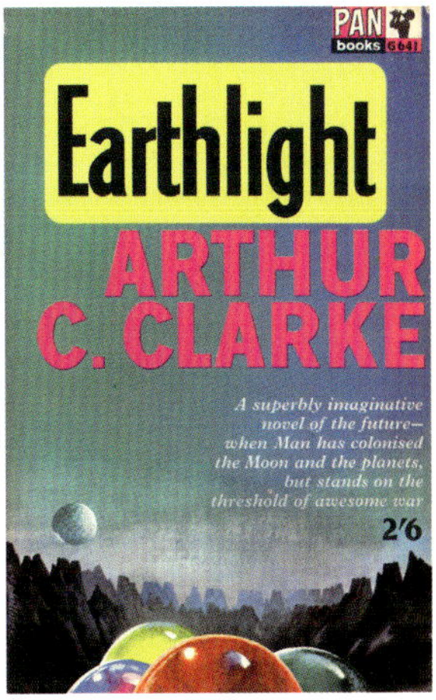

Arthur C. Clarke | *Earthlight*
Pan Books, 1963 | Art **William F. Phillipps**

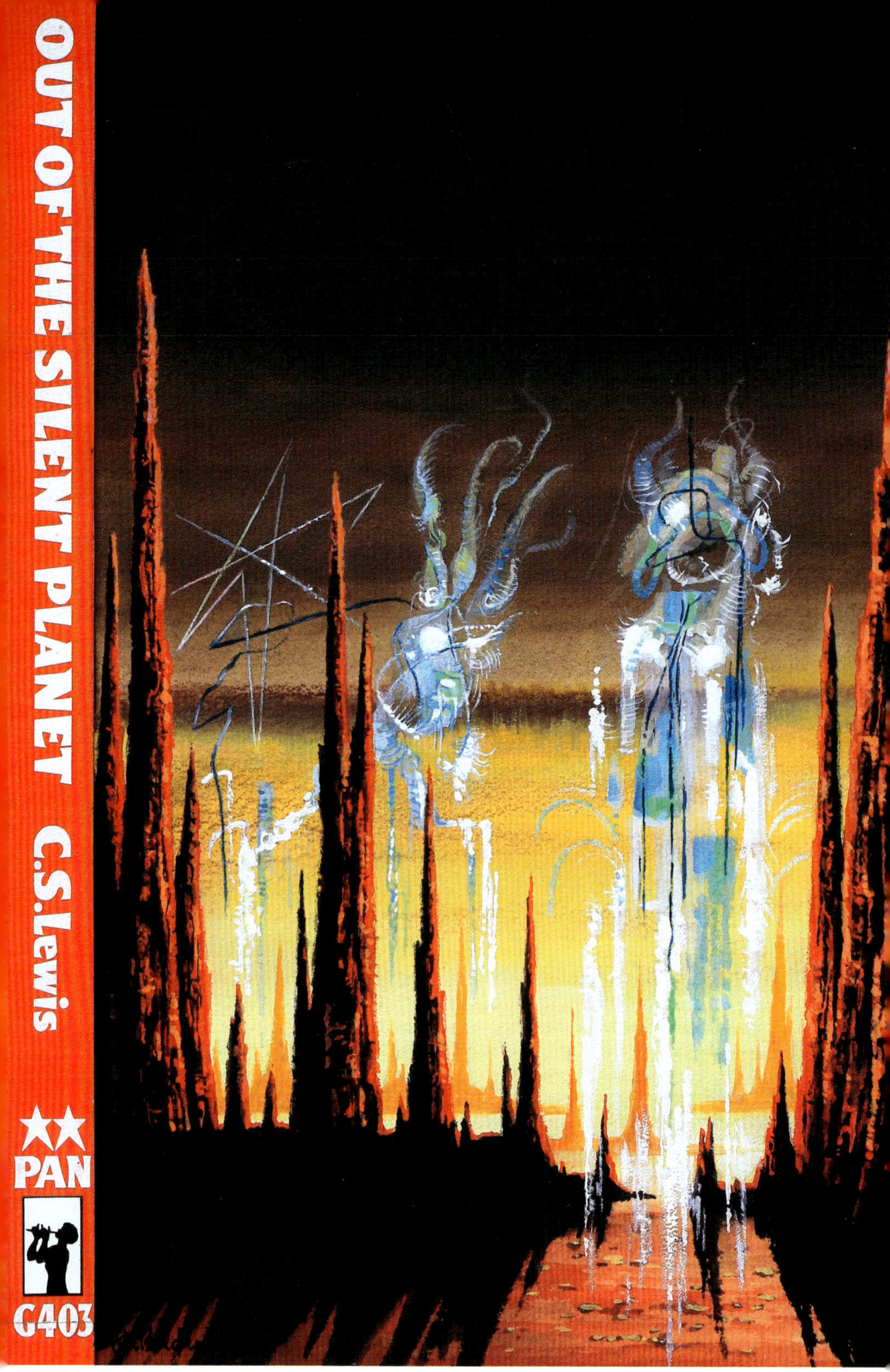

C. S. Lewis | *Out of the Silent Planet* | Pan Books, 1960
Original Art **S. R. Boldero** | From the collection of Colin Larkin, used by permission

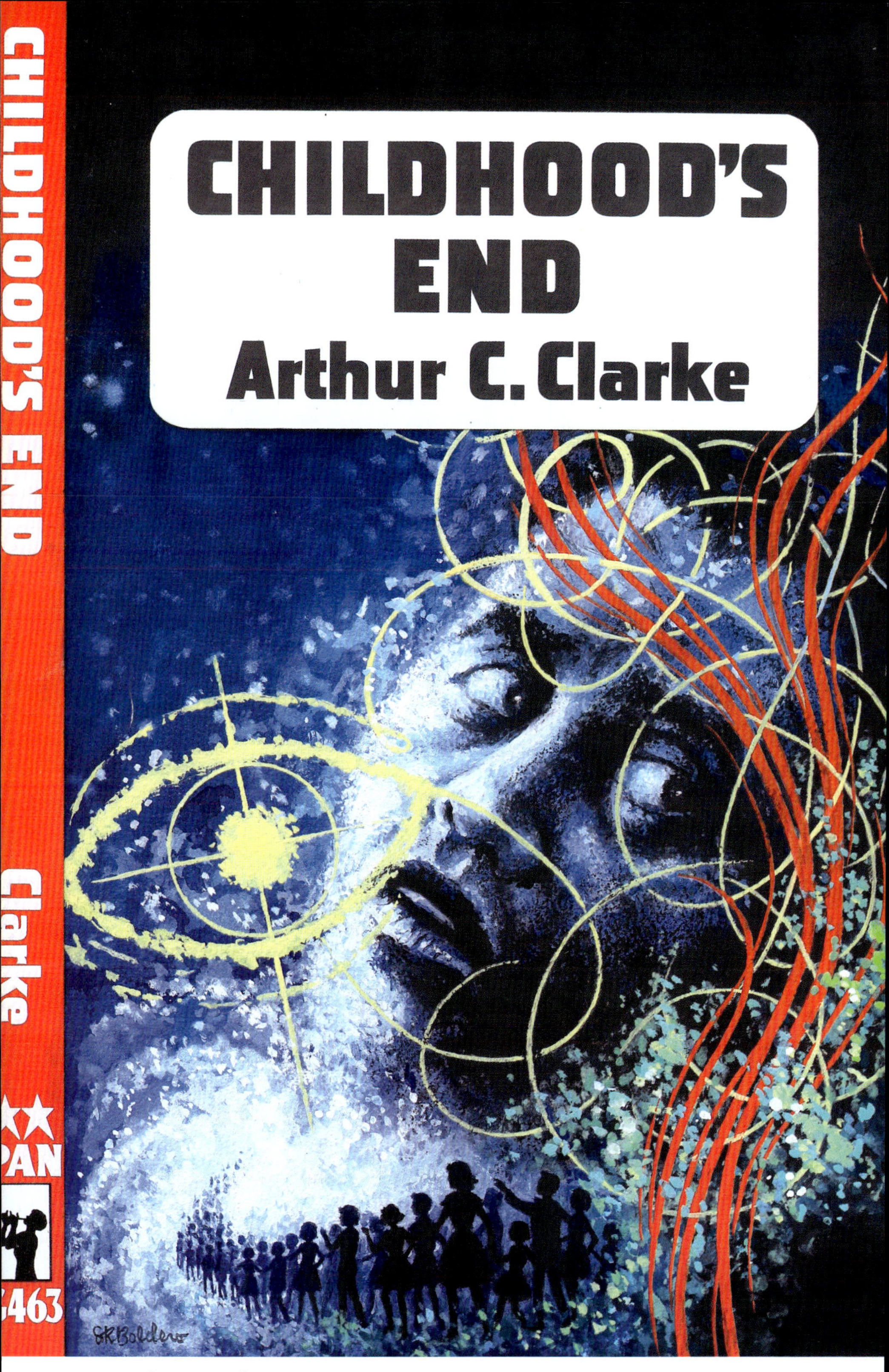

Arthur C. Clarke | *Childhood's End* | Pan Books, 1961
Original art **S. R. Boldero** | From the collection of Colin Larkin, used by permission

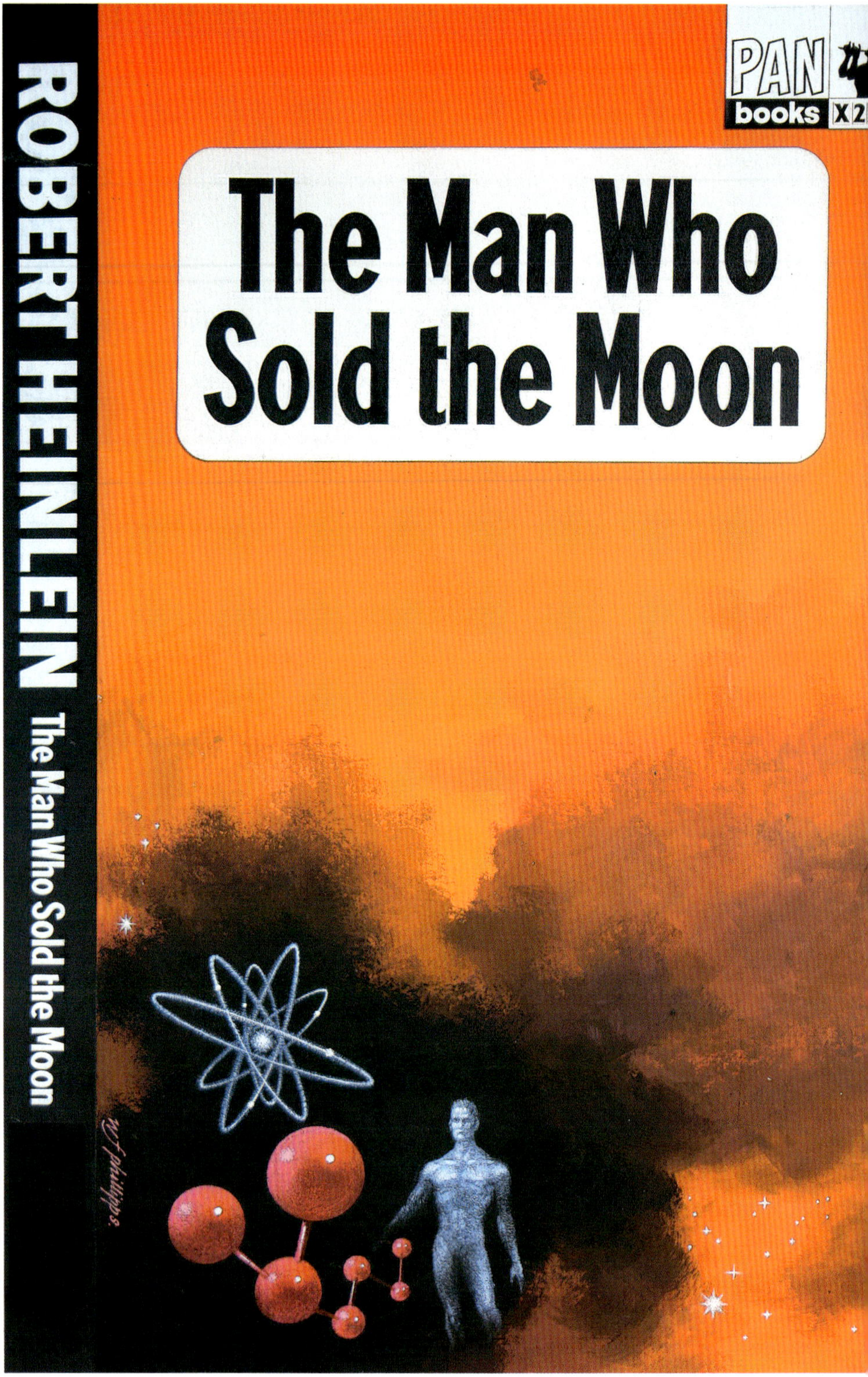

Robert Heinlein | *The Man Who Sold the Moon* | Pan Books, 1963
Original art **William F. Phillipps** | From the collection of Colin Larkin, used by permission

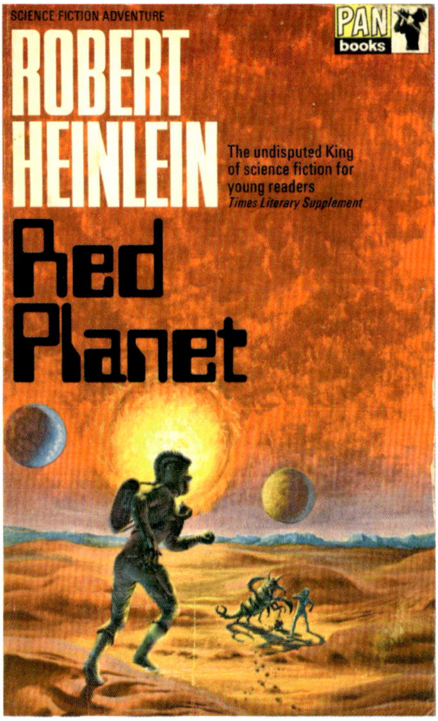

Robert A. Heinlein | Red Planet
Pan Books, 1967 | Art **Edward Mortelmans**

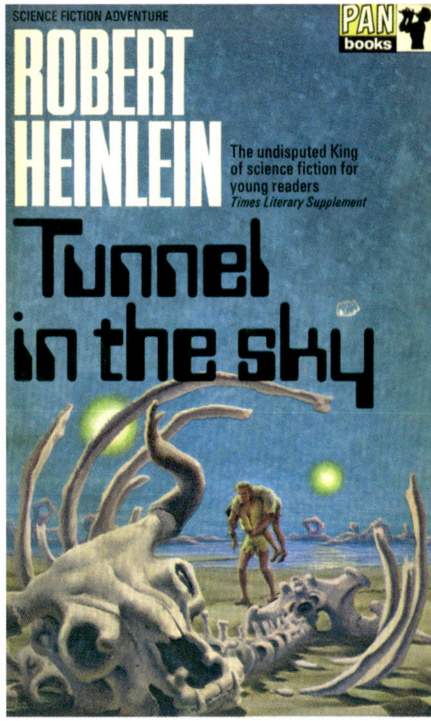

Robert A. Heinlein | Tunnel in the Sky
Pan Books, 1968 | Art **Edward Mortelmans**

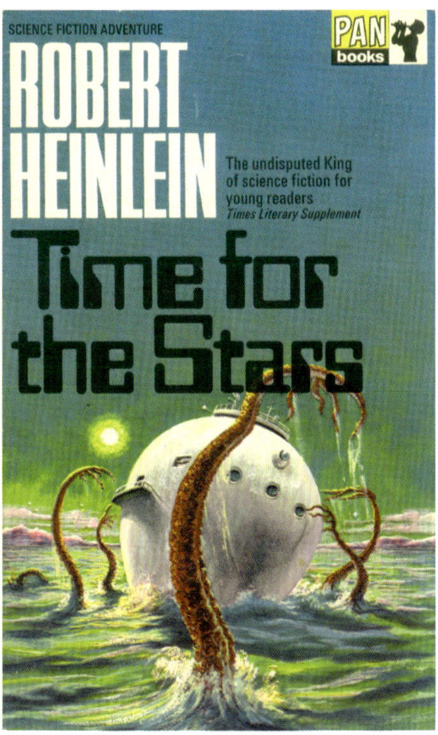

Robert A. Heinlein | Time for the Stars
Pan Books, 1968 | Art **Edward Mortelmans**

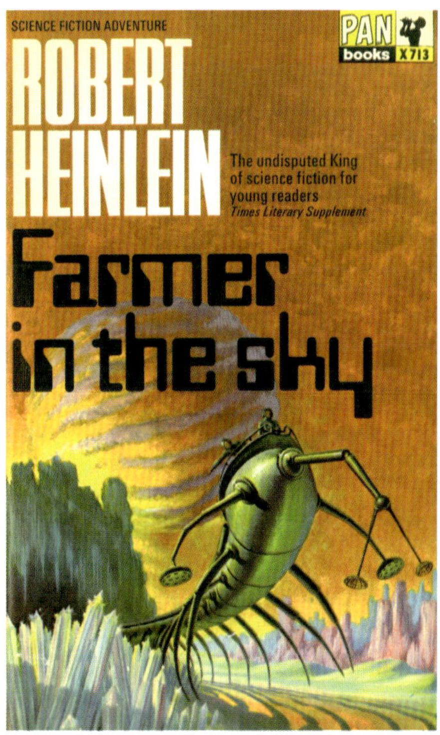

Robert A. Heinlein | Farmer in the Sky
Pan Books, 1967 | Art **Edward Mortelmans**

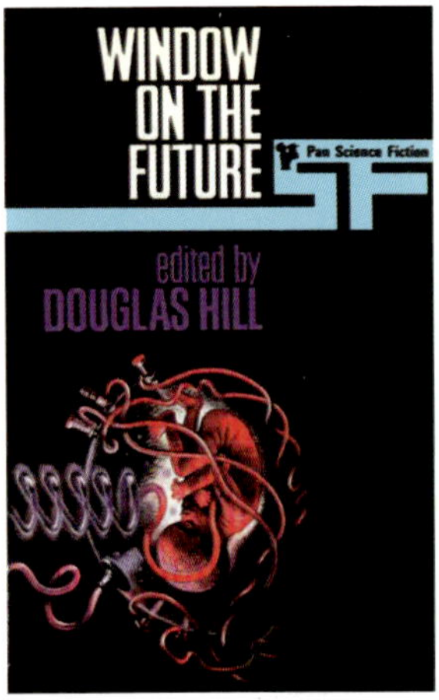

Douglas Hill
Window on the Future
Pan Books, 1970 | Art **William F. Phillipps**

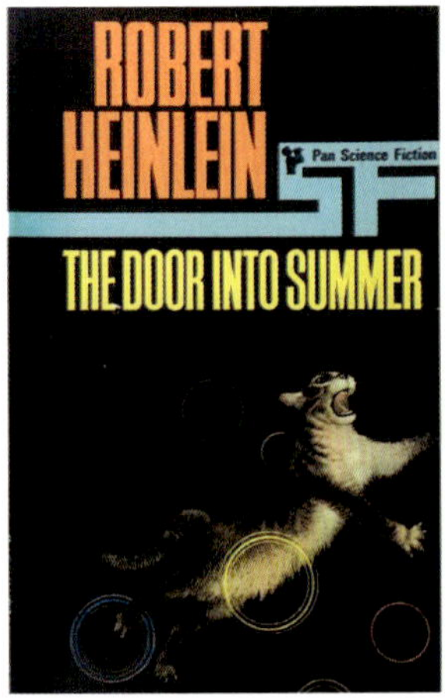

Robert A. Heinlein
The Door Into Summer
Pan Books, 1970 | Art **William F. Phillipps**

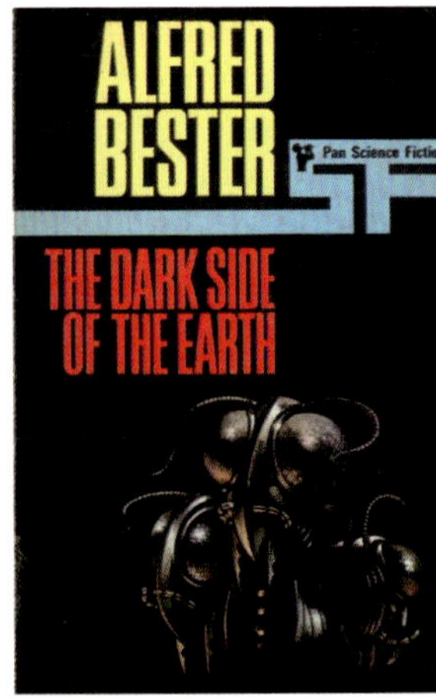

Alfred Bester
The Dark Side of the Earth
Pan Books, | Art **William F. Phillipps**

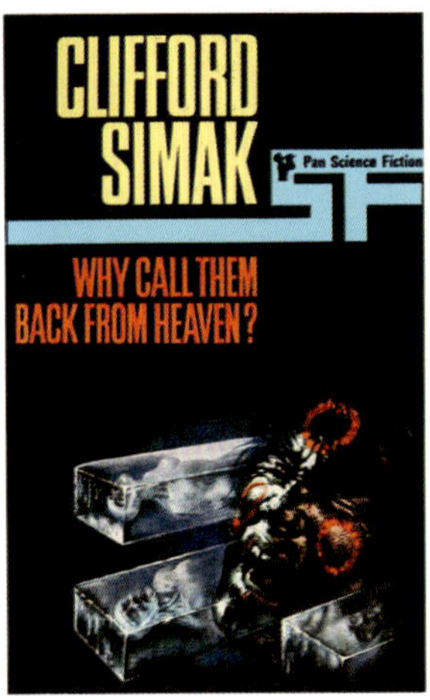

Clifford Simak
Why Call Them Back from Heaven?
Pan Books, 1970 | Art **William F. Phillipps**

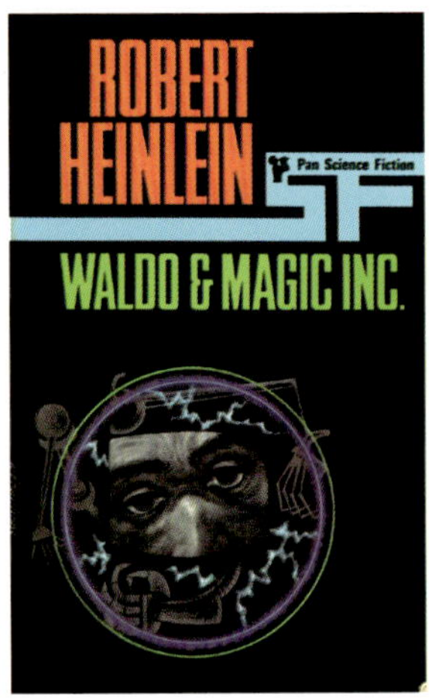

Robert A. Heinlein
Waldo & Magic, Inc.
Pan Books, 1969 | Art **William F. Phillipps**

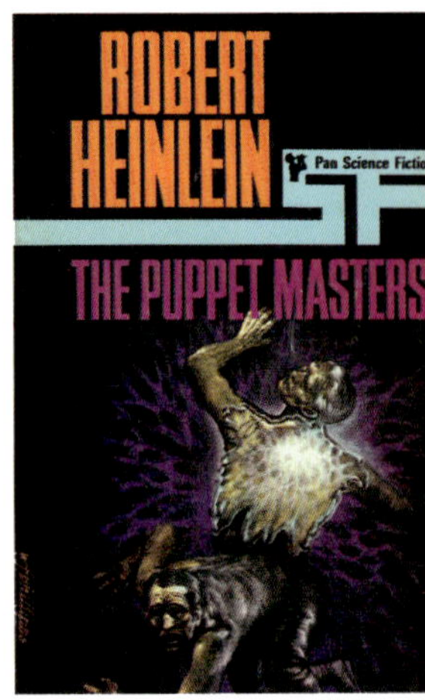

Robert A. Heinlein
The Puppet Masters
Pan Books, 1969 | Art **William F. Phillipps**

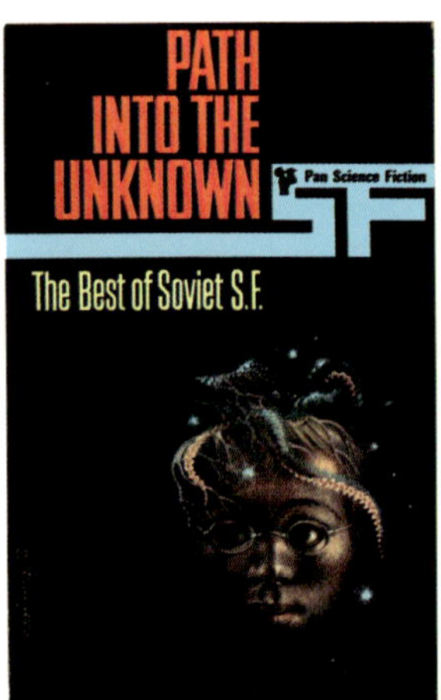

Path Into the Unknown:
The Best Soviet Science Fiction
Pan Books, 1969 | Art **William F. Phillipps**

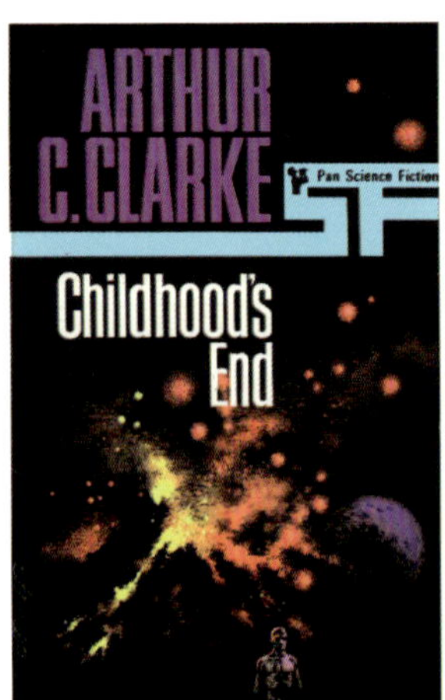

Arthur C. Clarke
Childhood's End
Pan Books, 1970 | Art **William F. Phillipps**

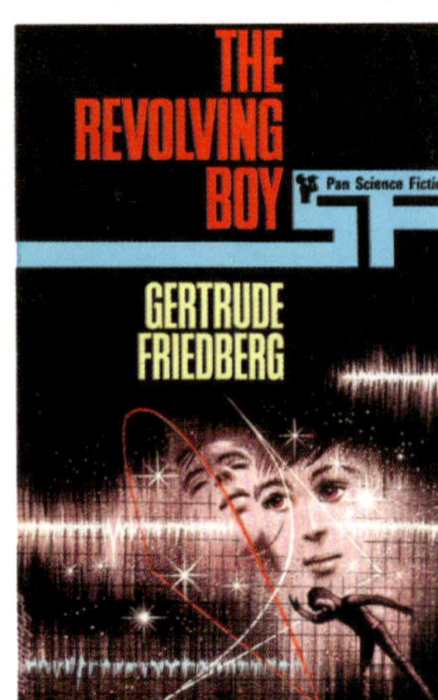

Gertrude Friedberg
The Revolving Boy
Pan Books, 1970 | Art **William F. Phillipps**

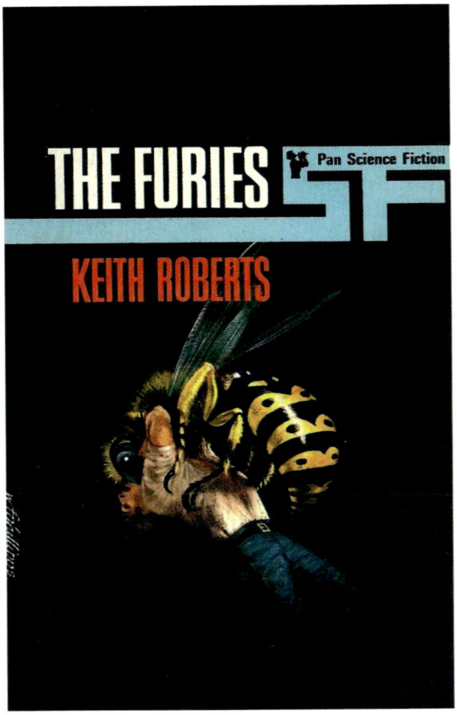

Keith Roberts | *The Furies*
Pan Books, 1969 | Art **William F. Phillipps**

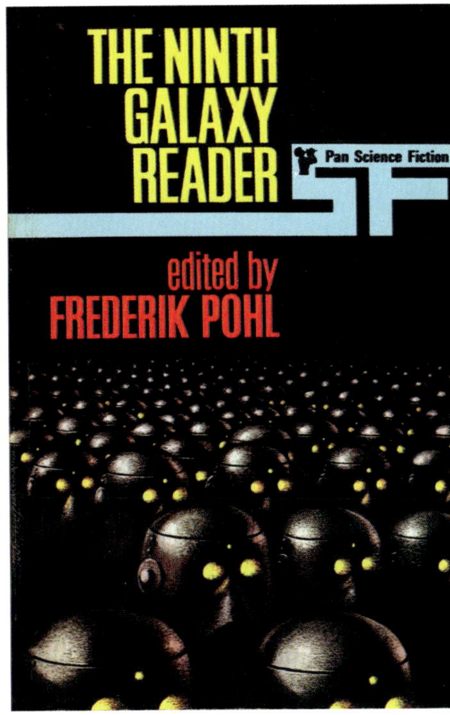

Frederik Pohl | *The Ninth Galaxy Reader*
Pan Books, 1970 | Art **William F. Phillipps**

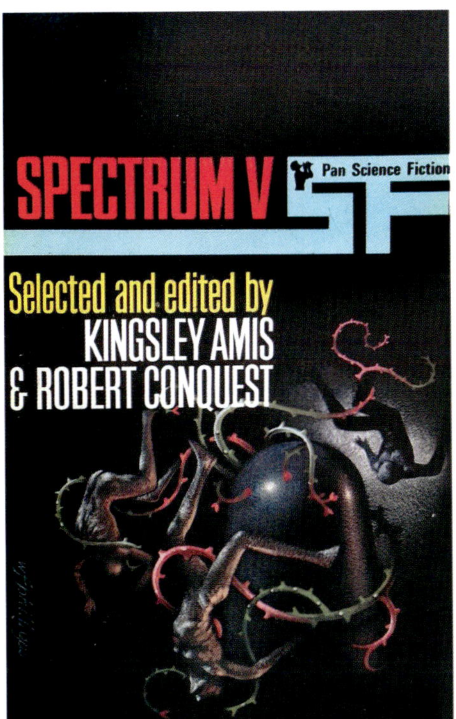

Kingsley Amis and Robert Conquest, eds. | *Spectrum V*
Pan Books 1969, | Art **William F. Phillipps**

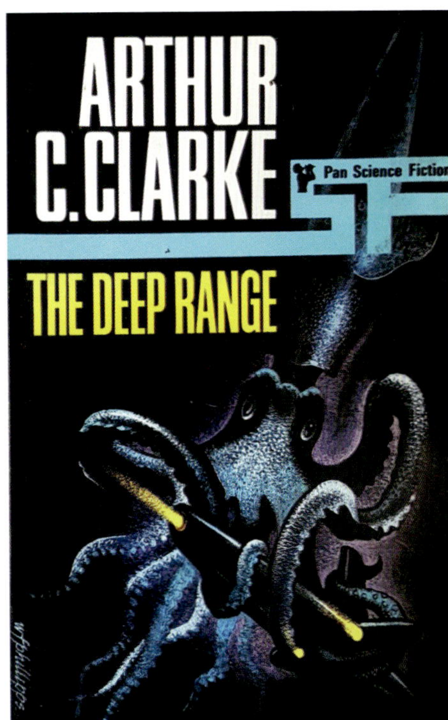

Arthur C. Clarke | *The Deep Range*
Pan Books, 1970 | Art **William F. Phillipps**

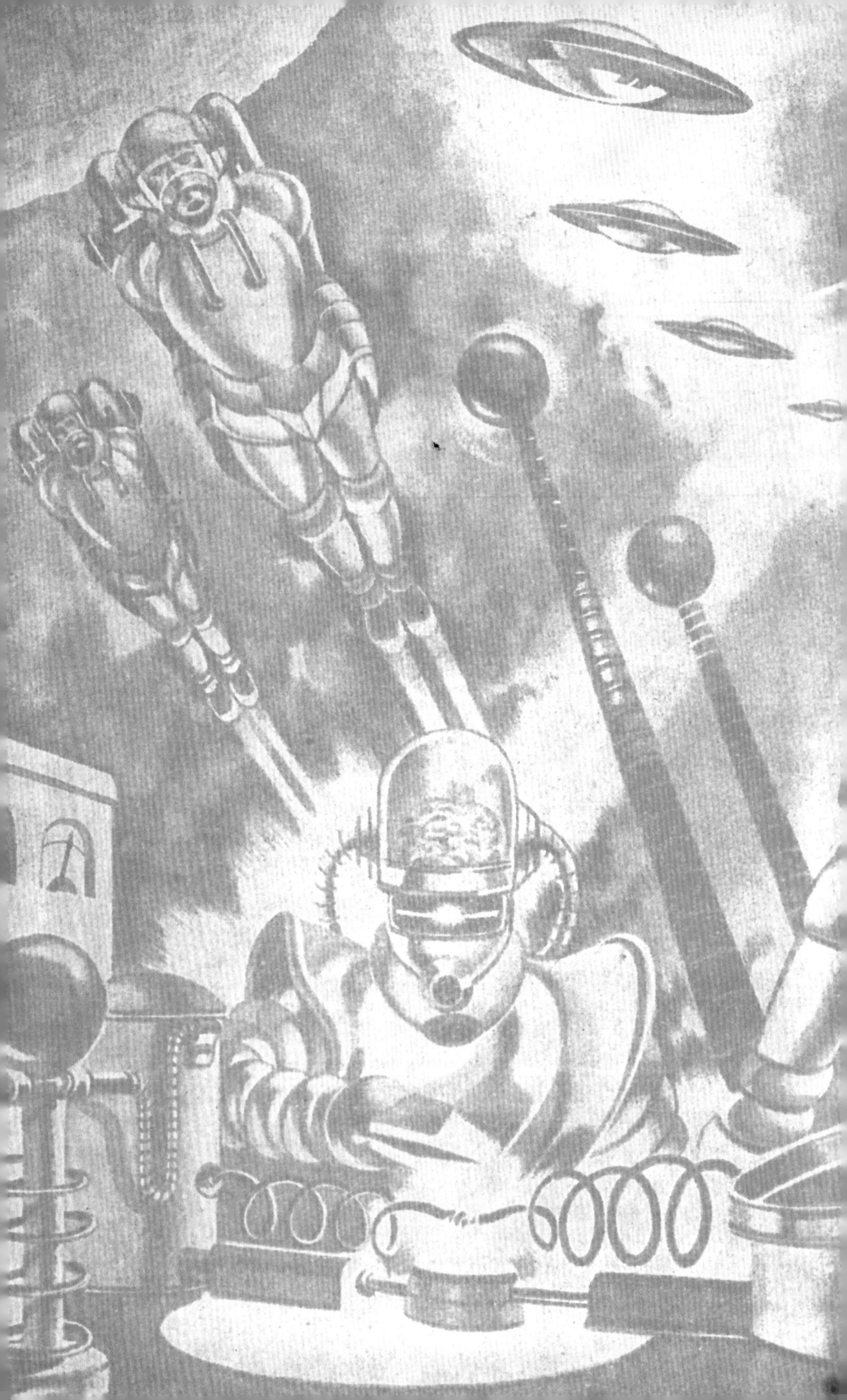

Endpapers from Hutchinson's hardcover juvenile science fiction series, c1954, by Ron Embleton

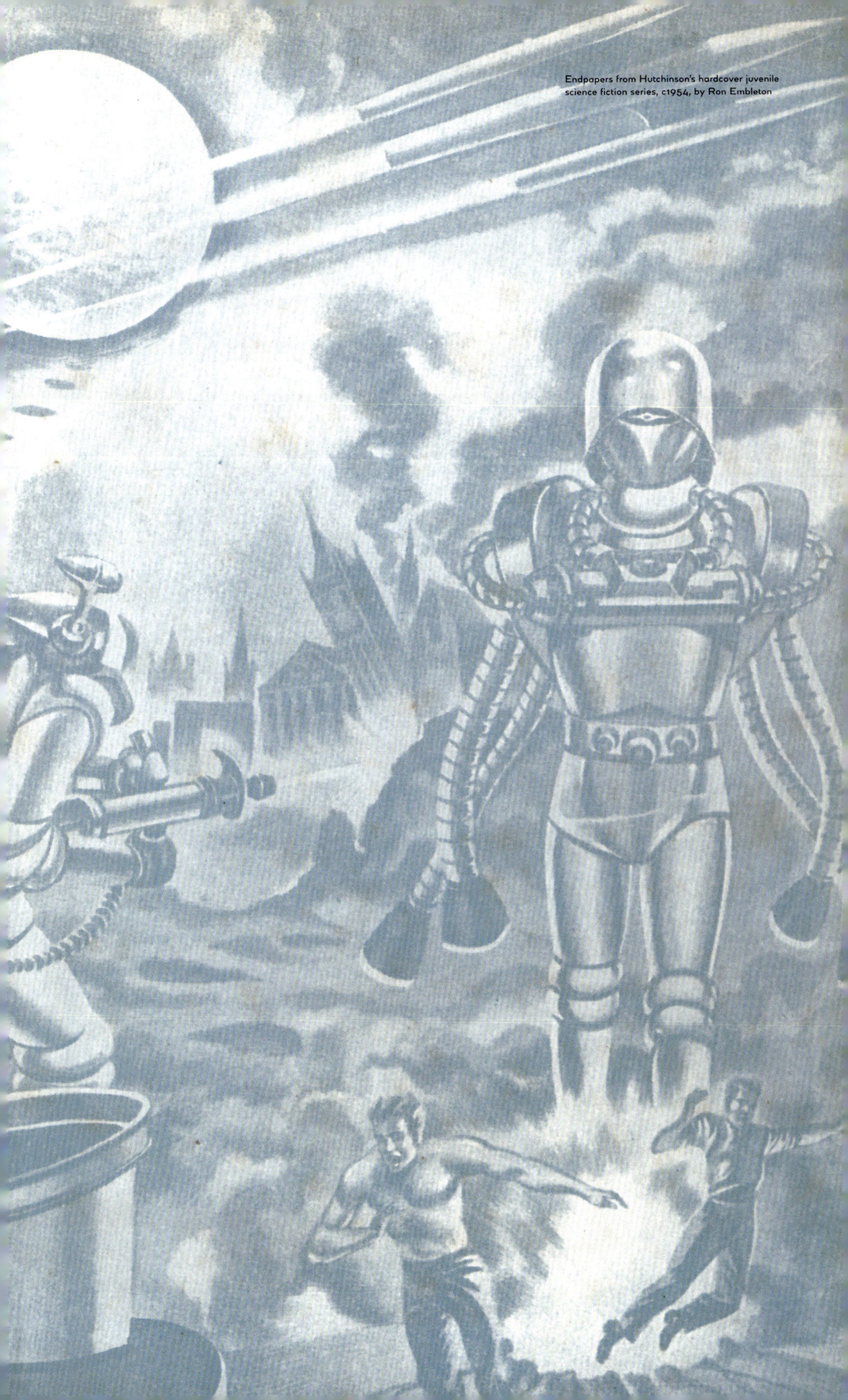

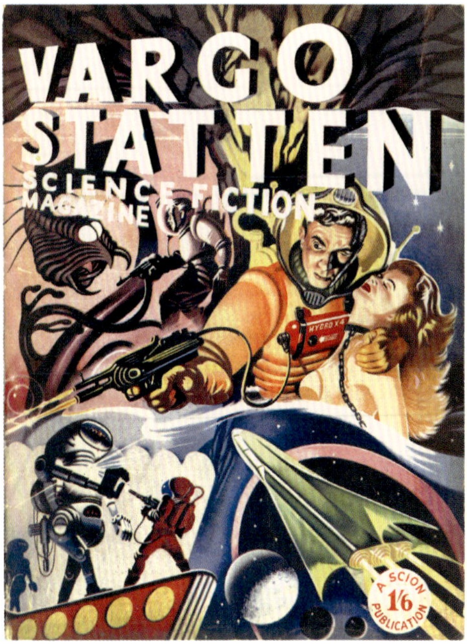

Vargo Statten | Vargo Statten Science Fiction Magazine, January 1954
Scion Ltd., 1954 | Art **Ron Turner**

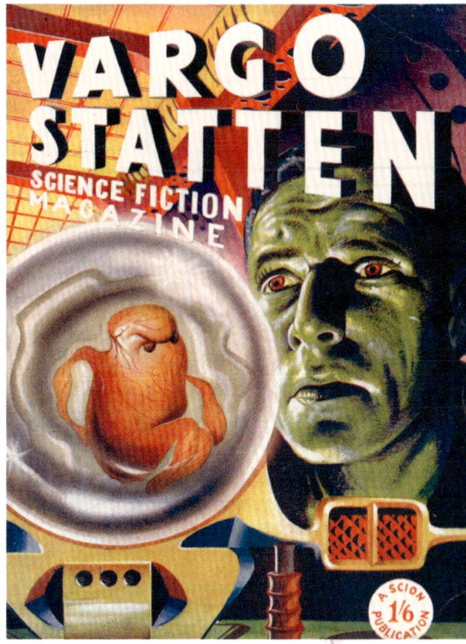

Vargo Statten | Vargo Statten Science Fiction Magazine, Vol 1 No 2
Scion Ltd., 1954 | Art **John Richards**

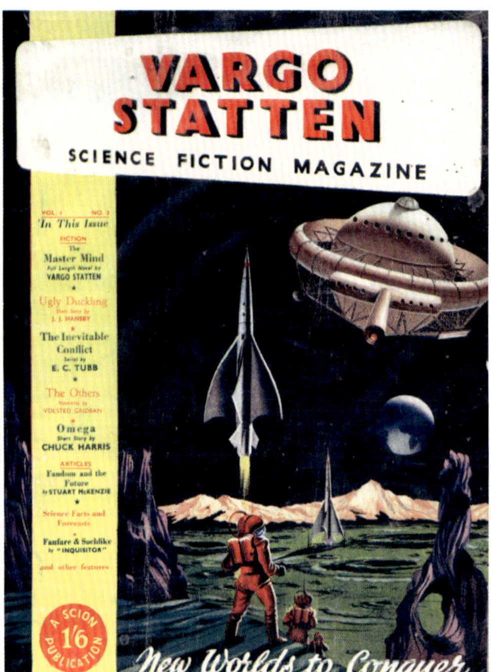

Vargo Statten | Vargo Statten Science Fiction Magazine, Vol 1 No 3
Scion Ltd., 1954 | Art **John Richards**

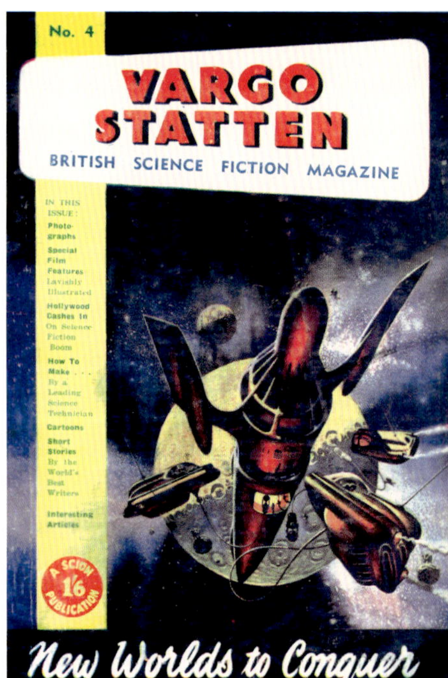

Vargo Statten | Vargo Statten British Science Fiction Magazine, Vol 1 No 4
Scion Ltd., 1954 | Art **Ron Turner**

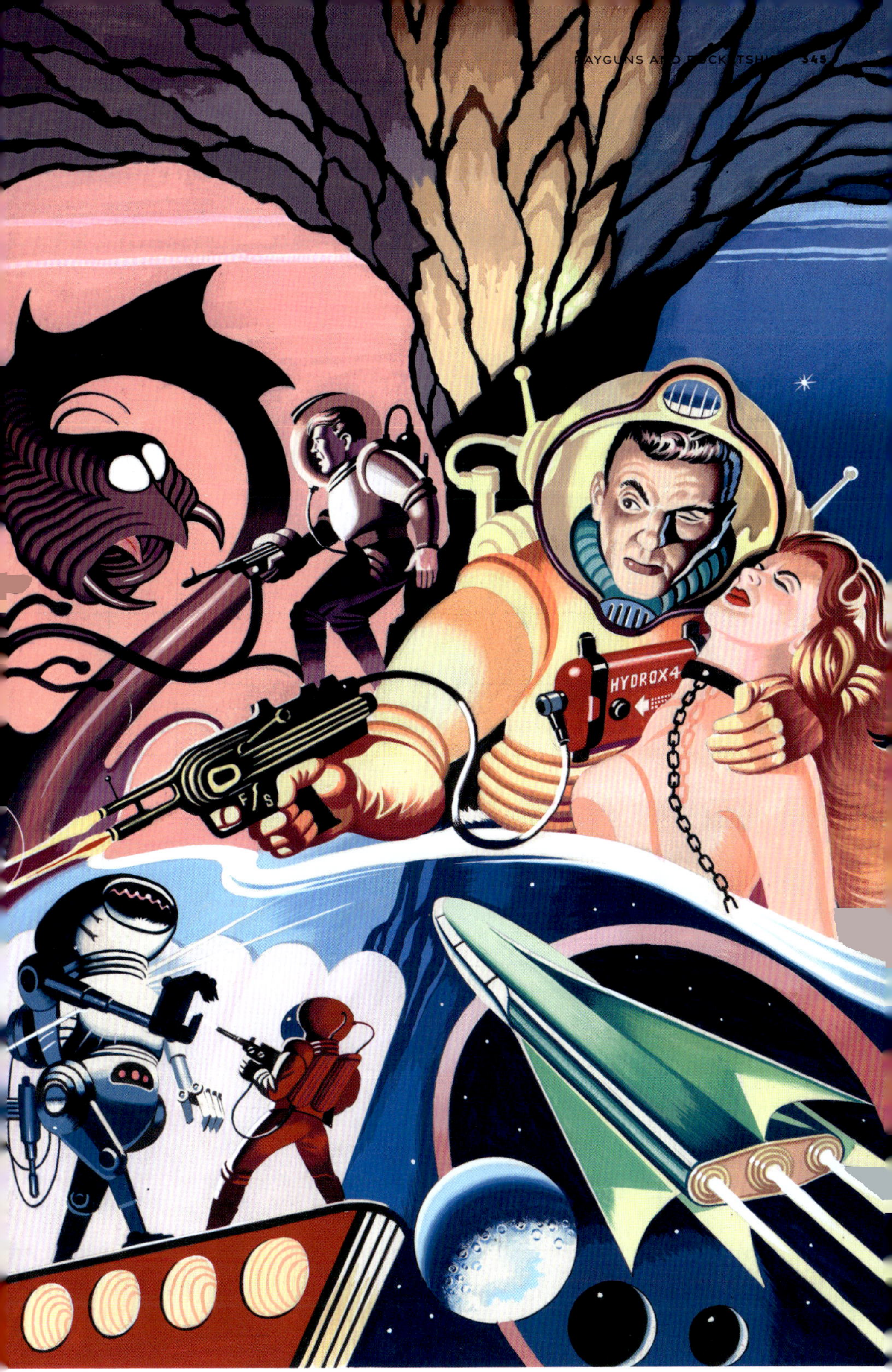

Vargo Statten | Vargo Statten Science Fiction Magazine, January 1954
Scion Ltd., 1954 | Art recreation c.1980s **Ron Turner**

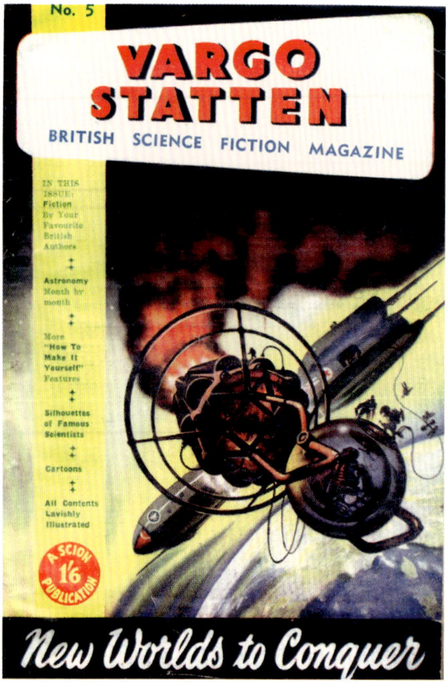

Vargo Statten | Vargo Statten British Science Fiction Magazine, Vol 1 No 5
Scion Ltd., 1954 | Art **Ron Turner**

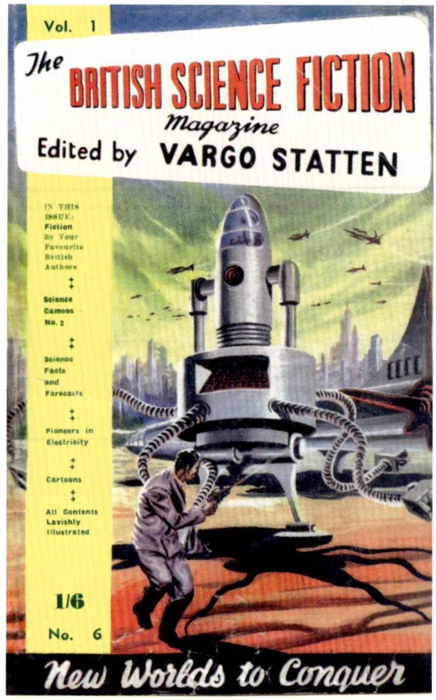

Vargo Statten | The British Science Fiction Magazine, Vol 1 No 6
Scion Ltd., 1954 | Art **John Richards**

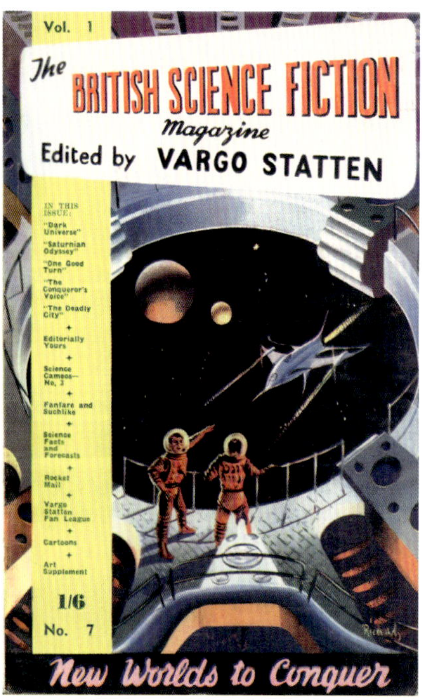

Vargo Statten | The British Science Fiction Magazine, Vol 1 No 7
Scion Ltd., 1954 | Art **John Richards**

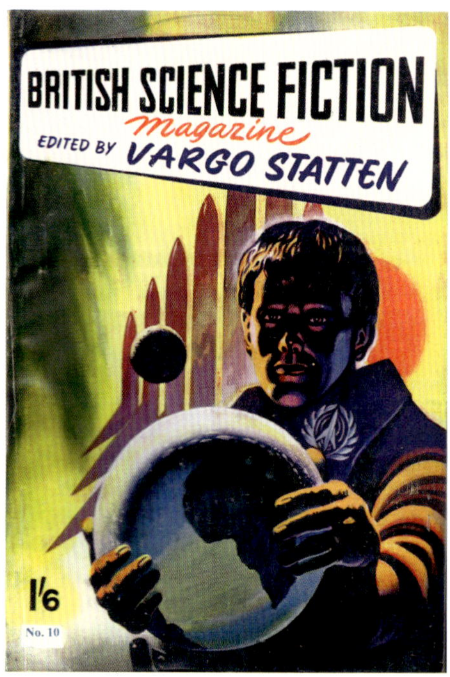

Vargo Statten | British Science Fiction Magazine, Vol 1 No 10
Scion Ltd., 1954 | Art **Ron Turner**

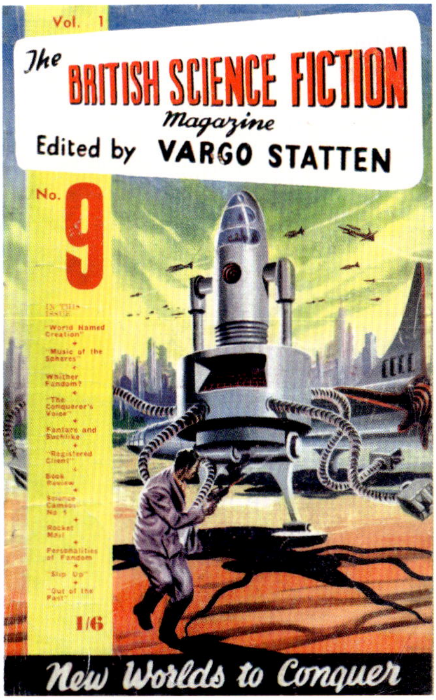

Vargo Statten | The British Science Fiction Magazine, Vol 1 No 9
Scion Ltd., 1955 | Art **John Richards**

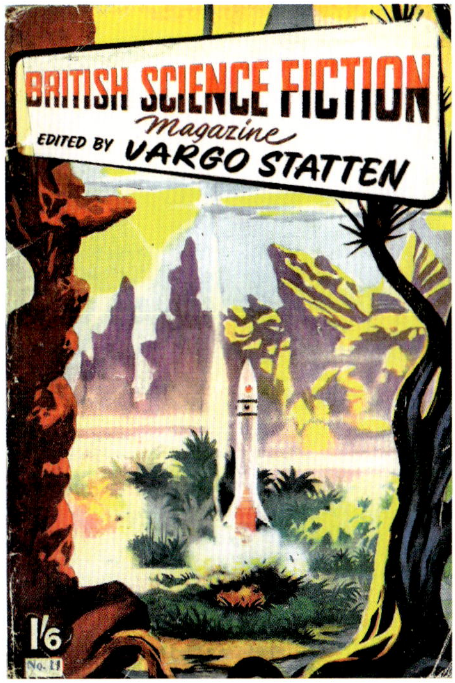

Vargo Statten | British Science Fiction Magazine, Vol 1 No 11
Scion Ltd., 1955 | Art **Ron Turner**

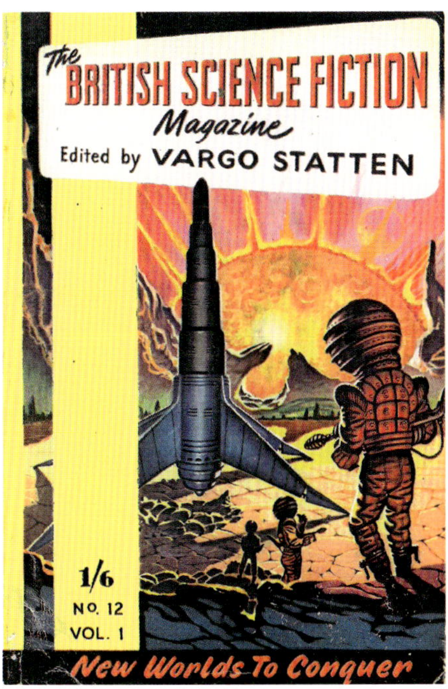

Vargo Statten | The British Science Fiction Magazine, Vol 1 No 12
Scion Ltd., 1955 | Art **Ron Turner**

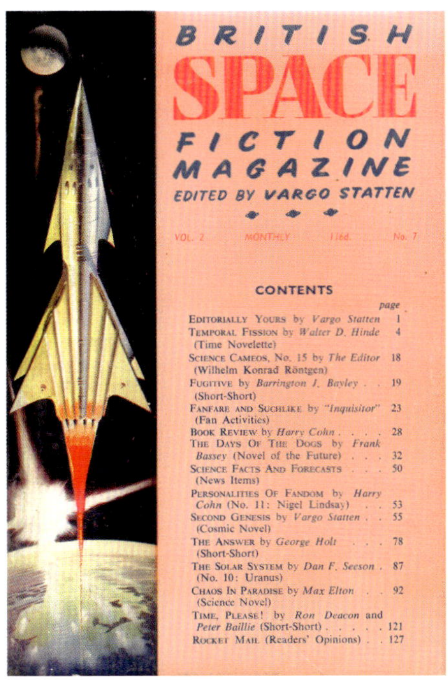

Vargo Statten | British Space Fiction Magazine, Vol. 2, No. 7
Scion Ltd., 1955 | Art **Ron Turner**

opposite **Richard Matheson** | *The Shores of Space*
Corgi Books S614, 1959 | Original art **John Richards**

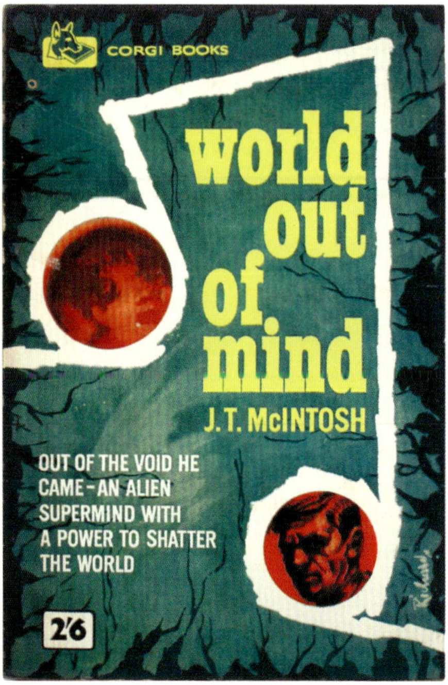

J. T. McIntosh | *World Out of Mind*
Corgi Books SS995, 1961 | Art **John Richards**

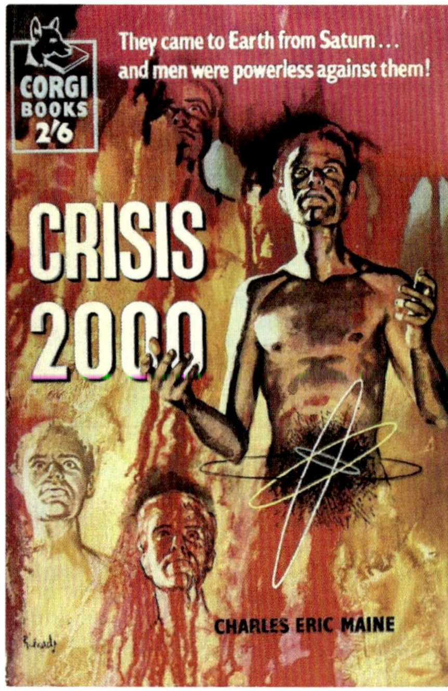

Charles Eric Maine | *Crisis 2000*
Corgi Books / Transworld Publishers S520, 1958 | Art **John Richards**

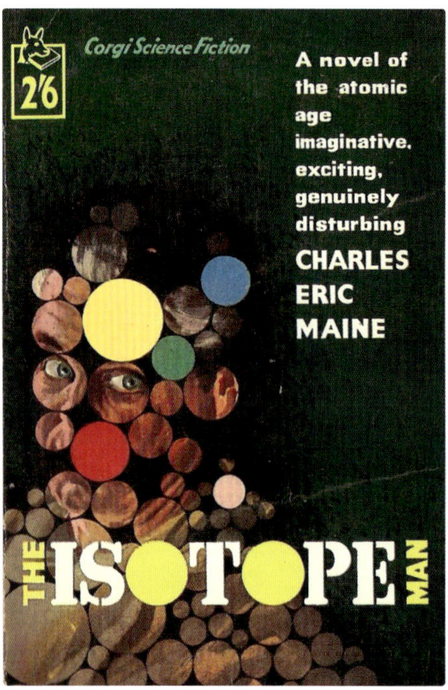

Charles Eric Maine | *The Isotope Man*
Corgi Books S631, 1959 | Art **John Richards**

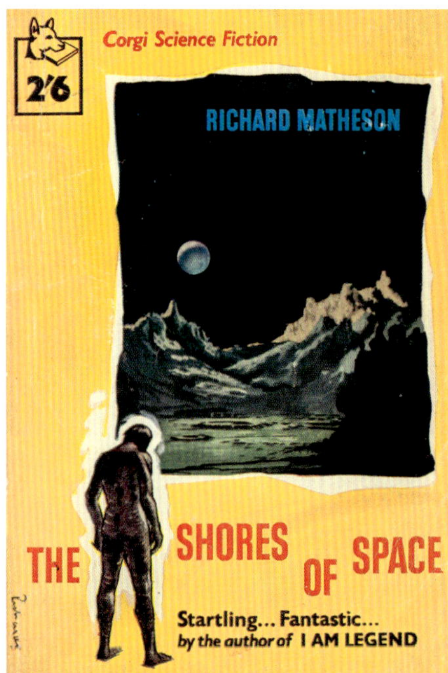

Richard Matheson | *The Shores of Space*
Corgi Books S614, 1959 | Art **John Richards**

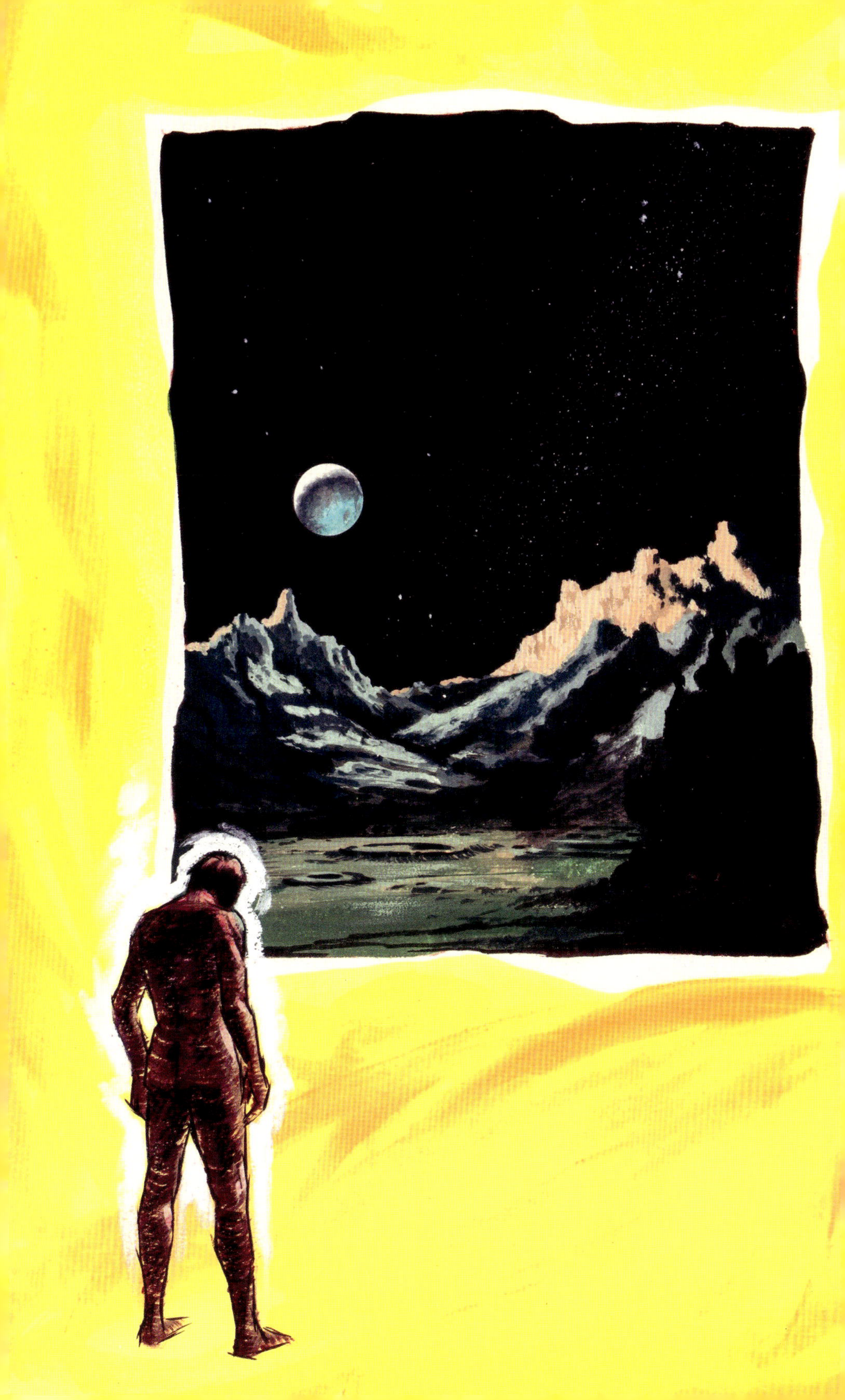

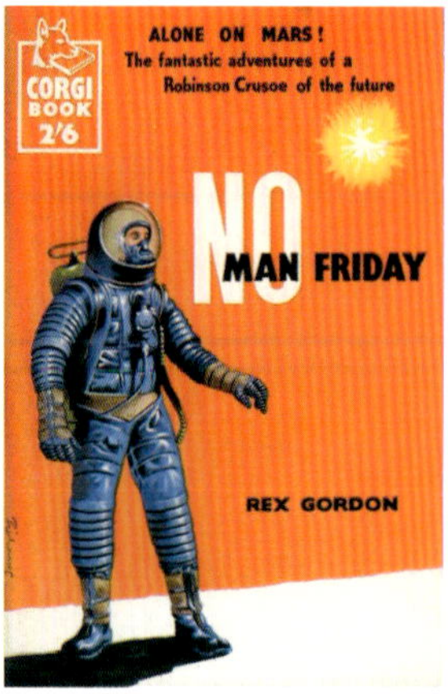

Rex Gordon | *No Man Friday*
Corgi Books S569, 1958 | Art **John Richards**

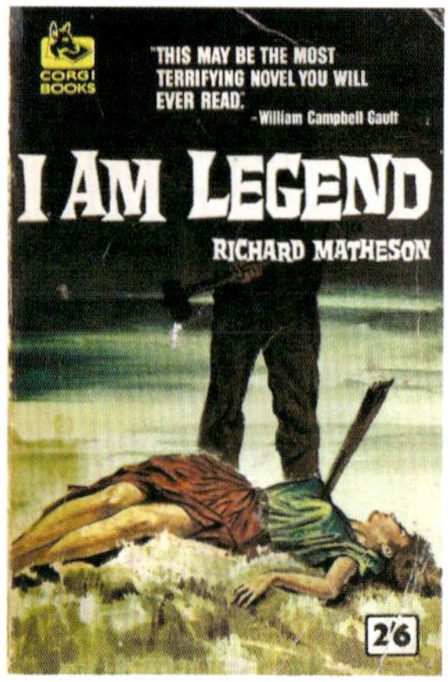

Richard Matheson | *I Am Legend*
Corgi Books S854, 1960 | Art **John Richards**

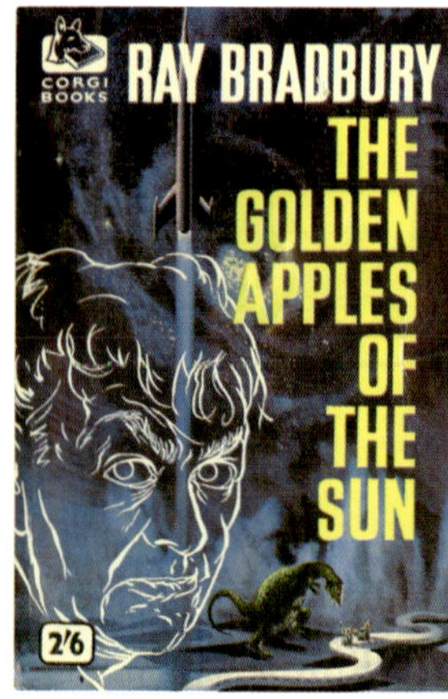

Ray Bradbury | *The Golden Apples of the Sun*
Corgi Books SS820, 1960 | Art **John Richards**

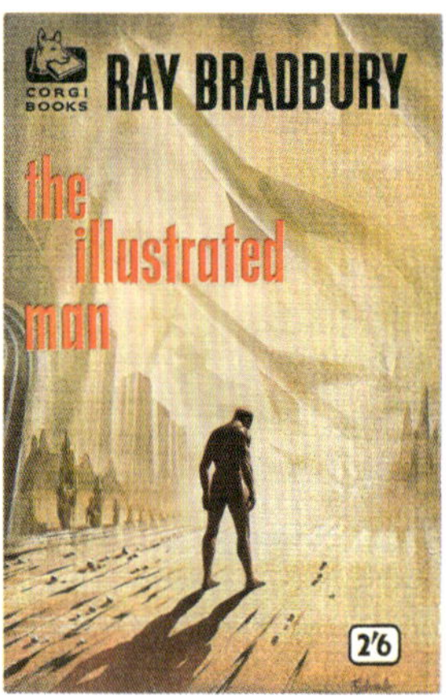

Ray Bradbury | *The Illustrated Man*
Corgi Books SS818, 1960 | Art **John Richards**

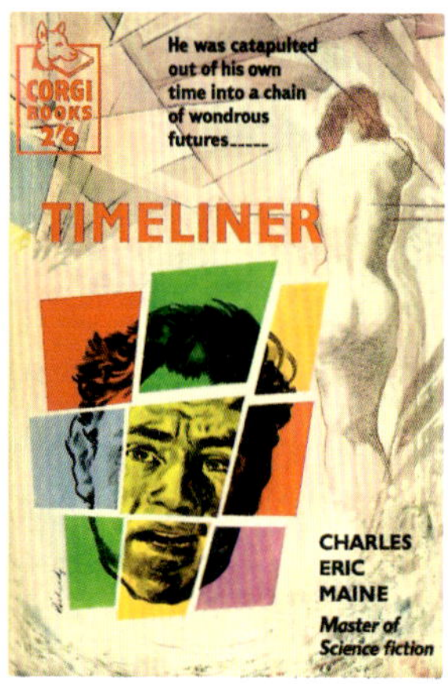

Charles Eric Maine | *Timeliner*
Corgi Books S554, 1958 | Art **John Richards**

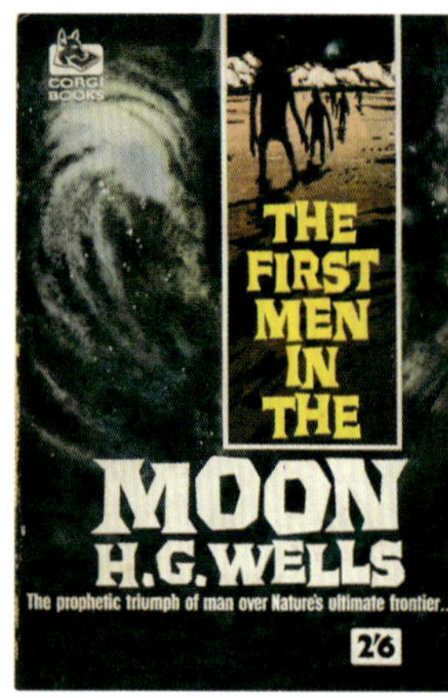

H. G. Wells | *The First Men in the Moon*
Corgi Books SS898, 1960 | Art **John Richards**

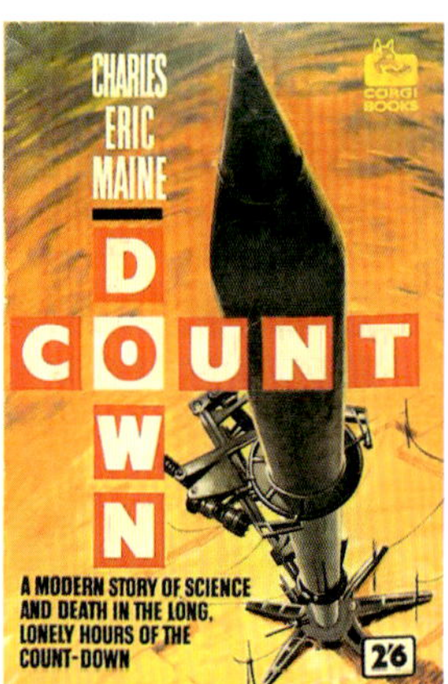

Charles Eric Maine | *Count-Down*
Corgi Books SS971, 1961 | Art **John Richards**

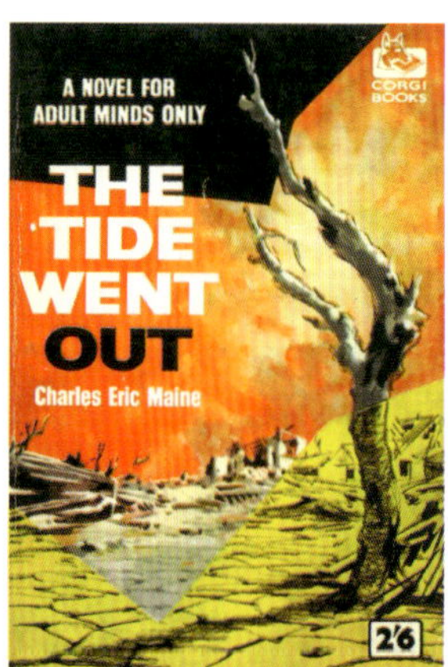

Charles Eric Maine | The Tide Went Out
Corgi Books SS873, 1960 | Art **John Richards**

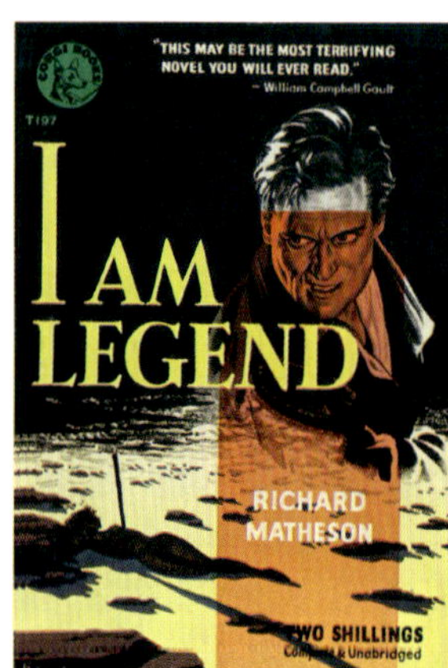

Richard Matheson | *I Am Legend*
Corgi Books T-197, 1956 | Art **John Richards**

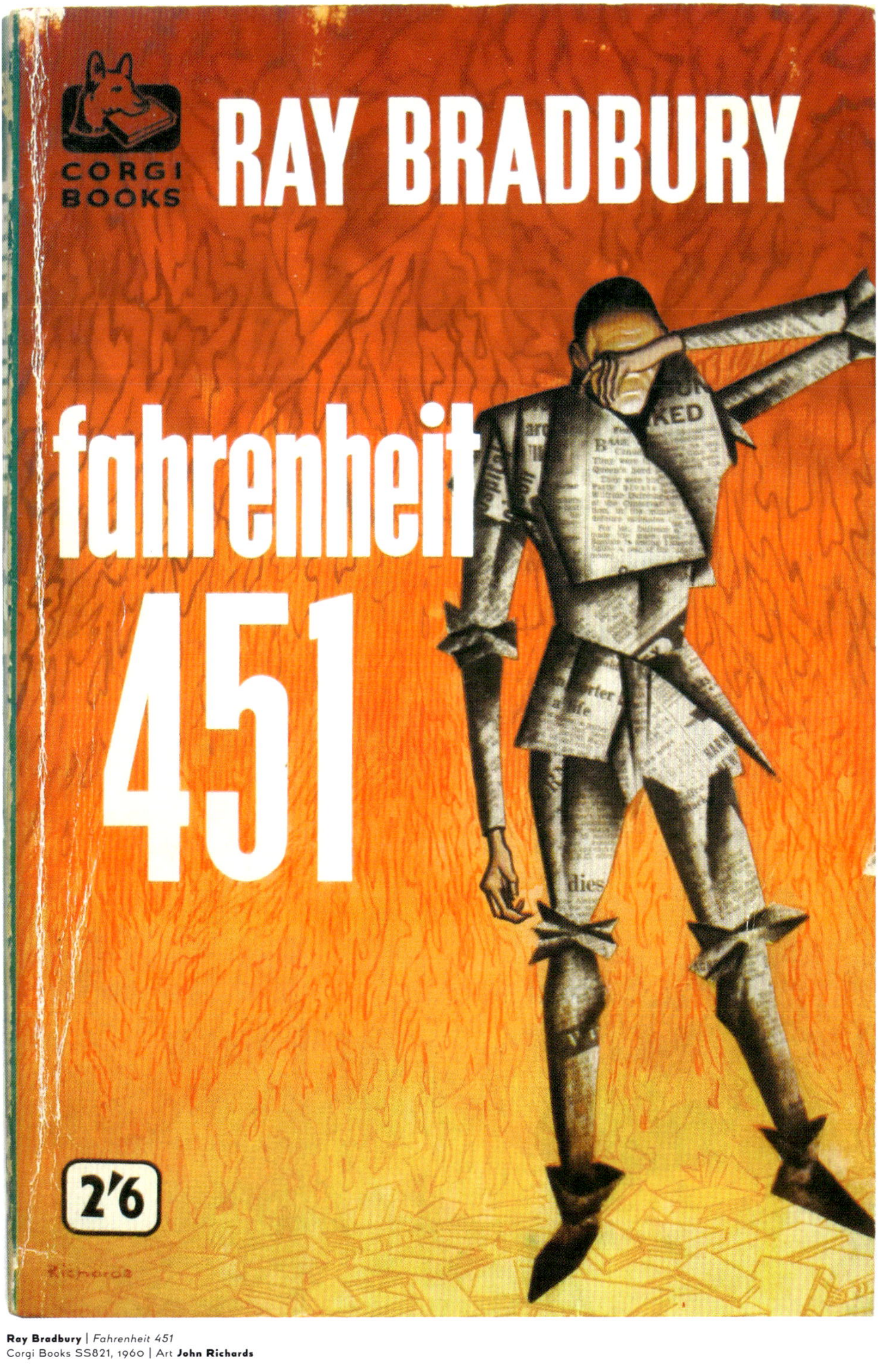

Ray Bradbury | *Fahrenheit 451*
Corgi Books SS821, 1960 | Art **John Richards**

opposite **Ray Bradbury** | *The Silver Locusts*
Corgi Books SS819, 1960 | Original art **John Richards**

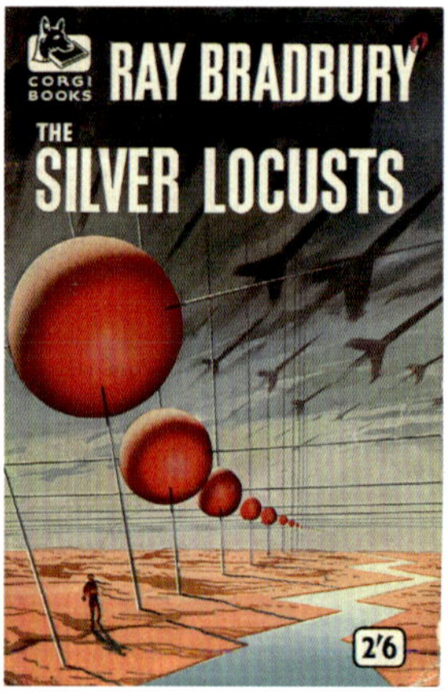

Ray Bradbury | *The Silver Locusts*
Corgi Books SS819, 1960 | Art **John Richards**

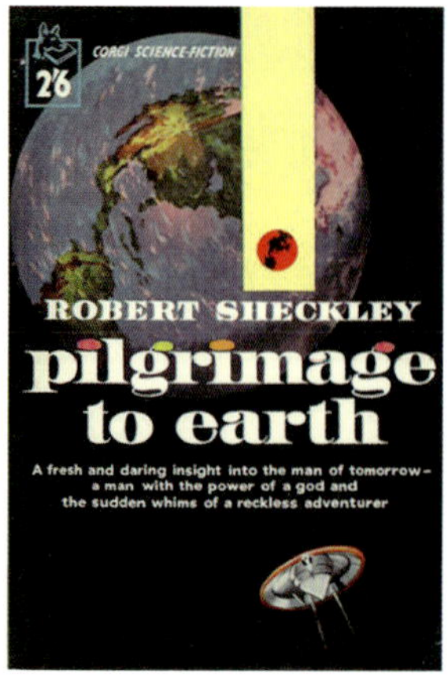

Robert Sheckley | *Pilgrimage to Earth*
Corgi Books SS746, 1959 | Art **Unknown**

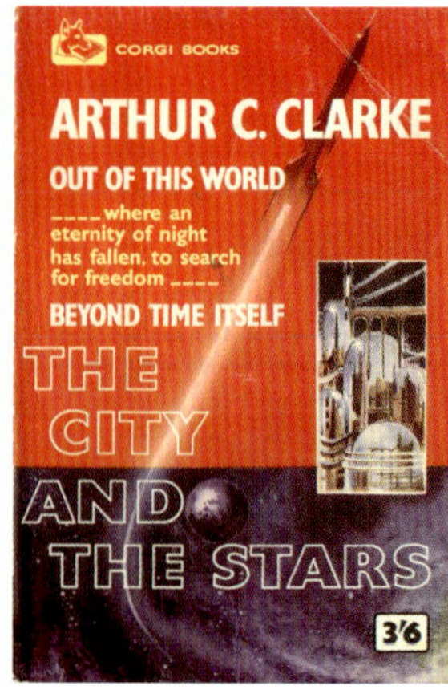

Arthur C. Clarke | *The City and the Stars*
Corgi Books GS933, 1960 | Art **John Richards**

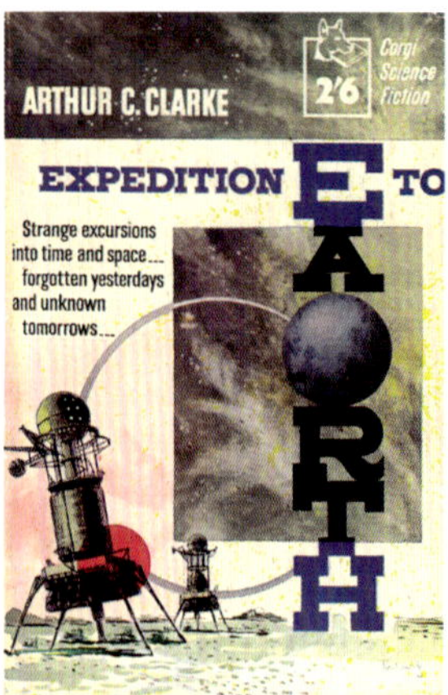

Arthur C. Clarke | *Expedition to Earth*
Corgi Books S650, 1959 | Art **John Richards**

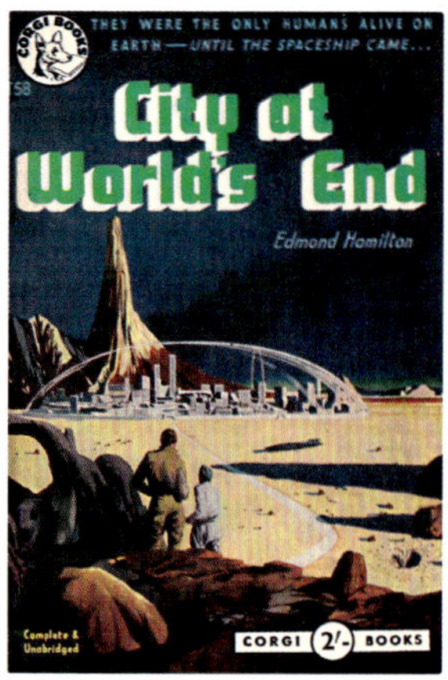

Edmond Hamilton | *City at World's End*
Corgi Books T58, 1954 | Art **John Richards**

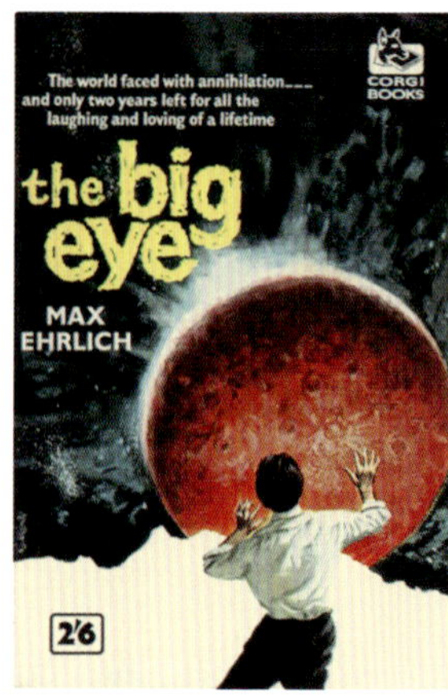

Max Ehrlich | *The Big Eye*
Corgi Books SS844, 1960 | Art **John Richards**

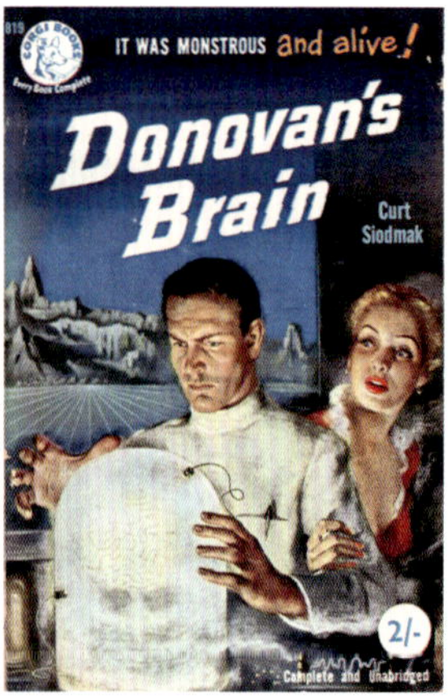

Curt Siodmak | *Donovan's Brain*
Corgi Books 819, 1952 | Art **Unknown**

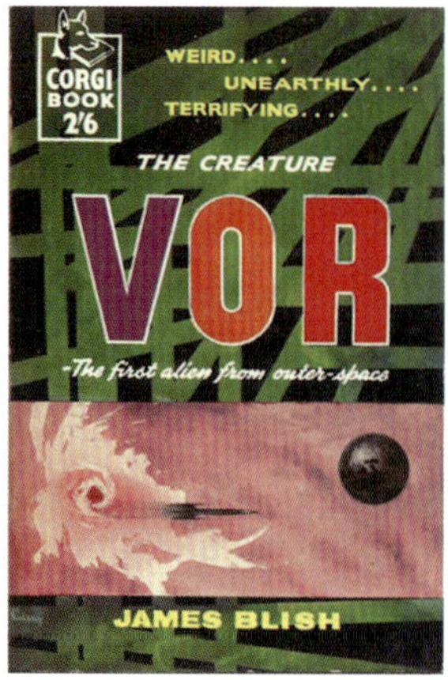

James Blish | *VOR*
Corgi Books S681, 1959 | Art **John Richards**

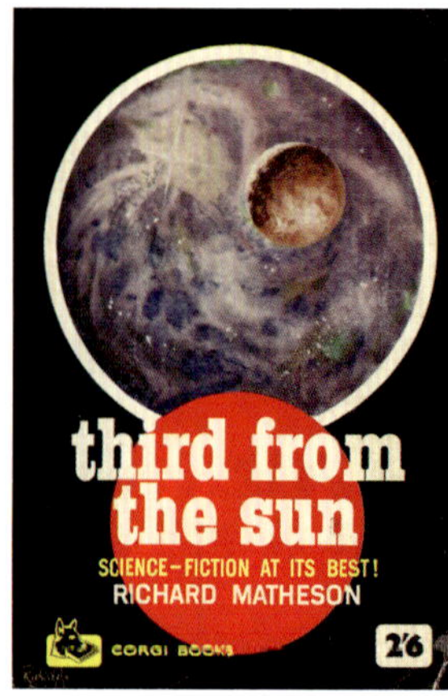

Richard Matheson | *Third from the Sun*
Corgi Books SS1027, 1961 | Art **John Richards**

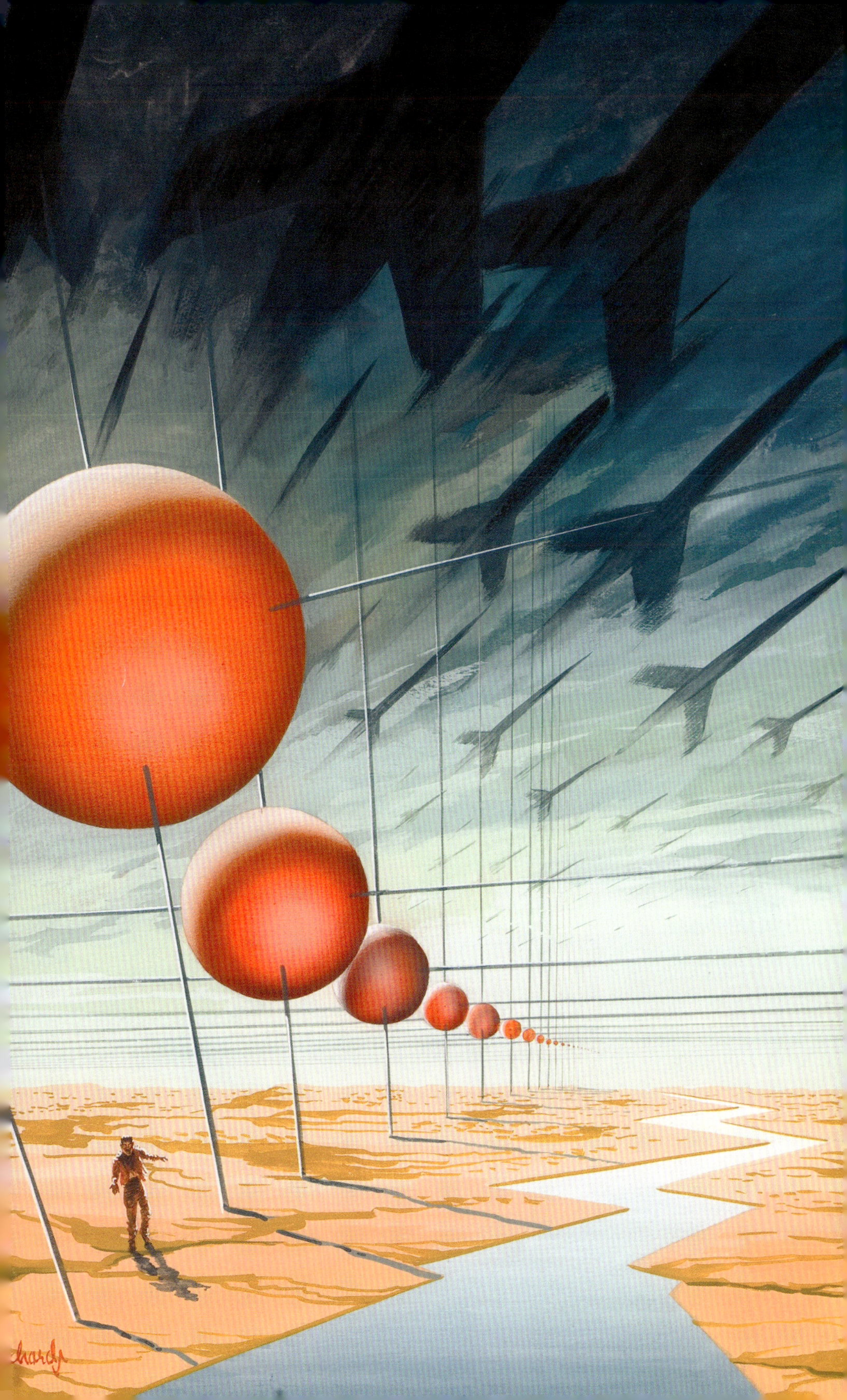
hardy

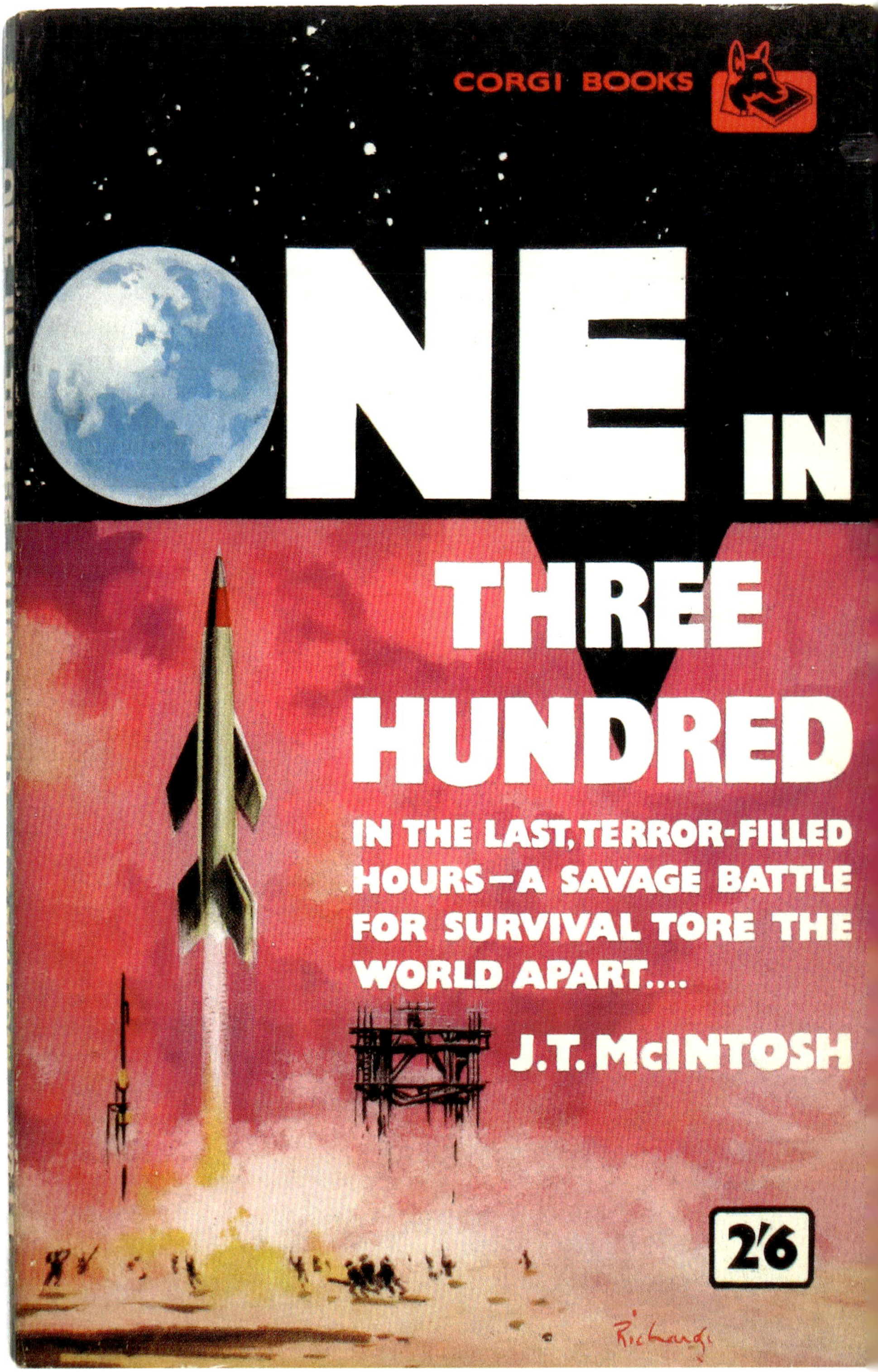

J. T. McIntosh | *One in Three Hundred*
Corgi Books SS960, 1961 | Art **John Richards**

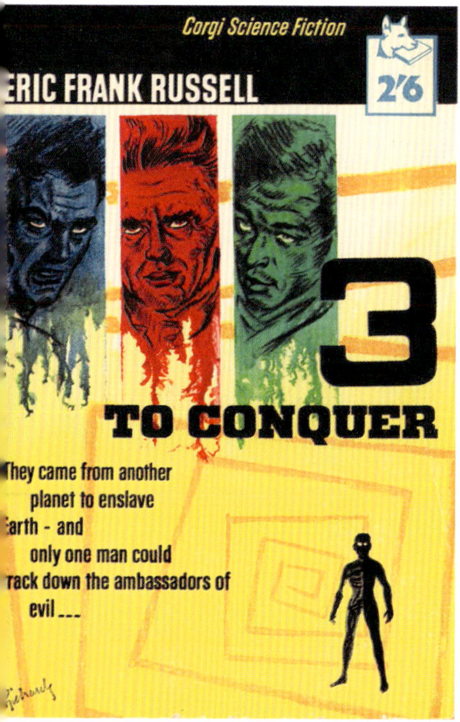

c Frank Russell | *Three to Conquer*
rgi Books S596, 1958 | Art **John Richards**

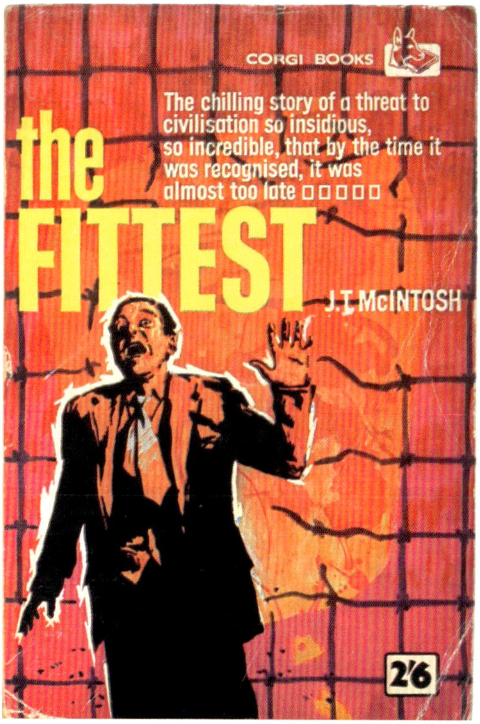

J. T. McIntosh | *The Fittest*
Corgi Books SS1051, 1961 | Art **John Richards**

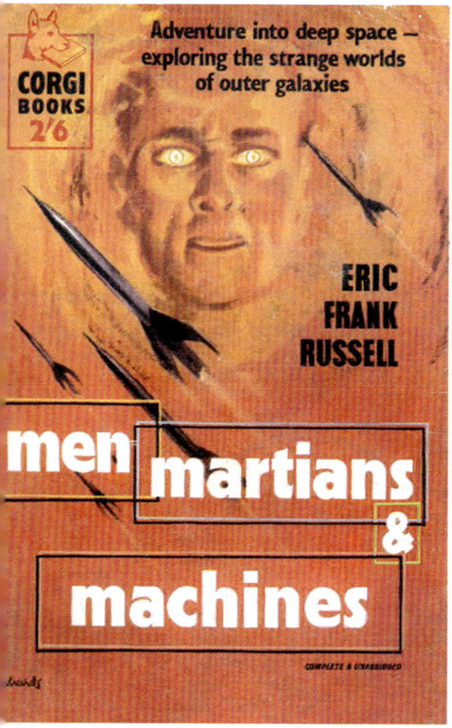

Frank Russell | *Men, Martians and Machines*
ji Books S424, 1957 | Art **John Richards**

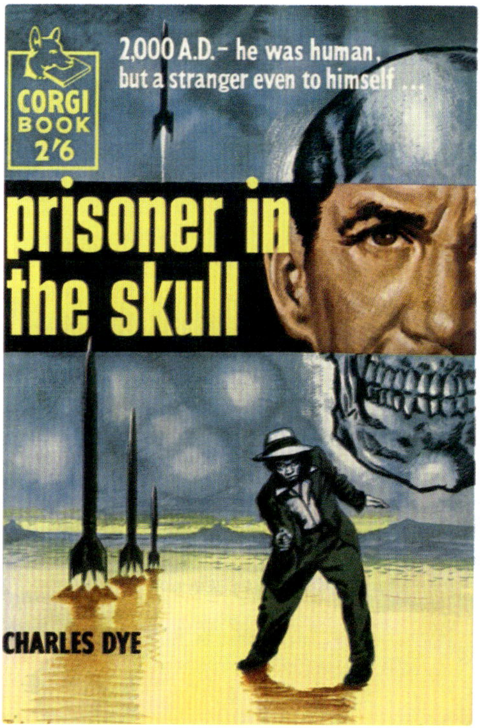

Charles Dye | *Prisoner in the Skull*
Corgi Books S486, 1957 | Art **John Richards**

opposite: **Robert Sheckley** | *Journey Beyond Tomorrow*
Corgi Books GS7365, 1966 | Original art **Josh Kirby**

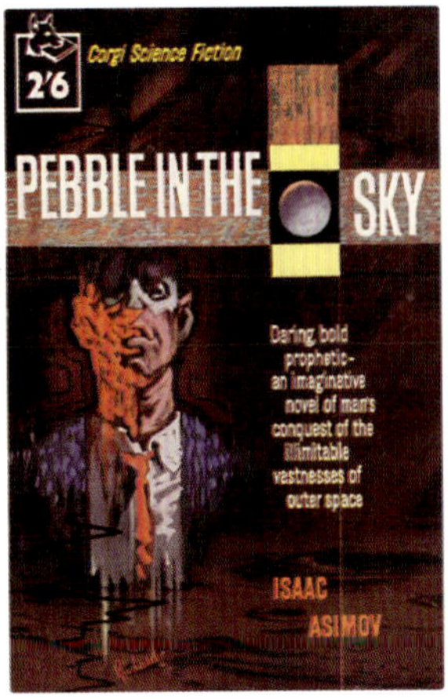

Isaac Asimov | *Pebble in the Sky*
Corgi Books S583, 1958 | Art **John Richards**

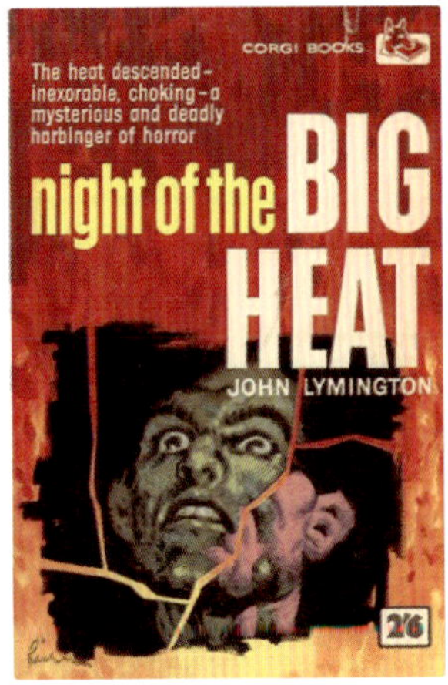

John Lymington | *Night of the Big Heat*
Corgi Books SS982, 1961 | Art **John Richards**

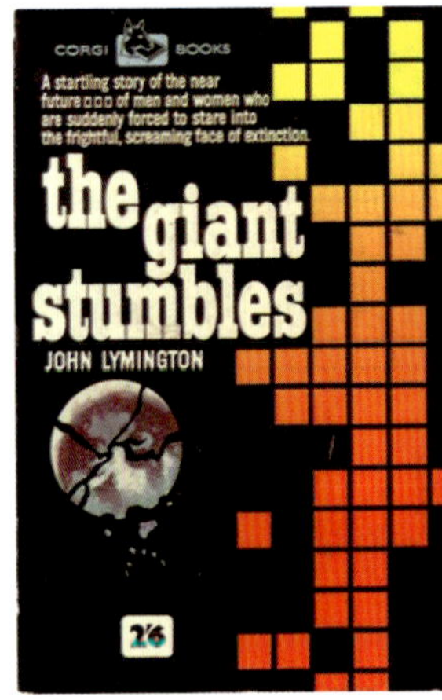

John Lymington | *The Giant Stumbles*
Corgi Books SS1063, 1961 | Art **John Richards**

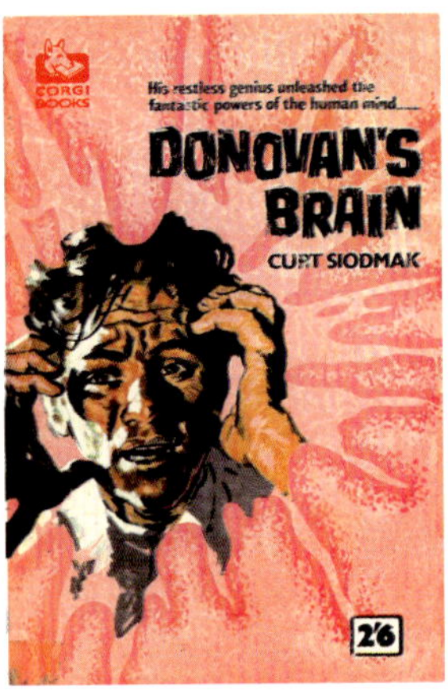

Curt Siodmak | *Donovan's Brain*
Corgi Books SS853, 1960 | Art **John Richards**

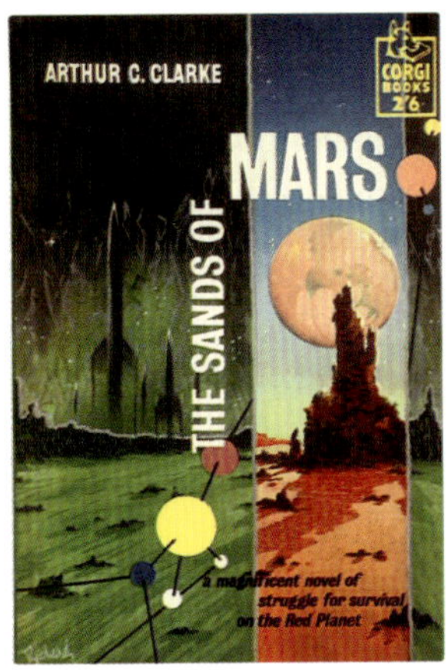

Arthur C. Clarke | *The Sands of Mars*
Corgi Books S564, 1958 | Art **John Richards**

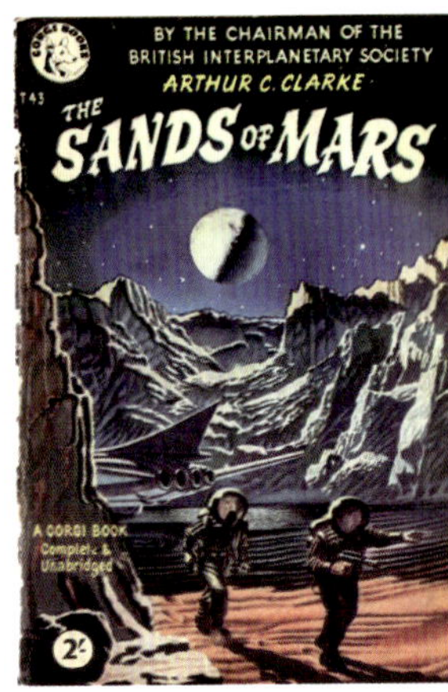

Arthur C. Clarke | *The Sands of Mars*
Corgi Books T43, 1954 | Art **John Richards**

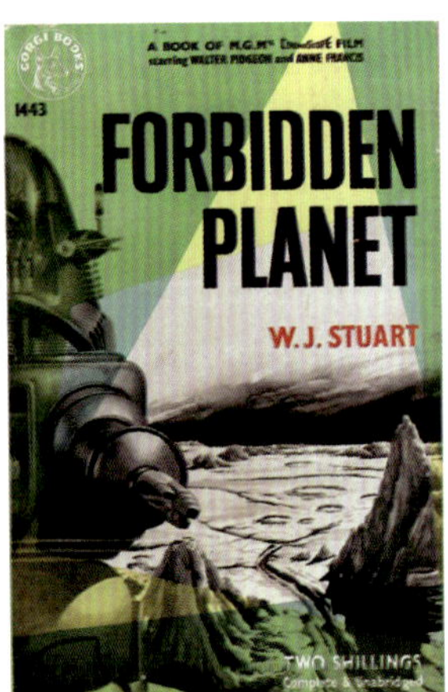

W. J. Stuart | *Forbidden Planet*
Corgi Books, 1956 | Art **John Richards**

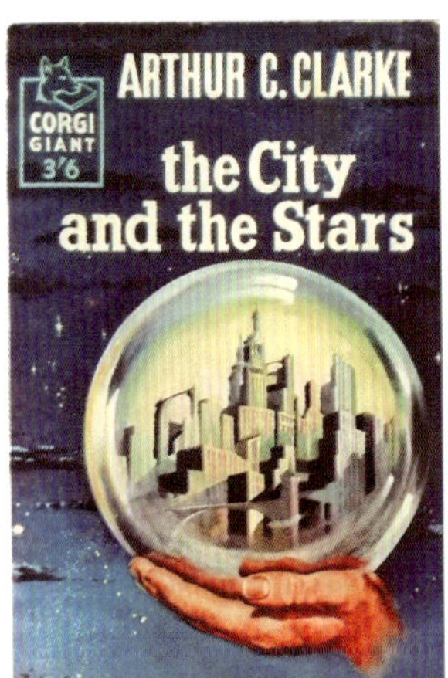

Arthur C. Clarke | *The City and the Stars*
Corgi Giant G443, 1957 | Art **John Richards**

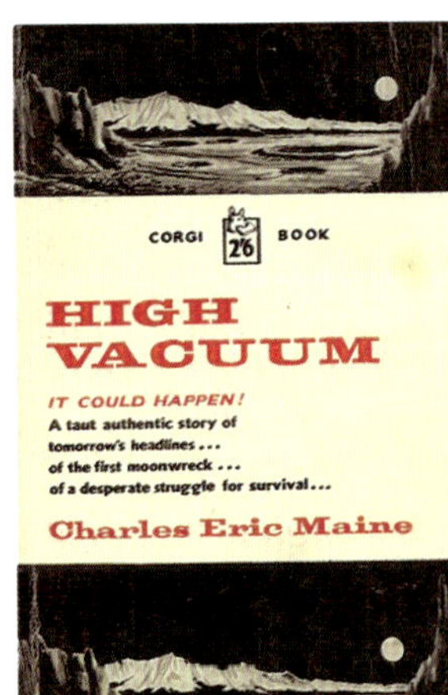

Charles Eric Maine | *High Vacuum*
Corgi Books SS714, 1959 | Art **John Richards**

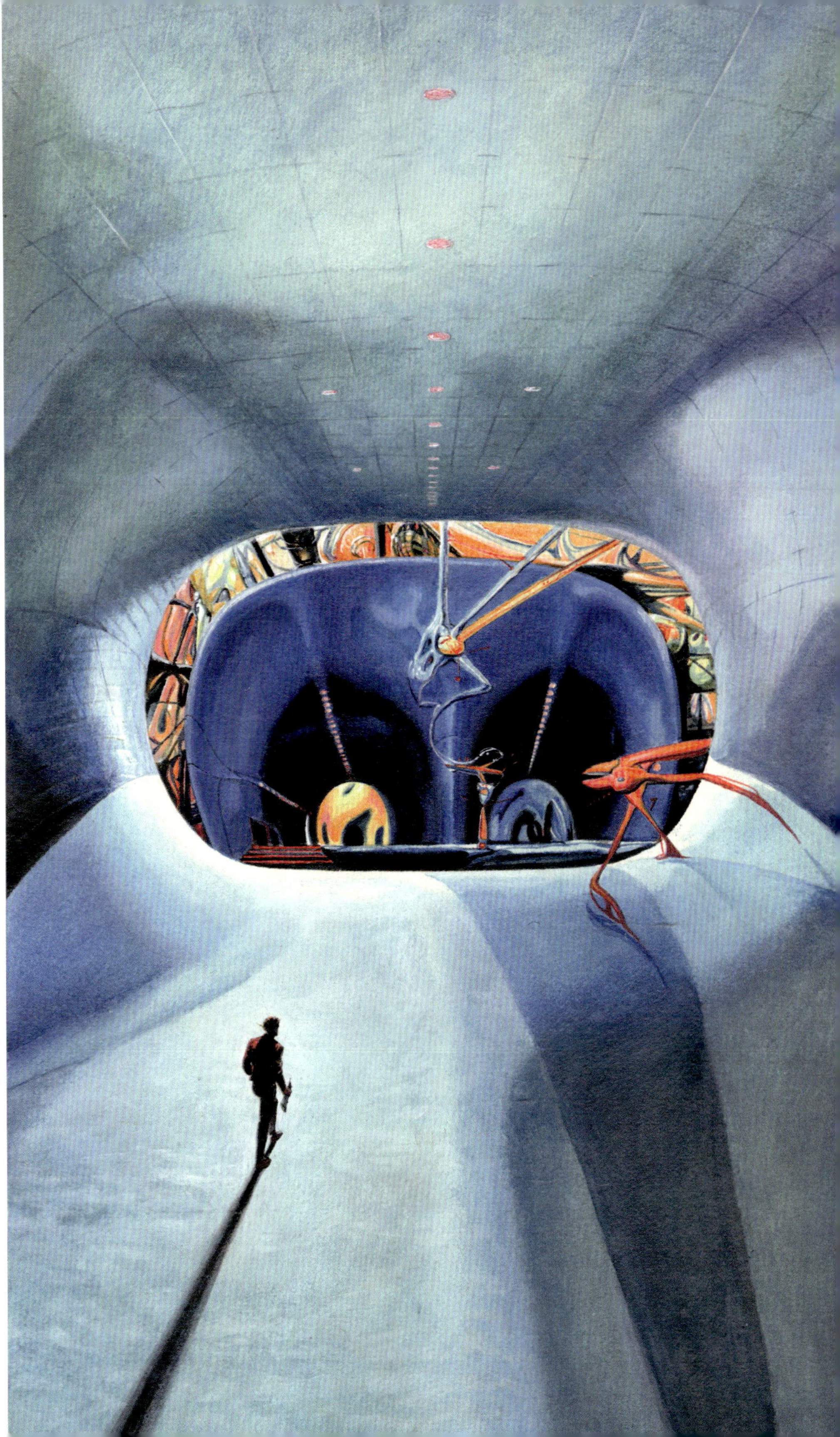

Ray Bradbury | *The Silver Locusts*
Corgi Books YS1350, 1963 | Original art **Josh Kirby**

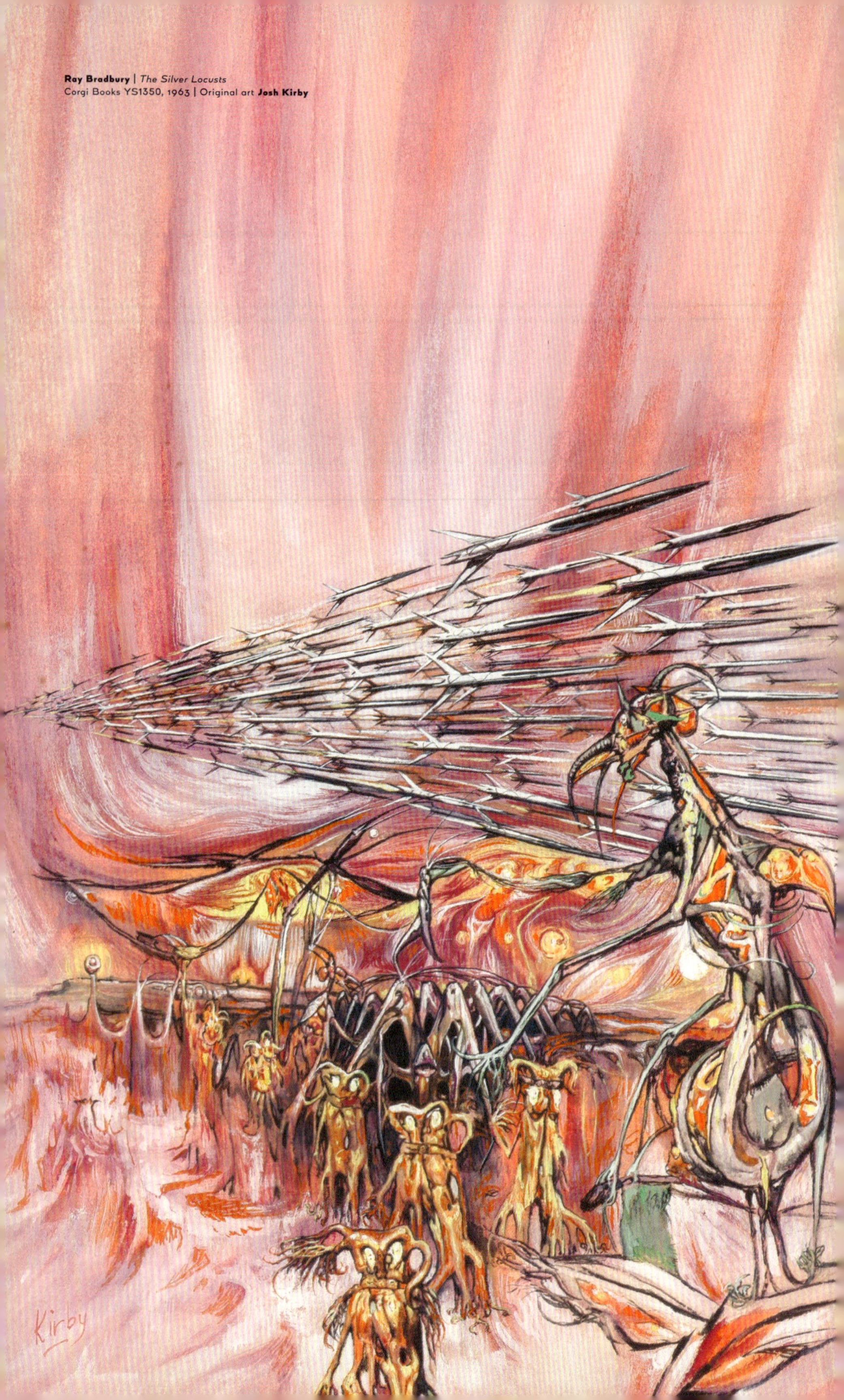

Ray Bradbury | *The Silver Locusts*
Corgi Books GS7185, 1965 | Original art **Josh Kirby**

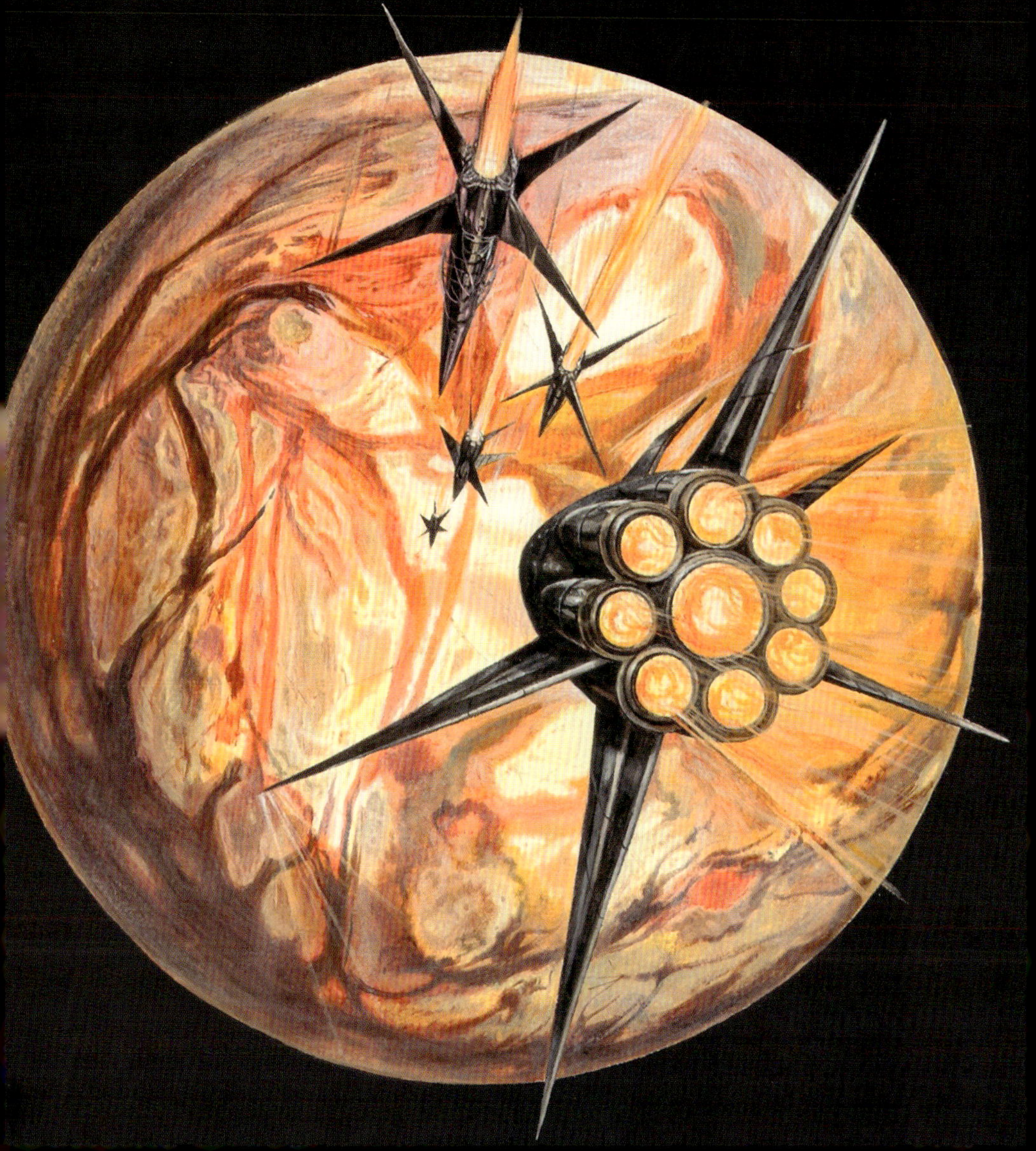

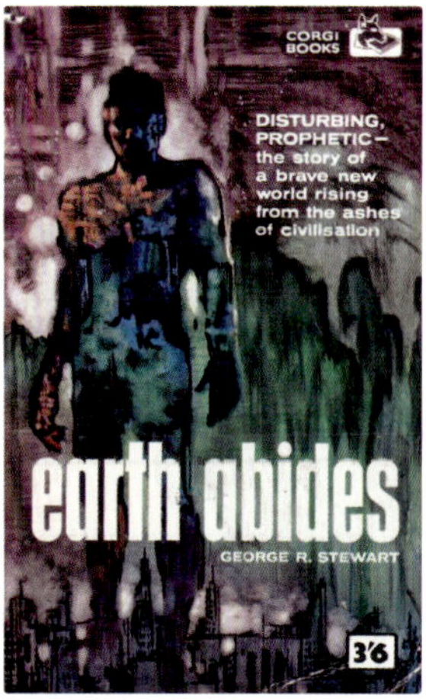

George R. Stewart | *Earth Abides*
Corgi Books GS1095, 1961 | Art **John Richards**

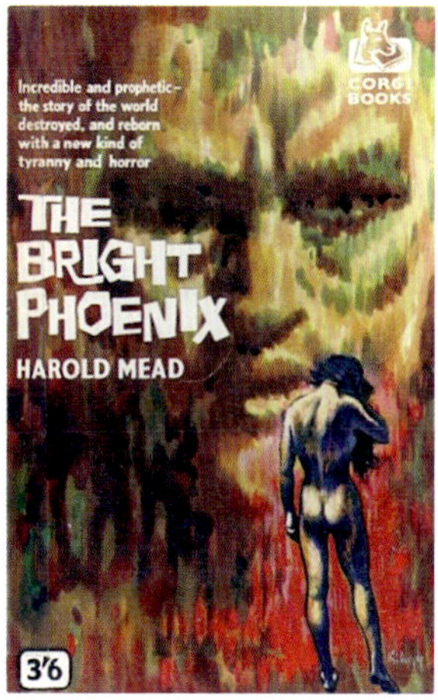

Harold Mead | *The Bright Phoenix*
Corgi Books GS784, 1960 | Art **John Richards**

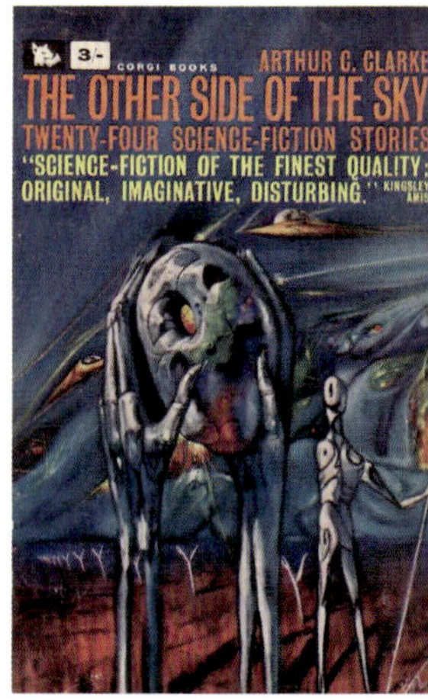

Arthur C. Clarke | *The Other Side of the Sky*
Corgi Books YS1289, 1963 | Art **Josh Kirby**

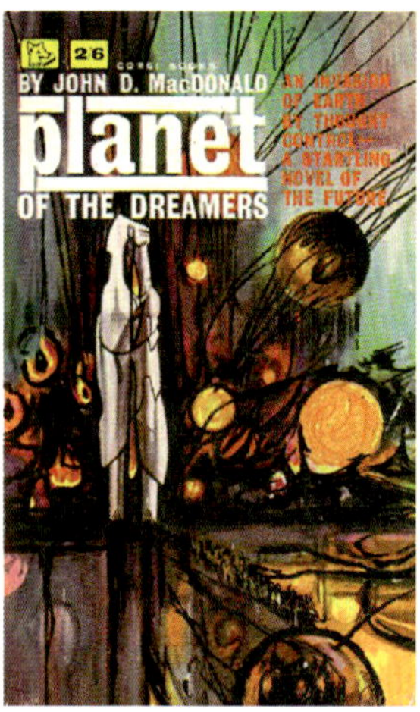

John D. MacDonald | *Planet of the Dreamers*
Corgi Books SS1143, 1962 | Art **Josh Kirby**

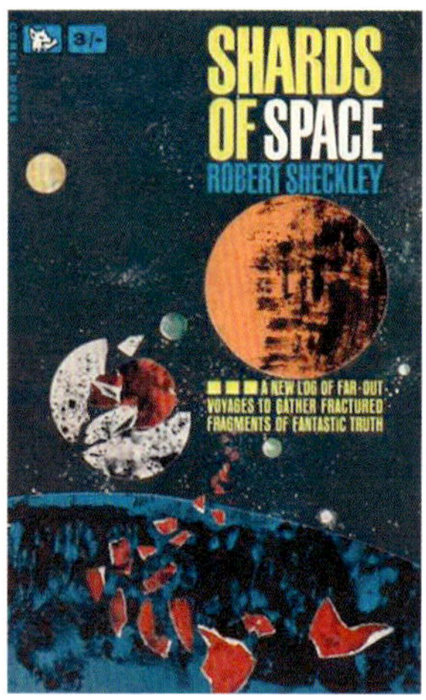

Robert Sheckley | *Shards of Space*
Corgi Books, 1962 | Art **Hoot von Zitzewitz**

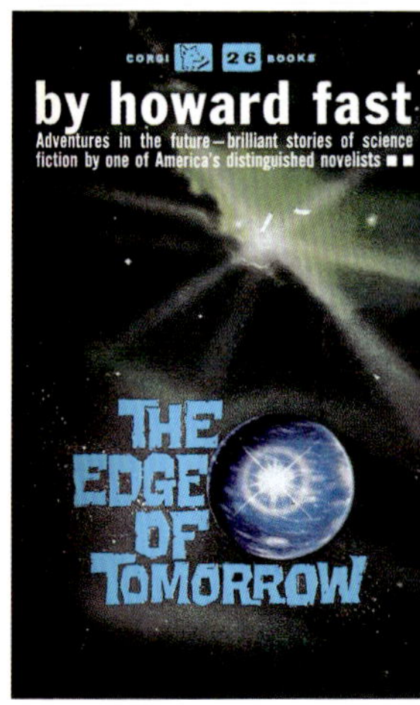

Howard Fast | *The Edge of Tomorrow*
Corgi Books SS1107, 1962 | Art **Unknown**

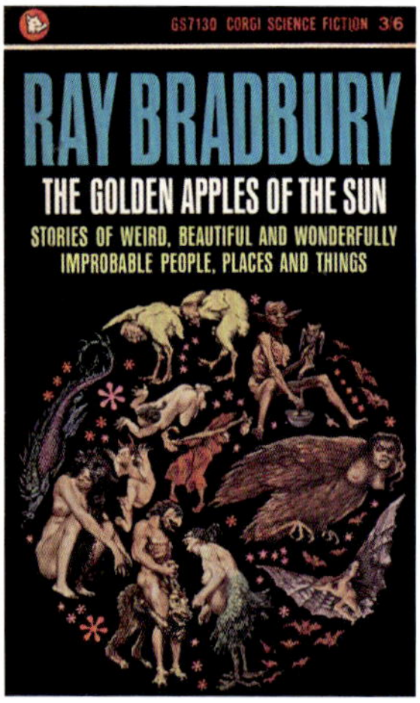

Ray Bradbury | *The Golden Apples of the Sun*
Corgi Books, 1965 | Art **Josh Kirby**

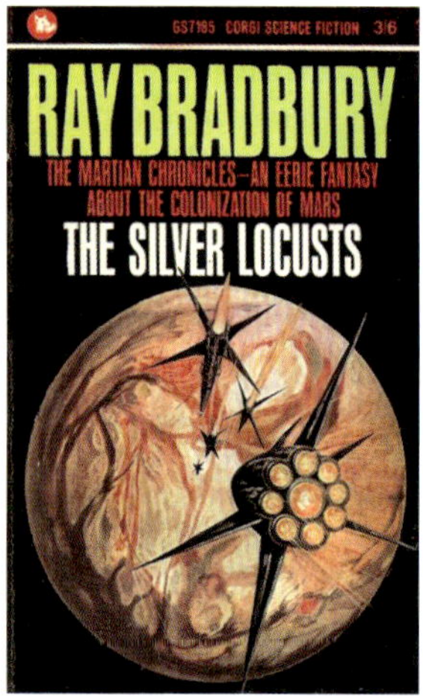

Ray Bradbury | *The Silver Locusts*
Corgi Books GS7185, 1965 | Art **Josh Kirby**

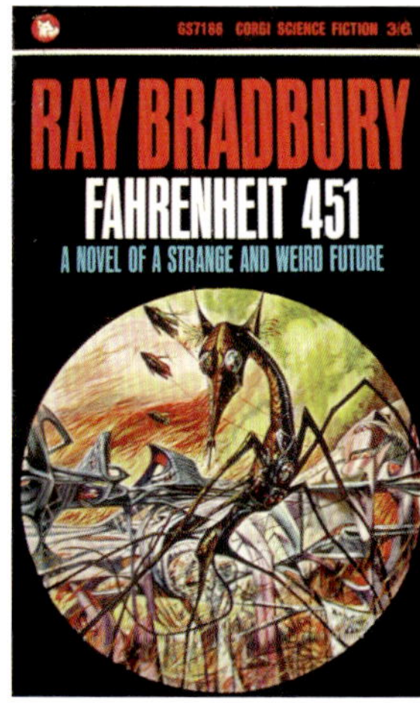

Ray Bradbury | *Fahrenheit 451*
Corgi Books GS7186, 1965 | Art **Josh Kirby**

Charles Eric Maine | *Timeliner*
Corgi Books GS1512, 1964 | Original art **Josh Kirby**

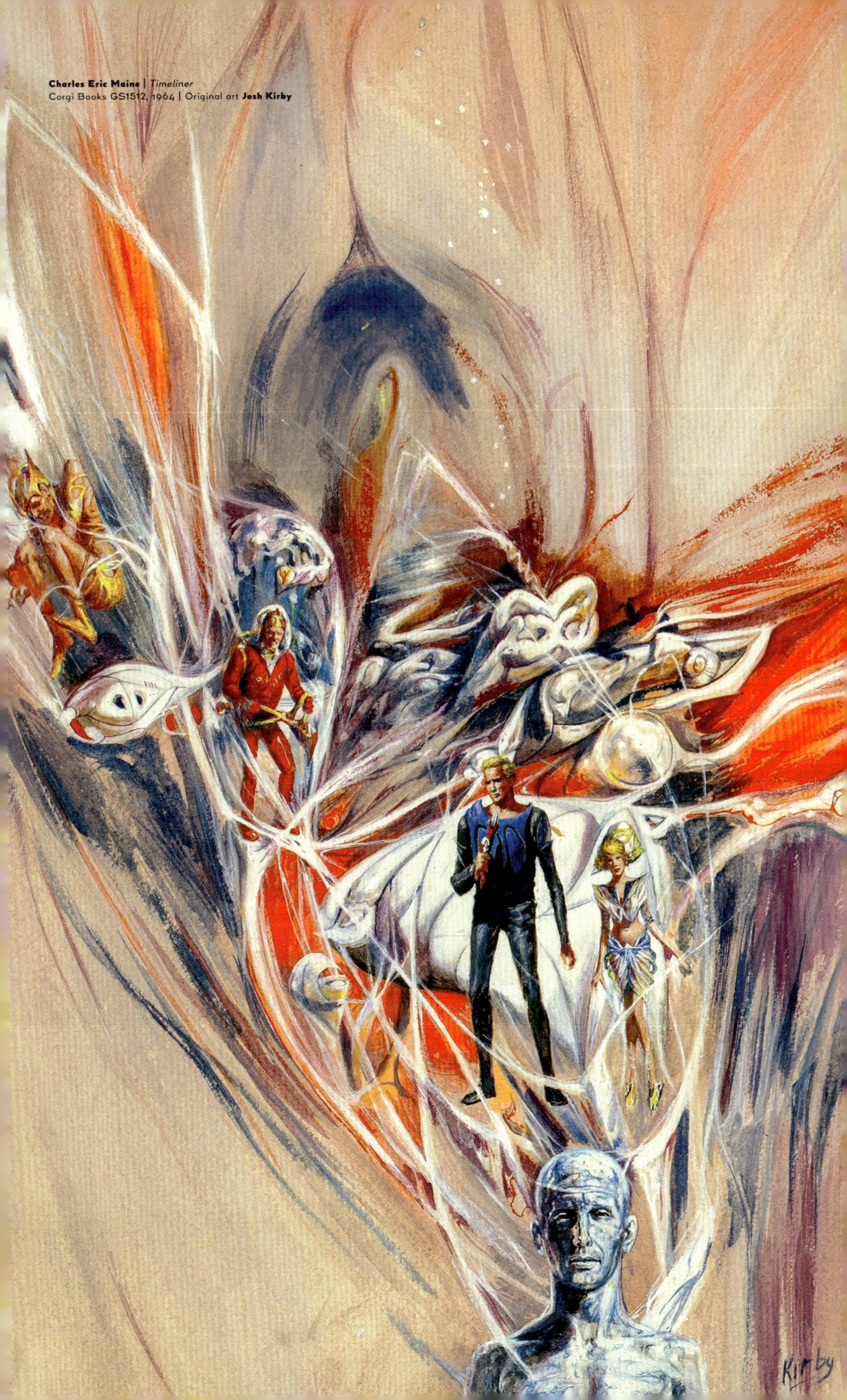

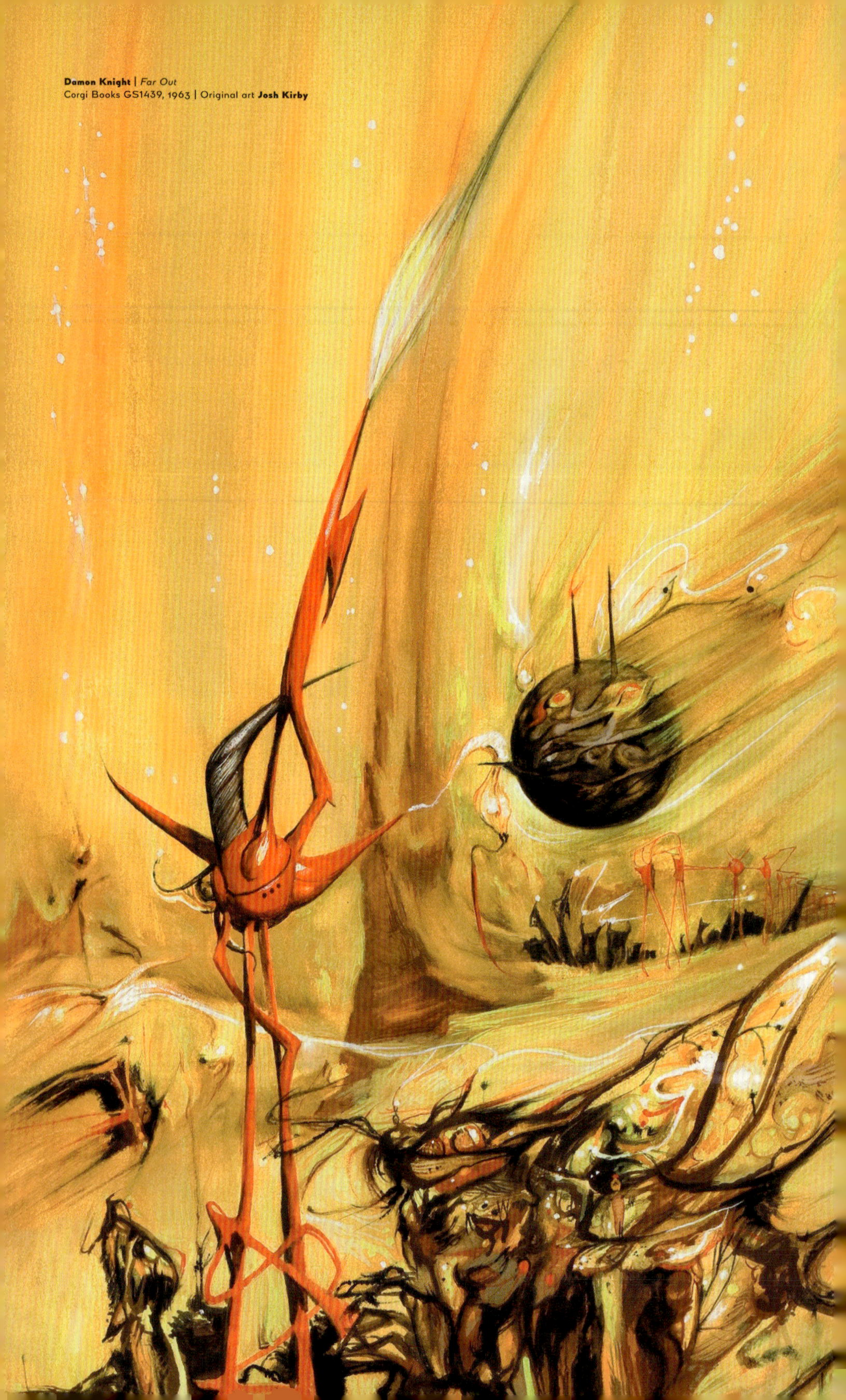

Damon Knight | *Far Out*
Corgi Books GS1439, 1963 | Original art **Josh Kirby**

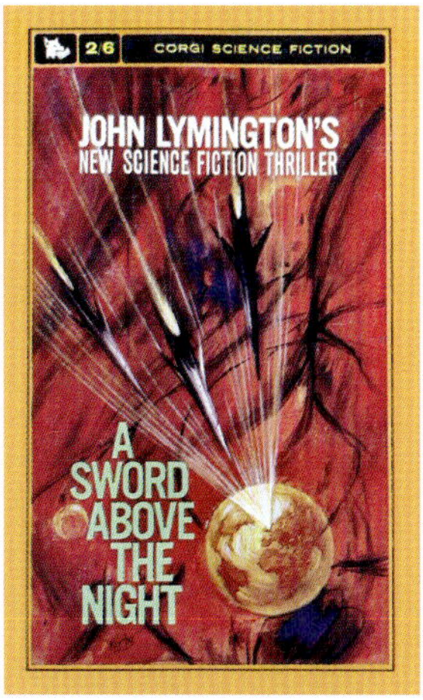

John Lymington | *A Sword Above the Night*
Corgi Books SS1334, 1963 | Art **Josh Kirby**

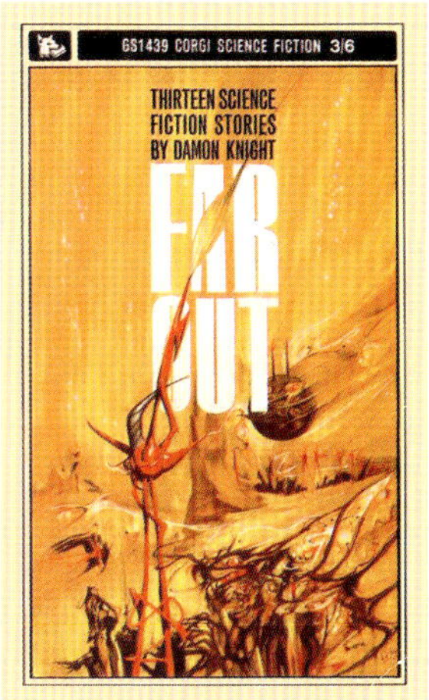

Damon Knight | *Far Out*
Corgi Books GS1439, 1963 | Art **Josh Kirby**

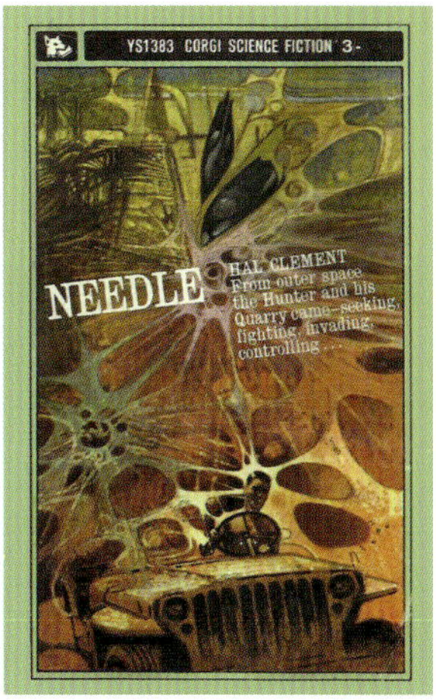

Hal Clement | *Needle*
Corgi Books YS1383, 1963 | Art **Josh Kirby**

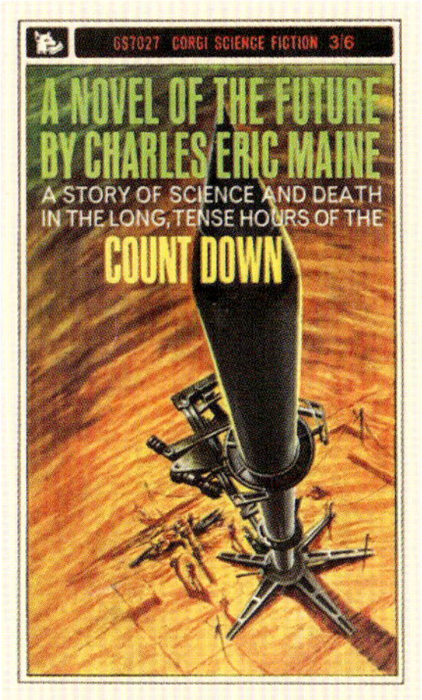

Charles Eric Maine | *Count Down*
Corgi Books GS7027, 1964 | Art **John Richards**

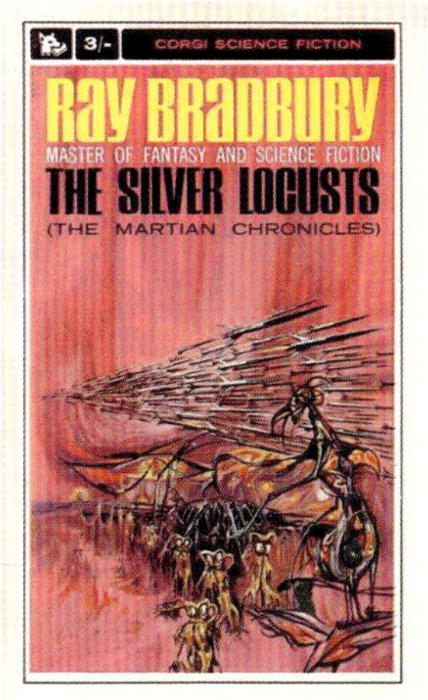

Ray Bradbury | *The Silver Locusts*
Corgi Books YS1350, 1963 | Art **Josh Kirby**

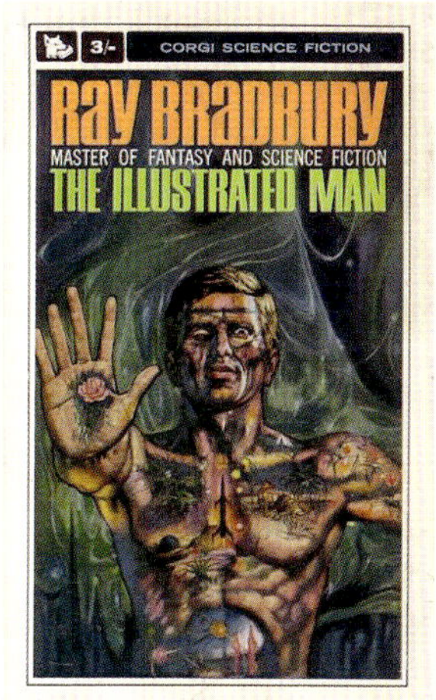

Ray Bradbury | *The Illustrated Man*
Corgi Books YS1349, 1963 | Art **Josh Kirby**

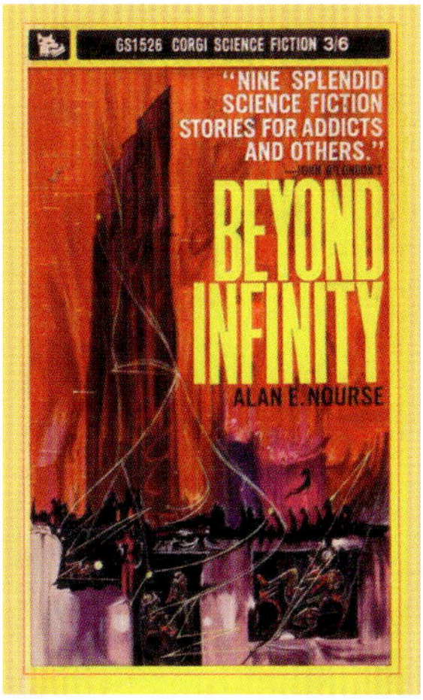

Alan E. Nourse | *Beyond Infinity*
Corgi Books GS1526, 1964 | Art **Josh Kirby**

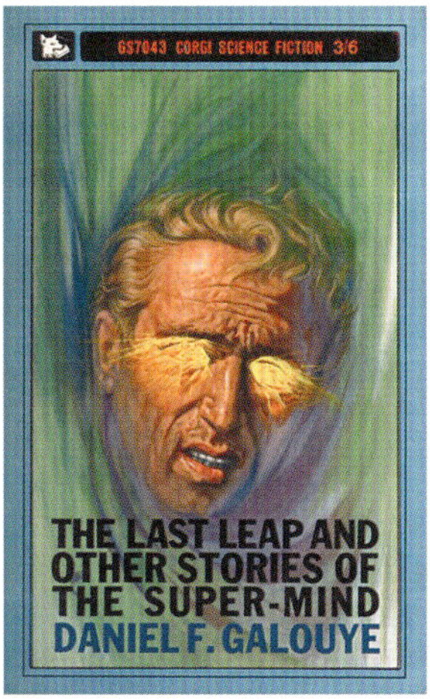

Daniel F. Galouye
The Last Leap and Other Stories of the Super-Mind
Corgi Books GS7043, 1964 | Art **Josh Kirby**

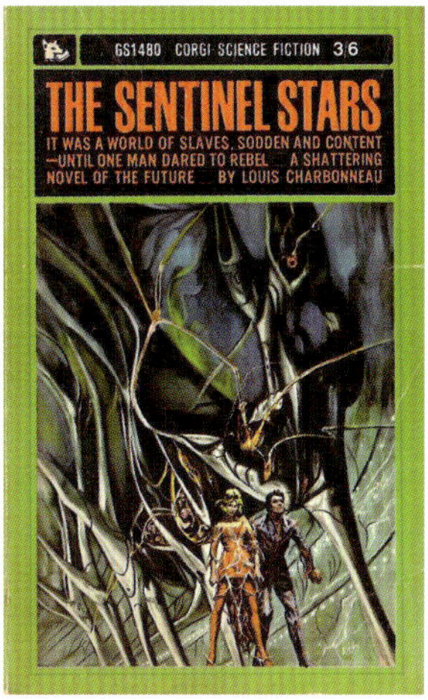

Louis Charbonneau | *The Sentinel Stars*
Corgi Books GS1480, 1964 | Art **Josh Kirby**

Louis Charbonneau | *The Sentinel Stars*
Corgi Books, 1964 | Original art **Josh Kirby**

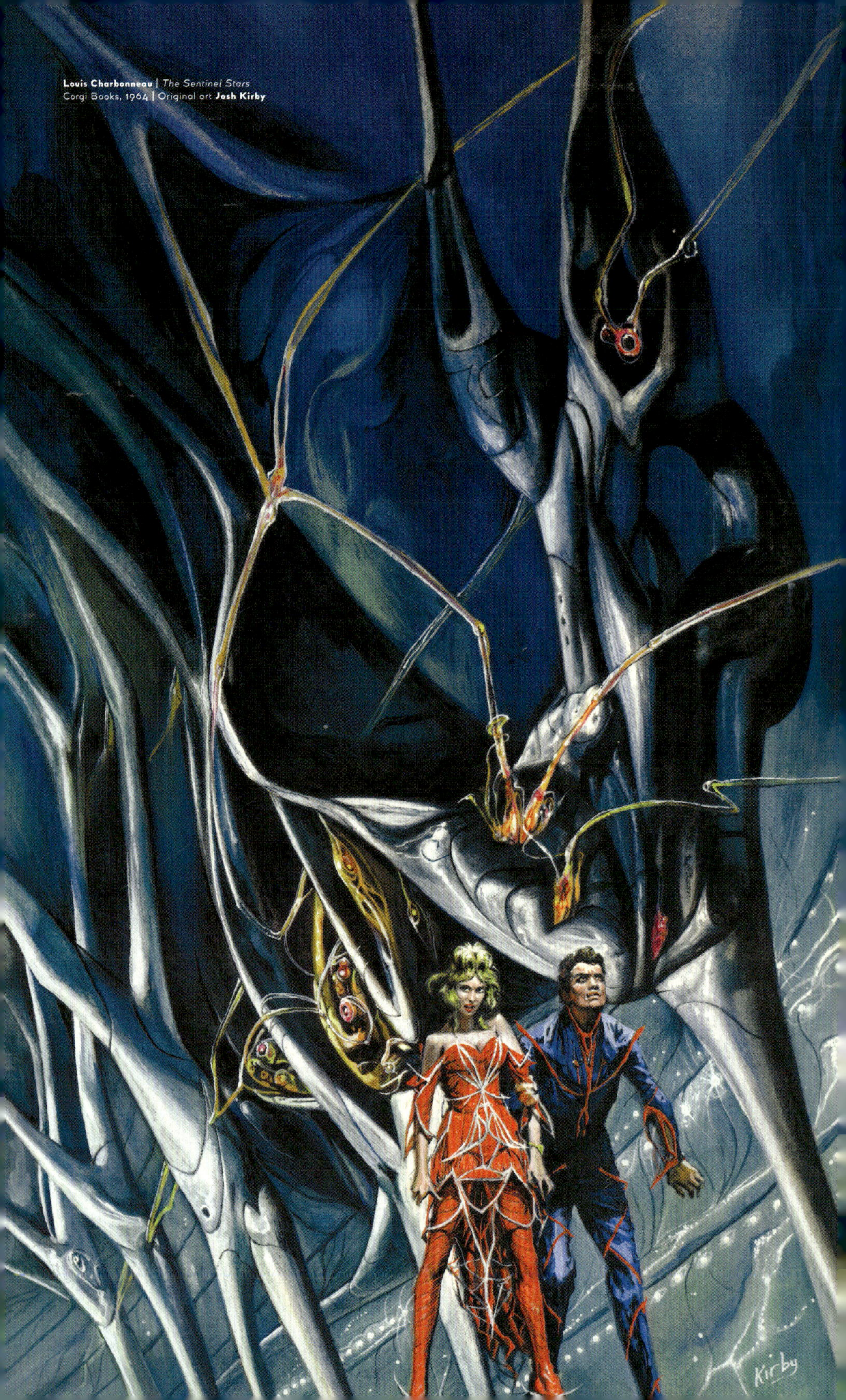

Damon Knight | *The Other Foot*
Corgi Books, 1968 | Original art **Josh Kirby**

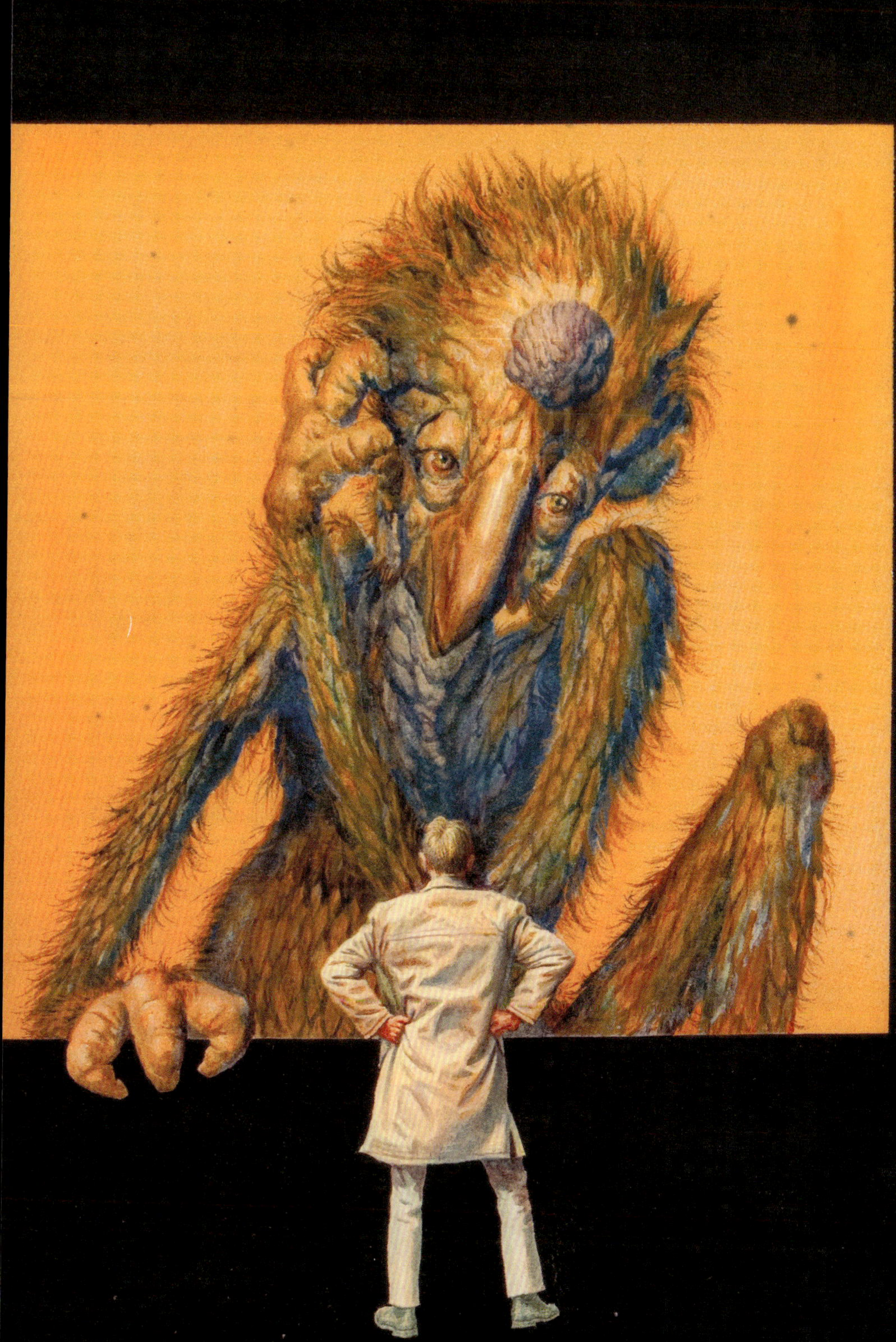

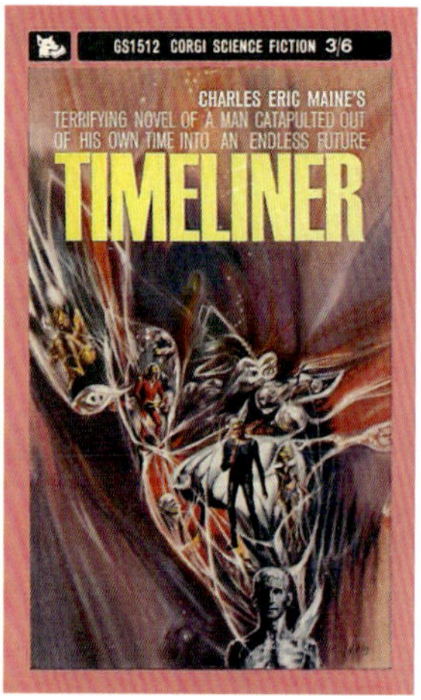

Charles Eric Maine | *Timeliner*
Corgi Books GS1512, 1964 | Art **Josh Kirby**

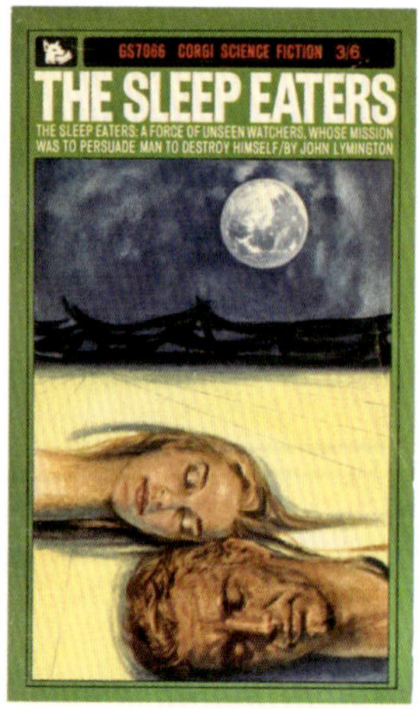

John Lymington | *The Sleep Eaters*
Corgi Books, 1963 | Art **Josh Kirby**

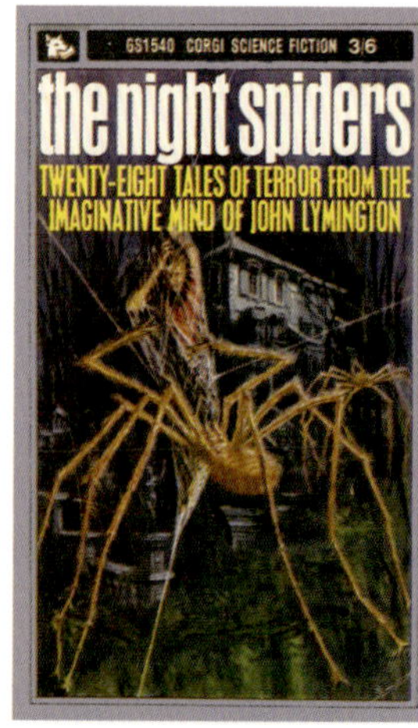

John Lymington | *The Night Spiders*
Corgi Books, 1964 | Art **Josh Kirby**

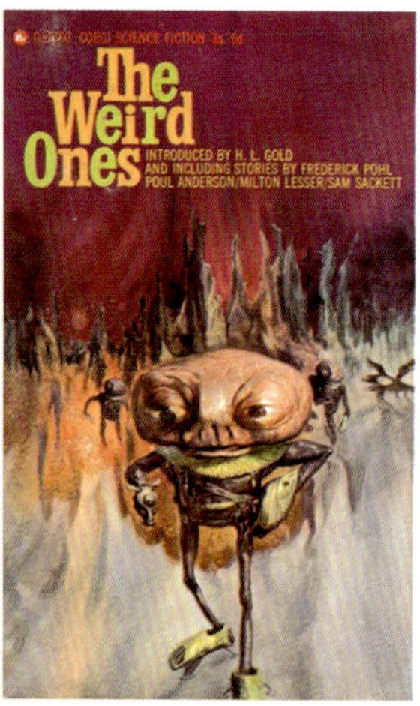

H. L. Gold, ed. | *The Weird Ones*
Corgi Books, 1967 | Art **Josh Kirby**

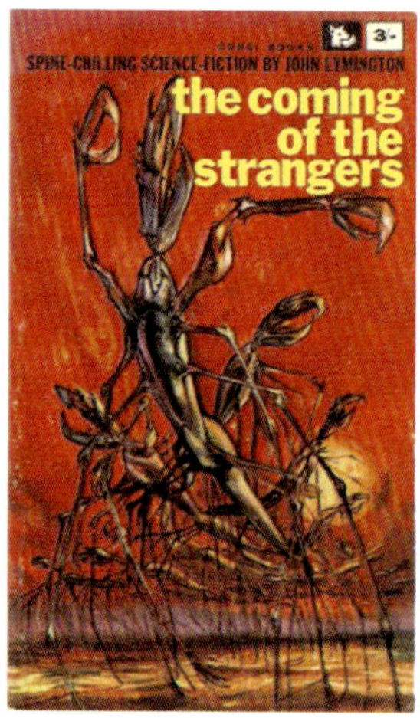

John Lymington | *The Coming of the Strangers*
Corgi Books YS1267, 1963 | Art **Josh Kirby**

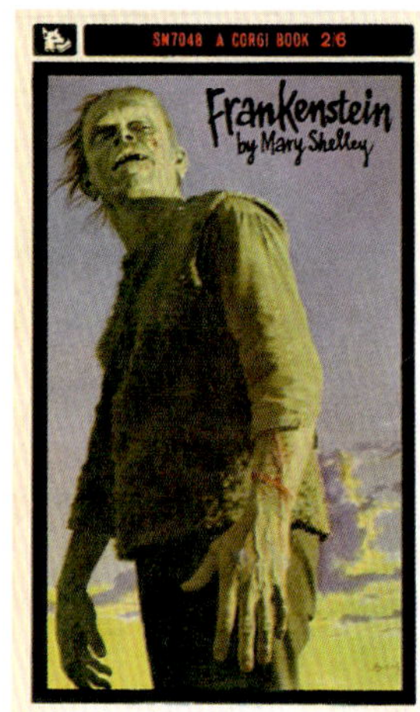

Mary Shelley | *Frankenstein*
Corgi Books, 1965 | Art **Jean-Leon Huens**

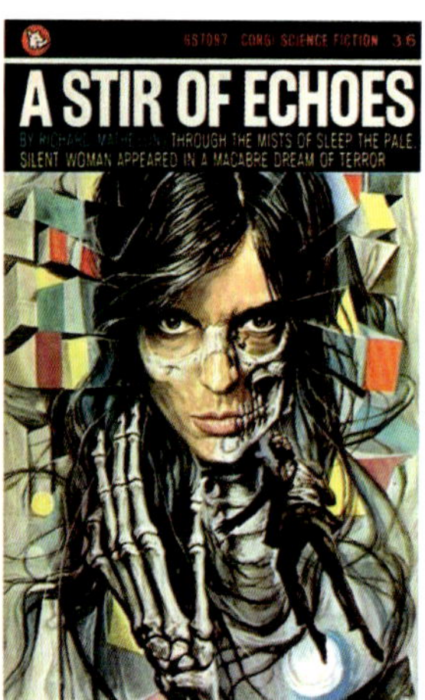

Richard Matheson | *A Stir of Echoes*
Corgi Books, 1965 | Art **Josh Kirby**

Colin Kapp | *The Dark Mind*
Corgi Books, 1965 | Art **Josh Kirby**

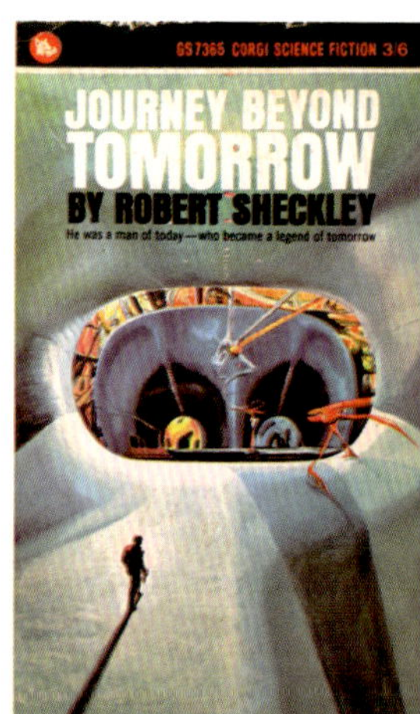

Robert Sheckley | *Journey Beyond Tomorrow*
Corgi Books GS7365, 1966 | Art **Josh Kirby**

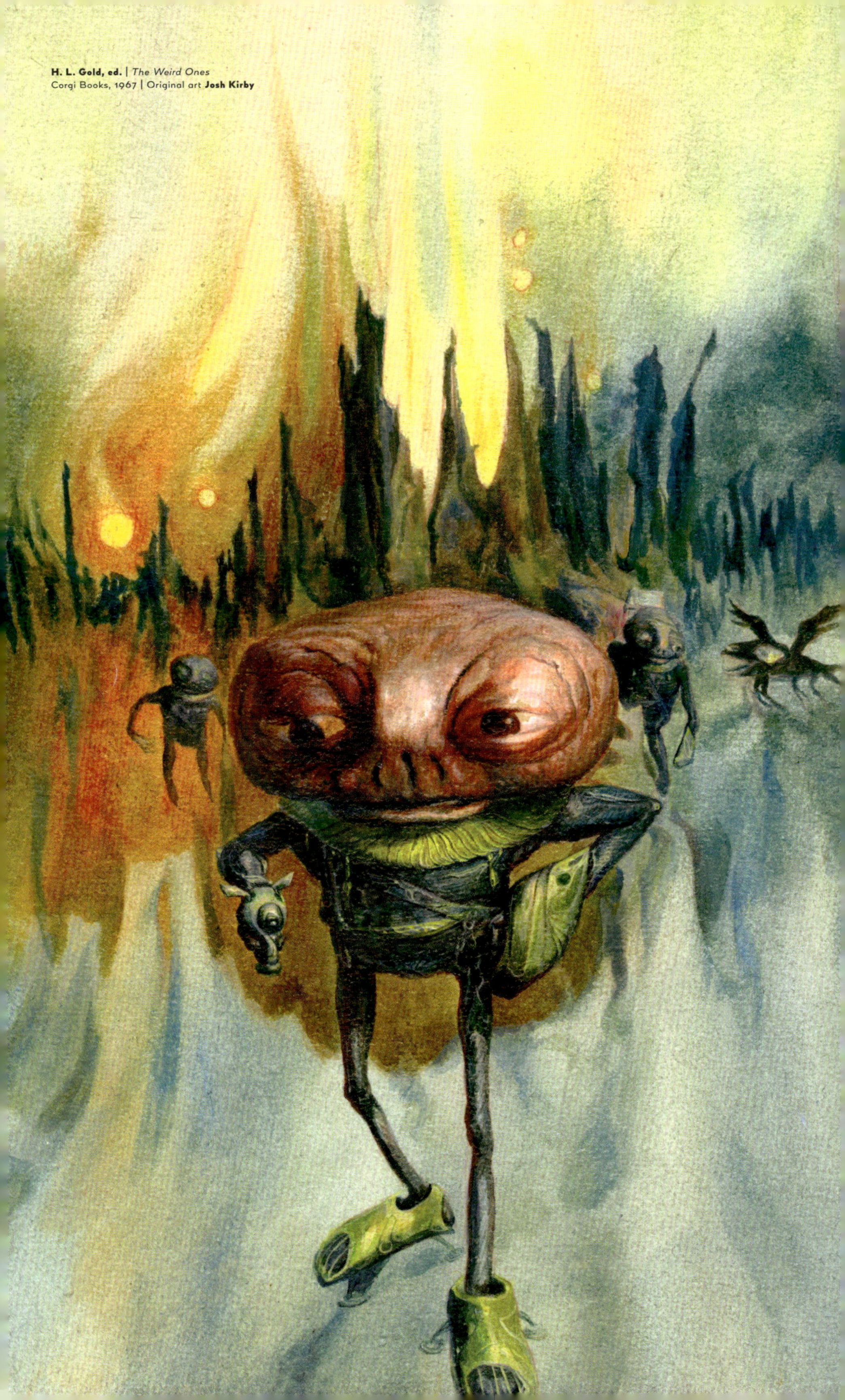

H. L. Gold, ed. | *The Weird Ones*
Corgi Books, 1967 | Original art **Josh Kirby**

Edgar Wallace and Merian C. Cooper | *King Kong*
Corgi Books, 1966 | Original art **Unknown**

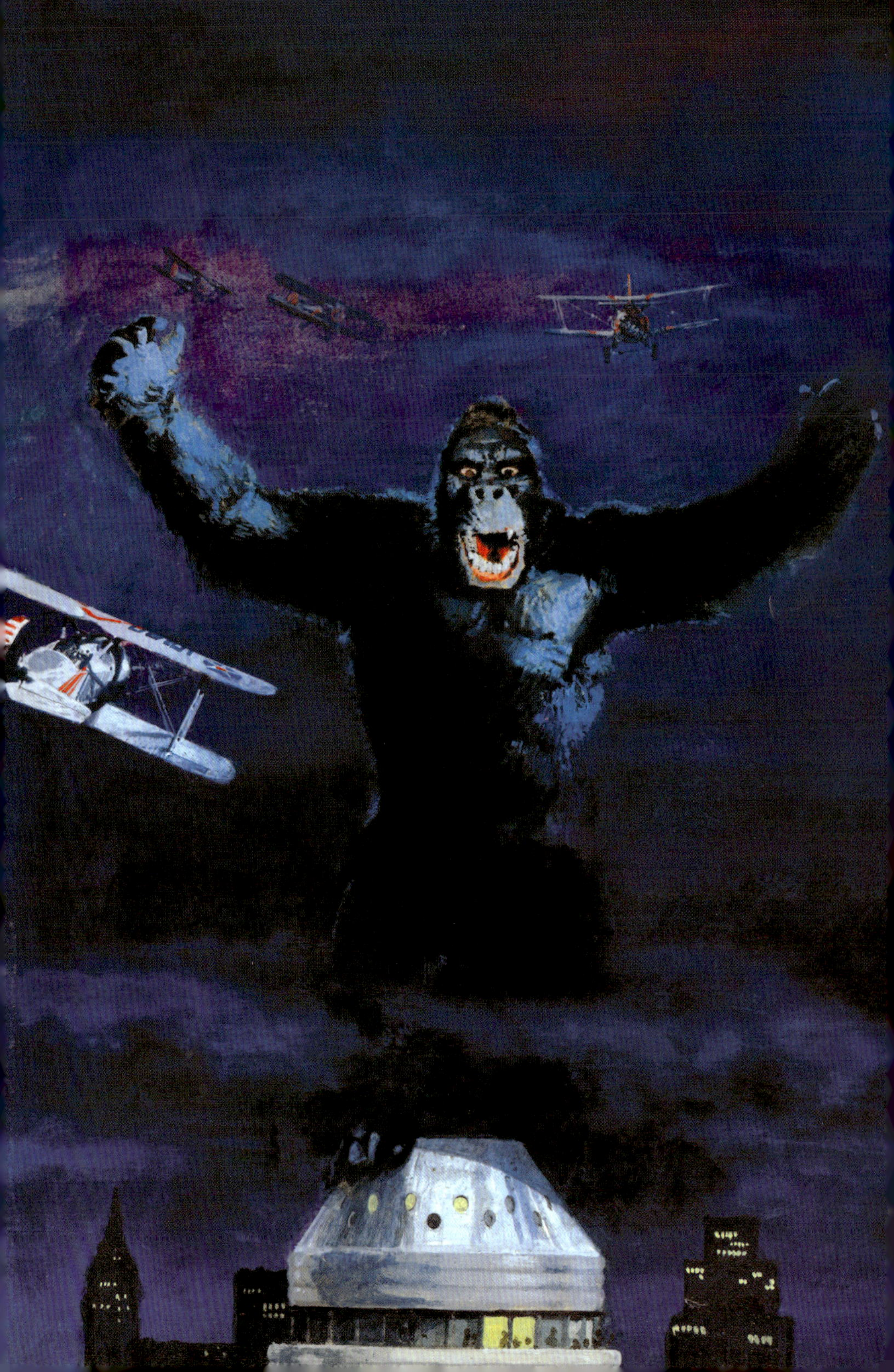

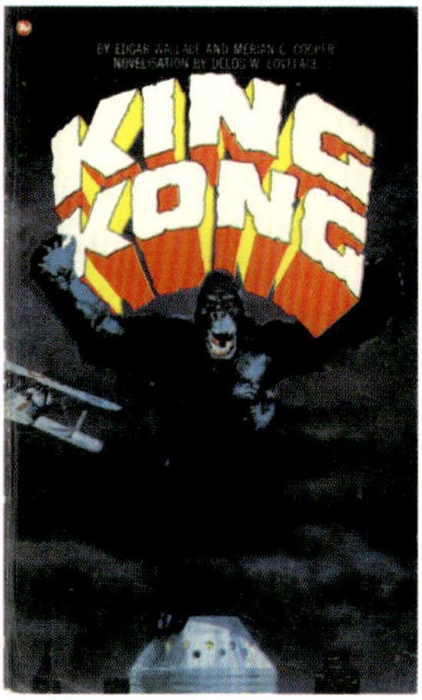

Edgar Wallace, Merian C. Cooper | *King Kong*
Corgi Books, 1966 | Art **Unknown**

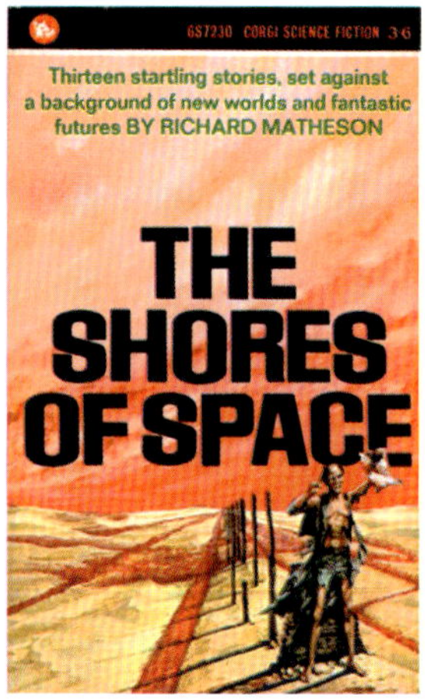

Richard Matheson | *The Shores of Space*
Corgi Books, 1965 | Art **Josh Kirby**

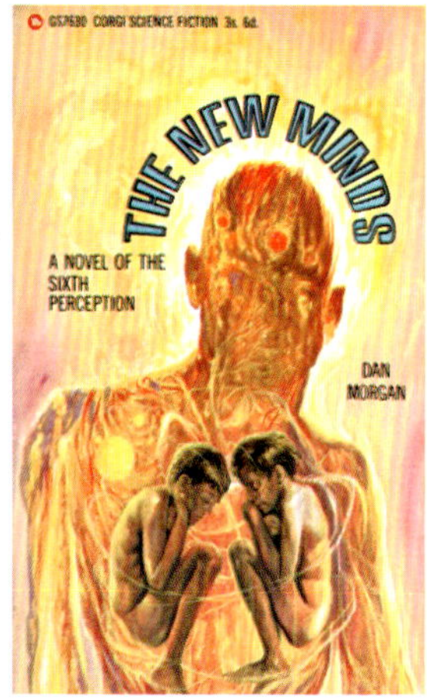

Dan Morgan | *The New Minds*
Corgi Books, 1967 | Art **Josh Kirby**

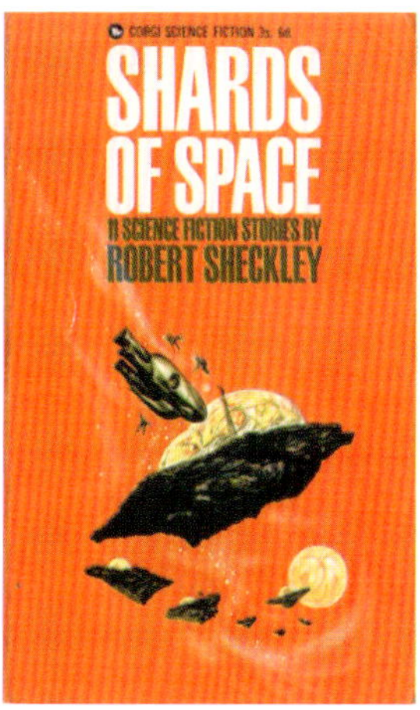

Robert Sheckley | *Shards of Space*
Corgi Books, 1966 | Art **Josh Kirby**

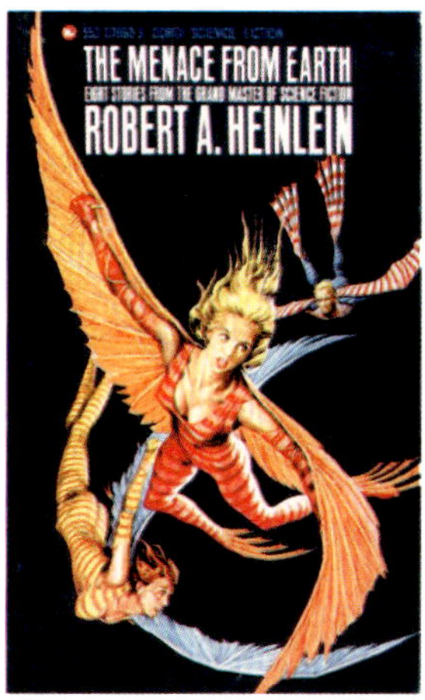

Robert A. Heinlein | *The Menace from Earth*
Corgi Books, 1968 | Art **Josh Kirby**

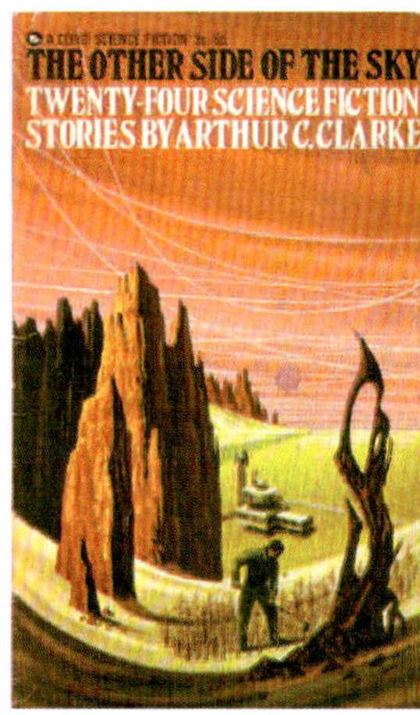

Arthur C. Clarke | *The Other Side of the Sky*
Corgi Books, 1966 | Art **Ralph Brillhart**

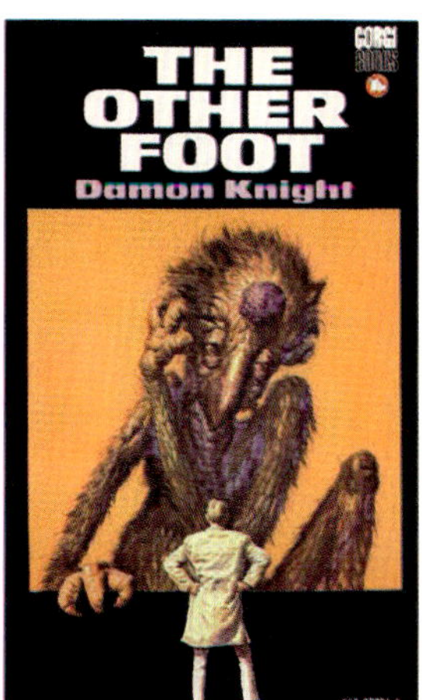

Damon Knight | *The Other Foot*
Corgi Books, 1968 | Art **Josh Kirby**

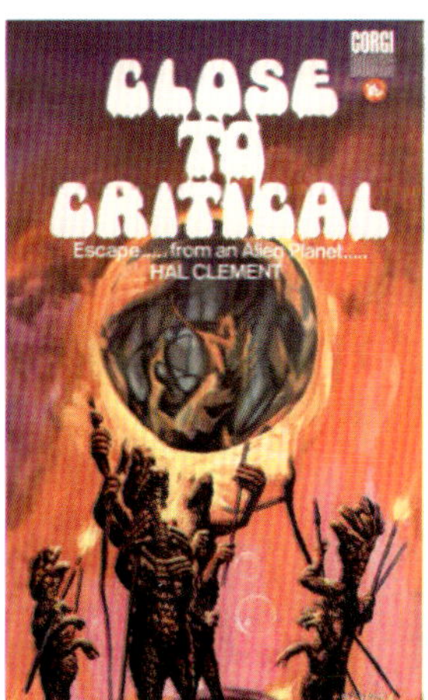

Hal Clement | *Close to Critical*
Corgi Books, 1968 | Art **Unknown**

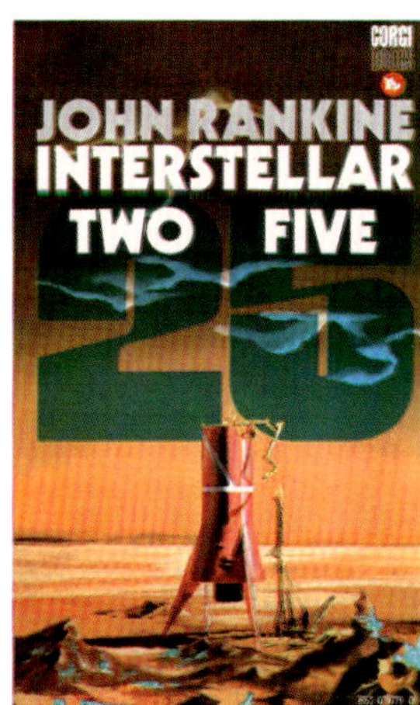

John Rankine | *Interstellar Two Five*
Corgi Books, 1968 | Art **Unknown**

Ray Bradbury | *Fahrenheit 451*
Corgi Books GS7186, 1965 | Original art **Josh Kirby**

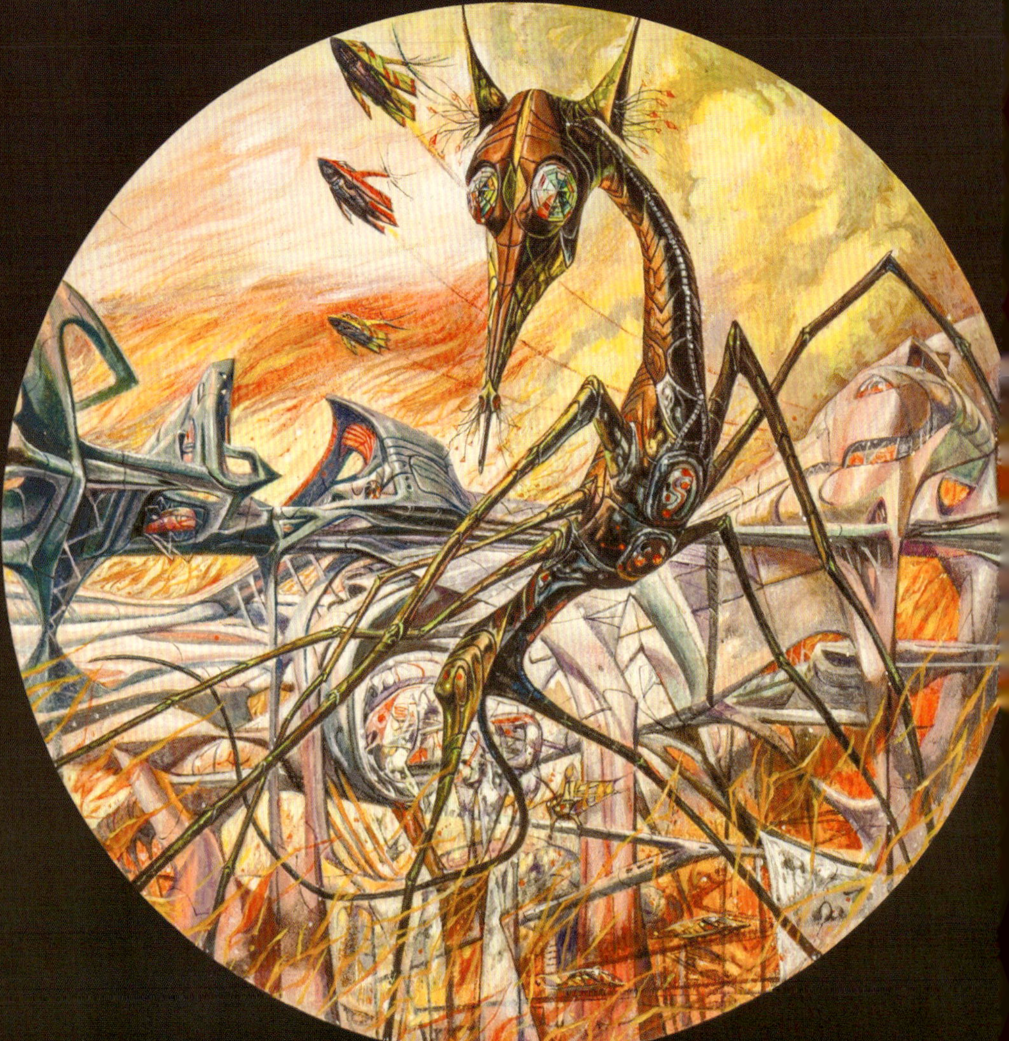

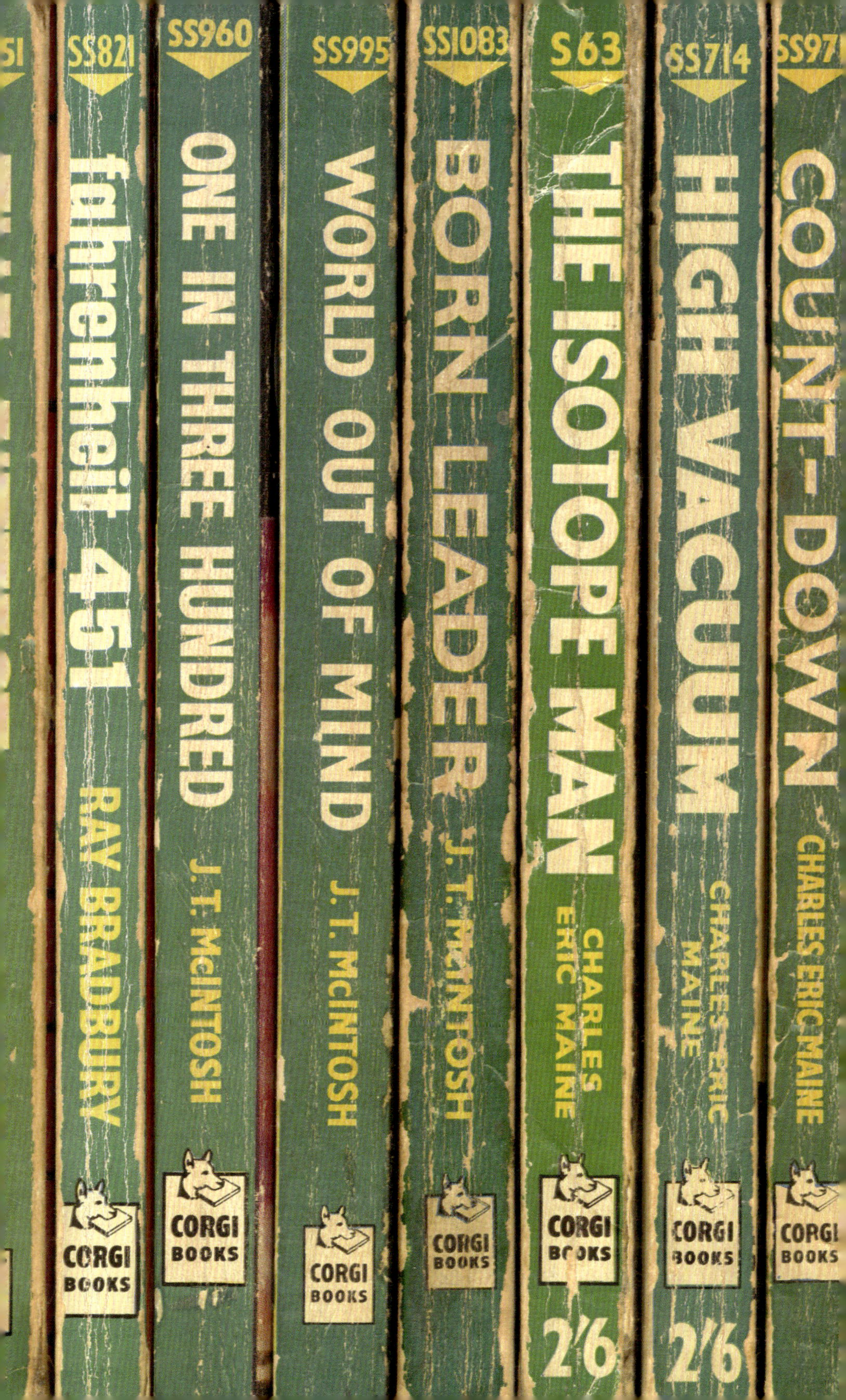
SS821
fahrenheit 451
RAY BRADBURY
CORGI BOOKS
SS960
ONE IN THREE HUNDRED
J. T. McINTOSH
CORGI BOOKS
SS995
WORLD OUT OF MIND
J. T. McINTOSH
CORGI BOOKS
SS1083
BORN LEADER
J. T. McINTOSH
CORGI BOOKS
S 63
THE ISOTOPE MAN
CHARLES ERIC MAINE
CORGI BOOKS
2'6
SS714
HIGH VACUUM
CHARLES ERIC MAINE
CORGI BOOKS
2'6
COUNT-DOWN
CHARLES ERIC MAINE
CORGI BOOKS

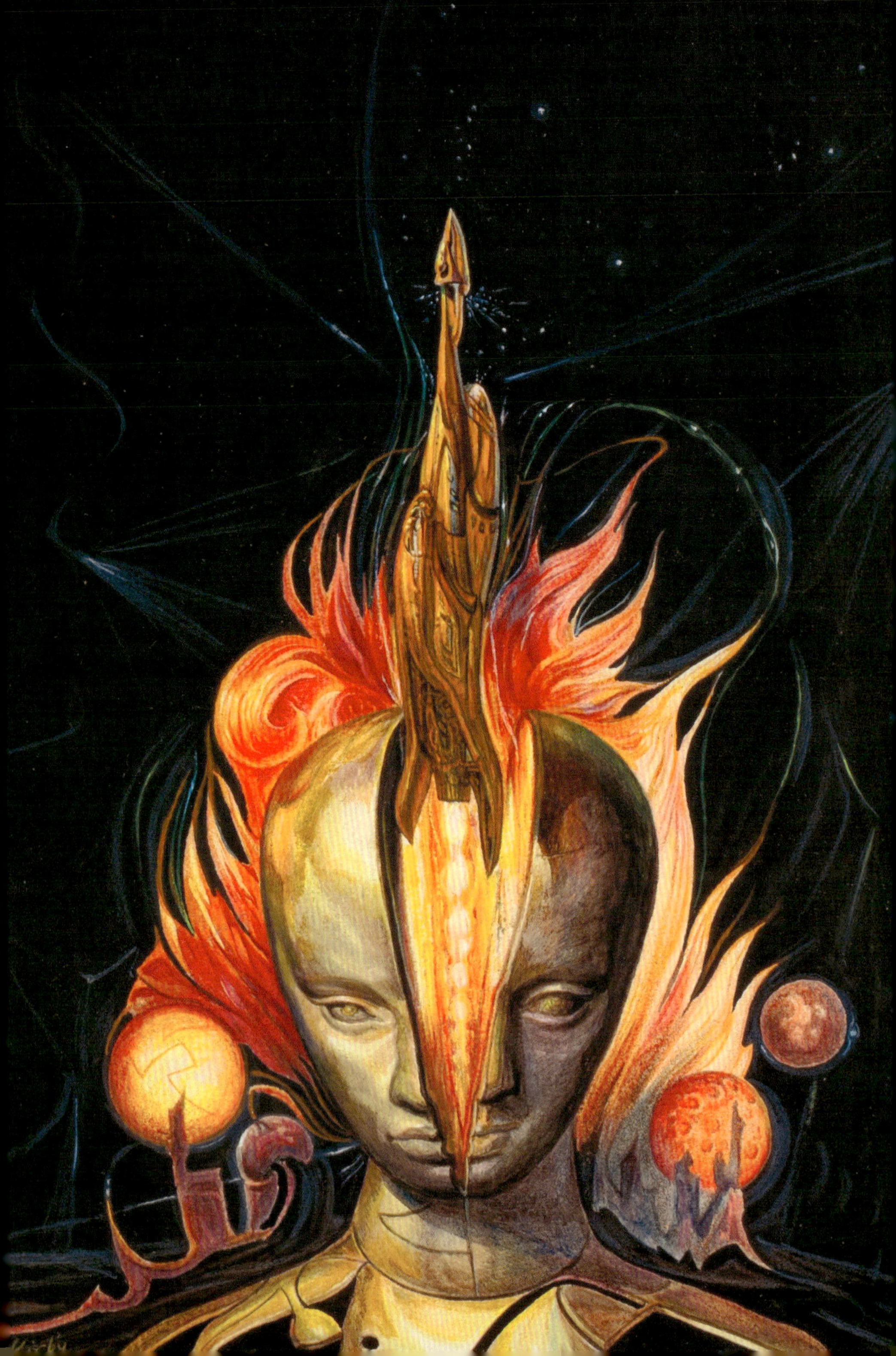

Wiship | Original art **Josh Kirby**
opposite **Charles Grey (E. C. Tubb)** | *I Fight for Mars*
Milestone Publications, Ltd., 1953 | Art **Ron Turner**

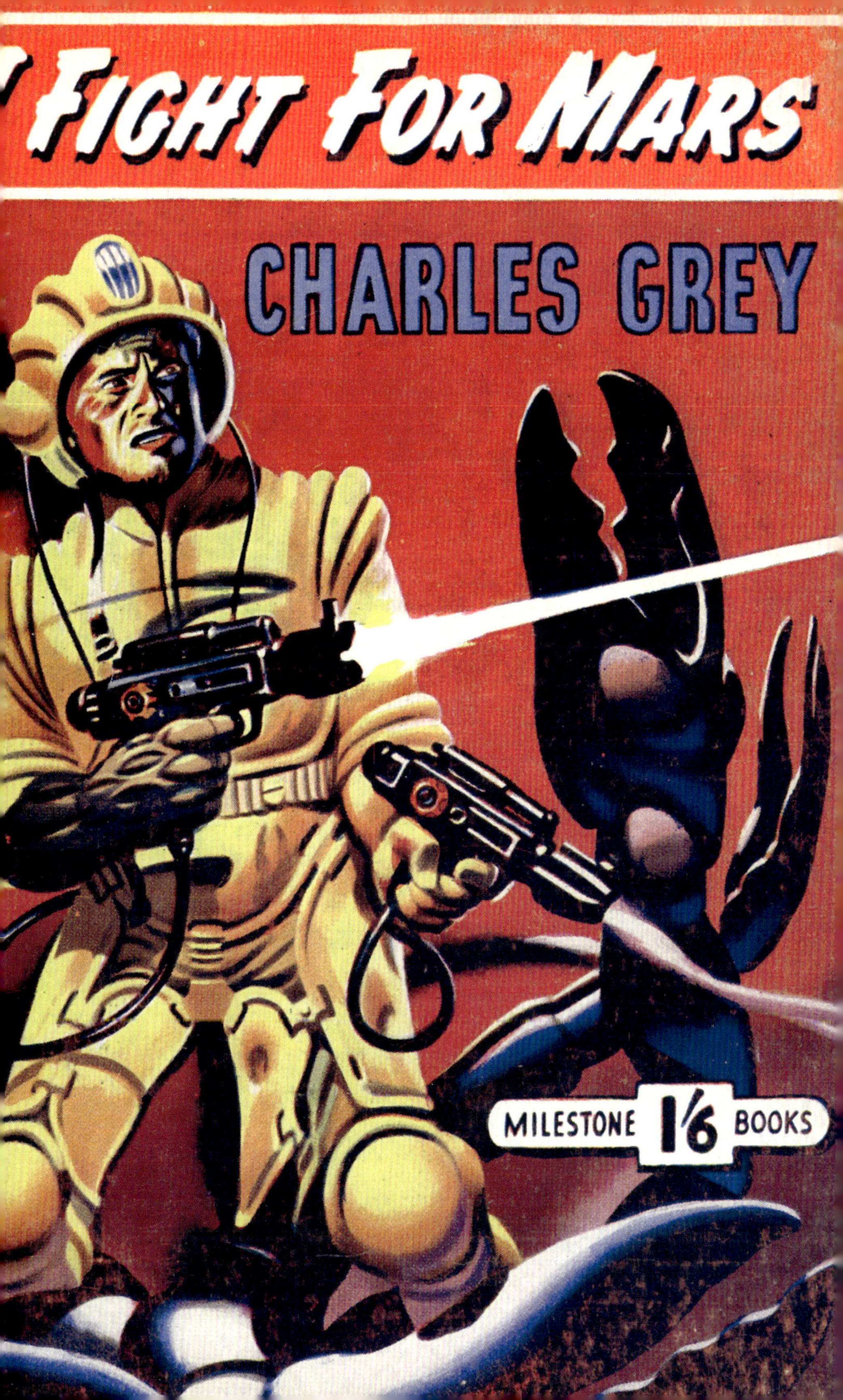
FIGHT FOR MARS
CHARLES GREY
MILESTONE 1/6 BOOKS

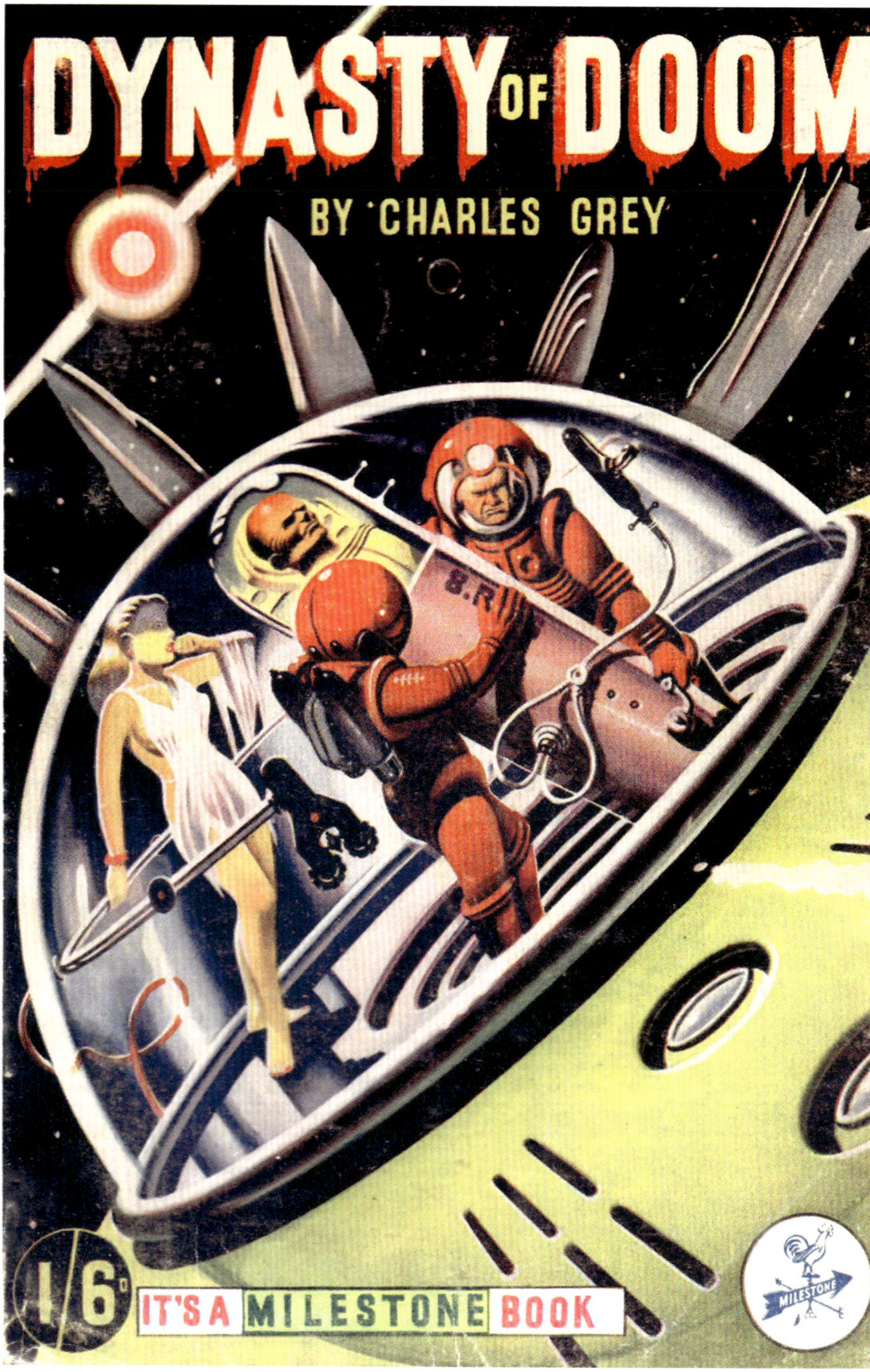

Charles Grey (E. C. Tubb) | *Dynasty of Doom*
Milestone Publications, Ltd., 1062, 1953 | Art **Ron Turner**

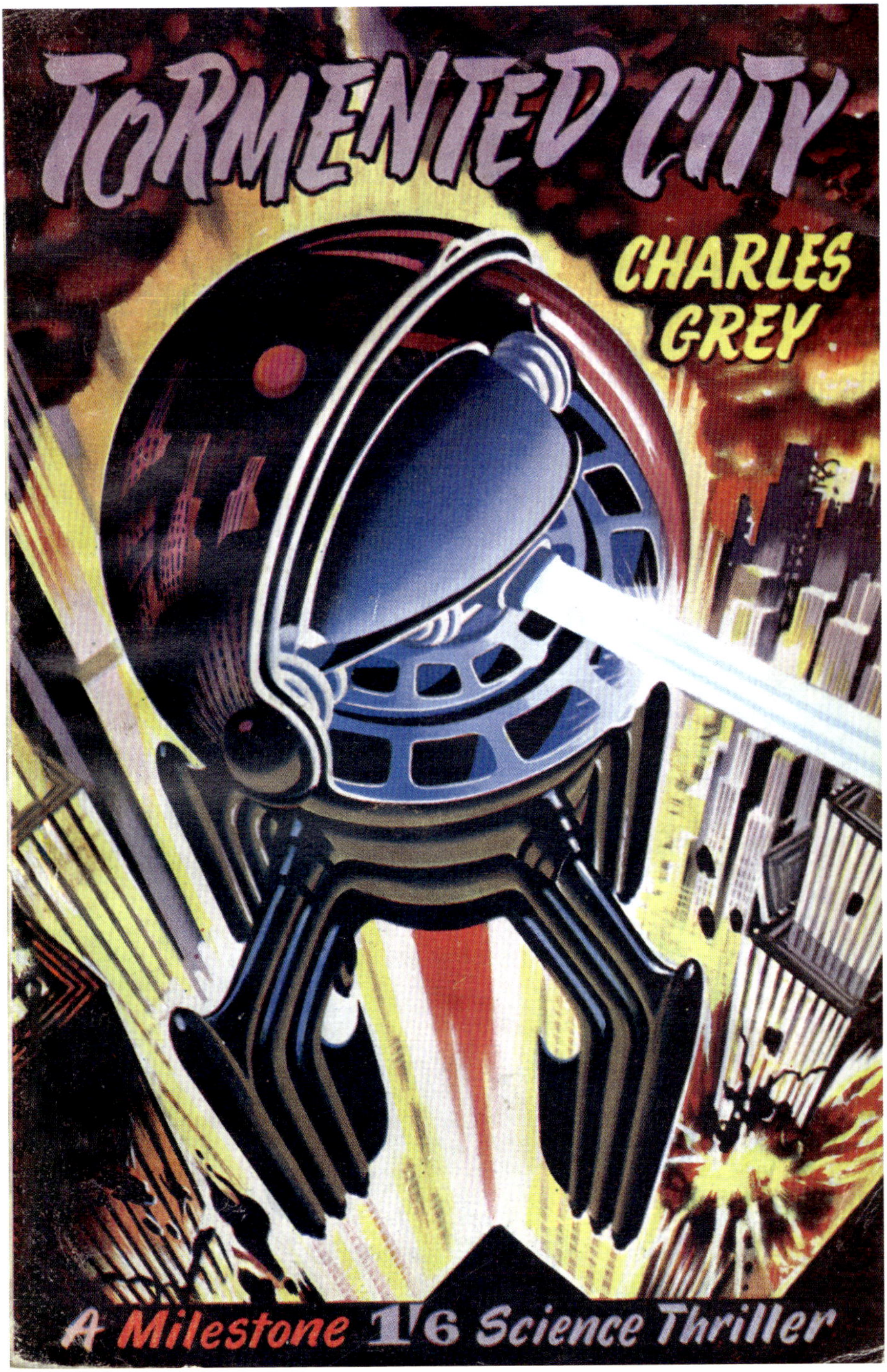

Charles Grey (E. C. Tubb) | *Tormented City*
Milestone Publications, Ltd., 1953 | Art **Ron Turner**

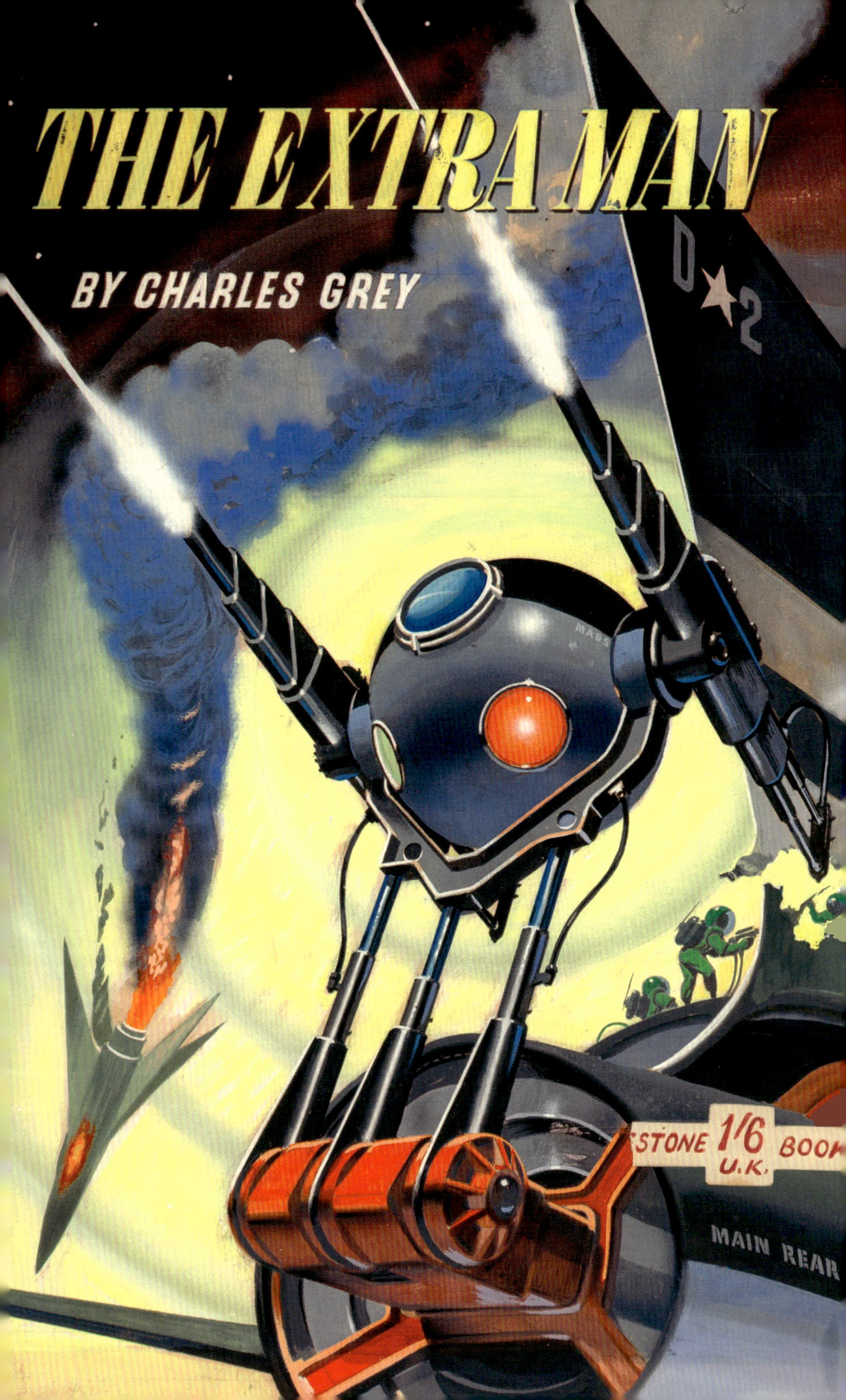
THE EXTRA MAN
BY CHARLES GREY
D★2
1/6
U.K.
MAIN REAR

Charles Grey (E. C. Tubb) | *The Extra Man*
Milestone Publications, Ltd., 1954 | Original art **Ron Turner**

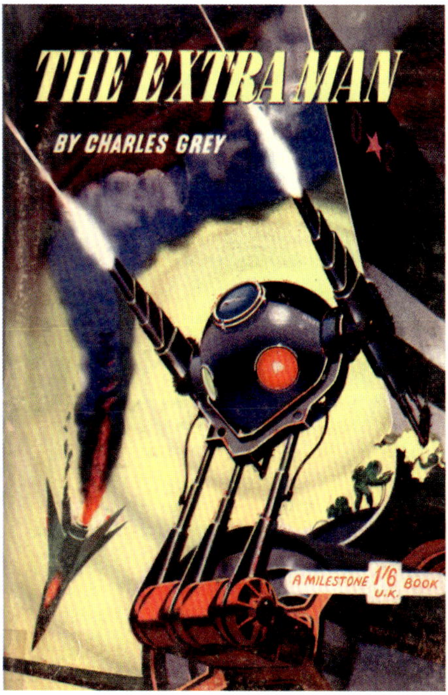

Charles Grey (E. C. Tubb) | *The Extra Man*
Milestone Publications, Ltd., 1954 | Art **Ron Turner**

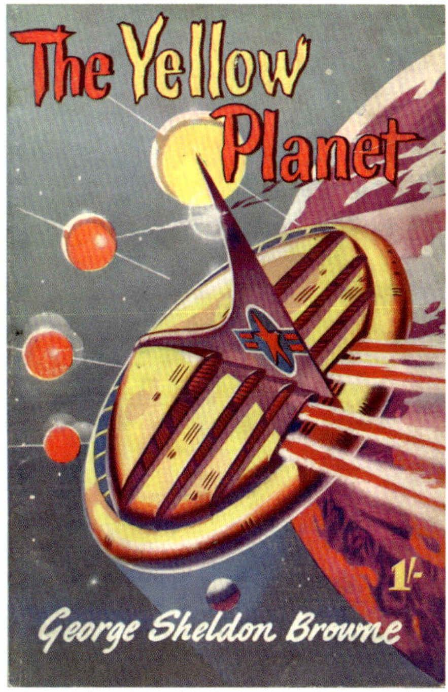

George Sheldon Browne (John Jennison) | *The Yellow Planet*
Edwin Self, 1954 | Art **Ron Turner**

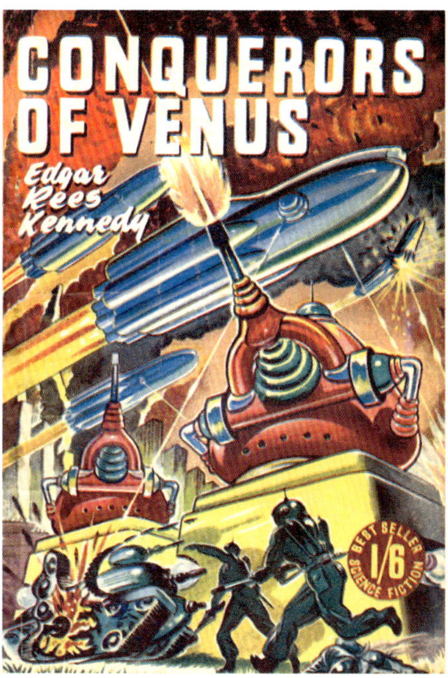

Edgar Rees Kennedy (John Jennison) | *Conquerors of Venus*
Edwin Self 7, 1951 | Art **Ron Turner**

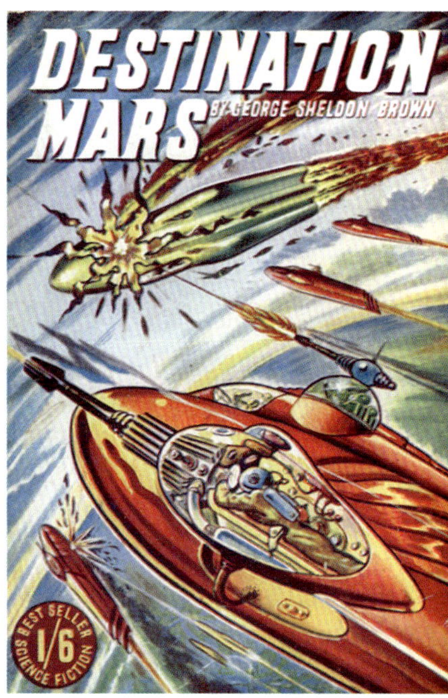

George Sheldon Brown (Denis Hughes) | *Destination Mars*
Edwin Self, 1951 | Art **Ron Turner**

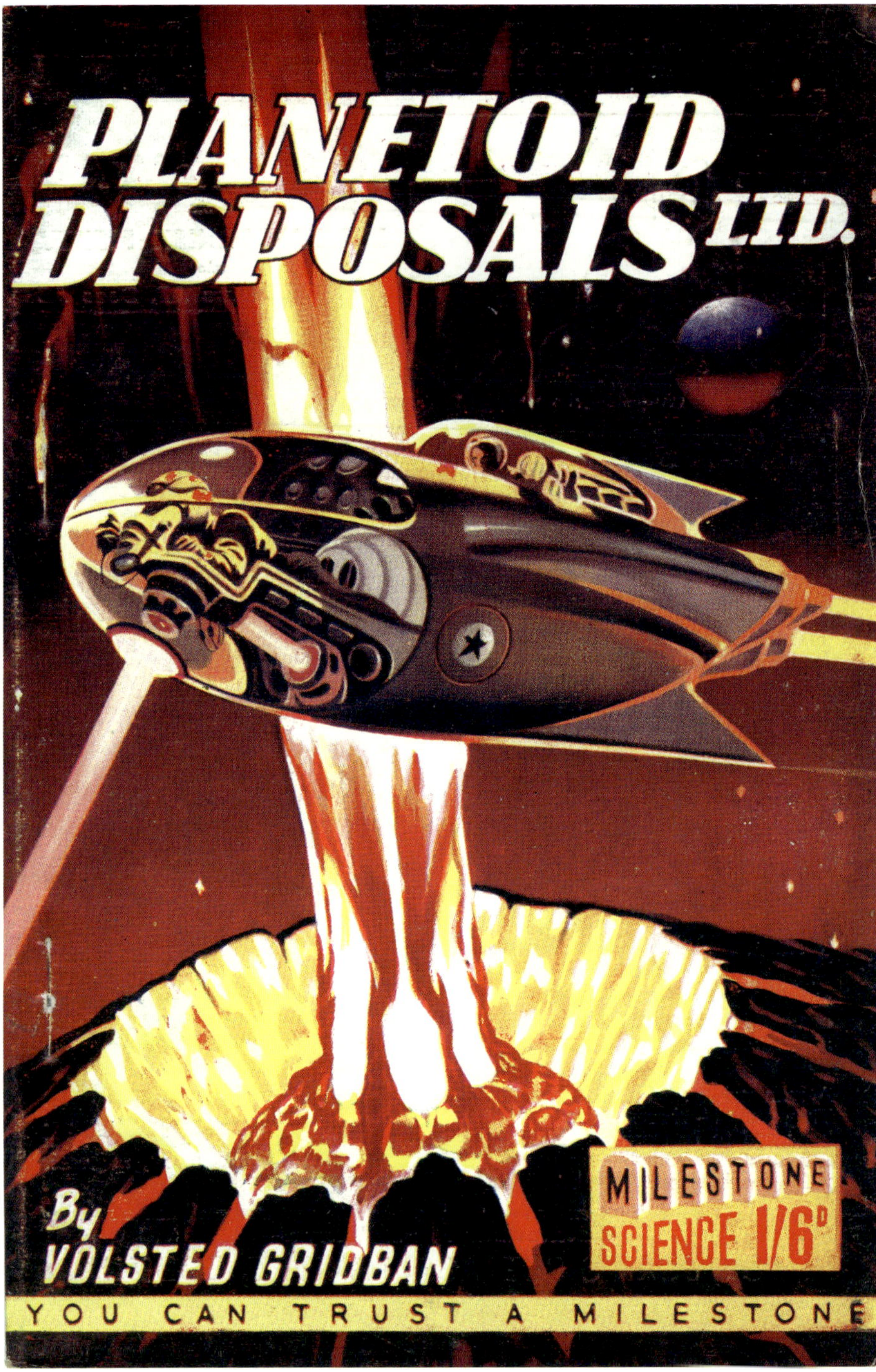

Volsted Gridban (E. C. Tubb) | *Planetoid Disposals Ltd.*
Milestone Publications, Ltd., 1953 | Art **Ron Turner**

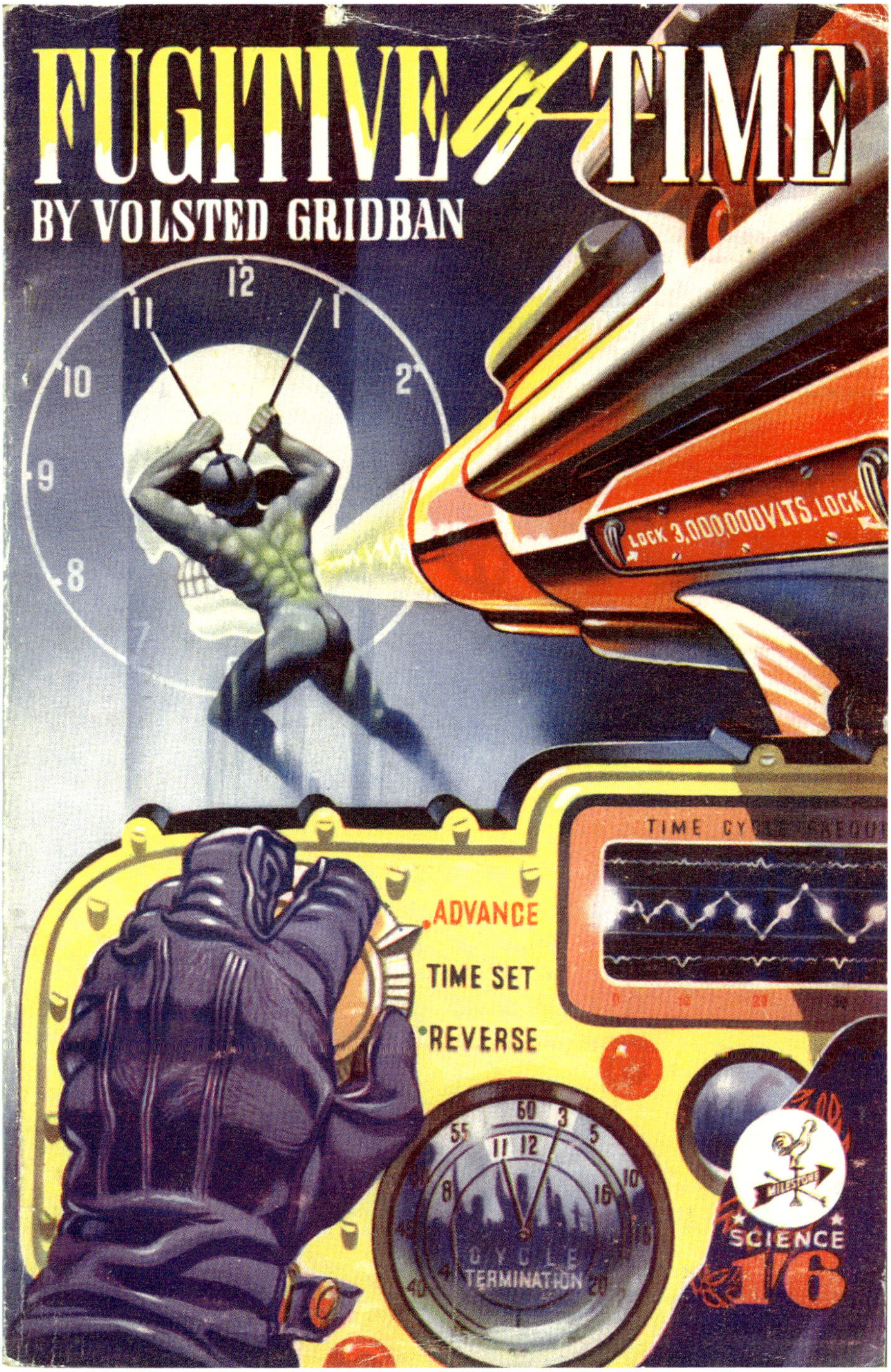

Volsted Gridban (E. C. Tubb) | *Fugitive of Time*
Milestone Publications, Ltd., 1953 | Art **Ron Turner**
Originally intended for *Zero Hour,* but used here instead. A new cover was then produced for *Zero Hour,* resulting in two Turners for the same title.

opposite: **Charles Grey (E. C. Tubb)** | *Space Hunger*
Milestone Publications, Ltd., 1953 | Original art **Ron Turner**

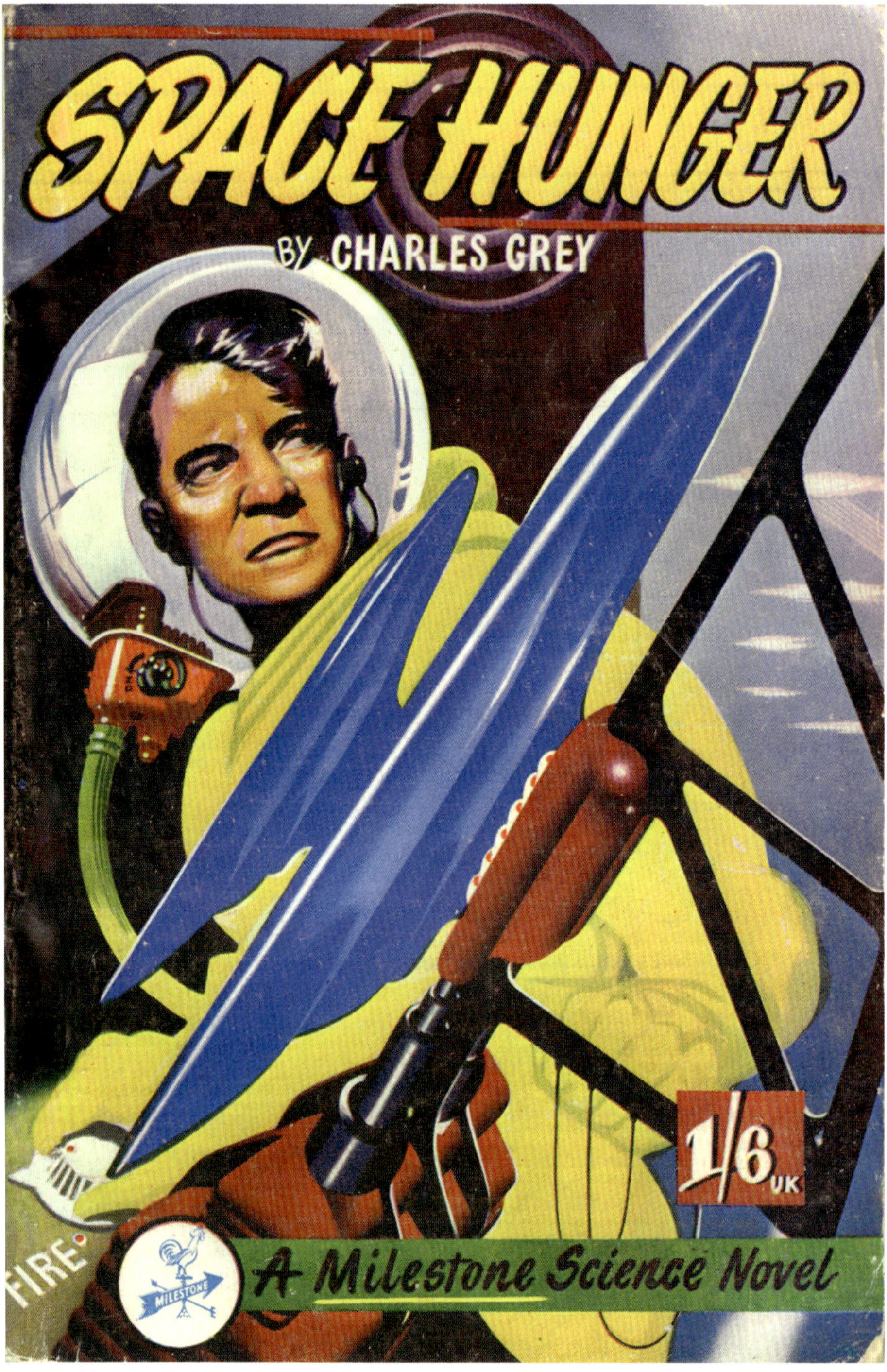

Charles Grey (E. C. Tubb) | *Space Hunger*
Milestone Publications, Ltd., 1953 | Art **Ron Turner**

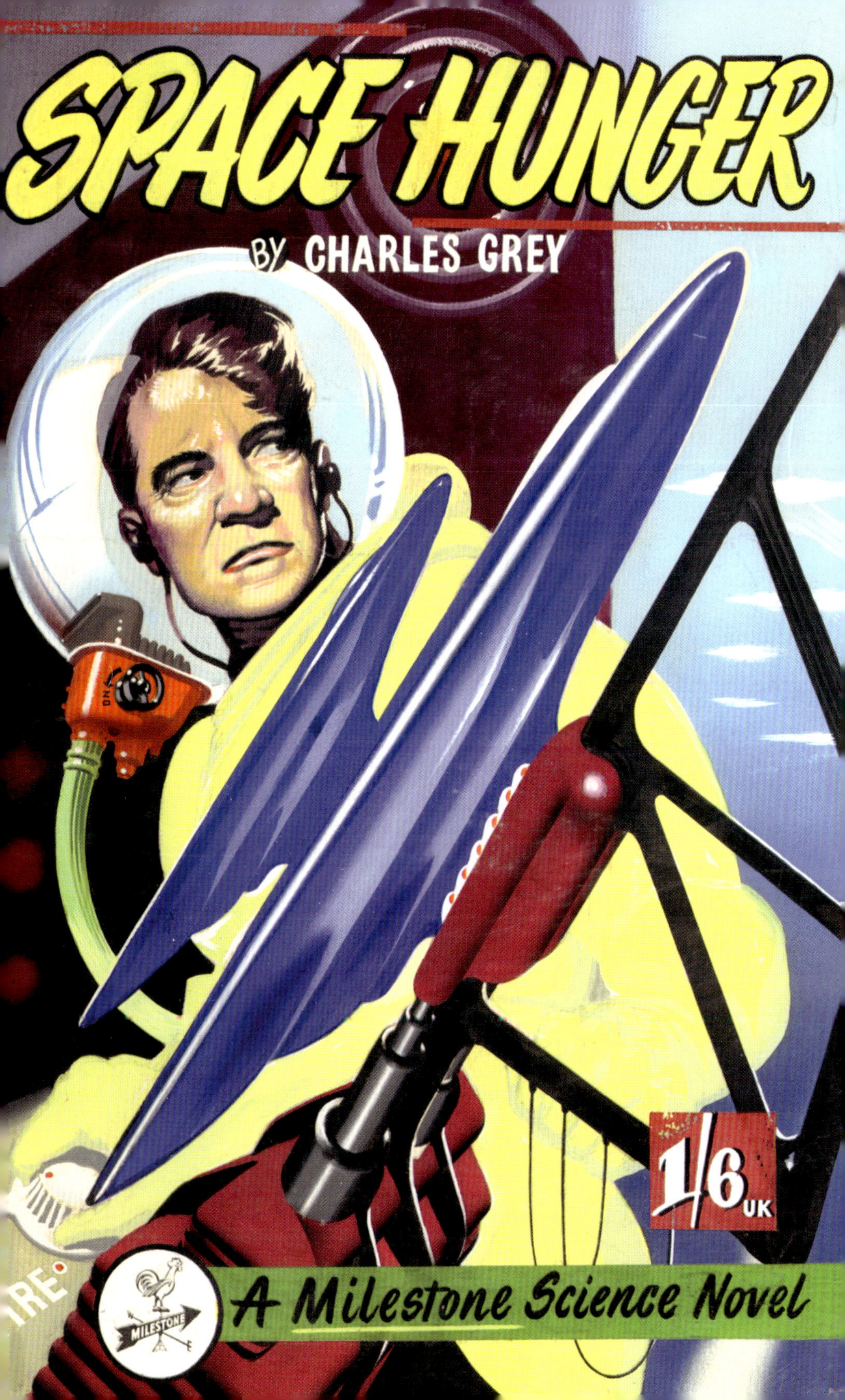
SPACE HUNGER
BY CHARLES GREY
1/6 UK
MILESTONE
A Milestone Science Novel

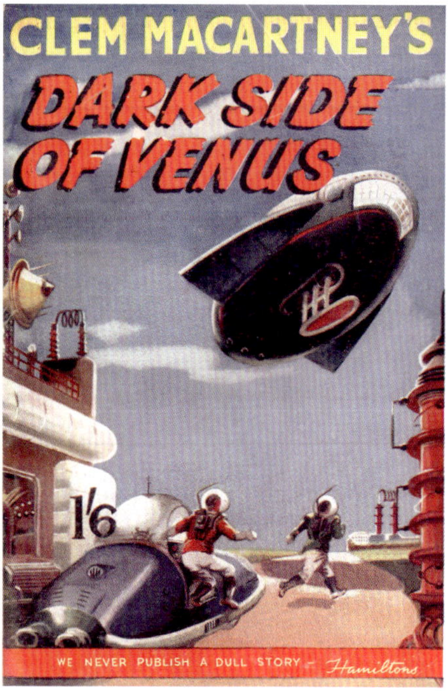

Clem Macartney (William David Flackes) | *Dark Side of Venus*
Hamilton & Co., 1951 | Art **George Ratcliffe**

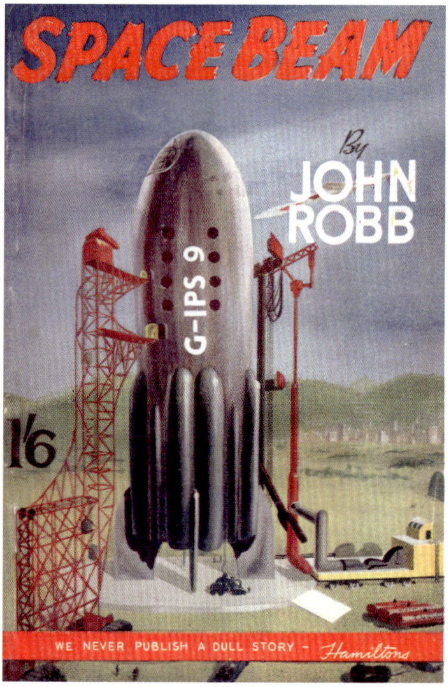

John Robb (Norman Robson) | *Space Beam*
Hamilton & Co., 1951 | Art **George Ratcliffe**

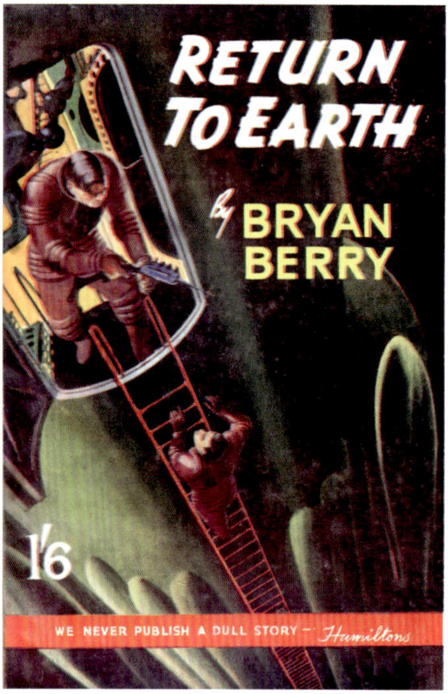

Bryan Berry | *Return to Earth*
Hamilton & Co., 1951 | Art **George Ratcliffe**

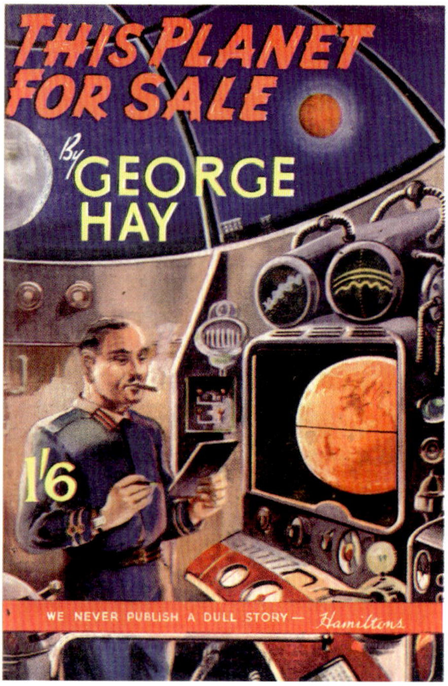

George Hay | *This Planet for Sale*
Hamilton & Co., 1951 | Art **George Ratcliffe**

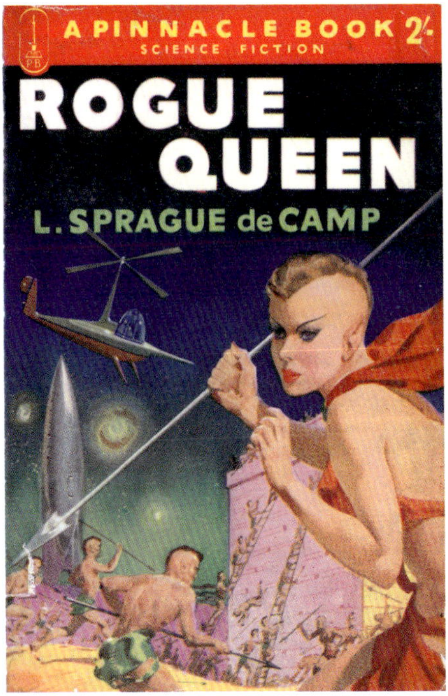

L. Sprague de Camp | Rogue Queen
Pinnacle Books, 1954 | Art **James McConnell**

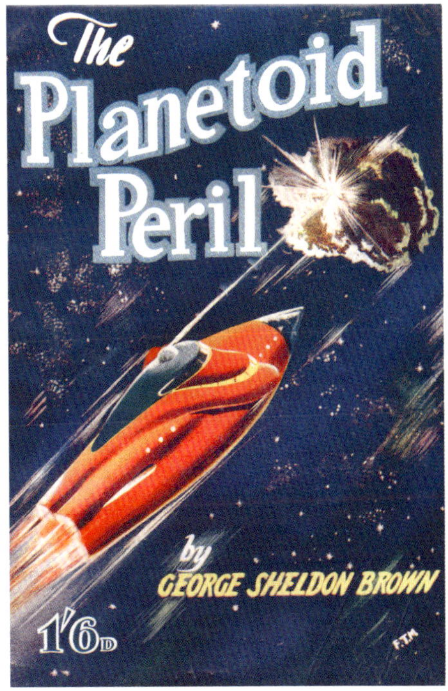

George Sheldon Brown (Denis Hughes) | *The Planetoid Peril*
Edwin Self, 1952 | Art **Terry Maloney**

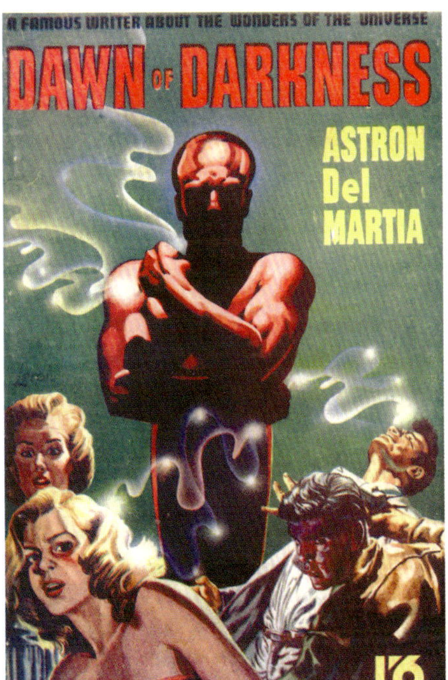

Astron del Martia | *Dawn of Darkness*
Gaywood Press, 1951 | Art **Leroi (R. A. Osborne)**

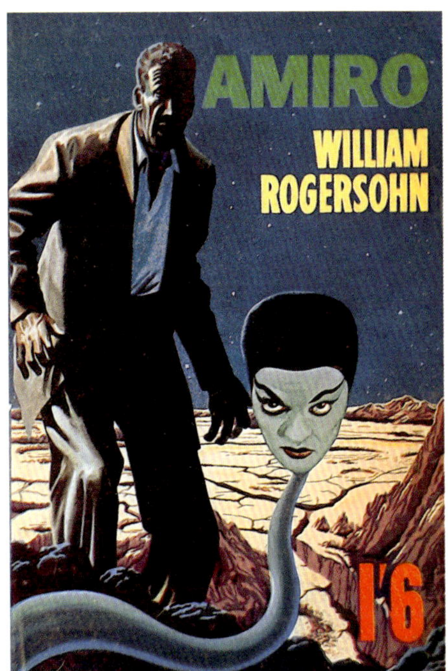

William Rogersohn (Denis Hughes) | *Amiro*
Brown, Watson, 1954 | Art **Leroi (R. A. Osborne)**

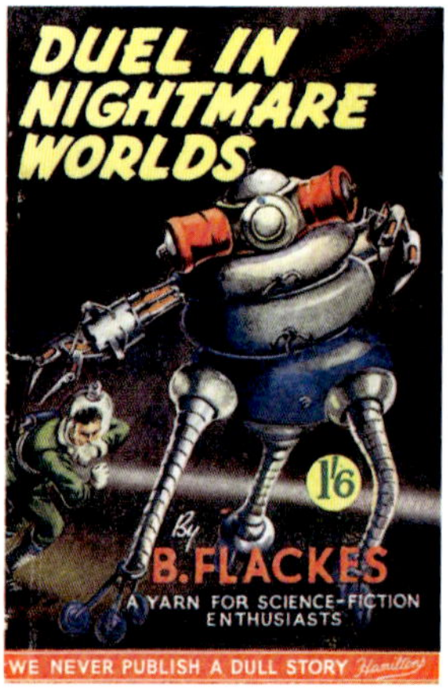

B. Flackes (William David Flackes)
Duel in Nightmare Worlds
Hamilton & Co., 1952 | Art **George Ratcliffe**

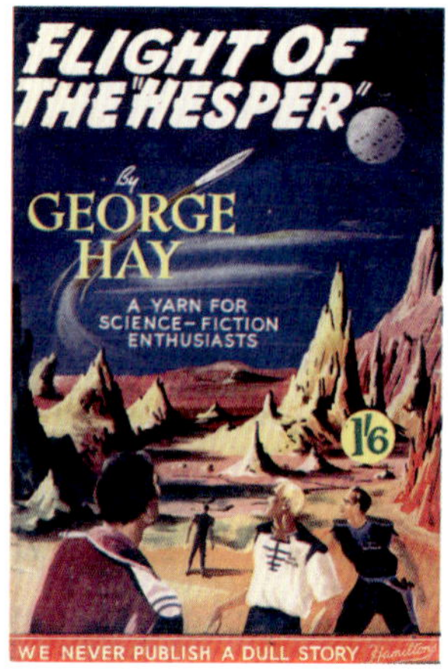

George Hay | *Flight of the "Hesper"*
Hamilton & Co., 1952 | Art **George Ratcliffe**

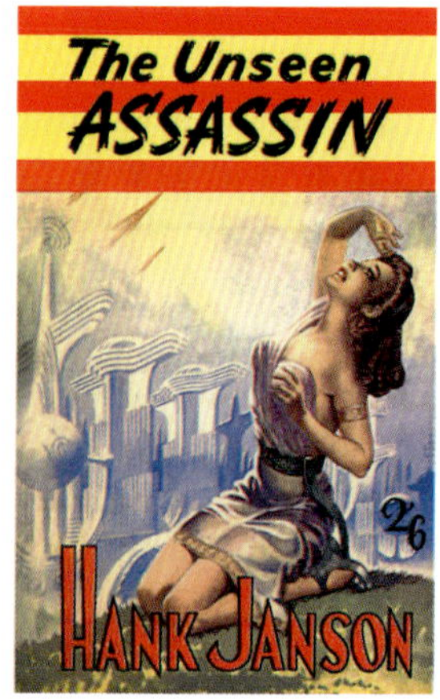

Hank Janson (Stephen Daniel Frances)
The Unseen Assasin | Alexander Moring, 1956
Art **Reginald Heade,** background **Ron Turner**

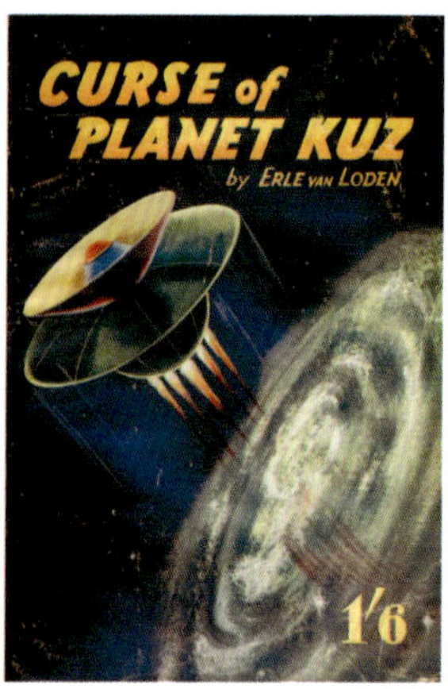

Erle Van Loden (Lisle Willis)
Curse of Planet Kuz
Edwin Self, 1953 | Art **Gerald Facey**

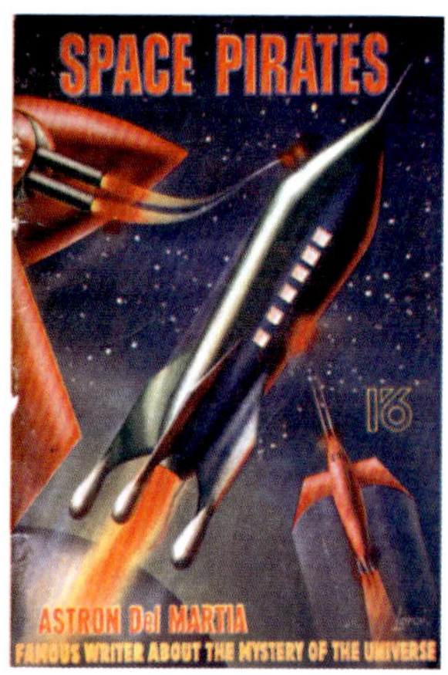

Astron del Martia (Franz Harkon) | *Space Pirates*
Gaywood Press, 1951 | Art **Leroi (R. A. Osborne)**

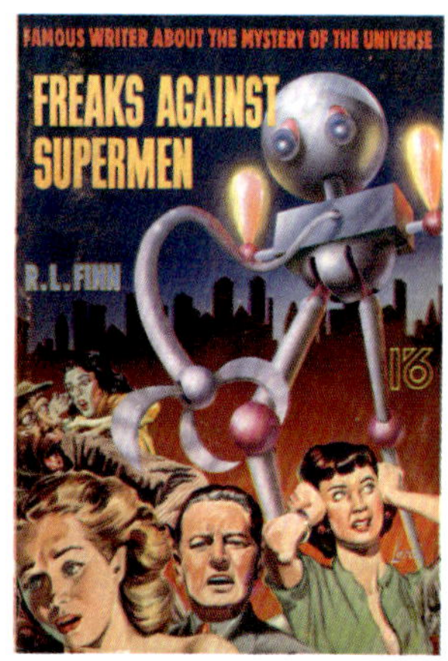

Ralph L. Finn | *Freaks Against Supermen*
Gaywood Press, 1950 | Art **Leroi (R. A. Osborne)**

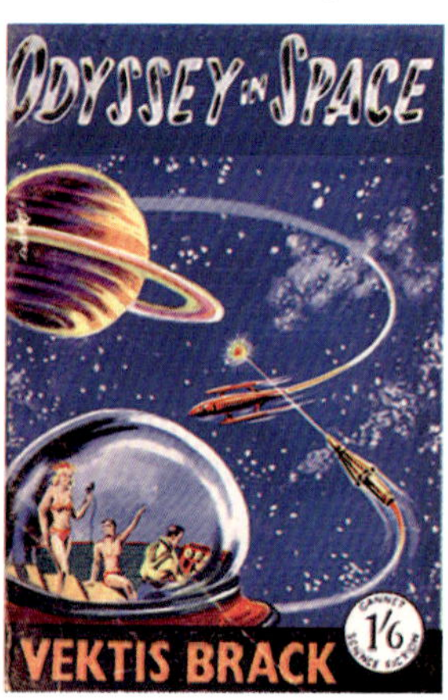

Vektis Brack (Leslie Humphrys)
Odyssey in Space
Gannet Press, 1954 | Art **Gerald Facey**

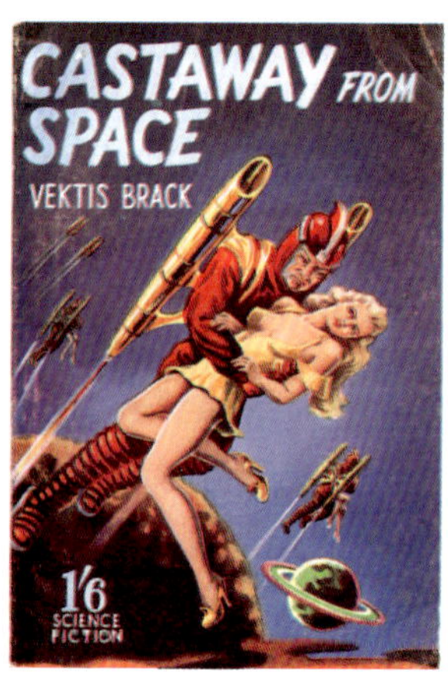

Vektis Brack | *Castaway from Space*
Gannet Press, 1953 | Art **Ray Theobald**

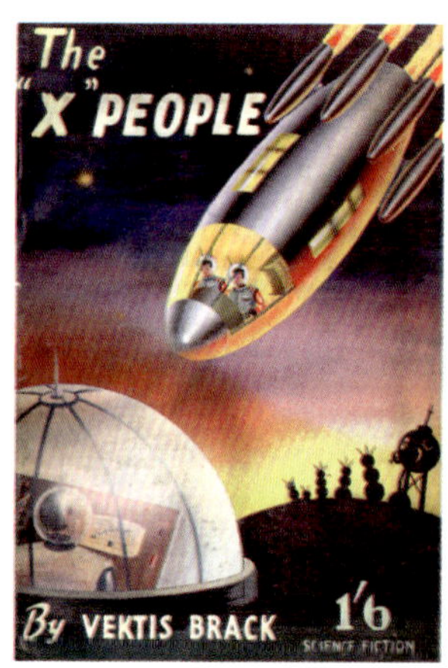

Vektis Brack | *The "X" People*
Gannet Press, 1953 | Art **Gerald Facey**

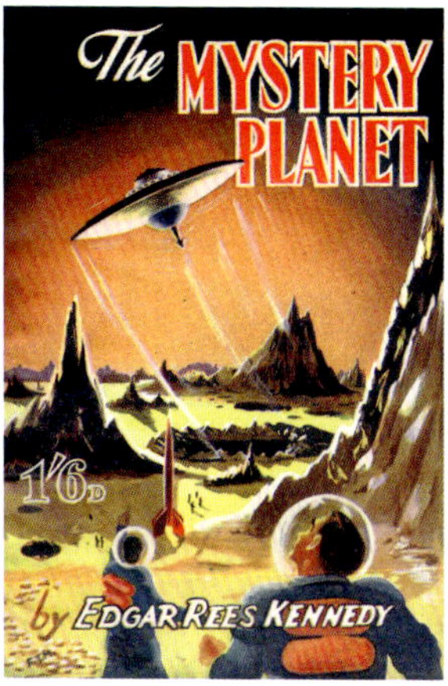

Edgar Rees Kennedy (John Jennison)
The Mystery Planet
Edwin Self, 1952 | Art **Terry Maloney**

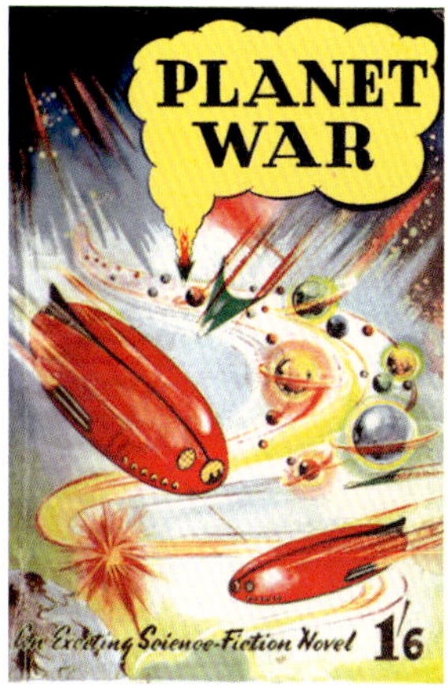

Fysh (Leonard G. Fish) | *Planet War*
Archer, 1952 | Art **Gerald Facey**

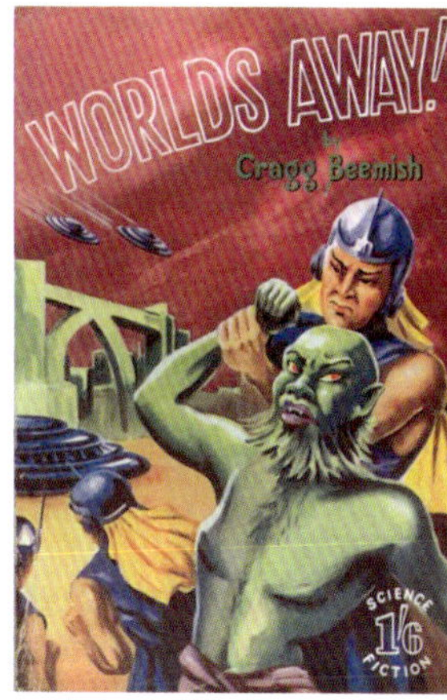

Cragg Beemish | *Worlds Away!*
Gannet Press, 1953 | Art **Ray Theobald**

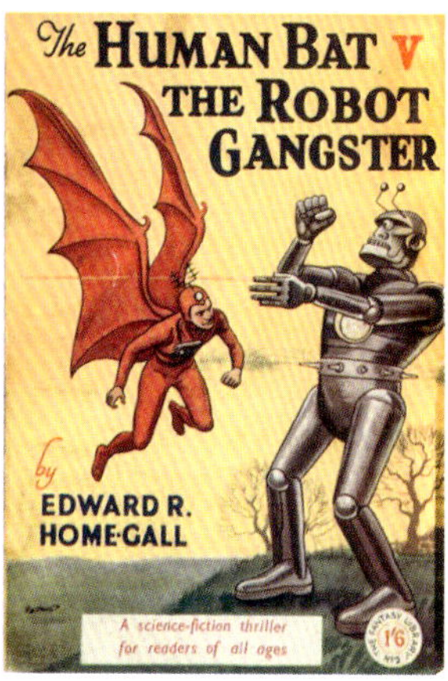

Edward R. Home-Gall
The Human Bat v the Robot Gangster
Mark Goulden Ltd., 1950 | Art **Roland G. Davies**

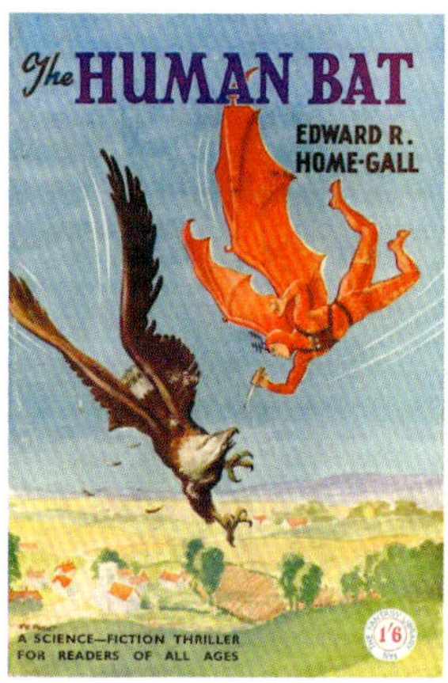

Edward R. Home-Gall | *The Human Bat*
Mark Goulden Ltd., 1950 | Art **Roland G. Davies**

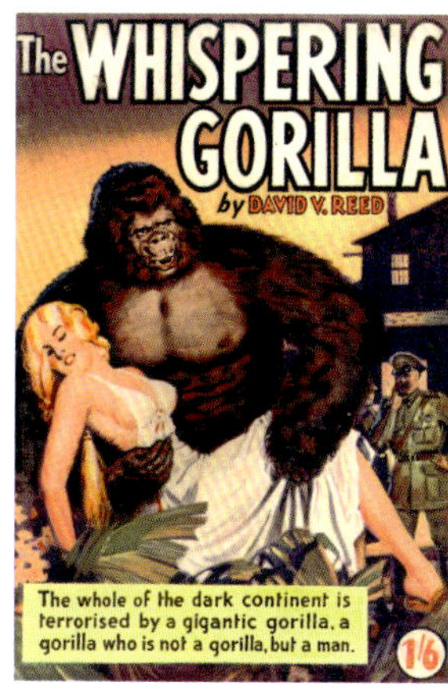

David V. Reed | *The Whispering Gorilla*
World Distributors/Sydney Pemberton, 1950
Art **R. A. Osborne** after **Robert Gibson Jones**

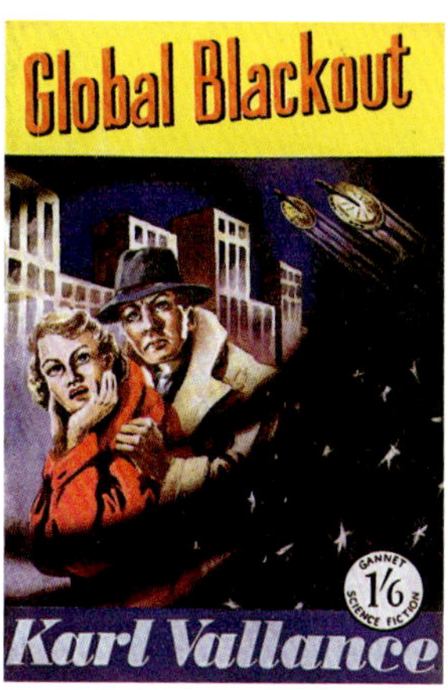

Karl Vallance | *Global Blackout*
Gannet Press, 1954 | Art **Ray Theobald**

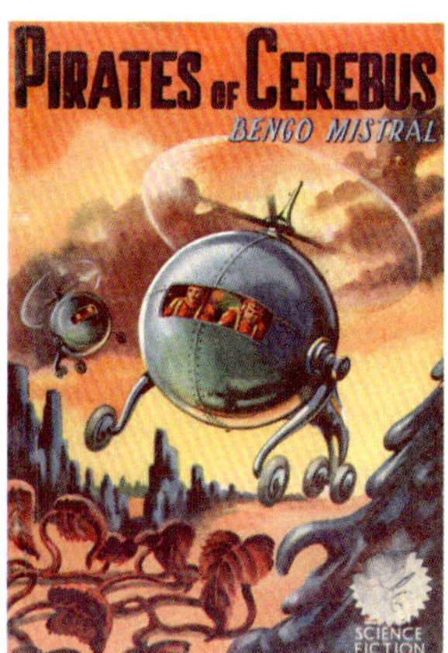

Bengo Mistral (Barney Ward) | *Pirates of Cerebus*
Gannet Press, 1953 | Art **Ray Theobald**
Perhaps "the worst sf novel ever published" [PH]

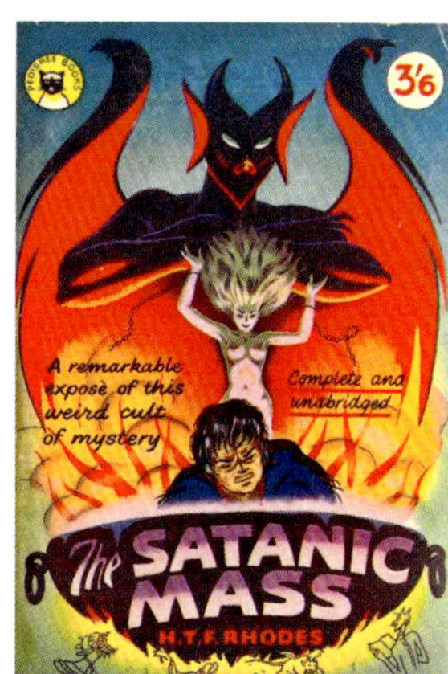

H. T. F. Rhodes | *The Satanic Mass*
Pedigree Books, 1957 | Art **Ron Turner**

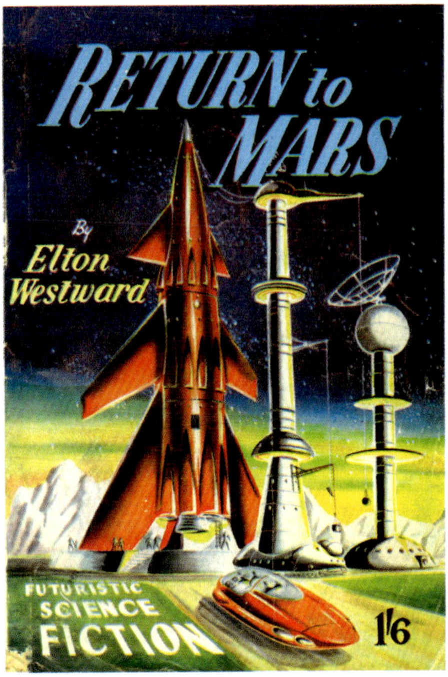

Elton Westward | *Return to Mars*
Brown, Watson, 1952 | Art **Gordon C. Davies**

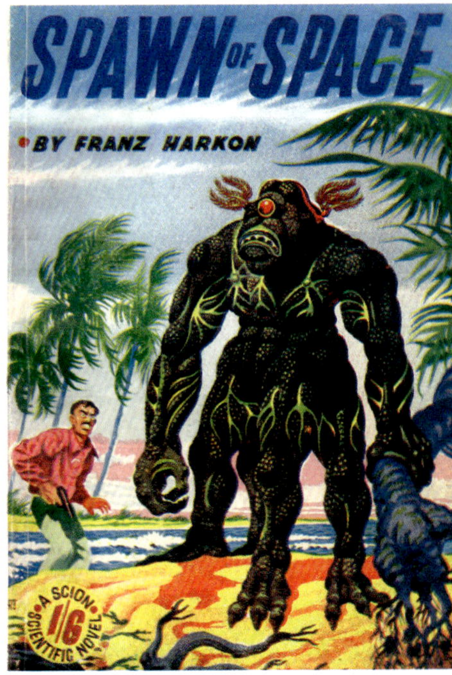

Franz Harkon | *Spawn of Space*
Scion Ltd., 1951 | Art **Ron Turner**

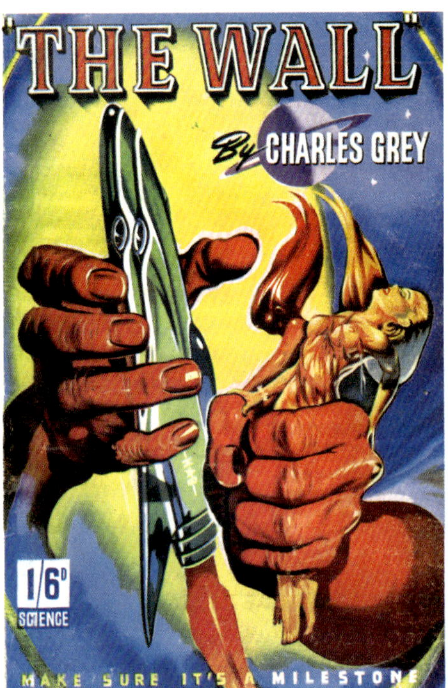

Charles Grey (E. C. Tubb) | *The Wall*
Milestone Publications, Ltd., 1953 | Art **Ron Turner**

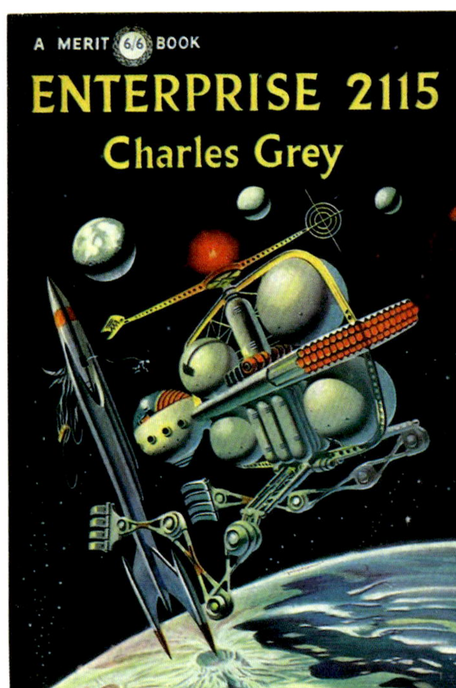

Charles Grey (E. C. Tubb) | *Enterprise 2115*
Merit Books (Milestone Publications), 1954 | Art **Ron Turner**

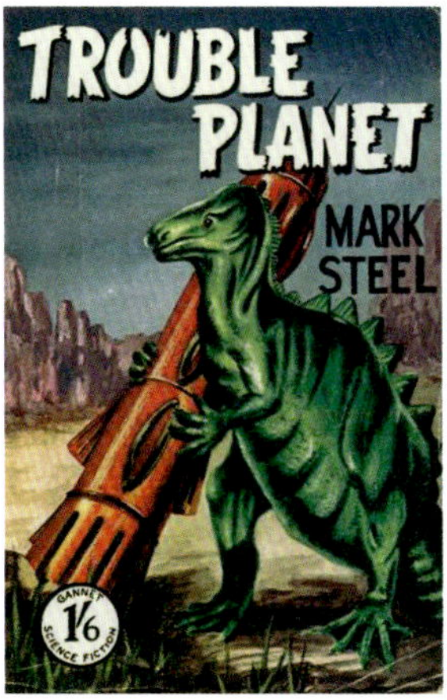

Mark Steel | *Trouble Planet*
Gannet Press, 1954 | Art **Gerald Facey**

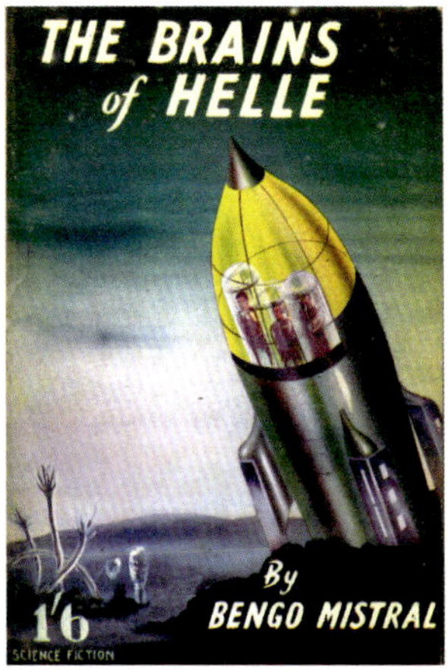

Bengo Mistral (Norman Lazenby)
The Brains of Helle
Gannet Press, 1953 | Art **Gerald Facey**

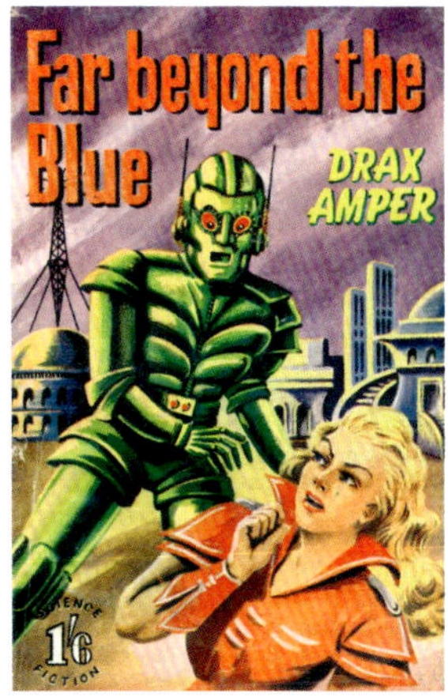

Drax Amper | *Far Beyond the Blue*
Gannet Press, 1953 | Art **Ray Theobald**

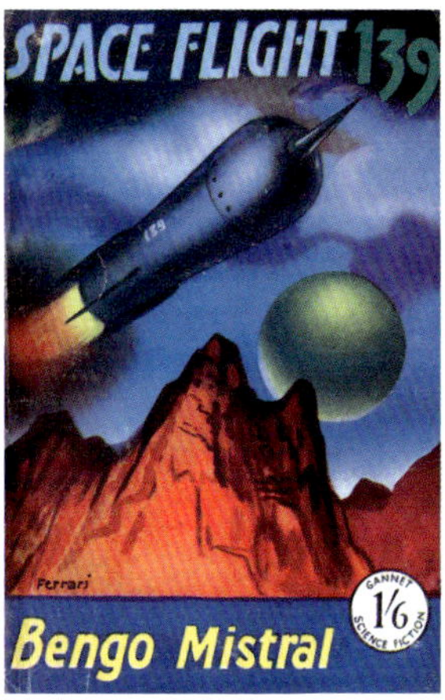

Bengo Mistral | *Space Flight 139*
Gannet Press, 1954
Art **Ferrari (Philip Mendoza)**

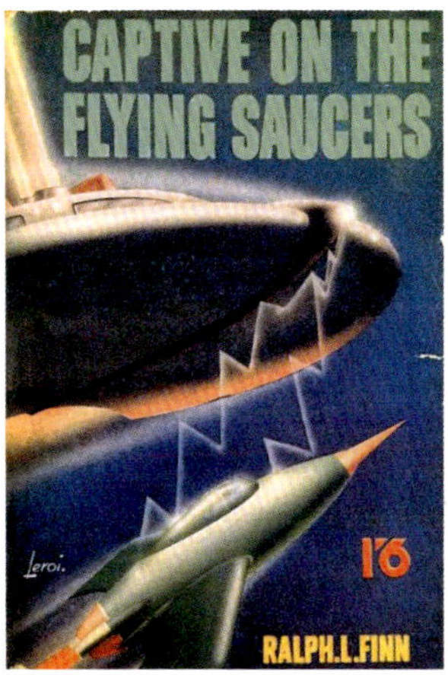

Ralph L. Finn | *Captive on the Flying Saucers*
Gaywood Press, 1951
Art **Leroi (R. A. Osborne)**

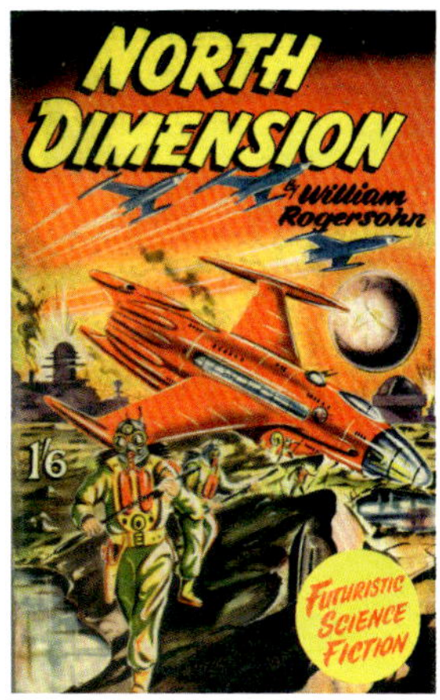

William Rogersohn (Denis Hughes)
North Dimension
Brown, Watson, 1954 | Art **Gordon C. Davies**

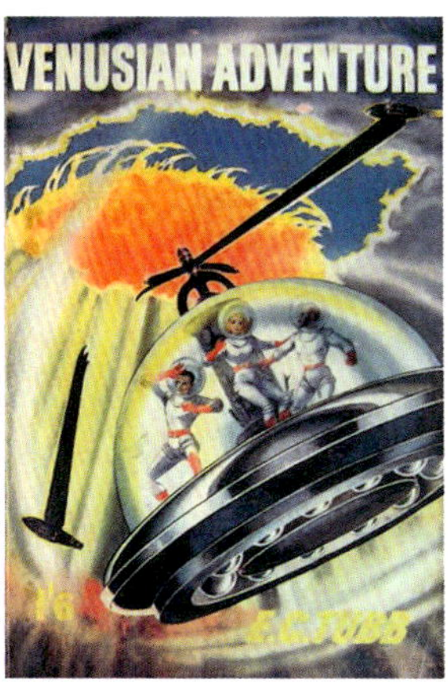

E. C. Tubb | *Venusian Adventure*
Comyns Ltd., 1953 | Art **George Ratcliffe**

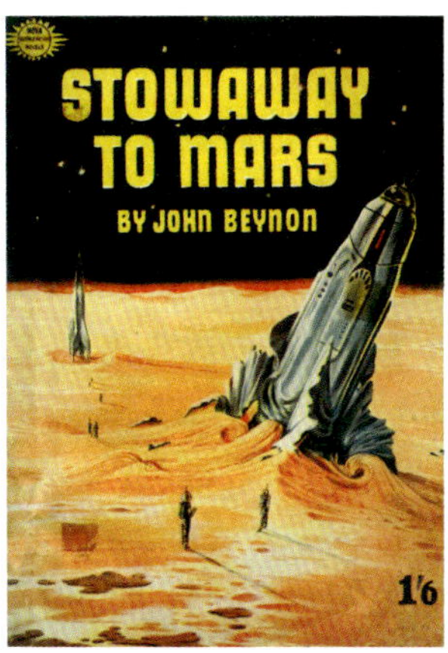

John Beynon | *Stowaway to Mars*
Nova Publications, 1953 | Art **Gordon Hutchings**

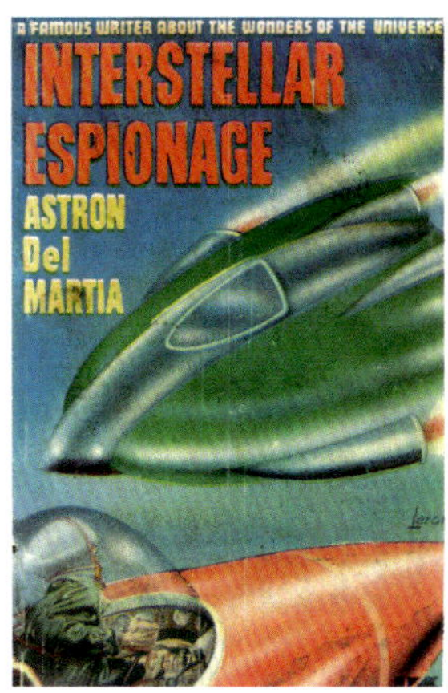

Astron del Martia (Franz Harkon)
Interstellar Espionage | Gaywood Press, 1952
Art **Leroi (R. A. Osborne)**

opposite **Alvin Westwood** | *Sinister Forces*
Brown, Watson, 1953 | Original art recreation, 1986 **Ron Turner**

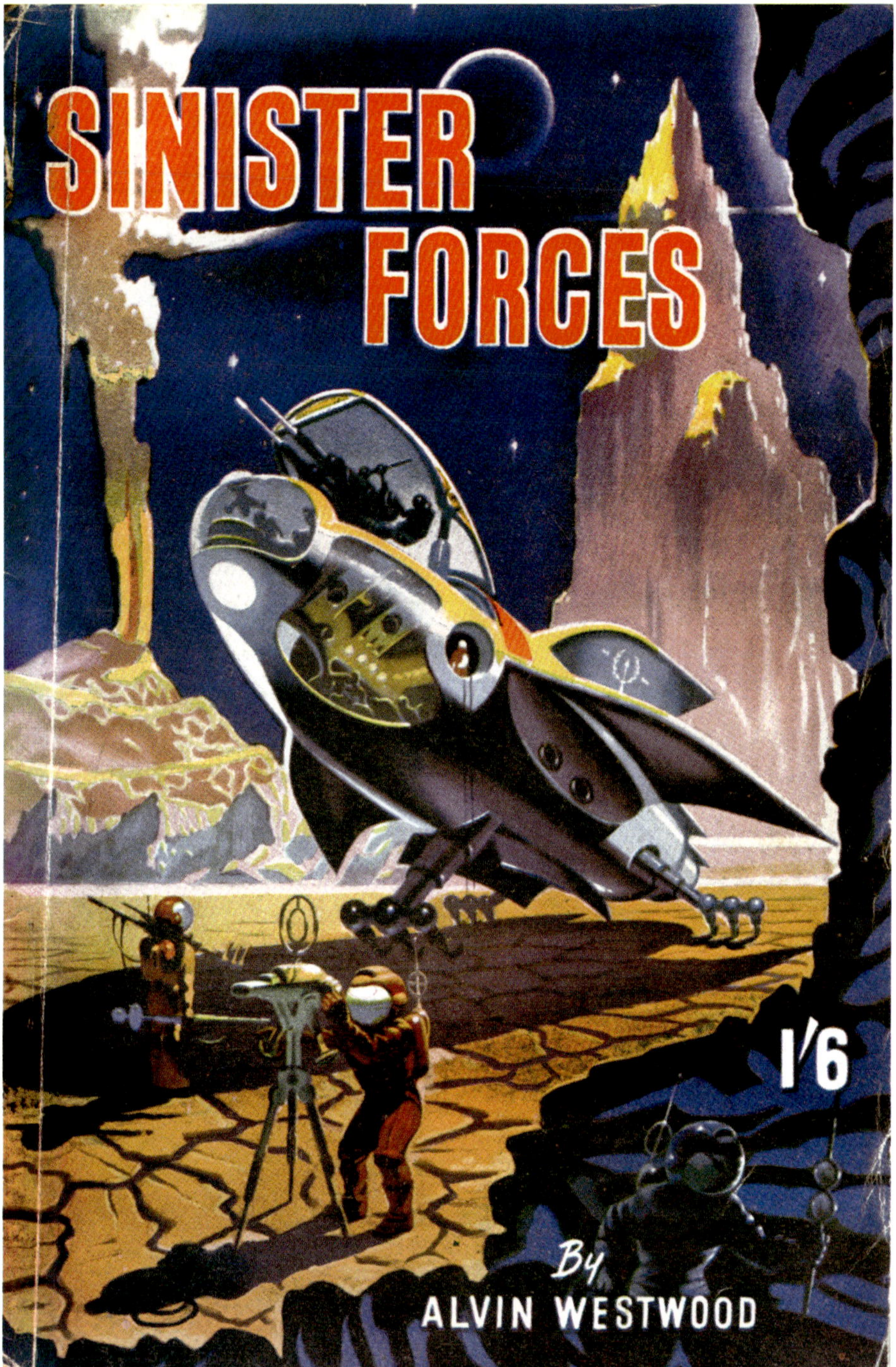

Alvin Westwood | *Sinister Forces*
Brown, Watson, 1953 | Art **Ron Turner**

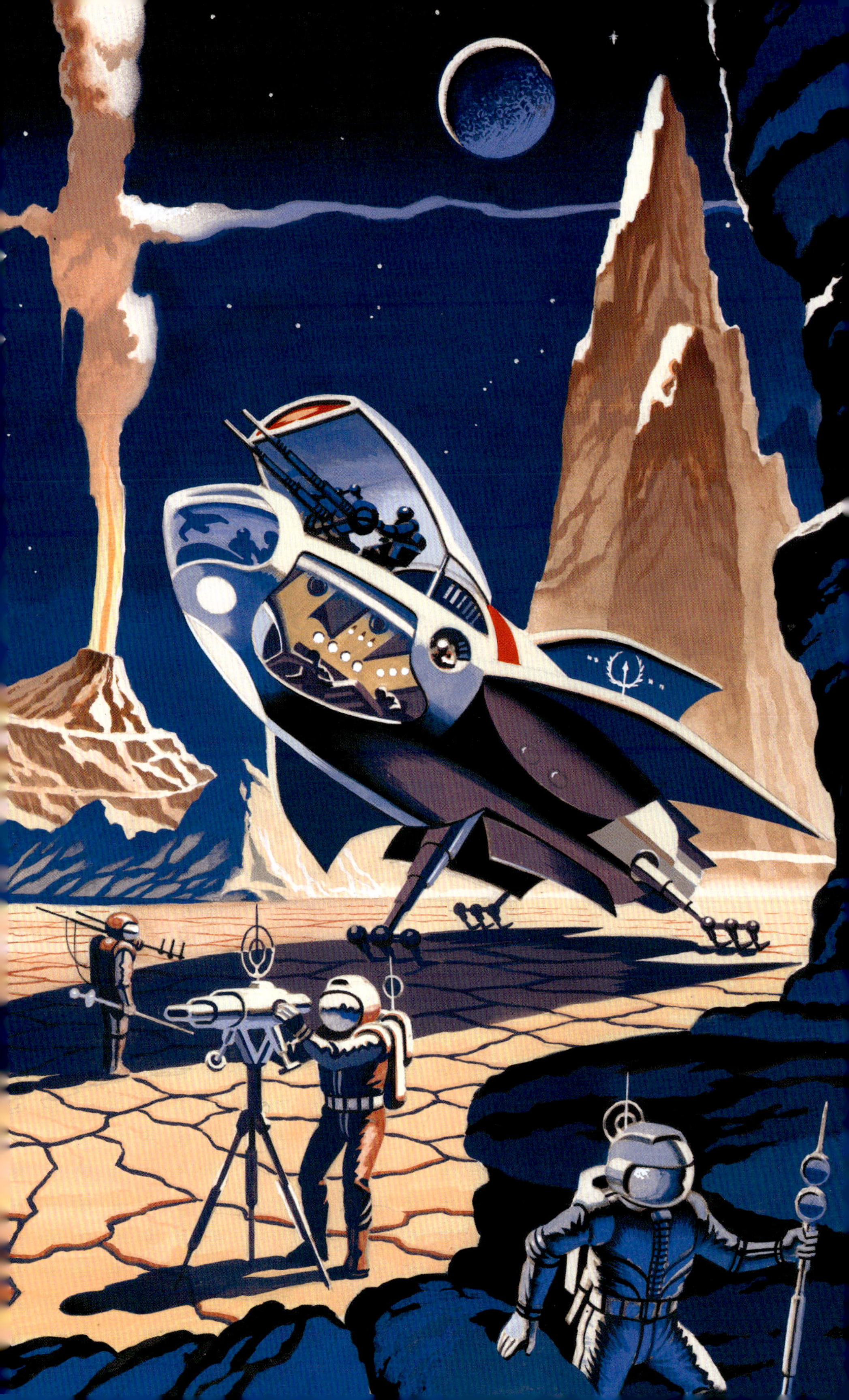

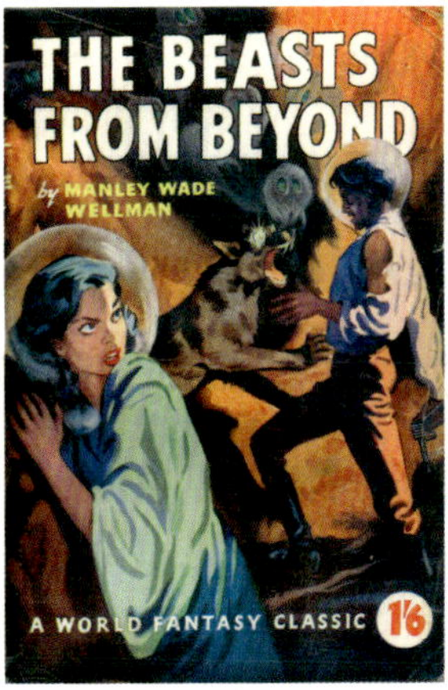

Manly Wade Wellman | *The Beasts from Beyond*
World Distributors/Sydney Pemberton, 1950
Art **A. J. Donnell**

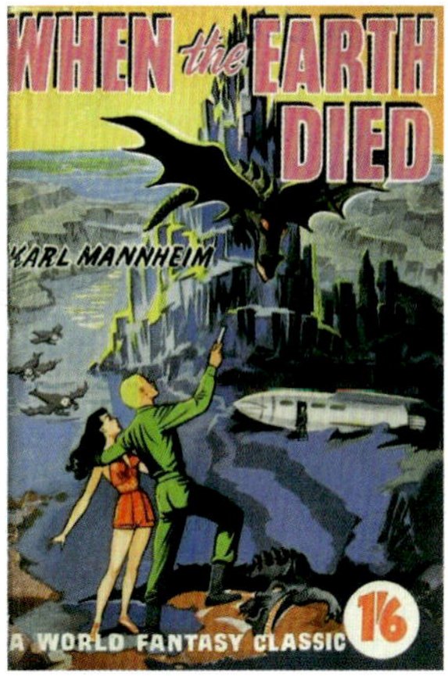

Karl Mannheim | *When the Earth Died*
World Distributors/Sydney Pemberton, 1951
Art **Unknown**

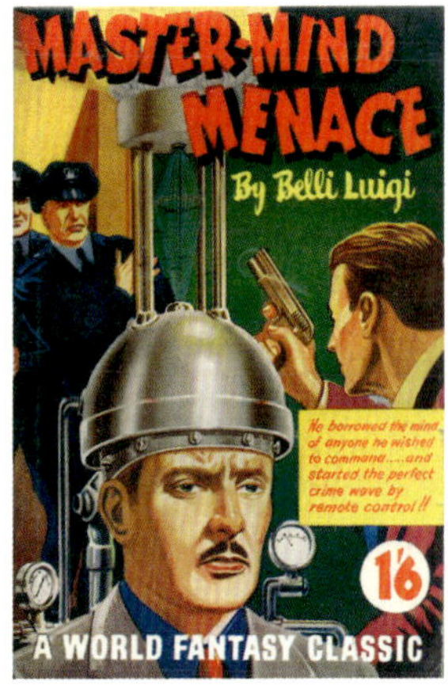

Belli Luigi | *Master-Mind Menace*
World Distributors/Sydney Pemberton, 1950
Art **Maurice Bramley**

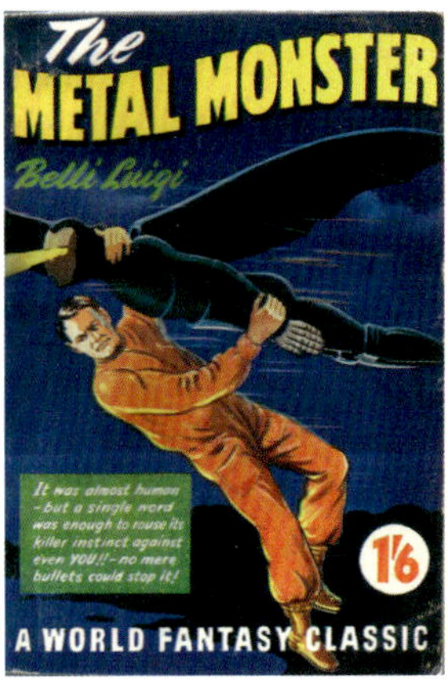

Belli Luigi | *The Metal Monster*
World Distributors/Sydney Pemberton, 1950
Art **Unknown**

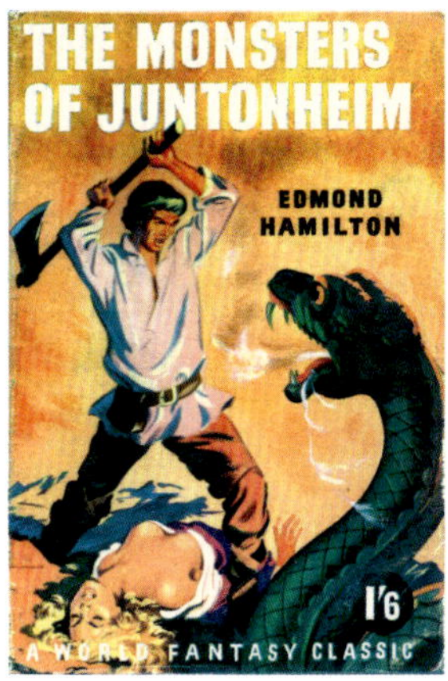

Edmond Hamilton | *The Monsters of Juntonheim*
World Distributors/Sydney Pemberton, 1950
Art **R. A. Osborne**

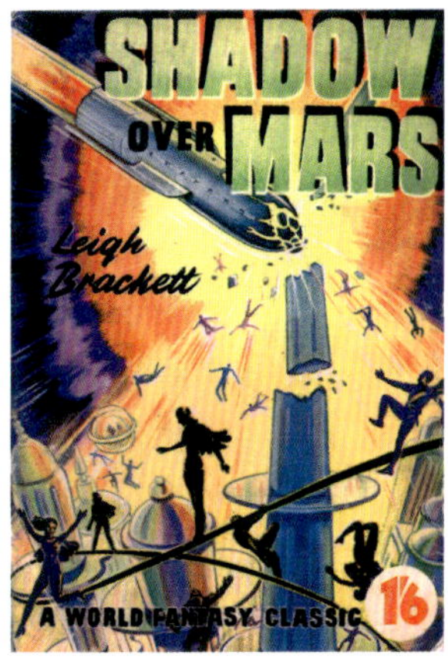

Leigh Brackett | *Shadow Over Mars*
World Distributors/Sydney Pemberton, 1951
Art **R. A. Osborne**

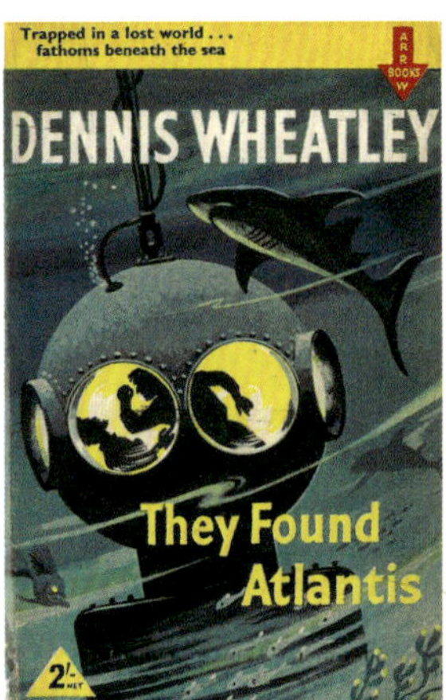

Dennis Wheatley | *They Found Atlantis*
Arrow Books, 1958 | Art **Unknown**

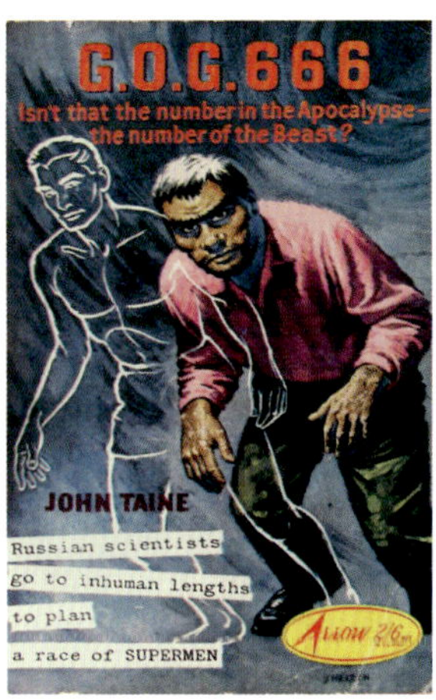

John Taine | *G.O.G. 666*
Arrow Books, 1963 | Art **Sheldon (Louis Shabner)**

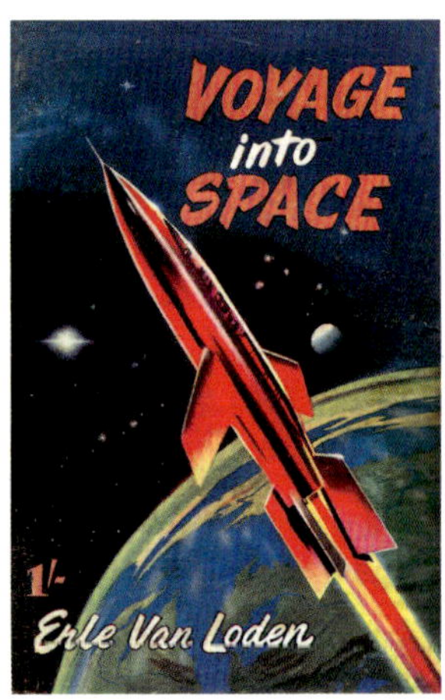

Erle van Loden (Lisle Willis) | *Voyage into Space*
Edwin Self, 1954 | Art **Ron Turner**

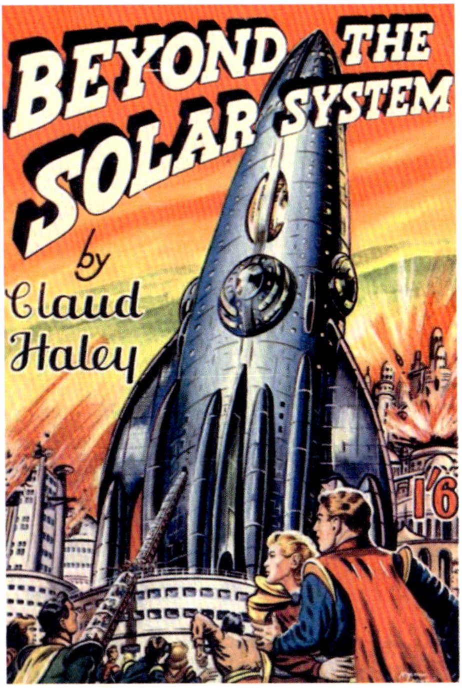

Claude Haley (Leonard G. Fish) | *Beyond the Solar System*
Arc Press, 1954 | Art **Norman Light**

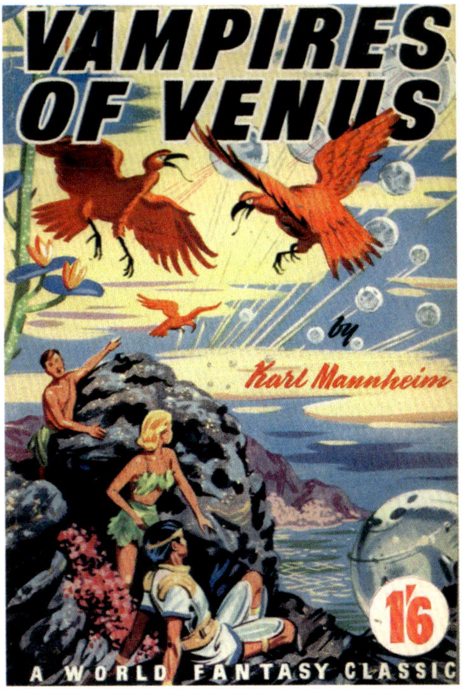

Karl Mannheim | *Vampires of Venus*
World Distributors/Sydney Pemberton, 1951 | Art **Unknown**

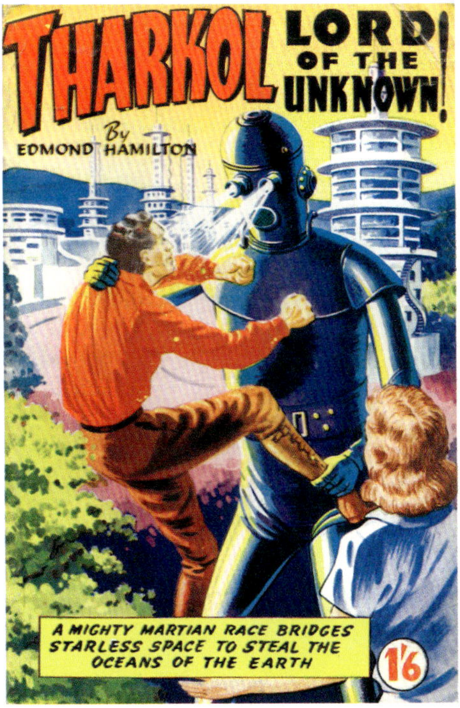

Edmond Hamilton | *Tharkol, Lord of the Unknown*
World Distributors/Sydney Pemberton, 1950
Art **R. A. Osborne** after **H. W. Wesso**

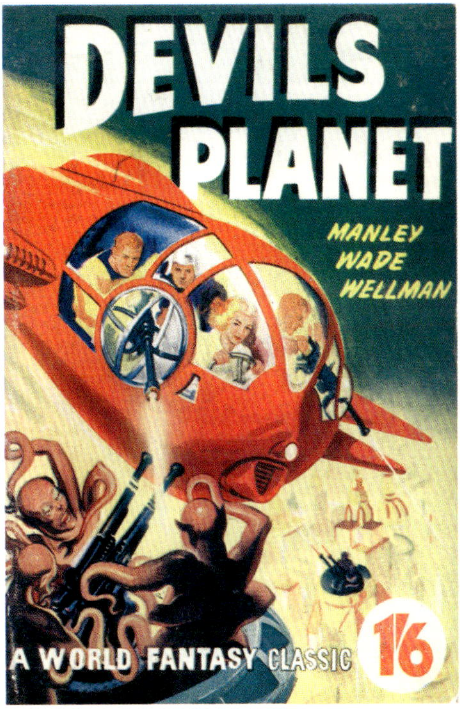

Manly Wade Wellman | *Devil's Planet*
World Distributors/Sydney Pemberton, 1951
Art **R. A. Osborne** after **Rudolph Belarski**

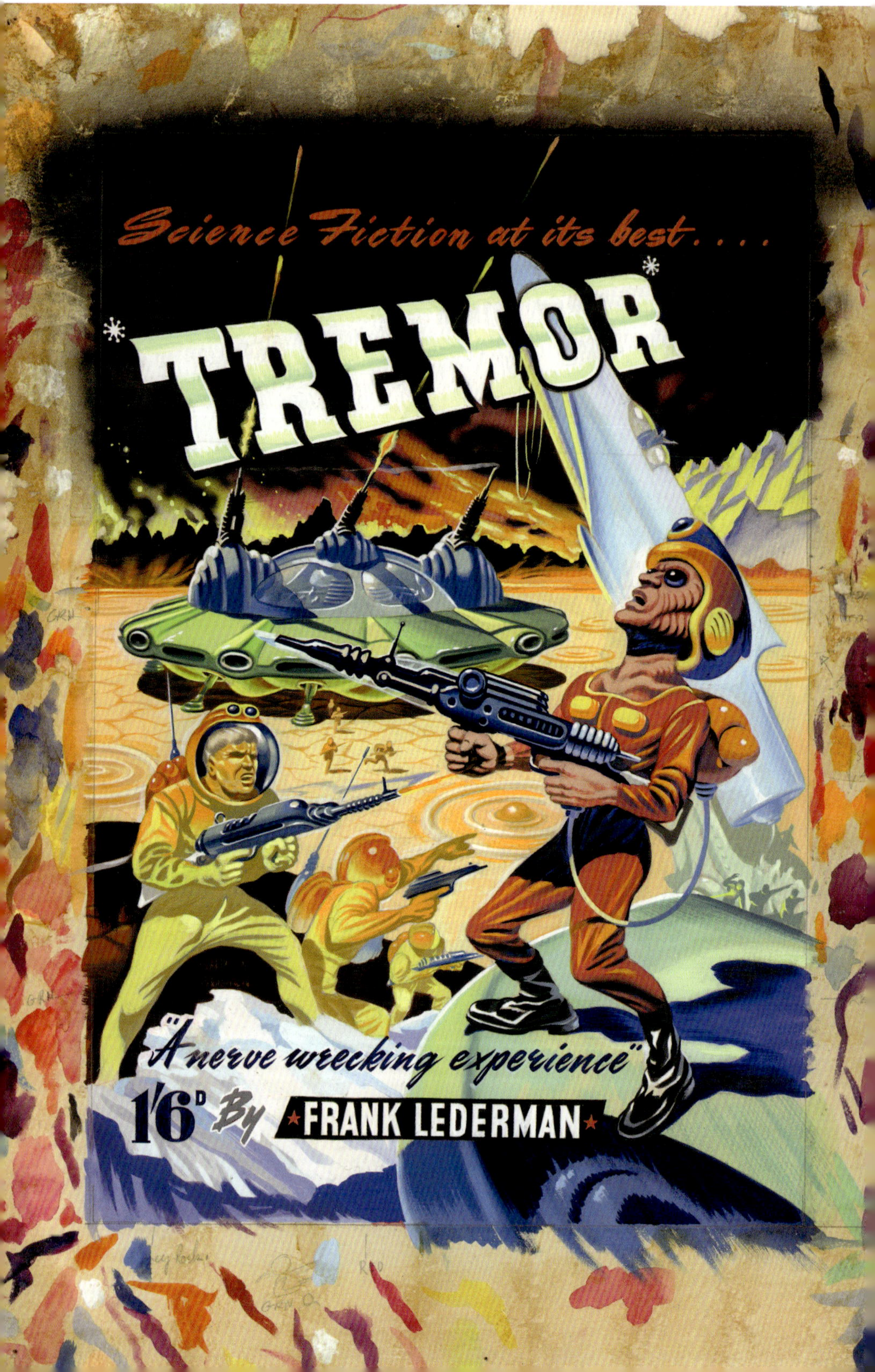
Science Fiction at its best....
TREMOR
"A nerve wrecking experience"
1'6D By
FRANK LEDERMAN

opposite **Frank Lederman** | *Tremor*
Kaye Publications, 1952 | Original art **Ron Turner**

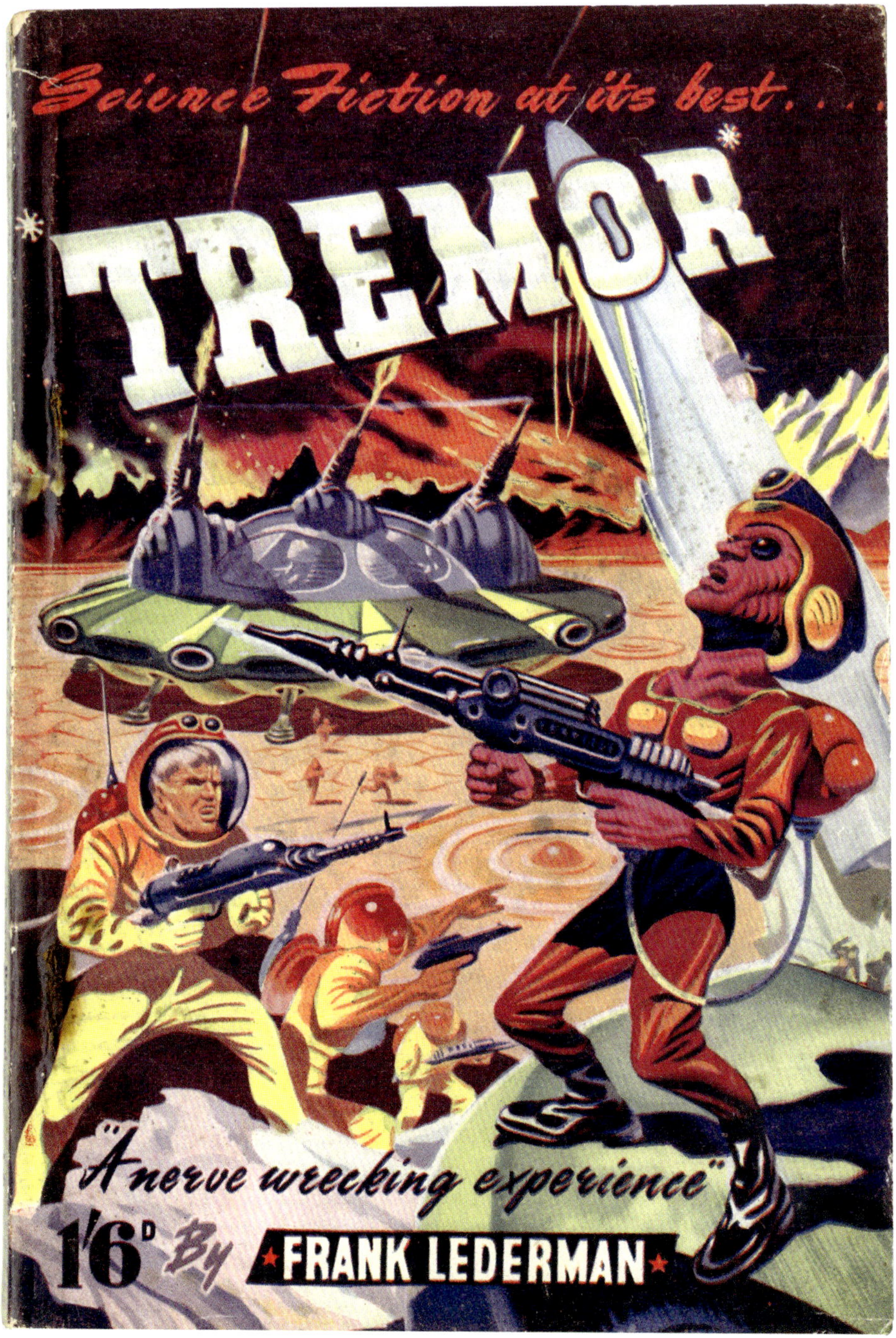

Frank Lederman | *Tremor*
Kaye Publications, 1952 | Art **Ron Turner**

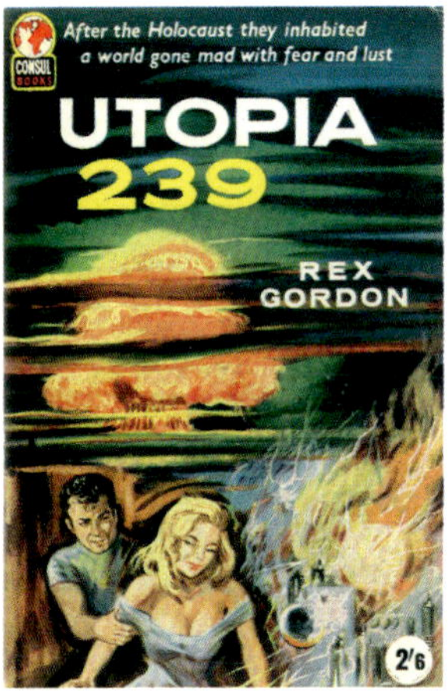

Rex Gordon | *Utopia 239*
Consul Books, 1961 | Art **John Richards**

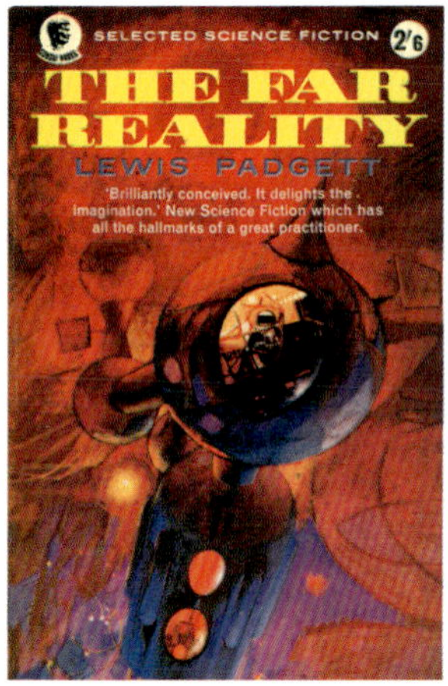

Lewis Padgett | *The Far Reality*
Consul Books, 1963 | Art **Josh Kirby**

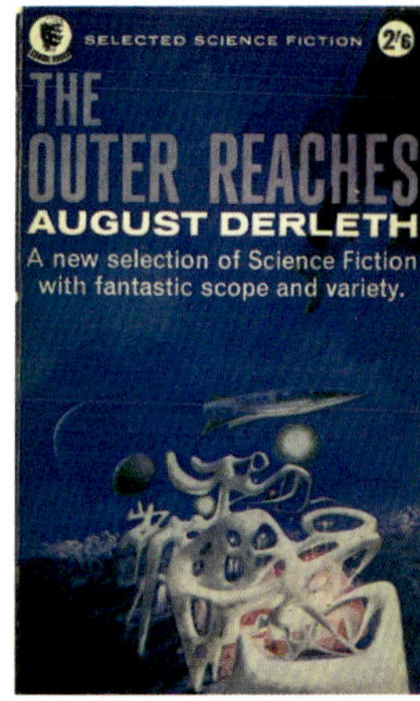

August Derleth | *The Outer Reaches*
Consul Books, 1963 | Art **Unknown**

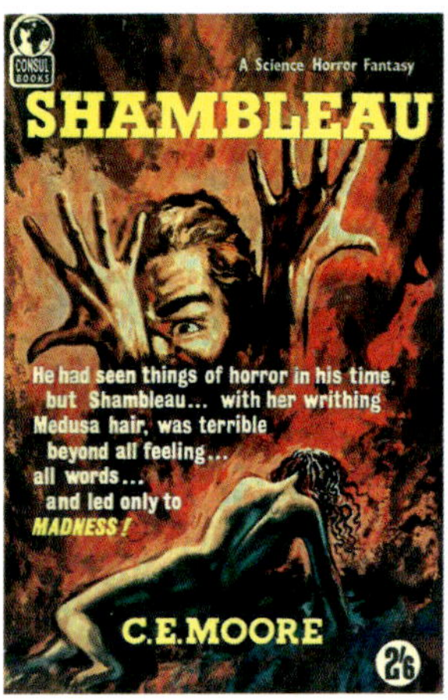

C. L. Moore | *Shambleau*
Consul Books, 1961 | Art **Unknown**

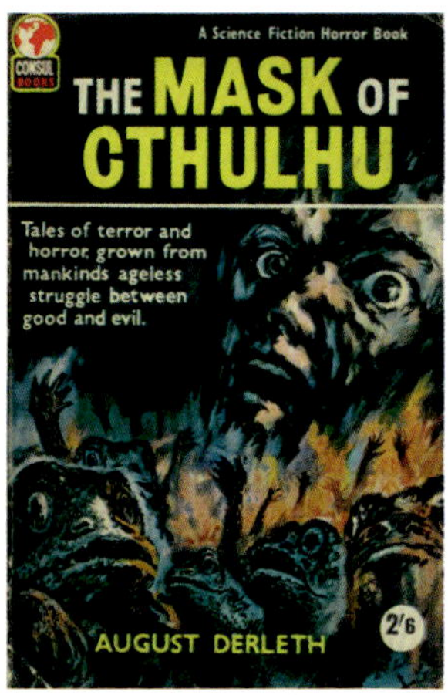

August Derleth | *The Mask of Cthulhu*
Consul Books, 1961 | Art **Unknown**

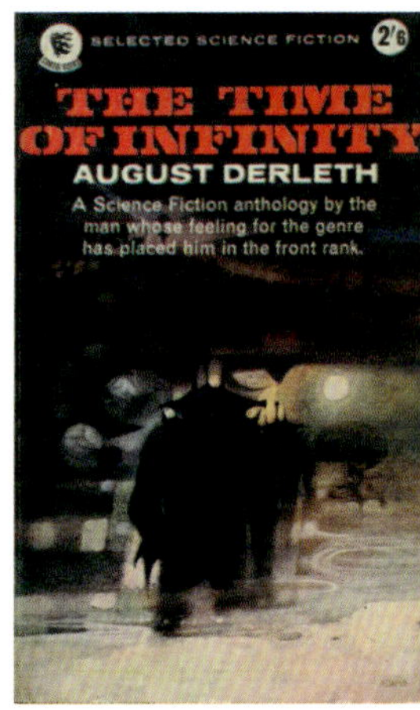

August Derleth | *The Time of Infinity*
Consul Books, 1963 | Art **Norman Adams**

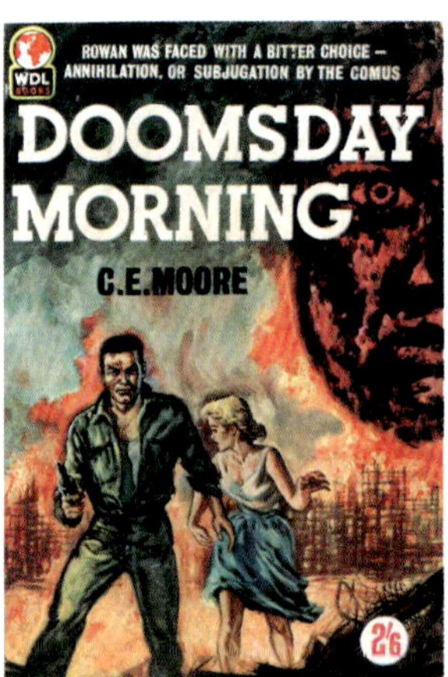

C. E. Moore (C. L. Moore) | *Doomsday Morning*
WDL Books, 1960 | Art **Unknown**

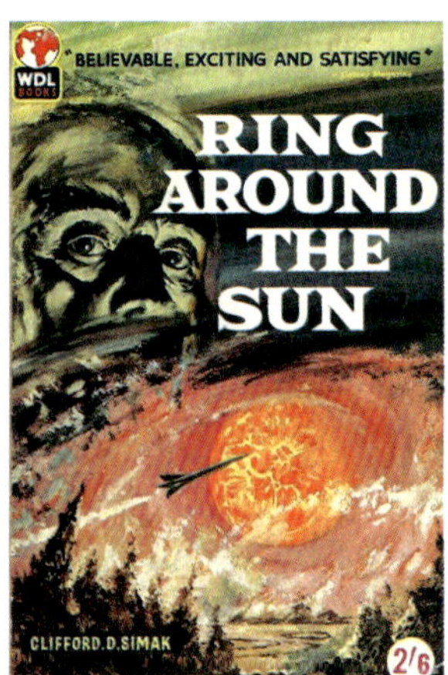

Clifford Simak | *Ring Around the Sun*
WDL Books, 1960 | Art **Edgar Hodges**

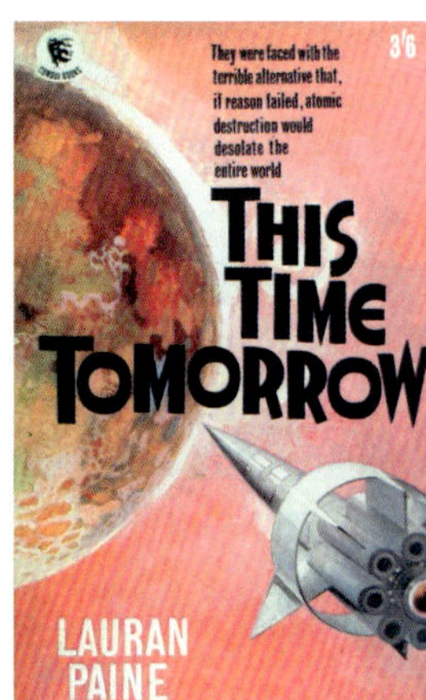

Lauran Paine | *This Time Tomorrow*
Consul Books, 1963 | Art **Unknown**

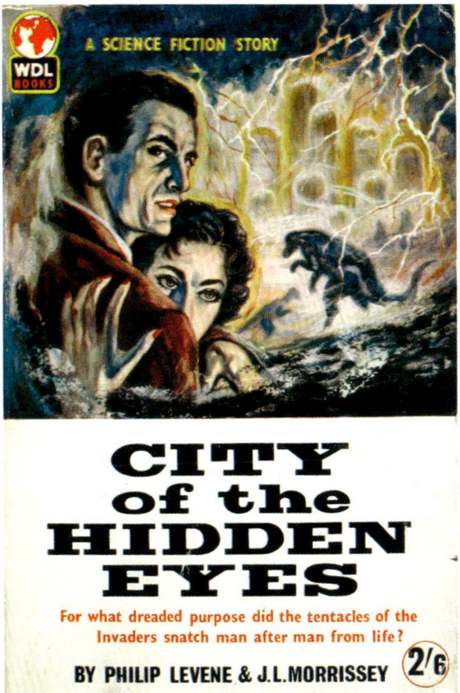

Philip Levene, J. L. Morrissey | *City of the Hidden Eyes*
World Distributors, 1960 | Art **Unknown**

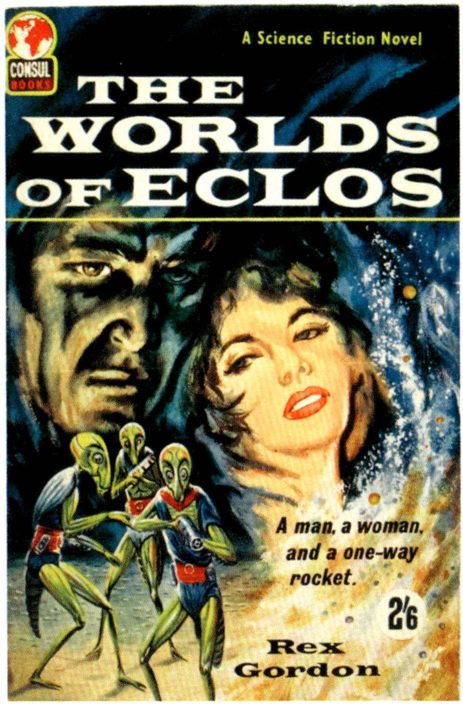

Rex Gordon | *The Worlds of Eclos*
Consul Books, 1961 | Art **Unknown**

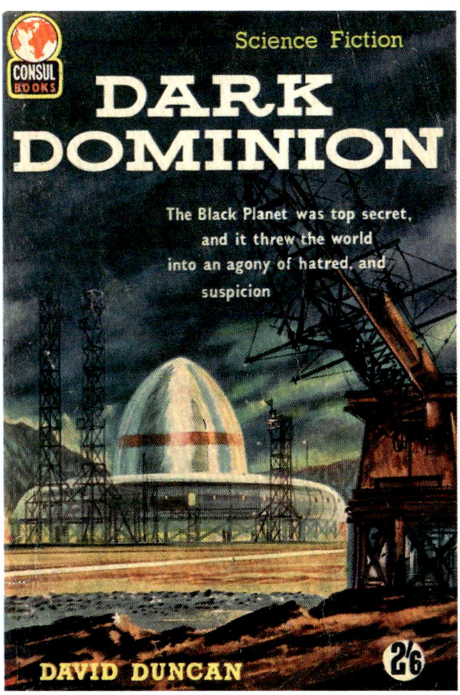

David Duncan | *Dark Dominion*
Consul Books, 1961 | Art **John Richards**

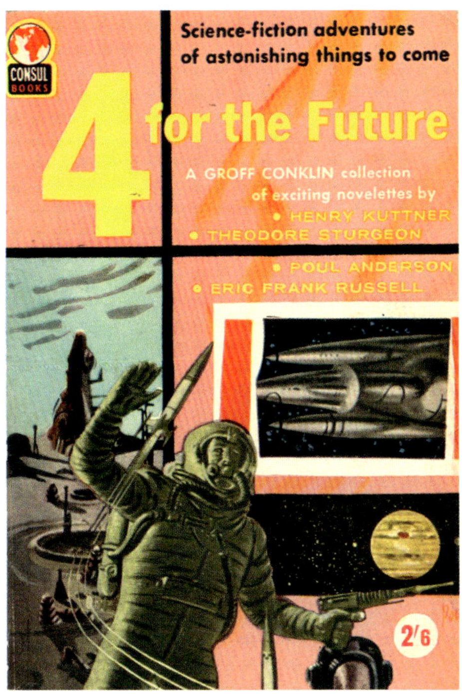

Groff Conklin | *4 for the Future*
Consul Books, 1961 | Art **Richard Powers** (see page 111)

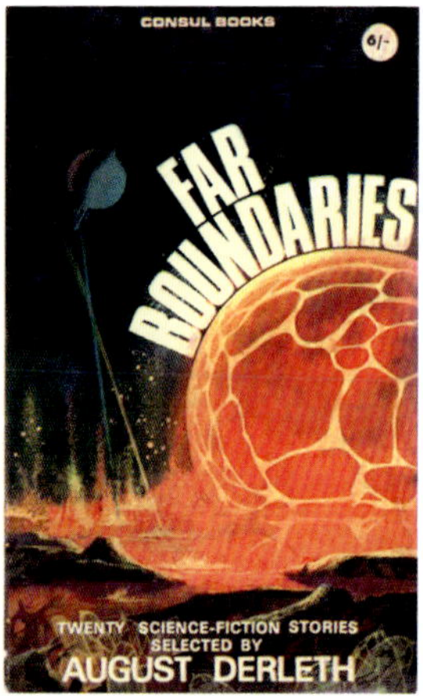

August Derleth, ed. | *Far Boundaries*
Consul Books, 1965 | Art **Unknown**

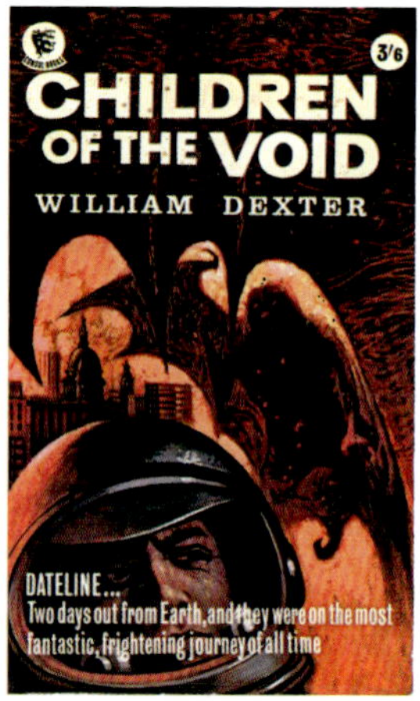

William Dexter | *Children of the Void*
Consul Books, 1963 | Art **Unknown**

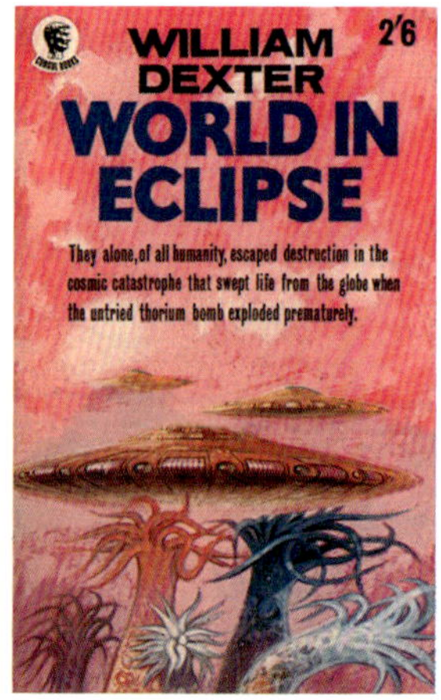

William Dexter | *World in Eclipse*
Consul Books, 1962 | Art **Adams**

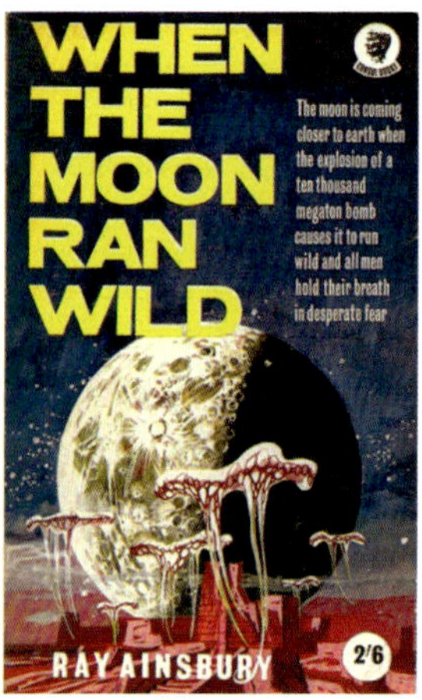

Ray Ainsbury | *When The Moon Ran Wild*
Consul Books, 1962 | Art **Unknown**

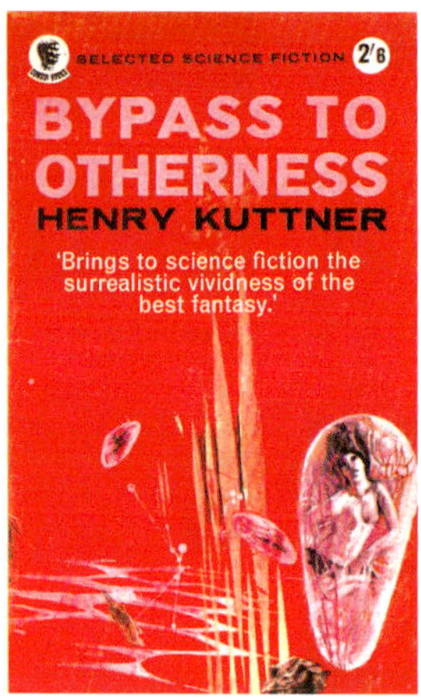

Henry Kuttner | *Bypass to Otherness*
Consul Books, 1963 | Art **Pino Dell'Orco**

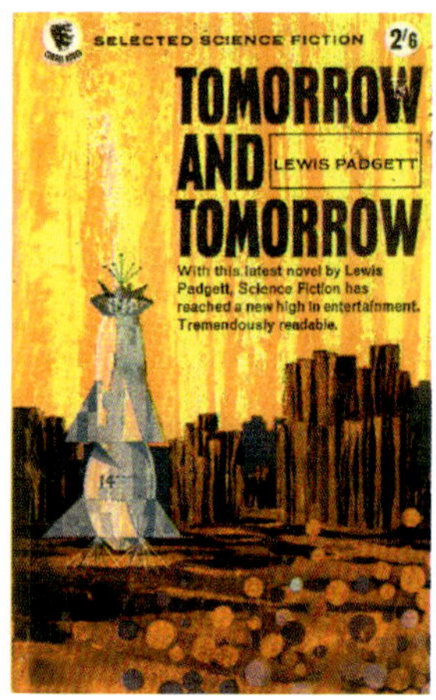

Lewis Padgett | *Tomorrow and Tomorrow*
Consul Books, 1963 | Art **Unknown**

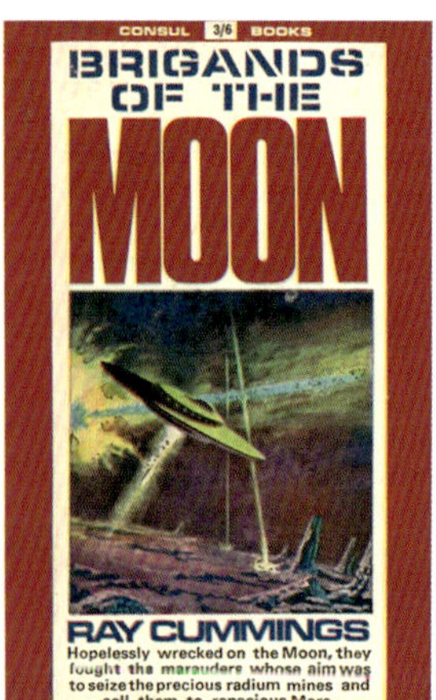

Ray Cummings | *Brigands of the Moon*
Consul Books, 1966 | Art **Ken Freeman**

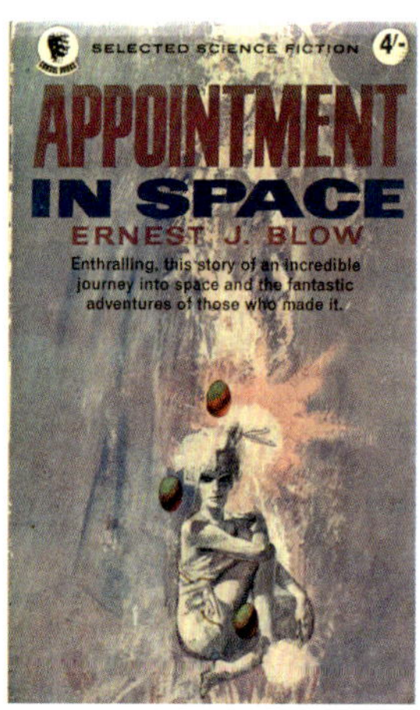

Ernest J. Blow | *Appointment in Space*
Consul Books, 1963 | Art **Pino Dell'Orco**

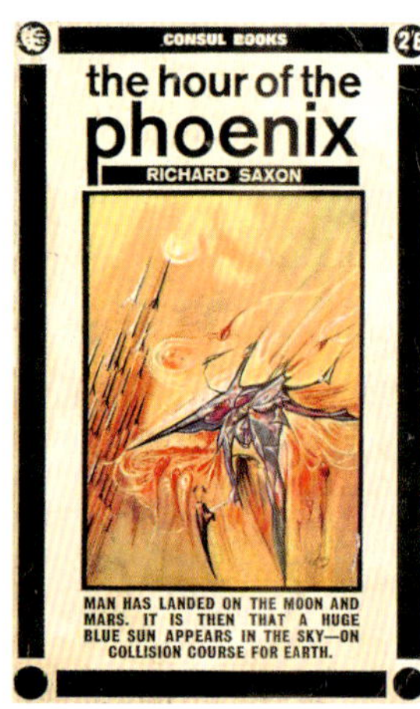

Richard Saxon | *The Hour of the Phoenix*
Consul Books, 1964 | Art **Josh Kirby**

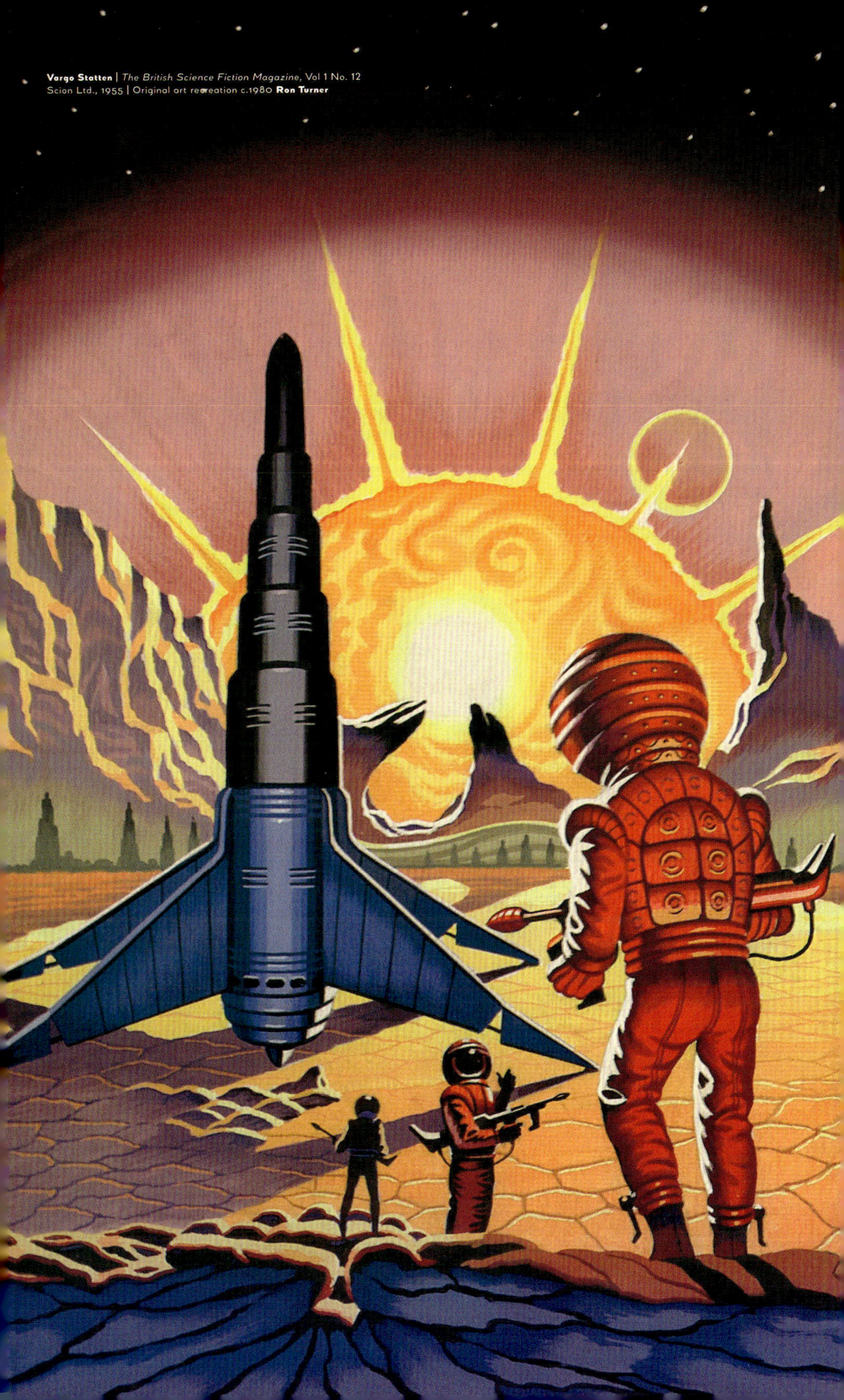

Vargo Statten | *The British Science Fiction Magazine*, Vol 1 No. 12
Scion Ltd., 1955 | Original art recreation c.1980 **Ron Turner**

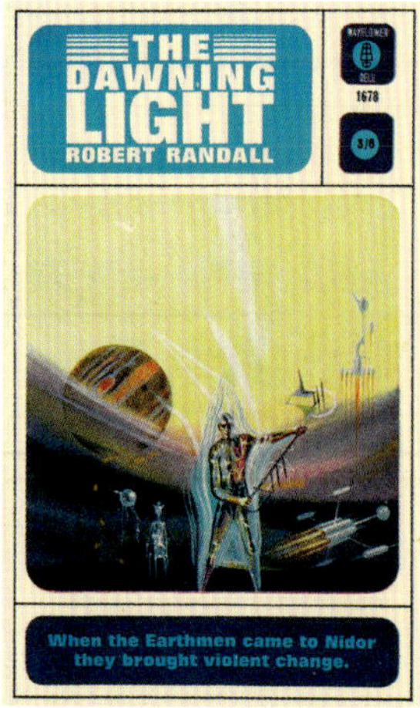

Robert Randall | *The Dawning Light*
Mayflower-Dell, 1964 | Art **Richard Powers**

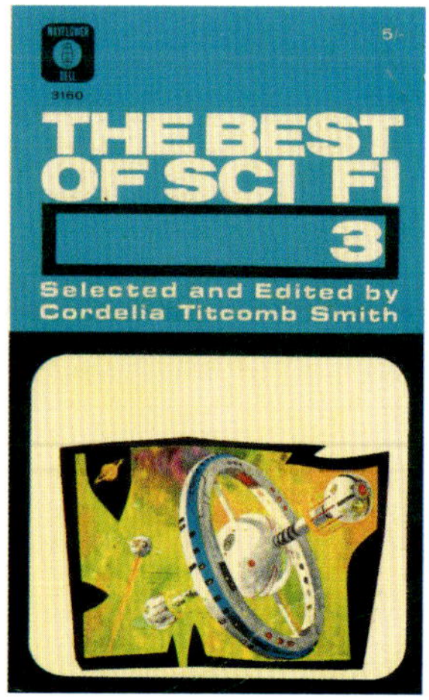

Cordelia Titcomb Smith | *The Best of Sci Fi 3*
Mayflower-Dell, 1964 | Art **Richard Powers**

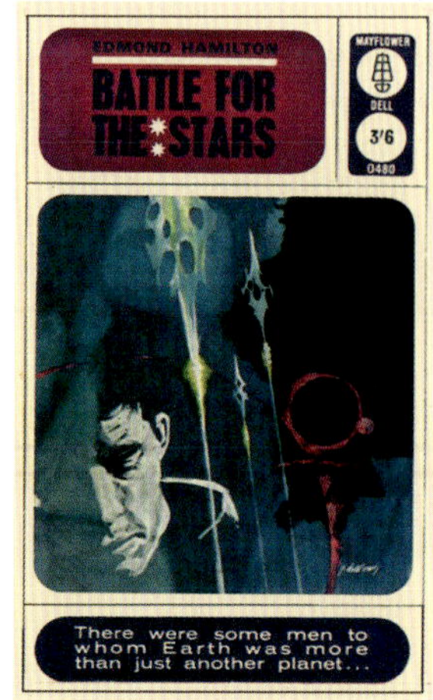

Edmond Hamilton | *Battle for the Stars*
Mayflower-Dell, 1963 | Art **Pino Dell'Orco**

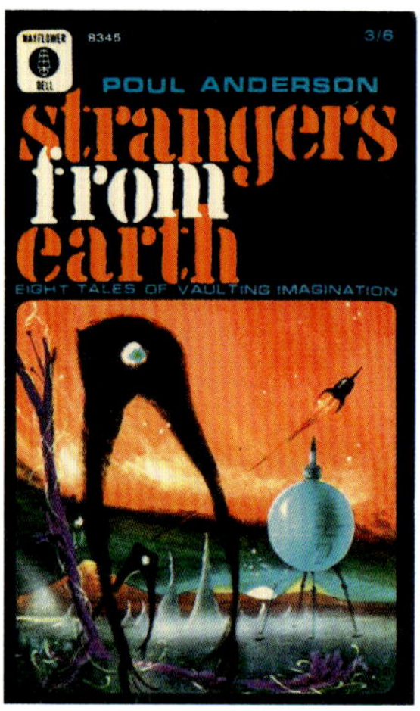

Poul Anderson | *Strangers from Earth*
Mayflower-Dell, 1965 | Art **Jacks**

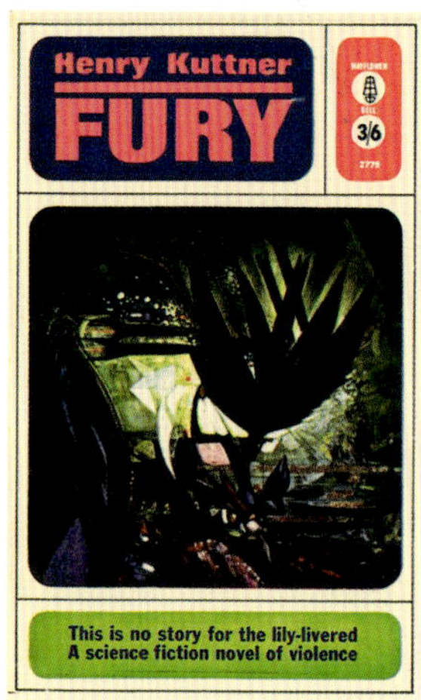

Henry Kuttner | *Fury*
Mayflower-Dell, 1963 | Art **Unknown**

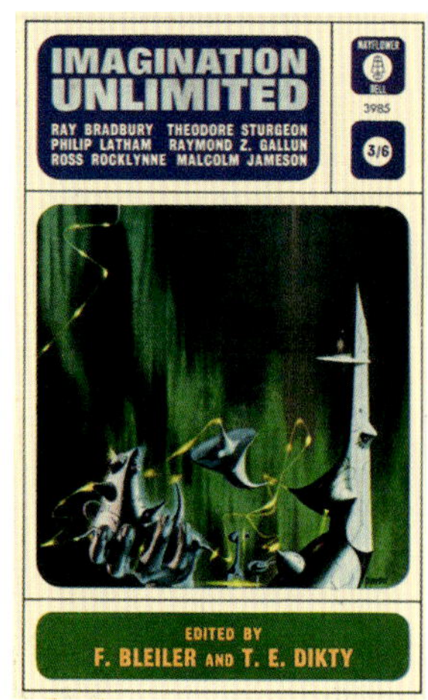

F. Bleiler, T. E. Dikty | *Imagination Unlimited*
Mayflower-Dell, 1964 | Art **Richard Powers**

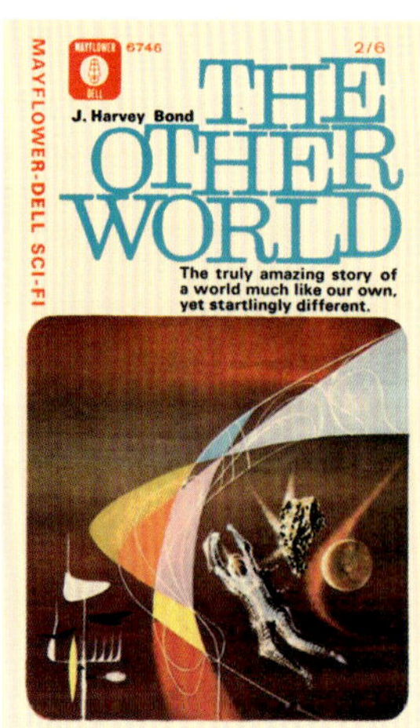

J. Harvey Bond | *The Other World*
Mayflower-Dell, 1964 | Art **Richard Powers**

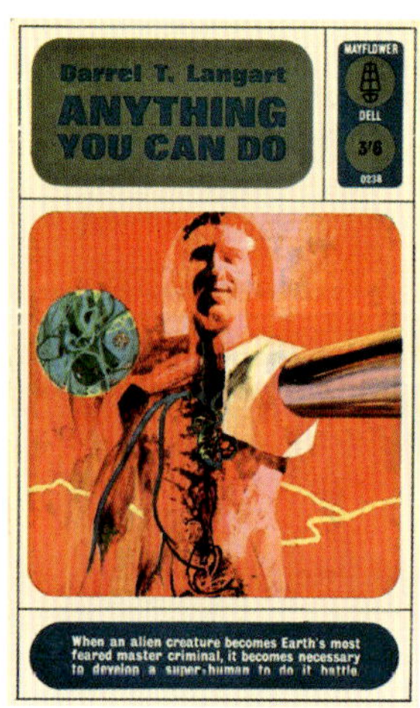

Darrel T. Langart | *Anything You Can Do*
Mayflower-Dell, 1963 | Art **Pino Dell'Orco**

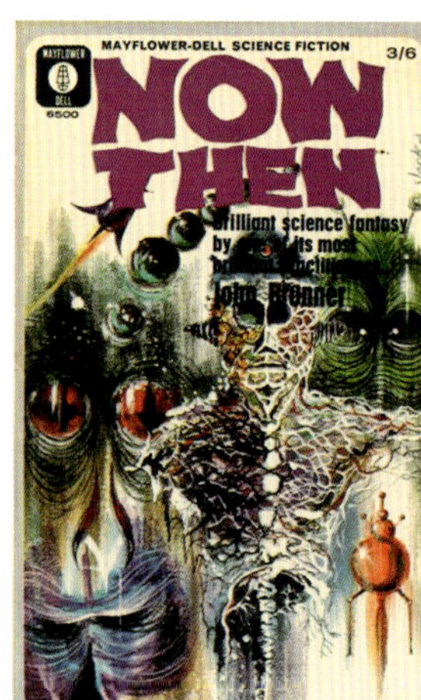

John Brunner | *Now Then*
Mayflower-Dell, 1965 | Art **Jacks**

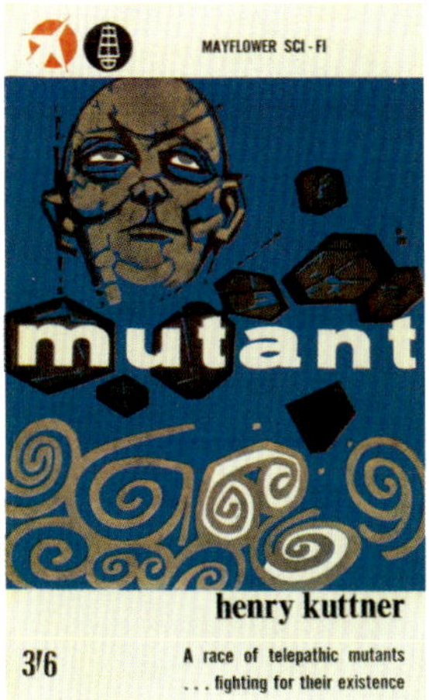

Henry Kuttner | *Mutant*
Mayflower, 1962 | Art **Unknown**

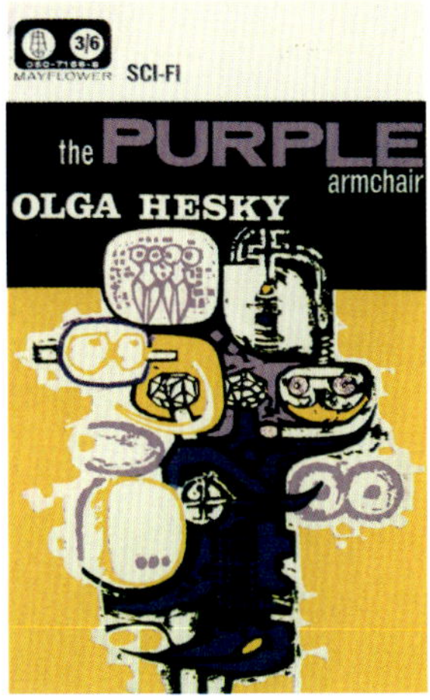

Olga Hesky | *The Purple Armchair*
Mayflower, 1963 | Art **Unknown**

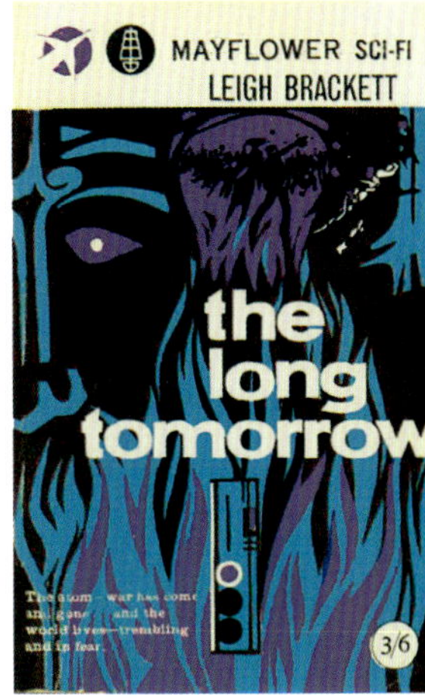

Leigh Brackett | *The Long Tomorrow*
Mayflower, 1962 | Art **Unknown**

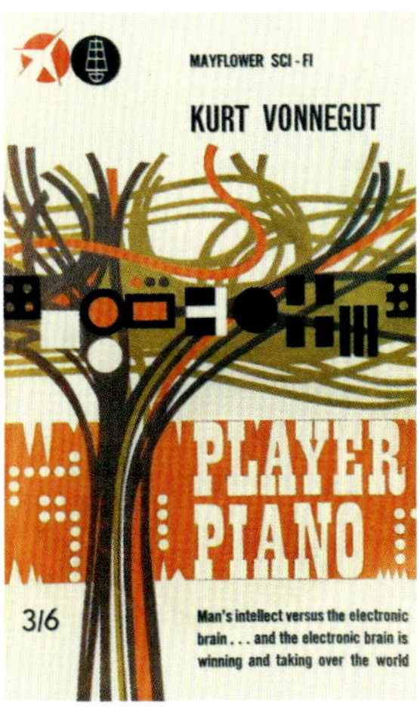

Kurt Vonnegut | *Player Piano*
Mayflower, 1962 | Art **Unknown**

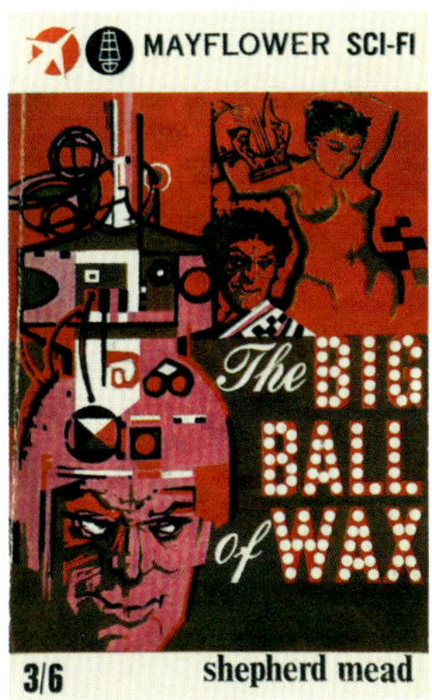

Shepherd Mead | *The Big Ball of Wax*
Mayflower, 1962 | Art **Unknown**

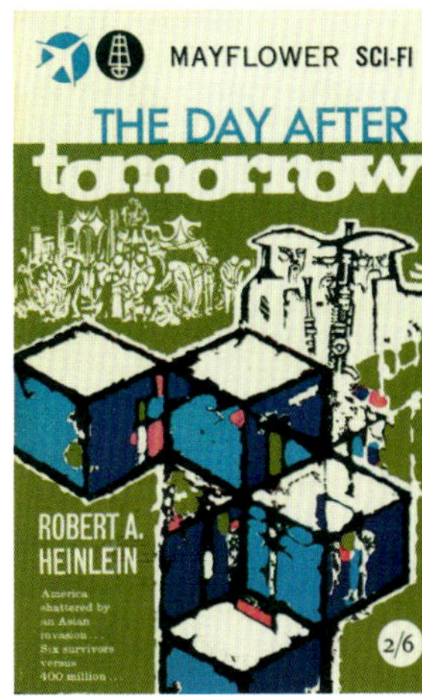

Robert A. Heinlein | *The Day After Tomorrow*
Mayflower, 1962 | Art **Unknown**

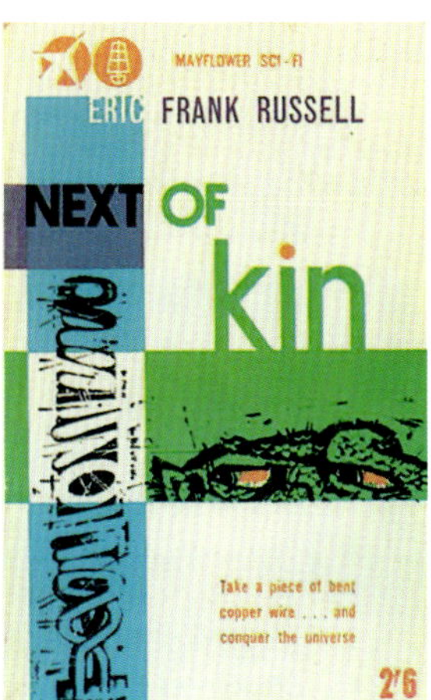

Eric Frank Russell | *Next of Kin*
Mayflower, 1962 | Art **Unknown**

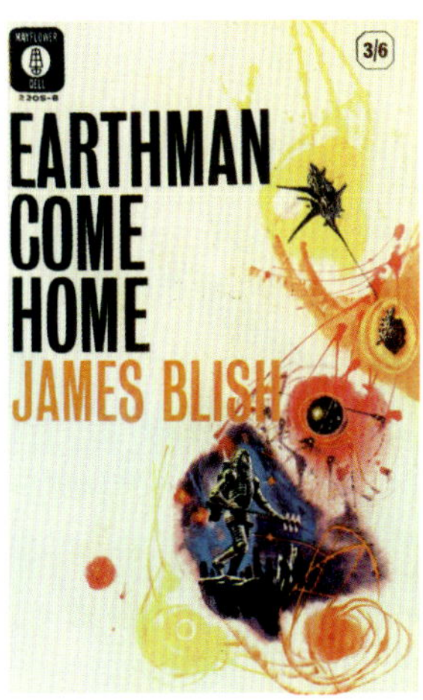

James Blish | *Earthman Come Home*
Mayflower, 1963 | Art **Richard Powers**

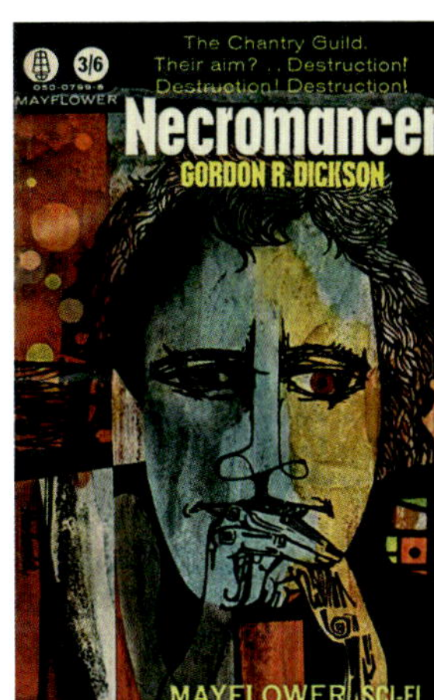

Gordon R. Dickson | *Necromancer*
Mayflower, 1963 | Art **John Bestwick**

opposite **Neal Barrett, Jr.** | *The Gates of Time*
Ace Books, 1970 | Original art **Josh Kirby**

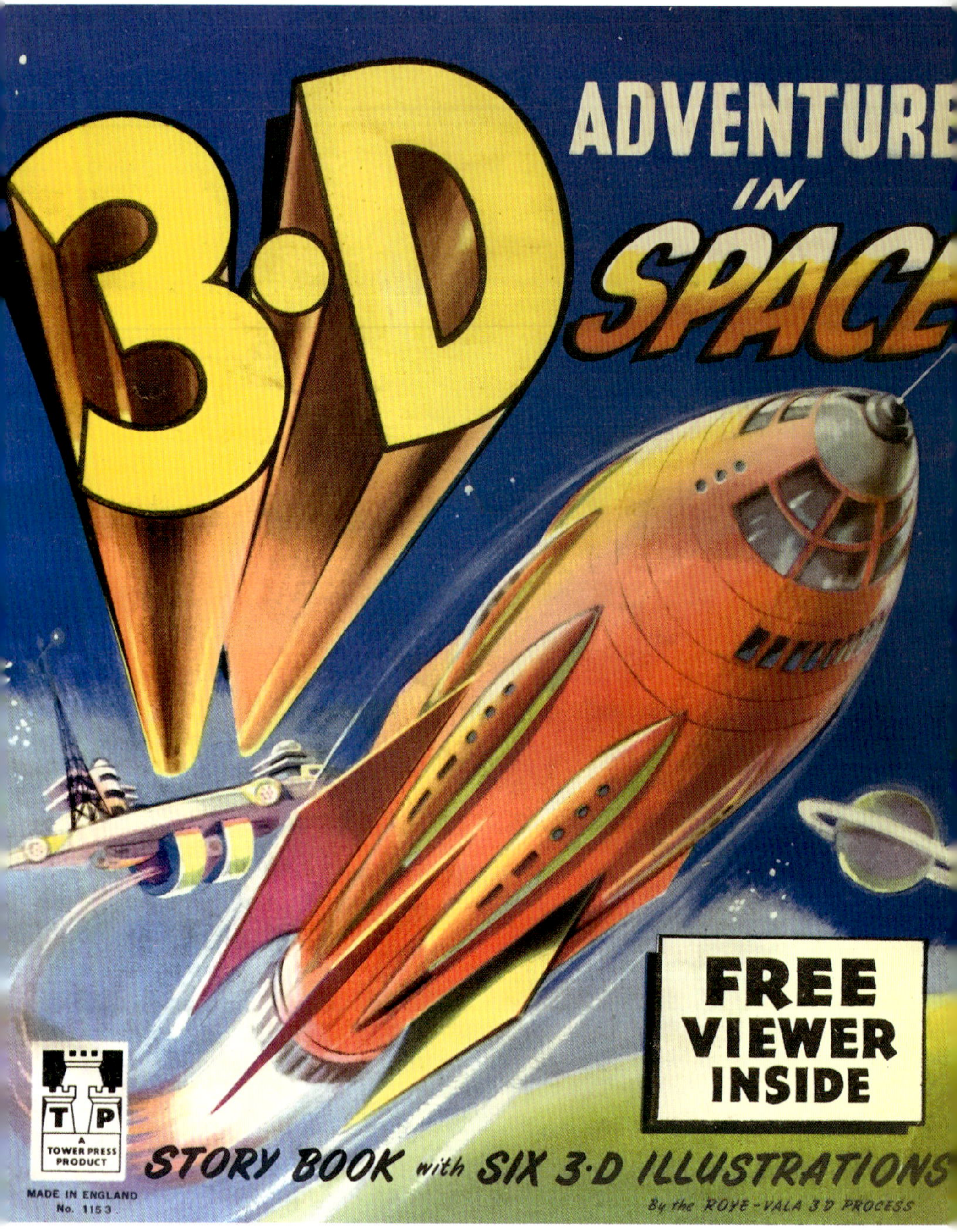

Natural Vision Studio Ltd | *3-D Adventure in Space*
Tower Press, 1950s | Art **Unknown**

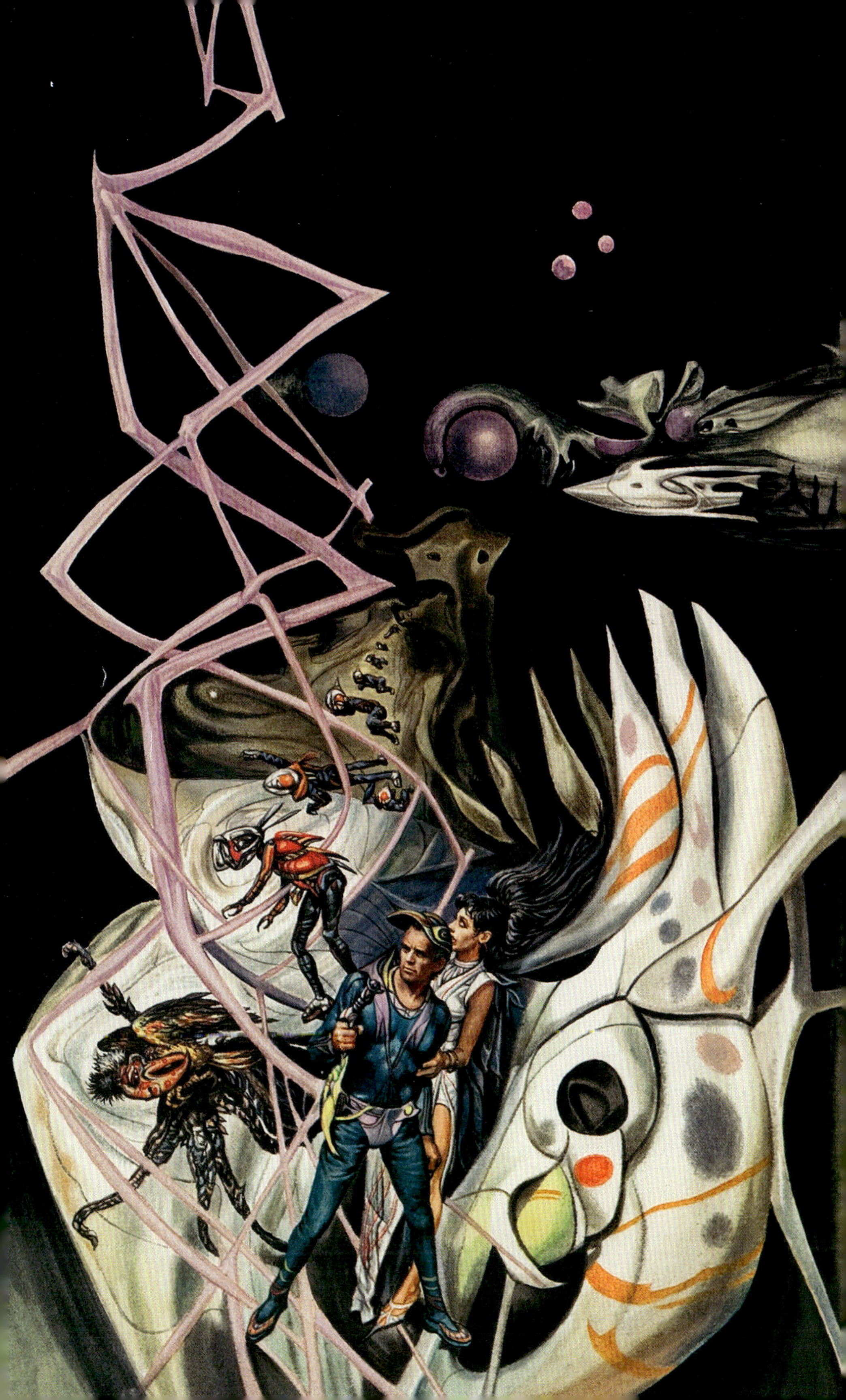

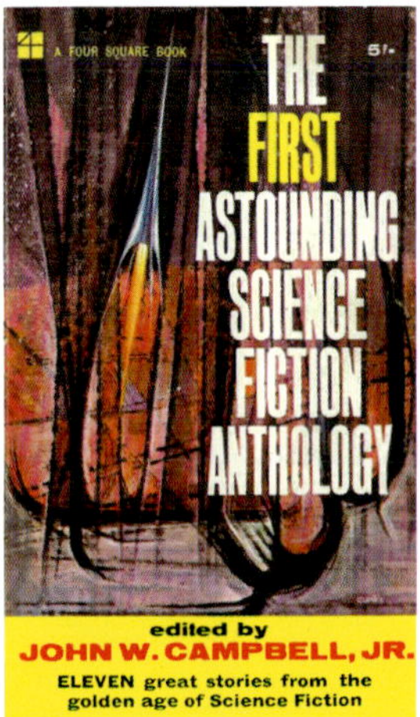

John W. Campbell, Jr.
The First Astounding Science Fiction Anthology
Four Square Books, 1964 | Art **Unknown**

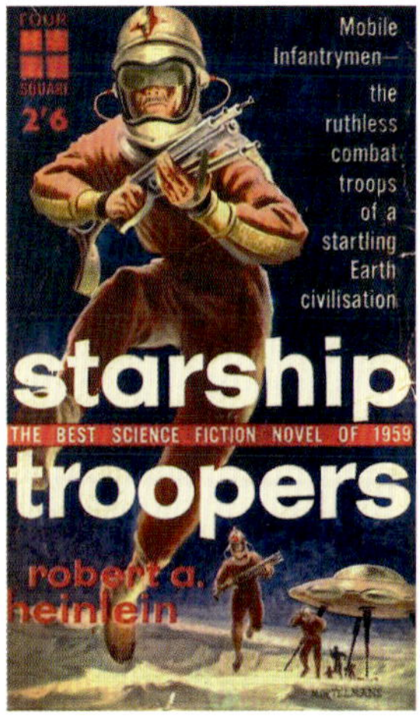

Robert Heinlein | *Starship Troopers*
Four Square Books, 1965
Art **Edward Mortelmans**

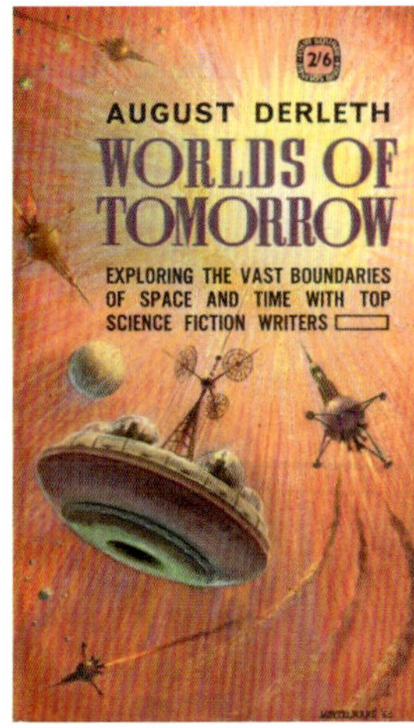

August Derleth, ed. | *Worlds of Tomorrow*
Four Square Books, 1963
Art **Edward Mortelmans**

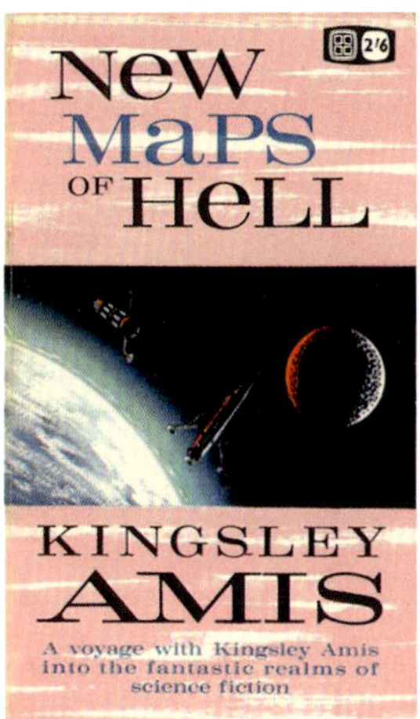

Kingsley Amis | *New Maps of Hell*
Four Square Books, 1963 | Art **Unknown**

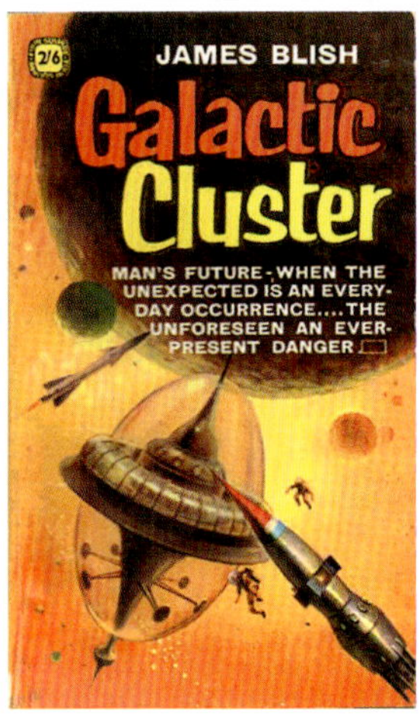

James Blish | *Galactic Cluster*
Four Square Books, 1963 | Art **Edward Mortelmans**

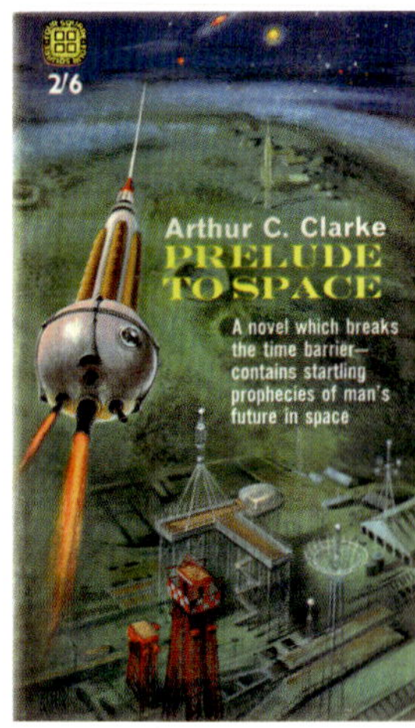

Arthur C. Clarke | *Prelude to Space*
Four Square Books, 1962 | Art **Unknown**

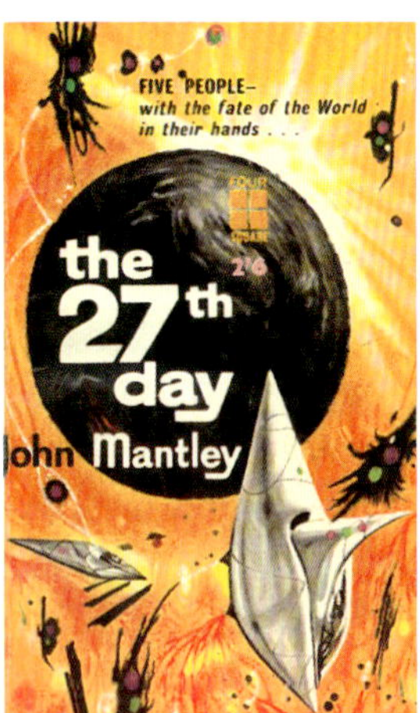

John Manley | *The 27th Day*
Four Square Books, 1961 | Art **Josh Kirby**

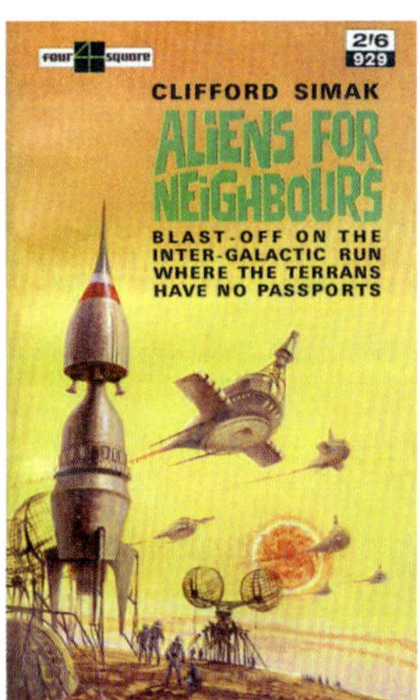

Clifford Simak | *Aliens for Neighbours*
Four Square Books, 1965 | Art **Unknown**

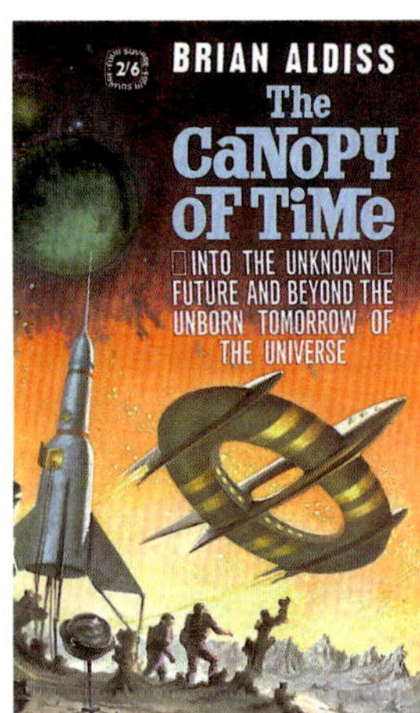

Brian Aldiss | *The Canopy of Time*
Four Square Books, 1964 | Art **Roy Carnon**

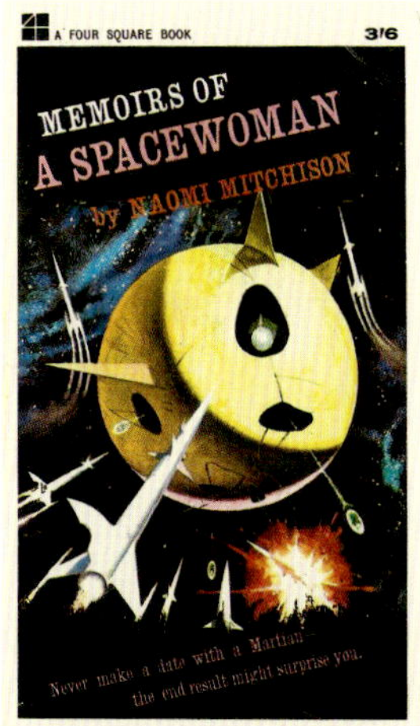

Naomi Mitchison | *Memoirs of a Spacewoman*
Four Square Books, 1964 | Art **R. S. Lonati**

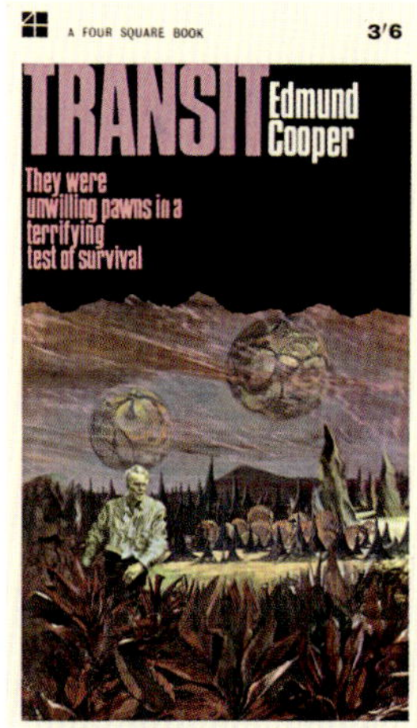

Edmund Cooper | *Transit*
Four Square Books, 1965 | Art **Unknown**

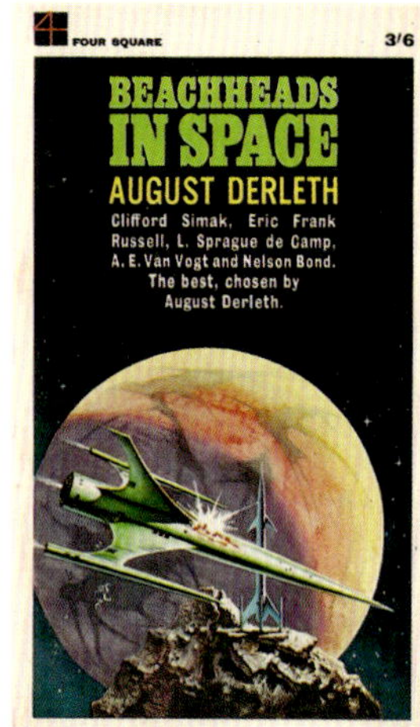

August Derleth | *Beachheads in Space*
Four Square Books, 1964 | Art **R. S. Lonati**

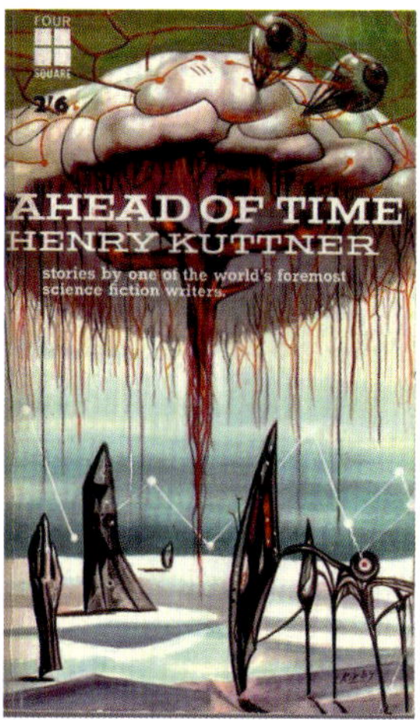

Henry Kuttner | *Ahead of Time*
Four Square Books, 1961 | Art **Josh Kirby**

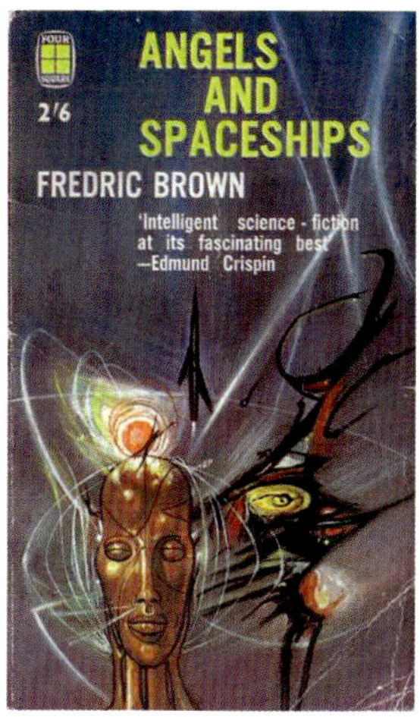

Frederic Brown | *Angels and Spaceships*
Four Square Books, 1962 | Art **Josh Kirby**

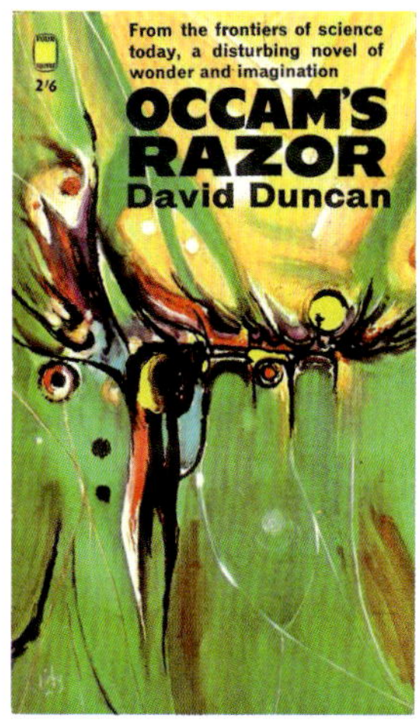

David Duncan | *Occam's Razor*
Four Square Books, 1962 | Art **Josh Kirby**

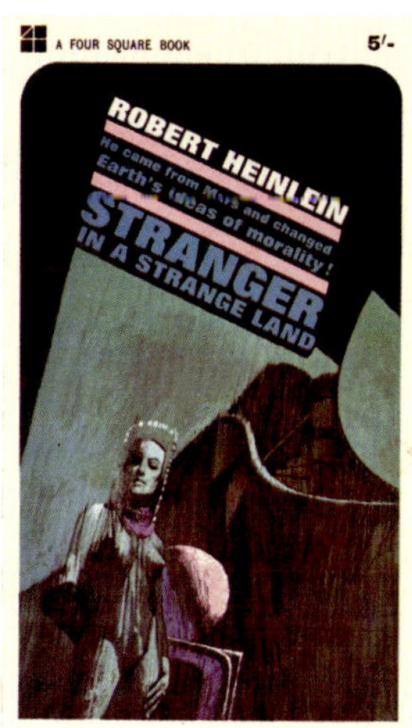

Robert Heinlein | *Stranger in a Strange Land*
Four Square Books, 1965 | Art **Unknown**

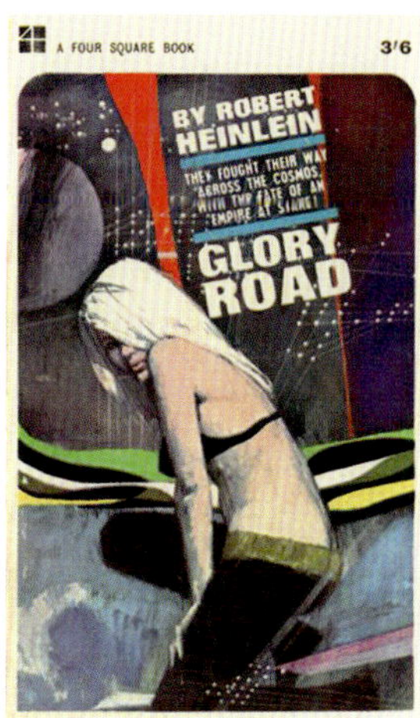

Robert Heinlein | *Glory Road*
Four Square Books, 1965 | Art **Unknown**

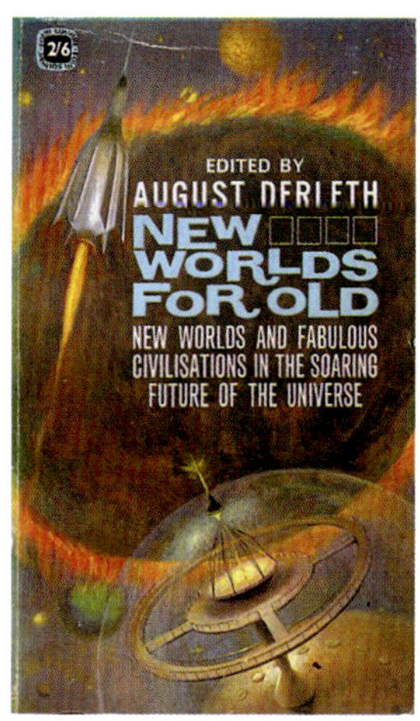

August Derleth, ed. | *New Worlds for Old*
Four Square Books, 1963 | Art **Roy Carnon**

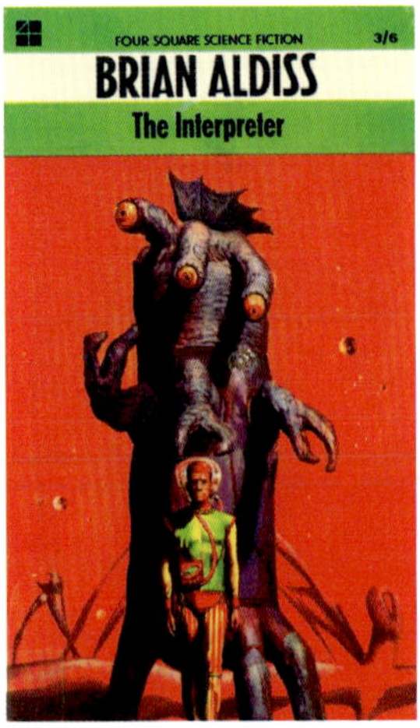

Brian Aldiss | *The Interpreter*
Four Square Books, 1967 | Art **Josh Kirby**

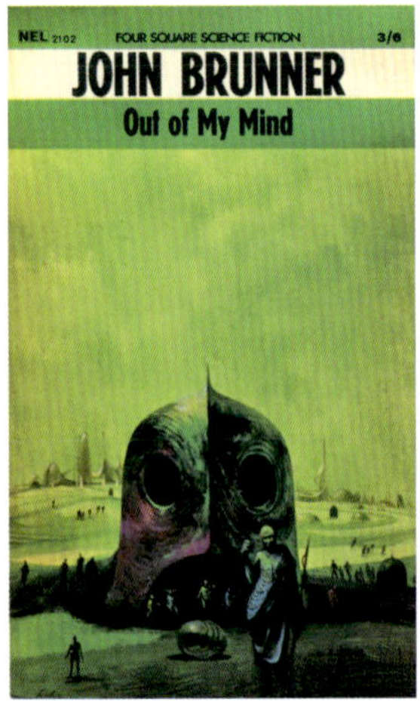

John Brunner | *Out of My Mind*
Four Square Books, 1968 | Art **Paul Lehr**

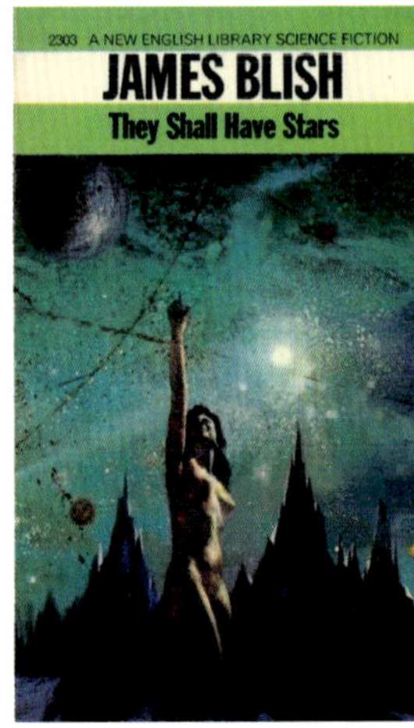

James Blish | *They Shall Have Stars*
New English Library, 1968 | Art **Unknown**

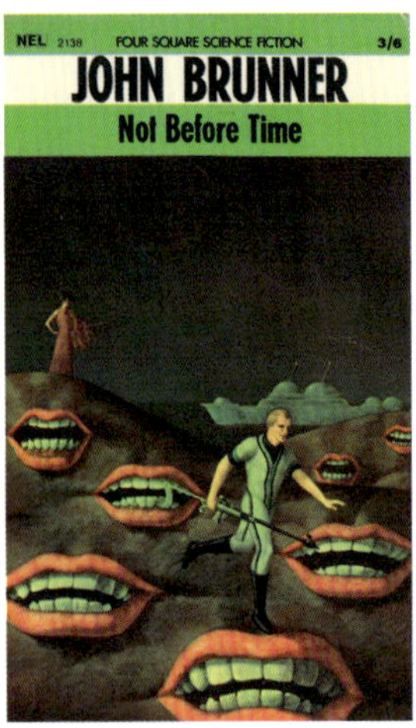

John Brunner | *Not Before Time*
Four Square Books, 1968 | Art **Don Punchatz**

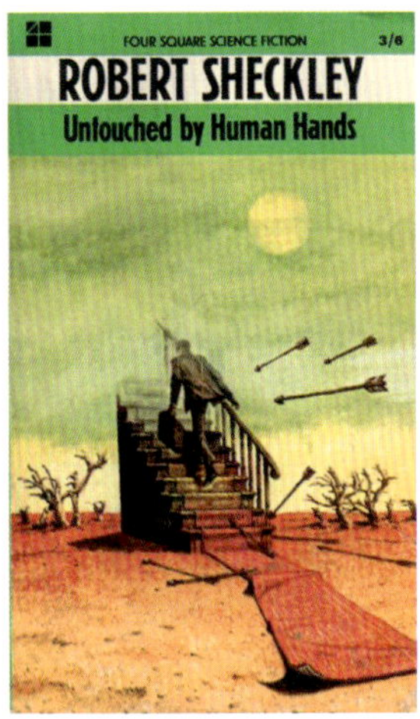

Robert Sheckley | *Untouched by Human Hands*
Four Square Books, 1967 | Art **Josh Kirby**

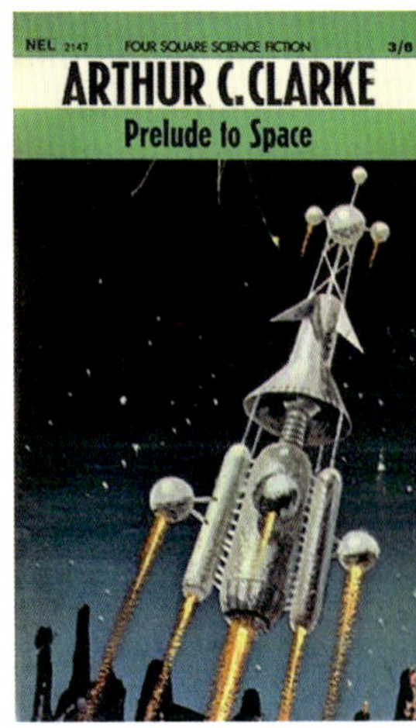

Arthur C. Clarke | *Prelude to Space*
Four Square Books, 1968 | Art **Richard Powers**

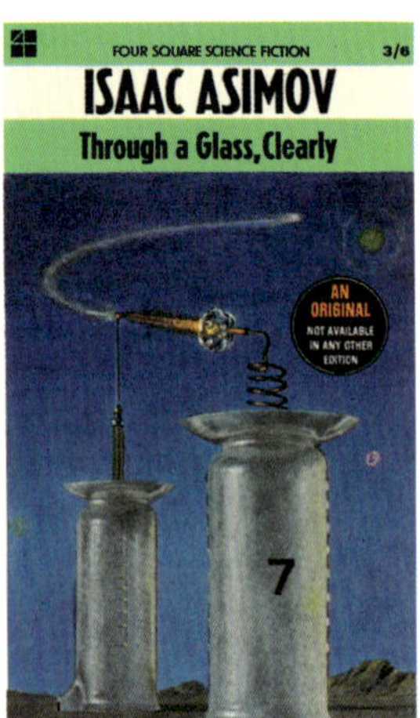

Isaac Asimov | *Through a Glass, Clearly*
Four Square Books, 1967 | Art **Josh Kirby**

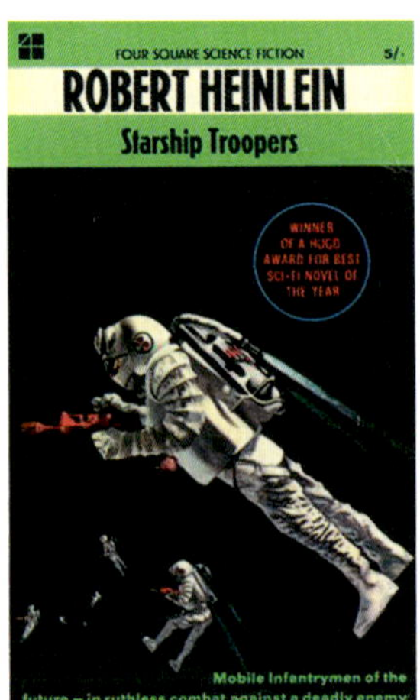

Robert A. Heinlein | *Starship Troopers*
Four Square Books, 1967 | Art **Karel Thole**

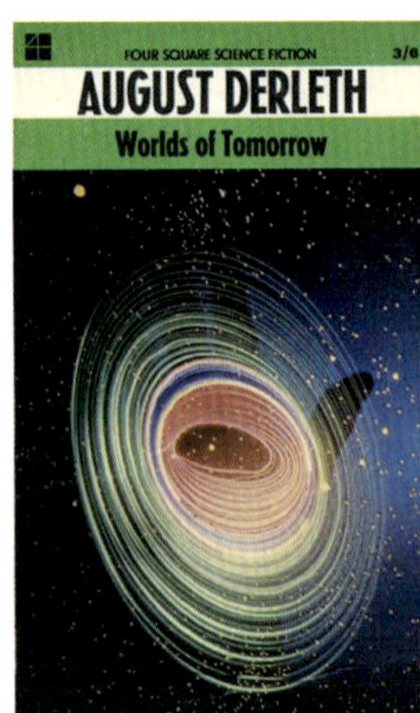

August Derleth | *Worlds of Tomorrow*
Four Square Books, 1967 | Art **Unknown**

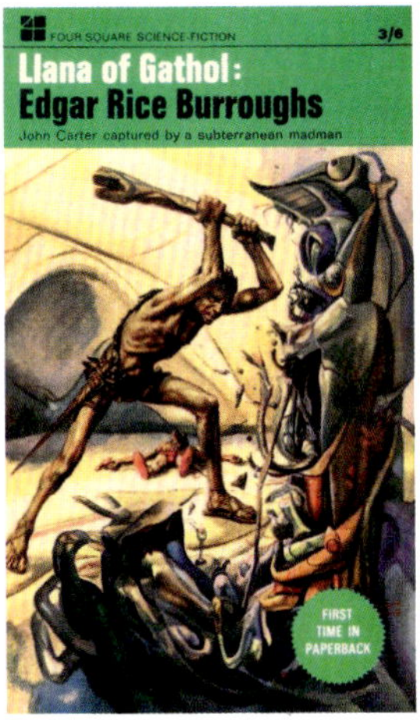

Edgar Rice Burroughs | *Llana of Gathol*
Four Square Books, 1967 | Art **Josh Kirby**

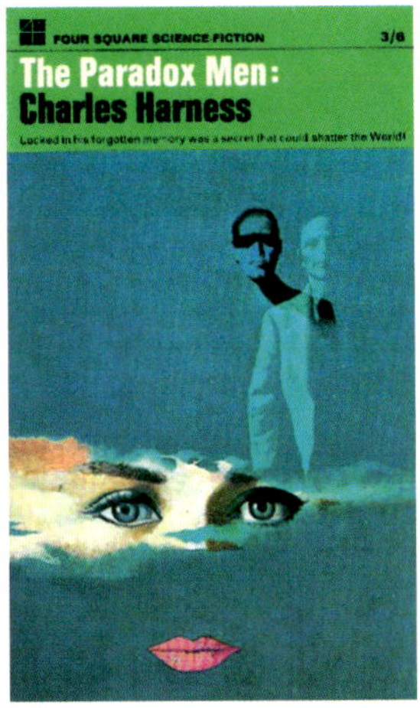

Charles L. Harness | *The Paradox Men*
Four Square Books, 1967 | Art **Unknown**

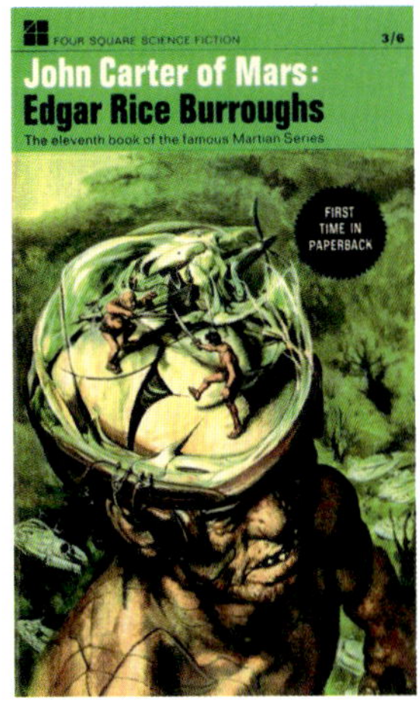

Edgar Rice Burroughs | *John Carter of Mars*
Four Square Books, 1968 | Art **Josh Kirby**

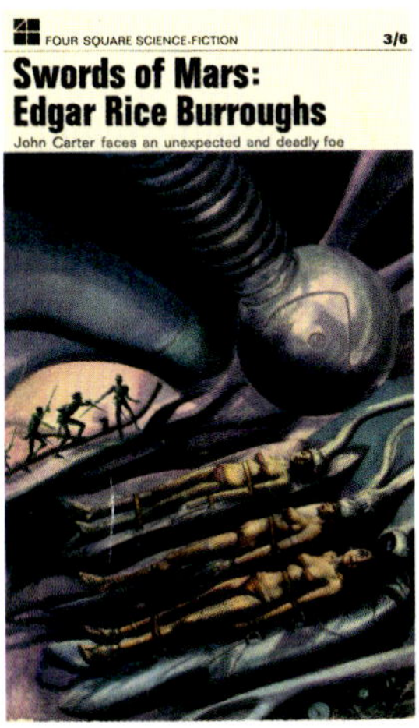

Edgar Rice Burroughs | *Swords of Mars*
Four Square Books, 1966 | Art **Josh Kirby**

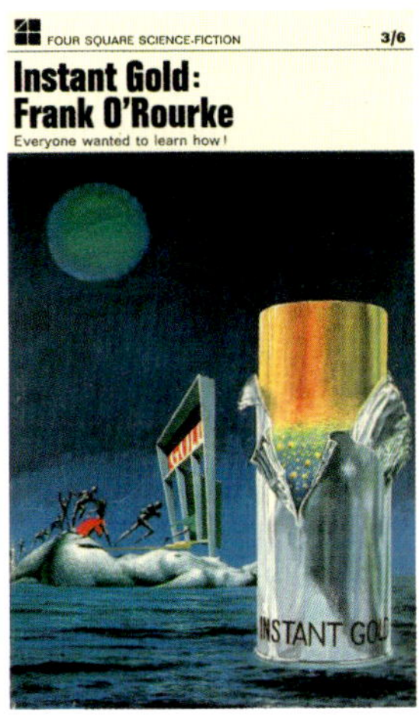

Frank O'Rourke | *Instant Gold*
Four Square Books, 1966 | Art **Unknown**

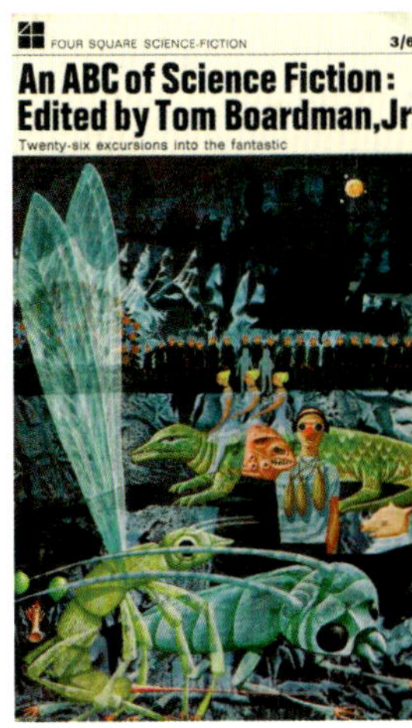

Tom Boardman, Jr. | *An ABC of Science Fiction*
Four Square Books, 1966 | Art **Barry Evans**

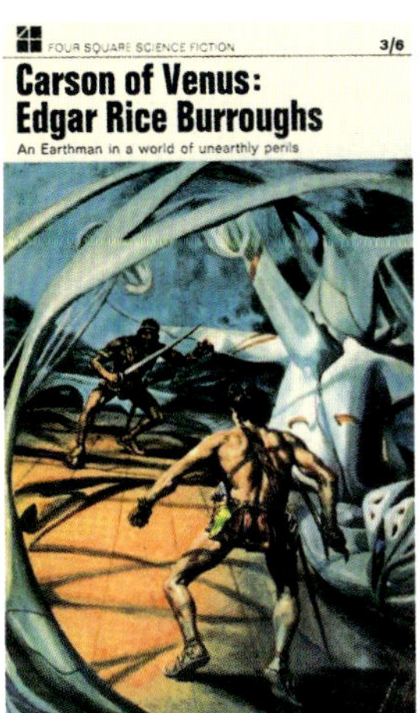

Edgar Rice Burroughs | *Carson of Venus*
Four Square Books, 1967 | Art **Josh Kirby**

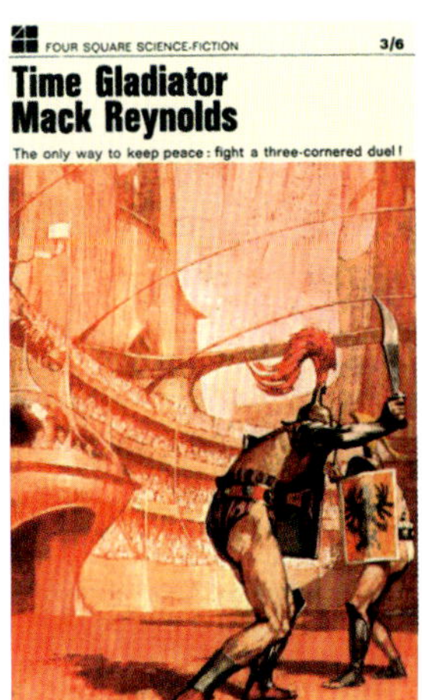

Mack Reynolds | *Time Gladiator*
Four Square Books, 1966 | Art **Leonard**

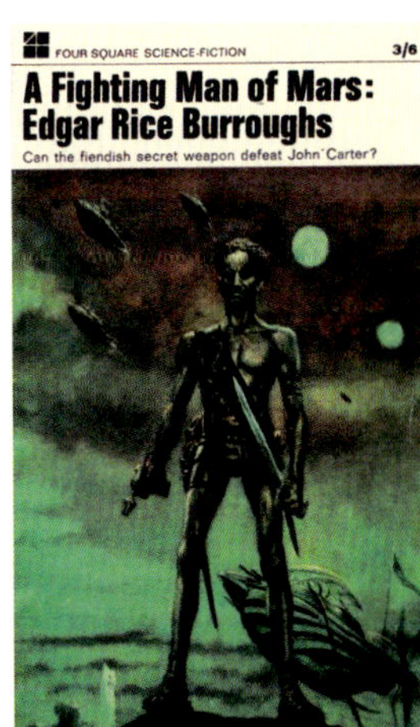

Edgar Rice Burroughs | *A Fighting Man of Mars*
Four Square Books, 1966 | Art **Josh Kirby**

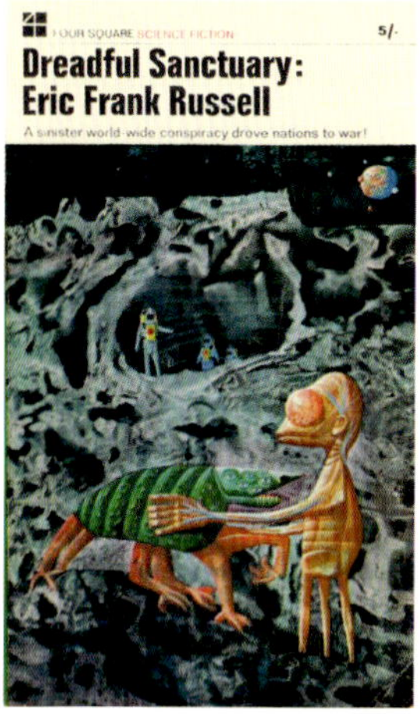

Eric Frank Russell | *Dreadful Sanctuary*
Four Square Books, 1967 | Art **Barry Evans**

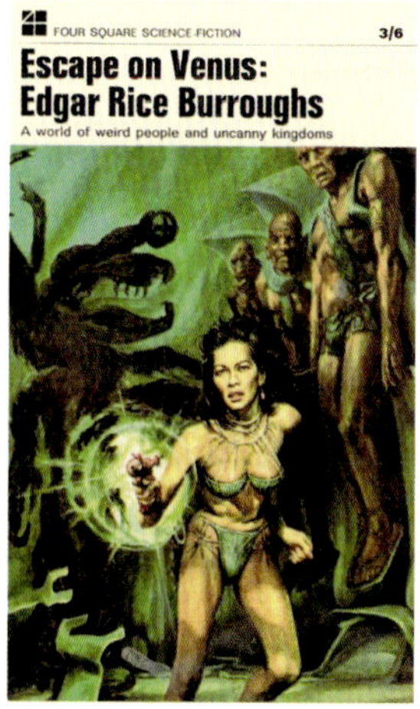

Edgar Rice Burroughs | *Escape on Venus*
Four Square Books, 1966 | Art **Josh Kirby**

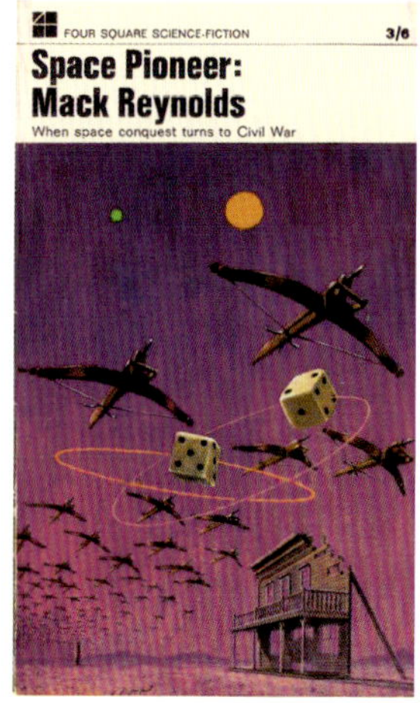

Mack Reynolds | *Space Pioneer*
Four Square Books, 1966 | Art **Unknown**

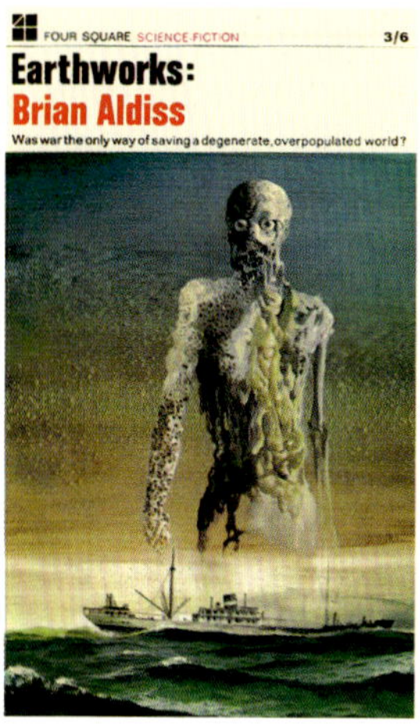

Brian W. Aldiss | *Earthworks*
Four Square Books, 1967 | Art **Karel Thole**

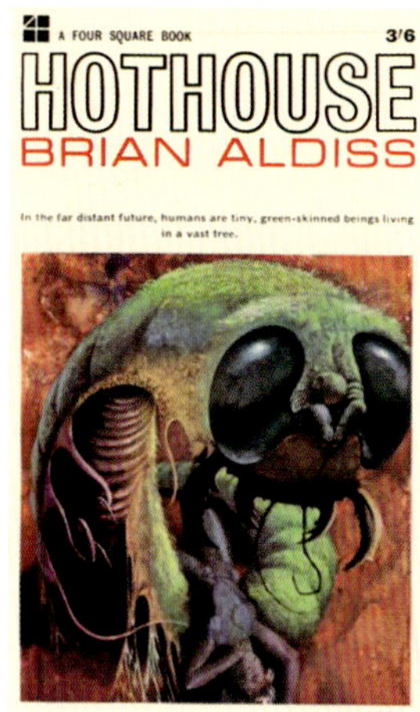

Brian W. Aldiss | *Hothouse*
Four Square Books, 1964 | Art **Unknown**

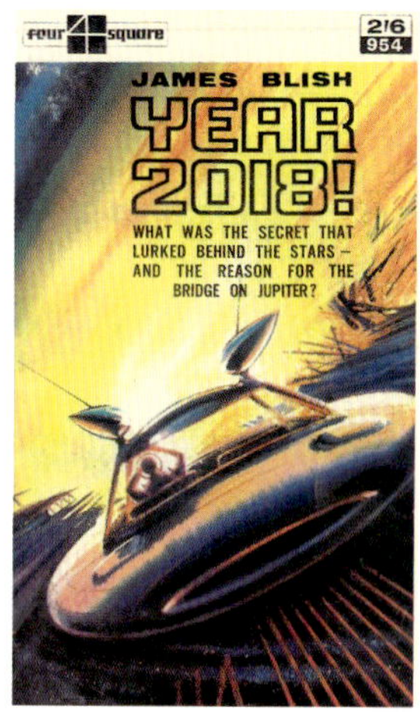

James Blish | *Year 2018!*
Four Square Books, 1964 | Art **Unknown**

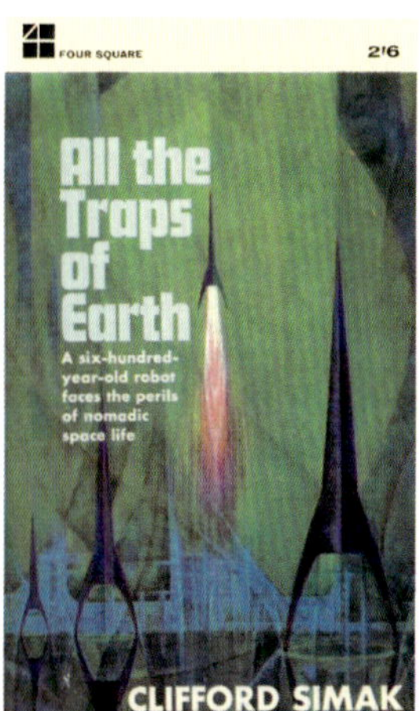

Clifford Simak | *All the Traps of Earth*
Four Square Books, 1964 | Art **Curtis**

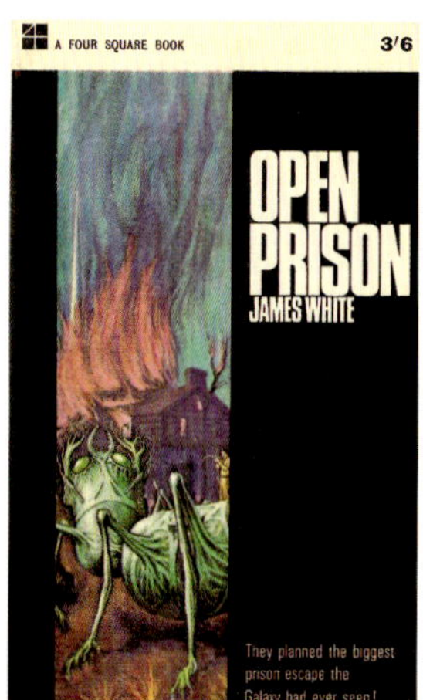

James White | *Open Prison*
Four Square Books, 1965 | Art **Josh Kirby**

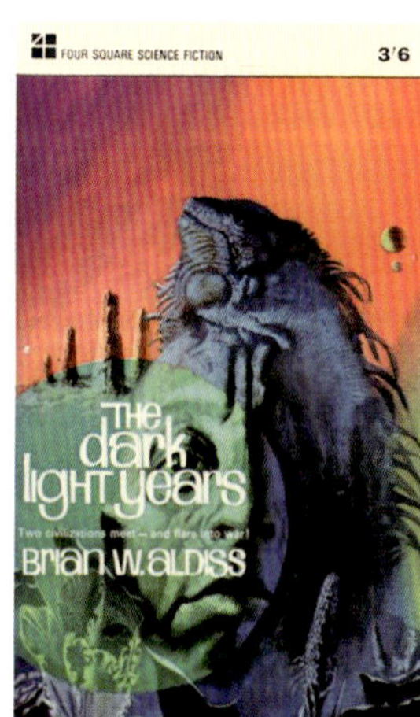

Brian W. Aldiss | *The Dark Light Years*
Four Square Books, 1966 | Art **Karel Thole**

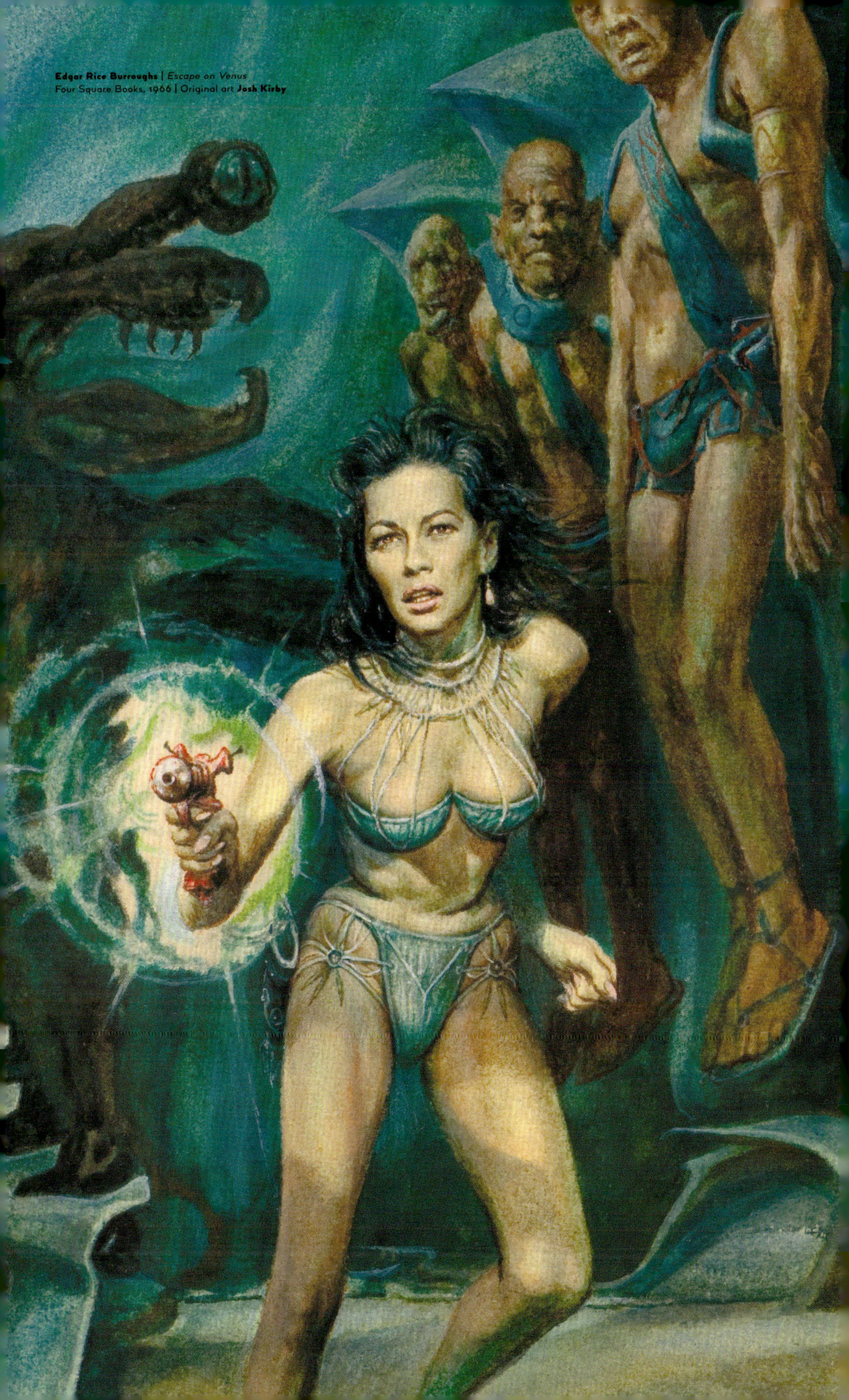

Edgar Rice Burroughs | *Escape on Venus*
Four Square Books, 1966 | Original art **Josh Kirby**

Frank Herbert | *Dune*
New English Library, 1968 | Original art **Bruce Pennington**

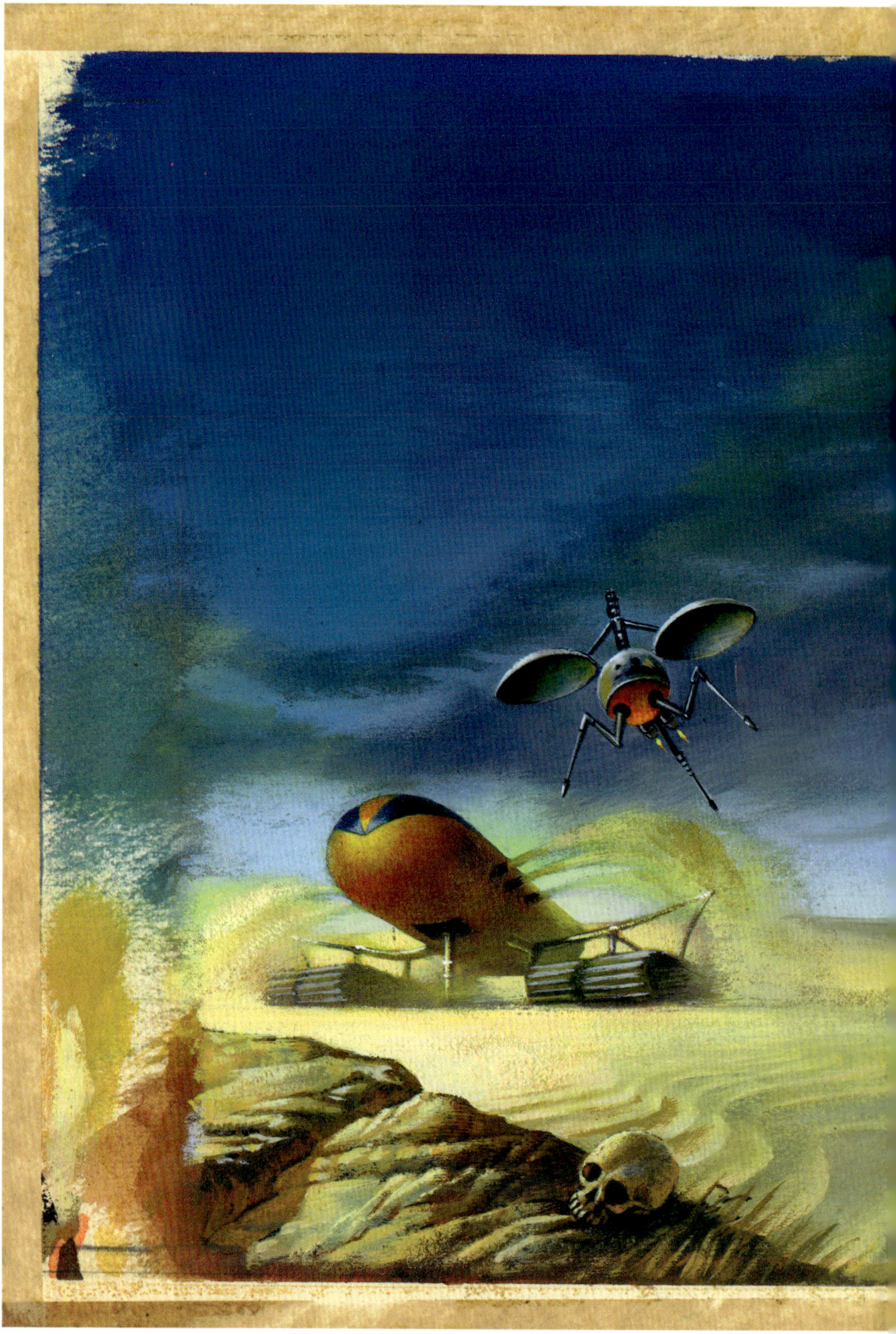

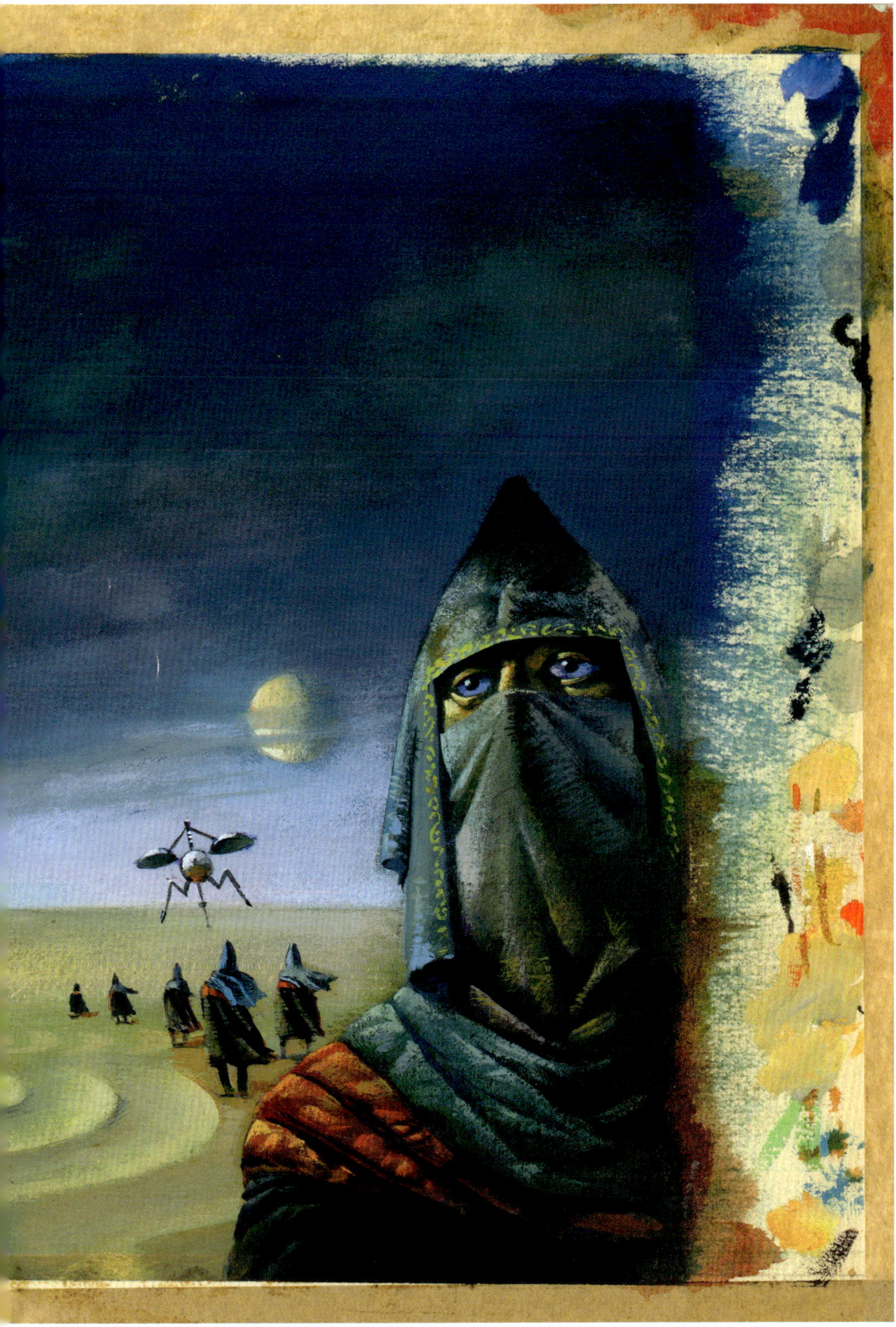

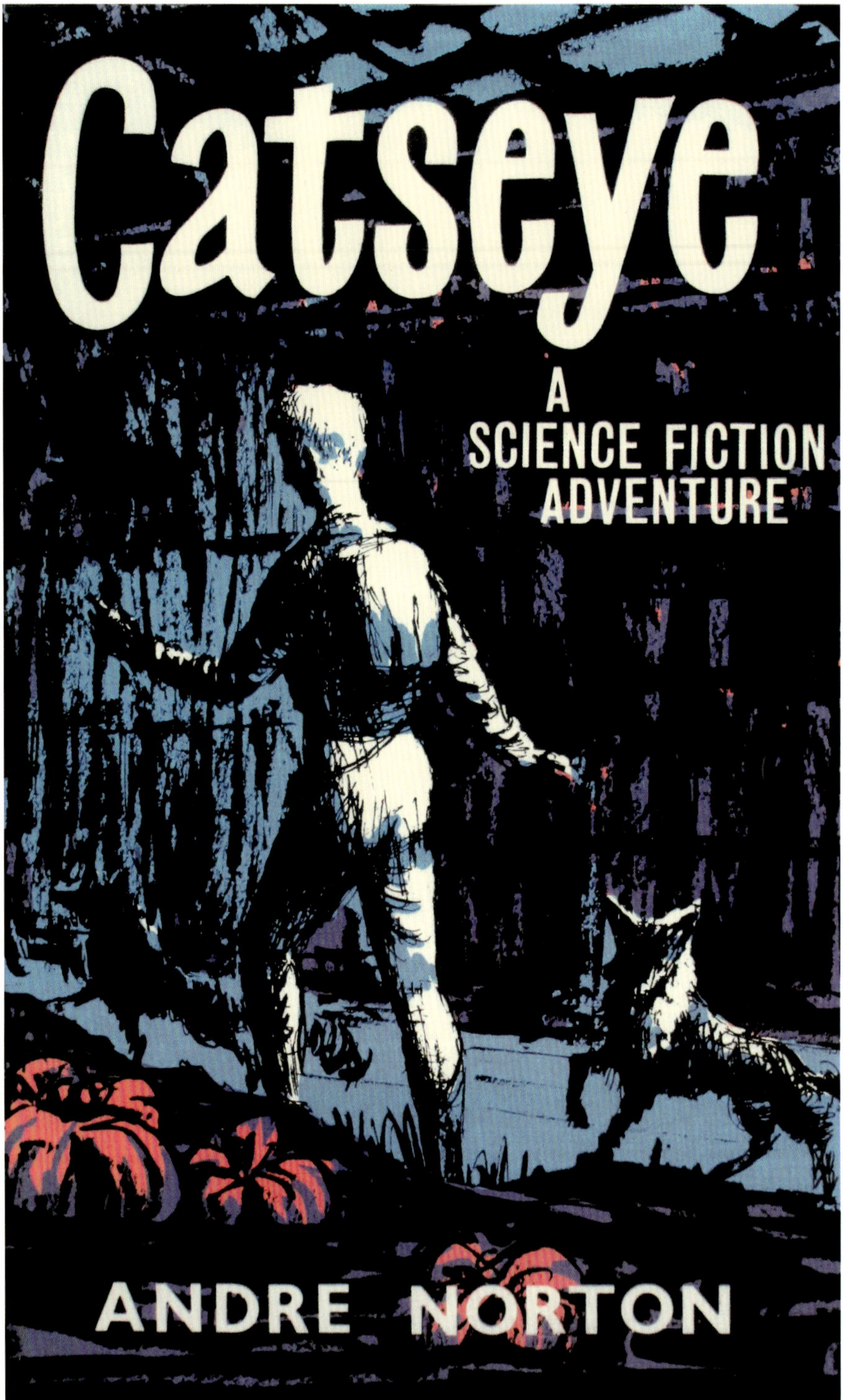

Andre Norton | *Catseye*
Gollancz, 1962 | Art **Alan Breese**

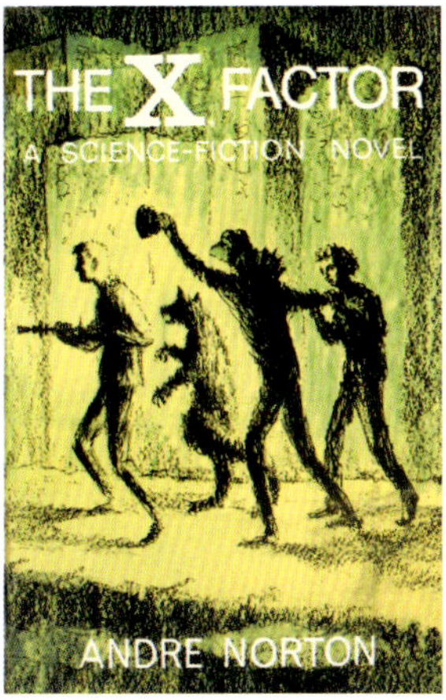

Andre Norton | *The X Factor*
Gollancz, 1967 | Art **Alan Breese**

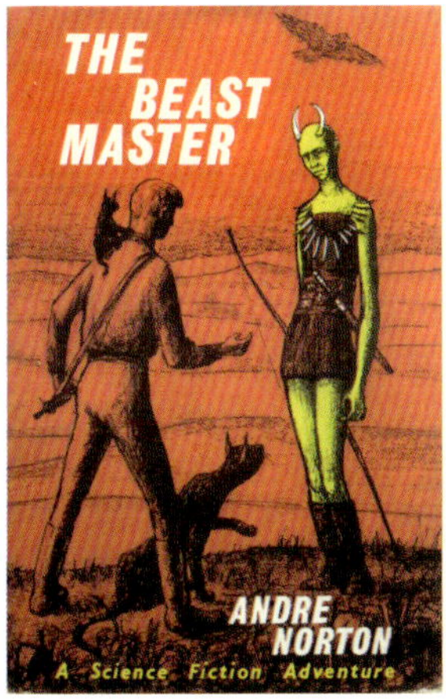

Andre Norton | *The Beast Master*
Gollancz, 1966 | Art **Alan Breese**

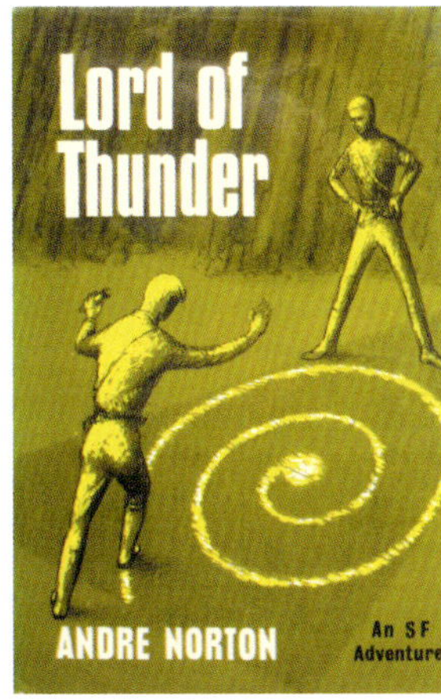

Andre Norton | *Lord of Thunder*
Gollancz, 1966 | Art **Alan Breese**

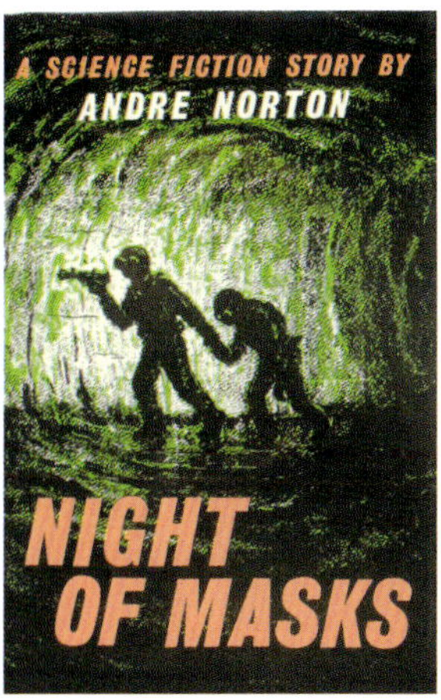

Andre Norton | *Night of Masks*
Gollancz, 1965 | Art **Alan Breese**

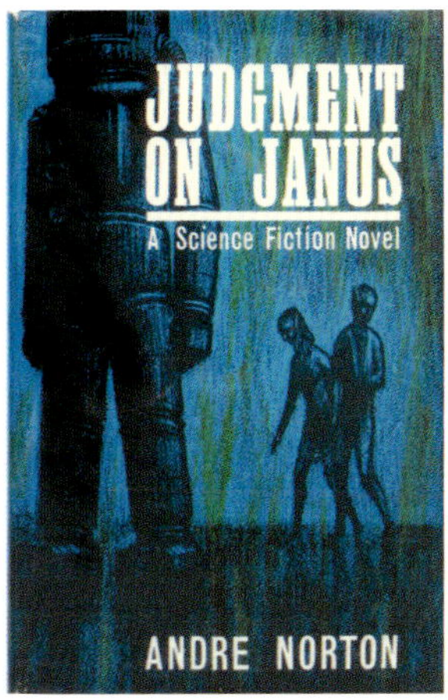

Andre Norton | *Judgment on Janus*
Gollancz, 1964 | Art **Alan Breese**

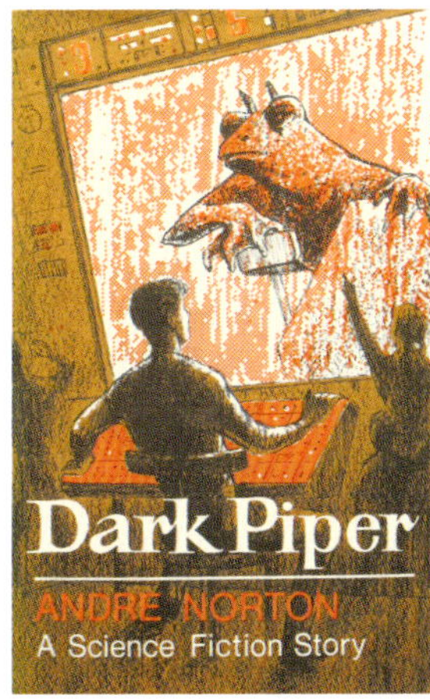

Andre Norton | *Dark Piper*
Gollancz, 1969 | Art **Alan Breese**

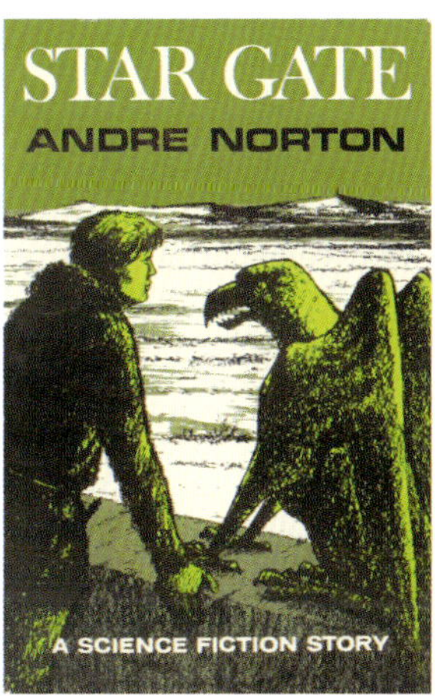

Andre Norton | *Star Gate*
Gollancz, 1970 | Art **Alan Breese**

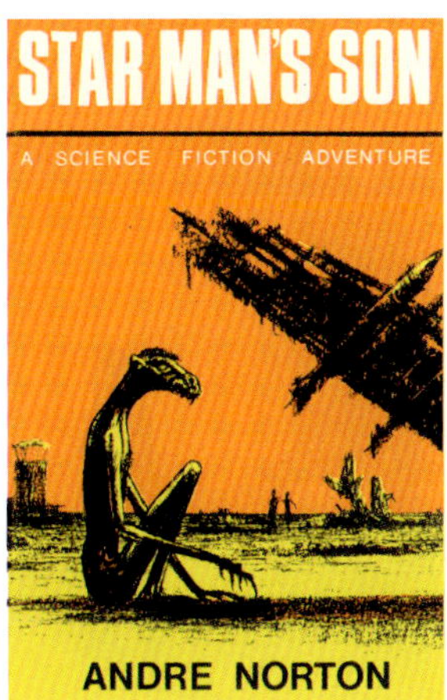

Andre Norton | *Star Man's Son, 2250 A.D.*
Gollancz, 1968 | Art **Alan Breese**

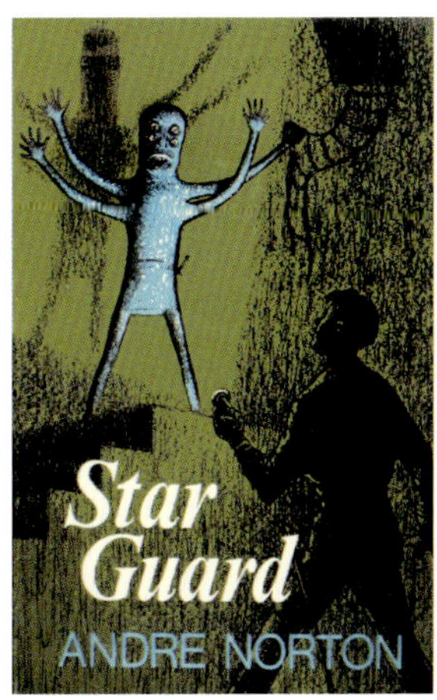

Andre Norton | *Star Guard*
Gollancz, 1969 | Art **Alan Breese**

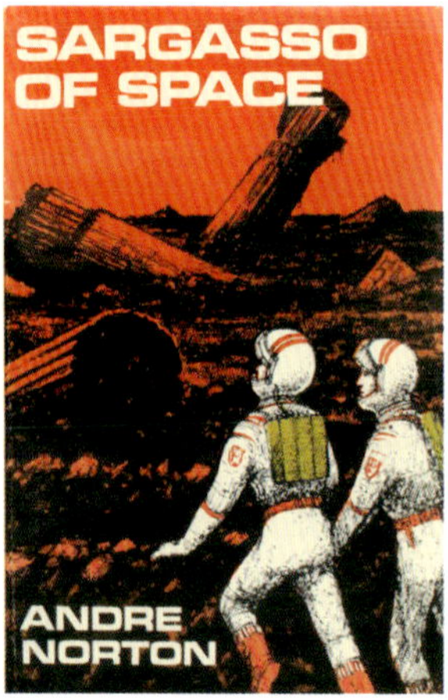

Andre Norton | *Sargasso of Space*
Gollancz, 1970 | Art **Alan Breese**

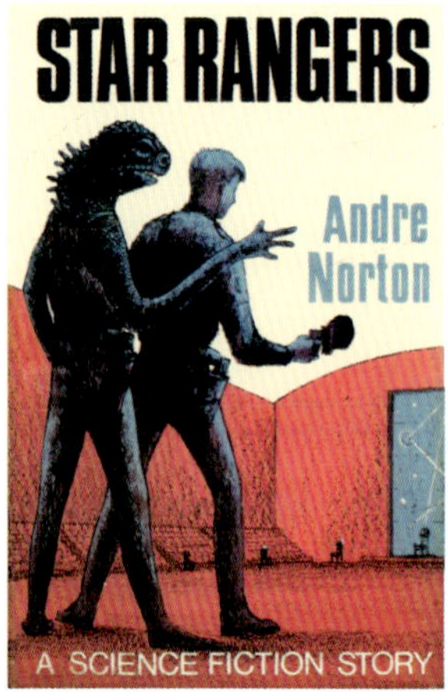

Andre Norton | *Star Rangers*
Gollancz, 1968 | Art **Alan Breese**

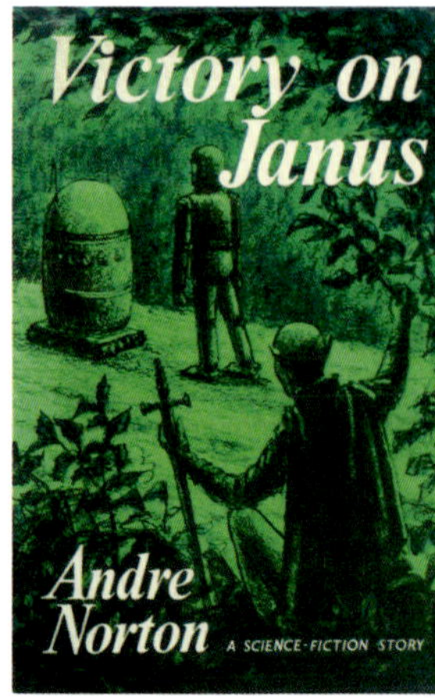

Andre Norton | *Victory on Janus*
Gollancz, 1967 | Art **Alan Breese**

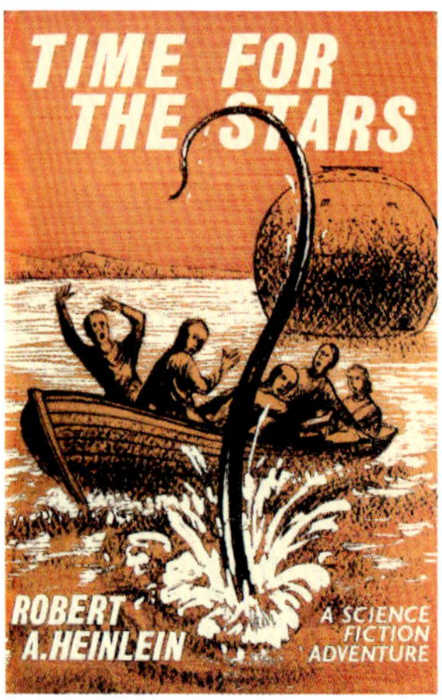

Robert A. Heinlein | *Time for the Stars*
Gollancz, 1963 | Art **Alan Breese**

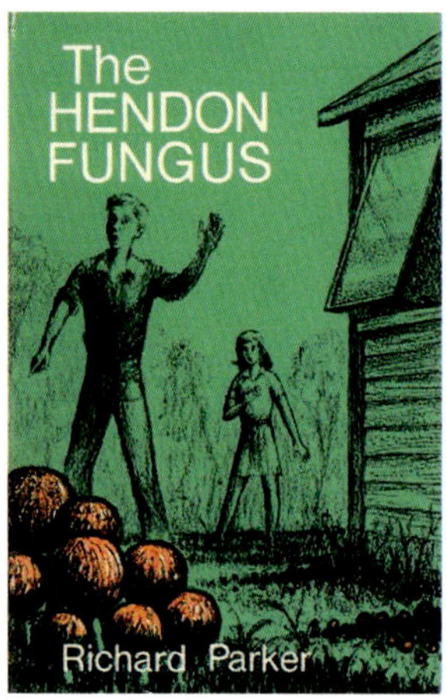

Richard Parker | *The Hendon Fungus*
Gollancz, 1967 | Art **Alan Breese**

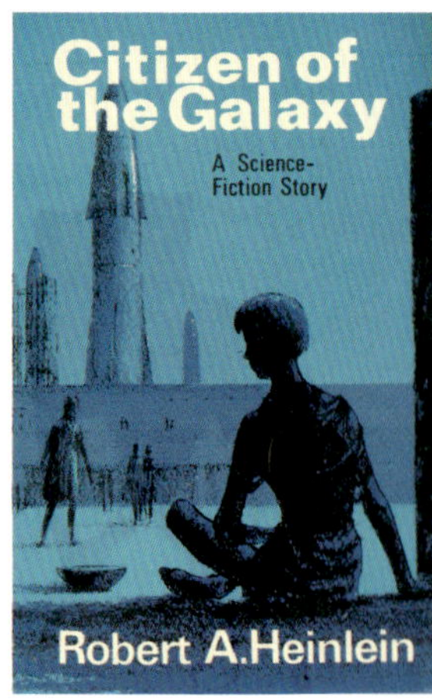

Robert A. Heinlein | *Citizen of the Galaxy*
Gollancz, 1969 | Art **Alan Breese**

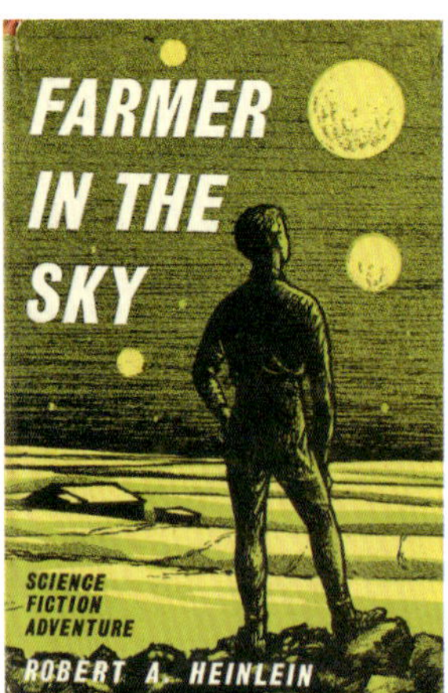

Robert A. Heinlein | *Farmer in the Sky*
Gollancz, 1962 | Art **Alan Breese**

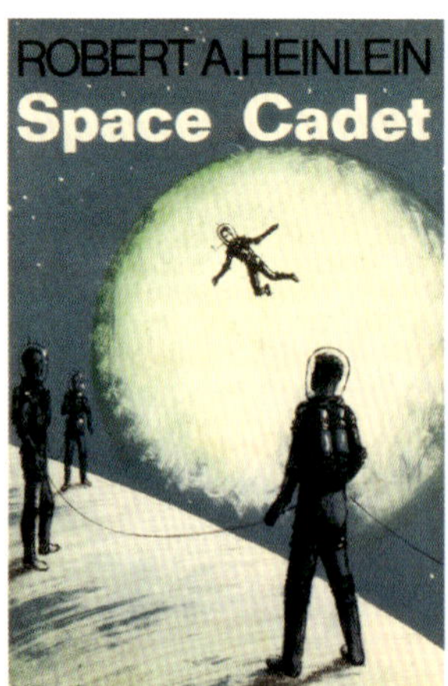

Robert A. Heinlein | *Space Cadet*
Gollancz, 1966 | Art **Alan Breese**

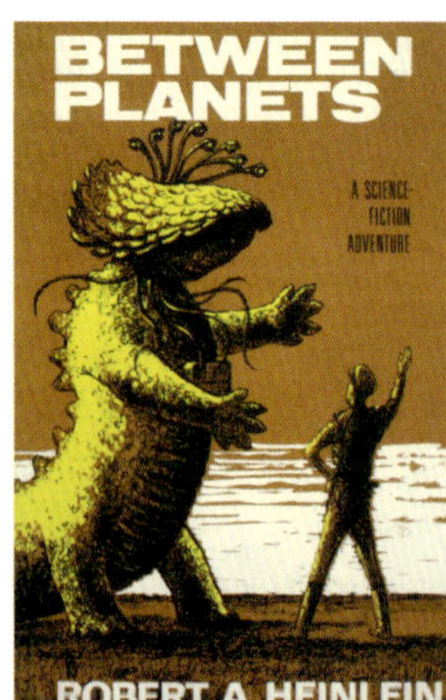

Robert A. Heinlein | *Between Planets*
Gollancz, 1968 | Art **Alan Breese**

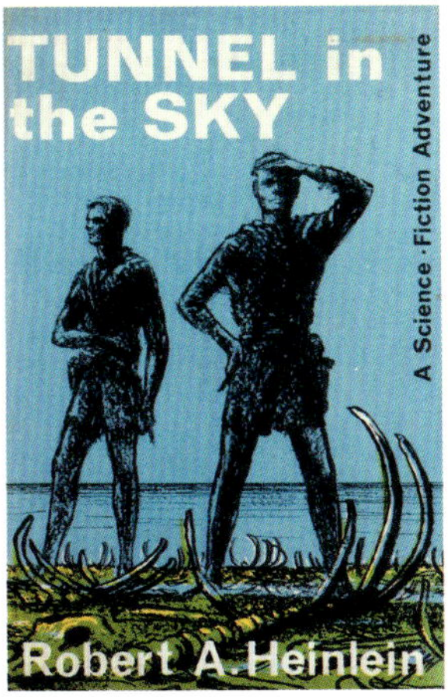

Robert A. Heinlein | *Tunnel in the Sky*
Gollancz, 1965 | Art **Alan Breese**

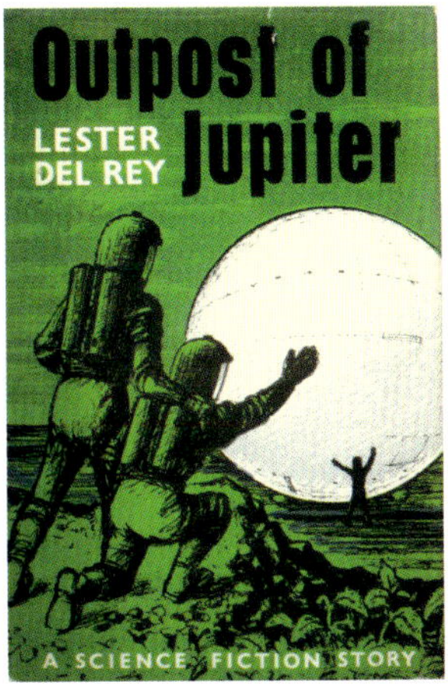

Lester del Rey | *Outpost of Jupiter*
Gollancz, 1964 | Art **Alan Breese**

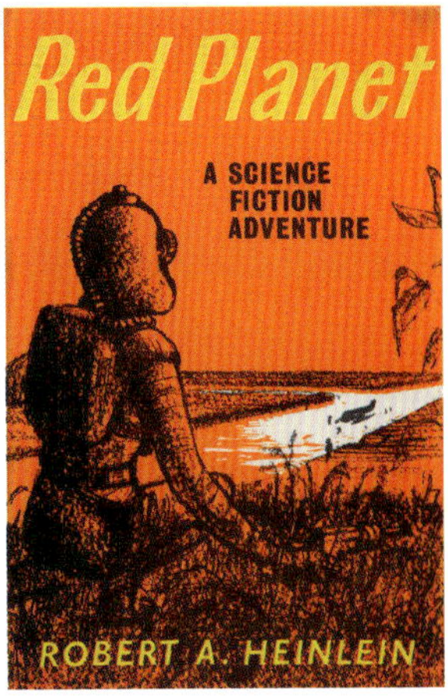

Robert A. Heinlein | *Red Planet*
Gollancz, 1963 | Art **Alan Breese**

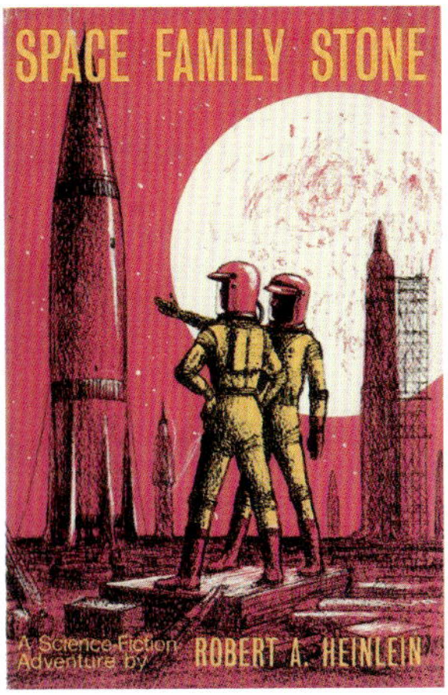

Robert A. Heinlein | *Space Family Stone*
Gollancz, 1969 | Art **Alan Breese**

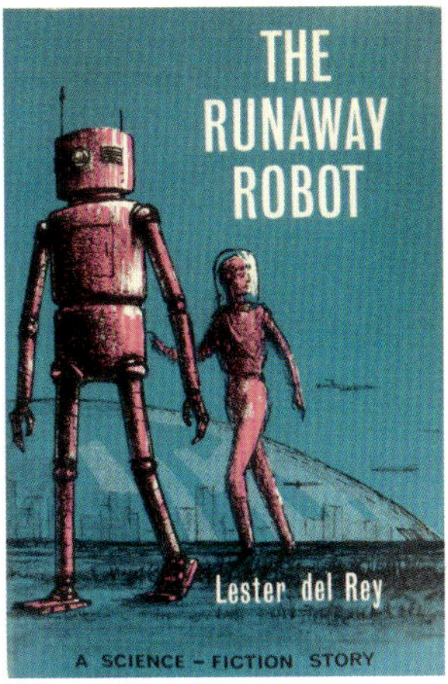

Lester del Rey | *The Runaway Robot*
Gollancz, 1967 | Art **Alan Breese**

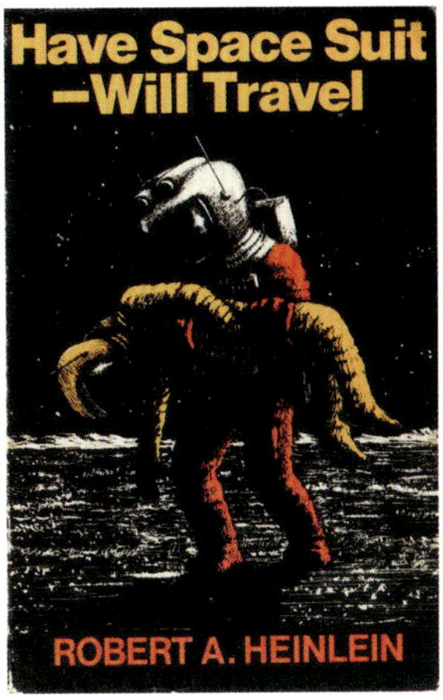

Robert A. Heinlein | *Have Space Suit–Will Travel*
Gollancz, 1970 | Art **Alan Breese**

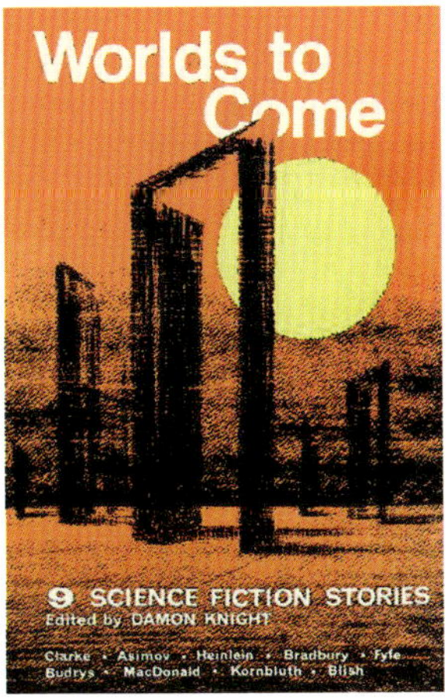

Damon Knight | *Worlds to Come*
Gollancz, 1969 | Art **Alan Breese**

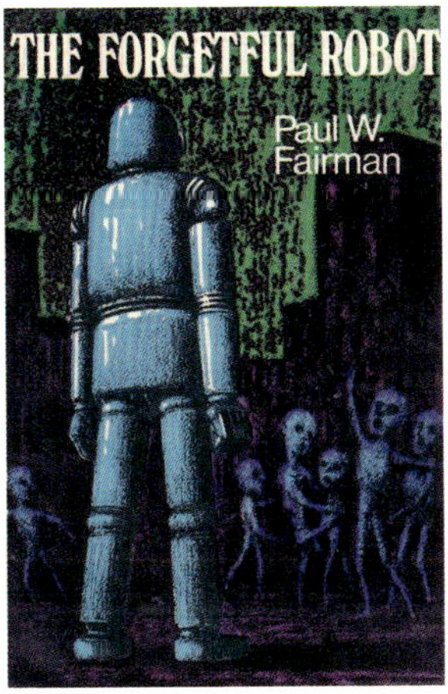

Paul W. Fairman | *The Forgetful Robot*
Gollancz, 1970 | Art **Alan Breese**

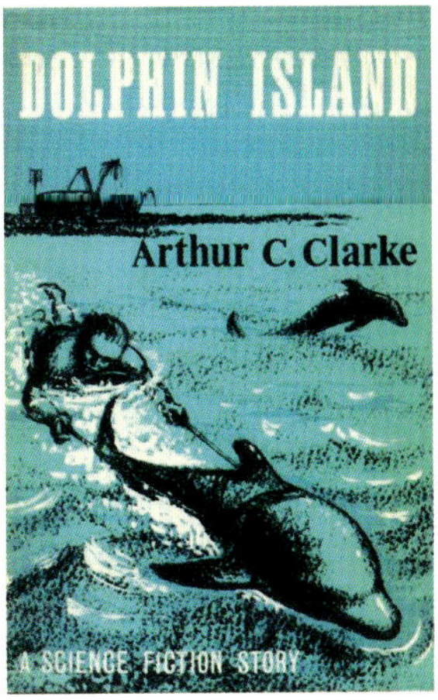

Arthur C. Clarke | *Dolphin Island*
Gollancz, 1963 | Art **Alan Breese**

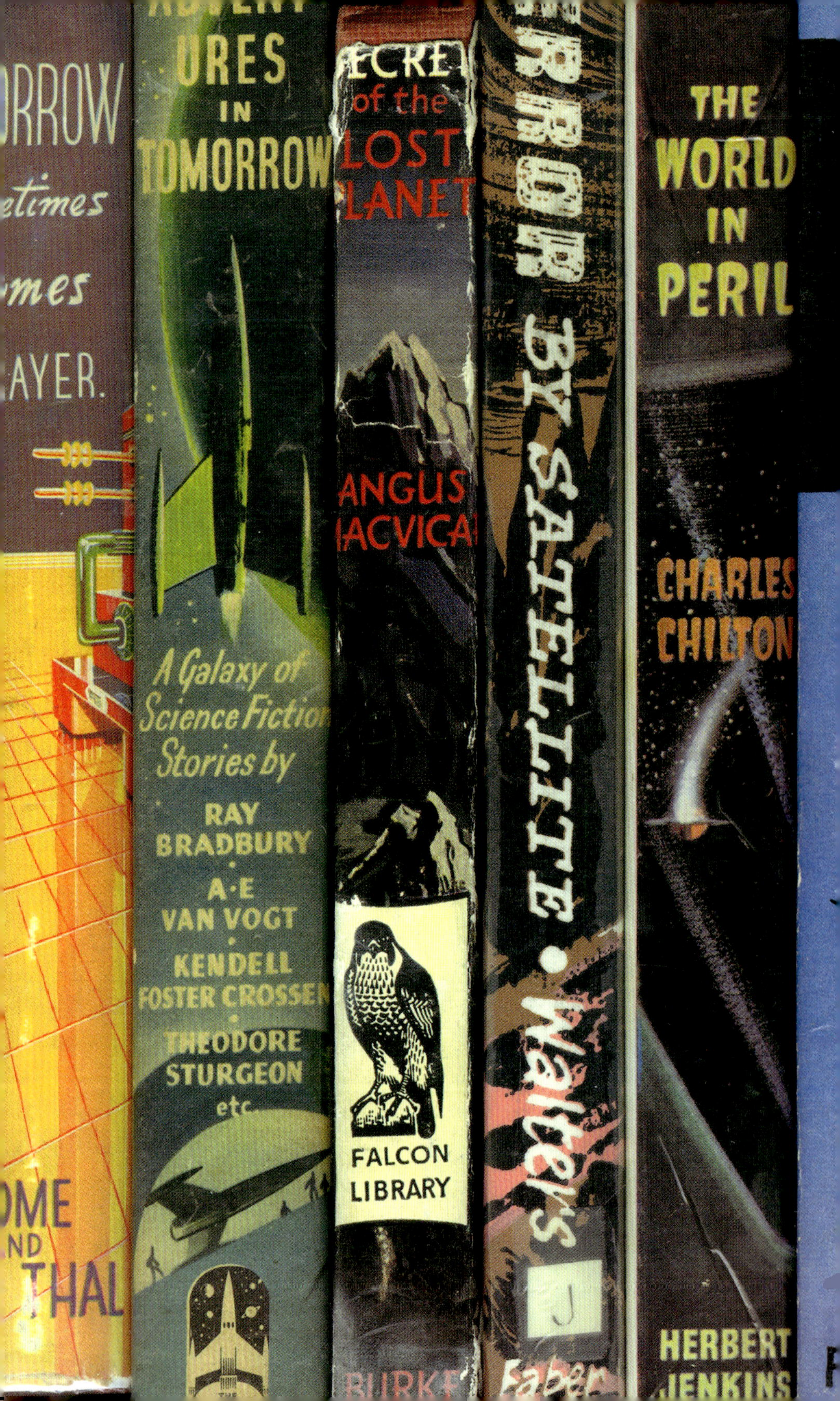
ORROW
etimes
mes
AYER.
OME
ND
THAL
URES
IN
TOMORROW
A Galaxy of Science Fiction Stories by
RAY BRADBURY
A·E VAN VOGT
KENDELL FOSTER CROSSEN
THEODORE STURGEON
etc.
ECRE
of the
LOST
LANET
ANGUS
ACVICA
FALCON
LIBRARY
RROR BY SATELLITE • Walters
Faber
THE WORLD IN PERIL
CHARLES CHILTON
HERBERT JENKINS

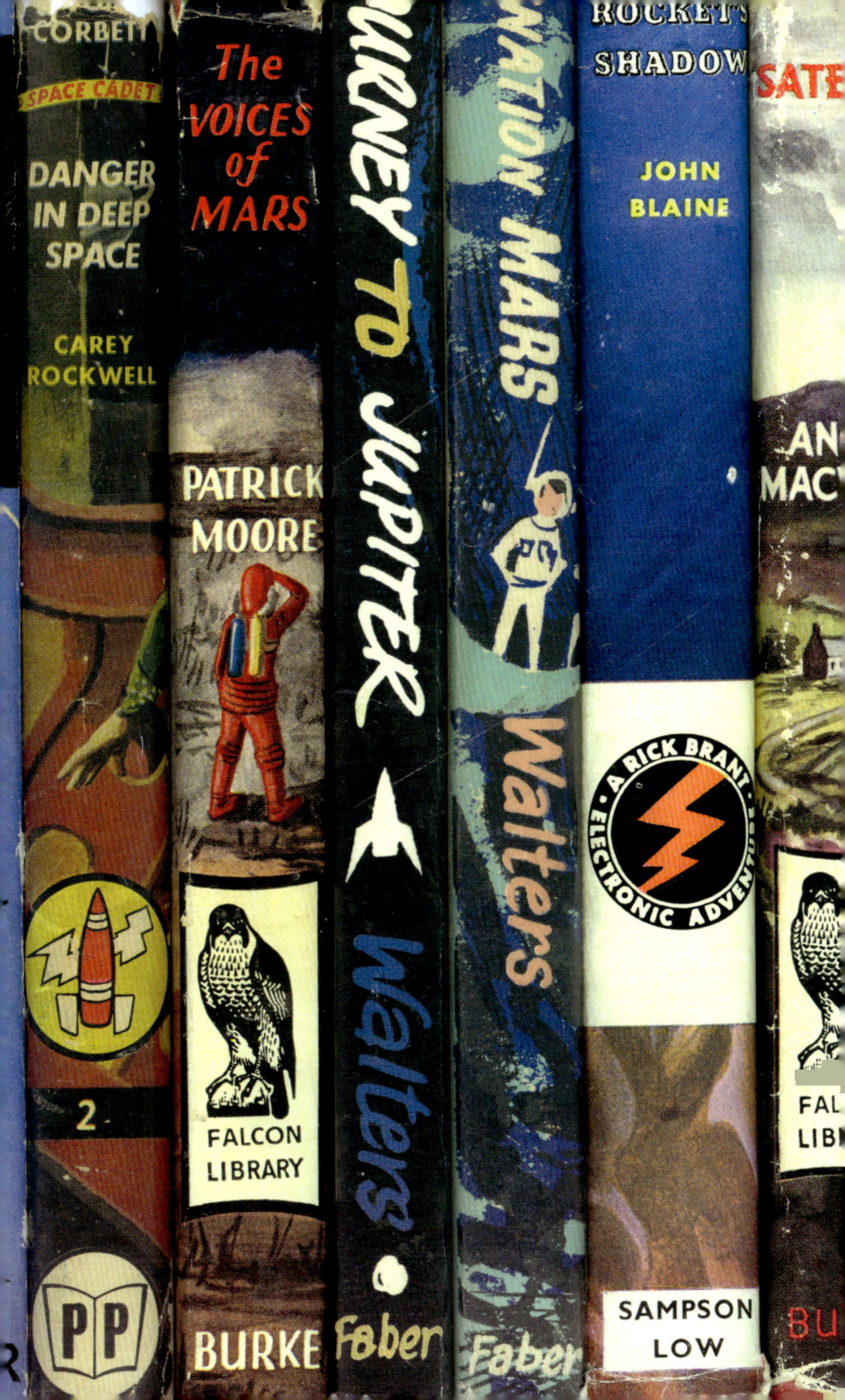

CORBETT
SPACE CADET
DANGER IN DEEP SPACE
CAREY ROCKWELL
2
PP
The VOICES of MARS
PATRICK MOORE
FALCON LIBRARY
BURKE
TO JUPITER
Walters
Faber
MARS
Walters
Faber
SHADOW
JOHN BLAINE
A RICK BRANT ELECTRONIC ADVENTURE
SAMPSON LOW

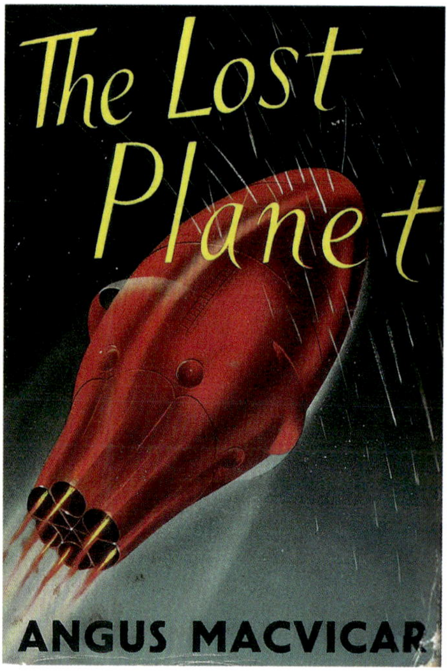

Angus MacVicar | *The Lost Planet*
Burke, 1953 | Art **C. W. Bacon**

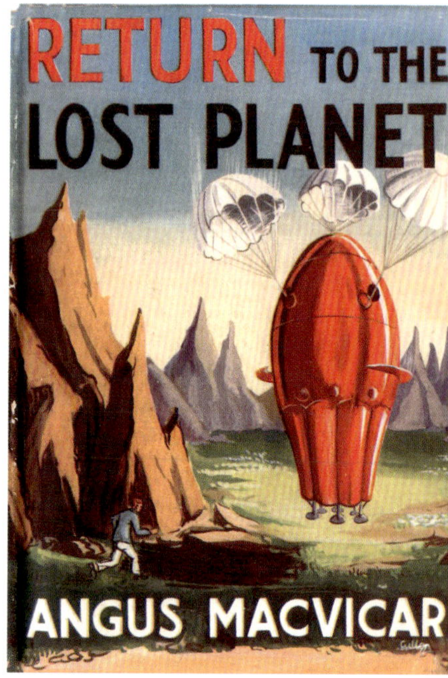

Angus MacVicar | *Return to the Lost Planet*
Burke, 1958 | Art **Patricia Cullen**

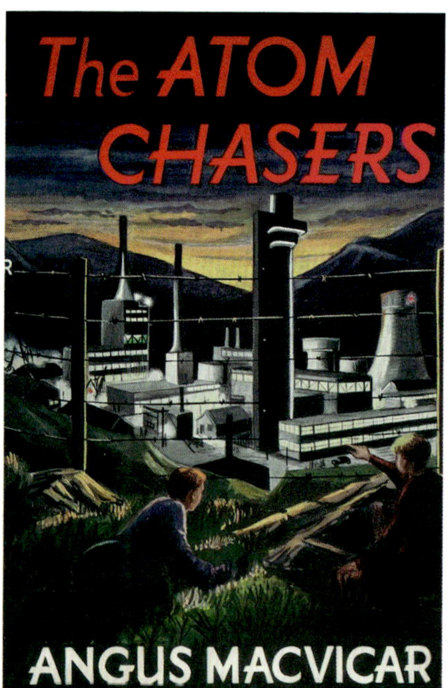

Angus MacVicar | *The Atom Chasers*
Burke, 1960 | Art **Patricia Cullen**

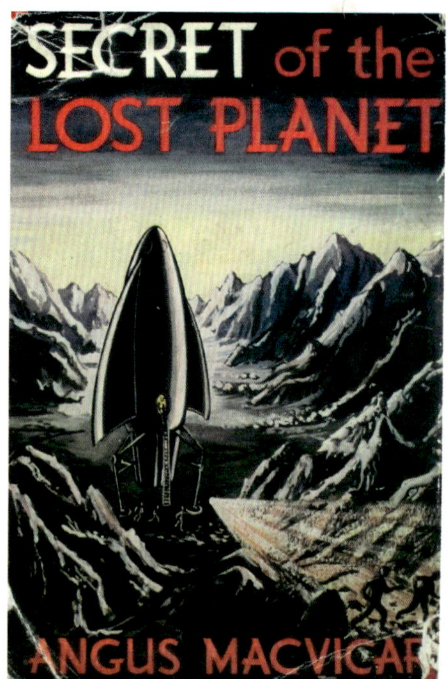

Angus MacVicar | *Secret of the Lost Planet*
Burke, 1955 | Art **Patricia Cullen**

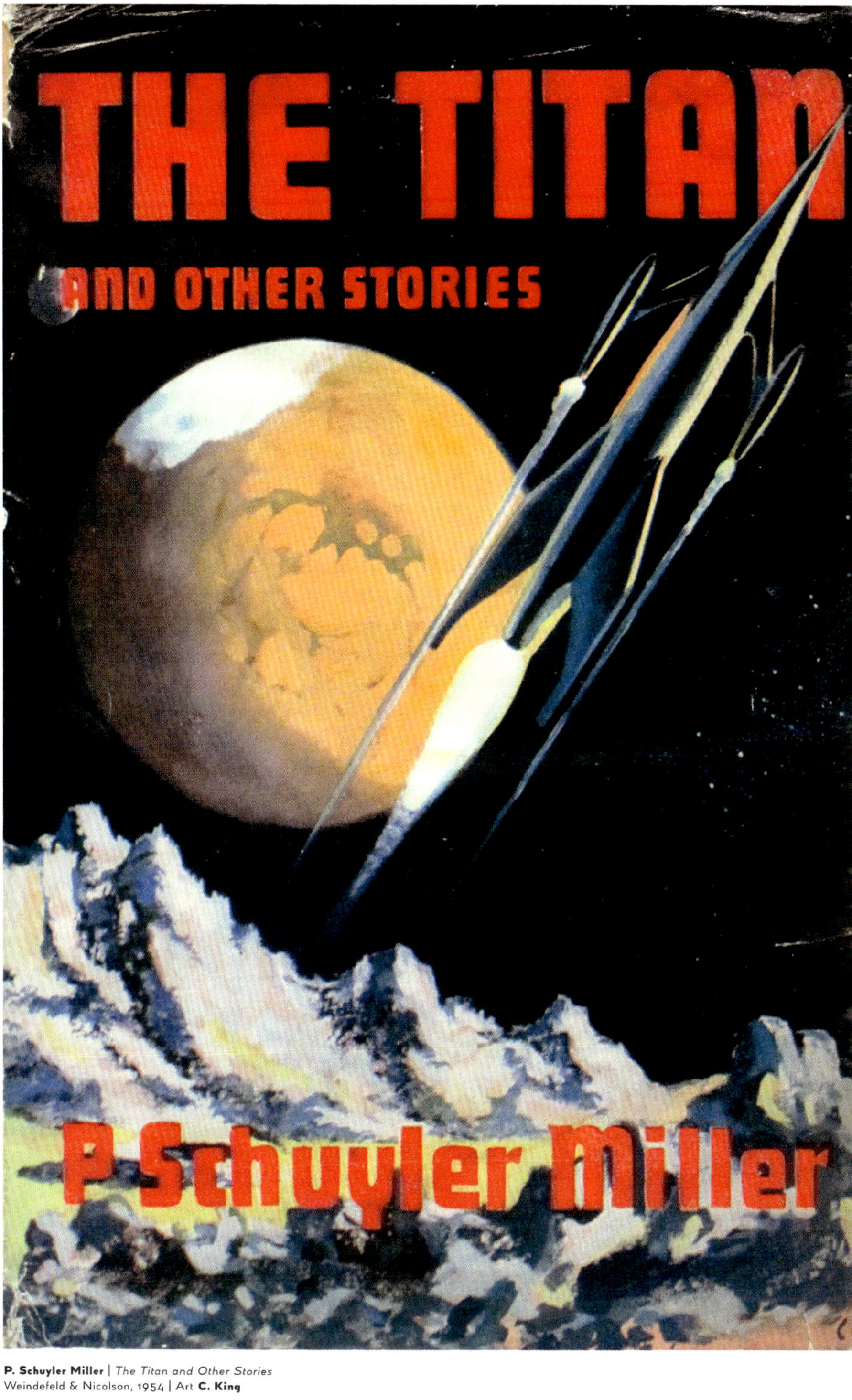

P. Schuyler Miller | *The Titan and Other Stories*
Weindefeld & Nicolson, 1954 | Art **C. King**

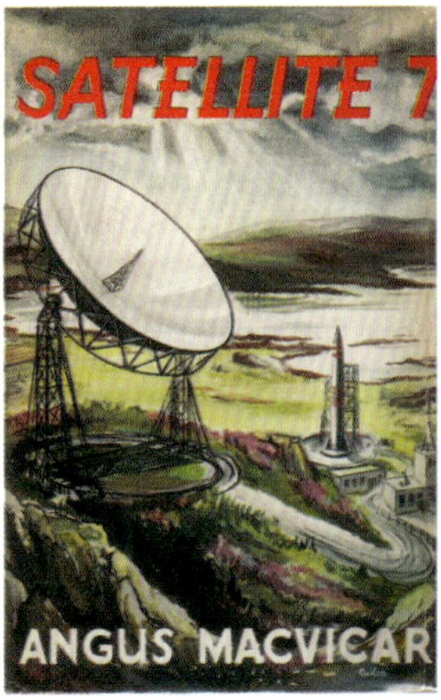

Angus MacVicar | *Satellite 7*
Burke, 1958 | Art **Patricia Cullen**

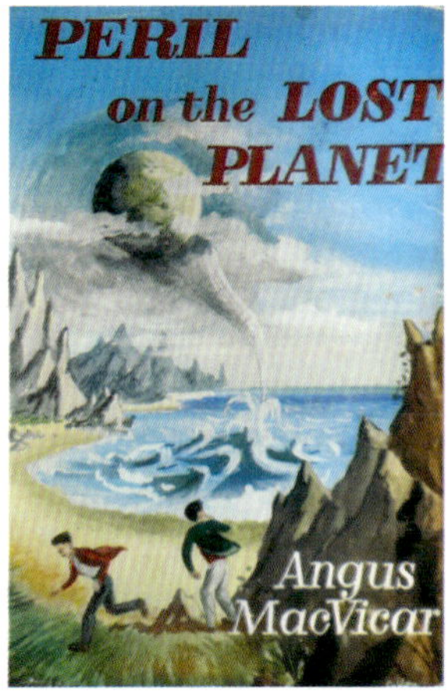

Angus MacVicar | *Peril on the Lost Planet*
Burke, 1960 | Art **Patricia Cullen**

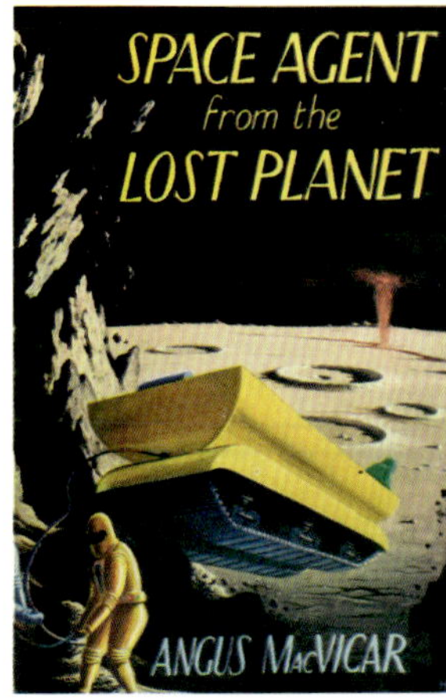

Angus MacVicar | *Space Agent from the Lost Planet*
Burke, 1961 | Art **David A. Hardy**

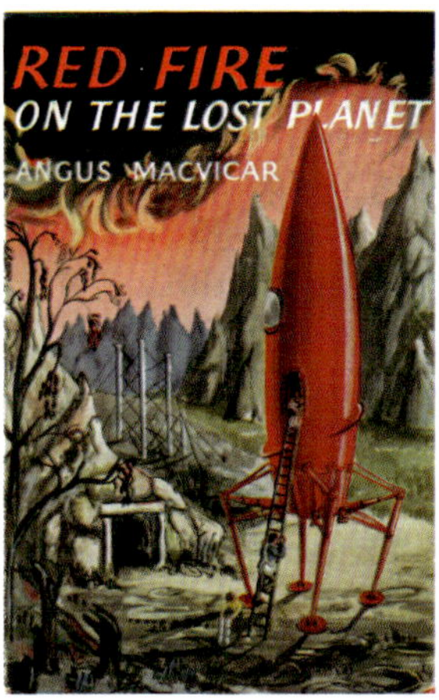

Angus MacVicar | *Red Fire on the Lost Planet*
Burke, 1959 | Art **Patricia Cullen**

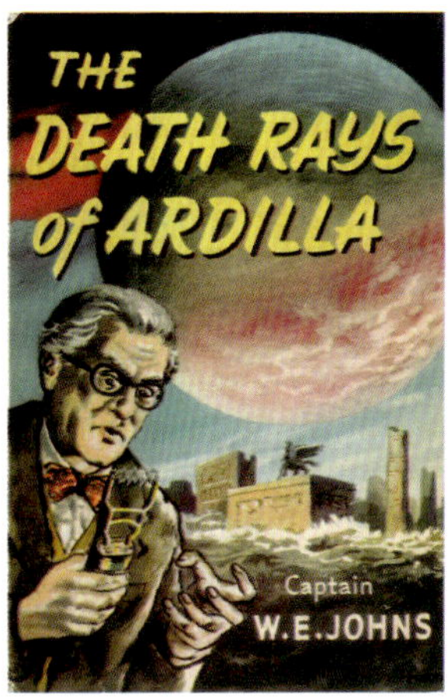

W. E. Johns | *The Death Rays of Ardilla*
The Children's Book Club, 1959 | Art **Unknown**

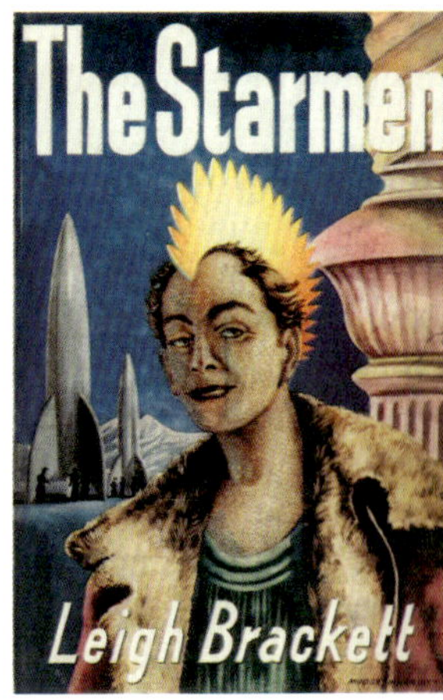

Leigh Brackett | *The Starmen*
Science Fiction Club, 1954 | Art **Mudge-Marriott**

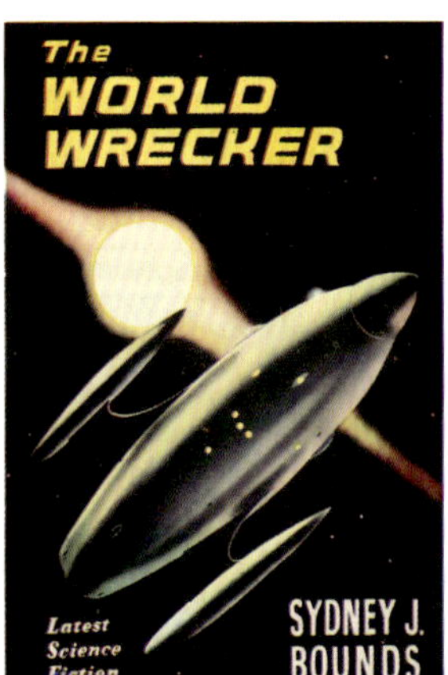

Sydney J. Bounds | *The World Wrecker*
W. Foulsham & Co., 1956 | Art **Blandford**

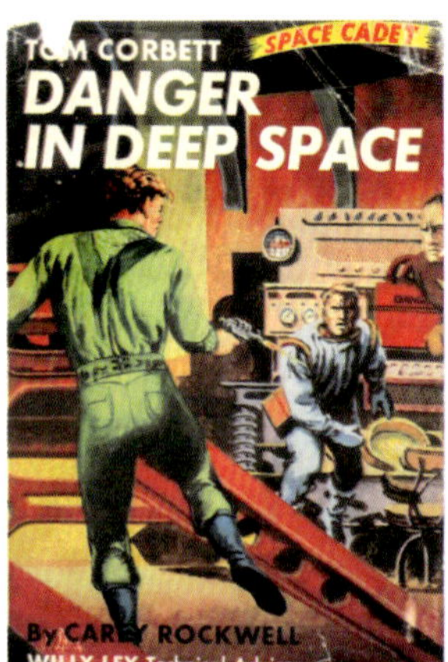

Carey Rockwell | *Danger in Deep Space*
Publicity Products, 1953 | Art **Unknown**

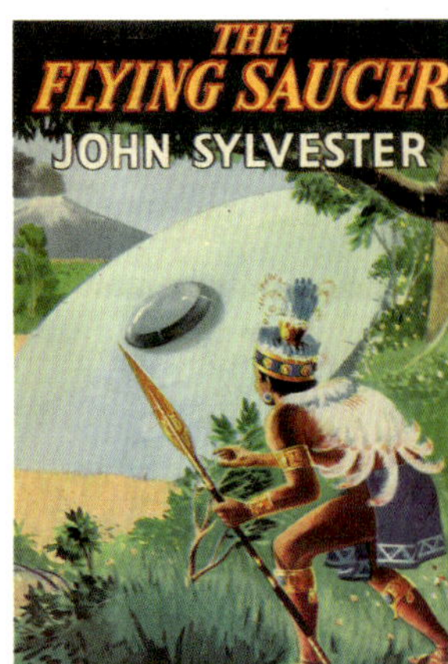

John Sylvester | *The Flying Saucer*
Ward, Lock, 1952 | Art **Ron Jobson**

Arthur C. Clarke, R. A. Smith | *The Exploration of the Moon*
Frederick Muller Ltd., 1954 | Art **R. A. Smith**

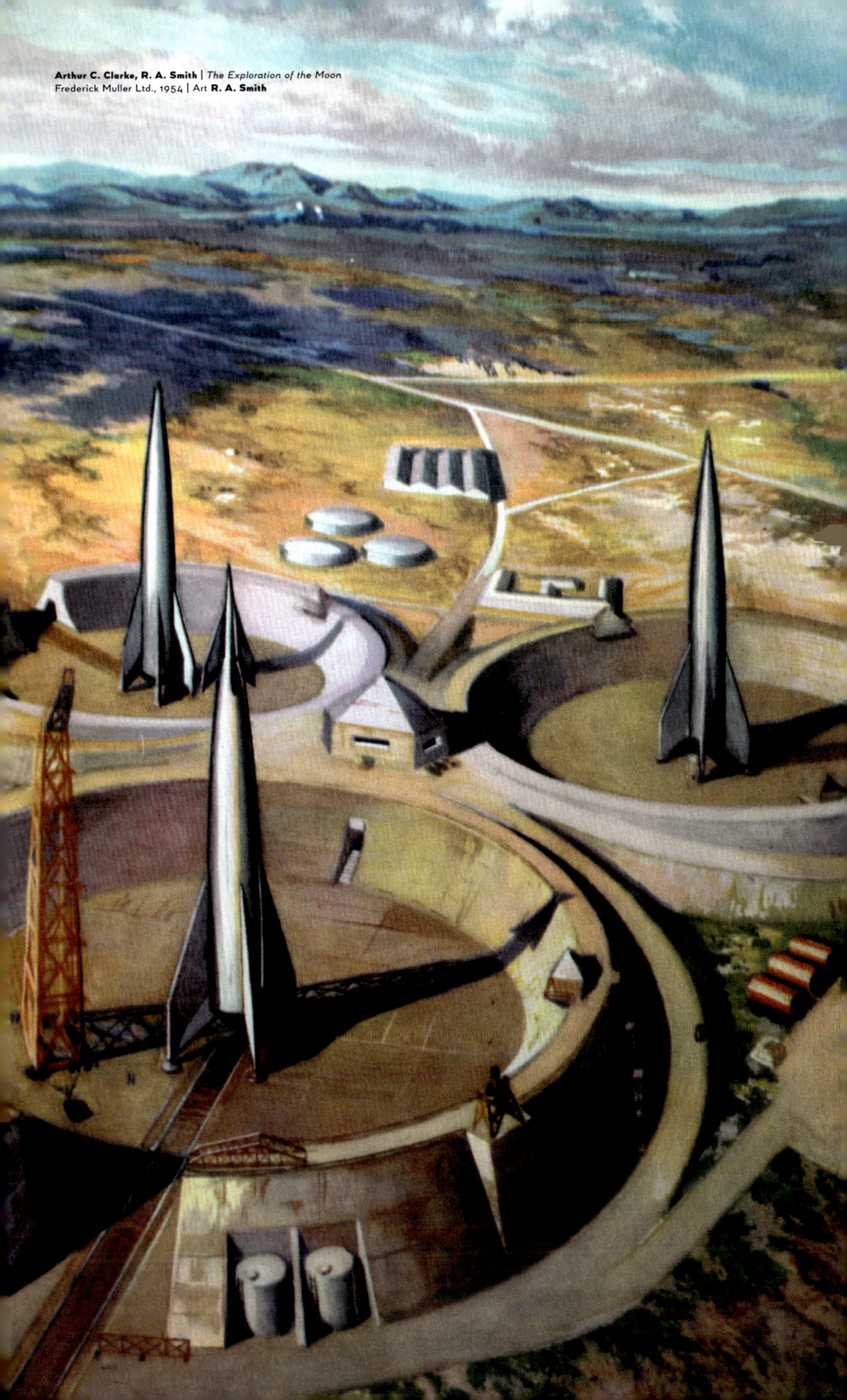

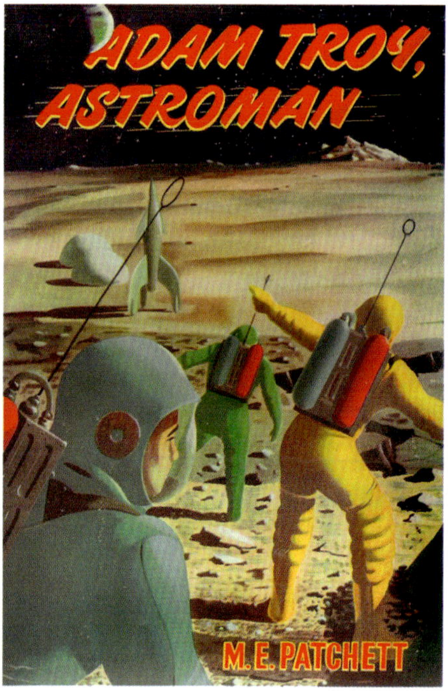

M. E. Patchett | *Adam Troy, Astroman*
Lutterworth Press, 1954 | Art **Unknown**

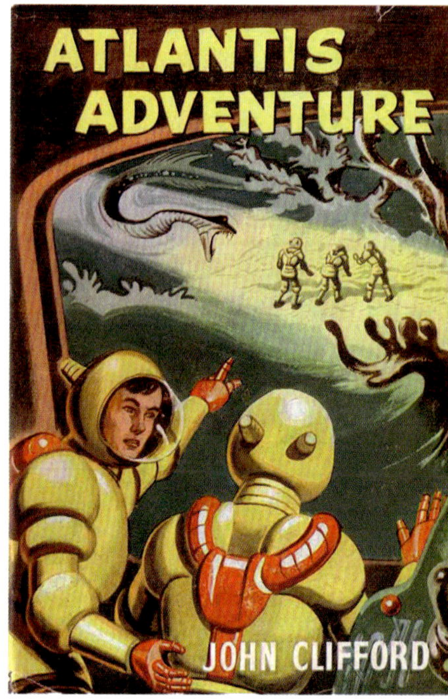

John Clifford | *Atlantis Adventure*
Ward, Lock, 1958 | Art **Unknown**

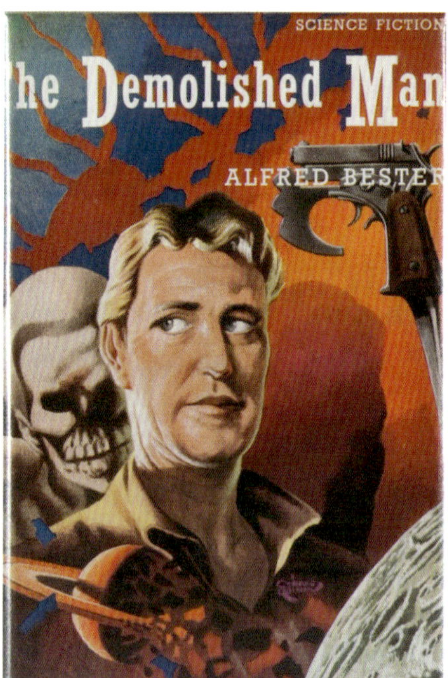

Alfred Bester | *The Demolished Man*
Sidgwick and Jackson, 1953 | Art **Gerard Quinn**

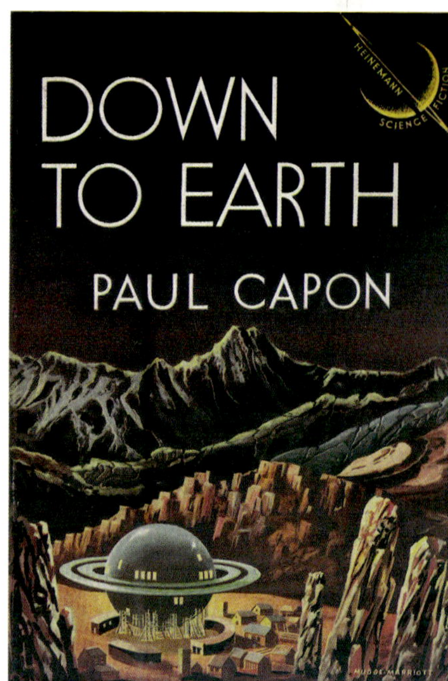

Paul Capon | *Down to Earth*
William Heinemann, 1954 | Art **Mudge-Marriott**

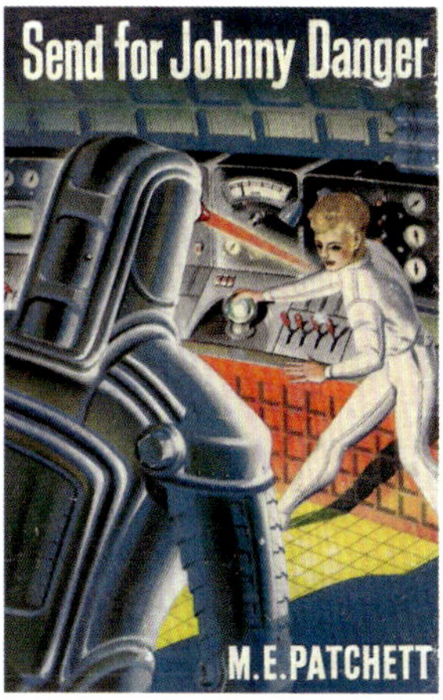

M. E. Patchett | *Send for Johnny Danger*
Lutterworth Press, 1956 | Art **Unknown**

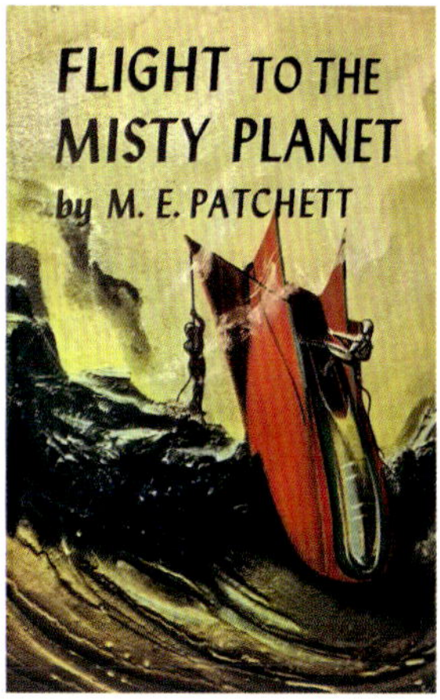

M. E. Patchett | *Flight to the Misty Planet*
Bobbs-Merrill Company, 1956 | Art **Unknown**

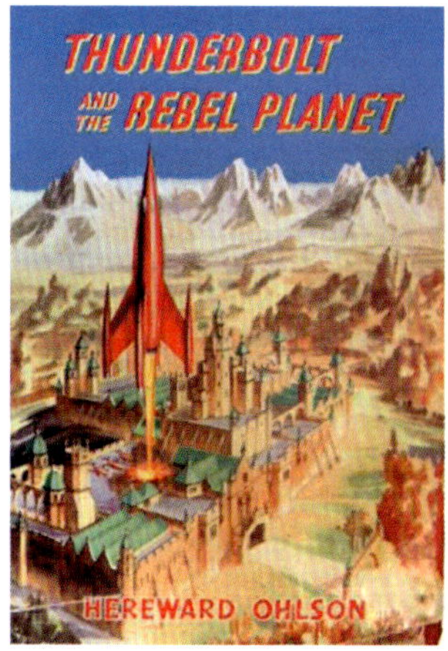

Hereward Ohlson | *Thunderbolt and the Rebel Planet*
Lutterworth Press, 1954 | Art **Unknown**

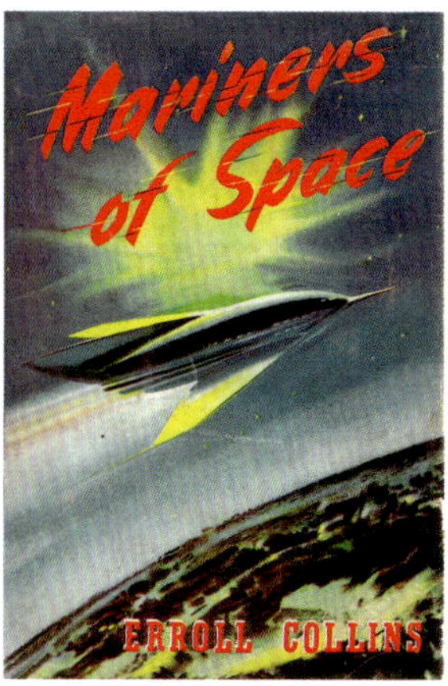

Erroll Collins | *Mariners of Space*
Lutterworth Press, 1949 | Art **Unknown**

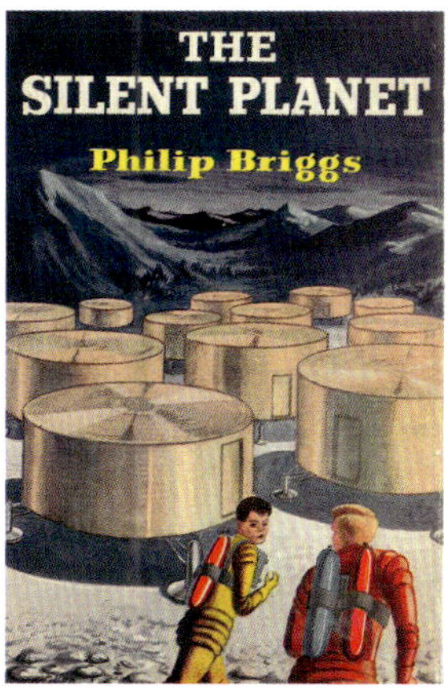

Philip Briggs | *The Silent Planet*
Lutterworth Press, 1957 | Art **Unknown**

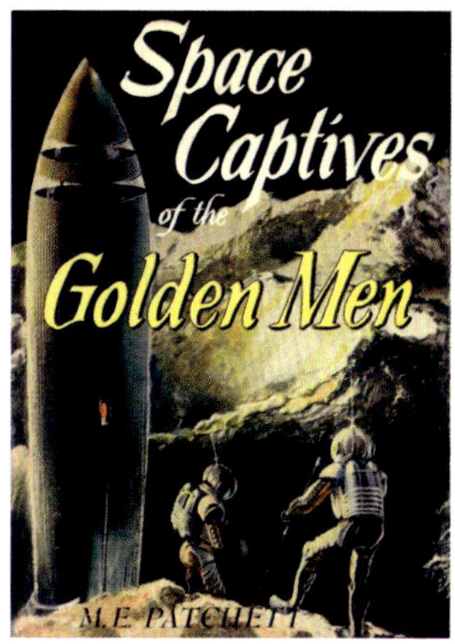

M. E. Patchett | *Space Captives of the Golden Men*
Bobbs-Merrill Company, 1955 | Art **Unknown**

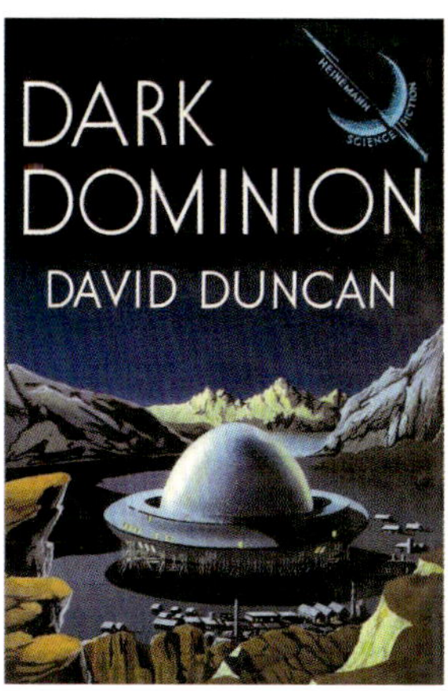

David Duncan | *Dark Dominion*
Heinemann, 1955 | Art **Mudge-Marriott**

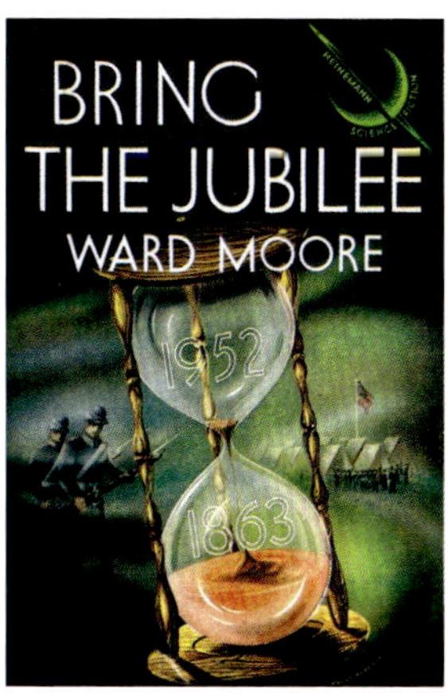

Ward Moore | *Bring the Jubilee*
Heinemann, 1955 | Art **Mudge-Marriott**

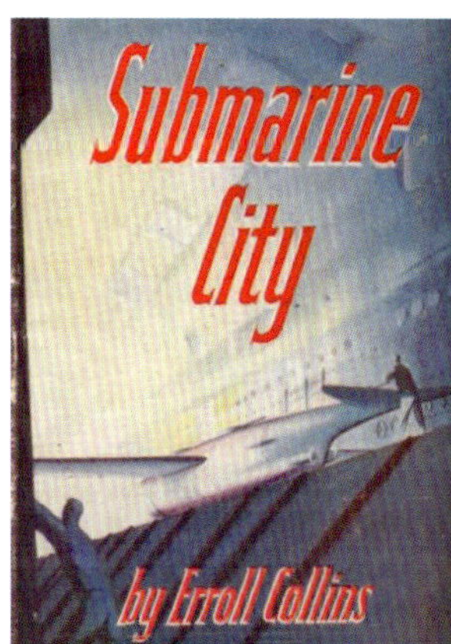

Erroll Collins | *Submarine City*
Lutterworth Press, 1946 | Art **Unknown**

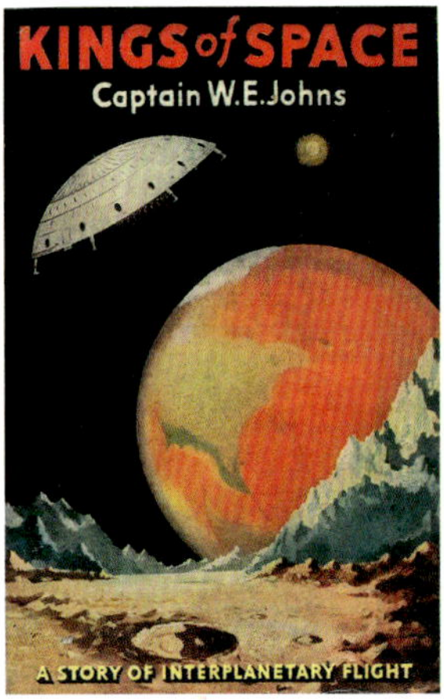

Captain W. E. Johns | *Kings of Space*
Hodder & Stoughton, 1954 | Art **Leslie Stead**

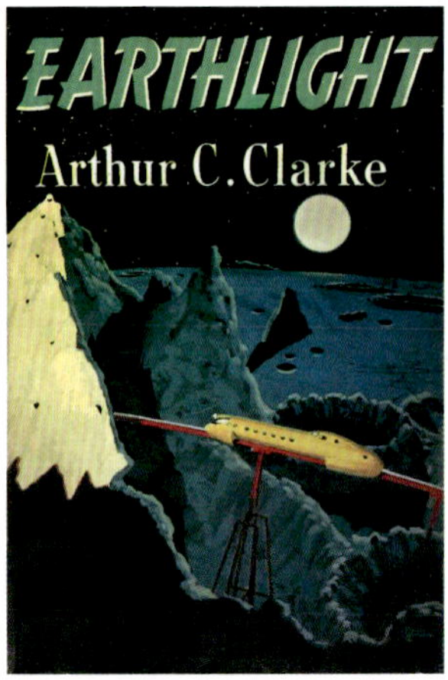

Arthur C. Clarke | *Earthlight*
Frederick Muller Ltd., 1955 | Art **Gerard Quinn**

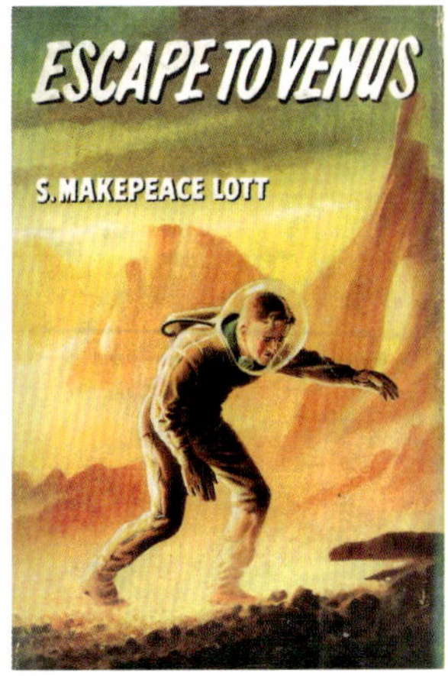

S. Makepeace Lott | *Escape to Venus*
Rich & Cowan, 1956 | Art **Ron Jobson**

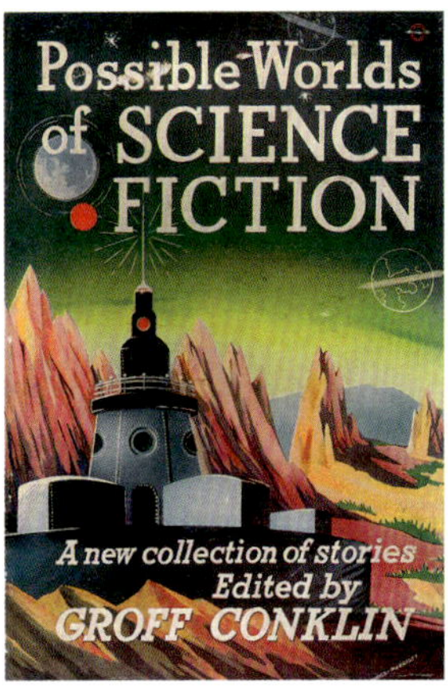

Groff Conklin | *Possible Worlds of Science Fiction*
Grayson & Grayson, 1952 | Art **Mudge-Marriott**

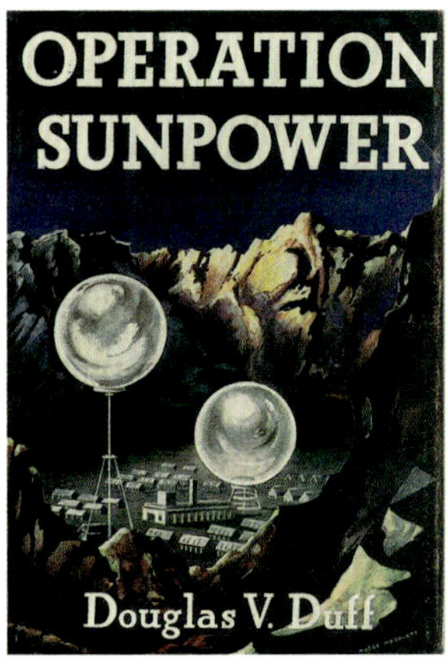

Douglas V. Duff | *Operation Sunpower*
Cassell, 1955 | Art **Mudge-Marriott**

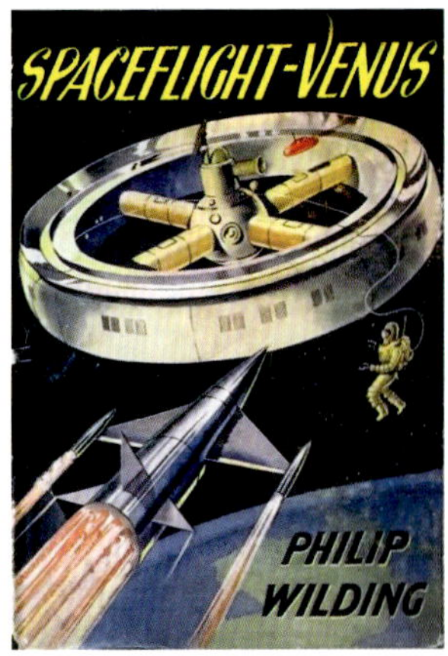

Philip Wilding | *Spaceflight Venus*
Hennel Locke, 1954 | Art **Unknown**

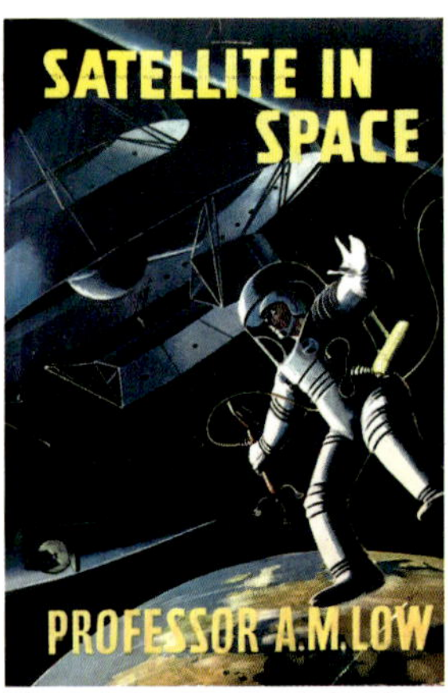

Professor A. M. Low | *Satellite in Space*
Herbert Jenkins, 1956 | Art **Ron Jobson**

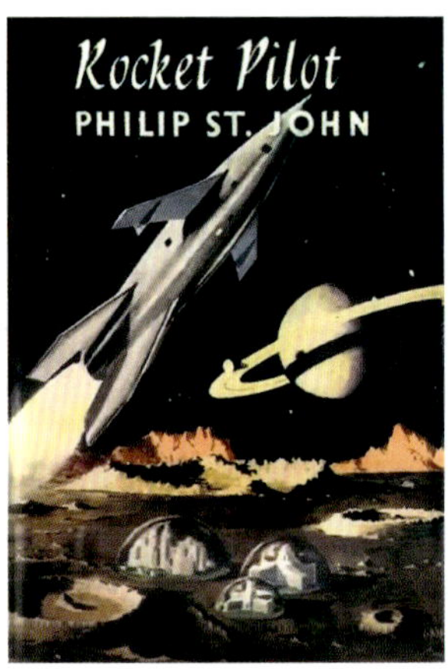

Philip St. John | *Rocket Pilot*
Hutchinson, 1955 | Art **C. King**

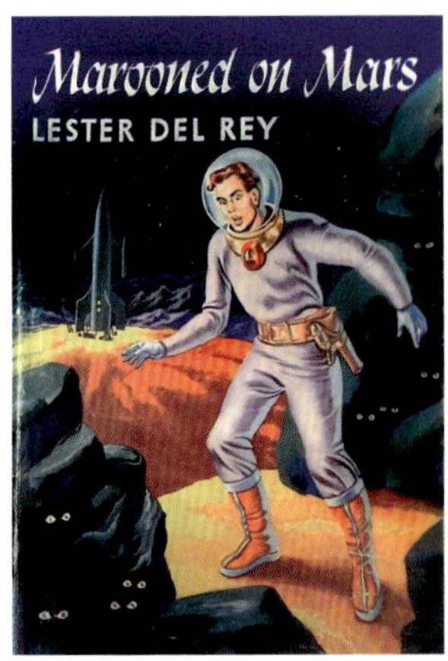

Lester Del Rey | *Marooned on Mars*
Hutchinson, 1954 | Art **Ron Embleton**

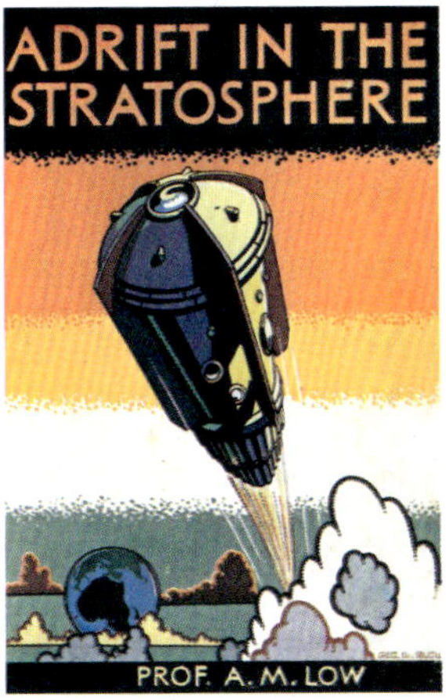

Prof. A. M. Low | *Adrift in the Stratosphere*
Blackie, date unknown | Art **Geo. W. Blow**

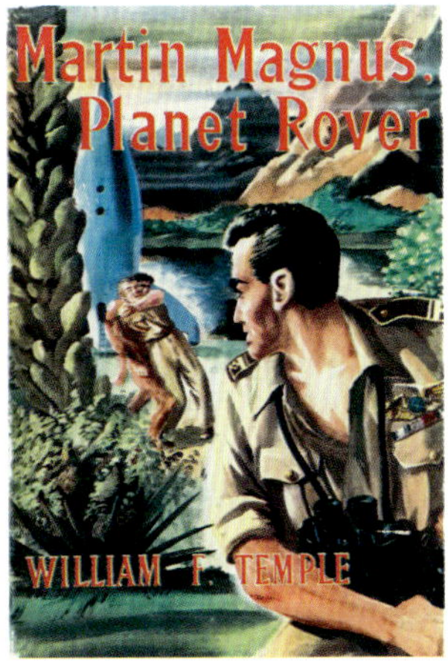

William F. Temple | *Martin Magnus, Planet Rover*
Frederick Muller, 1954 | Art **Unknown**

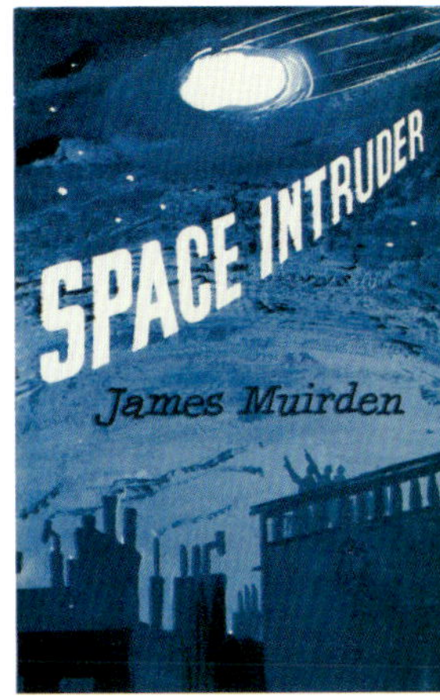

James Muirden | *Space Intruder*
Hamish Hamilton, 1965 | Art **Leslie Wood**

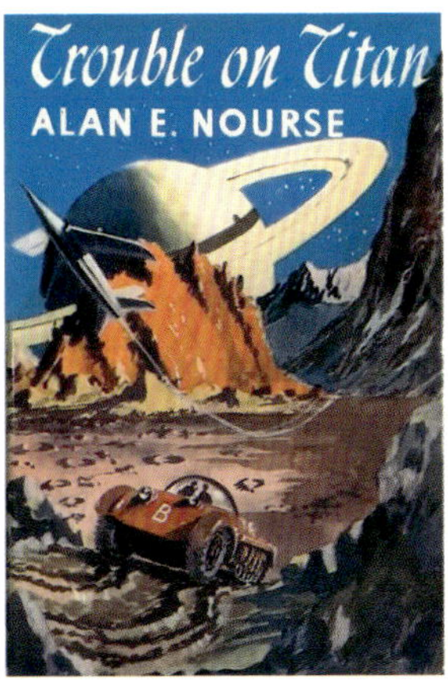

Alan E. Nourse | *Trouble on Titan*
Hutchinson, 1954 | Art **C. King**

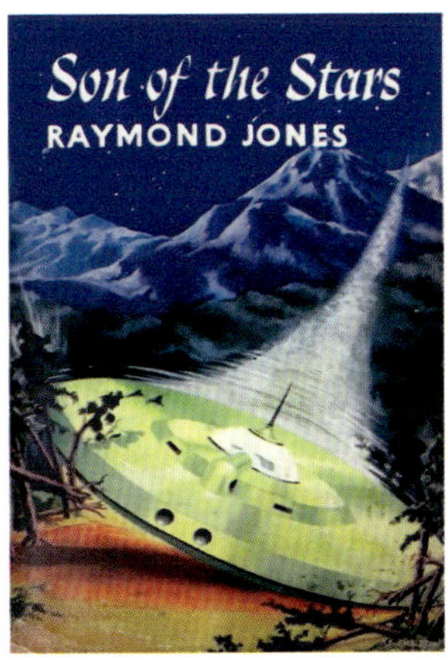

Raymond Jones | *Son of the Stars*
Hutchinson, 1954 | Art **Ron Embleton**

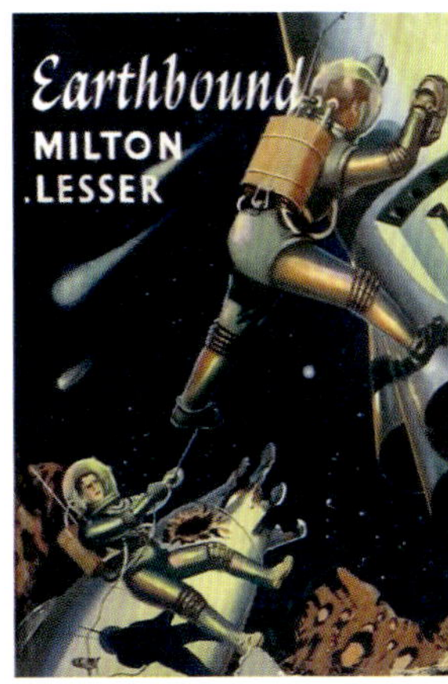

Milton Lesser | *Earthbound*
Hutchinson, 1954 | Art **C. King**

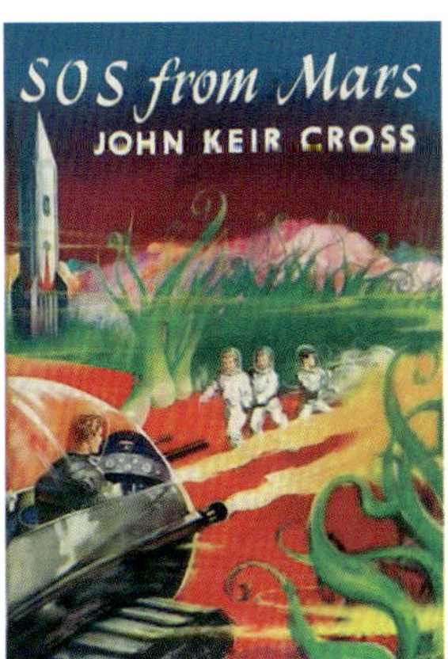

John Kier Cross | *SOS From Mars*
Hutchinson, 1954 | Art **C. King**

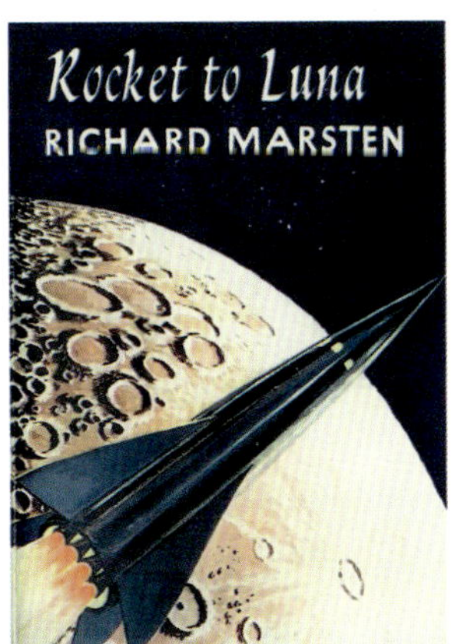

Richard Marsten | *Rocket to Luna*
Hutchinson, 1954 | Art **C. King**

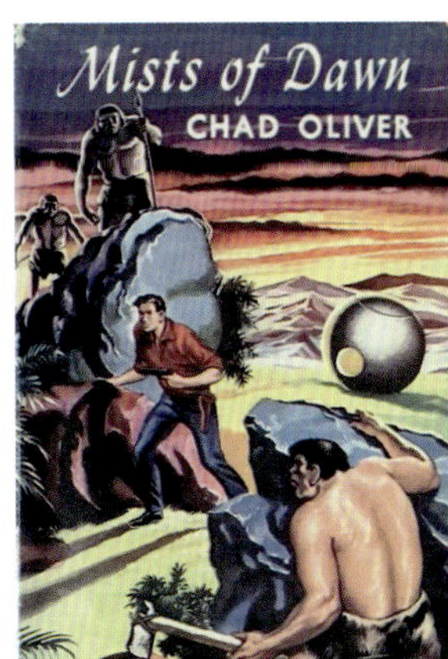

Chad Oliver | *Mists of Dawn*
Hutchinson, 1955 | Art **Ron Embleton**

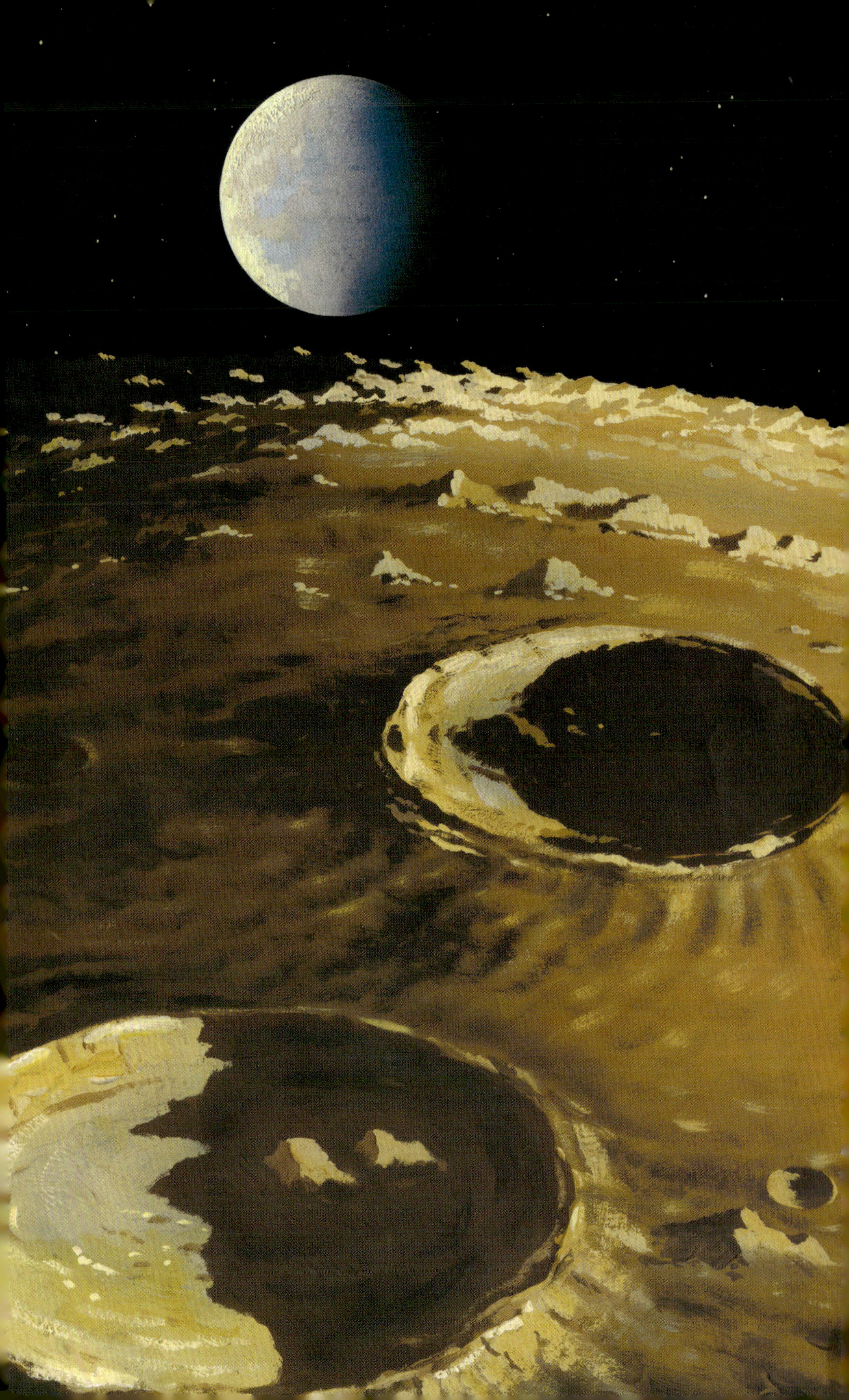

opposite **Captain W. E. Johns** | *Kings of Space*
Hodder & Stoughton, 1954 | Original interior art **Leslie Stead**

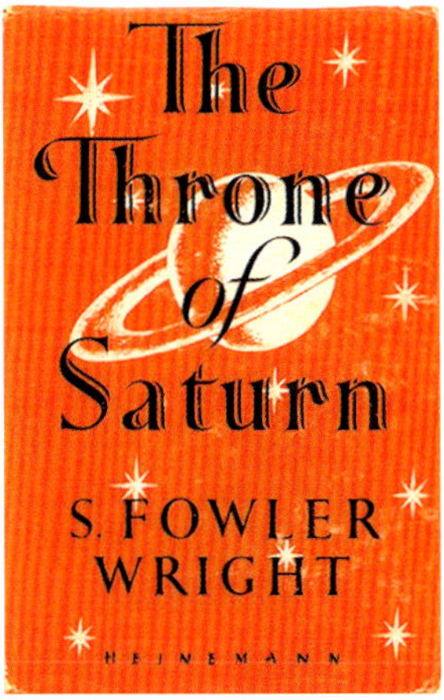

S. Fowler Wright | *The Throne of Saturn*
Heinemann, 1951 | Art **Unknown**

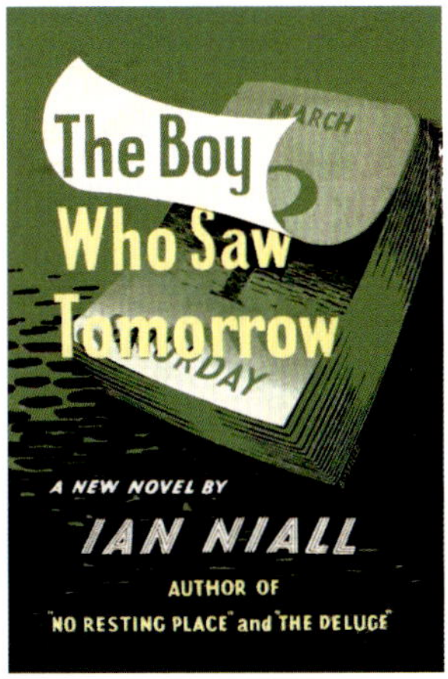

Ian Niall | *The Boy Who Saw Tomorrow*
Heinemann, 1952 | Art **Busfield**

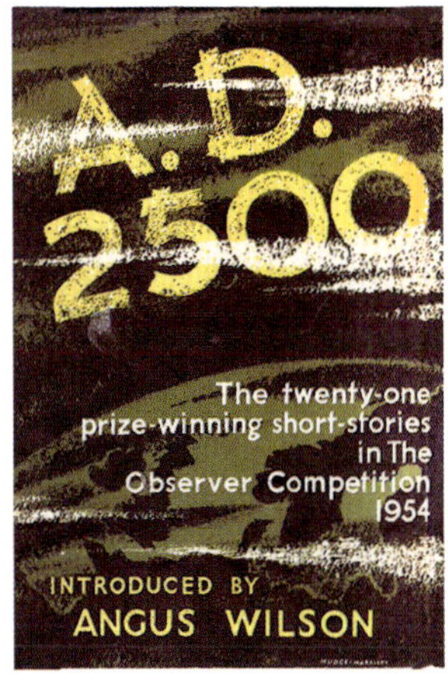

Angus Wilson | *A. D. 2500*
Heinemann,, 1955 | Art **Mudge-Marriott**

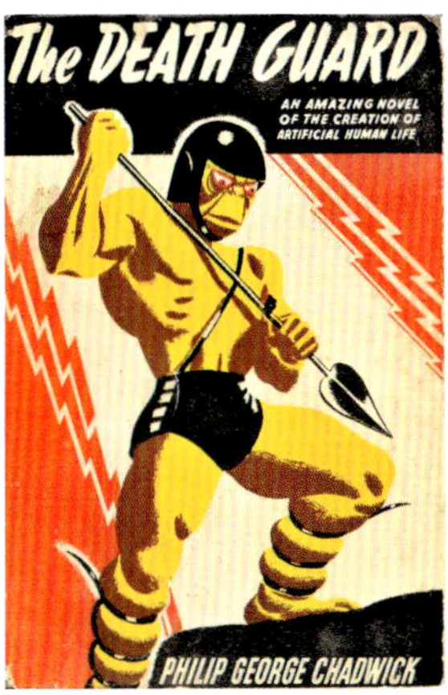

Philip George Chadwick | *The Death Guard*
Hutchinson, 1939 | Art **Unknown**

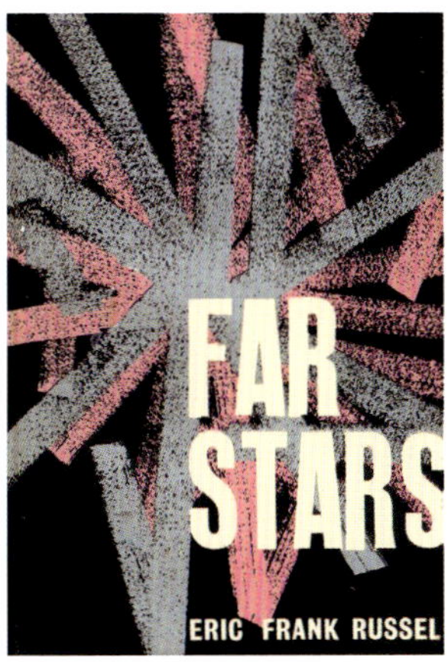

Eric Frank Russel | *Far Stars*
Dinnis Dobson, 1961 | Art **Unknown**

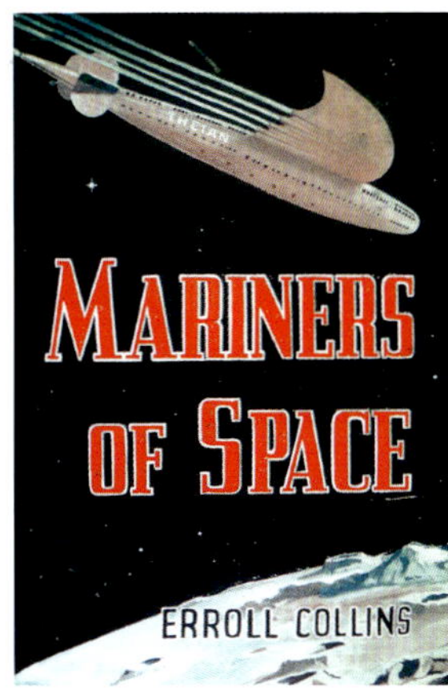

Erroll Collins | *Mariners of Space*
Lutterworth Press, 1944 | Art **Unknown**

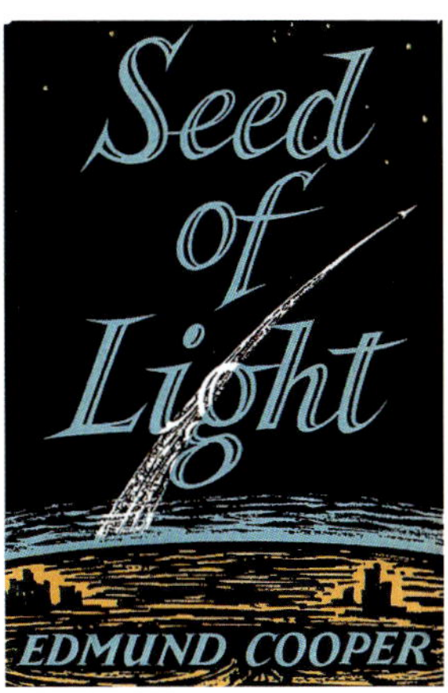

Edmund Cooper | *Seed of Light*
Hutchinson, 1959 | Art **Peter Curl**

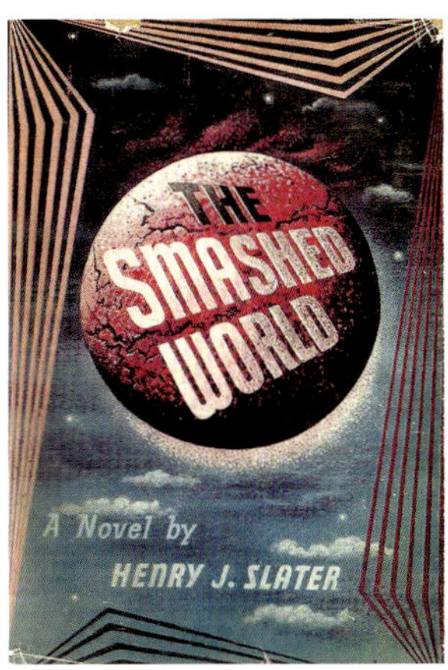

Henry J. Slater | *The Smashed World*
Jarrolds, 1952 | Art **Unknown**

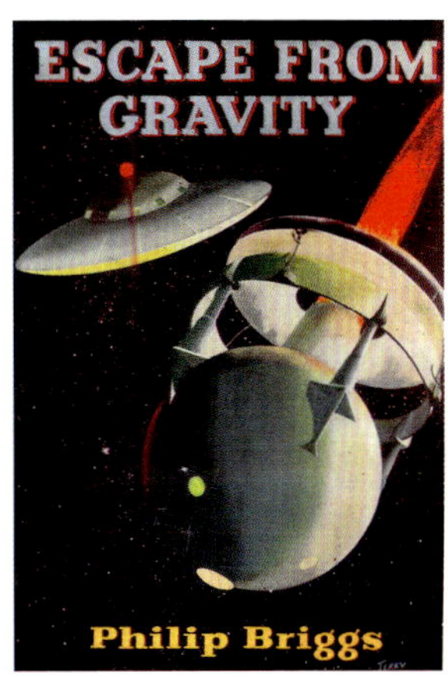

Philip Briggs | *Escape from Gravity*
Lutterworth Press, 1955 | Art **Unknown**

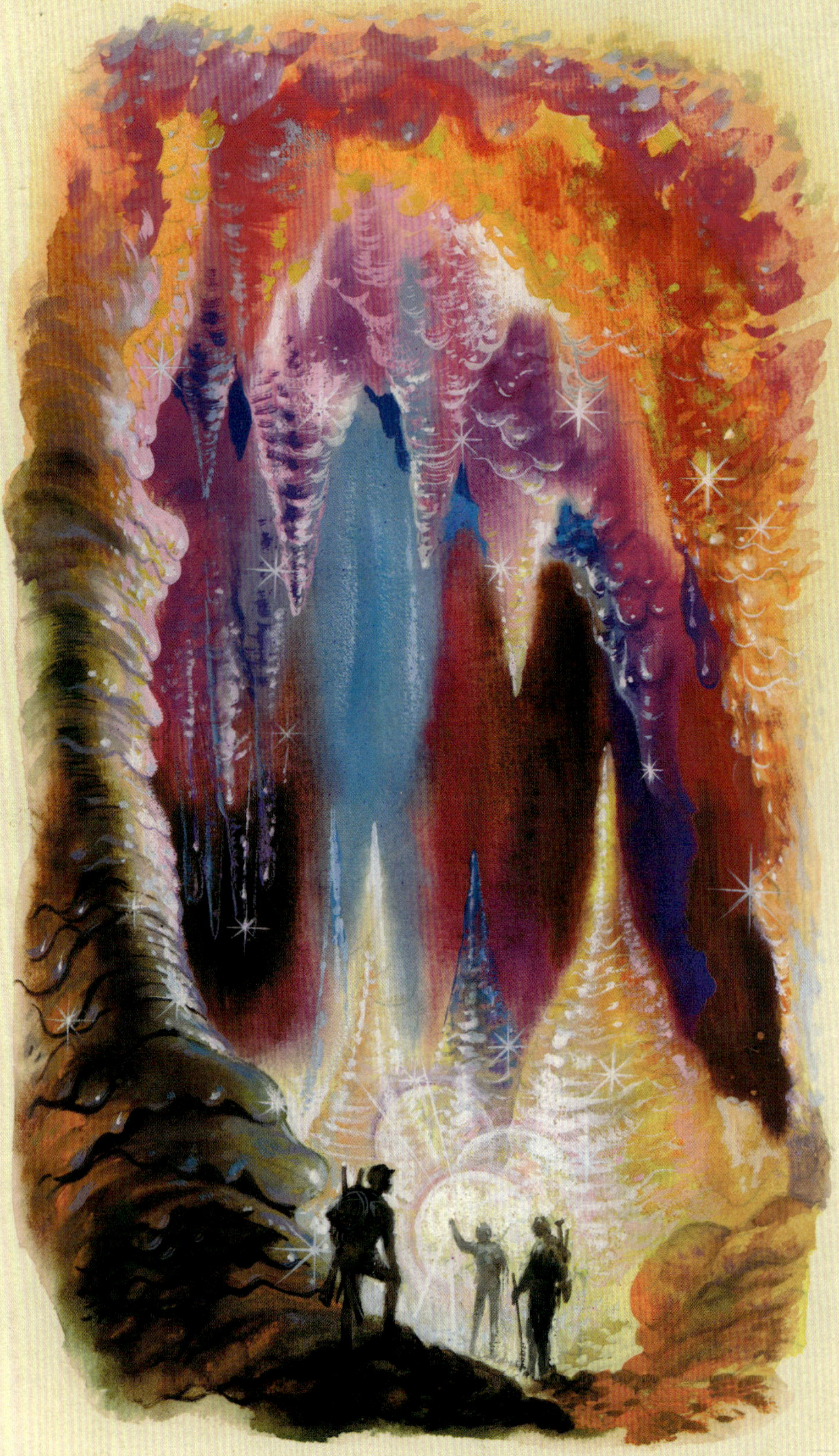

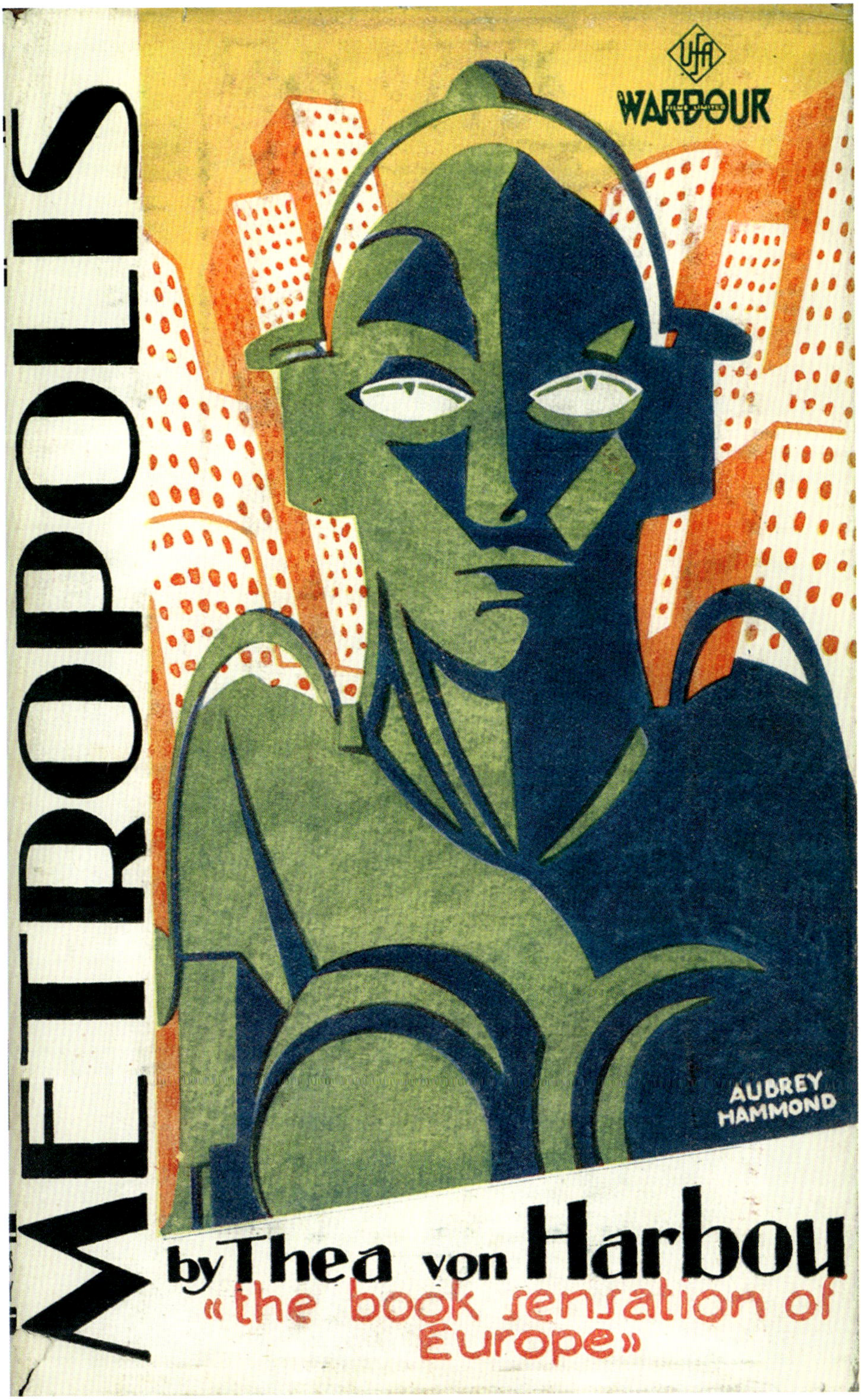

opposite **Jules Verne** | *Journey to the Centre of the Earth*
Dent, 1970 | Original art **William F. Phillipps**

Thea von Harbou | *Metropolis*
The Readers Library Publishing Company Ltd., 1927 | Art **Aubrey Hammond**

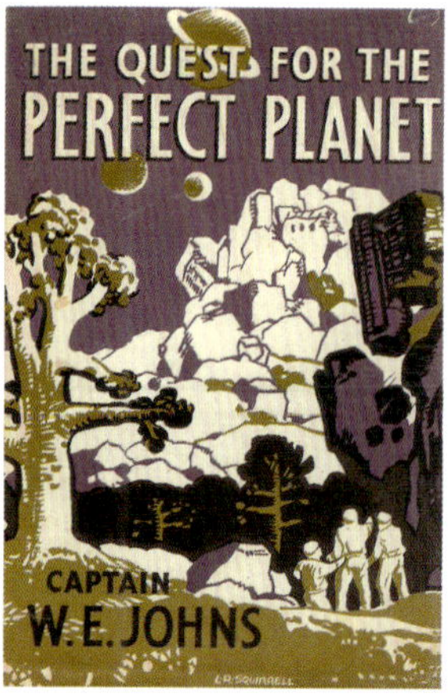

Captain W. E. Johns
The Quest for the Perfect Planet
Hodder & Stoughton, 1961 | Art **L. R. Squirrell**

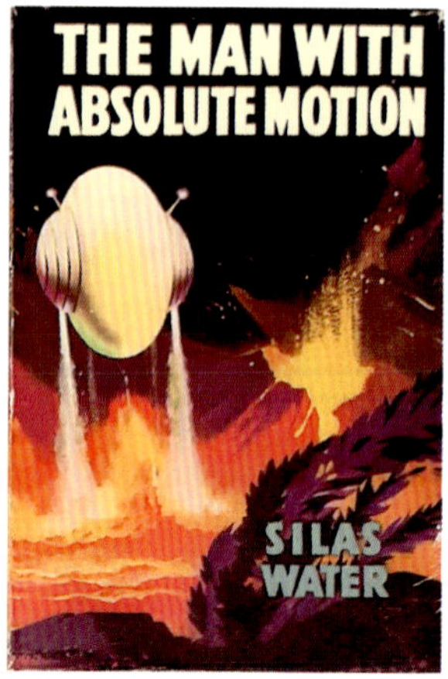

Silas Water | *The Man With Absolute Motion*
Rich and Cowan, 1955 | Art **Ron Turner**

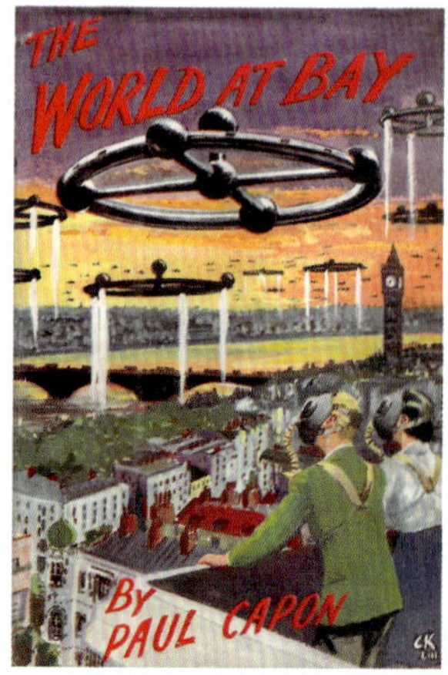

Paul Capon | *The World at Bay*
William Heinemann, 1953 | Art **C. King**

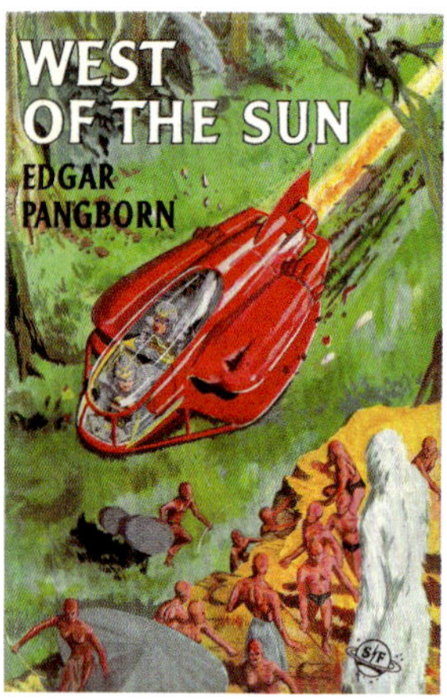

Edgar Pangborn | *West of the Sun*
Robert Hale, 1953 | Art **Unknown**

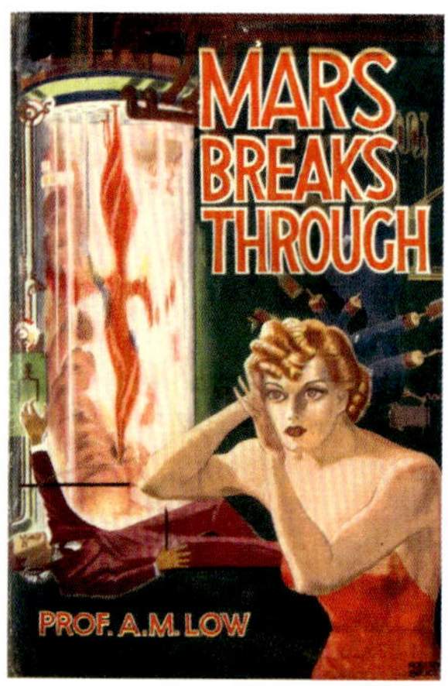

Prof. A. M. Low | *Mars Breaks Through*
Herbert Joseph, 1937 | Art **Robert Bruce**

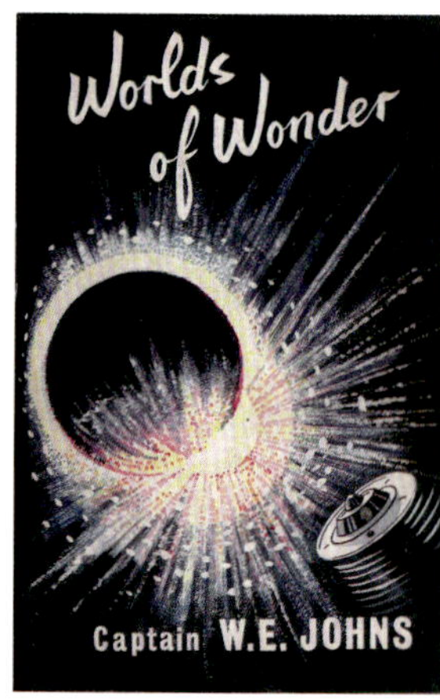

Captain W. E. Johns | *Worlds of Wonder*
Children's Book Club, 1962 | Art **R. W. W.**

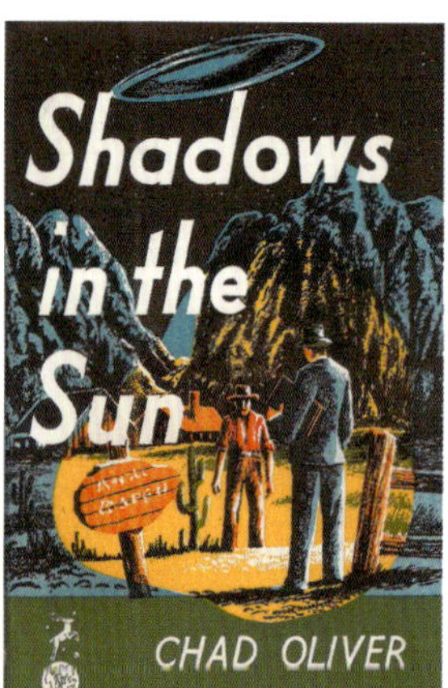

Chad Oliver | *Shadows in the Sun*
Max Reinhardt, 1955 | Art **Mudge-Marriott**

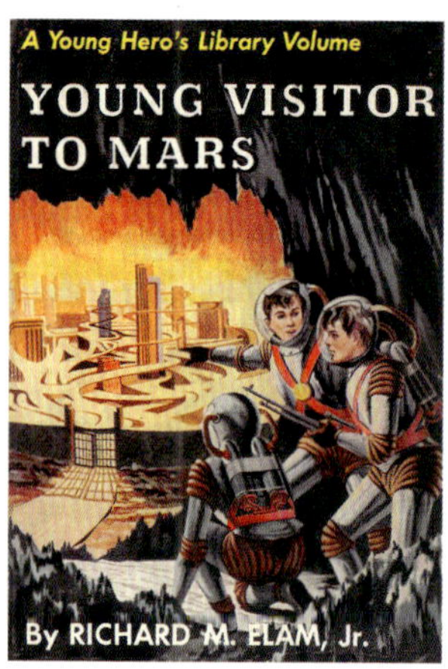

Richard M. Elam, Jr. | *Young Visitor to Mars*
Lantern Press, 1953 | Art **Charles Geer**

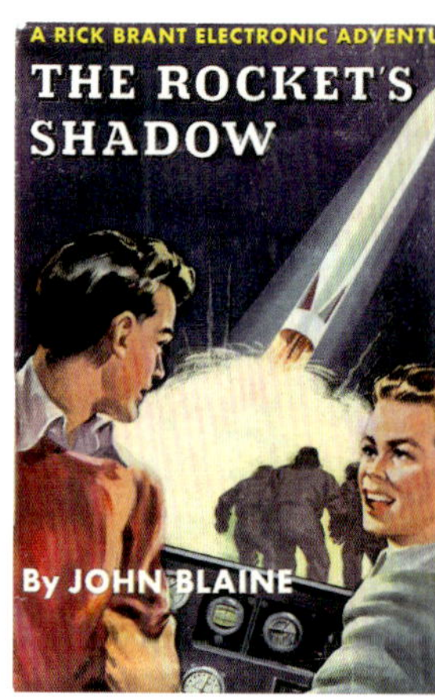

John Blaine | *The Rocket's Shadow*
Grosset & Dunlap, 1947 | Art **Unknown**

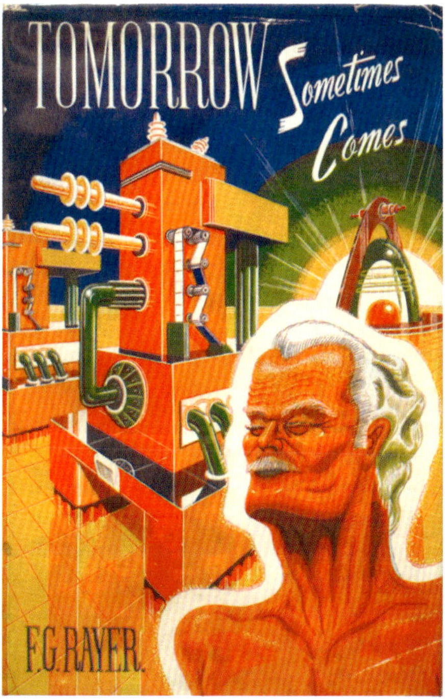

F. G. Rayer | *Tomorrow Sometimes Comes*
Home & Van Thal, 1951 | Art **Bob Clothier**

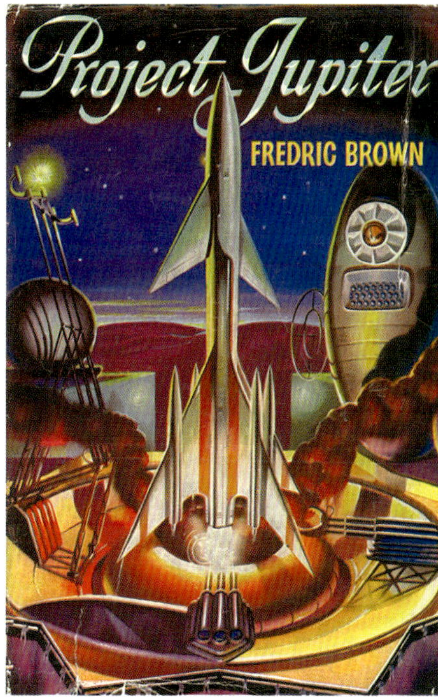

Fredric Brown | *Project Jupiter*
T. V. Boardman, 1954 | Art **Ron Turner**

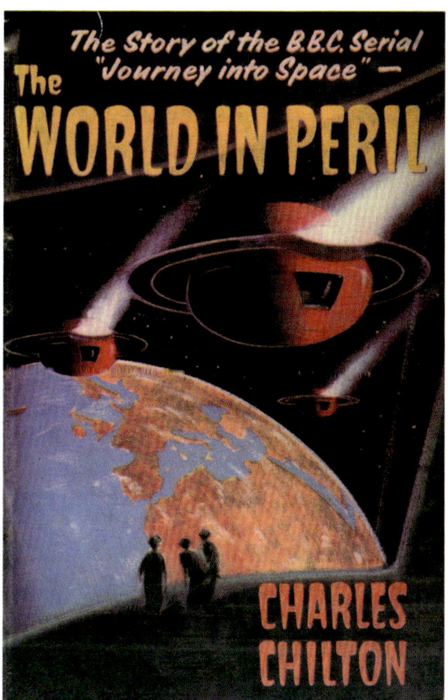

Charles Chilton | *The World in Peril*
Herbert Jenkins, 1960 | Art **J. W. Jobson**

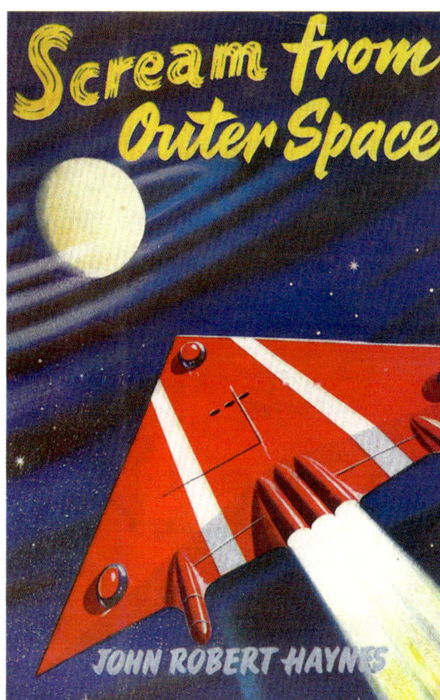

John Robert Haynes | *Scream from Outer Space*
Rich & Cowan, 1955 | Art **Ron Jobson**

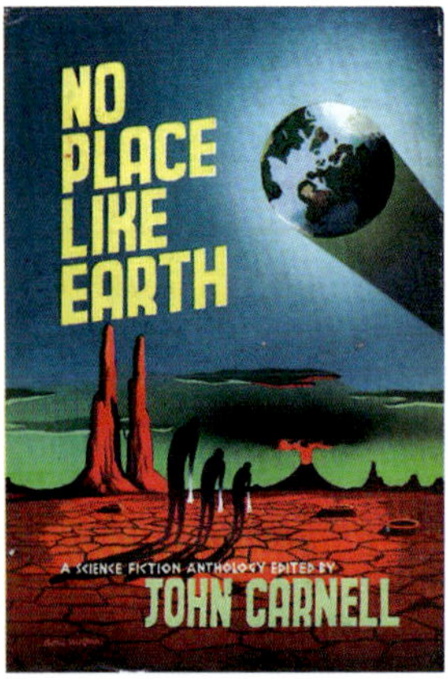

John Carnell | *No Place Like Earth*
T. V. Boardman, 1952 | Art **Denis McLoughlin**

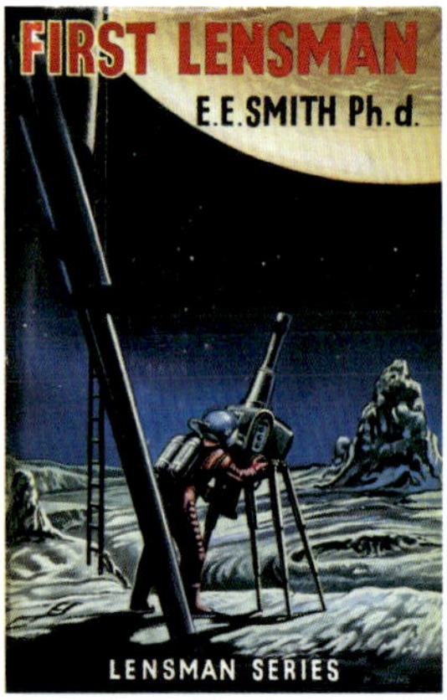

Edward E. Smith, Ph.D. | *First Lensman*
T. V. Boardman, 1955 | Art **Harold Johns**

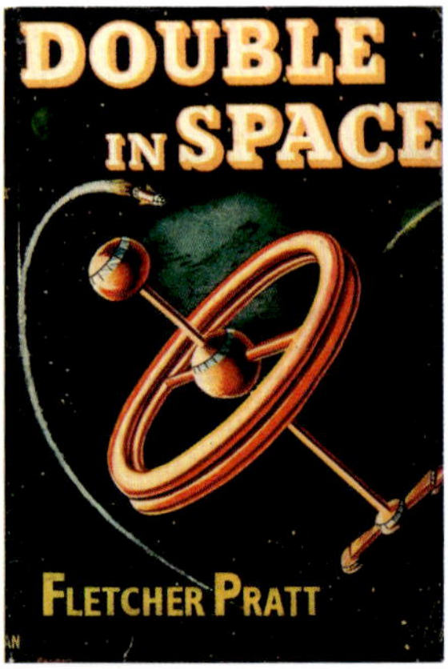

Fletcher Pratt | *Double in Space*
T. V. Boardman, 1954 | Art **E. J. Pagram**

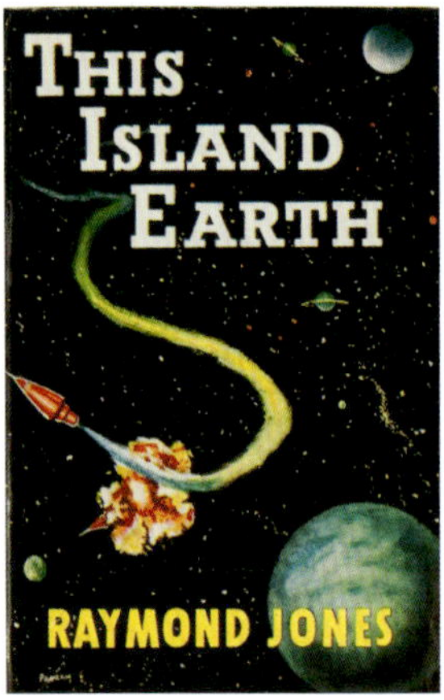

Raymond F. Jones | *This Island Earth*
T. V. Boardman, 1955 | Art **E. J. Pagram**

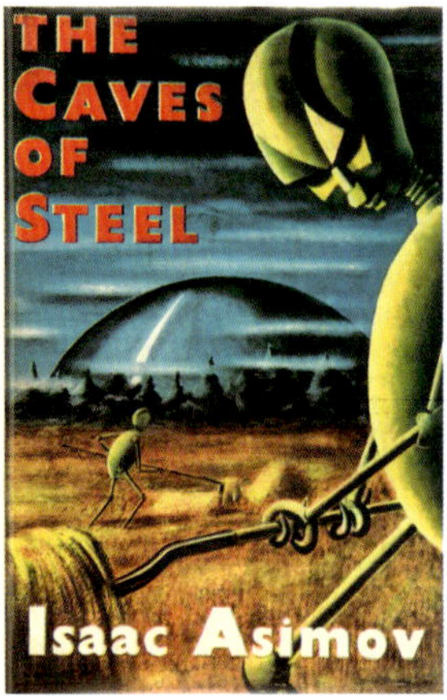

Isaac Asimov | *The Caves of Steel*
T. V. Boardman, 1954 | Art **E. J. Pagram**

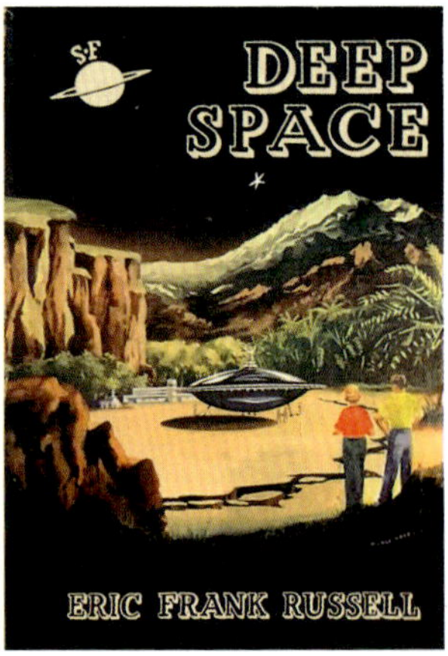

Eric Frank Russell | *Deep Space*
Eyre and Spottiswoode, 1956 | Art **Mudge-Marriott**

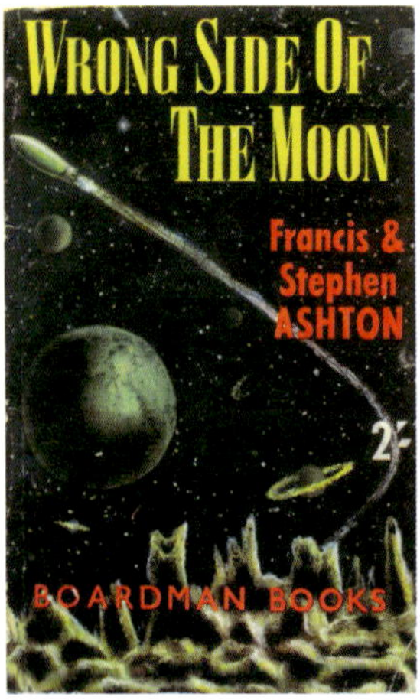

Francis & Stephen Ashton
Wrong Side of the Moon
T. V. Boardman 159, 1955 | Art **E. J. Pagram**

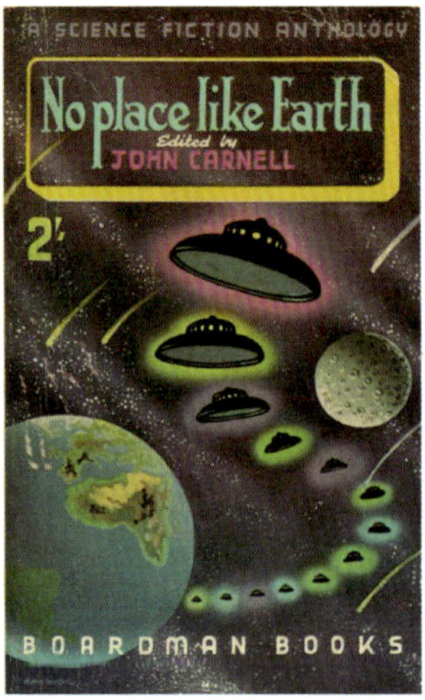

John Carnell | *No Place Like Earth*
T. V. Boardman, 1954 | Art **Denis McLoughlin**

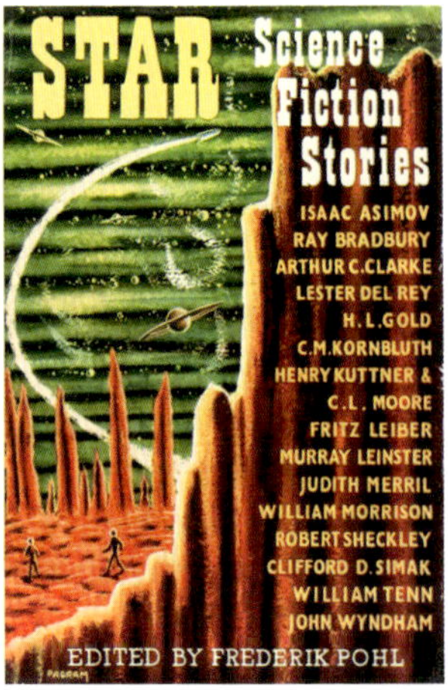

Frederik Pohl | *Star Science Fiction Stories*
T. V. Boardman, 1954 | Art **E. J. Pagram**

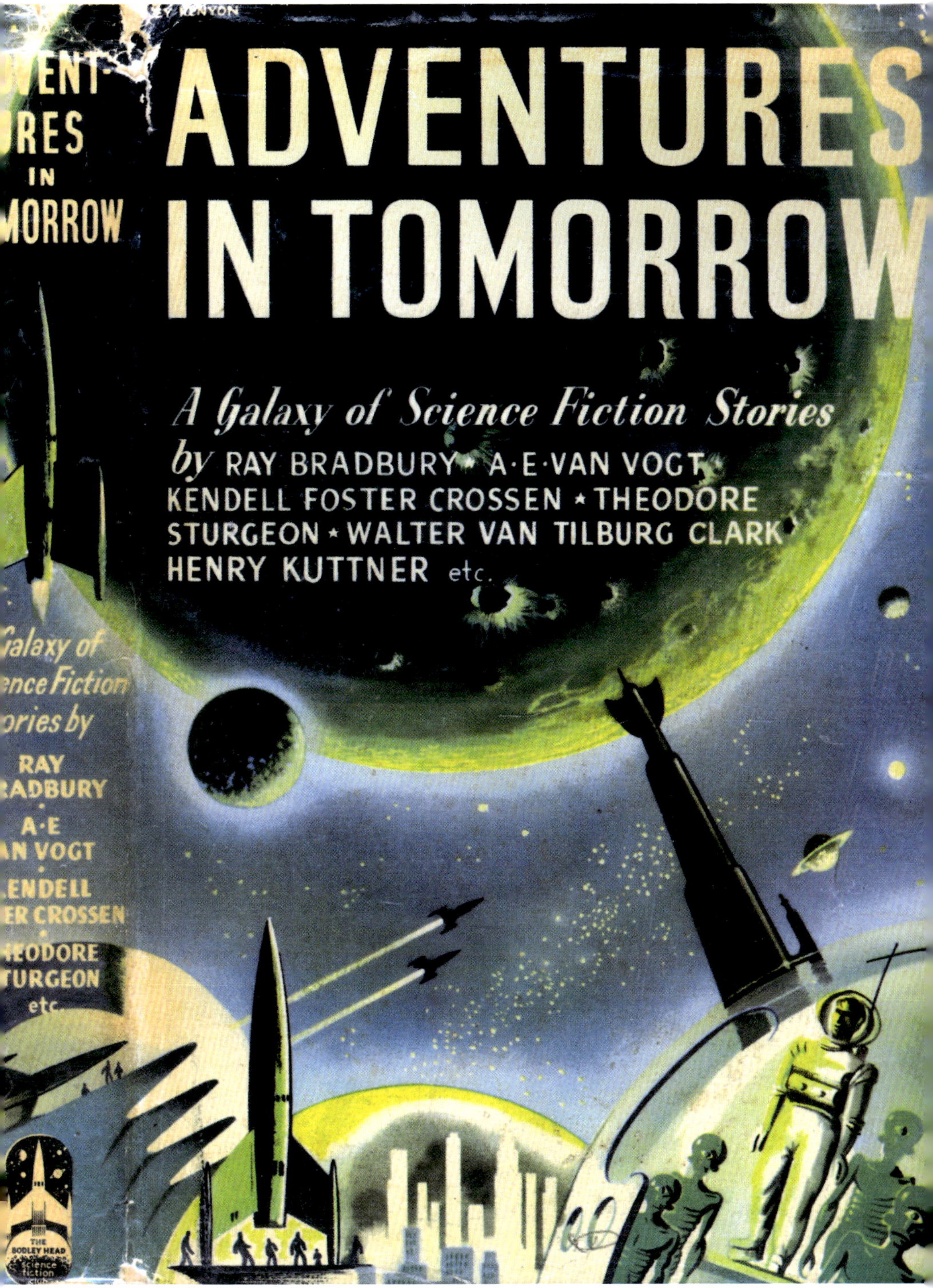

Kendell F. Crossen, ed. | *Adventures in Tomorrow*
The Bodley Head, 1953 | Art **Ley Kenyon**

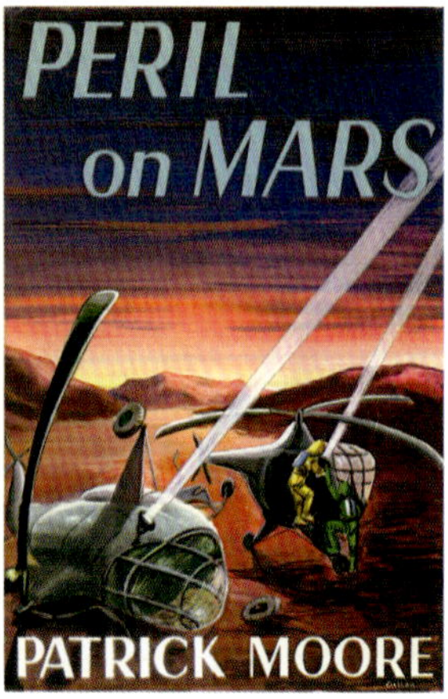

Patrick Moore | *Peril on Mars*
Burke, 1958 | Art **Patricia Cullen**

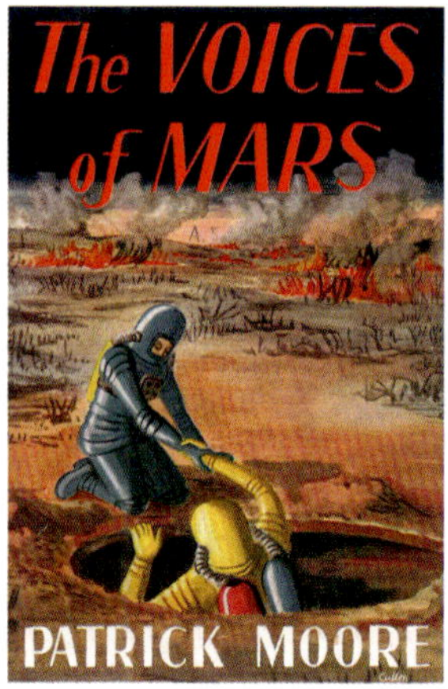

Patrick Moore | *The Voices of Mars*
Burke, 1957 | Art **Patricia Cullen**

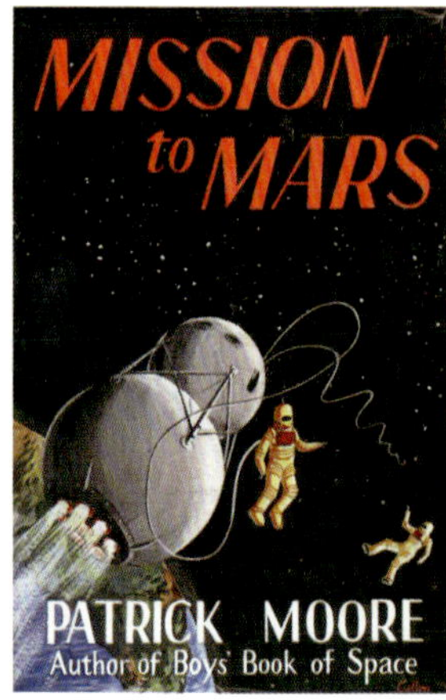

Patrick Moore | *Mission to Mars*
Burke, 1955 | Art **Patricia Cullen**

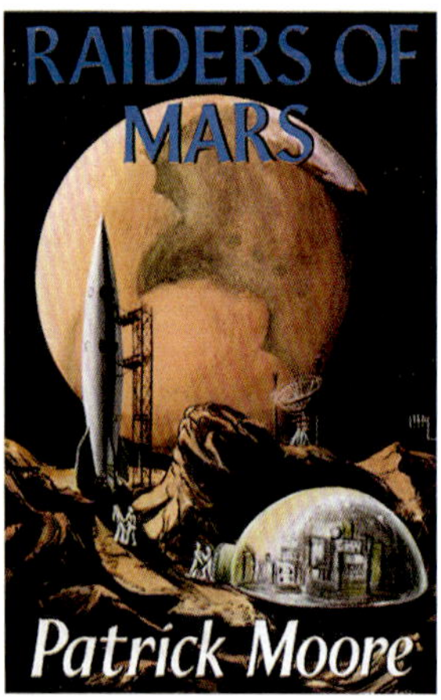

Patrick Moore | *Raiders of Mars*
Burke, 1959 | Art **Patricia Cullen**

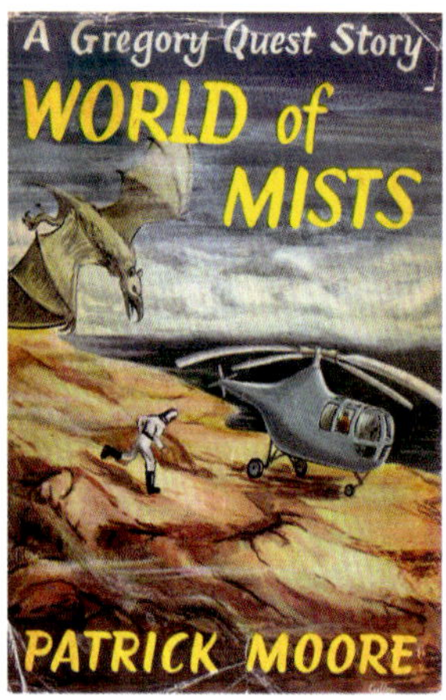

Patrick Moore | *World of Mists*
Frederick Muller Ltd., 1956 | Art **Patricia Cullen**

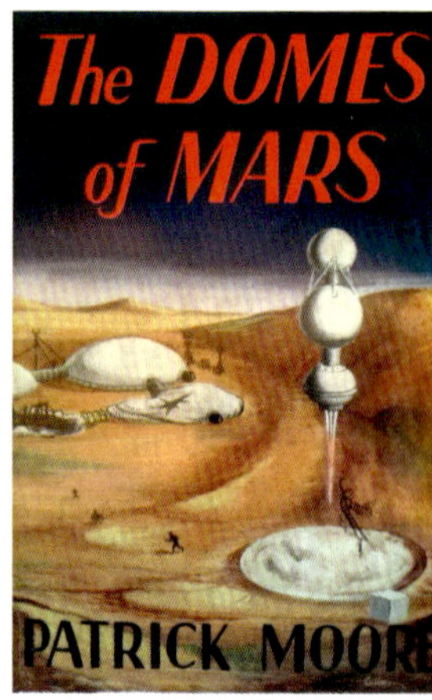

Patrick Moore | *The Domes of Mars*
Burke, 1956 | Art **Patricia Cullen**

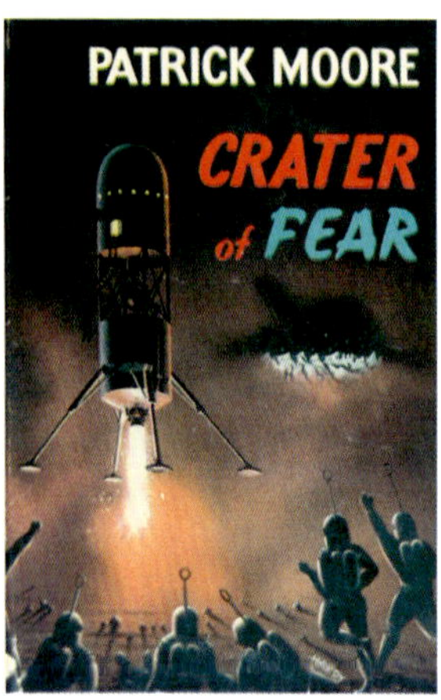

Patrick Moore | *Crater of Fear*
Burke, 1900 | Art **David A. Hardy**

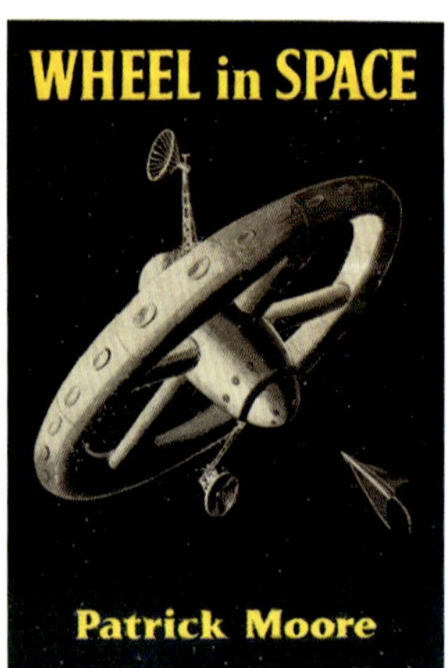

Patrick Moore | *Wheel in Space*
Lutterworth Press, 1956 | Art **Patricia Cullen**

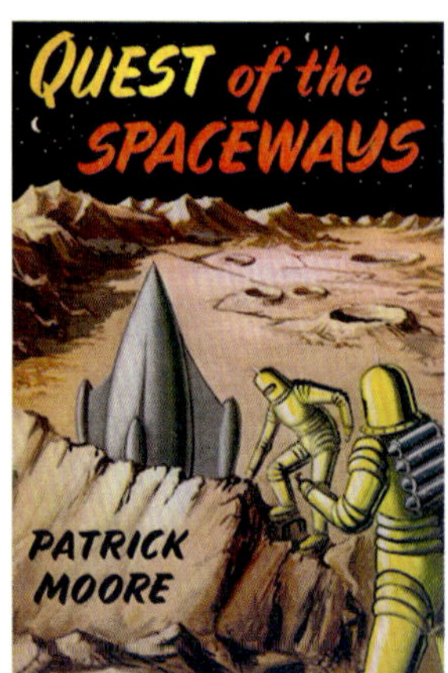

Patrick Moore | *Quest of the Spaceways*
Frederick Muller Ltd., 1955 | Art **Patricia Cullen**

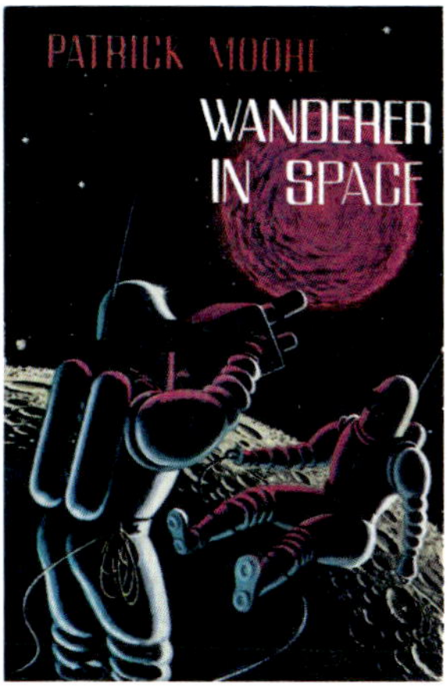

Patrick Moore | *Wanderer in Space*
Burke, 1961 | Art **David A. Hardy**

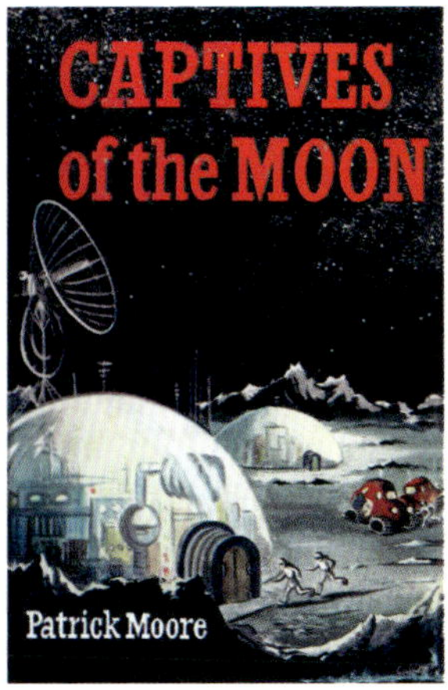

Patrick Moore | *Captives of the Moon*
Burke, 1960 | Art **Patricia Cullen**

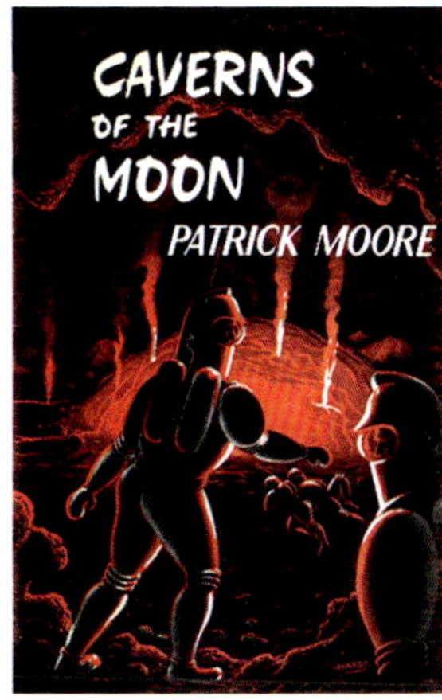

Patrick Moore | *Caverns of the Moon*
Burke, 1964 | Art **David A. Hardy**

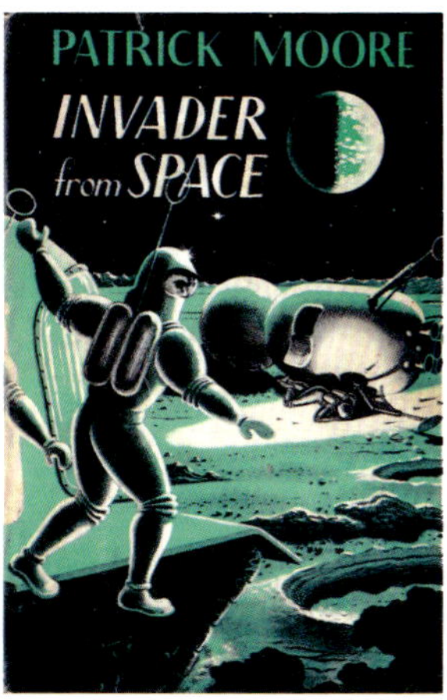

Patrick Moore | *Invader from Space*
Burke, 1963 | Art **David A. Hardy**

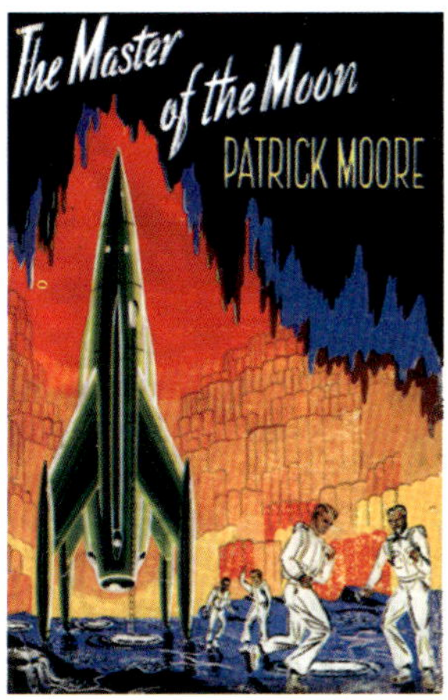

Patrick Moore | *The Master of the Moon*
Museum Press, 1952 | Art **Unknown**

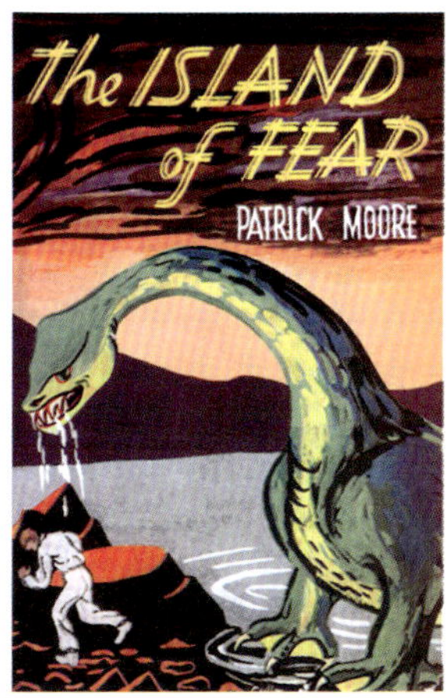

Patrick Moore | *The Island of Fear*
Museum Press, 1954 | Art **Unknown**

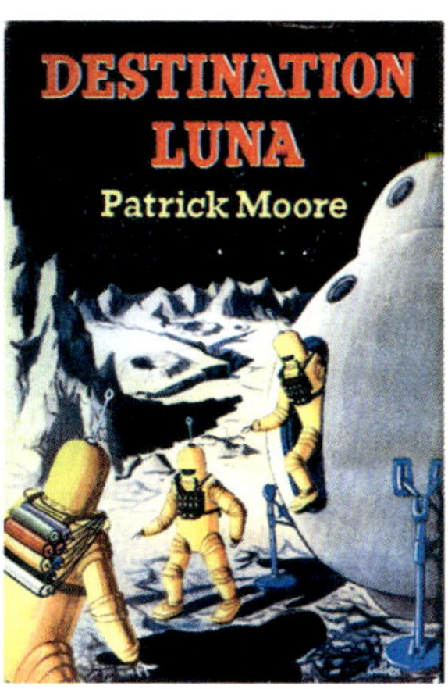

Patrick Moore | *Destination Luna*
Lutterworth Press, 1955 | Art **Patricia Cullen**

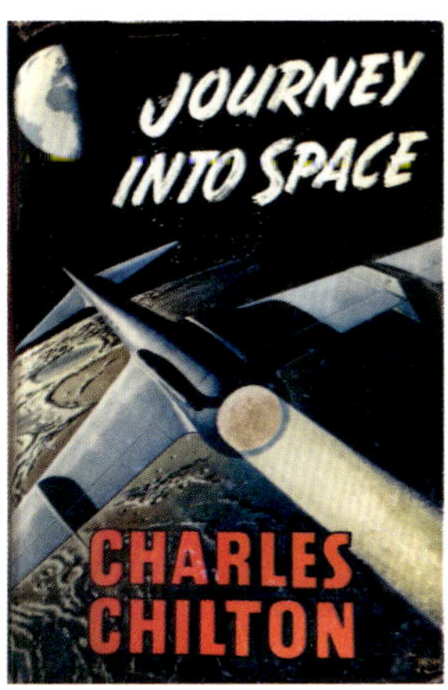

Charles Chilton | *Journey Into Space*
Herbert Jenkins, 1954 | Art **J. W. Jobson**

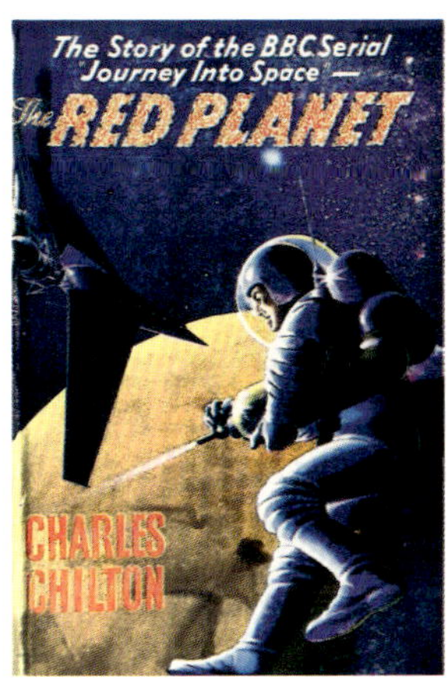

Charles Chilton | *The Red Planet*
Herbert Jenkins, 1956 | Art **J. W. Jobson**

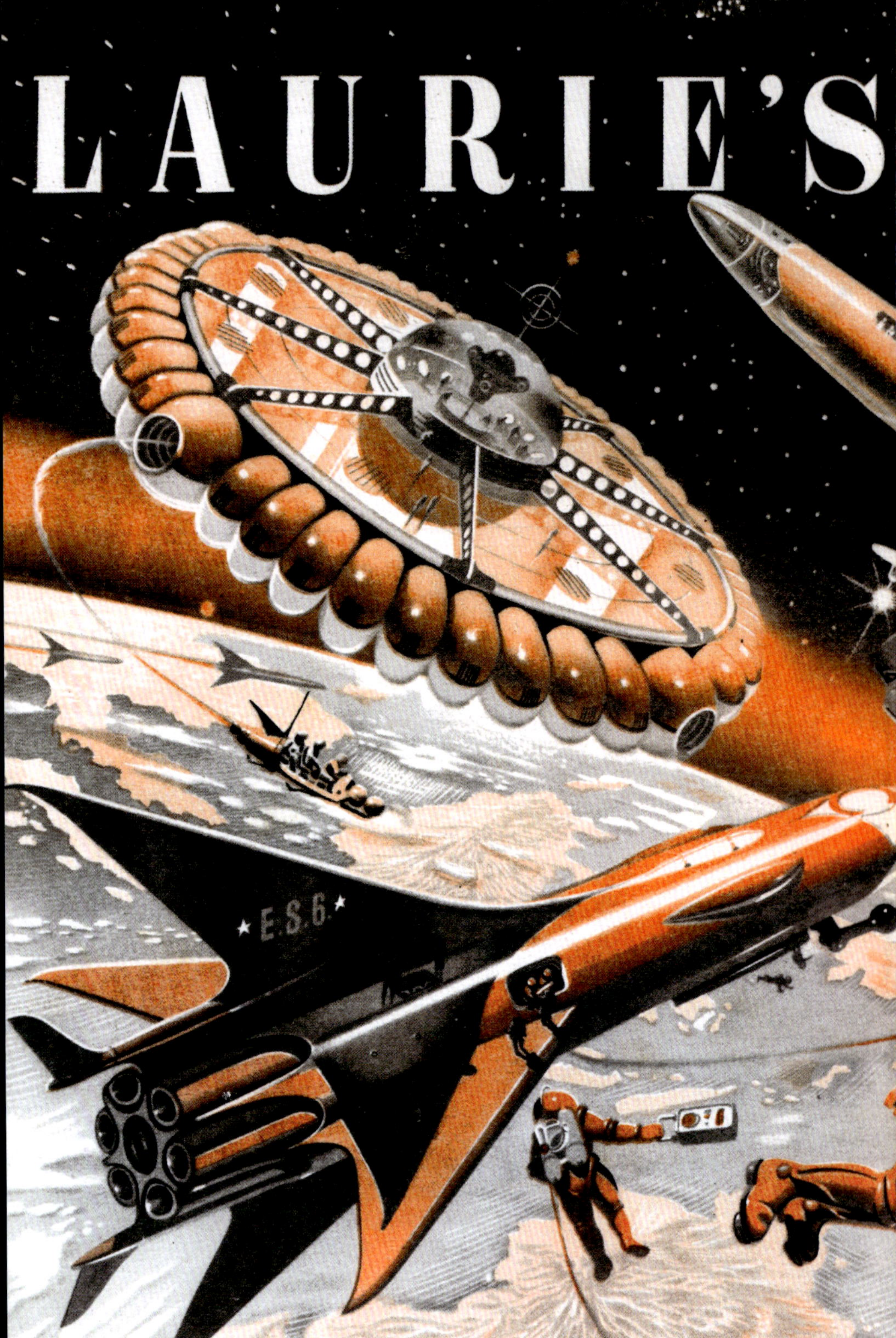

Laurie's Space Annual
T. Werner Laurie Ltd., 1953 | Art **Ron Turner**

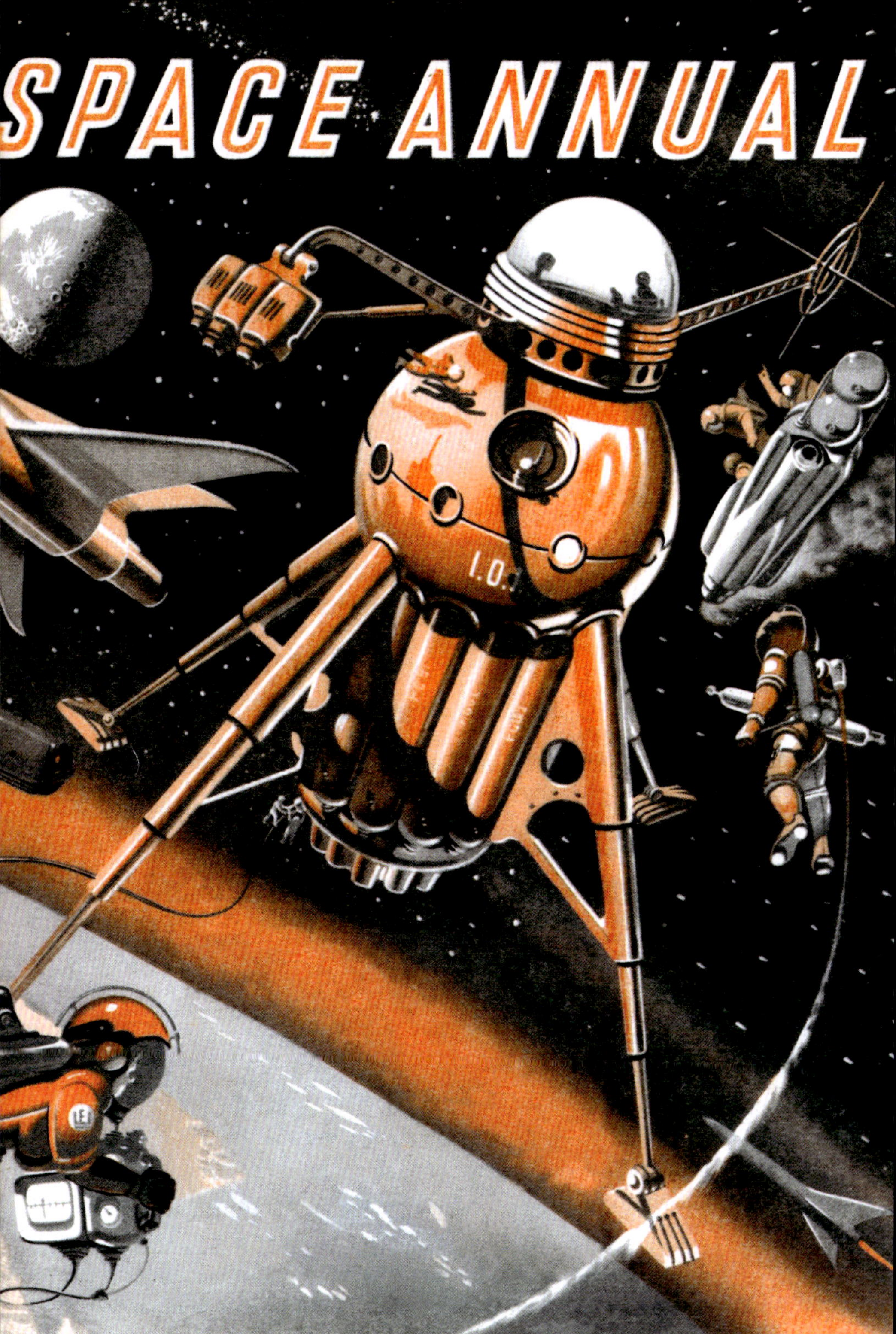
SPACE ANNUAL

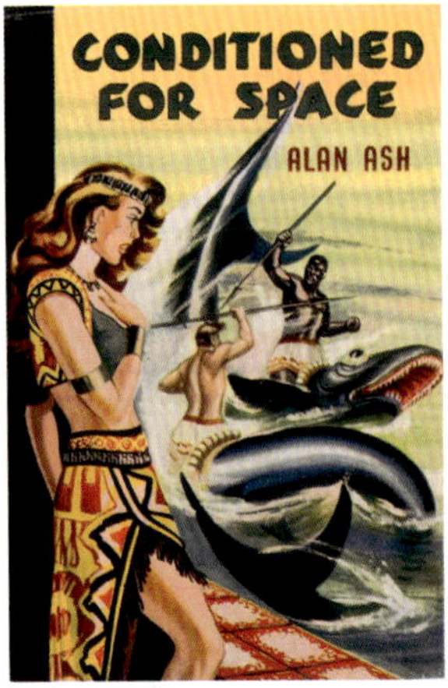

Alan Ash | *Conditioned for Space*
Ward, Lock, 1955 | Art **Ron Embleton**

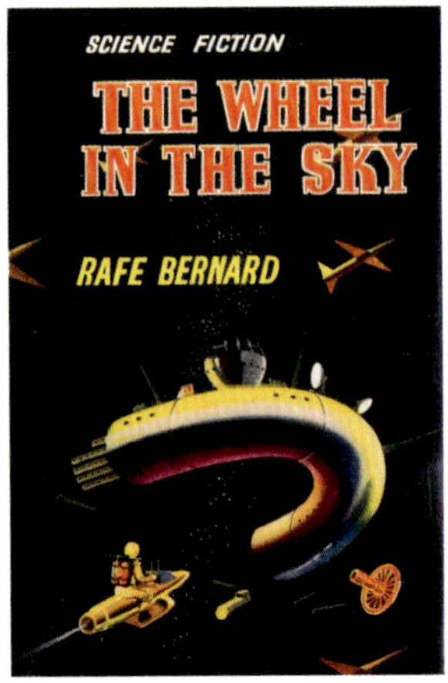

Rafe Bernard | *The Wheel in the Sky*
Ward, Lock, 1954 | Art **Harold Johns**

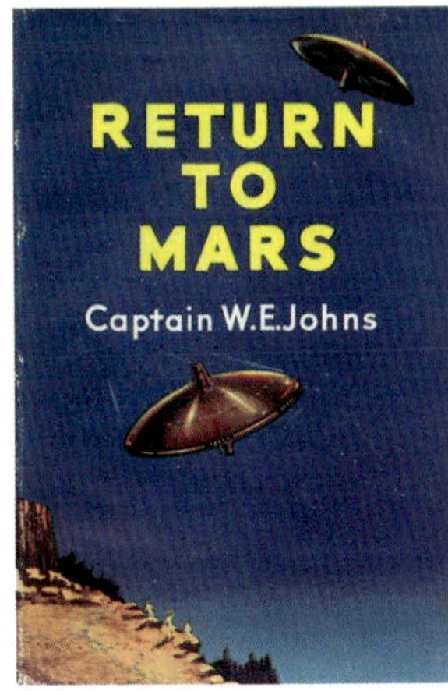

Captain W. E. Johns | *Return to Mars*
Hodder & Stoughton, 1955 | Art **Leslie Stead**

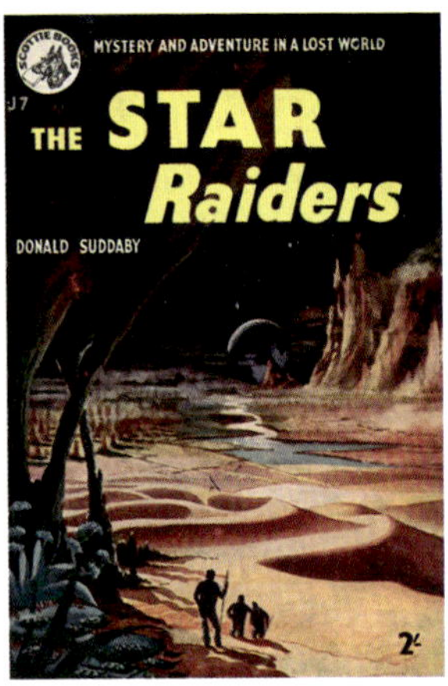

Donald Suddaby | *The Star Raiders*
Scottie Books, 1955 | Art **John Richards**

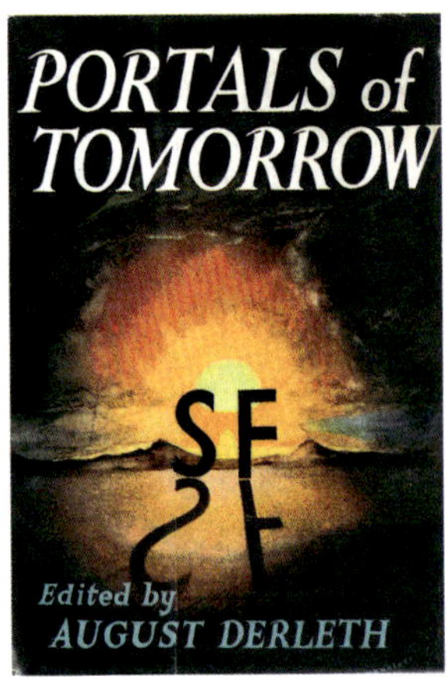

August Derleth | *Portals of Tomorrow*
Cassell & Company, 1956 | Art **Mudge-Marriott**

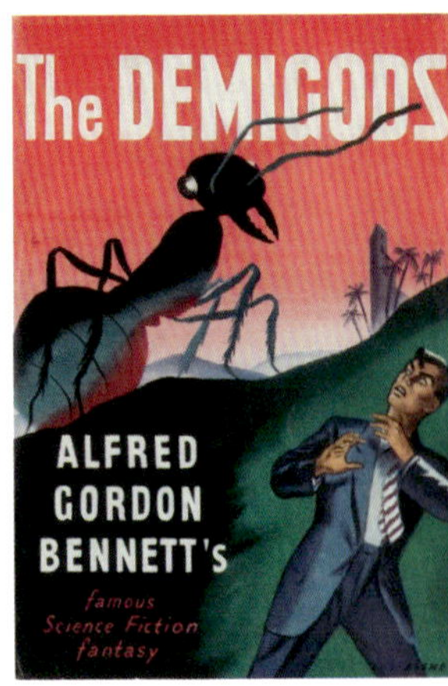

Alfred Gordon Benett | *The Demigods*
Rich and Cowan, 1955 | Art **Eisner**

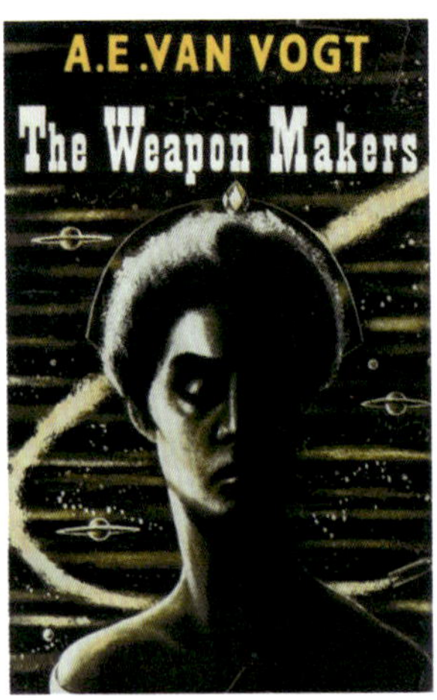

A. E. van Vogt | *The Weapon Makers*
Weidenfeld & Nicolson, 1954 | Art **E. J. Pagram**

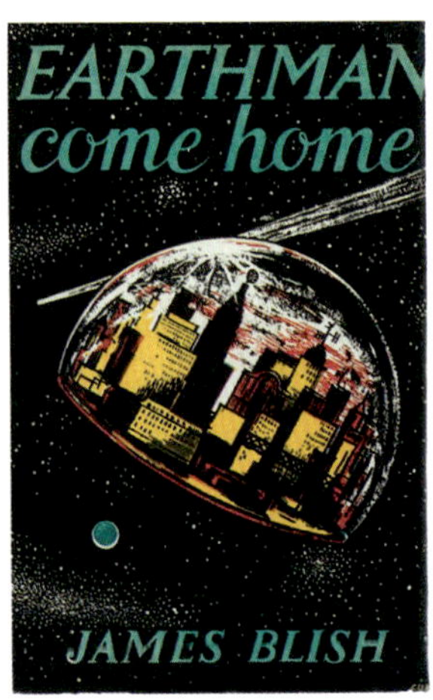

James Blish | *Earthman, Come Home*
Faber and Faber, 1956 | Art **Peter Curl**

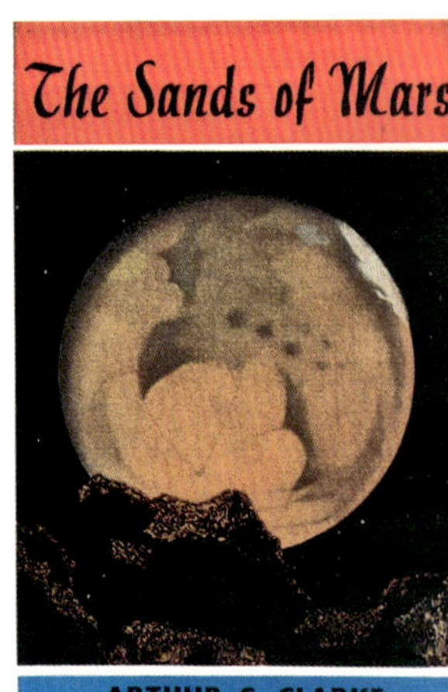

Arthur C. Clarke | *The Sands of Mars*
Sidgwick & Jackson, 1951 | Art **Chesley Bonestell**

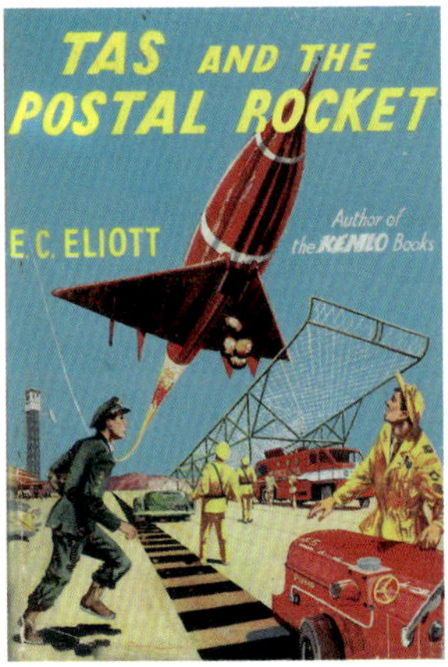

E. C. Eliott | *Tas and the Postal Rocket*
Thomas Nelson & Sons, 1955 | Art **Bruce Cornwell**

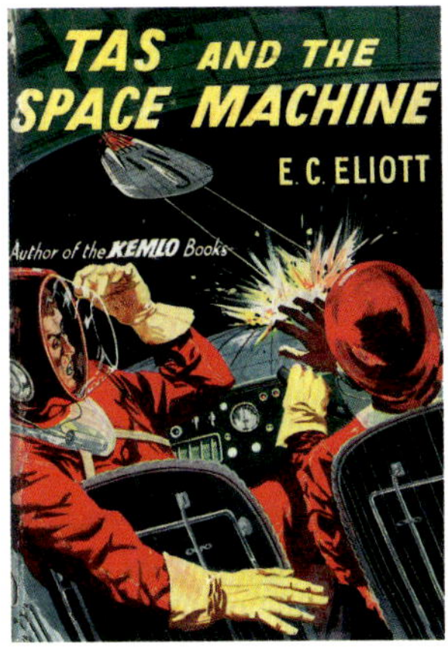

E. C. Eliott | *Tas and the Space Machine*
Thomas Nelson & Sons, 1955 | Art **Bruce Cornwell**

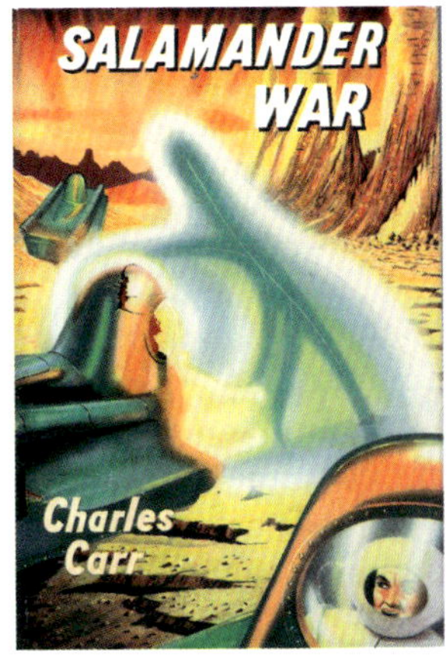

Charles Carr | *Salamander War*
Ward, Lock, 1955 | Art **Harold Johns**

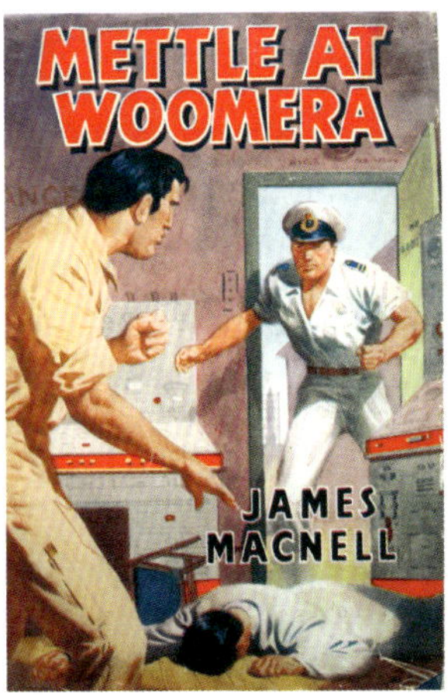

James Macnell | *Mettle at Woomera*
The Children's Press, 1958 | Art **Unknown**

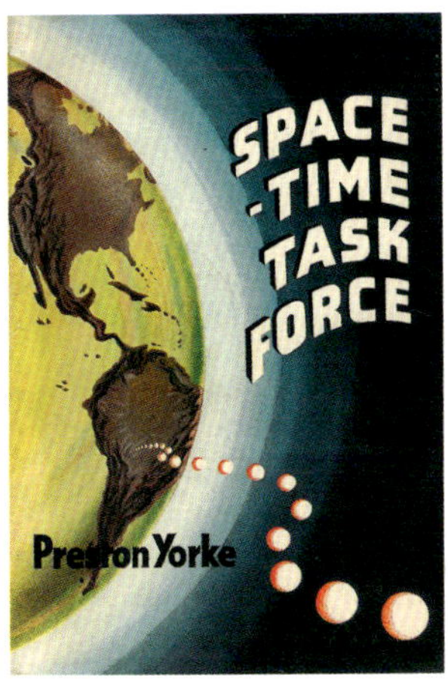

Preston Yorke (Harold Ernest Kelly)
Space-Time Task Force
Hector Kelly, 1953 | Art **James McConnell**

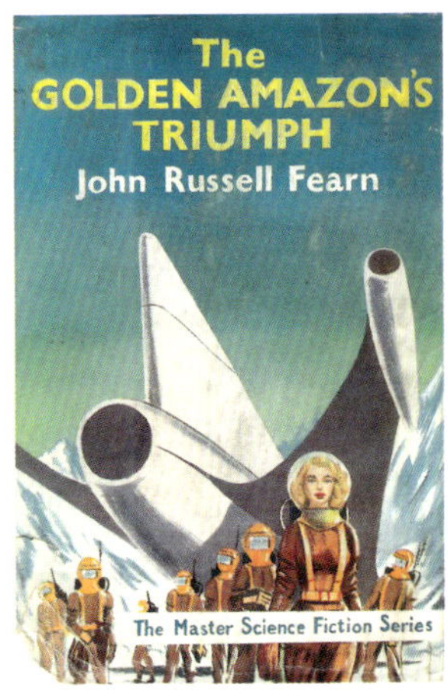

John Russell Fearn | *The Golden Amazon's Triumph*
World's Work 1, 1953 | Art **D.S.K.**

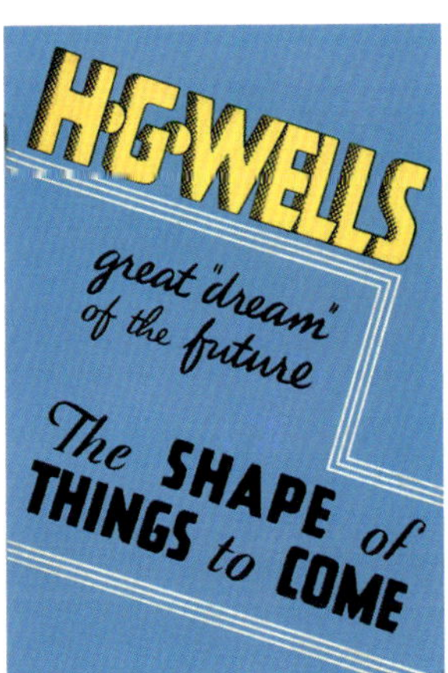

H. G. Wells | *The Shape of Things to Come*
Hutchinson, 1933 | Art **Unknown**

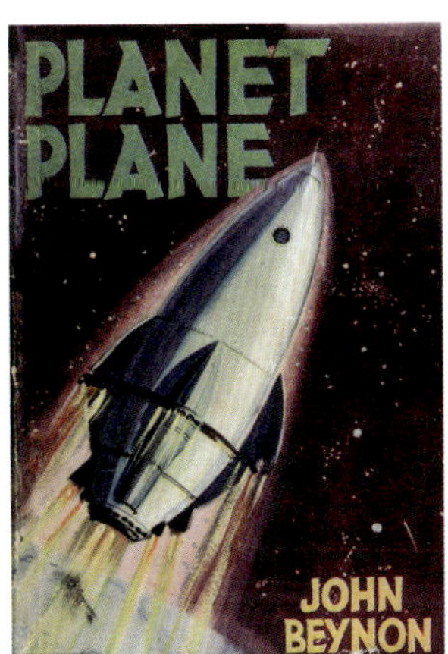

John Beynon (John Wyndham) | *Planet Plane*
George Newnes, 1936 | Art **Unknown**

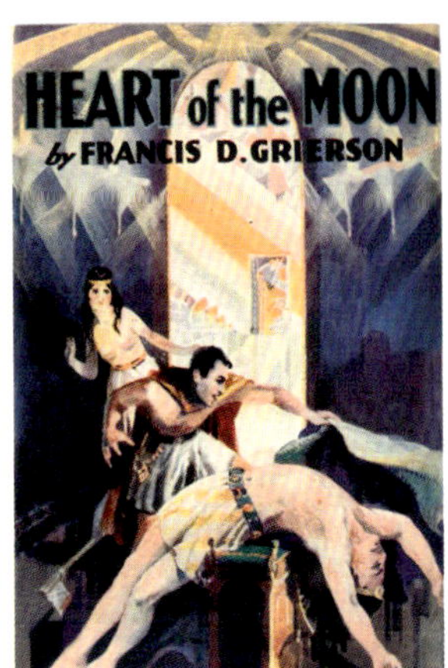

Francis D. Grierson | *Heart of the Moon*
Alston Rivers, 1928 | Art **Unknown**

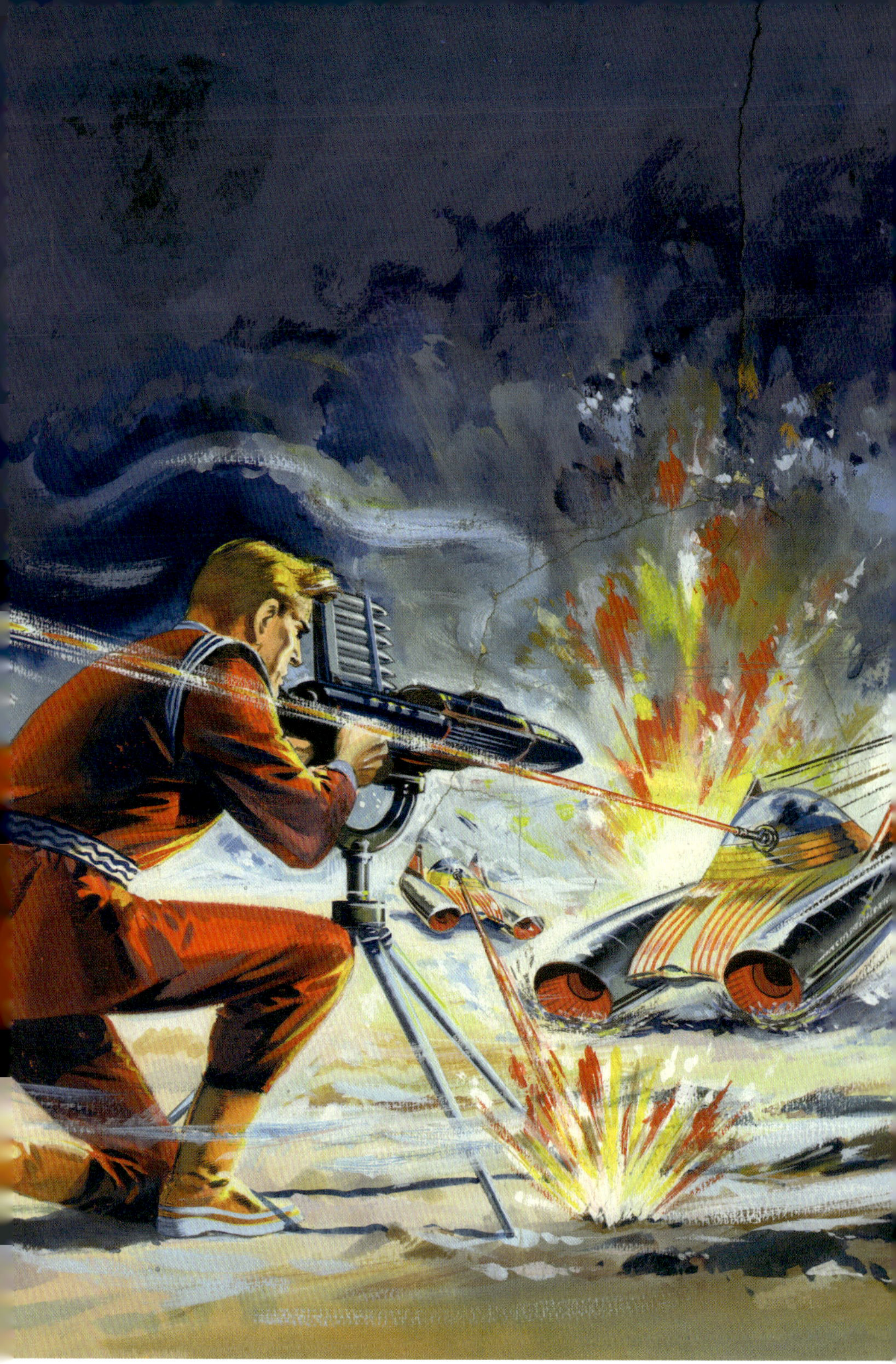

Rick Random and the Kidnapped Planet
Super Detective Library 163, Fleetway, 1959 | Original art **James McConnell** or **Nino Caroselli**

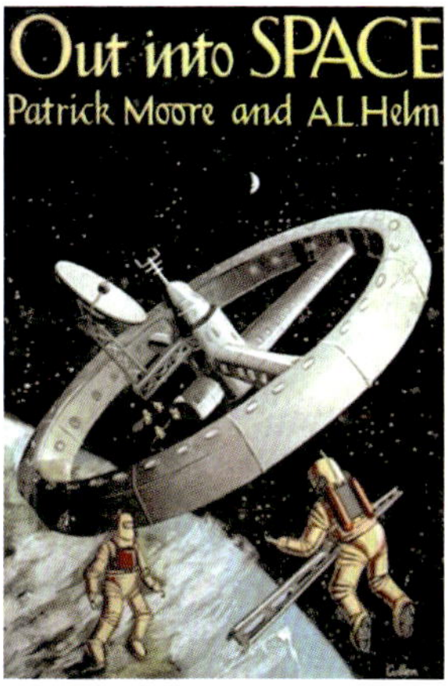

Patrick Moore and A. L. Helm | *Out into Space*
Museum Press, 1954 | Art **Patricia Cullen**

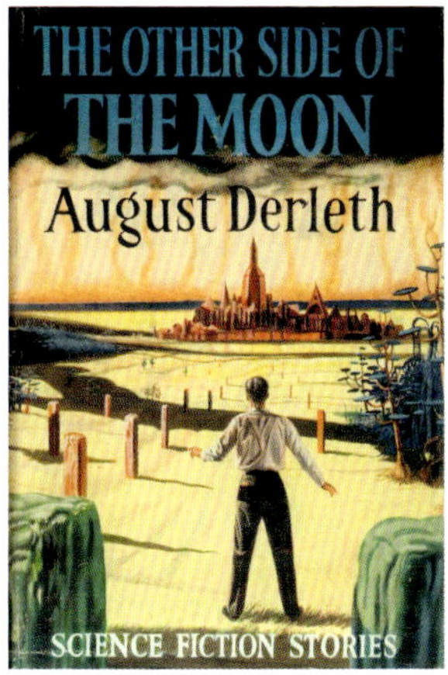

August Derleth | *The Other Side of the Moon*
Grayson and Grayson, 1956 | Art **Harold Johns**

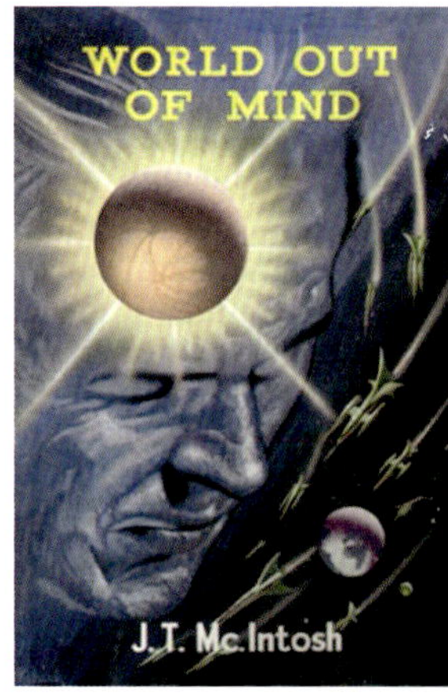

J. T. McIntosh | *World out of Mind*
Grayson and Grayson, 1955 | Art **John Richards**

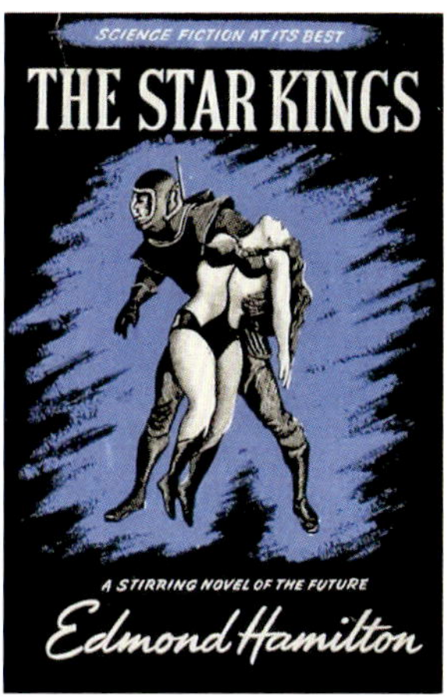

Edmond Hamilton | *The Star Kings*
Museum Press, 1951 | Art **Unknown**

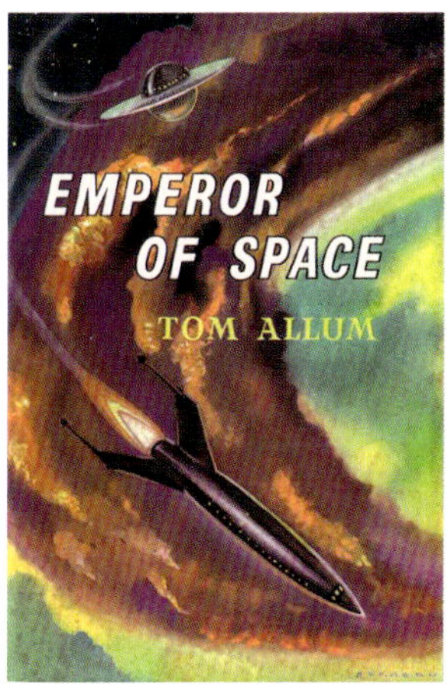

Tom Allum | *Emperor of Space*
Blackie, 1959 | Art **Charles Sargeant**

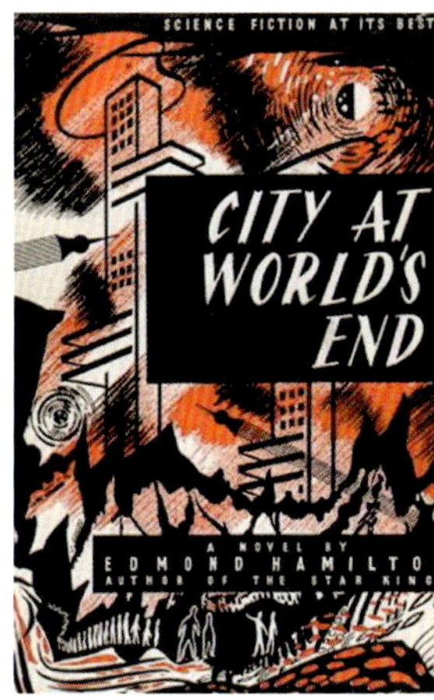

Edmond Hamilton | *City at World's End*
Museum Press, 1952 | Art **Unknown**

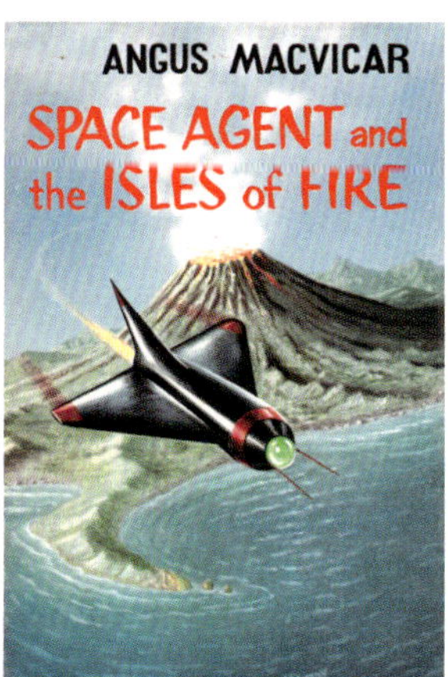

Angus MacVicar
Space Agent and the Isles of Fire
Burke, 1952 | Art **David Hardy**

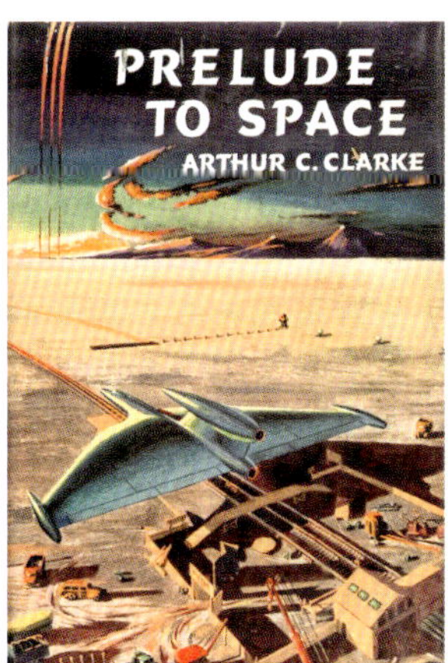

Arthur C. Clarke | *Prelude to Space*
Sidgwick and Jackson, 1953 | Art **Gerard Quinn**

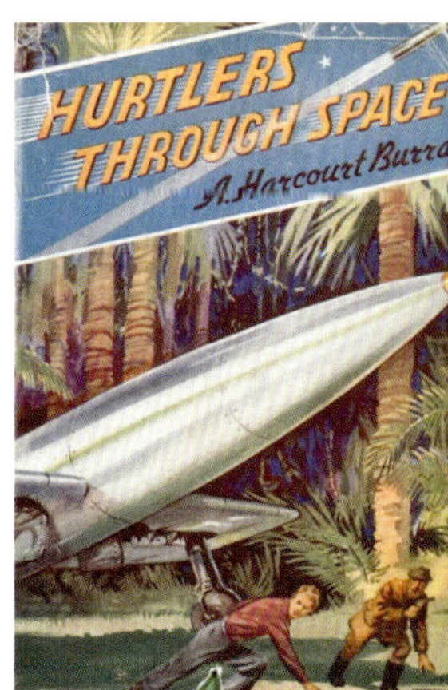

A Harcourt Burrage | *Hurtlers Through Space*
Frederick Warne & Co., 1951 | Art **Leslie Shepherd**

Space Wars | Octopus, nd | Original art **Gerald Wood**

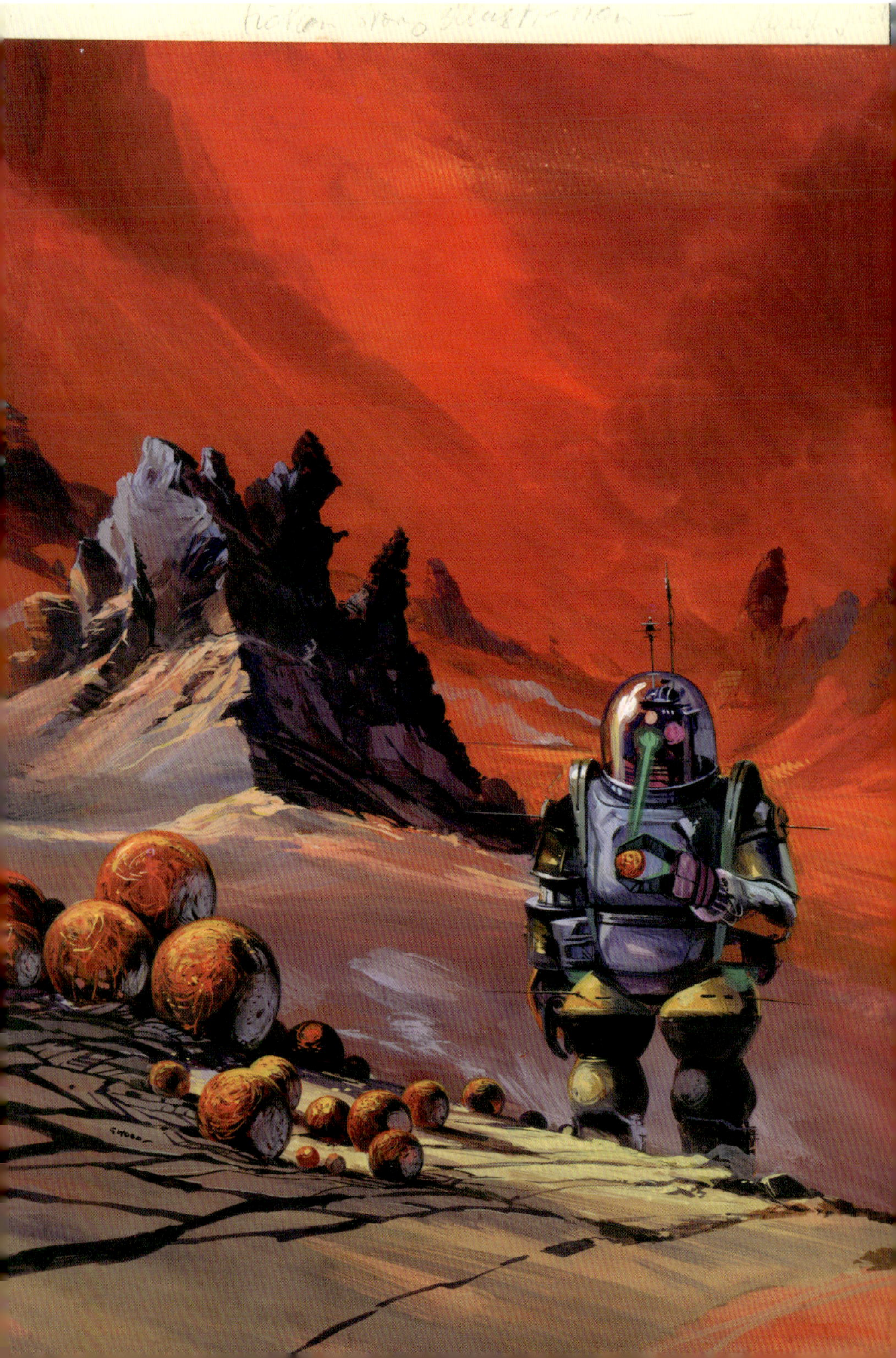

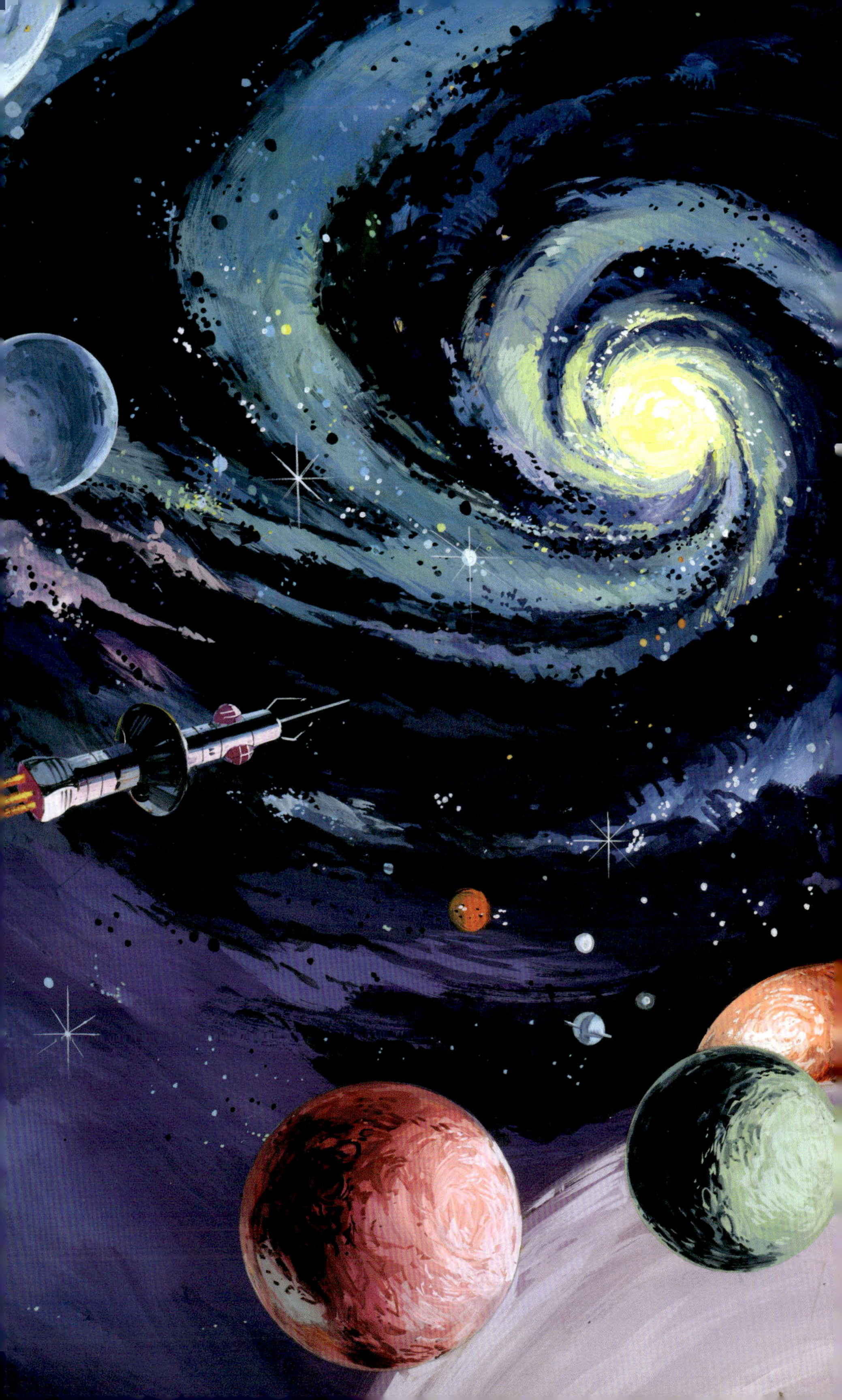

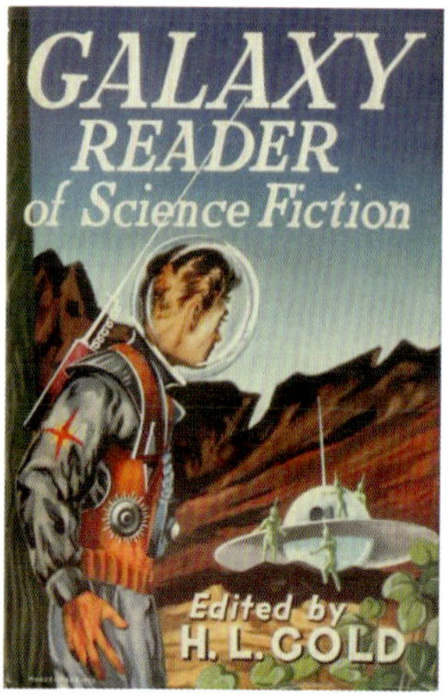

H. L. Gold, ed.
Galaxy Reader of Scisence Fiction
Grayson & Grayson, 1953 | Art **Mudge-Marriott**

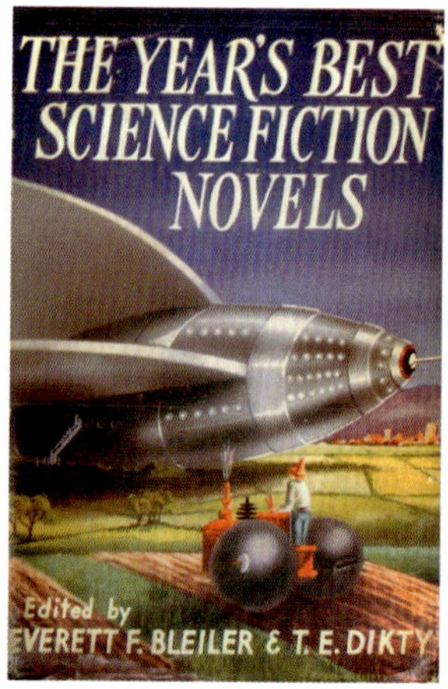

Everett F. Bleiler and T. E. Ditky, ed.
The Year's Best Science Fiction Novels
Grayson & Grayson, 1954 | Art **Mudge-Marriott**

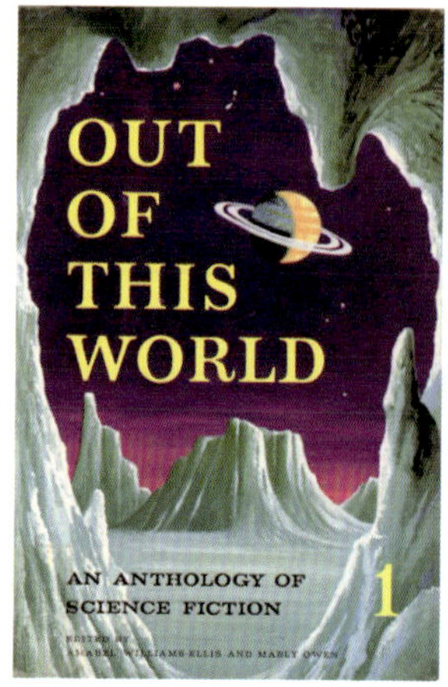

Amabel Williams-Ellis & Mably Owen
Out of This World 1
Blackie, 1960 | Art **Unknown**

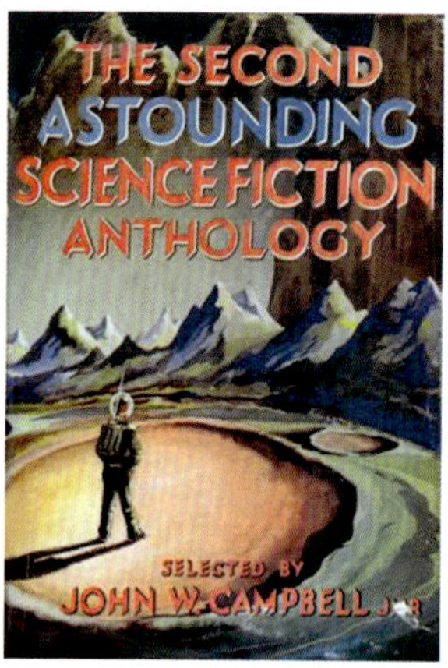

John W. Campbell Jr., ed.
The Second Astounding Science Fiction Anthology
Grayson & Grayson, 1953 | Art **Mudge-Marriott**

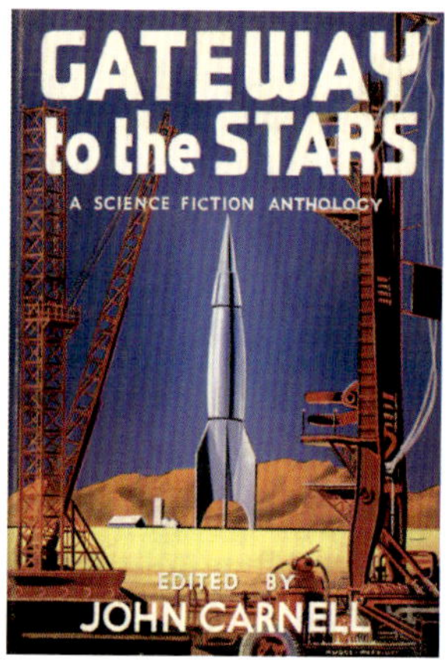

John Carnell, ed. | *Gateway to the Stars*
Cassell & Company, 1956 | Art **Mudge-Marriott**

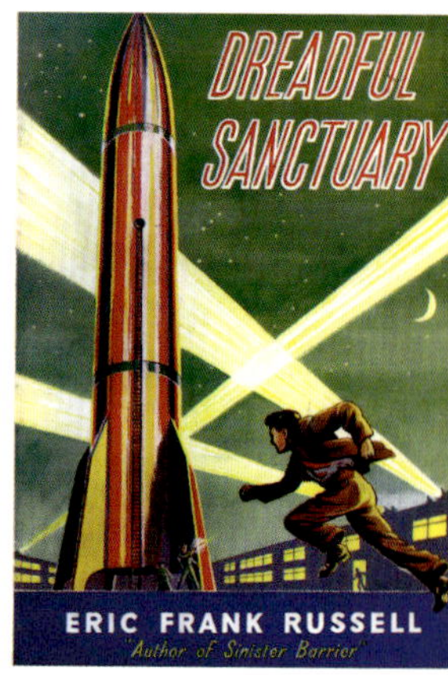

Eric Frank Russell | *Dreadful Sanctuary*
Museum Press, 1955 | Art **Harry Turner**

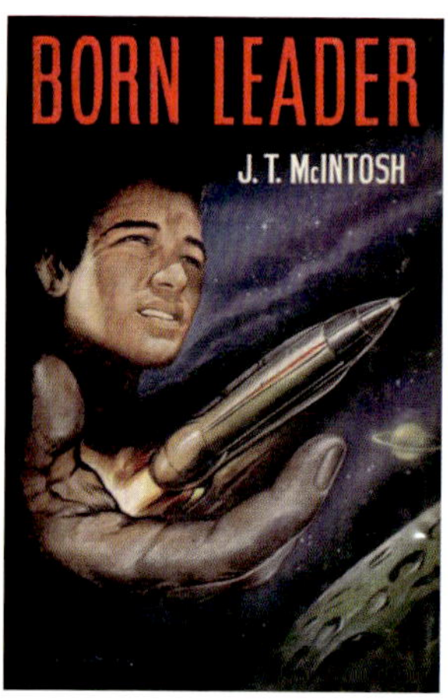

J. T. McIntosh | *Born Leader*
Museum Press, 1955 | Art **John Pollack**

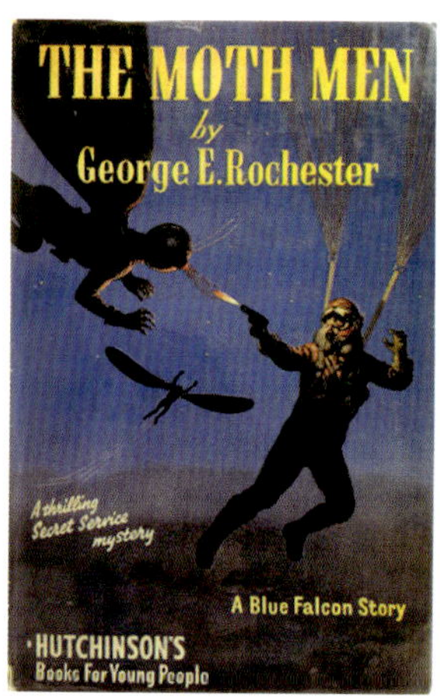

George E. Rochester | *The Moth Men*
Hutchinson's, 1950 | Art **Unknown**

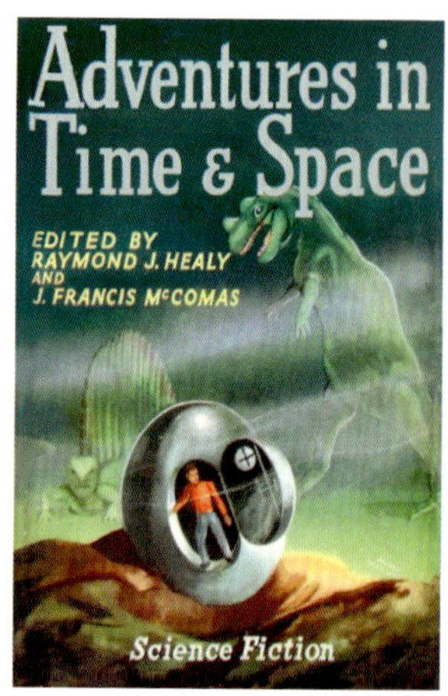

Raymond J. Healy & J. Francis McComas, ed.
Adventures in Time and Space
Grayson & Grayson, 1952 | Art **Mudge-Marriott**

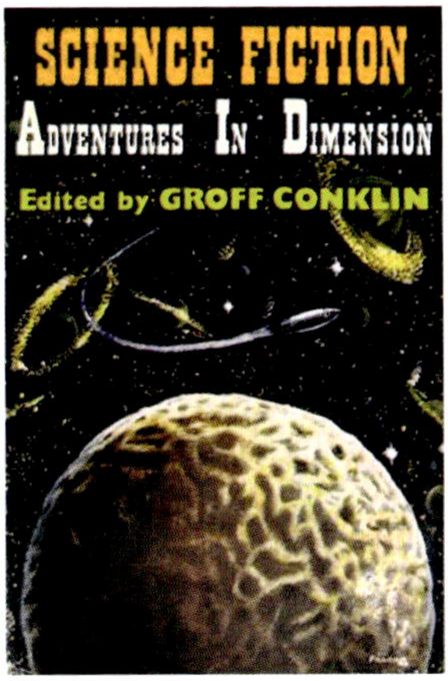

Groff Conklin, ed.
Science Fiction Adventures in Dimension
Grayson & Grayson, 1953 | Art **E. J. Pagram**

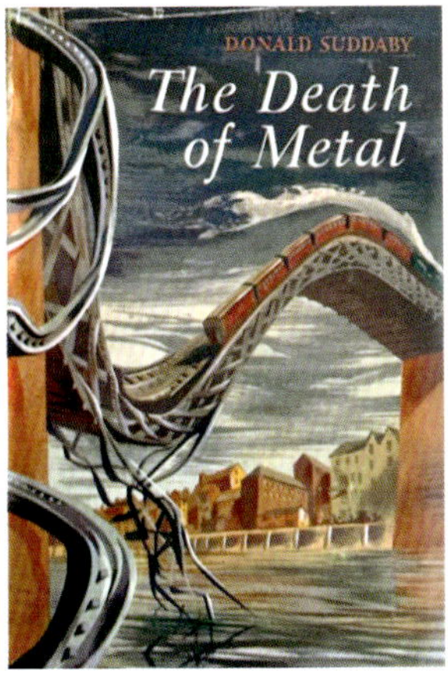

Donald Suddaby | *The Death of Metal*
Oxford University Press, 1952
Art **William Stobbs**

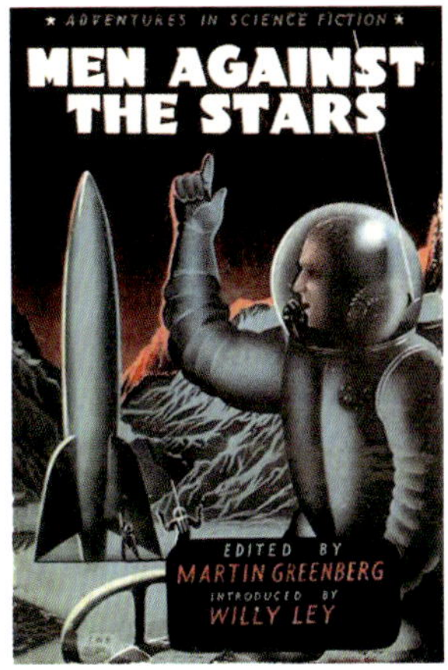

Martin Greenberg, ed. | *Men Against the Stars*
Grayson & Grayson, 1951 | Art **C.W.B.**

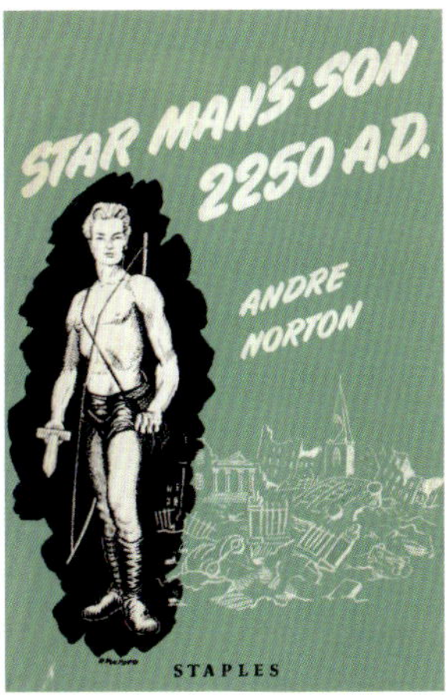

Andre Norton
Star Man's Son 2250 A.D.
Staples Press, 1953 | Art **R. Dulford**

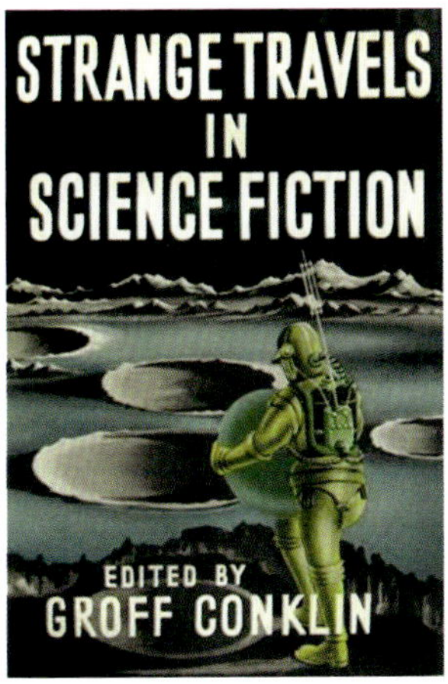

Groff Conklin, ed.
Strange Travels in Science Fiction
Grayson & Grayson, 1954 | Art **Unknown**

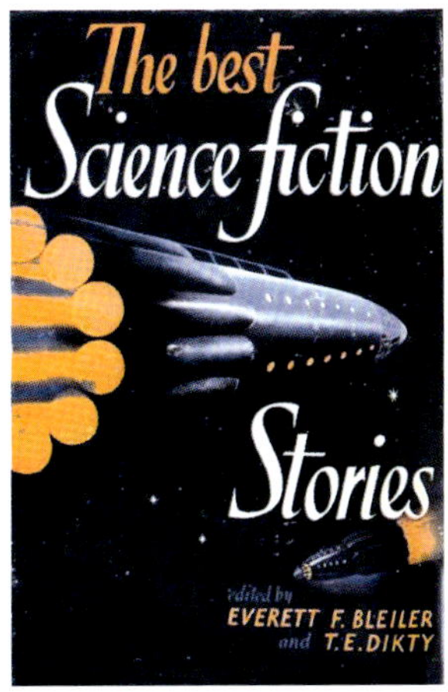

Everett F. Bleiler and T. E. Ditky, ed.
The Best Science Fiction Stories
Grayson & Grayson, 1951 | Art **Unknown**

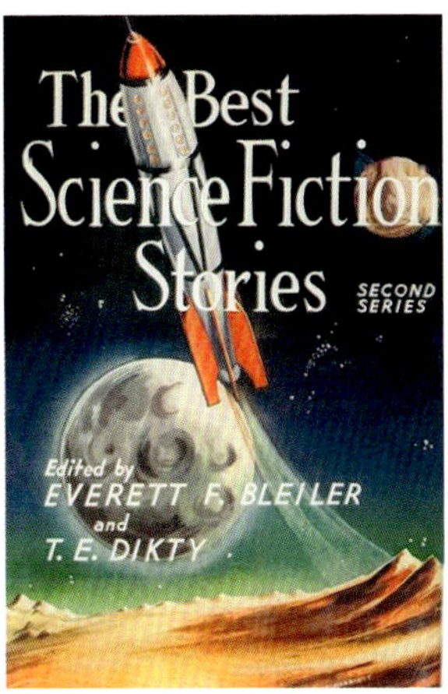

Everett F. Bleiler and T. E. Ditky, ed.
The Best Science Fiction Stories, second series
Grayson & Grayson, 1952 | Art **Mudge-Marriott**

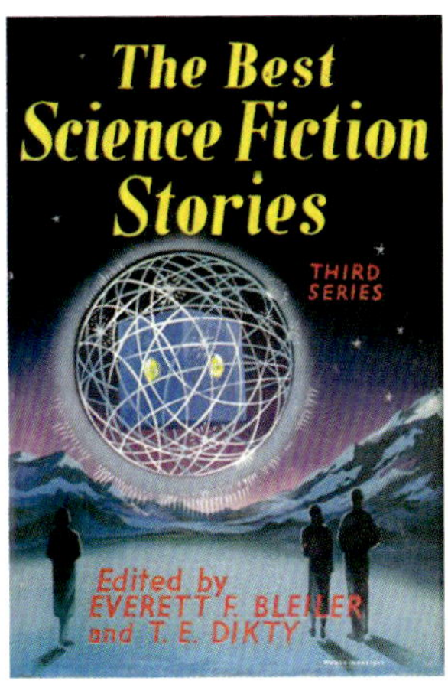

Everett F. Bleiler and T. E. Ditky, ed.
The Best Science Fiction Stories, third series
Grayson & Grayson, 1953 | Art **Mudge-Marriott**

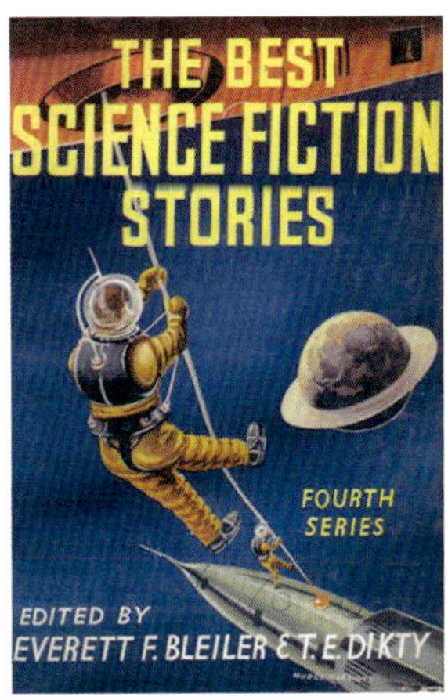

Everett F. Bleiler and T. E. Ditky, ed.
The Best Science Fiction Stories, fourth series
Grayson & Grayson, 1955 | Art **Mudge-Marriott**

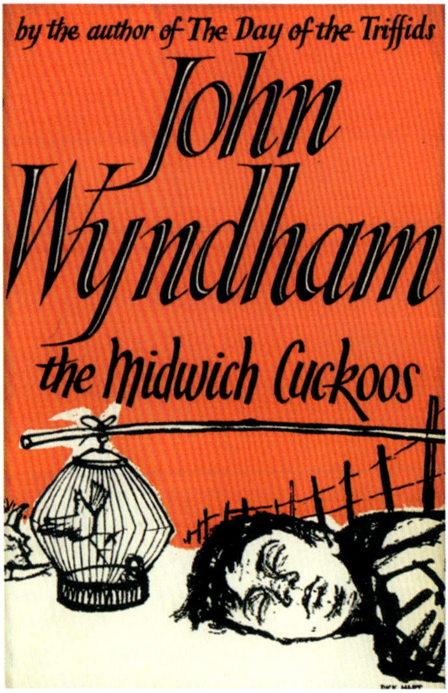

John Wyndham | *The Midwich Cuckoos*
Michael Joseph, 1957 | Art **Dick Hart**

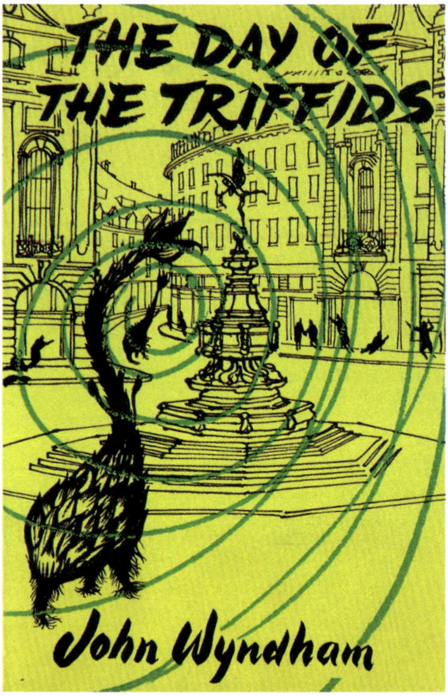

John Wyndham | *The Day of the Triffids*
Michael Joseph, 1951 | Art **Patrick Gierth**

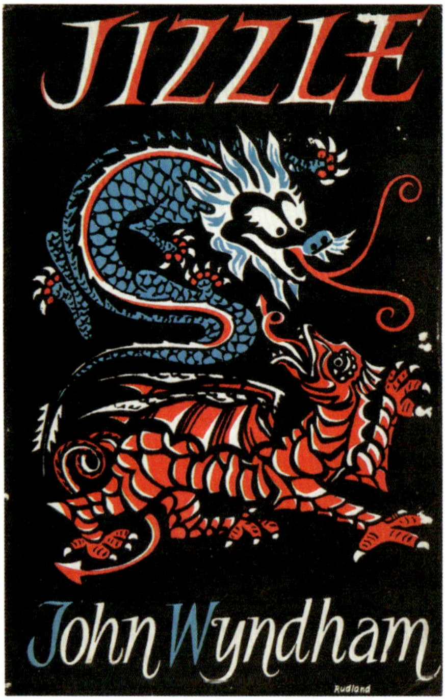

John Wyndham | *Jizzle*
Dennis Dobson, 1954 | Art **Peter Rudland**

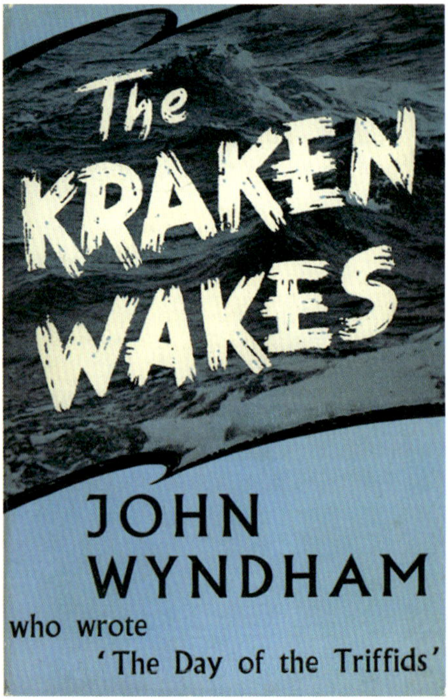

John Wyndham | *The Kraken Wakes*
Michael Joseph, 1953 | Art **Unknown**

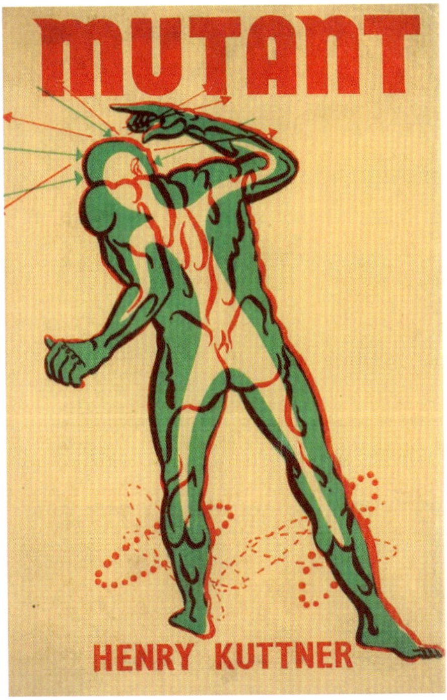

Henry Kuttner | *Mutant*
Weidenfeld and Nicholson, 1954 | Art **Unknown**

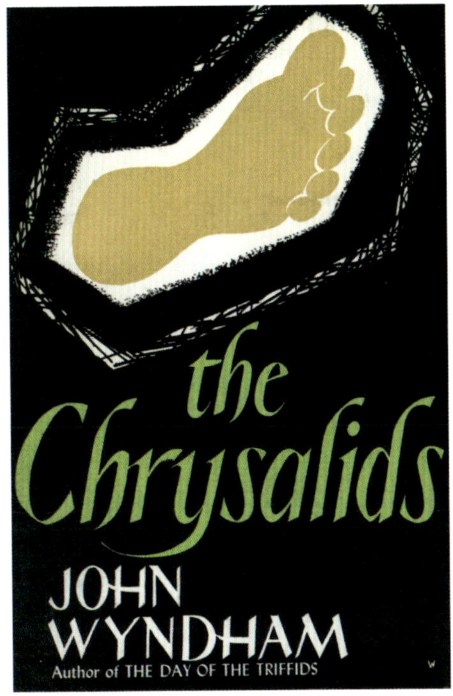

John Wyndham | *The Chrysalids*
Michael Joseph, 1955 | Art **Brian Wildsmith**

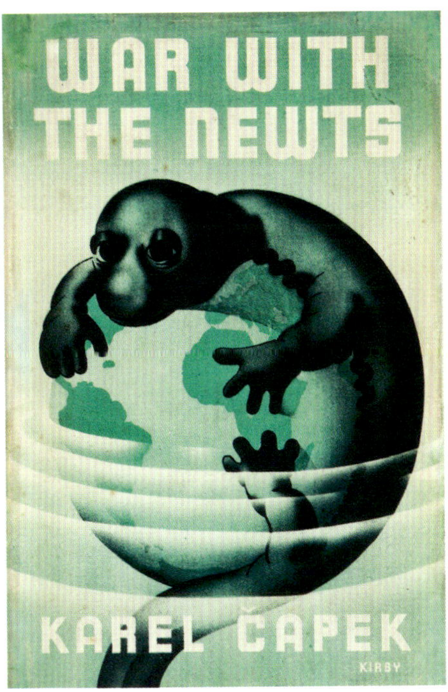

Karel Čapek | *War with the Newts*
George Allen & Unwin, 1936 | Art **Kirby**

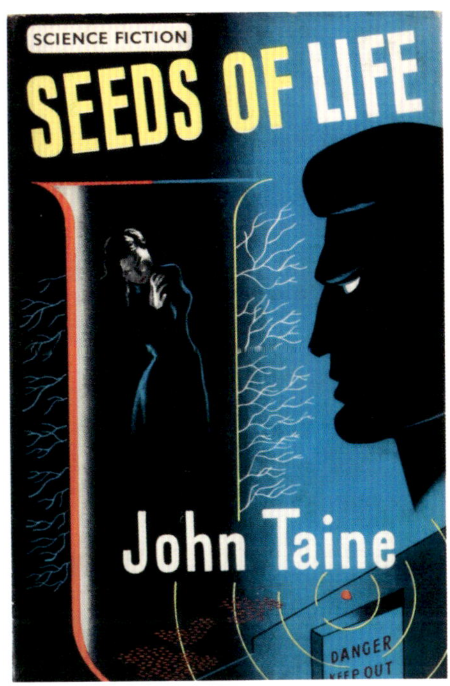

John Taine | *Seeds of Life*
Rich and Cowan, 1955 | Art **Unknown**

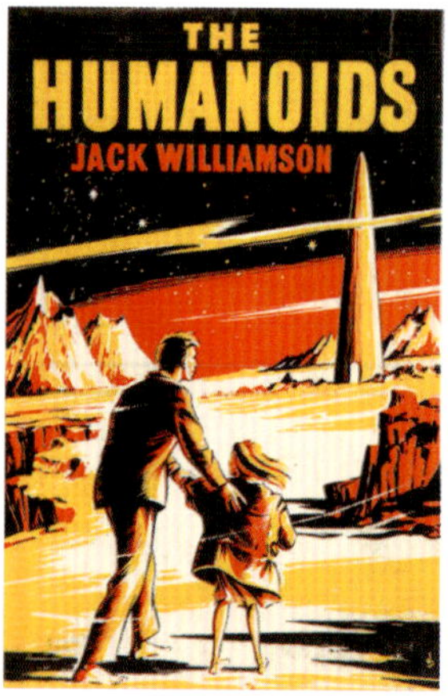

Jack Williamson | *The Humanoids*
Museum Press, 1953 | Art **Ron Jobson**

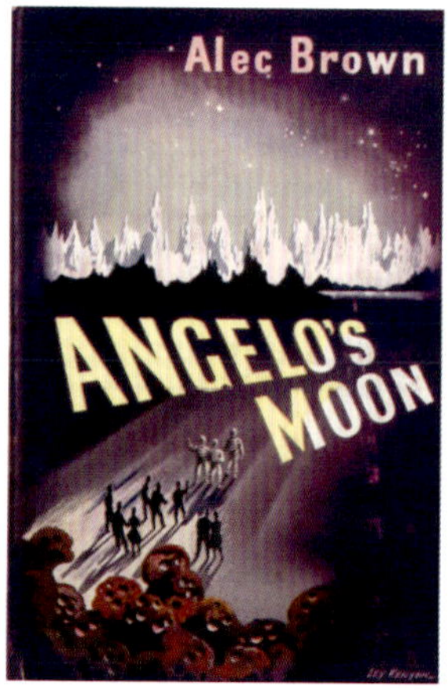

Alec Brown | *Angelo's Moon*
The Bodley Head, 1955 | Art **Ley Keynon**

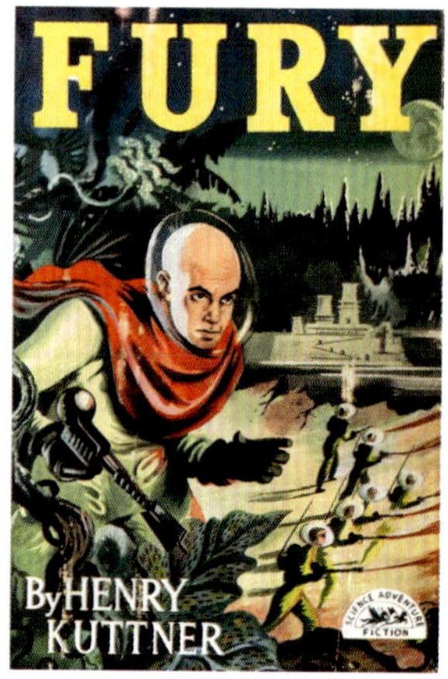

Henry Kuttner | *Fury*
Dennis Dobson, 1954 | Art **Ley Kenyon**

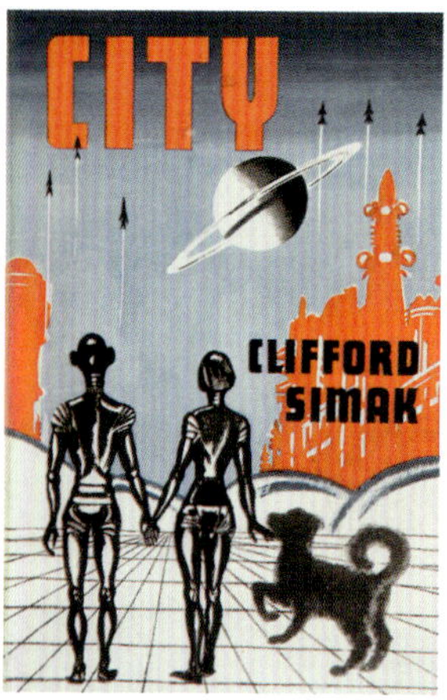

Clifford D. Simak | *City*
Weidenfeld & Nicolson, 1954 | Art **C. King**

Jonathan Burke | *Alien Landscapes*
Museum Press, 1955 | Art **Unknown**

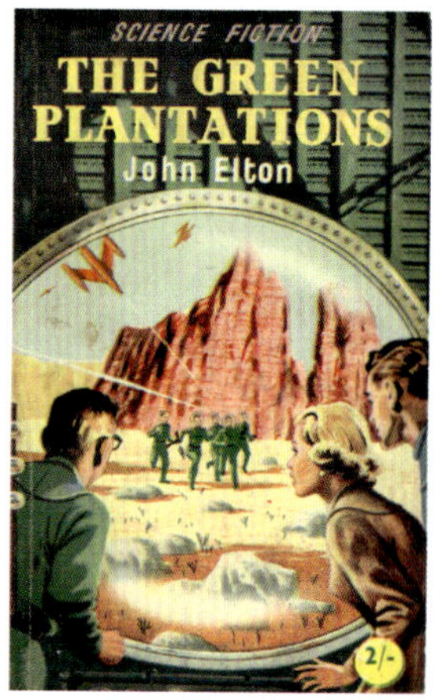

John Elton | *The Green Plantations*
Ward, Lock 37, 1956 | Art **Harold Johns**

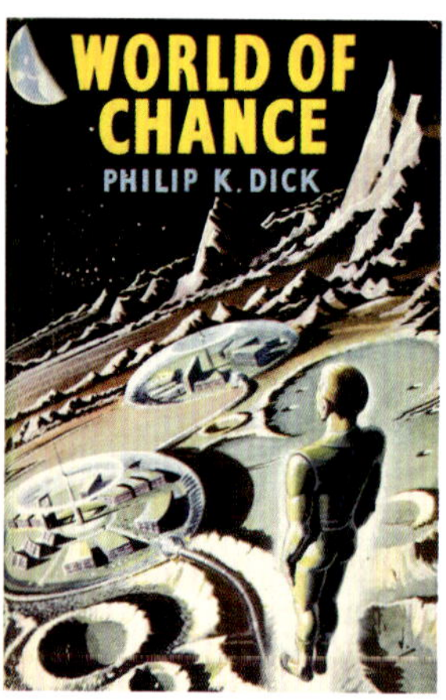

Philip K. Dick | *World of Chance*
Rich & Cowan, 1956 | Art **Ron Jobson**

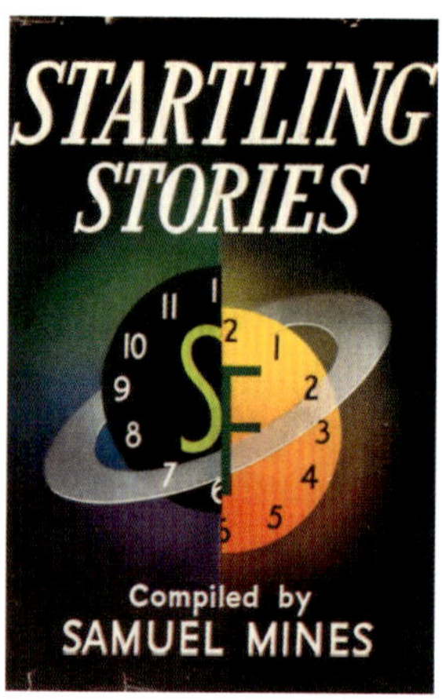

Samuel Mines | *Startling Stories*
Cassell, 1954 | Art **Unknown**

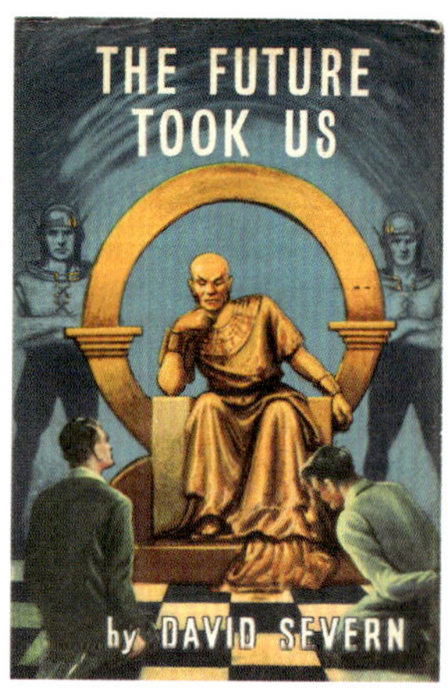

David Severn | *The Future Took Us*
Children's Book Club, 1958 | Art **Unknown**

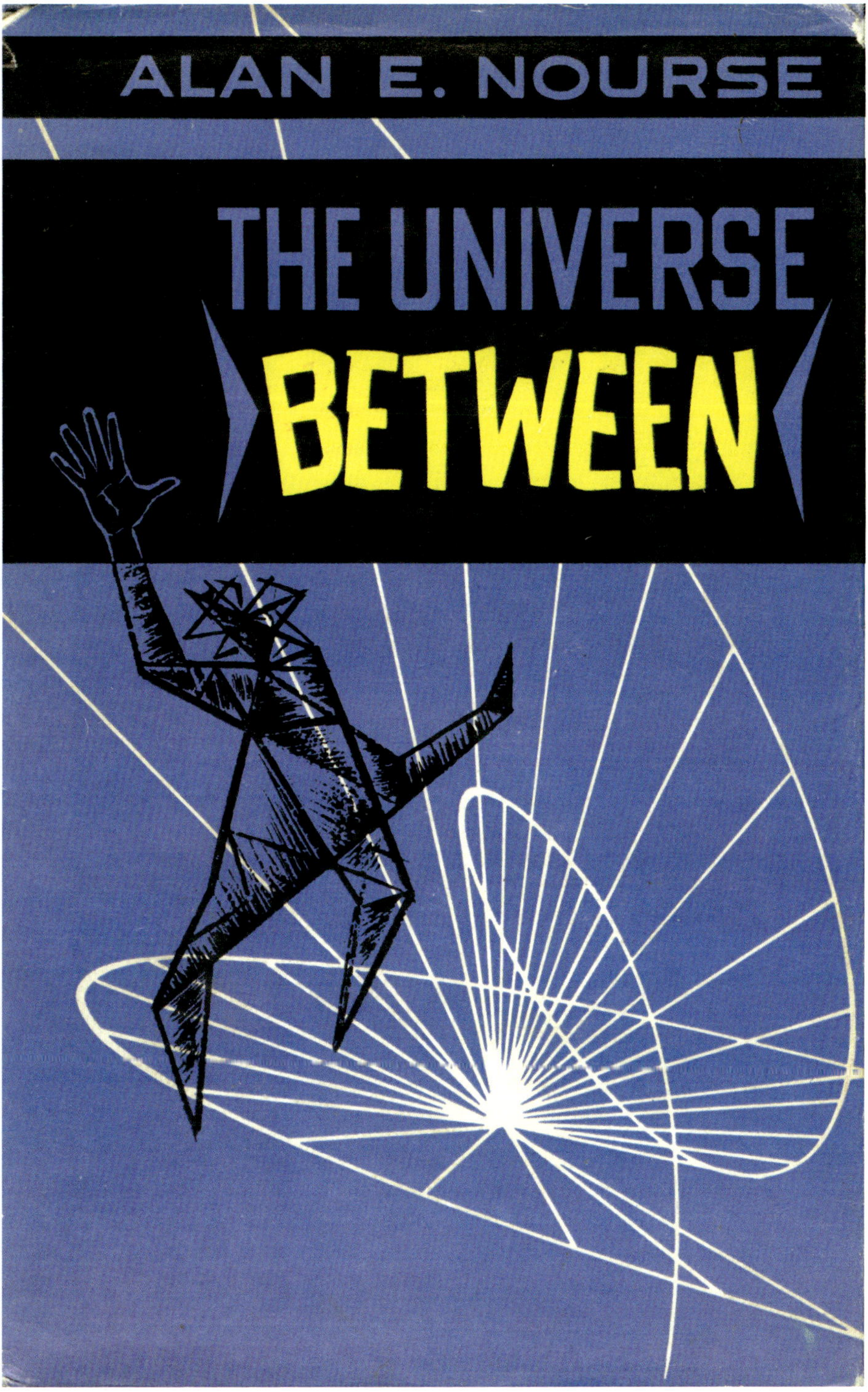

Alan E. Nourse | *The Universe Between*
Faber and Faber, 1966 | Art **Mel Hunter**

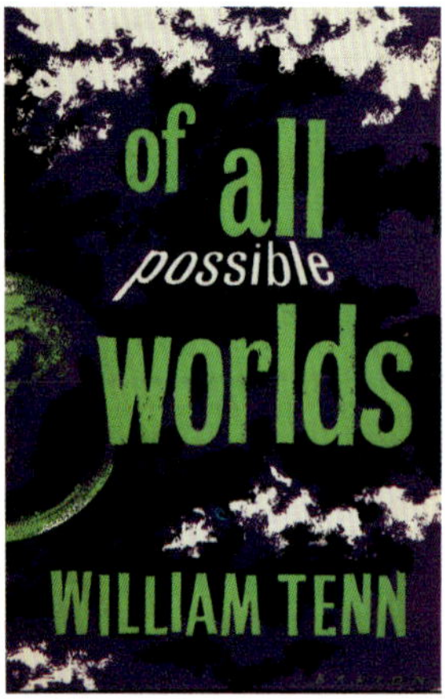

William Tenn | *Of All Possible Worlds*
Michael Joseph, 1956 | Art **Richard Barton**

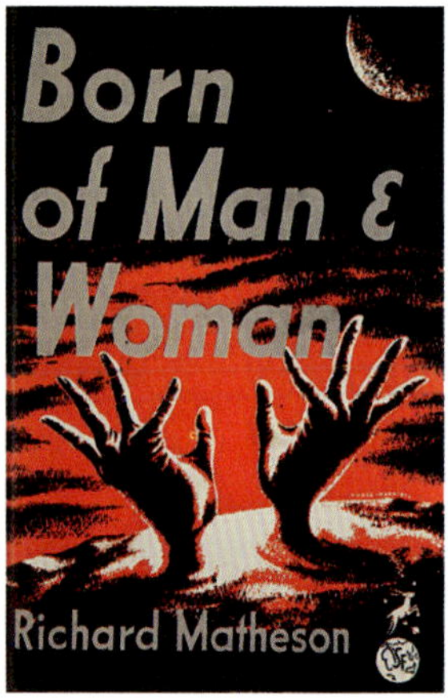

Richard Matheson | *Born of Man & Woman*
Max Reinhardt, 1954 | Art **Mudge-Marriott**

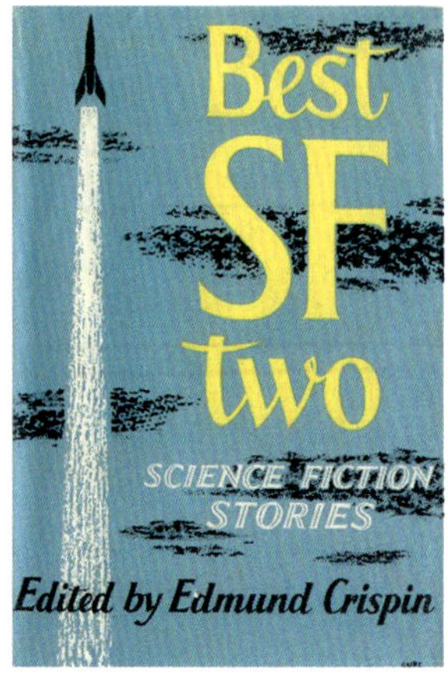

Edmund Crispin, ed. | *Best SF Two*
Faber and Faber, 1956 | Art **Peter Curl**

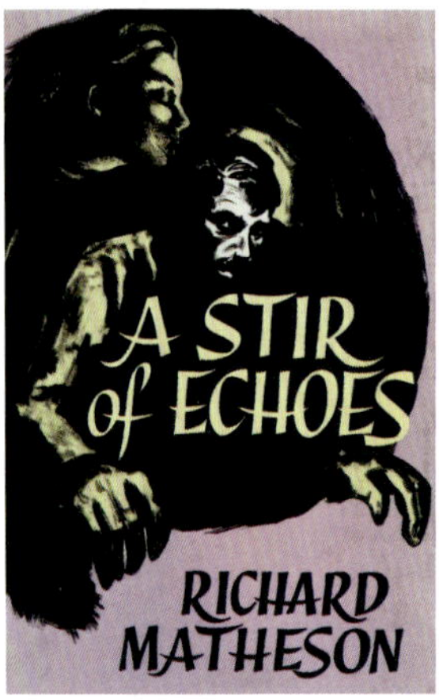

Richard Matheson | *A Stir of Echoes*
Cassell, 1958 | Art **Unknown**

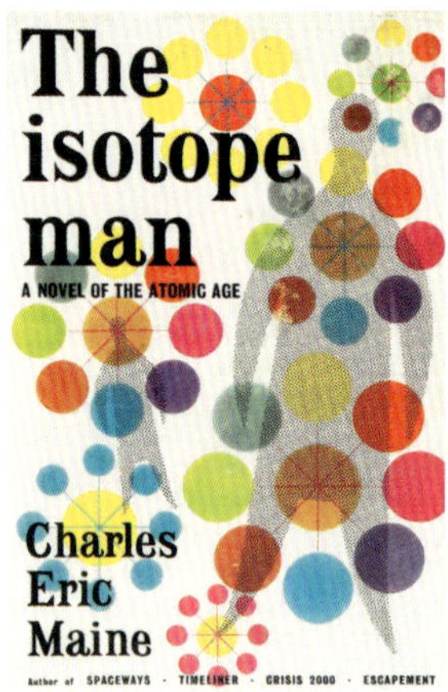

Charles Eric Maine | *The Isotope Man*
Hodder and Stoughton, 1957 | Art **Martin Kaye**

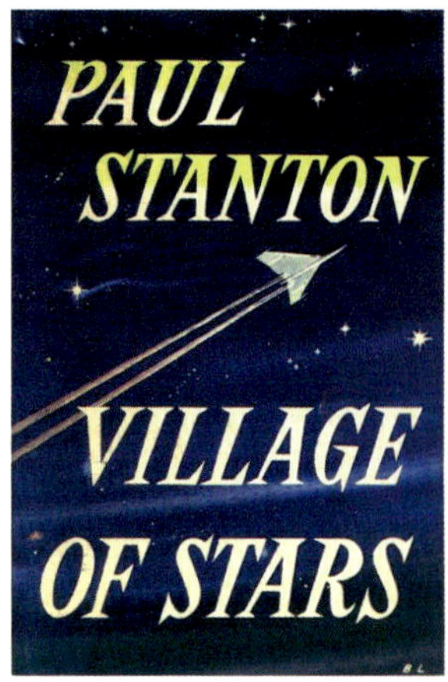

Paul Stanton | *Village of Stars*
Michael Joseph, 1960 | Art **B. L.**

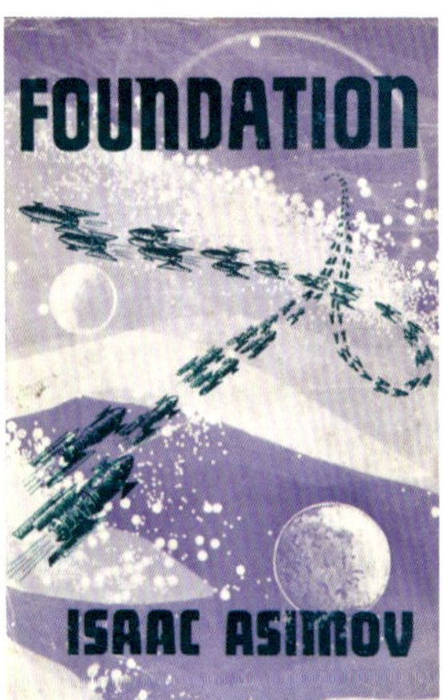

Isaac Asimov | *Foundation*
Weidenfeld & Nicolson, 1953 | Art **Unknown**

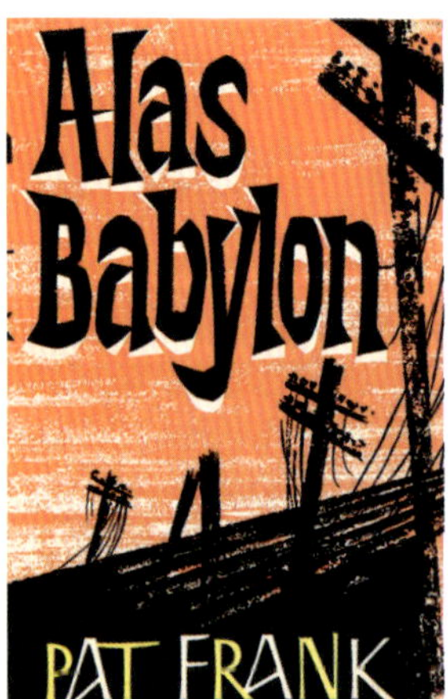

Pat Frank | *Alas Babylon*
Constable, 1959 | Art **Unknown**

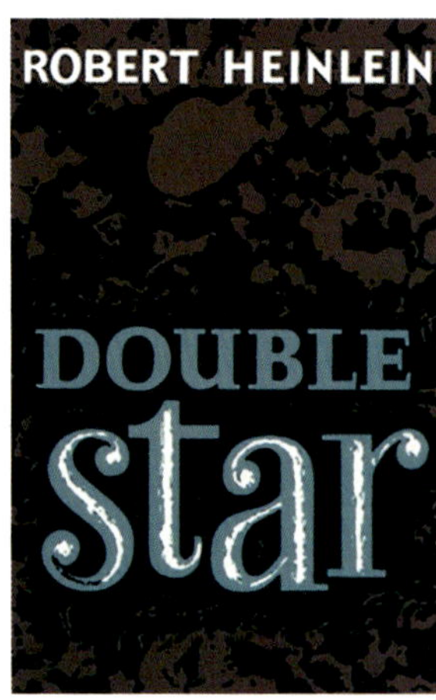

Robert Heinlein | *Double Star*
Michael Joseph, 1958 | Art **Unknown**

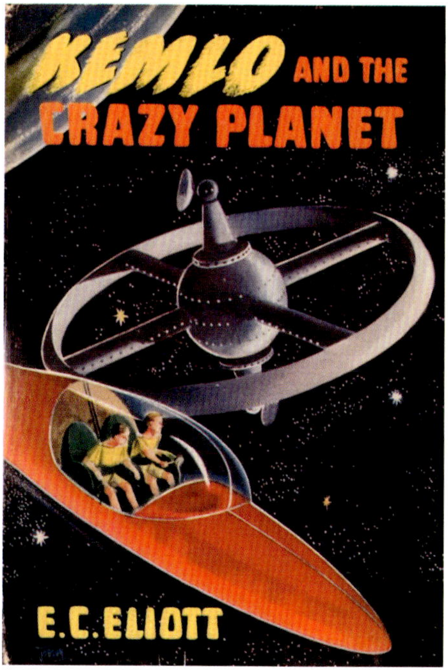

E. C. Eliott | *Kemlo and the Crazy Planet*
Thomas Nelson & Sons, 1954 | Art **Ron Jobson**

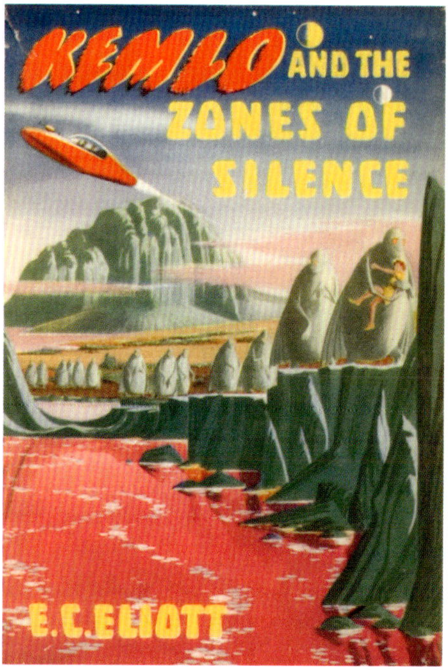

E. C. Eliott | *Kemlo and the Zones of Silence*
Thomas Nelson & Sons, 1954 | Art **Ron Jobson**

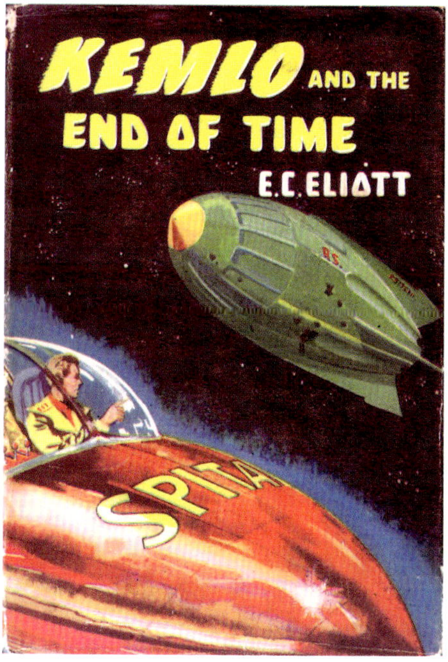

E. C. Eliott | *Kemlo and the End of Time*
Thomas Nelson & Sons, 1957 | Art **Bruce Cornwell**

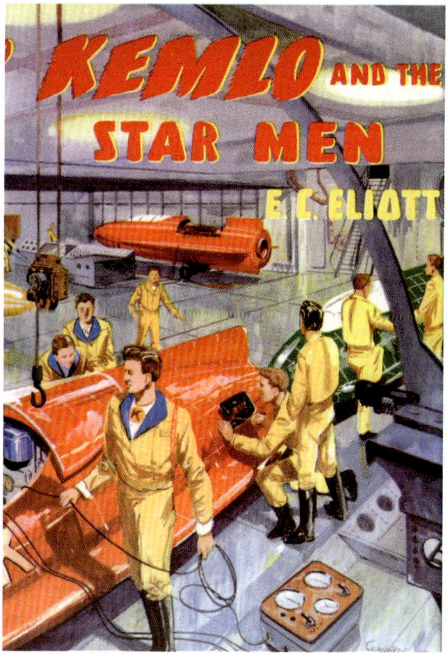

E. C. Eliott | *Kemlo and the Star Men*
Thomas Nelson & Sons, 1955 | Art **Bruce Cornwell**

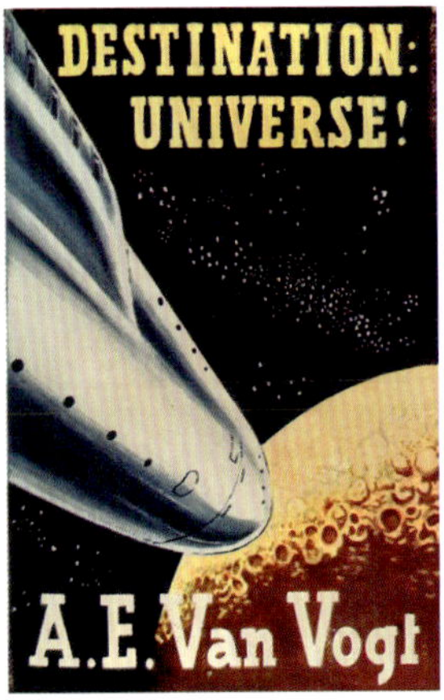

A. E. Van Vogt | *Destination: Universe!*
Eyre and Spotiswoode, 1953 | Art **Craig**

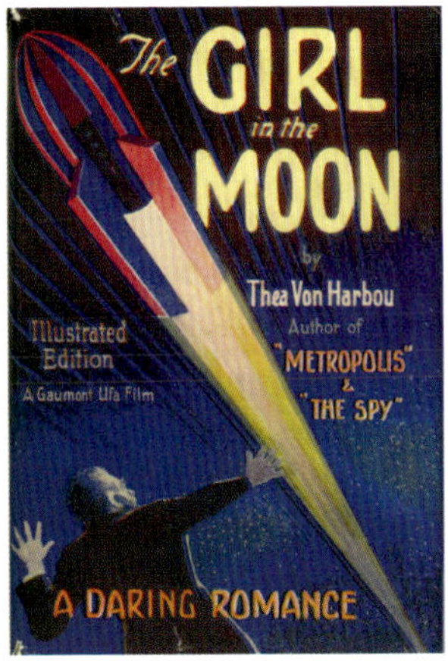

Thea Von Harbou | *The Girl in the Moon*
Readers Library Pub. Co., 1930 | Art **Unknown**

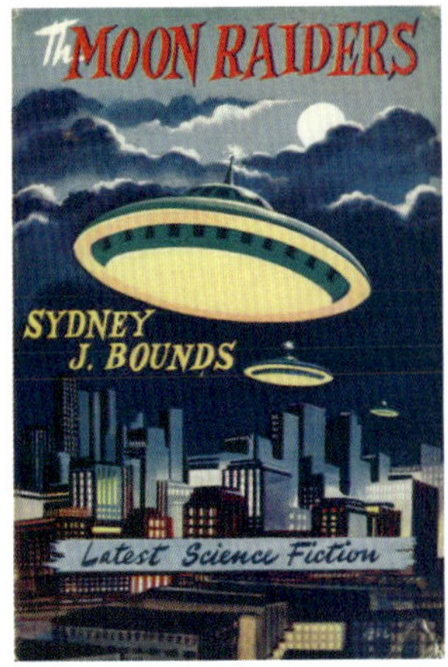

Sydney J. Bounds | *The Moon Raiders*
W. Foulsham & Co., 1955 | Art **Unknown**

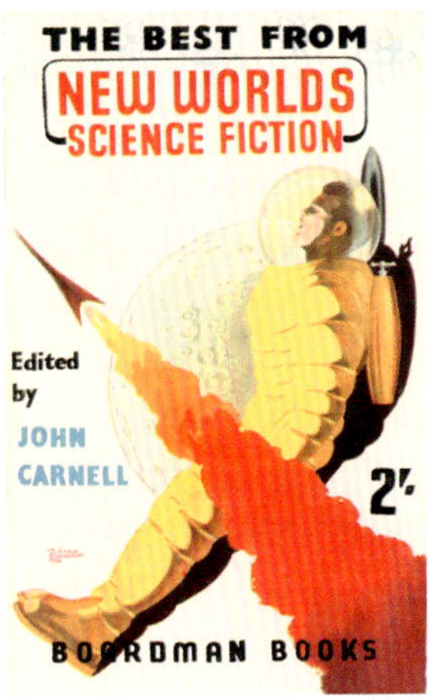

John Carnell, ed. | *The Best from New Worlds*
T. V. Boardman, 1955 | Art **Gerard Quinn**

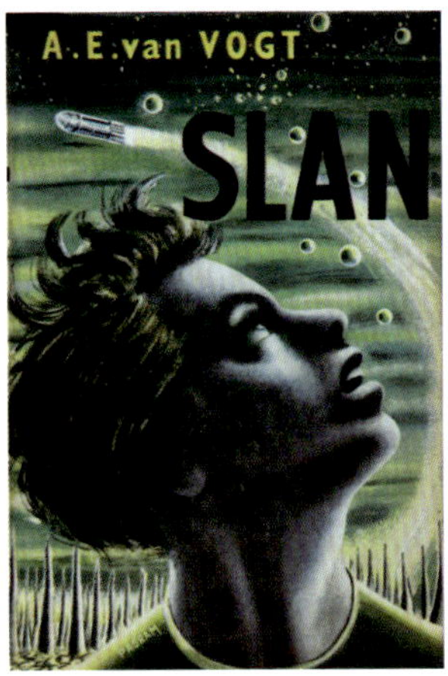

A. E. van Vogt | *Slan*
Weidenfeld & Nicolson, 1953 | Art **E. J. Pagram**

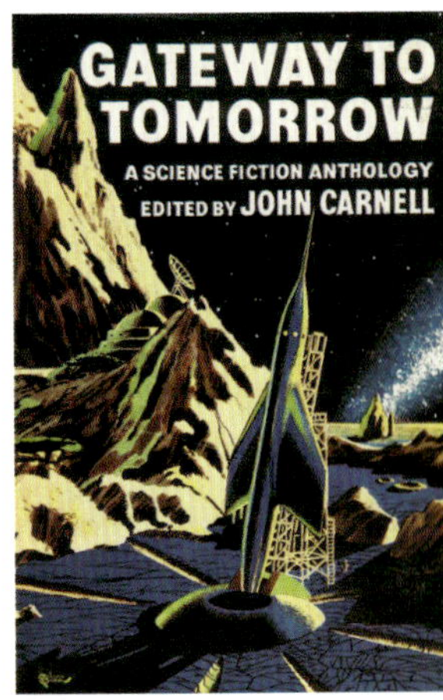

John Carnell, ed. | *Gateway to Tomorrow*
Museum Press, 1954 | Art **Gerard Quinn**

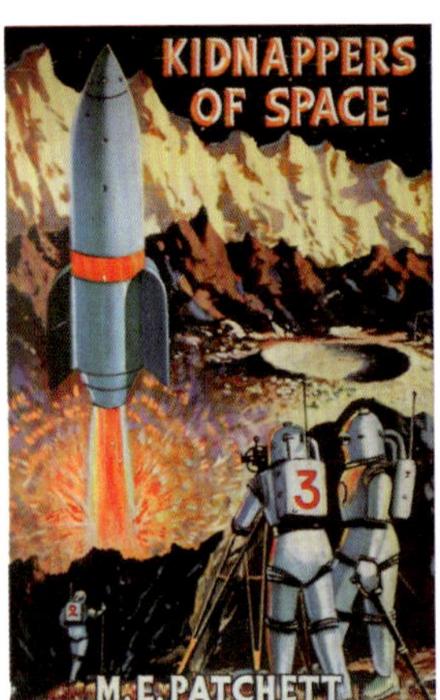

M. E. Patchett | *Kidnappers of Space*
Lutterworth Press, 1953 | Art **Unknown**

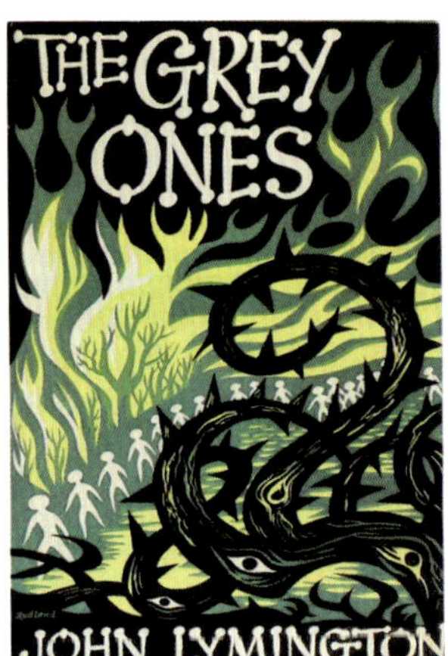

John Lymington | *The Grey Ones*
Hodder & Stoughton, 1960 | Art **Peter Rudland**

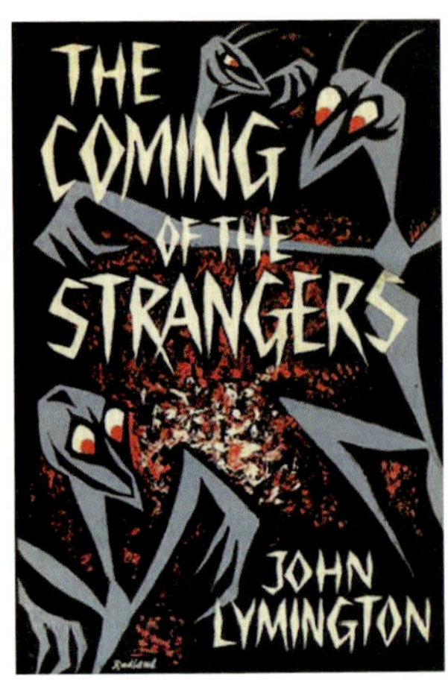

John Lymington | *The Coming of the Strangers*
Hodder & Stoughton, 1961 | Art **Peter Rudland**

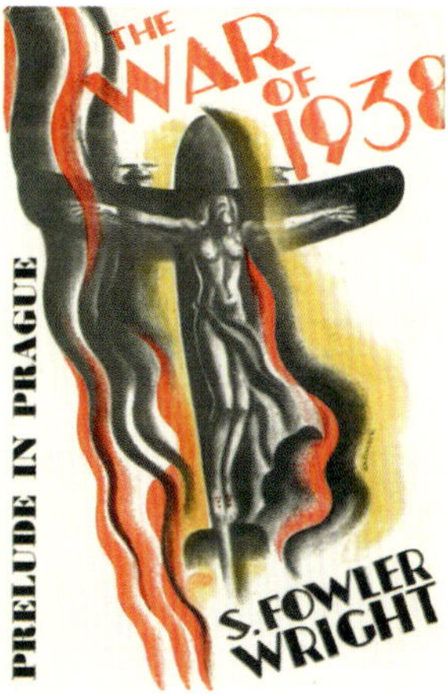

S. Fowler Wright | *The War of 1938*
George Newnes, 1935 | Art **J. M. Pollock**

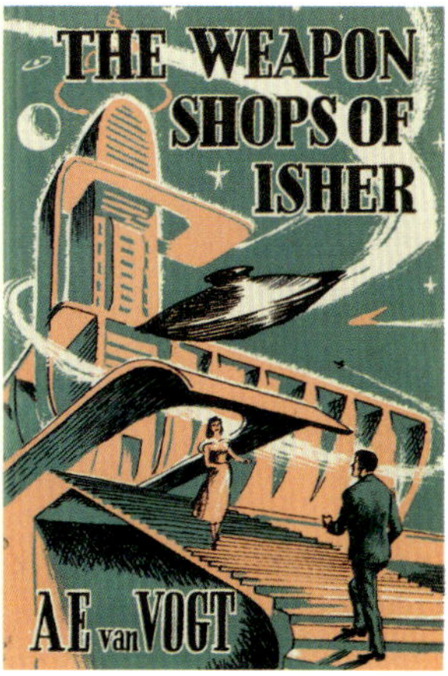

A. E. Van Vogt | *The Weapon Shops of Isher*
Weidenfeld & Nicolson, 1952 | Art **Unknown**

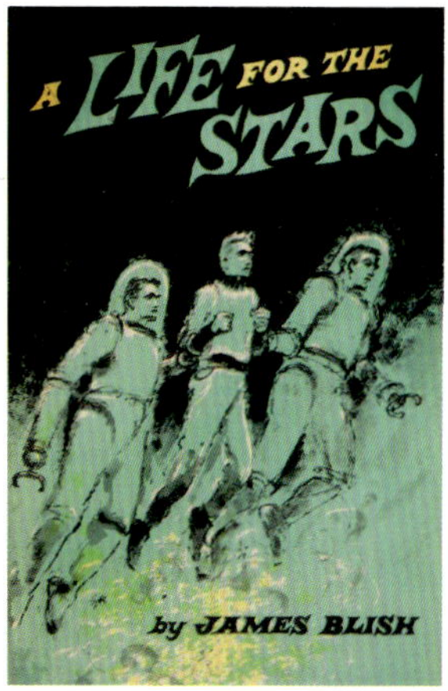

James Blish | *A Life for the Stars*
Faber and Faber, 1964 | Art **Robert MacLean**

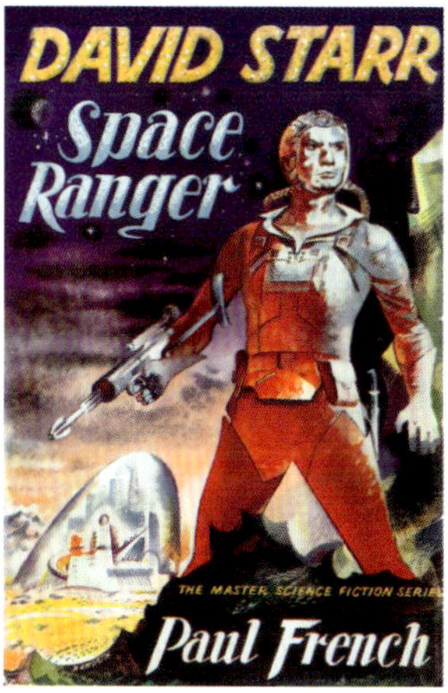

Paul French (Issac Asimov)
David Starr Space Ranger
World's Work, 1953 | Art **Haworth**

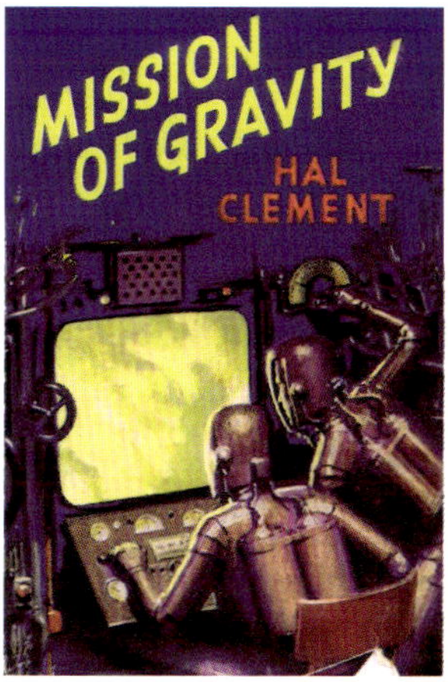

Hal Clement | *Mission of Gravity*
Robert Hale, 1955 | Art **Unknown**

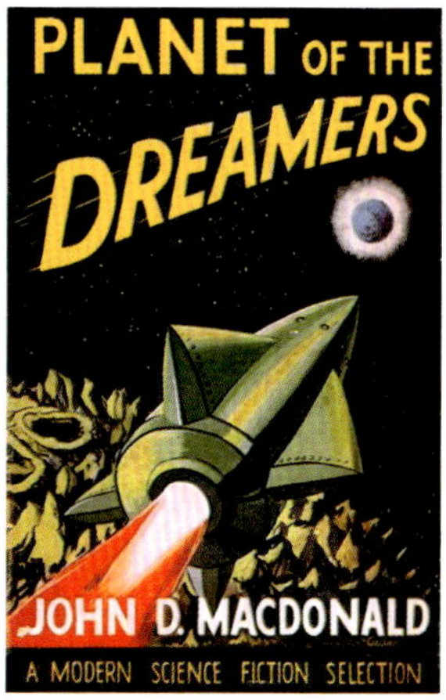

John D. Macdonald | *Planet of the Dreamers*
Robert Hale, 1954 | Art **Patricia Cullen**

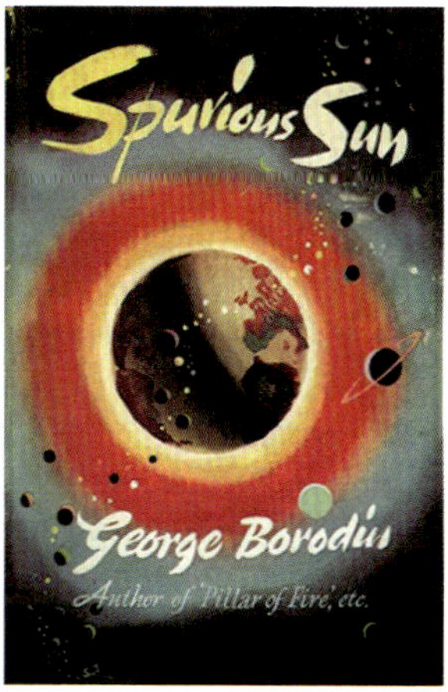

George Borodin | *Spurious Sun*
T. Werner Laurie, 1948 | Art **S. J.**

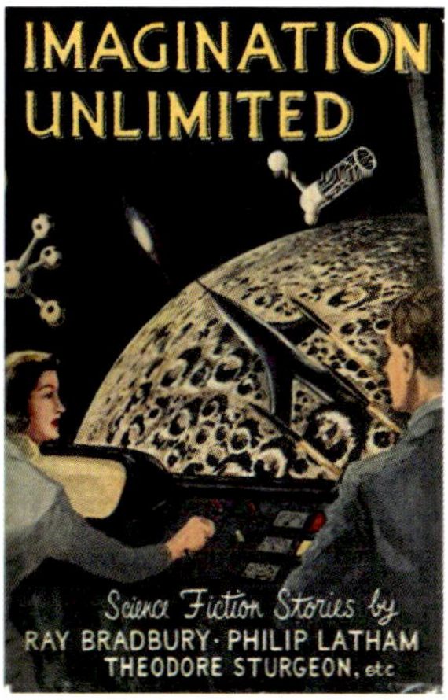

Everett F. Bleiler and T. E. Dikty, eds
Imagination Unlimited
The Bodley Head, 1954 | Art **Unknown**

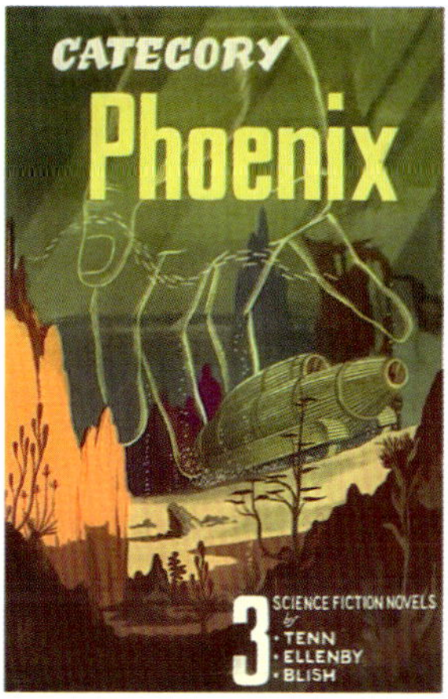

Everett F. Bleiler and T. E. Dikty, eds
Category Phoenix
The Bodley Head, 1954 | Art **C. Stewart**

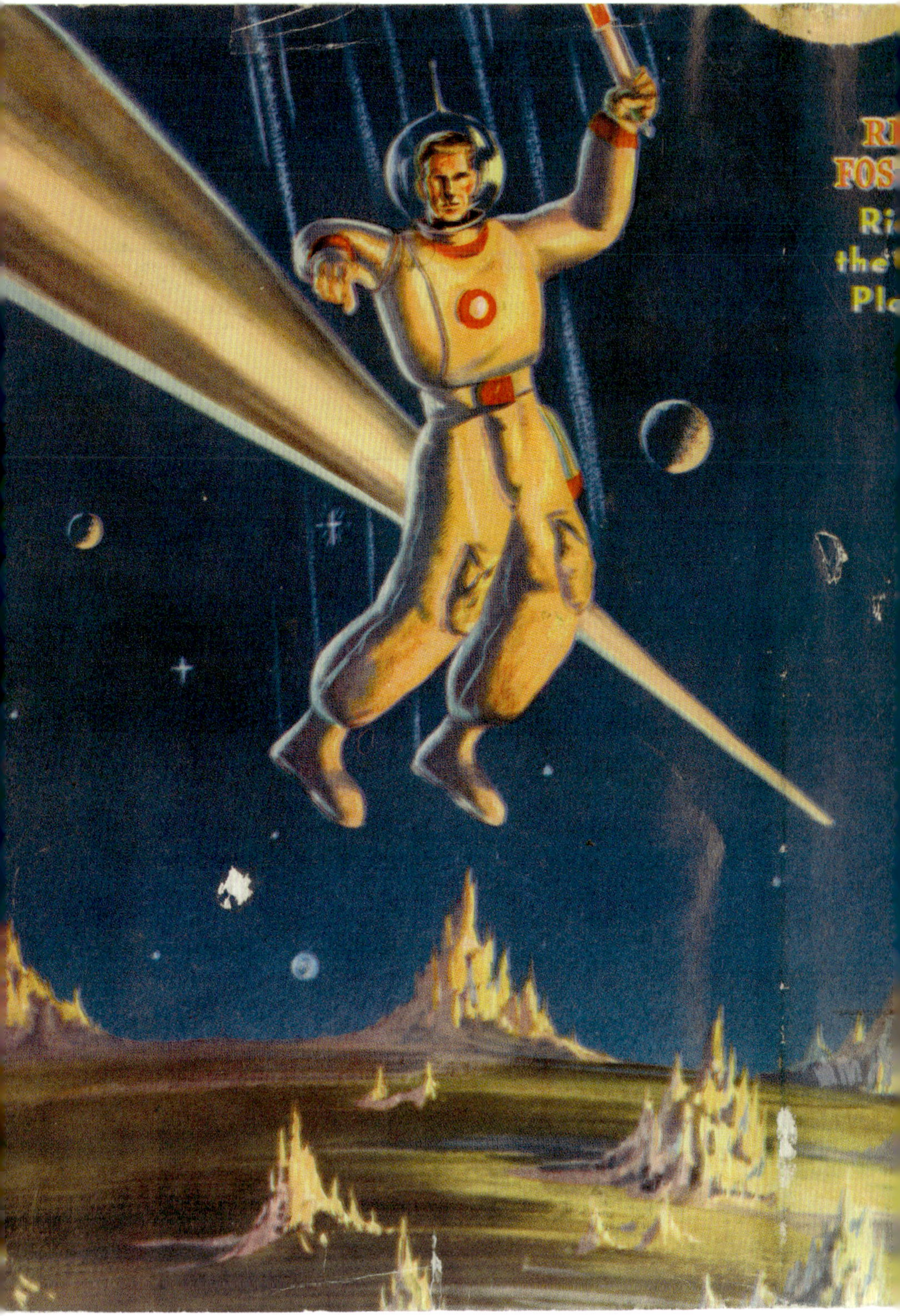

Blake Savage | *Rip Foster Rides the Grey Planet*
Publicity Products, 1952 | Art **E. Deane Cate**

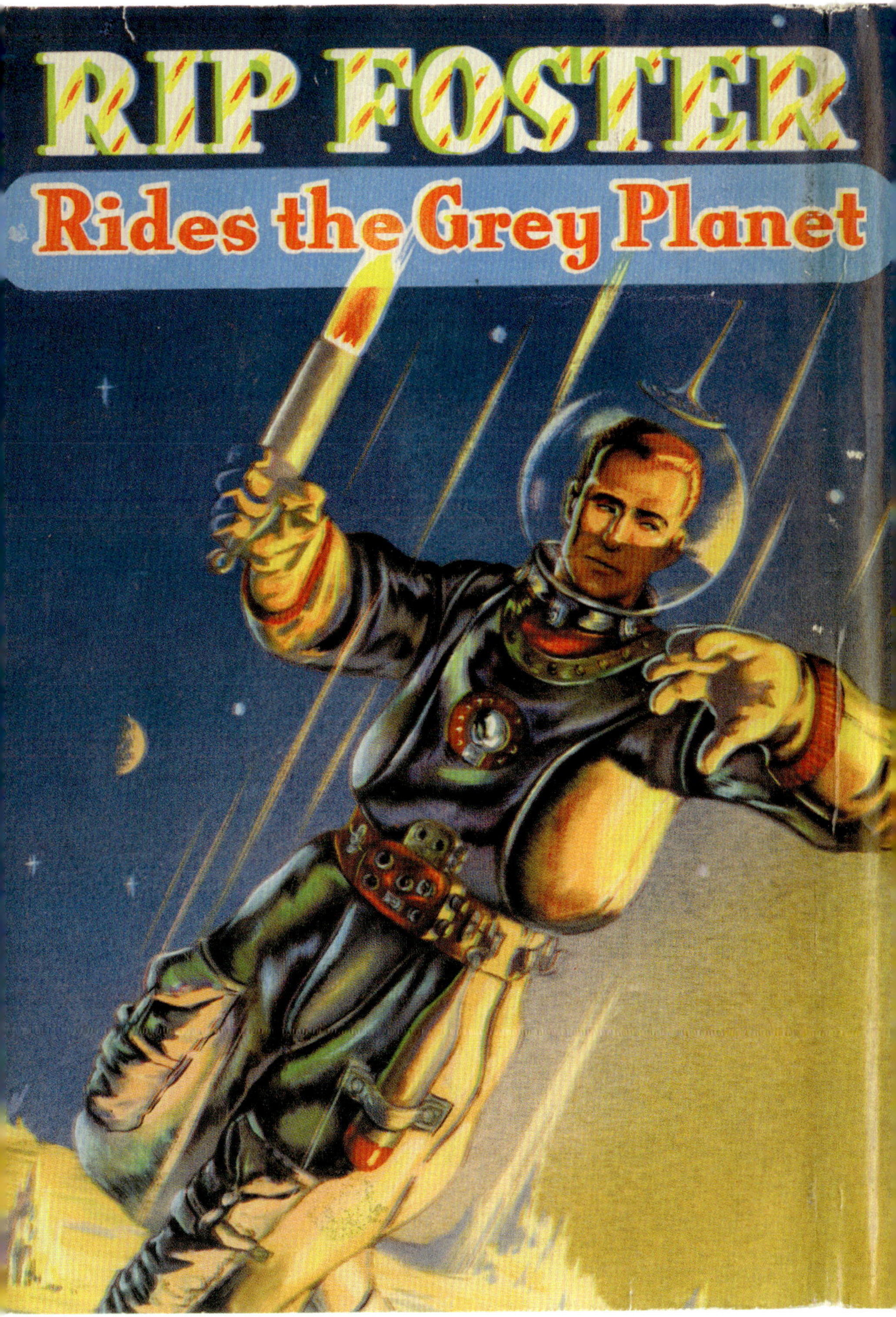
RIP FOSTER
Rides the Grey Planet

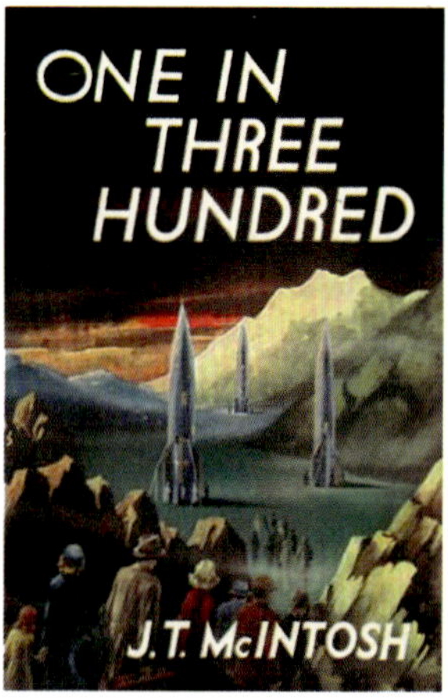

J. T. McIntosh | *One in Three Hundred*
Museum Press, 1956 | Art **Mudge-Marriott**

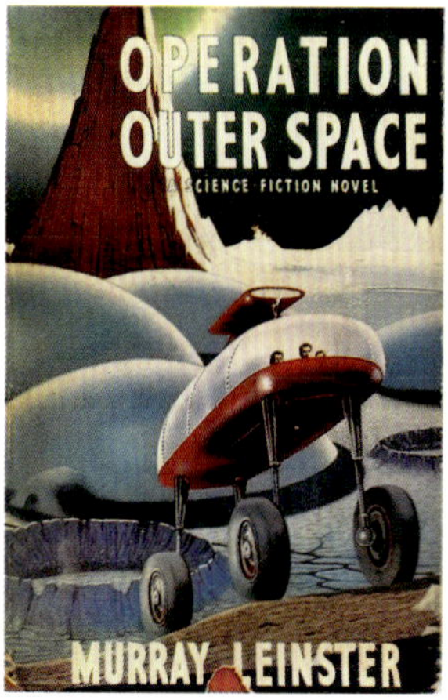

Murray Leinster | *Operation Outer Space*
Grayson & Grayson, 1957 | Art **Unknown**

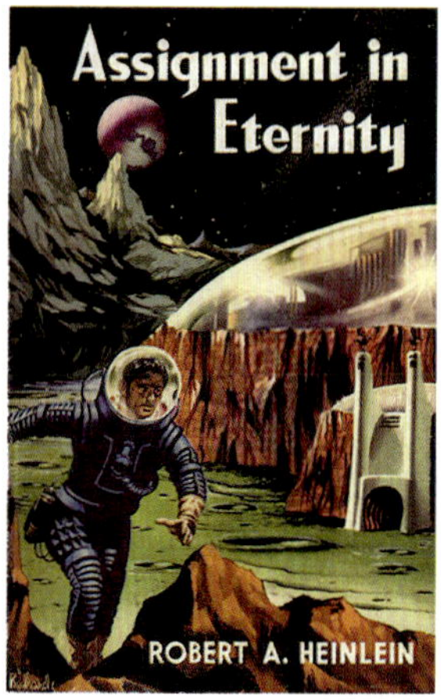

Robert A. Heinlein | *Assignment in Eternity*
Museum Press, 1954 | Art **John Richards**

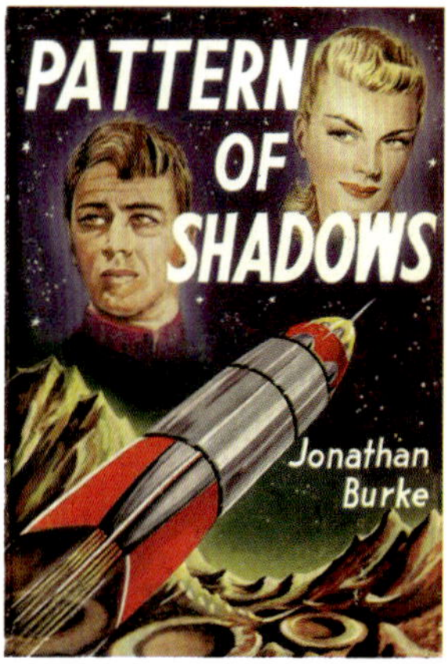

Jonathan Burke | *Pattern of Shadows*
Museum Press, 1954 | Art **Unknown**

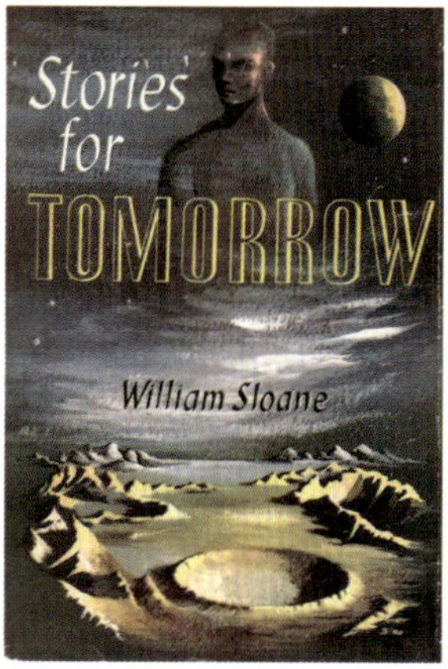

William Sloane | *Stories for Tomorrow*
Eyre and Spottiswoode, 1955 | Art **Val Biro**

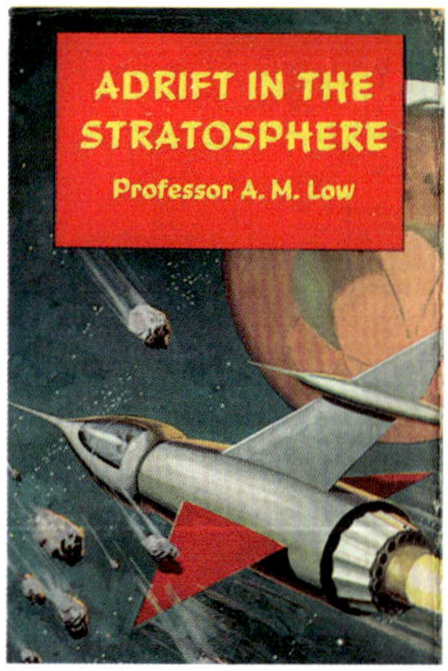

Professor A. M. Low | *Adrift in the Stratosphere*
Peal Press, c.1960 | Art **Ed Valigursky**

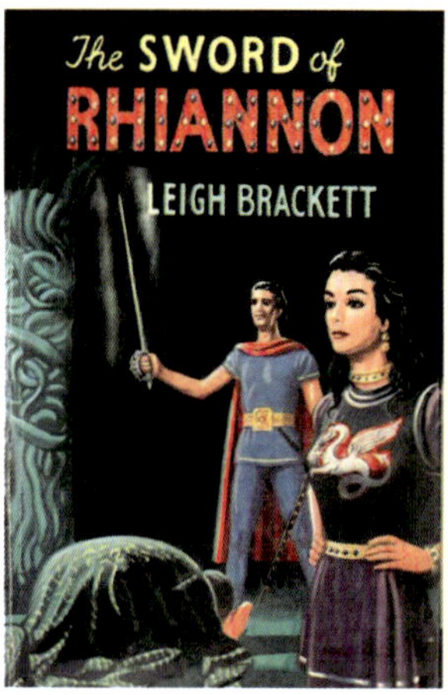

Leigh Brackett | *The Sword of Rhiannon*
T. V. Boardman, 1955 | Art **Harold Johns**

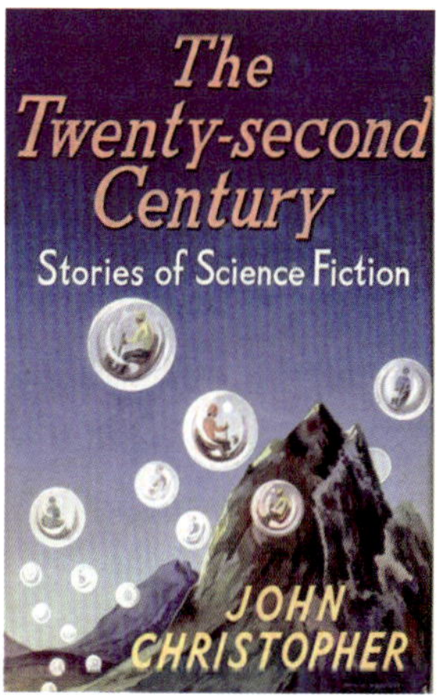

John Christopher | *The Twenty-second Century*
Grayson & Grayson, 1954 | Art **Mudge-Marriott**

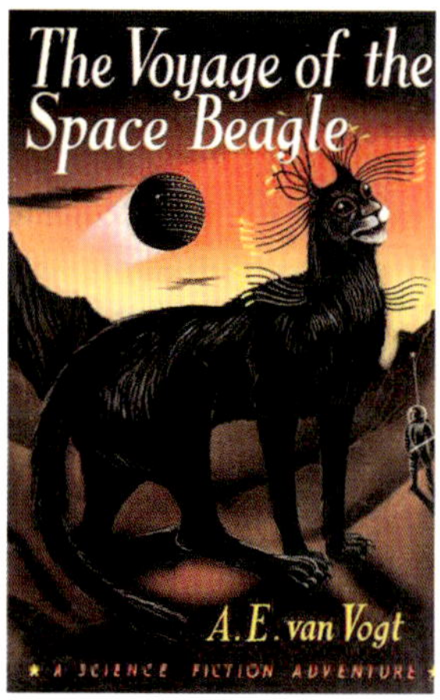

A. E. Van Vogt | *The Voyage of the Space Beagle*
Grayson & Grayson, 1951 | Art **Unknown**

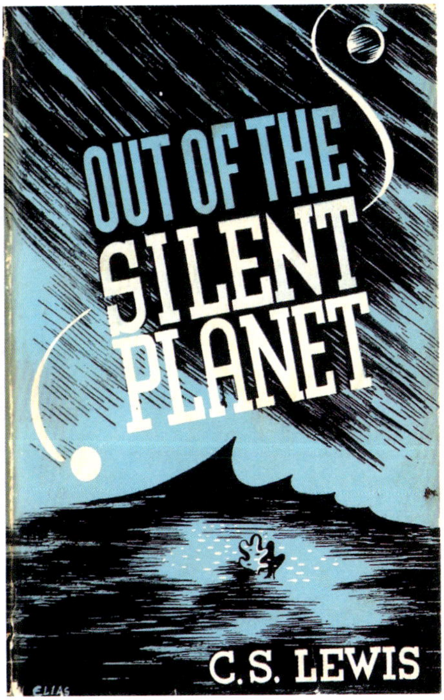

C. S. Lewis | *Out of the Silent Planet*
The Bodley Head, 1951 | Art **Elias**

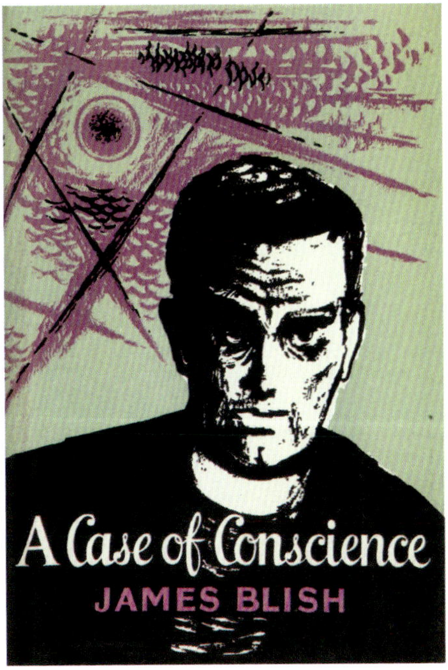

James Blish | *A Case of Conscience*
Faber and Faber, 1959 | Art **Peter Curl**

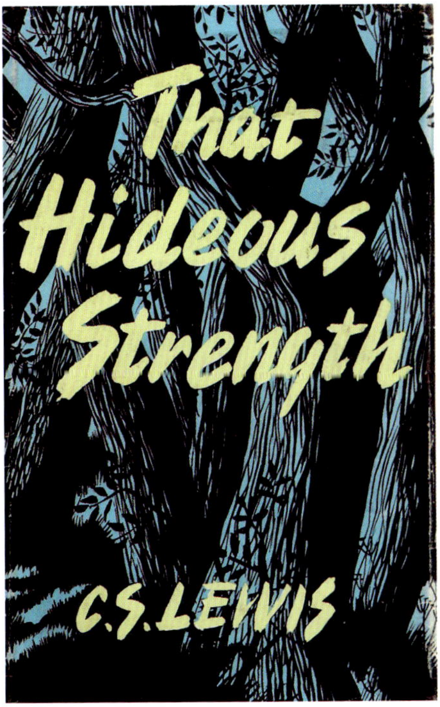

C. S. Lewis | *That Hideous Strength*
The Bodley Head, 1945 | Art **Unknown**

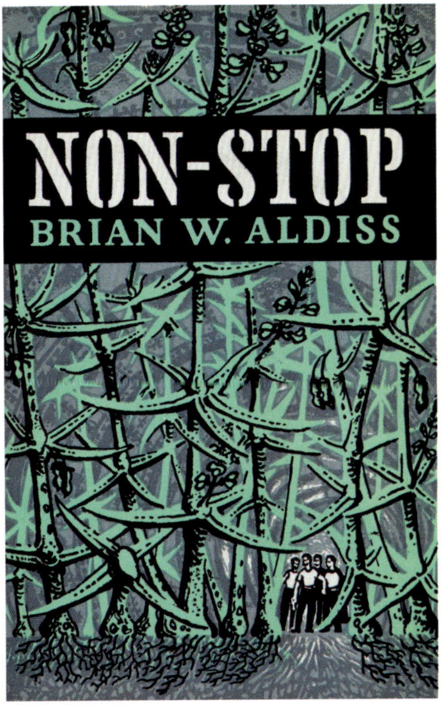

Brian W. Aldiss | *Non-Stop*
Faber and Faber, 1958 | Art **Peter Curl**

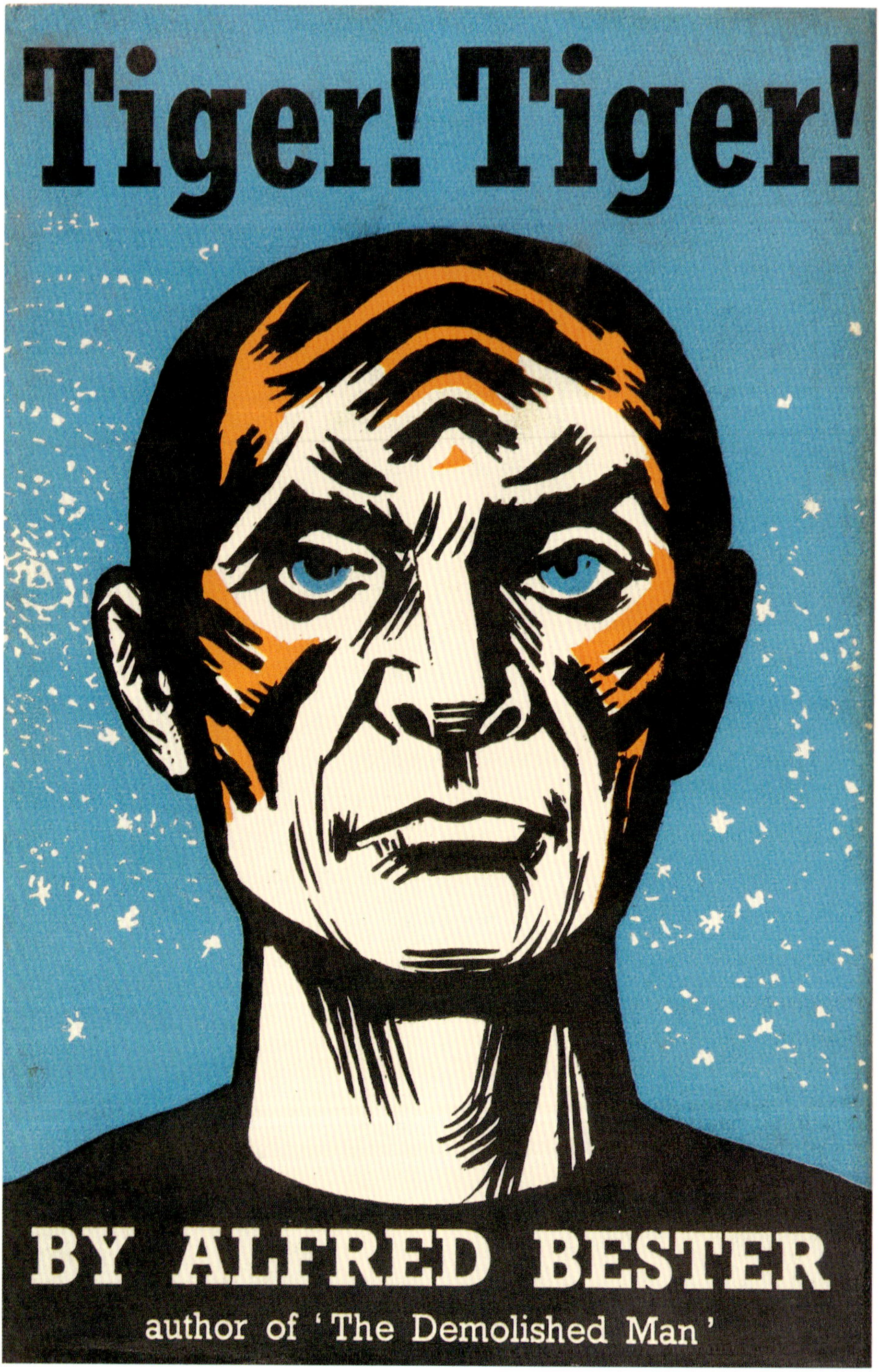

Alfred Bester | *Tiger! Tiger!*
Sidgwick & Jackson, 1956 | Art **Unknown**

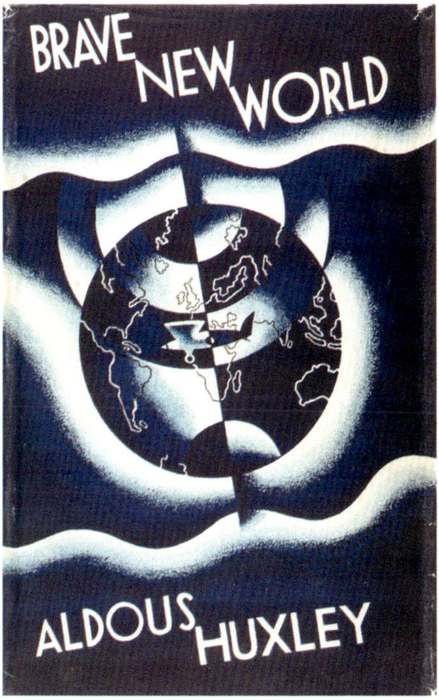

Aldous Huxley | *Brave New World*
Chatto & Windus, 1932 | Art **Leslie Holland**

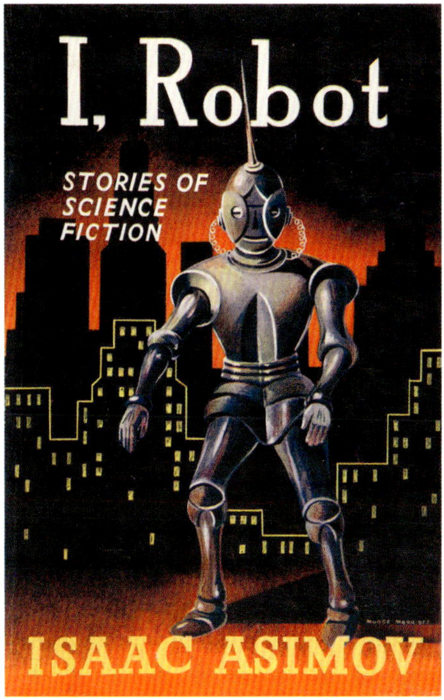

Isaac Asimov | *I, Robot*
Grayson & Grayson, 1952 | Art **Mudge-Marriott**

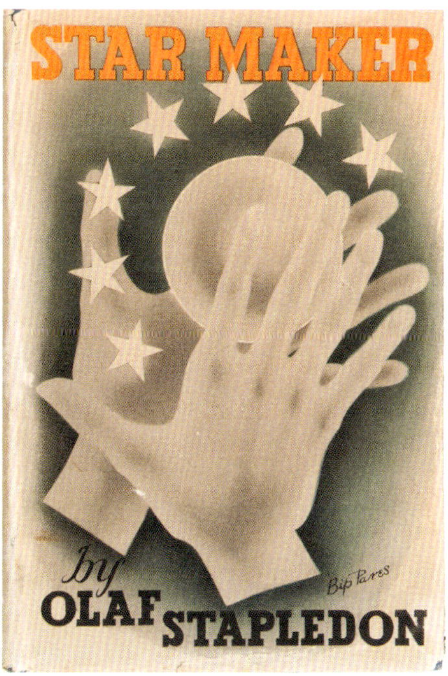

Olaf Stapledon | *Star Maker*
Methuen, 1937 | Art **Bip Pares**

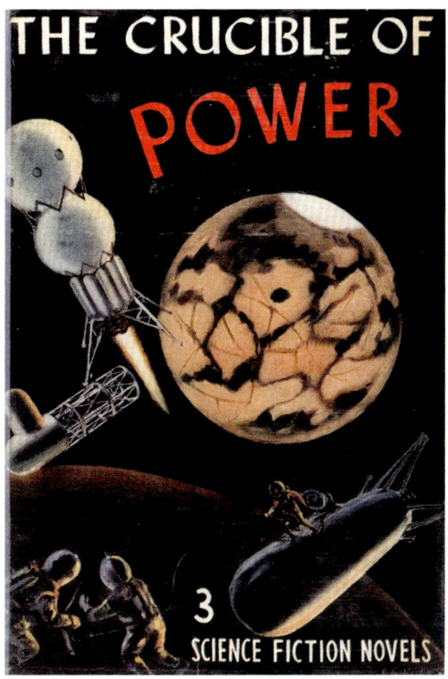

Martin Greenberg | *The Crucible of Power*
The Bodley Head, 1953 | Art **C. King**

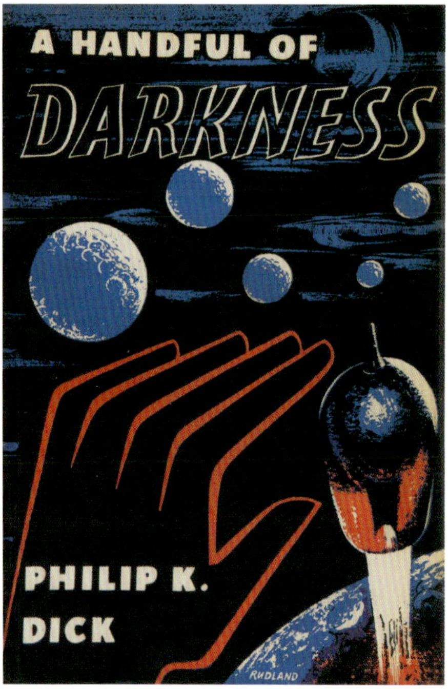

Philip K. Dick | *A Handful of Darkness*
Rich & Cowan, 1955 | Art **Peter Rudland**

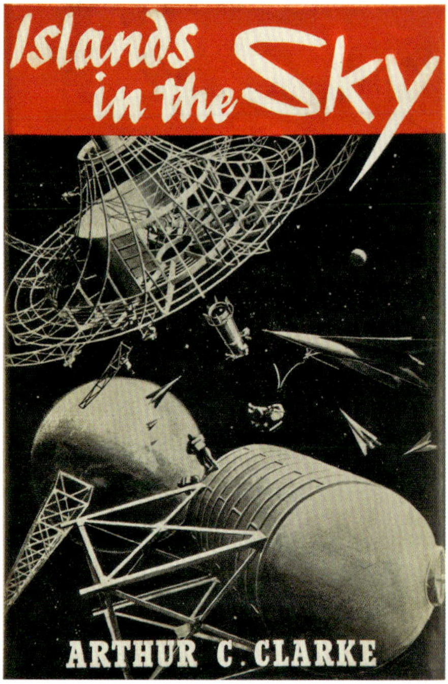

Arthur C. Clarke | *Islands in the Sky*
Sidgwick & Jackson, 1952 | Art **Gerard Quinn**

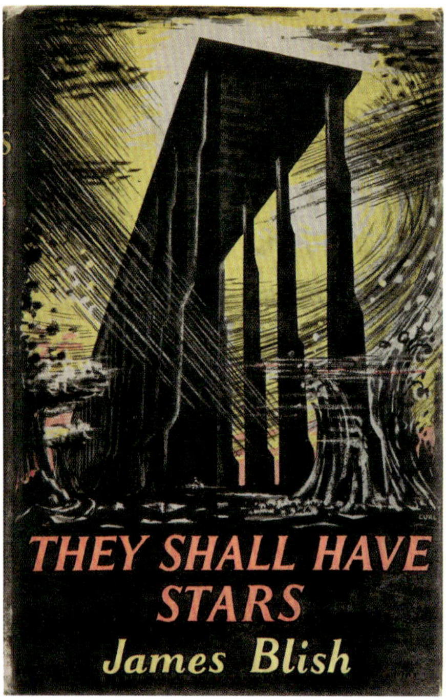

James Blish | *They Shall Have Stars*
Faber and Faber, 1956 | Art **Peter Curl**

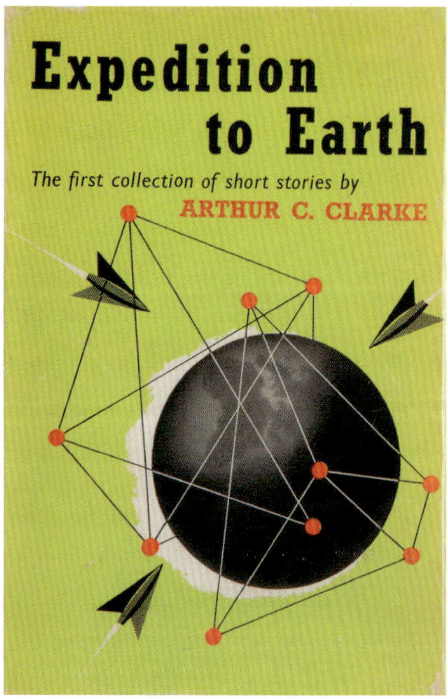

Arthur C. Clarke | *Expedition to Earth*
Sidgwick & Jackson, 1954 | Art **Unknown**

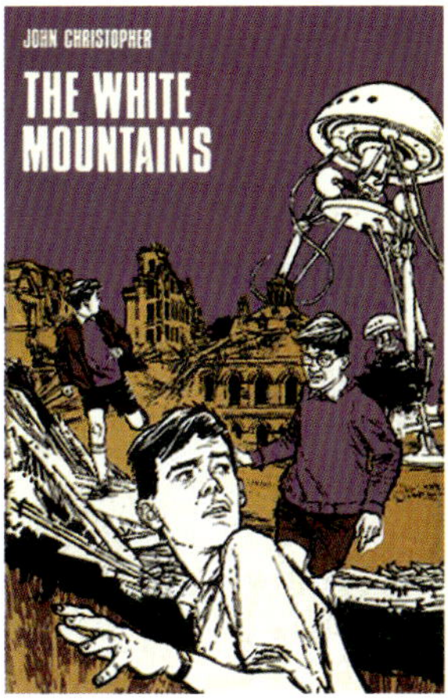

John Christopher | *The White Mountains*
Hamish Hamilton 1967 | Art **Roger Payne**

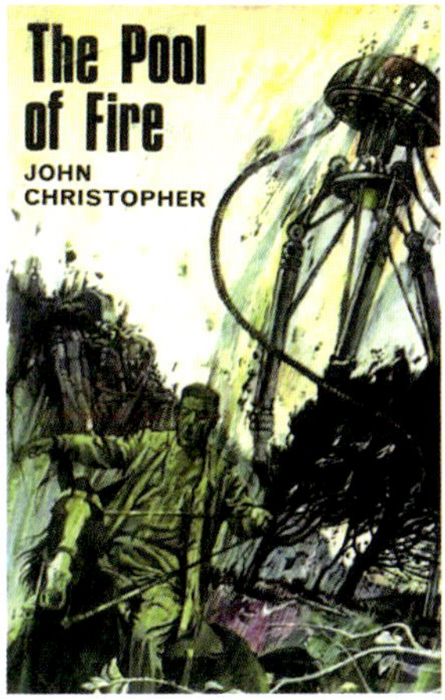

John Christopher | *The Pool of Fire*
Hamish Hamilton 1968 | Art **Michael Heslop**

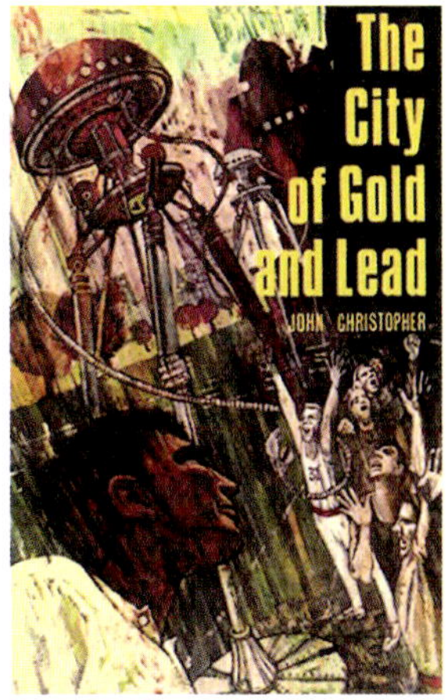

John Christopher | *The City of Gold and Lead*
Hamish Hamilton 1967 | Art **Michael Heslop**

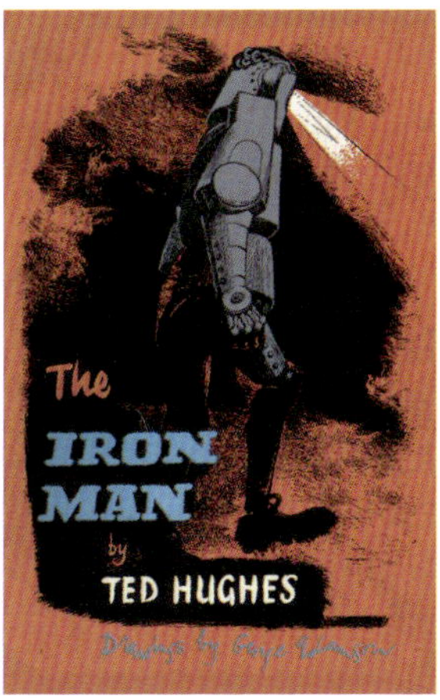

Ted Hughes | *The Iron Man*
Faber and Faber, 1965 | Art **George Adamson**

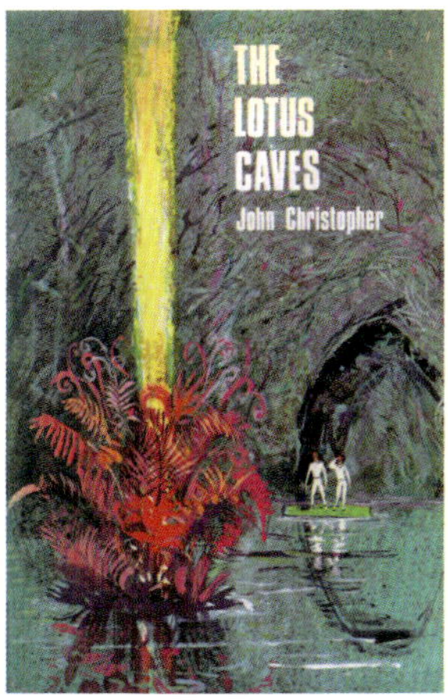

John Christopher | *The Lotus Caves*
Hamish Hamilton 1969 | Art **Unknown**

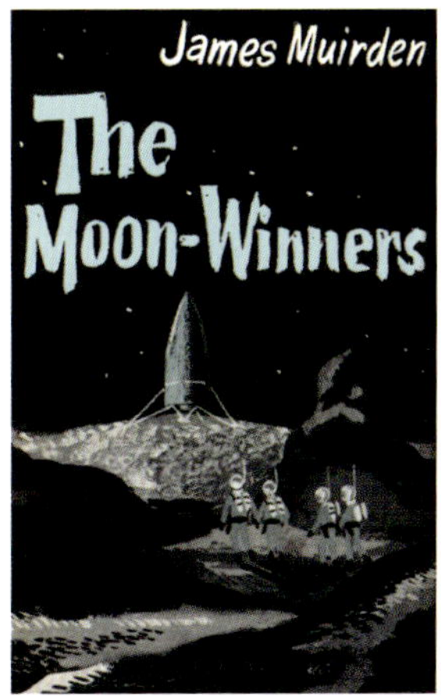

James Muirden | *The Moon Winners*
Hamish Hamilton 1965 | Art **Leslie Wood**

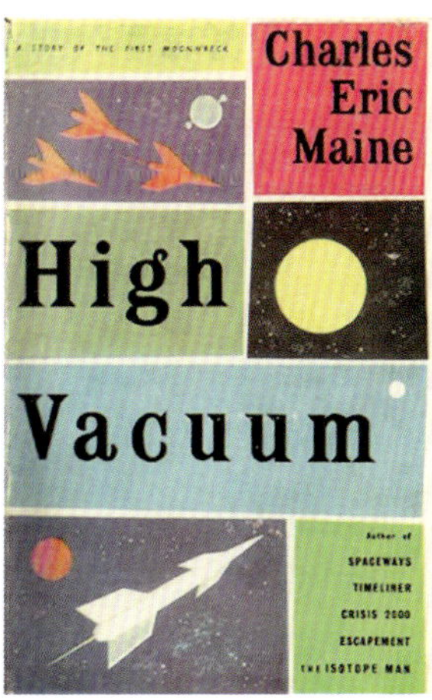

Charles Eric Maine | *High Vacuum*
Hodder and Stoughton, 1957 | Art **Martin Kaye**

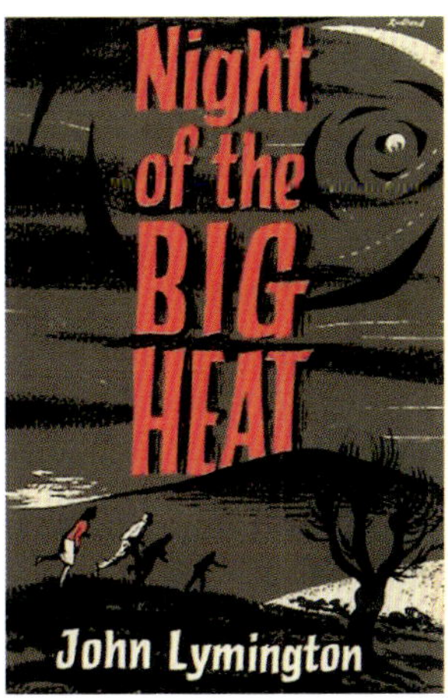

John Lymington | *Night of the Big Heat*
Hodder and Stoughton, 1959 | Art **Peter Rudland**

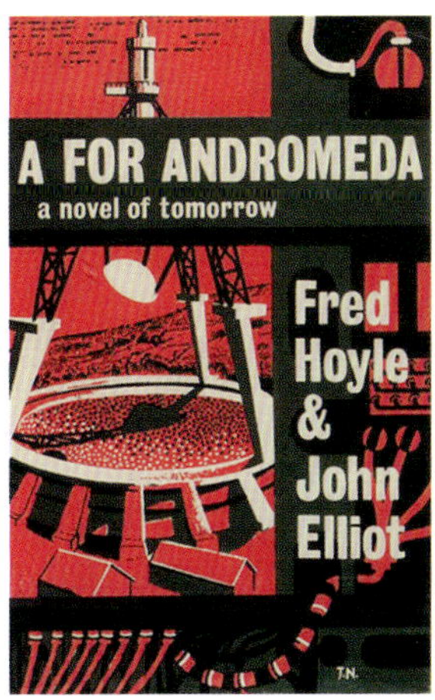

Fred Hoyle and John Elliot | *A For Andromeda*
Souvenir Press, 1962 | Art **J. N.**

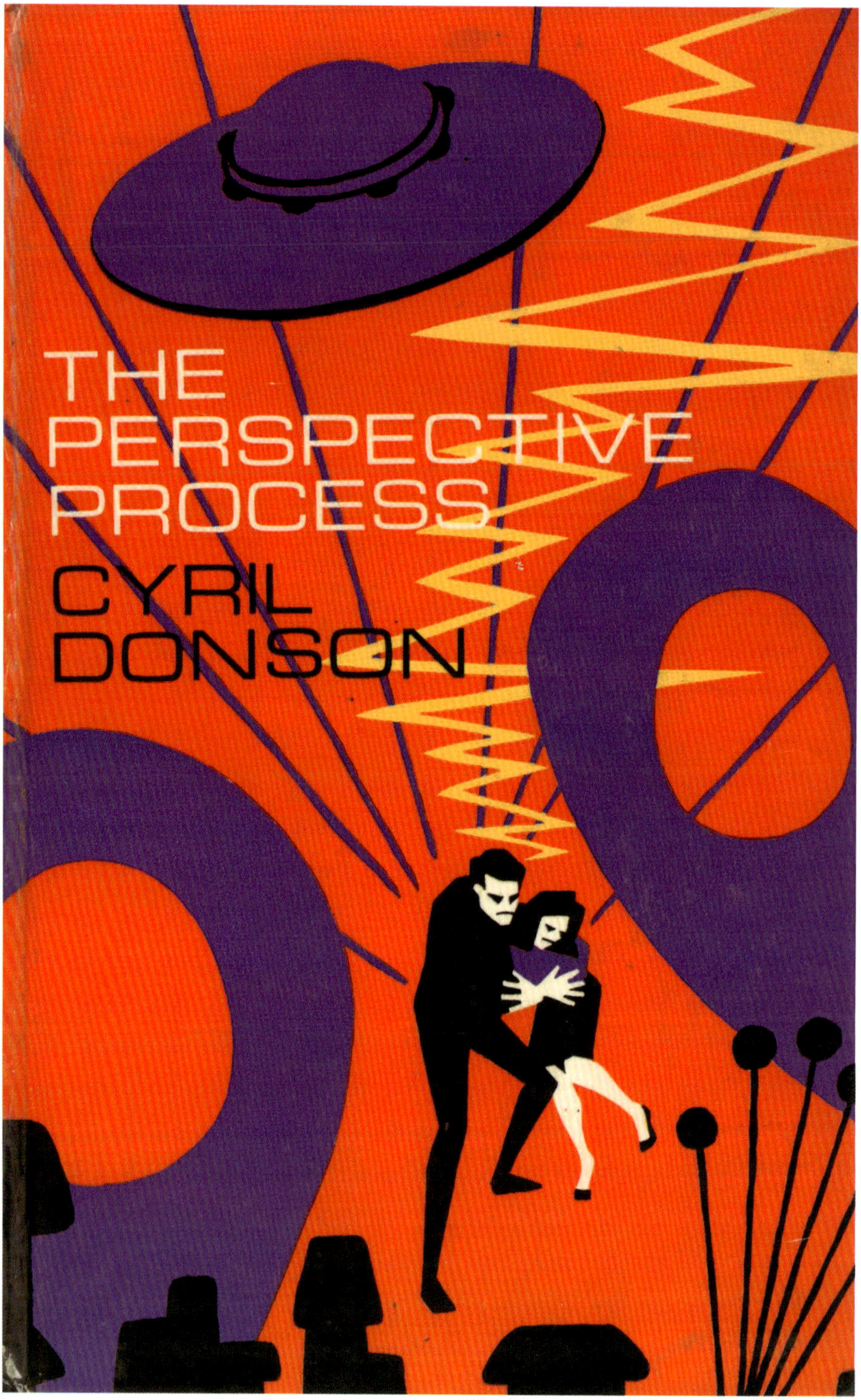

Cyril Donson | *The Perspective Process*
Hale SF, 1969 | Art **Barbera Walton**

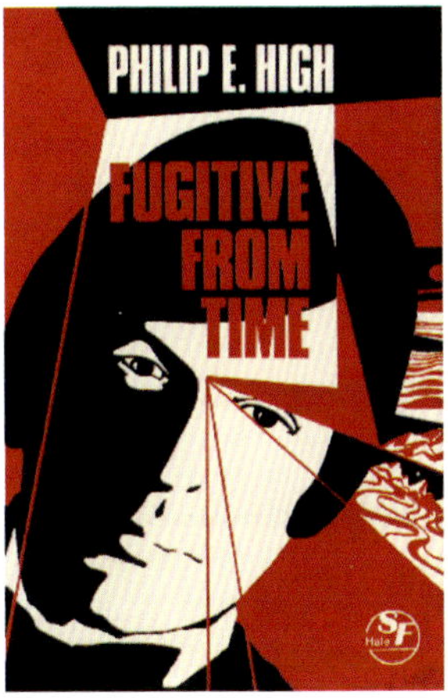

Philip E. High | *Fugitive From Time*
Hale SF, 1969 | Art **Barbera Walton**

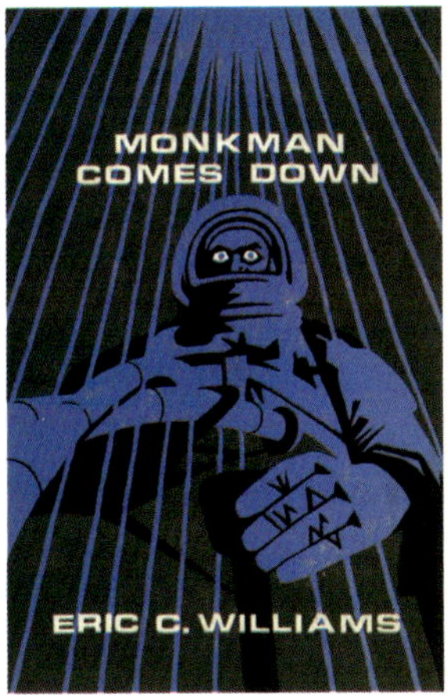

Eric C. Williams | *Monkman Comes Down*
Hale SF, 1969 | Art **Barbera Walton**

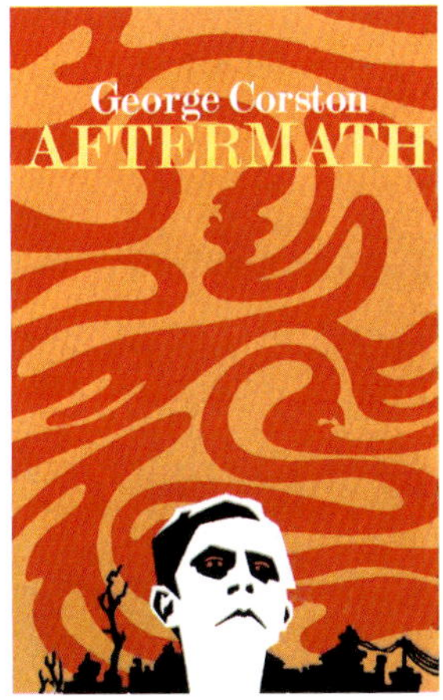

George Corston | *Aftermath*
Hale SF, 1968 | Art **Barbera Walton**

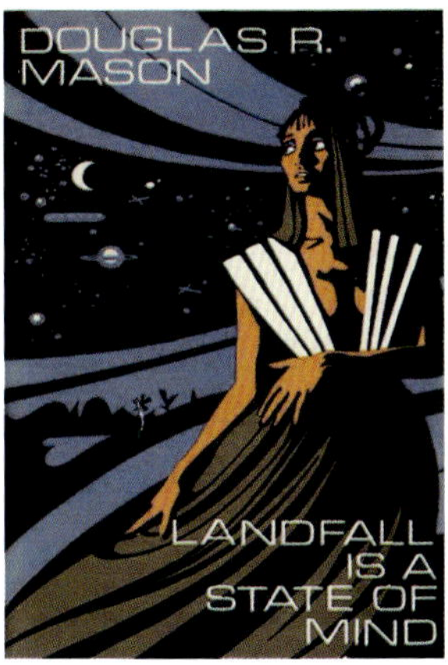

Douglas R. Mason | *Landfall is a State of Mind*
Hale SF, 1968 | Art **Barbera Walton**

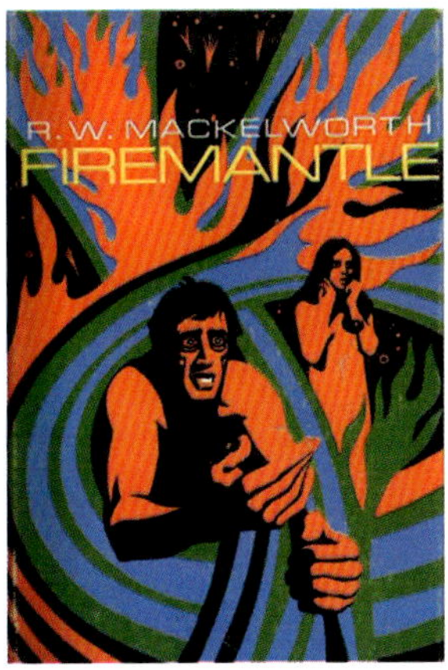

R. W. Mackelworth | *Firemantle*
Hale SF, 1968 | Art **Barbera Walton**

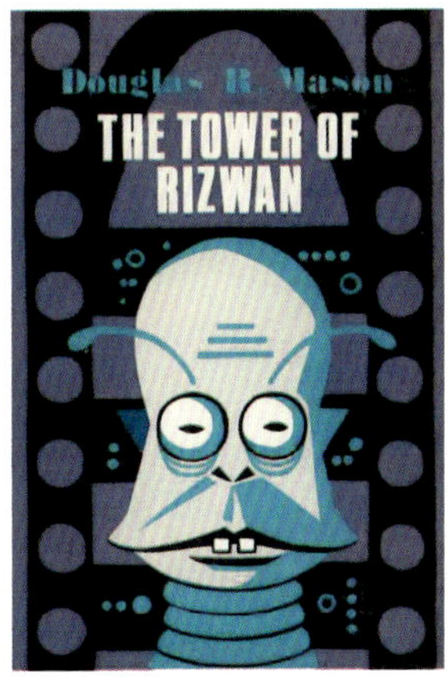

Douglas R. Mason | *The Tower of Rizwan*
Hale SF, 1968 | Art **Barbera Walton**

Kenneth Bulmer | *The Patient Dark*
Hale SF, 1969 | Art **Barbera Walton**

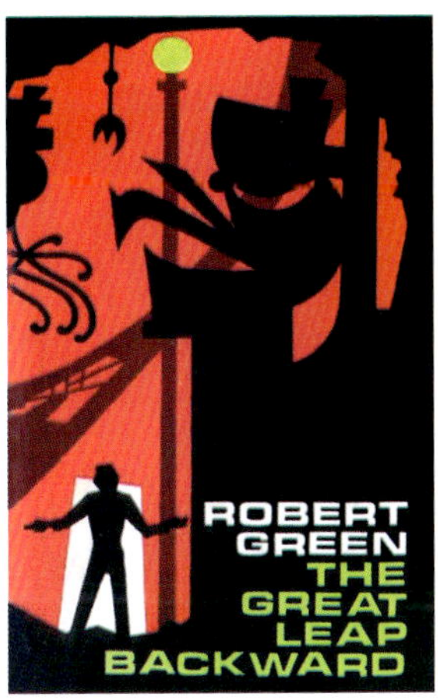

Robert Green | *The Great Leap Backward*
Hale SF, 1968 | Art **Barbera Walton**

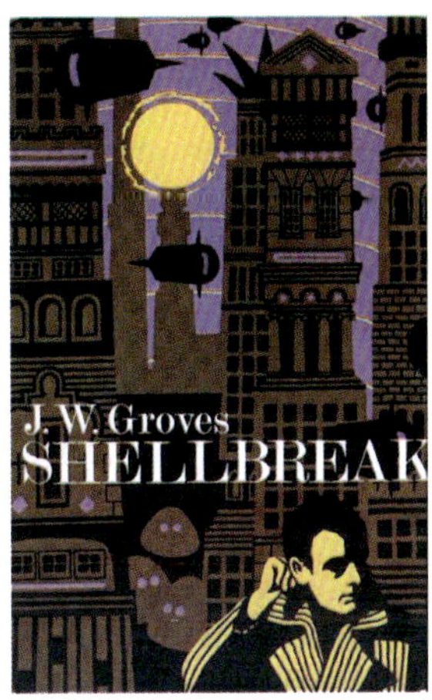

J. W. Groves | *Shellbreak*
Hale SF, 1968 | Art **Barbera Walton**

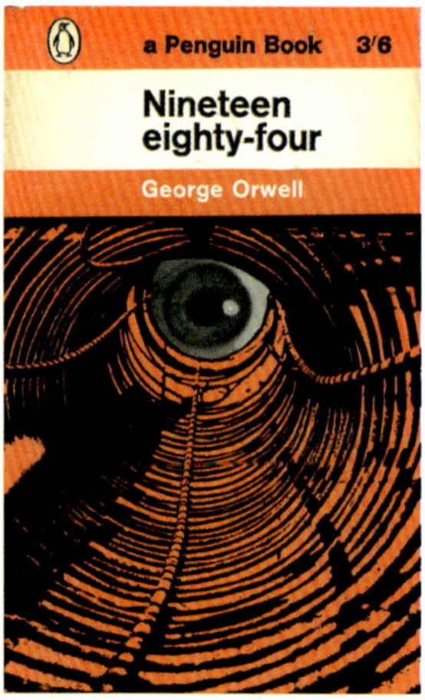

George Orwell | *Nineteen Eighty-Four*
Penguin, 1962 | Art **Germano Facetti**

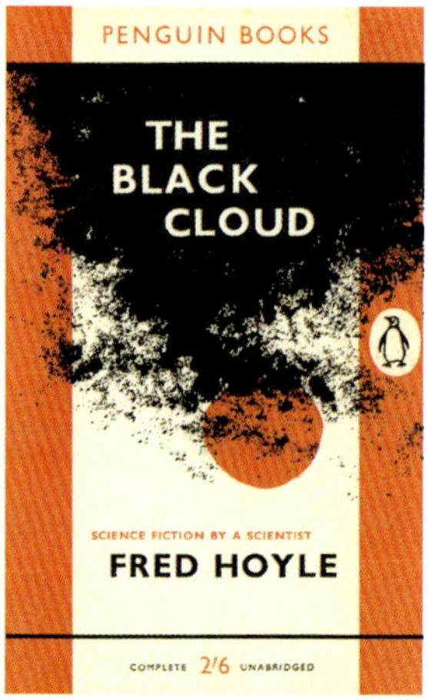

Fred Hoyle | *The Black Cloud*
Penguin, 1963 | Art **John Griffiths**

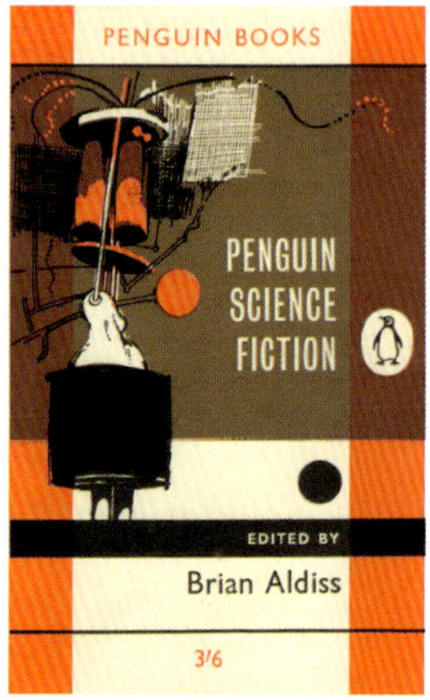

Brian Aldiss, ed. | *Penguin Science Fiction*
Penguin, 1962 | Art **Brian Keogh**

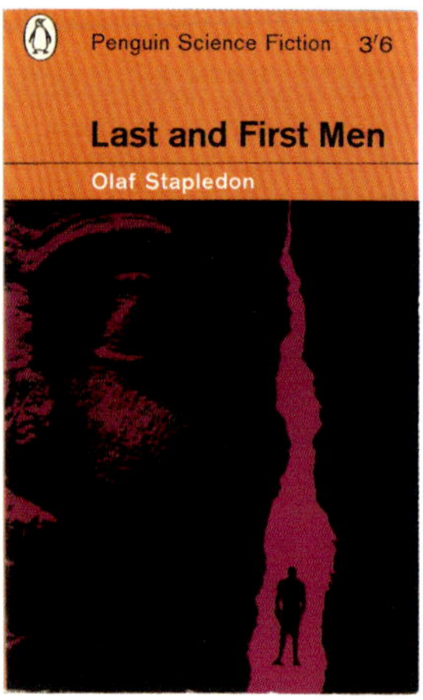

Olaf Stapledon | *First and Last Men*
Penguin, 1963 | Art **Geoffrey Martin**

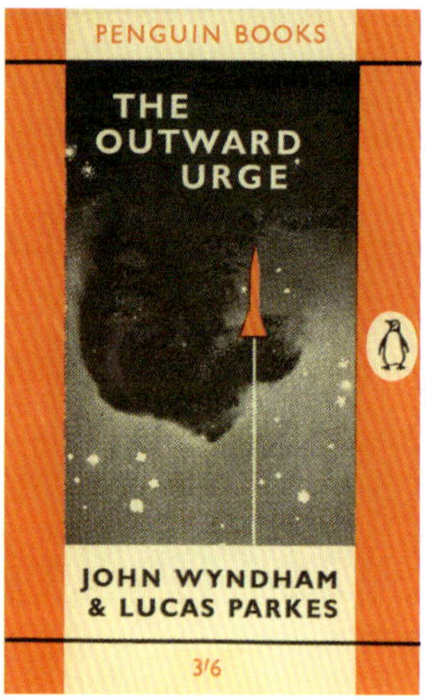

John Wyndham and **Lucas Parkes**
The Outward Urge
Penguin, 1959 | Art **John Griffiths**

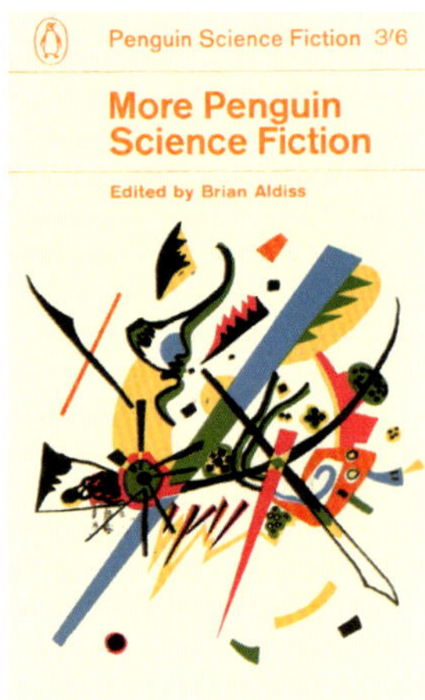

Brian Aldiss, ed. | *More Penguin Science Fiction*
Penguin, 1964 | Art **Vassily Kandinsky**

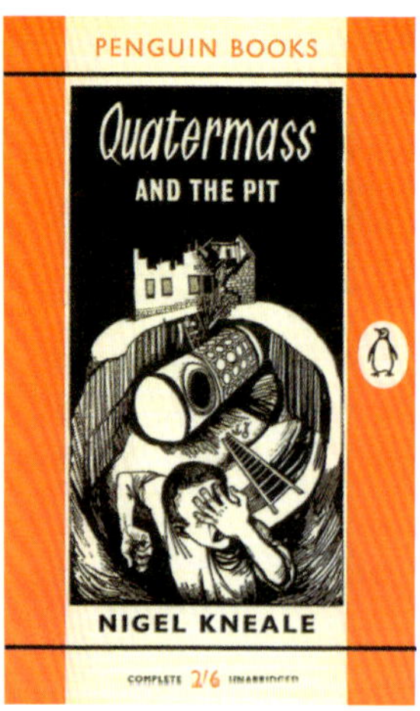

Nigel Kneale | *Quatermass and the Pit*
Penguin, 1960 | Art **Bryan Kneale**

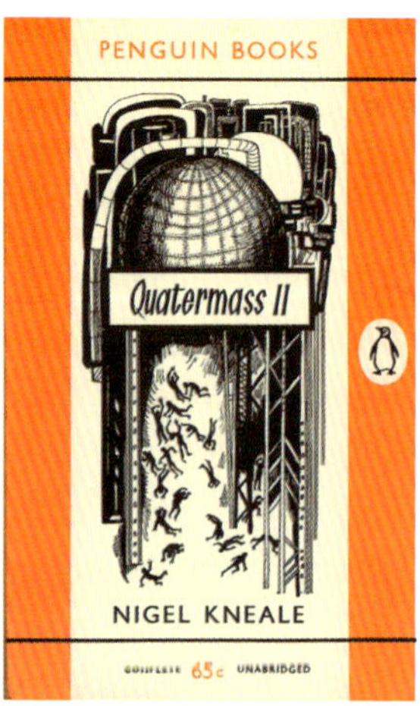

Nigel Kneale | *Quatermass II*
Penguin, 1960 | Art **Bryan Kneale**

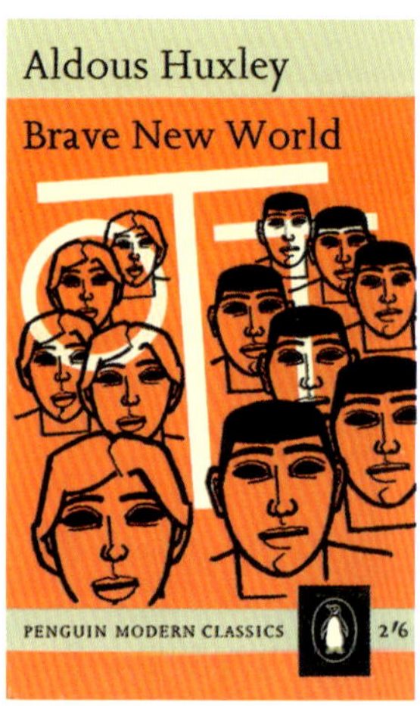

Aldous Huxley | *Brave New World*
Penguin, 1961 | Art **Denis Piper**

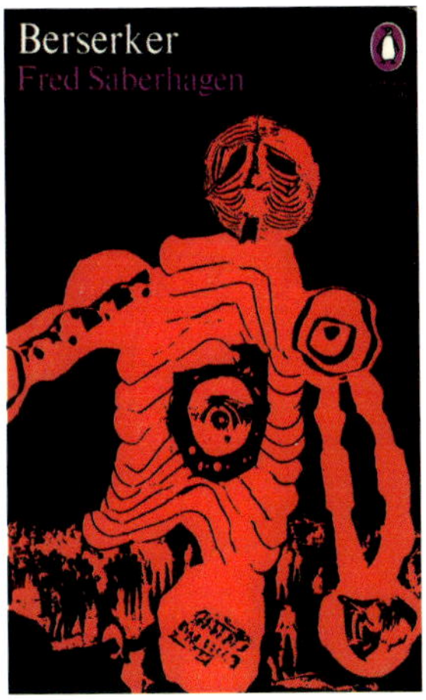

Fred Saberhagen | *Berserker*
Penguin, 1970 | Art **Franco Grignani**

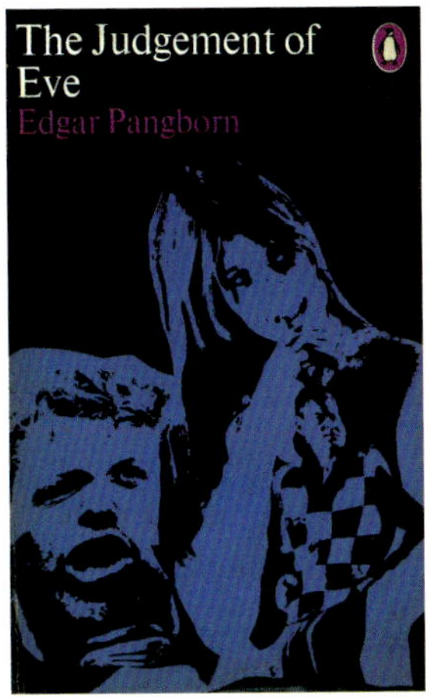

Edgar Pangborn | *The Judgement of Eve*
Penguin, 1970 | Art **Franco Grignani**

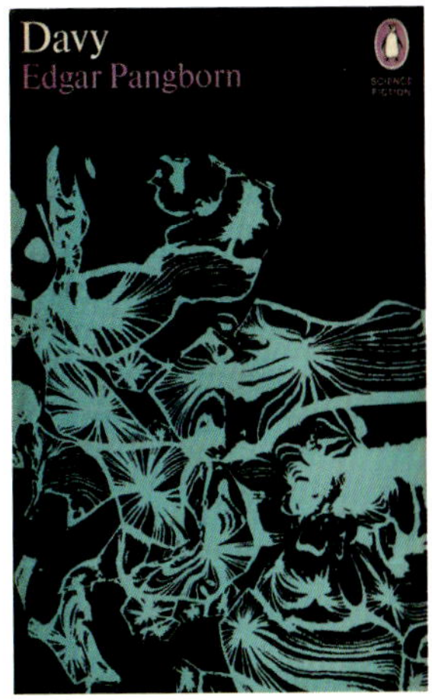

Edgar Pangborn | *Davy*
Penguin, 1969 | Art **Franco Grignani**

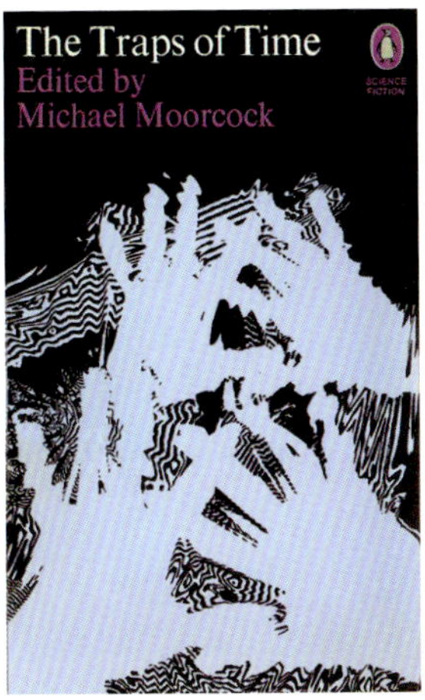

Michael Moorcock | *The Traps of Time*
Penguin, 1970 | Art **Franco Grignani**

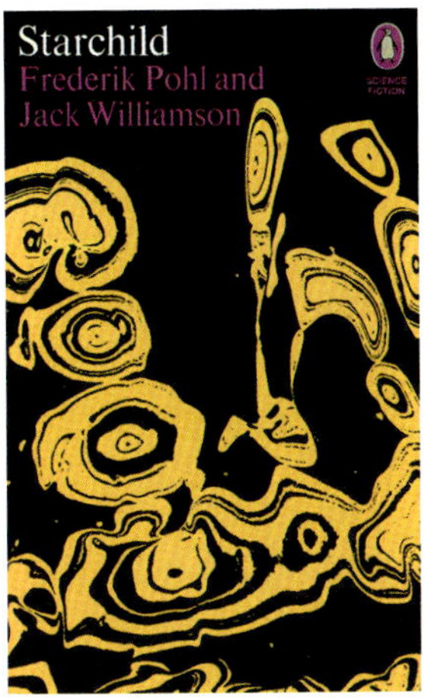

Frederik Pohl & Jack Williamson | *Starchild*
Penguin, 1970 | Art **Franco Grignani**

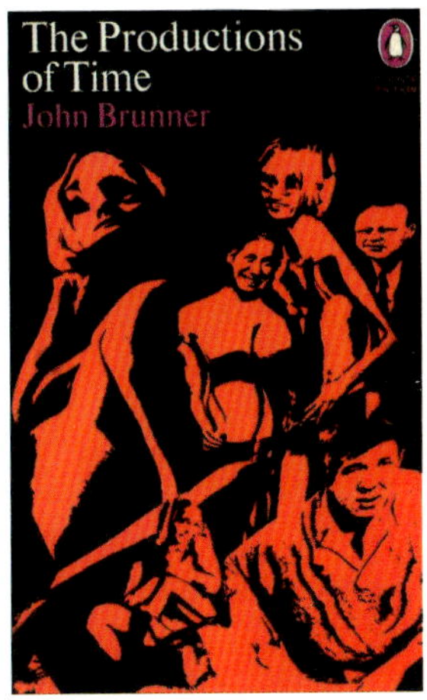

John Brunner | *The Productions of Time*
Penguin, 1970 | Art **Franco Grignani**

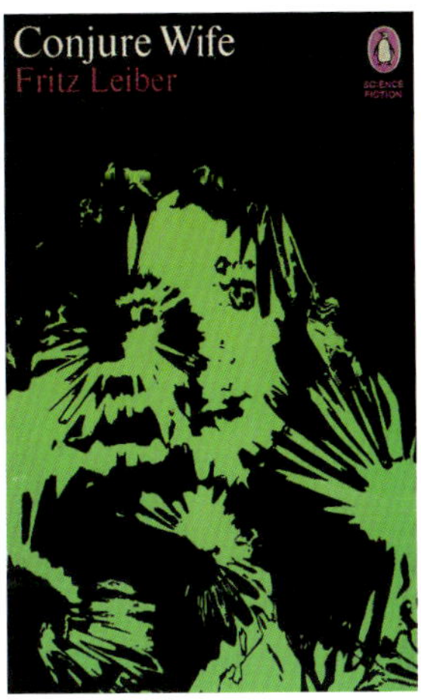

Fritz Leiber | *Conjure Wife*
Penguin, 1969 | Art **Franco Grignani**

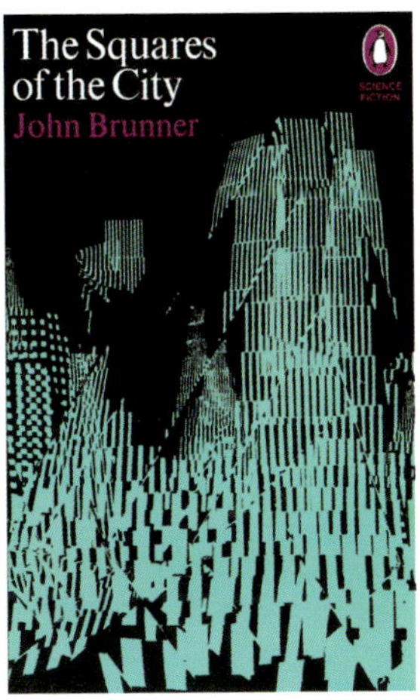

John Brunner | *The Squares of the City*
Penguin, 1969 | Art **Franco Grignani**

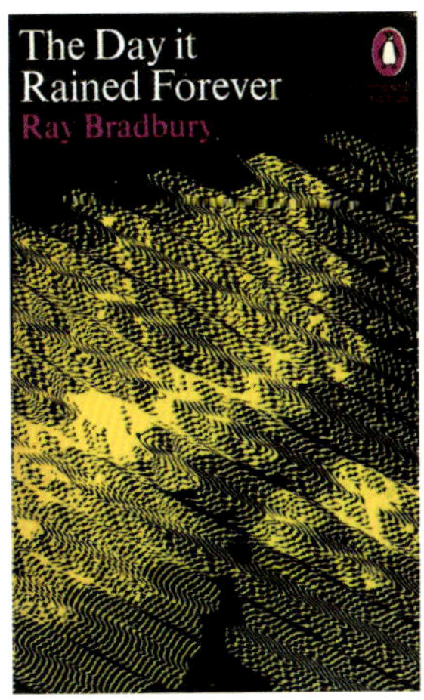

Ray Bradbury | *The Day It Rained Forever*
Penguin, 1969 | Art **Franco Grignani**

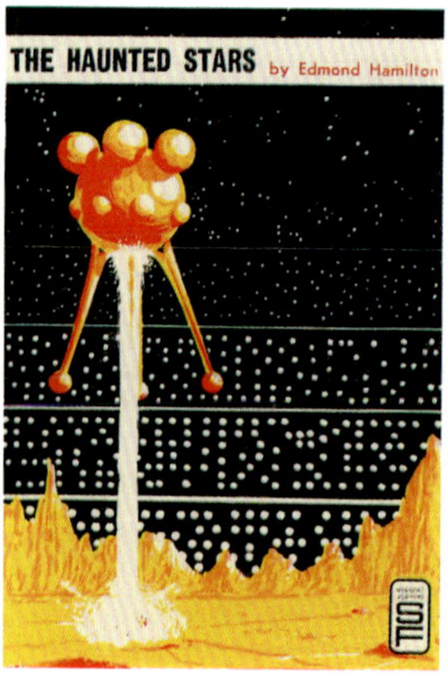

Edmond Hamilton | *The Haunted Stars*
Herbert Jenkins, 1965 | Art **Brian Lewis**

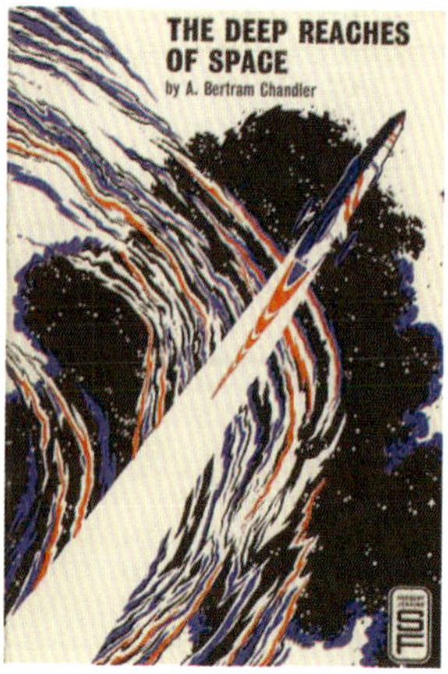

A. Bertram Chandler | *The Deep Reaches of Space*
Herbert Jenkins, 1965 | Art **Brian Lewis**

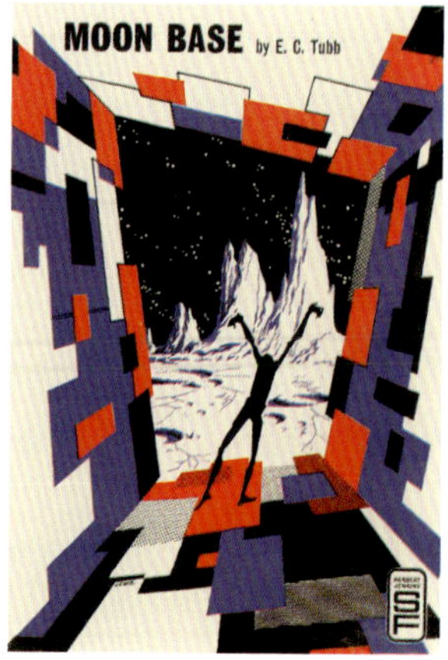

E. C. Tubb | *Moon Base*
Herbert Jenkins, 1965 | Art **Brian Lewis**

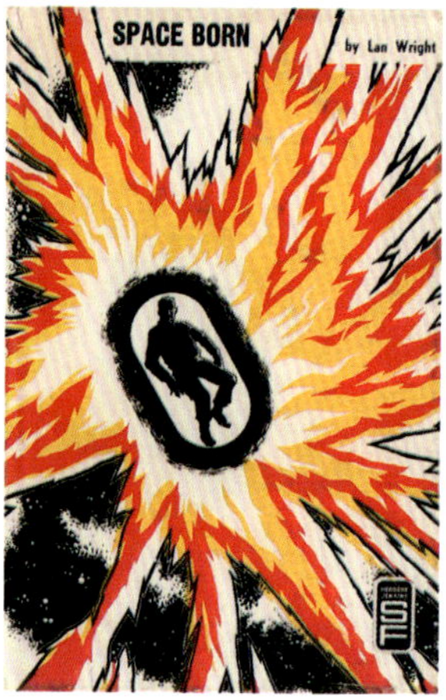

Lan Wright | *Space Born*
Herbert Jenkins, 1964 | Art **Brian Lewis**

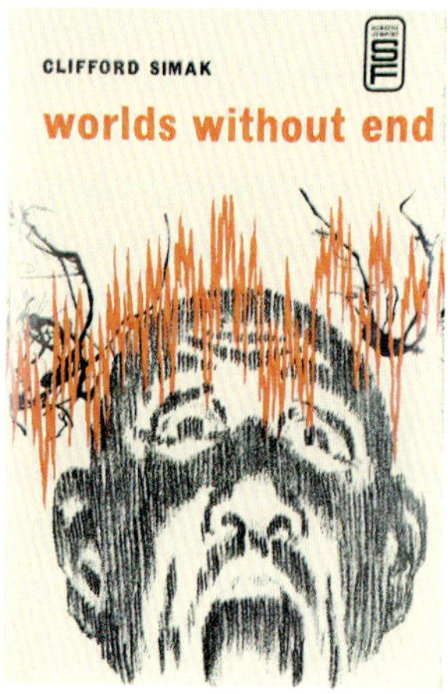

Clifford Simak | *Worlds Without End*
Herbert Jenkins, 1965 | Art **Brian Lewis**

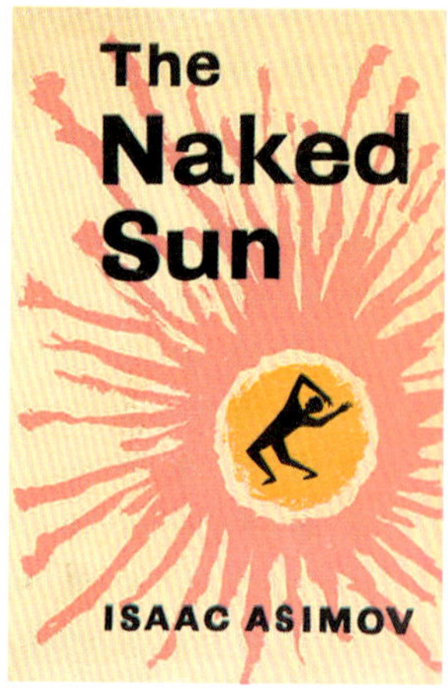

Isaac Asimov | *The Naked Sun*
Michael Joseph, 1958 | Art **Unknown**

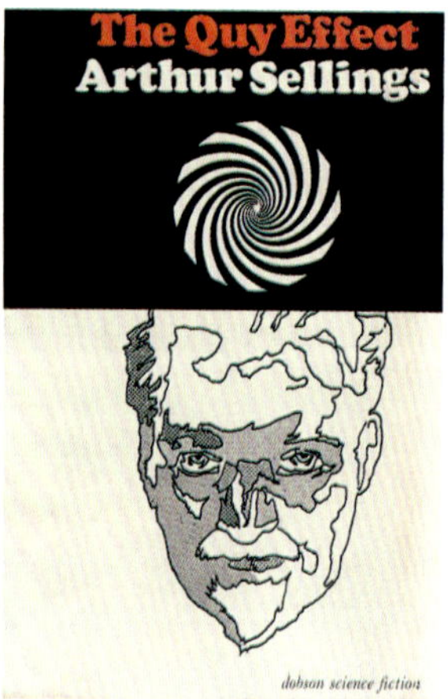

Arthur Sellings | *The Quy Effect*
Dennis Dobson, 1966 | Art **Richard Weaver**

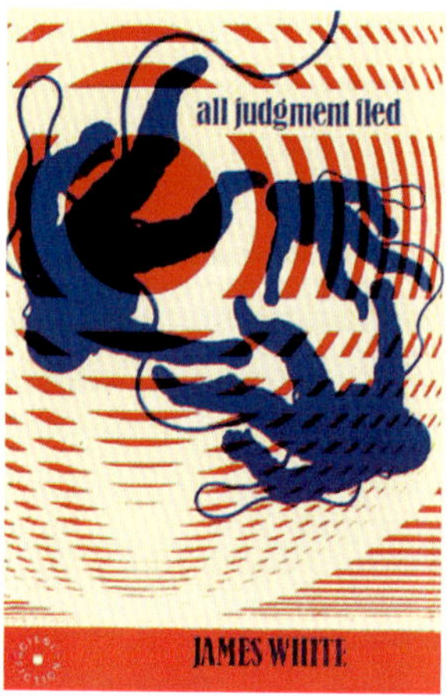

James White | *All Judgement Fled*
Rapp & Whiting, 1968 | Art **Lawrence Edwards**

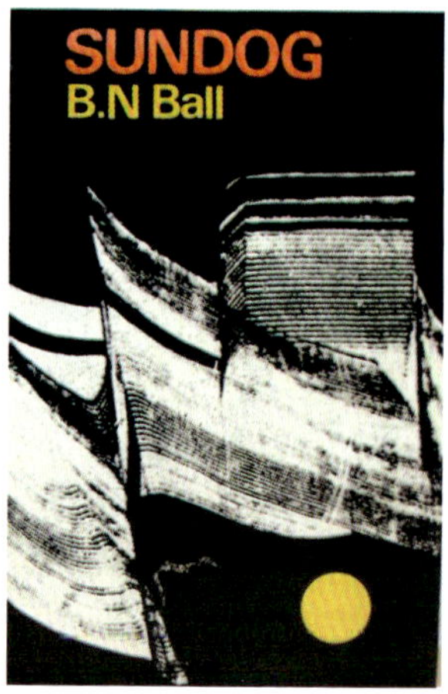

B. N. Ball | *Sundog*
Dennis Dobson, 1965 | Art **William Belcher**

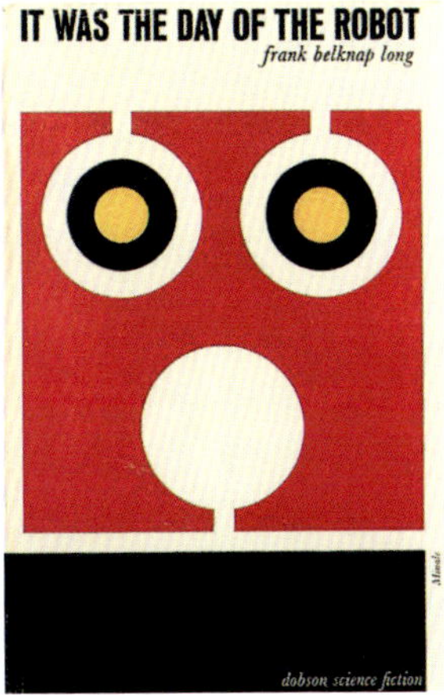

Frank Belknap Long
It Was The Day of the Robot
Dennis Dobson, 1964 | Art **Marcello Minale**

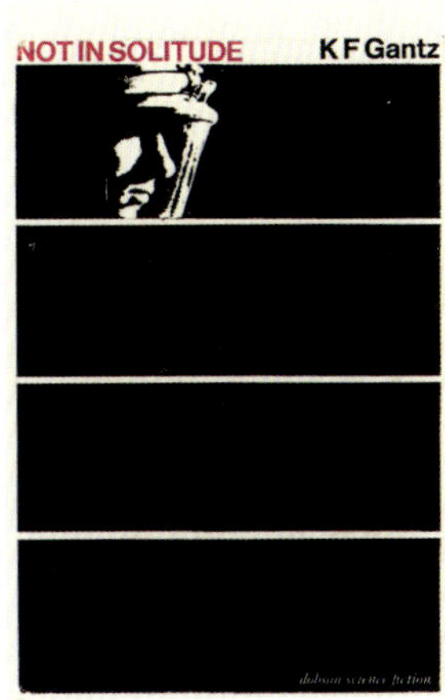

K. F. Gantz | *Not In Solitude*
Dennis Dobson, 1966 | Art **Richard Weaver**

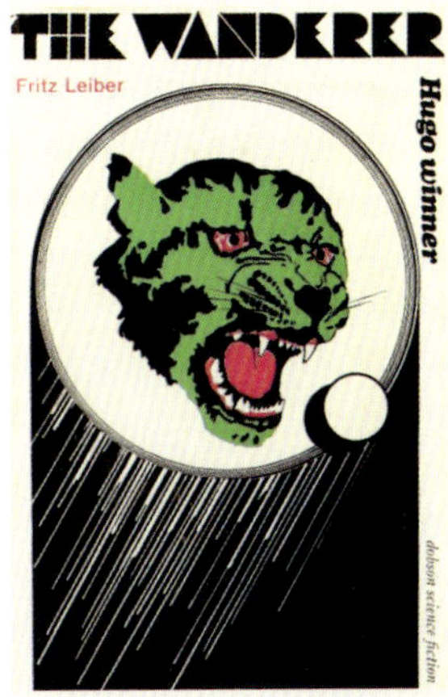

Fritz Leiber | *The Wanderer*
Dennis Dobson, 1967 | Art **Richard Weaver**

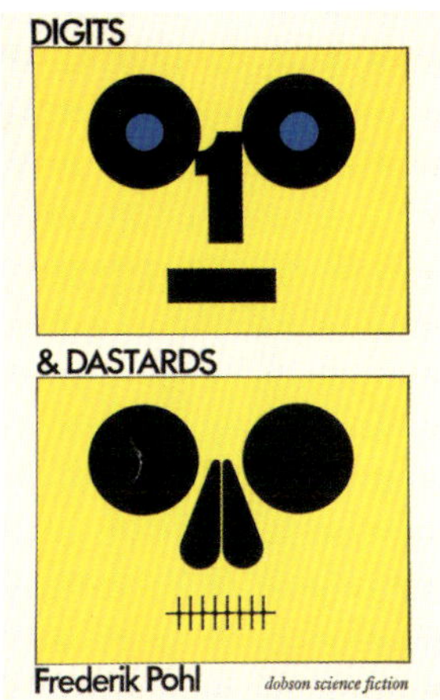

Frederik Pohl | *Digits and Dastards*
Dennis Dobson, 1968 | Art **Richard Weaver**

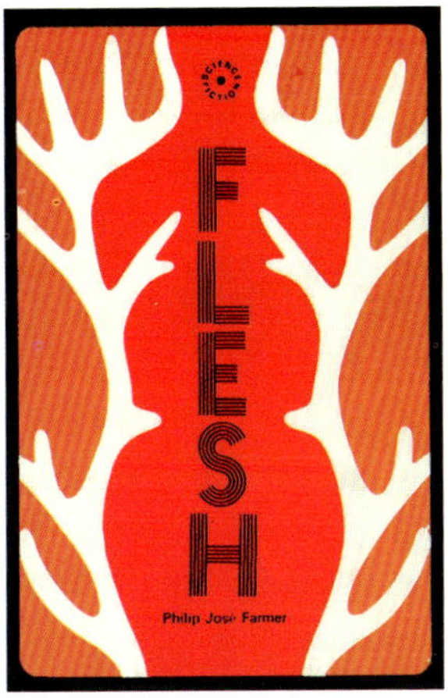

Philip José Farmer | *Flesh*
Rapp & Whiting, 1969 | Art **Lawrence Edwards**

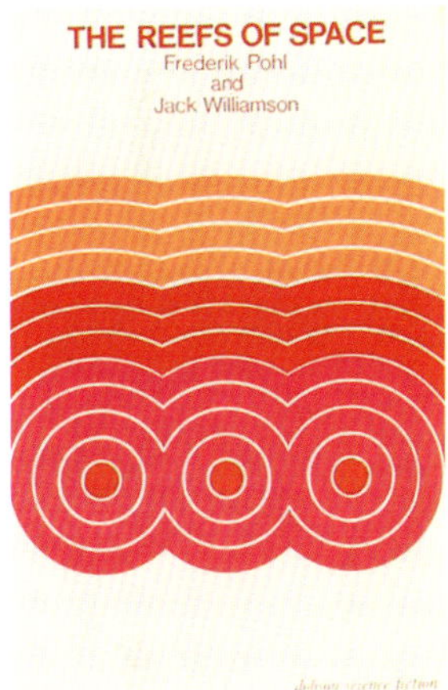

Frederik Pohl and Jack Williamson
The Reefs of Space
Dennis Dobson, 1965 | Art **Unknown**

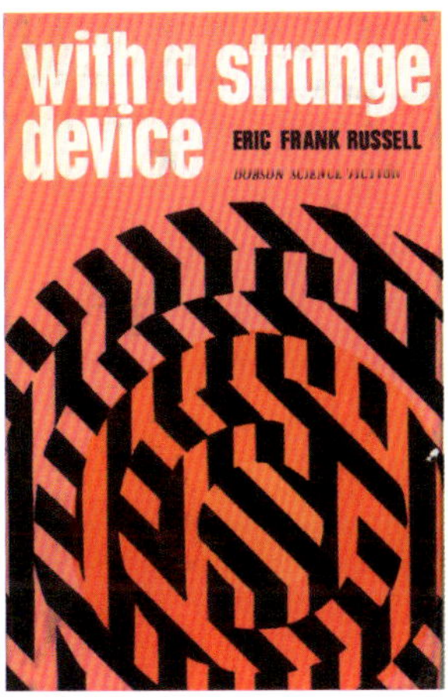

Eric Frank Russell | *With A Strange Device*
Dennis Dobson, 1964 | Art **Unknown**

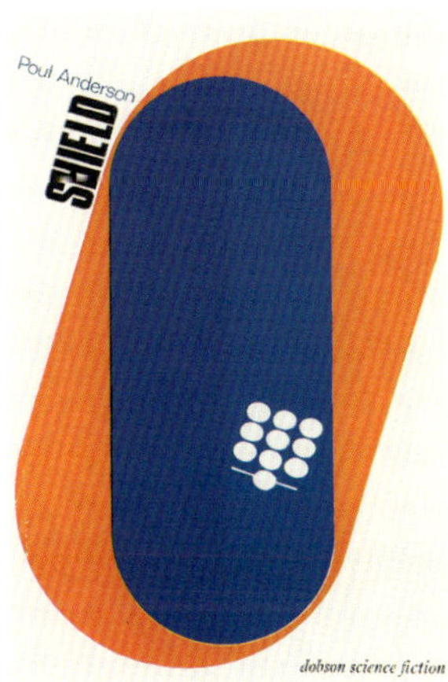

Poul Anderson | *Shield*
Dennis Dobson, 1965 | Art **Richard Weaver**

Keith Laumer | *Galactic Odyssey*
Dennis Dobson, 1968 | Art **Richard Weaver**

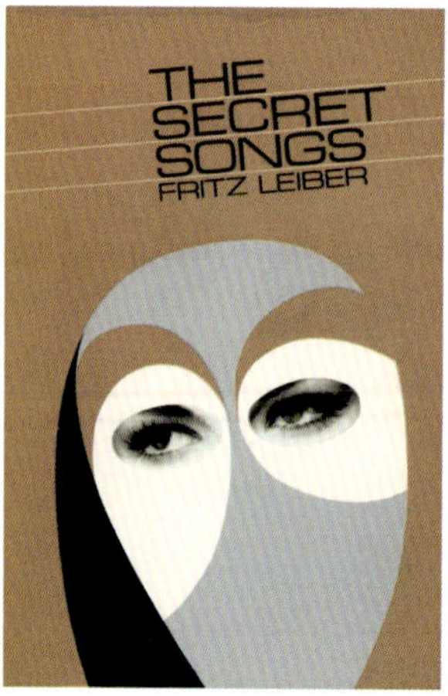

Fritz Leiber | *The Secret Songs*
Hart-Davis, 1968 | Art **Ken Reilly**

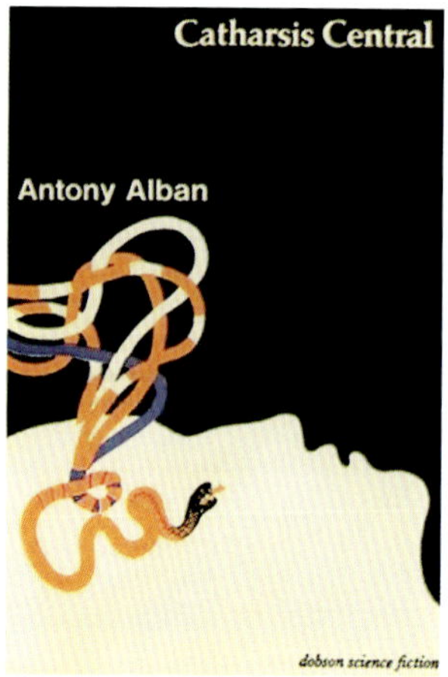

Anthony Alban | *Catharsis Central*
Dennis Dobson, 1968 | Art **Unknown**

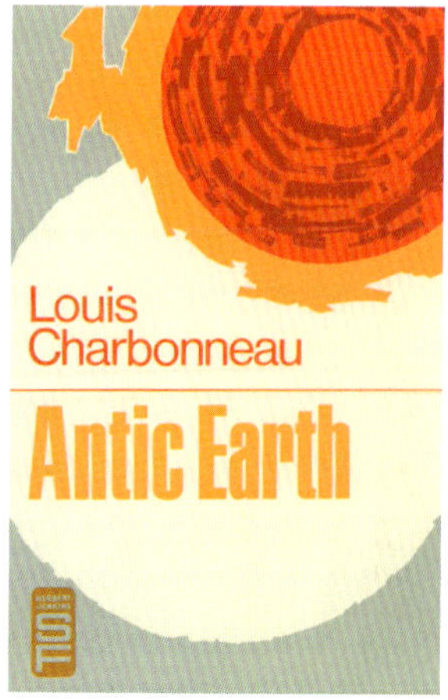

Louis Charbonneau | *Antic Earth*
Herbert Jenkins, 1967 | Art **Unknown**

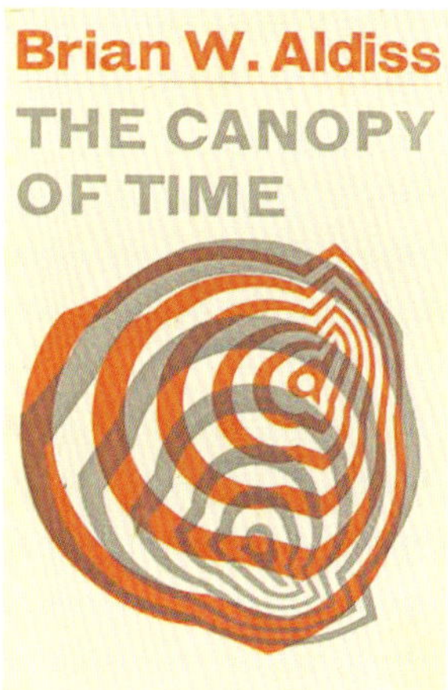

Brian W. Aldiss | *The Canopy of Time*
Faber and Faber, 1966 | Art **Unknown**

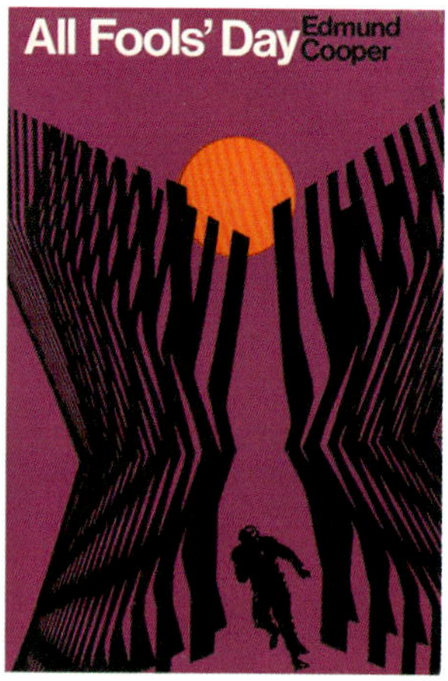

Edmund Cooper | *All Fool's Day*
Hodder and Stoughton, 1966 | Art **Brian Keogh**

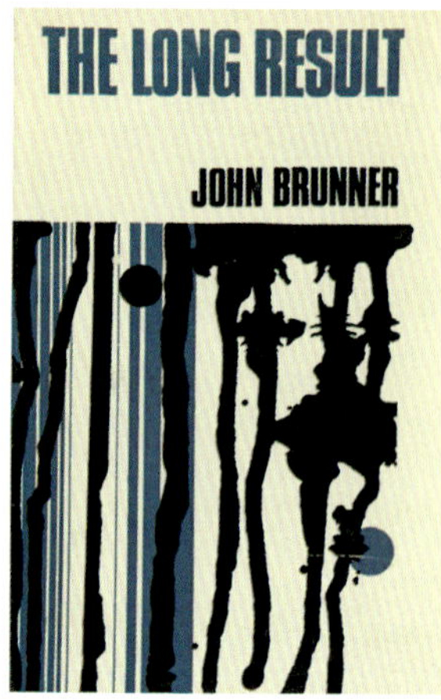

John Brunner | *The Long Result*
Faber and Faber, 1965 | Art **Unknown**

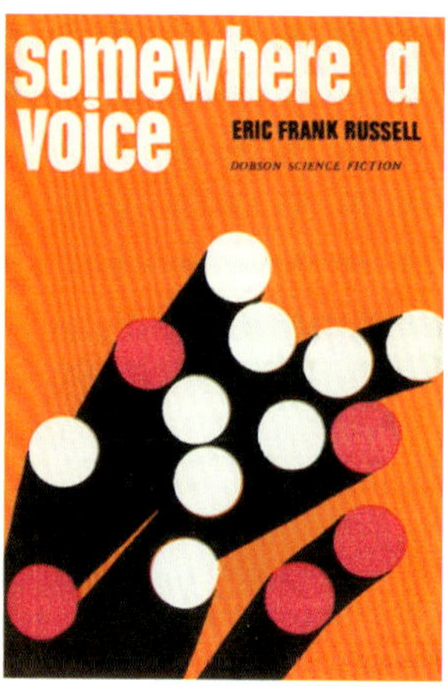

Eric Frank Russel | *Somewhere a Voice*
Dennis Dobson, 1965 | Art **Unknown**

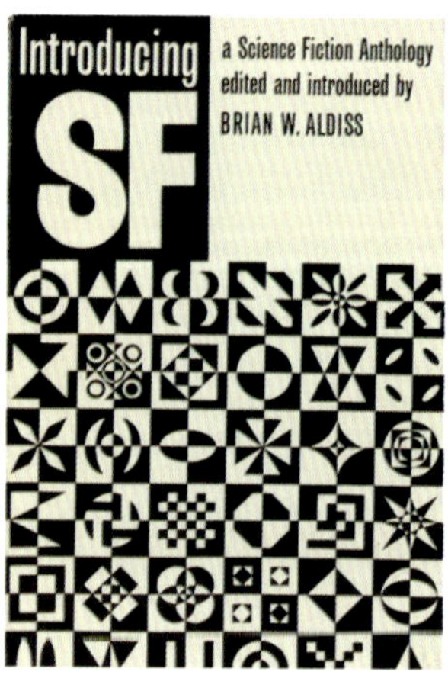

Brian W. Aldiss, ed. | *Introducing SF*
Faber and Faber, 1964 | Art **Bridget Riley**

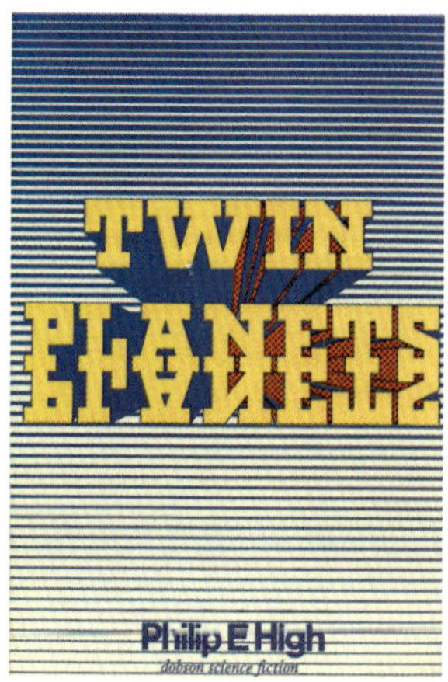

Philip E. High | *Twin Planets*
Dennis Dobson, 1968 | Art **Richard Weaver**

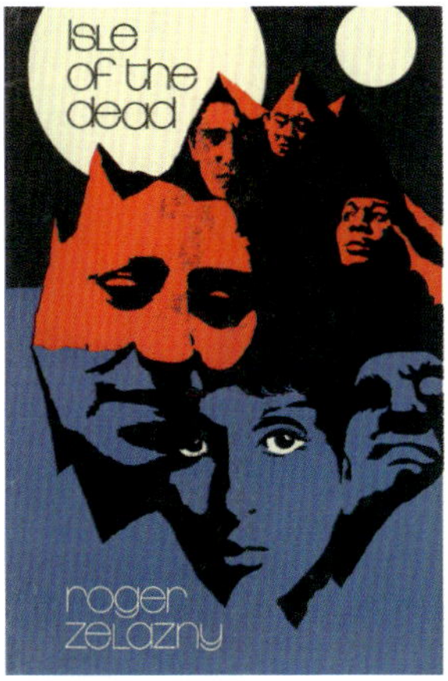

Roger Zelazny | *Isle of the Dead*
Rapp & Whiting, 1970 | Art **Lawrence Edwards**

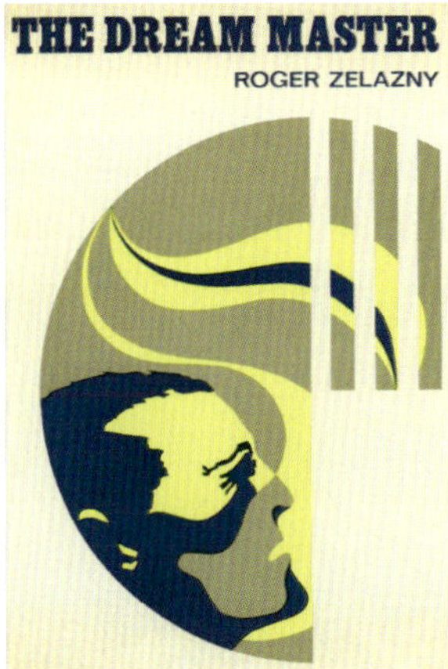

Roger Zelazny | *The Dream Master*
Hart-Davis, 1968 | Art **Ken Reilly**

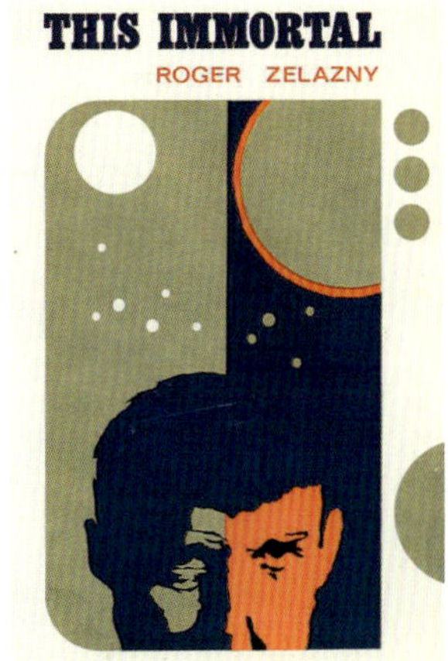

Roger Zelazny | *This Immortal*
Hart-Davis, 1967 | Art **Ken Reilly**

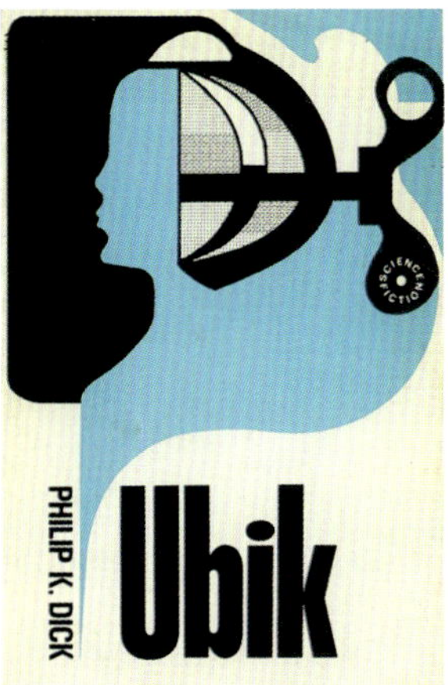

Philip K. Dick | *Ubik*
Rapp & Whiting, 1970 | Art **John Richards**

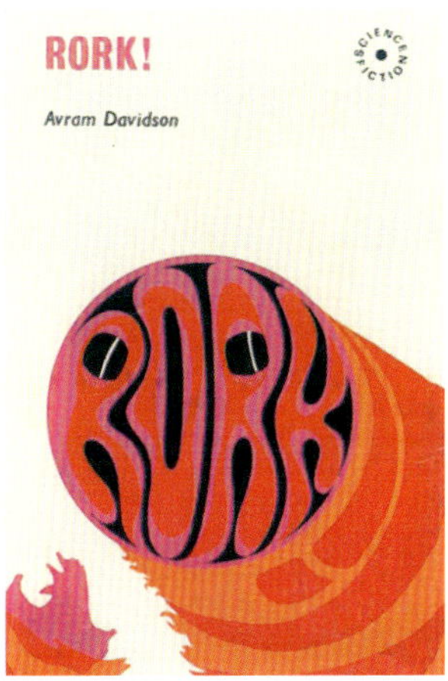

Avram Davidson | *Rork!*
Rapp & Whiting, 1968 | Art **Lawrence Edwards**

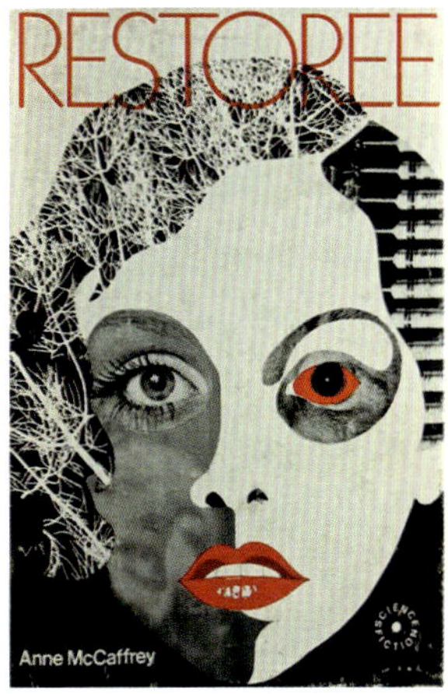

Anne McCaffrey | *Restoree*
Rapp & Whiting, 1967 | Art **Lawrence Edwards**

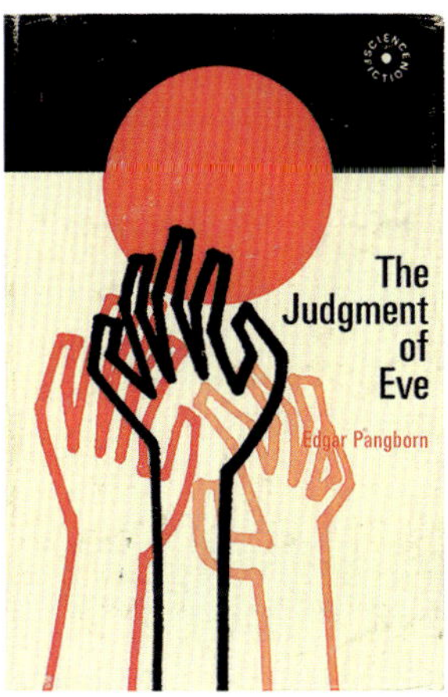

Edgar Pangborn | *The Judgment of Eve*
Rapp & Whiting, 1968 | Art **Lawrence Edwards**

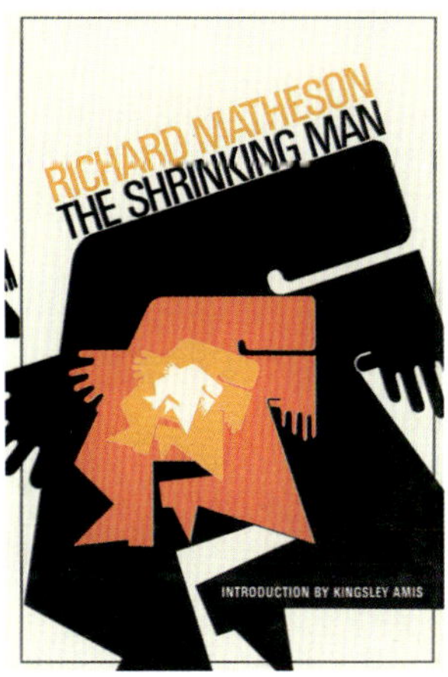

Richard Matheson | *The Shrinking Man*
Dennis Dobson, 1973 | Art **Bill Botten**

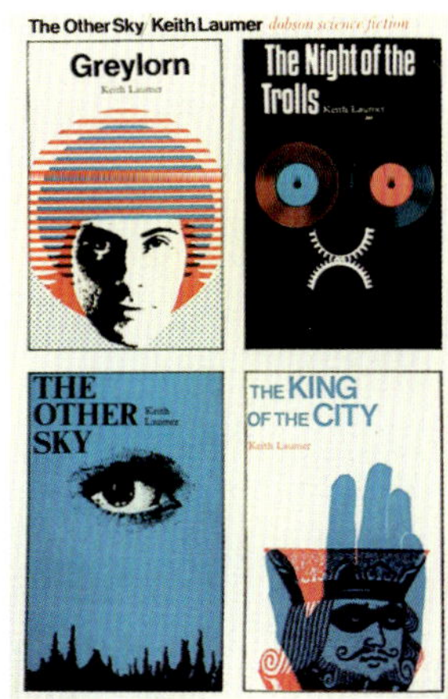

Keith Laumer | *The Other Sky*
Dennis Dobson, 1968 | Art **Richard Weaver**

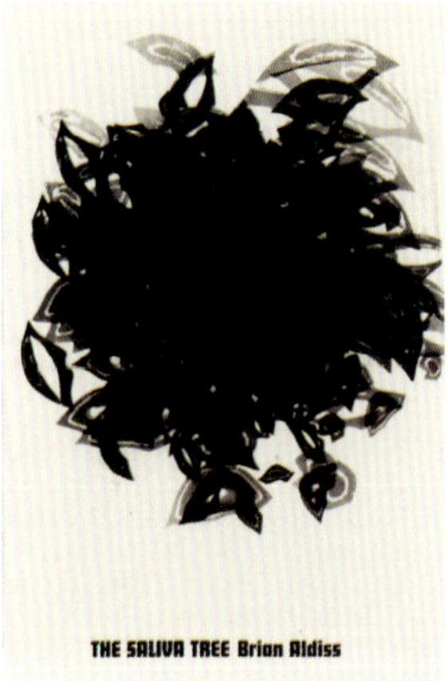

Brian Aldiss | *The Saliva Tree*
SFBC, 1967 | Art **Terry James**

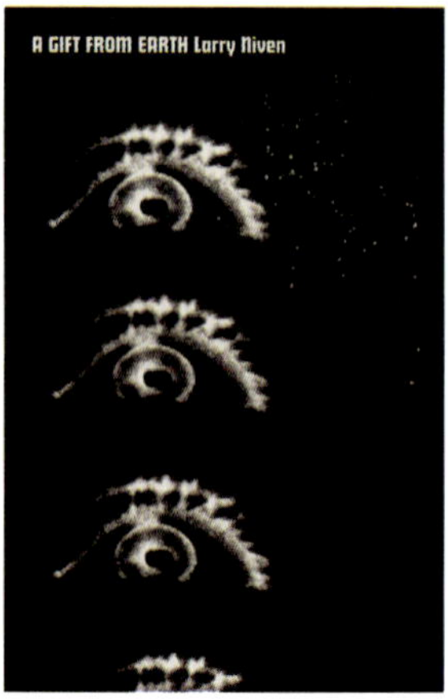

Larry Niven | *A Gift From Earth*
SFBC, 1970 | Art **Terry James**

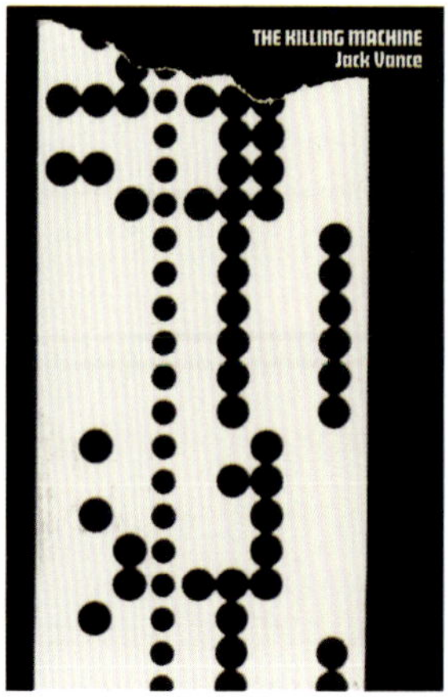

Jack Vance | *The Killing Machine*
SFBC, 1968 | Art **Terry James**

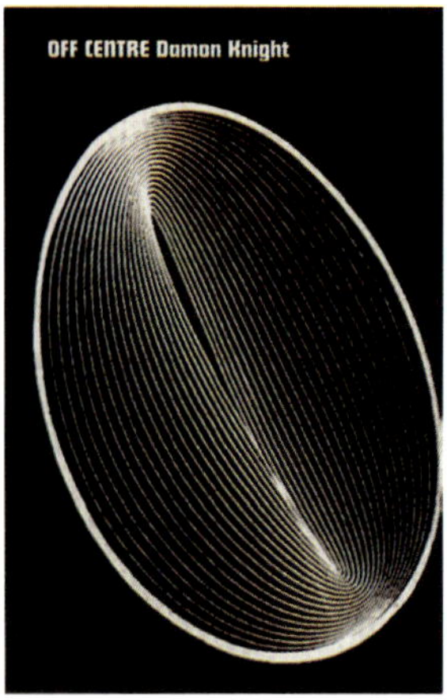

Damon Knight | *Off Centre*
SFBC, 1971 | Art **Terry James**

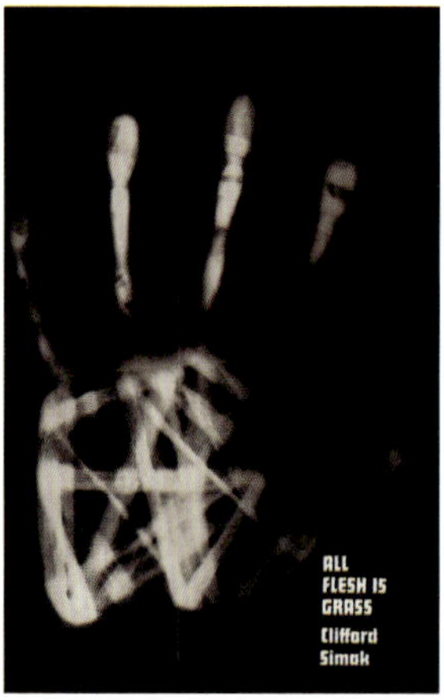

Clifford Simak | *All Flesh is Grass*
SFBC, 1967 | Art **Terry James**

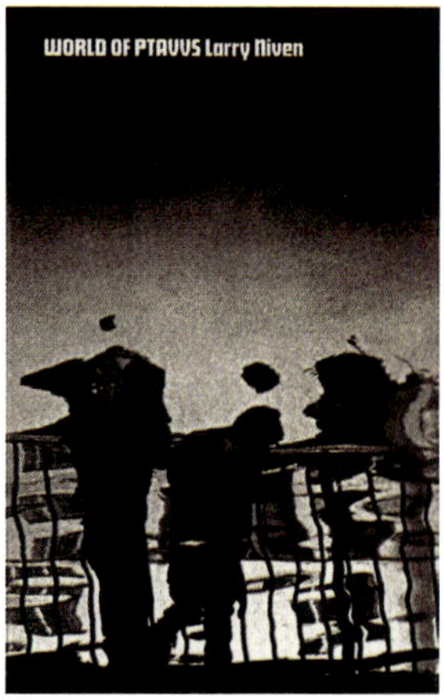

Larry Niven | *World of Ptavvs*
SFBC, 1969 | Art **Terry James**

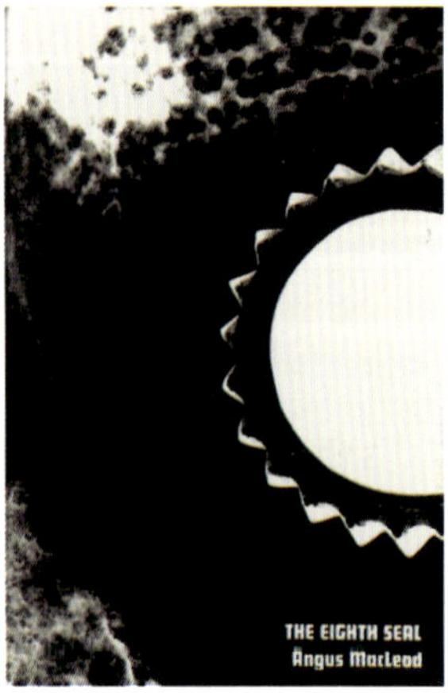

Angus MacLeod | *The Eighth Seal*
SFBC, 1967 | Art **Terry James**

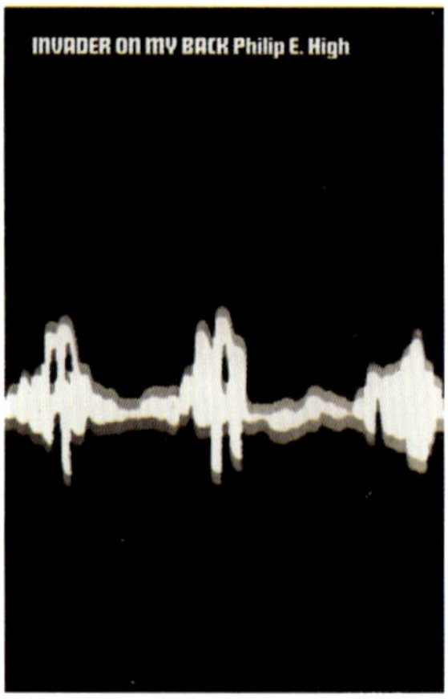

Philip E. High | *Invader On My Back*
SFBC, 1969 | Art **Terry James**

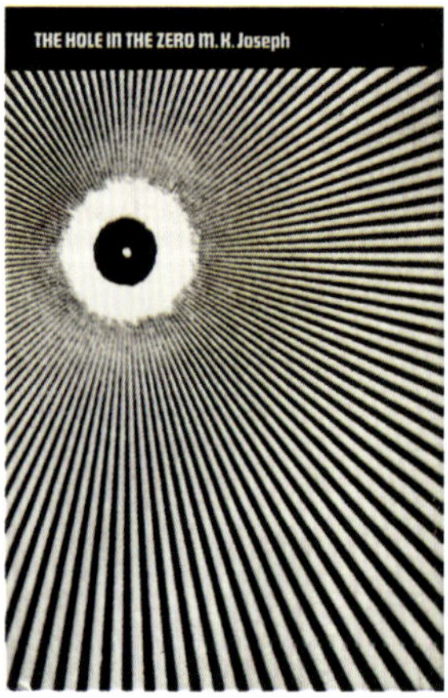

M. K. Joseph | *The Hole in the Zero*
SFBC, 1968 | Art **Terry James**

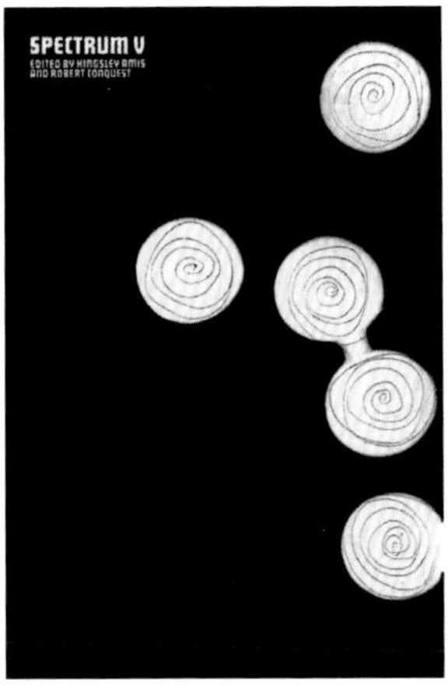

Kingsley Amis and Robert Conquest | *Spectrum V*
SFBC, 1967 | Art **Terry James**

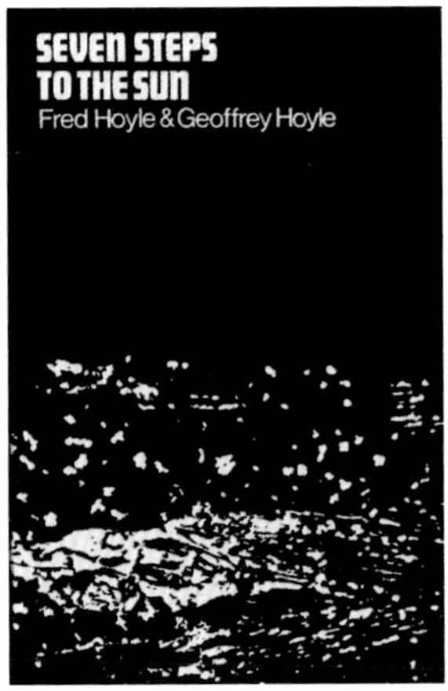

Fred & Geoffrey Hoyle | *Seven Steps to the Sun*
SFBC, 1971 | Art **Terry James**

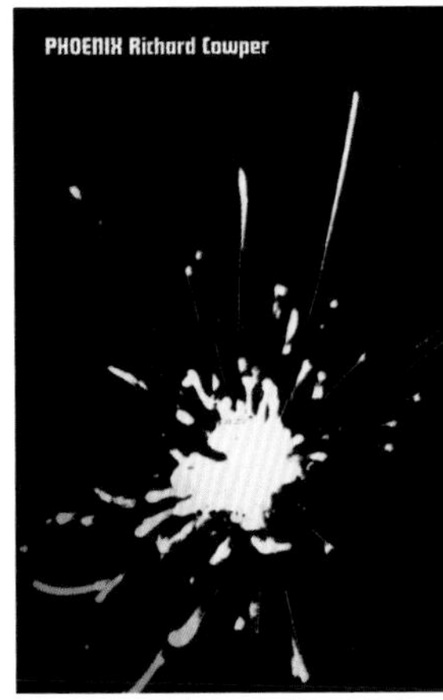

Richard Cowper | *Phoenix*
Burke, 1969 | Art **Terry James**

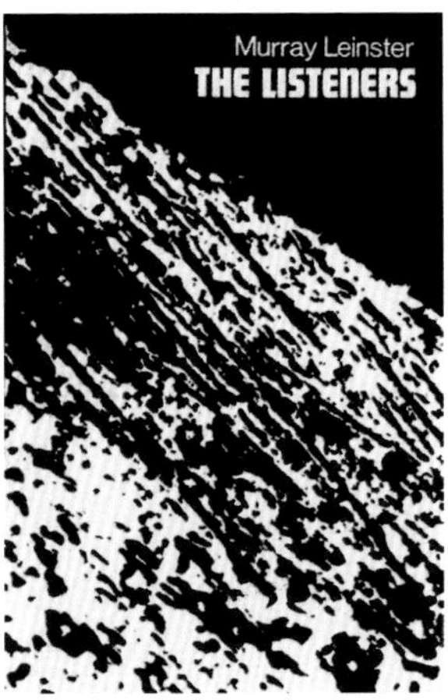

Murray Leinster | *The Listeners*
SFBC, 1971 | Art **Terry James**

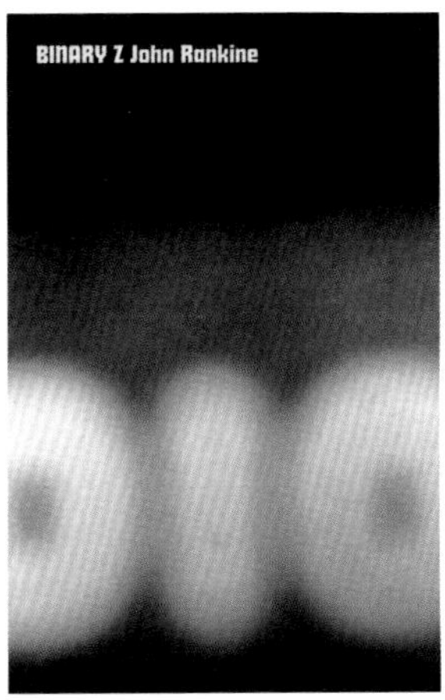

John Rankine | *Binary Z*
SFBC, 1970 | Art **Terry James**

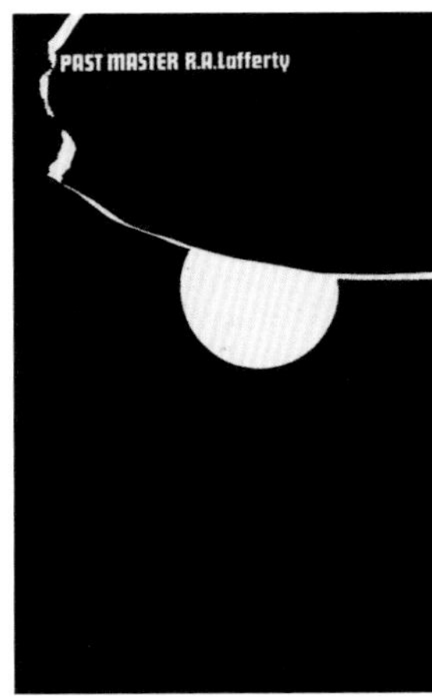

R. A. Lafferty | *Past Master*
SFBC, 1970 | Art **Terry James**

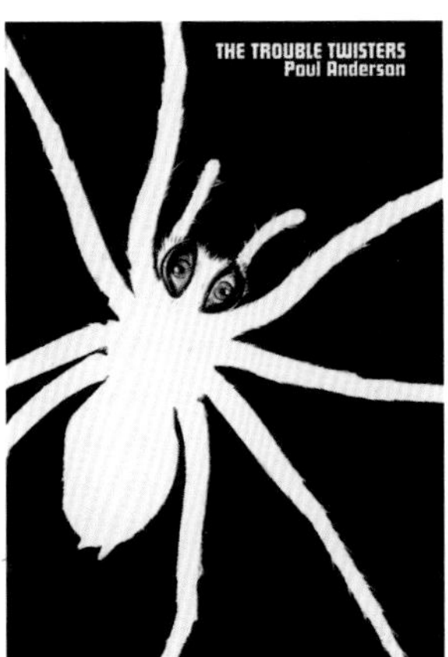

Poul Anderson | *The Trouble Twisters*
SFBC, 1969 | Art **Terry James**

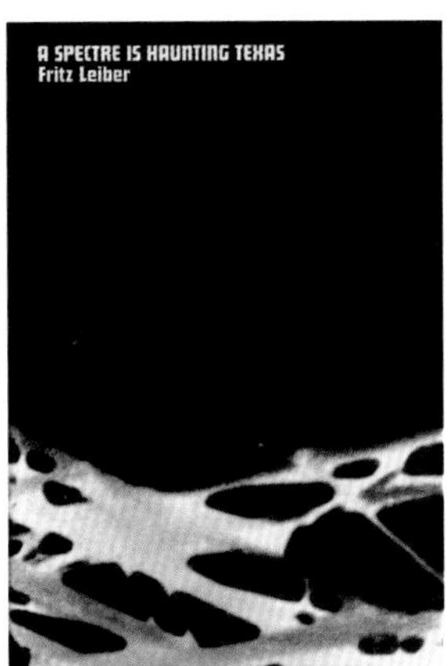

Fritz Leiber | *A Spectre is Haunting Texas*
SFBC, 1970 | Art **Terry James**

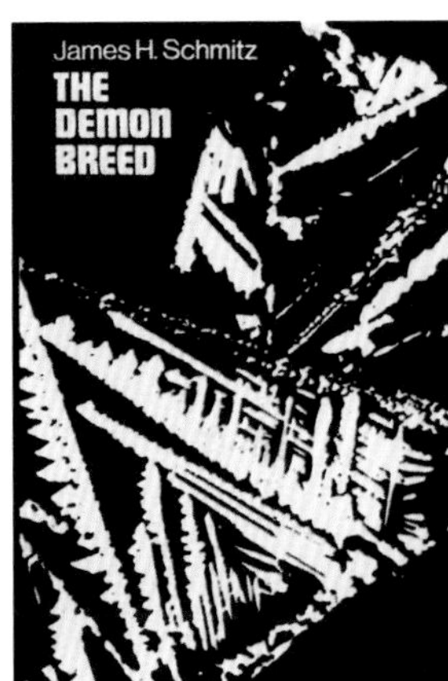

James H. Schmitz | *The Demon Breed*
SFBC, 1971 | Art **Terry James**

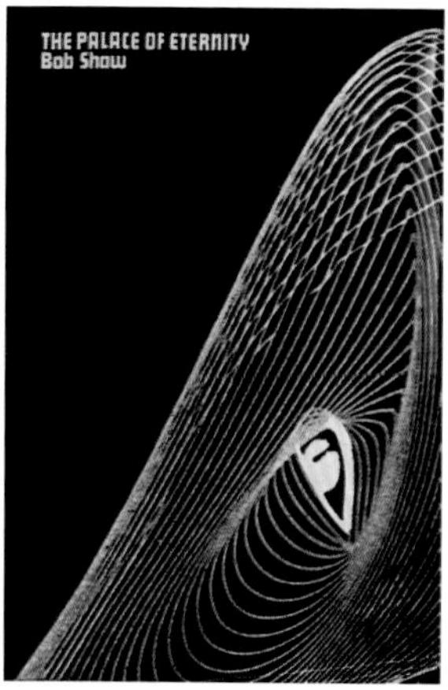

Bob Shaw | *The Palace of Eternity*
SFBC, 1971 | Art **Terry James**

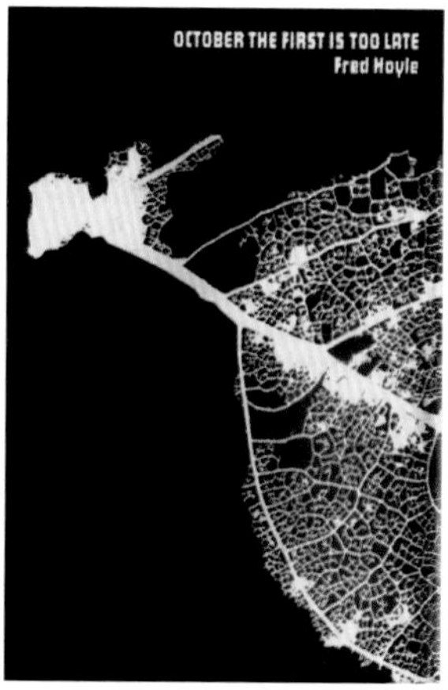

Fred Hoyle | *October the First is Too Late*
SFBC, 1967 | Art **Terry James**

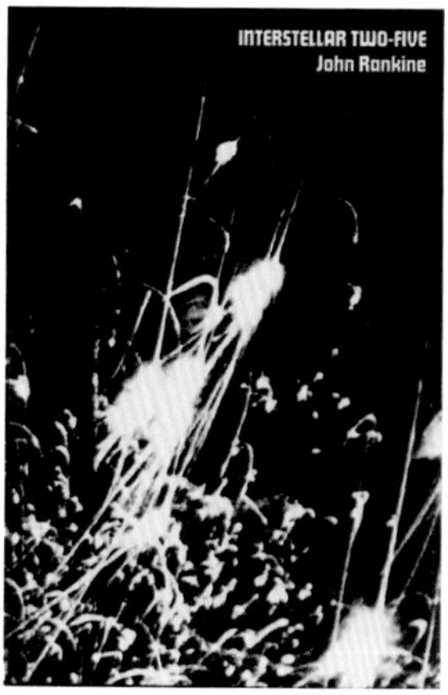

John Rankine | *Interstellar Two-Five*
SFBC, 1967 | Art **Terry James**

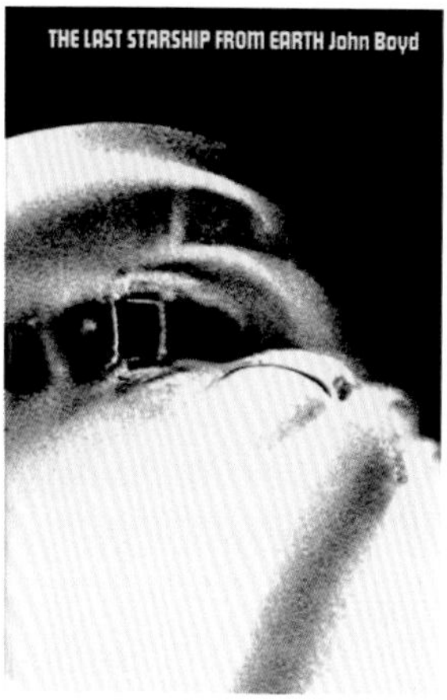

John Boyd | *The Last Starship From Earth*
SFBC, 1970 | Art **Terry James**

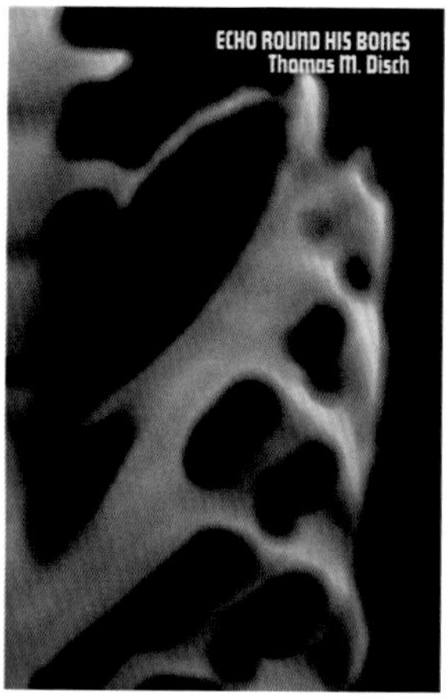

Thomas M. Disch | *Echo Round His Bones*
SFBC, 1970 | Art **Terry James**

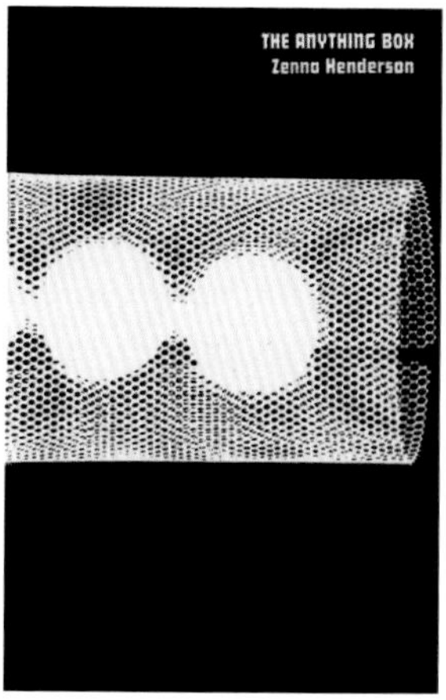

Zenna Henderson | *The Anything Box*
SFBC, 1967 | Art **Terry James**

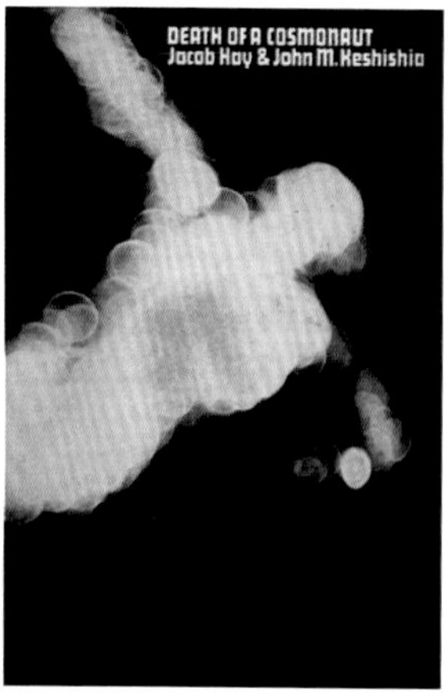

Jacob Hay & John M. Keshishia
Death of a Cosmonaut
SFBC, 1971 | Art **Terry James**

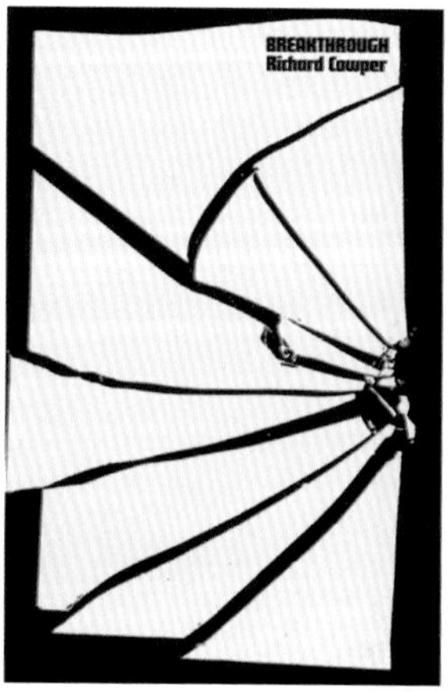

Richard Cowper | *Breakthrough*
SFBC, 1968 | Art **Terry James**

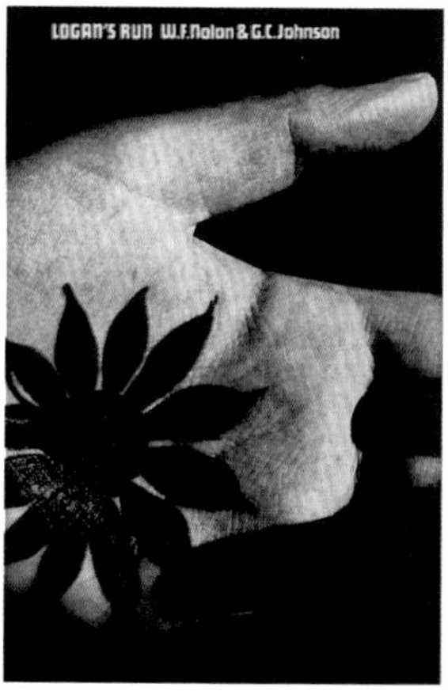

William F. Nolan & George Clayton Johnson
Logan's Run
SFBC, 1969 | Art **Terry James**

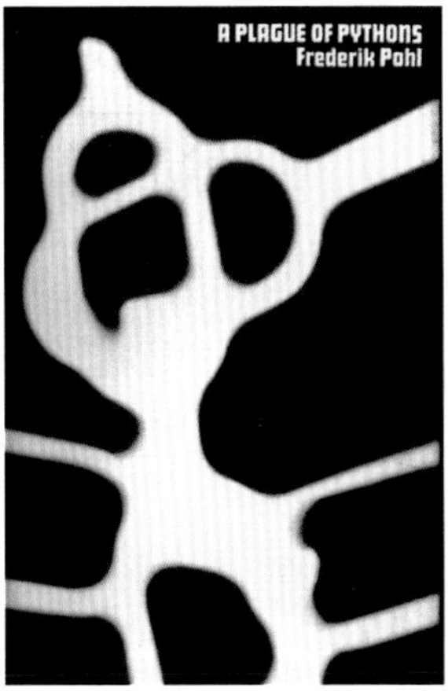

Frederik Pohl | *A Plague of Pythons*
SFBC, 1967 | Art **Terry James**

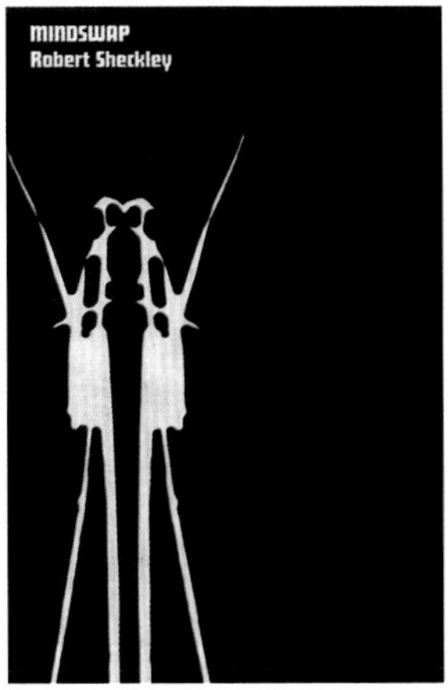

Robert Sheckley | *Mindswap*
SFBC, 1967 | Art **Terry James**

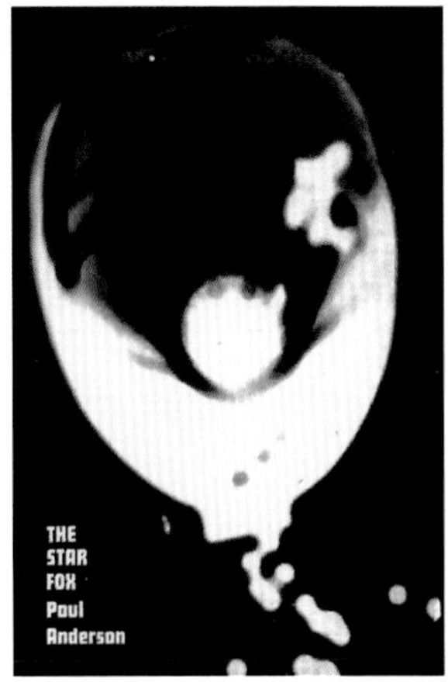

Poul Anderson | *The Star Fox*
SFBC, 1967 | Art **Terry James**

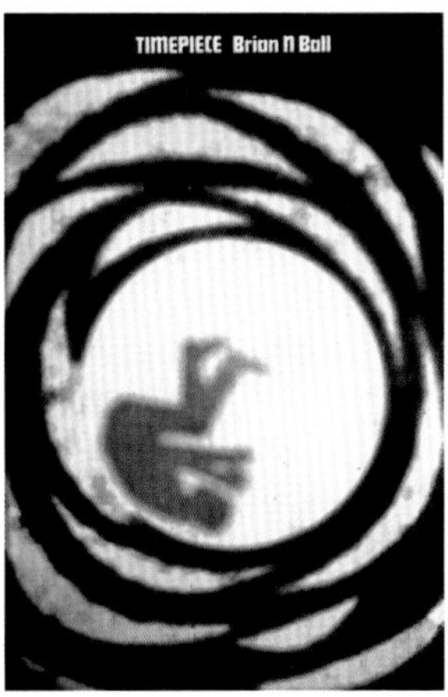

Brian N. Ball | *Timepiece*
SFBC, 1970 | Art **Terry James**

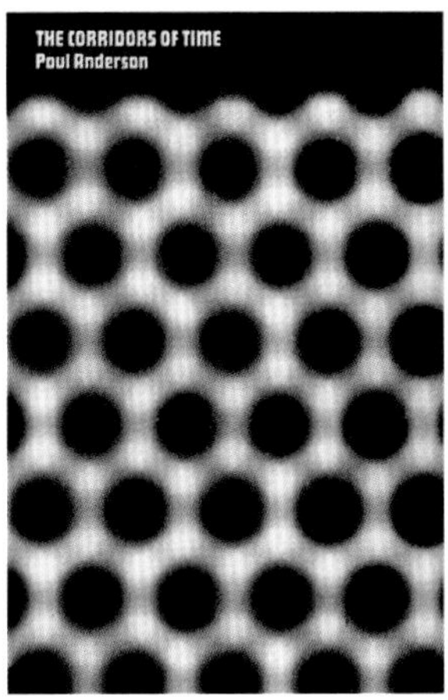

Poul Anderson | *The Corridors of Time*
SFBC, 1967 | Art **Terry James**

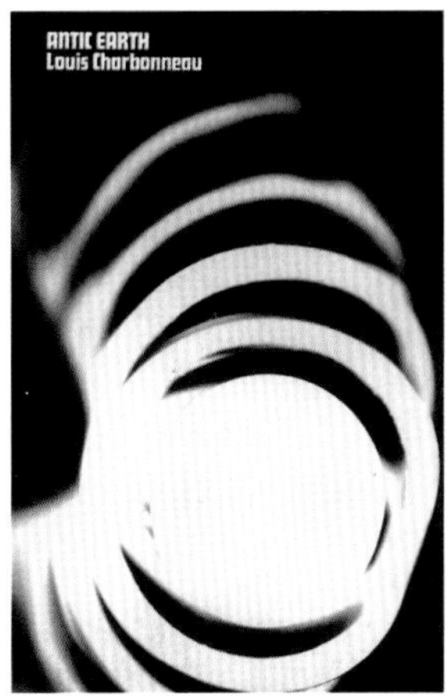

Louis Charbonneau | *Antic Earth*
SFBC, 1968 | Art **Terry James**

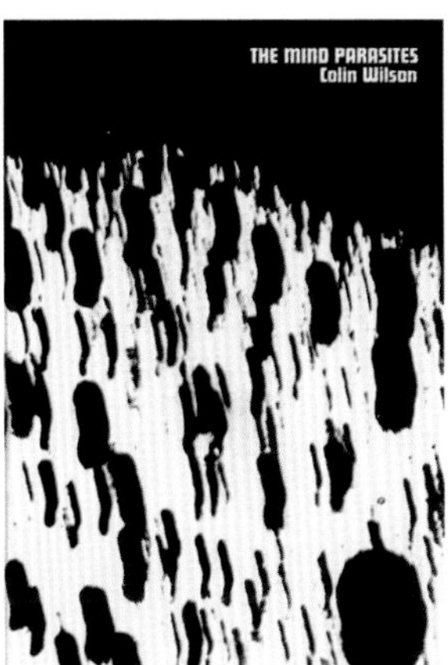

Colin Wilson | *The Mind Parasites*
SFBC, 1968 | Art **Terry James**

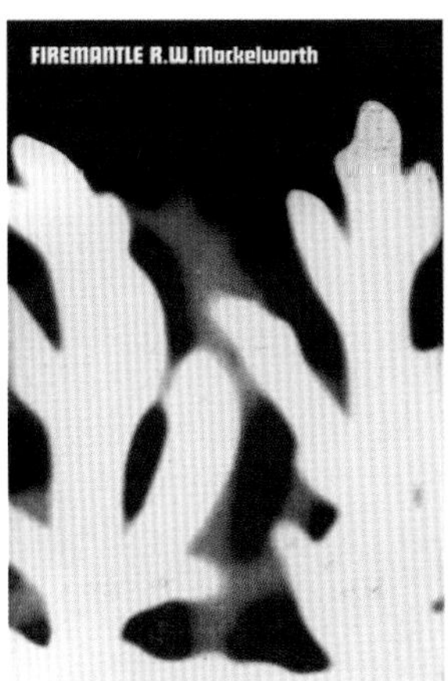

R. W. Mackelworth | *Firemantle*
SFBC, 1969 | Art **Terry James**

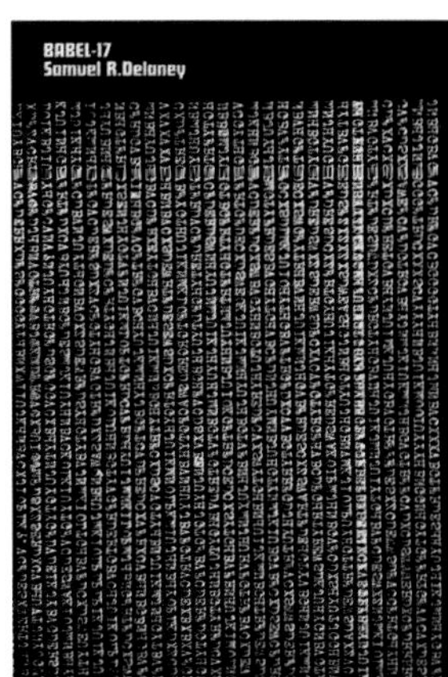

Samuel R. Delany | *Babel-17*
SFBC, 1968 | Art **Terry James**

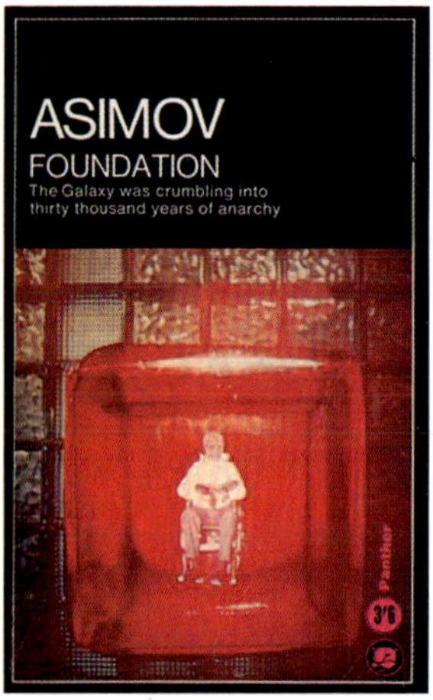

Issac Asimov | *Foundation*
Panther Books, 1965 | Art **Unknown**

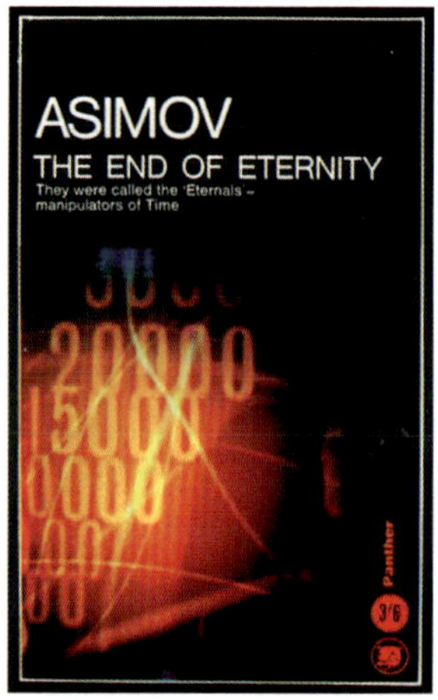

Issac Asimov | *The End of Eternity*
Panther Books, 1965 | Art **Unknown**

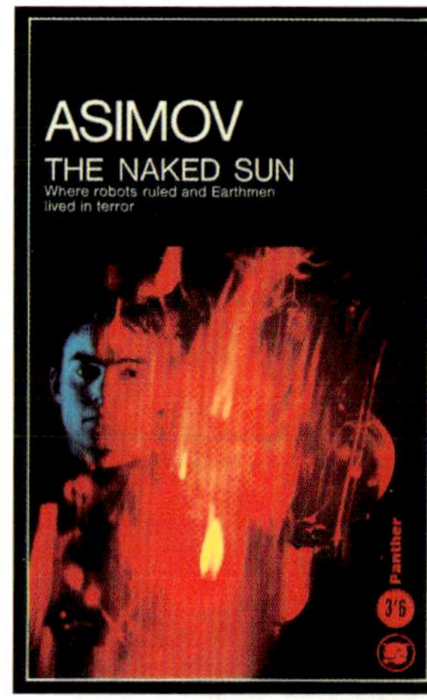

Issac Asimov | *The Naked Sun*
Panther Books, 1965 | Art **Unknown**

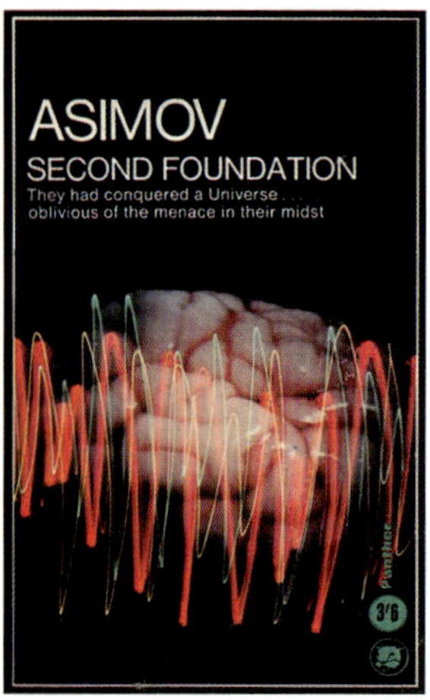

Issac Asimov | *Second Foundation*
Panther Books, 1965 | Art **Unknown**

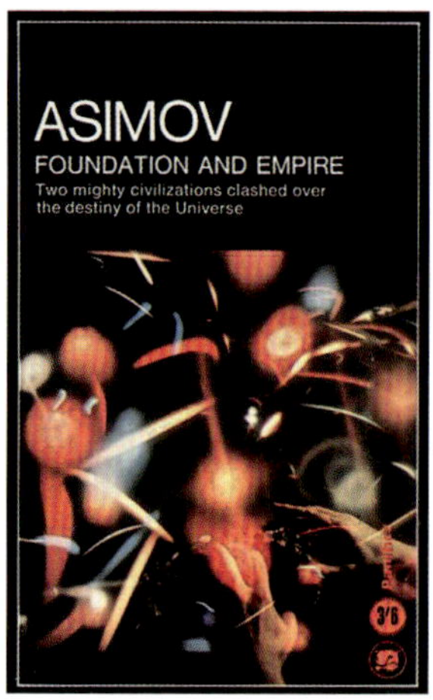

Issac Asimov | *Foundation and Empire*
Panther Books, 1965 | Art **Unknown**

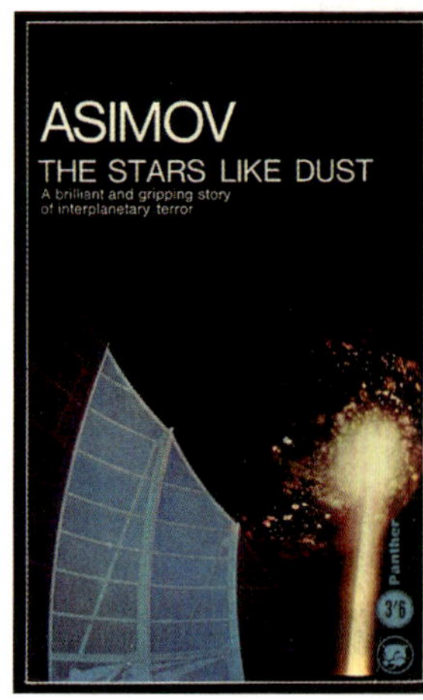

Issac Asimov | *The Stars like Dust*
Panther Books, 1965 | Art **Unknown**

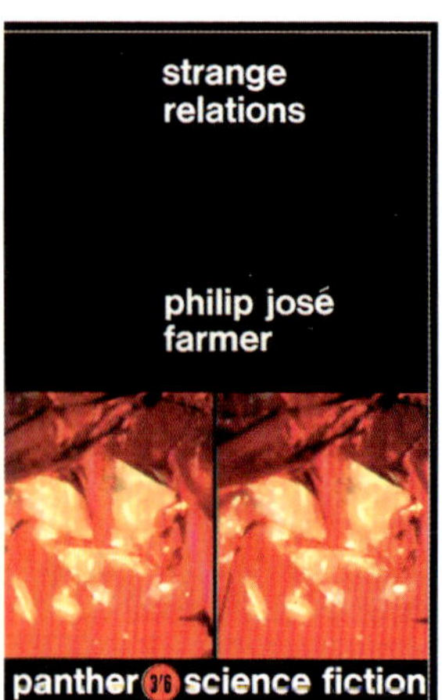

Philip José Farmer | *Strange Relations*
Panther Books, 1966 | Art **Unknown**

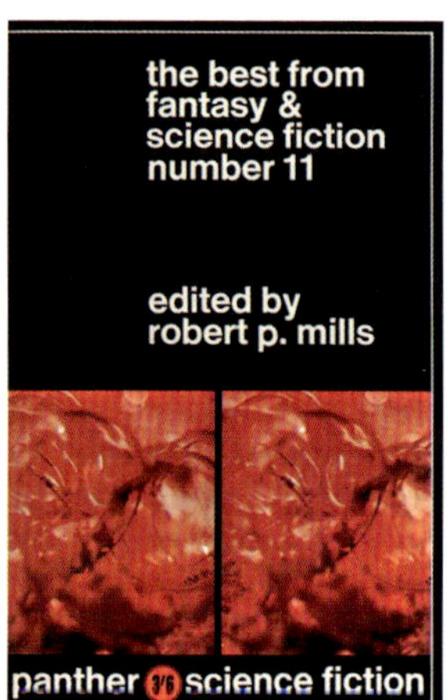

Robert P. Mills, ed.
The Best from Fantasy and Science Fiction 11
Panther Books, 1966 | Art **Unknown**

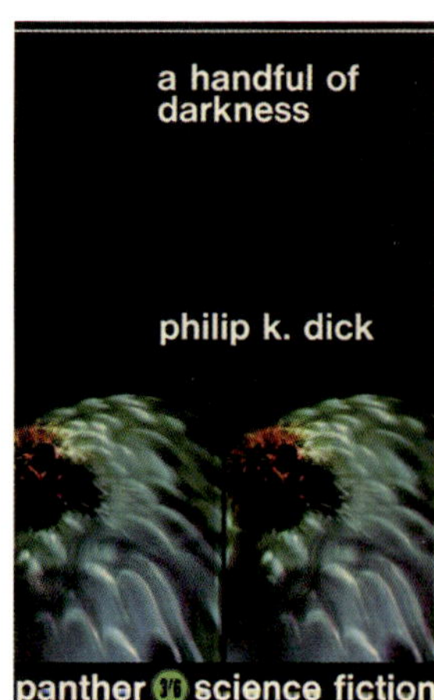

Philip K. Dick | *A Handful of Darkness*
Panther Books, 1966 | Art **Unknown**

A Perfect Bust

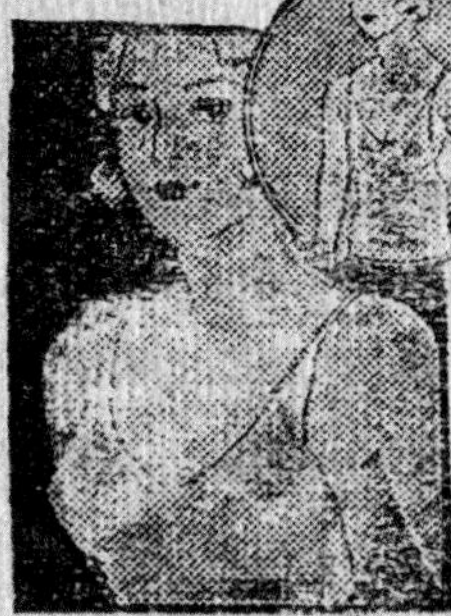

You can obtain perfect, fascinating curves with BEAUTIPON the **amazing** Vegetable Flesh Former—or money back. Simply rub this **harmless** cream into the skin last thing at night, and in a few weeks you will have a glorious figure. Develops bust 3-6 ins. Adds healthy flesh anywhere. Guaranteed harmless. Miss G.A. writes: *"I have actually developed my bust 4½ inches, and my breasts are now a lovely shape, high and firm. It is a joy to me to be told how young I look."* You, too, can increase your bust and have lovely rounded feminine curves. 30 days' Course, **5/6.** Full Course, **10/-. Money back if not delighted in 7 days.** Details **2d.** Sent under plain sealed cover. **Beautipon, 28 (J.S.11), Dean Road, London, N.W.2.** (Established 25 years.)

Losing Hair?

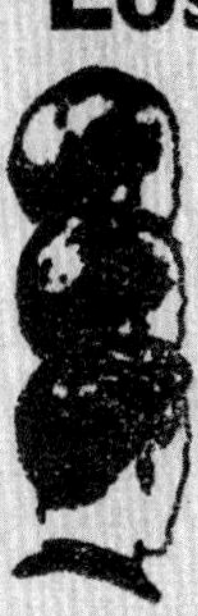

You can have thicker, healthier, lustrous hair in 2-6 weeks—or money back. NEW Nature Treatment grows strong hair, ends falling, scurf, etc. 30 days' treatment, **10/-.** Full Intensive Course **25/-. Nature Treatment, 28 (J.S.11), Dean Road, London, N.W.2.**

STOP SMOKING

IN THREE DAYS or MONEY BACK

Safe, pleasant, permanent. The only scientific way. **No Will Power necessary.** Save pounds. Recommended by leading journals. *"Within two days I was rid of the tobacco habit."—W.G. "After 15 years of heavy smoking, up to forty a day, I stopped smoking . . . It is now five weeks since I had a cigarette."—G.A. "Was a smoker for two years and broke the habit in two days."—F.N.*

Complete Course, **6/6.** Sent under plain cover. Write now. — **Nature Remedies, 28 (J.S.11), Dean Road, London, N.W.2.**

Be Taller

You can be inches taller in 14 days or money back! The unique Safe System activates the Growth Glands and quickly brings a permanent gain in height of 1-5 inches, also lively "pep" and energy. Guaranteed safe. No drugs. The first original and the one Guaranteed System. R. M. Patel gains 2 in.; L.P., age 25, gains 3 in.; S.J., age 17, gains 4 in.; A.J., age 63, gains 2 in.; C.T., age 34, gains 3½ in. Complete Course, **10/-.** Details **2d.** Sent under plain cover. **Safe System, 28 (J.S.11), Dean Road, London, N.W.2.**

Why Be Skinny, Run Down?

Gain Weight

in 10 days or Money Back

Amazing new way enables you to put on firm pounds and inches on your body, chest, arms, thighs and legs. Guaranteed . . . or your **money back.** There's no need to be afraid to strip for sports or go to parties . . . you can put on up to **a pound a day** without exercise . . . harmful drugs . . . or special diet . . . with **Beautipon Vitamin Tablets.** They contain the "Sunshine Vitamin" . . . nourishing, revitalising haemoglobin . . . flesh-forming malt . . . and pure yeast. If you are **skinny, nervy and run down,** get started now. If after 10 days your mirror doesn't tell you that you have put on weight and look better, money will be refunded. Only **5/-** and **15/-** (Full Course) from: **Beautipon Tablets 28 (J.S.11), Dean Road, London, N.W.2.**

A Slim Bust

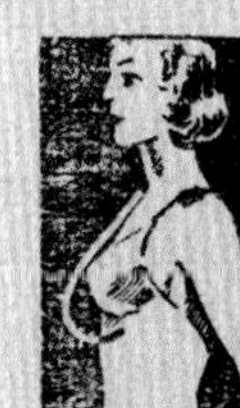

You can reduce 3-5 inches and obtain alluring slim loveliness with SLIM CREAM, the remarkable Vegetable Reducing Cream —or money back. Simply rub this harmless cream into the bust last thing at night and in a few weeks you will have a youthful, slim figure. **Reduces fat anywhere.** Guaranteed safe. *"Bust was 40 ins., and hips 45. Bust now 36, hips 41."*—Miss G.L. *"It is really wonderful the way it banishes unwanted flesh in so short a time,"* writes Miss Joan C. *"I measured my bust after 14 days and I had already reduced 2 ins. . . . after 30 days my bust was reduced another 2 ins."* —Miss V.D. 30 days' Course, **5/-.** Complete Course, **10/-. Money back if not delighted in 7 days.** Sent under plain cover. **Slimcream, 28 (J.S.11), Dean Road, London, N.W.2.** (Established 19[illegible])

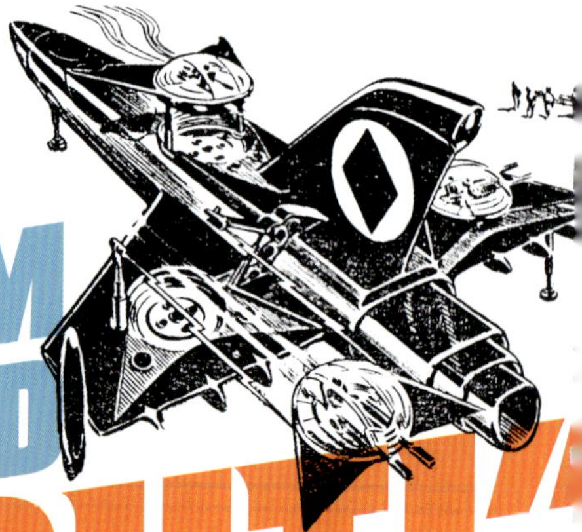

BRITAIN DISCOVERS SCIENCE FICTION

"MUSHROOM CLOUD FALLOUT!"

AFTERWORD by PHILIP HARBOTTLE

I was born in 1941, and soon after starting school discovered the world of comics through friends and classmates. Numerous British and Australian reprints of American sf and fantasy superhero comics were published in postwar Britain, including *Superman* and *Captain Marvel* [1], and I became an avid fan.

In May 1950 I became a regular reader of the new weekly *Eagle* comic, primarily for Frank Hampson's *Dan Dare* [2]. I also followed Steve Dowling's *Garth*, the newspaper strip cartoon strongman then appearing in the *Daily Mirror,* whose adventures by 1950 had settled into a distinctly science fiction mode with the interplanetary story *Journey to Jason* [3].

Then one glorious Saturday in 1954 a school friend told me that his grandfather had let him read a "science fiction pocket book". He enthusiastically described the plot, about "a man who saw into the future, and knew when he was going to die". (I would later identify this as *Zero Hour* by Vargo Statten [page 249], a pseudonym of John Russell Fearn). He gave me the location of a local second-hand bookshop about half a mile away where these fabulous items could be bought. I soon found the dingy premises of Joseph Storm: Book Seller. "Do you have any science fiction books please?" I asked hopefully.

A small pile of paperbacks was placed on the counter. "One shilling each, sixpence trade-in when you bring them back." I chose three titles, all published by Scion Ltd., which bore the legend "science fiction" prominently on the covers. I handed over my week's pocket money for *A Thing of the Past* [page 246] by Volsted Gridban, *The Dust Destroyers* [page 224] by Vargo Statten, and *The Resurrected Man* [page 231] by E. C. Tubb.

A Thing of the Past had the most splendidly lurid cover: a man and a scantily clad girl confronting a fearsome dinosaur. *The Dust Destroyers* showed two space-suited men standing on the hull of their spaceship, in orbit above the Earth. *The Resurrected Man* had the most restrained cover: tiny space-suited figures jetting through space towards a spaceship airlock. And that was the order in which I read the books.

To say that I read *A Thing of the Past* is an understatement – I *devoured* it! This was *real* science fiction, completely eclipsing all of the childish flimflam of the comic strips. I quickly read the other two books, which made a tremendous and lasting impression.

I thereafter introduced "science fiction pocket books" to my comic-reading friends, who also graduated to the new form. Then came the fateful day when I read in quick succession two other Scion epics, *Operation Venus* [page 241] by John Russell Fearn and *Reverse Universe* [page 227] by Volsted Gridban. I enjoyed *Operation Venus,* and was electrified to see a house ad on the back cover urging readers to "*look out for the next*

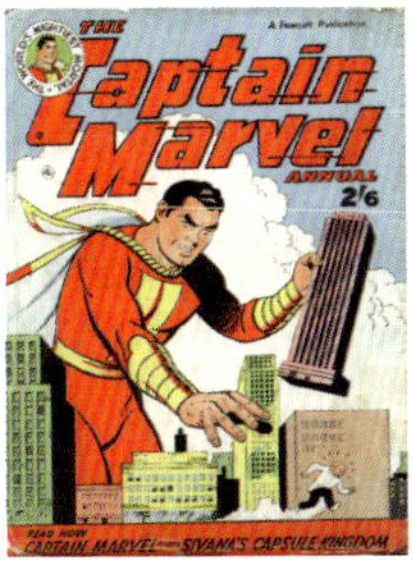

1

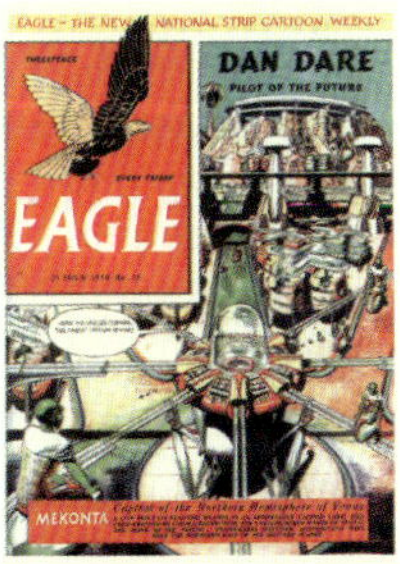

2

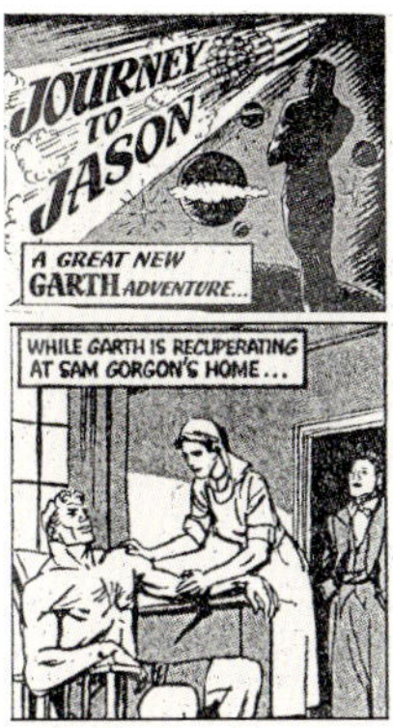

3

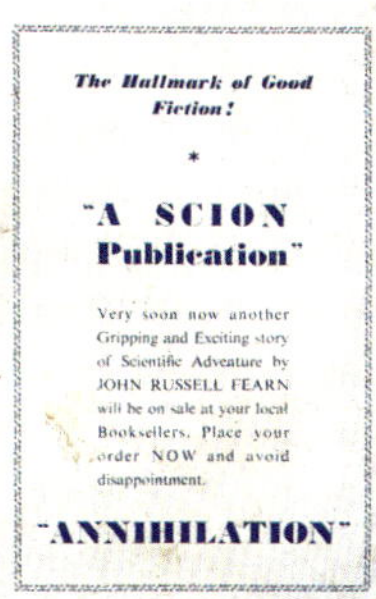
The Hallmark of Good Fiction!

*

"A SCION Publication"

Very soon now another Gripping and Exciting story of Scientific Adventure by JOHN RUSSELL FEARN will be on sale at your local Booksellers. Place your order NOW and avoid disappointment.

"ANNIHILATION"

4

title by John Russell Fearn – Annihilation!" [4]. I already had a copy of *Annihilation*, and knew it to have been written by Vargo Statten. The penny dropped immediately: Fearn and Statten were one and the same person, and his real name was probably Fearn, since I'd never met anyone called "Vargo"! I then realized that the tongue-twisting "Volsted Gridban" must be another made-up name, and that was probably Fearn too, which was why I enjoyed his stories so much.

Delighted, I then settled into reading *Reverse Universe*. Anticipating another Fearn epic, I was to receive a shock – the style was nothing like Fearn's. If Fearn had not written this book, then who had? By the time I reached the end, I had recognized who the author was: none other than my other great favourite, E. C. Tubb!

The hunt was on!

I knew then that I would just *have* to read every other similar science fiction book I could find to see if I could discover any other pen names of Fearn and Tubb, and also to unravel three profound mysteries: why different authors could write under the same name, why some novels were excellent whilst others from the same publishers were rotten, and why, by 1956, most of the sf books and magazines I had only recently discovered seemed to have abruptly ceased publication. It was not until I was appointed editor of the new British science fiction magazine *Vision of Tomorrow* in 1969 [5] that I learned the whole story, through meeting and becoming friends with many of my favourite authors and artists who became contributors.

In building my science fiction collection, I had grown to love some of the cover artwork, especially the covers of an artist I would eventually identify as Ron Turner.

Turner had fond memories of his 1950s science fiction cover work. Asked about his influences, he told me: "I was always a great admirer of the work of *Flash Gordon* creator Alex Raymond. No one, of course, could help but admire the breathtaking work of astronomical artist Chesley Bonestell, and the photographic realism of his 'I am a camera' technique; probably the most emulated artist of all in this particular field."

Turner's interest in science fiction secured him commissions from Scion in 1950 to paint the paperback covers for their new series. His second cover, for Vargo Statten's *Annihilation*, was outstanding and contributed to the success of the line. It showed a rocket ship blasting into space to escape a doomed Earth wracked by solar storms, and typified all Turner's subsequent covers: dramatic, realistic, beautifully coloured, and featuring an accurate depiction of the story.

Turner recalled: "All my work, starting with the Scion publications, was handled by Greg Hall [his agent] who passed on manuscripts for me to read and select a suitable episode to illustrate. I was inspired by a combination of Fearn's imagination and descriptive capacity and my own inherent interest in the subject matter. This got me off on the right foot. Had I started off working on inferior material it might have been a different story! The only time I can remember Fearn making contact was when he wrote to congratulate me on the Scion cover for his *The Genial Dinosaur* story [page 234]. I think I had about four days to complete each cover – some, but not all, lettered by myself. I think the going rate was about fifteen guineas, with perhaps an extra five for the lettering."

After the British mushroom paperback boom began to falter in 1955, Turner switched to comic strips and became famous for the *Rick Random* series, illustrating several scripts by Harry Harrison, and for his colour artwork for *The Daleks* in *TV21* comic. In the 1980s, working with myself and John Lawrence, Turner created *Nick Hazard* [6], a science fiction

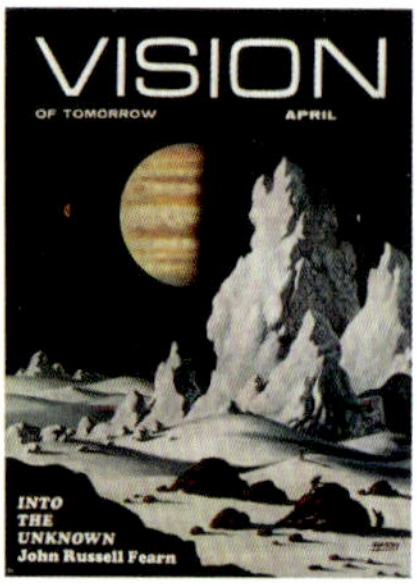

5

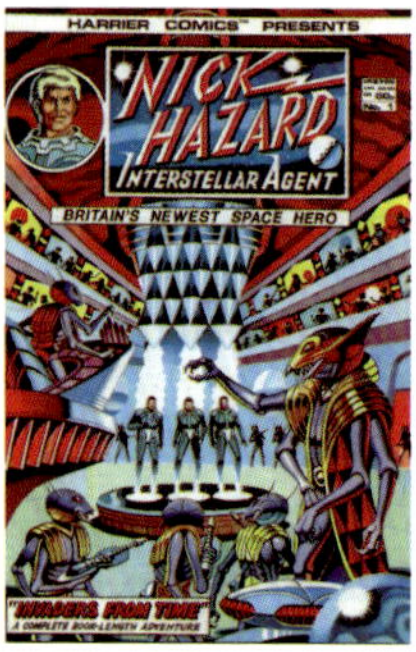

6

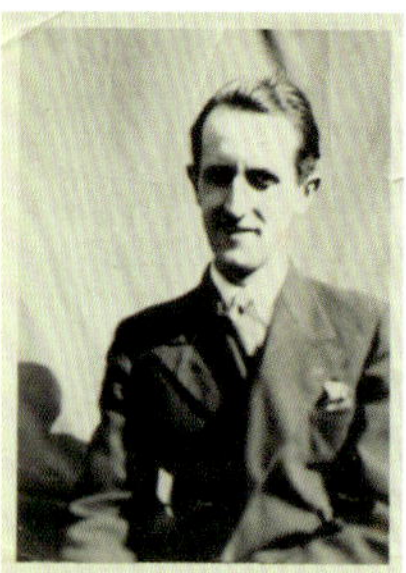
7

strip hero based on Fearn's stories, and a full-length graphic version of one of his *Golden Amazon* novels. They are currently being reprinted in *Spaceship Away*, coloured by Martin Baines.

I was also privileged to know and interview author E. C. Tubb, who went on record about his own experiences.

"In the 1930s, sf was restricted to a few imported American magazines. The war came, fans got scattered, and when they got back together, they had a Great Dream. 'Let's produce our own sf magazine, let's get a British magazine going.' But it wasn't easy. First you had to find a lot of money!

"Starved of magazines because of the paper shortage, the breakthrough came when British business restrictions started to be lifted, and your wide boys got in on the act. The pocket book – the paperback – was born. Now it wasn't born in the sense of it never having been known before, but it took off after the war. People were eager to make money, printers wanted to print, publishers wanted to publish, shops wanted to sell. But there was a sudden dearth of writers who could produce all this stuff. The only real source for science fiction writing was science fiction fandom, because they knew it all, didn't they? They were steeped in the background. So there was a scurrying round by publishers wanting people who could write this stuff.

"Some people could: John Russell Fearn [7], for example, was a past master. Others were established writers. A lot of new writers came in on the wave, myself amongst them, and what had been a hobby became a business.

"And it just grew; publishers flowered, they proliferated. Scion, Panther, Curtis Warren, Paladin, Milestone... They were all there. Most of them (at least initially) paid low rates. So, in order to survive, you had to be prolific. Turning out work quickly meant, of course, that some of it was poor quality. But one quality they did have was enthusiasm – a zest. I mean, 90 per cent of all writing is poor, even today's writing is poor. But at least then there was more of an excuse for it.

"The publishers set certain limits: the story was so long, you were paid so much for it, and let's go to town. And this kind of publishing expanded and grew, until the collapse came with the scandal of Hank Janson, and sado-masochistic detective stories. For fear of being prosecuted for selling obscene material, the sellers simply refused to accept anything from these publishers. So your gangsters and your sf and westerns wouldn't sell. End of boom!

"And that hit me very hard at the time, because I'd just bought a house. I was left with a mortgage and no job and no publishers, which meant I had to scurry around like the proverbial blue-arsed fly to get a job, and keep the wolf from the door. So that's what happened to me, and to others.

"But I have happy memories of that boom, of the exuberance of it. I was asked by publishing houses to produce books – or sometimes I went to them. They'd tell me that they'd pay so much, and some of them would offer a little more than the other chap. So you sat down and did whatever you did as quickly as you could. Now, because publishers were nasty, and grasping and mean (they still are!) the house name came in. If someone became very popular, the publisher owned the house name, and that's where the *nom de plumes* started.

"With Curtis Warren you were 'King Lang', or whatever – half a dozen authors all using the same name. These bylines were distinct from the *nom de plume* you deliberately chose because you had two stories in one issue of the magazine, so in that case you became 'Charles Grey' or somebody else. But the novels started that way, and then of course by the laws of the marketplace, you became that publisher's author, until somebody else wanted to use you and invented a different name. It became a kind of merry-go-round.

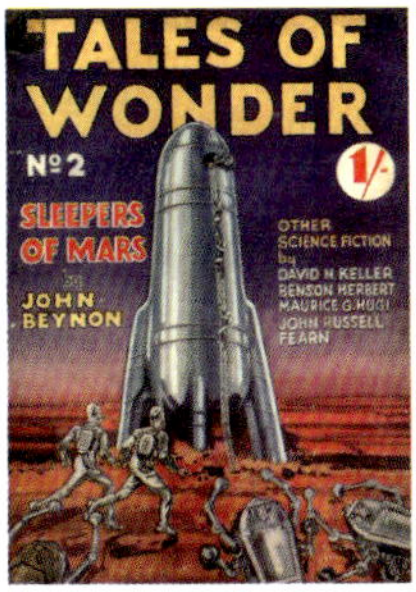

8

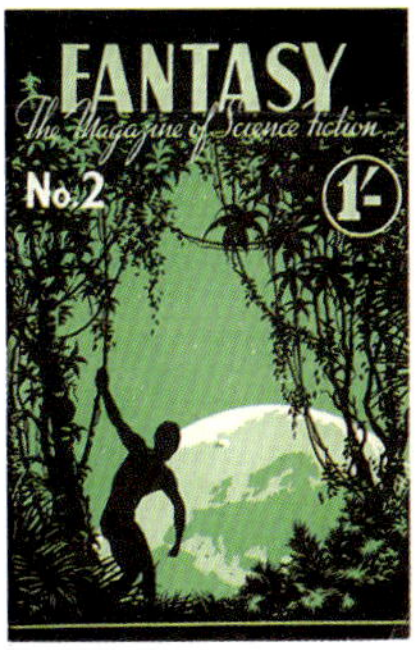

9

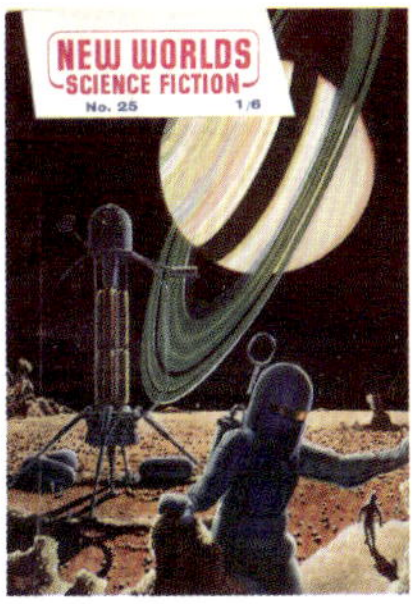

10

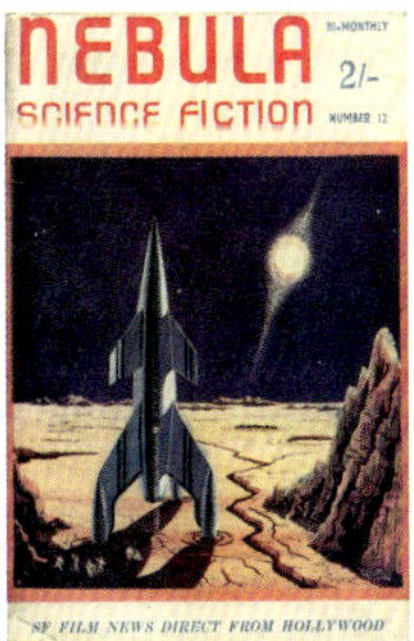

11

"I was fortunate in having been well-grounded in science fiction. I knew about space... I knew you couldn't breathe on the moon without a helmet. So I had an edge – I was up on the rest of the crowd. I knew how a rocket worked. I knew there was a little bit of a difference between a solar system and an intergalactic system. I knew my stuff, so I became quite popular in the science fiction pocket book field, writing for Milestone, Scion, and others. I proliferated, and that was it – until the boom busted. And that's another story.

"Publishers wouldn't take anything for fear of prosecution, frightened that in the pile there was some sadomasochistic stuff. Tame by our present-day standards, but it was there. So the bubble burst. The cycle of trust, of credit, borrowing, paying for the last one after you'd done the six... it was like a bank collapsing. There was a hell of a flap, which was rather disastrous for authors in on the scheme at the time."

During the Second World War opportunists had begun to exploit various shortages, paper included. Any publisher who could lay hands on paper stood to make money. The public had been so starved of reading matter that anything printed would sell. But the new "mushroom" publishers themselves had deplorable tastes, which they believed were shared by the general public. So for years they issued a profusion of westerns and gangster thrillers laced with sex. Occasionally a western or a thriller writer would be commissioned to try science fiction. The results were insultingly bad, and science fiction in post-war Britain struggled to get off the ground.

That it eventually did so was largely due to the efforts of two science fiction fans, Walter Gillings and John Carnell. A professional journalist, Gillings had edited Britain's first adult science fiction magazine, *Tales of Wonder*, from 1937 until 1942 [8], until wartime austerity killed it. Although he managed to interest another publisher in 1944, publication of his planned new sf magazine *Fantasy* [9] was held up because of paper rationing.

Carnell had been a print salesman who'd had useful pre-war experience editing *New Worlds*, then an amateur sf fanzine. In 1940 he'd been hired to edit a new professional version, only for his publisher to suddenly go into liquidation. Carnell himself was later called up. But soon after being demobbed, Carnell was introduced to Stephen Frances, the Director of Pendulum Publications. On the strength of his unused 1940 portfolio, Carnell was hired to edit a new science fiction magazine to be called *New Worlds*. When Gillings' *Fantasy* was eventually published in December 1946, it had been pipped to the post in July by *New Worlds*.

Although it had sold out, Gillings' *Fantasy* was terminated after three issues because its publisher decided to use its paper quota for another more profitable magazine. Pendulum's *New Worlds* also lasted only three issues. Pendulum were under-capitalized and wartime austerity conditions forced them into liquidation in 1947.

Carnell and Gillings published early stories by such authors as Arthur C. Clarke and John Wyndham, who were later to become world-famous, and their magazines laid a foundation for British science fiction. Carnell's *New Worlds* was resurrected by a consortium of its authors in 1949, and became a great success. *New Worlds*, together with the new magazines that followed it, most notably *Authentic Science Fiction* and *Nebula Science Fiction*, created a market for talented new young British writers such as E. C. Tubb and his contemporaries. The likes of Sydney J. Bounds, Ken Bulmer, John Burke, Peter Hawkins and others all followed Tubb's example and gradually infiltrated the mushroom novels market themselves, raising its standards immeasurably and replacing the hacks.

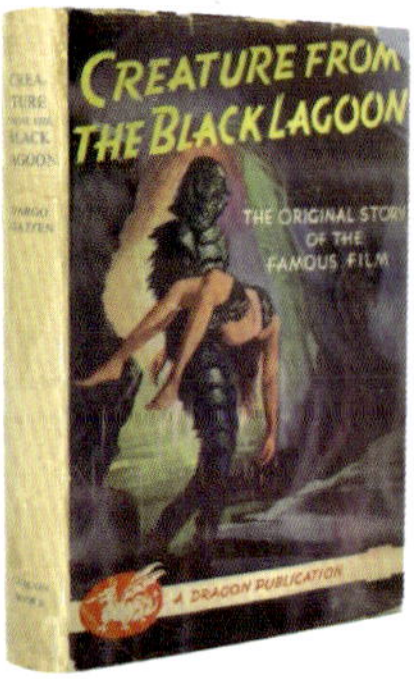

12

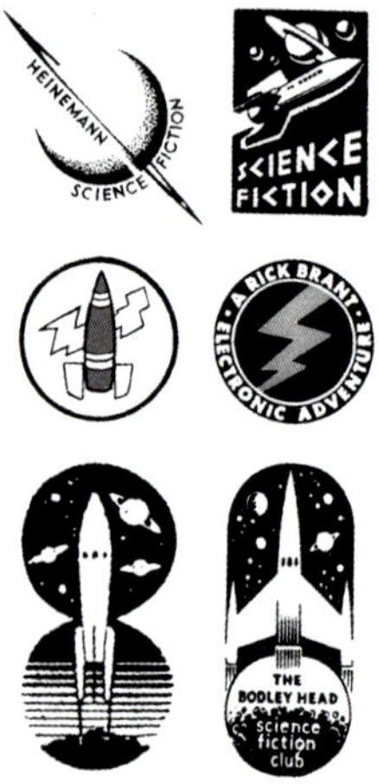

13

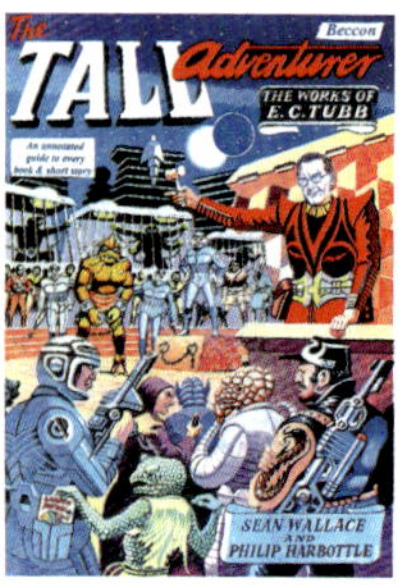

14

The new magazines also provided a market for emerging cover artists Gerard Quinn [10], Josh Kirby [see original art herein] and Bob Clothier [11].

Back in 1947, following the collapse of Pendulum Publications, Stephen Frances started a new publishing company S. D. Frances Ltd., which issued his own line of gangster novels written under the "Hank Janson" pseudonym. Francis' books were modelled on the tough and risqué best-selling novels of James Hadley Chase, but the Janson novels had an unhealthy undercurrent of brutal sex and sadism.

Before the war lots of quality fiction magazines had flourished, employing good artists. But wartime austerity killed these quality markets, and the artists then had to accept whatever work they could find with the mushroom publishers. Frances had been able to secure the services of a very experienced cover artist, Reginald Heade, who was adept at painting beautiful women. The Janson novels quickly became best-sellers, which led to a tremendous boom in the mushroom publishing industry.

All of the small independent publishers rushed to deliberately imitate Janson, bringing out their own line of so-called "sophisticated" gangster novels – there were suddenly hundreds of them. The post-war mushroom publishers had engineered their own downfall. It was all too much, and eventually the Watch Committees began to prosecute these publishers for obscenity, leading to a number of destruction orders for their books and crippling fines and jail sentences for the worst offenders.

Paradoxically, these cheap books are avidly collected today, and even sell for eye-watering prices. A few of the mushroom publishers even experimented with hardcovers as well as paperbacks, and some of these are now rare and valuable. Panther Books issued their early titles in both paperback and hardback "library editions", the latter replacing the 1/6 price with a "P" [page 163, spines page 155], and published the only editions of *L. Sprague De Camp's New Anthology* [page 167]. The few surviving copies of Dragon Press's hardback and paperback editions of Vargo Statten's *Creature From the Black Lagoon* [12], a unique novelization of the famous Hollywood movie, can fetch well over a thousand pounds. Other British edition movie tie-ins attracting big money from American collectors are Cherry Tree's paperback of *The Thing From Another World* [page 258] and Corgi Books' *Forbidden Planet* [page 356]. Publishers would often give their sf lines special logos to set them apart from their mystery or crime titles [13].

But the main reason for their collectability lies with their covers, most of which were painted by talented and imaginative artists. This wonderful book, *Rayguns and Rocketships*, is proof of that!

PHILIP JAMES HARBOTTLE discovered J. R. Fearn's "Vargo Statten" novels as a teenager. Researching their history led to his editing the sf magazine *Vision of Tomorrow* in 1969, and contributing to many sf reference books. His own non-fiction books include *The Multi-Man* and *The Tall Adventurer* (cover by Ron Turner) [14], bio-bibliographies of Fearn and E. C. Tubb respectively. He has published numerous posthumous novel collaborations with Fearn, and has edited several sf anthologies. His latest non-fiction book is *Vultures of the Void: the Legacy* (2011), a unique personalized history of British post-war science fiction publishing, which he is currently adapting for video on his YouTube channel.

As well as pursuing his own writing he runs the Cosmos Literary Agency, specialising in sf, detective and westerns.

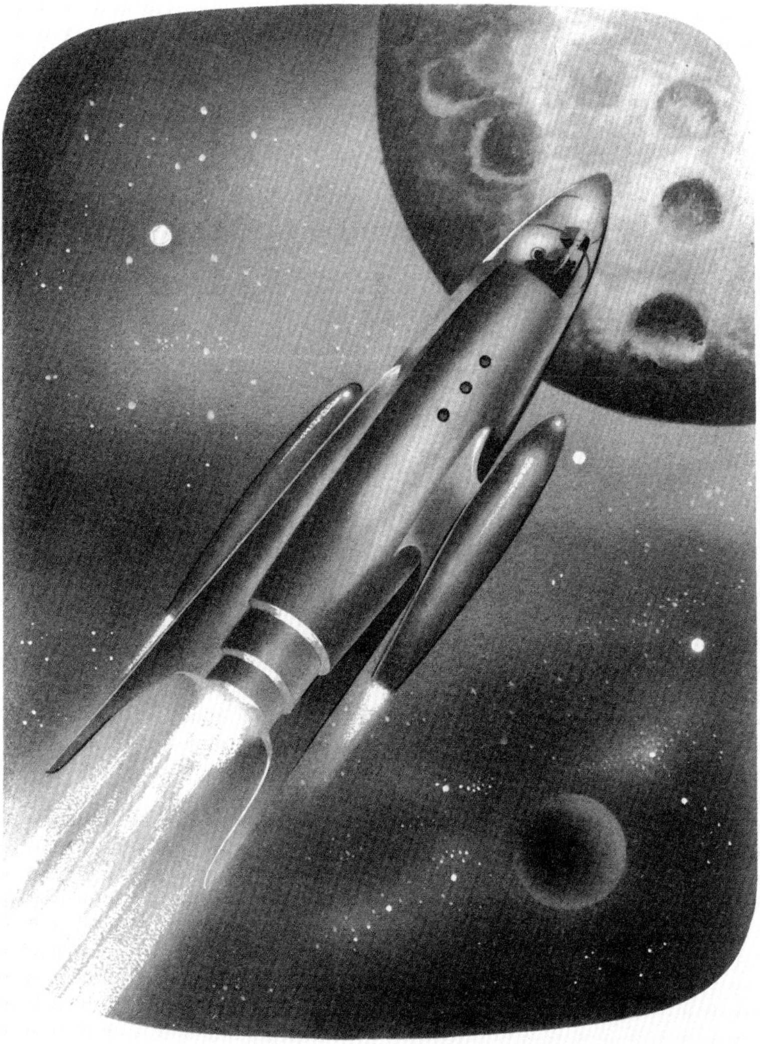

SCIENCE FICTION

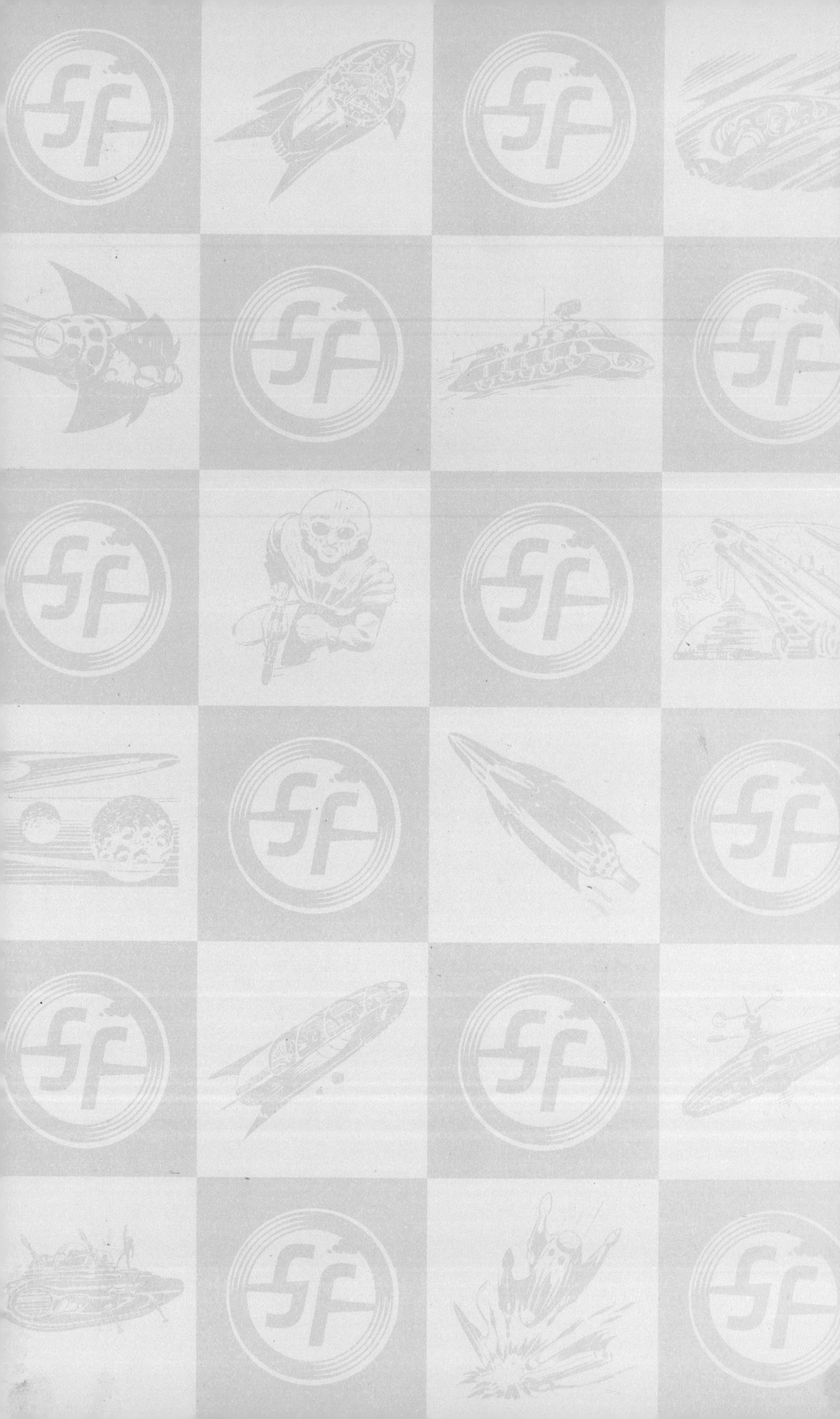